D1523017

The Kentucky Anthology

Two Hundred Years of Writing in the Bluegrass State

Edited by
Wade Hall

THE UNIVERSITY PRESS OF KENTUCKY

Publication of this volume was made possible in part by a grant
from the National Endowment for the Humanities.

Scholarly publisher for the Commonwealth,
serving Bellarmine University, Berea College, Centre
College of Kentucky, Eastern Kentucky University,
The Filson Historical Society, Georgetown College,
Kentucky Historical Society, Kentucky State University,
Morehead State University, Murray State University,
Northern Kentucky University, Transylvania University,
University of Kentucky, University of Louisville,
and Western Kentucky University.

Editorial and Sales Offices: The University Press of Kentucky
663 South Limestone Street, Lexington, Kentucky 40508-4008
www.kentuckypress.com

05 06 07 08 09   5 4 3 2 1

Cataloging-in-Publication data available from
the Library of Congress

This book is printed on acid-free paper meeting
the requirements of the American National Standard
for Permanence in Paper for Printed Library Materials.

Manufactured in the United States of America.

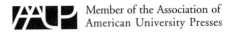

Member of the Association of
American University Presses

Contents

Politicians, Teachers, Preachers, and Occasional Poets: Writing as an Avocation   129

Turning the Century:
Kentucky Writing Comes of Age 157

The Dramatic Tradition in Kentucky   567

Contemporary Nonfiction   585

A Shower of Poets: Contemporary Kentucky Poetry   719

Acknowledgments

I wish to thank my editor, Gena Henry, a knowledgeable, affirming literary companion and guide; David Cobb, whose editorial expertise and hawk-eye diligence kept us on the straight and narrow paths and bypaths; Danielle Dove, who took a mountain of words and created a design that makes this book both attractive and readable; Stephen Wrinn, the visionary director of the University Press of Kentucky, who set us on our way with godspeed and sufficient supplies and directions; Gregg Swem, the native Kentuckian who has provided invaluable aid and encouragement every step of the way. I send warm thanks especially to the thousands of Kentucky students with whom I have made many Kentucky journeys for more than forty years. Enjoy now the fruits of our labors.

This volume is dedicated to Dr. Thomas D. Clark (1903–2005). I had the good sense to follow his lead to Kentucky from the lower South, thirty-one years later.

Introduction

Come with me on a journey of exploration and discovery. It's a Kentucky journey you can take anytime it pleases you—day or night, winter or summer, in sunshine or rain. Open this book and join the adventure at any point—from Daniel Boone's account of his early years in the Kentucky wilderness to Bobbie Ann Mason's memoir of her mother's heroic contest with a fish of epic proportions in western Kentucky. It is a journey that will titillate, irritate, educate, delight, and enlighten you, a journey with a Kentucky accent that has been in the making for over two centuries. Our Kentucky trip is not only geographical and historical but social, political, economic, racial, religious, and literary. It chronicles our interests and aspirations, our achievements and failures, our comedies and tragedies. Indeed, this collection of Kentucky writing seeks to cover a wide spectrum of subjects and events that have made our state unique and American.

Some of the landscape you will recognize as we pass through. Some you will not know, for we will be exploring new ground as we seek to redefine Kentucky's heritage by claiming territories heretofore shunned or unknown. You will find a road filled with potholes, alluring diversions, and occasional epiphanies. In fact, during our Kentucky journey you will hear Whitmanesque voices of human aspirations, failures, and achievements that are common to us all.

A motley crew of writers will be your guides. In the early years they are hunters, soldiers and adventurers, travelers and tourists, land speculators and Indian fighters, even outlaws; later, they are farmers, lawyers, preachers, physicians, and educators; and more recently they are journalists, historians, playwrights, novelists, and poets. In May 1780 John Adams described the beauties of Paris in a letter to his wife, Abigail, while he was on a diplomatic mission, then added wistfully: "I must study Politicks and War that my sons may have liberty to study Painting and Poetry, Mathematics and Philosophy, Geography, natural History, Naval Architecture, navigation, Commerce and Agriculture, in order to give their Children a right to study Painting, Poetry, Musick, Architecture, Statuary, Tapestry and Porcelaine." Likewise, the early Kentuckians were occupied with basic human needs for the better part of their first century and had little time for the arts.

This is not to say that Kentuckians as early as the 1770s were not writing. In fact, they were writing diaries, letters, laws, sermons, and legal documents. Squire Boone, the preacher brother of Daniel, is alleged to have written a crude couplet. As you will see in the early chapters of this collection, most of their early writing was utilitarian: military, political, promotional, and religious. It was not until the latter part of the nineteenth century that Kentuckians had the wealth and leisure, as well as a usable past, to produce a large body of fine poetry, fiction, and nonfiction. But let us put state chauvinism aside and be honest. Kentucky produced no world-class literary talent before Robert Penn Warren. The last six chapters, however, showcase how well Kentucky writers have fared during the state's second century, when some of the most acclaimed writers of the twentieth century called Kentucky home. Joy Bale Boone once reported gleefully that tiny Todd County, in southwestern Kentucky, had produced within a single life span three literary luminaries—Dorothy Dix, Caroline Gordon, and Robert Penn Warren. It is a legacy that any state would be proud to claim.

In 1913 John Wilson Townsend published a two-volume anthology called *Kentucky in American Letters 1784–1912,* which surveyed Kentucky writers from John Filson to James Lane Allen. In his introduction Townsend reported that he had identified more than 1,000 Kentucky writers but that he could choose only 196 for his collection. He promised that he would eventually publish a dictionary of Kentucky writers, in which he would honor all 1,000 of them, as well as all the scattered "crossroads poets" that he could find. Sadly, his grandiose plans never came to fruition. Even though we would not consider most of the writers included in his volumes serious writers at all, my task has been more daunting than his because, as the twentieth century ran its course, great numbers of Kentucky writers began producing prose and poetry good enough to compete with that of writers anywhere. I have, consequently, been forced to make this anthology representative and selective.

Thus, I have sought to make it a representation of the people who have left a meaningful and eloquent record and thereby contributed to our Kentucky patchwork quilt. The result is a gathering together of many voices, some of which you will love and will agree with, and some which you may not approve of or like, but all of which contribute to the strength, richness, and beauty of our national fabric.

I have searched for good, effective writing in many places, some of them nontraditional. Good writing can be discovered almost anywhere, from hastily scribbled Civil War letters and local columns in weekly newspapers to a finely honed poem by Charles Semones or an epic whaling novel by Sena Jeter Naslund. Good writing is good writing, whether it appears in the *New Yorker* or *Open 24 Hours,* Brescia University's literary magazine. It may be found daily on the editorial page of the *Courier-Journal* or in the features section of the *Lexington Herald-Leader* or in the sports pages of the *Paducah Sun.* Good writing is published not only by Knopf and William Morrow in New York but also by Algonquin Books in Chapel Hill, North Carolina; NewSouth Books in Montgomery, Alabama; Sarabande Books in Louisville, Kentucky; Plum Lick Publishing in North Middletown, Kentucky; and Wind Publications in Nicholasville, Kentucky.

My Kentucky journey began long before I had the good fortune to move here just after Christmas 1962. It began with stories of Daniel Boone and the drama of exploring and settling the Kentucky wilderness that I heard in grade school, before I could locate Kentucky on the map. It continued as I studied American history and read about Abraham Lincoln, who not only freed the slaves but also built a moral base for the whole nation. When I learned that Jefferson Davis, the president of the Confederacy, was also born in Kentucky, I began to see that Kentucky's place in our nation's history has, indeed, been central, ironic, and contradictory. From its founding during the American Revolution, it has served as a crossroads state for the nation—geographically, historically, and symbolically. Jesse Stuart worded it eloquently in "Kentucky Is My Land":

Kentucky is neither southern, northern, eastern or western,
It is the core of America.
If these United States can be called a body,
Kentucky can be called its heart.

My Kentucky journey continued in high school and college, where I read stories and poems by such vintage Kentucky writers as James Lane Allen, John Fox Jr., Janice Holt Giles, Harriette Simpson Arnow, Robert Penn Warren, James Still, and Elizabeth Madox Roberts. It was not, however, until I was teaching in a small junior high school in south Alabama that my life was changed by reading a Kentucky book. I was a nineteen-year-old first-year English teacher and was becoming thoroughly discouraged by having to manage and teach my recalcitrant seventh- and eighth-grade scholars. One day after classes I moped into the school library and put my head on a reading table to rest. The librarian walked over and asked me if I was sick. "No, ma'am," I said. "I just think I have failed as a teacher." She smiled at me and said, "Honey, you're too young to be a failure at anything. Wait a minute. I've got something for you." I expected her to return with an aspirin. Instead, she came back with a book in her hand. "Here," she said. "Read this book. It will make you feel better." Indeed, it did. After the first page I was hooked and spent the rest of the day and evening reading *The Thread That Runs So True,* Jesse Stuart's inspiring account of his experiences taming and teaching a schoolhouse full of rough country pupils in Greenup County, Kentucky, in the late 1920s.

Some ten years after that day, when he came to lecture at the University of Florida, where I was teaching, I was able to tell Stuart in person that he had saved my career. At that time I could not know that within a year I would be moving north and spending most of my life and career in Kentucky. Neither did I dream that I would get to know Jesse Stuart and dozens of other Kentucky writers personally as well as professionally—or that I would be bringing them together in this book.

What qualifies a writer to be a part of this anthology? Who is a Kentucky writer? Does any writer born in the state qualify? When someone asked Robert Penn Warren to define a Southern writer, he responded that "the work will tell us all we need to know." Wendell Berry once defined Kentucky writing as "local life aware of itself." My definition is broad and applies mainly to creative works, whether fiction or nonfiction: A Kentucky writer is one who was born in Kentucky or has lived in the state long enough to relate intimately to the Kentucky land, heritage, or history and whose writing in obvious or subtle ways reflects this relationship. This does not mean, of course, that a "Kentucky" piece of writing has to be about Kentucky, only that in some way, usually intangible, the writing has been affected by the author's having lived in the state—whether he or she is a native or not. These definitions, however, do not apply to such perceptive travelers to Kentucky as Charles Dickens and Alexis de Tocqueville, whose outside experiences and impressions are also valid.

Writers who are born in Kentucky naturally have a head start on outlanders who move in. A writer's earliest experiences are usually the most important. In a story by Elizabeth Madox Roberts, "On the Mountainside," this point is made vividly by an old native mountaineer who is going home, at last, after many years lived in the flatlands. He meets a young mountain boy going the other way and says:

The places you knowed when you was a little shirt-tail boy won't go outen your head or outen your recollections. . . . Your insides is made that way, and you'll find it so. Your dreams of a night and all you pine to see will go back. You won't get shed so easy of hit. You won't get shed. . . . You may go far, but mark me as I say it, the places ye knowed when you was a little tad will be the strongest in your remembrance. It's true, whoever you are and whatever land you come from. Your whole insides is made outen what you done first.

I do not mean to suggest that a longtime resident, such as Jim Wayne Miller, could not write a convincing poem about Kentucky because he was not a native—in fact, he wrote many good poems about Kentucky—but I think that his instinctive inclination was to think first of words, images, and experiences from his boyhood in North Carolina.

Most of the writers assembled in this collection had the good fortune to be born in this state. Some of them proudly trace their Kentucky roots back five, six, even seven generations. Like Daniel Boone, however, Sena Jeter Naslund, James Still, Janice Holt Giles, and even Annie Fellows Johnston, author of *The Little Colonel* books, and many other Kentucky writers, including me, were not born here. One might say that we are Kentuckians by choice. We were fortunate to have moved to Kentucky and spent large portions of our lives and careers in this wondrous, richly cultured, hospitable state. Perhaps our status as naturalized citizens of this commonwealth, moreover, has given us a special perspective and lent us a stranger's objectivity as we enjoy and exploit the incredible literary and historical riches of this first offspring of the American West.

Kentuckians, whether native-born or naturalized, are fiercely proud of where they live. Indeed, it is an American trait that Kentuckians celebrate with great passion in prose and poetry. We are all proud of our homeland— from nation to state to county to city to neighborhood—and as a nation have fought to protect it in numerous ways and wars. Even when the country seemed to be splitting in half with civil war in the 1860s, both sides argued that they were fighting for their country. Needless to say, the American Indians, although their definition of land and ownership differed from their invaders', fought bravely to keep their land unencumbered, the way it had always been. For most of the newcomers from Europe, however, the love of homeland was a literal love of home land—the deep thirst to own the place where they lived, be it a home or land or both. It was the kind of home ownership that immigrant Americans had usually been denied in their native countries. In our brash new world, people at last had at least a fighting chance actually to own a piece of this earth. For the common people, it was truly something new under the sun; for Kentuckians it became a passion.

Nowhere has the love of land and place been more pronounced than in this "great meadow," this "new Eden" carved out of the virgin wilderness. For more than two hundred years Kentuckians have cherished, criticized, fought for, and litigated over their homeland in deeds and in words. "Dark and Bloody Ground" is an epithet well suited to this state. From Daniel Boone's loving descriptions of the new land to James H. Mulligan's praise poem, "In Kentucky," Lee Pennington's "Of Earth," Patricia Ramsey's lament, "Harlan County Cat," and Jane Gentry's anticipation of spring, "A Garden in Kentucky," the care and love for this Kentucky homeland is a leitmotif that runs through our literature. A reviewer of Chris Offutt's *Out of the Woods* in the *New York Times Book Review* calls his collection of stories "a lean and brilliant examination of romantic obsession." The reviewer then adds, "But the love object isn't a girl; it's the state of Kentucky."

Alas, as Offutt himself can attest, we often flee the thing we love; and for generations Kentuckians have been running away from home to seek fame and fortune and freedom elsewhere—then returning in fact or, at least, in their fiction. James Lane Allen, who first put Kentucky on the national literary map in the 1880s with his Kentucky-based local-color stories, set the pattern when he spent the final thirty-two years of his life in New York. Harriette Simpson Arnow and Robert Penn Warren spent most of their lives outside their native state, Arnow in Michigan and Warren in Louisiana, Minnesota, and Connecticut; but when they sat down to write fiction or poetry they came home to Kentucky for their subjects, characters, and themes. Bobbie Ann Mason hit the road for New York soon after graduating from the University of Kentucky in 1962; but when she began writing fiction, she located her stories in Mayfield and western Kentucky, the very places she had left. Indeed, Kentucky's history and heritage make rich grist for the writer's mill.

Kentuckians love their state, but contemporary writers, especially, do not overlook its faults: they write about them freely in their poems, stories, and essays. The dark side of the American Dream is very much present in Kentucky's history and lore. Kentucky's role in the dispossession of the American Indians and the abuse of minorities is a popular subject. When Kentucky became a state in 1792, women and all minorities were, in varying degrees, denied their full human rights. The landowning white male was king. This anthology reflects the gradual democratizing of Kentucky life, from the shame revealed in antebellum slave narratives to the glowing rainbow of fresh and vibrant voices that today celebrate our differences and our similarities.

I have tried to select complete works, but often space limitations have forced me to use excerpts from longer works, especially fiction. I have, however, provided context for these. Each selection is included because it is a worthwhile example of the writer's work. My introductions are designed to orient you to each selection. The 179 writers who are included in this anthology are represented by selections ranging from a few lines of poetry to more than a dozen pages of fiction. Although such internationally known authors as Robert Penn Warren, Barbara Kingsolver, Wendell Berry, Sue Grafton, Bobbie Ann Mason, James Still, and Guy Davenport are represented with multiple pages from their works, there is no correlation between the length of a selection and its author's critical reputation or popularity.

These selections have another objective: they were chosen to tantalize you to read additional works by the writers in this book as well as other Kentucky writers who are worthy of your time and patronage. Let us consider this collection but the first course for a banquet of delights that Kentucky's writers have waiting for you in libraries and bookstores.

Many of these authors you already know. I used to say that Jesse Stuart was so well known and popular throughout Kentucky that he could sell his books to illiterates. Some of these writers, however, will be new to you. All of them are worth knowing and reading. The biographical appendix at the back of this book gives their vital statistics and lists a couple of their representative works. If you do not find your favorite author included, please keep in mind that this collection is not exhaustive. There are many other good writers whose works you may want to become acquainted with, and I mention a number of them in the pages that follow.

In "There Is No Frigate Like a Book," Emily Dickinson likens reading a book to taking a voyage. When you open a book, you embark upon a trip that will take you wherever the author's words carry you. The trip awaiting you in this book is navigated by many authors. These guides I now call into service as we embark together through the thickets and prairies, the smooth waters and the rapids, the barrens and the bluegrass of our Kentucky journey. The route is easy, for I have arranged the selections generally in chronological order. By the end, you will know Kentucky and its people better. And, more important, you'll know yourself better and recognize the humanity that is common to us all.

When Kentucky
Was Wilderness
The Early Years

In the mid-eighteenth century, to the west, beyond the English colonies that bordered the Atlantic Ocean and were struggling to become independent, lay a vast, uncharted wilderness of great promise and wealth. Although this land was declared off limits to His Majesty George III's subjects by the Proclamation of 1763, many hunters, adventurers, land speculators, and land-hungry settlers—especially from Pennsylvania, Virginia, and North Carolina—ignored the king's edict and began trekking over the Allegheny Mountains into the new territory that some people, despite the hardships and dangers that awaited them, had dubbed the New Eden. The country was simply too alluring to resist.

It is appropriate, therefore, that we start our journey with those intrepid adventurers who defied wild animals, hostile terrain, alarmed Indians, the indifferent elements, even their own human reason and limitations, and ventured forth by foot, horse and wagon, and boat to claim a share of this wondrous place already being called Kentucky.

From George Rogers Clark and his secret mission during the American Revolution to dismantle the British posts in the Illinois country to John James Audubon, the bird-obsessed painter and inept merchant, we read the words of the witnesses to this bold migration. In addition, through the words of one contemporary author and two latter-day fiction writers, we can relive those pioneer times in our imaginations. For more than two hundred years the early settlement of Kentucky has been a perennial subject for numerous fiction writers, poets, and playwrights, beginning with Gilbert Imlay's novel, *The Emigrant*. A generation later, Robert Montgomery Bird, a native of Delaware, sojourned in Kentucky in the 1830s and wrote a popular novel about the Western frontier. Bird's *Nick of the Woods, or The Jibbenainosay, A Tale of Kentucky,* published in London in 1837, tells of the incredible feats of a mythical giant or spirit who protects the white settlers from Indian attacks in 1782. Other novelists who have written of early Kentucky include Elizabeth Madox Roberts, whose *The Great Meadow* (1930) is perhaps the best novel about the migration into Kentucky. Gene Markey, a novelist, screenwriter, and producer, was born in Michigan but became a Kentuckian after 1952, when he married Lucille Parker Wright, the owner of Calumet Farm. *The Far Paradise* (1960) tells of the trials and triumphs of a wealthy Virginia family who, with their servants, furniture, and livestock, move en masse down the Ohio River to Kentucky in 1794 and settle in Lexington. Two novels that tell the epic story of the pioneer family of Roman and Kitty Gentry are Betty Layman Receveur's *Oh, Kentucky!* (1990) and *Kentucky Home* (1995). A seventh-generation Kentuckian, Receveur once said of Kitty Gentry, "She is all my ancestors." Last but hardly least are Robert Emmett McDowell and Jude Deveraux. All these writers open vivid windows on this howling and croaking but exhilarating land.

John Filson

from *The Discovery, Settlement, and Present State of Kentucke*

It is appropriate that we start with a real man who became a myth. No man's name says Kentucky and the early American West better than that of Daniel Boone, a native of Pennsylvania and onetime resident of North Carolina who, as he tells us in the "auto-biography" written for him by Kentucky's first historian, John Filson, came to Kentucky in 1769 with a band of friends to hunt and explore. Filson's description of the new country begins after an introductory paragraph from Boone's autobiography.

It was on the 1st of May, in the year 1769, that I resigned my domestic happiness for a time, and left my family and peaceable habitation on the Yadkin river, in North Carolina, to wander through the wilderness of America, in quest of the country of Kentucke, in company with John Finley, John Stewart, Joseph Holden, James Monay, and William Cool. We proceeded successfully; and after a long and fatiguing journey, through a mountainous wilderness, in a westward direction, on the seventh day of June following we found ourselves on Red river, where John Finley had formerly been trading with the Indians, and, from the top of an eminence, saw with pleasure the beautiful level of Kentucke. Here let me observe, that for some time we had experienced the most uncomfortable weather as a prelibation of our future sufferings. At this place we encamped, and made a shelter to defend us from the inclement season, and began to hunt and reconnoiter the country. We found everywhere abundance of wild beasts of all sorts, through this vast forest. The buffaloe were more frequent than I have seen cattle in the settlements, browzing on the leaves of the cane, or cropping the herbage on those extensive plains, fearless, because ignorant, of the violence of man. Sometimes we saw hundreds in a drove, and the numbers about the salt springs were amazing. In this forest, the habitation of beasts of every kind natural to America, we practiced hunting with great success, until the 22d day of December following. . . .

Among the native animals are the urus, bison, or zorax, described by Cesar, which we call a buffalo, much resembling a large bull, of a great size, with a large head, thick, short, crooked horns, and broader in his forepart than behind. Upon his shoulder is a large lump of flesh, covered with a thick boss of long wool and curly hair, of a dark brown color. They do not rise from the ground as our cattle, but spring up at once upon their feet; are of a broad make, and clumsy appearance, with short legs, but run fast, and turn not aside for any thing when chased, except a standing tree. They weigh from 500 to 1000 weight, are excellent meat, supplying the inhabitants in many parts with beef, and their hides make good leather. I have heard a hunter assert, he saw above 1000 buffaloes at the Blue Licks at once; so numerous were they before the first settlers had wantonly sported away their lives. There still remains a great number in the exterior parts of the settlement. They feed upon cane and grass, as other cattle, and are innocent, harmless creatures.

There are still to be found many deer, elks, and bears, within the settlement, and many more on the borders of it. There are also panthers, wild cats, and wolves.

The waters have plenty of beavers, otters, minks, and muskrats: nor are the animals common to other parts wanting, such as foxes, rabbits, squirrels, racoons, ground-hogs, pole-cats, and opossums. Most of the species of the domestic quadrupeds have been introduced since the settlement, such as horses, cows, sheep, and hogs, which are prodigiously multiplied, suffered to run in the woods without a keeper, and only brought home when wanted. . . .

This country is more temperate and healthy than the other settled parts of America. In summer it has not the sandy heats which Virginia and Carolina experience, and receives a fine air from its rivers. In winter, which at most lasts three months, commonly two, and is but seldom severe, the people are safe in bad houses; and the beasts have a goodly supply without fodder. The winter begins about Christmas, and ends about the first of March, at farthest does not exceed the middle of that month. Snow seldom falls deep or lies long. The west winds often bring storms, and the east winds clear the sky; but there is no steady rule of weather in that respect, as in the northern states. The west winds are sometimes cold and nitrous. The Ohio running in that direction, and there being mountains on that quarter, the westerly winds, by sweeping along their tops, in the cold regions of the air, and over a long tract of frozen water, collect cold in their course, and convey it over the Kentucke country; but the weather is not so intensely severe as these winds bring with them in Pennsylvania. The air and seasons depend very much on the winds, as to heat and cold, dryness and moisture.

Colonel James Smith

from *An Account of the Remarkable Occurrences in the Life and Travels of Col. James Smith*

Colonel James Smith, a native of Pennsylvania, in May 1755 went with a party of three hundred men to cut a wagon road from Fort Loudon to Braddock's Road, near the present-day town of Connellsville in Fayette County, Pennsylvania. His capture by the Canasatauga and Delaware Indians, his travels and uncertain life with them, and his eventual escape are true-life adventures that still have the power to freeze the blood. Afterward, Smith settled in Bourbon County, Kentucky, and in 1799 published a book about his harrowing experiences.

In May 1755, the province of Pennsylvania, agreed to send out three hundred men, in order to cut a waggon road from Fort Loudon, to join Braddock's road, near the Turkey Foot, or three forks of Yohogania. My brother-in-law, William Smith esq. of Conococheague, was appointed commissioner, to have the oversight of these road-cutters.

Though I was at that time only eighteen years of age, I had fallen violently in love with a young lady, whom I apprehended was possessed of a large share of both beauty and virtue;—but being born between Venus and Mars, I concluded I must also leave my dear fair one, and go out with this company of road-cutters, to see the event of this campaign; but still expecting that some time in the course of this summer, I should again return to the arms of my beloved.

We went on with the road, without interruption, until near the Allegheny Mountain; when I was sent back, in order to hurry up some provisions waggons that were on the way after us; I proceeded down the road as far as the crossings of Juniata, where, finding the waggons were coming on as fast as possible, I returned up the road again towards the Allegheny Mountain, in company with one Arnold Vigoras. About four or five miles above Bedford, three Indians had made a blind of bushes, stuck in the ground, as though they grew naturally, where they concealed themselves, about fifteen yards from the road. When we came opposite to them, they fired upon us, at this short distance, and killed my fellow traveller, yet their bullets did not touch me; but my horse making a violent start, threw me, and the Indians immediately ran up, and took me prisoner. The one that laid hold on me was a Canasatauga, the other two were Delawares. One of them could speak English, and asked me if there were any more white men coming after? I told them, not any near, that I knew of. Two of these Indians stood by me, whilst the other scalped my comrade: they then set off and ran at a smart rate, through the woods, for about fifteen miles, and that night we slept on the Allegheny Mountain, without fire.

The next morning they divided the last of their provision which they had brought from Fort DuQuesne, and gave me an equal share, which was about two or three ounces of mouldy biscuit—this and a young Ground-Hog, about as large as a Rabbit, roasted, and also equally divided, was all the provision we had until we came to the Loyal-Hannan, which was about fifty miles; and a great part of the way we came through exceeding rocky Laurel-thickets, without any path. When we came to the West side of Laurel-Hill, they gave the scalp halloo, as usual, which is a long yell or halloo, for every scalp or prisoner they have in possession; the last of these scalp halloos were followed with quick and sudden shrill shouts of joy and triumph. On their performing this, we were answered by the firing of a number of guns on the Loyal-Hannan, one after another, quicker than one could count, by another party of Indians, who were encamped near where Ligoneer now stands. As we advanced near this party, they increased with repeated shouts of joy and triumph; but I did not share with them in their excessive mirth. When we came to this camp, we found they had plenty of Turkeys and other meat, there; and though I never before eat venison without bread or salt, yet as I was hungry, it relished very well. There we lay that night, and the next morning the whole of us marched on our way for Fort DuQuesne. The night after we joined another camp of Indians, with nearly the same ceremony, attended with great noise, and apparent joy, among all, except one. The next morning we continued our march, and in the afternoon we came in full view of the fort, which stood on the point, near where Fort Pitt now stands. We then made a halt on the bank of the Allegheny, and repeated the scalp halloo, which was answered by the firing of all the firelocks in the hands of both Indians and French who were in and about the fort, in the aforesaid manner, and also the great guns, which were followed by the continued shouts and yells of the different savage tribes who were then collected there.

As I was at this time unacquainted with this mode of firing and yelling of the savages, I concluded that there were thousands of Indians there, ready to receive General Braddock; but what added to my surprize, I saw numbers running towards me, stripped naked, excepting breech-clouts, and painted in the most hideous manner, of various colours, though the principal color was vermillion, or a bright red; yet there was annexed to this, black, brown, blue, &c. As they approached, they formed themselves into two long ranks, about two or three rods apart. I was told by an Indian that could speak English, that I must run betwixt these ranks, and that they would flog me all the way, as I ran, and if I ran quick, it would be so much the better, as they would quit when I got to the end of the ranks. There appeared to be a general rejoicing around me, yet, I could find nothing like joy in my breast; but I started to the race with all the resolution and vigor I was capable of exerting, and found that it was as I had been told, for I was flogged the whole way. When I had got near the end of the lines, I was struck with something that appeared to me to be a stick, or the handle of a tommahawk, which caused me to fall to the ground. On my recovering my senses, I endeavored to renew my race: but as I arose, some one cast sand in my eyes, which blinded me so, that I could not see where to run. They continued beating me most intolerably, until I was at length insensible; but before I lost my senses, I remember my wishing them to strike the fatal blow, for I thought they intended killing me, but apprehended they were too long about it.

The first thing I remember was my being in the fort, amidst the French and Indians, and a French doctor standing by me, who had opened a vein in my left arm: after which, the interpreter asked me how I did, I told him I felt much pain; the doctor then washed my wounds, and the bruised places of my body, with French brandy. As I felt faint, and the brandy smelt well, I asked for some inwardly, but the doctor told me, by the interpreter, that it did not suit my case.

When they found I could speak, a number of Indians came around me, and examined me, with threats of cruel death, if I did not tell the truth. The first question they asked me, was, how many men were there in the party that were coming from Pennsylvania, to join Braddock? I told them the truth, that there were three hundred. The next question was, were they well armed? I told them they were all well armed, (meaning the arm of flesh) for they had only about thirty guns among the whole of them; which, if the Indians had known, they would certainly have gone and cut them all off; therefore, I could not in conscience let them know the defenceless situation of these road-cutters. I was then sent to the hospital, and carefully attended by the doctors, and recovered quicker than what I expected.

Some time after I was there, I was visited by the Delaware Indian already mentioned, who was at the taking of me, and could speak some English. Though he spoke but bad English, yet I found him to be a man of considerable understanding. I asked him if I had done any thing that had offended the Indians, which caused them to treat me so unmercifully? He said no, it was only an old custom the Indians had, and it was like how do you do; after that he said I would be well used. I asked him if I should be admitted to remain with the French? He said no—and told me that as soon as I recovered, I must not only go with the Indians, but must be made an Indian myself. I asked him what news from Braddock's army? He said the Indians spied them every day, and he showed me by making marks on the ground with a stick, that Braddock's army was advancing in very close order, and that the Indians would surround them, take trees, and (as he expressed it) *shoot um down all one pigeon.*

Shortly after this, on the 9th day of July 1755, in the morning I heard a great stir in the fort. As I could then walk with a staff in my hand, I went out of the door which was just by the wall of the fort, and stood upon the wall and viewed the Indians in a huddle before the gate, where were the barrels of powder, bullets, flints &c. and every one taking what suited; I saw the Indians also march off in rank, intire—likewise the French Canadians, and some regulars. After viewing the Indians and French in different positions, I computed them to be about four hundred, and wondered that they attempted to go out against Braddock with so small a party. I was then in high hopes that I would soon see them fly before the British troops, and that General Braddock would take the fort and rescue me.

I remained anxious to know the event of this day; and in the afternoon I again observed a great noise and commotion in the fort, and though at that time I could not understand French, yet I found that it was the voice of Joy and triumph, and feared that they had received what I called bad news.

I had observed some of the old country soldiers speak Dutch, as I spoke Dutch I went to one of them, and asked him, what was the news? he told me that a runner had just arrived, who said that Braddock would certainly be defeated; that the Indians and French had surrounded him, and were concealed behind trees and in gullies, and kept a constant fire upon the English, and that they saw the English falling in heaps, and if they did not take the river which was the only gap, and make their escape, there would not be one man left alive before sun down. Some time after this I heard a number of scalp halloo's and saw a company of Indians and French coming in. I observed they had a great many bloody scalps, grenadiers' caps, British canteens, bayonets &c. with them. They brought the news that Braddock was defeated. After that, another company came in, which appeared to be about one hundred, and chiefly Indians, and it seemed to me that almost every one of this company was carrying scalps; after this came another company with a number of waggon-horses, and also a great many scalps. Those that were coming in, and those that had arrived, kept a constant firing of small arms, and also the great guns in the fort, which were accompanied with the most hedious shouts and yells from all quarters; so that it appeared to me as if the infernal regions had broke loose.

About sun down I beheld a small party coming in with about a dozen prisoners, stripped naked, with their hands tied behind their backs, and their faces and part of their bodies blacked—these prisoners they burned to death on the bank of Allegheny River opposite to the fort. I stood on the fort wall until I beheld them begin to burn one of these men, they had him tied to a stake, and kept touching him with fire-brands, red-hot irons &c. and he screeming in a most doleful manner,—the Indians in the mean time yelling like infernal spirits. As this scene appeared too shocking for me to behold, I retired to my lodgings both sore and sorry. . . .

A few days after this the Indians demanded me and I was obliged to go with them. I was not yet well able to march, but they took me in a canoe, up the Allegheny River to an Indian town that was on the north side of the river, about forty miles above Fort DuQuesne. Here I remained about three weeks, and was then taken to an Indian town on the west branch of Muskingum, about twenty miles above the forks, which was called Tullihas, inhabited by Delawares, Caughnewagos and Mohicans.—On our rout betwixt the aforesaid towns, the country was chiefly black-oak and white-oak land, which appeared generally to be good wheat land, chiefly second and third rate, intermixed with some rich bottoms.

The day after my arrival at the aforesaid town, a number of Indians collected about me, and one of them began to pull the hair out of my head. He had some ashes on a piece of bark, in which he frequently dipped his fingers in order to take the firmer hold, and so he went on, as if he had been plucking a turkey, until he had all the hair clean out of my head, except a small spot about three or four inches square on my crown; this they cut off with a pair of scissors, excepting three locks, which they dressed up in their own mode. Two of these they wraped round with a narrow beaded garter made by themselves for that purpose, and the other they platted at full length, and then stuck it full of silver broches. After this they bored my nose and ears, and fixed me off with ear rings and nose jewels, then they ordered me to strip off my clothes and put on a breech-clout, which I did; they then painted my head, face and body in various colours. They put a large belt of wampom on my neck, and silver bands on my hands and right arm; and so an old chief led me out in the street and gave the alarm halloo, *coo-wigh,* several times repeated quick, and on this all that were in the town came running and stood round the old chief, who held me by the hand in the midst.—As I at that time knew nothing of their mode of adoption, and had seen them put to death all they had taken, and as I never could find that they saved a man alive at Braddock's defeat, I made no doubt but they were about putting me to death in some cruel manner. The old chief holding me by the hand, made a long speech very loud, and when he had done he handed me to three young squaws, who led me by the hand down the bank into the river until the water was up to our middle. The squaws then made signs to me to plunge myself into the water, but I did not understand them; I thought that the result of the council was that I should be drowned, and that these young ladies were to be the executioners. They all three laid violent hold of me, and I for some time opposed them with all my might, which occasioned loud laughter by the multitude that were on the bank of the river. At length one of the squaws made out to speak a little English (for I believe they began to be afraid of me) and said, *no hurt you*; on this I gave myself up to their ladyships, who were as good as their word; for though they plunged me under water, and washed and rubbed me severely, yet I could not say they hurt me much.

These young women then led me up to the council house, where some of the tribe were ready with new cloths for me. They gave me a new ruffled shirt, which I put on, also a pair of leggins done off with ribbons and beads, likewise a pair of mockasons, and garters dressed with beads, Porcupine-quills, and redhair—also a tinsel laced cappo. They again painted my head and face with various colors, and tied a bunch of red feathers to one of these locks they had left on the crown of my head, which stood up five or six inches. They seated me on a bear skin, and gave me a pipe, tomahawk, and polecat skin pouch, which had been skinned pocket fashion, and contained tobacco, killegenico, or dry sumach leaves, which they mix with their tobacco,—also spunk, flint and steel. When I was thus seated, the Indians came in dressed and painted in their grandest manner. As they came in they took their seats and for a considerable time there was a profound silence, every one was smoking,—but not a word was spoken among them.—At length one of the chiefs made a speech, which was delivered to me by an interpreter,—and was as followeth:—"My son, you are now flesh of our flesh, and bone of our bone. By the ceremony which was performed this day, every drop of white blood was washed out of your veins; you are taken into the Caughnewago nation, and initiated into a warlike tribe; you are adopted into a great family, and now received with great seriousness and solemnity in the room and place of a great man; after what has passed this day, you are now one of us by an old strong law and custom—My son, you have now nothing to fear, we are now under the same obligations to love, support and defend you, that we are to love and to defend one another, therefore you are to consider yourself as one of our people."—At this time I did not believe this fine speech, especially that of the white blood being washed out of me; but since that time I have found that there was much sincerity in said speech,— for, from that day I never knew them to make any distinction between me and themselves in any respect whatever until I left them.—If they had plenty of cloathing I had plenty, if we were scarce we all shared one fate.

After this ceremony was over, I was introduced to my new kin, and told that I was to attend a feast that evening, which I did. And as the custom was, they gave me also a bowl and wooden spoon, which I carried with me to the place, where there was a number of large brass kettles full of boiled venison and green corn; every one advanced with his bowl and spoon and had his share given him.—After this, one of the chiefs made a short speech, and then we began to eat.

The name of one of the chiefs in this town was Tecanyaterighto, alias Pluggy, and the other Asallecoa, alias Mohawk Solomon.—As Pluggy and his party were to start the next day to war, to the frontiers of Virginia, the next thing to be performed was the war dance, and their war songs. At their war dance they had both vocal and instrumental music. They had a short hollow gum closed in one end, with water in it, and parchment stretched over the open end thereof, which they beat with one stick, and made a sound nearly like a muffled drum,—all those who were going on this expedition collected together and formed. An old Indian then began to sing, and timed the music by beating on this drum, as the ancients formerly timed their music by beating the tabor. On this the warriors began to advance, or move forward in concert, like well disciplined troops would march to the fife and drum. Each warrior had a tomahawk, spear or warmallet in his hand, and they all moved regularly towards the east, or the way they intended to go to war. At length they all stretched their tomahawks towards the Potomack, and giving a hideous shout or yell, they wheeled quick about, and danced in the same manner back. The next was the war song. In performing this, only one sung at a time, in a moving posture, with a tomahawk in his hand, while all the other wariors were engaged in calling aloud *he-uh, he-uh*, which they constantly repeated, while the war song was going on. When the warior that was singing had ended his song, he struck a war-post with his toma-hawk, and with a loud voice told what warlike exploits he had done, and what he now intended to do: which were answered by the other warriors with loud shouts of applause. Some who had not before intended to go to war, at this time were so animated by this performance, that they took up the tomahawk and sung the war song which was answered with shouts of joy, as they were then initiated into the present marching company. The next morning this company all collected at one place, with their heads and faces painted with various colors, and packs upon their backs: they marched off, all silent, except the commander, who, in the front, sung the travelling song, which began in this manner: *hoo caugh-tainte heegana.* Just as the rear passed the end of the town, they began to fire in their slow manner, from the front to the rear, which was accompanied with shouts and yells from all quarters.

This evening I was invited to another sort of dance, which was a kind of promiscuos dance. The young men stood in one rank, and the young women in another, about one rod apart, facing each other. The one that raised the tune, or started the song, held a small gourd or dry shell of a squash, in his hand, which contained beads or small stones, which rattled. When he began to sing, he timed the tune with his rattle; both men and women danced and sung together, advancing towards each other, stooping until their heads would be touching together, and then ceased from dancing, with loud shouts, and retreated and formed again, and so repeated the same thing over and over, for three or four hours, without intermission. This exercise appeared to me at first, irrational and insipid; but I found that in singing their tunes, they used *ya ne no hoo wa ne*, &c. like our *fa sol la*, and though they have no such thing as jingling verse, yet they can intermix sentences with their notes, and say what they please to each other, and carry on the tune in concert. I found that this was a kind of wooing or courting dance, and as they advanced stooping with their heads together, they could say what they pleased in each others ear, without disconcerting their rough music, and the others, or those near, not hear what they say. . . .

Tontileaugo left us a little before Christmas, and from that until some time in February, we had always plenty of bear meat, venison, &c. During this time I killed much more than we could use, but having no horses to carry in what I killed, I left part of it in the woods. In February there came a snow, with a crust, which made a great noise when walking on it, and frightened away the deer; and as bear and beaver were scarce here, we got entirely out of provision. After I had hunted two days without eating any thing, and had very short allowance for some days before, I returned late in the evening faint and weary. When I came into our hut, Tecaughretanego asked what success? I told him not any. He asked me if I was not very hungry? I replied that the keen appetite seemed to be in some measure removed, but I was both faint and weary. He commanded Nunganey his little son, to bring me something to eat, and he brought me a kettle with some bones and broth,—after eating a few mouthfuls, my appetite violently returned, and I thought the victuals had a most agreable relish, though it was only fox and wild-cat bones, which lay about the camp, which the ravens and turkey-buzzards had picked—these Nunganey had collected and boiled, until the sinews that remained on the bones would strip off. I speedily finished my allowance, such as it was, and when I had ended my sweet repast, Tecaughretanego asked me how I felt? I told him that I was much refreshed. He then handed me his pipe and pouch, and told me to take a smoke. I did so. He then said he had something of importance to tell me, if I was now composed and ready to hear it. I told him that I was ready to hear him. He said the reason why he deferred his speech till now, was because few men are in a right humor to hear good talk, when they are extremely hungry, as they are then generally fretful and discomposed; but as you appear now to enjoy calmness and serenity of mind, I will now communicate to you the thoughts of my heart, and those things that I know to be true.

"*Brother,*

"As you have lived with the white people, you have not had the same advantage of knowing that the great being above feeds his people, and gives them their meat in due season, as we Indians have, who are frequently out of provisions, and yet are wonderfully supplied, and that so frequently that it is evidently the hand of the great Owaneeyo that doth this: whereas the white people have commonly large stocks of tame cattle, that they can kill when they please, and also their barns and cribs filled with grain, and therefore have not the same opportunity of seeing and knowing that they are supported by the ruler of Heaven and Earth.

"*Brother,*

"I know that you are now afraid that we will all perish with hunger, but you have no just reason to fear this.

"*Brother,*

"I have been young, but am now old—I have been frequently under the like circumstances that we now are, and that some time or other in almost every year of my life; yet, I have hitherto been supported, and my wants supplied in time of need.

"*Brother,*

"Owaneeyo sometimes suffers us to be in want, in order to teach us our dependance upon him, and to let us know that we are to love and serve him: and likewise to know the worth of the favors that we receive, and to make us more thankful.

"*Brother,*

"Be assured that you will be supplied with food, and that just in the right time; but you must continue diligent in the use of means—go to sleep, and rise early in the morning and go a hunting—be strong and exert yourself like a man, and the great spirit will direct your way."

The next morning I went out, and steered about an east course. I proceeded on slowly for about five miles, and saw deer frequently, but as the crust on the snow made a great noise, they were always running before I spied them, so that I could not get a shoot. A violent appetite returned, and I became intolerably hungry;—it was now that I concluded I would run off to Pennsylvania, my native country. As the snow was on the ground, the Indian hunters almost the whole of the way before me, I had but a poor prospect of making my escape, but my case appeared desperate. If I staid here I thought I would perish with hunger, and if I met with Indians, they could but kill me.

I then proceeded on as fast as I could walk, and when I got about ten or twelve miles from our hut, I came upon fresh buffaloe tracks,—I pursued after, and in a short time came in sight of them, as they were passing through a small glade—I ran with all my might, and headed them, where I lay in ambush, and killed a very large cow. I immediately kindled a fire and began to roast meat, but could not wait till it was done—I ate it almost raw. When hunger was abated I began to be tenderly concerned for my old Indian brother, and the little boy I had left in a perishing condition. I made haste and packed up what meat I could carry, secured what I left from the wolves, and returned homewards.

I scarcely thought on the old man's speech while I was almost distracted with hunger, but on my return was much affected with it, reflected on myself for my hard-heartedness and ingratitude, in attempting to run off and leave the venerable old man and little boy to perish with hunger. I also considered how remarkably the old man's speech had been verified in our providentially obtaining a supply. I thought also of that part of his speech which treated of the fractious dispositions of hungry people, which was the only excuse I had for my base inhumanity, in attempting to leave them in the most deplorable situation.

As it was moon-light, I got home to our hut, and found the old man in his usual good humor. He thanked me for my exertion, and bid me sit down, as I must certainly be fatigued, and he commanded Nunganey to make haste and cook. I told him I would cook for him, and let the boy lay some meat on the coals, for himself—which he did, but ate it almost raw, as I had done. I immediately hung on the kettle with some water and cut the beef in thin slices, and put them in:—when it had boiled awhile, I proposed taking it off the fire, but the old man replied, "let it be done enough." This he said in as patient and unconcerned a manner, as if he had not wanted one single meal. He commanded Nunganey to eat no more beef at that time, least he might hurt himself; but told him to sit down, and after some time he might sup some broth—this command he reluctantly obeyed.

When we were all refreshed, Tecaughretanego delivered a speech upon the necessity and pleasure of receiving the necessary supports of life with thankfulness, knowing that Owaneeyo is the great giver. Such speeches from an Indian, may be tho't by those who are unacquainted with them, altogether incredible; but when we reflect on the Indian war, we may readily conclude that they are not an ignorant or stupid sort of people; or they would not have been such fatal enemies. When they came into our country they outwitted us—and when we sent armies into their country, they outgeneralled, and beat us with inferior force. Let us also take into consideration that Tecaughretanego was no common person, but was among the Indians, as Socrates in the ancient Heathen world; and it may be, equal to him—if not in wisdom and in learning, yet, perhaps, in patience and fortitude.

George Rogers Clark

Letter from Patrick Henry

George Rogers Clark, the founder of Louisville on Corn Island at the Falls of the Ohio in 1778, was a soldier who was directed by Virginia's Governor Patrick Henry to attack the British forts at Kaskaskia, Vincennes, and Detroit to eliminate the British presence in lands that would be claimed, should the American Revolution prove successful, by the new independent nation. Clark's expedition was spectacularly successful—and so was the Revolution. In 1781 he was made a brigadier general by Governor Thomas Jefferson and established Fort Nelson at the Falls. He spent most of the rest of his life in the Louisville area and died in 1818. The first document relating to General Clark's early career in Kentucky is the orders from Governor Henry, dated January 2, 1778, to undertake the expedition to the British outposts.

✑

VIRGINIA SCт.

In Council, Wmsbug, Jan. 2, 1778.

LIEUT. COLONEL GEORGE ROGERS CLARK:

You are to proceed with all convenient Speed to raise Seven Companies of Soldiers to consist of fifty men each officered in the usual manner & armed most properly for the Enterprise, & with this Force attack the British post at Kaskasky.

It is conjectured that there are many pieces of Cannon & military Stores to considerable amount at that place, the taking & preservation of which would be a valuable acquisition to the State. If you are so fortunate therefore as to succeed in your Expectation, you will take every possible Measure to secure the artillery & stores & whatever may advantage the State.

For the Transportation of the Troops, provisions &c., down the Ohio, you are to apply to the Commanding Officer at Fort Pitt for Boats, &c. during the whole Transaction you are to take especial Care to keep the true Destination of your Force secret. Its success depends upon this. Orders are therefore given to Capt[n] Smith to secure the two men from Kaskasky. Similar conduct will be proper in similar cases.

It is earnestly desired that you show Humanity to such British Subjects and other persons as fall in your hands. If the white Inhabitants at the post

& the neighbourhood will give undoubted Evidence of their attachment to this State (for it is certain they live within its Limits) by taking the Test prescribed by Law and by every other way & means in their power, Let them be treated as fellow Citizens & their persons & property duly secured. Assistance & protection against all Enemies whatever shall be afforded them, & the commonwealth of Virginia is pledged to accomplish it. But if these people will not accede to these reasonable Demands, they must feel the Miseries of War, under the direction of that Humanity that has hitherto distinguished Americans, & which it is expected you will ever consider as the Rule of your Conduct, & from which you are in no Instance to depart.

The Corps you are to command are to receive the pay & allowance of Militia & to act under the Laws & Regulations of this State now in Force as Militia. The Inhabitants at this Post will be informed by you that in Case they accede to the offers of becoming Citizens of this Commonwealth a proper Garrison will be maintained among them & every Attention bestowed to render their Commerce beneficial, the fairest prospects being opened to the Dominions of both France & Spain.

It is in Contemplation to establish a post near the Mouth of Ohio. Cannon will be wanted to fortify it. Part of those at Kaskasky will be easily brought thither or otherwise secured as circumstances will make necessary.

You are to apply to General Hand for powder & Lead necessary for this Expedition. If he can't supply it the person who has that which Capt Lynn bro^t from Orleans can. Lead was sent to Hampshire by my orders & that may be delivered you. Wishing you success, I am

Sir,

Your h'ble Serv.,

P. HENRY.

Letter from Clark to the Indians

This is Clark's explanation to the Indian tribes in the Detroit area near Lake Erie warning them not to support the British.

Nothing destroys Your Interest among the Savages so soon as wavering sentiments or speeches that shew the least fear. I consequently had observed one steady line of conduct among them: Mr. Hamilton, who was almost Deifyed among them being captured by me, it was a sufficient confirmation to the Indians of every thing I had formerly said to them and gave the greatest weight to the Speeches I intended to send them; expecting that I should shortly be able to fulfill my threats with a Body of Troops sufficient to penetrate into any part of their Country; and by Reducing Detroit bring them to my feet. I sent the following Speech to the different Tribes near the Lakes that was at war with us, to-wit:

To the Warriers of the different Nations.

Men and Warriers: it is a long time since the Big Knives sent Belts of peace among You Siliciting of You not to listen to the bad talks and deceit of the English as it would at some future day tend to the Destruction of Your Nations. You would not listen, but Joined the English against the Big Knives and spilt much Blood of Women & Children. The Big Knives then resolved to shew no mercy to any People that hereafter would refuse the Belt of Peace which should be offered, at the same time One of War. You remember last summer a great many People took me by the hand, but a few kept back their Hearts. I also sent Belts of Peace and War among the nations to take their choice, some took the Peace Belt, others still listned to their great father (as they call him) at Detroit, and Joined him to come to War against me. The Big Knives are Warriers and look on the English as old Women and all those that Join him and are ashamed when they fight them because they are no Men.

I now send two Belts to all the Nations, one for Peace and the other for War. The one that is for War has your great English fathers Scalp tied to it, and made red with his Blood; all You that call yourselves his Children, make your Hatchets sharp & come out and Revenge his Blood on the Big Knives, fight like Men that the Big Knives may not be ashamed when they fight you; that the old Women may not tell us that we only fought Squaws. If any of You is for taking the Belt of Peace, send the Bloody Belt back to me that I may know who to take by the hand as Brothers, for you may be Assured that no peace for the future will be granted to those that do not lay down their Arms immediately. Its as you will I dont care whether You are for Peace or War; as I Glory in War and want Enemies to fight us, as the English cant fight us any longer, and are become like Young Children begging the Big Knives for mercy and a little Bread to eat; this is the last Speech you may ever expect from the Big Knives, the next thing will be the Tomahawk. And You may expect in four Moons to see Your Women & Children given to the Dogs to eat, while those Nations that have kept their words with me will Flourish and grow like the Willow Trees on the River Banks under the care and nourishment of their father, the Big Knives.

Letter from Francis to Clark

The final document relating to Clark is the letter of concession to Clark from Francis, the son of Tobacco, grand chief of the regional tribes.

❦

By the TOBACOES SON, *Grand Chief of all the Peankeshaws Nations and of all the Tribes, Grand Dore to the Ouabache as ordered by the Master of Life, holding the Tomahawk in one hand and Peace in the other: Judging the Nations, giving entrance for those that are for Peace, and making them a clear road, &c.*

DECLARATION.

WHEREAS for many Years past, this once Peaceable Land hath been put in confusion by the English encouraging all People to Raise the Tommahawk Against the Big Knives, saying that they were a bad People, Rebellious, and ought to be put from under the Sun, and their names to be no more.

But as the Sky of our Councils was always Misty, and never Clear we still was at a loss to know what to do, hoping that the Master of Life would one Day or other make the Sky Clear and put us in the right Road. He taking Pitty on us sent a father among us (Col°. George Rogers Clark) that has cleared our eyes And made our Paths straight defending our Lands, &c., So that we now enjoy Peace from the Rising to the Setting of Sun; and the Nations even to the heads of the great River (meaning the Messicippi) are happy and will no more listen to Bad Birds; but abide by the Councils of their great father, A Chief of the Big Knives that is now among us.

AND whereas it is our desire that he should long remain among us, that we may take his Council and be happy, it also being our desire to give him Lands to reside on in our Country that we may at all times speak to him. After many Silicitations to him to make choice of a Tract, he chusing the Lands adjoining the falls of Ohio on the west side of said River.

I do hereby in the names of all the Great Chiefs and Warriers of the Ouabash and their Allies, Declare that so much Lands at the falls of Ohio contained in the following bounds, to-wit, Begining opposite the middle of the first Island below the falls, Bounded upwards by the west Bank of the River so far as to include two Leagues and half on a straight line from the begining, thence at right angles with said line two Leagues & half in Breadth, in all its Parts shall hereafter and ever be the sole property of our great father (Col°. Clark) with all things thereto belonging, either above or below the Earth shall be and is his; except a Road through said Land to his Door, which shall remain ours, and for us to walk on to speak to our father. All Nations from the Rising to the setting of the Sun, that are not in alliance with us are hereby warned to esteem the said gift as sacred and not to make that Land taste of Blood; that all People either at peace or War may repair in safety to get Council of our father. Whoever first darkens that Land shall no longer have a Name. This declaration shall forever be a Witness between all Nations and our Present G^r father; that the said Lands are forever hereafter his Property. In witness whereof I do in the name of all the Great Chiefs and Warriers of the Ouabash in open Council affix my mark and Seal done at St. Vincents this 16th day of June 1779.

(Signed) FRANCIS SON OF TOBACCO.

Thomas Perkins

"Letter from Kentucky"

A rare and choice travel narrative is the following letter written by an anonymous visitor to Kentucky describing his dangerous trip through the Cumberland Gap, one of the two main avenues into the new land (the other was the water route down the Ohio River). The preponderance of evidence suggests that the author of the letter was Thomas Perkins, a Massachusetts-born lawyer who moved to Danville in 1784 from Fredericksburg, Virginia. It is a delightful eyewitness narrative by a close observer and good writer. Published in the September 1785 issue of the *Boston Magazine,* it is prefaced by this note: "By Publishing the following Letter from a Gentleman in Kentucky to his Friend in this State [Massachusetts], you will oblige G.B."

❈

Danville, Kentucky, March 1st, 1785

Some time in December last I sent an account of my tour, for the amusement of my friends, to Fredericksburg in Virginia by the hand of Mr. B___; but have lately heard that the whole company in which Mr. B___was, were attacked by a party of Indians in crossing Clinch River, and the best accounts say they were all killed or taken prisoners.

As I presume the Cherokees will not be polite enough to forward your packet, I embrace this opportunity of conveying you the substance of it in a letter. I left Major M's family in Orange county on the 27th of September, and set off for Kentucky without the prospect of a single person to accompany me. Twice I had appointed to go with company. They failed of going. Therefore, fearing that another disappointment might prevent my going before spring, I resolved to risque the journey alone, knowing that, as this was the time of year in which the people move, it would hardly be possible but what I should fall in with company before I arrived at the Block house, which is the last settlement of consequence on the eastern side of the wilderness.

I crossed the blue ridge at a place called Rock Fish Gap. A man must be insensible not to be charmed with the beauties of that mountain, especially on the eastern side. I was five hours and an half ascending the mountain, which, in some places, is too steep to ride with safety. The soil of it is extremely fertile, and is delightfully watered by an almost infinite variety of rivulets which run down its side, falling in many places near fifty feet per-pendicular. The murmuring of these streams, the variety of fowls and birds, the prodigious herds of cattle and horses which graze on this mountain, the different kinds of wild fruit with which it abounds, and a thousand nameless beauties peculiar to such places, almost made me imagine myself on en-chanted ground. On the top of it is a large spring which breaks out from under a cliff of rocks, and affords many kinds of fish. This has given the passage over it in that place the name of Rock Fish Gap. The growth pecu-liar to the mountains is honey locust, paupau, chinquopins, black walnut and wild cherry: these are in common with such other trees and shrubs as are found usually on the mountains of New England. On the western side of the mountain the inhabitants appear altogether different from what they call the lowlanders, i.e., the people on the east side. They have but few slaves, are more industrious, and instead of raising tobacco, turn their whole attention to corn and grain. The county of Rockbridge, which is the first you go through after crossing the mountain, took its name from a natural stone bridge over one of the branches of James River, which is, perhaps, one of the greatest natural curiosities in Virginia. The bridge is about eighty feet long, and forty or fifty feet wide, and is supported by a well turned arch, from the top of which to the water, is two hundred and forty three feet. There is soil enough on the bridge to produce small trees and bushes, which grow so thick on its sides, that strangers often ride over the bridge without knowing it.

The next day after crossing the mountain I met a company from Ken-tucky, who confirmed the accounts I had before heard that the Indians were growing very troublesome in the wilderness: that the Cheekomangres, a tribe of the Cherokees, thought themselves neglected in the late treaty, and were therefore determined to do us all the mischief they could. They informed me that the week before, while they were in the wilderness, there were seventeen armed men in company with five women and three children on their way to Kentucky. They were attacked in the night by nine Indians, on which the men instantly fled, leaving the women and children a prey to the savages. If cowardice ever deserved the gibbet it was in this instance.

The tract of country which lies between the Blue Ridge and the Alliganey mountains is, I think, less fertile than any part of Virginia. Near the Alliganey it is settled chiefly by the Scotch and Irish, who, on account of the cheapness of the land, have removed hither in prodigious shoals from the back part of Pennsylvania and Maryland.

The Alliganey mountain is the dividing ridge between the eastern & western waters. The ascent, except in a very few places, is not difficult: you seem to be rising gradually for near thirty miles. The mountain is thickly inhabited, by all sorts of indolent ignorant people, who raise a little corn, but depend chiefly on hunting for their support. They live in little log huts, destitute of every convenience of life; but as they never were acquainted with any other kind of living, they do not appear unhappy. Their only wants are salt and whiskey.

October 5. I crossed New River, the first stream that runs west. This is a branch of the Ohio and empties into it about 250 miles below fort Pitt, where it is called the big Connoway [Kanawha].

Having arrived at the place where all the roads which lead to Kentucky meet, I kept an account of the number of souls I overtook in one day going to that country; and though I was the whole day in riding about thirty miles, but very little faster than a waggon would drive, I overtook two hundred and twenty one. They seemed absolutely infatuated by something like the old crusading spirit to the holy land. West of the mountain, the land, though stony, appears good. The growth is sycamore alias button wood, sugar tree, cherry, walnut, lucust, oak, &c. &c.

Saturday 10. I arrived at the block house, the last house on this side the wilderness, except a few scattering huts, which are possessed alternately by hunters and Indians. Col. A. The gentleman who keeps the house informed me that a very agreeable company left that place the day before: and that as there were a number of families in it, they would move slow, that I might overtake them in one day; and, therefore, advised me to push after them as fast as I could.

At 7 in the evening, Col. B. Arrived there from the Cherokee tribe. He was formerly our minister plenipotentiary, and resided a considerable time at their court.

In consequence of the mischief which had lately been done, he went there to enquire into the reasons of it, and to demand the horses and cattle they had stolen.

He told me, that on the 3^d day, they refused to admit him in to their public council, which much alarmed him. One of his Indian friends came to him privately and told him the subject of debate was, whether they should roast him that day, or put it off a few days longer; on which he made his escape.

His friend also assured him, that many of the Indians, were much disposed for war, and that a large party of near 300 were then on the Kentucky road hunting horses and hares, as they term it; and his business there was to inform the people of the danger on the road and to warn them against attempting the wilderness, unless in large companies well armed. This was most unwelcome information. I was, however, under a necessity of going on; and being informed that there was but little danger in the first day's march. I set off alone on Sunday at break of day, to overtake the companies before. The wilderness is 195 miles from the block house to the first settlement in Kentucky, though for 40 or 50 miles, there are a number of little huts, with small pieces of cleared land, where the hunters have endeavoured to raise corn.

The badness of the road from the block house is not easily described. From the rugged ascents and descents, which seemed absolutely impassible; and from the mire, which was every step up to my horse's knees, occasioned by heavy rains, which had fallen a few days before, I had hard work to go a mile in an hour. I however made the best of my time 'til sunset, but could hear nothing of the company. As marching in the dark was out of the question, I began to look out for a place to sleep, or rather to stay, for I did not expect to sleep. Some little apprehension of danger from the Indians, the loneliness of my situation, the howling of wolves and croaking of ravens on every side, made me feel some what gloomy. I turned aside from the road about a quarter of a mile, by the side of a steep rock, where I found green grass for my horse, and after giving him my hat full of corn, tied him to a tree, then bringing my saddle, my bag of corn and wallet of provision by the side of the rock, I wrapped myself in my blanket, and with a large horseman's pistol in each hand, I set down to guard him and myself. About one o'clock I fell asleep, and forgot the danger of my situation 'til morning.

Monday about noon I overtook the company. It consisted of upwards of 500 souls, 134 of which were active men, well armed; the rest were old men, women, children and negroes. Tuesday we spent in making regulations, chusing officers, &c. We found, that evening, that a number of the families had on the road been exposed to the measles and were then beginning to break out. This was a difficulty for which we were unprepared. To go back with them was out of the question, to leave them behind certain death. We agreed to keep with them and move on slowly encamping every night by the roadside, and keeping a guard of thirty men, who by keeping a great number of fires round the encampment, and crying every five minutes as loud as they can "all is well," would endeavour to terrify the savages. We turned our horses out to graze every night. The woods afford cane, wild pea vines, grass, &c. in great plenty.

In a few days we found our company too large to move with any convenience; and that we must either divide or perish with famine. We divided our company at Cumberland river taking 54 guns.

I believe no company ever had so disagreeable a time of it through the wilderness. Out of 22 days we had only 4 in which it did not rain and thunder most excessively.

We, however, all got safe through, notwithstanding many of the company, while sick, rode from morning 'til evening in the rain. We generally marched about ten miles in a day. Were never disturbed by the Indians, except once they fired on some of our company, who were out a hunting; but we frequently saw the effects of their cruelties. Scarce a day but we found the marks of a defeated company. The last summer and the beginning of the fall, the people supposing the Indians to be at peace, ventured through the wilderness in small companies, which fell an easy prey to them. It is supposed they have killed more than a hundred on that road since last July. Some whole companies have never been heard of. The encampments of those who have been destroyed by them, exhibit a scene too horrid to be described.

My situation, and prospects, with respect to business, are as good as could reasonably be expected, considering the time I have been in the country. I hold my office in this place [Danville], a small trading town, containing about 15 families, who live in little log huts, and seem quite sociable. I am here however but a small part of my time, having the courts to attend in four counties, each of which is held once a month; so that I have one court to attend every week, besides a circle of about 250 miles to ride every month, from county to county. I had almost forgotten to observe, that this is Lincoln county, about 95 miles from the falls of Ohio [Louisville].

I have now given you quite a circumstantial account of myself for the last six months; and although a dry narration, without so much as one philosophical observation or wise speech to set it off to advantage, am in hopes it may serve for the amusement of a leisure hour.

Gilbert Imlay

from *Topographical Description of the Western Territory of North America*

The life of Gilbert Imlay, another early visitor to Kentucky, reads like an adventure novel. A native of New Jersey and a veteran of the American Revolution, he came to Louisville in 1784 and failed as a land speculator. He left in 1792 and moved to London, where he published his *Topographical Description of the Western Territory of North America*, one of the most readable and accurate descriptions of early Kentucky life. His novel, *The Emigrants,* published in London in 1793, is the sentimental story of an English merchant and his family who move to Louisville. In a series of letters the novel tells of the hardships they experience on the rough frontier, including his daughter's capture by the Indians and her eventual rescue. It is usually accorded the honor of being called the first Kentucky novel. The excerpt below, from his first book, describes early Kentucky "stations," or small settlements, the log houses, the soil, the domestic animals and crops, and country amusements.

In some of my first letters I gave you an account of the first settlement of this country. The perturbed state of that period, and the savage state of the country, which was one entire wilderness, made the object of the first emigrants that of security and sustenance, which produced the scheme of several families living together in what were called Stations. These stations were a kind of quadrangular, or sometimes oblong forts, formed by building log-houses connectedly only leaving openings for gate-ways to pass as they might have occasion. They were generally fixed in a favourable situation for water, and in a body of good land. Frequently the head of some party of connections who had a settlement and pre-emption right, seized upon these opportunities to have his land cleared, which was necessary for the support of the station; for, it was not only prudent to keep close in their forts at times, but it was also necessary to keep their horses and cows up, otherwise the Indians would carry off the horses, and shoot and destroy the cattle.

Under such circumstances, the first settlement of Kentucky was formed, which soon opened a considerable quantity of land in the county of Lincoln, which lies in the upper part of the state, and contiguous to the wilderness, which ends in this delectable region.

As the country gained strength, the stations began to break up in that part of the country, and their inhabitants to spread themselves, and settle upon their respective estates. But the embarrassment they were in for most of the conveniences of life, did not admit of their building any other houses but of logs, and of opening fields in the most expeditious way for planting the Indian corn; the only grain which was cultivated at that time.

A log-house is very soon erected, and in consequence of the friendly disposition which exists among those hospitable people, every neighbour flew to the assistance of each other upon occasions of emergency. Sometimes they were built of round logs entirely, covered with rived ash shingles, and the interstices stopped with clay, or lime and sand, to keep out the weather. The next object was to open the land for cultivation. There is very little under-wood in any part of this country, so that by cutting up the cane, and girdling the trees, you are sure of a crop of corn. The fertility of the soil amply repays the labourer for his toil; for if the large trees are not very numerous, and a large proportion of them the sugar maple, it is very likely from this imperfect cultivation, that the ground will yield from 50 to 60 bushels of corn to the acre. The second crop will be more ample; and as the shade is removed by cutting the timber away, great part of our land will produce from 70 to 100 bushels of corn from an acre. This extraordinary fertility enables the farmer who has but a small capital to increase his wealth in a most rapid manner (I mean by wealth the comforts of life). His cattle and hogs will find sufficient food in the woods, not only for them to subsist upon, but to fatten them. His horses want no provender the greatest part of the year except cane and wild clover; but he may afford to feed them with corn the second year. His garden, with little attention, produces him all the culinary roots and vegetables necessary for his table; and the prolific increase of his hogs and poultry, will furnish him the second year, without fearing to injure his stock, with a plenty of animal food; and in three or four years his flock of cattle and sheep will prove sufficient to supply him with both beef and mutton; and he may continue his plan at the same time of increasing his stock of those useful animals. By the fourth year, provided he is industrious, he may have his plantation in sufficient good order to build a better house, which he can do either of stone, brick, or a framed wooden building, the principal articles of which will cost him little more than the labour of himself and domestics; and he may readily barter or sell some part of the superfluous productions of his farm, which it will by this time afford, and procure such things as he may stand in need of for the completion of his building. Apples, peaches, pears, &c. &c. he ought to plant when he finds a soil or eligible situation to place them in, as that will not hinder, or in any degree divert, him from the object of his aggrandizement. I have taken no notice of the game he might kill, as it is more a sacrifice of time to an industrious man than any real advantage.

Such has been the progress of the settlement of this country, from dirty stations or forts, and smoaky huts, that it has expanded into fertile fields, blushing orchards, pleasant gardens, luxuriant sugar groves, neat and commodious houses, rising villages, and trading towns. Ten years have produced a difference in the population and comforts of this country, which to be pourtrayed in just colours would appear marvellous. To have implicit faith or belief that such things have happened, it is first necessary to be (as I have been) a spectator of such events.

Emigrations to this country were mostly from the back parts of Virginia, Maryland, Pennsylvania, and North Carolina, until 1784: in which year many officers who had served in the American army during the late war came out with their families; several families came also from England, Philadelphia, New Jersey, York, and the New England States. The country soon began to be chequered after that æra with genteel men, which operated both upon the minds and actions of back woods people, who constituted the first emigrants. A taste for the decorum and elegance of the table was soon cultivated; the pleasures of gardening were considered not only as useful but amusing. These improvements in the comforts of living and manners, awakened a sense of ambition to instruct their youth in useful and accomplished arts. Social pleasures were regarded as the most inestimable of human possessions—the genius of friendship appeared to foster the emanations of virtue, while the cordial regard, and sincere desire of pleasing produced the most harmonizing effects. Sympathy was regarded as the essence of the human soul, participating of celestial matter, and as a spark engendered to warm our benevolence and lead to the raptures of love and rational felicity.

With such sentiments our amusements flow from the interchange of civilities, and a reciprocal desire of pleasing. That sameness may not cloy, and make us dull, we vary the scene as the nature of circumstances will permit. The opening spring brings with it the prospect of our summer's labour, and the brilliant sun actively warms into life the vegetable world, which blooms and yields a profusion of aromatic odours. A creation of beauty is now a feast of joy, and to look for amusements beyond this genial torrent of sweets, would be a perversion of nature, and a sacrilege against heaven.

The season of sugar making occupies the women, whose mornings are cheered by the modulated buffoonery of the mocking bird, the tuneful song of the thrush, and the gaudy plumage of the parroquet.—Festive mirth crowns the evening.—The business of the day being over, the men join the women in the sugar groves where inchantment seems to dwell.—The lofty trees wave their spreading branches over a green turf, on whose soft down the mildness of the evening invites the neighbouring youth to sportive play; while our rural Nestors, with calculating minds, contemplate the boyish gambols of a growing progeny, they recount the exploits of their early age, and in their enthusiasm forget there are such things as decrepitude and misery. Perhaps a convivial song or a pleasant narration closes the scene.

Christian Schultz

from *Travels of an Inland Voyage*

In the two volumes of his *Travels of an Inland Voyage,* Christian Schultz, apparently a native of New York City, takes us on an 1807–8 journey from New York through Pennsylvania, Virginia, and Ohio into Kentucky and on down to New Orleans. His travels through Kentucky are detailed and colorful and filled with marvelous stories and anecdotes, meetings with fellow travelers, and data regarding distances between various towns. In these selections he tells about the different kinds of boats seen on the Western waters, his encounters with wild animals and wild people, a visit to Big Bone Lick, and an up-close description of the Falls at Louisville.

In my last I promised to give you some account of the different kinds of boats made use of on these waters, and shall now proceed to gratify your curiosity on that subject. The smallest kind of craft in use are simple log canoes; next follow perrogues, which are a larger kind of canoes, but sufficiently strong and capacious to carry from twelve to fifteen barrels of salt. Skiffs are built of all sizes, from five hundred to twenty thousand pounds weight burthen. Batteaux are the same as the larger kind of skiffs, and indifferently known by either name. Arks are not much in use on these waters; what few I have noticed were similar to those you have seen on the Susquehanna. Kentucky boats are strong frames of an oblong form, varying in size from twenty to fifty feet in length, and from ten to fourteen in breadth; they are built of stout square timber, and, before they are sided and roofed in, have much the appearance of old graving scows, excepting that the front part or bow has somewhat of a rake. The gunwales are generally from twelve to twenty-four inches high, and from three to six inches thick; on the top of these are mortised square joist of three or four feet in length, and four or five inches thick, which are sided up like a house with ordinary boards; on the top of these studs are secured the foot of each rafter, over which the roof is laid, which likewise answers the purpose of a main and quarter deck; they are steered by a long swing oar of the whole length of the boat, and generally have from one to three hands to manage a boat, having frequent occasion, when heavily loaded, to use their unwieldy oars, in order to keep nearly in the middle of the river. Some of these floating machines, with a shed roof, bear a very striking resemblance to what you daily see in the streets of New-York, where new houses are building, and generally denominated a lime-house.

New-Orleans boats are built upon the same model as the Kentucky boats, excepting that they are generally much larger and stronger, with an arched roof fore and aft. When I first saw a row of these boats lying high and dry on the shore at Pittsburgh, I really concluded they were detached pieces of some large rope-walk which had been carried off by the freshes from above. The largest boats of this kind will carry four hundred and fifty barrels of flour. Keel boats are very different from what their name would seem to imply to a stranger who has never seen one, especially to an inhabitant of a sea-port, where the name is always applied to sailing boats, particularly those kinds that can beat up against a wind. Here, however, it is given to a species of the Schenectady boats, which you will find particularly described in my account of the navigation of the Mohawk River. The principal difference consists in this, that the timbers or knees of these are built upon a small keel, about three inches in depth, and four or five in width; from which circumstance they are denominated keel boats. I have no doubt but the keel is an additional strength to the boat, as it receives the first shock of any obstruction in the navigation, which otherwise would fall immediately upon the planking; but at the same time it makes a draft of three inches more water than Schenectady boats of the same size and burthen. These boats are generally built from forty to eighty feet in length, and from seven to nine feet in width; the largest kind require but one hand to steer and two to row, in descending the Ohio, and will carry about one hundred barrels of salt; but, to ascend the stream, they will require at least six or eight hands to make any considerable progress.

The last and best kind of boats used on the Ohio and Mississippi is what is called a barge. You will have a tolerable correct idea of this kind when you see a ship's long boat, or those used at the ferry from the city of New-York to Long Island, adding thereto about three times the length and a proportionable depth, their width being generally between seven and ten feet. These boats are steered by a rudder, and are easily managed while they have any *way* upon them; but when descending with the force of the current alone, are not so easily twisted and turned as a keel boat is by her long steering oar. A barge will carry from forty to sixty thousand weight, and requires four hands besides the helmsman to descend the river; but, to return with a loading, from eight to twelve become necessary. Barges, as well as keel boats, generally carry a moveable mast a-midships, and, whenever the wind will permit, set a square-sail, and some few top-sails. A small fleet of six or seven of these vessels coming up before a wind, at a distance of three or four miles, is equally as pleasing a sight in this country, as an equal number of the largest square-rigged vessels entering the harbour of New-York.

The prices of the various kinds of boats already described are as follows: Canoes from one to three dollars; perrogues from five to twenty; small skiffs from five to ten dollars; large skiffs or batteaux from twenty to fifty; arks one dollar a foot in length; Kentucky and New-Orleans boats from one dollar to one and a half a foot; keel boats from two and a half to three dollars a foot, and barges from four to five dollars a foot. These are the customary prices for new boats; but, from the constant influx of boats of every description down the Monongahela and Alleghany Rivers, whose destination is no farther than Pittsburgh, boats may often be had at very reduced prices.

The land from the Kentucky line, at Big Sandy River, to this place, which is a distance of seventy miles, presents a rough and hilly country, as far as can be seen from the river, excepting some small bottoms, alternately found, first on one side and then on the other.

This country appears to be completely overrun with innumerable quantities of black and grey squirrels. The river, since we left Marietta, has afforded us an abundant supply of these animals, without any trouble on our part, as our boat had continually five or six of them on board, who clambered up the oars in order to rest themselves. I have counted no less than forty-seven at one time swimming across the river in different directions. The shores on each side of the river are literally lined with drowned squirrels; and I suppose that one third at least of those who take to the river perish in the water. They all appear to be migrating to the southward. Higher up the river we found them very fat, and they afforded us many delicious repasts; but they have now become too poor to be eatable.

Although, in one of my former letters, I described the navigation of the Ohio to be perfectly safe, yet experience has shewn me it is at least necessary to keep a constant *look out*. We were about three miles below Salt Lick Creek when our boat drifted very gently against a pointed log or snag, which was barely covered with water. The boat was under such moderate way, that we had not the least idea that she was injured, as she wheeled around and continued her course. I soon, however, perceived the water rising fast over the timbers, and at the same time heard a rippling noise, which I at first supposed was occasioned by the current, but was soon convinced that it proceeded from the leaking of the boat. I removed some of the baggage, and perceiving the water gushing in with violence, thrust an old great coat into the hole, and directed my men to make for the shore, where we unloaded, and drew the boat out of the water. On examination we found one of the plank stove through; but by means of a thin piece of board and a few nails, we soon covered the fracture, and payed it over with some of the rich mud of the Ohio, which, on this occasion, answered all the purposes of tar, without the trouble of boiling.

After repairing the boat, and reloading our trumpery, we set forward again, when, just as we turned a short bend in the river, we discovered a bear that had taken to the water, with an intention of crossing to the opposite side. We immediately manned our oars with all hands in order to come up with him, but all to no purpose, for as soon as he perceived our intention, he prudently turned about, and recovered the shore he had left before we could come within gun shot. We had better luck, however, in the afternoon: seeing a deer make the same attempt, we despatched two hands in our light canoe after him, who, after cutting him off from the shore, and forcing him again to the middle of the river, determined not to shoot him, but give him fair play, and either take him alive or suffer him to escape: after a chase of nearly five miles, they seized him by the horns and dragged him ashore.

Limestone is said to be the oldest settlement in the State of Kentucky. The town, which consists of about eighty houses, is built on a flat in a bend of the river, and commands a pleasing view of the stream both above and below; and, from the great number of boats of every description lying along the shore, must have a very considerable share of business. Ship building, I was informed, is likewise carried on with much spirit, but I saw nothing of the kind going on while I was there.

The river had made very considerable encroachments upon the town, by washing away the banks; so that in some places there is barely room between the houses and the edge of the bank for a passable road. A year or two more, especially if assisted by any extraordinary freshes, will either swallow up those on the margin of the bank, or oblige their inhabitants to remove them to some more permanent foundation.

Lexington, which is the largest town in the State of Kentucky, is only sixty-five miles distant from this place; it is said to be nearly five times as large as Limestone, and situated in one of the finest countries in the world.

Limestone Creek falls into the Ohio immediately above the town. I understand that this is sometimes a considerable stream; but, at present, its bed, which is at least six feet above the surface of the river, is perfectly dry. This is the case with most of the creeks which empty into the Ohio, although at other times they rush down with all the appearance of large and permanent rivers.

After leaving Limestone six miles, we came in sight of Charlestown, likewise in the State of Kentucky. This place contains about forty houses, and makes a respectable appearance from the river. Twelve miles lower we passed the town of Augusta, situated on the right bank of the river, in the State of Ohio, and containing about thirty houses. Thirty-seven miles below Augusta, the Little Miami River puts in from the right; immediately above which, is the site of a small town called Columbia, consisting of about one dozen scattered houses. Seven miles further down stands the town of Cincinnati, the largest town on the Ohio below Pittsburgh, from whence it is distant about four hundred and eighty miles, and lies in latitude 39. 6. N. and 84. 18. W. . . .

Descending thence twenty-four miles, we arrived at Big Bone Lick Creek, in the State of Kentucky.

Big Bone Lick is celebrated for the incredibly large bones found in its vicinity, which have not only amazed and astonished, but likewise puzzled the learned world. Horns have been found here measuring fifteen feet in length, fifteen inches in circumference, and weighing nearly one hundred pounds; teeth or grinders from five to twelve pounds weight, and other bones in proportion.

That this animal, which has been denominated the mammoth, is now extinct, is, I believe, the generally received opinion, although, I am informed, the Indians cherish a tradition that he still exists unknown in the west.

"That in ancient times a herd of them came to Big Bone Lick, and began a universal destruction of the bears, deer, elks, buffaloes, and other animals which had been created for the use of the Indians; that the Great Man above, looking down and seeing this, was so enraged that he seized his lightning, descended to the earth, seated himself upon a neighbouring mountain on a rock, on which his seat and the print of his feet are still to be seen, and hurled his bolts among them, until the whole were slaughtered except the big bull, who presented his forehead to the shafts and shook them off as they fell; but at length missing one, it wounded him in the side; whereupon, springing round, he bounded over Ohio, the Wabash and the Illinois, and finally over the Great Lakes, where he is living to this day."

Col. Morgan informs us, that upon putting similar queries to a chief of the Iroquois tribe, whom he saw at the Lick, he delivered himself as follows: "After the Great Spirit first formed the world he made the various birds and beasts which now inhabit it. He also made man; but having formed him *white*, and finding him imperfect and ill tempered, he placed him on one side of the earth, from whence he lately found a passage across the great water to be a plague to *us*. As the Great Spirit was not pleased with this work, he took some black clay, and made what you call a negro, with a woolly head. This black man was much better than the white man, but still he did not please the Great Spirit. At last the Great Spirit, having found a piece of pure red clay, formed of it the red man, perfectly to his mind; and was so well pleased with him that he placed him on this great island, separate from the white and black men, and gave him rules for his conduct. He increased ex- ceedingly, and was perfectly happy for ages; but the foolish young people at length despising his rules, became very wicked. In consequence of this, the Great Spirit created the great buffalo, the bones of which you now see before us; these made war upon the human species, and destroyed all but a few, who repented, and promised the Great Spirit to live according to his laws in future; whereupon he sent thunder and lightning, and destroyed the whole race in this spot, two excepted, a male and female, which he shut up in yonder mountain, ready to let loose again, should occasion require."

Thirty miles below Big Bone Lick Creek, and on the same side, you perceive the Kentucky River, which, after having traversed the State in its widest part, and passing through innumerable tracts of the finest lands, here discharges its waters into the general receiver, the Ohio. This river is one hundred and fifty yards wide, and is navigable for one hundred and sixty miles during a great part of the year; but in dry seasons it is frequently obstructed with shallows. Immediately at the mouth of Kentucky River, which lies in latitude 38. 39. N. and 85. 2. W. is situated a thriving little town named Port William, consisting at present of about forty houses. Frankfort, which is the seat of government, although not the capital of the State, is situated on this river, about sixty-five miles from its mouth, and is said to be in a very flourishing condition, containing already about two hundred houses. Several large vessels have been launched on this river, and descended to New-Orleans. Westport is forty-eight miles below Port William, and contains only six houses. I have observed, during my whole course down this river, that the land rises and falls alternately on each side: whenever you see a flat on one side you will always find a corresponding elevation on the opposite shore.

In descending the Ohio River you frequently pass what are here called floating mills; they are of a very simple construction, and consequently the more valuable in a country so destitute of mill-seats as this. The mill is supported by two large canoes, with the wheel between them; this is moored wherever they can find the strongest current nearest to the shore, by the force of which alone the mill is put into operation. You have seen a razor-grinder wheeling his machine from house to house in the city of New-York—this is exactly the case with the mills I am now describing; for they are literally floated up and down the stream, wherever a customer calls. Should I ever again attempt farming, it will most probably be in this new country, for I well remember I lost nearly one half of all my time and labour by *sending to mill*; for let me call for whom I would, he was always "gone to the mill." Here, therefore, I may flatter myself with a better prospect of success, in that particular at least, for instead of the farmer's *going* to mill, the mill *comes* to him.

After leaving Westport we descended twenty miles, and found ourselves at the head of the Falls of Ohio, before the town of Louisville, six hundred and thirty miles below Pittsburgh. This town is very handsomely situated on an elevated bank on the left side of the river, in the State of Kentucky, about eight hundred yards above the commencement of the rapids, and contains one hundred and twenty houses; it is the county town, and carries on ship and boat-building with considerable spirit; several large vessels have already been built, and the many advantages which it enjoys in this respect, over all the towns above the falls, bids fair to give it all the encouragement it can wish. The country around Louisville is perfectly level for some miles, and the elevation of the town commands a beautiful prospect of the smooth and gentle stream above, as well as the rough and foaming billows of the falls below. Louisville has lately been erected into a port of entry and clearance, and lies in latitude 38. 14. N. and 85. 29. W.

The river at this place appears to have acquired a breadth of about one mile and a quarter; and, as the passage of the falls is dangerous to strangers unacquainted with the navigation, the court appoints able and experienced pilots, who conduct you over in safety. Our pilot informed us that he received the same pilotage for a ship of three hundred tons as for a canoe, which you may carry on your shoulder, for, according to the act, "*every boat shall pay two dollars for pilotage.*"

These falls, which may be considered as the only real obstruction in the navigation of the Ohio throughout a distance of nearly eleven hundred miles, are occasioned by a bed of solid rocks extending from one side of the river to the other. The water was low when we passed them, and according to the pilot's account, no more than twenty inches of water over them. I have, however, seen too much water roll not to be able to form a reasonable conjecture of the quantity necessary to raise so violent a commotion as is here found, and shall therefore venture to say there could not have been less than three feet, but probably more. You will perhaps be surprised at my stupidity in not sounding the falls on our passage over them. I certainly intended it, but, by beginning too soon, I lost my pole, and before I could procure another, it being entangled under the rowers' oars, we had passed the shoalest part of the fall.

When the river is high, I am told, there is not the least appearance of any fall, except that the current is somewhat swifter at this place than ordinary; but when low, as at present, nearly two thirds of the breadth of the river may be walked over without wetting your ancle. There are three different passages or shoots over these falls, all depending, however, on the state of the water. The principal is nearest the Indiana shore; the middle is the next best; and the third, or Kentucky shoot, is only passable with the larger vessels during the highest stage of the water. Two fine large ships, of two hundred and fifty and three hundred tons burthen, were lying upon the falls as we descended the river, having attempted to pass without a sufficient rise of the water; they had their keels knocked out, and were otherwise considerably damaged. Their situations were considered so very precarious that the one which ought to have been worth ten thousand dollars, was sold at public auction for fifteen hundred only.

The descent of these falls appears to have been accurately surveyed, and found to be twenty-two feet and a half in two miles. The legislature of Kentucky have incorporated a company for the purpose of opening a canal from the mouth of Bear Grass Creek, which runs in front of the town to the foot of the falls below. The ground has been bored, and every way examined for the purpose, and it is considered as practicable. The only difficulty remaining, is that of raising a sufficient capital to undertake it. When, therefore, this is once effected, the only serious obstruction in the navigation of the Ohio will be removed.

It may be of some service to you, should you ever take a *trip* this way, and become a "captain," like myself, that I have attained that *honour* before you; for although I may not be able to instruct you what you ought to do, yet my experience will enable me to inform you what you ought *not* to do. You must never, on any account, advance money to your boatmen. One of my hands, being arrested by a constable for a debt of eight or ten dollars, at the moment we were leaving the shore, I paid the money without the least hesitation, thinking to deduct it from his wages. After descending a mile or two, I observed a fine stream of spring-water on the shore, and expressing a desire to have a keg filled with it, this fellow was ready in an instant; we accordingly landed him, and, after waiting near an hour, and receiving no answer to our repeated calls, I sent our pilot after him; but the fellow had left the keg at the spring, and escaped to the woods. Another agreed with me at Cincinnati to go the whole voyage down to New-Orleans, or up the Mississippi, as I should think proper, at twenty-five dollars a month. Just as we were ready to start, his wife came down to see him off—She had no money—she might want a little before Josey returned—and, finally, could not I oblige her with one month's advance, as Josey would probably continue with me three or four months? I let her have the twenty-five dollars, and the second night after, the rascal ran away!

After having proceeded about thirty miles through this flat country, you pass the mouth of Green River, which falls into the Ohio from the left shore. This is a beautiful stream, being about one hundred and eighty yards in breadth, navigable for one hundred and sixty miles, and presenting to the eye a far greater degree of transparency than the Ohio itself. Its mouth lies in lat. 37. 59. N. and long. 37. 13. W. Twenty-two miles below Green River, and likewise in the State of Kentucky, you arrive at the town of Henderson, or, as it is more commonly called, Red Banks. This village, which contains about forty houses, is situated on the second bank, about one quarter of a mile from the river, owing to the nearest banks being subject to be over-flowed with every ordinary rise of the river; which still continues its breadth of about one mile and a quarter, rather increasing. Green River, before mentioned, is no more than seven miles distant from Henderson by land, but owing to an extraordinary bend in the river, it is twenty-five miles by water.

One evening, a little after sunset, below a place called Diamond Island, as we were landing on the shore, we discovered a bear which had just entered the river about one quarter of a mile above us, on the opposite shore, with the intention of crossing over to our side. I have ever been anxious, while on these waters, to shoot at least one of these animals, but have always been disappointed. This I thought a most favourable opportunity; accordingly I took a rifle, and proceeded, under cover of the willows, to the spot where I concluded the current would land him. I soon found myself conveniently posted; and at the moment he stood still to shake himself, I fired, and shot him down. He, however, recovered sufficiently to ascend the bank, and passed me so close, that in a fright I jumped down, with the intention of retreating to the river. But finding he made no pursuit, I reloaded my piece, followed his trail, which was covered with blood, and found him dead about one hundred yards distant from the place where he passed me. We afterwards found the ball had entered in at the breast and passed out at the left flank.

John James Audubon

John James Audubon, the most famous bird painter in history, moved to Louisville in 1808 and lived off and on in Louisville and Henderson for more than a quarter of a century. He spent his Kentucky years trying to be a good merchant and sawmill operator and roaming the woods in pursuit of birds he could shoot and stuff and paint. He was more successful with the birds, his bird prints, and his autobiographical books than with his business enterprise. He had mixed feelings about his Kentucky sojourn, but the selections below show him in a more positive mood—first his tribute to Louisville and its people, followed by an amusing account of a friend's affair with a pole cat, a visit to a corn shucking, and a Fourth of July barbecue.

⊗

from "Louisville in Kentucky"

Louisville in Kentucky has always been a favourite place of mine. The beauty of its situation, on the banks of *La Belle Rivière,* just at the commencement of the famed rapids, commonly called the Falls of the Ohio, had attracted my notice, and when I removed to it, immediately after my marriage, I found it more agreeable than ever. The prospect from the town is such that it would please even the eye of a Swiss. It extends along the river for seven or eight miles, and is bounded on the opposite side by a fine range of low mountains, known by the name of the Silver Hills. The rumbling sound of the waters, as they tumble over the rock-paved bed of the rapids, is at all times soothing to the ear. Fish and game are abundant. But, above all, the generous hospitality of the inhabitants, and the urbanity of their manners, had induced me to fix upon it as a place of residence; and I did so with the more pleasure when I found that my wife was as much gratified as myself, by the kind attentions which were shewn to us, utter strangers as we were, on our arrival.

No sooner had we landed, and made known our intention of remaining, than we were introduced to the principal inhabitants of the place and its vicinity, although we had not brought a single letter of introduction, and could not but see, from their unremitting kindness, that the Virginian spirit of hospitality displayed itself in all the words and actions of our newly-formed friends. I wish here to name those persons who so unexpectedly came forward to render our stay among them agreeable, but feel at a loss with whom to begin, so equally deserving are they of our gratitude. The CROGHANS, the CLARKS (our great traveller included), the BERTHOUDS, the GALTS, the MAUPINS, the TARASCONS, the BEALS, and the BOOTHS, form but a small portion of the long list which I could give. The matrons acted like mothers towards my wife, the daughters proved agreeable associates, and the husbands and sons were friends and companions to me. If I absented myself on business or otherwise, for any length of time, my wife was removed to the hospitable abode of some friend in the neighbourhood until my return, and then, kind reader, I was several times obliged to spend a week or more with these good people, before they could be prevailed upon to let us return to our own residence. We lived for two years at Louisville, where we enjoyed many of the best pleasures which this life can afford; and whenever we have since chanced to pass that way, we have found the kindness of our former friends unimpaired.

During my residence at Louisville, much of my time was employed in my ever favourite pursuits. I drew and noted the habits of every thing which I procured, and my collection was daily augmenting, as every individual who carried a gun, always sent me such birds or quadrupeds as he thought might prove useful to me.

"The Traveler and the Pole-Cat"

On a journey from Louisville to Henderson in Kentucky, performed during very severe winter weather, in company with a foreigner, the initials of whose name are D. T., my companion spying a beautiful animal, marked with black and a pale yellow, and having a long and bushy tail, exclaimed, "Mr. Audubon, is not that a beautiful squirrel?" "Yes," I answered, "and of a kind that will suffer you to approach, and lay hold of it if you are well gloved." Mr. D. T. dismounting, took up a dry stick, and advanced toward the pretty animal, with his large cloak floating in the breeze. I think I see him approach, and laying the stick gently across the body of the animal, try to secure it; and I can yet laugh almost as heartily as I then did, when I plainly saw the discomfiture of the traveller. The Pole-cat (for a true Pole-cat it was, the *Mephitis americana* of zoologists), raised its fine bushy tail, and showered such a discharge of the fluid given him by nature as a defence, that my friend, dismayed and infuriated, began to belabour the poor animal. The swiftness and good management of the Pole-cat, however, saved its bones, and as it made its retreat towards its hole, kept up at every step a continued ejectment, which fully convinced the gentleman that the pursuit of such squirrels as these was at the best an unprofitable employment.

This was not all, however. I could not suffer his approach, nor could my horse; it was with difficulty he mounted his own; and we were forced to continue our journey far asunder, and he much to leeward. Nor did the matter end here. We could not proceed much farther that night; as, in the first place, it was nearly dark when we saw the Pole-cat, and as, in the second place, a heavy snow-storm began, and almost impeded our progress. We were forced to make for the first cabin we saw. Having asked and obtained permission to rest for the night we dismounted and found ourselves amongst a crowd of men and women who had met for the purpose of *corn-shucking*.

To a European who has not visited the western parts of the United States, an explanation of this corn-shucking may not be unacceptable. Corn (or you may prefer calling it maize) is gathered in the husk, that is, by breaking each large ear from the stem. These ears are first thrown into heaps in the field, and afterwards carried in carts to the barn, or, as in this instance, and in such portions of Kentucky, to a shed made of the blades or long leaves that hang in graceful curves from the stalk, and which, when plucked and dried, are used instead of hay as food for horses and cattle. The husk consists of several thick leaves rather longer than the corn-ear itself, and which secure it from the weather. It is quite a labour to detach these leaves from the ear, when thousands of bushels of the corn are gathered and heaped together. For this purpose, however, and in the western country more especially, several neighbouring families join alternately at each other's plantations, and assist in clearing away the husks, thus preparing the maize for the market or for domestic use.

The good people whom we met with at this hospitable house, were on the point of going to the barn (the farmer here being in rather good condition) to work until towards the middle of the night. When we had stood the few stares to which strangers must accustom themselves, no matter where, even in a drawing-room, we approached the fire. What a shock for the whole party! The scent of the Polecat, that had been almost stifled on my companion's vestments by the cold of the evening air, now recovered its primitive strength. The cloak was put out of the house, but its owner could not be well used in the same way. The company, however, took to their heels, and there only remained a single black servant, who waited on us until supper was served.

I felt vexed at myself, as I saw the traveller displeased. But he had so much good breeding as to treat this important affair with great forbearance, and merely said he was sorry for his want of knowledge in zoology. The good gentleman, however, was not only deficient in zoological lore, but, fresh as he was from Europe, felt more than uneasy in this out-of-the-way dwelling, and would have proceeded towards my own house that night, had I not at length succeeded in persuading him that he was in perfect security.

We were shown to bed. As I was almost a stranger to him, and he to me, he thought it a very awkward thing to be obliged to lie in the same bed with me, but afterwards spoke of it as a happy circumstance, and requested that I should suffer him to be placed next the logs, thinking, no doubt, that there he should run no risk.

We started by break of day, taking with us the frozen cloak, and after passing a pleasant night in my own house, we parted. Some years after I met my Kentucky companion in a far distant land, when he assured me, that whenever the sun shone on his cloak, or it was brought near a fire, the scent of the Pole-cat became so perceptible, that he at last gave it to a poor monk in Italy.

The animal commonly known in America by the name of Pole-cat is about a foot and a half in length, with a large bushy tail, nearly as long as the body. The colour is generally brownish-black, with a large white patch on the back of the head; but there are many varieties of colouring, in some of which the broad white bands of the back are very conspicuous. The Pole-cat burrows, or forms a subterranean habitation among the roots of trees, or in rocky places. It feeds on birds, young hares, rats, mice, and other animals, and commits great depredations on poultry. The most remarkable peculiarity of this animal is the power, alluded to above, of squirting for its defence a most nauseously scented fluid contained in a receptacle situated under the tail, which it can do to the distance of several yards. It does not, however, for this purpose, sprinkle its tail with the fluid, as some allege, unless when extremely harassed by its enemies. The Pole-cat is frequently domesticated. The removal of the glands prevents the secretion of the nauseous fluid, and when thus improved, the animal becomes a great favourite, and performs the offices of the common cat with great dexterity.

"Kentucky Barbecue on the Fourth of July"

Beargrass Creek, which is one of the many beautiful streams of the highly cultivated and happy State of Kentucky, meanders through a deeply shaded growth of majestic beech woods, in which are interspersed various species of walnut, oak, elm, ash, and other trees, extending on either side of its course. The spot on which I witnessed the celebration of an anniversary of the glorious Proclamation of our Independence is situated on its banks, near the city of Louisville. The woods spread their dense tufts towards the shores of the fair Ohio on the west, and over the gently rising grounds to the south and east. Every open spot forming a plantation was smiling in the luxuriance of a summer harvest. The farmer seemed to stand in admiration of the spectacle: the trees of his orchards bowed their branches, as if anxious to restore to their mother earth the fruit with which they were laden; the flocks leisurely ruminated as they lay on their grassy beds; and the genial warmth of the season seemed inclined to favour their repose.

The free, single-hearted Kentuckian, bold, erect, and proud of his Virginian descent, had, as usual, made arrangements for celebrating the day of his country's Independence. The whole neighbourhood joined with one consent. No personal invitation was required where every one was welcomed by his neighbour, and from the governor to the guider of the plough all met with light hearts and merry faces.

It was indeed a beautiful day; the bright sun rode in the clear blue heavens; the gentle breezes wafted around the odours of the gorgeous flowers; the little birds sang their sweetest songs in the woods, and the fluttering insects danced in the sunbeams. Columbia's sons and daughters seemed to have grown younger that morning. For a whole week or more, many servants and some masters had been busily engaged in clearing an area. The undergrowth had been carefully cut down, the low boughs lopped off, and the grass alone, verdant and gay, remained to carpet the sylvan pavilion. Now the waggons were seen slowly moving along under their load of provisions, which had been prepared for the common benefit. Each denizen had freely given his ox, his ham, his venison, his turkeys, and other fowls. Here were to be seen flagons of every beverage used in the country; "La belle Rivière" had opened her finny stores; the melons of all sorts, peaches, plums and pears, would have sufficed to stock a market. In a word, Kentucky, the land of abundance, had supplied a feast for her children.

A purling stream gave its water freely, while the grateful breezes cooled the air. Columns of smoke from the newly kindled fires rose above the trees; fifty cooks or more moved to and fro as they plied their trade; waiters of all qualities were disposing the dishes, the glasses, and the punch-bowls, amid vases filled with rich wines. "Old Monongahela" filled many a barrel for the crowd. And now, the roasted viands perfume the air, and all appearances conspire to predict the speedy commencement of a banquet such as may suit the vigorous appetite of American woodsmen. Every steward is at his post, ready to receive the joyous groups that at this moment begin to emerge from the dark recesses of the woods.

Each comely fair one, clad in pure white, is seen advancing under the protection of her sturdy lover, the neighing of their prancing steeds proclaiming how proud they are of their burdens. The youthful riders leap from their seats, and the horses are speedily secured by twisting their bridles round a branch. As the youth of Kentucky lightly and gaily advanced towards the Barbecue, they resembled a procession of nymphs and disguised divinities. Fathers and mothers smiled upon them, as they followed the brilliant *cortège*. In a short time the ground was alive with merriment. A great wooden cannon, bound with iron hoops, was now crammed with home-made powder; fire was conveyed to it by means of a train, and as the explosion burst forth, thousands of hearty huzzas mingled with its echoes. From the most learned a good oration fell in proud and gladdening words on every ear, and although it probably did not equal the eloquence of a Clay, an Everett, a Webster, or a Preston, it served to remind every Kentuckian present of the glorious name, the patriotism, the courage, and the virtue, of our immortal Washington. Fifes and drums sounded the march which had ever led him to glory; and as they changed to our celebrated "Yankee Doodle," the air again rang with acclamations.

Now the stewards invited the assembled throng to the feast. The fair led the van, and were first placed around the tables, which groaned under the profusion of the best productions of the country that had been heaped upon them. On each lovely nymph attended her gay beau, who in her chance or sidelong glances ever watched an opportunity of reading his happiness. How the viands diminished under the action of so many agents of destruction I need not say, nor is it neccessary that you should listen to the long recital. Many a national toast was offered and accepted, many speeches were delivered, and many essayed in amicable reply. The ladies then retired to booths that had been erected at a little distance, to which they were conducted by their partners, who returned to the table, and having thus cleared for action, recommenced a series of hearty rounds. However, as Kentuckians are neither slow nor long at their meals, all were in a few minutes replenished, and after a few more draughts from the bowl, they rejoined the ladies, and prepared for the dance.

Double lines of a hundred fair ones extended along the ground in the most shady part of the woods, while here and there smaller groups awaited the merry trills of reels and cotillons. A burst of music from violins, clarionets, and bugles, gave the welcome notice, and presently the whole assemblage seemed to be gracefully moving through the air. The "hunting-shirts" now joined in the dance, their fringed skirts keeping time with the gowns of the ladies, and the married people of either sex stepped in and mixed with their children. Every countenance beamed with joy, every heart leaped with gladness; no pride, no pomp, no affectation, were there; their spirits brightened as they continued their exhilarating exercise, and care and sorrow were flung to the winds. During each interval of rest, refreshments of all sorts were handed round, and while the fair one cooled her lips with the grateful juice of the melon, the hunter of Kentucky quenched his thirst with ample draughts of well-tempered punch.

I know, reader, that had you been with me on that day, you would have richly enjoyed the sight of this national *fête champêtre*. You would have listened with pleasure to the ingenious tale of the lover, the wise talk of the elder on the affairs of the state, the accounts of improvement in stock and utensils, and the hopes of continued prosperity to the country at large, and to Kentucky in particular. You would have been pleased to see those who did not join the dance, shooting at distant marks with their heavy rifles, or watched how they shewed off the superior speed of their high bred "old Virginia" horses, while others recounted their hunting-exploits, and at intervals made the woods ring with their bursts of laughter. With me the time sped like an arrow in its flight, and although more than twenty years have elapsed since I joined a Kentucky Barbecue, my spirit is refreshed every 4th of July by the recollection of that day's merriment.

But now the sun has declined, and the shades of evening creep over the scene. Large fires are lighted in the woods, casting the long shadows of the living columns far along the trodden ground, and flaring on the happy groups, loath to separate. In the still clear sky, began to sparkle the distant lamps of heaven. One might have thought that Nature herself smiled on the joy of her children. Supper now appeared on the tables, and after all had again refreshed themselves, preparations were made for departure. The lover hurried for the steed of his fair one, the hunter seized the arm of his friend, families gathered into loving groups, and all returned in peace to their happy homes.

And now, Reader, allow me also to take my leave and wish you good night, trusting that when I again appear with another volume, you will be ready to welcome me with a cordial greeting.

Robert Emmett McDowell

from *Tidewater Sprig*

One of the Kentucky novelists who have written fiction about Kentucky's pioneer period is Robert Emmett McDowell. McDowell, a historian who wrote history and historical fiction, is the author of *Tidewater Sprig* (1961), the story of Todd Medford, a ne'er-do-well from an aristocratic Virginia family who comes to Kentucky on an Ohio River flatboat, debarks at Louisville, and winds up working at the saltworks in Bullitt County. This excerpt describes Todd's arrival in Louisville.

Todd wasn't disappointed by the settlement at the Falls of the Ohio for the simple reason that he hadn't expected it to amount to anything. Louisville, for such was its official name, consisted of a scattering of rude log hovels set down in the midst of ponds and swampy ground that gave the place an unhealthy appearance. There was a new, raw-looking stockade, where he understood General George Rogers Clark made his headquarters; a short walk downstream he discovered a second, older fortification that already was beginning to fall into a state of disrepair.

Since the Andrews and the Collings tribes were leaving the river at this point, planning to journey inland to Caleb's improvement a short distance above the saltworks, Todd found himself faced with the necessity of hiring hands to work the boat. He made his way to the lower fort where, he had learned, there was a public house.

This fort, unlike the new one where Clark made his headquarters, was a typical Kentucky station. Since it was the first that Todd had seen, he studied it curiously. It had been built in the form of a rectangle, the backs of the cabins making up the walls, the space between the individual cabins stockaded in with pickets. The cabins themselves were but one story high, with flat shed roofs sloping in toward the compound. Todd counted eight to the long sides of the roofs rectangle and four at the ends; at the corner nearest him a two-story blockhouse reared itself above the stockade, the second floor projecting about three feet beyond the walls.

The gates stood open, and the compound was ankle-deep in mire, the musky odor of cattle droppings mingling with the sharper scents of urine and wood smoke. He located the ordinary and stepped inside to find a small, gloomy, dirt-floored chamber where a number of men were drinking and playing cards, laughing and joking boisterously. They were as fine a parcel of rogues as Todd had yet seen, unshaven for the most part, clad in dirty buckskins or linsey-woolsey. A man was snoring drunkenly on the floor in a corner; the stink in the place must have risen to high heaven.

Jude Deveraux

from *River Lady*

River Lady is a modern historical romance by the best-selling novelist Jude Deveraux, a native of Louisville. It is the story of Wesley Stanford, a handsome, wealthy philanderer from Virginia who moves his family to the wilderness of Kentucky in 1803. His unconventional family includes Leah, whom he marries in Virginia after she becomes pregnant, and his new girlfriend, Kimberly, whom he plans to marry after they reach their new Kentucky home and he divorces Leah. His plans don't quite work out that way. Like many of the newcomers to the West, he finds that a new land opens up all kinds of new possibilities.

There were many travelers on the road heading for Kentucky and even farther west. They were drawn by the enticement of riches beyond belief, of fertile, virgin land that was theirs for the asking. There was no longer an Indian problem and Kentucky was a state, so they felt safe, protected from hardship. Some of the travelers were well prepared, their wagons loaded with goods. They'd sold their farms and had money to buy new land in the west. But too many others had merely walked away from where they'd lived, their families trailing behind them with no more than the clothes on their backs and a sackful of food.

Leah trudged along behind Wesley through the silent, roaringly loud forest. Her eyes kept darting this way and that, trying to see behind trees and bushes. A sound in the distance made her jump. Ahead of her, Wesley didn't even turn at Leah's sound.

In the morning he'd turned every time she'd given a little squeal of fright, then smiled smugly and turned back around. Leah swore she'd be quiet from now on, but she broke her vow constantly. Never had she been so far away from people. She'd grown up surrounded by brothers and sisters and the only time she'd left was to live at Wesley's plantation, where there'd been even more people near her. On the trip toward Kentucky, they'd never been out of sight and sound of many people.

Now for the first time in her life she was alone—or at least very close to it. The way she felt now, Wesley didn't count as a human being. Very early that morning they'd loaded goods into packs.

"Which horses do you plan to take?" John Hammond asked.

"We're going where a horse can't go," Wesley answered, slinging the pack on his back.

Refusing to comment or even look at Wesley, she put on her much smaller pack. She was swearing to herself that she'd show no fear.

Kimberly stayed close to John and it was unusual to see her up so early in the morning. Usually she stayed in bed until breakfast was cooked. Leah wasn't sure if Kim wanted to be near John or if he was insisting she stay there. But Leah was too caught up in her own problems to worry about Kim.

"Ready, Mrs. Stanford?" Wes asked.

Leah wouldn't look at him, but when he started walking, she was behind him.

Now they'd been walking for hours. Leah was tired, and long ago they'd left all sights and sounds of other people. Only she and the buckskin-clad man in front of her seemed to be left on the earth.

"Can you climb up there?" Wes asked, stopping and pointing.

Leah looked up at the steep climb to what seemed to be a cave opening. Curtly she nodded, but she wouldn't look at Wes.

"Give me your pack."

"I can carry it," she said, starting forward.

Wesley caught her pack and half pulled it from her back. "I told you to give me your pack and that's what I meant. You give me any more trouble and I'll throw you over my shoulder and carry you."

Still without looking at him, she slipped out of the pack and handed it to him. It wasn't an easy climb, especially in her long skirt, but every time she had difficulty, Wes was there with a hand freeing her skirt edge, steadying her at her waist, and once giving her a boost on her seat.

When she reached the top, she didn't thank him but stood on the ledge, flattened against the stone wall and peering into the blackness that was the cave. "Do you think there are any bears in there?" she whispered.

"Maybe," Wes answered unconcerned as he put their packs on the ground. "I'll have a look."

"Be . . . be careful," she murmured.

"Worried about me, are you?"

She met his eyes. "I don't want to be left here alone."

"I guess I deserved that," he half grunted, removing a heavy knife from the sheath at his side and a candle from his pack.

"Shouldn't you take the rifle?" she asked, aghast.

"Rifles are useless in close combat. How about a kiss before I enter?"

"I'm to reward you for putting us in the middle of nowhere in front of a bear's den? Maybe there's a whole family of bears in there and we'll both die."

His eyes twinkled. "If I could but die with your kiss on my lips . . ."

"Go on! Get it over with."

Wesley's face turned serious as he disappeared into the cave. "It's bigger than I thought," he said, his voice sounding hollow. "There're some Indian paintings on the walls and some signs of camp fires."

She could hear him moving in the cave and when he spoke again his voice sounded farther away.

"Doesn't look like there are any signs of bears. A few bones. Looks like lots of people have camped here."

For a few minutes he said nothing else and Leah began to relax from her rigid stance and took a step closer to the cave opening. She could hear Wesley walking about and now and then see the flicker of his candle flame.

"Is it safe?" she called.

"Sure," he yelled back. "Clean as a whistle."

In the next few seconds everything happened at once.

Wesley said, "Uh oh," then bellowed, "run, Leah! Hide!"

Instantly, Leah froze right where she was, smack in the middle of the wide cave opening.

In a lightning flash of buckskin fringe, Wesley came tearing out of the cave, and inches behind him was a big old black bear, its fat rippling as it lumbered after Wesley.

The bear brushed past Leah so closely that her nostrils flared at the smell of it. But she could no more move than the rock behind her could.

The bear didn't seem to notice her at all in its pursuit of Wes.

Only her eyes able to move, Leah watched Wes tear down the hillside.

"Climb a tree, Leah," he yelled back at her.

Tree, Leah thought. What is a tree? What does it look like?

She was still wondering this when she heard a loud splash to her left.

"Move, Leah," she commanded herself. But nothing happened. "Move!"

When she did move, it was quickly. She ignored Wes's order to climb a tree and took off, running toward the sound of the splash. She stopped, chest heaving, by a little pool of water that was surrounded by rock. Everything was perfectly quiet. There was no sign of Wesley or the bear. Just the birds singing, the late afternoon sunshine, the smell of grasses.

The next thing she knew her ankle had been grabbed and she was being dragged downward. Instinctively she began to struggle.

"Stop kicking!" Wes's voice hissed—his voice alone, because Leah still saw no one.

When she paused in her struggles, Wes jerked her into the water.

"What—?" She gasped just as Wes put his hand on the top of her head and pushed her underwater.

Her breath held, furious, she saw him submerge and she glared at him through the clear water.

He pointed and she looked. There above them, sniffing the air, was the bear. Wes motioned for her to follow him underwater and she did.

He swam to the opposite side of the little pool and stuck his head up behind some hanging greenery. Leah came up struggling for breath and instantly Wes put his fingers to her lips.

With a sideways glance Leah saw the bear in the same place and she moved away from the animal, which happened to be nearer Wesley. His arms opened and he pulled her to him, her back against his front. She couldn't struggle because the sound might carry to the bear.

Wesley caught her earlobe between his teeth and began to nibble on it.

She tried to move away.

He released her ear and nodded meaningfully toward the bear.

She tried to tell him with her eyes that she almost preferred the bear's mauling, but Wes's grip wouldn't let her move.

He began to nuzzle her neck, his kisses trailing upward to her hairline.

The water was warm, heated all day by the sun, and it was relaxing Leah's tired muscles. As Wes continued to explore her neck and the side of her face, Leah leaned back into him, turning her head to give him freer access.

"The bear's gone," he murmured.

"Mmm?" Leah said, her eyes closed.

Carolyn Lott Monohan

"Virginia Woman: 1775"

Poets who have written about pioneer Kentucky are legion. The Louisville poet Carolyn Lott Monohan speaks about the strong women who accompanied their men into the wilderness and often suffered more than they did.

Bright hunter, speak to her of Ken-tuck-ee.
"Imagine!
There are woodcocks there
with ivory bills;
beaver, deer and waterfoul
abound.
And cane there is,
great meadows of it
shining in the sun;
woodlands watered green
and wondrous caves all dripping
alabaster ice.
Seven rivers ravel
from blue mountain skeins
and over all there lies
the sheen of Eden!"
She listens, hunter!
She will risk the Gap with you
to Ken-tuck-ee.
In her hands is will enough
and strength
to mold you to the fertile land.

Charles Dickens

from *American Notes*

One of the most famous visitors to Kentucky was Charles Dickens, who, accompanied by his wife, visited the United States and Canada between January and June 1842. As a passenger on a steamboat between Cincinnati and Louisville, he met Chief Pitchlynn of the Choctaw Indians, who impressed him with his intelligence and learning. He arrived about midnight in Louisville and went immediately to the Galt House, with which he was much impressed. Indeed, he liked it so much that he later spent a second night there on his way back to Cincinnati from St. Louis. On his way to board the boat in the canal below Louisville near Portland, he commented on the coal-blackened buildings and the pigs in the streets. Onboard the *Fulton,* he entertained Jim Porter, the Kentucky Giant, who, unlike the dull, leaden people he traveled with on the boat, impressed him with his height of seven feet eight inches and his hospitality. As this selection indicates, by the time of Dickens's visit in 1842, Kentucky was almost out of the wilderness.

Leaving Cincinnati at eleven o'clock in the forenoon, we embarked for Louisville in the Pike steamboat, which, carrying the mails, was a packet of a much better class than that in which we had come from Pittsburg. As this passage does not occupy more than twelve or thirteen hours, we arranged to go ashore that night: not coveting the distinction of sleeping in a state-room, when it was possible to sleep anywhere else.

There chanced to be on board this boat, in addition to the usual dreary crowd of passengers, one Pitchlynn, a chief of the Choctaw tribe of Indians, who *sent in his card* to me, and with whom I had the pleasure of a long conversation.

He spoke English perfectly well, though he had not begun to learn the language, he told me, until he was a young man grown. He had read many books; and Scott's poetry appeared to have left a strong impression on his mind: especially the opening of The Lady of the Lake, and the great battle scene in Marmion, in which, no doubt from the congeniality of the subjects to his own pursuits and tastes, he had great interest and delight. He appeared to understand correctly all he had read; and whatever fiction had enlisted his sympathy in its belief, had done so keenly and earnestly. I might almost say fiercely. He was dressed in our ordinary every-day costume, which hung about his fine figure loosely, and with indifferent grace. On my telling him that I regretted not to see him in his own attire, he threw up his right arm, for a moment, as though he were brandishing some heavy weapon, and answered, as he let it fall again, that his race were losing many things besides their dress, and would soon be seen upon the earth no more: but he wore it at home, he added proudly.

He told me that he had been away from his home, west of the Mississippi, seventeen months: and was now returning. He had been chiefly at Washington on some negotiations pending between his Tribe and the Government: which were not settled yet (he said in a melancholy way), and he feared never would be: for what could a few poor Indians do, against such well-skilled men of business as the whites? He had no love for Washington; tired of towns and cities very soon; and longed for the Forest and the Prairie.

I asked him what he thought of Congress? He answered, with a smile, that it wanted dignity, in an Indian's eyes.

He would very much like, he said, to see England before he died; and spoke with much interest about the great things to be seen there. When I told him of that chamber in the British Museum wherein are preserved household memorials of a race that ceased to be, thousands of years ago, he was very attentive, and it was not hard to see that he had a reference in his mind to the gradual fading away of his own people.

This led us to speak of Mr. Catlin's gallery, which he praised highly: observing that his own portrait was among the collection, and that all the likenesses were "elegant." Mr. Cooper, he said, had painted the Red Man well; and so would I, he knew, if I would go home with him and hunt buffaloes, which he was quite anxious I should do. When I told him that supposing I went, I should not be very likely to damage the buffaloes much, he took it as a great joke and laughed heartily.

He was a remarkably handsome man; some years past forty I should judge; with long black hair, an aquiline nose, broad cheek-bones, a sunburnt complexion, and a very bright, keen, dark, and piercing eye. There were but twenty thousand of the Choctaws left, he said, and their number was decreasing every day. A few of his brother chiefs had been obliged to become civilised, and to make themselves acquainted with what the whites knew, for it was their only chance of existence. But they were not many; and the rest were as they always had been. He dwelt on this: and said several times that unless they tried to assimilate themselves to their conquerors, they must be swept away before the strides of civilised society.

When we shook hands at parting, I told him he must come to England, as he longed to see the land so much: that I should hope to see him there, one day: and that I could promise him he would be well received and kindly treated. He was evidently pleased by this assurance, though he rejoined with a good-humoured smile and an arch shake of his head, that the English used to be very fond of the Red Men when they wanted their help, but had not cared much for them, since.

He took his leave; as stately and complete a gentleman of Nature's making, as ever I beheld; and moved among the people in the boat, another kind of being. He sent me a lithographed portrait of himself soon afterwards; very like, though scarcely handsome enough; which I have carefully preserved in memory of our brief acquaintance.

There was nothing very interesting in the scenery of this day's journey, which brought us at midnight to Louisville. We slept at the Galt House; a splendid hotel; and were as handsomely lodged as though we had been in Paris, rather than hundreds of miles beyond the Alleghanies.

The city presenting no objects of sufficient interest to detain us on our way, we resolved to proceed next day by another steamboat, the Fulton, and to join it, about noon, at a suburb called Portland, where it would be delayed some time in passing through a canal.

The interval, after breakfast, we devoted to riding through the town, which is regular and cheerful: the streets being laid out at right angles, and planted with young trees. The buildings are smoky and blackened, from the use of bituminous coal, but an Englishman is well used to that appearance, and indisposed to quarrel with it. There did not appear to be much business stirring; and some unfinished buildings and improvements seemed to intimate that the city had been overbuilt in the ardour of "going ahead," and was suffering under the reaction consequent upon such feverish forcing of its powers.

On our way to Portland, we passed a "Magistrate's office," which amused me, as looking far more like a dame school than any police establishment: for this awful Institution was nothing but a little lazy, good-for-nothing front parlour, open to the street; wherein two or three figures (I presume the magistrate and his myrmidons) were basking in the sunshine, the very effigies of languor and repose. It was a perfect picture of Justice retired from business for want of customers; her sword and scales sold off; napping comfortably with her legs upon the table.

Here, as elsewhere in these parts, the road was perfectly alive with pigs of all ages; lying about in every direction, fast asleep; or grunting along in quest of hidden dainties. I had always a sneaking kindness for these odd animals, and found a constant source of amusement, when all others failed, in watching their proceedings. As we were riding along this morning, I observed a little incident between two youthful pigs, which was so very human as to be inexpressibly comical and grotesque at the time, though I dare say, in telling, it is tame enough.

One young gentleman (a very delicate porker with several straws sticking about his nose, betokening recent investigations in a dunghill) was walking deliberately on, profoundly thinking, when suddenly his brother, who was lying in a miry hole unseen by him, rose up immediately before his startled eyes, ghostly with damp mud. Never was pig's whole mass of blood so turned. He started back at least three feet, gazed for a moment, and then shot off as hard as he could go: his excessively little tail vibrating with speed and terror like a distracted pendulum. But before he had gone very far, he began to reason with himself as to the nature of this frightful appearance; and as he reasoned, he relaxed his speed by gradual degrees; until at last he stopped and faced about. There was his brother, with the mud upon him glazing in the sun, yet staring out of the very same hole, perfectly amazed at his proceedings! He was no sooner assured of this; and he assured himself so carefully that one may almost say he shaded his eyes with his hand to see the better; than he came back at a round trot, pounced upon him, and summarily took off a piece of his tail; as a caution to him to be careful what he was about for the future, and never to play tricks with his family any more.

We found the steamboat in the canal, waiting for the slow process of getting through the lock, and went on board, where we shortly afterwards had a new kind of visitor in the person of a certain Kentucky Giant whose name is Porter, and who is of the moderate height of seven feet eight inches, in his stockings.

There never was a race of people who so completely gave the lie to history as these giants, or whom all the chroniclers have so cruelly libelled. Instead of roaring and ravaging about the world, constantly catering for their cannibal larders, and perpetually going to market in an unlawful manner, they are the meekest people in any man's acquaintance: rather inclining to milk and vegetable diet, and bearing anything for a quiet life. So decidedly are amiability and mildness their characteristics, that I confess I look upon that youth who distinguished himself by the slaughter of these inoffensive persons, as a falsehearted brigand, who, pretending to philanthropic motives, was secretly influenced only by the wealth stored up within their castles, and the hope of plunder. And I lean the more to this opinion from finding that even the historian of those exploits, with all his partiality for his hero, is fain to admit that the slaughtered monsters in question were of a very innocent and simple turn; extremely guileless and ready of belief; lending a credulous ear to the most improbable tales; suffering themselves to be easily entrapped into pits; and even (as in the case of the Welsh Giant) with an excess of the hospitable politeness of a landlord, ripping themselves open, rather than hint at the possibility of their guests being versed in the vagabond arts of sleight-of-hand and hocus-pocus.

The Kentucky Giant was but another illustration of the truth of this position. He had a weakness in the region of the knees, and a trustfulness in his long face, which appealed even to five-feet nine for encouragement and support. He was only twenty-five years old, he said, and had grown recently, for it had been found necessary to make an addition to the legs of his inexpressibles. At fifteen he was a short boy, and in those days his English father and his Irish mother had rather snubbed him, as being too small of stature to sustain the credit of the family. He added that his health had not been good, though it was better now; but short people are not wanting who whisper that he drinks too hard.

I understand he drives a hackney-coach, though how he does it, unless he stands on the footboard behind, and lies along the roof upon his chest, with his chin in the box, it would be difficult to comprehend. He brought his gun with him, as a curiosity. Christened "The Little Rifle," and displayed outside a shopwindow, it would make the fortune of any retail business in Holborn. When he had shown himself and talked a little while, he withdrew with his pocket-instrument, and went bobbing down the cabin, among men of six feet high and upwards, like a lighthouse walking among lamp-posts.

Within a few minutes afterwards, we were out of the canal, and in the Ohio river again.

The arrangements of the boat were like those of the Messenger, and the passengers were of the same order of people. We fed at the same times, on the same kind of viands, in the same dull manner, and with the same observances. The company appeared to be oppressed by the same tremendous concealments, and had as little capacity of enjoyment or lightheartedness. I never in my life did see such listless, heavy dulness as brooded over these meals: the very recollection of it weighs me down, and makes me, for the moment, wretched. Reading and writing on my knee, in our little cabin, I really dreaded the coming of the hour that summoned us to table; and was as glad to escape from it again, as if it had been a penance or a punishment. Healthy cheerfulness and good spirits forming a part of the banquet, I could soak my crusts in the fountain with Le Sage's strolling player, and revel in their glad enjoyment: but sitting down with so many fellow-animals to ward off thirst and hunger as a business; to empty, each creature, his Yahoo's trough as quickly as he can, and then slink sullenly away; to have these social sacraments stripped of everything but the mere greedy satisfaction of the natural cravings; goes so against the grain with me, that I seriously believe the recollection of these funeral feasts will be a waking nightmare to me all my life.

There was some relief in this boat, too, which there had not been in the other, for the captain (a blunt good-natured fellow) had his handsome wife with him, who was disposed to be lively and agreeable, as were a few other lady-passengers who had their seats about us at the same end of the table. But nothing could have made head against the depressing influence of the general body. There was a magnetism of dulness in them which would have beaten down the most facetious companion that the earth ever knew. A jest would have been a crime, and a smile would have faded into a grinning horror. Such deadly leaden people; such systematic plodding weary insupportable heaviness; such a mass of animated indigestion in respect of all that was genial, jovial, frank, social, or hearty; never, sure, was brought together elsewhere since the world began.

The Scourges of Slavery
and Civil War

It is hard to believe that less than a century and a half ago—when my great-grandparents were living—most people, north and south, in this "land of the free" still accepted human slavery as a part of civil society. There had been abolitionist sentiments and movements throughout the colonial and early national periods, but none of them had been effective enough to abolish slavery as a matter of national policy. Indeed, all the so-called Northern states had officially outlawed slavery by the time of the Civil War; but all the states that had been English colonies had at one time permitted slavery. Even President Abraham Lincoln was ambivalent about the practice. Although he personally found slavery repugnant, he said at the beginning of the Civil War that his major objective was to save the Union and that if he could preserve the Union by freeing all of the slaves, he would do so; that if he could preserve the Union by freeing some of the slaves, he would do so; and that if he could preserve the Union by freeing none of the slaves, he would do so. In fact, his Emancipation Proclamation, issued on January 1, 1863, specifically freed only those slaves in states or parts of states that were "in rebellion against the United States." It was not until the adoption of the Thirteenth Amendment to the U.S. Constitution in 1865 that all the slaves in the nation were officially freed.

In this section of our Kentucky journey, we address slavery, the most important moral issue that the nation and Kentucky have had to resolve, and the war that probably had to be fought to resolve it. Although Southern apologists sometimes still justify their states' secessions from the Union in the name of states' rights, it is apparent to any objective reader of American history that the bottom line was slavery. For Lincoln and even for most of his Northern supporters, the war may have been about saving the Union; but it wasn't until Lincoln issued the Emancipation Proclamation that the war took on the moral dimension it needed for the continued support that led to ultimate victory for the Union side.

These fifteen selections pertain to the intertwining of slavery and war in Kentucky: commentary on slavery by Tocqueville; the reality of slavery as seen in the slave narratives; documents relating to the Civil War by Jefferson Davis and Abraham Lincoln, the Kentucky-born presidents of the Confederacy and the Union; fiction and nonfiction responses to slavery and the war by Harriet Beecher Stowe, the author of *Uncle Tom's Cabin,* who witnessed slavery in Kentucky while she was living in Cincinnati; and four twentieth-century Kentucky writers, Clara Rising, Alfred Leland Crabb, Charles Bracelen Flood, and Allen Tate.

Alexis de Tocqueville

from *Democracy in America*

Alexis de Tocqueville (1805–1859) was born into a prominent French aristocratic family with royal connections, but he developed liberal, democratic ideas and came to America in May 1831, ostensibly to study our prisons but actually to gather information on our political institutions that might be useful in democratizing France. His American journey took him from New England and Canada through almost all the states east of the Mississippi River. The Kentucky portion of his trip took him from Pittsburgh down the Ohio River to Wheeling, Cincinnati, and Louisville, then on to the lower south and finally back to New York, where he embarked for France in February 1832. The first volume of *Democracy in America* was published in 1835, and the second in 1840. In the following piece he contrasts the industry and thriving economy of "free labor" in Ohio with the sloth and violence he said characterized Kentucky, a slave state.

. . . why did the Americans abolish slavery in the North and why have they kept it and increased its hardships in the South?

The answer is easy. Slavery is being abolished in the United States not in the interest of the Negro but in that of the white man.

The first Negroes were imported into Virginia around 1621. In America as in the rest of the world, servitude was therefore born in the South. From there it spread gradually, but as slavery moved northward, the number of slaves tended to diminish. There have always been very few Negroes in New England.

The colonies were founded; a century had already elapsed when everyone began to be struck by an extraordinary fact. In provinces where people owned virtually no slaves, population, wealth, and prosperity were increasing more rapidly than in provinces where people did own slaves.

In the former, however, residents were obliged to cultivate the soil themselves or else to hire the services of others. In the latter, they could avail themselves of the services of workers who were not compensated for their efforts. Thus, labor and expense on the one hand, leisure and economy on the other: yet the advantage lay with the former.

This result was difficult to explain, all the more so in that the immigrants, all belonging to the same European race, shared the same habits, civilization, and laws and differed only in rather subtle ways.

More time passed: leaving the shores of the Atlantic Ocean behind, Anglo-Americans daily plunged deeper into the solitudes of the West. There they encountered new terrain and new climates. They had to overcome obstacles of various kinds. Their races mingled: men from the South went north, and men from the North went south. With all these various causes at work, the same phenomenon recurred at every stage, and, in general, colonies where there were no slaves became more populous and prosperous than colonies where slavery was in force.

The farther they went, the more they began to see that servitude, so cruel to the slave, was also fatal to the master.

The ultimate demonstration of this truth came when they reached the banks of the Ohio.

The river that the Indians called the Ohio, or Beautiful River par excellence, waters one of the most magnificent valleys ever settled by man. The rolling land that stretches into the distance on both sides of the river is for the farmer a constant source of inexhaustible riches. On both banks the air is healthy and the climate temperate. The river forms the boundary between two vast states. The one that lies to the left as one travels downstream through the thousand twists and turns described by the Ohio River is called Kentucky; the one that lies to the right takes its name from the river itself. The two states differ in only one respect: Kentucky allows slaves, whereas Ohio has expelled them from its midst.

Thus the traveler who lets the current of the Ohio carry him to the point where it joins the Mississippi navigates, as it were, between freedom and servitude, and he has only to look around to judge at a glance which is more propitious for humanity.

On the left bank of the river, the population is sparse. From time to time, a group of slaves can be seen ambling in their carefree way through half-cleared fields. The virgin forest never disappears for long. Society seems to slumber. Man appears idle, whereas nature is the very image of activity and life.

By contrast, the confused hum emanating from the right bank proclaims from afar the presence of industry. Rich harvests fill the fields. Elegant homes hint at the taste and fastidiousness of the farmers. Prosperity is apparent everywhere. Man seems rich and content: he is at work.

The state of Kentucky was founded in 1775, the state of Ohio not until twelve years later: twelve years in America is more than half a century in Europe. Today the population of Ohio already exceeds that of Kentucky by 250,000.

The contrasting effects of freedom and slavery are easy to understand. They suffice to explain many of the differences that one finds between ancient civilization and civilization today.

Labor is identified south of the Ohio with the idea of slavery, north of the Ohio with the idea of well-being and progress. To the south it is degraded, to the north honored. On the left bank of the river it is impossible to find workers of the white race; they would be afraid of looking like slaves. For labor, people must rely on the Negro. On the right bank one would search in vain for an idle person. The White applies his industriousness and intelligence to labor of every kind.

Hence those whose task it is to exploit the natural riches of the soil in Kentucky are neither eager nor enlightened, while those who could be both either do nothing or else cross over into Ohio so as to put their industriousness to good use in conditions where they need not be ashamed of it.

To be sure, masters in Kentucky make their slaves work without being obliged to pay them, but they derive little fruit from the slaves' efforts, whereas money paid to free workers would be returned with interest in the price of their products.

The free worker is paid, but he works more quickly than the slave, and speed of execution is an important factor in the economy. The White sells his services, but he finds buyers only when those services are useful. The Black has no claim on a price for his services, but he must be fed regularly. He must be supported in old age as well as in maturity, in barren childhood as well as in the fertile years of youth, in sickness and in health. Thus the work of both the White and the Black must be paid for: the free worker receives wages; the slave receives an upbringing, food, care, and clothing. The money that the master spends on the upkeep of the slave is meted out for specific purposes a little at a time; it is barely noticed. The wage paid to the worker is distributed in a lump sum and seems to enrich only the person to whom it is paid. In reality, however, the slave costs more than the free man, and his labor is less productive.

The influence of slavery extends still further. It penetrates the master's very soul and imparts a particular direction to his ideas and tastes.

Nature has given man an enterprising and energetic character on both banks of the Ohio, but the uses to which these common qualities are put differ from one side to the other.

The White on the right bank, who must support himself through his own efforts, has made material well-being the principal goal of his existence. Because he lives in a region that offers inexhaustible resources to his industry and endless incentives to his activity, his ardor to acquire has surpassed the ordinary limits of human cupidity: tormented by the desire for wealth, he boldly explores every path that fortune uncovers. He is equally ready to become a sailor, pioneer, manufacturer, or farmer, and equally willing to persevere in the face of the rigors and dangers with which these various occupations confront him. There is something wonderful about his ingenious resourcefulness and a kind of heroism in his avidity for profit.

The American of the left bank is contemptuous not only of labor but of all enterprises that succeed by virtue of labor. Living in idle comfort, he has the tastes of idle men. Money has lost part of its value in his eyes. What he seeks is not so much fortune as excitement and pleasure, and to that end he invests energy that his neighbor employs elsewhere. He has a passionate love of hunting and war. He enjoys the most violent forms of physical exercise. He is familiar with the use of arms, and as a child he learned to risk his life in single combat. Thus slavery not only prevents the White from making a fortune but diverts his will to other ends.

For two centuries, these factors, tending in opposite directions, have been constantly at work in the English colonies of North America, and they have led to a prodigious difference in the commercial abilities of southerners and northerners. Today, only the North has ships, factories, railroads, and canals.

This difference is apparent not only when the North is compared to the South but also when southerners are compared to one another. Almost all the men who engage in commercial enterprises and seek to use slavery in the southernmost states of the Union come from the North. Every day, northerners spread throughout this part of the country, where they have less to fear from competition. They discover resources that the residents had failed to notice and, adapting to a system of which they disapprove, capitalize on it more effectively than the people who founded it and still support it.

Were I inclined to press this parallel further, I could easily demonstrate that nearly all the evident differences between the southern and northern characters stem from slavery, but to do so would take me away from my subject: right now I am looking not at the effects of servitude in general but at the effects of servitude on the material prosperity of those who permit it.

Antiquity could have had only an imperfect understanding of this influence of slavery on the production of wealth. Servitude then existed throughout the civilized world; only among barbarian peoples was it unknown.

Accordingly, Christianity destroyed slavery solely by insisting on the rights of the slave. Today, one can attack it in the name of the master: on this point interest and morality are in accord.

As these truths became clear in the United States, slavery began slowly to recede in the face of enlightenment born of experience.

Servitude began in the South and expanded northward. Today it is receding. Freedom, emanating from the North, has been moving steadily southward. Among the large states, Pennsylvania today constitutes the extreme northern limit of slavery, but within its borders the institution is shaky. Maryland, which is just south of Pennsylvania, is on the point of abolishing it, and in Virginia, the next state to the south after Maryland, there is debate about its usefulness and dangers.

Whenever a great change in human institutions occurs, the law of inheritance always figures among the causes.

When unequal division of estates was the law in the South, every family had as its representative a wealthy man, who felt neither the desire nor the need to work. Surrounding him like so many parasitic plants were the members of his family, who were legally barred from a share of the common inheritance and lived as he did. In those days all southern families resembled the noble families that one still sees today in certain countries of Europe, where younger sons, though not as wealthy as the eldest, nevertheless lead lives just as idle. Similar effects sprang from entirely analogous causes in America and Europe. In the southern United States, the entire white race constituted an aristocratic body headed by a number of privileged individuals whose wealth was permanent and leisure hereditary. The leaders of the American nobility perpetuated the traditional prejudices of the white race in the body they represented and continued to set a high value on idleness. Within this aristocracy there were poor men but not workers; misery seemed preferable to industry. Negro workers and slaves therefore had no competitors, and no matter what opinion one might have held as to the utility of their efforts, one had to employ them, because there was no one else.

William Wells Brown

from *Narrative of William W. Brown, a Fugitive Slave*

Slave narratives were based on the true stories told by escaped or emancipated slaves about their experiences. Many of them were told to educated writers who doctored them up to conform to literary standards and to give them dramatic flair. This is the way that William Wells Brown's autobiography begins:

I was born in Lexington, Ky. The man who stole me as soon as I was born recorded the births of all the infants which he claimed to be born his property in a book which he kept for that purpose. My mother's maiden name was Elizabeth. She had seven children, viz: Solomon, Leander, Benjamin, Joseph, Millford, Elizabeth, and myself. No two of us were children of the same father. My father's name, as I learned from my mother, was George Higgins. He was a white man, a relative of my master, and connected with some of the first families in Kentucky.

Josiah Henson

from *Father Henson's Story of His Own Life*

Josiah Henson, the presumed model for Uncle Tom in Harriet Beecher Stowe's *Uncle Tom's Cabin,* was born a slave in 1789 in Charles County, Maryland, and grew up to become a trusted overseer and servant to his owner. His master put him in charge of a group of slaves being transported from Maryland to Owensboro, Kentucky, where Henson became a Methodist preacher. Here he also gained the confidence of his new master, who took him on a trading trip down the Mississippi River to New Orleans, where he planned to sell him. Had not his owner become disabled from an illness and needed Henson's care, he would have been sold into the harsher slavery of the lower south. It was this experience that convinced Henson that all forms of slavery were evil and that eventually he must run away. In October 1830 he escaped with his family and fled to Canada; there he helped to establish a thriving fugitive slave colony and became a leading spokesman for the emancipation of slaves. In these excerpts Henson (with the obvious aid of a writing teacher), speaks of how slaves managed to survive and even have some fun; then he recalls his family's escape to Cincinnati, the first leg of the road to freedom.

I have no desire to represent the life of slavery as an experience of nothing but misery. God be praised, that however hedged in by circumstances, the joyful exuberance of youth will bound at times over them all. Ours is a light-hearted race. The sternest and most covetous master cannot frighten or whip the fun out of us; certainly old Riley never did out of me. In those days I had many a merry time, and would have had, had I lived with nothing but moccasins and rattle-snakes in Okafenoke swamp. Slavery did its best to make me wretched; I feel no particular obligation to it; but nature, or the blessed God of youth and joy, was mightier than slavery. Along with memories of miry cabins, frosted feet, weary toil under the blazing sun, curses and blows, there flock in others, of jolly Christmas times, dances before old massa's door for the first drink of egg-nog, extra meat at holiday times, midnight visits to apple orchards, broiling stray chickens, and first-rate tricks to dodge work. The God who makes the pup gambol, and the kitten play, and the bird sing, and the fish leap, was the author in me of many a light-hearted hour. True it was, indeed, that the fun and freedom of Christmas, at which time my master relaxed his front, was generally followed up by a portentous back-action, under which he drove and cursed worse than ever; still the fun and freedom were fixed facts; we had had them and he could not help it.

Besides these pleasant memories I have others of a deeper and richer kind. I early learned to employ my spirit of adventure for the benefit of my fellow-sufferers. The condition of the male slave is bad enough; but that of the female, compelled to perform unfit labor, sick, suffering, and bearing the peculiar burdens of her own sex unpitied and unaided, as well as the toils which belong to the other, is one that must arouse the spirit of sympathy in every heart not dead to all feeling. The miseries which I saw many of the women suffer often oppressed me with a load of sorrow.

During the bright and hopeful days I spent in Ohio, while away on my preaching tour, I had heard much of the course pursued by fugitives from slavery, and became acquainted with a number of benevolent men engaged in helping them on their way. Canada was often spoken of as the only sure refuge from pursuit, and that blessed land was now the desire of my longing heart. Infinite toils and perils lay between me and that haven of promise; enough to daunt the stoutest heart; but the fire behind me was too hot and fierce to let me pause to consider them. I knew the North Star—blessed be God for setting it in the heavens! Like the Star of Bethlehem, it announced where my salvation lay. Could I follow it through forest, and stream, and field, it would guide my feet in the way of hope. I thought of it as my God-given guide to the land of promise far away beneath its light. I knew that it had led thousands of my poor, hunted brethren to freedom and blessedness. I felt energy enough in my own breast to contend with privation and danger; and had I been a free, untrammeled man, knowing no tie of father or husband, and concerned for my own safety only, I would have felt all difficulties light in view of the hope that was set before me. But, alas! I had a wife and four dear children; how should I provide for them? Abandon them I could not; no! not even for the blessed boon of freedom. They, too, must go. They, too, must share with me the life of liberty.

It was not without long thought upon the subject that I devised a plan of escape. But at last I matured it. My mind fully made up, I communicated the intention to my wife. She was overwhelmed with terror. With a woman's instinct she clung to hearth and home. She knew nothing of the wide world beyond, and her imagination peopled it with unseen horrors. We should die in the wilderness,—we should be hunted down with blood-hounds, —we should be brought back and whipped to death. With tears and supplications she besought me to remain at home, contented. In vain I explained to her our liability to be torn asunder at any moment; the horrors of the slavery I had lately seen; the happiness we should enjoy together in a land of freedom, safe from all pursuing harm. She had not suffered the bitterness of my lot, nor felt the same longing for deliverance. She was a poor, ignorant, unreasoning slave-woman.

I argued the matter with her at various times, till I was satisfied that argument alone would not prevail. I then told her deliberately, that though it would be a cruel trial for me to part with her, I would nevertheless do it, and take all the children with me except the youngest, rather than remain at home, only to be forcibly torn from her, and sent down to linger out a wretched existence in the hell I had lately visited. Again she wept and entreated, but I was sternly resolute. The whole night long she fruitlessly urged me to relent; exhausted and maddened, I left her, in the morning, to go to my work for the day. Before I had gone far, I heard her voice calling me, and waiting till I came up, she said, at last, she would go with me. Blessed relief! my tears of joy flowed faster than had hers of grief.

Our cabin, at this time, was near the landing. The plantation itself extended the whole five miles from the house to the river. There were several distinct farms, all of which I was over-seeing, and therefore I was riding about from one to another every day. Our oldest boy was at the house with Master Amos; the rest of the children were with my wife.

The chief practical difficulty that had weighed upon my mind, was connected with the youngest two of the children. They were of three and two years, respectively, and of course would have to be carried. Both stout and healthy, they were a heavy burden, and my wife had declared that I should break down under it before I had got five miles from home. Sometime previously I had directed her to make me a large knapsack of tow cloth, large enough to hold them both, and arranged with strong straps to go round my shoulders. This done, I had practised carrying them night after night, both to test my own strength and accustom them to submit to it. To them it was fine fun, and to my great joy I found I could manage them successfully. My wife's consent was given on Thursday morning, and I resolved to start on the night of the following Saturday. Sunday was a holiday; on Monday and Tuesday I was to be away on farms distant from the house; thus several days would elapse before I should be missed, and by that time I should have got a good start.

At length the eventful night arrived. All things were ready, with the single exception that I had not yet obtained my master's permission for little Tom to visit his mother. About sundown I went up to the great house to report my work, and after talking for a time, started off, as usual, for home; when, suddenly appearing to recollect something I had forgotten, I turned carelessly back, and said, "O, Master Amos, I most forgot. Tom's mother wants to know if you won't let him come down a few days; she wants to mend his clothes and fix him up a little." "Yes, boy, yes; he can go." "Thankee, Master

Amos; good night, good night. The Lord bless you!" In spite of myself I threw a good deal of emphasis into my farewell. I could not refrain from an inward chuckle at the thought—how long a good night that will be! The coast was all clear now, and, as I trudged along home, I took an affectionate look at the well-known objects on my way. Strange to say, sorrow mingled with my joy; but no man can live anywhere long without feeling some attachment to the soil on which he labors.

It was about the middle of September, and by nine o'clock all was ready. It was a dark, moonless night, when we got into the little skiff, in which I had induced a fellow slave to set us across the river. It was an anxious moment. We sat still as death. In the middle of the stream the good fellow said to me, "It will be the end of me if this is ever found out; but you won't be brought back alive, Sie, will you?" "Not if I can help it," I replied; and I thought of the pistols and knife I had bought some time before of a poor white. "And if they're too many for you, and you get seized, you'll never tell my part in this business?" "Not if I'm shot through like a sieve." "That's all," said he, "and God help you." Heaven reward him. He, too, has since followed in my steps; and many a time in a land of freedom have we talked over that dark night on the river.

In due time we landed on the Indiana shore. A hearty, grateful farewell, such as none but companions in danger can know, and I heard the oars of the skiff propelling him home.

There I stood in the darkness, my dear ones with me, and the all unknown future before us. But there was little time for reflection. Before daylight should come on, we must put as many miles behind us as possible, and be safely hidden in the woods. We had no friends to look to for assistance, for the population in that section of the country was then bitterly hostile to the fugitive. If discovered, we should be seized and lodged in jail. In God was our only hope. Fervently did I pray to him as we trudged on cautiously and steadily, and as fast as the darkness and the feebleness of my wife and boys would allow. To her, indeed, I was compelled to talk sternly; she trembled like a leaf, and even then implored me to return.

For a fortnight we pressed steadily on, keeping to the road during the night, hiding whenever a chance vehicle or horseman was heard, and during the day burying ourselves in the woods. Our provisions were rapidly giving out. Two days before reaching Cincinnati they were utterly exhausted. All night long the children cried with hunger, and my poor wife loaded me with reproaches for bringing them into such misery. It was a bitter thing to hear them cry, and God knows I needed encouragement myself. My limbs were weary, and my back and shoulders raw with the burden I carried. A fearful dread of detection ever pursued me, and I would start out of my sleep in terror, my heart beating against my ribs, expecting to find the dogs and slave-hunters after me. Had I been alone I would have borne starvation, even to exhaustion, before I would have ventured in sight of a house in quest of food. But now something must be done; it was necessary to run the risk of exposure by daylight upon the road.

The only way to proceed was to adopt a bold course. Accordingly, I left our hiding-place, took to the road, and turned towards the south, to lull any suspicion that might be aroused were I to be seen going the other way. Before long I came to a house. A furious dog rushed out at me, and his master following to quiet him, I asked if he would sell me a little bread and meat. He was a surly fellow. "No, he had nothing for niggers!" At the next I succeeded no better, at first. The man of the house met me in the same style; but his wife, hearing our conversation, said to her husband, "How can you treat any human being so? If a dog was hungry I would give him something to eat." She then added, "We have children, and who knows but they may some day need the help of a friend." The man laughed, and told her that she might take care of niggers, he wouldn't. She asked me to come in, loaded a plate with venison and bread, and, when I laid it into my handkerchief, and put a quarter of a dollar on the table, she quietly took it up and put it in my handkerchief, with an additional quantity of venison. I felt the hot tears roll down my cheeks as she said "God bless you;" and I hurried away to bless my starving wife and little ones.

A little while after eating the venison, which was quite salty, the children become very thirsty, and groaned and sighed so that I went off stealthily, breaking the bushes to keep my path, to find water. I found a little rill, and drank a large draught. Then I tried to carry some in my hat; but, alas! it leaked. Finally, I took off both shoes, which luckily had no holes in them, rinsed them out, filled them with water, and carried it to my family. They drank it with great delight. I have since then sat at splendidly furnished tables in Canada, the United States, and England; but never did I see any human beings relish anything more than my poor famishing little ones did that refreshing draught out of their father's shoes. That night we made a long run, and two days afterward we reached Cincinnati.

Harry Smith

from *Fifty Years of Slavery*

Another Kentucky slave, Harry Smith, paints a vivid portrait of the infamous slave pens in Louisville and the nefarious work of the "patrollers," who preyed upon runaway slaves.

Atkinson and Richardson were two southern men, living in New Orleans. They made annual tours to Kentuckey in the spring attending all the resorts of Tennessee and Kentuckey buying all the slaves they could find, large and small, they could get. When the planters would learn of their presence in the vicinity they would tell their negroes who would not toe the line that they would sell them to go south and drink Mississippi water.

When the slaves were aware of the presence of these two slave buyers a number of them would run away to the hills and remain often a year before they returned. Some would reach Canada for fear of being sold.

Going to New Orleans was called the Nigger Hell, few ever returning who went there. Usually those who ran away when caught were sold. As fast as they were brought back by Richardson and Atkins, they were taken to Louisville and placed in the negro pen and guarded until fall, when they were fettered, chained together and started on their long journey South.

Mr. Smith's old Massa Midcalf, as the reader is aware, kept a large hotel and when they were on their way with droves of negroes every negro that would stop there that night would be ordered not to leave the plantation under penalty of death. All night long chains would rattle. Some were crying for a mother left behind, some for an only child, and altogether it made a scene almost indescribable; and all the consolation they could hear would be the crack of the bull-whip of some watchman and floods of profanity. Some were tired out by their bloody feet walking on the frozen ground, and were compelled to dry up. "I will take you where it is warm enough—where you d——m backs will crack instead of your feet." Many were so crippled they could not walk and were thrown into some old wagon and conveyed in this manner to their journey's end. Water and mud made no difference; they were compelled to move right along.

At that time there were no turnpikes. The roads were all dirt and rock roads. After reaching Louisville they were put in a negro pen—barracks where they could not get away. Then these traders had them all washed and each one had a new suit of clothes, consisting of hard time cotton, this was for the man's breeches and shirts; and then cheap calico for the woman and a hard-time shirt constituted the woman's clothing. No shoes on any of them. There were two negro pens in Louisville. Nat Garrison owned one of them and Artiburn owned the other. They were marched out hundreds at a time after dressing and put on the steam boats and taken down the river.

Finally Magroo, who lived on the Bargetown turnpike, turned out to be a patroller. He was cruel and wicked to the colored folks. He owned a large steam distillery. He caught a colored man out one night and undertook to whip him, he resisted and it took six men to accomplish it, but they succeeded in cutting his flesh all into pieces, striking him over six hundred lashes. He finally reached home and was confined to his bed six weeks before he was able to resume work. Dick said nothing until the next fall. Then he repeated he would fix old Magroo for whipping him. When Magroo commenced making whiskey in the fall, he had a fine colored girl who Dick was paying some attention to. Magroo happened in one night when Dick was there and ordered him home; Dick started at the word. A few nights following, Magroo's still house and mill was all on fire. There was another great excitement among the colored folks, as it was all laid to them. So they had about a week's whipping to find out who fired the mill. All the clue they could get on Dick, some of the colored people heard him say he would fix Magroo. Uncle Dick was taken before Squire Salone, his sentence was to place him in jail, and in a few days send him down the river. The patrollers still continued in their nefarious business.

The next encounter the patrollers got into, was with a colored man belonging to old John Hycus, Harrison was his name, and he was away visiting his girl, where they found him and took him out to whip him. Harrison resisted them. They struck him as usual with their iron canes. Harrison was getting the best of them. One of them stabbed him. Harrison whipped out his knife and the wildest excitement ensued. The man who owned the girl Harrison called to see, saw the whole affair, also his three sons and his wife. In the fight at that time the darkies wore their hair long, many took great pains with their hair. In the melee that ensued, one of the first party struck Harrison on the head with his iron cane and cut off a large tuft of hair, clearing the skin from the scalp. They succeeded in getting the advantage of him at last, and leaving him for dead they quit the bloody scene. Immediately his owner, John Hycus, was informed and he came down with a conveyance and took him home. When Harrison got a little better, the patrollers sued John Hycus for injuring some of them, then he sued them for barberously using his colored man. For each man Harrison cut with his knife, the court granted them $700 each. For every hair they knocked and cut off from Harrison's head it cost the patrollers the sum of $100, which amounted to a good many thousand dollars.

The hairs were counted in the court house at Louisville. John Hycus won the suit after one year. This tragic affair forever ended in Kentuckey the nefarious work of the patrollers.

Milton Clarke

from *Narrative of the Suffering of Lewis and Milton Clarke*

Milton Clarke, a Lexington slave, describes the gruesome reality of slave auctions, broken families, and floggings, giving a graphic portrayal of slave driving.

When I was about six years of age, the estate of Samuel Campbell, my grandfather, was sold at auction. His sons and daughters were all present at the sale, except Mrs. Banton. Among the articles and animals put upon the catalogue, and placed in the hands of the auctioneer, were a large number of slaves. When every thing else had been disposed of, the question arose among the heirs, "What shall be done with Letty (my mother) and her children?" John and William Campbell came to mother, and told her they would divide her family among the heirs, but none of them should go out of the family. One of the daughters—to her everlasting honor be it spoken—remonstrated against any such proceeding. Judith, the wife of Joseph Logan, told her brothers and sisters, "Letty is our own half sister, and you know it; father never intended they should be sold." Her protest was disregarded, and the auctioneer was ordered to proceed. My mother, and her infant son Cyrus, about one year old, were put up together and sold for $500!! Sisters and brothers selling their own sister and her children!! My venerable old father, who was now in extreme old age, and debilitated from the *wounds* received in the war of the Revolution, was, nevertheless, roused by this outrage upon his rights and upon those of his children.

"He had never expected," he said, "when fighting for the liberties of this country, to see his own wife and children sold in it to the highest bidder." But what were the entreaties of a quivering old man, in the sight of eight or ten hungry heirs? The bidding went on; and the whole family, consisting of mother and eight children, were sold at prices varying from $300 to $800. Lewis, the reader will recollect, had been previously given to that paragon of excellence, Mrs. Banton. It was my fortune, with my mother, brother Cyrus, and sister Delia, to fall into the hands of aunt Judith; and had she lived many years, or had her husband shared with her the virtues of humanity, I should probably have had far less to complain of, for myself and some of the family.

She was the only one of all the family that I was ever willing to own, or call my aunt.

The third day after the sale, father, mother, Delia, Cyrus, and myself, started for our home at Lexington, with Mr. Joseph Logan, a tanner. He was a tall, lank, gray-eyed, hard-hearted, cruel wretch; coarse, vulgar, debauched, corrupt and corrupting; but in good and regular standing in the Episcopalian church. We were always protected, however, from any very great hardships during the life of his first wife.

At her death, which happened in about two years, we were sincere mourners; although her husband was probably indulging far other emotions than those of sorrow. He had already entered, to a considerable extent, into arrangements for marrying a younger sister of his wife, Miss Minerva Campbell. She was a half fool, besides being underwitted. If any body falls into such hands, they will know what Solomon meant, when he said, "Let a bear robbed of her whelps meet a man, rather than a *fool* in his folly." There are a great many bears in Kentucky, but none of them quite equal to a slaveholding woman.

I had a regular battle with this young mistress, when I was about eleven years old. She had lived in the family while her sister was alive, and from the clemency of Judith, in protecting the slaves, the authority of Miss Minerva was in a very doubtful state when she came to be installed mistress of the house. Of course, every occasion was sought to show her authority. She attempted to give me a regular breaking-in, at the age above stated. I used the weapons of defence "God and nature gave me;" I bit and scratched, and well nigh won the battle; but she sent for Logan, whose shadow was more than six feet, and I had to join the *non-resistance* society right off. It was all day with me then. He dashed me down upon my head, took the raw hide and ploughed up my young back, and that grinning fool, his wife, was looking on; this was a great aggravation of the flogging, that she should see it and rejoice over it.

When I was about twelve years old, I was put to grinding bark in the tannery. Not understanding the business, I did not make such progress as Logan thought I ought to make. Many a severe beating was the consequence. At one time, the shoulder of the horse was very sore, and Logan complained that I did not take good care of him. I tried to defend myself as well as I could, but his final argument was thumping my head against the post. Kings have their *last* argument, and so have slaveholders. I took the old horse into the stable, and, as I had no one else to talk with, I held quite a dialogue with old Dobbin. Unluckily for me, Logan was hid in another stall, to hear his servant curse him. I told the horse, "Master complains that I don't grind bark enough; complains that I work you too hard; don't feed you enough; now, you old rascal, you know it is a lie, the whole of it; I have given you fifteen ears of corn three times a day, and that is enough for any horse; Cæsar says that is enough, and Moses says that is enough; now eat your corn, and grow fat." At the end of this apostrophe, I gave the old horse three good cuts on the face, and told him to walk up and eat the corn. I then stepped out into the floor and threw in fifteen ears more, and said, "See if the old man will think that is enough."

Scarcely had the words passed my lips, when I heard a rustling in the next stall, and Joe Logan was before me, taller than ever I saw him before, and savage as a cannibal. I made for the door, but he shut it upon me, and caught me by one leg. He began kicking and cuffing, till, in my despair, I seized him, like a young bear, by the leg, with my teeth, and, with all his tearing and wrenching, he could not get me off. He called one of the white hands from the tanyard, and just as he came in, Logan had his knife out, and was about to cut my throat. The man spoke, and told him not to do that. They tied me and gave me *three hundred lashes*; my back was peeled from my shoulders to my heels.

Mother was in the house, and heard my screams, but did not dare to come near me. Logan left me weltering in my blood; mother then came and took me up, and carried me into her own room. About 8 o'clock that evening, Logan came out and asked mother if I was alive or dead. She told him I was alive. I laid there four weeks, before I went out of the door. Let fathers and mothers think what it would be to see a child whipped to the very gate of death, and not be permitted to say a word in their behalf. Words can never tell what I suffered, nor what mother suffered. I shuddered at the countenance of Joseph Logan for many months after. The recollection now makes me shudder, as I go back to that bitter day.

Jefferson Davis

from "Farewell Address to the U.S. Senate"

Born in Fairview, in Todd County, Kentucky, Jefferson Davis attended St. Thomas Catholic School in Springfield and later Transylvania University; he graduated from West Point in 1828. When he was two years old, his family moved to Louisiana and then Mississippi, which became Davis's political base. After the collapse of the Confederacy, he moved his family to Beauvoir, an estate on the Mississippi Gulf coast.

The following is Davis's farewell not only to the Senate but also to the Union; he was soon to become the first and only president of the Confederate States of America.

I am sure I feel no hostility towards you, Senators from the North. I am sure there is not one of you, whatever sharp discussion there may have been between us, to whom I cannot now say, in the presence of my God, I wish you well; and such, I am sure, is the feeling of the people whom I represent towards those whom you represent. I, therefore, feel that I but express their desire when I say I hope, and they hope, for peaceable relations with you, though we must part. They may be mutually beneficial to us in the future, as they have been in the past, if you so will it. The reverse may bring disaster on every portion of the country; and, if you will have it thus, we will invoke the God of our fathers, who delivered them from the power of the lion, to protect us from the ravages of the bear; and thus, putting our trust in God and in our own firm hearts and strong arms, we will vindicate the right as best we may. . . .

Mr. President and Senators, having made the announcement which the occasion seemed to me to require, it only remains for me to bid you a final adieu. . . .

Letter to Governor Magoffin

Davis wrote this letter to Governor Beriah Magoffin of Kentucky regarding the state's attempt to remain neutral.

To the Hon. B. Magoffin, Governor of Kentucky, etc.

Sir.—I have received your letter informing me that "since the commencement of the unhappy difficulties yet pending in the country, the people of Kentucky have indicated a steadfast desire and purpose to maintain a position of strict neutrality between the belligerent parties." In the same communication you express your desire to elicit "an authoritative assurance that the government of the Confederate States will continue to respect and observe the neutral position of Kentucky."

In reply to this request, I lose no time in assuring you, that the government of the Confederate States of America neither intends nor desires to disturb the neutrality of Kentucky. The assemblage of troops in Tennessee, to which you refer, had no other object than to repel the lawless invasion of that State by the forces of the United States, should their government seek to approach it through Kentucky without respect for its position of neutrality. That such apprehensions were not groundless has been proved by the course of that government in the States of Maryland and Missouri, and more recently in Kentucky itself, in which, as you inform me, "a military force has been enlisted and quartered by the United States authorities."

The government of the Confederate States had not only respected most scrupulously the neutrality of Kentucky, but has continued to maintain the friendly relations of trade and intercourse which it has suspended with the people of the United States generally.

In view of the history of the past, it can scarcely be necessary to assure your Excellency that the government of the Confederate States will continue to respect the neutrality of Kentucky so long as her people will maintain it themselves.

But neutrality, to be entitled to respect, must be strictly maintained between both parties; or if the door be opened on the one side for aggressions of one of the belligerent parties upon the other, it ought not to be shut to the assailed when they seek to enter it for the purpose of self-defense.

I do not, however, for a moment believe that your gallant State will suffer its soil to be used for the purpose of giving an advantage to those who violate its neutrality and disregard its rights, over others who respect them both.

In conclusion, I tender to your Excellency the assurance of my high consideration and regard.

And am, Sir, very respectfully yours, etc.,

Jefferson Davis

Abraham Lincoln

Letter to Governor Magoffin

Abraham Lincoln was born into a humble family in a log cabin in Kentucky in 1809, near Hodgenville, and he had the good fortune to remain in the state until he was seven, when his family moved westward, first across the Ohio River to Indiana, and later to Illinois, which now claims him as a native son. He became a lawyer, then courted and married the aristocratic Mary Todd from Lexington. His best friend was Joshua Speed of Louisville. He helped to found the Republican Party in 1856, which selected him as its candidate for president in 1860. He was elected, and then re-elected in 1864; he was assassinated by a South-sympathizing actor in 1865. He was easily this nation's greatest president and possibly the best writer to be elected to that office. This, the first of two superb letters, is written to the Confederate-leaning governor of Kentucky.

To his Excellency B. Magoffin, Governor of the State of Kentucky.

Sir.—Your letter of the 19th inst., in which you "urge the removal from the limits of Kentucky of the military force now organized, and in camp within said State," is received.

I may not possess full and precisely accurate knowledge upon this subject, but I believe it is true that there is a military force in camp within Kentucky, acting by authority of the United States, which force is not very large, and is not now being augmented.

I also believe that some arms have been furnished to this force by the United States.

I also believe that this force consists exclusively of Kentuckians, having their camp in the immediate vicinity of their own homes, and not assailing or menacing any of the good people of Kentucky.

In all I have done in the premises, I have acted upon the urgent solicitation of many Kentuckians, and in accordance with what I believed, and still believe, to be the wish of a majority of all the Union-loving people of Kentucky.

While I have conversed on this subject with many eminent men of Kentucky, including a large majority of her members of congress, I do not remember that any one of them, or any person, except your Excellency and the bearers of your Excellency's letter, has urged me to remove the military force from Kentucky, or to disband it. One other very worthy citizen of Kentucky did solicit me to have the augmenting for the force suspended for a time.

Taking all the means within my reach to form a judgment I do not believe it is the popular wish of Kentucky that this force should be removed beyond her limits, and, with this impression, I must respectfully decline to so remove it.

I most cordially sympathize with your Excellency in the wish to preserve the peace of my own native State, Kentucky, but it is with regret I search, and cannot find, in your not very short letter any declaration or intimation that you entertain any desire for the preservation of the Federal Union.

Your obedient servant,
A. Lincoln

Letter to Mr. Hodges

Another fine letter, this is one Lincoln wrote to a Kentuckian in the spring of 1864 about his hatred of slavery and his love of the Union.

⌇⧖⌇

My dear Sir: You ask me to put in writing the substance of what I verbally said the other day in your presence, to Governor Bramlette and Senator Dixon. It was about as follows:

"I am naturally antislavery. If slavery is not wrong, nothing is wrong. I cannot remember when I did not so think and feel, and yet I have never understood that the presidency conferred upon me an unrestricted right to act officially upon this judgment and feeling. It was in the oath I took that I would, to the best of my ability, preserve, protect, and defend the Constitution of the United States. I could not take the office without taking the oath. Nor was it my view that I might take an oath to get power, and break the oath in using the power. I understood, too, that in ordinary civil administration this oath even forbade me to practically indulge my primary abstract judgment on the moral question of slavery. I had publicly declared this many times, and in many ways. And I aver that, to this day, I have done no official act in mere deference to my abstract judgment and feeling on slavery. I did understand, however, that my oath to preserve the Constitution to the best of my ability imposed upon me the duty of preserving, by every indispensable means, that government—that nation, of which that Constitution was the organic law. Was it possible to lose the nation and yet preserve the Constitution? By general law, life and limb must be protected, yet often a limb must be amputated to save a life; but a life is never wisely given to save a limb. I felt that measures otherwise unconstitutional might become lawful by becoming indispensable to the preservation of the Constitution through the preservation of the nation. Right or wrong, I assumed this ground, and now avow it. I could not feel that, to the best of my ability, I had even tried to preserve the Constitution, if, to save slavery or any minor matter, I should permit the wreck of government, country, and Constitution all together. When, early in the war, General Fremont attempted military emancipation, I forbade it, because I did not then think it an indispensable necessity. When, a little later, General Cameron, then Secretary of War, suggested the arming of the blacks, I objected because I did not yet think it an indispensable necessity. When, still later, General Hunter attempted military emancipation, I again forbade it, because I did not yet think the indispensable necessity had come. When in March and May and July, 1862, I made earnest and successive appeals to the border States to favor compensated emancipation, I believed the indispensable necessity for military emancipation and arming the blacks would come unless averted by that measure. They declined the proposition, and I was, in my best judgment, driven to the alternative of either surrendering the Union, and with it the Constitution, or of laying strong hand upon the colored element. I chose the latter. In choosing it, I hoped for greater gain than loss; but of this, I was not entirely confident. More than a year of trial now shows no loss by it in our foreign relations, none in our popular sentiment, none in our white military force—no loss by it anyhow or anywhere. On the contrary it shows a gain of quite a hundred and thirty thousand soldiers, seamen, and laborers. These are palpable facts, about which, as facts, there can be no cavilling. We have the men; and we could not have had them without the measure.

"And now let any Union man who complains of the measure test himself by writing down in one line that he is for subduing the rebellion by force of arms; and in the next, that he is for taking these hundred and thirty thousand men from the Union side, and placing them where they would be but for the measure he condemns. If he cannot face his case so stated, it is only because he cannot face the truth."

I add a word which was not in the verbal conversation. In telling this tale I attempt no compliment to my own sagacity. I claim not to have controlled events, but confess plainly that events have controlled me. Now, at the end of three years' struggle, the nation's condition is not what either party, or any man, devised or expected. God alone can claim it. Whither it is tending seems plain. If God now wills the removal of a great wrong, and wills also that we of the North, as well as you of the South, shall pay fairly for our complicity in that wrong, impartial history will find therein new cause to attest and revere the justice and goodness of God.

Yours, A. Lincoln

"Second Inaugural Address"

I have included my favorite of Lincoln's public speeches, his "Second Inaugural Address," in which, with his characteristic eloquence and succinctness, he reviews the stark tragedy of war, God's possible role in the conflict, and, finally, his hope for reconciliation with the breakaway South. He extends to his enemies the hand of fellowship and generosity.

❧

Fellow-Countrymen:—At this second appearing to take the oath of the presidential office there is less occasion for an extended address than there was at the first. Then a statement somewhat in detail of a course to be pursued seemed fitting and proper. Now, at the expiration of four years, during which public declarations have been constantly called forth on every point and phase of the great contest which still absorbs the attention and engrosses the energies of the nation, little that is new could be presented. The progress of our arms, upon which all else chiefly depends, is as well known to the public as to myself, and it is, I trust, reasonably satisfactory and encouraging to all. With high hope for the future, no prediction in regard to it is ventured.

On the occasion corresponding to this four years ago all thoughts were anxiously directed to an impending civil war. All dreaded it, all sought to avert it. While the inaugural address was being delivered from this place, devoted altogether to *saving* the Union without war, insurgent agents were in the city seeking to *destroy* it without war—seeking to dissolve the Union and divide effects by negotiation. Both parties deprecated war, but one of them would *make* war rather than let the nation survive, and the other would *accept* war rather than let it perish, and the war came.

One eighth of the whole population was colored slaves, not distributed generally over the Union, but localized in the southern part of it. These slaves constituted a peculiar and powerful interest. All knew that this interest was somehow the cause of the war. To strengthen, perpetuate, and extend this interest was the object for which the insurgents would rend the Union even by war, while the Government claimed no right to do more than to restrict the territorial enlargement of it. Neither party expected for the war the magnitude or the duration which it has already attained. Neither anticipated that the *cause* of the conflict might cease with or even before the conflict itself should cease. Each looked for an easier triumph, and a result less fundamental and astounding. Both read the same Bible and pray to the same God, and each invokes His aid against the other. It may seem strange that any men should dare to ask a just God's assistance in wringing their bread from the sweat of other men's faces, but let us judge not, that we be not judged. The prayers of both could not be answered. That of neither has been answered fully. The Almighty has His own purposes. "Woe unto the world because of offenses: for it must needs be that offenses come, but woe to that man by whom the offense cometh." If we shall suppose that American slavery is one of those offenses which, in the providence of God, must needs come, but which, having continued through His appointed time, He now wills to remove, and that He gives to both North and South this terrible war, as the woe due to those by whom the offense came, shall we discern therein any departure from those divine attributes which the believers in a living God always ascribe to Him? Fondly do we hope, fervently do we pray, that this mighty scourge of war may speedily pass away. Yet, if God wills that it continue until all the wealth piled by the bondsman's two hundred and fifty years of unrequited toil shall be sunk, and until every drop of blood drawn with the lash shall be paid by another drawn with the sword, as was said three thousand years ago, so still it must be said, "The judgments of the Lord are true and righteous altogether."

With malice toward none, with charity for all, with firmness in the right as God gives us to see the right, let us strive on to finish the work we are in, to bind up the nation's wounds, to care for him who shall have borne the battle and for his widow and his orphan, to do all which may achieve and cherish a just and lasting peace among ourselves and with all nations.

Harriet Beecher Stowe

from *Uncle Tom's Cabin*

Harriet Beecher Stowe was not a Kentucky writer, but she wrote the most influential book ever written in this country and set it in Kentucky. She did live close to Kentucky, just across the Ohio River in Cincinnati, where her husband taught in a theological seminary. Moreover, she apparently made a number of visits into Kentucky's slavocracy, with trips to Maysville, Paint Lick, and Daviess County, where the slave Josiah Henson lived, who may have been a model for Uncle Tom in her novel *Uncle Tom's Cabin* (1852). Stowe did a considerable amount of research before writing her big book, including field research and reading such works as Josiah Henson's and Milton Clarke's slave narratives. As the legend goes, when Mrs. Stowe met Mr. Lincoln, he remarked that, ah, so she was the little lady whose book had caused the big war. I have chosen from her book one of its best-known and most loved passages, the episode in which the slave Eliza, after discovering that her son has been sold, spirits him away to freedom across the frozen Ohio River, one ice floe at a time. Stowe was not a great writer, but her story, even in the twenty-first century, is heartbreaking.

In consequence of all the various delays, it was about three-quarters of an hour after Eliza had laid her child to sleep in the village tavern that the party came riding into the same place. Eliza was standing by the window, looking out in another direction, when Sam's quick eye caught a glimpse of her. Haley and Andy were two yards behind. At this crisis, Sam contrived to have his hat blown off, and uttered a loud and characteristic ejaculation, which startled her at once; she drew suddenly back; the whole train swept by the window, round to the front door.

A thousand lives seemed to be concentrated in that one moment to Eliza. Her room opened by a side door to the river. She caught her child, and sprang down the steps towards it. The trader caught a full glimpse of her, just as she was disappearing down the bank; and throwing himself from his horse, calling loudly on Sam and Andy, he was after her like a hound after a deer. In that dizzy moment her feet to her scarce seemed to touch the ground, and a moment brought her to the water's edge. Right on behind they came; and, nerved with strength such as God gives only to the desperate, with one wild cry and flying leap, she vaulted sheer over the turbid current by the shore, on to the raft of ice beyond. It was a desperate leap—impossible to anything but madness and despair; and Haley, Sam, and Andy, instinctively cried out, and lifted up their hands, as she did it.

The huge green fragment of ice on which she alighted pitched and creaked as her weight came on it, but she stayed there not a moment. With wild cries and desperate energy she leaped to another and still another cake;—stumbling—leaping—slipping—springing upwards again! Her shoes are gone—her stockings cut from her feet—while blood marked every step; but she saw nothing, felt nothing, till dimly, as in a dream, she saw the Ohio side, and a man helping her up the bank.

"Yer a brave gal, now, whoever ye ar!" said the man, with an oath.

Eliza recognized the voice and face of a man who owned a farm not far from her old home.

"O Mr. Symmes!—save me—do save me—do hide me!" said Eliza.

"Why, what's this?" said the man. "Why, if 'tan't Shelby's gal!"

"My child!—this boy!—he'd sold him! There is his Mas'r," said she, pointing to the Kentucky shore. "O Mr. Symmes, you've got a little boy!"

"So I have," said the man, as he roughly, but kindly drew her up the steep bank. "Besides, you're a right brave gal. I like grit, wherever I see it."

When they had gained the top of the bank the man paused.

"I'd be glad to do something for ye," said he; "but then thar's nowhar I could take ye. The best I can do is to tell ye to go *thar*," said he, pointing to a large white house which stood by itself, off the main street of the village. "Go thar; they're kind folks. Thar's no kind o' danger but they'll help you,—they're up to all that sort o' thing."

"The Lord bless you!" said Eliza earnestly.

"No 'casion, no 'casion in the world," said the man. "What I've done's of no 'count."

"And, oh, surely, sir, you won't tell any one!"

"Go to thunder, gal! What do you take a feller for? In course not," said the man. "Come, now, go along like a likely, sensible gal, as you are. You've arnt your liberty, and you shall have it, for all me."

The woman folded her child to her bosom, and walked firmly and swiftly away. The man stood and looked after her.

"Shelby, now, mebbe won't think this yer the most neighborly thing in the world; but what's a feller to do? If he catches one of my gals in the same fix, he's welcome to pay back. Somehow I never could see no kind o' critter a-strivin' and pantin', and trying to clar theirselves, with the dogs arter 'em, and go agin 'em. Besides, I don't see no kind of 'casion for me to be hunter and catcher for other folks, neither."

So spoke this poor, heathenish Kentuckian, who had not been instructed in his constitutional relations, and consequently was betrayed into acting in a sort of Christianized manner, which, if he had been better situated and more enlightened, he would not have been left to do.

Haley had stood a perfectly amazed spectator of the scene, till Eliza had disappeared up the bank, when he turned a blank, inquiring look on Sam and Andy.

"That ar was a tol'able fair stroke of business," said Sam.

"The gal's got seven devils in her, I believe!" said Haley. "How like a wildcat she jumped!"

"Wal, now," said Sam, scratching his head, "I hope Mas'r'll 'scuse us tryin' dat ar road. Don't think I feel spry enough for dat ar, no way!" and Sam gave a hoarse chuckle.

"*You* laugh!" said the trader with a growl.

"Lord bless you, Mas'r. I couldn't help it, now," said Sam, giving way to the long pent-up delight of his soul. "She looked so curi's, a leapin' and springin'—ice a crackin'—and only to hear her,—plump! ker chunk! ker splash! Spring! Lord! how she goes it!" and Sam and Andy laughed till the tears rolled down their cheeks.

"I'll make ye laugh t'other side yer mouths!" said the trader, laying about their heads with his riding-whip.

Both ducked, and ran shouting up the bank, and were on their horses before he was up.

"Good-evening, Mas'r!" said Sam, with much gravity. "I berry much 'spect Missis be anxious 'bout Jerry. Mas'r Haley won't want us no longer. Missis wouldn't hear of our ridin' the critters over 'Lizy's bridge to-night;" and, with a facetious poke into Andy's ribs, he started off, followed by the latter, at full speed,—their shouts of laughter coming faintly on the wind.

Eliza made her desperate retreat across the river just in the dusk of twilight. The gray mist of evening, rising slowly from the river, enveloped her as she disappeared up the bank, and the swollen current and floundering masses of ice presented a hopeless barrier between her and her pursuer. Haley therefore slowly and discontentedly returned to the little tavern, to ponder further what was to be done. The woman opened to him the door of a little parlor, covered with a rag-carpet, where stood a table with a very shining black oil-cloth, sundry lank, high-backed wood chairs, with some plaster images in resplendent colors on the mantel-shelf, above a very dimly-smoking grate; a long hard-wood settle extended its uneasy length by the chimney, and here Haley sat him down to meditate on the instability of human hopes and happiness in general.

"What did I want with the little cuss, now," he said to himself, "that I should have got myself treed like a coon, as I am, this yer way?" and Haley relieved himself by repeating over a not very select litany of imprecations on himself, which, though there was the best possible reason to consider them as true, we shall, as a matter of taste, omit.

He was startled by the loud and dissonant voice of a man who was apparently dismounting at the door. He hurried to the window.

"By the land! if this yer an't the nearest, now to what I've heard folks call Providence," said Haley. "I do b'lieve that ar's Tom Loker."

Haley hastened out. Standing by the bar, in the corner of the room, was a brawny, muscular man, full six feet in height, and broad in proportion. He was dressed in a coat of buffalo-skin, made with the hair outward, which gave him a shaggy and fierce appearance, perfectly in keeping with the whole air of his physiognomy. In the head and face every organ and lineament expressive of brutal and unhesitating violence was in a state of the highest possible development. Indeed, could our readers fancy a bull-dog come unto man's estate, and walking about in a hat and coat, they would have no unapt idea of the general style and effect of his physique. He was accompanied by a travelling companion, in many respects an exact contrast to himself. He was short and slender, lithe and cat-like in his motions, and had a peering mousing expression about his keen black eyes, with which every feature of his face seemed sharpened into sympathy; his thin, long nose ran out as if it was eager to bore into the nature of things in general; his sleek, thin, black hair was stuck eagerly forward, and all his motions and evolutions expressed a dry, cautious acuteness. The great big man poured out a big tumbler half full of raw spirits, and gulped it down without a word. The little man stood tiptoe, and putting his head first to one side then to the other, and snuffing considerately in the directions of the various bottles, ordered at last a mint julep, in a thin and quivering voice, and with an air of great circumspection. When poured out, he took it and looked at it with a sharp, complacent air, like a man who thinks he has done about the right thing, and hit the nail on the head, and proceeded to dispose of it in short and well-advised sips.

"Wal, now, who'd a thought this yer luck'd come to me? Why, Loker, how are ye?" said Haley, coming forward, and extending his hand to the big man.

"The devil!" was the civil reply. "What brought you here, Haley?"

The mousing man, who bore the name of Marks, instantly stopped his sipping, and, poking his head forward, looked shrewdly on the new acquaintance, as a cat sometimes looks at a moving dry leaf, or some other possible object of pursuit.

"I say, Tom, this yer's the luckiest thing in the world. I'm in a devil of a hobble, and you must help me out."

"Ugh? aw! like enough!" grunted his complacent acquaintance. "A body may be pretty sure of that, when *you're* glad to see 'em; something to be made off of 'em. What's the blow now?"

"You've got a friend here?" said Haley, looking doubtfully at Marks; "partner, perhaps?"

"Yes, I have. Here, Marks! here's that ar feller that I was in with in Natchez."

"Shall be pleased with his acquaintance," said Marks, thrusting out a long, thin hand, like a raven's claw. "Mr. Haley, I believe?"

"The same, sir," said Haley. "And now, gentlemen, seein' as we've met so happily, I think I'll stand up to a small matter of a treat in this here parlor. So, now, old coon," said he to the man at the bar, "get us hot water, and sugar, and cigars, and plenty of the *real stuff,* and we'll have a blow-out."

Behold, then, the candles lighted, the fire stimulated to the burning point in the grate, and our three worthies seated round a table, well spread with all the accessories to good-fellowship enumerated before.

Haley began a pathetic recital of his peculiar troubles. Loker shut up his mouth, and listened to him with gruff and surly attention. Marks, who was anxiously and with much fidgeting compounding a tumbler of punch to his own peculiar taste, occasionally looked up from his employment, and, poking his sharp nose and chin almost into Haley's face, gave the most earnest heed to the whole narrative. The conclusion of it appeared to amuse him extremely, for he shook his shoulders and sides in silence, and perked up his thin lips with an air of great internal enjoyment.

"So, then, ye'r fairly sewed up, ain't ye?" he said; "he! he! he! It's neatly done, too."

"This yer young-un business makes lots of trouble in the trade," said Haley, dolefully.

"If we could get a breed of gals that didn't care, now, for their young uns," said Marks; "tell ye, I think 'twould be 'bout the greatest mod'rn improvement I knows on,"—and Marks patronized his joke by a quiet introductory sniggle.

"Jes so," said Haley; "I never couldn't see into it; young uns is heaps of trouble to 'em; one would think, now, they'd be glad to get clar on 'em; but they arn't. And the more trouble a young un is, and the more good for nothing, as a gen'l thing, the tighter they sticks to 'em."

"Wal, Mr. Haley," said Marks, "jest pass the hot water. Yes, sir; you say jest what I feel and all'us have. Now, I bought a gal once, when I was in the trade,—a tight, likely wench she was, too, and quite considerable smart,—and she had a young un that was mis'able sickly; it had a crooked back, or something or other; and I jest gin't away to a man that thought he'd take his chance raising on't, being it didn't cost nothin';—never thought, yer know, of the gal's takin' on about it,—but, Lord, yer oughter seen how she went on. Why, re'lly, she did seem to me to valley the child more 'cause 'twas sickly and cross and plagued her; and she wan't making b'lieve, neither,—cried about it, she did, and lopped round, as if she'd lost every friend she had. It re'lly was droll to think on't. Lord, there an't no end to women's notions."

"Wal, jest so with me," said Haley. "Last summer, down on Red River, I got a gal traded off on me, with a likely lookin' child enough, and his eyes looked as bright as yourn; but come to look, I found him stone blind. Fact— he was stone blind. Wal, ye see, I thought there warn't no harm in my jest passing him along, and not sayin' nothin'; and I'd got him nicely swapped off for a keg o' whiskey; but come to get him away from the gal, she was jest like a tiger. So 'twas before we started, and I hadn't got my gang chained up; so what should she do but ups on a cotton-bale, like a cat, ketches a knife from one of the deck hands, and, I tell ye, she made all fly for a minit, till she saw 'twan't no use; and she jest turns round, and pitches head first, young un and all, into the river,—went down plump, and never ris."

"Bah!" said Tom Loker, who had listened to these stories with ill-repressed disgust,—"shif'less, both on ye! *my* gals don't cut up no such shines, I tell ye!"

"Indeed! how do you help it?" said Marks, briskly.

"Help it? why, I buys a gal, and if she's got a young un to be sold, I jest walks up and puts my fist to her face, and says, 'Look here, now, if you give me one word out of your head, I'll smash yer face in. I won't hear one word— not the beginning of a word.' I says to 'em, 'This yer young un's mine, and not yorn, and you've no kind o' business with it. I'm going to sell it, first chance; mind, you don't cut up none o' yer shines about it, or I'll make ye wish ye'd never been born. I tell ye, they sees it an't no play, when I gets hold. I makes 'em as whist as fishes; and if one on 'em begins and gives a yelp, why,—" and Mr. Loker brought down his fist with a thump that fully explained the hiatus.

"That ar's what ye may call *emphasis*," said Marks poking Haley in the side, and going into another small giggle. "An't Tom peculiar? he! he! he! I say, Tom, I s'pect you makes 'em *understand*, for all niggers' heads is woolly. They don't never have no doubt o' your meaning, Tom. If you an't the devil, Tom, you's his twin brother, I'll say that for ye!"

Tom received the compliment with becoming modesty, and began to look as affable as was consistent, as John Bunyan says, "with his doggish nature."

Haley, who had been imbibing very freely of the staple of the evening, began to feel a sensible elevation and enlargement of his moral faculties—a phenomenon not unusual with gentlemen of a serious and reflective turn, under similar circumstances.

"Wal, now, Tom," he said, "ye re'lly is too bad, as I al'ays have told ye; ye know, Tom, you and I used to talk over these yer matters down in Natchez, and I used to prove to ye that we made full as much, and was as well off for this yer world, by treatin' on 'em well, besides keepin' a better chance for comin' in the kingdom at last, when wust comes to wust, and thar an't nothing else left to get, ye know."

"Boh!" said Tom, "*don't* I know?—don't make me too sick with any yer stuff,—my stomach is a leetle riled now;" and Tom drank half a glass of raw brandy.

"I say," said Haley, and leaning back in his chair and gesturing impressively, "I'll say this now, I al'ays meant to drive my trade so as to make money on't, *fust and foremost*, as much as any man; but, then, trade an't everything, and money an't everything, 'cause we's all got souls. I don't care, now, who hears me say it,—and I think a cussed sight on it,—so I may as well come out with it. I b'lieve in religion, and one of these days, when I've got matters tight and snug, I calculates to tend to my soul and them ar matters; and so what's the use of doin' any more wickedness than's re'lly necessary?—it don't seem to me it's 'tall prudent."

"Tend to your soul!" repeated Tom, contemptuously; "take a bright lookout to find a soul in you,—save yourself any care on that score. If the devil sifts you through a hair sieve, he won't find one."

"Why, Tom, you're cross," said Haley; "why can't ye take it pleasant, now, when a feller's talking for your good?"

"Stop that ar jaw o' yourn, there," said Tom, gruffly. "I can stand 'most any talk o' yourn but your pious talk,—that kills me right up. After all, what's the odds between me and you? 'Tan't that you care one bit more, or have a bit more feelin',—it's clean, sheer dog meanness, wanting to cheat the devil and save your own skin; don't I see through it? And your 'gettin' religion,' as you call it, arter all, is too p'isin mean for any crittur;—run up a bill with the devil all your life, and then sneak our when paytime comes! Boh!"

"Come, come, gentlemen, I say; this isn't business," said Marks. "There's different ways, you know, of looking at all subjects. Mr. Haley is a very nice man, no doubt, and has his own conscience; and, Tom, you have your ways, and very good ones, too, Tom; but quarrelling, you know, won't answer no kind of purpose. Let's go to business. Now, Mr. Haley, what is it?—you want us to undertake to catch this yer gal?"

"The gal's no matter of mine—she's Shelby's; it's only the boy. I was a fool for buying the monkey!"

"You're generally a fool!" said Tom, gruffly.

"Come, now, Loker, none of your huffs," said Marks, licking his lips; "you see, Mr. Haley's a-puttin' us in a way of a good job, I reckon; just hold still,—these yer arrangements is my forte. This yer gal, Mr. Haley, how is she? what is she?"

"Wal! white and handsome—well brought up. I'd a gin Shelby eight hundred or a thousand and then made well on her."

"White and handsome—well brought up!" said Marks, his sharp eyes, nose, and mouth all alive with enterprise. "Look here, now, Loker, a beautiful opening. We'll do a business here on our own account;—we does the catchin'; the boy, of course, goes to Mr. Haley,—we takes the gal to Orleans to speculate on. An't it beautiful?"

Tom, whose great heavy mouth had stood ajar during this communication, now suddenly snapped it together, as a big dog closes on a piece of meat, and seemed to be digesting the idea at his leisure.

"Ye see," said Marks to Haley, stirring his punch as he did so, "ye see, we has justices convenient at all p'ints along shore, and does up any little jobs in our line quite reasonable. Tom, he does the knockin' down and that ar; and I come in all dressed up—shining boots—everything first chop, when, the swearin' 's to be done. You oughter see, now," said Marks, in a glow of professional pride, "how I can tone it off. One day, I'm Mr. Twickem, from New Orleans; 'nother day, I'm just come from my plantation on Pearl River, where I works seven hundred niggers; then, again, I come out a distant relation of Henry Clay, or some old cock in Kentuck. Talents is different, you know. Now, Tom's a roarer when there's any thumping or fighting to be done; but at lying he an't good, Tom an't,—ye see it don't come natural to him; but, Lord, if thar's a feller in the country that can swear to anything and everything, and put in all the circumstances and flourishes with a longer face, and carry 't through better'n I can, why, I'd like to see him, that's all! I b'lieve my heart, I could get along and snake through, even if justices were more particular than they is. Sometimes, I rather wish they was more particular: 'twould be a heap more relishin' if they was,—more fun, yer know."

Tom Loker, who, as we have made it appear, was a man of slow thoughts and movements, here interrupted Marks by bringing his heavy fist down on the table, so as to make all ring again. *"It'll do!"* he said.

"Lord bless ye, Tom, ye needn't break all the glasses!" said Marks; "save your fist for time o' need."

"But, gentlemen, an't I to come in for a share of the profits?" said Haley.

"An't it enough we catch the boy for ye?" said Loker. "What do ye want?"

"Wal," said Haley, "if I gives you the job, it's worth something,—say ten percent on the profits, expenses paid."

"Now," said Loker, with a tremendous oath, and striking the table with his heavy fist, "don't I know *you*, Dan Haley? Don't you think to come it over me! Suppose Marks and I have taken up the catchin' trade, jest to 'commodate gentlemen like you, and get nothin' for ourselves?—Not by a long chalk! we'll have the gal out and out, and you keep quiet, or, ye see, we'll have both,—what's to hinder? Han't you show'd us the game? It's as free to us as you, I hope. If you or Shelby wants to chase us, look where the partridges was last year; if you find them or us, you're quite welcome."

"O, wal, certainly, jest let it go at that," said Haley, alarmed; "you catch the boy for the job;—you allers did trade *far* with me, Tom, and was up to yer word."

"Ye know that," said Tom; "I don't pretend none of your snivelling ways, but I won't lie in my 'counts with the devil himself. What I ses I'll do, I will do,—you know *that*, Dan Haley."

"Jes so, jes so,—I said so, Tom," said Haley; "and if you'd only promise to have the boy for me in a week, at any point you'll name, that's all I want."

"But it an't all I want, by a long jump," said Tom. "Ye don't think I did business with you, down in Natchez, for nothing, Haley; I've learned to hold an eel, when I catch him. You've got to fork over fifty dollars, flat down, or this child don't start a peg. I know yer."

"Why, when you have a job in hand that may bring a clean profit of somewhere about a thousand or sixteen hundred, why, Tom, you're onreasonable," said Haley.

"Yes, and hasn't we business booked for five weeks to come,—all we can do? And suppose we leaves all, and goes to bush-whacking round arter yer young'un, and finally doesn't catch the gal,—and gals allers is the devil *to* catch,—what's then? would you pay us a cent—would you? I think I see you a-doin' it—ugh! No, no; flap down your fifty. If we get the job, and it pays, I'll hand it back; if we don't, it's for our trouble,—that's far, an't it, Marks?"

"Certainly, certainly," said Marks, with a conciliatory tone; "it's only a retaining fee, you see,—he! he! he!—we lawyers, you know. Wal, we must all keep good-natured,—keep easy, yer know. Tom'll have the boy for yer, any-where ye'll name; won't ye, Tom?"

"If I find the young'un, I'll bring him on to Cincinnati, and leave him at Granny Belcher's, on the landing," said Loker.

Marks had got from his pocket a greasy pocket-book, and taking a long paper from thence, he sat down, and fixing his keen black eyes on it, began mumbling over its contents: "Barnes—Shelby County—boy Jim, three hundred dollars for him, dead or alive.

"Edwards—Dick and Lucy—man and wife, six hundred dollars; wench Polly and two children—six hundred for her or her head.

"I'm jest a-runnin' over our business, to see if we can take up this yer handily. Loker," he said, after a pause, "we must set Adams and Springer on the track of these yer; they've been booked some time."

"They'll charge too much," said Tom.

"I'll manage that ar; they's young in the business, and must spect to work cheap," said Marks, as he continued to read. "Ther's three on 'em easy cases, 'cause all you've got to do is to shoot 'em, or swear they is shot; they couldn't, of course, charge much for that. Them other cases," he said, folding the paper, "will bear puttin' off a spell. So now let's come to the particulars. Now, Mr. Haley, you saw this yer gal when she landed?"

"To be sure,—plain as I see you."

"And a man helpin' on her up the bank?" said Loker.

"To be sure, I did."

"Most likely," said Marks, "she's took in somewhere; but where, 's a question. Tom, what do you say?"

"We must cross the river to-night, no mistake," said Tom.

"But there's no boat about," said Marks. "The ice is running awfully, Tom; an't it dangerous?"

"Don'no nothing 'bout that,—only it's got to be done," said Tom, decidedly.

"Dear me," said Marks, fidgeting, "it'll be—I say," he said, walking to the window, "it's dark as a wolf's mouth, and, Tom——"

"The long and short is, you're scared, Marks; but I can't help that,— you've got to go. Suppose you want to lie by a day or two, till the gal's been carried on the underground line up to Sandusky or so, before you start."

"O, no; I an't a grain afraid," said Marks, "only——"

"Only what?" said Tom.

"Well, about the boat. Yer see there an't any boat."

"I heard the woman say there was one coming along this evening, and that a man was going to cross over in it. Neck or nothing; we must go with him," said Tom.

"I s'pose you've got good dogs," said Haley.

"First rate," said Marks. "But what's the use? you han't got nothin' o' hers to smell on."

"Yes, I have," said Haley, triumphantly. "Here's her shawl she left on the bed in her hurry; she left her bonnet, too."

"That ar's lucky," said Loker; "fork over."

"Though the dogs might damage the gal, if they come on her unawares," said Haley.

"That ar's a consideration," said Marks. "Our dogs tore a feller half to pieces, once, down in Mobile, 'fore we could get 'em off."

"Well, ye see, for this sort that's to be sold for their looks, that ar won't answer, ye see," said Haley.

"I do see," said Marks. "Besides, if she's got took in, 'tan't no go, neither. Dogs is no 'count in these yer up states where these critters gets carried; of course, ye can't get on their track. They only does down in plantations, where niggers, when they runs, has to do their own running, and don't get no help."

"Well," said Loker, who had just stepped out to the bar to make some inquiries, "they say the man's come with the boat; so, Marks——"

That worthy cast a rueful look at the comfortable quarters he was leaving, but slowly rose to obey. After exchanging a few words of further arrangement, Haley, with visible reluctance, handed over the fifty dollars to Tom, and the worthy trio separated for the night.

If any of our refined and Christian readers object to the society into which this scene introduces them, let us beg them to begin and conquer their prejudices in time. The catching business, we beg to remind them, is rising to the dignity of a lawful and patriotic profession. If all the broad land between the Mississippi and the Pacific becomes one great market for bodies and souls, and human property retains the locomotive tendencies of this nineteenth century, the trader and catcher may yet be among our aristocracy.

❧ ❧ ❧

While this scene was going on at the tavern, Sam and Andy, in a state of high felicitation, pursued their way home.

Sam was in the highest possible feather, and expressed his exultation by all sorts of supernatural howls and ejaculations, by divers odd motions and contortions of his whole system. Sometimes he would sit backward, with his face to the horse's tail and sides, and then, with a whoop and a somerset, come right side up in his place again, and, drawing on a grave face, begin to lecture Andy in high-sounding tones for laughing and playing the fool. Anon, slapping his sides with his arms, he would burst forth in peals of laughter, that made the old woods ring as they passed. With all these evolutions, he contrived to keep the horses up to the top of their speed, until, between ten and eleven, their heels resounded on the gravel at the end of the balcony. Mrs. Shelby flew to the railings.

"Is that you, Sam? Where are they?"

"Mas'r Haley's a-restin' at the tavern; he's drefful fatigued, Missis."

"And Eliza, Sam?"

"Wal, she's clar 'cross Jordan. As a body may say, in the land o' Canaan."

"Why, Sam, what *do* you mean?" said Mrs. Shelby, breathless, and almost faint, as the possible meaning of these words came over her.

"Wal, Missis, de Lord he parsarves his own. 'Lizy's done gone over the river into 'Hio, as 'markably as if de Lord took her over in a charrit of fire and two hosses."

Sam's vein of piety was always uncommonly fervent in his mistress' presence; and he made great capital of Scriptural figures and images.

Harriet Beecher Stowe 103

"Come up here, Sam," said Mr. Shelby, who had followed on to the verandah, "and tell your mistress what she wants. Come, come, Emily," said he, passing his arm around her, "you are cold and all in a shiver; you allow yourself to feel too much."

"Feel too much! Am not I a woman,—a mother? Are we not both responsible to God for this poor girl? My God! lay not this sin to our charge."

"What sin, Emily? You see yourself that we have only done what we were obliged to."

"There's an awful feeling of guilt about it, though," said Mrs. Shelby, "I can't reason it away."

"Here, Andy, you nigger, be alive!" called Sam, under the verandah; "take these yer hosses to der barn; don't yer hear Mas'r a-callin'?" and Sam soon appeared, palm-leaf in hand, at the parlor door.

"Now, Sam, tell us distinctly how the matter was," said Mr. Shelby. "Where is Eliza, if you know?"

"Wal, Mas'r, I saw her, with my own eyes, a-crossin' on the floatin' ice. She crossed most 'markably; it wasn't no less nor a miracle; and I saw a man help her up the 'Hio side, and then she was lost in the dusk."

"Sam, I think this rather apocryphal,—this miracle. Crossing on floating ice isn't so easily done," said Mr. Shelby.

"Easy! couldn't nobody a done it, widout the Lord. Why, now," said Sam, "'twas jist dis yer way. Mas'r Haley, and me, and Andy, we comes up to de little tavern by the river, and I rides a leetle ahead,—(I's so zealous to be a cotchin' 'Lizy, that I couldn't hold in, no way),—and when I comes by the tavern winder, sure enough, there she was right in plain sight, and dey diggin' on behind. Wal, I loses off my hat, and sings out 'nuff to raise the dead. Course 'Lizy she hars, and she dodges back when Mas'r Haley he goes past the door; and then, I tell ye, she clared out de side door; she went down the river-bank;—Mas'r Haley he seed her, and yelled out, and him, and me, and Andy, we took arter. Down she come to the river, and thar was the current running ten feet wide by the shore, and over t'other side ice a-sawin' and a-jiggling up and down, kinder as 'twere a great island. We come right behind her, and I thought my soul he'd got her sure enough,—when she gin sich a screech as I never hearn, and thar she was, clar over t'other side the current, on the ice, and then on she went, a-screeching and a-jumpin'—the ice went crack! c'wallop! cracking! chunk! and she a-boundin' like a buck! Lord, the spring that ar gal's got in her an't common, I'm o' 'pinion."

Mrs. Shelby sat perfectly silent, pale with excitement, while Sam told his story.

"God be praised, she isn't dead!" she said; "but where is the poor child now?"

"De Lord will pervide," said Sam, rolling up his eyes piously. "As I've been a-sayin', dis yer's a providence and no mistake, as Missis has allers been a-instructin' on us. Thar's allers instruments ris up to do de Lord's will. Now, if 't hadn't been for me to-day, she'd a been took a dozen times. Warn't it I started off de hosses, dis yer mornin', and kept 'em chasin' till nigh dinner time? And didn't I car' Mas'r Haley nigh five miles out of de road, dis evening, or else he'd a come up with 'Lizy as easy as a dog arter a coon. These yer's all providences."

"They are a kind of providence that you'll have to be pretty sparing of, Master Sam. I allow no such practices with gentlemen on my place," said Mr. Shelby, with as much sternness as he could command, under the circumstances.

Clara Rising

from *In the Season of the Wild Rose*

Kentucky's own Clara Rising wrote a fact-filled novel about Kentucky's dashing Confederate raider, John Hunt Morgan. *In the Season of the Wild Rose* resurrects her hero and clothes him in the burnished armor of doomed chivalry. (Another twentieth-century Kentucky novelist, Gene Markey, wrote about the family of one of Morgan's raiders and the harsh realities of Reconstruction in *Kentucky Pride* [1956].) Here are two passages from Rising's magnificent reenactment of the Battle of Shiloh, one of the war's crucial turning points, which occurred near a little country church on a cliff overlooking the Tennessee River, close to where the states of Tennessee, Alabama, and Mississippi come together. The first excerpt is a lyrical paean to the foolish courage of warriors on both sides. The second is a macabre postmortem on the wasted lives of young men lost in battle.

Shiloh! *Shiloh.* The sound of that name, like the vibrato of a chill wind, would blow everything, everything before it. A silent, sacred, secret place for tabernacles to wait, as in the days of Samuel: *And the whole congregation of the children of Israel assembled. . . . And the land was subdued before them.*

Shiloh.

A little log church in Tennessee.

An insignificant country meeting place surrounded by a tumbled, upended land of vine-choked woods and ravines with sheer drops of a hundred feet or more, of forests and fields where more than a hundred thousand men would struggle and scream and leave more Americans dead in two days than the Revolution, the War of 1812 and the Mexican War combined. Where the thunder of cannon, like a mad giant hammering the sky, his feet mired in blood-soaked mud, would annihilate valor, however brave, however individual.

From the river and across trembling peach blossoms and peaceful ponds and the dark, haunted mounds of dead Indians the roar would deafen and drown and finally silence the groans of the wounded and dying, and the giant would laugh at those onrushing lines with their flags fluttering and their notion of honor and wait for the fear that would numb and the pain that would blind all human hope. Like a monster lifting his head above the clouds, War would watch the miscalculation and error, the orders received too late or sent too soon, nameless boys dying and a general with steel-blue eyes and a square jaw, under vines and in the shade of April leaves, laughing at the wound that would kill him.

No grave, however deep, can bury you, O Shiloh.

No wind, however strong, can blow the memory of you away. . . .

The retreating lines stretched for almost ten miles, long lines of wagons loaded with wounded, piled like sacks, groaning and cursing the lurching wheels that stuck in axle-deep mud. Exhausted horses and mules strained forward, some sinking in their harnesses, which were removed, in some cases carefully placed in other wagons, or on the limbers of gun-carriages. Behind the wagons came the infantry, too tired to curse, staggering, supporting each other or a dangling, broken arm. About nightfall a cold, drizzling rain became a pitiless hail, as if the sky itself were bombarding them with vindictiveness.

In Corinth the ghastly trains arrived, dripping blood on the streets as the wounded were carried up the steps of houses, onto sidewalks, or laid out at the depot platform, where shocked ladies received, made comfortable, nursed and by daylight slumped, exhausted themselves, in a nightmare of dead and dying. For two weeks mothers appeared, from little towns like Bolivar and Middleburg and Hickory Valley and Rogers Springs, to gather their wounded, to take their boys home, in most cases to die. Chest and stomach wounds were the worst; mercifully, the pain would not last long. Amputees had, the doctors knew, a 10 percent chance. As for the others, they managed, and a slow exodus began.

The generals made proclamations. The Battle of Shiloh was a Confederate success. Braxton Bragg's first act was to assemble his troops, the brave men of Shiloh and Elkhorn (for by now Van Dorn's troops had arrived from Arkansas), to tell them that "A few more days of needful preparation and organization and I shall give your banners to the breeze." He would lead them "to additional honors to those you have already won on other fields." Then he added: "But be prepared to undergo privations and labor with cheerfulness and alacrity." Strangely, insanely, they cheered.

Underneath, Morgan knew why. Something had happened. After Shiloh, nothing, not even the well-intentioned speeches of its own generals, could have told the Confederate soldier what he knew in his bowels, in his soul: that a gut-deep determination to survive had been born.

For three days Breckinridge, with the rear guard, camped on the Corinth Road, burying the dead from the "hospital," collecting straggling wounded and sending on to Beauregard scavanged Yankee guns. Morgan's squadron remained in the vicinity of the battlefield for more than a week. But the Federals were quiet, busy burning dead horses and burying their dead. An acrid, incredible stench blew in with the smoke. Before dawn Tuesday Morgan received an order from Beauregard's headquarters to send a courier for permission to gather the Confederate dead and wounded from the battlefield.

Sam Morgan and Gus Magee volunteered to go. Morgan watched them leave just as daylight began lifting mist in the woods. Sam carried the white flag and galloped forward, his body bent in a V. Three hours later they returned. When Magee dismounted, Morgan saw the answer written on his face.

"They're burying their own. Neat rows. Separate graves. The Confederates . . ."

"The Confederates?"

"General Grant refuses," Sam spoke up, "to release them. Claims the climate . . . health reasons." He looked down at his boots, scuffing the trampled grass under his feet.

Magee cleared his throat. "The Confederates are being buried seven deep in open trenches. Or where they fell, where convenient."

So. James, beloved West. Standing so straight when he took the oath at Woodsonville. And Jim Geslin. Behind his mother, so full of trust, in the terror of retreat through Nashville. And Buckner, just a boy. They were all just boys. Buckner chopping down that flagpole for Alice. They should be courting somewhere. Flung down like dogs in a common grave. He would never know where. He prayed they were dead.

It rained constantly, threatening to wash away the mud from shallow graves. Mounted Confederate vedettes, shifting on their horses, watched the reeking, mud-running, corpse-strewn battlefield in disbelief. For four days the smoke kept rising from those mounds of horseflesh. In the distance squads of bent forms, carrying dead and wounded, looked like giant, misshapen ants against the underbrush. Morgan, late one afternoon, rode near Fraley Field with Tom. They heard voices, and Morgan held up his hand for silence. Two Yankee infantrymen were laughing and talking not fifty feet away. They soon saw what their joke was: A hand and half an arm had escaped a grave, and one of the soldiers had stuck a piece of hardtack between the fingers.

"Wouldn't want this feller to go to the next world empty-handed, now would we? Might get a mite hongry before he gets thar!"

Tom sank back in his saddle, his face white. Tears cut through rage: The sleeve on the arm was gray.

Alfred Leland Crabb

from *Peace at Bowling Green*

No one has written more historical novels about the Civil War than Alfred Leland Crabb, who was born in Plum Springs, in Warren County, Kentucky, in 1916. Six of his novels are set in Tennessee, and only one—his most popular and best—takes place in Kentucky. Although focused on the war, *Peace at Bowling Green* (1955) presents a grand panorama of the history of Bowling Green, from the town's founding in 1803 through the Civil War, Reconstruction, and Reconciliation. Briefly designated the Confederate capital of Kentucky, Bowling Green was a hotbed of passion and violence, which was quelled at last by an early peace. These excerpts from the novel bring together historical characters such as Confederate general Simon Bolivar Buckner, who had refused a commission in the Union Army, and a host of fictional but genuine Bowling Green citizens.

Early in November, General Buckner sent notice of his intention to occupy Bowling Green with his army. He planned to erect such fortifications as were necessary to protect the section in case of invasion from the north. He promised the citizens the least possible interruption to their daily routines. Under the existing conditions, he could not permit any hindrance to the army in its assigned tasks. It had been the plan of the South to respect Kentucky's neutrality, but the status of neutrality had been violated by Northern forces, and consequently the South could hardly be expected to regard with fidelity the state's border lines.

On a Monday morning, the leading citizens gathered in the courthouse to consider solemnly their plans for the future. Rumsey Skiles acted as chairman. And that was fitting. No one had heard him speak a partisan word in the whole unhappy issue. He read aloud General Buckner's message and proclamation.

"It all means," he said in his cool, precise way, "that Kentucky is at war. I have never thought there would be any way to stay out of it. We have a great many people who favor the South. That has been their way of life and thought. We have a great many friends and neighbors who favor the North. We have already contributed soldiers to both armies. Undoubtedly, there will be a great many more. But our homes are here. We are neighbors. Undoubtedly, there will be friction and strained relations. But we must let the battles be fought by soldiers on the fields, and we must learn to abide by both defeat and victory. We must come to realize that a man can favor either side and still be a gentleman. We want no spies here sending out reports to either side.

"We learn that General Buckner is coming up from Tennessee with a detachment of Kentucky troops to occupy our town. All of us hate to have the town so disturbed by the activities of war, but there is nothing we can do to prevent it. We will be fortunate indeed if General Buckner's is the only army brought to Bowling Green. Our very location will tempt armies. It is my strong suggestion that those who stay here as citizens play the part of citizens, and no other part. Are there any questions, or does any citizen wish to make a statement?"

Frisbee Cherry, a known Northern sympathizer, stood. "We have been told time and again that Kentucky is a neutral state, and that we would not be invaded by either army."

"We have indeed been told that," said the chairman gravely, "but as a matter of fact, Northern troops have already invaded Kentucky and established a camp on our soil. It is possible that Kentucky will take neither side officially, but both sides will use Kentucky, and we might just as well face it. There is no earthly way to keep them out."

"All right," said Cherry, "but are we to pay the bills of both sides while they are in the state? Will these Rebels—" he looked about him and decided to change the word—"Southerners raid our cribs to feed their horses? Will they take the meat from our smokehouses?"

"We have been promised that they will not. In war promises are usually kept at first, but forgotten if it goes on long enough. I do not anticipate any pillage under General Buckner. My information is that, while he is a soldier, his word can be trusted."

"Why are we meeting if there is nothing we can do?" asked Ed Hampton.

"So that we may understand the situation, so that under this stress we may behave with due discretion. It will be annoying, of course, to have the work of this army going on near us. We may be stopped from using some of our streets. A great many objectionable things may arise. It is plain good sense to accept them with all the grace we can summon. Anything else will only make matters worse."

"How long is this army expected to be here?"

"I have no idea. Maybe just a little while, maybe as long as the war lasts. You can have no less knowledge of that than I, Ed." He paused, thinking, then was speaking again, "I might say that I have lived here all of my life. This century and I were born the same year. I came here with my parents when I was three years old. Except for the time I spent in Transylvania College, I have not been away from here many days. I speak both modestly and truthfully when I say that my father and mother helped build this town. My wife and I have reared our children here. Almost all of our friends live here. This is our home. We do not plan ever to have another one. I cannot conceive of a section more gravely stricken by war than this. Most of us have blood kin on both sides. All of us have dear friends in both armies, and we will have more. For us, there can be no real victory except peace. For us, divided as we are, there can be no good news except that our friends still live. We shall have to play this war out with such restraint and dignity and good will as we can possibly have."

He sat down and the minister of the Baptist church arose. "I have only a weak, human mind," he said, and his voice was hoarse from emotion, "and so I do not understand God. I do not comprehend His purposes till in the fullness of time they stand revealed. I do not know toward what end God is moving us now, but I do know that God is not wasting His time, nor piddling with the substance of our lives. Every word that Brother Skiles has said is good. Hearken to it and leave the end in God's hands."

They went soberly back to their homes, and to the work that waited them there. Rumsey Skiles found that Bill Willie Blewett was burying cabbages and turnips, except those he had stored in a cool place in the cellar for immediate use. The potatoes were already in the great ridge that was to be their winter home.

"It has been a good cabbage season," said Bill Willie. "Taters and turnips fair, but it's the best cabbage year I ever seen. There's five crocks of kraut in your cellar, and better kraut I never tasted. Kraut goes mighty good with backbones and spareribs. We got at least ten bushels of cabbage in there now." He pointed to the fresh mound. "I guess we're jest about ready for winter to set in: plenty o' firewood ready, barn loft filled with fust-rate hay, two cribs o' corn, more'n a bushel o' shelled beans, four bushels o' dried apples, and one o' dried peaches, fifty gallons o' sorghum———"

"Anything in the smokehouse?" asked Skiles, smiling faintly.

"Enough to last till we get good hog-killin' weather. We'll have fifteen hogs ready when it turns cold."

"Plenty of feed for the cattle, I suppose?"

"Plenty. I'm a-goin' to start haulin' the fodder to the sheds tomorrer. I bet you don't know what's been goin' on here lately."

"Working a little on the side maybe." Again the faint smile.

"I'm a bread eater. I could live offn bread by itself, corn bread or flour bread, it don't make me no difference. But I jest natchelly got to have my bread. There's a lot o' scalawags in any army, and you can't tell when they'll be thievin' aroun'. So I got that carpenter that helped build the crib out in the woods, and while you and Miz Ella was gone to preachin' Sunday, we fixed a secret place in the attic to hide meal and flour in. You might say the ox was in the ditch, and this carpenter knows when to keep his mouth shet. You let me get three or four sacks o' meal and flour and put it up there, and I'll feel a lot safer about my bread."

"Take all the corn and wheat you need to the mill. I wouldn't want you to be stunted, Bill Willie. Better take it right away."

"Had a visitor while you was gone to town."

"Anybody I know?"

"Trez Covington. He wants to buy that red bull. His bull has got the hollow horn, or somethin', so he needs another one. I told him he would have to see you, and he said he would rather trade with me, said you was liable to cheat him out of his last dollar, said he knowed he could trust me."

"So can I," Rumsey said. "We don't need that bull—anyhow, that is what I heard you say a month ago. You go ahead and trade him. I will try to do what is right by whichever one is left alive."

"It'd be right amusin' to cheat that old buzzard out o' the last strand o' hair he's got left on his head."

"You'll run a risk, Bill Willie. Don't forget that he is my wife's uncle."

Ella Skiles had come out on the veranda in time to hear the reference to the prospective sale of the bull. She was laughing heartily. "Virgil is the only man who ever beat Uncle Trez in a trade. You two youngsters would be no match for him."

"That red bull is a mighty good bull," said Bill Willie meditatively. "That is a long sight better bull than Trez Covington is used to. I think it would be a right good thing if we could fix it so afore he dies he could say that he had had one bull that wasn't a scrub."

"When is he coming back?" asked Rumsey Skiles.

"Tomorrer. I told him I'd ast you what you'd take."

"Whatever you do, Bill Willie, will suit me fine. I have an important case in court tomorrow afternoon, but I'll hurry home to hear about it."

Bill Willie and two of the hands were replacing some rotted posts in the garden fence when Trezevant Covington arrived the following morning. Bill Willie told the men to continue with their work and went out to meet his visitor. It was a clear day and the feel of frost was in the air. Covington flung himself from the horse with all the sprightliness of youth. Bill Willie asked him if he wouldn't come into the house. "A glass o' milk is mighty refreshin' after a hard ride."

"You call three miles a hard ride? But I reckon it would be for a man as old as you."

"I walked out to Providence Knob to preachin' Sunday. Had a real good time. Got to feelin' sorry for people that have to use a hoss every time they leave home."

"Why didn't you say something to me? I'd have lent you a horse. That is too long a walk for a man that is feeble." Trez Covington's eyes were twinkling.

"Didn't want a hoss. Had a good time jest a-walkin' along and a-thinkin' about things. How about you walkin' out there with me sometime? Preachin' is real good."

"I always go to my own church."

"I don't blame you. It's close. Besides, I guess you ride even to it. The folks both done gone to town. He had some business he couldn't put off, and she's gone to visit awhile with Miz Robin Rodes. From what I hear, she's ailin' some."

"Worrying about that boy of hers in the army. Did you ask Rumsey about that bull?"

"Yessir, and he said that seein' as how that bull would still be in the family, for me to make you a special price of thirty-five dollars."

"Thirty-five dollars!" Trez almost shouted. "You misunderstood me. I didn't say anything about buying all the stock he has got. You ought to have told him I just wanted the bull."

"That bull has got blood in it. And another thing, that bull has got sense. That bull took it mighty hard when Lincoln was elected. I thought for a while we was a-goin' to lose it."

"I wouldn't pay thirty-five dollars for Lincoln himself."

Bill Willie sighed. "It's jest like Rumsey Skiles said: your stock is a-lookin' a little run-down, and here's a good chance for you to sort o' build it up. That bull can practically read and write. You would be surprised how smart that bull is."

"How did it find out that Lincoln was elected? Read it in the New York *Tribune*?"

"We don't get that paper. I told it, and jest like I am tellin' you, it made that bull mighty unhappy. That's a real Southern bull."

"Why don't you sell it to Jeff Davis?"

"He ain't no good man with a real fine bull. You want me to show you what a Southern bull this one is?"

"Bill Willie Blewett, what are you talking about? You sound to me like old age has got you."

"I'll prove it to you what a real Southern bull that is. Now you look at that gate. You can see it opens out due south. Yonder is the rest of the cattle." He pointed to the right. "Natchelly, you'd think that bull would go up where the others are. And he would if I didn't remind him what direction that is. I am goin' to put this rope on him so he can't get away, and I'm a-goin' to ast him what kind o' bull he is. You jest watch."

He looped the rope around the bull's horns. He opened the gate, holding firmly to the end of the rope. "His name is Ginral Jackson," Bill Willie explained to Covington. "Now, Ginral, I'm goin' to ast you which kind o' bull you is. Ifn you're a Northern bull, you turn to the right when you go through that gate. Ifn you're a Southern bull you keep goin' straight ahead. I'm a-leavin' it to you."

"And you'll jerk a little the way you want it to go."

"You jest watch close and see ifn I make a sign. Now, take your choice, Ginral."

The bull didn't even look at the other cattle grazing up to the right. It continued exactly as it had come through the gate.

"Wait a minute. That just happened. Try it again."

Bill Willie led the bull back into the lot. "Now, Ginral, I am givin' you another chance to show this gentleman that you ain't got a drap o' Yankee blood in you. I'm a-goin to open that gate agin, and ifn you a real Southern bull you keep goin' straight ahead. You understand me, don't you?"

General Jackson walked majestically through the gate, and kept going with not a fractional shift in course. Trezevant Covington looked at the cattle grazing up on the rise to the right. Then he looked at General Jackson, and then at Bill Willie Blewett.

"You put on a good show, Bill Willie. I'll buy that bull though I think I am being cheated out of the nine teeth I have got left. You are a strong young fellow. You walk out to Providence Knob to preaching. I guess you wouldn't mind just walking along and thinking a little, and help me get that bull to my place."

"No trouble a-tall. I need me a little stroll. I expect you'll find it right tiresome, jest a-settin' on that hoss, but I guess it's about your only chance to get there. I'll get the Ginral there for you. Wait here till I get my hat."

He hitched General Jackson to the gate and went inside the house. A minute later, he was back, wearing his hat, and in his hand he held a lump of salt which he gave to a very eager General Jackson.

"Don't you reckon you ought to have a little snack to eat?" asked Bill Willie. "You look all frazzled out to me."

Trezevant Covington grinned. "This horse of mine has got real Southern blood in it. It's a real Rebel horse. It will carry double in case you give plumb out."

Bill Willie Blewett handed Rumsey Skiles the thirty-five dollars. "I mighta got a little more, but I let Trez off easy, seein' he's a member of the family."

"I didn't need that bull. Twenty-five dollars would have been enough. How did you raise Uncle Trez that high?"

"You might say that the saltin' place had sumpin' to do with it. I'd been keerful not to let that bull have any salt since yesterday mornin'."

౷ ౷ ౷

One morning a week later, Nat Grider passed by with sacks of wheat flour in his spring wagon. Rumsey Skiles was starting to town as Grider drove by the gate.

"You have made an early trip to the mill."

"I didn't want to take any chances. The soldiers got to town last night."

"General Buckner's soldiers?" Rumsey asked.

"The town is filled with them. I was afraid they would take over the mill, so I hurried to get my grinding done."

"That was commendable foresight, Nat. I think I will ask Bill Willie to take some corn and wheat to the mill sometime today. Were there many there?"

"They were coming in when I left. I saw Tom Henry Hines on the street. He was wearing a gray uniform. Here for a last visit to his folks, he said. We spent a few minutes very pleasantly. He told me he was leaving tonight, but of course he didn't say where he was going. I am glad it wasn't Motley he met. They never did like each other."

Skiles left word for Bill Willie to make the trip to the mill. Then he rode on to town. Nat had been right. The place was crowded with soldiers. They were dressed in a wild scramble of uniforms, with little exactness in color and not much concern about fit. But they seemed cheerful enough, and twice they broke ranks for Skiles to pass through. He went directly to his office and wrote a letter to General Buckner, asking whether he might assume that his coming to and going from work would be unhindered. He then settled into the legal work before him. For a while his mind held to its proper focus, and the questions that arose were quickly answered. Then his attention weakened. His lawsuits faded out and in their place were the soldiers he had passed that morning. What were they doing in Bowling Green? Their presence on the streets of the city was incredible. Such a state of things must not be permitted. Then his mind cleared, and he knew there was nothing unreasonable about the presence of those ill-clothed soldiers. It was war that was unreasonable, incredible, unthinkable. But incredible or not, war was their lot. God alone knew when strife would cease and the happy days of peace return. He couldn't get his mind back to those legal forms on his desk before him. So he closed the desk and rode up Bridge Street to Vinegar Hill to see what was going on there.

A great deal was going on. The brow of the hill lying nearest town had been cleared of the fine cedars that had been there for generations. The boughs had been chopped off and burned in great, roaring, crackling fires. The logs were being stacked for further use. Skiles dismounted from his horse and stood watching the soldiers put the logs into stacks. An officer, obviously in charge, saw him and came up.

"I played on this hill when I was a small lad," said Skiles. "I imagine that I have been up in most of those trees. Am I trespassing?"

"Why, not at all, as long as you don't get in the way. I like trees, and I hate like fury to cut one down. War is bad medicine, any way you take it. I wish the Yanks had not forced this on us, but people have to defend themselves. My name is Happy Watts. I can't complain because I have been trained for war. I am the youngest graduate West Point ever turned out."

"My name is Rumsey Skiles. I am a lawyer here."

"A good one, I dare say from your looks. Well, I have a hundred men up here and half of them don't know which end of an ax you cut with till you show them. I suppose I'd better get to showing them."

He smiled pleasantly and moved on. Skiles looked about him and flinched at the terrible wound that a hundred men had inflicted upon his favorite hill. The sounds of shouting and chopping were deafening. Skiles mounted his horse to ride away. At the head of Bridge Street, he reined in his horse and sat there looking at the town beneath him. He could hear chopping and shouting on Grider Hill, farther in toward town, and to his right. Skiles flinched again. That was a beautiful elevation, not so high as Vinegar Hill, but more suited to homes. He knew that they were at work on College Hill, but the view was obstructed and it was too far away for the sounds of chopping to be heard. They would be making fortifications on Baker's Hill across the river. To the right of Baker's Hill he could see Mount Ayr, on the summit of which was the home of Warner Underwood. It was one of the country's finest homes. The site was well suited for fortifying, though it was not likely of much military significance. It would, Skiles thought, be sheer vandalism to require it, so gracious and fine was the home on its crest. But Underwood had been frank and unrestrained in his partisanship for the North. His position was well understood. The place might be in danger.

The courthouse clock struck four. It was time for him to be on his way to Three Springs. Supper would be ready by the time he reached there. As he rode down Bridge Street, he met Shade Gossom, the owner of the mill.

"Have you done any grinding for Bill Willie today?" he asked.

"A fair wagonful. There will be bread at Three Springs, Mr. Skiles, war or no war. I was just going up to see what they are doing on Vinegar Hill. Have you been up there?"

"I almost wish I hadn't gone. They have destroyed the finest cedars in south Kentucky, and I don't know for what."

"It will be more than trees, Mr. Skiles. This place has got its share of head-strong Northerners. I am going to run my mill as long as I can get grinding for it, and not open my mouth about anything except meal and flour. It would be a lot safer for the milling business if everybody was on one side or the other."

"Better for everybody. Better for the town. Any other news except the forts they are building?"

"Yes, the recruiting office on the square is filled. It looks like every Southerner came in town to enlist just as soon as he got word the army had got here. There is a full company of them already in down there now."

It was only a few squares out of his way, so Skiles rode by the recruiting office. Shade Gossom was right. The enlistment station was doing a flourishing business. He pulled his horse to one side and stopped. Fully fifty men were lounging there outside the office. There was Franklin Beck, whom a dozen times he had helped out of fighting scrapes. The boy wasn't good for much besides fighting, but for his father's sake—his father was a steady and industrious farmer out in the county—Skiles had been able to keep him out of jail. Franklin had always called him judge.

He saw Rumsey sitting there on his horse and grinned. "This is one thing you won't have to get me out of, Judge. This time I got the law on my side."

"That's fine. Keep it there."

"Don't expect to be in more'n three months, six at the most. The Yankees ain't got a chance."

"Not many of us have," said Skiles soberly. "I wish you good luck, Franklin. Make them a good soldier."

"All I ask, Judge, is a chance in a good battle."

"Franklin Beck!" bawled an orderly. "Inside." The boy grinned at Skiles and disappeared inside the office.

"Remember me, Mr. Skiles?" The young man had arisen from the curb and was standing close to him. Skiles could not at the moment identify him, though the face was familiar. "My name is Phillip Chandler. I have preached at the Methodist Church here several times."

Then Skiles remembered the man. He had met and talked briefly with him at a Methodist conference held at Woodburn the year before. Brother Tully Napier, of the Bowling Green Methodist church, had invited him out to the conference, and had driven by Three Springs and taken him in his gig. Brother Napier was a hale and hearty man, and loved a joke dearly. He told Skiles that he had asked him to go because the blood of the Methodists was getting too thick and needed a little Presbyterian thinning.

The faint smile appeared on Skiles's face. "Have you ever tried sassafras-root tea? It is a good thinner."

"It's our favorite drink, and it leaves our blood thicker."

"Then I'll stand by my Presbyterian doctrine that your blood is predestined to a thickness. But I'll be delighted to go to your conference with you."

Rumsey Skiles had found the conference refreshing both to his body and spirit. The basket dinner spread by the ladies of Rockfield was well prepared and of great quantity. He had told his wife that evening that in all of his sixty years of life he had never seen so much fried chicken as was in plain view at Rockfield that day.

"I imagine you altered the view some, Rumsey."

"What would you have done with that chicken so good and those Rockfield ladies urging you on?"

The main sermon at the conference had been delivered by the great Dr. John B. McFerrin of Nashville. Its thunderous eloquence had set Rumsey Skiles's thin Presbyterian blood to coursing through his veins at unwonted speed. It was then that he had seen Phillip Chandler, sitting one row ahead and just across the aisle. The young man sat there transfixed. There was upon his face the look of one exalted, and his eyes shone like stars.

The episode came back to Rumsey Skiles, as he sat there on his horse. Chandler had preached a sermon at the Methodist Church at Bowling Green, but Skiles had not known of it till later.

"I wish I had known of your engagement here. I would have deserted the Presbyterian church that day."

"I didn't blame people from staying away who did know of it. Brother Frogge is a much better preacher than I will be for a long time, maybe ever. I can preach a little and I know a good deal about sickness. I want the army to take me as a chaplain."

"How is it that you are so well acquainted with sickness?"

"I felt there was a war coming on and I have gone with Dr. Strother on all of his trips for the last two months. There has been a lot of sickness. I have studied the Bible between trips," he added proudly. "Do you think they will take me?"

"I don't see how they can refuse. When you have time write me a letter."

Skiles turned his horse and started away. Then he stopped, dismounted, and hitched his horse to a paling fence. He walked into the recruiting room past the orderly, who looked at him in some astonishment but said nothing in protest. An officer sat behind a table.

Skiles spoke to him. "I am an attorney in the city here. My name is Rumsey Skiles. I wish to speak with you about a man waiting outside to enlist."

"Yes? I am Colonel Lillard."

"The man's name is Phillip Chandler. He wishes to enlist as a chaplain and as a medical attendant. I recommend him strongly."

"How long have you known him?"

"A little more than a year."

"Is he related to you?"

"Not in the least."

Colonel Lillard made some notes on a paper. "We have not enlisted any as chaplains, and I am not sure that we have any official instructions about them. Perhaps we have been negligent there. When he comes in I shall give him special thought because of what you have said." . . .

Spring was at its best that day. The sky was clean-swept, but its deep blue was dimmed and softened by a purple-tinged haze that was everywhere—against the hills and thickets, over the fields, hanging gently and caressingly against the sky. It softened the stark white of the dogwoods that gave brightness to an April world. The graveyard vine that lay heavily upon and between the Shobe graves had lost its winter dinginess, and again was alive with the buoyant green of spring and thick with purple, star-shaped flowers. Everywhere the trees were clad in the garments of spring or poised to put them on. The birds that thronged the trees, or hopped gaily about on the ground, knew that it was spring again, and their songs swelled into a chorus of praise. All of the sounds that greeted the ears were tuned to spring: the plowmen calling to their teams, the tinkle of a cowbell in a meadow, somewhere in the distance the casual, deep-throated bay of a foxhound, a train engine sounding long and mournfully for the station at Oakland—all fused into the unity of spring.

A wooden bench had been placed in the graveyard. The grave nearest it did not bear the maturity of the other graves about. On the bench sat Jane Shobe and at her side a boy nearing three. He did not understand what the graves meant, but he did understand that his mother did not want him to run and scamper about, as was his way at home. For some reason she wished him to sit quietly at her side. She held in her hand some lilac blooms that she had broken from a hedge at the side of her yard, less than a half mile away. A cardinal sat on a maple bough not a dozen feet distant, its head cocked to one side, and watched with bright eyes.

"Listen, Jackson," Jane said to the child, "I want to tell you something. You will not understand what I am saying. Maybe you will understand better than I think. Anyhow, I want to talk to you a little while. That is your father's grave there. You never saw him, but I am going to tell you about him so often that you will almost think you did. I don't want you to grow up thinking that he is somebody far, far off. He believed in the South very deeply, and so did I. We married after the war started, but neither of us thought it would last very long, a year at the most. Things got worse, and he decided that it was his duty to enlist. I thought it was too. He went away to the army, son, but once he came back to see me. We talked a great deal about you, what you would look like and how we would love you. Your father didn't come back any more, son. My father came home one day with the news that he had been wounded. Bill Willie took me to Fort Donelson where your father was. You know Bill Willie, don't you?"

"Bill Willie," said the boy, his eyes bright with recognition.

"I don't know how we got there, Jackson. I don't want you ever to forget Bill Willie, son. I don't believe anyone else could have got me there in time. And we did get there in time. Your father was still alive. I know that he was spared that long so I could see him once more. We talked mostly about you. He was weak, and he would rest awhile so that we could talk again. And then the time came when he wouldn't ever talk any more. It was Bill Willie who brought us back."

"Bill Willie," said the boy again, nodding his head.

"And we buried him in that grave there. It was very cold that day, and the sun wasn't showing at all. I was terribly tired and heartbroken, and sometimes when Dr. Smoot was talking I thought I would die too. Then I knew that I wouldn't. I would live for you. I knew that your father would want me to. And then the sun came out, and that was a sign to me that you would soon be here and that everything would be better. We have had a hard time of it, Jackson, and there have been some very bad days for me. If it hadn't been for you, I don't suppose that I would ever have got through them. But everything seems all right now. The war is over and I don't think you will ever see another one. I pray to God you won't. I don't know what is going to happen, but you and I will be together. Sunday we are going to see your grandfather and grandmother. They are good people, son. You are going to be proud of them. You are going to be proud of the Shobes too. You look like the Shobes. You are one of them. Take these flowers and put them on your father's grave. Right over there. Put them down right there. That's right, Jackson. We must go back to the house now. There is a lot of work to be done."

Far in the distance, all but hidden by the haze, were the Edmonson County hills. In the southwest, Cook's Knob stood in faint outline. There seemed fitness in the scene: the haze, the hills and knobs, everywhere the white dogwoods, the misty spring sky above, the plows threading patiently across the fields, the birds throbbing their joy from meadow and bough. Spring had come, and not only spring, but the beginnings of peace.

Charles Bracelen Flood

from *Lee: The Last Years*

Charles Bracelen Flood, a naturalized Kentucky citizen who has lived in Richmond for some thirty years, has written popular and acclaimed fiction and nonfiction about numerous wars, from the American Revolution to World War II, Korea, and Vietnam. His biography *Lee: The Last Years* (1981) includes this moving portrait of General Robert E. Lee at his finest hour, when he chose to surrender to Grant and end the war, thereby helping the South to pick up the pieces and survive.

General Robert E. Lee stood on a hilltop, studying the fog-covered woods ahead. Listening to the artillery fire and musketry, he tried to judge the progress of the crucial attack that his men were making. It was shortly after eight o'clock in the morning on Palm Sunday, April 9, 1865, and the shattered remnants of Lee's Army of Northern Virginia were in a column strung along four miles of road near the village of Appomattox Court House.

A few minutes earlier, Lee had ordered Lieutenant Colonel Charles Venable of his staff to ride forward through these woods and find Major General John B. Gordon, the able and aggressive Georgian whose corps was making this assault. When Venable returned through the mist, the report he brought would determine whether this army was to fight on or surrender.

After four years of war, the northern front of the Confederate States of America had collapsed. A week before, unable to hold their overextended lines against the massive Union forces being thrown at them by General Ulysses S. Grant, Lee's battered, worn-out army had evacuated both Petersburg and the Confederate capital, Richmond. Since then they had slogged westward across Virginia through a hundred miles of spring mud, marching and fighting in an effort to break away from pursuing Federal columns. Lee's plan was to move west parallel to the railroad lines, and pick up food that was to await his army at supply depots. Then they would turn south to join the Confederate army under Joseph E. Johnston that was opposing Sherman's march north through the Carolinas from Savannah.

That turn to the south had never come. The march west became a nightmare retreat under incessant attacks that produced terrible losses—three days before this Palm Sunday, in the rout at Sayler's Creek, eight thousand of Lee's men were captured at one stroke. The food had not materialized. Starving horses collapsed and died in the mud. Reeling from hunger, soldiers who had won amazing victories in the past threw away their muskets and lay down in the fields, waiting to be picked up as prisoners. At its peak, this once-fearsome army had numbered seventy thousand men. A week before, thirty thousand began this withdrawal to the west, with sixty to seventy thousand Union Army soldiers on their heels. On this misty morning, the Army of Northern Virginia was reduced to eleven thousand gaunt, tenacious veterans. During the night, Federal troops had thrown themselves in strength across the Confederate line of march, and Lee's army was at last surrounded. At five this morning Lee had launched this final drive to break out to the west and continue the retreat.

Waiting for Lieutenant Colonel Venable to return with the message that would tell him whether further fighting would be useless, Lee stood silent amidst a few of his staff officers. He was a strikingly handsome man of fifty-eight, nearly six feet tall, with grey hair and a trim silver beard. Years of campaigning had burnt his clear ruddy skin to a deep red-brown; there were crow's-feet at the corners of his luminous brown eyes. He had a broad forehead, prominent nose, short thick neck, big shoulders and deep chest, and stood erect as the West Point cadet he once had been. Because he thought he might end this day as General Grant's prisoner, Lee was not wearing his usual grey sack coat. To represent his thousands of mud-caked scarecrows who were still ready to fight on, this morning Lee was resplendent in a double-breasted grey dress coat with gilt buttons. Around his waist was a deep red silk sash, and over that was a sword belt of gold braid. At his side hung a dress sword in a leather and gilt scabbard; on the blade was an inscription in French, *Aide toi et Dieu t'aidera*—Help yourself and God will help you.

Standing on this hillside, Lee knew the consequences of the choice he must soon make. In the past forty-eight hours Ulysses S. Grant had opened a correspondence with him, sending messages under flags of truce, urging him to surrender this army. If he surrendered these men now, the other armies of the Confederacy might stagger on briefly, but his action would mean the end of the war.

For Lee, there was a special problem faced by no other Confederate officer. He was not only the field commander of this army, but he was the general in command of all Confederate forces. If the rider coming back through the woods brought him reason to think he could get his men through to Johnston's army in North Carolina and assume direct command of both armies, it might be his duty to continue the bloodshed. He had produced near-miracles before; if he could fashion one more sharp blow, it might ease the terms of the inevitable surrender.

Everything was converging. Two days before, he had sent a message to his son Major General W. H. Fitzhugh Lee, a young cavalry commander who had served in the United States Army before the war: "Keep your command together and in good spirits, General; don't let it think of surrender. I will get you out of this." Earlier in the war he had written this same son, whose nickname was Rooney, "If victorious, we have every thing to live for in the future. If defeated, nothing will be left for us to live for."

All the hopes were crashing now, in a way that affected his flesh and blood. Rooney was up there in the fighting in those misty trees; so was another Major General Fitzhugh Lee, his nephew. His oldest son, Major General Custis Lee, a West Pointer like himself, had been missing since Sayler's Creek; there were rumors that he was dead. His youngest son, Captain Robert E. Lee, Jr., had been missing in action for a week.

Those were the bonds of family, but this entire army was filled with love for Lee. They were proud of his appearance, proud of his brilliant leadership, but their hearts went out to him because he shared their risks and hardships, constantly showing them how much he admired them and appreciated their sacrifices. Thousands of them referred to him as "Uncle Robert." His soldiers saw their cause embodied in him; one of his generals told him, "You are the country to these men." In the horrendous confusion of the defeat at Sayler's Creek, Lee had cantered into the midst of his scattered troops. Facing the enemy, he grabbed up a red Confederate battle flag and held it high in the dusk, the banner waving against the flames of destroyed supplies. A staff officer told what happened next.

> . . . The sight of him aroused a tumult. Fierce cries resounded on all sides and, with hands clinched violently and raised aloft, the men called on him to lead them against the enemy. "It's General Lee!"
>
> "Uncle Robert!" "Where's the man who won't follow Uncle Robert?" I heard on all sides—the swarthy faces full of dirt and courage, lit up every instant by the glare of the burning wagons.

⁙ ⁙ ⁙

Lieutenant Colonel Venable emerged from the misty woods and rode up the slope to Lee. He had an oral message from Major General Gordon on the front line: "I have fought my corps to a frazzle, and I fear I can do nothing unless I am heavily supported by Longstreet's corps."

Longstreet's corps. Lee knew that Gordon could not have the reinforcements he said he needed to break through; they were committed and fighting as the army's rear guard, holding off twice their numbers. There were no reserves left, and no hope of breaking out.

Lee said in his deep voice, addressing no one, "Then there is nothing left me but to go and see General Grant, and I would rather die a thousand deaths."

His words broke the respectful silence and dignified bearing of the officers near him. Years of dedication, of comrades killed, had come to naught in an instant. "Convulsed with passionate grief," an artilleryman said, "many were the wild words we spoke as we stood around him."

As the fog began to lift and Lee finally could see his last battlefield, he spoke again, this time in what an officer beside him called a voice "filled with hopeless sadness."

"How easily I could be rid of this," Lee said, again addressing no one, "and be at rest! I have only to ride along the line and all will be over!" He meant that it would be easy to commit suicide by riding in front of his lines, drawing enemy fire. Lee crossed his arms over his chest, his hands gripping his biceps; an inward battle was being fought to a decision. Finally he said with a deep sigh: "But it is our duty to live. What will become of the women and children of the South if we are not here to protect them?"

Allen Tate

"Ode to the Confederate Dead"

Finally, we come to what is probably the most eloquent tribute to those who did not survive the Civil War, or any war, Allen Tate's "Ode to the Confederate Dead." The poem contrasts egocentric, materialistic visitors to the cemetery, who cannot comprehend dedication to cause and duty, with the young men who are buried there. People of the modern age are incapable, Tate suggests, of such sacrifice because they are guilty of the unpardonable sin of total self-centeredness—"narcissism," he called it. Tate was born near Winchester and attended Vanderbilt University, where he studied with John Crowe Ransom and became one of the luminaries of "The Fugitives" and "The Agrarians," which were overlapping neoconservative groups of poets, novelists, and historians who promoted a return to a true humanism and a concern for classical form. Tate also wrote a highly valued biography of a Confederate icon, Stonewall Jackson, who was killed by friendly fire at the Battle of Chancellorsville.

Row after row with strict impunity
The headstones yield their names to the element,
The wind whirrs without recollection;
In the riven troughs the splayed leaves
Pile up, of nature the casual sacrament
To the seasonal eternity of death;
Then driven by the fierce scrutiny
Of heaven to their election in the vast breath,
They sough the rumour of mortality.

Autumn is desolation in the plot
Of a thousand acres where these memories grow
From the inexhaustible bodies that are not
Dead, but feed the grass row after rich row.
Think of the autumns that have come and gone!—
Ambitious November with the humors of the year,
With a particular zeal for every slab,
Staining the uncomfortable angels that rot

On the slabs, a wing chipped here, an arm there:
The brute curiosity of an angel's stare
Turns you, like them, to stone,
Transforms the heaving air
Till plunged to a heavier world below
You shift your sea-space blindly
Heaving, turning like the blind crab.

    Dazed by the wind, only the wind
    The leaves flying, plunge

You know who have waited by the wall
The twilight certainty of an animal,
Those midnight restitutions of the blood
You know—the immitigable pines, the smoky frieze
Of the sky, the sudden call: you know the rage,
The cold pool left by the mounting flood,
Of muted Zeno and Parmenides.
You who have waited for the angry resolution
Of those desires that should be yours tomorrow,
You know the unimportant shrift of death
And praise the vision
And praise the arrogant circumstance
Of those who fall
Rank upon rank, hurried beyond decision—
Here by the sagging gate, stopped by the wall.

    Seeing, seeing only the leaves
    Flying, plunge and expire

Turn your eyes to the immoderate past,
Turn to the inscrutable infantry rising
Demons out of the earth—they will not last.
Stonewall, Stonewall, and the sunken fields of hemp,
Shiloh, Antietam, Malvern Hill, Bull Run.
Lost in that orient of the thick-and-fast
You will curse the setting sun.

    Cursing only the leaves crying
    Like an old man in a storm

You hear the shout, the crazy hemlocks point
With troubled fingers to the silence which
Smothers you, a mummy, in time.

                                    The hound bitch
Toothless and dying, in a musty cellar
Hears the wind only.

                          Now that the salt of their blood
Stiffens the saltier oblivion of the sea,
Seals the malignant purity of the flood,

What shall we who count our days and bow
Our heads with a commemorial woe
In the ribboned coats of grim felicity,
What shall we say of the bones, unclean,
Whose verdurous anonymity will grow?
The ragged arms, the ragged heads and eyes
Lost in these acres of the insane green?
The gray lean spiders come, they come and go;
In a tangle of willows without light
The singular screech-owl's tight
Invisible lyric seeds the mind
With the furious murmur of their chivalry.

    We shall say only the leaves
    Flying, plunge and expire

We shall say only the leaves whispering
In the improbable mist of nightfall
That flies on multiple wing;
Night is the beginning and the end
And in between the ends of distraction
Waits mute speculation, the patient curse
That stones the eyes, or like the jaguar leaps
For his own image in a jungle pool, his victim.
What shall we say who have knowledge
Carried to the heart? Shall we take the act
To the grave? Shall we, more hopeful, set up the grave
In the house? The ravenous grave?

                                    Leave now
The shut gate and the decomposing wall:
The gentle serpent, green in the mulberry bush,
Riots with his tongue through the hush—
Sentinel of the grave who counts us all!

Politicians, Teachers, Preachers, and Occasional Poets
Writing as an Avocation

Throughout most of the nineteenth century most Kentucky writing was done by men and a few women whose vocation was elsewhere—politics, law, business, education, journalism, ministry, or soldiering. There were few if any professional writers. Except for writing connected with literary-based professions such as the law, the ministry, and journalism, a person simply couldn't make a living from his or her pen. Even so, fine writing was practiced by Kentuckians, usually after they had done the day's practical chores. In the privacy of their offices or kitchens or bedrooms, they wrote poems, essays, orations, and autobiographies—most of which were never published. Newspapers and magazines, however, welcomed legions of would-be poets and fictionists.

This chapter samples the range of writing by unexpected belletrists. Here are men and women who write poetry and prose that is valued more for its form and style than for its content or moral lessons. Of course, fine writing can be found in unusual places, from the courts of justice to the halls of ivy, from the halls of Congress to the battlefield.

The most famous American physician-poet is New Jersey's William Carlos Williams, but Kentucky has produced Daniel Drake, who was born in New Jersey in 1785 but moved with his family to Mayslick, in Mason County, when he was three. After studying medicine at the University of Pennsylvania, he returned to Kentucky and practiced and taught medicine at several regional universities. In addition to medical treatises, he wrote *Pioneer Life in Kentucky* (1870), a popular book about early Kentucky life. A lesser-known poet is Elisha Bartlett, who taught medicine at Transylvania University in Lexington and authored *Simple Settings,* a collection of verse in triplets about characters in the novels of Dickens. Another physician-poet is John M. Harney, who was born in 1789 in Delaware but wound up practicing medicine in Bardstown. One of his jingles, "The Whippowil," begins, "There is a strange, mysterious bird, / Which few have seen, but all have heard . . . Whippowil." A more recent writer of note is Abraham Flexner, a native of Kentucky, a pioneer in medical education, and the author of a delightful autobiography, *I Remember* (1940), in which he recalls his Jewish boyhood in Louisville.

Many educators are called to be writers, but few are chosen. One of the chosen ones is Mary Jane Holmes, a native of Massachusetts who taught for several years in Woodford County and in 1854 published *Tempest and Sunshine, or Life in Kentucky*, a novel based in part on a farm near Versailles. After she moved to New York State, she continued to write popular sentimental novels, including four more with Kentucky characters and settings: *Homestead on the Hillside, Lena Rivers, Marian Grey*, and *Hugh Worthington*.

Lawyers and politicians seem to go together, perhaps because so many lawyers become politicians. Since the beginning, Kentucky has been blessed (or cursed) with an abundance of both. Good lawyers are usually good speakers, and good speakers make good, or at least successful, politicians. These men lived during the Golden Age of Spread-Eagle Oratory, and a roll call of effective lawyers who were also politicians and orators includes John J. Crittenden, born in 1787 near Versailles and later a governor and a senator; Thomas F. Marshall, a Kentuckian who preached temperance and practiced inebriety, and who, when he was a congressman, gave an impassioned oration in Washington on temperance before the Total Abstinence and Vigilance Society; and Richard H. Menefee, born in 1809 at Owingsville, a congressman who in 1838 gave a toast in response to a salute to Kentucky by Daniel Webster: "Kentucky," he orated, "stands by the Union in her living efforts; she means to hold fast to it in her expiring groans. With Massachusetts she means to perish, if perish she must, with hands clenched, in death, upon the Union."

Another proud Kentucky orator was George Robertson, born near Harrodsburg in 1790. He was a congressman and later chief justice of the Kentucky Court of Appeals; in an 1855 anniversary address on the settlement of Kentucky, he concluded his remarks with a model of spread-eagle oratory: "Let us, come what may, be true to God, true to ourselves, and faithful to our children, our country and mankind. And then, whenever or wherever it may be our doom to look, for the last time, on earth, we may die justly proud of the title of 'Kentuckian,' and, with our expiring breath, may cordially exclaim—Kentucky, as she was—Kentucky, as she is—Kentucky, as she will be—Kentucky forever."

We've had journalists in Kentucky almost as long as we've had politicians and lawyers. The *Kentucky Gazette* published its first issue—the first issue of any newspaper in Kentucky—on August 11, 1787. In 1818 Shadrach Penn established in Louisville the *Public Advertiser*, and in 1830 George D. Prentice started the *Louisville Journal*. The *Advertiser* was Democratic and the *Journal* was Whig. Soon the two Louisville papers were at political war with each other. The *Louisville Courier* was established by Walter N. Haldeman in 1844, and that same year James Guthrie started the *Louisville Democrat*. In 1868 the *Democrat*, the *Journal*, and the *Courier* were merged into the *Courier-Journal*, edited by one of the most influential journalists of the post–Civil War period, Henry Watterson. In Lexington the *Herald-Leader* traces its origins to 1870, when Hart Foster and Henry Duncan founded the *Lexington Daily Press*. Meanwhile, throughout the state other towns began their own weekly and daily papers.

Two of the most prominent editors were Prentice and Watterson. Prentice came to Kentucky from his home state of Connecticut in 1830 to write the campaign biography of Henry Clay; he started the *Journal* the same year. The biography was a good promotional book, but it failed to get Clay elected. He was much more successful with his newspaper. He made the *Journal* famous for its witty prose and sentimental poetry, mostly written by his "stable of female poets," including the worst one of the lot, the "Sweet Singer of Louisville," Amelia B. Welby. Prentice himself was a bad poet, but she was worse. She is so bad that she is fun to read.

Kentucky preachers wrote poems, autobiographies, essays, and in other literary genres, but mostly they wrote sermons—unless they preached not from notes but from inspiration. There is in fact much good historical and social material buried in the numerous personal narratives and memoirs written by Kentucky's ministers. A good example is *Will Makes Way; or, Autobiography of Rev. S. Noland,* published in 1887. He was born in Wayne County, Indiana, but after his mother's death when he was seven, he moved to Kentucky to live with relatives. He worked and studied hard and became a lawyer (and, yes, a politician), a banker, and finally a Methodist minister. His is a Horatio Alger story for the pulpit.

The first Roman Catholic priest in Kentucky, Stephen T. Badin, was born in France and wrote poetry—in Latin! His best-known Latin poem is an elegy on the death of Colonel Joseph H. Daviess, who fell at the Battle of Tippecanoe in November 1811. Fortunately, he provided his nonscholarly readership an English translation, which contains this rhyming summation: "The noblest act the patriot's fame can tell, / Is that he bravely for his country fell." Father Badin had obviously never been in combat.

One of Kentucky's earliest poets, Hew Ainslie, was a Scotsman born in the old country in 1792, the year Kentucky became a state; he arrived in Kentucky in 1829. He became a prominent builder and wrote poems frequently in Scottish dialect, including a tribute to his adopted state, "The Haughs o' Auld Kentucky," which opens, "Welcome, Edie, owre the sea, / Welcome to this lan' an' me."

Unlike Amelia Welby, who was bad enough to be entertaining, most of Kentucky's nineteenth-century poets were just bad enough to be boring, and I shall not bore you with many of their verses; there is, however, always gold hidden somewhere in the hills. I close this early gathering of poets with three soldier-poets, William O. Butler, Henry T. Stanton, and Theodore O'Hara.

Julia A. Tevis

from *Sixty Years in a School-Room*

Julia A. Tevis, born in 1799 near Winchester, founded Science Hill Academy for young women in Shelbyville in 1825. Her autobiography is *Sixty Years in a School-Room* (1878), from which this selection is taken. Here she describes the custom of crowning a May queen each year and the year the crowning almost didn't take place because the winner came down with measles.

For many years we kept up the custom of crowning a "Rose Queen" in May, and enjoying a holiday in the woods. Happily for the girls, I greeted the return of the festival day with a gladness almost equal to theirs, for I retained enough of the freshness of youth in my heart to enable me to participate with zest in the joys of childhood.

"Once upon a time," after a long severe Winter, followed by a Spring of unusual beauty, it was determined to celebrate the day with great rejoicings. The girls were wild with delight at the prospect of a whole day's release from slates, books, and blackboards—a charming episode in the drudgery of their everyday life. Ah, happy children! to whom every glimpse of nature is beautiful, and every blade of grass a marvel! Give them ever so small a bit of green meadow checkered with sunshine and shade upon which to revel among buttercups and daisies, and "little they'll reck" how the world goes on.

There was but little opportunity for canvassing or intrigue in the election of Queen. Fanny Henning was chosen by acclamation as best fitted to grace the regal authority. Fanny possessed a mind and a character as transparent as a clear brook. Her ingenuous face, her self-forgetting and amiable bearing towards her companions made her the loved and cherished of them all. She also held a distinguished place in the estimation of her teachers for superior excellence, dutiful affection, and modest deportment. Thus it was universally conceded that "Fair-handed Spring" might well resign to Fanny her sovereignty for one day over the brilliant treasures of garden, glade, and forest, awakened into life and brightened into beauty by her magic wand.

The rosy hours followed each other in quick succession until within a few days of the anticipated time, when lo! the "queen elect" broke out with

measles. The whole school was filled with dismay, bitter tears of disappointment were shed by some; others predicted that she would be well enough to
go through the ceremony. Fanny, uniting in their hopeful aspirations, prepared her coronation speech and rehearsed it to perfection, for, though confined to her room, she was not really ill. On the eve of the appointed day,
however, the doctor pronounced her too feeble to endure the fatigue. What
was to be done? The trophies of many loyal hearts were ready to be laid at the
feet of the queen. Spirit hands seemed dispensing blessings, and guardian
angels extending their wings over these healthful, happy girls as they dili-
gently wrought sparkling wreaths and arranged beautiful bouquets.

The banners were prepared, the white dresses were trimmed with evergreen. The Seasons, the maids of honor, and all the officials were in waiting,
but *"Hamlet"* could not be left out of the play. One modest little girl, after
listening in silence to the suggestions of the others, raised her eyes to my face
and said hesitatingly:

"Can't Emma Maxwell be queen in Fanny's place?"

"Oh, no!" said another; "she could not possibly learn the speech in time."

"No, indeed!" exclaimed several voices at once, "that would be impossible; but she might read it."

"Yes, yes! let her read it; the queen's speeches are read in Parliament!"

"Will you accept the proposition?" said I, turning to Emma.

"I think I can learn it," she replied, "and will try if you wish it."

The coronation was to take place the next morning at ten o'clock. A
previous rehearsal would be impossible; but what Emma proudly determined
to do was generously accomplished.

The evening star looked out bright and clear in the blue deep, thrilling
the hearts of these young girls with the prospect of a pleasant morrow.

Most of them were stirring before sunrise. "Is it clear?" "Are we going?"
And from every room issued the sound of cheerful voices; and then such shouts,
such hurrying and bathing and dressing as was seldom known before.

Ten o'clock came, and the yard, where the temporary throne was erected,
was soon filled with spectators and invited guests, mingling with the children and participating in their pleasure. The proxy queen bore her blushing
honors meekly, going through all the coronation ceremonies with a charming dignity. She stood Calypso-like among her train of attendants in full
view of the audience who listened in breathless silence to her address. I watched
her closely; she seemed to plant her feet firmly, as if to still the beatings of her
heart; no gesture except a gentle motion of the right arm as she swayed her
scepter majestically around, her eyes steadily fixed upon some object beyond, with which she seemed completely absorbed. Not a word was mis-
placed, not a sentence omitted, of a speech long enough for a Parliamentary

harangue. No one prompted, nor did she once turn her eyes toward the scroll she held in her left hand. Enthusiastic and excessive were the rejoicings of her juvenile auditors.

Fanny witnessed the whole ceremony through a convenient window which framed for her a living picture of ineffable beauty, and on this clear day, with only a few white Spring clouds floating over the bluest of skies, it was a sight of earth that makes one understand heaven.

Henry Clay

"Reply to John Randolph"

Kentucky's most famous citizen before the Civil War was undoubtedly Henry Clay, a master lawyer and a master politician who offered himself in vain three times for the presidency. He was born in Virginia in 1777, moved to Lexington to practice law at twenty, and then became a Kentucky congressman and senator. His political oratory in Congress was unmatched. During an 1824 debate with Senator John Randolph of Virginia, he responded to Randolph's attack on him in words that would have crushed even a worthy opponent.

Sir, I am growing old. I have had some little measure of experience in public life, and the result of that experience has brought me to this conclusion, that when business, of whatever nature, is to be transacted in a deliberative assembly, or in private life, courtesy, forebearance, and moderation, are best calculated to bring it to a successful conclusion. Sir, my age admonishes me to abstain from involving myself in personal difficulties; would to God that I could say, I am also restrained by higher motives. I certainly never sought any collision with the gentleman from Virginia. My situation at this time is peculiar, if it be nothing else, and might, I should think, dissuade, at least, a generous heart from any wish to draw me into circumstances of personal altercation. I have experienced this magnanimity from some quarters of the house. But I regret, that from others it appears to have no such consideration. The gentleman from Virginia was pleased to say that in one point at least he coincided with me—in an humble estimate of my grammatical and philological acquirements. I know my deficiencies. I was born to no proud patrimonial estate; from my father I inherited only infancy, ignorance, and indigence. I feel my defects; but, so far as my situation in early life is concerned, I may, without presumption, say they are more my misfortune than my fault. But, however I regret my want of ability to furnish to the gentleman a better specimen of powers of verbal criticism, I will venture to say, it is not greater than the disappointment of this committee as to the strength of his argument.

"Address to Lafayette"

On December 10, 1824, during a triumphal tour of the nation he had helped to birth some fifty years earlier, the aged Marquis de Lafayette was welcomed to the House of Representatives by Speaker Clay, who pulled out all the stops with the following grand oration.

⌒∞⌒

General,

The house of representatives of the United States, impelled alike by its own feelings, and by those of the whole American people, could not have assigned to me a more gratifying duty than that of presenting to you cordial congratulations upon the occasion of your recent arrival in the United States, in compliance with the wishes of Congress, and to assure you of the very high satisfaction which your presence affords on this early theatre of your glory and renown. Although but few of the members who compose this body shared with you in the war of our revolution, all have, from impartial history, or from faithful tradition, a knowledge of the perils, the sufferings, and the sacrifices, which you voluntarily encountered, and the signal services, in America and in Europe, which you performed for an infant, a distant, and an alien people; and all feel and own the very great extent of the obligations under which you have placed our country. But the relations in which you have ever stood to the United States, interesting and important as they have been, do not constitute the only motive of the respect and admiration which the house of representatives entertain for you. Your consistency of character, your uniform devotion to regulated liberty, in all the vicissitudes of a long and arduous life, also commands its admiration. During all the recent convulsions of Europe, amidst, as after the dispersion of, every political storm, the people of the United States have beheld you, true to your old principles, firm and erect, cheering and animating with your well-known voice, the votaries of liberty, its faithful and fearless champion, ready to shed the last drop of that blood which here you so freely and nobly spilt, in the same holy cause.

The vain wish has been sometimes indulged, that Providence would allow the patriot, after death, to return to his country, and to contemplate the intermediate changes which had taken place; to view the forest felled, the cities built, the mountains levelled, the canals cut, the highways constructed, the progress of the arts, advancement of learning, and the increase of population. General, your present visit to the United States is a realization of the consoling object of that wish. You are in the midst of posterity. Every where, you must have been struck with the great changes, physical and moral, which have occurred since you left us. Even this very city, bearing a venerated name, alike endeared to you and to us, has since emerged from the forest which then covered its site. In one respect you behold us unaltered, and this is in the sentiment of continued devotion to liberty, and of ardent affection and profound gratitude to your departed friend, the father of his country, and to you, and to your illustrious associates in the field and in the cabinet, for the multiplied blessings which surround us, and for the very privilege of addressing you which I now exercise. This sentiment, now fondly cherished by more than ten millions of people, will be transmitted, with unabated vigor, down the tide of time, through the countless millions who are destined to inhabit this continent, to the latest posterity.

J. Proctor Knott

from "The Duluth Speech"

Perhaps the most famous speech ever made in the U.S. Congress by a Kentuckian is J. Proctor Knott's "Duluth Speech," which he delivered before a roaring audience on January 27, 1871, during a debate on a land grant that would pay for a railroad to the northern Minnesota town of Duluth. Knott would serve in Congress for several more terms and then become governor of Kentucky, but this was his finest hour. His "Duluth Speech" is a comic masterpiece of mock-seriousness and irony.

. . . But with regard to the transcendent merits of the gigantic enterprise contemplated in this bill I never entertained the shadow of a doubt.

(Laughter.)

Years ago, when I first heard that there was somewhere in the vast *terra incognita*, somewhere in the bleak regions of the great Northwest, a stream of water known to the nomadic inhabitants of the neighborhood as the river St. Croix, I became satisfied that the construction of a railroad from that raging torrent to some point in the civilized world was essential to the happiness and prosperity of the American people, if not absolutely indispensable to the perpetuity of republican institutions on this continent. (Great laughter.) I felt instinctively that the boundless resource of that prolific region of sand and pine shrubbery would never be fully developed without a railroad constructed and equipped at the expense of the Government, and perhaps not then. (Laughter.) I had an abiding presentiment that, some day or other, the people of this whole country, irrespective of party affiliations, regardless of sectional prejudices, and "without distinction of race, color, or previous condition of servitude," would rise in their majesty and demand an outlet for the enormous agricultural productions of those vast and fertile pine barrens, drained in the rainy season by the surging waters of the turbid St. Croix. (Great laughter.) . . .

Now, sir, I repeat I have been satisfied for years that if there was any portion of the inhabited globe absolutely in a suffering condition for want of a railroad it was these teeming pine barrens of the St. Croix. (Laughter.) At what particular point on that noble stream such a road would be commenced I knew was immaterial, and so it seems to have been considered by the draughtsman of this bill. It might be up at the spring or down at the foot-log, or the water gate, or the fish-dam, or anywhere along the bank, no matter where. (Laughter.) But in what direction should it run, or where it should terminate, were always to my mind questions of the most painful perplexity. . . .

Hence, as I have said, sir, I was utterly at a loss to determine where the terminus of this great and indispensable road should be, until I accidentally overheard some gentleman the other day mention the name of "Duluth." (Great laughter.) Duluth! The word fell upon my ear with peculiar and indescribable charm, like the gentle murmur of a low fountain stealing forth in the midst of roses, or the soft, sweet accents of an angel's whisper in the bright, joyous dream of sleeping innocence. Duluth! 'Twas the name for which my soul had panted for years, as the hart panteth for the water-brooks. (Renewed laughter.) But where was Duluth? Never, in all my limited reading, had my vision been gladdened by seeing the celestial word in print. (Laughter.) And I felt a profounder humiliation in my ignorance that its dulcet syllables had never before ravished my delighted ear. (Roars of laughter.) I was certain the draughtsman of this bill had never heard of it, or it would have been designated as one of the termini of this road. I asked my friends about it, but they knew nothing of it. I rushed to the Library and examined all the maps I could find. (Laughter.) I discovered in one of them a delicate, hair-like line, diverging from the Mississippi near a place marked Prescott, which I supposed was intended to represent the river St. Croix, but I could nowhere find Duluth.

Nevertheless, I was confident it existed somewhere, and that its discovery would constitute the crowning glory of the present century, if not of all modern times. (Laughter.) I knew it was bound to exist in the very nature of things; that the symmetry and perfection of our planetary system would be incomplete without it, (renewed laughter;) that the elements of material nature would long since have resolved themselves back into original chaos if there had been such a hiatus in creation as would have resulted from leaving out Duluth. (Roars of laughter.) In fact, sir, I was overwhelmed with the conviction that Duluth not only existed somewhere, but that wherever it was it was a great and glorious place. I was convinced that the greatest calamity that ever befell the benighted nations of the ancient world was in their having passed away without a knowledge of the actual existence of Duluth; that their fabled Atlantis, never seen save by the hallowed vision of inspired poesy, was, in fact, but another name for Duluth; that the golden orchard of the Hesperides was but a poetical synonym for the beer-gardens in the vicinity of Duluth. (Great laughter.) I was certain that Herodotus had died a miserable death because in all his travels and with all his geographical research he had never heard of Duluth. (Laughter.) I knew that if the immortal spirit of Homer could look down from another heaven than that created by his own celestial genius upon the long lines of pilgrims from every nation of the earth to the gushing fountain of poesy opened by the touch of his magic wand, if he could be permitted to behold the vast assemblage of grand and glorious productions of the lyric art called into being by his own inspired strains, he would weep tears of bitter anguish that instead of lavishing all the stores of his mighty genius upon the fall of Ilion it had not been his more blessed lot to crystallize in deathless song the rising glories of Duluth. (Great and continued laughter.) Yet, sir, had it not been for this map, kindly furnished me by the Legislature of Minnesota, I might have gone down to my obscure and humble grave in an agony of despair, because I could nowhere find Duluth. (Renewed laughter.) Had such been my melancholy fate, I have no doubt that with the last feeble pulsation of my breaking heart, with the last faint exhalation of my fleeting breath, I should have whispered, "Where is Duluth?" (Roars of laughter.) . . .

Sir, I might stand here for hours and hours, and expatiate with rapture upon the gorgeous prospects of Duluth, as depicted upon this map. But human life is too short and the time of this House far too valuable to allow me to linger longer upon the delightful theme. (Laughter.) I think every gentlemen on this floor is as well satisfied as I am that Duluth is destined to become the commercial metropolis of the universe, and that this road should be built at once. I am fully persuaded that no patriotic Representative of the American people, who has a proper appreciation of the associated glories of Duluth and the St. Croix, will hesitate a moment to say that every able-bodied female in the land between the ages of eighteen and forty-five who is in favor of "women's rights" should be drafted and set to work upon this great work without delay. (Roars of laughter.) Nevertheless, sir, it grieves my very soul to be compelled to say that I cannot vote for the grant of lands provided for in this bill.

Ah! sir, you can have no conception of the poignancy of my anguish that I am deprived of that blessed privilege! (Laughter.) There are two insuperable obstacles in the way. In the first place my constituents, for whom I am acting here, have no more interest in this road than they have in the great question of culinary taste now perhaps agitating the public mind of Dominica, as to whether the illustrious commissioners who recently left this capital for that free and enlightened republic would be better fricasseed, boiled, or roasted, (great laughter;) and in the second place these lands, which I am asked to give away, alas, are not mine to bestow! My relation to them is simply that of trustee to an express trust. And shall I ever betray that trust? Never, sir! Rather perish Duluth! (Shouts of laughter.) Perish the paragon of cities! Rather let the freezing cyclones of the bleak Northwest bury it forever beneath the eddying sands of the raging St. Croix! (Great laughter.)

Henry Watterson
"On the Death of Carrie Nation"

Henry Watterson did not, to my knowledge, write poetry; but he was a genius with editorials, which were read and copied all over the country. Here is his hard-hitting *Courier-Journal* editorial of July 13, 1911, on the death of Carrie Nation, the antiliquor crusader who was born in Kentucky and attacked saloons with her hatchet. The Meg Merrilies whom Watterson refers to is a crazed Scottish folk figure featured in a poem by John Keats and a novel by Sir Walter Scott.

Yesterday all that was mortal of poor, old Carrie Nation was laid to rest in an obscure Missouri churchyard. Poor, old Carrie Nation! She was a crazy Jane, wasn't she? How many drunkards did she reform, how many would-be drunkards did she rescue, how many innocents turn away from the dram-shop? She seems to have done very well in the business of saloon-smashing and hatchet-selling. If mad at all, there was a method in her madness. Did she really suffer from the hysteria into which she threw herself, or enjoy the excitement and notoriety? Who shall tell? Poor, old hag! Peace to her ashes. Witches of the blasted heath, spirits of dead priestesses of pagan fable—maybe the soul of Meg Merrilies herself—attended her wanderings from Dan to Beersheba, which she did not find all barren, and they will e'en follow her to her grave. Born in Kentucky, 'twas fitting that she should die in Kansas. "I shall come again," said Meg Merrilies, "I shall come again, long, long after these crazed old bones have lain whitening beneath the mould." Will Carrie Nation come again? Not to Kentucky. Here at least emotional politics is beginning to yield to sanity and common sense at last.

Amelia B. Welby

"The Rainbow"

"The Sweet Singer of Louisville," Amelia B. Welby, was born in Maryland in 1819 but moved to Louisville with her family when she was fifteen. In 1837, with his wonderful nose for finding female poets, the editor George D. Prentice invited her to publish a poem in his *Louisville Journal*. There was no stopping her after that, and soon she was publishing poems in newspapers all over the nation; her fans demanded a collected edition, which they got in 1845, when *Poems by Amelia* came out. By 1870, when she had been dead for eighteen years, the book was in its seventeenth printing. Even Edgar Allan Poe praised it. Mark Twain had popular poets like Amelia Welby in mind when he created Emmeline Grangerford in *Huckleberry Finn*. Welby was a bad artist and a bad poet. She was always in love with death, as the titles of several of her poems attest: "The First Death of the Household," "The Dying Girl," "The Dying Mother," "The Bereaved," "Sudden Death," and "The Mournful Heart." Huck says of Grangerford: "She warn't particular, she could write about anything you choose to give her to write about, just so it was sadful." Here is Welby's most famous and most beloved poem, "The Rainbow"—all six stanzas of it. Try reading it aloud; you'll be glad you did.

I sometimes have thoughts, in my loneliest hours,
That lie on my heart like the dew on the flowers,
Of a ramble I took one bright afternoon
When my heart was as light as a blossom in June;
The green earth was moist with the late fallen showers,
The breeze fluttered down and blew open the flowers,
While a single white cloud, to its haven of rest
On the white-wing of peace, floated off in the west.

As I threw back my tresses to catch the cool breeze,
That scattered the rain-drops and dimpled the seas,
Far up the blue sky a fair rainbow unrolled
Its soft-tinted pinions of purple and gold.
'Twas born in a moment, yet, quick as its birth
It had stretched to the uttermost ends of the earth,
And, fair, as an angel, it floated as free,
With a wing on the earth and a wing on the sea.

How calm was the ocean! how gentle its swell!
Like a woman's soft bosom it rose and it fell;
While its light sparkling waves, stealing laughingly o'er,
When they saw the fair rainbow, knelt down on the shore.
No sweet hymn ascended, no murmur of prayer,
Yet I felt that the spirit of worship was there,
And bent my young head, in devotion and love,
'Neath the form of the angel, that floated above.

How wide was the sweep of its beautiful wings!
How boundless its circle! how radiant its rings!
If I looked on the sky, 'twas suspended in air;
If I looked on the ocean, the rainbow was there;
Thus forming a girdle, as brilliant and whole
As the thoughts of the rainbow, that circled my soul.
Like the wing of the Deity, calmly unfurled,
It bent from the cloud and encircled the world.

There are moments, I think, when the spirit receives
Whole volumes of thought on its unwritten leaves,
When the folds of the heart in a moment unclose
Like the innermost leaves from the heart of a rose.
And thus, when the rainbow had passed from the sky,
The thoughts it awoke were too deep to pass by;
It left my full soul, like the wing of a dove,
All fluttering with pleasure, and fluttering with love.

I know that each moment of rapture or pain
But shortens the links in life's mystical chain;
I know that my form, like that bow from the wave,
Must pass from the earth, and lie cold in the grave;
Yet O! when death's shadows my bosom encloud,
When I shrink at the thought of the coffin and shroud,
May Hope, like the rainbow, my spirit enfold
In her beautiful pinions of purple and gold.

William Shakespeare Hays
"Mollie Darling"

An unlikely poet is William Shakespeare Hays, whose day job was serving as captain of steamboats on the Ohio River. He penned the words for one of the most popular songs of the late nineteenth century—and it's still sung today—"Mollie Darling." During his lifetime he published more than 350 songs, including "The Drummer Boy of Shiloh" and "The Union Forever." He was the most successful songwriter with Kentucky roots until Haven Gillespie (1888–1975), a Covington-born writer whose songs include "Breezin' Along with the Breeze," "Lucky Old Sun," and "Santa Claus Is Coming to Town."

Won't you tell me, Mollie, darling,
    That you love none else but me?
For I love you, Mollie, darling,
    You are all the world to me.
O! tell me, darling, that you love me,
    Put your little hand in mine,
Take my heart, sweet Mollie, darling,
    Say that you will give me thine.

    CHORUS—
        Mollie, fairest, sweetest, dearest,
            Look up, darling, tell me this:
        Do you love me, Mollie, darling?
            Let your answer be a kiss.

Stars are smiling, Mollie, darling,
    Thro' the mystic vail of night;
They seem laughing, Mollie, darling,
    While fair Luna hides her light.
O! no one listens but the flowers,
    While they hang their heads in shame,
They are modest, Mollie, darling,
    When they hear me call your name.

I must leave you, Mollie, darling,
  Tho' the parting gives me pain;
When the stars shine, Mollie, darling,
  I will meet you here again.

O! good-night, Mollie, good-bye, loved one,
  Happy may you ever be,
When you're dreaming, Mollie, darling,
  Don't forget to dream of me.

Thomas Johnson Jr.

Thomas Johnson Jr. was born in Virginia about 1760 and came to Danville in 1785. By 1789 he had published a collection of his poems, *The Kentucky Miscellany*, a satire on just about everything in Danville: the town itself, all the churches, most of the professions, and human nature. He is known as one of the two Drunken Poets of Danville, for reasons that probably need no explanation.

"Danville"

Accursed Danville, vile, detested spot,
Where knaves inhabit, and where fools resort—
Thy roguish cunning, and thy deep design,
Would shame a Bluebeard or an Algerine.
O, may thy fatal day be ever curst,
When by blind error led, I entered first.

"Kentucky"

I hate Kentucky, curse the place,
And all her vile and miscreant race!
Who make religion's sacred tie
A mask thro' which they cheat and lie.
Proteus could not change his shape,
Nor Jupiter commit a rape
With half the ease these villains can
Send prayers to God and cheat their man!
I hate all Judges here of late,
And every Lawyer in the State.
Each quack that is called Physician,
And all blockheads in Commission—
Worse than the Baptist roaring rant,
I hate the Presbyterian cant—
Their Parsons, Elders, nay, the whole,
And wish them gone with all my soul.

"The Poet's Epitaph"

Underneath this marble tomb,
In endless shades lies drunken Tom;
Here safely moored, dead as a log,
Who got his death by drinking grog.
By whiskey grog he lost his breath—
Who would not die so sweet a death?

William F. Marvin

"The Bee"

Another Drunken Poet of Danville was William F. Marvin (1804–1879), a shoemaker by day and a drunkard by night. He was a veteran of the Mexican War and published in 1851 *The Battle of Monterey and Other Poems.* A short poem from this collection will give a good sample of his wit and style.

A bee, while hovering round a lip,
Where wit and beauty hung,
Mistook its bloom, and flew to sip,
But ah, the bee got stung.

William O. Butler

"The Boatman's Horn"

William O. Butler was born in 1791 in Nicholasville, fought in the War of 1812, and was with General Jackson at the Battle of New Orleans. His most famous poem is not about the military. It is a sentimental tribute to a bygone era when ferries were the only bridges across rivers.

O, boatman! wind that horn again,
   For never did the list'ning air
   Upon its lambent bosom bear
So wild, so soft, so sweet a strain!
What though thy notes are sad and few,
   By every simple boatman blown,
Yet is each pulse to nature true,
   And melody in every tone.

How oft, in boyhood's joyous day,
   Unmindful of the lapsing hours,
I've loitered on my homeward way
   By wild Ohio's bank of flowers;
While some lone boatman from the deck
   Poured his soft numbers to the tide,
As if to charm from storm and wreck
   The boat where all his fortunes ride!

Delighted, Nature drank the sound,
Enchanted; Echo bore it round
In whispers soft and softer still,
From hill to plain and plain to hill,
Till e 'en the thoughtless frolic boy,
Elate with hope and wild with joy,
Who gambolled by the river's side
And sported with the fretting tide,
Feels something new pervade his breast,

Change his light steps, repress his jest,
Bends o'er the flood his eager ear,
To catch the sounds far off, yet dear—
Drinks the sweet draught, but knows not why
The tear of rapture fills his eye.
And can he now, to manhood grown,
Tell why those notes, simple and lone,
As on the ravished ear they fell,
Bind every sense in magic spell?

There is a tide of feeling given
To all on earth, its fountains, heaven,
Beginning with the dewy flower,
Just ope'd in Flora's vernal bower,
Rising creation's orders through,
With louder murmur, brighter hue—
That tide is sympathy! its ebb and flow
Give life its hue, its joy, and woe.

Music, the master-spirit that can move
Its waves to war, or lull them into love—
Can cheer the sinking sailor 'mid the wave,
And bid the warrior on! nor fear the grave,
Inspire the fainting pilgrim on the road,
And elevate his soul to claim his God.

Then, boatman, wind that horn again!
Though much of sorrow mark its strain,
Yet are its notes to sorrow dear;
What though they wake fond memory's tear?
Tears are sad memory's sacred feast,
And rapture oft her chosen guest.

Henry T. Stanton

"The Moneyless Man"

Henry T. Stanton was born in 1834 in Virginia but moved with his parents to Maysville; he attended West Point and became a major in the Confederate Army. After the war he practiced law, journalism, and politics and, from time to time, wrote sentimental poems. "The Moneyless Man" is a melodramatic portrait in irregular couplets of poor people who find themselves not welcome in society. The moneyless man, alas, must wait for his reward in Heaven.

Is there no secret place on the face of the earth,
Where charity dwelleth, where virtue has birth?
Where bosoms in mercy and kindness will heave,
When the poor and the wretched shall ask and receive?
Is there no place at all, where a knock from the poor,
Will bring a kind angel to open the door?
Ah, search the wide world wherever you can
There is no open door for a Moneyless Man!

Go, look in yon hall where the chandelier's light
Drives off with its splendor the darkness of night,
Where the rich-hanging velvet in shadowy fold
Sweeps gracefully down with its trimmings of gold,
And the mirrors of silver take up, and renew,
In long lighted vistas the 'wildering view:
Go there! at the banquet, and find, if you can,
A welcoming smile for a Moneyless Man!

Go, look in yon church of the cloud-reaching spire,
Which gives to the sun his same look of red fire,
Where the arches and columns are gorgeous within,
And the walls seem as pure as a soul without sin;
Walk down the long aisles, see the rich and the great
In the pomp and the pride of their worldly estate;
Walk down in your patches, and find, if you can,
Who opens a pew to a Moneyless Man.

Go, look in the Banks, where Mammon has told
His hundreds and thousands of silver and gold;
Where, safe from the hands of the starving and poor,
Lies pile upon pile of the glittering ore!
Walk up to their counters—ah, there you may stay
'Til your limbs grow old, 'til your hairs grow gray,
And you'll find at the Banks not one of the clan
With money to lend to a Moneyless Man!

Go, look to yon Judge, in his dark-flowing gown,
With the scales wherein law weighteth equity down;
Where he frowns on the weak and smiles on the strong,
And punishes right whilst he justifies wrong;
Where juries their lips to the Bible have laid,
To render a verdict—they've already made:
Go there, in the court-room, and find, if you can,
Any law for the cause of a Moneyless Man!

Then go to your hovel—no raven has fed
The wife who has suffered too long for her bread;
Kneel down by her pallet, and kiss the death-frost
From the lips of the angel your poverty lost:
Then turn in your agony upward to God,
And bless, while it smites you, the chastening rod,
And you'll find, at the end of your life's little span,
There's a welcome above for a Moneyless Man!

Theodore O'Hara

"The Bivouac of the Dead"

Theodore O'Hara, remembered for one poem only, was probably born in Danville. He wrote a poem to honor the Kentuckians who had lost their lives in the Mexican War. "The Bivouac of the Dead" is generally considered the greatest military poem in the English language, and it has come to encompass and celebrate the sacrifices of all men in all wars. Its lines can be seen on tablets in cemeteries and at Civil War battlefields.

The muffled drum's sad roll has beat
The soldier's last tattoo;
No more on life's parade shall meet
That brave and fallen few.
On Fame's eternal camping-ground
Their silent tents are spread,
And Glory guards, with solemn round,
The bivouac of the dead.

No rumor of the foe's advance
Now swells upon the wind;
No troubled thought at midnight haunts
Of loved ones left behind;
No vision of the morrow's strife
The warrior's dreams alarms,
No braying horn nor screaming fife
At dawn shall call to arms.

Their shivered swords are red with rust
Their plumed heads are bowed;
Their haughty banner, trailed in dust,
Is now their martial shroud;
And plenteous funeral tears have washed
The red stains from each brow,
And the proud forms, by battle gashed,
Are free from anguish now.

The neighing troop, the flashing blade,
The bugle's stirring blast,
The charge, the dreadful cannonade,
The din and shout are past;
Nor war's wild note, nor glory's peal,
Shall thrill with fierce delight
Those breasts that nevermore may feel
The rapture of the fight.

Like the fierce northern hurricane
That sweeps his great pleateau,
Flushed with the triumph yet to gain,
Came down the serried foe.
Who heard the thunder of the fray
Break o'er the field beneath,
Knew well the watchword of that day
Was "Victory or death."

Long did the doubtful conflict rage
O'er all that stricken plain,
For never fiercer fight did wage
The vengeful blood of Spain.
And still the storm of battle blew,
Still swelled the gory tide—
Not long our stout old chieftain knew
Such odds his strength could bide.

'Twas at that hour his stern command
Called to a martyr's grave
The flower of his own loved land,
The Nation's flag to save,
By rivers of their father's gore
His first-born laurels grew,
And well he deemed the sons would pour
Their lives for glory too.

Full many a norther's breath has swept
O'er Angostura's plain—
And long the pitying sky has wept
Above its mouldering slain.
The raven's screams, or eagle's flight,

Or shepherd's pensive lay,
Alone awakens each sullen height
That frowned o'er that dread fray.

Sons of the Dark and Bloody Ground,
Ye must not slumber there,
Where stranger steps and tongues resound
Along the heedless air.
Your own proud land's heroic soil
Shall be your fitter grave;
She claims from War its richest spoil—
The ashes of her brave.

Thus 'neath their parent turf they rest,
Far from the gory field,
Borne to a Spartan mother's breast
On many a bloody shield;
The sunshine of their native sky
Smiles sadly on them here,
And kindred eyes and hearts watch by
The heroes' sepulcher.

Rest on, embalmed and sainted dead,
Dear as the blood ye gave,
No impious footstep here shall tread
The herbage of your grave;
Nor shall your glory be forgot
While Fame her record keeps,
Or Honor points the hallowed spot
Where Valor proudly sleeps.

Yon marble minstrel's voiceful stone
In deathless song shall tell,
When many a vanquished age hath flown,
The story how ye fell;
Nor wreck, nor change, nor winter's blight,
Nor Time's remorseless doom,
Shall dim one ray of Glory's light
That gilds your deathless tomb.

Turning the Century
Kentucky Writing Comes of Age

We are now about one hundred years through our Kentucky literary journey. In this chapter we will begin to see glimmers of major talent in the works of minor writers. To James Lane Allen and John Fox Jr. we owe gratitude for opening the great literary treasury of central Kentucky and the mountains and showcasing it to the world. Annie Fellows Johnston and Alice Hegan Rice put the Louisville area on the national literary map with *The Little Colonel* and *Mrs. Wiggs of the Cabbage Patch*. Other parts of Kentucky, from Florence in the north to Bowling Green and Owensboro in the south and west, were beginning to discover and celebrate their history and culture. African Americans were awakening to the riches of their own heritage. By the 1920s Irvin S. Cobb was writing some of the nation's most popular short stories and novels about the people he knew as a boy in Paducah. Many of the plots and characters in the poetry and prose we are about to read are stereotypical; but these writers were preparing the way for the great ones to follow.

James Lane Allen
from "Two Gentlemen of Kentucky"

Both James Lane Allen and John Fox Jr. were a part of the literary movement following the Civil War known as local color, which exploited the culture and folkways of people in "odd corners" of the nation. Most of Allen's fiction and nonfiction portrays the gentry and their servants in the antebellum and postwar Bluegrass region of central Kentucky, where Allen was born on a farm near Lexington in 1849. After graduating from Transylvania University in 1872, he taught in several high schools and colleges for a decade or more, then turned his time and talents to writing stories and articles for such popular magazines as the *Atlantic, Harper's,* and *Century,* which made his name known nationally. Many of the stories were collected in *Flute and Violin* in 1891, and the articles in *The Blue-Grass Region of Kentucky* in 1892. "Two Gentlemen of Kentucky," a signature piece by Allen, is a story based on a real-life landowner and his servant, neither of whom adjusted very well to the changes wrought by the Civil War and the emancipation of slaves.

It was near the middle of the afternoon of an autumnal day, on the wide, grassy plateau of Central Kentucky.

The Eternal Power seemed to have quitted the universe and left all nature folded in the calm of the Eternal Peace. Around the pale-blue dome of the heavens a few pearl-colored clouds hung motionless, as though the wind had been withdrawn to other skies. Not a crimson leaf floated downward through the soft, silvery light that filled the atmosphere and created the sense of lonely, unimaginable spaces. This light overhung the far-rolling landscape of field and meadow and wood, crowning with faint radiance the remoter low-swelling hill-tops and deepening into dreamy half-shadows on their eastern slopes. Nearer, it fell in a white flake on an unstirred sheet of water which lay along the edge of a mass of sombre-hued woodland, and nearer still it touched to spring-like brilliancy a level, green meadow on the hither edge of the water, where a group of Durham cattle stood with reversed flanks near the gleaming trunks of some leafless sycamores. Still nearer it caught the top of the brown foliage of a little bent oak-tree and burned it into a silvery flame. It lit on the back and the wings of a crow flying heavily in the path of its rays, and made his blackness as white as the breast of a swan. In the immediate foreground, it sparkled in minute gleams along the stalks of the coarse, dead weeds that fell away from the legs and the flanks of a white horse, and slanted across the face of the rider and through the ends of his gray hair, which straggled from beneath his soft black hat.

The horse, old and patient and gentle, stood with low-stretched neck and closed eyes half asleep in the faint glow of the waning heat; and the rider, the sole human presence in all the field, sat looking across the silent autumnal landscape, sunk in reverie. Both horse and rider seemed but harmonious elements in the panorama of still-life, and completed the picture of a closing scene.

To the man it was a closing scene. From the rank, fallow field through which he had been riding he was now surveying, for the last time, the many features of a landscape that had been familiar to him from the beginning of memory. In the afternoon and the autumn of his age he was about to rend the last ties that bound him to his former life, and, like one who had survived his own destiny, turn his face towards a future that was void of everything he held significant or dear.

The Civil War had only the year before reached its ever-memorable close. From where he sat there was not a home in sight, as there was not one beyond the reach of his vision, but had felt its influence. Some of his neighbors had come home from its camps and prisons, aged or altered as though by half a lifetime of years. The bones of some lay whitening on its battlefields. Families, reassembled around their hearth-stones, spoke in low tones unceasingly of defeat and victory, heroism and death. Suspicion and distrust and estrangement prevailed. Former friends met each other on the turnpikes without speaking; brothers avoided each other in the streets of the neighboring town. The rich had grown poor; the poor had become rich. Many of the latter were preparing to move West. The negroes were drifting blindly hither and thither, deserting the country and flocking to the towns. Even the once united church of his neighborhood was jarred by the unstrung and discordant spirit of the times. At affecting passages in the sermons men grew pale and set their teeth fiercely; women suddenly lowered their black veils and rocked to and fro in their pews; for it is always at the bar of Conscience and before the very altar of God that the human heart is most wrung by a sense of its losses and the memory of its wrongs. The war had divided the people of Kentucky as the false mother would have severed the child.

It had not left the old man unscathed. His younger brother had fallen early in the conflict, borne to the end of his brief warfare by his impetuous valor; his aged mother had sunk under the tidings of the death of her latest-born; his sister was estranged from him by his political differences with her husband; his old family servants, men and women, had left him, and grass and weeds had already grown over the door-steps of the shut, noiseless cabins. Nay, the whole vast social system of the old régime had fallen, and he was henceforth but a useless fragment of the ruins.

All at once his mind turned from the cracked and smoky mirror of the times and dwelt fondly upon the scenes of the past. The silent fields around him seemed again alive with the negroes, singing as they followed the ploughs down the corn-rows or swung the cradles through the bearded wheat. Again, in a frenzy of merriment, the strains of the old fiddles issued from crevices of cabin-doors to the rhythmic beat of hands and feet that shook the rafters and the roof. Now he was sitting on his porch, and one little negro was blacking his shoes, another leading his saddle-horse to the stiles, a third bringing his hat, and a fourth handing him a glass of ice-cold sangaree; or now he lay under the locust-trees in his yard, falling asleep in the drowsy heat of the summer afternoon, while one waved over him a bough of pungent walnut leaves, until he lost consciousness and by-and-by awoke to find that they both had fallen asleep side by side on the grass and that the abandoned fly-brush lay full across his face.

From where he sat also were seen slopes on which picnics were danced under the broad shade of maples and elms in June by those whom death and war had scattered like the transitory leaves that once had sheltered them. In this direction lay the district schoolhouse where on Friday evenings there were wont to be speeches and debates; in that, lay the blacksmith's shop where of old he and his neighbors had met on horseback of Saturday afternoons to hear the news, get the mails, discuss elections, and pitch quoits. In the valley beyond stood the church at which all had assembled on calm Sunday mornings like the members of one united family. Along with these scenes went many a chastened reminiscence of bridal and funeral and simpler events that had made up the annals of his country life.

The reader will have a clearer insight into the character and past career of Colonel Romulus Fields by remembering that he represented a fair type of that social order which had existed in rank perfection over the blue-grass plains of Kentucky during the final decades of the old régime. Perhaps of all agriculturists in the United States the inhabitants of that region had spent the most nearly idyllic life, on account of the beauty of the climate, the richness of the land, the spacious comfort of their homes, the efficiency of their negroes, and the characteristic contentedness of their dispositions. Thus nature and history combined to make them a peculiar class, a cross between the aristocratic and the bucolic, being as simple as shepherds and as proud as kings, and not seldom exhibiting among both men and women types of character which were as remarkable for pure, tender, noble states of feeling as they were commonplace in powers and cultivation of mind.

It was upon this luxurious social growth that the war naturally fell as a killing frost, and upon no single specimen with more blighting power than upon Colonel Fields. For destiny had quarried and chiselled him, to serve as an ornament in the barbaric temple of human bondage. There *were* ornaments in that temple, and he was one. A slave-holder with Southern sympathies, a man educated not beyond the ideas of his generation, convinced that slavery was an evil, yet seeing no present way of removing it, he had of all things been a model master. As such he had gone on record in Kentucky, and no doubt in a Higher Court; and as such his efforts had been put forth to secure the passage of many of those milder laws for which his State was distinguished. Often, in those dark days, his face, anxious and sad, was to be seen amid the throng that surrounded the blocks on which slaves were sold at auction; and more than one poor wretch he had bought to save him from separation from his family or from being sold into the Southern plantations— afterwards riding far and near to find him a home on one of the neighboring farms.

But all those days were over. He had but to place the whole picture of the present beside the whole picture of the past to realize what the contrast meant for him.

At length he gathered the bridle reins from the neck of his old horse and turned his head homeward. As he rode slowly on, every spot gave up its memories. He dismounted when he came to the cattle and walked among them, stroking their soft flanks and feeling in the palm of his hand the rasp of their salt-loving tongues; on his sideboard at home was many a silver cup which told of premiums on cattle at the great fairs. It was in this very pond that as a boy he had learned to swim on a cherry rail. When he entered the woods, the sight of the walnut-trees and the hickory-nut trees, loaded on the topmost branches, gave him a sudden pang.

Beyond the woods he came upon the garden, which he had kept as his mother had left it—an old-fashioned garden with an arbor in the centre, covered with Isabella grape-vines on one side and Catawba on the other; with walks branching thence in four directions, and along them beds of jump-up-johnnies, sweet-williams, daffodils, sweet-peas, larkspur, and thyme, flags and the sensitive-plant, celestial and maiden's-blush roses. He stopped and looked over the fence at the very spot where he had found his mother on the day when the news of the battle came.

She had been kneeling, trowel in hand, driving away vigorously at the loamy earth, and, as she saw him coming, had risen and turned towards him her face with the ancient pink bloom on her clear cheeks and the light of a pure, strong soul in her gentle eyes. Overcome by his emotions, he had blindly faltered out the words, "Mother, John was among the killed!" For a moment she had looked at him as though stunned by a blow. Then a violent flush had overspread her features, and then an ashen pallor; after which, with a sudden proud dilating of her form as though with joy, she had sunk down like the tenderest of her lily-stalks, cut from its root.

Beyond the garden he came to the empty cabin and the great wood-pile. At this hour it used to be a scene of hilarious activity—the little negroes sitting perched in chattering groups on the topmost logs or playing leap-frog in the dust, while some picked up baskets of chips or dragged a back-log into the cabins.

At last he drew near the wooden stiles and saw the large house of which he was the solitary occupant. What darkened rooms and noiseless halls! What beds, all ready, that nobody now came to sleep in, and cushioned old chairs that nobody rocked! The house and the contents of its attic, presses, and drawers could have told much of the history of Kentucky from almost its beginning; for its foundations had been laid by his father near the beginning of the century, and through its doors had passed a long train of forms, from the veterans of the Revolution to the soldiers of the Civil War. Old coats hung up in closets; old dresses folded away in drawers; saddle-bags and buck-skin-leggins; hunting-jackets, powder-horns, and militiamen hats; looms and knitting-needles; snuffboxes and reticules—what a treasure-house of the past it was! And now the only thing that had the springs of life within its bosom was the great, sweet-voiced clock, whose faithful face had kept unchanged amid all the swift pageantry of changes.

He dismounted at the stiles and handed the reins to a gray-haired negro, who had hobbled up to receive them with a smile and a gesture of the deep-est respect.

"Peter," he said, very simply, "I am going to sell the place and move to town. I can't live here any longer."

With these words he passed through the yard-gate, walked slowly up the broad pavement, and entered the house.

On the disappearing form of the colonel was fixed an ancient pair of eyes that looked out at him from behind a still more ancient pair of silver-rimmed spectacles with an expression of indescribable solicitude and love.

These eyes were set in the head of an old gentleman—for such he was—named Peter Cotton, who was the only one of the colonel's former slaves that had remained inseparable from his person and his altered fortunes. In early manhood Peter had been a wood-chopper; but he had one day had his leg broken by the limb of a falling tree, and afterwards, out of consideration for his limp, had been made supervisor of the wood-pile, gardener, and a sort of nondescript servitor of his master's luxurious needs.

Nay, in larger and deeper characters must his history be writ, he having been, in days gone by, one of those ministers of the gospel whom conscientious Kentucky masters often urged to the exercise of spiritual functions in behalf of their benighted people. In course of preparation for this august work, Peter had learned to read and had come to possess a well-chosen library of three several volumes—*Webster's Spelling-Book, The Pilgrim's Progress,* and the Bible. But even these unusual acquisitions he deemed not enough; for being touched with a spark of poetic fire from heaven, and enthused by the African's fondness for all that is conspicuous in dress, he had conceived for himself the creation of a unique garment which should symbolize in perfection the claims and consolations of his apostolic office. This was nothing less than a sacred blue-jeans coat that he had had his old mistress make him, with very long and spacious tails, whereon, at his further direction, she embroidered sundry texts of Scripture which it pleased him to regard as the fit visible annunciations of his holy calling. And inasmuch as his mistress, who had had the coat woven on her own looms from the wool of her finest sheep, was, like other gentlewomen of her time, rarely skilled in the accomplishments of the needle, and was moreover in full sympathy with the piety of his intent, she wrought of these passages a border enriched with such intricate curves, marvellous flourishes, and harmonious letterings, that Solomon never reflected the glory in which Peter was arrayed whenever he put it on. For after much prayer that the Almighty wisdom would aid his reason in the difficult task of selecting the most appropriate texts, Peter had chosen seven—one for each day in the week—with such tact, and no doubt heavenly guidance, that when braided together they did truly constitute an eloquent epitome of Christian duty, hope, and pleading.

From first to last they were as follows: "Woe is unto me if I preach not the gospel;" "Servants, be obedient to them that are your masters according to the flesh;" "Come unto me, all ye that labour and are heavy laden;" "Consider the lilies of the field, how they grow; they toil not, neither do they spin;" "Now abideth faith, hope, and charity, these three; but the greatest of these is charity;" " I would not have you to be ignorant, brethren, concerning them which are asleep;" "For as in Adam all die, even so in Christ shall all be made alive." This concatenation of texts Peter wished to have duly solemnized, and therefore, when the work was finished, he further requested his mistress to close the entire chain with the word "Amen," introduced in some suitable place.

But the only spot now left vacant was one of a few square inches, located just where the coat-tails hung over the end of Peter's spine; so that when any one stood full in Peter's rear, he could but marvel at the sight of so solemn a word emblazoned in so unusual a locality.

Panoplied in this robe of righteousness, and with a worn leathern Bible in his hand, Peter used to go around of Sundays, and during the week, by night, preaching from cabin to cabin the gospel of his heavenly Master.

The angriest lightnings of the sultriest skies often played amid the darkness upon those sacred coat-tails and around that girdle of everlasting texts, as though the evil spirits of the air would fain have burned them and scattered their ashes on the roaring winds. The slow-sifting snows of winter whitened them as though to chill their spiritual fires; but winter and summer, year after year, in weariness of body, often in sore distress of mind, for miles along this lonely road and for miles across that rugged way, Peter trudged on and on, withal perhaps as meek a spirit as ever grew foot-sore in the paths of its Master. Many a poor overburdened slave took fresh heart and strength from the sight of that celestial raiment; many a stubborn, rebellious spirit, whose flesh but lately quivered under the lash, was brought low by its humble teaching; many a worn-out old frame, racked with pain in its last illness, pressed a fevered lip to its hopeful hem; and many a dying eye closed in death peacefully fixed on its immortal pledges.

When Peter started abroad, if a storm threatened, he carried an old cotton umbrella of immense size; and as the storm burst, he gathered the tails of his coat carefully up under his armpits that they might be kept dry. Or if caught by a tempest without his umbrella, he would take his coat off and roll it up inside out, leaving his body exposed to the fury of the elements. No care, however, could keep it from growing old and worn and faded; and when the slaves were set free and he was called upon by the interposition of Providence to lay it finally aside, it was covered by many a patch and stain as proofs of its devoted usage.

One after another the colonel's old servants, gathering their children about them, had left him, to begin their new life. He bade them all a kind good-bye, and into the palm of each silently pressed some gift that he knew would soon be needed. But no inducement could make Peter or Phillis, his wife, budge from their cabin. "Go, Peter! Go, Phillis!" the colonel had said time and again. "No one is happier that you are free than I am; and you can call on me for what you need to set you up in business." But Peter and Phillis asked to stay with him. Then suddenly, several months before the time at which this sketch opens, Phillis had died, leaving the colonel and Peter as the only relics of that populous life which had once filled the house and the cabins. The colonel had succeeded in hiring a woman to do Phillis's work; but her presence was a strange note of discord in the old domestic harmony, and only saddened the recollections of its vanished peace.

Peter had a short, stout figure, dark-brown skin, smooth-shaven face, eyes round, deep set and wide apart, and a short, stub nose which dipped suddenly into his head, making it easy for him to wear the silver-rimmed spectacles left him by his old mistress. A peculiar conformation of the muscles between the eyes and the nose gave him the quizzical expression of one who is about to sneeze, and this was heightened by a twinkle in the eyes which seemed caught from the shining of an inner sun upon his tranquil heart.

Sometimes, however, his face grew sad enough. It was sad on this afternoon while he watched the colonel walk slowly up the pavement, well overgrown with weeds, and enter the house, which the setting sun touched with the last radiance of the finished day.

About two years after the close of the war, therefore, the colonel and Peter were to be found in Lexington, ready to turn over a new leaf in the volumes of their lives, which already had an old-fashioned binding, a somewhat musty odor, and but few written leaves remaining.

After a long, dry summer you may have seen two gnarled old apple-trees, that stood with interlocked arms on the western slope of some quiet hillside, make a melancholy show of blooming out again in the autumn of the year and dallying with the idle buds that mock their sapless branches. Much the same was the belated, fruitless efflorescence of the colonel and Peter.

John Fox Jr.

"Through the Gap"

John Fox Jr. was from the Bluegrass country (he was born in 1862 at Stony Point, in Bourbon County), but he took his literary material from the Kentucky mountains, which he explored in the mid-1880s when he accompanied his father and brother on visits to their mining interests in the Cumberland Mountains. He began to study the folklife of the mountain people and write stories about them. After James Lane Allen read the draft of one of Fox's stories, he encouraged him to complete it and send it to *Century Magazine*. "A Mountain Europa," which appeared in two installments in 1892, became his first publication. He received a check for $262, a princely amount for those times. Two of his novels, *The Little Shepherd of Kingdom Come* (1903) and *The Trail of the Lonesome Pine* (1908), as well as a number of his short stories are still widely and enthusiastically read. "Through the Gap" is an apt introduction to the strange ways of the hill people. It is a comedy of mountain manners that almost becomes a tragedy. The dark-skinned Malungians (also Melungians) in the story are thought to be descendants of Portuguese immigrants who were early settlers in the southern mountains of Kentucky. (Jesse Stuart wrote a novel, *Daughter of the Legend,* which is a sympathetic treatment of these misunderstood people.)

When thistles go adrift, the sun sets down the valley between the hills; when snow comes, it goes down behind the Cumberland and streams through a great fissure that people call the Gap. Then the last light drenches the parson's cottage under Imboden Hill, and leaves an after-glow of glory on a majestic heap that lies against the east. Sometimes it spans the Gap with a rainbow.

Strange people and strange tales come through this Gap from the Kentucky hills. Through it came these two, late one day—a man and a woman—afoot. I met them at the footbridge over Roaring Fork.

"Is thar a preacher anywhar aroun' hyeh?" he asked. I pointed to the cottage under Imboden Hill. The girl flushed slightly and turned her head away with a rather unhappy smile. Without a word, the mountaineer led the way towards town. A moment more and a half-breed Malungian passed me on the bridge and followed them.

At dusk the next day I saw the mountaineer chopping wood at a shanty under a clump of rhododendron on the river-bank. The girl was cooking supper inside. The day following he was at work on the railroad, and on Sunday, after church, I saw the parson. The two had not been to him. Only that afternoon the mountaineer was on the bridge with another woman, hideously rouged and with scarlet ribbons fluttering from her bonnet. Passing on by the shanty, I saw the Malungian talking to the girl. She apparently paid no heed to him until, just as he was moving away, he said something mockingly, and with a nod of his head back towards the bridge. She did not look up even then, but her face got hard and white, and, looking back from the road, I saw her slipping through the bushes into the dry bed of the creek, to make sure that what the half-breed told her was true.

The two men were working side by side on the railroad when I saw them again, but on the first pay-day the doctor was called to attend the Malungian, whose head was split open with a shovel. I was one of two who went out to arrest his assailant, and I had no need to ask who he was. The mountaineer was a devil, the foreman said, and I had to club him with a pistol-butt before he would give in. He said he would get even with me; but they all say that, and I paid no attention to the threat. For a week he was kept in the calaboose, and when I passed the shanty just after he was sent to the county-seat for trial, I found it empty. The Malungian, too, was gone. Within a fortnight the mountaineer was in the door of the shanty again. Having no accuser, he had been discharged. He went back to his work, and if he opened his lips I never knew. Every day I saw him at work, and he never failed to give me a surly look. Every dusk I saw him in his doorway, waiting, and I could guess for what. It was easy to believe that the stern purpose in his face would make its way through space and draw her to him again. And she did come back one day. I had just limped down the mountain with a sprained ankle. A crowd of women was gathered at the edge of the woods, looking with all their eyes to the shanty on the river-bank. The girl stood in the door-way. The mountaineer was coming back from work with his face down.

"He hain't seed her yit," said one. "He's goin' to kill her shore. I tol' her he would. She said she reckoned he would, but she didn't keer."

For a moment I was paralyzed by the tragedy at hand. She was in the door looking at him when he raised his head. For one moment he stood still, staring, and then he started towards her with a quickened step. I started too, then, every step a torture, and as I limped ahead she made a gesture of terror and backed into the room before him. The door closed, and I listened for a pistol-shot and a scream. It must have been done with a knife, I thought, and quietly, for when I was within ten paces of the cabin he opened the door again. His face was very white; he held one hand behind him, and he was nervously fumbling at his chin with the other. As he stepped towards me I caught the handle of a pistol in my side pocket and waited. He looked at me sharply.

"Did you say the preacher lived up thar?" he asked.

"Yes," I said, breathlessly.

In the door-way just then stood the girl with a bonnet in her hand, and at a nod from him they started up the hill towards the cottage. They came down again after a while, he stalking ahead, and she, after the mountain fashion, behind. And after this fashion I saw them at sunset next day pass over the bridge and into the mouth of the Gap whence they came. Through this Gap come strange people and strange tales from the Kentucky hills. Over it, sometimes, is the span of a rainbow.

"Grayson's Baby"

"Grayson's Baby" is a heartrending story of a starving family's pitiful pride and stoicism, as well as the attempts of outsiders to help them.

⌀

The first snow sifted in through the Gap that night, and in a "shack" of one room and a low loft a man was dead, a woman was sick to death, and four children were barely alive; and nobody even knew. For they were hill people, who sicken, suffer, and sometimes die, like animals, and make no noise.

Grayson, the Virginian, coming down from the woods that morning, saw the big-hearted little doctor outside the door of the shack, walking up and down, with his hands in his pockets. He was whistling softly when Grayson got near, and, without stopping, pointed with his thumb within. The oldest boy sat stolidly on the one chair in the room, his little brother was on the floor hard by, and both were hugging a greasy stove. The little girl was with her mother in the bed, both almost out of sight under a heap of quilts. The baby was in a cradle, with its face uncovered, whether dead or asleep Grayson could not tell. A pine coffin was behind the door. It would not have been possible to add to the disorder of the room, and the atmosphere made Grayson gasp. He came out looking white. The first man to arrive thereafter took away the eldest boy, a woman picked the baby girl from the bed, and a childless young couple took up the pallid little fellow on the floor. These were step-children. The baby boy that was left was the woman's own. Nobody came for that, and Grayson went in again and looked at it a long while. So little, so old a human face he had never seen. The brow was wrinkled as with centuries of pain, and the little drawn mouth looked as though the spirit within had fought its inheritance without a murmur, and would fight on that way to the end. It was the pluck of the face that drew Grayson. "I'll take it," he said. The doctor was not without his sense of humor even then, but he nodded. "Cradle and all," he said, gravely. And Grayson put both on one shoulder and walked away. He had lost the power of giving further surprise in that town, and had he met every man he knew, not one of them would have felt at liberty to ask him what he was doing. An hour later the doctor found the child in Grayson's room, and Grayson still looking at it.

"Is it going to live, doctor?"

The doctor shook his head. "Doubtful. Look at the color. It's starved. There's nothing to do but to watch it and feed it. You can do that."

So Grayson watched it, with a fascination of which he was hardly conscious. Never for one instant did its look change—the quiet, unyielding endurance that no faith and no philosophy could ever bring to him. It was ideal courage, that look, to accept the inevitable but to fight it just that way. Half the little mountain town was talking next day—that such a tragedy was possible by the public road-side, with relief within sound of the baby's cry. The oldest boy was least starved. Might made right in an extremity like his, and the boy had taken care of himself. The young couple who had the second lad in charge said they had been wakened at daylight the next morning by some noise in the room. Looking up, they saw the little fellow at the fireplace breaking an egg. He had built a fire, had got eggs from the kitchen, and was cooking his breakfast. The little girl was mischievous and cheery in spite of her bad plight, and nobody knew of the baby except Grayson and the doctor. Grayson would let nobody else in. As soon as it was well enough to be peevish and to cry, he took it back to its mother, who was still abed. A long, dark mountaineer was there, of whom the woman seemed half afraid. He followed Grayson outside.

"Say, podner," he said, with an unpleasant smile, "ye don't go up to Cracker's Neck fer nothin', do ye?"

The woman had lived at Cracker's Neck before she appeared at the Gap, and it did not come to Grayson what the man meant until he was half-way to his room. Then he flushed hot and wheeled back to the cabin, but the mountaineer was gone.

"Tell that fellow he had better keep out of my way," he said to the woman, who understood, and wanted to say something, but not knowing how, nodded simply. In a few days the other children went back to the cabin, and day and night Grayson went to see the child, until it was out of danger, and afterwards. It was not long before the women in town complained that the mother was ungrateful. When they sent things to eat to her the servant brought back word that she had called out, "'Set them over thar,' without so much as a thanky." One message was that "she didn' want no second-hand victuals from nobody's table." Somebody suggested sending the family to the poor-house. The mother said "she'd go out on her crutches and hoe corn fust, and that the people who talked 'bout sendin' her to the po'house had better save their breath to make prayers with." One day she was hired to do some washing. The mistress of the house happened not to rise until ten o'clock. Next morning the mountain woman did not appear until that hour. "She wasn't goin' to work a lick while that woman was a-layin' in bed," she said, frankly. And when the lady went down town, she too disappeared. Nor would she, she explained to Grayson, "while that woman was a-struttin' the streets."

After that, one by one, they let her alone, and the woman made not a word of complaint. Within a week she was working in the fields, when she should have been back in bed. The result was that the child sickened again. The old look came back to its face, and Grayson was there night and day. He was having trouble out in Kentucky about this time, and he went to the Blue Grass pretty often. Always, however, he left money with me to see that the child was properly buried if it should die while he was gone; and once he telegraphed to ask how it was. He said he was sometimes afraid to open my letters for fear that he should read that the baby was dead. The child knew Grayson's voice, his step. It would go to him from its own mother. When it was sickest and lying torpid it would move the instant he stepped into the room, and, when he spoke, would hold out its thin arms, without opening its eyes, and for hours Grayson would walk the floor with the troubled little baby over his shoulder. I thought several times it would die when, on one trip, Grayson was away for two weeks. One midnight indeed, I found the mother moaning, and three female harpies about the cradle. The baby was dying this time, and I ran back for a flask of whiskey. Ten minutes late with the whiskey that night would have been too late. The baby got to know me and my voice during that fortnight, but it was still in danger when Grayson got back, and we went to see it together. It was very weak, and we both leaned over the cradle, from either side, and I saw the pity and affection—yes, hungry, half-shamed affection—in Grayson's face. The child opened its eyes, looked from one to the other, and held out its arms to *me*. Grayson should have known that the child forgot—that it would forget its own mother. He turned sharply, and his face was a little pale. He gave something to the woman, and not till then did I notice that her soft black eyes never left him while he was in the cabin. The child got well; but Grayson never went to the shack again, and he said nothing when I came in one night and told him that some mountaineer—a long, dark fellow—had taken the woman, the children, and the household goods of the shack back into the mountains.

"They don't grieve long," I said, "these people."

But long afterwards I saw the woman again along the dusty road that leads into the Gap. She had heard over in the mountains that Grayson was dead, and had walked for two days to learn if it was true. I pointed back towards Bee Rock, and told her that he had fallen from a cliff back there. She did not move, nor did her look change. Moreover, she said nothing, and, being in a hurry, I had to ride on.

At the foot-bridge over Roaring Fork I looked back. The woman was still there, under the hot mid-day sun and in the dust of the road, motionless.

"Preachin' on Kingdom-Come"

In "Preachin' on Kingdom-Come," Fox has a native narrate the story of how a strange new preacher comes into a primitive mountain community and miraculously brings peace between two feuding families.

I've told ye, stranger, that Hell fer Sartain empties, as it oughter, of co'se, into Kingdom-Come. You can ketch the devil 'most any day in the week on Hell fer Sartain, an' sometimes you can git Glory everlastin' on Kingdom-Come. Hit's the only meetin'-house thar in twenty miles aroun'.

Well, the reg'lar rider, ole Jim Skaggs, was dead, an' the bretherin was a-lookin' aroun' fer somebody to step into ole Jim's shoes. Thar'd been one young feller up thar from the settlemints, a-cavortin' aroun', an' they was studyin' 'bout gittin' him.

"Bretherin' an' sisteren," I says, atter the leetle chap was gone, "he's got the fortitood to speak an' he shorely is well favored. He's got a mighty good hawk eye fer spyin' out evil—an' the gals; he can outholler ole Jim; an' *if,*" I says, "any *idees* ever comes to him, he'll be a hell-rouser shore—but they ain't comin'!" An', so sayin', I takes my foot in my hand an' steps fer home.

Stranger, them fellers over thar hain't seed much o' this world. Lots of 'em nuver seed the cyars; some of 'em nuver seed a wagon. An' atter jowerin' an' noratin' fer 'bout two hours, what you reckon they said they aimed to do? They believed they'd take that ar man Beecher, ef they could git him to come. They'd heerd o' Henry endurin' the war, an' they knowed he was agin the rebs, an' they wanted Henry if they could jes git him to come.

Well, I snorted, an' the feud broke out on Hell fer Sartain betwixt the Days an' the Dillons. Mace Day shot Daws Dillon's brother, as I rickollect—somep'n's al'ays a-startin' up that plaguey war an' a-makin' things frolicsome over thar—an' ef it hadn't a-been fer a tall young feller with black hair an' a scar across his forehead, who was a-goin' through the mountains a-settlin' these wars, blame me ef I believe thar ever would 'a' been any mo' preachin' on Kingdom-Come. This feller comes over from Hazlan an' says he aims to hold a meetin' on Kingdom-Come. "Brother," I says, "that's what no preacher have ever did whilst this war is a-goin' on." An' he says, sort o' quiet, "Well, then, I reckon I'll have to do what no preacher have ever did." An' I ups an' says: "Brother, an ole jedge come up here once from the settlemints to hold couht. 'Jedge,' I says, 'that's what no jedge have ever did without soldiers since this war's been a-goin' on.' An', brother, the jedge's words was yours, p'int-blank. 'All right,' he says, 'then I'll have to do what no other jedge have ever did.' An', brother," says I to the preacher, "the jedge done it shore. He jes laid under the couht-house fer two days whilst the boys fit over him. An' when I sees the jedge a-makin' tracks fer the settlemints, I says, 'Jedge,' I says, 'you spoke a parable shore.'"

Well, sir, the long preacher looked jes as though he was a-sayin' to hisself, "Yes, I hear ye, but I don't heed ye," an' when he says, "Jes the same, I'm a-goin' to hold a meetin' on Kingdom-Come," why, I jes takes my foot in my hand an' ag'in I steps fer home.

That night, stranger, I seed another feller from Hazlan, who was a-tellin' how this here preacher had stopped the war over thar, an' had got the Marcums an' Braytons to shakin' hands; an' next day ole Tom Perkins stops in an' says that *wharas* there mought 'a' been preaching somewhar an' sometime, thar nuver had been *preachin'* afore on Kingdom-Come. So I goes over to the meetin' house, an' they was all thar—Daws Dillon an' Mace Day, the leaders in the war, an' Abe Shivers (you've heerd tell o' Abe) who was a-carryin' tales from one side to t'other an' a-stirrin' up hell ginerally, as Abe most al'ays is; an' thar was Daws on one side o' the meetin'-house an' Mace on t'other, an' both jes a-watchin' fer t'other to make a move, an' thar'd 'a' been billy-hell to pay right thar! Stranger, that long preacher talked jes as easy as I'm a-talkin' now, an' hit was p'int-blank as the feller from Hazlan said. You jes ought 'a' heerd him tellin' about the Lawd a-bein' as pore as any feller thar, an' a-makin' barns an' fences an' ox-yokes an' sech like; an' not-a-bein' able to write his own name—havin' to make his mark mebbe—when he started out to save the world. An' how they tuk him an' nailed him onto a cross when he'd come down fer nothin' but to save 'em; an' stuck a spear big as a corn-knife into his side, an' give him vinegar; an' his own mammy a-standin' down thar on the ground a-cryin' an' a-watchin' him; an' he a-fergivin' all of 'em then an' thar!

Thar nuver had been nothin' like that afore on Kingdom-Come, an' all along I heerd fellers a-layin' thar guns down; an' when the preacher called out fer sinners, blame me ef the fust feller that riz wasn't Mace Day. An' Mace says, "Stranger, 'f what you say is true, I reckon the Lawd 'll fergive me too, but I don't believe Daws Dillon ever will," an' Mace stood thar lookin' around fer Daws. An' all of a sudden the preacher got up straight an' called out, "Is thar a human in this house mean an' sorry enough to stand betwixt a man an' his Maker"? An' right thar, stranger, Daws riz. "Naw, by God, thar hain't!" Daws says, an' he walks up to Mace a-holdin' out his hand, an' they all busts out cryin' an' shakin' hands—Days an' Dillons—jes as the preacher had made 'em do over in Hazlan. An' atter the thing was over, I steps up to the preacher an' I says:

"Brother," I says, "*you* spoke a parable, shore."

Annie Fellows Johnston

from *The Little Colonel*

No one who has ever seen Shirley Temple in the 1935 screen version of *The Little Colonel* can forget the famous opening scene in which two members of an estranged family, the little colonel and her grandfather, meet each other; the old colonel is an unreconstructed rebel who has given his son and his right arm to the Southern cause. Annie Fellows Johnston, the author of this most Southern of novels, was born in Evansville, Indiana, in 1863, and moved to Pewee Valley in Oldham County to live with her stepchildren and her aunt after the death of her husband. Immediately popular with children and adults, the novel was so successful that Johnston wrote eleven more volumes in the series.

It was one of the prettiest places in all Kentucky where the Little Colonel stood that morning. She was reaching up on tiptoes, her eager little face pressed close against the iron bars of the great entrance gate that led to a fine old estate known as "Locust."

A ragged little Scotch and Skye terrier stood on its hind feet beside her, thrusting his inquisitive nose between the bars, and wagging his tasselled tail in lively approval of the scene before them.

They were looking down a long avenue that stretched for nearly a quarter of a mile between rows of stately old locust-trees.

At the far end they could see the white pillars of a large stone house gleaming through the Virginia creeper that nearly covered it. But they could not see the old Colonel in his big chair on the porch behind the cool screen of vines.

At that very moment he had caught the rattle of wheels along the road, and had picked up his field-glass to see who was passing. It was only a coloured man jogging along in the heat and dust with a cart full of chicken-coops. The Colonel watched him drive up a lane that led to the back of the new hotel that had just been opened in this quiet country place. Then his glance fell on the two small strangers coming through his gate down the avenue toward him. One was the friskiest dog he had ever seen in his life. The other was a child he judged to be about five years old.

Her shoes were covered with dust, and her white sunbonnet had slipped off and was hanging over her shoulders. A bunch of wild flowers she had gathered on the way hung limp and faded in her little warm hand. Her soft, light hair was cut as short as a boy's.

There was something strangely familiar about the child, especially in the erect, graceful way she walked.

Old Colonel Lloyd was puzzled. He had lived all his life in Lloydsborough, and this was the first time he had ever failed to recognize one of the neighbours' children. He knew every dog and horse, too, by sight if not by name.

Living so far from the public road did not limit his knowledge of what was going on in the world. A powerful field-glass brought every passing object in plain view, while he was saved all annoyance of noise and dust.

"I ought to know that child as well as I know my own name," he said to himself. "But the dog is a stranger in these parts. Liveliest thing I ever set eyes on! They must have come from the hotel. Wonder what they want."

He carefully wiped the lens for a better view. When he looked again he saw that they evidently had not come to visit him.

They had stopped half-way down the avenue, and climbed up on a rustic seat to rest.

The dog sat motionless about two minutes and began to sniff the air, as if some delicious odour had blown across the lawn.

"Fritz," she exclaimed, in delight, "I 'mell 'trawberries!"

The Colonel, who could not hear the remark, wondered at the abrupt pause in the game. He understood it, however, when he saw them wading through the tall grass, straight to his strawberry bed. It was the pride of his heart, and the finest for miles around. The first berries of the season had been picked only the day before. Those that now hung temptingly red on the vines he intended to send to his next neighbour, to prove his boasted claim of always raising the finest and earliest fruit.

He did not propose to have his plans spoiled by these stray guests. Laying the field-glass in its accustomed place on the little table beside his chair, he picked up his hat and strode down the walk.

Colonel Lloyd's friends all said he looked like Napoleon, or rather like Napoleon might have looked had he been born and bred a Kentuckian.

He made an imposing figure in his suit of white duck.

The Colonel always wore white from May till October.

There was a military precision about him, from his erect carriage to the cut of the little white goatee on his determined chin.

No one looking into the firm lines of his resolute face could imagine him ever abandoning a purpose or being turned aside when he once formed an opinion.

Most children were afraid of him. The darkies about the place shook in their shoes when he frowned. They had learned from experience that "ole Marse Lloyd had a tigah of a tempah in him."

As he passed down the walk there were two mute witnesses to his old soldier life. A spur gleamed on his boot heel, for he had just returned from his morning ride, and his right sleeve hung empty.

He had won his title bravely. He had given his only son and his strong right arm to the Southern cause. That had been nearly thirty years ago.

He did not charge down on the enemy with his usual force this time. The little head, gleaming like sunshine in the strawberry patch, reminded him so strongly of a little fellow who used to follow him everywhere,—Tom, the sturdiest, handsomest boy in the county,—Tom, whom he had been so proud of, whom he had so nearly worshipped.

Looking at this fair head bent over the vines, he could almost forget that Tom had ever outgrown his babyhood, that he had shouldered a rifle and followed him to camp, a mere boy, to be shot down by a Yankee bullet in his first battle.

The old Colonel could almost believe he had him back again, and that he stood in the midst of those old days the locusts sometimes whispered about.

He could not hear the happiest of little voices that was just then saying, "Oh, Fritz, isn't you glad we came? An' isn't you glad we've got a gran'fathah with such good 'trawberries?"

It was hard for her to put the *s* before her consonants.

As the Colonel came nearer she tossed another berry into the dog's mouth. A twig snapped, and she raised a startled face toward him.

"Suh?" she said, timidly, for it seemed to her that the stern, piercing eyes had spoken.

"What are you doing here, child?" he asked, in a voice so much kinder than his eyes that she regained her usual self-possession at once.

"Eatin' 'trawberries," she answered, coolly.

"Who are you, anyway?" he exclaimed, much puzzled. As he asked the question his gaze happened to rest on the dog, who was peering at him through the ragged, elfish wisps of hair nearly covering its face, with eyes that were startlingly human.

"'Peak when yo'ah 'poken to, Fritz," she said, severely, at the same time popping another luscious berry into her mouth.

Fritz obediently gave a long yelp. The Colonel smiled grimly.

"What's *your* name?" he asked, this time looking directly at her.

"Mothah calls me her baby," was the soft-spoken reply, "but papa an' Mom Beck they calls me the Little Cun'l."

Alice Hegan Rice

from *Mrs. Wiggs of the Cabbage Patch*

Alice Hegan Rice was born in Shelbyville in 1870, but she spent most of her life in Louisville, where she met and married a popular and good-looking poet, Cale Young Rice, whose own illustrious career was later eclipsed by his wife's. In Louisville she also found the characters and the settings for a number of books, including the one that brought her wealth and fame, *Mrs. Wiggs of the Cabbage Patch* (1901), which became a major motion picture in 1934, starring W. C. Fields, Pauline Lord, and ZaSu Pitts. It had already been filmed twice, in 1914 and 1919, and would be filmed again in 1942. It is the happy mixture of humor and pathos that has made the novel and the movies so popular for so long. In this excerpt it is about 1900 when we visit Mrs. Wiggs in the Cabbage Patch, one of Louisville's poorest neighborhoods. Mrs. Wiggs has just awakened and adjusted her rose-colored glasses, and she now explains her supremely optimistic view of life.

"My, but it's nice an' cold this mornin'! The thermometer's done fell up to zero!"

Mrs. Wiggs made the statement as cheerfully as if her elbows were not sticking out through the boy's coat that she wore, or her teeth chattering in her head like a pair of castanets. But, then, Mrs. Wiggs was a philosopher, and the sum and substance of her philosophy lay in keeping the dust off her rose-colored spectacles. When Mr. Wiggs traveled to eternity by the alcohol route, she buried his faults with him, and for want of better virtues to extol she always laid stress on the fine hand he wrote. It was the same way when their little country home burned and she had to come to the city to seek work; her one comment was: "Thank God, it was the pig instid of the baby that was burned!"

So this bleak morning in December she pinned the bed-clothes around the children and made them sit up close to the stove, while she pasted brown paper over the broken window-pane and made sprightly comments on the change in the weather.

The Wiggses lived in the Cabbage Patch. It was not a real cabbage patch, but a queer neighborhood, where ramshackle cottages played hop-scotch over the railroad tracks. There were no streets, so when a new house was built the owner faced it any way his fancy prompted. Mr. Bagby's grocery, it is true, conformed to convention, and presented a solid front to the railroad track, but Miss Hazy's cottage shied off sidewise into the Wiggses' yard, as if it were afraid of the big freight-trains that went thundering past so many times a day; and Mrs. Schultz's front room looked directly into the Eichorns' kitchen. The latter was not a bad arrangement, however, for Mrs. Schultz had been confined to her bed for ten years, and her sole interest in life consisted in watching what took place in her neighbor's family.

The Wiggses' house was the most imposing in the neighborhood. This was probably due to the fact that it had two front doors and a tin roof. One door was nailed up, and the other opened outdoors, but you would never guess it from the street. When the country house burned, one door had been saved. So Mrs. Wiggs and the boys brought it to the new home and skilfully placed it at the front end of the side porch. But the roof gave the house its chief distinction; it was the only tin roof in the Cabbage Patch. Jim and Billy had made it of old cans which they picked up on the commons.

Jim was fifteen and head of the family; his shoulders were those of a man, and were bent with work, but his body dwindled away to a pair of thin legs that seemed incapable of supporting the burden imposed upon them. In his anxious eyes was the look of a bread-winner who had begun the struggle too soon. Life had been a tragedy to Jim: the tragedy that comes when a child's sensitive soul is forced to meet the responsibilities of manhood, yet lacks the wisdom that only experience can bring.

Billy Wiggs was differently constituted; responsibilities rested upon him as lightly as the freckles on his nose. When occasion or his mother demanded he worked to good purpose, with a tenacity that argued well for his future success, but for the most part he played and fought and got into trouble with the aptitude characteristic of the average small boy.

It was Mrs. Wiggs's boast that her three little girls had geography names; first came Asia, then Australia. When the last baby arrived, Billy had stood looking down at the small bundle and asked anxiously: "Are you goin' to have it fer a boy or a girl, ma?" Mrs. Wiggs had answered: "A girl, Billy, an' her name's Europena!"

Virginia Cary Hudson

from *O Ye Jigs and Juleps!*

A short drive from Louisville to Versailles will take you to a fine neighborhood, the home of a ten-year-old girl named Virginia. She is a delightful girl who goes to the best church in town and is somewhat of a snob, but you will like her anyway. Virginia's clever little essays about life among the gentry were written about 1904, but it was not until 1962 that her family published them under the title *O Ye Jigs and Juleps!*

⋘∞⋙

Before I go into the house of the Lord with praise and thanksgiving, I lift up mine eyes unto the town clock from whence cometh the time to see if I am late. It is not etiquette to be late.

Do not hop, skip, jump or slide in the church vestibule. Tip. Tip all the way to your seat. Be sure and do not sit in other people's pews. Jesus wouldn't care, but other people would. Paying money makes it yours to sit in. The first thing you do is kneel down and thank the Lord for your mother and your father and your breakfast and your lunch and your dinner and your lovely wallpaper and your new pink garter belt. Then you can sit and look around just a little bit. Don't turn around and look. That is not etiquette.

Kneel when you pray, stand when you sing, and sit when you listen. On communion Sunday take off your right glove and leave it in your pew. Don't wait until you get to the rail and the Body and the Blood comes around. Don't try to drink up all of the wine. That is not etiquette. Leave some for other people.

Never punch people in church, or giggle or cross your legs. Crossing your legs is as bad as scratching or walking in front of people or chewing gum or saying damn. Don't lose your place in the prayer book. Bow for the cross and for the Father, Son and Holy Ghost. When the choir marches back to the Vestry room and the minister calls out goodbye to the Lord until next Sunday, then you can speak to people.

The Baptist church is next door to our church. They sing as loud as they can all the time we are trying to pray. I bet the Lord can't hear one word we say. The Baptists sing about plunging sinners in a bloody fountain drawn from Emmanuel's veins. We sing about Crown Him Lord of All. I think it is much more ladylike to crown the King than to be plunging around in a bloody fountain. I took the cotton off my sore finger once and stuffed it in my ear on the Baptist side. But just once. My mother attended to that.

Of all people who come to church I love Mrs. Harris best. Mrs. Harris is Mrs. Porter's auntie and that makes her important, but Mrs. Harris doesn't care. She just goes on picking beans. She taught me to tell the young ones from the old ones, just like people. She says I am a good picker. When I ride my pony out to Mrs. Harris, she plays for me. She plays See the train go round the bend, goodbye my lover goodbye. I bet she plays that because she knows I am with the railroad. Mrs. Harris is cute and when she dies I am going to cry and cry.

Mrs. Harris takes me fishing and I carry the worms and the lunch. But not in the same box. The worms are in a can. She stops the buckboard in front of my house and hollers Yoohoo. That's for me. Mrs. Harris is crippled and it is hard for her to get out. When I am with her I boost her. She says I am the best booster in town. When we get to the Meadows Creek where we fish I climb out over the shafts and let down the horse's check rein. Mrs. Harris says letting down the check rein is just like getting home and taking off your Sunday corset. But I am not a horse and I don't have a corset so I wouldn't know. When I had the measles Mrs. Harris brought me the most darling June bug with a red thread on his leg and tied him to my bed post.

Mrs. Harris lets me churn. She has a lot of cows that give milk and one that doesn't and is mean. I asked her why she kept that one and she said, "He is a necessity." All the other cows have names but that one and everything should have a name, so I got me a shingle and painted Mr. Necessity on it and nailed it on the gate where the gentleman cow stays and Mrs. Harris said she just didn't understand why she didn't think of that herself.

Etiquette is what you are doing and saying when people are looking and listening. What you are thinking is your business. Thinking is not etiquette. Hallelujah, thine the glory. Revive us again.

P.S. If you want to stay awake in church, go to bed early Saturday night. You can't go to the Altar rail until you are 12. That is God's etiquette. You can't put on perfume until you are 16. That is Leesville etiquette. After you are confirmed your sponsors in Baptism can't be blamed for what you do. You are on your own then and if the devil gets you, it is your own fault and serves you just right.

Amen and the Lord have mercy.

John Uri Lloyd

from *Stringtown on the Pike*

John Uri Lloyd (1849–1936), a local-colorist of note, took as his literary domain his home turf of Boone and the surrounding counties of northern Kentucky; he was by profession a pharmaceutical chemist. Indeed, he was a prolific writer of scientific books and papers, but it was his Stringtown cycle of books, which chronicles the folklore and history of Florence and Boone County, that merits him a spot in this anthology. The following excerpt from *Stringtown on the Pike* (1900) sets the stage for the love stories and Civil War tales he told.

Stringtown is situated eight miles from the "county seat" of Stringtown County, where stood the county jail. In order to reach this important spot, the traveller from Stringtown follows the Mt. Carmel pike to Mt. Carmel Church, and then branches to the Turkey Foot road, which follows a creek bed four miles to its source. On the summit of this rise stands the village honoured by holding the court-house of Stringtown County.

Like other county seats in Kentucky, at the time under consideration this was subject several times a year to the flow and ebb of a human tide. The tide was high in Court week, but during the intermediate periods stagnation prevailed.

At the time of Quarterly Court, in June, from every section of the county, on the first day of Court week, men on horseback could be seen "going to Court." These as a rule started in pairs, or parties of three or four; but as they journeyed onward the byways merged into main roads and the isolated groups upon them coalesced until, when the village was reached, a steady stream of horsemen came pouring into its main avenue.

In this county seat, even to the very day before Court convened, stagnation ruled supreme. The two grocery stores were open for traffic between Court periods, but attracted none but home patrons; the two taverns were ready for business, but even their bar-rooms were quiet and the long rows of shed stalls adjacent to each tavern were empty, and the horse racks in front of the groceries and the taverns were vacant. The court-house, built like a church, excepting that it was the proud possessor of a second story and four white-washed round brick pillars in front, stood, the day before Court, with closed eyes; the iron gate was locked, the pepper-grass and shepherd's-purse grew high and luxuriant between the flat-rock paving stones, and the dog-fennel covered the edges and far into the street unmolested even about the long rows of horse racks that bounded "Court-House Square."

In the early morning, each hot summer day, a little business was done in each store; the barkeepers found occasion to wash a few glasses and bruise a little mint; the barefooted boy drove his cow to and from the pasture, and a smell of frying ham or bacon and browning corn-bread or biscuit hung at breakfast time about each residence. But as the sun mounted into the sky a universal lethargy settled over the scorching village, and not until the slanting shadows of evening fell did life reappear.

The idle sojourner might spend his time in this lazy village, and between Court periods, even to the day before Court, find nothing more exciting than an occasional dog fight, unless, perchance, it were a quarrel between the owners of the dogs.

Lazily the sun came up the day before Court; lazily the inhabitants of this sluggish village moved, when they did move; lazily the stray pig meandered along the side of the unpaved streets, picking up an occasional morsel; lazily a flock of gabbling geese waddled through the dusty road seeking the nearly dried creek bed adjacent to the village; lazily the unshaven barkeeper, with closed eyes, sat before the inn on the flat stone pavement in his tipped-back chair. One could not easily have found a creature in this village that was not infected by the lazy sun, which, day after day, crept through the sky and leisurely sank toward the earth into the tree tops, glowing a second through the branches, seemingly undetermined whether it were not best to pause awhile upon earth's edge before dropping over and rolling out of sight.

Opening of Court day brought a change. Bustle in and confusion about the tavern. The long dining-room tables were "set" by break of day; the kitchen stove was red and furious, the negro servants moved as if they actually enjoyed motion; piles of vegetables, a quarter of beef and several boiled hams spoke of the coming feast. The freshly shaven barkeeper, with freshly filled bottles and a pile of freshly cleaned glasses, no longer sat beside the door in the tipped-back chair; he too was ready for action. The iron gates that barred the main entrance of the court-house yard were open and the windows to that "Hall of Justice" were unshuttered. Even the stray geese had moved to other scenes, the wandering pig had not been loosed that morning, and the boy had come and gone with his cow before the sun had risen. The village was awake and the very buildings themselves took on a different air—the residents were in touch with life again and eager for the coming fray. The word fray is not inappropriate, for many were the men who had ridden to this court-house on horseback and returned home in an improvised spring wagon hearse; many have been the feuds that, argued in the Court of Stringtown County's capital by the mouths of the lawyers, have been settled, immediately after the Court adjourned, in the street by the mouths of pistols.

Men came to Court, antagonists led to enmity by some trifling incident, and grouped themselves into clusters; one clan went to Jim White's tavern, the other went to Jo Sweet's. They stood in separate groups about the streets, and scowled, but did not speak when first they chanced to meet; they visited their respective barrooms again, and grew surlier and thought meaner things with each uplifted glass; now they growled when group met group and looked defiantly at each other; another visit to the tavern, and when the antagonistic groups next came together their tongues were loosened, pistols flashed in the sunlight, and another "case" was made for the opposing lawyers to beat the air over at the next term of Court.

Eliza Calvert Hall

from *Aunt Jane of Kentucky*

A character who became a Kentucky icon in the early twentieth century, along with Mrs. Wiggs and the Little Colonel, was Aunt Jane, the garrulous old woman who tells stories of olden times in the Pennyrile area of western Kentucky. Writing under her maiden name, Eliza Calvert Hall (she married a Mr. Obenchain) lived all her life in the country she wrote about. She was also an advocate of women's rights, including the right to vote, and, for her time and place, held views that were at least liberal if not radical. In her fiction, however, she was traditional, sentimental, and very religious, as shown in this selection in which Aunt Jane explains her flower garden to a young visitor in words that personify the flowers as if they had human feelings.

⧉

"Do you see that row o' daffydils over yonder by the front fence, child—all leaves and no blossoms?"

I looked in the direction of her pointing finger and saw a long line of flowerless plants, standing like sad and silent guests at the festival of spring.

"It's been six years since I set 'em out there," said Aunt Jane impressively, "and not a flower have they had in all that time. Some folks say it's because I moved 'em at the wrong time o' the year. But the same week I moved these I moved some from my yard to Elizabeth Crawford's, and Elizabeth's bloom every year, so it can't be that. Some folks said the place I had 'em in was too shady, and I put 'em right out there where the sun strikes on 'em till it sets, and still they won't bloom. It's my opinion, honey, that they're jest homesick. I believe if I was to take them daffydils back to Aunt Matilda's and plant 'em in the border where they used to grow, alongside o' the sage and lavender and thyme, that they'd go to bloomin' again jest like they used to. You know how the children of Israel pined and mourned when they was carried into captivity. Well, every time I look at my daffydils I think o' them homesick Israelites askin', 'How can we sing the songs o' Zion in a strange land?'

"You needn't laugh, child. A flower is jest as human as you and me. Look at that vine yonder, takin' hold of everything that comes in its way like a little child learnin' to walk. And calycanthus buds, see how you've got to hold 'em in your hands and warm 'em before they'll give out their sweetness, jest like children that you've got to love and pet, before they'll let you git acquainted with 'em. You see that pink rose over by the fence?" pointing to a La France heavy with blossoms. "Well, that rose didn't do anything but put out leaves the first two years I had it. A bud might come once in a while, but it would blast before it was half open. And at last I says to it, says I, 'What is it you want, honey? There's somethin' that don't please you, I know. Don't you like the place you're planted in, and the hollyhocks and lilies for neighbors?' And one day I took it up and set it between that white tea and another La France, and it went to bloomin' right away. It didn't like the neighborhood it was in, you see. And did you ever hear o' people disappearin' from their homes and never bein' found any more? Well, flowers can disappear the same way. The year before I was married there was a big bed o' pink chrysanthemums growin' under the dinin'-room windows at old Dr. Pendleton's. It wasn't a common magenta pink, it was as clear, pretty a pink as that La France rose. Well, I saw 'em that fall for the first time and the last. The next year there wasn't any, and when I asked where they'd gone to, nobody could tell anything about 'em. And ever since then I've been searchin' in every old gyarden in the county, but I've never found 'em, and I don't reckon I ever will.

"And there's my roses! Just look at 'em! Every color a rose could be, and pretty near every kind there is. Wouldn't you think I'd be satisfied? But there's a rose I lost sixty years ago, and the ricollection o' that rose keeps me from bein' satisfied with all I've got. It grew in Old Lady Elrod's gyarden and nowhere else, and there ain't a rose here except grandmother's that I wouldn't give up forever if I could jest find that rose again.

"I've tried many a time to tell folks about that rose, but I can't somehow get hold of the words. I reckon an old woman like me, with little or no learnin', couldn't be expected to tell how that rose looked, any more'n she could be expected to draw it and paint it. I can say it was yeller, but that word 'yeller' don't tell the color the rose was. I've got all the shades of yeller in my garden, but nothin' like the color o' that rose. It got deeper and deeper towards the middle, and lookin' at one of them roses half-opened was like lookin' down into a gold mine. The leaves crinkled and curled back towards the stem as fast as it opened, and the more it opened the prettier it was, like some women that grow better lookin' the older they grow,—Mary Andrews was one o' that kind,—and when it comes to tellin' you how it smelt, I'll jest have to stop. There never was anything like it for sweetness, and it was a different sweetness from any other rose God ever made.

"I ricollect seein' Miss Penelope come in church one Sunday, dressed in white, with a black velvet gyirdle 'round her waist, and a bunch o' these roses, buds and half-blown ones, and full-blown ones, fastened in the gyirdle, and that bunch o' yeller roses was song and sermon and prayer to me that day. I couldn't take my eyes off 'em; and I thought that if Christ had seen that rose growin' in the fields around Palestine, he wouldn't 'a' mentioned lilies when he said Solomon in all his glory was not arrayed like one of these.

"I always intended to ask for a slip of it, but I waited too long. It got lost one winter, and when I asked Old Lady Elrod about it she said, 'Mistress Parrish, I cannot tell you whence it came nor whither it went.' The old lady always used mighty pretty language.

"Well, honey, them two lost flowers jest haunt me. They're like dead children. You know a house may be full o' livin' children, but if there's one dead, a mother'll see its face and hear its voice above all the others, and that's the way with my lost flowers. No matter how many roses and chrysanthemums I have, I keep seein' Old Lady Elrod's yeller roses danglin' from Miss Penelope's gyirdle, and that bed o' pink chrysanthemums under Dr. Pendleton's dinin'-room windows."

"Each mortal has his Carcassonne!" Here was Aunt Jane's, but it was no matter for a tear or even a sigh. And I thought how the sting of life would lose its venom, if for every soul the unattainable were embodied in nothing more embittering than two exquisite lost flowers.

One afternoon in early June I stood with Aunt Jane in her garden. It was the time of roses; and in the midst of their opulent bloom stood the tall white lilies, handmaidens to the queen. Here and there over the warm earth old-fashioned pinks spread their prayer-rugs, on which a worshiper might kneel and offer thanks for life and spring; and towering over all, rows of many-colored hollyhocks flamed and glowed in the light of the setting sun like the stained glass windows of some old cathedral.

Across the flowery expanse Aunt Jane looked wistfully toward the evening skies, beyond whose stars and clouds we place that other world called heaven.

"I'm like my grandmother, child," she said presently. "I know I've got to leave this country some day soon, and journey to another one, and the only thing I mind about it is givin' up my gyarden. When John looked into heaven he saw gold streets and gates of pearl, but he don't say anything about gyardens. I like what he says about no sorrer, nor cryin', nor pain, and God wipin' away all tears from their eyes. That's pure comfort. But if I could jest have Abram and the children again, and my old home and my old gyarden, I'd be willin' to give up the gold streets and glass sea and pearl gates."

The loves of earth and the homes of earth! No apocalyptic vision can come between these and the earth-born human heart.

Life is said to have begun in a garden; and if here was our lost paradise, may not the paradise we hope to gain through death be, to the lover of nature, another garden in a new earth, girdled by four soft-flowing rivers, and watered by mists that arise in the night to fall on the face of the sleeping world, where all we plant shall grow unblighted through winterless years, and they who inherit it go with white garments and shining faces, and say at morn and noon and eve: *My soul is like a watered garden?*

Irvin S. Cobb

from *Old Judge Priest*

West of Louisville, on the lower Ohio River, lived one of Kentucky's best-known writers, Irvin S. Cobb. Born in 1876 in Paducah, in western Kentucky, Cobb wrote about his hometown with a deep, almost filial affection. There we find a typical Kentucky character from the early years of the twentieth century, the backward-looking (he's a Confederate veteran) but noble and gracious country judge who will go against the local grain if a woman (who is not even a lady) is in distress. In this case, she is dead and greatly in need of a decent Christian funeral. Unfortunately, none of the decent Christian churches in town will open their doors for her funeral—so says the madam for whom she has worked. Enter Irvin S. Cobb's Judge Priest to the rescue.

Following his initial introduction to American readers in such popular magazines as the *Saturday Evening Post,* then in book form in *Back Home* in 1912, the Judge became almost a folk hero and was featured in many new adventures—all set in Cobb's beloved Paducah and the Jackson Purchase area; there was even a 1934 film starring Will Rogers. Cobb's careers as a journalist, humorist, scriptwriter, and actor took him to Louisville, to New York, and finally to Hollywood, but he never really left home. He once said that he'd rather be an orphan in Kentucky than a twin anywhere else. In fact, he requested that his grave be marked with a simple stone and a plate with his name and dates and the line "I Have Come Back Home."

This story begins with Judge Priest sitting at his desk at his chambers at the old courthouse. He strains to reach an especially itchy spot between his shoulder blades and addresses words to Jeff Poindexter, coloured, his body servant and house boy.

"They ain't so very purty to look at—red flannels ain't," said the judge. "But, Jeff, I've noticed this—they certainly are mighty lively company till you git used to 'em. I never am the least bit lonely fur the first few days after I put on my heavy underwear."

There was no answer from Jeff except a deep, soft breath. He slept. At a customary hour he had come with Mittie May, the white mare, and the buggy to take Judge Priest home to supper, and had found the judge engaged beyond his normal quitting time.

That, however, had not discommoded Jeff. Jeff always knew what to do with his spare moments. Jeff always had a way of spending the long winter evenings. He leaned now against a book-rack, with his elbow on the top shelf, napping lightly. Jeff preferred to sleep lying down or sitting down, but he could sleep upon his feet too—and frequently did.

Having, by brisk scratching movements, assuaged the irritation between his shoulder blades, the judge picked up his pen and shoved it across a sheet of legal cap that already was half covered with his fine, close writing. He never dictated his decisions, but always wrote them out by hand. The pen nib travelled along steadily for awhile. Eventually words in a typewritten petition that rested on the desk at his left caught the judge's eye.

"Huh!" he grunted, and read the quoted phrase, "'True Believers' Afro-American Church of Zion, sometimes called—" Without turning his head he again hailed his slumbering servitor: "Jeff, why do you-all call that there little church-house down by the river Possum Trot?"

Mightily well Jeff understood the how and the why and the wherefore of the True Believers. He could have traced out step by step, with circumstantial detail, the progress of the internal feud within the despised congregation that led to the upspringing of rival sets of claimants to the church property, and to the litigation that had thrown the whole tangled business into the courts for final adjudication. But except in company of his own choosing and his own colour, wild horses could not have drawn that knowledge from Jeff, although it would have pained him to think any white person who had a claim upon his friendship suspected him of concealment of any detail whatsoever. . . .

Further discussion of the affairs of the strange faith that was divided against itself might have ensued but that an interruption came.

Judge Priest swung about to find a woman in his doorway. She was a big, upstanding woman, overfleshed and overdressed, and upon her face she bore the sign of her profession as plainly and indubitably as though it had been branded there in scarlet letters.

The old man's eyes narrowed as he recognised her. But up he got on the instant and bowed before her. No being created in the image of a woman ever had reason to complain that in her presence Judge Priest forgot his manners.

"Howdy do, ma'am," he said ceremoniously. "Will you walk in? And mout I enquire the purpose of this here call?"

"Yes, sir, I'm a-goin' to tell you what brought me here without wastin' any more words than I can help," said the woman. "No, thank you, Judge," she went on as he motioned her toward a seat; "I guess I can say what I've got to say, standing up."

Her voice was coarsened and flat; it was more like a man's voice than a woman's, and she spoke with a masculine directness.

"There was a girl died at my house early this mornin'," she told him. "Viola St. Claire was the name she went by here. I don't know what her real name was—she never told anybody what it was. She wasn't much of a hand to talk about herself. She must have been nice people though, because she was always nice and ladylike, no matter what happened. From what I gathered off and on, she came here from some little town down near Memphis. I certainly liked that girl. She'd been with me nearly ten months. She wasn't more than nineteen years old.

"Well, all day yestiddy she was out of her head with a high fever. But just before she died she come to and her mind cleared up.

"She called me, and I leaned over her and asked her what it was she wanted, and she told me. She knew she was dyin'. She told me she'd been raised right, which I knew already without her tellin' me, and she said she'd been a Christian girl before she made her big mistake. And she told me she wanted to be buried like a Christian, from a regular church, with a sermon and flowers and music and all that.

⟋⟍⟋ ⟋⟍⟋ ⟋⟍⟋

"She made me promise that I'd see it was done just that way. She made me put my hand in her hand and promise her. She shut her eyes then, like she was satisfied, and in a minute or two after that she died, still holdin' on tight to my hand."

"Well, ma'am, I'm very sorry for that poor child. I am so," said Judge Priest, and his tone showed he meant it; "yit still I don't understand your purpose in comin' to me, without you need money to bury her."

"It's something else I wanted to speak with you about. I've rid miles on the street cars, and I've walked afoot until the bottoms of my feet both feel like boils right this minute, tryin' to find somebody that was fitten to preach a sermon over that dead girl. But every last one of them preachers said no."

"Do you mean to tell me that not a single minister in this whole city is willin' to hold a service over that dead girl?" Judge Priest shrilled at her with vehement astonishment—and something else—in his voice.

"No, no, not that," the woman made haste to explain. "There wasn't a single one of 'em but said he'd come to my house and conduct the exercises. They was all willin' enough to go to the grave too. But you see that wouldn't do. I explained to 'em, until I almost lost my voice, that it had to be a funeral in a regular church, with flowers and music and all. That poor girl got it into her mind somehow, I think, that she'd have a better chance in the next world if she went out of this one like a Christian should ought to go. I explained all that to 'em, and from explainin' I took to arguin' with 'em, and then to pleadin' and beggin'. I bemeaned myself before them preachers. I was actually ready to go down on my knees before 'em.

"So finally, when I was about to give up, I thought about you and I come here as straight as I could walk."

"But, ma'am," he said, "I'm not a regular church member myself. I reckin I oughter be, but I ain't. And I still fail to understand why you should think I could serve you, though I don't mind tellin' you I'd be mighty glad to ef I could."

"Maybe you don't remember it, Judge, but two years ago this comin' December that there Law and Order League fixed up to run me out of this town. They didn't succeed, but they did have me indicted by the Grand Jury, and I come up before you and pleaded guilty—they had the evidence on me all right. You fined me, you fined me the limit, and I guess if I hadn't 'a' had the money to pay the fine I'd 'a' gone to jail. But the main point with me was that you treated me like a lady.

"I ain't forgot that. I ain't ever goin' to forget it. And awhile ago, when I was all beat out and discouraged, I said to myself that if there was one man left in this town who could maybe help me to keep my promise to that dead girl, Judge William Priest was that man."

"Was it stated—was it specified that a preacher must hold the funeral service over that dead girl?" he inquired.

Ꙭ Ꙭ Ꙭ

The woman caught eagerly at the inflection that had come into his voice.

"No, sir," she answered; "all she said was that it must be in a church and with some flowers and some music. But I never heard of anybody preachin' a regular sermon without it was a regular preacher. Did you ever, Judge?" Doubt and renewed disappointment battered at her just-born hopes.

"I reckin mebbe there have been extryordinary occasions where an amateur stepped in and done the best he could," said the judge. "Mebbe some folks here on earth couldn't excuse sech presumption as that, but I reckin they'd understand how it was up yonder."

He stood up, facing her, and spoke as one making a solemn promise:

"Ma'am, you needn't worry yourself any longer. You kin go on back to your home. That dead child is goin' to have whut she asked for. I give you my word on it."

She strove to put a question, but he kept on:

"I ain't prepared to give you the full details yit. You see I don't know myself jest exactly whut they'll be. But inside of an hour from now I'll be seein' the undertaker and he'll notify you in regards to the hour and the place and the rest of it. Kin you rest satisfied with that?"

She nodded, trying to utter words and not succeeding. Emotion shook her gross shape until the big gold bands on her arms jangled together.

"So, ef you'll kindly excuse me, I've got quite a number of things to do betwixt now and suppertime. I kind of figger I'm goin' to be right busy."

For a fact the judge was a busy man during the hour which followed upon all this, the hour between twilight and night. Over the telephone he first called up M. Jansen, our leading undertaker; indeed at that time our only one, excusing the coloured undertaker on Locust Street. He had converse at length with M. Jansen. Then he called up Doctor Lake, a most dependable person in sickness, and when you were in good health too. Then last of all he called up a certain widow who lived in those days, Mrs. Matilda Weeks by name; and this lady was what is commmonly called a character. Mrs. Weeks was daily guilty of acts that scandalised all proper people. But the improper ones worshipped the ground her feet touched as she walked. She was much like that disciple of Joppa named Tabitha, which by interpretation is called Dorcas, of whom it is written that she was full of good works and almsdeeds which she did. Yes, you might safely call Mrs. Weeks a character.

With her, back and forth across the telephone wire, Judge Priest had extended speech. Then he hung up the receiver and went home alone to a late and badly burnt supper.

⁓ ⁓ ⁓

Oh, we've had funerals and funerals down our way. But the funeral that took place on an October day that I have in mind will long be talked about.

It came as a surprise to most people, for in the daily papers of that morning no customary black-bordered announcement had appeared. Others had heard of it by word of mouth. In dubious quarters, and in some quarters not quite so dubious, the news had travelled, although details in advance of the event were only to be guessed at.

Anyhow, the reading and talking public knew this much: That a girl, calling herself Viola St. Claire and aged nineteen, had died. It was an accepted fact, naturally, that even the likes of her must be laid away after some fashion or other. If she were put under ground by stealth, clandestinely as it were, so much the better for the atmosphere of civic morality. That I am sure would have been disclosed as the opinion of a majority, had there been inquiry among those who were presumed to have and who admitted they had the best interests of the community at heart.

So you see a great many people were entirely unprepared against the coming of the pitiably short procession that at eleven o'clock, or thereabout, turned out of the little street running down back of the freight depot into Franklin Street, which was one of our main thoroughfares. First came the hearse, drawn by M. Jansen's pair of dappled white horses and driven by M. Jansen himself, he wearing his official high hat and the span having black plumes in their head stalls, thus betokening a burial ceremony of the top cost. Likewise the hearse was M. Jansen's best hearse—not his third best, nor yet his second best.

The coffin, showing through the glass sides, was of white cloth and it looked very small, almost like a coffin for a child. However, it may have looked so because there was little of its shape to be seen. It was covered and piled and banked up with flowers. These were such flowers as, in our kindly climate, grew out of doors until well on into November: late roses and early chrysanthemums, marigolds and gladioluses, and such. They lay there loosely, with their stems upon them, just as Mrs. Weeks had sheared them, denuding every plant and shrub and bush that grew in her garden, so a girl whom Mrs. Weeks had never seen might go to her grave with an abundance of the blossoms she had coveted about her.

Behind the hearse came a closed coach. We used to call them coaches when they figured in funerals, carriages when used for lodge turnouts, and plain hacks when they met the trains and boats. In the coach rode four women. The world at large had a way of calling them painted women; but this day their faces were not painted nor were they garishly clad. For the time they were merely women—neither painted women nor fallen women—but just women.

ড়ঢ়ড়

And that was nearly all, but not quite.

At one side of the hearse, opposite the slowly turning front wheels, trudged Judge Priest, carrying in the crook of one bent arm a book. It wouldn't be a law book, for they commonly are large books, bound in buff leather, and this book was small and flat and black in colour. On the other side of the hearse, with head very erect and eyes fixed straight ahead and Sunday's best coat buttoned tightly about his sparse frame, walked another old man, Doctor Lake.

And that was all. At least that was all at first. But as the procession—if you could call it that—swung into Franklin Street I know that some men stood along the curbstones and stared and that other men, having first bared their heads, broke away to tail in at the end of the marching figures. And I know that of those who did this there were more than of those who merely stood and stared. The padding of shoe soles upon the gravel of the street became a steadily increasing, steadily rising thump-thump-thump; the rhythm of it rose above the creak and the clatter of the hearse wheels and the hoofs of the horses.

Heralded by the sound of its own thumping tread and leaving in its wake a stupefaction of astonishment, the procession kept straight on down Franklin Street, until it reached the very foot of the street. There it swung off at right angles into a dingy, ill-kempt little street that coursed crookedly along the water front, with poor houses rising upon one side and the raw mud banks of the river falling steeply away upon the other.

It followed this street until the head of it came opposite a little squat box-and-barn of a structure, built out of up-and-down planking; unpainted, too, with a slatted belfry, like an overgrown chicken coop, perched midway of the peak of its steeply pitched tin roof.

Now this structure, as all knew who remembered the history of contemporary litigation as recorded in the local prints, was the True Believers' Afro-American Church of Zion, sometimes termed in derision Possum Trot, being until recently the place of worship of that newest and most turbulent of local negro sects, but now closed on an injunction secured by one of the warring factions within its membership.

Technically it was still closed. Actually and physically it was at this moment open—wide open. The double doors were drawn back, the windows shone clean, and at the threshold of the swept and garnished interior stood Judge Priest's Jeff, with his broom in his hand and his mop and bucket at his side. Jeff had concluded his share of the labors barely in time.

As M. Jansen steered his dappled span close up alongside the pavement and brought them to a standstill, Judge Priest looked back and with what he saw was well content. He knew that morbid curiosity might account for the presence of some among this multitude who had come following after him, but not for all, and perhaps not for very many. He nodded to himself with the air of one who is amply satisfied by the results of an accomplished experiment.

∽ ∽ ∽

When the crowd was in and seated—all of it that could get in and get seated—a tall, white-haired woman in a plain black frock came silently and swiftly through a door at the back and sat herself down upon a red plush stool before a golden-oak melodeon. But Mrs. Matilda Weeks' finger ends fell with such sanctifying gentleness upon the warped keys, and as she sang her sweet soprano rose so clearly and yet so softly, filling this place whose walls so often had resounded to the lusty hallelujahs of shouting black converts, that to those who listened now it seemed almost as though a Saint Cecilia had descended from on high to make this music.

When she finished singing, Judge Priest got up from a front pew where he had been sitting and went and stood alongside the flower-piled coffin, with his back to the little yellow-pine pulpit and his prayer book in his hands, a homely, ungraceful figure, facing an assemblage that packed the darky meeting house until it could hold no more.

I deem it to have been characteristic of the old judge that he made no explanation for his presence before them and no apology for his assumption of a role so unusual. He opened his blackbound volume at a place where his plump forefinger had been thrust between the leaves to mark the place for him, and in his high, thin voice he read through the service for the dead, with its promise of the divine forgiveness. When he had reached the end of it he put the book aside, and spoke to them in the fair and grammatical English that usually he reserved for his utterances from the bench in open court:

"Our sister who lies here asked with almost her last conscious breath that at her funeral a sermon should be preached. Upon me, who never before attempted such an undertaking, devolves the privilege of speaking a few words above her. I had thought to take for my text the words: 'He that is without sin among you, let him first cast a stone at her.'

"But I have changed my mind. I changed it only a little while ago. For I recalled that once on a time the Master said: 'Suffer little children to come unto Me, and forbid them not: for of such is the kingdom of Heaven.' And I believe, in the scheme of everlasting mercy and everlasting pity, that before the eyes of our common Creator we are all of us as little children whose feet stumble in the dark. So I shall take that saying of the Saviour for my text."

Perhaps it would be unjust to those whose business is the preaching of sermons to call this a sermon. I, for one, never heard any other sermon in any other church that did not last longer than five minutes. And certainly Judge Priest, having made his beginning, did not speak for more than five minutes; the caressing fingers of the sunlight had not perceptibly shifted upon the flower-strewn coffin top when he finished what he had to say and stood with his head bowed. After that, except for a rustle of close-packed body and a clearing of men's huskened throats, there was silence for a little time.

෴ ෴ ෴

Then Judge Priest's eyes looked about him and three pews away he saw Ashby Corwin. It may have been he remembered that as a young man Ashby Corwin had been destined for holy orders until another thing—some said it was a woman and some said it was whisky, and some said it was first the woman and then the whisky—came into his life and wrecked it so that until the end of his days Ashby Corwin trod the rocky downhill road of the profligate and the waster. Or it may have been the look he read upon the face of the other that moved Judge Priest to say:

"I will ask Mr. Corwin to pray."

At that Ashby Corwin stood up in his place and threw back his prematurely whitened head, and he lifted his face that was all scarified with the blighting flames of dissipation, and he shut his eyes that long since had wearied of looking upon a trivial world, and Ashby Corwin prayed.

There are prayers that seem to circle round and round in futile rings, going nowhere; and then again there are prayers that are like sparks struck off from the wheels of the prophet's chariot of fire, coursing their way upward in spiritual splendour to blaze on the sills of the Judgment Seat. This prayer was one of those prayers.

After that Judge Priest bowed his head again and spoke the benediction.

⸎⸎ ⸎⸎ ⸎⸎

On the morning of the day following the day of this funeral Judge Priest sat putting the last words to his decision touching upon the merits of the existing controversy in the congregation of the True Believers' Afro-American Church of Zion. The door opened and in walked Beck Giltner, saloon keeper, sure-thing gambler, handy-man-with-a-gun, and, according to the language of a resolution unanimously adopted at a mass meeting of the Law and Order League, force-for-evil.

"Good mornin', Beck," said the judge. "Well?"

"Judge Priest," said Giltner, "as a rule I don't come to this courthouse except when I have to come. But to-day I've come to tell you something. You made a mistake yesterday!"

"A mistake, suh?" The judge's tone was sharp and quick.

"Yes, suh, that's what you did," returned the tall gambler. "I don't mean in regards to that funeral you held for that dead girl. You probably don't care what I think one way or the other, but I want to tell you I was strong for that, all the way through. But you made a mistake just the same, Judge; you didn't take up a collection.

"So last night I took it on myself to get up a collection for you. I started it with a bill or so off my own roll. Then I passed the hat round at several places where you wouldn't scarcely care to go yourself. And I didn't run across a single fellow that failed to contribute. Some of 'em don't move in the best society, and there's some more of 'em that you'd only know of by reputation. But every last one of 'em put in something. There was one man that didn't have only seven cents to his name—he put that in. So here it is—four hundred and seventy-five dollars and forty-two cents, accordin' to my count."

From one pocket he fetched forth a rumpled packet of paper money and from the other a small cloth sack, which gave off metallic clinking sounds. He put them down together on the desk in front of Judge Priest.

"I appreciate this, ef I am right in my assumption of the motives which

196   *The Kentucky Anthology*

actuated you and the purposes to which you natchally assumed this here money would be applied," said Judge Priest as the other man waited for his response. "But, son, I can't take your money. It ain't needed. Why, I wouldn't know whut to do with it. There ain't no outstandin' bills connected with that there funeral. All the expense entailed was met—privately. So you see—"

"Wait just a minute before you say no!" interrupted Giltner. "Here's my idea and it's the idea of all the others that contributed: We-all want you to take this money and keep it—keep it in a safe, or in your pocket, or in the bank to your credit, or anywheres you please, but just keep it. And if any girl that's gone wrong should die and not have any friends to help bury her, they can come to you and get the cash out of this fund to pay for puttin' her away. And if any other girl should want to go back to her people and start in all over again and try to lead a better life, why you can advance her the railroad fare out of that money too.

"You see, Judge, we are aimin' to make a kind of a trust fund out of it, with you as the trustee. And when the four seventy-five forty-two is all used up, if you'll just let me know I'll guarantee to rustle up a fresh bankroll so you'll always have enough on hand to meet the demands. Now then, Judge, will you take it?"

Judge Priest took it. He stretched out and scooped in currency and coin sack, using therefor his left hand only. The right was engaged in reaching for Beck Giltner's right hand, the purpose being to shake it.

Lucy Furman

from *Mothering on Perilous*

Not far from Paducah, in Henderson, lived Lucy Furman. Except for the last five years, she lived her entire life in Kentucky. Born in Henderson in 1870, she lost both parents when she was very young and was reared by an aunt. Early in her twenties she began publishing stories in *Century Magazine;* in 1897 she published *Stories of a Sanctified Town,* set in nearby Robards, which had recently experienced a huge religious awakening. In 1907 she joined the faculty of the Hindman Settlement School in the mountain county of Knott, where she taught for seventeen years and served as housemother in the small boys' cottage. She resumed her local-color stories, now writing about her new home in the mountains; she published them first in the *Atlantic Monthly,* then in such collections as *Mothering on Perilous* (1913) and *The Quare Women* (1923). Until James Still moved to the same area in the early 1930s and began to claim it for his own poetry and fiction, Lucy Furman's authentic, sensitive, and respectful renderings of Kentucky mountain life went unchallenged. In *Mothering on Perilous,* she uses a diary format to record her arrival at Hindman and her initiation into student life and culture.

JOSLIN, KY.
Last Thursday in July.

Here I am at the end of the railroad, waiting to begin my two-days' wagon-trip across the mountains. But the school wagon has not arrived,— my landlady says it is delayed by a "tide" in the creeks. By way of cheering me, she has just given a graphic account of the twenty-year-old feud for which this small town is notorious, and has even offered to take me around and show me, on walls, floors and courthouse steps, the blood-spots where seven or eight of the feudists have perished. I declined to go,—it is sad enough to know such things exist, without seeing them face to face. Besides, I have enough that is depressing in my own thoughts.

When I locked the doors of the old home day before yesterday, I felt as a ghost may when it wanders forth from the tomb. For a year I had not been off the place; it seemed I should never have the courage to go again. For I am one whom death has robbed of everything,—not only of my present but of my future. In the past seven years all has gone; and with Mother's passing a year ago, my very reason for existence went.

And yet none knows better than I that this sitting down with sorrow is both dangerous and wrong; if there is any Lethe for such pain as mine, any way of filling in the lonely, dreaded years ahead of me, I must find it. It would be better if I had some spur of necessity to urge me on. As it is, I am all apathy. If there is anything that could interest me, it is some form of social service. A remarkable settlement work being done in the mountains of my own state recently came to my attention; and I wrote the head-workers and arranged for the visit on which I am now embarked. I scarcely dare to hope, however, that I shall find a field of usefulness,—nothing interests me any more, and also, I have no gifts, and have never been trained for anything. My dearest ambition was to make a home, and have a houseful of children; and this, alas, was not to be!

Night.

Howard Cleves, a big boy from the settlement school, has just arrived with the wagon—he says he had to "lay by" twenty-four hours on account of the "tide"—and we are to start at five in the morning.

SETTLEMENT SCHOOL ON PERILOUS.

Sunday, In Bed.

I have passed through two days of torture in that wagon. When we were not following the rocky beds of creeks, or sinking to the hubs in mudholes, we were winding around precipitous mountainsides where a misstep of the mules would have sent us hundreds of feet down. Nowhere was there an actual road,—as Howard expressed it, "This country is intended for nag-travel, not for wagons." The mules climbed over logs and bowlders, and up and down great shelves of rock, the jolting, crashing, banging were indescribable, my poor bones were racked until I actually wept from the pain and would have turned back long before noon of the first day if I could; the thirteen hours—during which we made twenty-six miles—seemed thirteen eons, and I fell into the featherbed at the stopover place that first night hat, dress, shoes and all. Yesterday, having bought two pillows to sit on, I found the jolting more endurable, and was able to see some of the beauty through which we were passing. There is no level land, nothing but creeks and mountains, the latter steep, though not very high, and covered mostly with virgin forest, though here and there a cornfield runs half-way up, and a lonely log house nestles at the base. There were looms and spinning-wheels in the porches of these homes, and always numbers of children ran out to see us pass. Just at noon we turned into Perilous Creek, the one the school is on. Here the bed was unusually wide and smooth, and I was enjoying the respite from racking and jolting, when Howard said with an anxious brow, "All these nice smooth places is liable to be quicksands,—last time I come over, it took four ox-teams to pull my span and wagon out. That's how it gets its name,—Perilous."

We escaped the quicks, thank heaven, and just at dark the welcome lights of the school shone out in the narrow valley. I was relieved to find I should be expected to remain in bed to-day.

Racked muscles, black-and-blue spots, and dislocated bones are not exactly pleasant; but physical pain is an actual relief after endless ache of heart and suffering of spirit.

A pretty, brown-eyed boy just brought in a pitcher of water, asked me if I came from the "level country" and how many times I had "rid" on the railroad train; and gave me the information that he was Philip Sidney Floyd, that his "paw" got his name out of a book, that his "maw" was dead, that he was "very nigh thirteen," and had worked for "the women" all summer.

Monday Night.

Early this morning I was taken around by Philip and a smaller boy named Geordie to see the buildings,—handsome ones of logs, set in a narrow strip of bottom land along Perilous Creek. The "big house" especially, a great log structure of two-dozen rooms, where the settlement work goes on, and the teachers and girls live, is the most satisfying building I ever saw. There are also a good workshop, a pretty loom-house, and a small hospital, and the last shingles are being nailed on the large new school-house. When I asked the boys why any school-term should begin the first of August, they explained that the children must go home and help their parents hoe corn during May, June and July.

All day the children who are to live in the school, and many more who hope to, were arriving, afoot or on nags, the boys, however small, in long trousers and black felt hats like their fathers, the girls a little more cheerfully dressed than their mothers, whose black sun-bonnets and somber homespun dresses were depressing. Many of the parents stayed to dinner. There is a fine, old-fashioned dignity in their manners, and great gentleness in their voices. I have always heard that, shut away here in these mountains, some of the purest and best Anglo-Saxon blood in the nation is to be found; now I am sure of it. It was pathetic to see the eagerness of these men and women that their children should get learning, and to hear many of them tell how they themselves had had no chance whatever at an education, being raised probably sixty or eighty miles from a school-house.

Late in the afternoon, as Philip, Geordie and I were fastening up straying rose-vines on the pine-tree pillars of the "big house" porch, a one-legged and very feeble man, accompanied by a boy, dismounted at the gate and came up the walk on a crutch. During the time he sat on the porch, my two assistants abandoned their work to stare open-mouthed at him. When he was called in to see the heads, Geordie inquired of his boy,

"How'd your paw git all lamed up that-away?"

The new arrival pulled his black hat down, frowned, and measured Geordie with gray, combative eyes, before replying, coldly,

"Warring with the Cheevers."

"Gee-oh, air you one of the Marrses from Trigger Branch of Powderhorn?"

"Yes."

"What's your name?"

"Nucky."

"How old air you?"

"Going-on-twelve."

"What kin is Blant Marrs to you?"

"My brother."

"You don't say so! Gee, I wisht I could see him! Have you holp any in the war?"

"Some." Here Nucky was called in, to the evident disappointment of his interlocutor. Later, I saw him at the supper-table, gazing disapprovingly about him.

After supper I had a few minutes talk with the busy head-workers, and placed myself at their disposal, with the explanation that I really knew very little about anything, except music and gardening. They said these things are just what they have been wanting,—that a friend has recently sent the school a piano (how did it ever cross these mountains!) and that some one to supervise garden operations is especially needed. "Besides, what you don't know you can learn," they said, "we are always having to do impossible and unexpected things here,—our motto is 'Learn by doing.'" I am very dubious; but I promised to try it a month.

They told me that between six and seven hundred children had been turned away to-day for lack of room,—only sixty can live in the school, though two hundred more attend the day-school, which begins to-morrow.

Friday Night.

What a week! Foraging expeditions and music-lessons to big girls in the mornings, and in the afternoons, gardening, with a dozen small boys to keep busy. This is an industrial school,—in addition to the usual common-school subjects, woodwork, carpentry, blacksmithing, gardening, cooking, sewing, weaving and home-nursing are all taught, and the children in residence also perform all the work on the place, indoors and out. But alas, my agricultural force is diminishing,—the small boys are leaving in batches. This is the first year any number have been taken to live in the school, and they are unable to endure the homesickness. Nucky Marrs left after one night's stay; three others followed Tuesday afternoon, and five on Wednesday; more were taken in, but left at once. Keats Salyer, a beautiful boy who has wept every minute of his stay, ran away a third time this morning. Yesterday Joab Atkins left when the housekeeper told him to help the girls pick chickens. Eight new boys came in to-day, but the veterans, Philip and Geordie, say these are aiming to leave to-morrow.

Friday is mill day in the mountains, and this morning, having had the boys shell corn, I took it to mill to be ground into meal, in a large "poke" (sack) slung across my saddle. When I had gone a mile up Perilous, the thing wriggled from under me and fell off in the road. Of course I was powerless to lift it, though equally of course I got off the school nag and tried. There was nothing to do but sit on the roots of a great beech until somebody came along. Two men soon rode up, and smiling, dismounted and politely set the poke and me on Mandy again, and I reached the mill in safety. When I got back, my black china-silk was ruined from sitting on the meal.

James H. Mulligan
"In Kentucky"

There were poets scribbling all over Kentucky at the turn of the century, but the quality of the poems had not improved much since the earlier generations of poets, despite the fact that several of them achieved national reputations. New voices were beginning to emerge, but they were mostly weak and imitative. Isaac Joseph Schwartz (1885–1971), for example, a Jewish immigrant from Lithuania, came to New York in 1906 and in 1918 moved to Lexington, where he opened a millinery shop and began writing poetry. He called his work "a Yiddish poet's love song to America." Nine of his poems that deal with Kentucky life from the viewpoint of an immigrant were gathered and published as *Kentucky* in 1990.

In this gathering of poets, I offer you a sampling of the best-known ones. I would be remiss if I didn't include James H. Mulligan's oft-quoted poetic tribute to his homeland. Mulligan, born in Lexington in 1844, served in the General Assembly, became a judge, and wrote many verses about real Kentucky places; but it was "In Kentucky," the booster poem he read before a dinner given for legislators by the Lexington Chamber of Commerce at the Phoenix Hotel in February 1902, that carved his name in Kentucky limestone forever. Seldom has hyperbole reached such dizzying depths of bathos.

The moonlight falls the softest
  In Kentucky;
The summer days come oftest
  In Kentucky;
Friendship is the strongest,
Love's light glows the longest,
Yet, wrong is always wrongest
  In Kentucky.

Life's burdens bear the lightest
  In Kentucky;
The home fires burn the brightest
  In Kentucky;
While players are the keenest,
Cards come out the meanest,

The pocket empties cleanest
    In Kentucky.

The sun shines ever brightest
    In Kentucky;
The breezes whisper lightest
    In Kentucky;
Plain girls are the fewest,
Their little hearts the truest,
Maiden's eyes the bluest
    In Kentucky.

Orators are the grandest
    In Kentucky;
Officials are the blandest
    In Kentucky;
Boys are all the fliest,
Danger ever nighest,
Taxes are the highest
    In Kentucky.

The bluegrass waves the bluest
    In Kentucky;
Yet, bluebloods are the fewest (?)
    In Kentucky;
Moonshine is the clearest,
By no means the dearest,
And, yet, it acts the queerest
    In Kentucky.

The dovenotes are the saddest
    In Kentucky;
The streams dance on the gladdest
    In Kentucky;
Hip pockets are the thickest,
Pistol hands the slickest,
The cylinder turns quickest
    In Kentucky.

The song birds are the sweetest
    In Kentucky;

The thoroughbreds are fleetest
        In Kentucky;
Mountains tower proudest,
Thunder peals the loudest,
The landscape is the grandest—
And politics—the damnedest
        In Kentucky.

Robert Burns Wilson

"Lovingly, to Elizabeth, My Mother"

Robert Burns Wilson, who was born in Pennsylvania in 1850 but moved to Kentucky in the 1870s, fell in love with the rivers and creeks and landscapes of central Kentucky and used them for his double calling of painter and poet. He was a much better painter than poet. Although acclaimed as an important nature poet, he wrote his best-known poem, "Battle Song," in 1898 as a response to the Spanish sinking of the American battleship the *Maine*. As the final three lines of the first stanza demonstrate, he loved rhymes: "From ship to ship, from lip to lip, / Pass on the quick refrain, / Remember, remember the Maine." The following sonnet on the loss of his mother is replete with his signature traits: archaic language, predictable images and rhymes, and unbridled emotion.

> The green Virginian hills were blithe in May,
> And we were plucking violets—thou and I.
> A transient gladness flooded earth and sky;
>   Thy fading strength seemed to return that day,
>   And I was mad with hope that God would stay
> Death's pale approach—Oh! all hath long passed by!
> Long years! Long years! and now, I well know why
>   Thine eyes, quick-filled with tears, were turned away.
>
>   First loved; first lost; my mother:—time must still
> Leave my soul's debt uncancelled. All that's best
>   In me, and in my art, is thine:—Me-seems,
> Even now, we walk afield. Through good and ill,
>   My sorrowing heart forgets not, and in dreams
> I see thee, in the sun-lands of the blest.

Joseph S. Cotter Sr.

One of Kentucky's first African American poets, Joseph S. Cotter Sr. was largely a man of his time, although he does attempt, sometimes successfully, to sound a new voice in Kentucky poetry. He was born in Nelson County in 1861; but when he was an infant his family moved to Louisville, where he grew up, became a prominent educator and pioneer in black education, and lived the rest of his life. His poems are typically written in the common three- or four-line stanzas in rhythms of iambic pentameter or tetrameter with recurring patterns of rhyme. The four poems that follow suggest the range of Cotter's subjects, from homage to early opponents of slavery, such as the journalist William Lloyd Garrison (who founded the antislavery newspaper the *Liberator* in 1831) and the Kentucky abolitionist Cassius M. Clay, to poems about black domestic life and racial progress. His poems provided a good foundation and inspiration for African American writers in Kentucky who would flourish later in the twentieth century.

"William Lloyd Garrison"

His country seared its conscience through its gain,
    And had not wisdom to behold the loss.
It held God partner in the hellish stain,
    And saw Christ dying on a racial cross.

What unto it the shackled fellow-man,
    Whose plea was mockery, and whose groans were
      mirth?
Its boasted creed was: "He should rule who can
    Make prey of highest heaven and dupe of earth."

From out this mass of century-tutored wrong
    A man stood God-like, and his voice rang true.
His soul was sentry to the dallying throng,
    His thought was watchword to the gallant few.

He saw not as his fellow-beings saw;
    He would not misname greed expediency,
He found no color in the nation's law,
    And scorned to meet it in its liberty.

He saw his duty in his neighbor's cause,
    And died that he might rise up strong and free—
A creature subject to the highest laws,
    And master of a God-like destiny.

The thunder of a million armed feet,
    Reverberating till the land was stirred,
Was but the tension of his great heart-beat,
    The distant echo of his spoken word.

He speaks again: "Such as would miss the rod
    That ever chastens insufficiency,
Must purge their lives and make them fit for God,
    Must train their liberty and make it free."

"Gen. Cassius M. Clay"

"Give me an heir," the Century plead,
    "With the brain of a man and the will of a god;
With a soul that will flash with the word that is said,
    And a hand that will strike, 'though the heavens
      nod.

"When the storm blows not, and the way is clear,
    And man is to man as star to star,
Let the sage come forth with his thought-bred fear,
    And plans that are meek as the grass blades are.

"When soul meets soul and disdains to hate,
    When thought meets thought and clashes not,
The priest may sweetly, sternly prate
    Of a saintly way and a Godless lot.

"When weal must lessen the cry of woe,
    And blood must sanction the will of heaven,
My heir must conquer the foremost foe;
    To slay, faith-spurred, is the age's leaven."

So the Century hurled thee, a living flame,
    To blaze thy way to the heart of man.
Now, at its end, thou art a name
    That shines wherever greatness can.

"The Negro's Educational Creed"

The Negro simply asks the chance to think,
    To wed his thinking unto willing hands,
And thereby prove himself a steadfast link,
    In the sure chain of progress through the lands.

He does not ask to loiter and complain
    While others turn their life blood into worth.
He holds that this would be the one foul stain
    On the escutcheon of this brave old earth.

He does not ask to clog the wheels of State
    And write his color on the Nation's Creed.
He asks an humble freedman's estimate,
    And time to grow ere he essays to lead.

"The Kiddies and the Christmas Tree"

Smiling, smiling kiddies we—
All with eyes and eyes to see
 Goodies on the Christmas tree.

Jolly, jolly kiddies we,
Two by two and three by three,
Marching 'round the Christmas tree.

Singing, singing kiddies we,
Tasting songs and sipping glee
From the playthings on the tree.

Thankful, thankful kiddies we,
And we hope this year will be
Ended with a Christmas tree.

Welcome, welcome, Maidens, ye
Who left love and jollity
Dangling from our Christmas tree.

Madison Cawein
"Conclusion"

Madison Cawein was better known and respected in his lifetime than he is now. He was a Louisville native who, despite considerable critical praise, never could seem to sell enough copies of his thirty-six books of poetry to support himself, his family, and his magnificent house on Louisville's St. James Court, which he finally had to give up. (The novelist Sena Jeter Naslund has in recent years restored the home to its former elegance and fame as the residence of a prominent writer.) As a boy Cawein learned to appreciate the beautiful parks and natural haunts in and around Louisville from his father, a respected herbalist, and used them as subject and inspiration for the poems in his first collection, *Blooms of the Berry* (1887). He died at forty-nine and his name, which used to be widely known, has declined into obscurity.

His poem "Conclusion" is conventional in its use of four-line stanzas of iambic tetrameter rhyming *abab* and its linking of love with nature and the seasons in a metaphor of loss and acceptance.

The songs Love sang to us are dead:
Yet shall he sing to us again,
When the dull days are wrapped in lead,
And the red woodland drips with rain.

The lily of our love is gone,
That touched our spring with golden scent;
Now in the garden low upon
The wind-stripped way its stalk is bent.

Our rose of dreams is passed away,
That lit our summer with sweet fire;
The storm beats bare each thorny spray,
And its dead leaves are trod in mire.

The songs Love sang to us are dead;
Yet shall he sing to us again,
When the dull days are wrapped in lead,
And the red woodland drips with rain.

The marigold of memory
Shall fill our autumn then with glow;
Haply its bitterness will be
Sweeter than love of long ago.

The cypress of forgetfulness
Shall haunt our winter with its hue;
The apathy to us not less
Dear than the dreams our summer knew.

"Waste Land"

The Louisville art historian and critic Madeline C. Covi has reminded us recently (in *The Encyclopedia of Louisville*) that Cawein may be restored at least to a literary footnote because one of his poems, "Waste Land," from his 1913 volume, *Minions of the Moon,* "antedates and likely influenced T. S. Eliot's poem of the same name (1922), linking Cawein to the early modern tradition." Indeed, it is very possible that Eliot read and was influenced by Cawein's poem. In early 1913 Eliot was waiting impatiently in London to see if his poem "The Love Song of J. Alfred Prufrock" would be chosen and published in the January issue of the prestigious Chicago magazine *Poetry.* It was not, but a poem was published in that issue by Madison Cawein, who was identified by the editor of *Poetry* as "too well known to need any introduction." And so this may have been the inspiration and source for one of the best-known poems in the English language and one of the landmarks of modern poetry.

Briar and fennel and chincapin,
And rue and ragweed everywhere,
The field seemed sick as a soul with sin,
Or dead of an old despair,
Born of an ancient care.

The cricket's cry and the locust's whirr,
And the note of a bird's distress,
With the rasping sound of the grasshopper,
Clung to the loneliness
Like burrs to a trailing dress.

So sad the field, so waste the ground,
So curst with an old despair,

A woodchuck's burrow, a blind mole's mount
And chipmunk's stony lair,
Seemed more than it could bear.

So lonely, too, so more than sad,
So droning loud with bees—
I wondered what more could Nature add
To the sum of its miseries . . .
And *then*—I saw the trees.

Skeletons gaunt that gnarled the place,
Twisted and torn they rose—
The tortured trees of a perished race
Of monsters no mortal knows,
They startled the mind's repose.

And a man stood there, as still as moss,
A lichen form that stared;
With an old blind hound that, at a loss,
Forever around him fared
With a snarling fang half bared.

I looked at the man; I saw him plain;
Like a dead weed, gray and wan,
Or a breath of dust. I looked again—
And man and dog were gone,
Like the wisps of a greying dawn. . . .

Were they a part of the grim death there,
Ragweed, fennel, and rue?
Or forms of the mind, an old despair,
That there into semblance grew
Out of a grief I knew?

Cale Young Rice

Cale Young Rice, an almost forgotten poet, was born in Dixon in 1872 and earned a master's degree at Harvard; he then settled in Louisville and married Alice Hegan, whose literary reputation would soon eclipse his, despite his lifetime production of some thirty-five books of poetry, verse drama, fiction, and autobiography. Most critics consider him a competent but uninspired poet. He was a traditionalist who would have nothing of the new poetry being encouraged and brought to light by Ezra Pound, Hart Crane, and T. S. Eliot. Rice was thirty when he married Alice Hegan, but he must have loved her very much. Less than a year after she died, in 1942, he shot himself dead. The two poems below are soothing and predictable and contain no surprises or original insights.

"When the Wind Is Low"

When the wind is low, and the sea is soft,
And the far heat-lightning plays
On the rim of the West where dark clouds nest
On a darker bank of haze;
When I lean at the rail with you that I love
And gaze to my heart's content;
I know the heavens are there above—
But you are my firmament.

When the phosphor-stars are thrown from the bow
And the watch climbs up the shroud;
When the dim mast dips as the vessel slips
Through the foam that seethes aloud;
I know that the years of our life are few,
And fain as a bird to flee,
That time is as brief as a drop of dew—
But you are eternity.

"West of Eden"

We have fared west of Eden, far from peace,
Westward of Eden, breeding and dying,

The old race of Adam, seeking surcease,
The children of Cain, cursing and crying.

Far west of Eden, bearing our burden,
Wearing our sorrow, tilling the earth,
Wondering what shall at length be our guerdon
When we have bettered the seed of our birth.

Eden was ignorance; tasting the apple
Stung us to testing atom and star.
Speech of the serpent was prompting to grapple
With life as it is, things as they are.

Over the world we have fared, westing,
Farther away from the bliss of the brute,
Wanting it, hating it, yet in our questing
Glad to have eaten the fatal fruit.

From Arnow to Warren

The Flowering of Kentucky Writing

We will now visit with world-class Kentucky authors. Resuming our metaphor of a dinner table laden with food, we have partaken of the finger food and several side dishes and are now ready for the main courses. They are rich and delicious—food for the body and the soul. Not all the writers in this chapter are major authors, but some of them are. Any state that can claim such talents as Elizabeth Madox Roberts, James Still, Harriette Simpson Arnow, Thomas Merton, and that master of all genres, Robert Penn Warren, can be justly proud. We are now in the midst of the first major flowering of Kentucky writing, and first-class writers may be found in every corner of the state.

At the same time, during the first half of the twentieth century, Kentucky's culture in traditional music—folk, country, bluegrass, and various blends with popular music—became popular on recordings and on the radio. Musicians such as Pee Wee King, Redd Stewart, Bill Monroe, and Tom T. Hall were also composers. John Jacob Niles, Jean Thomas, and Jean Ritchie were pioneers in collecting and celebrating traditional folk music of Scottish-Irish-English origins. Thomas, known as the "Traipsin' Woman" because she traveled around the counties near her home in Ashland as a court stenographer while she also collected folksongs and folklore, founded the American Folk Festival in 1930. The author of several books on mountain music and folklore, she died in 1982 at the age of 101. Jean Ritchie was born in 1922 in the Perry County coal town of Viper and began singing as a child. With a degree in social work from the University of Kentucky in 1947, she moved to New York and worked in a settlement house and quickly became an important figure in the New York folk scene. In addition to recording more than thirty albums of folk music, she is a composer ("Sorrow in the Wind" is her best-known song) and an accomplished author of such books as *The Swapping Song Book* (1952) and *Singing Family of the Cumberlands* (1955). But it is as a performing musician playing on her mountain dulcimer that she is best known.

Elizabeth Madox Roberts

from *The Great Meadow*

Elizabeth Madox Roberts was born in Perryville in 1881 but spent most of her life in nearby Springfield and the rolling fields and knobs of Boyle, Washington, and Nelson Counties. Here she found the landscapes, the people, and the history for her fiction and poetry. Descended from pioneers herself, she had for many years the desire to write a novel about the westward migration into Kentucky. She published *The Great Meadow* in 1930, when she was almost fifty, and it is the best novel written so far about Kentucky's early history. Beginning in 1774 and ending in 1781, the story centers on the emigration of Berk Jarvis and his wife, Diony Hall, from her aristocratic family home in Virginia to Fort Harrod, the first permanent settlement in Kentucky. Against the larger backdrop of the American Revolution as it was played out in the West and the constant threat of Indian attacks, the plot focuses on Berk and Diony and how they survive the deprivations and dangers in the new land. The novel is actually about two journeys—the emigrants' search for new land and wealth and Diony's search for selfhood. In the opening of the novel, Diony repeats her name, "I, Diony Hall," as if to say, "Who am I?" The novel is about her attempt to answer this perennial question of human existence.

1774, and Diony, in the spring, hearing Sam, her brother, scratching at a tune on the fiddle, hearing him break a song over the taut wires and fling out with his voice to supply all that the tune lacked, placed herself momentarily in life, calling mentally her name, Diony Hall. "I, Diony Hall," her thought said, gathering herself close, subtracting herself from the diffused life of the house that closed about her. Sam was singing, flinging the song free of the worried strings, making a very good tune of it:

> There was a ship sailed for the North Amer-i-kee—
> Crying, O the lonesome lowlands low—
> There was a ship sailed for the North Amer-i-kee,
> And she went by the name of the Golden Van-i-tee,
> And she sailed from the lowlands low. . . .

"I, Diony Hall," her hands said back to her thought, her fingers knitting wool. Beyond her spread the floor which was of hard smooth wood, and beyond again arose the walls of the house, and outside reached the clearings of the plantation, Five Oaks the name her father called it by. Then came the trees and the rolling hills of Albemarle County and the upper waters of the James—Rockfish Creek, the Tye, Fluvanna, Rivanna. The world reached straight then, into infinity, laid out beyond the level of herself in a far-going horizontal, although report said of it that it bent to a round and made a globe. She was aware of infinity outward going and never returning. "I, Diony," she said, throwing the little strand of wool over her needle and making a web. Back then from infinity, having recovered herself, and the house stood close, intimately sensed. Sam's music:

There was a ship sailed for the North Amer-i-kee—
Crying, O the lonesome lowlands low . . .

The house was of two log parts standing near together, a covered passage lying between which the boys of the family had named the dog alley because the dogs lay there to sleep. One of the buildings was called the "old house" and this was used now for the kitchen and for the weaving. There was a loft above this room, reached by a corner stairway, and above in the loft were two rooms where the boys and their visitors slept. The dog alley was closed overhead and floored beneath. Beyond it lay the "new house," a building of equal size with the old and flanked by a great chimney at the front as the other was flanked by a similar chimney at the rear. Below in the new house was the great room where the heads of the family slept, where the elegant life of the plantation was enacted, where Thomas Hall, the father of the house, kept his books on a shelf. A corner stairway led to rooms above, two chambers. When the dogs, hearing a wildcat or a fox, would run through the dog alley on their way to the edge of the clearing, the boards of the puncheoned floor of the passage would rattle with a great clatter and then lie still. Thus the house stood about Diony.

"That land, hit belongs to the Indians," Polly said.

Her mouth drew in to a fine hardness, a protest against the wilderness. "Hit belongs," she said again, grimly. Diony saw the reason of all Polly uttered as it smote Berk and Sam and Reuben until they sat stilled, their food neglected. Berk made a movement as if he would speak, but he was abashed before Polly's anger, seeing the right in what she said through the power of her skillful mouth that flowed from moment to moment into newer ways of loveliness. She did not yield, but sat in uncompromising beauty, erect in her chair, her head lifted when she spoke.

"Hit's Indian property. The white man has got no rights there. Hit's owned already, Kentuck is. Go, and you'll be killed and skulped by savages, your skulp to hang up in a dirty Indian house or hang on his belt. Hit's already owned. White men are outside their rights when they go there."

Indetermination settled over the board and distress visited the young men. Outrageous battle, fire, burning at the stake, rapine, plunder, the jackals eating the dead. They saw all these and right divided itself from wrong anew. Thomas Hall spoke then. Striking the table over which he leaned with a great blow, his fist clenched, bringing decision back to their thought.

"If the Indian is not man enough to hold it let him give it over then," he said. "It's a land that calls for brave men, a brave race. It's only a strong race can hold a good country. Let the brave have and hold there."

"Yes, sir, yes," Berk joined him then. "If he can't hold, if he's afeared and frighted to stay there, let him cry for't. If he sees ghosts there and hears noises and is frighted by the Alleghewi . . . Dead men's bones! If he can't keep it he can leave it alone. Stronger men are bound to go in there, more enduren men."

The young men leaped to support the opening Thomas and Berk had made. Right settled to new ground and reared itself in new places. Their voices cracked sharply over the board, one after another.

"The most enduren will take . . ."

"You couldn't hold it safe for weak men until they think it safe to go there."

"The Long Knives are the strong men you named. The Long Knife is bound to win there."

"The Big Knife."

"Who is it calls the Virginians the Long Knives?"

"Hit's the Shawnees. They call all Virginia the Big Knife."

"I look to see the Long Knives take Kentuck."

"You couldn't hold a land safe for weak men."

"Strong men will go in and take."

"Strong men will win there."

When she waked, the light of day had begun to spread over the trees. All the men were astir, being scattered about the camp as a guard. No fire was allowed, and so their breakfast was of parched corn which they had at hand, but in the brush there were a few ripe berries. Diony milked her cow although there was little left in the animal's body that was of the softness of milk. The women prepared the children for the march and the packs were given to the beasts. The order of their going was established, and all moved off slowly, taking the even pace of their habitual travel. They moved up the narrow canyon along the faint trace, Boone's Trace, over stones and brambles, but here and there logs had been thrown from the way or a tree felled to make the passage clear. Together, men and women, they went slowly forward, the men to the fore, the man's strength being in the thrust, the drive, in action, the woman's lateral, in the plane, enduring, inactive but constant. They marched forward, taking a new world for themselves, possessing themselves of it by the power of their courage, their order, and their endurance. They went forward without bigotry and without psalm-singing to hide what they did. They went through the Gateway into Kentuck. They walked quietly, being subdued by the greatness about them in the great cliffs and the fine mountain rises that lifted upward from the pass.

She would sit in the cabin at twilight, resting on a stiff little chair she had bought from a wood-workman of the fort. The supper waited on the hearth, ready baked before the fire, and her few wooden vessels were ready to contain it. She would prolong her reverie until it fell into a clearly defined desire.

This was a new world, the beginning before the beginning. Sitting thus alone in the cabin, while Berk looked for the cow on the snowy creekside and brought her safely to the fort, while he, with the other men of the stockade, dragged fodder inside the wall, getting the wood, closing the gates—sitting thus she would see a vision of fields turned up by the plow. A moist loam rolls up to take the seeds and the rain into itself. Over the field some birds would go swiftly, darting here and there, calling now one and now all together, plovers tossing over a made field to go to the creekside beyond a low rising shoulder of turned loam. A field! This would be a great happiness.

Or again: A vision of sheep sprinkled over a pasture or turned in on a hillside to crop the stubble and glean a fine rich eatage for themselves. On their backs would grow round fat fleeces of fine wool to be sheared away in the spring, to be spun into yarn and woven. The sheep stand in a strange stillness, each one bent to the earth, or they lift their heads and look off toward the south, all looking together. Their small thin faces are pointed toward some invisible which they discern as if they examined it carefully, their small feet sunk into the low herbs, the wool put over their backs in a soft round coat. The odor of wool floats lightly about them as a more subtle coat they wear over their fleeces. To make them run forward to obey some command the farmer would cry out a musical "hou-ee," and "sheep-ah, sheep-ah!" It was a vision. She saw thus in the embers in her cabin within Fort Harrod in the cold season of the early year, 1778, wolves howling on the hill beyond the burying place.

A vision of stone walls and rail fences setting bounds to the land, making contentment and limitations for the mind to ease itself upon. The wearying infinitives of the wilderness come to an end. The land stands now, in vision, as owned, this man's farm beside that man's, all contained now, bounded, divided, and shared, and one sinks into the security and lies down to rest himself. Through the farms run lanes and well pounded roads, making a further happiness, ways to go to meet a neighbor at his own house.

A vision of neighbors, a man living to the right, a man to the left, each in his own land, their children meeting together to walk down the road to a schoolhouse or a church. Or the women learn of one another, each one using the best of her skill to make the food or the clothing a little better than they were before, each one wishing to do as well as the others, and some, those with skillful hands, excelling the rest.

A vision of places to sell the growth of the farms, there being farms now, a vision of some market place off in some town beyond the fields, where iron and glass could be had for the surplus of the harvest, where could be had books and journals and tools, clocks and vessels of earthenware, pewter spoons and vessels of brass, steel knives and smooth shoes for their feet, needles for their fingers . . . It was a happiness to think of.

Berk delayed coming and she knew that the cows must be lost. The little children in the next cabin were crying for milk, being unable to eat the harsh corn-pones and the jerked meats. She heard bobcats screaming in the stony places toward the west, and Gyp, her dog, whined at the door, wanting to be let in. Men at Harrod's cabin fired a rifle, a signal to those outside. There were more than a hundred men in the fort now, and some of them being wary hunters, there was always wild meat enough, but the turnips and pumpkins were gone. The children would gather into the mother's cabin at nightfall, and the sounds of the fort were then subdued under cabin rafters. Tears gathered through her entire being to hear the little children cry for their supper, wanting milk.

A vision of bridges over streams so that their horses or oxen need not be imperiled in flood waters and their goods lost, so that they might cross easily over and take no thought of the matter, so that they need not lash logs together to make a raft. The road runs smoothly down through settled fields and comes at last to a river where it runs lightly over a structure of smooth logs neatly trimmed and jointed, placed on stone pillars that stand well out of the flood. It was a wonder to dream on in the mind.

A vision of fine cattle in the pastures giving a rich yield of milk and cream, well chosen beasts that stand secure in good barns, not the wiry little scrub sort that run on the open range and live in constant fear of wild creatures and savages. In the pastures too are good horses, graceful riding beasts, easy in hand, smooth carriers, strong and sound.

Bees, then, in hives set in neat rows near a dwelling. They gather sweet from the wild growth in the uncleared places and from the pollen of the corn, from the white clover. It would be a civil picture, the hives cut out of well sawed logs and left to their own devices until the honey made a rich, sweet fatness within. Then a man, Berk Jarvis perhaps, goes among the hives and robs the bees of their harvest, and a woman, herself, Diony, stores the honey in earthen jars of which there would be a plenty.

A dream of letters written between one and another, of messages sent freely through long miles of travel. A courier waits at the door, his horse pawing the earth, ready to go hence. One folds the pages together and writes a name on the outer page, writing "Mister Thomas Hall," writing "Mistress Polly Hall," writing "Mistress Betty Hall." . . . The courier takes the letter into his hand and goes swiftly, carrying the letter to the one named. The vision grew dim because of the long, scarcely broken tangles of trees and stones that reared themselves in the way, but it cleared itself and was renewed to become a vision of messages received, of word sent to her. A letter comes to her hands that are now folded in her lap. She feels the crisp edges of the paper and reads eagerly what is inscribed within, messages from a man, Thomas Hall, telling her how all fared in Albemarle. It was a vision: there were no letters; no word had ever come to her.

A dream of knowledge, of wisdom brought under beautiful or awful sayings and remembered, kept stored among written pages and brought together then as books. Books stand in a row on a shelf where a narrow beam of light falls through a high casement over a desk where one might rest a volume, where one might sit for an hour and search the terrible pages, looking for beauty, looking for some final true way of life. In them, the books, Man walks slowly down through the centuries, walking on the stairs of the years. . . .

Berk came at last, white with new-fallen frost. The children had become quiet, their cries now soft and full of content. Her vision went with the flare of a fresh stick among the embers. She set the supper on the board and their hungers were satisfied.

from *The Time of Man*

In 1926, when Roberts was forty-five, she published her finest novel, *The Time of Man,* about a hero who, like Diony Hall Jarvis, is seeking self-fulfillment. In the first line of the novel, Ellen Chesser writes her name in the air as she begins her arduous journey to selfhood. It is rural Kentucky in the 1920s, and Ellen is the daughter of a poor itinerant farmer. The family is on the move again, looking for the bare essentials of life—food for survival, a roof that doesn't leak too much, and sufficient clothes to protect them from the elements. The entire novel is about Ellen's search for a modestly good life. It is a hard journey littered with an unfaithful lover, unremitting labor, childbearing, a near suicide, a child's death, and even a nightriders' attack on her husband. But she is a survivor. As she tells her husband, "I'll go where you go and live where you live, all my enduren life." Indeed, *The Time of Man* is a great American novel about the triumph of the human spirit.

⁓

Ellen wrote her name in the air with her finger, *Ellen Chesser*, leaning forward and writing on the horizontal plane. Beside her in the wagon her mother huddled under an old shawl to keep herself from the damp, complaining, "We ought to be a-goen on."

"If I had all the money there is in the world," Ellen said, slowly, "I'd go along in a big red wagon and I wouldn't care if it taken twenty horses to pull it along. Such a wagon as would never break down." She wrote her name again in the horizontal of the air.

"Here's a gypsy wagon broke down!" Some little boys ran up to the blacksmith shop, coming out of the field across the road. "Oh, Alvin, come on, here's horse-swappers broke down," one called.

Ellen's father was talking with a farmer, and the boys were staring, while the blacksmith pecked from time to time with his tools, the sounds muffled in the wet air. A voice complained, "We ought to be a-goen on."

The farmer said that he would pay three dollars a day for work that week. Henry Chesser stood with one foot on the hub of the wagon, thinking over the offer, drifting, his slow speech a little different from the farmer's slow speech.

"I look for rain again tonight," the farmer said, "and tomorrow will be a season. This is likely the last season we'll have, and so, as I say, I'll pay for help and I'll pay right. But the man I hire has got to work. Three dollars a day you can have. You can take it or leave it. As I say you can have three dollars and that-there house over in the place to stay in. It's a good tight house. Leaks a little, hardly to speak of."

Ellen and her mother sat still on the wagon while Henry decided. Later they drove up the wet road, following the farmer, who rode a sleek horse.

As night came they brought the bedding in from the wagon and prepared to sleep on the floor. Henry tied his two horses to a locust tree off by the creek and these began at once to eat the grass about their feet, biting hurriedly. Ellen was told to lie beside her mother on the quilts, her father lying beyond. The strangeness of the house troubled her, the smell of rats and soot. When she lay on the floor in the dark beside her snoring parents, she thought of Tessie, gone on in the wagon with Jock, sleeping she could not think where that night but not far off, on the road to Rushfield, in some open space by a bridge, perhaps, with the Stikes wagon near, and Screw Brook and Connie a little way on down the pike, the horses grazing about wherever they could. She would have something to tell Tessie when her father's wagon overtook the others. She recited in her mind the story of the adventure as she would tell it. Her thin, almost emaciated body fitted flat against the cabin floor, lying flatter and thinner than the tall bent woman stretched out beside her.

"After you-all went the blacksmith worked on our wagon tongue a long spell before he got it fixed. A farmer came up alongside the wagon and talked to Pappy about work in his patch. You could smell the iron when it went in the tub red hot and you could smell horse hoof. I saw you-all's wagon go on down the road till it got round and a sight littler and seemed like anybody's wagon a-goen anywheres. The country all around got little and narrow and I says to myself, 'The world's little and you just set still in it and that's all there is. There ain't e'er ocean,' I says, 'nor e'er city nor e'er river nor e'er North Pole. There's just the little edge of a wheat field and a little edge of a black-smith shop with nails on the ground, and there's a road a-goen off a little piece with puddles of water a-standen, and there's mud,' I says. When it rained Mammy pulled up the storm sheet. The farmer kept a-walken up and down and a-looken at the sky. 'I need a hand tomorrow and I'm a-goen to pay well,' he says. He'd put his hands inside his pockets and say, 'You can take it or leave it.' And then he climbed up on his big black critter and made like he was gone. 'If that-there gal's any good a-worken she can have twenty-five cents a hour, and the woman too.' Pappy said, 'I don't allow to work my old woman. The youngone can. She can do a sight in a day.' Then towards dark we went down the pike and off up a little dirt road to the house the farmer said we could have all night, and we dragged our bed in on the floor. It was a poor trash house. There was water a-runnen down the wall by the chimney flue and a puddle on the floor off on the yon side of the fireplace, but we kept dry. You could hear the rain all night a-fallen on the roof and a-drippen on the floor, and it was a fair sound. The house was a one-room house, an o'nary place, but before night I saw a cubbyhole against the chimney and a cubbyhole is good to put away in. The chimney was made outen rocks and it had soot smells a-comen outen it, and there was Negro smells a-comen out from back in the corners. When it came on to rain Pappy went out and put the critters under a shed."

The next morning a mist was spreading over the farm, but the rain was over. As soon as he had eaten from the supply of food in the wagon, Henry went off without a word. Ellen watched him cross the creek at the watergap and go up the fencerow toward the farmhouse. Her mother sat in the door of the cabin and waited.

"If you're a mind to drap you better be a-goen up there," she said. "You better leave your shoes behind you. Baccer setten is a muddy time."

Ellen hid her shoes in the wagon. She took off her outer skirt, a dark blue garment, and folded it neatly over the shoes, for Tessie had given her the skirt. The garment removed, she stood clothed in a drab-green waist and a short gray cotton petticoat. She went up the fencerow, the way her father had gone, shy at being between fences, at being penned in a field, a little uncomfortable for the beans and bacon she had eaten, uncertain as to which way to go and as to what was expected of her.

At the top of the field she found the laborers assembled. The farmer had drawn plants out of the bed earlier in the morning, and he gave a basket of these to Ellen, showing her how to drop them along the rows, how to space them by an accurate guess. The men who set the plants into the ground followed her. They made a hole in the soft earth with a round stick and pushed the plant into the hole, squeezing the mud about it with the left hand, bending along the rows, almost never straightening from row end to row end. Ellen walked ahead of the men, dropping a plant first to right and then to left, completing the farmer's field and leading a procession over a rolling hill, her bare feet, red from the sun and the dew, sinking into the mud where the field lay lowest. Her father and a grown boy named Ezra were those who worked behind her. In the mid-morning her mother came slowly, aimlessly, up the fencerow. The farmer offered her twenty-five cents an hour to take his place at the plant bed. " You could sit here on this board and be right comfortable and be earnen a little pin money besides. There won't be more'n a hour or two of it and then a rest."

"I might work for a spell," she said.

At noon they sat under a tree by a fence and waited until food was brought from the farmhouse. The farmer himself came with a basket, his wife following with a coffeepot and some cups. The farmer displayed his offering, bread and pieces of ham dripping hot. There was milk to go in the cups after the coffee and there were fried potatoes and stewed peas. The farmer's wife stayed only a moment, mopping her face, and the farmer said, pointing to the basket, "Here's a pie when you-all are ready for it, and if anybody wants any more helpens all he has to do is to ask. I always feed my hands well." Then he too went back up to the house.

Their fingers were brown on the white bread. They ate shyly, making at first as if they hardly cared to eat at all, picking meagerly at the bread, letting the peas stand untasted in the tin pail. Ezra said:

"I allow you-all are foreigners."

"We are on our way a-travelen. We are a-looken for a good place to settle down," Henry said.

"Is the place where you-all come from a far piece from here?"

"A right far piece."

"I allow you-all been all the way maybe to Green County, or maybe to Hardin or Larue."

"Larue! I been all the way to Tennessee and then on to Georgia."

An expression of wonder.

"I been all the way to Tennessee and then on to Georgia and back once and on to Tennessee once again. Me and my old woman and that-there gal there, all three of us. Say, old woman, I'm plum a fool about peas. Let's have some outen that bucket there."

"But before that I lived in Taylor County," Henry said after the peas had been eaten.

After the hour spent by the tree the work went forward again. Ellen caught the rhythm of her task and rested upon it, gaining thus a chance to look about her a little. The farmhouse stood off among tall trees, a yellow shape with points here and there, two red chimneys budding out of the roof. In her mind the house touched something she almost knew. The treetops above the roof, the mist in the trees, the points of the roof, dull color, all belonging to the farmer, the yellow wall, the distance lying off across a rolling cornfield that was mottled with the wet and traced with lines of low corn—all these touched something settled and comforting in her mind, something like a drink of water after an hour of thirst, like a little bridge over a stream that ran out of a thicket, like cool steps going up into a shaded doorway. That night she lay again on the quilts on the cabin floor beside her mother. Her shoulders ached from carrying the basket all day and her feet were sore from the sun and the mud. Until two weeks before, when her father had bought her shoes at a country store, she had gone barefoot for many months, and her feet were tough and hard, but the mud had eaten into the flesh. When she had returned from the field at sundown she had found that someone had stolen her shoes from the wagon. Her folded skirt had been thrown aside and the shoes were gone, but nothing else had been taken. Lying on the quilts she thought again of Tessie. Her closed eyes saw again the objects of the day in the field, the near mud over which she bent, her feet pulling in and out of it, little grains of soil swimming past her tired eyes. The farmer was there with his stiff legs and square butt, bending over the plant bed, urging everyone forward, trying to be both familiar and commanding. Across the mud and the swimming grains of soil ran his yellow house, off past trees, ran mist, roof-shapes, bobolinks over a meadow, blackbirds in locust trees, bumblebees dragging their bodies over red clover.

"Nine hours I worked and made two dollars and a quarter, but shoes cost two dollars. I'll have a heap to tell Tessie."

ᓚᓓᔓ ᓚᓓᔓ ᓚᓓᔓ

Before autumn Ellen was fifteen. During the summer there had always been food and she had grown less thin. Her bones had withdrawn under the flesh and her eyes were no longer hollow. Signs of woman began to appear on her meager body; woman took possession of her although she was hard like spines and sharp like flint. She looked at herself in the mirror of the creek, for she dared not unrobe herself in the house before the eyes of her mother. She thought that with the change of one or two externals everything might change—a room to sleep in where there would be pink and blue, herself reading a book by the window. Things to put in drawers and drawers to put things in, she would like, and people to say things to. Her mother would sit in a gay chair on a gallery sewing a seam, the little stitches falling up and down, her mother saying gentle things. Or even suppose they were poor, then she would be sitting with her hair clean and combed, and she would call out, "Ellen, come see the sparks, they're in the chimney a-flyen like geese here and yon," or "Come look at the cherry tree; it's like a little girl dressed up for summer."

She wanted to sit beside Tessie and talk about a house. She wanted to talk about a desert where camels walk in long lines, or about glaciers where men explore for poles, or about men walking into mines with little lights on their hats—about the wonders of the world.

"If I only had things to put in drawers and drawers to put things in. That's all I'd ask for a time to come." She could feel herself stooping to pull out a drawer, taking out a garment, at first vague and soft and fine, lace and ribbon and sweet smells, but she let it turn to coarse cotton in her hands, for when it took shape and grew definite there was no other way. She remembered a place where she and Irene had begged. "Could you give us some old clothes, Lady?" And then a tall dark lady before a chest, bending to open a drawer with a faint stooping gesture, bending a little forward, a woman like slow water, a slim fine lady with dark hair and flowing hands.

One evening in August one of the turkey hens failed to bring her brood back to the pasture, and Ellen searched the near-lying fields all through the dusk crying "pee, pee, pee," and looking into the fence corners. She thought the hen would be sitting with her chickens huddled about her. "Some varment will get you-all for certain if you stay out all night," she whispered over and over.

The next morning the hen had not come and Ellen went off across the fields as soon as she had milked the cow and cut the wood for the dinner fire. She looked anxiously through the oat stubble and down the tobacco rows. Beyond the tobacco field lay a stretch of lightly wooded hillside sloping down toward the north, and when this had been searched she came to strange fences and other fields belonging to neighboring farms. She retraced her way to the tobacco field again, climbing on fences to peer out over the land, but later she went down the wooded hill again, drawn by the strange vistas seen through the trees, framed by the trees, and climbed a stone wall which ran up one side of a cut grain field. It was a clear day with blue sky and wind and a hot sun shining. The wind and the sun were one. The sun flowed in waves over her and throbbed in the mesh of her cotton dress. The sun quivered in waves over the stubble and over the moist pasture. She walked through crab grass and timothy and wild barley, the way leading down a creek toward the north, a little creek that lay against the side of the hill and was crossed at each fencerow by a watergap. She broke a long withe and with this she switched at her ankles as she walked quickly down the creekside. The angles of the hills turned in strange ways and the white stones of a strange creek lay wide in the sun. She began to sing a song she had heard Ben mumbling.

> Oh, little Blue Wing is a pretty thing,
> All dressed out so fine.
> Her hair comes a-tribblen down her back
> And the boys can't beat her time.

She went over a watergap where a little willow grew, swaying down into the heart of the willow tree with a sweep of bent branches. Emerged from that she walked on gravel and rank creek grass and frightened the snake doctors away from a still pool as she pranced quickly by.

"Not a-goen anywheres, just a-goen . . ." She crossed the creek on a sandy bar, murmuring a little to herself as she went. "You're spiderwort. You're tansy. I know you. I'm as good as you. I'm no trash. I got no lice on me."

A path lay under her feet, a path cattle took to go to the deeper water holes and she saw the little steps of cattle in the pale soil. The beaten ground made walking easy, and when the way swerved away from the creek she followed although it drifted into an upland, an undulation of pasture where strange cattle grazed, black and white beasts lividly spotted. They made vivid color against the green of the hill and they drifted in the quivering air, raising a head now and then to see her as she passed. She sang loud in the face of the cattle as they stood on their up-sloping pasture.

> Liddy Marget died like it might be today,
> Like it might be today, like it might be today,
> And he saw the bones of a thousand men.

"Saw the bones of a thousand men. Saw with his eyes, that is. I thought till just now when I studied about it he sawed the bones with a saw. Sawed the bones of a thousand men. I saw that-there man there a-sawen with a big saw and bone saw-dust a-siften down. I'm a fool for sure."

In the enclosure beyond the pasture of the black-and-white cows she came to a tobacco field, a struggling crop unevenly growing on worn-out soil. She sat on the fence and marveled at the ill-conditioned plants, jeering at them.

"Gosh, what a crop! Durned if I ever see such runty trash a-growen in a field. What you call yourself nohow? Sallet?"

She inspected the tobacco for worms, a habitual action, as she passed down a row. Struggling clover grew between the drills and wild grass inched out from the fencerow.

Beyond the tobacco field she saw that there was a graveyard set beside an old church. She came upon it from the rear, walking down a path through brush tangles, and when she had climbed a high rail fence she stood among the abandoned graves. She parted the growth and twisted her body through the brush snarls until she came to the part that was grassy and well kept, some of the mounds adorned with blossoming flowers. There were no trees and thus the graves and the gravestones were open to the sun and were blown over by the wind. The sun came down more freely here than in the fields for it had the stones to play over, white and shining marble. The wind swayed the grass and the sun vibrated over the white monuments. "Erected to the Memory of," she read. "To the Memory of," or some held simply the legend of a family name, as Wakefield, in large stiff letters blocked out of the stone. On one a high winged creature stood holding a lily and a book.

"How would you buy a tombstone, now?" her mind chattered within itself. "Would you go to the store and say . . . But it would have to be some other kind of store beside Kelly's at the road corners. Say it's a tombstone store somewheres, and say he has a sign out, 'Tombstones cheap today.' You go inside the store and there the tombstones are all up and down the big counters, counters made big on purpose, and on the big shelves. You say to the man, 'I want to buy a tombstone' and he says, 'Would you like one that says "To the memory of" or would you rather have "Erected to?" Here's one that you can have cheap if you taken it offen my hands today. It's nicked a little at the corner and it says "Pray for the soul of" and that's not the latest style. But if you don't care so much about style and if you want something that'll wear you long, you'll never be sorry for a-buyen this-here one.'"

She laughed a little at the thought and walked about in the swaying grass and felt the hot waves of air as they rolled back off the large marbles. She came to a tall stone marked Gowan. It glittered in the sun where the small flecks like fine silver lay under the surface that shone in some places like glass. She read the legend slowly:

JAMES BARTHOLOMEW GOWAN
Born August 3, 1839
Departed this life May 17, 1906
An honored citizen, a faithful husband, a loving father, a true Christian. . . . Five times elected judge of the Country Court. . . . Fulfilling all trusts with . . .

"That's Judge Gowan," she whispered, awed by the personality erected by the legend against the tall stone. "He owned the Gowan farm and the Gowan horses and the Gowan peacocks . . . across the road from Mr. Al's place . . . and he left Miss Anne, his wife, all he had when he died, and people a-goen to law about it big in court. And when he died there was marchen and white plumes on hats and a band a-playen, and his picture is a-hangen up in the courthouse, life-size, they say. . . . And when he was a-liven he used to ride up to town in a high buggy with a big shiny horse, a-steppen up the road and him a-sitten big, and always had a plenty to eat and a suit of clothes to wear and a nigger to shine his shoes for him of a weekday even. Ben told me. And he was a-willen money big to his wife when he died and always a-sitten judge in court. A big man, he was. That's you." Her voice was whispering the words. And then after a long pause she added. "He's Judge Gowan in court, a-sitten big, but I'm better'n he is. I'm a-liven and he's dead. I'm better. I'm Ellen Chesser and I'm a-liven and you're Judge James Bartholomew Gowan, but all the same I'm better. I'm a-liven."

The sun came down white on the gravestones and beat back upon the hot air. The wind blew down from the west field and bent the grass. Ellen's eyes shone brighter when a new memory came to her mind. She lifted her head suddenly and her sunbonnet fell back, swept off by the breeze. She was calling aloud now, her shout growing into a song.

"Up in town on court day, it is, and a mighty big crowd is a-comen in the roads and horses are a-rampen up the street, and such a gang you can't stir withouten you watch where you go. And sheep a-bawlen and cows, and a man says loud and fast . . .

> *Fifteen fifteen who'll make it twenty*
> *Fifteen now come on with the twenty*
> *Who'll make it twenty*
> *Who'll make it twenty*
> *Fifteen now come on with the eighteen*
> *Fifteen fifteen*
> *Come on with the eighteen. . . .*

And bells a-ringen and banners go by and people with things in pokes to sell and apples a-rollen out on the ground and butter in buckets and lard to sell and pumpkins in a wagon, and sheep a-cryen and the calves a-cryen for their mammies, and little mules a-cryen for their horse mammies, and a big man comes to the courthouse door and sings out the loudest of all:

> *O yes! O yes!*
> *The honorable judge*

James Bartholomew Gowan
(It must 'a' been)
Is now a-sitten. . . .

That's just what he said, that man in the door of the courthouse that time.

O yes! O yes!
The honorable judge
James Bartholomew Gowan
Is now a-sitten . . .
Come all ye . . .
And you shall be heared.

"Powerful big county court today, they said. But I'm better'n he is. I'm better'n you. I'm a-liven and you ain't! I'm a-liven and you're dead! I'm better! I'm a-liven! I'm a-liven!"

"The Battle of Perryville"

Before she was a novelist, Roberts was a poet. "The Battle of Perryville" is about the pivotal battle of the Civil War in Kentucky. It was fought on October 8, 1862, in Roberts's hometown, fewer than twenty years before her birth. The scars were still there, and people remembered the day of carnage.

᭥

"They went by all day long," he said,
"From sun-up till the lamps were lit."
He leaned against an ellum tree
And looked far off to tell of it.

I stood beside him as he told
And tried to hear the feet of men.
I hushed my breath and stilled my thought
To hear the armies march again.

He said, "They went along this street,
Men marching east along the road.
All day long I saw them go . . .
Our men," he said.

"And on the next day other men
Came up the pike, a more than those.
'Twas such another day as this,
October, it was."

I laid my finger on the bark
Beside him . . . I looked up to see.
His face was bent and turned to tears.
I plucked at the ellum tree.

"The Butterbean Tent"

Roberts also wrote delightful lighter poems. "Butterbeans" is what she called them
when she enclosed copies in letters to friends. In many of them she recalls incidents
of her girlhood in Springfield. "The Butterbean Tent" is a poem about children for
children and adults.

All through the garden I went and went,
And I walked in under the butterbean tent.

The poles leaned up like a good tepee
And made a nice little house for me.

I had a hard brown clod for a seat,
And all outside was a cool green street.

A little green worm and a butterfly
And a cricket-like thing that could hop went by.

Hidden away there were flocks and flocks
Of bugs that could go like little clocks.

Such a good day it was when I spent
A long, long while in the butterbean tent.

Caroline Gordon

"All Lovers Love the Spring"

Caroline Gordon was born in 1895 in Todd County. She was homeschooled by her father, and she then attended his school for boys in nearby Clarksville, Tennessee. After graduating from Bethany College in West Virginia, she taught school for several years before becoming a critic for a newspaper in Chattanooga. Through her family friend Robert Penn Warren she met members of the literary movement "The Fugitives" at Vanderbilt University. These included her fellow Kentuckian Allen Tate, whom she married in 1924 and divorced in 1959. Her first novel was *Penhally* (1931), in which she follows a Kentucky family like her own through several generations, from the antebellum period through the Civil War and Reconstruction and into the early twentieth century. Another novel, *Aleck Maury, Sportsman* (1934), is based on her father, who preferred the agrarian days of the preindustrial Old South. One of her expertly crafted short stories is "All Lovers Love the Spring," a dramatic monologue by an unmarried lady who, like the author, is a member of one of the town's first families. Her straightforward, unsentimental delivery reveals a woman who somehow failed to live her life fully.

My third cousin, Roger Tredwell, is the president of the First National Bank in our town, Fuqua, Kentucky. He is also president of the Chamber of Commerce and permanent treasurer of the Community Chest and chairman of the board of directors of the hospital. People say that if you want anything done for the community you turn it over to the busiest man in town. I imagine Roger serves on a lot of other committees I never even heard of. I don't belong to any more organizations than I can help, but, after all, my family has lived here ever since there was a town and there are some things you can't get out of. I won't have anything to do with Kiwanis or Rotary but I serve on the women's auxiliary to the hospital and I'm a member of the Y.W.C.A. board and chairman of the board of the Florence Crittenden Home. Some people think they ought to have a married woman for that and I always say that anybody that wants the job can have it but I notice nobody ever takes me up on it.

Nowadays if as many as six women—or men—form an organization they have got to have a dinner at least once a year. Minnie Mayhew, who runs the Women's Club, caters for ours and always serves green peas, no matter what time of year it is. I often sit next to Roger at these dinners. He is the most prominent man in town and, after all, I am a Fuqua—have been one for forty-two years. There are some of my stocks never came back after the Depression; I always wear the same dress to these dinners: a black crepe de chine, with narrow white piping on neck and sleeves. It was a good dress when I bought it and it still fits perfectly but I never looked well in black.

Roger's wife says she is sure he wears out more white shirts and black ties than any man in town. He has taken on weight since he got middle-aged, and the Tredwells turn bald early. When a man gets those little red veins in his cheeks and his neck gets thick, so that it spreads out over his collar, there is something about a dinner jacket that makes him look like a carp. Or, as my father used to say, a grinnell. He was quite a learned man but always preferred to use the local name for a thing instead of the one you get out of the encyclopedia.

When I was thirteen years old my father got tired of living in town and moved back to the old Fuqua homestead on the Mercersville pike. The government set fire to the house the other day, after it bought a hundred and thirty thousand acres of land on the Mercersville pike for an army camp. But in those days it was still standing. Rather a handsome old brick house, set back from the road in a grove of silver poplars. When we went there to live tenants had been farming the place for twenty years. The yard was grown up in dog fennel as high as your waist and silver poplars had sprung up everywhere. They are like banyan trees; you have one poplar and a hundred shoots will spring up around it. The underside of the poplar leaf is white, like cotton, and shines. In the least little breeze all those leaves will turn and show their undersides. It's easy to see why you call them "silver poplars."

A perfect thicket of silver poplars had come up right back of the house but in amongst them were trees that had been grown when my father was a boy. There was one big tree that we children called "ours." It had four branches sticking up like the fingers on a hand, and one stout branch that had been half lopped off was the thumb. Each of us Fuquas claimed a finger for our special seat; Roger Tredwell, who was fifteen years old then and used to come out from town and spend every weekend with us, claimed the thumb.

The boys got hold of some old planks and built a platform high up in the branches of that tree. Then they made walls to it and we called it our "tree house." We used to haul up "supplies" in a bucket tied on to a rope. Joe—he was eight years old—was the one that had to sneak ginger cakes and cold biscuits and ham away from the cook to put in the bucket. The older boys, Tom and Ed, did most of the carpentering for the house but it was Roger's idea. He got tired of it, though, as soon as it was finished and never wanted to just play in it but was always adding something. Like the pulleys that went from that tree to a big maple. There were four wires stretched tight, and five things that looked like saddles slipped along on them, pads made out of tow sacks. You were supposed to hold on to them and swing over to the sugar tree. But the wires were stretched too tight or something and the whole thing broke the first time we tried it.

Roger was never disappointed or upset when anything like that happened but just went on to some other idea he had had in the back of his mind all the time. I don't believe he came out a single time that year that he didn't have some perfectly splendid idea, like nailing tobacco sticks onto mallets and playing croquet from horseback—I couldn't help laughing the first time I saw a polo game, thinking about me up on Old Eagle, trying to send the blue ball through the wicket!

Tom was fifteen that summer and Roger was almost sixteen, that tall, lean kind of boy; it was hard to imagine that he could ever get fat. They never paid much attention to me unless they needed me, for something like starter in the chariot races or, when we were younger, to help make up Robin Hood's band. Roger was always Robin, of course, and Tom was Little John. I had to be Allan-a-Dale. I remember their telling me he was the only one of the band that knew how to write his name. I had to be Chingachgook, too. I forget what excuse they gave for foisting him off on me.

But unless they needed me real bad they didn't want me along and when they started out for the stable would pretend they were going to see a man about a dog or even that some animal was being bred out in the stable lot, to keep me in the house. Every Friday night before I went to sleep I used to make up my mind that I wouldn't have anything to do with them, but when Saturday morning came I'd get out and follow them, far enough behind so that they wouldn't notice, pretending I was playing something by myself. Do you remember that when you were a child there were some people you couldn't stay away from because it seemed like there wasn't any use in being anywhere else?

I went off to school when I was sixteen, to Bardstown Academy, where Mama went. Roger went to Webb. He asked me for a date the first night he got home. It was a lawn party at the Harpers'. Mrs. Harper was the kind that like to play charades and was always asking the young people why they didn't get up a play. That night they had Japanese lanterns strung between the trees, and in the back yard Eleanor Harper was a witch, telling fortunes in a little hut made all of green boughs. But there weren't very many young people there. For some reason they didn't much like to go to the Harpers'. Maybe they were afraid Mrs. Harper would make them get up and dance the Virginia reel. I had on a blue dress that had white eyelets worked in the ruffles and I had had a big fuss with Mama before I left home. She thought that I ought to get in by eleven o'clock at the latest. But we got home by ten-thirty.

Roger was the one who suggested going, said he didn't like peach ice cream and we could stop by Shorty Raymond's and get a sandwich and a Coke on the way home. I knew I ought not to go inside a place like Shorty Raymond's at that time of night, but the Negro boy brought a tray out and we had a sandwich apiece and Roger had a Coke and I had an orangeade.

ᥩᥩ᠎ ᥩᥩ᠎ ᥩᥩ᠎

The next night Esther Morrison had a party for a girl that was visiting her from Paducah. . . . I was never specially pretty when I was young, but there were two or three men wanted to marry me. I see them around town now, and I can't say I ever passed one of them on the street and felt I'd made a mistake when I didn't take him. . . . Mamie Tredwell—Mamie Reynolds she was when she came to visit Esther—was a heap prettier at seventeen than she is at forty-three. She had the prettiest skin I ever saw on anybody except a baby, and that soft, brown hair that has a natural wave in it and can't fall any way that isn't graceful. But her eyes were always too wide apart and had that tiresome look in them, and she had that habit then that she has now of starting out to tell you something and taking in the whole universe. I have to go to dinner there once or twice a year and I always dread it. The other night I was there and she was telling me about old Mr. Wainwright falling off the roof when he was trying to fix his gutter and she got off on the guttering that new tinsmith did for them—it wasn't satisfactory and they had to have Roberts and Maxwell rip it all off and put it up again. "What was I saying?" she asked me when she got to how much it cost them; money's one thing that'll always bring her up short. "I don't know," I said, "but I've already heard what Mr. Wainwright said when he hit the ground: 'Ain't it just my luck? To fall off the roof and not break but one leg!'" He's a happy old soul. I always liked him.

Mama will be eighty-three this March. She's not as independent as she was a few years ago. Breaking her hip seemed to take all the spirit out of her. She wants to be read to a lot and she's crazy to know everything that's going on. I went to the post office the other day and when I got back I told her that I hadn't passed a soul but three boys shooting craps, and didn't talk to any-body but a bullfrog that was sitting in a puddle, and all he had to say was that things had come to a pretty pass. . . . Mama says that I don't take after her people, that I'm all Fuqua.

They say a person ought to have a hobby. I always thought that was all foolishness, until last fall, when my niece, Cora, came to visit and left that mushroom book behind. It cost twenty dollars—and no wonder. The illus-trations are something to look at, in beautiful colors, and some of the mush-rooms have the most extraordinary shapes. Like one that's called a Bear's Head Mushroom that grows out of the trunk of a tree and has white, spiny hairs that look like a polar bear's fur hanging down, and inside is all white and soft, like marshmallow. I started hunting for that one first because Cora told me it was good to eat.

The folks in town all say that I'm going to poison myself, of course, but I don't pay any attention. In our climate there's some mushroom that you can hunt almost every day of the year. But, of course, when the earth gets steamy and hot in the spring is the best time. I start in April—you can find the sponge mushroom then—and go every day I can get a little Negro girl to sit with Mama.

Yesterday I was out in the Hickman woods, about three miles from town. There is a swampy place in those woods where things come out earlier than anywhere else. The honeysuckle vines go up to the tops of the trees. Sometimes a vine will climb out to the end of a limb and then hang down in a great spray. I had to push a lot of those sprays aside before I got in there. But I was glad I went. On a mound of earth, in that black, swampy water, a tame pear tree was in bloom. An apple tree will bend to one side or fall if you don't prop it up, and peach trees don't care which way their boughs go, but pear branches rise up like wands. Most of the blossoms hadn't unfolded yet; the petals looked like seashells. I stood under the tree and watched all those festoons of little shells floating up over my head, up, up, up into the bluest sky I've ever seen, and wished that I didn't have to go home. Mama's room always smells of camphor. You notice it after you've been out in the fresh air.

Ben Lucien Burman

"Cumberland Justice," from *It's a Big Country: America off the Highways*

Ben Lucien Burman was born in 1895 in Covington, Kentucky, just across the Ohio River from Cincinnati. He was a traveler and an adventurer and seemed to live more than one life. In his eighty-eight years he wrote twenty-two books, most of them based on his love for rivers and his travels around the world. During World War II he covered the Free French forces in Africa; that experience resulted in *Miracle on the Congo* and his being awarded the French Legion of Honor. Late in his career he began a hugely popular series of children's books set in Catfish Bend, a mythical spot on the lower Mississippi River inhabited by such talking animals as Doc Raccoon and Judge Black, a vegetarian blacksnake. Several of his books were made into films, including *Mississippi* and *Steamboat Round the Bend,* which starred Will Rogers. The book that is closest to his Kentucky roots is *The Four Lives of Mundy Tolliver* (1953), which features a mountain protagonist from Coal Creek, Kentucky, who has just been released from the service after World War II and is hitchhiking in the Deep South in search of maturity, love, and happiness. About a year before Burman died (in New York in 1984), I received a card he'd sent me from Brazil, where he had been living with a tribe of headhunters. It read, "Getting marvelous material for a new Catfish Bend book here in the Amazon jungle, the most exciting place I've struck since the Congo in 1941." "Cumberland Justice" is a seriocomic vignette about how justice was served, home-style, in the Kentucky mountains of yore.

"It's what you call mountain justice," said Judge Honey.

We were sitting in his court at the little town of Manchester, deep in the Kentucky Cumberlands. Every American has his own picture of the Kentucky mountains. It is usually a comic strip idea of a rural people who are among America's finest citizens. But nothing is known to the world outside of what is perhaps the most remarkable feature of the mountain culture—the methods of the mountain judges as they sit on their worn benches, and the execution of the mountain law.

An officer who was at once the Manchester police chief and the entire police force came into the little courtroom with an overalled farmer in tow.

Judge Honey studied the newcomer a moment. He spoke with deep regret. "Honey. I hate to do this to you. But you been drunk. It'll be twelve fifty, honey."

The farmer grew troubled. His lean hands searched in vain through his pockets. "Judge, looks like I sure ain't got no money. Kin I pay you after I sell my tobacco?"

Judge Honey became thoughtful. He had earned the nick-name from his habit of addressing any offender before him by this term of affection on the theory that it made the punishment easier to bear. "Be all right with me, honey. But the city council's kind of hard right now about money. I got to have something stronger than after the tobacco, honey."

The police chief stepped forward as though to take the prisoner back to jail.

The farmer's voice choked with emotion. "That tobacco's sure going to rot if I git locked up again, Judge. And it's the prettiest patch of tobacco between here and Lexington."

Judge Honey shifted his stoutish body in his chair and looked out the window. The courtroom was on the second floor. Below us the life of the little town flowed steadily past, the coal trucks rumbling in from a near-by mineshaft with a blackened miner sitting beside the driver, the jeeps crowded with mountain families come to do their shopping, the occasional hillman on horseback.

Judge Honey turned to the prisoner again. "If I let you go out in town and talk to people, you think you can get some body who'll go on your bond for the $12.50?"

The farmer brightened. "I figure maybe I kin, Judge."

"All right. You do it, honey. I know what it is to have nice tobacco."

I watched the farmer go down the stairs and thought how letting a prisoner wander off to find his own bond would have horrified a jurist in a city court where often an accused man is not even allowed to use the telephone.

In fifteen minutes the prisoner was back with a friend to guarantee his fine and was free.

The court ended. I took my car and spent the day driving across the hazy ridges. More huge coal trucks lumbered along the roads where I had once ridden muleback, and expensive automobiles constantly raced past. But now and then a log cabin was visible, where tall mountain women went about their household chores and gaunt hillmen toiled in the sloping fields beyond, as they had toiled a hundred years before.

I stopped to see a sheriff I knew in a drowsy little village, and waited while a mountaineer in from a distant hollow came to discuss some property up for auction. The visitor was about to leave when the sheriff spoke to him amiably. "Mace, I just heard Will Scoggins shot a fellow up the creek this morning. Stop in at his cabin on your way back home and tell him I want to see him tomorrow, will you? And tell him to bring some clothes 'cause he's got to stay in jail for a while."

I drove on to Hyden, seat of Leslie County. I mounted the stairs of the weatherbeaten courthouse, and passing through the crowd of tobacco-chewing loungers gathered at the entrance, found Judge Begley, a dark, reserved man with thoughtful eyes that seemed always to be gazing at the distant hills. I sat in his office and watched the troubled procession moving in and out his door, an anxious mountaineer charged with moonshining, a pale youth accused of stealing a neighbor's hunting hound, a stern-eyed farmer charged with toting a pistol. As I watched and listened I realized the difficulties and perils of being a judge in this hill country, where in the remoter areas the ancient violence still lies close to the surface.

More than once a dangerous killer has been terrorizing some far-off valley, with no deputy available to make the arrest. Judge Begley has taken a horse, and riding alone to the murderer's cabin, has brought him back singlehanded, just as his forebears had done when Kentucky was the American frontier.

But the older customs continue in less perilous ways as well.

"Tell him about the dog trial, Judge," a genial hillman prompted.

Judge Begley's dark face lighted with the humor rarely absent in a jurist of the hills. "We try dogs here same as people," he explained. "Try 'em for killing sheep. Have lawyers for the state and lawyers for the defense and giving bond and juries. Just like a trial for murder. Have alibis, too, with a family and friends talking for hours to prove the dog not guilty. All the time, they say, he was five miles off, sleeping in his owner's cabin. But once in a while they find wool in his teeth. Then it isn't easy."

He stopped a moment to give a legal document to a passing deputy. "Had four dogs on trial a while ago. The farmers swore they killed some lambs and showed some tooth-wool they said proved it. Jury let three dogs go but sentenced the other to death by shooting. A beautiful young dog with big eyes like a deer, wasn't much more than a puppy. The evidence was pretty bad, and I didn't think he was guilty. So I put him on probation and ordered him out of the county. He's over in Clay County now. They say he's doing fine."

I returned to Manchester toward evening and sat in the pleasant little Royal Hotel. The streets were quieter now. The rumble of the coal trucks had ceased. Only in the bus cafe opposite a juke box was blaring, now playing a mournful mountain hymn, now some hit tune from distant Broadway. I had supper and walked up the steep hill that led to the Manchester jail. As I climbed by easy stages in the darkness I thought of the other mountain jails I knew, where like the courts all stiffness was lacking. In these little prisons where arrested men await trial or serve minor sentences there was none of the gloom, the mechanized grimness of a penitentiary. Most of the prisoners had been the jailer's friends since childhood. Any thought of brutality was impossible. I had often met a jailer who would not hesitate to let his charges go home for a night when there was a baby coming. I knew one, who when an inmate's father lay desperately ill with no relative at hand to aid him, permitted the prisoner to spend every night at the sick man's bedside on only one condition: he must return by court time in the morning to learn if he was to go on trial that day.

I saw a light in the barred building behind the courthouse and knocked loudly on the iron gate. As I waited for someone to open I could see figures upstairs moving behind a grating; I could hear a harmonica playing gaily. A moment later the jailer appeared, a towering Western-looking figure known as Cowboy, who had campaigned for his office on horseback, dressed in full cattle-punching regalia.

The gate swung open and he led me into his gray-walled office. We sat talking of his prisoners. Upstairs there came always the sound of tapping feet, following the rhythmic beat of the musician.

"I treat 'em right and they treat me right," said Cowboy. "Once in a while they'll do you wrong. But ain't often. This Jail's so old you can cut your way out quicker than a raccoon chews through a egg crate, and about a year back a fellow they called Black Jack sawed some bars and ran away. I went down the creek where his family was living. 'It ain't right the way Black Jack did me, Ace,' I told his brother. 'I gave him plenty of privileges and now he's run off like that it's going to hurt my reputation bad.'

"The brother didn't answer for a minute. 'Guess he didn't think nothing about that, Cowboy,' he said. 'I'm going out in the woods where he's hiding and tell him right away.'

"When I get up next morning Black Jack's sitting on the jail step. He was mighty sorry."

In the barred room upstairs the merry playing of the harmonica grew louder, then became a mournful blues.

Cowboy listened with approval. "Like to hear a harmonica or a fiddle going," he declared. "Never had trouble yet with a fellow that plays music."

He went out the door a moment.

A grizzled prisoner who had come in with a pile of supper dishes gazed after him with affection. "I been in jails all over," he told me. "From New Orleans to Chicago. You can't beat Cowboy nowhere for running a jail."

I glanced through the weekly newspaper lying on a table and found an advertisement of a rival seeking Cowboy's office at the next election. His platform read crisply: "If elected meals served to anyone confined will be the same as I have at my table. If you elect me you will not be sorry."

I stayed in the hills visiting many courts and sheriffs and jailers. I found always the same humanity and the lack of legal rigidity. In the lower courts some of the informality arises from the fact that the older judges rarely have been lawyers. They are simple citizens, often lacking even an eighth-grade education, but possessed of a deep native wisdom; like the old tribal leaders they have been chosen by their fellows to arbitrate their quarrels. Their favorite law-book is the Bible; their Supreme Court right and wrong.

I strolled over toward Judge Honey's court again, and climbed the worn steps to the courtroom. The little chamber was crowded and the air thick with tobacco smoke. Judge Honey tried each case with a generous admixture of wisdom and philosophy, varied now and then by an occasional recitation from McGuffey's *Reader* apt to the occasion.

The court business slackened. The judge began to sing a favorite hymn of the hills, *Amazing Grace*. Those present joined him. "A judge I knew when I was young used to open his court with hymn singing," said Judge Honey. "He always asked me to start 'em going."

The police chief came in with a farmer who could not read or write.

The judge let him off with a warning. He leaned over to me. "What we know is what we'll be tried for. I make the punishment fit the education. If a man don't know any better, I'm going to be easy on him. But if he's got plenty of learning, I'm going to make it twice as hard."

His round face grew sad. "My own son was standing here once. Wasn't much he did and I reckon if he'd been somebody else's boy I'd have let him go free. But he had learning and everything I could give him. So I fined him twenty-nine dollars."

I saw a pistol just taken from a prisoner and spoke of the hazards of being a hill-country officer.

Judge Honey sorted some letters. "If a man has a gun pointing at you saying he'll shoot, you needn't do any worrying. He's passed the time for shooting and he'll never pull the trigger. Time to look out is before he's got the gun pointing."

"Talking about judges, brother, you should have knowed a old judge we had here," declared a black-bearded visitor sitting before the bench. "He was sorry one time for a pretty woman in court didn't have nobody to go her bond, so the judge went it himself. And then one night he heard she'd skipped out to Hyden and wasn't ever coming back. Old Judge got hot as a turkey that's ate a quart of red pepper and jumped on his horse and rode off in the dark to get her. It was pretty near cockcrow when he got there and 'course she was dead asleep. But Judge was so mad he didn't wait for nothing. He jerked her out of bed, and sat her on the horse beside him, and locked her up in the Manchester jail with his own hands."

"Had another judge, Lew Lewis, used to be a card," put in Judge Honey.

"Judge Lew was talking to the Grand Jury, making indictments, and he said to 'em, 'If you see a fellow going down the road leading a hound dog and carrying a banjo or a guitar, indict him. 'Cause if he ain't done nothing yet, he sure is going to.'"

"What about Judge Lew and that awful tough fellow named Big Harm they had over in Leslie County?" remarked the bearded man, aiming expertly at a cuspidor. "Big Harm was going all around Hyden saying he was going to kill three men was just about the top fellows in town. Judge Lew didn't want none of them three to get hurt, and he knew the sheriffs couldn't handle Big Harm when he got drunk and started shooting. So instead of trying anything with Big Harm he put the three other fellows under a peace bond to keep out of his way."

A stout country woman from far back in the hills bustled into the room, breathless from climbing the stairs. "My sister Goldie ain't coming in today with her boy way you told her to, Judge," she panted. "She was going to get a tooth pulled the same time and when she looked at the almanac she seen this week the signs is in the legs and it'd bleed mighty bad. She says she'll come in next week when the signs is in the back."

I strolled around the town and listened to an old blind ballad singer droning away the verses of *Wild Bill Jones* as he accompanied himself on a cracked guitar. I climbed the hill again to the county courthouse. It was a quiet morning and only a few mountaineers were present in the bleak courtroom. The serious judge on the bench called the name of a defendant. The man failed to appear and by ordinary procedure his bond would have been instantly forfeited. But not by the code of the mountains.

"Guess he's getting in his corn, Judge," a clerk explained. "Been raining hard and today's first chance he's had to get to it."

The judge agreed and postponed the case until the crop was harvested.

The city dweller may be born and die without ever seeing a courtroom. It is a rare mountaineer who has never attended a trial, often as witness or direct participant. For along with the hillman's individuality goes a fierce and lasting stubbornness; he lands in court over a trifle. I have seen two mountain families spend every penny they had managed to save from the earnings of their pathetic farms in an argument over a skinny hog worth almost nothing. "It ain't the pig, it's the principle," the stern chief of one of the warring clans told me. Their interest is great in any trial, even where they have no personal concern; going to court is a break in their lonely lives, as city people go to the movies.

As I continued to ride up the rocky creeks and hollows, I constantly came on some new picturesque character. I found a deeply religious judge who if a man is arrested on Saturday night will release him on Sunday morning to attend church unescorted. Not a single prisoner has run away in the many years of his judgeship. Though one case came to an odd conclusion.

A sleepy-eyed hillman from a distant valley was asked by the jurist as usual if he cared to go to Sunday worship.

The prisoner looked at him with skepticism. "I sure do, Judge. But why you figuring I'll come back?"

"I ain't worrying," countered the judge.

The prisoner went off to church and returned to jail promptly with his fellows. But that night he broke some bars from a cell window and fled. For he was no longer on his honor.

It is this sense of honor which is perhaps the mountaineer's most remarkable quality. No matter how hardened a criminal a hillman may be, his promise once given will never be broken.

I was sitting one day at the window of the Royal Hotel with a mountain attorney. Outside in the street a hill family of three rode slowly past, all mounted on the back of a single muddy horse, as they might have ridden in the days of the earliest settlers; in the bus cafe the juke box blared the strident tones of the latest rhumba.

"I know a queer story about a man making a promise," the attorney remarked. "He made it fifty years ago. Now we wish we could get him to break it."

His fingers idly folded a newspaper lying on the window sill. "You know the man I mean. You met him on your jeep trip yesterday. A fine old mountaineer. Call him Pappy John." He pushed the paper away. "Back around 1900, Pappy was a young fellow feeling gay, with a new pistol and a new suit of clothes and a fine horse to take him in to town. Well, he drank a little when he got there and then he drank some more. And pretty soon he was shooting out windows in the schoolhouse, and then he woke up in jail. 'Judge, I done wrong,' he said when they brought him to the courtroom. 'If you let me go home, I'll make you a promise. I'll never set foot in Manchester again, if I live to be a hundred years.'"

The attorney called a greeting to a breezy traveling salesman just come into the hotel lobby. "That was over fifty years ago, and a lot of things have happened. The judge died a long time back and Pappy John's up in his seventies. He's different now than when he was a boy. One of the smartest men in the mountains. Asks all the time what's going on in Manchester, and his eyes shine when he talks about coming in, and seeing his first picture show and all the cars and new buildings. But he gave his word he'd stay away and nothing on earth can shake him. If you pass in a jeep he'll ride with you right to the edge of town, and then he'll jump out and go home. I talked to him once, and when he wouldn't listen, got the judge's son to see what he could do. The son told Pappy John that the judge would have released him from the promise long ago, and that he, the son, was releasing him now.

"But the old man still wouldn't pay any attention. 'Ain't nobody can free me now excepting the Lord,' he answered. 'And when Him and me meet, He's going to have plenty of other things to talk about besides going to Manchester.'"

Some other legal friends came in to join us. They were fascinating to watch, these mountain lawyers, dry, humorous, educated, capable of matching wits with their fellows anywhere, yet never having lost their simple touch or the deep understanding of their people. There was the usual banter of attorneys, the stories of mountain old timers with two sets of fees, one for simply taking a case, the other a double fee for also supplying the evidence. There were jovial remarks how the best mountain lawyer is not the one who knows the law, but the one who knows how to pick a jury: "Hang the jury, not the man" is his favorite motto.

"Talking about juries," drawled a lanky attorney known as Pleaz, famous throughout the hills. "A funny one happened in Owsley county. Man was on trial for being drunk and the judge couldn't find an unprejudiced jury. Fellow had too many friends and too many people didn't like him, and after combing the town there was only one man left said he was neutral. So the judge decided on a one-man jury. The trial ended and the judge sent off the jury to consider its verdict. An hour went by without any word and the judge told a clerk to go see what was happening. The thirteen jurymen all rolled into one sent a message in a hurry. 'We ain't decided, Judge.' The judge kept sending new messengers every hour, and always got the same answer. Finally about midnight he was pretty mad and went off to the jury room to see for himself. The fellow was sitting there, looking worried. 'Judge, I was just coming to tell you,' he said. 'The jury can't agree.'"

They discussed how the informality of mountain law continues to the final stages, even when a prisoner has been sentenced and is on his way to the state penitentiary.

A gentle-mannered individual who had come in with the others and whom I knew to be a noted ex-sheriff, spoke up quietly. His voice and looks gave him the air of a kindly preacher instead of one who had captured some of the most desperate killers in the hills. "Never used a handcuff all my life," he said. "And never once had a fellow that ran off. Fact is, it was just the other way. Had a man here they called Easy Joe killed somebody and the judge sentenced him to Frankfort Pen for life. I had five other prisoners to go down the same time with him and if I took 'em all they'd have packed my car mighty tight. Easy Joe stood there looking a minute. 'Sheriff, I sure hate to crowd you,' he said. 'My brother's driving down to Frankfort today to see a fellow. How about my going along with him to the Walls?'

"'All right, Joe,' I answered. 'You go on down with him. If you get there before I do, just wait till I come.'

"His brother's car was faster than mine. When I got there he was standing out in front of the gate."

The sheriff smiled in reminiscence. "Had another murderer once. A fellow we nicknamed Possum Tom. Judge gave him life, like the other. I was taking him to the Pen on the train and we had to change trains at Corbin. I left him down at the end of the platform so I could go off and buy our tickets. 'You wait right here, Possum,' I told him. 'I figure I'll be gone just about five minutes.' But there were a lot of people at the window and there was some kind of mixup, so it was over half an hour before I was through. When I got near the end of the platform again, I saw Possum pacing up and down, looking mighty nervous. His face lit up like the break of day when he saw me. 'Golly, where you been all this time, Sheriff?' he said. 'You sure had me worried you wasn't coming back.'"

My guests left soon after and I strolled over to Judge Honey's court for a final visit before my departure. The police force of one was bringing forward an awkward, burly man who was a stranger to the area.

Judge Honey studied the prisoner. "What you been doing, honey?"

The burly man shifted uneasily. "Had some liquor on me I bought in Louisville, Judge. I'm sure sorry."

The police force produced a pint flask of bonded whiskey.

The judge leaned forward in his chair. "Was the top broken open?"

The police force examined the cork with care. "It was fixing to be broke."

Judge Honey shook his round head. "Fixing to be broke ain't broken."

He remained silent a moment, then studied the prisoner again. "Let me see your hands, honey," he demanded.

The other obeyed in wonder.

The judge examined the toil-calloused palms. "You're a hardworking man all right, honey." He turned to the police chief. "Let him go."

I made my farewells and packed my car to leave the mountains. In the square, muddy jeeps rattled past and tall mountain men stood chewing tobacco. The mail carrier, astride a shiny black horse, clattered noisily down the road on his way to the dark hills.

I drove past the courthouse. From Cowboy's jail came the sound of a harmonica, playing merrily.

Harriette Simpson Arnow
from *The Dollmaker*

Harriette Simpson Arnow was a little woman who wrote a very big book, *The Dollmaker,* a classic of Kentucky writing and of American writing. When I met her some thirty years ago, I was astounded that such a modest and unpretentious woman had created one of the strongest and most enduring characters in American fiction. Indeed, Gertie Nevels is a woman who can commandeer a military car to take her ailing son Amos to a doctor and then, before they can get under way, perform a lifesaving tracheotomy on him using a pocket knife. It is Gertie's love of the Kentucky land, where she has lived her entire life, that strengthens her to do whatever is necessary. It is a gift that she will have as long as she stays close to the land. Significantly, *The Dollmaker* takes place during World War II, when many mountain families moved to industrial cities to do war work. Gertie's family is eventually uprooted in a migration north to Detroit.

Arnow was born in Wayne County in 1908 and grew up in Burnside and in Lee County, where her father worked in the oil fields. She attended Berea College and the University of Louisville, from which she graduated in 1930. She taught school for several years and then worked as a waitress in Cincinnati while she wrote and published short stories. After marrying the journalist Harold Arnow, she lived in Detroit and in Ann Arbor until her death in 1986.

Dock's shoes on the rocks up the hill and his heavy breathing had shut out all sound so that it seemed a long while she had heard nothing, and Amos lay too still, not clawing at the blanket as when they had started. They reached the ridge top where the road ran through scrub pine in sand, and while the mule's shoes were soft on the thick needles she bent her head low over the long bundle across the saddle horn, listening. Almost at once she straightened, and kicked the already sweat-soaked mule hard in the flanks until he broke into an awkward gallop. "I know you're tired, but it ain't much furder," she said in a low tight voice.

She rode on in silence, her big body hunched protectingly over the bundle. Now and then she glanced worriedly up at the sky, graying into the thick twilight of a rainy afternoon in October; but mostly her eyes, large, like the rest of her, and the deep, unshining gray of the rain-wet pine trunks, were fixed straight ahead of the mule's ears, as if by much looking she might help the weary animal pull the road past her with her eyes.

They reached the highway, stretching empty between the pines, silent, no sign of cars or people, as if it were not a road at all, but some lost island of asphalt coming from no place, going nowhere. The mule stopped, his ears flicking slowly back and forth as he considered the road. She kicked him again, explaining, "It's a road fer automobiles; we'll have to ride it to stop a car, then you can git back home."

The mule tried to turn away from the strange black stuff, flung his head about, danced stiff-leggedly back into the familiar sanctuary of soft ground and pine trees. "No," the woman said, gripping his thin flanks with her long thighs, "no, you've got to git out in th middle so's we can stop a car a goen toward th doctor's. You've got to." She kicked him again, turned him about. He tried one weary, half-hearted bucking jump; but the woman only settled herself in the saddle, gripped with her thighs, her drawn-up knees, her heels. Her voice was half pleading, half scolding: "Now, Dock, you know you cain't buck me off, not even if you was fresh—an you ain't. So git on."

The great raw-boned mule argued with his ears, shook the bridle rein, side-stepped against a pine tree, but accepted soon the fact that the woman was master still, even on a strange road. He galloped again, down the middle of the asphalt that followed a high and narrow ridge and seemed at times like a road in the sky, the nothingness of fog-filled valleys far below on either side.

A car passed. Dock trembled at the sound, and side-stepped toward the edge, but the woman spoke gently and held him still. "It won't hurt you none. It's a car like th coal truck; we ain't a stoppen it. It's a goen th wrong way."

The mule, in spite of all the woman's urging, was slow in getting through his fright from the passing of the car. He fought continually to stay on the edge of the road, which was beginning to curve sharply and down so that little of it could be seen in either direction. The woman's head was bent again, listening above the bundle, when the mule plunged wildly toward the pines. She jerked hard on the bridle, so swiftly, so fiercely, that he whirled about, reared, came down, then took a hard, stiff-legged jump that landed him for an instant crosswise in the road.

The roar of a car's coming grew louder. Terrified by the strange sound, the unfamiliar road, and the strangeness of the woman's ways, the mule fought back toward the pines. The woman gripped with her legs, pulled with her hand, so that they seemed to do some wild but well rehearsed dance, round and round in the road, the mule rearing, flinging his head about, fighting to get it down so that he could buck.

She eased her hold an instant, jerked hard with all her strength. He reared but stayed in the road. Yellow fog lights, pale in the gray mists, washed over them, shone on the red sandy clay on one of the woman's shoes, a man's shoe with cleats holding leather thongs, pressed hard against the mule's lifted body as if it pointed to a place in the bridle mended with a piece of rawhide. It seemed a long time she sat so, the mule on his hind legs, the car lights washing over her, the child unshaken in the crook of her left arm while she talked to the mule in the same low urgent voice she had used to get him onto the highway: "Don't be afeared, Dock. They'll stop. We'll make em stop. They dasn't take these downhill curves too last. They'll have to stop. We'll all go over th bluff together."

There was a loud, insistent honking; brakes squealed and rubber squeaked while the fingers of light swept away from the woman and out into the fog above the valley. Then, as the car skidded, the lights crossed the woman again, went into the pines on the other side of the road, swept back, as the car, now only a few feet behind her but on the other side of the road, came out of its skid. The woman's voice was low, pressed down by some terrible urgency as she begged under the screaming of the horn, "Crosswise, crosswise; it'll git by us on t' other side."

She jerked, kicked the mule, until he, already crazed with fright, jumped almost directly in front of the car, forcing it to swerve again, this time so sharply that it went completely off the road. It plowed partway into a thicket of little pines, then stopped on the narrow sandy shoulder above the bluff edge. The woman looked once at the car, then away and past the trembling mule's ears; and though she looked down it was like searching the sky on a cloudy day. There was only fog, thickened in splotches, greenish above a pasture field, brownish over the corn far down in the valley below the tree tops by the bluff edge.

"You done good, real good," she whispered to the mule. Then all in one swift motion she swung one long leg over the mule's back, looped the bridle over the saddle horn, turned the dazed mule southward, slapping him on the shoulder. "Git," she said. She did not look after him as he leaped away, broken ribbons of foam flying down his chin, and blood oozing from a cut on his left hind leg where the car had grazed him.

She hurried the few steps along the bluff edge to the car as if afraid it would be off again; but her hand was reaching for the front door handle before the door opened slowly, cautiously, and a soldier, his head almost to her chin, got out. He stared up at her and did not answer when she begged all in a breath: "I've got tu have a lift. My little boy he's . . ."

The soldier was no longer looking at her. His eyes, blue, and with the unremembering look of a very old man's eyes, were fixed on the poplar tops rising above the bluff edge. He looked past them down into the valley, then slowly taking his glance away he reached for the handle of the back door, but dropped his hand when he saw that the window in the door was opening.

The woman turned to the down-dropping window and watched impatiently while first a hard and shiny soldier's cap rose above it, then a man's face, straight and neat and hard-appearing as the cap, but flushed now with surprise and anger. The mouth was hardly showing before it spoke, quickly, but with a flat, careful pronunciation of the words. "You realize you've run me off the road. If you can't manage a horse, don't ride one on the highway. Don't you know there's a war and this road carries . . ."

The woman had listened intently, watching the man's lips, her brows drawn somewhat together like one listening to a language only partly understood. "I know they's a war," she said, reaching for the door handle. "That's why th doctor closest home is gone. It was a mule," she went on. "I managed him. I had to make you stop. I've got to git my little boy to a doctor—quick." She had one foot inside the door, the child held now in her two hands as she prepared to lay him on the seat.

The man, plainly irritated because he had neglected to hold the door shut, continued to sit by it, his legs outspread, barring her way. His hand moved slowly, as if he wanted her to see it touch the pistol in a polished holster by his side, let the pistol speak to her more than his toneless, unruffled words when he said, "You must use other means of getting your child to the doctor." He reached swiftly, jerked the door so that she, bent as she was, and with the heavy bundle in her two hands, staggered. Her head flopped downward to his knees, but she righted herself and kept one foot in the door.

"If my business were not so urgent," he said, not taking his hand from the door, "I would have you arrested for sabotage. I travel from"—he hesitated—"an important place on urgent business." The voice still was not a man's voice, but the shiny cap, the bright leather, the pistol. It sharpened a little when he said, turning from her to the driver, "Get back into the car and drive on." He looked once at the bundle where one small sun-burned but blue-nailed hand waved aimlessly out of the blanket folds. Then, letting the door swing wide, he jerked it swiftly so that it struck hard against the woman's back, bent again as she searched for his eyes.

She straightened, put the hand under the blanket, but continued to stand between door and car. "I'm sorry you're th army; frum Oak Ridge, I reckon, but I'd a stopped you enyhow." Her voice was quiet as the voice below the cap. "You can shoot me now er give me an this youngen a lift to th closest doctor." And even in the man's work shoes, the long and shapeless coat, green-tinged with age, open, giving glimpses of a blue apron faded in strange squares as if it might have at one time been something else—a man's denim trousers or overall jumper—she held herself proudly, saying: "You want my name; I'm Gertie Nevels frum Ballew, Kentucky. Now, let me lay my little boy down. You cain't go . . ."

The officer had flung the door suddenly outward again. Still she did not fall when he banged it back against her, though in her attempts to keep from falling forward into the car and onto the child she dropped to her knees, her feet sliding through the gravel to the bluff edge. The officer gripped the pistol butt, and his voice shrilled a little as he said to the young soldier who had stood stiff and silent, staring at the woman: "Get in and drive on. She'll have to drop off then."

The other took his eyes from the blanket, still now. He saluted, said, "Yes, sir," but continued to stand, his body pressed against the car, his glance going again to the treetops below his feet.

"Back up on the road and drive on," the other repeated, his face reddening, his eyes determinedly fixed straight in front of him.

"Yes, sir?" the other said again, unmoving. There was in his questioning acceptance of the command some slight note of pleasure. He looked up at the tall woman as if he would share it with her. Their glances crossed, but the trouble, the urgency of her need would let nothing else come into her eyes.

She looked again at the other. "You want him to go over th bluff?" And her voice was weary to breaking, like an overwrought mother speaking to a stubborn child.

The older man for the first time looked past the woman and realized that what he had taken for a continuation of the brush and scrub pine was the tops of tall-growing trees below a bluff. He looked quickly away and began a rapid edging along the seat to the opposite door. It was only when he was out of the car and a few feet from the bluff edge that he was able to speak with the voice of polished leather and pistol handle, and command the other to back out.

The woman, as soon as the officer moved, had laid the child on the seat, then stood a moment by the door, watching the driver, shaking her head slowly, frowning as he raced the motor until the car shivered and the smoking rear wheels dug great holes in the sandy shoulder. "That'll do no good," she said, then more loudly, her voice lifted above the roaring motor, "Have you got a ax?"

He shook his head, smiling a little, then his eyes were blank, prim like his mouth when the other told him to turn off the motor. The woman picked up a large sandrock, dropped it behind one of the deeply sunken rear wheels. "Have you got a jack?" she asked the officer. "You could heist it up with a jack, git rocks under them wheels, an back up on th road."

"Take your child out of the car and get on," he said, his voice no longer smooth. "We may be stuck here until I can get a tow truck. You'll be arrested."

She glanced at him briefly, smoothed back her straight dark brown hair with a bended arm, then drawing the bottom of her apron into one hand to form a kind of sack, she began gathering rocks with the other hand, going in a quick squatting run, never straightening in her haste, never looking up.

The young soldier had by now got out of the car and stood by it, his back and shoulders very straight, his hands dropped by his sides so that a band of colored ribbon was bright on his dull uniform. The woman glanced curiously at it as she dumped a load of rocks by a wheel. The officer looked at him, and his voice was shrill, akin to an angry woman's. "Hatcher, you're not on the parade ground."

"Yes, sir," the other said, drawing himself up still more rigidly.

"Get out the jack," the officer said, after frowning a moment at the woman as if loath to repeat her suggestion.

"Yes, hurry, please," the woman begged, not pausing in her rock gathering, but looking toward the child on the back seat. It had struggled until the blanket had fallen away from its head, showing dark hair above a face that through the window shone yellowish white, contorted with some terrible effort to cry or vomit or speak. Like the woman as she ran squatting through the mud, the struggling child seemed animal-like and unhuman compared to the two neatly dressed men.

The woman hurried up again with another apronful of rocks, dumped them, then went at her darting, stooping run along the bluff edge searching for more. The young soldier in the awkward, fumbling way of a man, neither liking nor knowing his business, got out the jack and set it in the sandy mud under the rear bumper. "That's no good," the woman said, coming up with more rocks; and with one hand still holding the apron she picked up the jack, put a flat rock where it had been, reset it, gave it a quick, critical glance. "That'll hold now," she said. She dumped her rocks by the wheel, but continued to squat, studying now the pines caught under the front of the car.

The officer stood at the edge of the asphalt, silent. Sometimes he looked up and down the road, and often he glanced at his wrist watch, but mostly his frowning glance was fixed on the car. He watched the woman now. Her hands had been busied with rocks and apron when she bent by the wheel; now one hand was still holding her emptied apron as she straightened, but in the other was a long knife, bright, thin, sharply pointed. The man, watching, took a quick step backward while his hand went again to the pistol butt. The woman, without looking at either man, knelt by the front of the car and, reaching far under with the knife, slashed rapidly at the entangled pine saplings while with the other hand she jerked them free and flung them behind her.

Finished with the pines, she went quickly along the bluff edge by the car, her glance searching through the window toward the child, still now, with the hand of one down-hanging arm brushing the floor. She watched only an instant and did not bend to listen, for clearly in the silence came the child's short choking gasps. She hurried on around the back of the car, and bent above the soldier, only now getting the jack into working position. "Hurry," she begged in the same tight, urgent voice she had used on the mule. "Please, cain't you hurry—he's a choken so," and in her haste to get a wheel on solid rock she began clawing at the muddy earth with her hands, pushing rocks under the tire as it slowly lifted.

In a moment the officer called, "That's enough; try backing out now."

Some of the woman's need for haste seemed to have entered the soldier. He straightened, glanced quickly toward the child, struggling with its head dangling over the edge of the seat, its eyes rolled back but unseeing. He turned quickly and hurried into the driver's seat without taking time to salute or say, "Yes, sir." The woman ran to the back wheel that had dug such a rut in the mud, and watched anxiously while the driver started the motor, raced it as he backed an inch or so. The car stopped, the motor roaring, the wheels spinning, smoking, flinging mud, rocks, and pine brush into the woman's face bent close above them in her frantic efforts with hands and feet to keep the brush and rocks under the wheel.

"Try rocking out," the officer said. "Pull up, then shift, quick, into reverse."

The soldier was silent, looking at the emptiness in front of him. With the bent young pines cut away, the bumper seemed to hang above the valley. He moved at last, a few inches forward, but slowly, while the woman pushed rocks behind the rear wheels, jumping from first one to the other as she tried to force the rocks into the earth with her heavy shoes. The car stopped. The driver shifted again into reverse. The woman stood waiting between the side of the car and the bluff, her long arms a little lifted, the big jointed fingers of her great hands wide spread, her eyes on the back fender, her shoulders hunched like those of an animal gathering itself for a spring.

The motor roared again, the back wheels bit an inch or so into the rocks and mud, then spun. The woman plunged, flinging her two hard palms against the fender. Her body arched with the push like a too tightly strung bow; her eyes bulged; the muscles of her neck and face writhed under the thin brown skin; her big shoes dug holes in the mud in their efforts to keep still against the power of the pushing hands. The car hung, trembling, shivering, and one of the woman's feet began to slide toward the bluff edge.

Then her body seemed slowly to lengthen, for the car had moved. The woman's hands stayed with the fender until it pulled away from them. She fell sideways by the bluff edge so that the front wheel scraped her hip and the bumper touched strands of the dark hair tumbled from the thick knob worn high on her head. She stayed a moment in the mud, her knees doubled under her, her hands dropped flat on the earth, her drooping head between her arms, her whole body heaving with great gasping breaths.

She lifted her head, shook it as if to clear some dimness from her eyes, smoothed back her hair, then got slowly to her feet. Still gasping and staggering a little, she hurried to the car, stopped again but ready to start with its wheels on the hard-packed gravel by the road.

She jerked the door open and started in, but with the awkwardness of one unused to cars she bumped her head against the doorframe. She was just getting her wide shoulders through, her eyes on the child's face, when the officer, much smaller and more accustomed to cars than she, opened the door on his side, stepped partway in, and tried to pick up the child. It seemed heavier than he had thought, and instead of lifting it he jerked it quickly, a hand on either shoulder, across the seat and through the door, keeping it always at arm's length as if it had been some vile and dirty animal.

The woman snatched at the child but caught only the blanket. She tried to jump into the car, but her long loose coattail got under her feet and she squatted an instant, unable to rise, trapped by the coattail. Her long, mud-streaked hair had fallen over her face, and through it her eyes were big, unbelieving, as the man said, straightening from pulling the child into the road a few feet from the car, "You've helped undo a little of the damage you've done, but"—he drew a sharp quick breath—"I've no time for giving rides. I'm a part of the Army, traveling on important business. If you must go with me, you'll leave your child in the road. He isn't so sick," he went on, putting his foot through the door, even though the woman, still crouching, struggled through the other door. "He seemed quite active, kicking around," and then to the driver, quietly now, with no trace of shrillness, "Go on."

The woman gave the driver a swift measuring glance, saw his stiff shoulders, his face turned straight ahead as if he were a part of the car to be stopped or started at the will of the other. The car moved slowly; the officer was in now, one hand on the back of the front seat, the other closing the door. She gave an awkward squatting lunge across the car, her hands flung palm outward as when she had flung herself against the fender. One hand caught the small man's wrist above his pistol, the other caught his shoulder, high up, close to the neck, pushing, grasping more than striking, for she was still entangled in her coat.

He half sat, half fell in the road, one foot across the child. She did not look at him, but reached from the doorway of the car for the child, and her voice came, a low breathless crying: "Cain't you see my youngen's choken tu death? I've got to git him to a doctor."

One of the child's hands moved aimlessly, weakly knocking the blanket from its face. She gave a gasping cry, her voice shrilling, breaking, as if all the tightness and calmness that had carried her through the ride on the mule and the stopping and the starting of the car were worn away.

"Amos, Amos. It's Mommie. Amos, honey, Amos?" She was whispering now, a questioning whisper, while the child's head dangled over her arm. His unseeing eyes were rolled far back; the whites bulged out of his dark, purplish face, while mucus and saliva dribbled from his blue-lipped swollen mouth. She ran her finger down his throat, bringing up yellow-tinged mucus and ill smelling vomit. He gave a short whispering breath that seemed to go no deeper than his choked-up throat. She blew in his mouth, shook him, turned him over, repeating the questioning whisper, "Amos, oh Amos?"

The driver, who had leaped from his seat when she pushed the other through the car, was still, staring at the child, his hands under the older man's elbows, though the latter was already up and straightening his cap. For the first time he really looked at the child. "Shake him by the heels—slap him on the back," the young soldier said.

"Yes, take him by the heels," the other repeated. "Whatever is choking him might come loose." And now he seemed more man than soldier, at once troubled and repelled by the sick child.

The woman was looking about her, shaking the child cradled in her arms with quick jerky motions. "It's a disease," she said. "They's no shaken it out." She saw what she had apparently been hunting. A few feet up the road was a smooth wide shelf of sandstone, like a little porch hung above the valley. She ran there, laid the child on the stone, begging of the men, "Help me; help me," meanwhile unbuttoning the little boy's blue cotton jumper and under it his shirt, straightening him on the stone as one would straighten the dead. "Bring me a rock," she said over her shoulder, "flat like fer a piller."

The young soldier gaped at her, looked around him, and at last picked up a squarish piece of sandrock. She slipped it high up under the child's shoulders so that the swollen neck arched upward, stretched with the weight of the head, which had fallen backward.

"Help me," she repeated to the young soldier. "You'll have to hold his head, tight." She looked up at the other, who had stopped a few feet away, and now stared at her, wondering, but no longer afraid. "You hold his hands and keep his feet down." She looked down at the blue swollen face, smoothed back the dark brown hair from a forehead high and full like her own. "He cain't fight it much—I think—I guess he's past feelen anything," and there was a hopefulness in her voice that made the officer give her a sharp appraising glance as if he were thinking she could be crazy.

"Wouldn't it be better," he said, "to go quickly to the nearest doctor? He's not—he still has a pulse, hasn't he?"

She considered, nodding her head a little like one who understood such things. "I kept a tryen to feel it back there—I couldn't on th mule—but his heart right now—it's not good." She looked at him, and said in a low voice:

"I've seen youngens die. He ain't hardly breathen," then looked down again at the child. "Hold his hands an keep his feet down; they's no use a talken a gitten to th doctor; th war got th closest; th next is better'n fifteen miles down th road—an mebbe out a his office."

"Oh," the officer said, and hesitantly drew closer and stooped above the child, but made no move to couch him.

"Hold him," the woman repeated, "his hands," her voice low again and tight, but with a shiver through it as if she were very cold. Her face looked cold, bluish like the child's, with all the color drained away, leaving the tanned, weather-beaten skin of her high cheekbones and jutting nose and chin like a brown freckled mask painted on a cold and frightened face with wide, frightened eyes. She looked again at the child, struggling feebly now with a sharp hoarse breath, all her eyes and her thoughts for him so that she seemed alone by the sloping sandrock with the mists below her in the valley and the little fog-darkened pines a wall between her and the road. She touched his forehead, whispering, "Amos, I cain't let th war git you too." Then her eyes were on his neck bowed up above the rock pillow, and they stayed there as she repeated, "Hold him tight now."

The older man, with the air of one humoring a forlorn and helpless creature, took the child's hands in one of his and put the other about its ankles. The young soldier, gripping the child's head, drew a sharp, surprised breath, but the other, staring down at patched overall knees, saw nothing until when he looked up there was the long bright knife drawing swiftly away from the swollen neck, leaving behind it a thin line that for an instant seemed no cut at all, hardly a mark, until the blood seeped out, thickening the line, distorting it.

The woman did not look away from the reddening line, but was still like a stone woman, not breathing, her face frozen, the lips bloodless, gripped together, the large drops of sweat on her forehead unmoving, hanging as she squatted head bent above the child. The officer cried: "You can't do that! You're—you're killing. You can't do that!"

He might have been wind stirring fog in the valley for all she heard. The fingers of her left hand moved quickly over the cut skin, feeling, pulling the skin apart, holding it, thumb on one side, finger on the other, shaping a red bowed mouth grinning up from the child's neck. "Please," the man was begging, his voice choked as if from nausea.

The knife moved again, and in the silence there came a little hissing. A red filmed bubble streaked with pus grew on the red dripping wound, rose higher, burst; the child struggled, gave a hoarse, inhuman whistling cry. The woman wiped the knife blade on her shoe top with one hand while with the other she lifted the child's neck higher, and then swiftly, using only the one hand, closed the knife, dropped it into her pocket, and drew out a clean folded handkerchief.

She gently but quickly wiped the blood and pus from the gaping hole, whispering to the child as it struggled, giving its little hoarse, inhuman cries. "Save yer breath, honey; thet little ole cut ain't nothen fer a big boy like you nigh four years old." She spoke in a low jerky voice like one who has run a long way or lifted a heavy weight and has no breath to speak. She lay down the handkerchief, hunted with her free hand an instant in her back hair, brought out a hairpin, wiped it on the handkerchief, inserted the bent end in the cut, and then slowly, watching the hole carefully, drew her hand from under the child's neck, all the while holding the hole open with the hairpin.

The young soldier, who had never loosened his grip on the child's head, drew a long shivering breath and looked with admiration at the woman, searching for her eyes; but finding them still on the child, he looked toward the officer, and at once gave an angry, whispering, "Jee-*sus*."

The woman looked around and saw the officer who had collapsed all in a heap, his head on Amos's feet, one hand still clutching the child's hands. "He's chicken-hearted," she said, turning back to the child, saying over her shoulder, "You'd better stretch him out. Loosen his collar—he's too tight in his clothes enyhow. Go on, I can manage."

The young soldier got up, smiling a secret, pleased sort of smile, and the woman, glancing quickly away from the child, gave him an uneasy glance. "Don't you be a letten him roll off the bluff edge."

"No?" the other said, smiling down at Amos, breathing hoarsely and quickly, but breathing, his face less darkly blue. The soldier looked past the officer crumpled on the stone down to the wide valley, then up and across to the rows of hills breaking at times through shreds and banks of the low-hanging fog, at other places hidden so that the low hills, seen through the fog, seemed vast and mysterious, like mountains rising into the clouds. He waved his hand toward the hills. "I'll bet hunting there is good."

The woman nodded without looking up. "Mighty good—now. They ain't hardly left us a man able to carry a gun er listen to a hound dog."

"Where is—" the soldier began, then stopped, for the officer's head was slowly lifting, and at once it was as if the other had never looked at the hills or spoken to her. He straightened his shoulders, pulled down his coat, watched an instant longer. As the head continued to lift, he stepped closer, and after a moment's hesitation, and with a swift glance at Gertie, put his hands under the other's arms, standing in front of him so that the officer was between him and the bluff.

The woman gave the two a quick, worried glance. "It's high there; watch out."

"I'm quite all right," the officer said, shaking the other's hands away. He lifted a greenish, watery-eyed face that seemed no soldier's face at all, only an old man's face. "How's the little one?" he asked, getting slowly to his feet.

"Breathen," the woman said.

from *Old Burnside*

Arnow's other books include *The Kentucky Trace* (1974), the nonfiction *Seedtime on the Cumberland* (1960), and *Old Burnside* (1977), from which the second selection is taken. It was, she said, a very difficult book to write. You will understand why when you read her recollection of a poignant visit to Burnside with her family in 1953, shortly after part of the town had been inundated by a huge lake formed by a dam on the Cumberland River.

Ann Arbor schools, like others in Michigan have long observed Easter with a week's vacation. During the Easter holiday of 1953, Husband took a week of his vacation in order to help take the children on the long-promised and overdue trip to see their grandmother Simpson at Burnside. Illness and vacations elsewhere had kept us away for more than three years. We would also see Lake Cumberland, one of the largest man-made lakes in the United States.

I had tourist material and newspaper clippings describing the dam, Lake Cumberland, and even the changes in Burnside. I knew Lake Cumberland began near the foot of Cumberland Falls and continued past Burnside and on down to Wolf Creek Dam, the largest earth-fill dam in the United States, over a mile long and 240 feet high. The lake it formed was 101 miles long with a shoreline of 1,255 miles. I thus knew everything and was ready to explain all to the children.

A few miles south of Somerset we came to a high bridge across a wide body of still water. "Children," I said, "this is what used to be Cumberland River; after Wolf Creek Dam was finished in 1950 it became Lake Cumberland."

Two voices came in chorus from the back seat: "The sign said 'Pitman Creek.'"

I sat in silent confusion, looking ahead to find Burnside. The children were the sign watchers, the backseat drivers. We passed a line of garish bedspreads flapping in the wind as our daughter said, "Cumberland River Bridge is just ahead. We're almost to Burnside."

We began to cross the long bridge. I could see little of the water near the bridge because of the head-high cement walls on either side of the two-lane road. Far away on the lake I could see here and there the same sort of pleasure craft I had seen in the Detroit River or Lake Erie. Was that point of land

Bunker Hill or Bronston? It looked too low for either. I tried to remember the figures I had learned; when the lake was high, as it now appeared to be, the surface of the water was more than 150 feet higher than the average surface of Cumberland River at Burnside had been.

The bridge ended. We were going past the white limestone and red earth of recent excavations. I remembered I had planned to show the children the road to Bronston and tell them it led to Monticello where the stagecoaches used to stay except when they were traveling back and forth to Burnside. I began: "Children, we'll soon be seeing the bridge across the South Fork to Bronston and Monticello. I remember——."

"Oh, Mother."

"Oh, Mothers" came frequently but with different meanings. I knew this one meant I had said something wrong. Our daughter continued, "We passed a sign for Monticello before we crossed the last bridge."

Our son said, "You mean Kentucky 90, don't you?"

I didn't know. The roads out from Burnside used to have names, not numbers, but maybe the Monticello Pike was now Kentucky 90. We were stopping for a red light. There had never been a traffic light in Burnside. I looked out and up to the shoulder of a hill that rose above the town. That must be Tyree's Knob where I had spent my childhood and our mother continued to live. The shape was different; still, no other hill had risen close above upper Burnside, and the redbud and the dogwood were in bloom to make pink and white patches over the hill as they had used to do.

I looked on either side of the road and saw nothing familiar. The light changed. I saw a sign—"Seven Gables Motel." That didn't mean anything. The building was nothing at all like the Seven Gables Hotel I had known in lower Burnside. Was this wide place in the road Burnside? A moment later I was certain. I saw a sign that said: "Grissom and Rakestraw Lumber." There had been a Grissom and Rakestraw Lumber Company in lower Burnside for many years; Grissoms had lived in the town before it had a name.

Past the name I glimpsed stacks of lumber; then both were behind us as we went through a cut several feet deep and made a sharp turn that brought us to a stretch of road with no buildings on either side. I looked out the window to see the lake with a causeway that ended on the side of a round-topped hill. I knew Bunker Hill even with its feet cut off. "Are you driving us to Tateville?" I asked.

The question angered Husband. He had driven around Burnside more than I. "You surely remember," he told me, "that U.S. 27 before reaching Tateville climbed that steep hill out of Burnside."

"We're on U.S. 27 South." "We've not been down in the valley." Our sign watchers sounded certain.

Traffic was heavy and fast, shoulders narrow. There was no turning back until we reached the parking space for a Tateville store. Nearing Burnside from the south, everybody saw the small sign that indicated the junction with another road, unnamed. We turned off here, though I was uncertain of our whereabouts. The cut and the curve for a new U.S. 27 had destroyed the homes that had stood above Antioch Road as it neared the lane I had walked on my way to and from school. Where was the lane?

I at last saw a familiar home ahead and knew we were on Antioch Road. The home belonged to Mrs. Robert Ellnor whom I had known since early childhood. I wanted to stop and speak with her, but now that we were off the main road with no restaurant in sight, the children declared they were starving to death and must have food.

Husband said we couldn't burst in on my old mother with two hungry children expecting food at once.

He turned around and drove back to the Seven Gables Motel where he had seen a restaurant sign. I told him and the children that I wasn't hungry. I planned, while they were eating, to hunt Burnside on foot.

I crossed U.S. 27 and soon found the upper end of a street with its sidewalk cracked and broken by the roots of old beech and maples. I had known this street as a child, though I had never lived on it. I walked down this sidewalk until I could see across the way a white-painted house which I knew as the place where the Harry Waits had brought up their three children. I wondered if the little log house the elder Waits had built behind their home was still there. They had arranged on the log walls, in cases, and on tables the swords and several varieties of firearms their ancestors had used in colonial wars, the American Revolution, the War of 1812, and later conflicts—all that for the school children and others curious to know what weapons their forebears had used.

The street I was on ended at the first street above the railway that had come through a cut in the hillside below. I turned right and walked to the far end of that street. The homes that stood surrounded by trees and shrubs in large lawns were only on the upper side of the street. All save two had been built before 1900, but still wore their gingerbread, wide verandas, and window shutters with an air of respectability. I had visited in many—some more often than others. I couldn't visit now; the people who had lived in them back in the used-to-be were dead or gone away.

I turned around and walked to the other end of the street, which brought me to the one road that had connected upper Burnside with the lower town by the rivers. I walked on the sidewalk on one side of the uphill road until I reached a side street. Here I stopped. Looking right along the side street I saw the Christian Church, and across from it the building that had once been Dr. Stigall's home and office, one in a row of other homes. Past the far end of this street I could see the Baptist Church. I turned to look up the hill road with homes on one side and on the other, the Methodist Church, the Masonic Temple, and past these the Burnside Graded and High School.

One part of Burnside still existed—the upper town that used to live chiefly from the business and industry in the lower town.

I turned around and followed the road down past the street I had been on, expecting to cross the railway tracks in a cut high on the hillside. Instead of the railway, the downhill road crossed a new road I have never seen. I was standing in the middle, trying to figure out where the passenger station and Burton's Restaurant had been, when a car honked. I scuttled to one side of the road and watched the long car towing a long boat on a trailer disappear around a curve in the new road.

I walked on, remembering that the railway had been moved. I decided after thinking over what I had read that both U.S. 27 and the railway had been moved a short distance up Cumberland River above Burnside. Going on down the hill, I was soon able to walk by the shore of the lake. It lay there, still and blue until I peered into it to see below the blue a murky nothingness.

I walked on down and onto the floating dock, not stopping until I had reached the end. Here the water was deeper, and I could see only murkiness. I looked across and around the lake, wider here. Burnside Veneer Company had been over there at the end of the line of anchored pleasure craft: the company's log boom had been on the South Fork above the steamboat landing. Where was the South Fork? It had flowed from behind Bunker Hill and on into the Cumberland. The rivers were all one now.

"Ma'am."

I turned around. A young man, the dock manager perhaps, spoke kindly, as if to warn a friend: "Be careful, lady. Don't fall in: the water's deep there, and cold. You go down, you might not come up—like that little boy friskin' around here two or three weeks ago."

I thanked the man and promised to be careful, but did not tell him I knew Cumberland River had been cold. This corpse of the Cumberland would be colder.

I looked again and saw a narrow band of shadow on the water by Bunker Hill. Lower Burnside hemmed by hills and river bluffs had been a place of long shadows that came early and stayed late. It was only an hour or so past noon, and the shadow of Bunker Hill lay on the water. The shadow was small now; it would grow longer but never fall so far as when Bunker Hill had stood tall and free of the lake; but it was there. The shadows would not be destroyed.

Robert Penn Warren

from *World Enough and Time*

In this anthology Robert Penn Warren is surrounded by great writers, but he stands above them all. As a master of all genres—short stories, essays, novels, plays, poems, criticism, memoirs—he won three Pulitzer Prizes. For the depth and breadth and artistry of his achievements in writing, he should also have won the Nobel Prize for Literature. Warren was born in 1905 in Todd County at Guthrie, on the Tennessee-Kentucky border, and studied at Vanderbilt University during the heyday of the "Fugitives" and the "Agrarians," both of which were conservative literary and political groups. He then studied at the University of California at Berkeley, at Yale, and at Oxford, where he was a Rhodes Scholar. During his long and productive writing career, he was a professor at Louisiana State University, the University of Minnesota, and Yale. His many honors include his appointment as the first poet laureate of the United States. Except for his best-known book, *All the King's Men* (1946), which is set in Louisiana, almost everything else he wrote has roots in his native Kentucky—from *World Enough and Time* (1950), a novel based on a sensational 1825 Kentucky murder case, to *Brother to Dragons* (1953), a poetic drama based on the 1811 butchery of a slave in Livingston County.

The last years of Warren's life were spent in West Redding, Connecticut. When he died in 1989, he left one of the great legacies in American literature. The first selection below is from *World Enough and Time,* a philosophical interlude following the murder of the attorney general Cassius Fort by Jeremiah Beaumont, who believed that he was duty-bound to slay the man who had sullied his wife's reputation. The real-life models for Beaumont and his wife were Jereboam O. Beauchamp and Ann Cook, who are buried together in a single grave in the cemetery at Bloomfield.

Cassius Fort had risen in the night and gone to John Saunders' bed to wake his kinsman and say that he had a plan to "reconcile all in justice." But he did not divulge his plan, and the steel of Jeremiah Beaumont found him soon, and things went on their way as though he had never lived.

Things went on their way, and the Commonwealth of Kentucky has, by the latest estimate, 2,819,000 inhabitants, and the only Shawnee in the country is in a WPA mural on a post-office wall, and Old Big Hump and his brass cannon are lost in the mud of the swamps, and tourists occasionally visit the grave of

Daniel Boone and the log cabin in Larue County where Abraham Lincoln was born and the log cabin in Todd County where Jefferson Davis was born and the Old Kentucky Home at Bardstown in Nelson County, and some 400,000,000 pounds of tobacco are grown annually, and in a good year over 60,000,000 tax gallons of whisky are distilled, and the State University now has 8000 students and a championship basketball team, and the literacy rate for the state is one of the lowest in the nation, and the thoroughbreds untrack to the roar of the crowd and the dainty galvanic legs flash like a blur of scimitars and the sun is on the colors and the parimutuels do a $40,000,000 business, and the Negro is emancipated and can vote and if he is smart he can even get paid for voting (just like white folks), and anyway he is free and can die of tuberculosis in a Louisville slum if he wants to and nobody will stop him (for it is his legal right and is damned near the only right the white folks will let him have) and as long as any man is not free, all men are slaves (and even the President of the Junior Chamber of Commerce of Louisville is a slave, but he probably doesn't care whether he is a slave or not), and from the white-columned portico you look across the gracious sweep of meadow to the sunset beyond the blue knobs and your heart almost breaks because it is so beautiful (and you love beauty), and there are 81,788 miles of improved highway and some of it passes through the little towns where if it is Sunday you can ride by the white gingerbread or lace-scrollwork houses or the new bungalows and see the old folks sitting under the maples, and some of the highways go back into the mountains (and you had better go there if you want to see it really quaint and old-timey and maybe pick up a hickory basket or patch-work quilt for a souvenir), and the teeth of the stalwart children of the hills tend to rot out by the age of thirty-five, but things are improving as all statistics show and civilization is making strides, and we can look forward to a great future for our state (if we accept the challenge, if we carry on our great tradition, if we pass on the torch), for it is a fair land and some people who live in it are happy, and many have the strength to endure without happiness and do not even think of the word, and only a few are so weak and miserable that they give up before their time, and in this fair land there is little enough justice yet, heart-justice or belly-justice, but that does not make Kentucky different from other places.

In the days before the white man came, the Indians called the land of Kentucky the Dark and Bloody Ground. But they also called it the Breathing Land and the Hollow Land, for beneath the land there are great caves. The Indians came here to fight and to hunt, but they did not come here to live. It was a holy land, it was a land of mystery, and they trod the soil lightly when they came. They could not live here, for the gods lived here. But when the white men came, the gods fled, either into the upper air or deeper into the dark earth. So there was no voice here to speak and tell the white men what justice is. Unless Cassius Fort *heard that voice in the night. That, of course, is unlikely, for Cassius Fort was only an ignorant back-county lawyer.*

But men still long for justice.

"I had longed for some nobility," Jeremiah wrote on the last sheet of his manuscript, by some huddled flame at night beside the trail back, "but did not know its name. I had longed to do justice in the world, and what was worthy of praise. Even if my longing was born in vanity and nursed in pride, is that longing to be wholly damned? For we do not damn the poor infant dropped by a drab in a ditch, but despite the mother's fault and tarnishment we know its innocence and human worth. And in my crime and vainglory of self is there no worth lost? Oh, was I worth nothing, and my agony? Was all for naught?"

Was all for naught?

"The Patented Gate and the Mean Hamburger"

This is a gothic short story about the consequences that follow the move of a man and his wife from their farm into the nearby town.

You have seen him a thousand times. You have seen him standing on the street corner on Saturday afternoon, in the little county-seat towns. He wears blue jean pants, or overalls washed to a pale pastel blue like the color of sky after a shower in spring, but because it is Saturday he has on a wool coat, an old one, perhaps the coat left from the suit he got married in a long time back. His long wrist bones hang out from the sleeves of the coat, the tendons showing along the bone like the dry twist of grapevine still corded on the stove-length of a hickory sapling you would find in his wood box beside his cookstove among the split chunks of gum and red oak. The big hands, with the knotted, cracked joints and the square, horn-thick nails, hang loose off the wrist bone like clumsy, home-made tools hung on the wall of a shed after work. If it is summer, he wears a straw hat with a wide brim, the straw fraying loose around the edge. If it is winter, he wears a felt hat, black once, but now weathered with streaks of dark gray and dull purple in the sunlight. His face is long and bony, the jawbone long under the drawn-in cheeks. The flesh along the jawbone is nicked in a couple of places where the unaccustomed razor has been drawn over the leather-coarse skin. A tiny bit of blood crusts brown where the nick is. The color of the face is red, a dull red like the red clay mud or clay dust which clings to the bottom of his pants and to the cast-iron-looking brogans on his feet, or a red like the color of a piece of hewed cedar which has been left in the weather. The face does not look alive. It seems to be molded from the clay or hewed from the cedar. When the jaw moves, once, with its deliberate, massive motion on the quid of tobacco, you are still not convinced. That motion is but the cunning triumph of a mechanism concealed within.

But you see the eyes. You see that the eyes are alive. They are pale blue or gray, set back under the deep brows and thorny eyebrows. They are not wide, but are squinched up like eyes accustomed to wind or sun or to measuring the stroke of the ax or to fixing the object over the rifle sights. When you pass, you see that the eyes are alive and are warily and dispassionately estimating you from the ambush of the thorny brows. Then you pass on, and he stands there in that stillness which is his gift.

With him may be standing two or three others like himself, but they are still, too. They do not talk. The young men, who will be like these men when they get to be fifty or sixty, are down at the beer parlor, carousing and laughing with a high, whickering laugh. But the men on the corner are long past all that. They are past many things. They have endured and will endure in their silence and wisdom. They will stand on the street corner and reject the world which passes under their level gaze as a rabble passes under the guns of a rocky citadel around whose base a slatternly town has assembled.

I had seen Jeff York a thousand times, or near, standing like that on the street corner in town, while the people flowed past him, under the distant and wary and dispassionate eyes in ambush. He would be waiting for his wife and the three towheaded children who were walking around the town looking into store windows and at the people. After a while they would come back to him, and then, wordlessly, he would lead them to the store where they always did their trading. He would go first, marching with a steady bent-kneed stride, setting the cast-iron brogans down deliberately on the cement; then his wife, a small woman with covert, sidewise, curious glances for the world, would follow, and behind her the towheads bunched together in a dazed, glory-struck way. In the store, when their turn came, Jeff York would move to the counter, accept the clerk's greeting, and then bend down from his height to catch the whispered directions of his wife. He would straighten up and say, "Gimme a sack of flahr, if'n you please." Then when the sack of flour had been brought, he would lean again to his wife for the next item. When the stuff had all been bought and paid for with the grease-thick, wadded dollar bills which he took from an old leather coin purse with a metal catch to it, he would heave it all together into his arms and march out, his wife and towheads behind him and his eyes fixed level over the heads of the crowd. He would march down the street and around to the hitching lot where the wagons were, and put his stuff into his wagon and cover it with an old quilt to wait till he got ready to drive out to his place.

For Jeff York had a place. That was what made him different from the other men who looked like him and with whom he stood on the street corner on Saturday afternoon. They were croppers, but he, Jeff York, had a place. But he stood with them because his father had stood with their fathers and his grandfathers with their grandfathers, or with men like their fathers and grandfathers, in other towns, in settlements in the mountains, in towns beyond the mountains. They were the great-great-great-grandsons of men who, half woodsmen and half farmers, had been shoved into the sand hills, into the limestone hills, into the barrens, two hundred, two hundred and fifty years before and had learned there the way to grabble a life out of the sand and the stone. And when the soil had leached away into the sand or burnt off the stone, they went on west, walking with the bent-kneed stride over the mountains, their eyes squinching warily in the gaunt faces, the rifle over the crooked arm, hunting a new place.

But there was a curse on them. They only knew the life they knew, and that life did not belong to the fat bottom lands, where the cane was head-tall, and to the grassy meadows and the rich swale. So they passed those places by and hunted for the place which was like home and where they could pick up the old life, with the same feel in the bones and the squirrel's bark sounding the same after first light. They had walked a long way, to the sand hills of Alabama, to the red country of North Mississippi and Louisiana, to the Barrens of Tennessee, to the Knobs of Kentucky and the scrub country of West Kentucky, to the Ozarks. Some of them had stopped in Cobb County, Tennessee, in the hilly eastern part of the county, and had built their cabins and dug up the ground for the corn patch. But the land had washed away there, too, and in the end they had come down out of the high land into the bottoms—for half of Cobb County is a rich, swelling country—where the corn was good and the tobacco unfurled a leaf like a yard of green velvet and the white houses stood among the cedars and tulip trees and maples. But they were not to live in the white houses with the limestone chimneys set strong at the end of each gable. No, they were to live in the shacks on the back of the farms, or in cabins not much different from the cabins they had once lived in two hundred years before over the mountains or, later, in the hills of Cobb County. But the shacks and the cabins now stood on somebody else's ground, and the curse which they had brought with them over the mountain trail, more precious than the bullet mold or grandma's quilt, the curse which was the very feeling in the bones and the habit in the hand, had come full circle.

Jeff York was one of those men, but he had broken the curse. It had taken him more than thirty years to do it, from the time when he was nothing but a big boy until he was fifty. It had taken him from sun to sun, year in and year out, and all the sweat in his body, and all the power of rejection he could muster, until the very act of rejection had become a kind of pleasure, a dark, secret, savage dissipation, like an obsessing vice. But those years had given him his place, sixty acres with a house and barn.

When he bought the place, it was not very good. The land was run-down from years of neglect and abuse. But Jeff York put brush in the gullies to stop the wash and planted clover on the run-down fields. He mended the fences, rod by rod. He patched the roof on the little house and propped up the porch, buying the lumber and shingles almost piece by piece and one by one as he could spare the sweat-bright and grease-slick quarters and half-dollars out of his leather purse. Then he painted the house. He painted it white, for he knew that that was the color you painted a house sitting back from the road with its couple of maples, beyond the clover field.

Last, he put up the gate. It was a patented gate, the kind you can ride up to and open by pulling on a pull rope without getting off your horse or out of your buggy or wagon. It had a high pair of posts, well braced and with a high cross-bar between, and the bars for the opening mechanism extending on each side. It was painted white, too. Jeff was even prouder of the gate than he was of the place. Lewis Simmons, who lived next to Jeff's place, swore he had seen Jeff come out after dark on a mule and ride in and out of that gate, back and forth, just for the pleasure of pulling on the rope and making the mechanism work. The gate was the seal Jeff York had put on all the years of sweat and rejection. He could sit on his porch on a Sunday afternoon in summer, before milking time, and look down the rise, down the winding dirt track, to the white gate beyond the clover, and know what he needed to know about all the years passed.

Meanwhile Jeff York had married and had had the three towheads. His wife was twenty years or so younger than he, a small, dark woman, who walked with her head bowed a little and from that humble and unprovoking posture stole sidewise, secret glances at the world from eyes which were brown or black—you never could tell which because you never remembered having looked her straight in the eye—and which were surprisingly bright in that sidewise, secret flicker, like the eyes of a small, cunning bird which surprise you from the brush. When they came to town she moved along the street, with a child in her arms or later with the three trailing behind her, and stole her looks at the world. She wore a calico dress, dun-colored, which hung loose to conceal whatever shape her thin body had, and in winter over the dress a brown wool coat with a scrap of fur at the collar which looked like some tattered growth of fungus feeding on old wood. She wore black high-heeled shoes, slippers of some kind, which she kept polished and which surprised you under that dress and coat. In the slippers she moved with a slightly limping, stealthy gait, almost sliding them along the pavement, as though she had not fully mastered the complicated trick required to use them properly. You knew that she wore them only when she came to town, that she carried them wrapped up in a piece of newspaper until their wagon had reached the first house on the outskirts of town, and that, on the way back, at the same point, she would take them off and wrap them up again and hold the bundle in her lap until she got home. If the weather happened to be bad, or if it was winter, she would have a pair of old brogans under the wagon seat.

It was not that Jeff York was a hard man and kept his wife in clothes that were as bad as those worn by the poorest of the women of the croppers. In fact, some of the cropper women, poor or not, black or white, managed to buy dresses with some color in them and proper hats, and went to the moving picture show on Saturday afternoon. But Jeff still owed a little money on his place, less than two hundred dollars, which he had had to borrow to rebuild his barn after it was struck by lightning. He had, in fact, never been entirely out of debt. He had lost a mule which had got out on the highway and been hit by a truck. That had set him back. One of his towheads had been sickly for a couple of winters. He had not been in deep, but he was not a man, with all those years of rejection behind him, to forget the meaning of those years. He was good enough to his family. Nobody ever said the contrary. But he was good to them in terms of all the years he had lived through. He did what he could afford. He bought the towheads a ten-cent bag of colored candy every Saturday afternoon for them to suck on during the ride home in the wagon, and the last thing before they left town, he always took the lot of them over to the dogwagon to get hamburgers and orange pop.

The towheads were crazy about hamburgers. And so was his wife, for that matter. You could tell it, even if she didn't say anything, for she would lift her bowed-forward head a little, and her face would brighten, and she would run her tongue out to wet her lips just as the plate with the hamburger would be set on the counter before her. But all those folks, like Jeff York and his family, like hamburgers, with pickle and onions and mustard and tomato catsup, the whole works. It is something different. They stay out in the country and eat hog-meat, when they can get it, and greens and corn bread and potatoes, and nothing but a pinch of salt to brighten it on the tongue, and when they get to town and get hold of beef and wheat bread and all the stuff to jack up the flavor, they have to swallow to keep the mouth from flooding before they even take the first bite.

So the last thing every Saturday, Jeff York would take his family over to Slick Hardin's *Dew Drop Inn Diner* and give them the treat. The diner was built like a railway coach, but it was set on a concrete foundation on a lot just off the main street of town. At each end the concrete was painted to show wheels. Slick Hardin kept the grass just in front of the place pretty well mowed and one or two summers he even had a couple of flower beds in the middle of that shirttail-size lawn. Slick had a good business. For a few years he had been a prelim fighter over in Nashville and had got his name in the papers a few times. So he was a kind of hero, with the air of romance about him. He had been born, however, right in town and, as soon as he had found out he wasn't ever going to be good enough to be a real fighter, he had come back home and started the dogwagon, the first one ever in town. He was a slick-skinned fellow, about thirty-five, prematurely bald, with his head slick all over. He had big eyes, pale blue and slick looking like agates. When he said something that he thought smart, he would roll his eyes around, slick in his head like marbles, to see who was laughing. Then he'd wink. He had done very well with his business, for despite the fact that he had picked up city ways and a lot of city talk, he still remembered enough to deal with the country people, and they were the ones who brought the dimes in. People who lived right there in town, except for school kids in the afternoon and the young toughs from the pool room or men on the night shift down at the railroad, didn't often get around to the dogwagon.

Slick Hardin was perhaps trying to be smart when he said what he did to Mrs. York. Perhaps he had forgotten, just for that moment, that people like Jeff York and his wife didn't like to be kidded, at least not in that way. He said what he did, and then grinned and rolled his eyes around to see if some of the other people present were thinking it was funny.

Mrs. York was sitting on a stool in front of the counter, flanked on one side by Jeff York and on the other by the three towheads. She had just sat down to wait for the hamburger—there were several orders in ahead of the York order—and had been watching in her sidewise fashion every move of Slick Hardin's hands as he patted the pink meat onto the hot slab and wiped the split buns over the greasy iron to make them ready to receive it. She always watched him like that, and when the hamburger was set before her she would wet her lips with her tongue.

That day Slick set the hamburger down in front of Mrs. York, and said, "Anybody likes hamburger much as you, Mrs. York, ought to git him a hamburger stand."

Mrs. York flushed up, and didn't say anything, staring at her plate. Slick rolled his eyes to see how it was going over, and somebody down the counter snickered. Slick looked back at the Yorks, and if he had not been so encouraged by the snicker he might, when he saw Jeff York's face, have hesitated before going on with his kidding. People like Jeff York are touchous, and they are especially touchous about the womenfolks, and you do not make jokes with or about their womenfolks unless it is perfectly plain that the joke is a very special kind of friendly joke. The snicker down the counter had defined the joke as not entirely friendly. Jeff was looking at Slick, and something was growing slowly in that hewed-cedar face, and back in the gray eyes in the ambush of thorny brows.

But Slick did not notice. The snicker had encouraged him, and so he said, "Yeah, if I liked them hamburgers much as you, I'd buy me a hamburger stand. Fact, I'm selling this one. You want to buy it?"

There was another snicker, louder, and Jeff York, whose hamburger had been about half way to his mouth for another bite, laid it down deliberately on his plate. But whatever might have happened at that moment did not happen. It did not happen because Mrs. York lifted her flushed face, looked straight at Slick Hardin, swallowed hard to get down a piece of the hamburger or to master her nerve, and said in a sharp, strained voice, "You sellen this place?"

There was complete silence. Nobody had expected her to say anything. The chances were she had never said a word in that diner in the couple of hundred times she had been in it. She had come in with Jeff York and, when a stool had come vacant, had sat down, and Jeff had said, "Gimme five hamburgers, if'n you please, and make 'em well done, and five bottles of orange pop." Then, after the eating was over, he had always laid down seventy-five cents on the counter—that is, after there were five hamburger-eaters in the family—and walked out, putting his brogans down slow, and his wife and kids following without a word. But now she spoke up and asked the question, in that strained, artificial voice, and everybody, including her husband, looked at her with surprise.

As soon as he could take it in, Slick Hardin replied, "Yeah, I'm selling it."

She swallowed hard again, but this time it could not have been hamburger, and demanded, "What you asken fer hit?"

Slick looked at her in the new silence, half shrugged, a little contemptuously, and said, "Fourteen hundred and fifty dollars."

She looked back at him, while the blood ebbed from her face. "Hit's a lot of money," she said in a flat tone, and returned her gaze to the hamburger on her plate.

"Lady," Slick said defensively, "I got that much money tied up here. Look at that there stove. It is a *Heat Master* and they cost. Them coffee urns, now. Money can't buy no better. And this here lot, lady, the diner sets on. Anybody knows I got that much money tied up here. I got more. This lot cost me moren . . ." He suddenly realized that she was not listening to him. And he must have realized, too, that she didn't have a dime in the world and couldn't buy his diner, and that he was making a fool of himself, defending his price. He stopped abruptly, shrugged his shoulders, and then swung his wide gaze down the counter to pick out somebody to wink to.

But before he got the wink off, Jeff York had said, "Mr. Hardin."

Slick looked at him and asked, "Yeah?"

"She didn't mean no harm," Jeff York said. "She didn't mean to be messen in yore business."

Slick shrugged. "Ain't no skin off my nose," he said. "Ain't no secret I'm selling out. My price ain't no secret neither."

Mrs. York bowed her head over her plate. She was chewing a mouthful of her hamburger with a slow, abstracted motion of her jaw, and you knew that it was flavorless on her tongue.

That was, of course, on a Saturday. On Thursday afternoon of the next week Slick was in the diner alone. It was the slack time, right in the middle of the afternoon. Slick, as he told it later, was wiping off the stove and wasn't noticing. He was sort of whistling to himself, he said. He had a way of whistling soft through his teeth. But he wasn't whistling loud, he said, not so loud he wouldn't have heard the door open or the steps if she hadn't come gumshoeing in on him to stand there waiting in the middle of the floor until he turned round and was so surprised he nearly had heart failure. He had thought he was there alone, and there she was, watching every move he was making, like a cat watching a goldfish swim in a bowl.

"Howdy-do," he said, when he got his breath back.

"This place still fer sale?" she asked him.

"Yeah, lady," he said.

"What you asken fer hit?"

"Lady, I done told you," Slick replied, "fourteen hundred and fifty dollars."

"Hit's a heap of money," she said.

Slick started to tell her how much money he had tied up there, but before he had got going, she had turned and slipped out of the door.

"Yeah," Slick said later to the men who came into the diner, "me like a fool starting to tell her how much money I got tied up here when I knowed she didn't have a dime. That woman's crazy. She must walked that five or six miles in here just to ask me something she already knowed the answer to. And then turned right round and walked out. But I am selling me this place. I'm tired of slinging hash to them hicks. I got me some connections over in Nashville and I'm gonna open me a place over there. A cigar stand and about three pool tables and maybe some beer. I'll have me a sort of club in the back. You know, membership cards to git in, where the boys will play a little game. Just sociable. I got good connections over in Nashville. I'm selling this place. But that woman, she ain't got a dime. She ain't gonna buy it."

But she did.

On Saturday Jeff York led his family over to the diner. They ate hamburgers without a word and marched out. After they had gone, Slick said, "Looks like she ain't going to make the invest-mint. Gonna buy a block of bank stock instead." Then he rolled his eyes, located a brother down the counter, and winked.

It was almost the end of the next week before it happened. What had been going on inside the white house out on Jeff York's place nobody knew or was to know. Perhaps she just starved him out, just not doing the cooking or burning everything. Perhaps she just quit attending to the children properly and he had to come back tired from work and take care of them. Perhaps she just lay in bed at night and talked and talked to him, asking him to buy it, nagging him all night long, while he would fall asleep and then wake up with a start to hear her voice still going on. Or perhaps she just turned her face away from him and wouldn't let him touch her. He was a lot older than she, and she was probably the only woman he had ever had. He had been too ridden by his dream and his passion for rejection during all the years before to lay even a finger on a woman. So she had him there. Because he was a lot older and because he had never had another woman. But perhaps she used none of these methods. She was a small, dark, cunning woman, with a sidewise look from her lowered face, and she could have thought up ways of her own, no doubt.

Whatever she thought up, it worked. On Friday morning Jeff York went to the bank. He wanted to mortgage his place, he told Todd Sullivan, the president. He wanted fourteen hundred and fifty dollars, he said. Todd Sullivan would not let him have it. He already owed the bank one hundred and sixty dollars and the best he could get on a mortgage was eleven hundred dollars. That was in 1935 and then farmland wasn't worth much and half the land in the country was mortgaged anyway. Jeff York sat in the chair by Todd Sullivan's desk and didn't say anything. Eleven hundred dollars would not do him any good. Take off the hundred and sixty he owed and it wouldn't be but a little over nine hundred dollars clear to him. He sat there quietly for a minute, apparently turning that fact over in his head. Then Todd Sullivan asked him, "How much you say you need?"

Jeff York told him.

"What you want it for?" Todd Sullivan asked.

He told him that.

"I tell you," Todd Sullivan said, "I don't want to stand in the way of a man bettering himself. Never did. That diner ought to be a good proposition, all right, and I don't want to stand in your way if you want to come to town and better yourself. It will be a step up from that farm for you, and I like a man has got ambition. The bank can't lend you the money, not on that piece of property. But I tell you what I'll do. I'll buy your place. I got me some walking horses I'm keeping out on my father's place. But I could use me a little place of my own. For my horses. I'll give you seventeen hundred for it. Cash."

Jeff York did not say anything to that. He looked slow at Todd Sullivan as though he did not understand.

"Seventeen hundred," the banker repeated. "That's a good figure. For these times."

Jeff was not looking at him now. He was looking out the window, across the alleyway—Todd Sullivan's office was in the back of the bank. The banker, telling about it later when the doings of Jeff York had become for a moment a matter of interest, said, "I thought he hadn't even heard me. He looked like he was half asleep or something. I coughed to sort of wake him up. You know the way you do. I didn't want to rush him. You can't rush those people, you know. But I couldn't sit there all day. I had offered him a fair price."

It was, as a matter of fact, a fair price for the times, when the bottom was out of everything in the section.

Jeff York took it. He took the seventeen hundred dollars and bought the dogwagon with it, and rented a little house on the edge of town and moved in with his wife and the towheads. The first day after they got settled, Jeff York and his wife went over to the diner to get instructions from Slick about running the place. He showed Mrs. York all about how to work the coffee machine and the stove, and how to make up the sandwiches, and how to clean the place up after herself. She fried up hamburgers for all of them, herself, her husband, and Slick Hardin, for practice, and they ate the hamburgers while a couple of hangers-on watched them. "Lady," Slick said, for he had money in his pocket and was heading out for Nashville on the seven o'clock train that night, and was feeling expansive, "lady, you sure fling a mean hamburger."

He wiped the last crumbs and mustard off his lips, got his valise from behind the door, and said, "Lady, git in there and pitch. I hope you make a million hamburgers." Then he stepped out into the bright fall sunshine and walked away whistling up the street, whistling through his teeth and rolling his eyes as though there were somebody to wink to. That was the last anybody in town ever saw of Slick Hardin.

The next day, Jeff York worked all day down at the diner. He was scrubbing up the place inside and cleaning up the trash which had accumulated behind it. He burned all the trash. Then he gave the place a good coat of paint outside, white paint. That took him two days. Then he touched up the counter inside with varnish. He straightened up the sign out front, which had begun to sag a little. He had that place looking spick and span.

Then on the fifth day after they got settled—it was Sunday—he took a walk in the country. It was along toward sun when he started out, not late, as a matter of fact, for by October the days are shortening up. He walked out the Curtisville pike and out the cut-off leading to his farm. When he entered the cut-off, about a mile from his own place, it was still light enough for the Bowdoins, who had a filling station at the corner, to see him plain when he passed.

The next time anybody saw him was on Monday morning about six o'clock. A man taking milk into town saw him. He was hanging from the main cross bar of the white patented gate. He had jumped off the gate. But he had propped the thing open so there wouldn't be any chance of clambering back up on it if his neck didn't break when he jumped and he should happen to change his mind.

But that was an unnecessary precaution, as it developed. Dr. Stauffer said that his neck was broken very clean. "A man who can break a neck as clean as that could make a living at it," Dr. Stauffer said. And added, "If he's damned sure it ain't ever his own neck."

∽∞ ∽∞ ∽∞

Mrs. York was much cut up by her husband's death. People were sympathetic and helpful, and out of a mixture of sympathy and curiosity she got a good starting trade at the diner. And the trade kept right on. She got so she didn't hang her head and look sidewise at you and the world. She would look straight at you. She got so she could walk in high heels without giving the impression that it was a trick she was learning. She wasn't a bad-looking woman, as a matter of fact, once she had caught on how to fix herself up a little. The railroad men and the pool hall gang liked to hang out there and kid with her. Also, they said, she flung a mean hamburger.

"A Confederate Veteran Tries to Explain the Event"

In this poem an old man tries hard to explain why a man commits suicide.

"But why did he do it, Grandpa?" I said
to the old man sitting under the cedar,
who had come a long way to that place, and that time
when that other man lay down in the hay

to arrange himself. And now the old man
lifted his head to stare at me.

"It's one of those things," he said, and stopped.
"What things?" I said. And he said: "Son—

"son, one of those things you never know."
"But there must be a why," I said. Then he
said: "Folks—yes, folks, they up and die."
"But, Grandpa—" I said. And he: "They die."

Said: "Yes, by God, and I've seen 'em die.
I've seen 'em die and I've seen 'em dead.
I've seen 'em die hot and seen 'em die cold.
Hot lead and cold steel—" The words, they stopped.

The mouth closed up. The eyes looked away.
Beyond the lawn where the fennel throve,
beyond the fence where the whitewash peeled,
beyond the cedars along the lane,

the eyes fixed. The land, in sunlight,
swam, with the meadow the color of rust,
and distance the blue of Time, and nothing—
of, nothing—would ever happen, and

in the silence my breath did not happen. But
the eyes, they happened, they found me, I
stood there and waited. "Dying," he said,
"hell, dying's a thing any fool can do."

"But what made him do it?" I said, again.
Then wished I hadn't, for he stared at me.
He stared at me as though I weren't there,
or as though I were dead, or had never been born,

and I felt like dandelion fuzz blown away,
or a word you'd once heard but never could spell,
or only an empty hole in the air.
From the cedar shade his eyes burned red.

Darker than shade, his mouth opened then.
Spit was pink on his lips, I saw the tongue move

beyond the old teeth, in the dark of his head.
It moved in that dark. Then, "Son—" the tongue said.

"For some folks the world gets too much," it said.
In that dark, the tongue moved. "For some folks," it said.

"Boy Wandering in Simms' Valley"

This poem portrays a boy's visit to an abandoned farm where a great tragedy occurred and how he tries to understand it.

Through brush and love-vine, well blooded by blackberry thorn
Long dry past prime, under summer's late molten light
And past the last rock-slide at ridge-top and stubborn,
Raw tangle of cedar, I clambered, breath short and spit white

From lung-depth. Then down the lone valley, called Simms' Valley still,
Where Simms, long back, had nursed a sick wife till she died.
Then turned out his spindly stock to forage at will,
And took down his twelve-gauge, and simply lay down by her side.

No kin they had, and nobody came just to jaw.
It was two years before some straggling hunter sat down
On the porch-edge to rest, then started to prowl. He saw
What he saw, saw no reason to linger, so high-tailed to town.

A dirt-farmer needs a good wife to keep a place trim,
So the place must have gone to wrack with his old lady sick.
And when I came there, years later, old furrows were dim,
And dimmer in fields where grew maples and such, a span thick.

So for years the farm had contracted: now barn down, and all
The yard back to wilderness gone, and only
The house to mark human hope, but ready to fall.
No buyer at tax-sale, it waited, forgotten and lonely.

I stood in the bedroom upstairs, in lowering sun,
And saw sheets hang spiderweb-rotten, and blankets a mass

Of what weather and leaves from the broken window had done,
Not to mention the rats. And thought what had there come to pass.

But lower was sinking the sun. I shook myself,
Flung a last glance around, then suddenly
Saw the old enameled bedpan, high on a shelf.
I stood still again, as the last sun fell on me,

And stood wondering what life is, and love, and what they may be.

James Still

from *River of Earth*

Nobody has written better poetry or prose about the southern mountains, particularly those in southeastern Kentucky, than James Still, the Alabama-born writer who, the people in Knott County used to say (according to Still), "just come in and sot down." Indeed, in 1932, in the depths of the Great Depression, he came in to be the librarian at Hindman Settlement School and sat down—after all, he needed a job—and stayed until his death in 2001. And he is still there, buried on the school campus. But he did more than sit down and stay. He observed the people and the land closely and decided that they were interesting and worthy of his time and talent as an aspiring writer. In many ways they were like his family and neighbors in Chambers County, Alabama, where he was born in 1906 and where his daddy was a horse doctor. He already knew a few Kentuckians, including Jesse Stuart, with whom he spent four years at Lincoln Memorial University in nearby Harrogate, Tennessee.

In Hindman he lived a polite but reserved and private life, much of it closed even to his friends. His emotional life seemed reserved for his poetry and fiction. Indeed, he lived most vitally through his characters, especially the young ones who cling to life through thick and thin. As a mature writer, even into his nineties, Still never lost his boyish sense of wonder at nature and at people. Despite his public persona (which he partly cultivated) as a quasi-hermit writing in seclusion in nearly inaccessible mountains, he liked people and he liked to travel. He served in North Africa and the Middle East during World War II and later made frequent trips to Europe and Latin America, where he was particularly attracted to the pre-Columbian ruins and relics. From these faraway places, from writers' workshops in New England, and from Knott County, the Hindman anchorite mailed me a stream of sometimes cryptic narratives of his travels and adventures.

Still was a slow, careful writer, always in control. He set no quotas. If he produced one good poem in a month, he was pleased. If he wrote a short story in a week—and it was good—he was pleased. If he had nothing to write and wrote nothing, that was all right too. Everything he published was accessible and as well crafted and honest as a Shaker chair. For a man who lived so long, however, his output may seem to be modest. Counting the posthumously published collection of his poems, *From the Mountain, From the Valley,* he has barely a baker's dozen of books. Yet he once said to me, "I've written what I wanted to write. In fact, I've already done more with my life and talents than I ever thought I would." His stories and poems have become not only a record of Kentucky's heritage but a vital part of our national literature.

The first selection of James Still's work comprises excerpts from *River of Earth* (1940), which introduce us to the boy narrator and his family in the mountain mining country and take us on a trip to a church meeting, where Brother Sim Mobberly preaches his famous sermon on the river of earth.

⌒∞⌒

The mines on Little Carr closed in March. Winter had been mild, the snows scant and frost-thin upon the ground. Robins stayed the season through, and sapsuckers came early to drill the black birch beside our house. Though Father had worked in the mines, we did not live in the camps. He owned the scrap of land our house stood upon, a garden patch, and the black birch that was the only tree on all the barren slope above Blackjack. There were three of us children running barefoot over the puncheon floors, and since the year's beginning Mother carried a fourth balanced on one hip as she worked over the rusty stove in the shedroom. There were eight in the family to cook for. Two of Father's cousins, Harl and Tibb Logan, came with the closing of the mines and did not go away.

"It's all we can do to keep bread in the children's mouths," Mother told Father. "Even if they are your blood kin, we can't feed them much longer." Mother knew the strings of shucky beans dried in the fall would not last until a new garden could be raised. A half-dozen soup bones and some meat rinds were left in the smokehouse; skippers had got into a pork shoulder during the unnaturally warm December, and it had to be thrown away. Mother ate just enough for the baby, picking at her food and chewing it in little bites. Father ate sparingly, cleaning his plate of every crumb. His face was almost as thin as Mother's. Harl and Tibb fed well, and grumblingly, upon beans and corn pone. They kicked each other under the table, carrying on a secret joke from day to day, and grimacing at us as they ate. We were pained, and felt foolish because we could not join in their laughter. "You'll have to ask them to go," Mother told Father. "These lazy louts are taking food out of the baby's mouth. What we have won't last forever." Father did not speak for a long time; then he said simply: "I can't turn my kin out." He would say no more. Mother began to feed us between meals, putting less on the table. They would chuckle without saying anything. Sometimes one of them would make a clucking noise in his throat, but none of us laughed, not even Euly. We would look at Father, his chin drooped over his shirt collar, his eyes lowered. And Fletch's face would be as grave as Father's. Only the baby's face would become bird-eyed and bright.

When Uncle Samp, Father's great-uncle, came for a couple of days and stayed on after the week-end was over, Mother spoke sternly to Father. Father became angry and stamped his foot on the floor. "As long as we've got a crust, it'll never be said I turned my folks from my door," he said. We children were frightened. We had never seen Father storm like this, or heard him raise his voice at Mother. Father was so angry he took his rifle-gun and went off into the woods for the day, bringing in four squirrels for supper. He had barked them, firing at the tree trunk beside the animals' heads, and bringing them down without a wound.

Uncle Samp was a large man. His skin was soft and white, with small pink veins webbing his cheeks and nose. There were no powder burns on his face and hands, and no coal dust ground into the heavy wrinkles of his neck. He had a thin gray mustache, over a hand-span in length, wrapped like a loose cord around his ears. He vowed it had not been trimmed in thirty years. It put a spell on us all, Father's cousins included. We looked at the mustache and felt an itching uneasiness. That night at the table Harl and Tibb ate squirrels' breasts and laughed, winking at each other as they brushed up brown gravy on pieces of corn pone. Uncle Samp told us what this good eating put him in mind of, and he bellowed, his laughter coming deep out of him. The rio lamp trembled on the table. We laughed, watching his face redden with every gust, watching the mustache hang miraculously over his ears. Suddenly my brother Fletch began to cry over his plate. His shins had been kicked under the table. Mother's face paled, her eyes becoming hard and dark. She gave the baby to Father and took Fletch into another room. We ate quietly during the rest of the meal, Father looking sternly down the table.

After supper Mother and Father took a lamp and went out to the smokehouse. We followed, finding them bent over the meat box. Father dug into the salt with a plow blade, Mother holding the light above him. He uncovered three curled rinds of pork. We stayed in the smokehouse a long time, feeling contented and together. The room was large, and we jumped around like savages and swung head-down from the rafters.

Father crawled around on his hands and knees with the baby on his back. Mother sat on a sack of black walnuts and watched us. "Hit's the first time we've been alone in two months," she said. "If we lived in here, there wouldn't be room for anybody else. And it would be healthier than that leaky shack we stay in." Father kept crawling with the baby, kicking up his feet like a spoiled nag. Fletch hurt his leg again. He gritted his teeth and showed us the purple spot where he had been kicked. Father rubbed the bruise and made it feel better. "Their hearts are black as Satan," Mother said. "I'd rather live in this smokehouse than stay down there with them. A big house draws kinfolks like a horse draws nitflies."

It was late when we went to the house. The sky was overcast and starless. During the night, rain came suddenly, draining through the rotten shingles.

Father got up in the dark and pushed the beds about. He bumped against a footboard and wakened me. I heard Uncle Samp snoring in the next room; and low and indistinct through the sound of water on the roof came the quiver of laughter. Harl and Tibb were awake in the next room. They were mightily tickled about something. They laughed in long, choking spasms. The sound came to me as though afar off, and I reckon they had their heads under the covers so as not to waken Uncle Samp. I listened and wondered how it was possible to laugh with all the dark and rain. . . .

On a July Sunday we went down Little Carr, turning up the ridge at the three linns, climbing the cowpath through the ivy. The heifer bawled dolesomely after us. We were going to Red Fox Creek. Mell Holder had brought word Saturday night of a letter in the post office there. "'Brack Baldridge' hit says on the kiver. Wore thin in mail pockets, searching for you," Mell said.

"Where now does that office set?" Father had asked. "L T Pennington keeps a-jumping it around on Red Fox."

Father carried the baby, Mother and Euly and Fletch following after, walking single along the narrow path. I hung behind. I diddled, slow-footed, taking my time. I peered into the brush on both sides of the way. Under the ivy the ferns were still wet. They waved like long green feathers; they breathed and trembled, smelling of leafrot. Something there had nibbled the mosses, something small-muzzled and shy, leaving no tracks. Higher, on the ivy tops where the sun burned, bees worked the sticky blossoms. I heard a wheedle-dee sing in the green dark. A sheaf of bark creaked on a chestnut tree.

Mother's voice dripped through the leaves. "We hain't got a letter in three years."

"Aye-oo, aye-oo!" Fletch had cupped hands over his mouth, calling down to me. I climbed to where they waited under a shagbark hickory.

"Yearlings drive better in front," Father said. "You chaps walk ahead." The baby slept in his arms.

Beyond, at the mouth of Defeated Creek, we came on folk walking toward Seldom Churchhouse. The men wore white shirts, with collars buttoned. One had a latch-pin at his throat, for the button was gone, and another fellow's neck was wrapped around with a tie, rooster-comb red. The women walked stiffly, dresses rustling like wind among corn blades, their hair balled on their necks. They carried yard flowers and wild blooms in their arms: honeysuckle and Easter flowers, and seasash.

"Look," Euly said. "The men are carrying blossoms too."

A few held flowers tight in their hands, grasping them awkwardly. One carried a stalk cut from a meat-hanger center, white with flower bells. A fellow held a bunch of red clover blossoms, circling the stems with thumb and forefinger.

"Must be Graveyard Decoration Day," Father said.

"It's the second Sunday in July," Mother said. "I reckon it's a funeralizing. They'll be preaching for sure. I'd give a pretty to hear a sermon. I would now."

We left the wagon ruts, coming onto the broad road. White pebbles, water-rounded and smooth, stuck between my toes. A horse went by, setting its feet down so quietly the rider hardly jiggled in the saddle. The church bell rang.

"We'll cool a spell in the churchhouse grove," Father said. "I'll take a look around to see if L T Pennington has come down from Red Fox."

Mother took the baby, and we sat down on a log.

A wagon drove among the poplars. The dry axles groaned, for one wheel was larger than the others, tilting the floor-bed. Three people sat on the spring seat, and six on chairs behind. The women held to the men's sleeves. The men had their hands latched to the siding. They drew up to the grave-yard fence.

Father came back to tell us Preacher Sim Mobberly from Troublesome Creek was going to preach. "Folks here all the way from Rockhouse to Pigeon Roost," he said. "Got so many blossoms in that church, hit's like a funeral meeting."

"When I was a girl Brother Sim preached every burying of my kin," Mother said. "He's a saint if ever one walked God's creation."

"I never found L T Pennington," Father said. "I'll just go along to Red Fox for that letter, and you all can stay for the preaching. No use dragging these chaps up thar and back."

"I've not got on a dress fitten," Mother said.

"I'm ashamed to go in barefoot," Euly complained.

Father grunted. He spat on the ground. "I don't reckon the Lord will be eying your clothes and feet. I'll be back against two hours." He went out of the grove to the pebbly road, striking upcreek.

We found an empty bench in a far corner of the churchhouse. Mother did not take us where the black-bonneted women gathered beside the pulpit. Men moved restlessly beside us; they sat before and behind, crossing and uncrossing their legs. Two whispered behind the flat of their hands. They were swapping knives, one taking boot in a cut plug of tobacco. The plug looked good enough to eat. It curled as though it had been sat upon in a hip pocket. The smell of it was heavier than the resin scent of the benches or the graveyard flowers.

An elder stood in the pulpit. He was lean as a martin pole, thinner even than Father. His cheek bones were large, angled from the nub of his chin. He lined a hymn, speaking the words before they were sung, holding the great stick of his arm in the air:

> Come, Holy Spirit, heavenly Dove,
> With all thy quickening powers,
> Kindle a flame of sacred love
> In these cold hearts of ours.

The words caught into the throats of the hearers, and were thrown out again, buried in the melody. The hollow under the ceiling shook. A wind of voices roared into the grove. The second verse was lined, the third. . . . The elder raised on his toes, growing upward, thinner, leaner.

> Dear Lord, and shall we ever live
> At this poor dying rate?
> Our love so faint, so cold to Thee,
> And Thine to us so great.

"O God, have mercy." A moan came from where the black bonnets were. I rose on the bench, looking. I could see only the beak end of white noses bobbing out of dark hoods, the fans waving before them. "O God . . . sinner . . . I am . . . Lord."

The singing ended. A fleece of beard rose behind the pulpit, blue-white, blown to one side as though it hung in a wind. A man stood alone, bowed, not yet ready to lift his eyes. He embraced the pulpit block. He pressed his palms gently upon the great Bible, touching the covers as though they were living flesh. His eyes shot up, green as water under a mossy bank, leaping over the faces turned to him.

"Brother Sim Mobberly," Mother whispered.

The preacher raised a finger. He plunged it into the Bible, his eyes roving the benches. When the text was spread before him on the printed page he looked to see what the Lord had chosen. He began to read. I knew then where his mouth was in the beard growth. "'The sea saw it and fled: Jordan was driven back. The mountains skipped like rams, and the little hills like lambs. Tremble, thou earth . . .'" He snapped the book to. He leaned over the pulpit. "I was borned in a ridge-pocket," he said. "I never seed the sun-ball withouten heisting my chin. My eyes were sot upon the hills from the beginning. Till I come on the Word in this good Book, I used to think a mountain was the standingest object in the sight o' God. Hit says here they go skipping and hopping like sheep, a-rising and a-falling. These hills are jist dirt waves, washing through eternity. My brethren, they hain't a valley so low but what hit'll rise agin. They hain't a hill standing so proud but hit'll sink to the low ground o' sorrow. Oh, my children, where air we going on this mighty river of earth, a-borning, begetting, and a-dying—the living and the dead riding the waters? Where air it sweeping us? . . ."

A barlow knife cut into the seat behind us, chipping, chipping. A boy whittled the soft pine. The baby slept again, and Fletch's head nodded. The preacher seemed to draw farther away, melting into his beard. Presently his words were strokes of sound falling without meaning on my ears. I leaned against Mother, closing my eyes, and suddenly Father was shaking me. He held the letter in his hands. We went out into the grove, walking toward home. A great voice walked with me, roaring in my head.

"Mrs. Razor"

This short story, "Mrs. Razor," is about childhood fantasy and a family's preposterous trip to Biggety Creek to meet their six-year-old daughter's husband.

"We'll have to do something about that child," Father said. We sat in the kitchen eating our supper, though day still held and the chickens had not yet gone to roost in the gilly trees. Elvy was crying behind the stove, and her throat was raw with sobbing. Morg and I paused, bread in hand, and glanced over our shoulders. The firebox of the Cincinnati stove winked, the iron flowers of the oven throbbed with heat. Mother tipped a finger to her lips, motioning Father to hush. Father's voice lifted:—

"I figure a small thrashing would make her leave off this foolish notion."

Elvy was six years old. She was married, to hear her tell it, and had three children and a lazy shuck of a husband who cared not a mite for his own and left his family to live upon her kin. The thought had grown into truth in her mind. I could play at being Brother Hemp Leckett, climb onto a chopblock and preach to the fowls; or I could be Round George Parks, riding the creeks, killing all who crossed my path; I could be any man body. Morg couldn't make-believe; he was just Morg. But Elvy had imagined herself old and thrown away by a husband, and she kept believing.

"A day will come," Elvy told us, "when my man's going to get killed down dead, the way he's living." She spoke hard of her husband and was a shrew of a wife who thought only of her children; she was as busy with her young as a hen with diddles. It was a dog's life she led, washing rags of clothes, sewing with a straw for needle, singing by the half hour to cradled arms, and keeping an eye sharp for gypsies. She jerked at loose garments and fastened and pinned, as Mother did to us.

Once we spied her in the grape arbor making to put a jacket on a baby that wouldn't hold still. She slapped the air, saying, "Hold up, young'un!" Morg stared, half believing. Later she claimed her children were stolen. It wasn't by the dark people. Her husband had taken them—she didn't know where. For days she sat pale and small, minced her victuals, and fretted in her sleep. She had wept, "My man's the meanest critter ever was. Old Scratch is bound to get him."

And now Elvy's husband was dead. She had run to Mother to tell this thing, the news having come in an unknown way. She waited dry-eyed and shocked until Father rode in from the fields in middle afternoon and she met him at the barn gate to choke out her loss.

"We've got to haste to Biggety Creek and fetch my young'uns ere the gypsies come," she grieved. "They're left alone."

"Is he doornail dead?" Father had asked. And he smiled to hear Biggety Creek named, the Nowhere Place he had told us of once at table. Biggety Creek where heads are the size of water buckets, where noses are turned up like old shoes, women wear skillets for hats, and men screw their breeches on, and where people are so proper they eat with little fingers pointing, and one pea at a time. Father rarely missed a chance to preach us a sermon.

"We've got to haste," Elvy pled.

"Do you know the road to Biggety Creek?"

Elvy nodded.

Father keened his eyes to see what manner of child was his own, his face lengthening and his patience wearing thin. He grabbed his hat off and clapped it angrily against his leg; he strode into the barn, fed the mules, and came to the house with Elvy tagging after and weeping.

"Fix an early supper," he told Mother.

Father's jaws were set as he drew his chair to the table. The day was still so bright the wall bore a shadow of the unkindled lamp. Elvy had hidden behind the stove, lying on the cat's pallet, crying. "Come and eat your victuals," Mother begged, for her idea was to humor children and let them grow out of their notions. But Elvy would not.

We knew Father's hand itched for a hickory switch. Disobedience angered him quicker than anything. Yet he only looked worried. The summer long he had teased Elvy, trying to shake her belief. Once while shaving he had asked, "What ever made you marry a lump of a husband who won't come home, never furnishes a cent?" Morg and I stood by to spread left-over lather on our faces and scrape it off with a kitchen knife. "I say it's past strange I've not met my own son-in-law. I hunger to shake his hand and welcome him to the family, ask him to sit down to our board and stick his feet under."

Father had glanced slyly at Elvy. "What's his name? Upon my honor, I haven't been told."

Elvy looked up. Her eyes glazed in thought. "He's called Razor."

"Given name or family?"

"Just Razor."

"Ask him to visit us," Father urged in mock seriousness. "Invite him up for Sunday dinner."

Elvy had promised that her husband would come. She had Mother fry a chicken, the dish he liked best, claiming the gizzard was his chosen morsel. Nothing less than the flax tablecloth was good enough, and she gathered day-eye blossoms for the centerpiece. An extra chair was placed, and we waited; we waited noon through, until one o'clock. Then she told us confidentially, "Go ahead and eat. Razor allus was slow as Jim Christmas."

She carried a bowl of soup behind the Cincinnati stove to feed her children. In the evening she explained, "I've learnt why my man stayed away. He hain't got a red cent to his pocket and he's scared of being lawed for not supporting his young'uns."

Father had replied, "I need help—need a workhand to grub corn ground. A dollar a day I'll pay, greenback on the barrel top. I want a feller with lard in his elbows and willing to work. Fighting sourwood sprouts is like going to war. If Razor has got the measure of the job, I'll hire him and promise not to law."

"I ought never to a-took him for a husband," Elvy confessed. "When first I married he was smart as ants. Now he's turned so lazy he won't even fasten his gallus buckles. He's slouchy and no 'count."

"Humn," Father had grunted, eying Morg and me, the way our clothes hung on us. "Sloth works on a feller," he preached. "It grows roots. He'll start letting his sleeves flare and shirttail go hang. One day he gets too sorry to bend and lace his shoes, and it's a *swarp, swarp* every step. A time comes he'll not latch the top button of his breeches—ah, when a man turns his potty out, he's beyond cure."

"That's Razor all over," Elvy had said.

Father's teasing had done no good. As we sat at supper that late afternoon, listening to Elvy sob behind the stove, Morg began to stare into his plate and would eat no more. He believed Elvy. Tears hung on his chin.

Father's face tightened, half in anger, half in dismay. He lifted his hands in defeat. "Hell's bangers!" he blurted. Morg's tears fell thicker. I spoke small into his ear, "Act it's not so," but Morg could never make-like.

Father suddenly thrust back his chair. "Hurry and get ready," he ordered, "the whole push of you. We're going to Biggety Creek." His voice was dry as a stick.

Elvy's sobbing hushed. Morg blinked. The room became so quiet I could hear flames eating wood in the firebox. Father arose and made long-legged strides toward the barn to harness the mules.

We mounted the wagon, Father and Mother to the spring seat, Elvy settling between; I stood with Morg behind the seat. Dusk was creeping out of the hollows. Chickens walked toward the gilly trees, flew to their roosts, sleepy and quarrelsome. Father gathered the reins and angled the whip to start the mules. "Now, which way?" he asked Elvy. She pointed ahead and we rode off.

The light faded. Night came. The shapes of trees and fences were lost and there were only the wise eyes of the mules to pick the road when the ground had melted and the sky was gone. Elvy nodded fitfully, trying to keep awake. We traveled six miles before Father turned back.

"Heritage"

Here begin three fabulous poems by James Still. The first, "Heritage," is Still's tribute to the everlasting hills of Knott County. Next comes "Leap, Minnows, Leap," an unnerving metaphor for nature's indifference. We close our reading of James Still with the poem that he kept adding to, "Those I Want in Heaven with Me, Should There Be Such a Place."

c◈ɔ

I shall not leave these prisoning hills
Though they topple their barren heads to level earth
And the forests slide uprooted out of the sky.
Though the waters of Troublesome, of Trace Fork,
Of Sand Lick rise in a single body to glean the valleys,
To drown lush pennyroyal, to unravel rail fences;
Though the sun-ball breaks the ridges into dust
And burns its strength into the blistered rock
I cannot leave. I cannot go away.

Being of these hills, being one with the fox
Stealing into the shadows, one with the new-born foal,
The lumbering ox drawing green beech logs to mill,
One with the destined feet of man climbing and descending,
And one with death rising to bloom again, I cannot go.
Being of these hills I cannot pass beyond.

"Leap, Minnows, Leap"

The minnows leap in drying pools.
In islands of water along the creekbed sands
They spring on drying tails, white bellies to the sun,
Gills spread, gills fevered and gasping.
The creek is sun and sand, and fish throats rasping.

One pool has a peck of minnows. One living pool
Is knuckle deep with dying, a shrinking yard
Of glittering bellies. A thousand eyes look, look,
A thousand gills strain, strain the water-air.
There is plenty of water above the dam, locked and deep,
Plenty, plenty and held. It is not here.
It is not where the minnows spring with lidless fear.
They die as men die. Leap minnows, leap.

"Those I Want in Heaven with Me, Should There Be Such a Place"

First, I want my dog Jack,
Granted that Mama and Papa are there,
And my nine brothers and sisters,
And "Aunt" Fanny who diapered me, comforted me, shielded me,
Aunt Enore who was too good for this world,
And the grandpa who used to bite my ears,
And the other one who couldn't remember my name—
There were so many of us;
And Uncle Edd—"Eddie Boozer" they called him—
Who had devils dancing in his eyes,
And Uncle Luther who laughed so loud in the churchyard
He had to apologize to the congregation,
And Uncle Joe who saved the first dollar he ever earned,
And the last one, and all those in between;
And Aunt Carrie who kept me informed:
"Too bad you're not good-looking like your daddy";
And my first sweetheart, who died at sixteen,
Before she got around to saying "Yes";

I want my dog Jack nipping at my heels,
Who was my boon companion,

Suddenly gone when I was six;
And I want Rusty, my ginger pony,
Who took me on my first journey—
Not far, yet far enough for the time;

I want the playfellows of my youth
Who gathered bumblebees in bottles,
Erected flutter mills by streams,
Flew kites nearly to heaven,
And who before me saw God.

Be with me there.

Jesse Stuart

from *The Thread That Runs So True*

Jesse Stuart was the first Kentucky writer I ever met in person. It was in the early 1960s, and I was a young assistant professor of English at the University of Florida. The head of the department had asked me to drive to the airport to pick up Jesse Stuart, who was scheduled to speak to our students. I was nervous about the prospect of being in a car for as much as an hour with a world-famous author. I should not have worried. Within ten minutes of our meeting, we were calling each other by our first names and sharing stories. When I moved to Kentucky a year later, I got to know Stuart and his wife, Naomi Deane, and, later, their grown daughter, Jane, also a writer. I visited them many times at their home at W-Hollow, where Stuart was born in 1907, in Greenup County in northeastern Kentucky. It was a friendship that I cherish.

Jesse Stuart was not only Kentucky's most prolific major author, with more than fifty books to his credit, but also Kentucky's friendliest and most generous author. Whether he was writing fiction or nonfiction or poetry, his subject was almost always his beloved homeland of Kentucky. Although Stuart was no sentimentalist and often wrote bitter satire, he loved the Appalachian people and their ways. Hundreds, perhaps thousands, of his readers considered themselves not only his literary fans but also his personal friends. Stuart was never too busy to write letters of thanks, to accept total strangers into his home, or to give words of advice and encouragement to fledgling writers. He spent so much time with his readers that it is incredible that he found time to write so many books, including *Trees of Heaven* (1940), *Taps for Private Tussie* (1943), *The Thread That Runs So True* (1949), and *The Year of My Rebirth* (1956).

Jesse Stuart was very much like Op, a larger-than-life character in *The Good Spirit of Laurel Ridge* (1953), who he once said was based on a real person, whom he had to "tone down" to make him believable. Although his national vogue in the 1930s as America's plowboy poet—the American Robert Burns—has waned as literary tastes have changed, Jesse Stuart has a safe niche in American literature as the author of well-crafted, authentic Appalachian fiction and autobiography. Today the Jesse Stuart Foundation, with historian and author James M. Gifford at the helm as executive-director, preserves and promotes the Stuart legacy as well as the larger Appalachian heritage and culture. The following selection from *The Thread That Runs So True* is a fictional rendering of Stuart's own teaching experiences.

⚜

Monday morning when I started on my way to school, I had with me Don Conway, a pupil twenty years of age, who had never planned to enter school again. I was the new teacher here at Lonesome Valley and I didn't know what kind of brains he had. He had left school when he was in the fourth grade. But I did know that he had two good fists and that he would be on my side. All day Sunday while I had worked at the schoolhouse, I was trying to think of a plan so I could stay at Lonesome Valley School. I knew I had to stay. I knew if one had to go it would be Guy Hawkins. I might have to use my head a little but that was why I had it.

It had taken a lot of persuasion to get Don Conway to return to school. He had planned to get married after his tobacco crop was sold. But I explained the value of an education to him in dollars and cents. I told him I would teach him how to measure a field and figure the number of acres, how to figure the number of bushels in a wagon bed, cornbin, and how many cubic yards of dirt one would have to remove to dig a cellar or a well. Don Conway was interested in this type of knowledge. I told him no man should be married and live on a farm unless he knew these simple things, for he could easily be cheated the rest of his days. I was interested in his learning these things all right, but I was interested in something else.

Don, his two small brothers, his sister Vaida, and I went to school together. I congratulated John Conway for sending all his children but one. I told him he should set the example for other farmers on the creek. It would have been hard on John to try to worm and sucker his ten acres of tobacco and care for his other crops if Flossie, his older daughter, had not volunteered to help him. And Bertha, his wife, assured him she would divide her time between the housework and work in the field.

Flossie, eighteen years old, who had left school six years ago, would gladly have started back to school if I had insisted. But I knew John and Bertha had to have someone left to help them. I insisted and almost begged Don to return to school when he and I were sitting on the porch late one Sunday afternoon and Ova Salyers and Guy Hawkins rode past on their horses. They glanced toward the porch for their first look at the new teacher, never spoke but rode silently down the road.

Don Conway looked at Guy Hawkins and Ova Salyers and then he looked at me. He didn't ask me how old I was. I didn't tell him in eighteen more days I would be seventeen. One had to be eighteen before he was old enough to teach school. Don Conway knew the fate of my sister when she was employed to teach the Lonesome Valley School. He knew how Guy Hawkins had blacked her eyes with his fists, had whipped her before the Lonesome Valley pupils. She was a fair-haired, beautiful blue-eyed girl of nineteen when she had come to Lonesome Valley. She went home a nervous wreck, long before her school was finished. After I'd seen the way my sister was beaten up, I begged to go to Lonesome Valley. My parents would have none of it. They thought if I went hunting trouble I would get more than my share.

But I made the mistake at Landsburgh High School of going to the wrong room. I'd forgotten the Greenwood County rural teachers were having "teacher's examination" in our American literature room. And when Superintendent Harley Staggers, who didn't know all his teachers, mistook me for a rural teacher an idea came to me. I knew the school I wanted if I passed the examination. I made a second-class certificate. Then I had John Hampton, a rural teacher and friend, contact John Conway and get the school for me. Superintendent Staggers didn't want me to go to Lonesome Valley. But there wasn't anything he could do about it after John Conway, Lonesome Valley District School trustee, recommended me. That was why I was here to teach school.

When Don and I reached the schoolhouse, at least thirty-five pupils were there waiting outside. Guy Hawkins and Ova Salyers were standing together near the coalhouse with their torn-and-tattered, first-grade books. They looked out of place with the other pupils. They were larger than either Don or me. They were older too. They looked at me when I said "Good morning" to them. Many of the pupils turned shyly away and did not speak. They were waiting for the schoolhouse to be unlocked so they could rush in and select their seats. Each had his dinner basket or bucket in his hand. The majority of them carried tattered-edged and backless books.

I thought we had reached the schoolhouse very early. It wasn't eight o'clock and school didn't start until eight-thirty. The July sun hadn't dried the dew from parts of the valley yet; dew was ascending in white formless clouds from the tobacco, cane, and corn patches. But the people in Lonesome Valley went to bed early and got up early. All of the pupils in Lonesome Valley came from farms.

The girls wore pigtails down their backs tied with all colors of ribbons. They wore clean print dresses and they were barefooted. Not one pupil in my school, large or small, boy or girl, wore a pair of shoes. I'd never seen in my life so many barefooted people, young, middle-aged, and old, as I had seen in Lonesome Valley. Wearing gloves on their hands in summer was the same to them as wearing shoes on their feet. They just didn't do it.

"Well, I'm opening the door," I said, to break the silence of my pupils.

When I opened the door they laughed, screamed, and raced for the schoolhouse. Their shyness was gone now. There was a mad scramble to get inside the schoolhouse for seats. Then there was some discussion among them as to who would sit by whom. Girls had selected their seatmates. There were a few controversies and a few hurt feelings. Often two pupils wanted to sit by the same person. No trouble with Guy and Ova. They walked inside reluctantly and sat down in a seat on the boys' side farthest from my desk.

"Now let me make an announcement to you before school starts," I said, after walking up to my desk. "There will not any longer be a girls' side and a boys' side. Sit anyplace you want to."

They looked strangely at one another. Not one boy would cross to the girls' side. Not one girl would cross to the boys' side. In Lonesome Valley it was hard to break a teaching tradition more than a century old. But after I had been to high school, where there were no such things as a girls' side and a boys' side in a schoolroom, I didn't see why it wouldn't work in Lonesome Valley. Little did I dream that what I had said here would make news in Lonesome Valley, that it would be talked about by everybody, and that many would criticize me and call my school "a courting school." Boys and girls sitting together? Who had ever heard tell of it?

The schedules were not made out for the teachers at the Superintendent's office. No one had ever heard of such routine. Each teacher had to make his own schedule. And that was what I had done long before I left home for Lonesome Valley. I knew what I had to teach and I went to work, making out my schedule and dividing my time as accurately as possible for my six hours of actual work. I had to conduct fifty-four classes in this time, for I had pupils from the chart class to and including the eighth grade.

When I walked down the broad center aisle and pulled on the bell rope, the soft tones sounded over the tobacco, corn, and cane fields and the lush green valley; with the ringing of this bell, my school had begun. I knew that not half the pupils in the school census were here. There were 104 in the school census, of school age, for whom the state sent per capita money to pay for their schooling. I had thirty-five pupils. I thought the soft tones of this school bell through the rising mists and over warm cultivated fields where parents and their children were trying to eke out a bare subsistence from the soil might bring back warm memories of happy school days. For I remembered the tones of the Plum Grove school bell, and how I had longed to be back in school after I had quit at the age of nine to work for twenty-five cents a day to help support my family. If I could have, I would have returned to school when I heard the Plum Grove bell. So I rang the bell and called the Lonesome Valley pupils back to school—back to books and play. For going to school had never been work to me. It had been recreation. And I hoped it would be the same for my pupils in Lonesome Valley.

During my first day all I did was enroll my pupils in their classes, call them up front to the recitation seat and give them assignments in the few textbooks they possessed. At that time, the textbooks were not furnished by the state. Each pupil had to furnish his own. If he didn't, there was a meager allotment of cash set aside by the Greenwood County School Board of Education to buy books for those whose parents were not able to buy them. I knew that many would buy books after the tobacco crops had been sold or the cane had been made into sorghum and sold. These were the money crops in Lonesome Valley.

While enrolling my pupils, I made some temporary changes in seating arrangements. I often put a pupil without books beside a pupil with books, if they were in the same grade. As I enrolled the pupils, I tried to remember and familiarize myself with each name. I tried to get acquainted with my pupils. I found them very shy. I was a stranger among them, though I had grown up under similar circumstances with equivalent opportunities. There were approximately thirty miles separating their Lonesome Valley from my W-Hollow. But I was a stranger here.

When I dismissed my pupils for the first recess, a fifteen-minute period between the beginning of the school day and the noon hour, I was amazed to see them all jump up from their seats at the same time and try to be the first out of the house. Big pupils pushed past the little ones and there was so much confusion and disorder, I knew they would never leave the room like this again. Why were they running? I wondered. I had a few minutes' work to do before I could join them on the playground. Before I had finished this work, I heard the tenor of their uneven voices singing these familiar words:

> The needle's eye that does supply,
> The thread that runs so true,
> Many a beau, have I let go,
> Because I wanted you.
>
> Many a dark and stormy night,
> When I went home with you,
> I stumped my toe and down I go,
> Because I wanted you.

I walked to the door and watched them. They had formed a circle, hand in hand, and around and around they walked and sang these words while two pupils held their locked hands high for the circle to pass under. Suddenly the two standing—one inside the circle and one outside—let their arms drop down to take a pupil from the line. Then the circle continued to march and sing while the two took the pupil aside and asked him whether he would rather be a train or an automobile. If the pupil said he'd rather be an automobile, he stood on one side; if a train, he stood on the other of the two that held hands. And when they had finished taking everybody from the circle, the two groups faced each other, lined up behind their captains. Each put his arms around the pupil in front of him and locked his hands. The first line to break apart or to be pulled forward lost the game.

Fifteen minutes were all too short for them to play "the needle's eye." I let recess extend five minutes so they could finish their second game. It had been a long time since I had played this game at Plum Grove. These words brought back pleasant memories. They fascinated me. And my Lonesome Valley pupils played this game with all the enthusiasm and spirit they had! They put themselves into it—every pupil in school. Not one stood by to watch. Because they were having the time of their lives, I hated to ring the bell for "books." I lined them up, smaller pupils in front and larger ones behind, and had them march back into the schoolroom.

Guy Hawkins and Ova Salyers were the last on the line. When they came inside the door, Guy asked permission to go with Ova after a bucket of water. We didn't have a well or a cistern at the schoolhouse. We had to get water from some home in the district. I told them they could go but not to be gone too long, for the pupils, after running and playing, were thirsty. The July sun beat down on the galvanized tin roof. This made the pine boards so hot inside they oozed resin. We raised all the windows but still the place was hot as the room in which I slept at Conways'. My little room upstairs with a high unscreened window of only one sash didn't cool off until about midnight. Then, I could go to sleep.

I knew the reason that all the rural schools had to begin in July, though the farmers had objected because they needed their children at home to help with farm work. Rural schools began early because coal was an added expense for winter months. The county schools all over the state had barely enough funds to keep them going, and if they could have school during the hot months it sheared away a great expense from their budgets. But it was hard on the children and the teachers.

The first bucket of water Guy and Ova brought didn't last five minutes. The majority of the pupils were still thirsty. I sent Guy and Ova back for more, telling them to borrow another bucket. I sent them in a hurry. And I knew I had to do something about the dipper problem. At Plum Grove, too, we had all drunk from the same dipper, but when I went to Landsburgh High School I was taught something different.

So I made "an important announcement" to my pupils. I told them each had to bring his own drinking cup the next day. It could be a glass, teacup, gourd, dipper, just so it was his own and no one else drank from it. My pupils looked at one another and laughed as if my announcement was funny. But I had seen sweat run from their faces into the dipper, and the next in line put his mouth where the sweat had run or where the other pupil had put his lips. I noticed, too, several pupils had put the rim up near the handle to their mouths, so I knew they didn't like to drink after the others.

On Tuesday they brought their dippers, tin cups, and glasses. Only a few had forgotten, and I stopped with my busy schedule of class work long enough to teach them how to make paper drinking cups. I showed them how to take a clean sheet of paper from a tablet and fold it to hold water. I gave them a lecture about drinking water. I told them never to drink from a stream. I told them how I had gotten typhoid fever twice: once from drinking cool water from a little stream, and once from drinking in a river. I had my pupils use the dipper to dip water from the bucket into their cups. They accepted my suggestion gladly. I also borrowed another water bucket from Bertha Conway and brought it to school. The one bucket allowed me for thirty-five pupils (and there would be more as soon as the farmers were through with their summer plowing and worming and suckering tobacco, stripping their cane and boiling the juice to syrup) was not enough. They played hard at recess and noon and in the "time of books" sat in a schoolroom almost as hot as a stove oven.

Tuesday when I stood beside Guy Hawkins and showed him how to hold his book when he read, my pupils laughed until I had to stop them. I was trying to teach Guy to read as he stumbled over the simple words in the *First Grade Reader*. My pupils laughed because Guy was taller by two inches than I was and heavier. He had a bullneck almost as large as his head, and a prominent jaw. His beard was so heavy that he had to shave every day.

Wouldn't Coach Wilson like to have him! I thought. He would make the best tackle Landsburgh High School ever had.

Guy had big hands. His right hand covered the back of his *First Reader*. And he had powerful arms. The muscles rippled under his clean blue-faded shirt. I measured him as I stood beside him. I knew that if I ever had to fight him, it would be a fight. And I knew that I wasn't going to fight him unless he forced me to fight. He was more powerful physically than I was. And the outcome of our fight might depend on the one who successfully landed the first haymaker to the other's jaw.

Then I looked down at Ova Salyers sitting on the recitation seat beside me. Another tackle for Coach Wilson, I thought. This pair would be a coach's dream. Pity some coach doesn't have 'em instead of me.

If it were not for these two young men, I wouldn't have had any trouble disciplining my school. All the other pupils played hard and they were obedient. They would have been good in their class work if they had had the proper training. I had ten-year-old pupils just starting to school. Nineteen-year-olds in the first grade. Fourteen-year-olds in the second grade. I had one twelve-year-old girl in the eighth grade. They had not been promoted because they had never attended a full school term. They had taken the same grade over and over until they could stand and recite some of the beginning lessons from memory.

"Guy, how long have you been in the first grade?" I asked.

"Oh, about eight years," he laughed.

"You're not going to be in it any longer," I said.

"Why?" he asked.

"Because I'm going to promote you," I said. "Tomorrow you start in the second grade."

Then I had Ova Salyers read. He had also been in the first grade eight years. I promoted him.

When these young men sat down again I saw them look at each other and laugh as if they thought my promoting them was funny. I knew they accepted school as a joke, a place to come and see people. A place where they could join a circle of smaller children and play "the needle's eye." And I knew there wasn't much chance of reasoning with either one. But I had a feeling that time would come. I didn't believe they were coming to school for any good. I felt that Guy was waiting his chance for me. I was not going to take any chances; I was going to give him the full benefit of the doubt.

I had doubted that my second-class certificate and my three years in high school qualified me to teach school. But now, when I measured my knowledge with my pupils', I knew without a doubt that I was an educated man. I had never known that youth could be so poorly trained in school as were my Lonesome Valley pupils. But unless I was chased out of the school, as my sister had been, I was determined to give them the best I had.

The following Monday I had stayed at the schoolhouse to do some work on my school records, and Don Conway had gone home with his sister and brothers. This was the first afternoon I had stayed at school after all my pupils had gone. The room was very silent and I was busy working when I heard soft footsteps walking around the building. I looked through the window on my left and I saw Guy Hawkins' head. His uncombed, tousled hair was ruffled by the Lonesome Valley wind.

I wondered why he was coming back. I wondered if he had forgotten something.

Then I realized this was the first time he had been able to catch me by myself. And I remembered a few other incidents in Greenwood County's rural schools where a pupil had come back to the school when the teacher was there alone, and had beaten hell out of him. I could recall three or four such incidents. But I didn't have time to think about them. Not now. Guy came in the door with his cap in his hand. I didn't want him to see me looking up at him, but I did see him coming down the broad middle aisle, taking long steps and swinging his big arms. He looked madder than any man or animal I had ever seen. He walked up to my desk and stood silently before me.

"Did you forget something, Guy?" I asked.

"Naw, I've never forgot nothin'," he reminded me.

"Then what do you want?" I asked.

"Whip you," he said.

"Why do you want to whip me?" I asked him.

"I didn't like your sister," he said. "You know what I done to her."

"Yes, I know what you did to her," I said.

"I'm a-goin' to do the same thing to you," he threatened.

"Why do you want to fight me?" I asked him. I dropped my pencil and stood up facing him.

"I don't like you," he said. "I don't like teachers. I said never another person with your name would teach this school. Not as long as I'm here."

"It's too bad you don't like me or my name," I said, my temper rising.

"I won't be satisfied until I've whipped you," he said.

"Can you go to another school?" I asked him. "The Valley School is not too far from where you live."

"Naw, naw," he shouted, "if anybody leaves, you'll leave. I was in Lonesome Valley first. And I ain't a-goin' to no other school because of you!"

"Then there's nothing left for us to do but fight," I said. "I've come to teach this school and I'm going to teach it!"

"Maybe you will," he snarled. "I have you penned in this schoolhouse. I have you where I want you. You can't get away! You can't run! I aim to whip you right where you stand! It's the same place where I whipped your sister!"

I looked at his face. It was red as a sliced beet. Fire danced in his pale-blue, elongated eyes. I knew Guy Hawkins meant every word he said. I knew I had to face him and to fight. There was no other way around. I had to think quickly. How would I fight him?

"Will you let me take my necktie off?" I said, remembering I'd been choked by a fellow pulling my necktie once in a fight.

"Yep, take off that purty tie," he said. "You might get it dirty by the time I'm through with you."

I slowly took off my tie.

"Roll up the sleeves of your white shirt too," he said. "But they'll be dirty by the time I sweep this floor up with you."

"Sweep the floor up with me," I said.

He shot out his long arm but I ducked. I felt the wind from his thrust against my ear.

I mustn't let him clinch me, I thought.

Then he came back with another right and I ducked his second lick. I came around with my first lick—a right—and planted it on his jaw, not a good lick but just enough to jar him and make him madder. When he rushed at me, I sidestepped. He missed. By the time he had turned around, I caught him a haymaker on the chin that reeled him. Then I followed up with another lick as hard as I had ever hit a man. Yet I didn't bring him down. He came back for more. But he didn't reach me this time. He was right. I did get my shirt dirty. I dove through the air with a flying tackle. I hit him beneath the knees. I'd tackled like this in football. I'd tackled hard. And I never tackled anybody harder than Guy. His feet went from under him, and I scooted past on the pine floor. I'd tackled him so quickly when he had expected me to come back at him with my fists, that he went down so fast he couldn't catch with his hands. His face hit flat against the floor and his nose was flattened. The blood spurted as he started to get up.

I let him get to his feet. I wondered if I should. For I knew it was either him or me. One of us had to whip. When he did get to his feet after that terrible fall, I waded into him. I hit fast and I hit hard. He swung wild. His fingernail took a streak of hide from my neck and left a red mark that smarted and the blood oozed through. I pounded his chin. I caught him on the beardy jaw. I reeled him back and followed up. I gave him a left to the short ribs while my right in a split second caught his mouth. Blood spurted again. Yet he was not through. But I knew I had him.

"Had enough?" I panted.

He didn't answer. I didn't ask him a second time. I hit him hard enough to knock two men down. I reeled him back against a seat. I followed up. I caught him with a haymaker under the chin and laid him across the desk. Then he rolled to the floor. He lay there with blood running from his nose and mouth. His eyes were rolled back. I was nearly out of breath. My hands ached. My heart pounded. If this is teaching school! I thought. If this goes with it! Then I remembered vaguely I had asked for it. I'd asked for this school. I would take no other.

Guy Hawkins lay there sprawled on the unswept floor. His blood was mingled with the yellow dirt carried into the schoolroom by seventy bare feet. I went back and got the water bucket. With a clean handkerchief, I washed blood from his mouth and nose. I couldn't wash it from his shirt. I put cool water to his forehead.

I worked over a pupil—trying to bring him back to his senses—who only a few hours before I had stood beside and tried to teach how to pronounce words when he read. "Don't stumble over them like a horse stumbles over frozen ground," I told him, putting it in a language he would understand. I had promoted him. I'd sent Guy and Ova after water when other pupils had wanted to go. On their way to get water, I knew they chewed tobacco and thought they were putting something over on me. I had known I couldn't allow them to use tobacco at school. I had known the time would eventually come. But I wanted to put it off as long as I could. Now I had whipped him and I wondered as I looked at him stretched on the floor how I'd done it. He was really knocked out for the count. I knew the place where we had fought would always be marked. It was difficult to remove bloodstain from pine wood. It would always be there, this reminder, as long as I taught school at Lonesome Valley.

When Guy Hawkins came to his senses, he looked up at me. I was applying the wet cool handkerchief to his head. When he started to get up, I helped him to his feet.

"Mr. Stuart, I really got it poured on me," he admitted. "You're some fighter."

This was the first time he had ever called me "Mr. Stuart." I had heard, but had pretended not to hear, him call me "Old Jess" every time my back was turned. He had never before, when he had spoken directly to me, called me anything.

"I'm not much of a fighter until I have to fight, Guy," I said. "You asked for it. There was no way around. I had to fight you."

"I know it," he said. "I've had in mind to whip you ever since I heard you's a-goin' to teach this school. But you win. You winned fair too," he honestly admitted. "I didn't think you could hit like that."

Guy was still weak. His nose and mouth kept bleeding. He didn't have a handkerchief and I gave him a clean one.

"Think you can make it home all right, Guy?"

"I think so," he said.

He walked slower from the schoolhouse than he had walked in. I was too upset to do any more work on my record-book. I stood by the window and watched him walk across the schoolyard, then across the foot log and down the Lonesome Creek Road until he went around the bend and was out of sight. Something told me to watch for Ova Salyers. He might return to attack me. I waited several minutes and Ova didn't come. Guy had come to do the job alone.

I felt better now that the fight was over, and I got the broom and swept the floor. I had quickly learned that the rural teacher was janitor as well, and that his janitor work was one of the important things in his school. I believed, after my brief experience, that the schoolhouse should be made a place of beauty, prettier and cleaner than any of the homes the pupils came from so they would love the house and the surroundings, and would think of it as a place of beauty and would want to keep it that way.

The floor was easy to sweep. But it was difficult to clean blood from the floor. I carried a coal bucket of sand and poured it on the blood and then shoveled up the sand and carried it out. I had the blood from the floor. Then I scrubbed the place but the stain was there. I could not get it from the oily, soft pine wood. I knew this was one day in my teaching career I would never forget.

from *The Year of My Rebirth*

The Year of My Rebirth is Stuart's inspiring journal of recovery from a near-fatal heart attack.

⬦

I met a minnow today who loved life.

This was the time to walk down the channel of the stream. Everywhere the land was dry and parched. There had not been rain for weeks. And across the long bottom where the yellow soybean leaves were dropping to the ground, gray soup-bean-colored clouds of dust arose. They swirled over and over trying to catch each automobile.

Gray dust had settled over the strips of late-summer green an acre in from either side of the lane road. Dust had settled in the tops of trees sixty feet tall. Dust had sifted down among the soap-bellied leaves that made a preening sound when the dry cottonmouth winds blew. This was the time for me to be hunting water down this dry creek channel in the midafternoon of this hot September day. This stream had stopped flowing for the first time in many years.

My shoes clicked against the bottom of the stream's channel on the rough rock floor. Dust rose up in tiny clouds where I stepped. This was very strange, to see dust coming from the bottom of the creek's channel. My eyes were just even with the soybean bottom, where I watched the yellow leaves dropping like rain and smelled the dust that had blown from the lane road. Dust had settled on soybean gold, poplar green, sourwood purple, and sumac red like a thin, gray snow.

Farther along, the stream had dropped over a strata of dark hard rock the color of pig iron. This rock had withstood centuries of flowing water. Below, there was a deep bowl where water had once poured over. Now this bowl was filled with water like some ancient iron vessel entrenched in solid earth.

This stagnant pool of water had an unpleasant smell in this sultry afternoon world under the high channel banks. Streams of perspiration were running from my face. But I had found water. Had the animals found this spot? Did they fight over this last water hole?

As I sat down on the hard dry bank, I saw one minnow in the water hole. He seemed greatly disturbed. He swam the length and breadth of this six-by-four-foot hole a half-dozen times. When a little ground squirrel came to the hole to drink, the minnow saw its shadow. He swam faster than ever in his decreasing world. He couldn't go upstream or down. He was the only occupant of this small pool. The butterflies sat back a few inches from the water's edge to drink from the soft sand. How much longer would this water last?

While the ground squirrel was drinking, he looked upstream and saw me sitting under the locusts. He gave a shrill bark, leaped across the sand bar, and scurried away. The butterflies, frightened, rose up like a bright cloud, their fragile wings bouncing on the waves of heat. They fluttered in the air scarcely a minute before descending again to their fountain of sand.

When the shadows from their wings fell onto the little pool, the lone minnow swam for his life. He raced forward, around, across, a single streak of living silver, three and a half inches long. Once this minnow and his family swam lazily in a clear pool of fresh water, waiting for a fly or bug to drop from the willow leaves. They could swim upstream or race down through their world without limitation.

I heard a rustle on the dry stems under the wilted bull grass. I sat so still I stopped breathing when I saw the long water moccasin emerge from under this wilted canopy of grass. What had he been doing under there? Waiting for a ground squirrel, perhaps, or getting the last frogs sitting by the pool catching the greenflies as they came to drink. The snake didn't see me. I sat like a statue of stone under the locust with the pods of wilted leaves. I sat thirsty in a land of thirst where the minnow ran wild in his limited world and the big snake crawled toward him.

When the butterflies saw the snake, his skin the color of gray dust, coming across the sand, they rose up in a cloud, though he didn't intend to disturb them. He knew where he was going all right. There was purpose in his movement toward the water hole. He put his head down into the water, sliding down like a long submarine. But he didn't stop, he went all the way in. He'd not come to get a drink. He had another purpose.

The long snake started chasing the minnow. He chased him around the pool, but the minnow was too fast. Then I knew the snake hadn't caught a frog or a ground squirrel. He was hungry. He had come for the last minnow. He had caught the other minnows in this family when they had come down the dwindling stream to be trapped in their last little world. He had feasted here at ease, for his prey couldn't go beyond these rock walls.

This water snake chased the minnow until I was sure he had caught him. It didn't matter a great deal to me. Among these wild creatures, it was life preying upon life. Then the flapping and flopping of the big snake ceased.

Already the pool was stirred until the brown sand rose up discoloring the water. The water snake had caught the minnow all right. Since this was the last one, perhaps I should have stopped him. But I was lazy, sitting under the locust shade in the hot dry-mouthed wind.

I kept my eyes glued on the pool. The snake was still under water, but I knew he would have to rise. He couldn't stand the muddy water too long. Maybe the sand in the water hurt his lidless eyes. He could stay under a long time without air, but still he had to come up to breathe. Watching for him, I thought about the times when I used to wait for a water snake to stick his head above the muddy water when I was a boy. I'd stand over the muddy pool with a stick. When he stuck his head up, I'd batter him over the head.

There was a lull, then a ripple in the pool where the hard lips broke the muddy surface. Slowly, the bulletlike head came up, the two eyes shining in the sweltering heat of the white sun. You feel satisfied now, I thought. You've eaten the minnow. He didn't have a chance. I ought to have got up, found me a stick, and finished you when you crawled over the sand. A stick?

I started looking around for one. It was too late now to save the minnow, but when a snake is near, it isn't a bad idea to have a stick anyway. I located one the length of a cane and as big around as the small end of a baseball bat. It was just across the channel on the bank where a swollen stream had once deposited it.

I looked back at the clearing water. To my surprise, I saw what appeared to be a quick movement across the pool again. I watched closely. Again the quick movement through the water. The sediment dropped more, and I saw the minnow still alive, a silver streak of life in the brown water. The minnow had been too fast for the snake, and too much in love with life, even in this stagnant remnant of a stream.

The snake saw, too. He gave a great lunge. Low sprays of sluggish water went up and fell back into the pool. This second lunge was filled with desperate effort. A ground squirrel came, saw the commotion in the sand-stirred water, and turned tail, running fast toward the wilted bullgrass.

How would I react to being in a cage with a tiger the size of an elephant? How would I like to be shut in a closet with something fifty times my size trying to swallow me? Just the two of us, my pursuer and I, locked in my small dark world? Would I lie still and wait to be devoured., or would I fight back? I began to feel active sympathy for the little minnow.

He was fighting for his survival while I sat under the locust and wondered if I would fight for mine. I had wondered a few times in the recent past if life was worth the fight. A few months back, under an oxygen tent that reminded me of my own grave, I had idly sought some handy exit. But the little minnow, by instinct, found life worth fighting for. He had thrown off

302 The Kentucky Anthology

one attack. If he could only survive this second . . . but the minnow didn't have a chance without me. I sat by watching.

The sun dipped under a black cloud that blew up from nowhere. A soft wind pressed against my flushed face. In the far distance I heard a sound like a road crew dynamiting a cliff. A distant sound. The sound that disturbed me now was the swishing water. I jumped up without thinking further and grabbed the stick. I stood over this pool of muddy water. Suddenly the snake gave up his chase. This time he'd surely caught the minnow, so frightened and bewildered. I watched for his head to come up. I waited and watched for a water snake, club in hand, like in the days of my youth.

Then I saw the hard lips rise up like a periscope. I held my club over my shoulder. When his head was two inches above the surface, I came down in an arc like striking at a golf ball. There was another flapping in the water, but it was brief this time. A creamlike substance like oily milk spread slowly over the water hole. With the end of my club, I raked the writhing snake out onto the bank. I beat him twice again with the stick, for I had suddenly become involved in this animal world of survival of the fittest. I was the minnow in the pool. This was my life. This was my enemy trying to take my only true possession.

Standing above the pool, I watched the water as sediment dropped for the third time. I watched for a flash of silver as the whole heavens above me darkened. I hadn't deliberately wanted to kill this snake. I hadn't wanted to take sides, to get excited.

I saw a silver flash in the murky water. The minnow who loved life had thrown off his enemy's third attack. And now rain had begun to fall. A storm was coming that might fill this channel. The dust would be washed from the leaves. The time of the cottonmouth winds had ended.

"Oh, Singing World"

This poem, "Oh, Singing World," is Jesse Stuart's letter to the world he loved.

Oh, singing world, you are too beautiful
Tonight—upon the misty moonlit hill
I hear the plaintive singing whippoorwill,
And down in white-top fields the beetles lull
A drowsy song—and jar-flies sing to rest
The sweaty mules that lie on pine-tree needles.
Oh, world of whippoorwills, jar-flies and beetles!

And now a corn-bird fluting from the nest!
The katydids are singing everywhere—
And down among the trees the night-hawk screams.
The pasture branch is fretting sod-grass seams.
The lazy cows lie under dew-drenched willows
And dream of calving time and better meadows.

Janice Holt Giles

from *The Believers,* Foreword

Janice Holt Giles was not a native Kentuckian; she was born in Arkansas in 1909 and grew up there and in Oklahoma. She married Otto Jackson Moore, with whom she had one daughter, Elizabeth. A couple of years after her divorce in 1939, she moved to Kentucky to work briefly as a church secretary and then as a secretary to the dean at the Louisville Presbyterian Seminary. In the summer of 1943 she met Henry Giles while riding a bus to visit her daughter in Texas. After a lengthy correspondence during the war, Henry returned to Kentucky, and they married in Louisville the day he arrived and soon moved to his home in rural Adair County, on Giles Ridge near Knifley and Columbia. Although she was an outsider, she was quickly smitten with her husband's people and their folk culture and began to write about them in novels, short stories, and nonfiction. The natives were polite and helpful enough, but they always looked upon her as an outsider, a person "from off," as they put it. Moreover, it was not easy for her to adjust to life under the primitive conditions she found. Nevertheless, by the time of her death in 1979, her hugely popular books about Henry's home county and people had made them known around the world.

Giles's novels fall into three distinct groups: the Piney Woods trilogy, consisting of *The Enduring Hills* (1950), *Miss Willie* (1951), and *Tara's Healing* (1952); the Kentucky trilogy, consisting of *The Kentuckians* (1953), *Hannah Fowler* (1956), and *The Believers* (1957); and the several novels she wrote about Arkansas and the western frontier. The Giles Foundation, established in 1996, is dedicated to preserving the literary legacy of Janice and Henry Giles, restoring their log home near Knifley, and collecting and disseminating materials relating to the Giles legacy.

The Believers is about the Shakers who came to Kentucky in the early 1800s and recruited converts into their celibate communities. In the selection that follows, her foreword to the novel, Giles explains the historical background for the characters and events. Since the time Giles wrote this foreword, the buildings in the community she describes have been converted into a Shaker museum.

Around 1800, a small fire was lit on the Gasper River in south-central Kentucky. It caught from the passionate zeal of two brothers, itinerant preachers from Tennessee, and quickly, with the heat, the rapidity and the intensity of a forest fire, it spread over all of the state, throughout Tennessee and on into much of the rest of the south. It was called "The Great Revival."

Such preaching, such passion and such zeal in religion had not before been experienced, and people were caught up in its emotional raptures, taken with the jerks and shakes, dancing like dervishes, speaking in unknown tongues, weeping, wailing, barking like animals, crawling, rolling, going into trances. So great was the interest, so fast the spread, that within two years crowds of ten, fifteen, twenty thousand were gathering for these revival experiences. It created schisms in established churches and created new denominations, and it left its mark so that even today, in the hill country of both Kentucky and Tennessee, there are strange, emotional sects whose religion is most strongly characterized by the emotions and raptures of the revival practices.

Hearing about this great revival "in the west" the queer, celibate group calling themselves The United Society of Believers in Christ's Second Coming, more commonly known as "Shakers," determined that this was the land seen in vision by their great leader and founder, Mother Ann Lee. They sent their missionary teams into the country and made converts. Eventually two communities were founded in Kentucky. One was located near Harrodsburg on Shawnee Run. It was called Pleasant Hill. The other was situated on the Gasper River, south and west of Bowling Green. Its name was South Union. This book concerns the latter.

All of the central characters are fictional, but Brother Benjamin, Brother Rankin, Sister Molly, the missionaries, are quite real. From journals, diaries, biographies, and from study of the actual location of the village, I have tried to recover the daily life as it was lived there. Most of the incidents which are worked into the plot have their origin in actual happenings. Not all of them occurred at South Union, but they did occur in some Shaker village, at some time in its history, to some person.

When the last ten Shakers left South Union, in the 1920s, the land and buildings were sold to the Bond Brothers, and for years it was run as a stock farm. More recently the Benedictine Order has bought several of the buildings, still as sturdy, as stout and as beautiful as they ever were, and a boys' school has been established there. It is a strange coincidence that what was begun as an experiment in communal living should again today be another experiment, though of a different nature, in communal living.

I have had great respect for the Shakers. They were a gentle, dedicated, innocent people, though in their dedication and innocence they perpetrated great wrongs because of their fanaticism. That is what this book is about.

from *The Believers*, Chapter 8

This selection shows how the fictional family of Richard Fowler is destroyed by his conversion to the Shaker faith. Rebecca, his wife, narrates the novel.

⌁⧂⌁

I should have known better, of course. I had too much experience with his ways not to know that not only he could, but he would, if he thought it was right. And he came to think it right.

It was only two days later that he told me of his conviction. We were eating supper. I had already laid out our clothes to go to the meeting and had to hurry a little to set out the meal. Richard walked about, waiting, and I thought it made him restless having to wait to eat. He was ever one to want food right off when his stomach demanded it. "I'll have it ready," I told him, "in a minute."

He didn't answer . . . just kept on with his pacing. When we sat down and he'd said the blessing, he took food on his plate, but he did not touch it. Instead he said bluntly and plainly, "Rebecca, I've made up my mind. I'm going to join up with them."

"With the Shakers?" I said, like an idiot, for it was plain who he meant.

"With the Shakers."

I leaned back in my chair feeling cold and hot at the same time, with a queer trembling set up inside of me, afraid, deeply afraid, a sinking coming over me so that I thought I would faint away. It made me sick and I felt as if the few bites I had taken were going to rise up in my throat. "No," I managed to say, past the woolly dryness and nausea. "No, Richard."

"Yes." He broke off a piece of piece of corn pone and buttered it, then sat staring at it, crumbling it between his fingers.

I watched the bread break into small pieces, shredded under his fingers, and it came over me that that was what he was doing to us . . . breaking us into little pieces. And suddenly a swift anger took hold of me and I stood, hanging on to the edge of the table, my body shaking as if I had an ague. "You'll not!" I yelled at him, and my voice was more a scream torn from me than a voice. I had never spoken so to him before, but I could not bear this thing he wanted to do. "You'll not do it," I shouted, hitting the table with my fist, making the dishes clatter. "They won't have you without me. They won't take a husband without his wife, or a wife without her husband. I heard them say so! And I'll *not* go in with you! Do you hear, Richard? I'll not do this thing!"

He put his hands up over his face and I could see how white he'd got. His hands were trembling, too. His mouth moved, but no words came. I stood and watched him, almost hating him for what he was willing to do. Finally he took his hands down. "I hoped I wouldn't have to say this." He stood up, too, then. "I didn't want to say it. But there's a way they'll take me. If I provide for you, so's you'll not come to want . . . if I leave . . ."

All my anger drained out of me, and my knees sagged so that I had to reach for a chair or fall. "You would do that?" I said, and all I could manage was a whisper.

He looked at me, pleadingly. "I don't want to."

"But you would . . . you would, wouldn't you?"

He locked his hands in front of him and raised them and a kind of shudder ran over him. "I'd *have* to! Don't you see, Becky? I'd *have* to!"

A sword piercing me could not have hurt worse. It seemed to me as if a deep breath would tear the walls of my chest and the pain would go flowing down my sides, like blood from the heart itself. Hot tears scalded my eyes. "Richard . . . ?"

"Don't," he said, turning away, "don't. Do you think it's easy for me?"

No . . . to do him justice, I didn't think it was easy. I had seen him get up from our bed, pace the floor, groan in his labor to see the truth, pray without ceasing through the hours. That afternoon I had tempted him, I had seen him turn away when he was spent, white-faced, angry, at me, at himself, and I had heard him mutter, "The woman Thou gavest me . . ."

No, I didn't think it was easy. But I did think it was wrong. "God made us the way we are, Richard," I pled, "male and female created He them. He intended men and women to join together, to live together, to have children . . ."

I stopped, knowing the moment I had said the word that I, myself, had condemned us. "But we have no children," Richard said, "and that's just it. It wouldn't be so hard to think it right if we had, or ever could have . . . and it's been plainly shown to us . . . the Bible says, 'in season and for the procreation of young.' There is no season for us, Becky. For us it is lust, and for us it is sin."

And I knew there would never be any shaking him.

Janie wrote to me. "Why did you do it? Why didn't you hold out against him?"

My parents wrote to me, "Why?"

Richard's folks wrote to me, "Why? What sense does it make?"

The only sense it made was that I had to go where Richard went. What else could I do? It was his conviction that the Believers had the final, the ultimate truth. It made him willing to set me aside. It was my conviction that nothing should part me from my husband. I might have to live apart from him, but I would be where he was, where I could see him, could, in some measure, watch over him.

That night, before meeting began, we, with Brother Rankin and two others, made confession to Richard McNemar. They made theirs joyously. I made mine in sorrow and pain. They had few sins to confess, but Brother McNemar, seeing my sadness, drew from me my own hurt and grief. He was gentle, but he was firm. "You must do this willingly, Sister Rebecca."

"I am willing."

"For whose sake, Richard's or your own?"

"For the sake of us both."

"But you do not believe?"

This was a confession and I could not lie. "No."

There was a moment of silence and then his voice came, very firm. "We can admit you to partial membership, Sister Rebecca, only if you are willing to try to believe. Are you willing?"

I had to go where Richard went. "I will try," I said, and I knew I *must* try.

Brother McNemar smiled at me. "That will be enough. We can't admit you or Richard to the Church Order, but you can come into the Novitiate. In time, when your efforts have borne fruit, and I have faith they will, you can come into the Church Family."

I did not know what he meant, what the terms he used meant, and I thought perhaps Richard would be unhappy over the limitation, but he was not. Instead he was pleased with me. "It will come," he said, "and we will be within the fold at any rate."

We joined in the exercises for the first time that night, publicly making it known we had confessed and been received. I was awkward and self-conscious, but Richard and Brother Rankin went forth as if they had always been accustomed to the slow shuffling step and the shaking. There was great rejoicing and weeping and singing, and Brother Rankin received the gift of tongues and sang and spoke in them.

There was no joy in me, but at least I had won a little peace. Many another wife or husband had to make that same choice I made, and to some a peace was given, and later, even joy . . . to some it was never given. Permilla was one of those, but then she never wanted peace, nor the kind of joy the Shakers knew.

She went in, for Thomas would have set her aside, but he had so little with which to endow her that with five children she hadn't much choice. "I'd let the old fool go," she told me in disgust, "if it warn't fer the younguns. But they'd have a hard way to go with jist me to do for 'em, no more'n he could pervide. This way they'll not go hungry, an' they'll do as good as the next 'uns." She laughed. "Hit won't misput me none not to have him botherin' me, I c'n tell you that. Hit'll be a relief. But I've got no likin' fer livin' amongst 'em so close. How is it they're aimin' to manage, Becky?"

The three missionaries had been among us a month, and twenty-three people had been converted. The last night before they left they had called us together and given us instructions. As best I could I explained it to Permilla, who evidently hadn't listened to a word. "We're to go on living on our places the way we do now, families together. But the men are to work for the common good, and everything they raise and sell or make in any way is to be put in a common fund. Brother Rankin is to be the head of us for a time, but they'll send down from Union Village somebody to preach and see to things from time to time. In time, as soon as it can be worked out, we'll be gathered in order."

"An' that," Permilla said, "is what I mainly don't understand."

I understood it all too well. When that happened, when we were gathered in order, it meant that families would be broken up. We would leave our homes, a community would be established, and we would go to live in Shaker families within the community. It would be here, on Gasper River, for Brother Rankin had given his farm as a start, and doubtless his home would be one of the houses used. But no longer would husbands and wives and children be a family. The Shakers classified their people into three main families . . . the Novitiate, in which Richard and I, Permilla and Thomas, any other married couples not dedicating both their property and themselves, would belong. There was the Junior Order . . . the unmarried people not yet ready for full membership, for one reason or another, and there was the Church Family, those who had committed themselves and all they owned to the church, never expecting to live outside its folds again, and had made full dedication. Brother Rankin had gone at once into full membership. Few of the rest of us could, or even wanted to, though it was I who held Richard back. He was ready. I, because of my unbelief, was not.

Gwen Davenport

from *Belvedere*

Not many authors have the talent or luck to create a fictional character who leaves the pages of a novel and assumes an independent life outside the book. Huck Finn and Scarlett O'Hara come to mind. Among Kentucky creations, there are the Little Colonel and Mrs. Wiggs and maybe a few others. What about Lynn Belvedere? He's the creation of Gwen Davenport, who was born in the Panama Canal Zone in 1910 but had the good fortune to marry a Louisville stockbroker, John Davenport, in 1931 and live in Kentucky until her death in 2002. Shortly after World War II, when domestic help was scarce, Davenport wrote a novel entitled *Belvedere* (1947) about a writer named Lynn Belvedere who answers an ad in the *Saturday Review of Literature* and obtains a job with an upper-middle-class family in Louisville as a nurse–baby-sitter. Actually, the wife who places the ad thinks that she's getting a female worker. A motion picture called *Sitting Pretty* based on the book came out in 1948 starring Clifton Webb and was followed by two more: *Mr. Belvedere Goes to College* in 1949 and *Mr. Belvedere Rings the Bell* in 1951. The character was again revived from 1985 until 1990, when *Mr. Belvedere* became a popular comedy series on ABC television. Although Davenport wrote some ten books of fiction and non-fiction, it is *Belvedere* that people remember. We join the Louisville couple Tacey and Harry as they await the arrival of the new nurse.

On the evening of August 20, Tacey put the children to bed after dinner while Harry got out the car to go down to the station. "I don't know how I'll recognize her," he said, "but if I just stand there and look respectable perhaps she'll accost me. You should have told her to wear a red carnation."

"Just look for someone with a typewriter," Tacey said.

"Oh, Lord—I'd forgotten about typewriters. I thought you were getting someone with a quiet talent."

"A typewriter is less noisy than a harp."

"One broken leg isn't so bad as two," said Harry as he departed.

Tacey waited in the living room. She picked up a book but was so nervous she could not settle down to read. Would Miss Belvedere like the maid's room? Tacey had moved into it some of her nicest furniture and had picked zinnias in Mr. Appleton's garden for the chest of drawers. There was a big table that would serve nicely as a writing desk, and a comfortable armchair. The room was not large, but it did have a private shower.

She went to the piano and opened a book of Beethoven sonatas that Harry amused himself with sometimes, turning the pages until she came to a passage that looked easy. It was not. Tacey stumbled along, making no effort to do more than pick out the melody, pausing frequently and going back over the more difficult places. Genius, she thought, could be defined as the ability to make impossible things look easy; that would apply equally to Beethoven and to those who knew how to play him.

In one of her frequent pauses she heard from the garden a familiar forgotten sound. "Hoo-hoo!"

Edna! Edna had sent a postcard saying she expected to get home today and Tacey had even called up her cleaning woman and milkman to apprise them of this, but in her own preoccupation with Miss Belvedere she had forgotten it herself.

"Hoo-hoo!"

"Edna! Come on in."

Edna rushed through the French door from the porch like a sudden squall. "Tace! How are you?"

They embraced with fervor and both began talking at once.

"Did you have a wonderful time?"

"How are the kids?"

"What's the news from Bill?"

"Tacey, I'm so thrilled to see you. How are you? How've you been? Where's Harry! And the children?"

"I've just got them down for the night. Don't wake them, for heaven's sweet sake! My, but I'm glad to see you, Edna. We missed you."

They sat on the sofa and Edna lighted a cigarette. "I shouldn't stay," she remarked. "There's nobody with the kids. I came over the minute I got them settled. What've you been doing lately?"

"Canning tomatoes, mostly."

"My family will just have to starve this winter. Well, dear, I'm *dying* to tell you all about it. The trip back was awful! It reminded me of something Bill said once—that the sardines were packed in there just like people. Isn't he a scream?"

Tacey thought she heard a car in the lane. She leaned forward, listening. It was an airplane, far overhead and at some distance. "You look well, Edna," she said automatically.

"Just because I'm sunburned, darling. I'm really rotten to the core underneath, but if your skin's brown everyone'll tell you you look the picture of health."

"I can't seem to get a good sun tan, myself," Tacey said. "I always just turn red and——"

"Turn red and peel. I know, dear. Well, what's your news? Where's Harry?"

Tacey was pacing the floor now like an expectant father. "That's my news, Edna. He went to the station to meet my new nurse."

Edna stared, her face a picture of disbelief. "*New nurse?* Why, you're not going to get rid of Harry, are you?"

Tacey laughed. "No, but I was afraid he'd leave me if I didn't get someone to help him. Oh, she's not really a nurse—just kind of a permanent sitter. A sort of squatter, you might say."

"But how in the world did you find her?" screamed Edna. "I could die of jealousy! Every time I go away there's a revolution at home."

"She's not an ordinary sitter at all," Tacey explained, enjoying the sensation she was causing. "She's an author." She rummaged in the desk for a copy of the advertisement to show Edna, explaining her idea. "I'll show you the letters I had. They're priceless. I just put an ad in the *Saturday Review* asking if there wasn't some author who'd like a nice quiet place to work."

"Say, you turned out a neat bit of fiction there, yourself."

Tacey found what she was looking for, the magazine and the letters of application. Edna read the ad and was impressed.

"Tacey King, you are smart! I always said you were—but now I'll never listen to any other opinion."

Tacey glanced sharply at her friend, but Edna's face was bland and guileless.

They settled down to read the letters from the rejected candidates.

"I want first whack at the ones you didn't take," Edna said. "My—there's going to be quite a literary renaissance on Hummingbird Hill!"

"One of them, Harry said, seemed to misunderstand the nature of her duties."

"I know one of our neighbors who's going to misunderstand, too," said Edna. "Especially if she's young and pretty."

"Wait a minute, Edna—was that Harry's car?"

They heard a car come along the lane, but instead of turning in at the driveway it seemed to hesitate by the front entrance.

"Somebody lost again," said Tacey. "I don't know why people who seem able to read the comics can never manage to read the sign at the corner that says DEAD END, NO THRU STREET."

"It's because they *can* read the sign that they come on down the lane," Edna said. "They want to see if it's right. I'll go as soon as we see Harry's car," she added reluctantly. "I suppose you want to be alone with your new-found friend. By the way, what's her name?"

"Lynn Belvedere. It doesn't sound like the name of a good writer. More like *True Revelations.*"

"Well, I certainly can't wait to see her. I do wish they'd come."

The doorbell rang imperiously.

"My God," said Edna, "I feel just like Aladdin!"

"Don't be dumb," Tacey said. "That's not them—uh—not they. I guess I'm going to have to start watching my grammar, with an author in the house."

"It must be them." Edna consulted her watch. "It's just on time." She rose with extreme reluctance. "I suppose really I'd better go. . . ."

Tacey went into the hall. "Harry has a key, Edna, and he wouldn't ring the bell of his own house. It couldn't be they." She switched on the light and opened the front door.

The illumination fell full on a man she had never seen before, and one she would certainly never forget, even if she were never to see him again. He was immensely tall, with a narrow, emaciated body terminating in a head that was altogether remarkable. Tacey was aware of deep-set, burning eyes in a pallid face, of high, slanted cheekbones and black hair that sprang back from a bulbous forehead with such vitality that it seemed to have independent life. He was hatless and carried a shabby, bulging brief case.

"Yes?" said Tacey. She thought this was a strange hour for a salesman and felt glad Edna was behind her in the living room in case of need. Instinctively, she narrowed the opening of the door, blocking ingress with her body.

"Mrs. King?"

"Why—yes, that's right."

He stepped onto the doorsill. "How do you do? I am Lynn Belvedere."

Tacey fell back as if he had struck her. She continued to regard him speechlessly.

"I am Lynn Belvedere," he repeated, fixing her with a burning glance. His voice was a very deep, full bass that seemed to come all the way up the whole length of him from his shoes.

Tacey still stared stupidly. "Oh, but you can't be," she said at last.

"Why not? Have you ever seen me before?"

"No, of course I haven't."

"Well, then." He walked past her and looked around appraisingly.

Tacey followed and urged him into the living room, where Edna was goggle-eyed in the middle of the floor. "Edna . . . this is . . . this man claims to be Miss Belvedere."

"Impossible!"

"But we weren't expecting . . . ." Tacey began. "I mean, I understood *you* were to be a woman. A novelist."

"Some men write novels too, Mrs. King," he said in a most reasonable tone.

Edna sank to the support of the sofa.

"Yes, of course they do," Tacey floundered. "But not you. That is, I mean to say, not Lynn Belvedere. Oh, this is awful! You're here under false pretenses."

He was colossally patient. "On the contrary," he explained, "if some woman were here calling herself Lynn Belvedere, *she* would be under false pretenses. It is I who have been exchanging letters with you for the past month."

"Yes, but I thought you were a woman. I advertised for a woman."

"Then don't you think you should have said so in your advertisement? *I* am the one who is here under false pretenses!"

"That's what I *said!*" wailed Tacey. "Didn't I, Edna? You heard me." She turned to face the man, craning her neck to look up at his extraordinary head. "You were supposed to be a woman. I may have neglected to mention it in the advertisement, but I certainly *thought* it in my mind. Besides," she added triumphantly, "in my letters I distinctly wrote 'Dear Miss Belvedere.'"

"And I answered, 'Dear Mrs. King.'"

"Well, I *am* Mrs. King!" cried Tacey, unable in her agitation to put her tongue on the fallacy in his reasoning.

"Delighted to meet you, Mrs. King," he said, and held out his hand with a stiff little bow.

Tacey stared at the outstretched hand, which was preternaturally long and thin. She noticed that his sleeve looked shabby and she felt sure he had not had enough to eat for some time past. After a moment she decided to stall until Harry got home. "This is my friend, Mrs. Philby," she said. "She knows all about you."

"Oh, no, I don't!" Edna said, backing away.

"Don't go!" Tacey said desperately and unnecessarily to Edna, who could not have been dislodged by a bomb.

Belvedere turned from one of the ladies to the other, including them both in a low bow from which it seemed he would never straighten. "I have a suitcase on the front steps. May I?"

Tacey bobbed assent. She thought he was asking for her permission to bring in the suitcase and had made up her mind not to cross him until Harry arrived. But he was waiting for her to step aside, out of his way. She did so. He bowed again, more briefly, passed her and went out.

Tacey rushed to Edna. "What'll we do?" she whispered. "Harry went to meet her and naturally he must have missed her. He never could have expected she'd look like that!"

"Why not try her out?" Edna whispered back. "Oh, I mean him. Why not try him out?"

"But it wouldn't do! I want him to wash dishes and help with the kids. Not a man's work at all!"

"Don't ever let Harry or Bill hear you say that!" said Edna.

"Sh-h-h! Here he comes!"

They jerked apart. Belvedere had come back into the hall.

Tacey decided to try keeping him there until Harry got home. "Is that all the luggage you have?" she asked, relieved to see only one battered, middle-sized suitcase and a portable typewriter.

"That is all," he said. "My material wants are few—sufficient food to maintain life, warm clothing, a place to lay my head. My other wants—far more pressing—I carry always with me." He indicated his brief case. "Now, Mrs. King, I suppose you are willing to admit a man can be a novelist?"

"Why, I never said——"

"Here is my manuscript. I have about six months to a year of work left to do on it."

"Six months to a year?" echoed Edna, who had moved to the hall also and sat now on a bench under the mirror.

"If it's only six months or a year," Tacey said doubtfully. She found it difficult to take her eyes from Lynn Belvedere's head. It was a head to make a sculptor's fingers itch: definite features, strong facial characteristics, a craggy nose and eyes set deep in their sockets under an overhanging brow. Yet somehow the head had a kind of grandeur; its creator had known when to stop and had stopped just short of the grotesque. What a portrait bust he would make! Tacey judged him to be around forty, but he could be any age between thirty and fifty. There was no gray in the extraordinarily vital hair and his almost translucent skin was stretched so tight over the bones as to preclude wrinkles.

Conversation came to a standstill with the two women staring covertly at Belvedere, who seemed unaware of their amazement. He stood in the middle of the hall, the light from the chandelier shining on his head and throwing the shadow of brow and nose over the lower part of his face.

"My husband went to the station, but he must have missed you," Tacey explained. "I'm sorry you had to take a cab." She wondered if he would be offended were she to offer reimbursement of the taxi fare.

"Perhaps I might see my room?" he suggested.

"But Mr. King—my husband—I thought we'd wait . . ."

"You can't send him back to town tonight," Edna said. "You know there's not a hotel room in the city of Louisville."

"It is very crowded," Tacey admitted. "Where *is* Harry? There are so many war plants here, Mr. Belvedere," she explained. "Not to mention Fort Knox and a huge Army airfield. There's Tube Turns and the boat works and a neoprene plant, and of course the bag plant across the river, and dozens of others that weren't even a gleam in an executive's eye before December 7, 1941."

"That's where all our maids went," Edna said, making conversation.

"You can't blame them," Tacey added. "I'd do the same thing myself."

Belvedere leaned down and repeated, with an air of infinite patience, "May I see my room?"

"Oh, dear . . ." said Tacey, irresolute. She was beginning to be worried about Harry.

He cleared his throat with an ominous effect, as if he were about to lose his temper. Tacey realized for the first time, with a little stirring of panic, that she knew absolutely nothing about him—had not, indeed, even asked the supposedly female Lynn Belvedere for a reference. She was appalled at herself for not having insisted on a reference; then she would at least have known the sex of her correspondent. Suppose this were an impostor? What if Harry were to walk in with the real Lynn Belvedere, a beautiful young girl—or what if this man had disposed of the real Lynn and intended to take her place here for dire reasons of his own?

"Where is my room?" Belvedere asked for the third time, in a strained voice like that of a man trying to hold on to himself.

Tacey was afraid not to humor him. "It's . . . upstairs. Next to the children. My husband and I sleep down here." She waved in the general direction of the downstairs bedroom without shifting her gaze from his face. "Since we haven't had any help staying in the house I've been sleeping up there sometimes myself, when it's too cold to keep everything open, you know, so I could hear the children if they cried in the night." She smiled desperately. "Of course I wouldn't do that if you were in it."

Edna snorted, but quickly became grave again in the face of Belvedere's continued solemnity.

"I must have a room to myself," he said. "I require solitude when I work. And quiet. Absolute quiet. You see, Mrs. King, I am a genius." He announced this in a tone as matter-of-fact as if he were announcing a propensity to suffer from hay fever.

"Suppose I show you the room, then," Tacey said, as if he had given himself the necessary reference and she would not have considered hiring anyone but a genius. "It's this way."

He picked up his suitcase and typewriter and followed her up the stairs. It was hotter here than on the ground floor and Tacey began hoping he would object to the situation of the room, its temperature or its equipment, and make for himself the decision not to stay.

"It's not much of a room for a genius," she said as she reached the landing. She opened the door and pressed the light switch. There was the room she had made ready that morning, with such high hopes, for the sympathetic and talented young woman who had been her dream Lynn Belvedere.

The actual Belvedere—or was he?—whose remarkable head nearly touched the ceiling, strode in and laid his suitcase on the bed without more than a casual glance around. "I shall have to have my writing table directly under the window" was all he said.

"Perhaps you want to wash up," Tacey suggested. She showed him the closet and the small lavatory. "Here are some clean towels. There's only a shower in here. If you want to take a tub bath, you have to use the children's bathroom, down the hall."

"Please do not trouble yourself about me," said Belvedere. "My physical wants are few and easily satisfied. The needs of the mind are another matter, but I am fortunately able to satisfy those myself."

Thomas Merton

Thomas Merton's life was of not much consequence until December 10, 1941, when he joined the Order of Cistercians of the Strict Observance, commonly called the Trappists, entered the Abbey of Our Lady of Gethsemani, near Bardstown, Kentucky, and began a life based on prayer, silence, and work. His spiritual journey led finally to his ordination as a priest on May 26, 1949, when he became Father Louis. Two years later he became an American citizen. It was an unlikely destination for this man who was born in 1915 in Prades, France, the son of Ruth Jenkins Merton, an American-born artist-designer, and Owen Merton, a New Zealand–born painter. He was educated in the United States, Bermuda, France, and England; he studied at Cambridge and Columbia, where he received an M.A. in English in 1938. After several years of a reputedly bohemian lifestyle, he converted from Anglicanism to Roman Catholicism. He had done some minor writing before he became a Trappist and continued to write as a part of his monastic vocation. His books include *Thirty Poems* (1944), *Seeds of Contemplation* (1949), *The Sign of Jonas* (1953), and *Conjectures of a Guilty Bystande*r (1966).

His best-known book is his spiritual autobiography, *The Seven Storey Mountain* (1948), which chronicles his pilgrimage from a youthful profligate life to his conversion and decision to enter the monastery. In the 1960s he wrote on many topics of social justice, including racial conflict, genocide, nuclear armament, and the Vietnam War. It is, however, as a poet that Merton did his best and most spiritual writing. In 1965 he received permission from his abbot to move into a small, isolated cabin—he called it "The Hermitage"—and live a life of solitude. His developing interest in non-Christian religions and cultures led him to attend a Buddhist-Christian conference on monasticism in 1968 near Bangkok, Thailand, where he apparently died an accidental death on December 10, electrocuted by a fan with faulty wiring. His body was sent home to be buried at the Abbey of Gethsemani. The Merton Collection at Bellarmine University in Louisville is the world's largest collection of books and manuscripts pertaining to his life and writings. The selection that follows, a portion of his *Seven Storey Mountain,* describes his second arrival at the monastery—this time to stay and become a monk. The four subsequent poems only begin to suggest the dimensions of his subject matter and style.

from *The Seven Storey Mountain*

When I finally got off in Bardstown, I was standing across the road from a gas station. The street appeared to be empty, as if the town were asleep. But presently I saw a man in the gas station. I went over and asked where I could get someone to drive me to Gethsemani. So he put on his hat and started his car and we left town on a straight road through level country, full of empty fields. It was not the kind of landscape that belonged to Gethsemani, and I could not get my bearings until some low, jagged, wooded hills appeared ahead of us, to the left of the road, and we made a turn that took us into rolling, wooded land.

Then I saw that high familiar spire.

I rang the bell at the gate. It let fall a dull, unresonant note inside the empty court. My man got in his car and went away. Nobody came. I could hear somebody moving around inside the Gatehouse. I did not ring again. Presently, the window opened, and Brother Matthew looked out between the bars, with his clear eyes and graying beard.

"Hullo, Brother," I said.

He recognized me, glanced at the suitcase, and said: "This time have you come to stay?"

"Yes, Brother, if you'll pray for me," I said.

Brother nodded, and raised his hand to close the window.

"That's what I've been doing," he said, "praying for you."

II

So Brother Matthew locked the gate behind me and I was enclosed in the four walls of my new freedom.

And it was appropriate that the beginning of freedom should be as it was. For I entered a garden that was dead and stripped and bare. The flowers that had been there last April were all gone. The sun was hidden behind low clouds and an icy wind was blowing over the gray grass and the concrete walks.

In a sense my freedom had already begun, for I minded none of these things. I did not come to Gethsemani for the flowers, or for the climate— although I admit that the Kentucky winters were a disappointment. Still, I had not had time to plan on any kind of a climate. I had been too busy with the crucially important problem of finding out God's will. And that problem was still not entirely settled.

There still remained the final answer: would I be accepted into this monastery? Would they take me into the novitiate, to become a Cistercian?

Father Joachim, the guest master, came out the door of the monastery and crossed the garden with his hands under his scapular and his eyes fixed on the cement walk. He only raised them when he was near me, and then he grinned.

"Oh, it's you," he said.

I did not give him a chance to ask if I had come to stay. I said: "Yes, Father, this time I want to be a novice—if I can."

He just smiled. We went into the house. The place seemed very empty. I put the suitcase down in the room that had been assigned to me, and hastened to the church.

If I expected any grand welcome from Christ and His angels, I did not get it—not in the sensible order. The huge nave was like a tomb, and the building was as cold as ice. However, I did not mind. Nor was I upset by the fact that nothing special came into my head in the way of a prayer. I just knelt there more or less dumb, and listened to the saw down at the sawmill fill the air with long strident complaints and the sound of labor.

That evening at supper I found that there was another postulant—an ancient, toothless, gray-haired man hunched up in a huge sweater. He was a farmer from the neighborhood who had lived in the shadow of the abbey for years and had finally made up his mind to enter it as a lay brother. However, he did not stay.

The next day I found out there was still a third postulant. He arrived that morning. He was a fat bewildered youth from Buffalo. Like myself, he was applying for the choir. Father Joachim put the two of us to work together washing dishes and waxing floors, in silence. We were both absorbed in our own many thoughts, and I dare say he was no more tempted to start a conversation than I was.

In fact every minute of the day I was secretly congratulating myself that conversations were over and done with—provided always I was accepted.

I could not be quite sure whether someone would call me and tell me to go down for an interview with the Father Abbot, or whether I was expected to go down to him on my own initiative, but that part of the problem was settled for me toward the end of the morning work.

I went back to my room and started puzzling my head over the copy of the *Spiritual Directory* that Father Joachim had brought me. Instead of settling down quietly and reading the chapter that directly concerned me, the one that said what postulants were supposed to do while they were waiting in the Guesthouse, I started leafing through the two thin volumes to see if I could not discover something absolutely clear and definite as to what the Cistercian vocation was all about.

It is easy enough to say, "Trappists are called to lead lives of prayer and penance," because after all there is a sense in which everybody is called to lead that kind of a life. It is also easy enough to say that Cistercians are called to devote themselves entirely to contemplation without any regard for the works of the active life: but that does not say anything precise about the object of our life and it certainly does not distinguish the Trappists from any of the other so-called "contemplative orders." Then the question always arises: "What do you mean by contemplation, anyway?"

From the *Spiritual Directory* I learned that "the Holy Mass, the Divine Office, Prayer and pious reading which form the exercises of the contemplative life occupy the major part of our day."

It was a frigid and unsatisfying sentence. The phrase "pious reading" was a gloomy one, and somehow the thought that the contemplative life was something that was divided up into "exercises" was of a sort that would have ordinarily depressed me. But I think I had come to the monastery fully resigned to the prospect of meeting that kind of language for the rest of my life. In fact, it is a good thing that I was resigned to it, for it is one of the tiresome minor details of all religious life today that one must receive a large proportion of spiritual nourishment dished up in the unseasoned jargon of transliterated French.

I had no way of saying what the contemplative life meant to me then. But it seemed to me that it should mean something more than spending so many hours a day in a church and so many more hours somewhere else, without having to go to the bother of preaching sermons or teaching school or writing books or visiting the sick.

A few lines further on in the *Directory* there were some cautious words about mystical contemplation which, I was told, was "not required" but which God sometimes "vouchsafed." That word "vouchsafe"! It almost sounded as if the grace came to you dressed up in a crinoline. In fact, to my way of interpreting it, when a spiritual book tells you that "infused contemplation is sometimes vouchsafed" the idea you are supposed to get is this: "infused contemplation is all right for the saints, but as for *you*: hands off!"

III

Dom Frederic was deep in a pile of letters which covered the desk before him, along with a mountain of other papers and documents. Yet you could see that this tremendous volume of work did not succeed in submerging him. He had it all under control. Since I have been in the monastery I have often had occasion to wonder by what miracle he manages to *keep* all that under control. But he does.

In any case, that day Father Abbot turned to us with just as much ease and facility as if he had nothing else whatever to do but to give the first words of advice to two postulants leaving the world to become Trappists.

"Each one of you," he said, "will make the community either better or worse. Everything you do will have an influence upon others. It can be a good influence or a bad one. It all depends on you. Our Lord will never refuse you grace. . . ."

I forget whether he quoted Father Faber. Reverend Father likes to quote Father Faber, and after all it would be extraordinary if he failed to do so on that day. But I have forgotten.

We kissed his ring as he blessed us both, and went out again. His parting shaft had been that we should be joyful but not dissipated, and that the Names of Jesus and Mary should always be on our lips.

At the other end of the long dark hall we went into a room where three monks were sitting at typewriters, and we handed over our fountain pens and wrist watches and our loose cash to the Treasurer, and signed documents promising that if we left the monastery we would not sue the monks for back wages for our hours of manual labor.

And then we passed through the door into the cloister.

"A Practical Program for Monks"

1

Each one shall sit at table with his own cup and spoon, and with his own
    repentance. Each one's own business shall be his most important
    affair, and provide his own remedies.
They have neglected bowl and plate.
Have you a wooden fork?
Yes, each monk has a wooden fork as well as a potato.

2

Each one shall wipe away tears with his own saint, when three bells hold
    in store a hot afternoon. Each one is supposed to mind his own
    heart, with its conscience, night and morning.
Another turn on the wheel: ho hum! And observe the Abbot!
Time to go to bed in a straw blanket.

3

Plenty of bread for everyone between prayers and the psalter: will you
    recite another?
Merci, and *Miserere*.
Always mind both the clock and the Abbot until eternity.
Miserere.

4

Details of the Rule are all liquid and solid. What canon was the first to
    announce regimentation before us? Mind the step on the way down!

Yes, I dare say you are right, Father. I believe you; I believe you.
I believe it is easier when they have ice water and even a lemon.
Each one can sit at table with his own lemon, and mind his conscience.

5

Can we agree that the part about the lemon is regular?
In any case, it is better to have sheep than peacocks, and cows rather
    than a chained leopard says Modest, in one of his proverbs.
The monastery, being owner of a communal rowboat, is the antecham-
    ber of heaven.
Surely that ought to be enough.

6

Each one can have some rain after Vespers on a hot afternoon, but *ne
    quid nimis,* or the purpose of the Order will be forgotten.
We shall send you hyacinths and a sweet millennium.
Everything the monastery provides is very pleasant to see and to sell for
    nothing.
What is baked smells fine. There is a sign of God on every leaf that
    nobody sees in the garden. The fruit trees are there on purpose, even
    when no one is looking. Just put the apples in the basket.
In Kentucky there is also room for a little cheese.
Each one shall fold his own napkin, and neglect the others.

7

Rain is always very silent in the night, under such gentle cathedrals.
Yes, I have taken care of the lamp. *Miserere.*
Have you a patron saint, and an angel?
Thank you. Even though the nights are never dangerous, I have one of
    everything.

"Evening: Zero Weather"

Now the lone world is streaky as a wall of marble
With veins of clear and frozen snow.
There is no bird song there, no hare's track
No badger working in the russet grass:
All the bare fields are silent as eternity.

And the whole herd is home in the long barn.
The brothers come, with hoods about their faces,

Following their plumes of breath
Lugging the gleaming buckets one by one.

This was a day when shovels would have struck
Full flakes of fire out of the land like rock:
And ground cries out like iron beneath our boots

When all the monks come in with eyes as clean as the cold sky
And axes under their arms,
Still paying out *Ave Marias*
With rosaries between their bleeding fingers.

We shake the chips out of our robes outside the door
And go to hide in cowls as deep as clouds,
Bowing our shoulders in the church's shadow, lean and whipped,
To wait upon your Vespers, Mother of God!

And we have eyes no more for the dark pillars or the freezing windows,
Ears for the rumorous cloister or the chimes of time above our heads:
For we are sunken in the summer of our adoration,
And plunge, down, down into the fathoms of our secret joy
That swims with indefinable fire.

And we will never see the copper sunset
Linger a moment, like an echo, on the frozen hill
Then suddenly die an hour before the Angelus.

For we have found our Christ, our August
Here in the zero days before Lent—
We are already binding up our sheaves of harvest
Beating the lazy liturgy, going up with exultation
Even on the eve of our Ash Wednesday,
And entering our blazing heaven by the doors of the Assumption!

"For My Brother: Reported Missing in Action, 1943"

Sweet brother, if I do not sleep
My eyes are flowers for your tomb;
And if I cannot eat my bread,
My fasts shall live like willows where you died.

If in the heat I find no water for my thirst,
My thirst shall turn to springs for you, poor traveler.

Where, in what desolate and smoky country,
Lies your poor body, lost and dead?
And in what landscape of disaster
Has your unhappy spirit lost its road?

Come, in my labor find a resting place
And in my sorrows lay your head,
Or rather take my life and blood
And buy yourself a better bed—
Or take my breath and take my death
And buy yourself a better rest.

When all the men of war are shot
And flags have fallen into dust,
Your cross and mine shall tell men still
Christ died on each, for both of us.

For in the wreckage of your April Christ lies slain,
And Christ weeps in the ruins of my spring:
The money of Whose tears shall fall
Into your weak and friendless hand,
And buy you back to your own land:

The silence of Whose tears shall fall
Like bells upon your alien tomb.
Hear them and come: they call you home.

"The Heavenly City"

City, when we see you coming down,
Coming down from God
To be the new world's crown:
How shall they sing, the fresh, unsalted seas
Hearing your harmonies!

For there is no more death,
No need to cure those waters, now, with any brine;

Their shores give them no dead,
Rivers no blood, no rot to stain them.

Because the cruel algebra of war
Is now no more.
And the steel circle of time, inexorable,
Bites like a padlock shut, forever,
In the smoke of the last bomb:

And in that trap the murderers and sorcerers and crooked leaders
Go rolling home to hell.
And history is done.

Shine with your lamb-light, shine upon the world:
You are the new creation's sun.
And standing on their twelve foundations,
Lo, the twelve gates that are One Christ are wide as canticles:
And Oh! Begin to hear the thunder of the songs within the crystal Towers,
While all the saints rise from their earth with feet like light
And fly to tread the quick-gold of those streets,

Oh, City, when we see you sailing down,
Sailing down from God,
Dressed in the glory of the Trinity, and angel-crowned
In nine white diadems of liturgy.

Elizabeth Hardwick

"Evenings at Home"

A Lexington native, Elizabeth Hardwick is not a household name in Kentucky—not even in the households where books are often read. Blame it on her decision to move to New York as soon as she finished her master's degree at the University of Kentucky in 1939 and then to maintain a rather cold distance from her family and hometown. During her time away from home, however, she has been busy creating a reputation for herself as a no-nonsense critic and author of essays and short stories and several novels, including her very promising first novel, *The Ghostly Lover* (1945). Despite her rather calculated decision to absent herself from her home, she has certainly earned a spot in this anthology by the quality of work she has produced, including this fine memoir-essay of a Jamesian return to Lexington, where she confronts some of the ghosts she left behind—some living, some dead, and some merely disfigured. There is a saying that Kentuckians some way or another, sooner or later, will always come home. Will Elizabeth Hardwick disprove the old Kentucky saying?

I am here in Kentucky with my family for the first time in a number of years and, naturally, I am quite uncomfortable, but not in the way I had anticipated before leaving New York. The thing that startles me is that I am completely free and can do and say exactly what I wish. This freedom leads me to the bewildering conclusion that the notions I have entertained about my family are fantastic manias, complicated, willful distortions which are so clearly contrary to the facts that I might have taken them from some bloody romance, or, to be more specific, from one of those childhood stories in which the heroine, ragged and castoff, roams the cold streets begging alms which go into the eager hands of a tyrannical stepmother.

I staggered a bit when I actually came face to face with my own mother: she carries no whips, gives no evidence of cannibalism. At night everyone sleeps peacefully. So far as I can judge they accuse me of no crimes, make no demands upon me; they neither praise nor criticize me excessively. My uneasiness and defensiveness are quite beside the point, like those flamboyant but unnecessary gestures of our old elocution teacher. My family situation is distinguished by only one eccentricity—it is entirely healthy and normal. This truth is utterly disarming; nothing I have felt in years has disturbed me so profoundly as this terrible fact. I had grown accustomed to a flat and

328

literal horror, the usual childhood traumas, and having been away from home for a long time I had come to believe these fancies corresponded to life, that one walked in the door, met his parents, his brothers and sisters, and there they were, the family demons, bristling, frowning, and leaping at one's throat. I was well prepared to enjoy the battle and felt a certain superiority because I was the only one among us who had read up on the simplicities and inevitabilities of family life, the cripplings and jealousies, the shock of birth and brutality of parenthood. When I did not find these hostilities it was just as if the laws of the universe had stopped and I became wary and confused. It is awful to be faced each day with love that is neither too great nor too small, generosity that does not demand payment in blood; there are no rules for responding, no schemes that explain what this is about, and so each smile is a challenge, each friendly gesture an intellectual crisis.

I cannot sit down to a meal without staring oft in a distraction and when they ask me what I am thinking I am ashamed to say that I am recalling my *analysis* of all of them, pacing again, in some amazement, the ugly, angry, damp alleys I think of as my inheritance. But now I look around the table and can see these family faces—my father's narrow skull, the sudden valley that runs down my mother's cheeks from the ears to the chin, my sister's smile which uncovers her large, crooked teeth and makes one think for the moment that she is as huge as an old work horse, though she is, except for her great teeth, very frail—everything I see convinces me that I have been living with a thousand delusions. The simple, benign reality is something else. (I have only one just complaint and that is that the radio is never turned off.) But where are the ancient misdeeds and brutish insufficiencies that have haunted me for years?

My nephew, a brown-haired boy of three, disconcerts me as much as anything else. When I take him on my lap I feel he is mocking me for the countless times I have lamented that he should be doomed to grow up *here*. Since the day of his birth I have been shuddering and sighing in his behalf; I have sung many requiems for him and placed sweet wreaths on his grave; but often he looks at me, perhaps noticing the lines on my face and the glaze on my eyes, as if he were returning my solicitude.

At least one thing I anticipated is true and it makes me happy to acknowledge that I am bored. The evenings are just as long as ever, dead, dead, "nothing going on." I take a deep breath and yearn for the morning so that I can go downtown to see how the old place is coming along. And when I get on the streets I see vigorous, cheerful faces which, in spite of the dark corners and violent frustrations in small-town life, beam with self-love and sparkle with pride. These magnificent countenances seem to be announcing: Look! I made it! And the wives—completely stunned by the marvelous possession of these blithe, busy husbands. They sigh tenderly under the delightful burdens of propitious marriages and smile at the less fortunate with queenly compassion. Some wan, sensitive souls carry the dreadful obligations of being "well-born" and do their noble penance by assuming an expert, affecting dowdiness, like so many rusty, brown, pedigreed dogs who do not dare to bark.

There is something false and perverse in my playing the observer, I who have lived here as long as anyone. Still these bright streets do not belong to me and I feel, not like someone who chose to move away, but as if I had been, as the expression goes, "run out of town." I can remember only one person to whom that disgrace actually happened and he was a dapper, fastidious little man who spoke in what we used to call a "cultured" voice and spent the long, beautiful afternoons in the park beside the wading pond in which the children under five played. No doubt he too went to New York, the exile for those with evil thoughts.

For the first week or so everything went well here and I was, during this sweet coma, under the impression that I might have a fine time. And suddenly a terrible thing happened. Just after dark I walked up to the mailbox, a few blocks away. On the way back home I passed a group of small, identical, red brick houses, four of them, each with a low concrete porch and a triangular peak at the top. In one of these houses I saw him, sitting alone on the porch, with a ray of light from the inside hallway shining behind his head. I stopped involuntarily and gasped because his face seemed with the years to have become much larger. It was incredibly ugly and brutal, a fierce face, rather like a crocodile's with wide, ponderous jaws, sleepy reptilian eyes, heavy, indolent features in horrible incompatibility with his fresh, pinkish skin. I walked on quickly without speaking, but my heart raced painfully, and I prayed that I had not been recognized. When I reached my own house I was almost out of breath and rushed into the living room, believing I would ask what he was doing here in our neighborhood, what had happened to him in the last years. But I did none of these things. Instead I looked suspiciously at my mother, trying to decide why she hadn't mentioned him or if she had forgotten that I once knew him.

"You devil, you witch!" I thought, enraged by her bland face and even despising the dark blue dress she wore with a frill of chaste white organdy at the neck.

"What's the matter, sister?" she asked.

"Don't call me *sister*," I said, "it makes me feel like a fool. And if you want to know what's wrong, I don't like that dress you're wearing. It isn't good for you."

"How funny. I'm always getting compliments on it. But, I don't care one way or another."

The face on the porch belonged to a young man I had not seen for years, but whom I had once thought myself in love with. Had he always looked so sinister, so bloated with ignorance and lethargy? I tried to remember a younger, healthier face with some brightness or pathos that had appealed to me, some gaiety and promise; anything except that large, iron, insentient image on the porch. But I remembered nothing comforting, not even one cool, happy afternoon in which he was different from the dark, hateful person living out some kind of life a few steps away from me. It was not love I had felt, not really love, I assured myself, but simply one of those incomprehensible youthful errors.

"Mama," I said, "forgive me. The funny thing is that I honestly like that dress *better* than any you have."

"Make up your mind," she said with good humor. I said good night, but on the steps I turned around and saw my father looking at me, his blue eyes dark and strange with an infinite sadness. *He knows, he knows,* I decided. Men can sense these things. Let me die now.

I went to bed and in the darkness and stillness I felt the mere existence of the man I had seen to be sickeningly important to me. I was appalled by the undeniable fact that I had once been his slave, had awakened each morning with no thoughts except how I might please him. As two numb beasts we had found each other and created a romance. It was somehow better to believe that in him I had simply recognized an equal than to answer the shocking question as to why, if I was in any way his superior, I had been so violently attached to him.

It all came back to me: I had not only been in love with him, but he had required courage, daring, and cunning on my part. It had not been easy and I cannot excuse myself by saying we were "thrown together" when the truth is that every effort was made to tear us apart and only my mad-dog determination prevented that. And I began to hate my brother, my own flesh and blood, now dead, poor boy. It was he who started interfering and I can still see him, his face twisted with wonder and fear, saying, "How could you?" My brother's case was weakened, even in his own mind, by his inability to accuse my friend of anything except frightening, depressing stupidity. Oh, is *that* all? I must have thought victoriously, because I continued to make clandestine engagements and took no interest in anyone else.

I heard my parents coming up the steps—thump, thump, closer and closer—and then like the killer in the movies they passed by the one marked for destruction and went to their own rooms. But this is impossible, impossible, I resolved; I must face it. (Self-analysis, bravery, objectivity. Is anything really *bad*?) Yet it was so difficult to recall those old days, almost beyond my powers to see myself again. I couldn't even remember when I had first met that terrible creature. It seemed to have been in high school, some dull, immoral season, a kind of Indian summer romance. On the other hand, I had the weird and disturbing notion that I had known him since infancy, which is quite possible since he has lived off and on in our neighborhood or else we could not have gone to the same schools. In any case I remembered that he was literally not interested in anything, did his lessons with minimum competence and never became involved in anything he learned, never preferred one subject to another, since he was equally mediocre in all of them. He played sports but was not first-rate in any game, even though he was physically powerful.

A few other mortifying things flashed through my mind. His behavior had only two variations: he either went blindly through the days like a stupefied giant or then quite suddenly, as if bored by his own apathy, he would laugh at everything, burst forth in this rocking strange sound as if some usually sluggish portion of his brain had flared up in a brief, dazzling moment. The laughter must have cost him great effort and he engaged in it only out of a rudimentary social instinct which at times told him that he owed the human race at least that raucous recognition. The other aspect of him I remembered was that, though he initiated nothing, things were always happening to him, one disaster after another. Violence erupted spontaneously in his presence and he was usually the victim. He was always either limping or wearing a bandage; he fell out of trees as a child, got shot in the leg when he was old enough to go hunting, lived through so many narrow escapes and calamities that finally shocks left no mark at all upon him.

But there must have been something else. What happened between us? No, no, merciful stars, not that! But yes, and on a gray November afternoon, mad and dark, and as though I had just come into the world, an orphan, responsible to no one, magnificently free. Embraces and queer devotions, ironically mixed with that fine, beguiling notion of those years in which one thinks himself chosen from all people on earth for happiness. "I'll love you always! Nothing can separate us!" And it was true, for in his anarchic face, in his non-human, reckless force, I saw the shadow of something lost, some wild, torrential passion lived out years and years before in my soul. How shameful! What unutterable, beautiful chaos! Yes, it was he, he, image of all the forgone sin that forever denies innocence. Nothing can ever separate us.

How I regretted that walk to the mailbox to send a letter to New York. If I hadn't done that there is at least a good possibility that I might never have seen him again and might have been spared that long night in which I tried to account for humiliating days and emotions. I couldn't sleep at all and yet I didn't want the night to pass because it seemed to me that once morning came everyone in town would remember what kind of man I first fell in love with.

I looked up the dark street in the direction of his house and thought, suppose, great heavens, that I had married him. This idea completely unnerved me because I had wanted to marry him and would have done so if he had not violated one of those rigid, adolescent, feminine laws. I finally broke with him only because he went away for three days and didn't write to me on each of them. His infidelity crushed me and with real anguish I forced myself to say, "My heart is utterly broken. If you don't care enough for me to keep your promises . . ." The thought of the risk I had taken chilled me to the bone. I might at this moment have been asleep in his house, my stupid head pressed against his chest, touching the stony curve of his chin.

At last I dozed off and when I awakened late the next morning there was great commotion downstairs. We were going on a picnic. I threw myself into the preparations so gleefully that my mother was taken aback and said, "If you like picnics so much I'm surprised you haven't mentioned them before."

꩜ ꩜ ꩜

Another week has passed and I have found the temerity to see some of my old friends. They are all somewhat skeptical of me but not for the right reasons. It is a great relief to learn that I am thought of only as "radical" and though I know that is not meant to be a compliment it seems quite the happiest way out and so I try to keep that aspect of my past in the public mind on the theory that nice people demand only one transgression and if they find a suitable sin they won't go snooping around for more. Perhaps I have overplayed it a little, become too dogmatic and angry. (Extremes of any sort embarrass small-town people. They are dead set against overexertion and for that reason even opera singers and violinists make them uncomfortable because it seems a pity the notes won't come forth without all that fuss and foolishness.)

Even I was taken in by my act and it did seem to me that when I lived here I thought only of politics. One afternoon, overwhelmed by nostalgia and yearning for the hopeful, innocent days in which we used to talk about the "vanguard of the future," I went to the old courthouse. Here our radical group, some six or seven snoring people on a good night, used to meet. I found the courthouse unchanged; it is still the same hideous ruin with the familiar dirt and odor of perspiring petitioners and badgered drunks who have filed in and out for a hundred years, the big spittoons, the sagging staircase. When I left I heard the beautiful bells ringing to announce that it was five o'clock and I went home in a lyrical mood, admitting that I had spent many happy, ridiculous days in this town.

For some reason I could not wait to reach the garage next to our house where my father keeps his fishing equipment. I saw there the smooth poles painted in red and green stripes and I intended to rush into the house, throw my arms around my father's neck, and tell him how many times in New York I had thought of him bent over his workbench, and that I despised myself for criticizing him for going fishing instead of trying to make money.

But just as I stepped upon the back porch I stopped and pretended to be admiring an old fat hen which the neighbors had intended to kill long ago but hadn't found the heart to do so because the hen has a human aspect and keeps looking at them gaily and as an equal. I was not thinking about the hen; I was wondering, of course, why my family hadn't mentioned that my friend was living on the street. We had spent many hours talking about the new tenants, deaths and births, who had become alcoholic or been sent to the asylum. It wasn't like my mother, a talented gossip, to forget such an arrival, and I concluded sorrowfully that she remembered all my lies and tricks and thought me guilty of the one, unforgivable wrong. Yet when I finally entered the house my family was in such a good mood I hadn't the nerve to mention my suspicions. Perhaps they want to forget me, I thought. Silly, proud people who must see the broad face of the boy on the street and recoil, thinking, "Oh, my sweet daughter! What dreadful horrors she was born with. . . . Some genes from an old Tennessee reprobate who cropped up in the family, passed on, and now wants to live again in her."

I will force nothing, I decided. It will all come out and then I shall leave forever, vanish, change my name, and begin over again in Canada.

෨෨ ෨෨ ෨෨

Several nights later I went to visit a friend in the neighborhood, a girl who weighs over two hundred pounds and who is so fearful of becoming a heavy, cheerful clown that she is, instead, a mean-spirited monster. And yet her malice, which is of a metropolitan order, is often quite entertaining, and I might have stayed longer if I had not begun to imagine the inspired tales she could tell on me. Her small eyes seemed to contain all my secrets and I could see her plump, luxurious mouth forming the syllables of misdeeds even I could not name. At nine o'clock I went home where I found the house dark and supposed my family had gone out for a few minutes, perhaps to the drugstore or across town to the ice-cream factory. This was the moment at last. I felt it acutely.

There he was, sitting on the steps, smoking a cigarette. I realized it was he the moment I saw the figure, the wide, slumping shoulders, the head turned somewhat to the side. Even in the dark I felt his slow, calm, somnolent gaze on me.

"Is that you?" he asked in a low, untroubled voice that is unlike any I have ever heard before. It seems to come at you from a great distance, rolling like a wave.

"Yes, it is," I answered lightly and in exactly the opposite way I had planned. But after I had spoken so hospitably I began to worry about my family. They might return at any moment, and I couldn't bear them to find him here, couldn't endure their curious glances, questions, and recollections of the past.

"Don't bother me!" I said rapidly. "I don't want to see you. What are you doing living around here anyway? It isn't fair for me to come home to this. . . . I'm different now."

I could see his face quite well now and apparently he too had changed because he actually registered an emotion. He looked at me with disgust, his mouth opening slowly and curiously, his lazy eyes blinking at me reproachfully.

"Bother you?" he said. "What do you mean? Come back to what?"

I began to tremble with impatience. "Don't you see?" I whispered desperately. "I don't want them to know I've seen you again. It would just start up the old argument."

He put his hand on my arm to steady me and I looked angrily into his wide, immobile face. It was not frightening, but simply infuriating for it had a kind of prehistoric, dumb strength, so that he looked like some Neanderthal ruler, superb and forceful in a savage way, and quite eternal. My ghastly darling.

"Never mind. Dear God, it's too late now," I said, because I saw the car driving up in front of the house and in a fit of weakness I sat down beside him on the steps and buried my face in my hands.

I did not look up when I heard my parents saying something dryly and politely, saying nothing much because they sounded tired and sleepy. The perspiration on my forehead dampened my hands, but somehow I was able to stand up and bid my old friend good night. I smiled at him and he returned this last gesture shyly, and turning away his eyes seemed in the evening light a soft, violet color.

As I went into the hall I stopped before the mirror and saw that my cheeks were burning and that there was something shady and subtly disreputable in my face. My mother was taking the hairpins out of her hair. The great mysterious drama had passed, but I knew that I could not stay at home any longer.

The next day I prepared to leave and I noted with astonishment that I had been at home nineteen days. We packed my bags, and my mother said that she thought the trip had done me good. "You're not quite as nervous as when you arrived," she observed.

"Not as nervous!" I said. "I'm a wreck!"

"Well, go on back to New York if it makes you feel better," she said wearily.

"I don't feel exactly wonderful there—"

"There's only one answer to that," my mother said, slamming the door as she walked out of the room. "There must be something wrong with *you!*"

I ran to the door and opened it so that she would be certain to hear me. "If there is something wrong with me it's your fault," I said triumphantly.

"Mine!" she called back. "What madness!"

For some reason this altercation put me in a good humor. Now that I was leaving my feelings shifted every five seconds from self-pity to the gushiest love and affection. I even began to think how nice it was at home, how placid. My father came in and I could tell from the serious expression on his face that he was thinking of important matters. I'm sure he meant to make me very happy but he had a way of expressing himself that was often misleading and so, with the most tender look in his eyes, he informed me that *in spite of everything* they all liked me very much. I graciously let that pass because I was, in my thoughts, already wondering whether once I was away, home would again assume its convenient sinister shape.

There was only one thing left to do in Kentucky, a little ritual which I always liked to put off until the end. My mother mistakenly believes that I mourn my dead brother and tomorrow morning there will still be time before the train leaves to drive out to the cemetery where he lies. The pink and white dogwood will be flowering and the graves will be surrounded by tulips and lilacs. At this time of year the cemetery is magnificent, and my mother will not let me miss the beauty. When we get there she will point to the family lot and say, "Sister, I hate to think of you alone in New York, away from your family. But you'll come back to us. There's a space for you next to Brother . . . In the nicest part . . . So shady and cool."

And so it is, as they say, comforting to have these roots.

Hollis Summers

"Herschell"

Hollis Summers wrote short stories, novels, and poems and wrote them very well—with humor, irony, and master craftsmanship. The son of a Baptist minister, he grew up in parsonages all over Kentucky, from Eminence, his birthplace in 1916, to Louisville and Campbellsville and Madisonville. Much of the subject matter of his fiction and poetry is taken from his own life as a preacher's boy and as a high school teacher and college professor at Georgetown College, the University of Kentucky, and Ohio University. *Brighten the Corner* (1952) is about the motley members of a Baptist church, from the former minister who still wants to run the church to the congregant who is always backsliding from one misdemeanor to another. Summers wrote until his death in 1987. "Herschell" is a haunting, subtle story of two close boyhood friends; one narrates the story with honesty and innocent longing, and the other is charming, handsome, and illegitimate. They eventually go their own unhappy ways.

⁖

I come from old Kentucky families.

I have been told since I was old enough to listen that I come from old families, my father's family, the Baxters, with a land grant in 1799; my mother's, the Archers, in 1832. Mother never forgave the Baxters for their earlier arrival.

"They were farmers. They worked other people's lands after they lost their own," Mother said and said. "But they were God-fearing people. There's nothing to be ashamed of in your father's lineage. It's just that he never took any interest in his forebears. I must admit, Archie Lee, I consider that a character flaw. But I'm not speaking against your father. I've never spoken against him. Isn't that true, Archie?"

"Yeah. Sure," I said and said, not wanting the conversation to continue.

The Archers were professional people, ministers, professors, lawyers, even a judge. "But you aren't to be vain about your inheritance on my side. Inheritance, like grace, is something we don't deserve. It's something to thank God for, but quietly."

The portrait of Great Great Great Grandmother Phoebe Essex is my earliest memory. Always, in the variously miserable houses we rented through my youth, Grandmother stood above a fireplace, over a couch, between windows, watching me. She is a young girl with an old woman's face. Her hands rest on a pedestal. Her background is blue and gray fog. She is contained within a frame of gold curlicues bumping into each other. Beneath her is a museum light. Every dusk of my life in those rented houses Mother turned on the light under Grandmother Phoebe's picture. The last person to bed was supposed to turn Grandmother out.

"Have you turned Grandmother out?" Mother called from her bedroom.

More often than I fumbled down dark stairs to make sure the water heater was turned off I went to check on Grandmother Phoebe.

Grandmother seemed to look at me, even after the light was out. It was only a trick of the moon or a streetlight, a trick of twelve-year-old eyes, my twenty-one-year-old eyes, twenty-five, the eyes of a man who lived in a house with his mother for thirty-five years.

As a child I often studied the picture. I stood on a chair to look at her. I lay with my head hanging over the edge of a couch, making the world upside down, imagining the light fixture a candelabra on the white floor of the ceiling, Grandmother and her pedestal standing on their heads.

There was something wrong with Grandmother from every angle.

Her right arm and hand were good enough, but her left arm didn't belong to her body. The left arm wasn't long enough to reach the pedestal, but it reached the pedestal.

I worried about Grandmother. Perhaps, with her young body and her old face, she was a dwarf. Perhaps she was painfully crippled. Perhaps I would inherit her body. Maybe I would never grow tall enough to be a man. Maybe my arm, my right arm—inheritances changed from women to men—would be so crippled I could never catch a baseball. Often, looking at her, I clenched my fists, imagining baseballs. It did not once enter my mind to ask Mother about Grandmother Phoebe's deformity.

෨෬ ෨෬ ෨෬

Mother never encouraged me to learn to fix, to mend or repair. I think she wanted to spare my hands, as if she nurtured Paderewski, Kreisler, Rodin. Mr. Barnes, my friend Herschell's father, was our handyman. Mother called on Mr. Barnes for everything from light switches to leaking faucets.

God knows my hands were not worth saving for any reason except for the convenience of having hands. For a year I studied violin with Mrs. Keeton next door in exchange for Mother's taking care of the Keeton twins twice a week. During fourth grade, after my father's death, I studied the piano. Mother took great pride in saying, "Arch is studying the piano now." There was a year of oboe with Mr. Fontaine at the Normal School. I have no memory of how the piano or oboe lessons were paid for. I remember only the shame I felt when Mother boasted of my studies. Feeling I owed her something, I practiced hard. But I never made the junior orchestra or the junior band. In the seventh grade I took a paper route, not without a painful scene with Mother. She almost cried, but, being an Archer, she did not cry.

"Your music, Arch! Music is the soul of man. You'll thank me some day for your music. If you had a paper route you wouldn't have time for practicing."

I said, "You work too hard. I ought to be working. I thank you very much for my music. I thank you right now. Everybody has a paper route."

"*Everybody* being Herschell Barnes, I suppose."

"Yeah, he has one. But that's not the reason. And, anyhow, Herschell's my friend."

"Archer, I have told you and told you and told you . . ."

Mother fretted over my being able to have only one friend at a time.

"You should have a dozen friends, at least a dozen. Or more."

I told her, again, that I didn't want that many friends; I wouldn't know what to do with them. "There's nothing wrong with Herschell."

"I didn't say there was. Perhaps Mr. Barnes is a little . . . well, a little feckless."

I asked what *feckless* meant. I was learning three new words a day. Mother told me to never mind. "There's no reason in the world for you to take a paper route."

"Are you telling me I can't?"

We were standing in front of the mantel in the house on Elm Street.

I have not thought of that house in years.

That moment under Grandmother Phoebe's portrait was a moment of triumph for me, but I hardly relish remembering it.

Mother said, "You're thirteen."

I said, "I was just going to say I was thirteen."

I thought, "She's not as tall as she used to be. Or I'm getting taller." I said, "I'm not going to take oboe lessons any more."

Mother said, "Very well," and went back to the kitchen. I went upstairs and practiced at "The Stars and Stripes Forever" for almost an hour. By suppertime we were acting as if the day were just any old day.

That fall was as fine a season as I can remember. At school we were seated alphabetically. All day I sat by Herschell. After school we went straight to the *Messenger* office. Most days old Mr. Roberts was late in getting the paper out. We horsed around. We raced each other to the post office and back; we stole each other's caps. Herschell sang sometimes. When Herschell decided to sing everybody listened. He had learned the songs from an old Victrola his granddaddy had willed him. Herschell sang "O Sole Mio," and "Funiculi, Funicula," and "The Volga Boatman," and "Loch Lomond."

Herschell could do everything well. Herschell knew what he was going to do with his life. Miss Grange, our Sunday School teacher, said we all should know what we were going to do with our lives, but Herschell was the only one of us who really knew. He was going to be a radio singer. And then he was going to Hollywood and be a movie star. When he was about thirty years old he was coming back to Graham and buy Major Thompson's house at the edge of town, the house on the hill with porches that looked all over Scott County.

We never doubted Herschell's future. "We'll come to see you."

"Sure," Herschell said, even to the black kid who delivered the Buttermilk Lane route. "I'll be having a party every night or so. You're all invited."

I courted Herschell. I helped him with his arithmetic. While we were friends his grade in English changed from *D* to *A*. I imagined myself in a tuxedo entering Major Thompson's house on the hill. "Hello, old friend." Herschell was dressed in a white tuxedo. "My, but I'm glad to see you," Herschell said.

രൈ രൈ രൈ

Monday's *Messenger* was the lightest paper of the week. One Monday, it was October still, a red and yellow October that made you catch your breath, Herschell came home with me after we had delivered our papers. "We'll make popcorn," I promised. "Maybe we'll even have cider. And fresh apple cake, maybe."

Mother was cordial enough to Herschell, as cordial as she ever was. There was fresh apple cake, and cider. Every grain of the popcorn popped as complete as a snowflake.

We played three games of carom. Herschell won, even though it was difficult to make him win.

In the kitchen Mother rattled dishes and pans. I knew we were going to have soup and hamburgers. Soup and hamburgers shouldn't have made that much noise. I kept hoping Mother would ask Herschell to stay for supper.

At five-thirty Mother came into the living room to turn on Grandmother.

Herschell leaned back in his chair. He slapped rhythmically at his stomach, making drum sounds. "Who in the world's that?" Herschell tossed his head, making his dark hair rise and fall.

"Phoebe Essex. You saw her before, that other time we played carom."

"Not with her light on. It don't look like anybody much."

"She's my three greats grandmother."

"What was the matter with her?"

Mother stood at the door to the dining room.

Herschell was my friend. I felt free to tell Herschell anything. I said, "She was crippled some way. I hope I don't catch it. I guess I won't, after all this time."

"I sure hope not."

"Archer Baxter!" Mother came into the living room, her hands on her hips. She looked like somebody angry in a comic strip. She was angry. "That is your great great great grandmother you are speaking of. She was not afflicted. She was a beautiful, cultured woman. All of the letters and diaries so attest. "

Attest. It was a word I could add. I tried to think about the word.

Herschell said, "She looks crippled to me. She looks pretty bad off." Herschell always spoke up to everybody.

We were having a bad time, I remember—the grocery bill; we owed the dentist for my wisdom teeth; we had charged for my school clothes; maybe we still owed Herschell's father for fixing the electric iron and Mother's sewing machine. I thought about feeling sorry for Mother. But she need not have said, "She is *who* we are. Many people are uncertain of their own parentage."

I had no notion of what she was talking about. Herschell seemed to know. He was standing. He said, "I knowed Pa Tate. He left me his Victrola." He and Mother were looking hard at each other.

"Which is very nice," Mother said. "Archie has told me you have a splendid singing voice."

"I guess I better be gettin' home."

"It *is* late," Mother said. "I expect your family will be waiting for you. And, oh yes, Herschell. Would you mind asking Mr. Barnes to drop in some time tomorrow? The furnace. And the nights are getting cold. You'll be sure and tell *Mr.* Barnes."

"My daddy."

"Mr. Barnes."

"I guess I'll tell him."

"Herschell!"

"O.K. I'll tell him. But Pa Tate was a good singer. I got it from him. Singin'."

"I'm sure you do. Good-bye Herschell."

I said, "I'll walk you part of the way."

Mother said, "Supper's almost ready."

I walked with Herschell to the comer of Elm and Fourth Street. We did not talk.

I said, "I'll see you tomorrow."

"Sure." Herschell broke into a run. I thought of calling, "Last look." We were always calling, "Last look," prolonging ourselves.

The soup that night was potato. The hamburger had gristle in it. I used the last of the mustard in the cut-glass jar. The milk was very cold.

I was ready to leave the table before I said, "I think you hurt Herschell's feelings. I don't know what you were talking about."

"There are certain subjects we do not discuss, Archie Lee."

"I got a right to know."

Mother said, "Evil communications corrupt good manners."

"I don't know what that means."

"I expect my son to be pure. The Barneses have values different from ours. Now, that's enough."

"For gosh sakes."

"That is a vulgar expression."

"Herschell's very nice. I don't know what you're talking about."

Mother said, "In the olden days itinerant artists visited country homes. They were not always master painters." She was making conversation as if I were company. "We are very fortunate that Grandmother Essex's portrait was done by a skilled craftsman. A number of years ago the museum in Cincinnati was quite interested in securing Grandmother for their permanent collection. I would not part with her."

"I know. I know that. What's the matter with Herschell?"

Mother patted her lips with her napkin. "You're excused, Arch. I'm sure you have homework to do. There's no need to help me with the dishes."

I didn't get to talk to Herschell at all the next day. While we were waiting for old man Roberts to bring out the *Messengers,* Herschell grabbed Eric Thompson's cap and raced him to the post office.

"How ya doing?" we kept asking each other.

꧁ ꧁ ꧁

That fall Herschell began working with his father, afternoons after school. Once—it was late December—Herschell came alone. The gas grate in my bedroom was broken.

I had had a terrible cold since Thanksgiving. Mother had insisted that I give up the paper route. I didn't mind giving it up.

I was glad to see Herschell. I stood in the doorway of my room and watched him. I dug my hands deep into the pockets of my corduroy pants. I was ashamed of my hands that couldn't play anything or fix anything.

Herschell hummed as he worked.

I said, "You tell me if I can help. Hold anything. Or anything?"

"I got it. It's coming all right."

I wanted to leave the doorway. I wished Mother would call me. She did not call.

I was coughing. I sounded like a dog barking.

Herschell said, "That's a pretty bad cough you got."

"Mother and I both have colds. I haven't been at school in a week."

"I thought I hadn't seen you around."

"I hope you don't catch anything from us."

Herschell laughed. "I never get a cold." He threw back his hair and smiled.

I said, "I hear Mother calling me. I got to go see what she wants." I hoped Herschell imagined he had heard Mother call. "You yell if I can do anything."

I was standing at the kitchen sink turning the water on and off when Herschell came downstairs. Mother was sewing in the dining room. I started to go up the back stairway. I changed my mind.

Mother was being polite to Herschell. "Now, you're sure you're charging me enough? I don't want to rob you."

"It wasn't anything very wrong. The valve. It was just clogged up."

I was in the dining room. Under Grandmother Phoebe's picture Mother was saying, "You must take this extra twenty cents. It means a great deal to me for Archie to be warm. I insist, Herschell."

I started to back into the kitchen. But Herschell was looking at me over Mother's shoulder. He didn't smile. Herschell dropped one of the dimes. Mother and Herschell and I looked at the dime's wobbling across the hearth. I imagined that it would never stop.

I walked over and picked up the dime and dropped it in Herschell's hand. Our hands did not touch.

I went with Herschell to the edge of the porch. I wanted to offer to walk part-way home with him.

Herschell said, "S'long."

I said, "See you."

My heart was beating hard. I was afraid Mother would come to the door. I was afraid she would say, "Arch Baxter, you'll catch your death. What on earth? What on earth are you thinking about?"

I was thinking that maybe Herschell would turn around and call to me. I was thinking maybe he would say, "What about some carom tomorrow?"

I hurried inside. Mother was in the kitchen. I started upstairs.

"Arch? Is that you?"

"It's me. It's I. I." I began coughing.

"Gargle. And take two aspirin. It's time for aspirin. Can you hear me, Arch? Are you hearing me?"

Herschell had left the stove lighted. After I had gargled and taken two aspirin, I sat close against the fire, wishing I were named Herschell Barnes, saying my own name. Miss Grange was always saying, "A man will lay down his life for his friend." I would have laid down my life for Herschell.

Archer Lee Baxter is a slow man.

⁓ ⁓ ⁓

It must have been six months before I pieced Mother's hints and innuendoes together with what Ed Hoskin told me one afternoon while we were trading stamps.

Mr. Barnes wasn't the real father of any of his children. When he was drunk he would go into Webster's barber shop or the pool hall and cry about the situation. Ed said Dr. Frank Martin was Herschell's father. Hadn't I noticed how much Herschell looked like Dr. Martin? "Everybody knows. It beats all, doesn't it?"

I confronted Mother with the story. She shook her head sadly. "I didn't want you to know, Arch. I wanted to protect you."

That was a dark day. The story of the Barneses was as devastating to me as newspaper stories about plane wrecks and hurricanes.

Had I turned into a novelist I would probably have written about Mr. Barnes, who was handy with his hands, who drank, who sometimes ushered at the First Presbyterian Church, who lived with four handsome children in a shotgun house down by the L and N station, who was married to a small woman with bright hair. I cannot remember the woman's face, or her first name, or the clothes she wore.

Ed Hoskin who, in the eighth grade, had a large collection of dirty comics, became lieutenant governor under a Republican administration.

Herschell quit school in the eleventh grade to marry Tooli Cooper. He was killed by the midnight train at Dead Man's curve, leaving Tooli and three small children. Mother said it was a great tragedy.

Cordia Greer Petrie

"Angeline Jines the Choir"

The Angeline Keaton stories by Cordia Greer Petrie are a variation of the ancient wise fool archetype: a naive country bumpkin goes to town (or court) speaking a rustic dialect but, under the cloak of ignorance and innocence, preaches good lessons to his or her betters. Sometimes he is a sidekick-servant to a master, such as Sancho Panza to Don Quixote; sometimes the comic moralist is a loner, like Angeline, who moves through a "superior" society and reveals its hypocrisy and hollowness. In most of her sketches the educated, affluent Cordia Greer Petrie assumes the mask of Angeline to take on urbane snobs of all kinds and undress them. Born at Merry Oaks in Barren County in 1872, Petrie attended Eminence College and later married a physician, Hazel G. Petrie, who practiced in eastern Kentucky for some ten years before moving to Louisville. She died in 1964. Most of her sketches focus on Angeline's adventures in polite society, but in the following one she satirizes herself as Angeline tries to join a sophisticated choir in the county seat.

She sat upon the edge of the veranda, fanning herself with her "split" sunbonnet, a tall, angular woman, whose faded calico gown "lost connection" at the waist line. Her spring being dry, she came to our well for water. Discovering that Angeline Keaton was a "character," I invariably inveigled her to rest awhile on our cool piazza before retracing her steps up the steep, rocky hillside to her cabin home.

"I missed you yesterday," I said as a starter.

"Yes'm," she answered in a voice harsh and strident, yet touched with a peculiar sibilant quality characteristic of the Kentucky backwoodsman, "and thar wuz others that missed me, too!"

Settling herself comfortably, she produced from some hidden source a box of snuff and plied her brush vigorously.

"We-all have got inter a wrangle over at Zion erbout the church music," she began. "I and Lum, my old man, has been the leaders ever since we moved here from Lick-skillet. We wuz alluz on hand—Lum with his tunin' fork and me with my strong serpraner. When it come to linin' off a song, Lum wuz pintedly hard to beat. Why, folks come from fur and near to hear us, and them city folks, at Mis' Bowles' last summer, lowed thar warn't nothing in New York that could tech us. One of 'em offered us a dollar to sing inter a phonygraf reckerd, but we wuz afeerd to put our lives in jopperdy by dabblin' in 'lectricerty. But even celebrerty has its drawbacks, and a 'profit is not without honor in his own country,' as the saying is. A passel of 'em got jellus, a church meeting was called, unbeknownst to us, and ermong 'em they agreed to make a change in the music at old Zion. That peaked-faced Betty Button wuz at the bottom of it. Ever since she tuk that normal course at Bowling Green she's been endeverin' to push herself inter promernence here at Bear Waller. Fust she got up a class in delsarty, but even Bear Waller warn't dull ernough to take to that foolishness! Then she canvassed the county with a cuttin' system and a book called 'Law at a Glance.' Now she's teaching vokle culshure. She orter know singers, like poits, is born, not made! Jest wantin' to sing won't do it. It takes power. It's give up mine's the powerfullest voice in all Bear Waller. I kin bring old Brindle in when she's grazing in the woods, back o' Judge Bowles' medder, and I simply step out on the portico and call Lum to dinner when he's swoppin' yarns down to the store quarter o' mile away. Fur that matter, though, a deef and dum man could fetch Lum to *vittles*.

"Do you know Bear Waller owes its muserkil educashun to me? Mine wuz the fust accordyon brought to the place, and I wuz allus ready to play fur my nabers. I didn't hafter be *begged*. I orgernized the Zobo band, I lent 'em my ballads, but whar's my thanks? At the battin' of an eye they're ready to drop me for that quavery-voiced Button gal and them notes o' hern that's no more'n that many peryids and commers.

"When the committee waited on me and Lum we jest flew mad and 'lowed we'd quit. Maybe we wuz hasty, but it serves 'em right. Besides, these Bear Wallerites ain't compertent to appreshiate a voice like mine, nohow. I decided I'd take my letter to Glasgow and jine that brag choir of their'n. It did me good to think how it 'ud spite some folks to see me leadin' the singin' at the county seat!

"Lum wuz dead set ergin it, but armin' myself with the rollin' pin and a skillet o' bilin grease, I finally pervailed on him to give in. Lum is of a yieldin' dispersishun if a body goes at 'im right.

"Jim Henry, that's my boy, an' I tuk a early start. We had tied up the colt in the cow shed and I wuz congratulatin' myself on bein' shet of the pesky critter when I heerd him nicker. Lookin' back, I saw him comin' in a gallerp, his head turned to one side, while he fairly obscured the landscape with great clouds o' pike dust!

"We wuz crossin' the railroad when old Julie heered that nicker, an' right thar she balked. Neither gentle persuasion from the peach tree switch which I helt in my hand, nor well-aimed kicks of Jim Henry's boots in her flanks could budge her till that colt come up pantin' beside her. We jest did clear the track when the accomerdashun whizzed by. Well, sir, when old Julie spied them kyars she began buck-jumpin' in a manner that would'er struck terror to a less experienced hosswoman. Jim Henry, who wuz gazin' at the train with childlike pleasure, wuz tuk wholly by suprise, and before he knowed what wuz up he wuz precippyatated inter the branches o' a red-haw tree. He crawled out, a wreck, his face and hands scratched and bleedin' and his britches hangin' in shreds, and them his Sundays, too! I managed to pin 'em tergether with beauty pins, and cautionin' him not to turn his back to the ordiance, we finally resumed our journey. That colt alluz tries hisself, and jest as we reached the square, in Glasgow, his appertite began clammerin', and Julie refused to go till the pesky critter's wants wuz appeased. Them Glasgowites is dear lovers of good hoss flesh, and quite a crowd gethered to discuss the good pints of the old mare and that mule colt.

"Some boys mistook Jim Henry for somebody they knowed and hollered, 'Say, Reube!' 'Hey, Reube!' at him. Jim Henry wuz fur explainin' to 'em their mistake, till one of 'em began to sing, 'When Reuben comes to town, he's shore to be done brown!' 'Jim Henry,' says I, sternly, 'you're no child o' mine ef you take *that*! Now, if you don't get down and thrash him I'm agoin' to set you afire when I get you home.'

"Jim Henry needed no second biddin'. He wuz off that nag in a jiffy, and the way he did wallerp that boy wuz a cawshun! He sellerbrated his victry by givin' the Bear Waller war-whoop. Then crawlin' up behind me, he said he wuz *now* ready fur meetin'. That boy's a born fiter. He gets it honest, for me and Lum are both experts, but then practice makes perfect, as the sayin' is.

"Our arrival created considerable stir in meetin'. Why is it that when a distinguished person enters a church it allus perduces a flutter? Owin' to the rent in Jim Henry's britches, I shoved him inter the back seat. Cautionin' him not to let me ketch him throwin' paper wads, I swept merjestercally up the ile and tuk a seat by the orgin. A flood of approvin' glances fastened themselves on my jet bonnet and fur-lined dolman. I wuz sorry I didn't know the fust song. It must have been a new one to that choir. Thar wuz four of 'em and each one wuz singin' it to a different tune, and they jest couldn't keep tergether! The coarse-voiced gal to my rear lagged dretfully. When the tall blonde, who wuz the only one of 'em that knowed the tune, when she'd sing,

"'Wake the song!'

that gal who lagged would echo,

"'Wake the song!'

in a voice as coarse as Lum's. She 'peared to depend on the tall gal for the words, for when the tall 'un would sing,

"'Song of Ju-ber-lee,'

the gal that lagged, and the two gents, would repeat, 'Of Ju-ber-lee.'

"I passed her my book, thinkin' the words wuz tore out o' hern, but, la! she jest glared at me, and she and them gents, if anything, bellered louder'n ever. I looked at the preacher, expecting to see him covered with shygrin, but, la! he wuz takin' it perfectly cam, with his eyes walled up at the ceilin' and his hands folded acrost his stummick like he might be havin' troubles of his own.

"I kept hopin' that tryo would either ketch up with the leader or jest have the curridge to quit. Goodness knows, I done what I could fur 'em, by beatin' time with my turkey wing.

"Somebody must have give 'em a tip, for the next song which the preacher give out as 'a solo,' that tryo jest pintedly giv it up and set thar is silent as clambs. The tall gal riz and commenced singin' and that tryo never pertended to help her out! My heart ached in symperthy fur her as she stood thar alone, singin' away with her voice quaverin', and not a human bein' in that house jined in, not even the *preacher*! But she had *grit*, and kept right on! Most people would'er giv right up. She's a middlin' good singer, but is dretfully handercapt by that laggin' tryo and a passel o' church members that air too triflin' to sing in meetin'. The song wuz a new 'un to me, but havin' a nacheral year for music, I soon ketched the tune and jined in on the last verse with a vim. Of course I could only hummit, not knowin' the words, but I come down on it good and strong and showed them folks that Angeline Keaton ain't one to shirk a duty, if they wuz. After the sermon the preacher giv out 'Thar Is a Fountain Filled with Blood.' Here wuz my chanct to show 'em what the brag-voice of Bear Waller wuz like!

"With my voice risin' and fallin', and dwellin' with extry force on the fust syllerbles of foun-tin and sin-ners, in long, drawn-out meeter, I fairly lost myself in the grand old melerdy. I wuz soarin' inter the third verse when I discovered I wuz the only one in the house that knowed it! The rest of 'em wuz singin' it to a friverlous tune like them Mose Beasley plays on his fiddle! What wuz more, they wuz titterin' like I wuz in errer! The very idy! That wuz too much fur me, and beckernin' Jim Henry to foller, I marched outer meetin'!

"We found the old mare had slipped the bridle and gone home, so thar wuz nothin' left fur us to do but foot it. The last thing I heered as we struck the Bear Waller pike and set out fur home wuz that coarse-voiced gal, still lagging behind, as she sang,

"'The Blood of the Lamb!'"

John Jacob Niles

Perhaps the best known of Kentucky's composer-collector-poets is John Jacob Niles, who was born in Louisville in 1892 into a musical family. After serving in World War I as a pilot, he became a popular singer in nightclubs and on concert stages. His favorite songs were the ballads, folksongs, and Christmas carols of the southern mountains that he collected during his tours of the Appalachians. He arranged or composed more than one thousand ballads and folksongs, some of which were gathered in 1961 in his *Ballad Book of John Jacob Niles*. In 1980 he died at his Boot Hill Farm near Lexington. One of his most popular songs is "I Wonder As I Wander," included below with two of his original poems.

"I Wonder As I Wander"

I wonder as I wander out under the sky
How Jesus our Saviour did come for to die,
For poor orn'ry people like you and like I . . .
I wonder as I wander out under the sky.

When Mary birthed Jesus, 'twas in a cow's stall,
With wise men and farmers and shepherds and all,
But high from God's heaven a star's light did fall,
And the promise of ages it then did recall.

If Jesus had wanted for any wee thing,
A star in the sky or a bird on the wing,
Or all of god's angels in heaven for to sing,
He surely could have had it, 'cause He was the King.

I wonder as I wander out under the sky,
How Jesus our Saviour did come for to die,
For poor orn'ry people like you and like I,
I wonder as I wander out under the sky.

"The Locusts"

The locusts have eaten nearly all of my years
And left the husks and hulls of endless days.

And now I must discover how to live with the bitter
Husks and the tattered fragile hulls
Of days I shall never see again.
So if you see me trying to piece the shards
Of broken days and tiny fragmented moments together
To brighten the dark night of my loneliness,
Be kind, be gentle, be affectionate to an old man
Who has given his years to the locusts: be kind.

"My Love for You"

My love for you, my very dearest dear,
Is not a thing that I can put aside
And say, I've many things to do, I fear.
'twould be as if some part of me had died.
Ah, but to know the sweetness and the peace
Of coming back to you for one brief rest,
The gesture of your love when in release
You cradle my tired body in a nest
Of your dear arms. Ah, but to lie unwaking,
Asleep and yet awake in love's abyss,
Close-locked within a world of lovers' making,
Dead to life but deathless to your kiss,
For life and death are things we cannot stay,
But you and I and love have had our way.

Edwin Carlile Litsey

"To John Keats"

Edwin Carlile Litsey was born in 1874 in Washington County; he grew up and lived the rest of his life in nearby Lebanon, in Marion County, where he worked in the Marion National Bank, first as a runner and later as a bank officer. He wrote romantic novels resembling those of Sir Walter Scott and composed verses that were much better, including the poem below, "To John Keats," written in traditional iambic pentameter couplets. (An interesting footnote to Kentucky literary history is that John Keats's brother George moved to the United States in 1818 and, after a year in Henderson, moved to Louisville, where he became a prosperous lumber merchant and spent the rest of his days.)

An hostler's son! What boots the lowly birth
When manger-born was King of Heaven and Earth!
Pale-featured youth; father of deathless song;
So frail of flesh, of spirit ever strong.
At thy nativity the stars above
Most surely sang for joy, and, sent by love,
A white-winged messenger brought thee a lyre,
And touched thy infant's tongue with poet's fire!
O pity! pity! that the gods of ruth
Should quench the flame immortal in thy youth!
Almost a boy, for six and twenty years
Are short enough to learn of hopes and fears;
Of love, and life, and death, and heaven and hell,
Whose mysteries and wonders thou didst tell.
Thy dying fear was useless—"Here lies one
Whose name was writ in water."—'Neath the sun
No name is more secure, John Keats, than thine,
O hostler's son, who sang with tongue divine!

Sarah Litsey

"Star Reaper"

Sarah Litsey, daughter of Edwin Carlile Litsey, was born in the home of her mother in Springfield in 1901. After a career as a teacher, she married Frank Wilson Nye in 1933 and lived the remainder of her life in Connecticut, writing novels and poetry, many of them about her native state. "Star Reaper" tells of a gruesome Kentucky tragedy in dialect and verse.

"Anny's mad an' seein' visions.
Ain't you never watched her eyes
Followin' of clouds that's pink-like
Out acrost the evenin' skies?"

Guess the cows are needin' milkin'
An' my old man's drunk in town.
God, but ain't it beautiful—
How the red sun's goin' down!

"She ain't been to Sunday meetin'
Since a year ago last June.
Parson seen her in the thicket
Sayin' prayers to the moon."

Light the lamps an' cook the supper,
Heat can make your eyeballs sore;
Moon's a-shinin' down the holler,
Whitenin' up the sycamore.

"Queer how Dan'el stands her doin's.
Never borned him but one child
An' they found her stranglin' that one
With her eyes all scairt an' wild."

Little baby—little baby—
How could I 'uv let you live

With your life all hard before you
An' me with no mite to give?

"Dan'el said she took to layin'
Out at nights down by the crick.
Couldn't do a blamed thing with her
Till he whupped her with a stick."

Walls has got me cramped an' chokin';
There's more room out in the night.
Christ—there's Dan'el comin' at me
With his lips all drawed an' tight!

"Found her naked as a jaybird
Runnin' down through Grundy's wood.
Folks as does the likes of such things
Ain't around for no great good."

Eat my body up with moonlight
Cool an' silver on my back
Where he beat me. Eat my skin an'
Lick my bones before they crack!

"Kilt herself for plain damfoolness
Jumpin' out of that there tree.
Never done no work for Dan'el,
Think he'd feel right glad an' free."

Ef I climbed jest one limb higher
I could maybe touch them stars.
Ooo—I burned my hands against 'em—
Awful dark—an' stars—an' stars——

Cotton Noe

"Umbrella Jim"

Cotton Noe was born in 1869 in Washington County near Springfield and attended Franklin College in Indiana, Cornell University, and the University of Chicago. After practicing law for several years, he became a professor and administrator, teaching at Williamsburg Institute, Lincoln Memorial University, and the University of Kentucky, where he was head of the Department of Education. He was made the first official poet laureate of Kentucky in 1926, an honor that he held until his death in 1953. "Umbrella Jim" is one of his popular, easy-to-read portrait poems.

Umbrella Jim,
About the time I knew him best,
Was probably somewhere between
Thirty and forty years of age,—
Tall and slim,
A fellow of the Whistler type,
With infinite depth of eyes
Blue and ripe
And healing as late June skies.
Nobody ever would have guessed,
Looking into that serene
Countenance,
That Jim was anything but a sage,
And that is how I classified him at a glance,—

That is in advance
Of any information concerning him
And his life's romance;
But Jim
Was something vastly more
Than just a sage.
Whether from heritage
Or long experience under the open sky,
I can not tell,
But like the recondite Tagore,

He was a poet as well,
And a poet, high
In Nature's councils and lore,
And intimate in her dreams,
As birds and trees and streams
Could testify.

Still, so far as I know,
Jim never wrote a line
Of poetry in all of his career.
But he read it everywhere,—
In flaming columbine,
In magic mistletoe,
In Tennyson and Keats and Poe,
In Shelley and Lanier,—
He read it everywhere;
In golden sheaf
And falling leaf,
In earth and sea and air.

Once I heard a fellow say,
Who really didn't know Jim,
"I can't find an adequate synonym
To express my contempt for such fellahs
As him,—
I mean that chap who fixes old umbrellahs,"
Referring, of course, to Umbrella Jim.
And Jim had that very day
Repaired this man's silk umbrella and charged him only
    a dime,
Although it took a lot of his time
He could have used in moving onward toward a warmer
    clime,—
For Jim always went south in the fall
Exactly like a migratory bird.
I think he must have felt or heard
The call
And turned southward early in September,
For I remember
That he always reached our town with the grackle;
And somehow I came to associate the cackle

Of the blackbirds with Umbrella Jim.
But nothing in my opinion, would have pleased him
Better than just that.
The only time I ever saw him lose his head
Was once when a fellow, blind as a bat
To everything that Jim was looking at,
Cursed and said:
"Why don't you get a job and go to work!"
It was a biting and unjust remark,
And Jim resented it.
His brow grew dark;
He dropped his tinker's kit,
And gave his vest an angry jerk;
But in a moment more was just himself again,
As he looked up and saw a little wren
Pirouetting from limb to limb,
And flirting, it seemed to me, with Umbrella Jim.

"I live my life," said Jim,
"The same as any other man.
Somebody must fix parasols, and why not I?
I serve as best I can.
The millionaires play half the year
And more; why not indulge my whim?
I love the changing clouds against the sky;
I love the landscape that the asters beautify;
I love the song of streamlet flowing near;
The figure and the rhyme of sonneteer;
I love the poets in the open all the year."

He ceased to speak and opened up his old tool kit.
I looked at him and then I looked in it,
And saw a grimy volume once my favorite.

Next day while I was playing golf and Jim
Was sitting where he always loved to sit,
Beside a stream, beneath an old elm tree,
1 placed my golf-ball on the tee
And drove,—
I drove it with terrific vim.
And then I watched the fleck of white till it grew dim.

Gaston exclaimed, "By Jove,
That drive was certainly a dream!"
Just as the ball dropped in the stream
Not more than ten feet distant from Umbrella Jim.
I hardly heard what my companion said.
Quite undisturbed the poet munched his crust of bread,
And as he munched he read.

Read many times a poem that I used to love
Before I ever heard of golf or tees.
It was the Ballad of the Master and the Trees.
That night I pondered long about Umbrella Jim,
And now I always tip my hat to him.

Olive Tilford Dargan

"We Creators"

Olive Tilford Dargan was born in Grayson County near Leitchfield in 1869 but spent most of her life in New York and North Carolina. Her earliest writings were long, poetic dramas that are almost unread today, but her proletarian novels written in North Carolina in the 1930s under the pseudonym of Fielding Burke have earned her considerable acclaim. She died in 1968. Her short poem "We Creators" is a tribute to writers and all artists who try—and try again.

Let us go on with experiments;
Let us dare and dream and do;
Some day we may make a world
With a buttercup in it,
Or a swallow's wing.

The Contemporary
Kentucky Writer

We have now arrived at a good stopping place, a virtual banquet of writing where new selections become available every day. Here we will meet writers who are still active, mostly men and women born after 1925 whose writing, for the most part, has been done since 1950. You will meet a tantalizing assortment of writers from tried and true traditions to those sporting new subjects and new styles. You may want to follow the advice of Sir Francis Bacon in his famous seventeenth-century essay on reading, wherein he suggests that some books are to be tasted, some to be swallowed, and some to be chewed and digested. Alas, even with a heavily laden table, I have not been able to include all the writers who deserve to be present. I hope that a good man, a good lawyer, and a good author such as Gerald R. Toner, for example, who writes wondrous Christmas stories, will get his place at the table another time. So perhaps will the talented essayist Dianne Aprile, whose book of words and pictures with Mary Lou Hess, *The Eye Is Not Enough* (2000), is worth twice its cost. Ditto for Georgia-born Gwyn Hyman Rubio of Versailles, author of *Icy Sparks* (1998) and *The Woodsman's Daughter* (2005), which Silas House has called "a completely transporting experience."

Most writers do not limit themselves to one form. Robert Penn Warren, for example, wrote poems, plays, short stories, nonfiction narratives and essays, memoirs, and novels—and he excelled in them all. Accordingly, in this chapter of primarily fiction selections, I also include pieces from other genres—especially for authors whose best writing is often found in poetry or nonfiction. I hope to present these contemporary storytellers at their strongest moments.

Billy C. Clark

"The Fiddle and the Fruit Jar"

Billy C. Clark was born in 1928 into a mostly illiterate family of eight children near the junction of the Big Sandy and the Ohio Rivers at Catlettsburg. As he once wrote, "In nineteen years of growing up in the valley, hunger was my most vivid memory and an education my greatest desire." In *A Long Row to Hoe* (1960) he tells his growing-up story through high school. Despite the straitened circumstances of his boyhood, his memories of struggle and survival are warm and gratifying. It was a boyhood that he would not have swapped with anyone. After high school, he spent four years in the military during the Korean War; he then enrolled at the University of Kentucky, where his writing teacher, Hollis Summers, told him, "You are the first natural-born writer I've ever met," and cautioned him against being influenced by the class. Fortunately, Clark kept his vision and his style and continued to write such books as *Song of the River* (1957) and *Sourwood Tales* (1968), which depict the life and lore of the Big Sandy region of northeastern Kentucky. This story from *Sourwood Tales* is about family love and his father's battered old fiddle.

Pa's fiddle hung in its case from a rusted nail on the wall of the bedroom. This had been its resting place since the day he and Ma had first gone to housekeeping in the valley of the Big Sandy. And through the years it had remained the only competition that my mother ever had. I say competition because it was often declared here by the hill folk that a fiddle player had a wanderer's foot. You could not change the ways of a fiddle player. Ma knew this. And so as a young bride she allowed the fiddle to become a part of their marriage. In all of Pa's travels over the valley the sweet music of his fiddle would be loved the most at home. Ma presented him with eight children, more than a good set for a square dance, and in all the years of our growing up I'm sure that the fiddle never caused her a jealous moment.

After Pa came home from work at his small cobbler's shop we used to gather in the center of the floor and wait for the music of his lonesome fiddle. We learned early that there was a story in each of his ballads. We couldn't afford books, but we learned to read each pull of his bow as if it were a printed page.

Each night ended the same way, with the eight of us quarreling for Pa to play a different ballad. And always Ma would scold and threaten to have Pa put the fiddle back in the battered case. Afraid he might, we quieted as Pa pat-patted his foot and struck up an old familiar song . . . Ma's favorite. He was sure to play this song as soon as a frown touched Ma's face, grinning and bringing a smile back to her face.

The song was a ballad of love, so bold that it made my older brothers and sisters blush. I was too young to understand love. I liked to hear Pa play it simply because it brought such smiles to Ma's face, and gave me courage to argue again for my favorite song.

By the time I was old enough to really know my father he had fiddled his hair white to match the white pine rosin dust that his bow had left under the strings. The fiddle had traveled with him over every foot of the Big Sandy country; to square dances where feet flew into the air like brown leaves in an autumn wind; to funerals where his fiddle hummed of death; to holy baptizings in the waters of the Big Sandy River. There had been ballads for all occasions. Pa had gained the reputation of being the greatest of the "old-time fiddlers" among the hills of Kentucky.

But now white-haired Pa was farther away from his fiddle than he had ever been. Only his dreams could touch it as it hung inside the battered case on the wall. He was bedfast from a stroke, the third within a year. He lay quarreling over the doctor bills coming, saying Ma needed the meager amount of money to buy food for the table.

The doctor had not given much promise. Either of the first two strokes had been great enough to have killed Pa. But he had proved by two recoveries that he was as stubborn and tough as the hills around him. This was the best encouragement the doctor could give.

But Ma had caught something in Pa's eyes that the doctor could not see. It was not the paralyzing of his body she saw there, but the paralyzing of his mind and spirit.

In the days that followed, Ma rested her eyes often on the battered fiddle case. She attributed untold powers to it, believing that if she could coax Pa to find courage to take it from the wall the pull of the bow over the strings would strengthen and mend his body. But Ma had less time now for coaxing. She left the house early to find housework. She scrubbed floors on her hands and knees, and stretched her little body to wash down walls. Of the evenings she brought home baskets of clothes and washed them with her hands into the late night. These hours of labor brought us food. And she sat on the edge of Pa's bed and fed him as she would have a small child, knowing that each bite he took reminded him of his helplessness and paralyzed him a little more.

It was not easy for Pa to remain flat on his back. He had worked hard all his life. He had begun in the small belly mines of the mountain country, then found his craft as a shoe cobbler. He had learned to work miracles with his hands. Weaving the needle in and out of leather that he had softened by hand, he built shoes for clubfooted children and covered scars and afflictions that couldn't be shod by machine-made shoes.

It shamed me to see an old man such as Pa have tears in his eyes as Ma fed him. Never once did it occur to me that he might have been looking at my mother's red hands, cracked until they bled over the rough washboard. Or that he might have been thinking it was a man's place to bring food to the table. I knew only that he had told me over the years that I should feel ashamed for crying. A *man* never cried.

One evening Ma came home from work and found the fiddle gone. She trembled as she spoke to Pa. "Where is the fiddle?"

Pa fought to raise his hand and Ma reached to take it in hers. And when they met Pa slipped something to her. She unfolded the wrinkled dollar bills and they fell to the floor.

"You . . . you had no right to do it," she sobbed. "I'm no better to provide than you've been doing all these years." And she could not say more.

Pa never was much of a talker. "A talking man never hears," he had always taught us kids. And without practice himself he failed miserably on this night. He could not convince Ma that he would remain paralyzed forever. She cried softly, believing that the only medicine to cure him was now gathering dust in the corner of the secondhand store—sold for little more than she could have earned with a few washings. Yet this pitiful sum had made Pa believe he had lightened Ma's burden. His eyes, wandering to rest on the rusted nail, sadly told us that what he had done had not been easy.

Often of the evenings I would go to meet Ma and help her carry the washings home. I was the smallest of four boys and the only one too young to be ashamed of being seen carrying them, telling all within sight that we were as poor as the red clay hills around us.

Each day Ma stopped at the secondhand store, leaving me outside guarding the clothes. This was one of Ma's queer new ways I could not understand. For instance, a few days earlier I had seen her stuffing something inside an empty fruit jar in the basement and then hiding the jar. After she had gone I sneaked the jar into the open and saw money in it. I just could not understand why she would be hiding money from us when there was so little to eat.

I sneaked each evening to see the jar until she finally caught me. She said, "What little money there is inside the jar wouldn't fill your tooth. It's the love tucked around it that fills the jar."

It just didn't make sense. I didn't know that old people had love. I thought it belonged only to the young, like my brother who was sparking a girl who lived nearby.

I went with Ma the morning she took the money from the jar. After we had picked up a heaping basket of clothes to be washed we stopped at the secondhand store. I stood guarding the basket and she went inside. When she came out she had the battered fiddle case under her arm. She tucked it under the clothes, and warned me not to speak of it when we reached home.

That night Pa quarreled at Ma for spending her hard-earned money to bring the fiddle back to just gather dust on the wall. But his tired old eyes had changed and they lied on him this time. There was tenderness inside them that we all recognized as we peeked around the door.

Ma scolded us back to bed and we cocked our ears hoping to hear the fiddle again. But no sound of music came. Since I was the smallest and the lightest on foot I was chosen to sneak again to the door and tell what I saw.

Here is what I told them: I saw my father lift his arm by his own strength and brush tears from my mother's eyes.

He tried to play the fiddle. He tried to play Ma's favorite . . . the one he always used to put her in a happy mood . . . the song he had first played many years ago when he had come to court her. And although we heard nothing but the squeak of the bow held by a crippled hand, I think that to them it was the softest, sweetest ballad he had ever played.

In the years that followed, Pa teased Ma about pulling him from the grave just to listen to his fiddle. Ma always blushed. She had little time for *foolishness*. She was always too busy spreading her love among us . . . the same sort of love she had tucked around the money inside the fruit jar.

Walter Tevis

from *The Color of Money*

Walter Tevis was born in San Francisco in 1928, but when he was ten his family moved to Lexington. He received bachelor's and master's degrees from the University of Kentucky and taught English at high schools in Science Hill, Hawesville, Carlisle, and Irvine. He later taught at Northern Kentucky University and Ohio University, from which he resigned in 1978; he lived in New York until his death in 1984. Throughout his teaching career he wrote stories and novels, many of which were made into excellent films, including *The Hustler* (1959) and *The Man Who Fell to Earth* (1963). The excerpt below is from *The Color of Money* (1984), which is a sequel to *The Hustler* and again opens up the world of high-stakes pool playing with Fast Eddie Felson and Minnesota Fats.

Back in Lexington, he tried it the first morning. Out to the closed poolroom at nine for eight hours of practice. When he unlocked the door he was shocked. There were only three tables in the room. He tried to shake off the dismay and began to shoot. It made him dizzy, walking around the table for hours in the near-empty room, bending, making a ball and going on to the next one. But he stayed with it doggedly, leaving for a few minutes at noon to get two hot dogs and a cup of coffee at Woolworth's. He shifted from straight pool to banks but got bored with that and started practicing long cut shots, slicing the colored balls parallel with the rail and into the corner pockets. His stroke began to feel smoother but his shoulder was tired. Was Fats right? Had his balls been shrivelling? He started shooting harder, making them slap against the backs of the pockets, rifling them in. Fats knew a lot. Loaded on junk food, his belly and ass enormous, over sixty years old, Fats shot pool beautifully; he had balls. Balls was what he, Eddie, had started playing pool for in the first place—that was what they all did. Mother's boys, some of them. He had been shy when he was twelve and thirteen, before he first picked up a pool stick. When he found out about pool and how well he could play it, it had changed him. He could not remember all of it, but it had even changed the way he walked. He smashed the orange five ball down the rail and into the pocket. Then the three, the fourteen, twelve, hitting them perfectly. He went on blasting at them, but missed the final ball. It came off the edge of the pocket, caromed its way around the table, bouncing off five cushions, and then rolled slowly to a stop. His back was hurting and he had a headache.

It was almost five o'clock. The phone at the room had been cut off for weeks. He went outside to the pay phone in the parking lot and called Arabella.

"I'd like to come over for a drink," he said.

"I'm going to a play at eight. You can come for a while."

"I'll bring wine," he said, and hung up.

༺ ༺ ༺

"Tell me about your husband," Eddie said. He was seated in one of the white armchairs. "Is his name Weems?"

"Harrison Frame."

"Haven't I heard of him?"

"It would be hard not to," Arabella said. "He used to do a television show on the university channel."

"You sound like you hate him."

"Do I?"

"Yes."

She took a thoughtful swallow from her wineglass. "I suppose you're right. Let's not talk about him. What have you been doing today?"

"Catching up on my homework."

"Did you?"

"Did I what?"

"Catch up?"

"I only started." He got up and went to the window, looking at the traffic in the street and the buildings across the street. "I like this apartment a lot," he said.

"Eddie," she said from the sofa, "I've been living in this one room for two months and I'm going crazy."

"It'll be better when you find a job."

"I'm not going to find a job. There's a recession going on. President Reagan speaks of recovery, but he's another one."

"Another what?"

"Another goddamned performer, like my former husband. He's only working the room, our president. Counting the house and working the room. The son of a bitch."

"*Hey,*" Eddie said, laughing. "You sound terrible. Are you drunk?"

"If three glasses of wine makes you drunk, I'm drunk."

"I'll get you something to eat." He left the window and went to the refrigerator. There was a wedge of Brie and four eggs. Nothing else. "What about a soft-boiled egg?"

"If you say so."

He boiled her two of them and, since there was no butter, merely put them in a bowl with salt and pepper and handed it to her. He heated some coffee and gave her a cup of it black.

She was a real cutie, eating her eggs on the sofa. She hunched over them with her silver hair glowing in the late afternoon light from the big window, spooning them in small bites. He sat across from her and watched, sipping his own coffee.

"Thanks, Eddie," she said when she finished. She held the bowl in her lap and smiled. "Why don't you tell me what you do for a living?"

He hesitated. "I was a poolroom operator until a few months ago. A long time ago I was a player." He felt relieved; it was time he told her about pool.

"A poolroom?" She didn't seem to understand.

"Yes."

"But what has that to do with Enoch Wax?"

"I'm doing exhibition games for Mid-Atlantic."

"Then you must be good."

"I lost the first two matches."

She didn't seem to notice what he said. She just kept looking at him. Finally she said, "Holy cow. A pool player." She sounded excited by the idea.

"My game isn't what it was. I practiced all day today and it bored the hell out of me."

She bit her lip a moment, then reached forward and set her empty bowl on the glass coffee table, next to a vase of orange gladiolas. "It must be better than sitting around an apartment."

"Not by much."

She stretched and yawned. "My God, Eddie! First you cheer me up, now I'm cheering you up. It could go on forever. Why don't you go to the play with us tonight? I can inveigle a ticket."

"I've never seen a play."

"All the more reason to go."

"Maybe you're right. What's the name of it?"

"*A Streetcar Named Desire.* At the university theater. The principal character bears some resemblance to you."

He looked at her. "Stanley Kowalski or Blanche DuBois?"

"*Well,*" she said, "a closet intellectual."

"I saw the movie."

"You didn't say Marlon Brando or Vivien Leigh."

"Look," he said, irritated, "I'll go to the play with you. But I'm tired of being figured out. I'm not a rube. I know who Tennessee Williams was. I just don't go to plays. Nobody asked me to before."

ↀ ↀ ↀ

They had dinner at the Japanese place, and this time Eddie ordered Sushi. He had practiced with a pair of pencils at Jean's apartment, picking up cigarettes. The trick was to hold the bottom one steady and use the top one like the jaw of a clamp. The Sushi was easy. Arabella watched him for a moment but made no comment.

They met the other couple outside the theater, in the Fine Arts Building. The Skammers, both of them professors. He was history and she was math. They were both thin people, both in running shoes and bright cotton sweaters, both easygoing and cordial. She had reddish hair and was pretty in an unexciting way. Eddie noticed the man was wearing a gold Rolex. The four of them had only a few minutes to chat before curtain time.

He had never seen even a high-school play and was uncertain what to expect. The actors were college students, and from his third-row seat he could see their makeup. It took him awhile, feeling self-conscious with real people on the stage in front of him, but after a few minutes he got into it. He liked Stanley; the student playing the part had the right swagger. And Blanche was a genuine loser—the real thing—with her talk and her posing. Arabella, sitting by him, laughed aloud at some of Blanche's lines, but he didn't find her funny. It would be frightening to be like that, in that kind of a fog. It was fascinating to listen to her talk, to hear her construct her version of her past and Stella's, and to watch her come apart. He had seen pool players come apart like that. "I have always depended on the kindness of strangers." You didn't have to be taken off by men in white suits to fail like that. You could stay home, drink beer, watch TV. There was a lot of it going around.

That was what he said when Skammer asked him, afterward, how he liked it. "There's a lot of that going around." They all stared at him and then laughed loudly.

"Eddie," Arabella said, "will you teach me to shoot pool?"

He was feeling good. "Right now?"

"Why not? Do you know a place?"

"Shoot pool?" Roy Skammer said. "That's a stunning idea."

"Oh boy!" Pat said. She had been crying at the play and her face was streaked from it. They were walking along the campus on their way to the car.

"Don't knock it," Roy said. "In my sophomore year I did little else. I was a veritable Fast Eddie."

Arabella looked at him. "A Fast Eddie?"

"Of the Princeton Student Union."

"There's a table at the Faculty Club," Pat said. "Roy is the eight-ball terror of arts and sciences."

"My my," Arabella said. And then to Eddie, "Will you teach me?"

Eddie shrugged. He was still feeling high from the play. It was a warm night and the light from mercury lamps was filtered through tall trees along the campus walk. He was not really interested in shooting pool. His right shoulder was sore from the eight hours at the room that day and he was not interested in seeing how well Roy Skammer shot eight-ball. Roy Skammer seemed amiable and smiled a lot, but Eddie did not like him. He did not like the man's glib way of talking.

"I'd like to learn," Arabella said.

"Okay. I'll show you how."

"If you'd like," Roy said, "I'll help."

Ed McClanahan

from *The Natural Man*

To secure his fame for all time, Ed McClanahan probably didn't need to write any other books after his first. *The Natural Man* (1983) is the sort of story that most writers dream about: a short novel that will surely be around when we, and most of the books of our times, will have turned to dust. It's the natural, honest story of a boy named Harry Eastep trying to grow up in the fictional town of Needmore, in the fictional county of Burdock, a boy very like McClanahan himself, who was born somewhere up there in northern Kentucky at Brooksville in Bracken County—such a natural, honest story that you would swear it was autobiographical. Harry longs for excitement and adventure that he is sure lies beyond the horizon. He never expects that it will come in the shape of an iconoclastic young stranger named Monk.

Thirteen years later McClanahan wrote another work of fiction, and he called it *A Congress of Wonders* (1996), which it is. Between those two books, he wrote a work of nonfiction called *Famous People I Have Known* (1985), which is something of a misnomer because most of the people therein are unfamous—but they are much more interesting than the famous ones. McClanahan completed a master's degree at the University of Kentucky in 1958 and has taught writing at Oregon State, Stanford, Montana, and Kentucky.

In the days of his youth, in the summertime, when school didn't interfere, Harry Eastep liked to spend a certain portion of his afternoons hanging around Marvin Conklin's drugstore, to catch the arrival of the Cincinnati–Lexington Greyhound. It wasn't that he was meeting anyone or going anywhere—scarcely anyone who needed meeting ever came to Needmore, and Harry scarcely ever went away. But the drugstore was the drop station for Needmore's daily supply of the Cincinnati *Morning Enquirer,* so the bus, which delivered the paper to the provinces, always stopped there. Nor was Harry more than most boys interested in the *Enquirer*'s already half-stale accounts of the affairs of whatever great world it was that lay beyond the narrow confines of Burdock County. The fact is, it was the bus driver himself that Harry came to see.

There were always two or three loafers sitting around in Conklin's, drinking fountain Cokes, when the bus roared up and stopped in the middle of the street between the drugstore and the Burdock County courthouse across the way. As if to inform the local yokels that he didn't intend to stay any longer than he damn well had to, the driver never bothered to cut off his engine; the bus sat there throbbing and muttering in flatulent impatience while the driver alighted through the fold-back door and came striding smartly across the street, a smallish banty rooster of a fellow, slim-hipped and natty in his tailored uniform, his cap cocked low and rakish on his brow, his nifty little Mandrake the Magician mustache already twitching in pleasurable anticipation, the thick log of newspapers balanced one-handed on his epauletted shoulder. Then, flinging open Marvin Conklin's screen door, he'd cry, in perfect rubbernecker tour-guide lookit-the-funny-natives-folks singsong, complete with an Ohio accent, "State of Kentucky, County of Burdock, City of Needmore, population 6 ⁷/₈ when they're all at home! Where prosperity is *a-a-always* just around the corner! *Heads up, hayseeds!*" With that, he'd heave the roll of papers end over end into the store, where it landed at the feet of the foremost loafer with a dreadful thud that shook the Coke glasses and patent-medicine bottles on the shelves; and the bus driver's scornful, mustachioed grin would hang there in the doorway till the screen door clapped shut after him and dispelled it. Moments later, as the Greyhound thundered off in a fulsome cloud of blue exhaust, the dumb-struck loafers would turn at last to one another, grousing bitterly about that high-handed little wisenheimer's latest effrontery. "Why, that smart-aleck snot!" they'd remind each other. "That cocky little s'rimp! That wise guy, that twerp, that . . ."

But to young Harry Eastep, lurking about the magazine rack in the drugstore's dimly lighted recesses, the bus driver was the hero, not the villain, of this brief yet curiously satisfying little matinee; he had, well, class, Harry guessed you'd call it; he was *suavay.* Harry didn't feel the least bit suavay himself, of course. As a matter of fact, he sometimes imagined himself to be the very object of the driver's scorn, the most egregiously obvious hayseed of all the 357 hayseed souls in Needmore. Harry, in the wisdom of his fifteen years, had come to suspect that there was a good deal more to the world than had so far met his eye, and to discover within himself a powerful itch to sally forth and See What It Was All About, to blow this one-horse jerkwater burg (as he imagined the bus driver might put it) and go where the Action was.

By that summer near the end of the 1940's, Harry Eastep and Needmore, Kentucky, had had the dubious pleasure of each other's company for six long years. Population 6 ⁷/₈, and Harry had been among that wretched number since his parents took him out of the fifth grade of the Wilbur Wright Elementary School in Dayton, Ohio, and trundled him down to Needmore with them to live with his aged, newly widowed, grim-visaged grandmother, "Miss" Lute Biddle, for the duration—theirs or hers. Miss Lute proved nothing if not durable, and six years later there they sat.

Needmore had changed not a hair in those six years, so far as Harry could determine; Harry, meanwhile, had changed most marvelously, from a plump, bespectacled, modestly precocious nine-year-old (an only child, with working parents and nothing better to do, he'd started school early, done his homework, and skipped the second grade) to a slouching, shambling, gangling tangle of ganglia, an almost-senior at Burdock County High, not yet sixteen, still bespectacled and modestly precocious, though not half so smart as he thought he was. Nearly six feet tall, he wore his height uneasily, like a new recruit in an ill-fitting uniform. He still looked up—literally and figuratively—to people who no longer needed looking up to, a habit which did little to improve his slouch or enhance his bearing, and indeed had caused more than one observer to liken his expression to that of a shit-eating dog. But Harry was going to make a nice-looking boy one of these days, most people said, when he filled out a little and his skin cleared up. Personally, Harry had his doubts.

So he took a certain discreet solace from the spectacle of his neighbors' humiliation: at least *he* had sense enough to recognize his own privation, at least he knew class when he saw it. The daily appearances of the bus driver, who was, to Harry's mind, the Action's harbinger as well as its pursuer, lent credence to Harry's tantalizing foreglimpse, gave substance to his hopes; and anyhow, Harry liked the driver's *style.*

As it happened, though, the Action came to Harry before he made his way to it; and, irony of ironies, that same bus driver was the one who bore it there, and abandoned it like an orphaned ogre on Needmore's doorstep. Because one stifling dog-days afternoon, as the din of the departing Greyhound died to a mumble in their ears, the loafers looked out through Marvin Conklin's plate-glass window and saw that they'd been delivered something they weren't sure they'd ordered. It stood six feet five inches tall, and weighed in at 238 pounds, and—Harry Eastep saw even while it was still shrouded in a pale swirl of evil blue exhaust fumes, like some unholy apparition the town had conjured up out of the abyss of its own ignorance—it was ugly as sin, and (unlike Harry) it plainly knew no fear, nor any shame.

It was fifteen years of age, and its name was Monk McHorning.

Pat Carr

"Bringing Travis Home"

Pat Carr taught at Western Kentucky University for only about seven years. She was born in Wyoming in 1932, educated at Rice and Tulane, from which she received a Ph.D., and taught at Rice, Texas Southern, Dillard, the University of New Orleans, the University of Texas at El Paso, and, from 1988 through the mid-1990s, at Western Kentucky; she is now at rest in Arkansas. In her years of moving about the country she learned a lot about writing. She is a superb poet and a master of the short story. Her several collections, including *The Women in the Mirror* (1977), *Beneath the Hill of the Three Crosses* (1993), and *Our Brothers' War* (1993, with Maureen Morehead), offer proof of her wondrous talent, which also shines clearly in this poignant story of the Civil War.

As soon as the clear air in my nostrils was overpowered by the odors of blood and rotting meat I knew they had sent me to the right place.

I swallowed hard a couple of times. A man, leaning in a chair just inside the door, was looking at me.

"They told me this was the hospital," I said and pulled the letter from my dress pocket.

"I came for my brother, Travis Woods."

I started unfolding the paper.

"We got this letter from a Doctor Simpson that said we could bring Travis home."

The man waved an arm toward the far end of the building which I could tell by then was a church.

"That's Doc Talbot up there. I don't know no Doc Simpson."

I looked where he was pointing. Rows of soldiers lined the floor, so close together that it didn't seem as if anyone could step between them without coming down on somebody. They were crowded in from both sides of the room with only a narrow passage between, and I'd have to walk the whole length of them to get up to the baldheaded doctor. I felt self-conscious standing there folding up the letter, so I kept it in my hand as I started up the narrow aisle.

I looked at the face of each soldier, trying not to see the brown seepage on the bandages, trying not to see the empty spaces where legs and arms should have been. A few of the eyes gazed back at me, but most of the soldiers lay with their faces clamped shut with pain. There was a constant rustling, gurgling, sort of panted moaning, and I didn't feel I was disturbing anyone as I clumped along the bare wood floor in my town shoes.

Autumn sunlight glared through the windows, and I found that the faces were all starting to look alike. What if I passed right by Travis and didn't know him? And he had been gone so long I probably couldn't recognize him from just a mouth and chin.

But then I saw that the soldier with the head bandage was in a Yankee uniform. He couldn't be Travis. And I noticed for the first time that Yankee and Confederate uniforms were side by side, mingled on the rickety cots. After I started separating out the blue and the gray uniforms, I calculated that maybe there were more blue ones on the cots, but then it was a Union hospital.

I got to the end of the church where the doctor was standing at what was probably the altar. He was scribbling in a ledger and didn't glance up but said in an irritated voice, "What do you want?"

I extended the letter.

"I came for my brother. Doctor Simpson wrote that we could bring Travis Home."

He looked up then, and his eyes were so blue, caught between his tanned cheeks and his tanned baldness, that it was as if they were in the wrong face.

"Doctor Simpson was killed in a field hospital a month ago. You took your sweet time coming," he said, the blue eyes narrowing.

"Pa had to get the harvest in before he could spare the wagon," I said, to let him know I wasn't one who did the deciding.

"It's always the same. If some of these boys could get home in time, they might stand a chance. But there's never enough money to come get them while they could save a limb, is there? Well, if Simpson said you could take your brother home, I suppose better late than never."

"I looked at all the soldiers in here and I didn't see him."

He made an impatient gesture.

"Well, if he improved enough, they might have sent him back into the field to complete the maiming and killing they didn't finish the first time."

"Travis was in the Confederate Army."

The doctor, who was about my height but stocky, peered at me sharply, not as angry.

"Well, if we have a rebel, the authorities may have taken your brother to a prison camp or exchanged him."

"Where's the prison camp?" I asked.

There was a pause as if he hadn't heard me.

"Or, in case your brother didn't get well, we have a temporary morgue out back where we stack the bodies until they get boxed and labelled."

The disgust and anger were back, but by then I knew they weren't aimed at me.

"May I check there?"

His hand came to rest on the page, but he didn't write anything.

"Have you got somebody to help you in case you find him?"

"Pa's boy, Archer."

"A slaveholding Reb, eh?"

"We only got one," I said.

"All right," making the impatient gesture again.

"I don't have anyone to send out there with you. Don't faint."

"I won't faint."

He gave me a long blue look.

"Go out this door. They're in back of the shed."

I folded up the letter and slid it in my pocket. Pa would need it to show some Yankee prison official to get Travis out.

He watched me go out. I walked around the side of the shed, and there they were, like the doctor said, laid out, not on top of each other exactly, but crammed together the same as stacked, from one end of the shed to the other.

A dead animal odor drifted around them, but the fall cold hadn't hurried the decay, and the smell in the sunlight wasn't half as bad as that inside the church hospital.

I walked along, keeping my skirt from dragging on their boots or on the socks of those without boots.

Their faces were stiffened yellow tan, a sort of murky uncoloredness like tallow, and they too, all looked alike. The gray jackets, blue jackets, gray undershirts, trousers were all so grimed and stained that I couldn't tell them apart either.

And then suddenly I saw Travis.

I knew him immediately, even among all the others that he resembled, and I didn't need to check the slip of paper showing from his pocket.

I could see he had both his arms and legs. His face was all right with the eyelids slightly ajar and a rim of white gleaming between the lashes. I hadn't had any trouble recognizing him. But there was something wrong with the way he looked. Not just the dead absence about him but something else besides.

And I realized it was his hair. Somebody had slicked it back away from his forehead. Mama would have seen it right away. She'd notice it first thing when I brought him home. She was always so proud of his hair, saying,

"None of you girls got that lovely curly hair" and adding, "What a shame—those beautiful curls are just wasted on a boy."

I carefully wedged my shoe between Travis and the soldier next to him and leaned down to pull the hair loose from its unfamiliar pompadour.

His skin was cold, but yielding somehow like day-old mush turned out of the pan. It felt almost moist as if it had broken out in a sweat one last time. I drew back my hand.

The hair hadn't fallen over his forehead in a curl, but was flared up, resisting and dead, more like arid grass than hair.

I didn't try to shape it again. I reached over and took the cap off the dead soldier beside my foot and put it on Travis.

That was better.

Jane Stuart

On August 22, 1942, a young Kentucky father in Riverton wrote to a friend in Cincinnati: "Born to us a daughter, 9 1/2 pounds, Jessica Jane Stuart, King's Daughters Hospital, Ashland, Ky., Aug. 20th, 11:14 A.M. . . . Our baby is one of the tallest born at the King's Daughters. She's a bundle of energy and joy." Thus did Jesse Stuart announce the birth of a daughter, who grew up to continue the Stuart family writing tradition. In many ways, she bettered the family tradition, earning degrees, including a Ph.D., from Case-Western and Indiana University. She went on to write fiction, including *Yellowhawk* (1973) and *Gideon's Children* (1976), and collections of poetry, including *Eyes of the Mole* (1967) and *White Barn* (1973). Like her father, Jane Stuart often looks no farther than W-Hollow and Greenup County for her inspiration and subjects, as the following story and poems attest.

⌒∞⌒

"Glory Train," from *Gideon's Children*

"Are you saved?" Brother Sugg cried out when the song had ended. "Are you saved?"

"Praise the Lord, yes," called back Thelma Fawver from the middle of the train. "Praise the Lord, yes."

Nobody paid much attention to Sister Thelma. She was always saying she was saved, and that she knew she was, and that she was happy and on her way to heaven. That was fine, but it didn't leave Brother Sugg much work to do with her, and Brother Sugg was a man who wanted to work. He wanted to go out and find the disturbed and the dying, the heretics and the indifferent, the lost souls that were taking up so much room that should be given over to the good Christians who needed more jobs, bigger homes, finer churches, and better schools.

"Are you saved, I asked you?" Brother Sugg cried out again, this time raising his guitar up and holding it like a sign, or a symbol. Music reached a lot of people, he knew, and some of them, just by looking at the guitar and remembering the songs they had been singing, might suddenly feel the spirit, rise up, and let salvation in.

"Hallelujah," Thelma Fawver cried out, looking at the guitar and remembering the fine music they had just had after their fried chicken picnic on the train Brother Sugg had rented to carry them from their hometown to the revival in Doxie.

"... saved and do you know it?" Brother Sugg went on, ignoring Sister Thelma. "Are you happy? Is God inside you? Has He spread His wings and grasped you to His breast? Has He taken you for one of His own? Are you no longer yourself, the sinner of the past, but are you now one of His, angel on earth, a better man, a finer woman, a child on the right way, the way to glory?"

"Yes!" They all cried out to him then. "Yes!"

"Amen." Brother Sugg cried, shaking his guitar with his right hand and then laying it down so he could wipe off the sweat that was pouring down his face like a fine sheet of rain. "Amen, brothers and sisters. We're on the glory train, all right. And it's a fine day for us to be here. We're going to be revived. We're going to pray to the Lord to *revive us again.*"

At once the forty-nine people on Car 1180 broke out into song. And Brother Sugg, when he had caught his breath, reached for his guitar and began to sing along as he played the old hymn that had done so much good for so many. From the corner of his left eye he could see Galen Millz's mouth twitching, and he thought that if he was going to catch a fish today this would be a good one for the pan. Galen had a lot on his conscience, everyone in Littlewood was talking about him. It was time that it all came out into the open and the air got cleared.

☙ ☙ ☙

Praise the fount of mannnnnny blessings, they were singing now, and Jeffy Titsworth had taken out his guitar from its fine case, and stood up to come to the front of the car and accompany Brother Sugg.

Brother Sugg motioned for him to come on, and Odle Knip followed, holding tight to his banjo as he tried to walk a straight line down the aisle. The train was lurching so that it was hard for anyone to walk straight, but then Odle had drunk so much in the years before he was saved that people often said now that he still couldn't walk a straight line. This bothered Odle so much that he had gone on an all-out campaign against drink, even giving up his beer which he'd held on to for years after he'd given up gin. Now he spent most of the time he was laid off from the plant out preaching in the streets and in the bars and trying to get every man and woman he could to take the oath that they'd never touch the stuff again. He hadn't saved anyone until Thelma Fawver had taken the oath—she agreed to anything—and that really made Odle feel like a man. He started courting Thelma off and on, when he wasn't working at the plant or preaching in the bars, and sometimes Brother Sugg thought that things might be going on there and that marriage was the best answer to their problem, even if they both were a little crazy.

☙ ☙ ☙

"Where I'm goin', the Lord is waitin',
    Got no fear of Man or Satan,"

they all sang now, the two guitars going fast and strong and the banjo keeping time. Thelma Fawver was patting her feet to the music, and Nevelyn Wente had taken out his harmonica to give a little treble to the singing.

Brother Sugg stole another look over toward Galen Millz and, sure enough, he could see the big tears welling up in Galen's eyes, and his thin red lips starting to tremble.

At once, Brother Sugg stopped playing and raised his right hand.

"Brothers and sisters," he said slowly and reverently, "I think we have someone here who wants to speak. Someone who wants to step forward and say what it is that's bothering him. Someone who wants to talk to the Lord, to pray to Him, to ask Him for forgiveness and help not in the future, but *now*, this minute, in the holy present."

"Amen," Thelma called.

"Amen," her sister Phon echoed.

"Amen," cried Jeffy Titsworth and Odle Knip, who had stopped their playing and were waiting to be told what to do.

"Sit down, brothers, sit down," Brother Sugg said. "Nevelyn, put aside your mouthpiece until you can play with joy and jubilation because we've brought a man to repentance and prepared him for the Judgment Day."

"Amen," they began calling out throughout the train car. "Amen. We're on the glory train, and we're going to glory. Stand up and speak. Stand up and testify."

"Stand up and speak."

"Stand up and testify."

"Be saved and get happy."

"Take joy in the comfort of the Lord."

"He's with us, let Him be with you."

"Be saved for the revival!"

"Be ready for Doxie!"

⸘ ⸘ ⸘

"Hallelujah!" Galen Millz cried out then, throwing aside the paper bag he'd been holding in his hand—the rest of his picnic lunch—and leaping to his feet. "Hallelujah and help me, brothers. Pray for me, sisters, for I'm a guilty man. I've sinned and there's no salvation for me unless it comes today. I know because the Lord has spoken and He's told me it's time. He's told me that, if I don't find it on the glory train, it'll never be there for me. Help me find it. Pray for me and bring me there a new man."

"Praise you, praise you!" Brother Sugg cried, holding his handkerchief to his face and wiping away the tears of emotion that were flowing down his red cheeks. "Praise you, Galen, for finding the courage and the strength to stand up and tell us all. Speak to us and we will listen. The Lord is surely with you, and He'll bring you through this trial."

Galen stood there holding onto the seat in front of him and almost pulling little Susie Rice's hair, his hands were clenching the seat back so hard.

"Oh, I've sinned, oh, Lord, I've sinned," he cried, and his voice was shaking.

"We all have at sometime or other," Brother Sugg said, quietly now, trying to give encouragement and understanding to the man who was speaking out to save his soul.

"But not the way I have," Galen said, and he began to sob. Little Susie started crying then, and her mother held her down in her lap and put her hands over her eyes so she couldn't see what was happening behind her.

"I have broken a commandment," Galen said. "Oh, I've broken them before. When I was a child, there were times when I did not honor my mother and my father. And once I stole, yes, brothers, I stole . . . I stole bread from the store when I was hungry, and I stole apples from the trees of another man's field. And there have been times when I didn't love my neighbor as I should have, times when I didn't want to build up my part of the fence, times when I didn't want to have to go to his house and help him when he was in need."

"Amen," someone called.

"It's happened to us all," another said.

"But I've done worse than that," Galen went on. "I've done worse. I've loved my neighbor too much, too. I've fornicated. I've done what I should never have done when I had the desire, the need, the lust for another man's wife."

Brother Sugg stood very still, holding onto the railing above him when the train lurched. He was watching Galen carefully, and he was watching the faces of the men and women in the train, watching them and waiting for someone to give himself away. It could be a man, the husband; it could be the guilty woman. Brother Sugg knew it was coming, and he couldn't tell which way the wind was blowing. It worried him that he couldn't tell, because he had a nose for finding out the truth, just like he'd known something was on Galen Millz's mind, and he'd known there was talk in town, and he'd known it all had to come out in the open or it would destroy them all and their faith in God.

⁂

"Galen," Brother Sugg said, "you are a brave man. You've come forth and confessed your guilt. You've said it here in front of us the way only a true man and a real believer could do. You're asking God's forgiveness just as you're asking ours. But there's one thing more you've got to do."

Galen shook his head slightly, but Brother Sugg went on.

"You've got to name the guilty party," Brother Sugg said. "You've got to help save a soul, in order for yours to be saved, too. You've got to bring it all out, wash it all out in the stream of forgiveness. How could you be saved if you left another adrift in the river of temptation? How could you get to heaven if you didn't help take another by the hand, in a right and holy way?"

"You're right, Brother Sugg," Galen said, his eyes now turned down to the seat. "You're right, I know. But I can't do it."

"Of course you can."

"Speak up, Brother Galen," Thelma Fawver cried.

"Speak up and name her," her sister Phon echoed.

"We're not stoning people," Mary Grace Blevins called. "We're forgiving ones. We won't laugh and call names, we won't point our fingers and say 'There she goes.' We'll say 'There she went. And there she is now, an angel, forgiven, a woman of the Lord.'"

"Her husband'll take her back, if he's a right man," Odle Knip cried. "If he won't take her back, he's the one who needs salvation more than she does."

"When you've sinned, you've sinned," called out an old lady. Brother Sugg couldn't see who it was, he had his eyes fixed on Galen Millz and he was waiting.

"I've sinned, too, in my time, hear me now!" she went on. "I've sinned and you all know who it was with, those of you as old as I am. There's no need to bring it up now, the man I sinned with is dead and gone to heaven and I've seen my own husband buried, but not before he forgave me and went off to heaven to live with the Lord and every man there in peace."

"There's no shame, when it's a sincere repentance," Brother Sugg said then.

Galen turned and looked at them all, looked at everyone riding the glory train, and shook his head. "I can't," he said, and his voice was a hoarse whisper.

"Then you've not truly repented," Brother Sugg said firmly, trying not to let the disappointment show. Time was running out. He could tell because the train was passing Grayson and in twenty minutes' time they'd be in Doxie.

"Speak," they all cried out, then, all forty-nine of them from the sound of it.

The conductor looked in, shook his head, and went out again. He knew about these revivalists, and he knew when to join them and when to leave them alone.

๛ ๛ ๛

"No, let him be," a woman cried out then. "Leave him alone. He won't name me, so I'll name myself."

And Amelia Sugg stood up from the corner of the front seat and faced her husband. "It was me," she said, the tears coming down her face. "I was the one."

Brother Sugg just stood there staring at her, and Galen Millz buried his head in his hands and fell back down into his seat.

"I was the one," Amelia went on. "Me, your wife and the mother of your children. I was the one, I was the one who bedded with him when you were gone so much preaching the word of the Lord and bringing others into the fold. I was the one."

Brother Sugg reached out and took her hand, and she began to sob.

"I wanted love," she cried. "I wanted love and some of the pleasures of the world before it was too late. I see now that I was wrong. I did wrong and I'm sorry. I'm sorriest, though, that it was you I did it with, Galen, because I see you're a weak man, too, with your fear of your fellow man more than your fear of God. It wasn't God's forgiveness you wanted, it was his"—and she looked at her husband—"and theirs"—she looked at them all—"because you knew there was talk and you were afraid."

Galen only shook his head and cried more into his hands.

"Well, I'm ashamed, and so you can be happy now. I'm ashamed because you've shamed me, and you've shamed my husband."

She tried to move away, but Brother Sugg held her to him very tightly, and she could feel him squeezing her harder than he needed to.

"Repent," he whispered in her ear. "Repent."

"No," she said.

"Amelia, you're my wife and my sister, but you're more than that. You're a child of God. Come back to his fold. Repent yourself of your pride and your shame and be forgiven."

She felt him pinching her side, and it hurt. He was pinching her as he held her to him, pinching her and no one could see.

"Be forgiven and come back to God. Come back to your home and your husband. Come back to your children. And let this man be forgiven, too. You've taken him farther than your bed. You've taken him to hell. Let him out."

"Amen," someone called.

"Take your sins to the Lord and pray, it's not too late to repent today," Mary Grace Blevins began to sing.

They all took up the song, and left Amelia standing there beside her husband, who was holding her tighter and pinching her harder.

"For the sake of us all, Amelia," Brother Sugg whispered in her ear. "I'll take you back. I'll give you back your home and your children. And I'll stay home with you more often, and give you the worldly pleasures that I've denied you."

❧ ❧ ❧

Then she shook her head, and began to cry again, and let loose all the feelings that had been pent up inside her since it had all happened, since her husband had left her so many times with only the children and then Galen Millz, who would come to see her when he could and love her and then cry about it before he even left.

"Praise the Lord" and "Glory, glory, glory," they all began to cry. Brother Sugg dropped to his knees and pulled Amelia with him, and they both buried their heads in the seats in front of them and cried and prayed together. Then Galen Millz stood up and made his way to them. He knelt down beside Brother Sugg, and he cried and prayed, and Brother Sugg put his arms around Galen and said, "I forgive you." Then he put his arms around Amelia and said, "I forgive you, too."

Everyone began singing and praying at the same time, even when they were crying. The spirit was with them. Brother Sugg was a fine man, a man who had proved that he was their leader and the right man to take them to God. He had forgiven his own wife, there in front of them all, and had brought her back to God. And he'd brought back Galen Millz, who was living in hell with his sins and had almost gone crazy from them.

Amelia cried and smiled into her hands at the same time, because it was all over now and she'd gotten her husband back home where he belonged.

Galen Millz just cried and cried because he knew he was a weak man and he would never have repented unless Amelia had made him take this trip on the glory train, knowing it would shame him into bringing everything out into the open.

And Brother Sugg smiled, too, as he held on to them both and thought what a great day it had been. They hadn't even got to Doxie and already he had brought two people home to the Lord.

"Plum Grove Cemetery"

They came from
everywhere
like a swarm
of bees,
photographers

reporters
newsmen
women with
tape recorders
men with cameras.

They stuck
microphones
into our mouths
and took pictures
of my mother's face
through the
car window.

I objected but
my mother said
my father would have
wanted it that way,
it was his final
public appearance;
it was my last one, too.

"Song of the Blackbirds"

I know a song
the blackbirds sing
when perched upon
a blue tipped wing
they peck at grains
of Indian corn
early on
an autumn morn
beneath a sleezy
sleepy sun
before cross scarecrows
have begun
to wave their tattered
blue stuffed sleeves
at shattered cornstalks,
falling leaves.

They sing of
their prosperity,
their fortune,
their longevity,
and of the good grain
they have found
thriving in
my river ground.

Leon Driskell

Leon Driskell was barely sixty-two when he died in 1995. It was a short life for one so talented—as a fiction writer, a poet, and a teacher. A native of Georgia, he earned degrees from the University of Georgia and a Ph.D. from the University of Texas. He served in the U.S. Army from 1956 to 1958, and when he became a civilian again he had teaching stints at the University of Texas, Birmingham-Southern College, and the University of Cincinnati; from 1964 until his death he taught at the University of Louisville. In 1971 he coauthored with Joan Brittain *The Eternal Crossroads,* a book about the life and works of Flannery O'Connor. In 1983 Driskell published *Passing Through,* a collection of connected short stories about a colorful family in Owen County. This first selection, "A Fellow Making Himself Up," introduces a family of Owen County citizens more believable than the real ones on the tax records. The two poems that follow are equally evocative of character and place.

"A Fellow Making Himself Up"

What uncle Lester liked most about Rosco was that he had named himself, and Lester thought he had picked the perfect name. He did not look like a Ralph, or Robert, or Rupert, but exactly like a Rosco. Audrey said she did not think it was so great to be named Rosco, for she could not think of a single movie star, or even TV personality, with that name. Uncle Lester admitted that Rosco had not exactly named himself all the way, for he had started out with what his parents had decided to call him, which was R.P. White.

To Lester what uncle Rosco had done was better than any story in a book, even the ones about the frog who turned into a prince or the poor boy who became Lord Mayor of London. Lester made Rosco tell him all the details many times, and even when he was a baby, or practically one, he would make Rosco go back and tell it again if he left out any part of it.

Lester mostly called Rosco, Rosco—without any uncle before it—and you could tell he liked the sound of it. He had looked in the Owenton phone book to see if he could find any other Roscoes. It took him a whole afternoon to read all the first names. He found four of them, but he felt better when he called up and learned that one of them was deceased and another had moved off to Henry County.

How it happened that Rosco got the name R.P. White was that he was the eighth baby, and, by the time he came along, his parents had run out of names along with practically everything else. They had used up some perfectly good names on babies who had died, and Rosco said he guessed they felt funny about using the same names twice, especially since the dead children were buried a hundred yards from the front porch.

Their names and dates were painted on slate stones, and they were also listed in the family Bible, which uncle Rosco said he would give a pretty to have so he could show it to Lester.

Sauie Garland White / Jan 9 1902 – Feb 2 1902
(At Rest Now)
Han. Leonidus White / June 11 1903 – Oct 7 1903
(God's own)
Eben. Ulysses White / Oct 30 1904
(Precious Moment)

Rosco knew what all was on the stones, and he said Han. stood for Hannibal which was too long to fit on the slate, and that Eben. stood for Ebenezer. Uncle Lester was glad that Rosco did not get either of those names, but he did not say so. He had seen an Ebenezer (and an Ichabod) on TV.

Rosco was stingy with nothing but words, and, with Lester, he was not even stingy with them. His hands hung a mile out of his sleeves, as Ichabod's did, but his shoulders were broad as a barn door, and Lester could not imagine him running from a headless horseman or anything else. Lester wasn't sure how he felt about the name Ulysses, for he knew that Ulysses was a hero and had traveled far as Rosco had, but he also knew that Ulysses was Greek—and the Greek who owned the cafe had been partly to blame for Lurline's going to the Women's Detention Center. Lester thought that since it was his name Lurline signed to a check he should have had some say about things, and not some Greek who wasn't even kin to Lurline.

Rosco said his Daddy had once worked at a textile mill in Walhalla, S.C., for a man named R.P. Swift, so when Rosco's Mama said *What can we name this one?* he came out with R.P.

"R.P.?" said Rosco's Mama. "What kind of name is that?"

They ended up writing it down in the family Bible anyhow—R.P. White, Dec. 6, 1917. That was how they named the children back then, at least in Walhalla. They wrote the name down in the Bible. None of them ever had a birth certificate, and uncle Rosco said that had caused him a world and all of trouble, though, as he said, you would think anybody with a grain of sense who saw him standing there would take it on faith that he had to have been born, even if he didn't have papers to show for it.

Until Rosco decided to name himself, lots of people said to him what his Mama had said to his Daddy.

"R.P.?" they would say. "What kind of name is that?"

His teachers would always tell him that he had to have more name than that. "You go home tonight," they told him, "and ask your Mama what those letters stand for so I can write it down." Uncle Rosco said he could never understand why certain people put so much stock in knowing things just so they could write them down.

One teacher told him that if he did not tell her his real name, she was going to call him Rastus—and how would he like answering to a nigger name? She called him that a time or two until he told her his Mama said that 'Rastus was short for Erastus and could not be what the R. stood for in his name—and besides, his Mama said *Erastus* was a lovely name. The teacher said she wondered who Mrs. White thought she was, but she stopped calling R.P. *Rastus* and took to calling him Robert, but he would answer to nothing but R.P.

Uncle Lester figured it was lucky that Rosco did not stay in school very long, for that teacher would have ended up naming him herself before he had a chance. Rosco said that he was never much for sitting indoors, and when his Daddy began to need him around the place, he just quit going to school though he did sometimes borrow books to read at night when the work was done.

By then, it was the Depression, though Rosco told Lester that the only difference he could see between the Depression and what come before was that the Federal Government began to notice that folks were poor. One of Rosco's brothers went off and joined the CCC. Rosco could not remember what the letters stood for, so Lester looked it up in the World Book and found out it was the Civilian Conservation Corps, and uncle Rosco said that was right. He said there was a CCC camp just below Franklin, N.C., and he had been there once. He said the boys there learned to plant trees and cut them down and how to build stone steps and walls on the National Park grounds. They had uniforms to wear and learned how to drive trucks and string electrical wires without hardly ever electrocuting themselves.

Another brother lied about his age so he could join the Navy and see the world, and what came of that was that he was at Pearl Harbor when the Japs made their sneak attack and he like to have been killed.

Rosco's sister, Rose Cameron White, took up with an older man and headed west not to be heard of for years. When Lester asked what happened to her, uncle Rosco shook his head. It seemed that Rose Cameron had prospered and now owned a large wheat ranch and had run through two more men. Another sister got herself married right off as soon as she was fifteen, though as Rosco's Daddy always said, she would have done better to head west too.

After a while Rosco's Mama died trying to have another baby. Rosco said she had already had eleven or twelve, he'd lost count, and was too old to have any more but didn't know what to do. His Daddy got married again soon so he would have somebody to look after the younger chaps.

"Chaps?" interrupted Lester.

"Chaps," uncle Rosco confirmed. "That's what Mama always called us children. Chaps, don't ask me why."

Rosco said he decided it was time for him to leave, and when Lester asked if his Daddy's new wife was a wicked stepmother, he said she was a good lady but that he did not feel at home with her. She was not much older than he was, and he felt funny every time he saw his Daddy hug and kiss her. He would think of his Mama and how old and tired seeming she had always been, and that made it hard for him to get used to a new, pretty Mama.

He did not get far the first time he ran away. Somebody in a buggy (he thought maybe it was the doctor) picked him up and brought him home before anybody even knew he was gone. They did not know he had run away until he told them, and he had time to help with the chores before he got his licking.

The next time he tried, he made it. He was fifteen and big for his age, and it was easy for him to find work even when all he got in exchange was his food and a pallet to sleep on. After a year or two, he took to sending an occasional postcard home, and once at Christmas he had sent a money order, but it was a long time before he saw any of his people again.

Mostly he bummed around, but he told Lester that he always kept himself neat and clean so nobody would think he was a hobo. He looked for work, and he sometimes settled in at a place for three or four months and then he would move on. He got all the way to California, and, though he liked the climate, he did not care for the people. None of the ones he met seemed to be where they ought to be, and most of them were trying to pretend they were not from where they came from. They were from all over, from North Dakota and Arkansas and Tennessee, but they all told him that California was God's country and they hoped they never had to go back to where they came from.

"Me," said Rosco, "I didn't think their Hoovervilles beat the mountain shacks I knew back home, and back there we at least didn't have guards walking around the fruit groves like they did in God's country. Every other person you'd meet would ask if you was an Oakie, and I said I didn't know that I was but I would answer to that name as soon as I would to 'cracker,' which is what they called people from Georgia."

Rosco was in Norfolk, Virginia, when the war broke out, so he just stayed there and worked in the shipyards. After a spell, he went from unskilled to skilled and joined the union and almost got himself married. If he had done that, he would never have come to Kentucky and met Mama Pearl, or any of them. He named himself there, in Norfolk, Virginia, at the place where his girlfriend worked.

The woman Rosco nearly married was named Irma and was a waitress at what Rosco called a greasy-spoon and pick-up joint. One night in 1942, Rosco was sitting at the counter in the eating half of the Gypsy Bar and Grill. "The *gyppy* bar and grill?" interrupted Lester.

"No," said uncle Rosco. "Though the words *gyp* and *gypsy* are probably kin, I have known a good many gypsies in my time and I have not found that they are any more likely to try and cheat you than other folks. Where Irma worked was called the Gypsy Bar and Grill because they had these round glass globes, like crystal balls, on the tables, and all the girls wore headrags and big loop earrings."

"Was Irma a gypsy?" uncle Lester wanted to know.

"I guess not," said Rosco. "I never noticed any of them was able to see much into the future, least of all Irma."

That night in 1942, uncle Rosco was feeling blue. The war was not looking good—Things Looked Bad for Democracy. He did not know if or when he would be drafted, and he did not know how he felt about killing people even if he did know that God was on our side. He was waiting for Irma to get off work at midnight, and he hoped they would have a few laughs together and he would start to feeling better.

Business slowed down in the cafe, and Irma began horsing around, first with one fellow and then another. Then she began razzing Rosco about his name.

She introduced him to a fellow she said was Angelo ("But don't let *that* fool you," she said winking at Angelo), and then she said, "Angelo, this here is R.P. White. Just don't ask me what that R.P. stands for, or I may tell you."

The men at the counter all laughed, and some of them started making up things that R.P. could stand for, and, though he tried, Rosco could not make himself laugh, and he said he felt his face going redder and redder. Pretty soon what they were saying got bad enough that it bothered even Irma, so she broke in and told them what she had read in the *Readers Digest* while she waited to get her hair fixed.

"It was in this part they call 'Humor in uniform,'" she told them. 'This hick from somewhere down south got drafted, and the sergeant told him to write down his full name—"

"It's a wonder he could write," Angelo said.

"He could write," Irma said, "but he didn't know what to do, because all he had was initials before his last name, which was Jones."

"What's wrong with that?" Rosco wanted to know, but nobody paid him any attention.

"Sooo," Irma concluded. "He wrote down R (only), P (only) Jones, and the next morning at roll-call, they called him Ronly Ponly Jones."

Everybody but Rosco screamed with laughter, Irma louder than anyone else. Then somebody called Rosco Ronly Ponly and they all laughed some more.

Rosco stood up then, and looked hard at Irma until she stopped laughing.

"My name is not Ronly Ponly or any of those other things you have been saying," he told them. He was going to say his name was R.P. White and what is wrong with that? but one of the men said, "If your name is not Ronly Ponly, then what is it?"

"Rosco," he said with sudden inspiration. "Rosco P. White."

He walked out of the Gypsy Bar and Grill then, and he never saw Irma again.

The next morning he signed on with the merchant marines and spent the next two years at sea. When the man in charge at the merchant marines gave him a form to fill out and told him to print his name in full, Rosco thought again of Private Ronly Ponly Jones. He stared at the sheet of paper for a minute, and the man said, "Go ahead. Put your full name right there on the page. Last name first, no initials."

Uncle Rosco said that he printed WHITE, ROSCO—and since he had never thought about what the P. could stand for, he wrote down PAGE. He was so pleased with his new name that he had his social security card changed, and, after he got out of the merchant marines, he went looking for Irma. He said he wanted to let her know who he was.

The short-order cook at the Gypsy Bar and Grill said he thought Irma had married somebody named Angelo, but somebody else said they didn't think so. And somebody else said the man Irma was living with might or might not be her husband, but she knew for certain that he was no angel— and, from the looks of Irma, she had found that out, too. The short-order cook said he had never noticed that Irma was what you could call perfect.

Uncle Rosco said, "What's in a name anyhow?"

At this point in the story, Lester would always scowl and say under his breath, "Plenty. There's plenty in a name."

One day Lester said it out loud. "There's plenty in a name," he told Rosco.

"If you had stayed R (only), P (only) White, Irma would have called you that all your life, and you would probably still be hanging around waiting for her to get off work and you would never have come to Kentucky and fallen in love with Mama Pearl, and we would never have known you or anything and we would not be a family."

Uncle Rosco thought hard about what Lester had said.

"Well," he said finally, "I just made up those names as I went along, but for a fellow making himself up, I guess I didn't do half bad, did I?"

He looked down over the barn and out to where the tobacco was yellowing in the field.

"Not half bad," he answered himself. "Let's go split some wood, so maybe we can have hot biscuits for supper."

"Like a Phoenix"

I rise in flame, claimed
Lawrence, and left Freida
a long time to be old alone.

And how does the Phoenix feel,
looking back at ash and
knowing it's all to be done again?

Much, I guess, like me,
chafing the heart, bracing
up for when breath begins.

Now, like a Phoenix,
I'll risk another start,
dusted gray with your ash.

"Owen County: August"

The cows won't believe the spring is dry.
I follow them to the blackberry tangles on the hillslope,
And find, among cow tracks, deer sign, coon tracks.
Skirting the empty hillside hole, the cows feign indifference,
Graze toward barn and creek. Later, I hear them bellowing
At the cedar-and-wire gap which keeps them out of the creek.
I cross Sawdridge Creek dry and recall its reputation:
"A wild creek," everyone told us.
"Washed out the bridge last winter,"
"Picked up Dave Hurt's truck
     Threw it at cedar creek,
      Broke it open like a turtle."
"A wild creek," everyone agreed.

Red True is laying irrigation pipe to save the tobacco.
He pumps our bathing hole dry.
The spurting fields look like the gardens at Versailles.
The snakes leave the drying creek. The fish cannot.
I interrupt turtles' weighty flight.
They pretend to be stones.

"Unless it rains, we pump at the bridge tomorrow."

When, at last, it rains, I climb the hill in the dark.
I anoint myself at the spring, and whisper needless
        to the whispering night:
"Sawdridge Creek is up."

Martha Bennett Stiles

from *Lonesome Road*

In 1933 Martha Bennett Stiles was born a Virginian. She finally made it through the Cumberland Gap into the promised land of Kentucky in 1977, where she lives on a thoroughbred horse farm in Bourbon County and writes delightful stories for children and adolescents and novels for adults, including *Lonesome Road* (1998), a sinister story of a little boy who quietly disappears one morning as he starts to school and the horror that builds inside his family after his disappearance. The reader enters this mystery on its very first page.

April frost glitters where the shadow of the mailbox and its post paints a gallows on the hard earth. A boy stands where the shadow almost touches his toes. He is considering climbing the fence that separates him from the field where a gray mare quietly grazes. She is due to foal soon; he would give his baseball not to be leaving her. Suddenly his head turns.

From the field a killdeer cries out. The boy's mother loves these boomerang-winged birds who, like her, were once creatures of the shore. The boy scarcely hears them; he is listening for danger.

The boy imagines that the mailbox is a tree which he has planted, and that at any moment men with axes may drive their Jeep into view over the rise where the big yellow Bourbon County bus appears at that hour every school day. The men will want to chop down the tree. He hears them shout first orders, then threats. He knows what they want, though they speak only Korean. When he stands resolute between them and the tree, they try to kill him. There are five of them. With his book bag he knocks their axes aside, one after another. When he gets his hands on one of these axes, the men scramble back into their Jeep.

The car that slows to a stop beside the boy is a 1980 Chevrolet with the battle flag of the Confederacy—the flag of half his great-great-grandfathers—fluttering from its antenna. The boy has stopped signaling base camp with his walkie-talkie.

The Chevrolet's idling engine is even louder than its radio. Born to lose, *the radio whines with belligerent self-pity. Despite the chill, the driver has rolled down his front windows. His car sits out at night, and he doesn't fool with wiping off the damn condensation.*

The driver is in his twenties. His jaw is lean and winter reddened; it has a sullen slackness. He wears a blue shirt faded from many launderings, none recent. His sleeves are rolled up, revealing muscular forearms, their hair too light to obscure the work of the Panama City tattoo artist who was probably the only person in that country who gave him his money's worth, though he spent all that he had. He eyes the boy through kinky bangs. "Hey Lang," he asks, "you talking to the mailbox?"

Lang's best friend Breck's bus stop is just around the corner. Lang chafes at his parents' rule that he may not walk there unescorted. Offered a lift, he barely hesitates.

Breck is still inside. He is telling his mother that he doesn't need his jacket and she is zipping it up on him when the rusty Chevrolet drives by without stopping.

Wendell Berry
"The Pleasures of Eating"

A perceptive comment by the critic Jack Hicks of the University of California at Davis is a good way to introduce Kentucky's preeminent writer about the human relationship to the land and, indeed, all of nature. Berry's own life and work, he says, "has nourished and been nourished by an extraordinarily rich metaphor: man as husband, in the oldest senses of the word, having committed himself in multiple marriage to wife, family, farm, community, and finally, to the great cycle of nature itself." It is, he says, "the central stream of Wendell Berry's writing." Berry's novels and short stories, his essays and poems, and his fiction and nonfiction center on the fragile but strong human bond to nature and humanity's good stewardship of the natural world—leitmotifs running like a river of life through them all. Although Berry probably wishes that he had been born at home in Port Royal in Henry County on the Kentucky River—a setting more in keeping with his agrarian vocation—he was born in a Louisville hospital on August 5, 1934. In his writing and in his life, he has more than made up for that missed symbolism. In 1965 he moved his family to a small farm near his ancestral home at Port Royal. Despite setbacks and false starts, it has been an awe-inspiring achievement in agrarian living. His works include *Nathan Coulter* (1960), a novel about farming the old way, *The Hidden Wound* (1970), a book of essays about the permanent wounds left by slavery on both the owners and the owned, and another collection of essays, *The Art of the Commonplace* (2002), from which the first selection is taken.

Many times, after I have finished a lecture on the decline of American farming and rural life, someone in the audience has asked, "What can city people do?"

"Eat responsibly," I have usually answered. Of course, I have tried to explain what I meant by that, but afterwards I have invariably felt that there was more to be said than I had been able to say. Now I would like to attempt a better explanation.

I begin with the proposition that eating is an agricultural act. Eating ends the annual drama of the food economy that begins with planting and birth. Most eaters, however, are no longer aware that this is true. They think of food as an agricultural product, perhaps, but they do not think of themselves as participants in agriculture. They think of themselves as "consumers." If they think beyond that, they recognize that they are passive consumers. They buy what they want—or what they have been persuaded to want—within the limits of what they can get. They pay, mostly without protest, what they are charged. And they mostly ignore certain critical questions about the quality and the cost of what they are sold: How fresh is it? How pure or clean is it, how free of dangerous chemicals? How far was it transported, and what did transportation add to the cost? How much did manufacturing or packaging or advertising add to the cost? When the food product has been manufactured or "processed" or "precooked," how has that affected its quality or price or nutritional value?

Most urban shoppers would tell you that food is produced on farms. But most of them do not know what farms, or what kinds of farms, or where the farms are, or what knowledge or skills are involved in farming. They apparently have little doubt that farms will continue to produce, but they do not know how or over what obstacles. For them, then, food is pretty much an abstract idea—something they do not know or imagine—until it appears on the grocery shelf or on the table.

The specialization of production induces specialization of consumption. Patrons of the entertainment industry, for example, entertain themselves less and less and have become more and more passively dependent on commercial suppliers. This is certainly true also of patrons of the food industry, who have tended more and more to be *mere* consumers—passive, uncritical, and dependent. Indeed, this sort of consumption may be said to be one of the chief goals of industrial production. The food industrialists have by now persuaded millions of consumers to prefer food that is already prepared. They will grow, deliver, and cook your food for you and (just like your mother) beg you to eat it. That they do not yet offer to insert it, prechewed, into your mouth is only because they have found no profitable way to do so. We may rest assured that they would be glad to find such a way. The ideal industrial food consumer would be strapped to a table with a tube running from the food factory directly into his or her stomach.

Perhaps I exaggerate, but not by much. The industrial eater is, in fact, one who does not know that eating is an agricultural act, who no longer knows or imagines the connections between eating and the land, and who is therefore necessarily passive and uncritical—in short, a victim. When food, in the minds of eaters, is no longer associated with farming and with the land, then the eaters are suffering a kind of cultural amnesia that is misleading and dangerous. The current version of the "dream home" of the future involves "effortless" shopping from a list of available goods on a television monitor and heating precooked food by remote control. Of course, this implies and depends on a perfect ignorance of the history of the food that is consumed. It requires that the citizenry should give up their hereditary and sensible aversion to buying a pig in a poke. It wishes to make the selling of pigs in pokes an honorable and glamorous activity. The dreamer in this dream home will perforce know nothing about the kind or quality of this food, or where it came from, or how it was produced and prepared, or what ingredients, additives, and residues it contains—unless, that is, the dreamer undertakes a close and constant study of the food industry, in which case he or she might as well wake up and play an active and responsible part in the economy of food.

There is, then, a politics of food that, like any politics, involves our freedom. We still (sometimes) remember that we cannot be free if our minds and voices are controlled by someone else. But we have neglected to understand that we cannot be free if our food and its sources are controlled by someone else. The condition of the passive consumer of food is not a democratic condition. One reason to eat responsibly is to live free.

But if there is a food politics, there are also a food esthetics and a food ethics, neither of which is dissociated from politics. Like industrial sex, industrial eating has become a degraded, poor, and paltry thing. Our kitchens and other eating places more and more resemble filling stations, as our homes more and more resemble motels. "Life is not very interesting," we seem to have decided. "Let its satisfactions be minimal, perfunctory, and fast." We hurry through our meals to go to work and hurry through our work in order to "recreate" ourselves in the evenings and on weekends and vacations. And then we hurry, with the greatest possible speed and noise and violence, through our recreation—for what? To eat the billionth hamburger at some fast-food joint hell-bent on increasing the "quality" of our life? And all this is carried out in a remarkable obliviousness to the causes and effects, the possibilities and the purposes, of the life of the body in this world.

One will find this obliviousness represented in virgin purity in the advertisements of the food industry, in which food wears as much makeup as the actors. If one gained one's whole knowledge of food from these advertisements (as some presumably do), one would not know that the various edibles were ever living creatures, or that they all come from the soil, or that they were produced by work. The passive American consumer, sitting down to a meal of pre-prepared or fast food, confronts a platter covered with inert, anonymous substances that have been processed, dyed, breaded, sauced, gravied, ground, pulped, strained, blended, prettified, and sanitized beyond resemblance to any part of any creature that ever lived. The products of nature and agriculture have been made, to all appearances, the products of industry. Both eater and eaten are thus in exile from biological reality. And the result is a kind of solitude, unprecedented in human experience, in which the eater may think of eating as, first, a purely commercial transaction between him and a supplier and then as a purely appetitive transaction between him and his food.

And this peculiar specialization of the act of eating is, again, of obvious benefit to the food industry, which has good reasons to obscure the connection between food and farming. It would not do for the consumer to know that the hamburger she is eating came from a steer who spent much of his life standing deep in his own excrement in a feedlot, helping to pollute the local streams, or that the calf that yielded the veal cutlet on her plate spent its life in a box in which it did not have room to turn around. And, though her sympathy for the slaw might be less tender, she should not be encouraged to meditate on the hygienic and biological implications of mile-square fields of cabbage, for vegetables grown in huge monocultures are dependent on toxic chemicals—just as animals in close confinement are dependent on antibiotics and other drugs.

The consumer, that is to say, must be kept from discovering that, in the food industry—as in any other industry—the overriding concerns are not quality and health, but volume and price. For decades now the entire industrial food economy, from the large farms and feedlots to the chains of supermarkets and fast-food restaurants, has been obsessed with volume. It has relentlessly increased scale in order to increase volume in order (presumably) to reduce costs. But as scale increases, diversity declines; as diversity declines, so does health; as health declines, the dependence on drugs and chemicals necessarily increases. As capital replaces labor, it does so by substituting machines, drugs, and chemicals for human workers and for the natural health and fertility of the soil. The food is produced by any means or any shortcut that will increase profits. And the business of the cosmeticians of advertising is to persuade the consumer that food so produced is good, tasty, healthful, and a guarantee of marital fidelity and long life.

It is possible, then, to be liberated from the husbandry and wifery of the old household food economy. But one can be thus liberated only by entering a trap (unless one sees ignorance and helplessness as the signs of privilege, as many people apparently do). The trap is the ideal of industrialism: a walled city surrounded by valves that let merchandise in but no consciousness out. How does one escape this trap? Only voluntarily, the same way that one went in: by restoring one's consciousness of what is involved in eating; by reclaiming responsibility for one's own part in the food economy. One might begin with the illuminating principle of Sir Albert Howard's *The Soil and Health*, that we should understand "the whole problem of health in soil, plant, animal, and man as one great subject." Eaters, that is, must understand that eating takes place inescapably in the world, that it is inescapably an agricultural act, and that how we eat determines, to a considerable extent, how the world is used. This is a simple way of describing a relationship that is inexpressibly complex. To eat responsibly is to understand and enact, so far as one can, this complex relationship. What can one do? Here is a list, probably not definitive:

1. Participate in food production to the extent that you can. If you have a yard or even just a porch box or a pot in a sunny window, grow something to eat in it. Make a little compost of your kitchen scraps and use it for fertilizer. Only by growing some food for yourself can you become acquainted with the beautiful energy cycle that revolves from soil to seed to flower to fruit to food to offal to decay, and around again. You will be fully responsible for any food that you grow for yourself, and you will know all about it. You will appreciate it fully, having known it all its life.

2. Prepare your own food. This means reviving in your own mind and life the arts of kitchen and household. This should enable you to eat more cheaply, and it will give you a measure of "quality control": you will have some reliable knowledge of what has been added to the food you eat.

3. Learn the origins of the food you buy, and buy the food that is produced closest to your home. The idea that every locality should be, as much as possible, the source of its own food makes several kinds of sense. The locally produced food supply is the most secure, the freshest, and the easiest for local consumers to know about and to influence.

4. Whenever possible, deal directly with a local farmer, gardener, or orchardist. All the reasons listed for the previous suggestion apply here. In addition, by such dealing you eliminate the whole pack of merchants, transporters, processors, packagers, and advertisers who thrive at the expense of both producers and consumers.

5. Learn, in self-defense, as much as you can of the economy and technology of industrial food production. What is added to food that is not food, and what do you pay for these additions?

6. Learn what is involved in the *best* farming and gardening.

7. Learn as much as you can, by direct observation and experience if possible, of the life histories of the food species.

The last suggestion seems particularly important to me. Many people are now as much estranged from the lives of domestic plants and animals (except for flowers and dogs and cats) as they are from the lives of the wild ones. This is regrettable, for these domestic creatures are in diverse ways attractive; there is much pleasure in knowing them. And farming, animal husbandry, horticulture, and gardening, at their best, are complex and comely arts; there is much pleasure in knowing them, too.

It follows that there is great *dis*pleasure in knowing about a food economy that degrades and abuses those arts and those plants and animals and the soil from which they come. For anyone who does know something of the modern history of food, eating away from home can be a chore. My own inclination is to eat seafood instead of red meat or poultry when I am traveling. Though I am by no means a vegetarian, I dislike the thought that some animal has been made miserable in order to feed me. If I am going to eat meat, I want it to be from an animal that has lived a pleasant, uncrowded life outdoors, on bountiful pasture, with good water nearby and trees for shade. And I am getting almost as fussy about food plants. I like to eat vegetables and fruits that I know have lived happily and healthily in good soil, not the products of the huge, bechemicaled factory-fields that I have seen, for example, in the Central Valley of California. The industrial farm is said to have been patterned on the factory production line. In practice, it looks more like a concentration camp.

The pleasure of eating should be an *extensive* pleasure, not that of the mere gourmet. People who know the garden in which their vegetables have grown and know that the garden is healthy will remember the beauty of the growing plants, perhaps in the dewy first light of morning when gardens are at their best. Such a memory involves itself with the food and is one of the pleasures of eating. The knowledge of the good health of the garden relieves and frees and comforts the eater. The same goes for eating meat. The thought of the good pasture and of the calf contentedly grazing flavors the steak. Some, I know, will think it bloodthirsty or worse to eat a fellow creature you have known all its life. On the contrary, I think it means that you eat with understanding and with gratitude. A significant part of the pleasure of eating is in one's accurate consciousness of the lives and the world from which food comes. The pleasure of eating, then, may be the best available standard of our health. And this pleasure, I think, is pretty fully available to the urban consumer who will make the necessary effort.

I mentioned earlier the politics, esthetics, and ethics of food. But to speak of the pleasure of eating is to go beyond those categories. Eating with the fullest pleasure—pleasure, that is, that does not depend on ignorance—is perhaps the profoundest enactment of our connection with the world. In this pleasure we experience and celebrate our dependence and our gratitude, for we are living from mystery, from creatures we did not make and powers we cannot comprehend. When I think of the meaning of food, I always remember these lines by the poet William Carlos Williams, which seem to me merely honest:

There is nothing to eat,
    seek it where you will,
        but of the body of the Lord.
The blessed plants
    and the sea, yield it
        to the imagination
intact.

from *A Timbered Choir:*
The Sabbath Poems, 1979–1997

Berry's essaylike short stories of what he calls the Port William Membership offer a vision of how the poison and wounds with which we have afflicted ourselves can be assuaged and perhaps undone. Considerably shorter works, these several poems will introduce you to his spoiled world and the possibilities of redemption.

"Another Sunday Morning Comes"

Another Sunday morning comes
And I resume the standing Sabbath
Of the woods, where the finest blooms
Of time return, and where no path

Is worn but wears its makers out
At last, and disappears in leaves
Of fallen seasons. The tracked rut
Fills and levels; here nothing grieves

In the risen season. Past life
Lives in the living. Resurrection
Is in the way each maple leaf
Commemorates its kind, by connection

Outreaching understanding. What rises
Rises into comprehension
And beyond. Even falling raises
In praise of light. What is begun

Is unfinished. And so the mind
That comes to rest among the bluebells

Comes to rest in motion, refined
By alteration. The bud swells,

Opens, makes seed, falls, is well,
Being becoming what it is:
Miracle and parable
Exceeding thought, because it is

Immeasurable; the understander
Encloses understanding, thus
Darkens the light. We can stand under
No ray that is not dimmed by us.

The mind that comes to rest is tended
In ways that it cannot intend:
Is borne, preserved, and comprehended
By what it cannot comprehend.

Your Sabbath, Lord, thus keeps us by
Your will, not ours. And it is fit
Our only choice should be to die
Into that rest, or out of it.

"Who Makes a Clearing Makes a Work of Art"

Who makes a clearing makes a work of art,
The true world's Sabbath trees in festival
Around it. And the stepping stream, a part
Of Sabbath also, flows past, by its fall
Made musical, making the hillslope by
Its fall, and still at rest in falling, song
Rising. The field is made by hand and eye,
By daily work, by hope outreaching wrong,
And yet the Sabbath, parted, still must stay
In the dark mazings of the soil no hand
May light, the great Life, broken, make its way
Along the stemmy footholds of the ant.
　　Bewildered in our timely dwelling place,
　　Where we arrive by work, we stay by grace.

"They Sit Together on the Porch, the Dark"

They sit together on the porch, the dark
Almost fallen, the house behind them dark.
Their supper done with, they have washed and dried
The dishes—only two plates now, two glasses,
Two knives, two forks, two spoons—small work for two.
She sits with her hands folded in her lap,
At rest. He smokes his pipe. They do not speak.
And when they speak at last it is to say
What each one knows the other knows. They have
One mind between them, now, that finally
For all its knowing will not exactly know
Which one goes first through the dark doorway, bidding
Goodnight, and which sits on a while alone.

"In Spring We Planted Seed"

In spring we planted seed,
And by degrees the plants
Grew, flowered, and transformed
The light to food, which we
Brought in, and ate, and lived.
The year grown old, we gathered
All that remained. We broke,
Manured, prepared the ground
For overwintering,
And thus at last made clear
Our little plot of time,
Tropical for a while,
Then temperate, then cold.

"I Would Not Have Been a Poet"

I would not have been a poet
except that I have been in love
alive in this mortal world,
or an essayist except that I
have been bewildered and afraid,

or a storyteller had I not heard
stories passing to me through the air,
or a writer at all except
I have been wakeful at night
and words have come to me
out of their deep caves
needing to be remembered.
But on the days I am lucky
or blessed, I am silent.
I go into the one body
that two make in making marriage
that for all our trying, all
our deaf-and-dumb of speech,
has no tongue. Or I give myself
to gravity, light, and air
and am carried back
to solitary work in fields
and woods, where my hands
rest upon a world unnamed,
complete, unanswerable, and final
as our daily bread and meat.
The way of love leads all ways
to life beyond words, silent
and secret. To serve that triumph
I have done all the rest.

Gurney Norman

"A Correspondence," from *Kinfolks*

Like a lot of readers, I was introduced to Gurney Norman through "Divine Right's Trip," a rite-of-passage story that appeared in *The Last Whole Earth Catalogue* in 1971 and documented the flower children and the drug-drenched counterculture of the 1960s. The central character is a young man from Kentucky who goes west to experience this culture and find himself, then returns home to find the meaning he was looking for. In 1977 Norman published *Kinfolks,* a collection of ten stories about Wilgus Collier that chronicle his maturation into adulthood through his relationships with members of his own family. At the beginning Wilgus is nine years old. At the end he is in his twenties, older and wiser and, in the words of Whitman, "a simple, separate person." Both books are at least semiautobiographical; the characters and events in the books parallel many similar people and events in Norman's life. The excerpt below chronicles the failed attempt, in a series of letters, of an estranged brother and sister to reconcile in their old age. Wilgus is the agent trying to bring them together.

Dear Brother Luther,

I know you will be surprised to hear from me it's been so long. How I found out you was yet living and where, was Wilgus Collier is from there, who came to rent my upstairs apartment, a nice young traveling man. He says he grew up within a mile of where your daughter lives in Knott County, that his aunt is her neighbor and for you to tell her hello. I call it the Lord's miracle that He sent Wilgus Collier to my house a messenger of the only good news I have had in many years. I pray to Him this will reach you and that you will answer and we will be in touch with one another again.

So it's been many years since we were all at home together hasn't it dear Brother? I often think of those old days and wish I was back at home with my loved ones instead of sitting in this lonesome place by myself. Did you know I lived in Phoenix? I have lived here eleven years. My husband Troy bought this house with two apartments and one other with three apartments and moved us here in 1954 when he retired and for my asthma. Then the next year he died of heart trouble and Bright's disease so I have a mighty load to carry by myself. Troy had a boy and girl by his first marriage but they have forgot their old stepmother, and I never had children of my own as you perhaps know. It is lonesome in Phoenix and I breathe with difficulty, and my tenants are the only ones I see and they are not always friendly except Wilgus Collier, a nice young traveling man who the Lord sent to me and put me in touch with you again and oh I hope how soon we can be together again dear Brother, like we were so many years ago when we lived on Cowan Creek. Join me in thanks to God and write soon.

Your loving sister,
Mrs. Drucilla Cornett Toliver

Sweet Sister,

Could not believe your letter at first. I thought it was another trick to torment me. I read it, read it again, then had daughter Cleo read it to me to be sure it was true. A big surprise, to think for years I have a sister living after all.

Yes, many years have gone under the bridge since we were all at home together and so happy. Now everything is down to a final proposition it appears like. I have the gout and cataracts. My wife Naomi died two years ago. My younguns are scattered here and yon, except daughter Blanche who died and son Romulus who lost his mind. I live first with one then the other, but mostly daughter Cleo, the others don't want me much. Bad business to be amongst ungrateful children.

Arizona. A mighty fine place I hear. Your man done good by you to leave you so well off. I seen Goldwater on television one night, speaking right from Phoenix. He strikes me as a scoundrel but it showed pictures of fine Arizona country, the desert and the sunset on some mountains so peaceful and quiet, it sure looked like where I want to be. And I hope how soon we can be together sweet sister, to keep each other company in these terrible times.

Your brother Luther Cornett,
Age 79 how old are you by now?

Dear Brother,

I am 72. I have asthma and artherites, bursitis and awful high blood pressure. My fingers hurts now to write this letter and I hope you will be able to read it.

But you have a nice hand write, Brother. You always was a good scholar at Little Engle School. I remember walking to school with you boys, and the way it set back against the hillside, the front end of it on stilts high enough to play under, and the way the willows and the sycamores leaned out over Engle Creek, and wading the creek and the Big Rock we played on that had mint growing around it. I remember an Easter egg hunt at the school. And the fight you had with Enoch Singleton. I know I have forgot a lot of old times but I do remember that school very well and hope to see it when I get back to dear Kentucky.

Which should not be too long now. My houses are not fancy but they are buying up property right and left here and I have buyers galore to pick from. But I want to get a good price so we can afford ourselves a nice place together somewhere there in Knott County. Do you ever hear of any places for sale in the Carr Fork section? Who owns the old homeplace now? Maybe we could buy it back and live there again and be like we used to be so many years ago.

I look forward to meeting your Cleo and all your grandchildren. You are so lucky to have grandchildren. I never did even have children but I guess I told you that. Until I learned you were yet living I cried myself to sleep every night with only Jesus for my comfort. But now He has sent me you, and soon we will be re-united in His love, sweet Brother.

In His Holy Name,
Drucilla Toliver

Sweet Sister,

So much racket going on here I can't hardly think what to write. It is this way all the time in this house, no peace and quiet. Cleo won't control her younguns. They all promised me my own room before I moved in, but then never give me one, it was all a lure and a trap. I turn the television up full blast to drown them out. After a while you don't hear a loud television but it is still a poor substitute for true quiet like you all must have out west.

The '27 flood got Engle School.

A flood can come and get the rest of this place for all I care. Kentucky is all tore up and gone, Sister. Soon they'll flood Carr Fork and that whole section, including the old homeplace, the government's doing it. You are fortunate to have your property. I used to have property on Hardburly Mountain, two hundred acres, with a good stand of white pine plus a well, dwelling house, barn and good-sized garden. But the strip miners got it all. I lawed the sons of bitches but couldn't do no good. So here I am stuck at Cleo's house, crowded up, no privacy, she can't cook, younguns gone wild, not enough heat, and they read my mail before I get it. (You be careful what you say!) Count your blessings in Arizona, sister, none in Kentucky to count. And keep your property, I'll be out there before long to help you run it and we'll get along good for ever more.

Your loving brother,
Luther

Dear Brother,

You would not like Arizona. It is not green and cool here like Kentucky, and Phoenix is difficult of living. I can't tell you too much about Phoenix except that Carson Avenue is a terrible place. I've only seen the downtown part once, in 1956 when the Presbyterians took me down and back one day for a good deed, but it wasn't much then and I doubt that it's any better now.

I want to pick blackberries again, and gather chestnuts and see the laurel when it blooms. I never see anything on Carson Avenue except the motorcycle gang go by. Taxes are awful and the heat and when you call the water company it takes it a month to come, and you can't see television because of this sarcastic neighbor Mr. Ortiz who pranks with the electricity.

So I'll be home in a month or two, soon as I settle up my business. You look for us a place to buy. Get it in the country, pick us out a cove off one of those cool hollows and have laurel on it if you can. It would be good to live close to Carr Creek or Troublesome, or maybe even over on North Fork River. I'm not much of a fisherman but you always were and I can cook fish. It would be handy if we could buy us a good house already built. But if you feel up to it, and some of your children would help, I'd like to buy a hillside with good timber on it and we could have us a house built out of our own wood, to suit us, and cheaper too. Wouldn't that be something? I'd like to be on the road to see people go by, nice Kentucky neighbors and kinfolks. Last Sunday I was sitting on my porch and a motorcycle man yelled an ugly thing at me and upset me terrible.

And I didn't exactly admire your using bad language in your last letter, Brother. That indicates you might not be saved, but I pray you are, but if you aren't tell me the truth about it.

Sister Drucilla

Drucilla,

Don't come to Kentucky. I tell you this is a terrible place. The union has pulled out. No work anywhere. They're gouging the hillsides down, stripping and augering. Ledford Pope's house got totally carried off by a mudslide. The streams are fouled, not a fish this side of Buckhorn Lake, not even any water to speak of except at flood time when there's more than anybody wants. The young folks have mostly moved to Ohio and Indiana to work, and them that's left have no respect for old people, they'd never help us build a house even if we had something to build it out of. Kentucky's timber has been gone since you have. Coal trucks make more racket than motorcycles, and there's no air fit to breathe for the slate dumps burning. Sure no place for asthma sufferers.

I've seen the pictures of Arizona, and read about it. It sounds like all the old folks in the country are retiring out there but me. Damn such business as that, I'm on my way soon as I can accumulate trainfare. If you've got some extra to send me for expenses I'd be grateful to you, and make it up to you once I got there. I'll rent two apartments from you myself, I want me some room to stretch in. And don't worry about getting downtown. Me and you will take right off the first thing and see all the sights and visit all the retired people in Phoenix and go to shows and ride buses and sit around the swimming pools drinking ice tea.

Sorry for the bad words. Yes, I'm saved. I was a terrible rip-roarer most of my life, but 12 years ago I seen the light and give up all bad habits except cussing. I'm ready to give that up too but see no way to go about it till I get somewhere where there ain't so much to cuss about.

Your brother,
Luther

Brother,

I'm not going to live in Arizona. That's all there is to it. You don't understand how it is here. Why do you not want me to come home? Are you making up all those bad tales on Kentucky, just to keep me from coming? I don't understand your attitude. A man that would cuss his sister would lie to her too, and the Bible admonishes against oaths and lies. I don't want to boss you but I'll not be bossed myself, and I absolutely will not stay in Arizona.

Drucilla Toliver

Sister,

You say you don't understand my attitude. Well I don't understand a sister that would have two fancy houses and yet turn out a suffering brother to suffer at the hands of mean children and a bad location. You talk like such a Christian. I say do unto others as you want them to do unto you and you're the one with two houses. I didn't cuss you. And I just wonder who is lying to who, for I have seen the pictures of Arizona and read of everybody moving there to retire and be happy. It sounds like you're all out there together plotting to keep me out. Well you won't get away with it and I have one question to ask: have you been getting secret letters from Cleo on the side? It wouldn't surprise me.

Luther Cornett

Brother,

I still refuse to stay in Arizona, in spite of your insults, and I suggest you read The Beatitudes.

Drucilla Cornett Toliver

Sister,

You and Cleo think you can lure and trap me into staying in Kentucky but you are wrong.

Luther Cornett

Luther,

You have turned out strange is all I can say, unmindful of the needs of others, and if you continue to curse me we might as well forget the whole business.

Drucilla Cornett Toliver

Drucilla,

I have not cussed you but I am about to get around to it. And Cleo and Emmit and Polly and Sarah and R.C. and Little Charles too if they all don't hush their racket. If you don't agree to my coming there then you are right, we might as well forget the whole thing for I absolutely refuse to stay in such a goddamn hell-hole as this.

Luther Cornett

Dear Luther,

Satan moves your tongue and I won't listen, or agree to stay here another week.

Drucilla Toliver

Dear Drucilla,

Then we just as well forget the whole thing.

Mr. Luther O. Cornett

Luther,

Suit yourself.

Mrs. Drucilla Toliver

"Death in Lexington"

This poem will have special significance for Kentucky Wildcat fans, even though it is a satire on their rabid behavior.

OBITUARY: A seventy-nine-year-old retired Lexington businessman passed away in Good Samaritan Hospital yesterday after a heart attack in Rupp Arena Wednesday night during the Kentucky-LSU basketball game.

Bart Haney, 1477 Glenway Avenue, was stricken in the tense final seconds of regulation play when it appeared that LSU had the victory sewed up with a 85–81 lead.

But the never-say-die Wildcats sent the game into overtime on back-to-back field goals by Cliff Hagen and Ralph Beard.

Beard's bucket came on a driving layup as the final horn was sounding.

Kentucky's Jack Givens opened the scoring in the overtime period with his patented one-hander from twelve feet out to put the Wildcats ahead, 87–85.

But the Bengals from the Bayou, who had led the Wildcats throughout the second half, drew even on a tap-in by center Lee Ferguson, his eleventh field goal of the game.

The score was tied three times during the overtime, and as the seconds ticked off, it appeared the game might go into yet another extra period.

But then Kentucky's hot-shooting guard Rex Chapman, who made string music from three-point land throughout the game, fouled Ferguson. The big LSU pivot man coolly sank two free-throws to give his team the lead, 92–91, with six seconds remaining.

After a time out and a brief strategy session, the Wildcats brought the ball into play near the center line. Richie Farmer passed to Tony Delk, who quickly fed the ball to Jamal Mashburn at the low post. Gliding across the paint Mashburn went high to loft a gentle shot over the reaching arms of Ferguson that swished through the net as the horn sounded to end the game.

The final score was Kentucky 93–LSU 92.

Mr. Haney will be buried in Laurel Hill Cemetery tomorrow afternoon at 2 p.m.

Sallie Bingham

"Apricots"

Sallie Bingham was born during the hugely destructive 1937 Ohio River flood that inundated most of downtown Louisville. Despite, and to some extent because of, the wealthy, powerful Bingham family into which she was born, she became a gifted writer of short stories, novels, poetry, and plays. As a successful writer she has in many ways been able to live out the dreams of her father, Barry Bingham Sr., who once told me that he had always wanted to write and publish a good book. Instead, he ran the family communications business, which included radio and television stations, two newspapers, and a printing company. Sallie Bingham has published a number of good books, including *After Such Knowledge* (1959), a novel, and three collections of short stories, *The Touching Hand* (1965), *The Way It Is Now* (1970), and *Transgressions* (2002). She has also written and published poems and plays of great originality and passion. Since she made Santa Fe her permanent home several years ago, she has exchanged—and to good advantage—the verdant Kentucky land-scapes of her earlier works for the arid deserts of the southwest. The following story of an older woman and her young, eager lover shows that her various talents have transferred to her new home very well.

That June Caroline's apricot tree finally bore fruit. In the six years she'd lived in the house behind the tree, late frost had nipped its buds in April and only a few dwarfed apricots had hung on the branches. Neighbors said the apricot trees were not native to northern New Mexico but were brought as seedlings in the saddlebags of the Spanish conquest; over the centuries they had not adapted to the harsh climate, but neither had they died. All along Caroline's dirt road, the tall conical shapes stood out in winter and, in a rare spring, were thickly hung with white blossoms and bees.

Living alone after a lifetime of living with other people granted Caroline time and leisure that had mystified and depressed her at first—where were the faces that used to surround her kitchen table, where were the feet that had pounded on her stairs?—but that lately had seemed the only real luxury life had ever, or could ever offer: to lie in bed late, dozing until the sun slid into her window and across her bed, a blade of hot brass; to eat alone off tray in this or that corner of the house or garden; to fall asleep, sometimes, on the porch, while a summer storm rattled overhead, then gave way to stars and the pondering moon. To Caroline at sixty-three it seemed all the nature that surrounded her sustained her—the moon in its silver cycles, the pink-red geraniums and long flowing native grasses in her garden, and now the apricot tree itself with its bridal finery that didn't droop and was replaced, overnight, it seemed, with an astonishing crop. All pondered, all watched from within their private and separate existences.

At first she picked all the apricots she could and filled bowls and baskets where the fruit fermented, giving off a sweet perfume that reminded her of the candy shops of her childhood. She hated to throw out all that luxury, that unprecedented generosity, but at first she could not think of an alternative. For a few days she let the fruit drop from the tree and ground it under the tires of her car every time she went in and out; that was an unacceptable waste. Finally she remembered another scene from her childhood, of women sweating, chatting, bending over pots on a stove, and she decided to do some canning.

For a city woman, once a New York City woman, at that, the idea of spending a day in a hot steamy kitchen was, at first, unthinkable, but she remembered all the friends who would prize squat jars of apricot jam, and how a few of those jars would blaze on her pantry shelf in the depths of winter. And so she went out and bought four large, light aluminum pots, bigger than any pots she had ever owned, and after some searching, discovered that the cardboard trays of quilted jam glasses she remembered were still available, along with the white oblongs of paraffin needed to seal the tops.

But the task was daunting and Caroline soon realized she would have to have help. The steps in her mother's cookbook were complicated, especially the dry insistence on blanching the fruit to remove the skins, then processing them to prevent darkening. (Caroline was not sure why the fruit should not darken since she did not remember anyone in the old days caring what color it was.)

She pondered the situation for several days, meanwhile accumulating more bowls and baskets of apricots, which she kept in her refrigerator. Going out early in the morning to pick up what had fallen during the night, she would stop for a moment and stand with her hands on her hips, looking at the huge, glittering thunderheads already piling up in the west. Then she would bend to the task, feeling for a moment not like a sophisticated older woman released at last from unproductive demands but like a nymph loose in some glade in Arcady. Her yard and drive were not equal to that picture but she herself was, she believed, with her ocher-colored hair and long limbs and alert, unlined face.

Then it occurred to her that one of the young men in the class she taught at the local college might be willing to help. The class had not been a particular success, from Caroline's point of view; the students were listless and her attempt to interest them in the poetry of the Modernists largely failed. But there was one among them who seemed to have a spark of willingness; sometimes she caught young Charles Cooper's eyes fixed upon her as she lectured.

The semester ended shortly, and when she met with her students to hand them their graded finals and speak—she hoped—a few words of wisdom about the importance of E. E. Cummings and H.D., Caroline had made up her mind. As the little group gathered itself to leave, she signaled to Charles who, as usual, was watching. He came to her desk promptly.

"I have a job I want to do—a domestic job," she added, realizing he would think it was something involving reading or writing. "My apricot tree is covered with fruit and I want to put up some jam."

He looked at her alertly. He was a slight, sharp-faced young man with brownish hair brushed straight back and oddly freckled green eyes. His hands and feet, she had already noticed, were small, but his legs were long and his arms, below the short sleeves of his shirt, were tanned and supple.

"Okay," he said, a little too quickly, she thought.

"Of course I'm planning to pay."

"That won't be necessary," he said, turning away. She had to call him back to explain that she needed a morning later that week, and to give him her address; as he listened, she felt sheepish. It was an unfamiliar sensation, not entirely unpleasant.

The day arrived with thunderheads, brilliant sun, and heat. Caroline got up early to gather the last windfalls; she now had seven containers of apricots, and her small kitchen soon filled with their sweet, narcotic perfume. She took a shower and dressed, then found herself, unaccountably, taking off her shorts and shirt and putting on a dress; she realized that if she had possessed such a thing as a house dress and apron, she would have put them on, not as a disguise (as she would have thought, even the day before) but as a proclamation of some kind. What the words in the proclamation were she did not know.

She filled the largest kettle and set it on the stove to boil water for the jam jars. As she took the jars off their tray, she felt their quilted sides and looked with admiration at the anonymous fruits that decorated their lids. The jars, which normally she would hardly have noticed, seemed like masterpieces of artistry to her; who could have devised the quilted pattern of the glass, or left such a cunning space on one side for a label?

Presently she heard a light knock, and went to let in Charles. She was struck by the fact that he came to the front door, obscured by walls and trees, rather than to the more accessible kitchen door. "That apricot tree is covered," he said by way of greeting, standing in front of her, poised as though to turn in any direction, or to leave.

"I've picked about all we can manage today," she said, gesturing toward the bowls. Charles put out his hand and picked up an apricot, which he slipped, whole, into his mouth. Smiling, he said, "That's the first one of those I've ever eaten. It's good!"

"Are you from around here?" It was, she realized, the first personal question she had ever asked him.

He shook his head. "Maine."

They set to the task at once; later, Caroline wondered if she should have offered him something, first—coffee, or a glass of water. She knew young men usually jumped out of bed and ran out with no breakfast to whatever the day offered; she had raised three sons herself, and remembered their mixture of lassitude and spontaneity, which had so baffled her at the time. Charles, she assumed, was hungry; but when, later on, she asked him, he said he had already cooked and eaten a perfectly adequate breakfast.

They quickly sorted out the tasks, working side by side at the counter as smoothly, Caroline thought, as though they had been working together for years. She undertook the blanching (the jars were sterilized by now and laid out to cool on a linen towel), dropping the apricots by handfuls into boiling water, then quickly lifting them out. Drained, the apricots went to Charles, who shucked off their skins; the pile of darkening yellow-and-orange skins grew by his elbow as the kitchen filled with the dense sweetness of the hot fruit.

"Do you really think darkening is the problem?" Caroline asked him as she studied the dogeared cookbook, its cover a map of kitchen stains.

"They look better light," he said with authority.

He began dropping the peeled apricots into a solution of salt, vinegar, and water, and the piercing smell of the vinegar was added to the apricots' sweetness.

"Oh dear, I'm afraid I should have reheated them first," Carolyn said after she had read the recipe again, but Charles reassured her that the fruit was still hot from the blanching process.

Caroline stopped for a moment to watch him. His small, tanned hands moved regularly across the counter as he shucked the apricots and dropped them into the solution; he was frowning with concentration, lost in the task, she thought, until he asked, gruffly, "What are you looking at?"

"You. I never thought I'd see any of you young men in my kitchen."

"Why not?"

"I only know you in terms of my class," she said.

"I used to help my mother a lot," he explained, as though this was not the most interesting answer to the question she implied.

"I expect she's about my age," Caroline said, returning to her blanching.

"I don't know. How old are you?"

"Sixty-three," she said proudly. She had never stooped to lying about her age.

"Why did you never bother to get to know any of us?" he asked abruptly.

Caroline was startled. It had not occurred to her that anything she had done, or not done, in the class had had a consequence.

"You never even learned all our names," Charles went on. "Last week you called Todd Franklin Frank."

"I always mix up those names that could be first or last," she equivocated. Really he had embarrassed her and she wished suddenly that he would go.

"That's not the reason you called him Frank," Charles said. "You just didn't care enough to figure us out."

Caroline stopped what she was doing and leaned on her hands. Looking down, she saw the age spots rise from her skin like the spots on the back of a toad; she saw the little sacks of skin around her knuckles and wondered when they had come there. "I did the best I could," she said and knew, instantly, that it was not true.

"Taste one of these," Charles said, and he handed her a peeled apricot.

Without its fuzzy skin, the apricot looked small and vulnerable, like a naked part of a person that would ordinarily be hidden. Caroline slipped it into her mouth and brought her teeth down lightly; the soft meaty flesh of the apricot fell away unto her tongue. It was deliciously sweet, and hot.

"You have one, too."

Charles slid an apricot into his mouth and smiled at her. "I forgive you," he said.

Instantly she was angry. "For what?"

"Not caring."

"Do all your other teachers care?" she asked.

"Some do, some don't. But I always find a way to tell the ones who don't. For their own good," he added mischievously. "I could tell you were disappointed in the class, you might want to know why it didn't work."

"I thought it was the reading list," she said.

"There's nothing wrong with those writers." To prove his point, he quoted one of them, but Caroline could not identify the line.

"I'm sorry," she said.

Charles seemed satisfied. "Let's save some of these last ones to eat later."

She agreed, and they sorted out several handfuls of the cooked apricots and put them on a china plate. The china plate was decorated with a stylized bird and a farmer, in blue on yellow, and Caroline remembered with a shock (she had not thought about this in years) that as a child she had often eaten her breakfast off this plate.

At last they put twelve filled jars to sterilize in the popping, boiling kettle. The kitchen windows were blind with steam and the heat was overpowering. Caroline suggested taking the saved apricots outside.

She and Charles sat on the doorstep and ate them. One by one, they fed them into their mouths, At some point, without a word, Charles pushed an apricot into her mouth, and Caroline laughed with surprise. "Why did you do that?"

"Just to see."

She spit the dark, smooth oval seed into her hand and studied it.

They finished the apricots—Caroline anticipated an upset stomach, she had eaten so many—and went back into the kitchen. Charles fished the hot jars out of the sterilizer and pulled up the rack, and Caroline inserted the remaining jars. As Charles lowered them into the boiling water, a plume of steam obscured his face. Then he slapped on the lid.

"So masterful," Caroline said, laughing. In the back of her mind a sort of clock was ticking, telling off the details of the plans she had made for the afternoon: a visit to the post office to mail her sister's birthday present, some cleaning to pick up. The clock ticked and ticked but it seemed to have removed itself to some other part of the house.

Charles laid his hand over her hand on the counter. "I think you're very attractive," he said.

"Oh, honestly. I'm old enough to be—"

"Why do you keep harping on age?"

"Because it's the truth. Or part of it," she added uneasily.

His hand slid up her arm to her shoulder, bare under the strap of her dress. "You have an amazing body."

She was speechless. The feel of his palm on her bare shoulder reminded her of the texture of her own skin, which she treated now like a commodity, washing and drying it mechanically. She tried to remember other touches, other times, but it seemed that the years between had blotted out the memory. She flushed and breathed deeply, trying to regain her balance. "What are you doing, Charles?" she asked.

His hand moved from her shoulder to her waist as he turned her. "Kissing you," he said, and did.

Later Caroline remember the flesh of the apricots, their slight graininess, the moisture that was not dripping like the sweetness of peaches but absorbed, contained. She remembered the wooly feel of the apricots' skins, and the smooth, shining brown pits. She even remembered the seam that ran up one side of each pit, and she also remembered the way the thick sweet smell of the cooking apricots had been cut by the tang of vinegar. And she longed to know what the apricots had meant, and continued to mean, even as she realized with dismay that her life was falling apart; the ticking of the clock had stopped and might never start again. With equal dismay and exhilaration, she remembered a line from one of the poets she had tried so unsuccessfully to teach her class that spring:

> that is why I am afraid;
> I look at you,
> I think of your song,
> I see the long trail of your coming.

That was said by an old poet of a young poet. Could it not also be said by an old woman of a young man?

Sue Grafton

from *"O" Is for Outlaw*

Kinsey Millhone may not yet be as well known as Poe's Auguste Dupin, Christie's Miss Marple, or Doyle's Sherlock Holmes, but give her time. Her creator, Sue Grafton, a Louisville native born in 1940 now living half the year in California and the other half back home, has cast Kinsey as the hero and private investigator par excellence in a series of "alphabet mysteries," beginning with *"A" Is for Alibi* and currently extending to *"R" Is for Ricochet*. By the time she gets to Z, we'll know Kinsey better than we know ourselves. Each new alphabetic installment of her life and career produces great joy among her myriad fans and a full-page ad in the *New York Times*. Kinsey lives in a studio apartment in southern California, drives a pale blue VW, and is addicted to McDonald's Quarter Pounders with Cheese. She investigates most of her crime cases in Santa Teresa and Montebello, the fictional versions of Santa Barbara and Montecito, where Grafton has a home. Her sleuthing, however, has taken her twice to Louisville and allowed Grafton to pay homage to her hometown. Kinsey's visit to Louisville in *"O" Is for Outlaw* shows just how exciting the old town can be.

My plane arrived in Louisville, Kentucky, at 5:20 P.M., at a gate so remote it appeared to be abandoned or under quarantine. I'd been in Louisville once before, about six months back, when a cross-country romp had ended in a cemetery, with my being the recipient of an undeserved crack on the head. In that case, as with this, I was out a substantial chunk of change, with little hope of recouping my financial losses.

As I passed through the terminal, I paused at a public phone booth and checked the local directory on the off chance I'd find Porter Yount listed. I figured the name was unusual and there couldn't be that many in the greater Louisville area. The high school librarian had told me the *Tribune* had been swallowed up by a syndicate some twenty years before. I imagined Yount old and retired, if he were alive at all. For once my luck held and I spotted the address and phone number of a Porter Yount, whom I assumed was the man I was looking for. According to the phone book, he lived in the 1500 block of Third Street. I made a note of the address and continued to the baggage claim level, where I forked over my credit card and picked up the keys to the rental car. The woman at Frugal gave me a sheet map and traced out my route: taking the Watterson Expressway east, then picking up I-65 North into the downtown area.

I found my car in the designated slot and took a moment to get my bearings. The parking lot was shiny with puddles from a recent shower. Given the low probability of rain any given day in California, I drank in the scent. Even the air felt different: balmy and humid with the late-afternoon temperatures in the low 70s. Despite Santa Teresa's proximity to the Pacific Ocean, the climate is desertlike. Here, a moist spring breeze touched at newly unfurled leaves, and I could see pink and white azaleas bordering the grass. I shrugged out of Mickey's jacket and locked it in the trunk along with my duffel.

I decided to leave the issue of a motel until after I'd talked to Yount. It was close to the dinner hour, and chances were good that I'd find him at home. Following instructions, I took one of the downtown off-ramps, cutting over to Third, where I took a right and crossed Broadway. I drove slowly along Third, scanning house numbers. I finally spotted my destination and pulled in at a bare stretch of curb a few doors away. The tree-lined street, with its three-story houses of dark red brick, must have been lovely in the early days of the century. Now, some of the structures were run-down, and encroaching businesses had begun to mar the nature of the area. The general population was doubtless abandoning the once-stately downtown for the featureless suburbs.

Yount's residence was two and a half stories of red brick faced with pale fieldstone. A wide porch ran along the front of the building. Three wide bay windows were stacked one to a floor. An air conditioner extended from an attic window. The street was lined with similar houses, built close to one another, yards and alleyways behind. In front, between the sidewalk and the street, a border of grass was planted with maples and oaks that must have been there for eighty to a hundred years.

I climbed three steps, proceeded along a short cracked walkway, and climbed an additional six steps to the glass door with its tiny foyer visible within. Yount's residence had apparently once been a single-family dwelling, now broken into five units, judging from the names posted on the mailboxes. Each apartment had a bell, connected to the intercom located near the entrance. I rang Yount's apartment, waiting two minutes before I rang again. When it became clear he wasn't answering, I tried a neighbor's bell instead. After a moment, the intercom crackled to life and an old woman clicked in, saying "Yes?"

I said, "I wonder if you can help me. I'm looking for Porter Yount."

"Speak up."

"Porter Yount in apartment three."

"What's the time?"

I glanced at my watch. "Six-fifteen."

"He'll be down yonder on the corner. The Buttercup Tavern."

"Thanks."

I returned to the sidewalk, where I peered up and down the street. Though I didn't see a sign, I spotted what looked like a corner tavern half a block down. I left my car where it was and walked the short distance through the mild spring air.

The Buttercup was dark, cloudy with cigarette smoke, and smelling of bourbon. The local news was being broadcast at low volume on a color TV set mounted in one corner of the room. The dark was further punctuated by neon signs in a series of advertisements for Rolling Rock, Fehr's, and Stroh's Beer. The tavern was paneled in highly varnished wood with red leather stools along the length of the bar. Most of the occupants at that hour seemed to be isolated individuals, all men, all smoking, separated from each other by as many empty stools as space allowed. Without exception, each turned to stare at me as I came in.

I paused just inside the door and said, "I'm looking for Porter Yount."

A fellow at the far end of the bar raised his hand.

Judging from the swiveling heads, my arrival was the most interesting event since the Ohio River flooded in 1937. When I reached Yount, I held my hand out, saying, "I'm Kinsey Millhone."

"Nice meeting you," he said.

We shook hands and I perched on the stool next to his.

I said, "How are you?"

"Not bad. Thanks for asking." Porter Yount was heavyset, raspy-voiced, a man in his eighties. He was almost entirely bald, but his brows were still dark, an unruly tangle above eyes that were a startling green. At the moment, he was bleary-eyed with bourbon and his breath smelled like fruitcake. I could see the bartender drift in our direction. He paused in front of us.

Yount lit a fresh cigarette and glanced in my direction. He was having trouble with his focus. His mouth seemed to work, but his eyeballs were rolling like two green olives in an empty relish dish. "What'll you have?"

"How about a Fehr's?"

"You don't want Fehr's," he said. And to the bartender, "Lady wants a shot of Early Times with a water back."

"The beer's fine," I corrected.

The bartender reached into a cooler for the beer, which he opened and placed on the bar in front of me.

Yount said peevishly, "Give the lady a glass. Where's your manners?"

The bartender set a glass on the bar and Yount spoke to him again. "Who's cooking tonight?"

"Patsy. Want to see a menu?"

"Did I say that? This lady and I could use some privacy."

"Oh, sure." The bartender moved to the other end of the bar, accustomed to Yount's manner.

Yount shook his head with exasperation and his gaze slid in my direction. His head was round as a ball, sitting on the heft of his shoulders with scarcely any neck between. His shirt was a dark polyester, probably selected for stain concealment and ease of laundering. A pair of dark suspenders kept his pants hiked high above his waist. He wore dark socks and sandals, with an inch of shinbone showing. "Outfit okay? If I'd knowed you was coming, I'd've wore my Sunday best," he said, deliberately fracturing his grammar.

I had to laugh. "Sorry. I tend to look carefully at just about everything."

"You a journalist?"

I shook my head. "A private investigator. I'm trying to get a line on Duncan Oaks. You remember him?"

"Of course. You're the second detective to come in here asking after him this month."

"You talked to Mickey Magruder?"

"That's the one," he said.

"I thought as much."

"Why'd he send you? He didn't take me at my word?"

"We didn't talk. He was shot last week and he's been in a coma ever since."

"Sorry to hear that. I liked him. He's smart. First fella I met who could match me drink for drink."

"He's talented that way. At any rate, I'm doing what I can to follow up his investigation. It's tough, since I don't really know what he'd accomplished. I hope this won't turn out to be a waste of your time."

"Drinking's a waste of time, not talking to pretty ladies. What's the sudden interest in Oaks?"

"His name's cropped up in connection with another matter . . . something in California, which is where I'm from. I know he once worked for the *Tribune*. Your name was on his press pass, so I thought I'd talk to you."

"Fool's errand if I ever heard one. He's been dead twenty years."

"So I heard. I'm sorry for the repetition, but if you tell me what you told Mickey, maybe we can figure out if he's relevant."

Yount took a swallow of whiskey and tapped the ash off his cigarette. "He's a 'war correspondent'—pretty fancy title for a paper like the *Trib*. I don't think even the *Courier-Journal* had a correspondent back then. This was in the early sixties."

"Did you hire him yourself?"

"Oh, sure. He's a local boy, a blueblood, high society: good looks, ambition, an ego big as your head. More charisma than character." His elbow slid off the bar, and he caught himself with a jerk that we both ignored. Mentally, he seemed sharp. It was his body that tended to slip out of gear.

"Meaning what?"

"Not to speak ill of the dead, but I suspect he'd peaked out. You must know people like that yourself. High school's the glory days; after that, nothing much. It's not like he did poorly, but he never did as well. He's a fellow cut corners, never really earned his stripes, so to speak."

"Where'd he go to college?"

"He didn't. Duncan wasn't school-smart. He's a bright kid, made good grades, but he never cared much for academics. He had drive and aspirations. He figured he'd learn more in the real world so he nixed the idea."

"Was he right about that?"

"Hard to say. Kid loved to hustle. Talked me into paying him seventy-five dollars a week—which, frankly, we didn't have. Even in those days, his salary was a pittance, but he didn't care."

"Because he came from money?"

"That's right. Revel Oaks, his daddy, made a fortune in the sin trades, whiskey and tobacco. That and real estate speculation. Duncan grew up in an atmosphere of privilege. Hell, his daddy would've given him anything he wanted: travel, the best schools, place in the family business. Duncan had other fish to fry."

"For instance?"

He waved his cigarette in the air. "Like I said, he wangled his way into a job with the *Trib,* mostly on the basis of his daddy's influence."

"And what did he want?"

"Adventure, recognition. Duncan was addicted to living on the edge. Craved the limelight, craved risk. He wanted to go to Vietnam and report on the war. Nothing would do until he got his way."

"But why not enlist? If you're craving life on the edge, why not the infantry? That's about as close to the edge as you can get."

"Military wouldn't touch him. Had a heart murmur sounded like water pouring through a sluice. That's when he came to us. Wasn't any way the *Trib* could afford his ticket to Saigon. Didn't matter to him. He paid his own way. As long as he had access, he's happy as a clam. In those days, we're talking Neil Sheehan, David Halberstam, Mal Browne, Homer Bigart. Duncan pictured his byline in papers all across the country. He did a series of local interviews with newlyweds, army wives left behind when their husbands went off to war. The idea was to follow up, talk to the husbands, and see the fighting from their perspective."

"Not a bad idea."

"We thought it had promise, especially with so many of his classmates getting drafted. Any rate, he got his press credentials and his passport. He flew from Hong Kong to Saigon and from there to Pleiku. For a while, he was fine, hitching rides on military transports, any place they'd take him. To give him credit, I think he might have turned into a hell of a journalist. He had a way with words, but he lacked experience."

"How long was he there?"

"Couple months is all. He heard about some action in a place called Ia Drang. I guess he pulled strings—maybe his old man again or just his personal charm. It was a hell of a battle, some say the worst of the war. After that came LZ Albany: something like three hundred fellas killed in the space of four days. Must have found himself caught in the thick of it with no way out. We heard later he was hit, but we never got a sense of how serious it was."

"And then what?"

Yount paused to extinguish his cigarette. He missed the ashtray altogether and stubbed out the burning ember on the bar. "That's as much as I know. He's supposed to be medevacked out, but he never made it back. Chopper took off with a bellyful of body bags and a handful of casualties. Landed forty minutes later with no Duncan aboard. His daddy raised hell, got some high Pentagon official to launch an investigation, but it never came to much."

"And that's it?"

"I'm afraid so. You hungry? Ask me, it's time to eat."

"Fine with me," I said.

Porter gestured to the bartender, who ambled back in our direction. "Tell Patsy to put together couple of Hot Browns. "

"Good enough," the man said. He set his towel aside, came out from behind the bar, and headed for a door I assumed led to Patsy in the kitchen.

Yount said, "Bet you never ate one."

"What's a Hot Brown?"

"Invented at the Brown Hotel. Wait and see. Now, where was I?"

"Trying to figure out the fate of Duncan Oaks," I said.

"He's dead."

"How do you know?"

"He's never been heard from since."

"Isn't it possible he panicked and took off on foot?"

"Absence of a body, anything's possible, I guess."

"But not likely?"

"I'd say not. The way we heard it later, the NVA were everywhere, scourin' the area for wounded, killing them for sport. Duncan had no training. He probably couldn't get a hundred yards on his own."

"I wonder if you'd look at something." I hauled up my bag from its place near my feet. I removed the snapshot, the press pass, and the dog tags embossed with Duncan's name.

Yount tucked his cigarette in the corner of his mouth, examining the items through a plume of smoke. "Same things Magruder showed me. How'd he come by them?"

"A guy named Benny Quintero had them. You know him?"

"Name doesn't sound familiar."

"That's him in the picture. I'm assuming this is Duncan."

"That's him. When's this taken?"

"Quintero's brother thinks Ia Drang. Benny was wounded November seventeenth."

"Same as Duncan," he said. "This'd have to be one of the last pictures of Duncan ever taken."

"I hadn't thought of that, but probably so."

Yount returned the snapshot, which I tucked in my bag.

"Benny's another Louisville boy. He died in Santa Teresa in 1972: probably a homicide, though there was never an arrest." I took a few minutes to detail the story of Benny's death. "Mickey didn't mention this?"

"Never said a word. How's Quintero tie in?"

"I can give you the superficial answer. His brother says he went to Manual; I'm guessing, at the same time Duncan went to Male. It seems curious he'd end up with Duncan's personal possessions."

Porter shook his head. "Wonder why he kept them?"

"Not a clue," I said. "They were in a lockbox in his room. His brother came across them maybe six months back. He brought them to California." I thought about it for a moment, and then I said, "What's Duncan doing with a set of dog tags if he was never in the service?"

"He had them made up himself. Appealed to his sense of theater. One more example of how he liked to operate: looking like a soldier was as good as being one. I'm surprised he didn't hang out in uniform, but I guess that'd be pushing it. Don't get me wrong. I liked Duncan, but he's a fella with shabby standards."

A woman, probably Patsy, appeared from the kitchen with a steaming ramekin in each of her oven-mitted hands. She put a dish in front of each of us and handed us two sets of flatware rolled in paper napkins. Yount murmured "thanks" and she said, "You're entirely welcome."

I stared at the dish, which looked like a lake of piping-hot yellow sludge, with a dusting of paprika and something lumpy underneath. "What *is* this?"

"Eat and find out."

I picked up my fork and tried a tiny bite. A Hot Brown turned out to be an open-faced sliced turkey sandwich, complete with bacon and tomatoes, baked with the most divine cheese sauce I ever set to my lips. I mewed like a kitten.

"Told you so," he said, with satisfaction.

When I was finished, I wiped my mouth and took a sip of beer. "What about Duncan's parents? Does he still have family in the area?"

Yount shook his head. "Revel died of a heart attack a few years back: 1974, if memory serves. His mother died three years later of a stroke."

"Siblings, cousins?"

"Not a one," he said. "Duncan was an only child, and his daddy was too. I doubt you'd find anyone left on his mother's side of the family either. Her people were from Pike County, over on the West Virginia border. Dirt poor. Once she married Revel, she cut all ties with them."

He glanced at his watch. It was close to 8 P.M. "Time for me get home. My program's coming on in two minutes."

"I appreciate your time. Can I buy your dinner?"

Yount gave me a look. "Obvious you haven't spent any time in the South. Lady doesn't buy dinner for a gent. That's his prerogative." He reached in his pocket, pulled out a wad of bills, and tossed several on the bar.

❧ ❧ ❧

At his suggestion, I spent the night at the Leisure Inn on Broadway. I might have tried the Brown Hotel, but it looked way too fancy for the likes of me. The Leisure Inn was plain, a sensible establishment of Formica, nylon carpet, foam rubber pillows, and a layer of crackling plastic laid under the bottom sheet in case I wet the bed. I put a call through to the airline and discussed the options for my return. The first (and only) seat available was on a 3 P.M. flight the next day. I snagged it, wondering what I was going to do with myself until then. I considered a side visit to Louisville Male High, where Duncan had graduated with the class of 1961. Secretly, I doubted there was much to learn. Porter Yount had painted an unappealing portrait of the young Duncan Oaks. To me, he sounded shallow, spoiled, and manipulative. On the other hand, he was just a kid when he died: twenty-two, twenty-three years old at the outside. I suspect most of us are completely self-involved at that age. At twenty-two, I'd already been married and divorced. By twenty-three, I was not only married to Daniel but I'd left the police department and was totally adrift. I'd *thought* I was mature, but I was foolish and unenlightened. My judgment was faulty and my perception was flawed. So who was I to judge Duncan? He might have become a good man if he'd lived long enough. Thinking about it, I felt a curious secondhand sorrow for all the chances he'd missed, the lessons he never learned, the dreams he'd had to forfeit with his early death. Whoever he was and whatever he'd been, I could at least pay my respects.

✥ ✥ ✥

At ten the next morning, I parked my rental car on a side street not far from Louisville Male High School, at the corner of Brook Street and Breckinridge. The building was three stories tall, constructed of dark red brick with white concrete trim. The surrounding neighborhood consisted of narrow red-brick houses with narrow walkways between. Many looked as if the interiors would smell peculiar. I went up the concrete stairs. Above the entrance, two gnomelike scholars were nestled in matching niches, reading plaques of some kind. The dates 1914 and 1915 were chiseled in stone, indicating, I supposed, the year the building had gone up. I pushed through the front door and went in.

The interior was defined by gray marble wainscoting, with gray-painted walls above. The foyer floor was speckled gray marble with inexplicable cracks here and there. In the auditorium, dead ahead, I could see descending banks of curved wooden seats and tiers of wooden flooring, faintly buckled with age. Classes must have been in session, because the corridors were empty and there was little traffic on the stairs. I went into the school office. The windows were tall. Long planks of fluorescent lighting hung from ceilings covered with acoustical tile. I asked for the school library and was directed to the third floor.

The school librarian, Mrs. Calloway, was a sturdy-looking soul in a calf-length denim skirt and a pair of indestructible walking shoes. Her iron-gray hair was chopped off in a fuss-free style she'd probably worn for years. Close to retirement, she looked like a woman who'd favor muesli, yoga, liniments, SAVE THE WHALES bumper stickers, polar-bear swims, and lengthy bicycle tours of foreign countries. When I asked to see a copy of the '61 yearbook, she gave me a look but refrained from comment. She handed me the *Bulldog* and I took a seat at an empty table. She returned to her desk and busied herself, though I could tell she intended to keep an eye on me.

I spent a few minutes leafing through the *Bulldog,* looking at the black-and-white portraits of the senior class. I didn't check for Duncan's name. I simply absorbed the whole, trying to get a feel for the era, which predated mine by six years. The school had originally been all male, but it had turned coed somewhere along the way. Senior pictures showed the boys wearing coats and ties, their hair in brush cuts that emphasized their big ears and oddly shaped heads. Many wore glasses with heavy black frames. The girls tended toward short hair and dark gray or black crew-neck sweaters. Each wore a simple strand of pearls, probably a necklace provided by the photog-

Sue Grafton   427

rapher for uniformity. By 1967, the year I graduated, the hairstyles were bouffant, as stiffly lacquered as wigs, with flipped ends sticking out. The boys had all turned into Elvis Presley clones. Here, in candid class photos, most students wore penny loafers and white crew socks, and the girls were decked out in straight or pleated skirts that hit them at the knee.

I breezed by the Good News Club, the Speech Club, the Art Club, the Pep Club, and the Chess Club. In views of classes devoted to industrial arts, home ec, and world science, students were clumped together pointing at wall maps or gathered around the teacher's desk, smiling and pretending to look interested. The teachers all appeared to be fifty-five and as dull as dust.

At Thanksgiving of that year, the fall of 1960, the annual Male–Manual game was played. Male High was victorious by a score of 20–6. "MALE BEATS MANUAL 20 TO 6, CLINCHES CITY & AAA CROWNS," the article said. "A neat, well-deserved licking of the duPont Manual Rams." Co-captains were Walter Morris and Joe Blankenship. The rivalry between the two high schools had been long and fierce, beginning in 1893 and doubtless continuing to the present. At that time, the record showed 39 wins for Male, 19 for Manual, and 5 games tied. At the bottom of the page, in the accompanying photograph of the Manual offense, I found a halfback named Quintero, weighing 162.

I went back to the first page and started through again. Duncan Oaks showed up in a number of photographs, dark-haired and handsome. He'd been elected vice president, prom king, and class photographer. His name and face seemed to crop up in many guises: the senior play, Quill and Scroll, Glee Club. He was a Youth Speaks delegate, office aide, and library assistant.

He hadn't garnered academic honors, but he had played football. I found a picture of him on the Male High team, a 160-pound halfback. Now that was interesting: Duncan Oaks and Benny Quintero had played the same position on opposing teams. They must have known each other, by reputation if nothing else. I thought about Porter Yount's comment that these were Duncan's glory years, that his life after this never approached the same heights. That might have been true for Quintero as well. In retrospect, it seemed touching that their paths had crossed again in Vietnam.

I turned to the front of the book and studied the picture of Duncan as prom king. He was wearing a tuxedo: shorn, clean-shaven, with a white boutonniere tucked into his lapel. I turned the page and studied the prom queen, wondering if they were boyfriend/girlfriend or simply elected separately and honored on the same occasion. Darlene LaDestro. Well, this was a type I'd known well. Long blond hair pulled up in a swirl on top, a strong nose, patrician air. She looked classy, familiar, like girls in my high school who came from big-time money. Though not conventionally pretty, Darlene was the kind of girl who'd age with style. She'd come back to class reunions having married her social equal, still thin as a rail, hair streaked tastefully with gray. Darlene LaDestro, what a name. You'd think she'd have dumped it the first chance she got, called herself Dodie or Dessie or—

A chill swept through me, and I made an involuntary bark of astonishment. Mrs. Calloway looked up; and I shook my head to indicate that I was fine . . . though I wasn't. No wonder Darlene looked familiar. She was currently Laddie Bethel, alive and well and living in Santa Teresa.

Hal Charles
(Harold Blythe
and Charlie Sweet)

"Horn of Plenty"

Harold Blythe and Charlie Sweet, two professors of English at Eastern Kentucky University who write as Hal Charles, have made quite a name for themselves among detective and mystery story lovers, from readers of *Ellery Queen Mystery Magazine* to readers of *Kentucky Monthly*. They've even contrived and solved mysteries all over the state in their 2001 collection, *Bloody Ground: Stories of Mystery and Intrigue from Kentucky*. A devilishly clever story appeared in the February 2005 issue of *Kentucky Monthly*, which proves that they're a talented twosome when it comes to dastardly crime and sweet revenge.

Julia Archer had just sat down in the Lexington Opera House lounge when a stranger slipped onto the seat beside her at the bar. He had on black pants and a black shirt like the orchestra's horn section wore, and he was carrying a battered instrument case.

"Enjoying our concert so far, hon?" he said, holding up two fingers and signaling the bartender.

"Yes," she said, glancing at her watch.

"Don't worry," he said. "The intermission lasts twenty minutes tonight. You alone?"

"My sister's waiting for me back at our seats," Julia said, feeling a sudden chill that her little black dress could not protect her from. She wasn't used to such frilly attire.

The bartender set down two white wine spritzers in front of them.

"My name's Chuck," he said. "Did I guess right?"

"Yes," she said, taking a sip; "I'm Julia, and the wine goes so well with such a lovely concert."

He looked around nervously, then opened his instrument case on the bar. "You're not from the city, are you, darlin'?"

"My accent." Julia couldn't help but notice how the scent from his clothing, what the folks back home called "wacky tobaccy," overpowered his cologne. "I'm from Tilghman County, down the interstate a bit."

"Listen, sweetheart, I don't usually do this."

"Pick up unattached women during intermission?" she said, gaining confidence.

He smiled. "No, make you a deal."

"I need three-hundred dollars fast . . . there are some guys . . . and I'm willing to let you have my practice trumpet cheap."

"Do I look like I play in a marching band?" she posed.

"Trust me, the horn's worth more than . . ." He shot a glance toward the entrance. "I see my 'friends.' I'll stall them and be right back. I really need that three-hundred, Julia."

She began tracing her finger over scratch marks on the instrument. It was certainly well used, and he certainly seemed desperate.

"That's a nice horn," said a man in a tuxedo who had suddenly materialized beside her. "Would you consider selling it?"

"I'm afraid I—"

"I'll give you, say, seven hundred for it. I love classic horns, and that one would look great in my collection." He glanced across the room and waved. "Think about it." He checked his watch. "I'll be back in ten minutes for your decision."

Everything, her mama always said, moved so fast up in the city. Maybe that's why Mama never left home, and why when Faith had moved up here to Lexington, Julia knew she was going to have to be the surrogate mom for her in-such-a-hurry-to-grow-up little sister. Julia clutched the black purse that matched her evening gown. She had the money and could see the opportunity to turn a fast profit of $400. Closing the trumpet case, she said to the bartender, "If the man who bought me this drink returns, tell him I've gone to the little girls' room."

When she got back to the bar, the house lights were flashing, announcing the concert was about to resume.

༺ ༻ ༺ ༻ ༺ ༻

Chuck, the trumpet's owner, was waiting at the bar for her. She put down the opened case and said, "I couldn't see the horn well in this semi-darkness, so I took it into the powder room where the bright lights let me inspect it a little closer."

"And what have you decided?" said the black-shirted man.

"Are you sure you want to sell?" Julia asked.

"Of course."

"Well, I'd be less than honest if I didn't point out some of the scratches . . ."

"I know, sweetheart. I told you it was my practice horn," he said with exasperation, glancing around nervously. "I need the money now. Do you want the horn or not?"

Julia reached into her purse and withdrew three crisp one-hundred-dollar bills. As he snatched the money, she shook his hand and said, "Deal."

As he started off, she said, "What do you think about the name etched inside the horn?"

"What . . . what are you talking about?" he stammered.

She pointed with her finger at the crude letters in the horn's flared bell. "S.A.T.C.H.M.O. I'm afraid my musical history's mostly bluegrass and country, but wasn't that the nickname of Louis Armstrong, the famous jazz musician?"

"Lem'me see," he said, looking carefully. After a momentary pause, he reached for the case. "Here's your money back," he said. "I know you . . ."

"I thought you needed the money so bad, and a deal's a deal," she said calmly. "I'm sure the bartender will back me up."

He scowled at her as he stormed off.

No sooner had he disappeared than the man in the tuxedo reappeared. "What about my offer?" he said.

"I've just discovered this may be a famous horn, a real classic," she said, pointing at the lettering. "I think it's easily worth more than $700."

"I might go a little higher," the gentleman said, glancing at the letters.

"Of course," Julia said, "the lettering could easily be a fake, and I wouldn't want that on my conscience."

"I'll tell you what," he said. "It might be worth more, but maybe less." He counted out ten one-hundred-dollar bills, then slapped them on the bar.

Julia motioned the bartender over. "You're trained to spot a phony. Is this money real?"

After looking it over, the bartender was certain it was; Julia handed the tuxedoed gentleman the trumpet and case, then placed the thousand dollars in her purse.

Julia sat down beside her sister in the back row. The dimming lights indicated a minute before the fourth concert she'd been to that week resumed.

"I'm starting to like this music," said Faith. "They got more instruments than we do back home."

Julia smiled at her little sister. "I told you if we came back to the Opera House often enough, Mr. Black Shirt and Mr. Tuxedo would try the same scam on me that they pulled on you."

"So you saw them," Faith said excitedly. "Did you demand my money back? Did you threaten to go to the police?"

"Men like that aren't afraid of threats, and Mama taught us back in

Tilghman County that we take care of ourselves. It's that Scots-Irish blood down deep in our veins."

"If you gave that musician the three hundred dollars you got from the bank, you can kiss it goodbye. That guy in the tuxedo isn't coming back with a higher offer. You'll be stuck the way I was, with an old pawn shop horn worth about $50."

Julia opened her purse. Pushing aside the electric etcher she had used in the powder room to scratch in the phony letters, S.A.T.C.H.M.O., she pulled out the wad of money. Faith's eyes grew wide as her sister peeled off three hundred-dollar bills and handed them to her. "After covering the cost of all the concert tickets we bought this week, we'll give the rest of the money those gentlemen gave me to Mama to cover the agony you put her through by being taken for the rent money you borrowed."

"How did you . . . I never could . . ."

"I'll explain it on the drive back to Mama's."

"I'm so sorry," Faith said. "Those men were so smooth. You know I haven't been up here long or had much experience with city folks."

As the maestro on stage raised his baton, Julia whispered, "The next time somebody toots their own horn with a deal too good to be true, it probably is."

Bobbie Ann Mason

"Shiloh"

Bobbie Ann Mason may not have as many murders and high crimes in her books as Sue Grafton, but the stories, novels, and memoirs she has based on the people and places in her home turf of Graves County are just as dramatic and interesting. I became aware of her work in 1980, when a friend called to tell me about a short story in the *New Yorker*. I read the story, which is reprinted below; it was clear that here was a writer to be reckoned with, a writer of great natural talent who had found her literary turf in the backyard of her own family and childhood. Indeed, with her subsequent publications, she has put western Kentucky on the contemporary literary map.

Her voice joins those of earlier writers from west of Interstate 65, such as Irvin Cobb, Robert Penn Warren, and Caroline Gordon. Moreover, in combination with her contemporaries Joe Ashby Porter of Madisonville, Louise Natcher Murphy of Bowling Green, Coleman Dowell of Franklin, Joy Bale Boone of Elizabethtown and Elkton, and Tony Crunk of Hopkinsville, she has made western Kentucky stories and accents heard and understood and admired around the world. Mason's books range from such novels as *In Country* (1985), the story of a young woman's obsession with her father, who was killed in Vietnam, to *Feather Crowns* (1993), which probes the sideshow consequences that destroyed a family with quintuplets in the early twentieth century. Mason's short stories have been collected in several books, but it was *Shiloh and Other Stories* (1982) that announced a new master of short fiction at work.

Leroy Moffitt's wife, Norma Jean, is working on her pectorals. She lifts three-pound dumbbells to warm up, then progresses to a twenty-pound barbell. Standing with her legs apart, she reminds Leroy of Wonder Woman.

"I'd give anything if I could just get these muscles to where they're real hard," says Norma Jean. "Feel this arm. It's not as hard as the other one."

"That's 'cause you're right-handed," says Leroy, dodging as she swings the barbell in an arc.

"Do you think so?"

"Sure."

Leroy is a truckdriver. He injured his leg in a highway accident four months ago, and his physical therapy, which involves weights and a pulley, prompted Norma Jean to try building herself up. Now she is attending a body-building class. Leroy has been collecting temporary disability since his tractor-trailer jackknifed in Missouri, badly twisting his left leg in its socket. He has a steel pin in his hip. He will probably not be able to drive his rig again. It sits in the backyard, like a gigantic bird that has flown home to roost. Leroy has been home in Kentucky for three months, and his leg is almost healed, but the accident frightened him and he does not want to drive any more long hauls. He is not sure what to do next. In the meantime, he makes things from craft kits. He started by building a miniature log cabin from notched Popsicle sticks. He varnished it and placed it on the TV set, where it remains. It reminds him of a rustic Nativity scene. Then he tried string art (sailing ships on black velvet), a macramé owl kit, a snap-together B-17 Flying Fortress, and a lamp made out of a model truck, with a light fixture screwed in the top of the cab. At first the kits were diversions, something to kill time, but now he is thinking about building a full-scale log house from a kit. It would be considerably cheaper than building a regular house, and besides, Leroy has grown to appreciate how things are put together. He has begun to realize that in all the years he was on the road he never took time to examine anything. He was always flying past scenery.

"They won't let you build a log cabin in any of the new subdivisions," Norma Jean tells him.

"They will if I tell them it's for you," he says, teasing her. Ever since they were married, he has promised Norma Jean he would build her a new home one day. They have always rented, and the house they live in is small and nondescript. It does not even feel like a home, Leroy realizes now.

Norma Jean works at the Rexall drugstore, and she has acquired an amazing amount of information about cosmetics. When she explains to Leroy the three stages of complexion care, involving creams, toners, and moisturizers, he thinks happily of other petroleum products—axle grease, diesel fuel. This is a connection between him and Norma Jean. Since he has been home, he has felt unusually tender about his wife and guilty over his long absences. But he can't tell what she feels about him. Norma Jean has never complained about his traveling; she has never made hurt remarks, like calling his truck a "widow-maker." He is reasonably certain she has been faithful to him, but he wishes she would celebrate his permanent homecoming more happily. Norma Jean is often startled to find Leroy at home, and he thinks she seems a little disappointed about it. Perhaps he reminds her too much of the early days of their marriage, before he went on the road. They had a child who died as an infant, years ago. They never speak about their memories of Randy, which have almost faded, but now that Leroy is home all the time, they sometimes feel awkward around each other, and Leroy wonders if one of them should mention the child. He has the feeling that they are waking up out of a dream together—that they must create a new marriage, start afresh. They are lucky they are still married. Leroy has read that for most people losing a child destroys the marriage—or else he heard this on *Donahue*. He can't always remember where he learns things anymore.

At Christmas, Leroy bought an electric organ for Norma Jean. She used to play the piano when she was in high school. "It don't leave you," she told him once. "It's like riding a bicycle."

The new instrument had so many keys and buttons that she was bewildered by it at first. She touched the keys tentatively, pushed some buttons, then pecked out "Chopsticks." It came out in an amplified fox-trot rhythm, with marimba sounds.

"It's an orchestra!" she cried.

The organ had a pecan-look finish and eighteen preset chords, with optional flute, violin, trumpet, clarinet, and banjo accompaniments. Norma Jean mastered the organ almost immediately. At first she played Christmas songs. Then she bought *The Sixties Songbook* and learned every tune in it, adding variations to each with the rows of brightly colored buttons.

"I didn't like these old songs back then," she said. "But I have this crazy feeling I missed something."

"You didn't miss a thing," said Leroy.

Leroy likes to lie on the couch and smoke a joint and listen to Norma Jean play "Can't Take My Eyes Off You" and "I'll Be Back." He is back again. After fifteen years on the road, he is finally settling down with the woman he loves. She is still pretty. Her skin is flawless. Her frosted curls resemble pencil trimmings.

∽ ∽ ∽

Now that Leroy has come home to stay, he notices how much the town has changed. Subdivisions are spreading across western Kentucky like an oil slick. The sign at the edge of town says "Pop: 11,500"—only seven hundred more than it said twenty years before. Leroy can't figure out who is living in all the new houses. The farmers who used to gather around the courthouse square on Saturday afternoons to play checkers and spit tobacco juice have gone. It has been years since Leroy has thought about the farmers, and they have disappeared without his noticing.

Leroy meets a kid named Stevie Hamilton in the parking lot at the new shopping center. While they pretend to be strangers meeting over a stalled car, Stevie tosses an ounce of marijuana under the front seat of Leroy's car. Stevie is wearing orange jogging shoes and a T-shirt that says CHATTAHOOCHEE SUPER-RAT. His father is a prominent doctor who lives in one of the expensive subdivisions in a new white-columned brick house that looks like a funeral parlor. In the phone book under his name there is a separate number, with the listing "Teenagers."

"Where do you get this stuff?" asks Leroy. "From your pappy?"

"That's for me to know and you to find out," Stevie says. He is slit-eyed and skinny.

"What else you got?"

"What you interested in?"

"Nothing special. Just wondered."

Leroy used to take speed on the road. Now he has to go slowly. He needs to be mellow. He leans back against the car and says, "I'm aiming to build me a log house, soon as I get time. My wife, though, I don't think she likes the idea."

"Well, let me know when you want me again," Stevie says. He has a cigarette in his cupped palm, as though sheltering it from the wind. He takes a long drag, then stomps it on the asphalt and slouches away.

Stevie's father was two years ahead of Leroy in high school. Leroy is thirty-four. He married Norma Jean when they were both eighteen, and their child Randy was born a few months later, but he died at the age of four months and three days. He would be about Stevie's age now. Norma Jean and Leroy were at the drive-in, watching a double feature *(Dr. Strangelove* and *Lover Come Back)*, and the baby was sleeping in the back seat. When the first movie ended, the baby was dead. It was the sudden infant death syndrome. Leroy remembers handing Randy to a nurse at the emergency room, as though he were offering her a large doll as a present. A dead baby feels like a sack of flour. "It just happens sometimes," said the doctor, in what Leroy always recalls as a nonchalant tone. Leroy can hardly remember the child anymore, but he still sees vividly a scene from *Dr. Strangelove* in which the President of the United States was talking in a folksy voice on the hot line to the Soviet premier about the bomber accidentally headed toward Russia. He was in the War Room, and the world map was lit up. Leroy remembers Norma Jean standing catatonically beside him in the hospital and himself thinking: Who is this strange girl? He had forgotten who she was. Now scientists are saying that crib death is caused by a virus. Nobody knows anything, Leroy thinks. The answers are always changing.

When Leroy gets home from the shopping center, Norma Jean's mother, Mabel Beasley, is there. Until this year, Leroy has not realized how much time she spends with Norma Jean. When she visits, she inspects the closets and then the plants, informing Norma Jean when a plant is droopy or yellow. Mabel calls the plants "flowers," although there are never any blooms. She always notices if Norma Jean's laundry is piling up. Mabel is a short, overweight woman whose tight, brown-dyed curls look more like a wig than the actual wig she sometimes wears. Today she has brought Norma Jean an off-white dust ruffle she made for the bed; Mabel works in a custom-upholstery shop.

"This is the tenth one I made this year," Mabel says. "I got started and couldn't stop."

"It's real pretty," says Norma Jean.

"Now we can hide things under the bed," says Leroy, who gets along with his mother-in-law primarily by joking with her. Mabel has never really forgiven him for disgracing her by getting Norma Jean pregnant. When the baby died, she said that fate was mocking her.

"What's that thing?" Mabel says to Leroy in a loud voice, pointing to a tangle of yarn on a piece of canvas.

Leroy holds it up for Mabel to see. "It's my needlepoint," he explains. "This is a *Star Trek* pillow cover."

"That's what a woman would do," says Mabel. "Great day in the morning!"

"All the big football players on TV do it," he says.

"Why, Leroy, you're always trying to fool me. I don't believe you for one minute. You don't know what to do with yourself—that's the whole trouble. Sewing!"

"I'm aiming to build us a log house," says Leroy. "Soon as my plans come."

"Like *heck* you are," says Norma Jean. She takes Leroy's needlepoint and shoves it into a drawer. "You have to find a job first. Nobody can afford to build now anyway."

Mabel straightens her girdle and says, "I still think before you get tied down y'all ought to take a little run to Shiloh."

"One of these days, Mama," Norma Jean says impatiently.

Mabel is talking about Shiloh, Tennessee. For the past few years, she has been urging Leroy and Norma Jean to visit the Civil War battleground there. Mabel went there on her honeymoon—the only real trip she ever took. Her husband died of a perforated ulcer when Norma Jean was ten, but Mabel, who was accepted into the United Daughters of the Confederacy in 1975, is still preoccupied with going back to Shiloh.

"I've been to kingdom come and back in that truck out yonder," Leroy says to Mabel, "but we never yet set foot in that battleground. Ain't that something? How did I miss it?"

"It's not even that far," Mabel says.

After Mabel leaves, Norma Jean reads to Leroy from a list she has made. "Things you could do," she announces. "You could get a job as a guard at Union Carbide, where they'd let you set on a stool. You could get on at the lumberyard. You could do a little carpenter work, if you want to build so bad. You could—"

"I can't do something where I'd have to stand up all day."

"You ought to try standing up all day behind a cosmetics counter. It's amazing that I have strong feet, coming from two parents that never had strong feet at all." At the moment Norma Jean is holding on to the kitchen counter, raising her knees one at a time as she talks. She is wearing two-pound ankle weights.

"Don't worry," says Leroy. "I'll do something."

"You could truck calves to slaughter for somebody. You wouldn't have to drive any big old truck for that."

"I'm going to build you this house," says Leroy. "I want to make you a real home."

"I don't want to live in any log cabin."

"It's not a cabin. It's a house."

"I don't care. It looks like a cabin."

"You and me together could lift those logs. It's just like lifting weights."

Norma Jean doesn't answer. Under her breath, she is counting. Now she is marching through the kitchen. She is doing goose steps.

ဢ ဢ ဢ

Before his accident, when Leroy came home he used to stay in the house with Norma Jean, watching TV in bed and playing cards. She would cook fried chicken, picnic ham, chocolate pie—all his favorites. Now he is home alone much of the time. In the mornings, Norma Jean disappears, leaving a cooling place in the bed. She eats a cereal called Body Buddies, and she leaves the bowl on the table, with the soggy tan balls floating in a milk puddle. He sees things about Norma Jean that he never realized before. When she chops onions, she stares off into a corner, as if she can't bear to look. She puts on her house slippers almost precisely at nine o'clock every evening and nudges her jogging shoes under the couch. She saves bread heels for the birds. Leroy watches the birds at the feeder. He notices the peculiar way goldfinches fly past the window. They close their wings, then fall, then spread their wings to catch and lift themselves. He wonders if they close their eyes when they fall. Norma Jean closes her eyes when they are in bed. She wants the lights turned out. Even then, he is sure she closes her eyes.

He goes for long drives around town. He tends to drive a car rather carelessly. Power steering and an automatic shift make a car feel so small and inconsequential that his body is hardly involved in the driving process. His injured leg stretches out comfortably. Once or twice he has almost hit something, but even the prospect of an accident seems minor in a car. He cruises the new subdivisions, feeling like a criminal rehearsing for a robbery. Norma Jean is probably right about a log house being inappropriate here in the new subdivisions. All the houses look grand and complicated. They depress him.

One day when Leroy comes home from a drive he finds Norma Jean in tears. She is in the kitchen making a potato and mushroom-soup casserole, with grated-cheese topping. She is crying because her mother caught her smoking.

"I didn't hear her coming. I was standing here puffing away pretty as you please," Norma Jean says, wiping her eyes.

"I knew it would happen sooner or later," says Leroy, putting his arm around her.

"She don't know the meaning of the word 'knock,'" says Norma Jean. "It's a wonder she hadn't caught me years ago."

"Think of it this way," Leroy says. "What if she caught me with a joint?"

"You better not let her!" Norma Jean shrieks. "I'm warning you, Leroy Moffitt!"

"I'm just kidding. Here, play me a tune. That'll help you relax."

Norma Jean puts the casserole in the oven and sets the timer. Then she plays a ragtime tune, with horns and banjo, as Leroy lights up a joint and lies on the couch, laughing to himself about Mabel's catching him at it. He thinks of Stevie Hamilton—a doctor's son pushing grass. Everything is funny. The whole town seems crazy and small. He is reminded of Virgil Mathis, a boastful policeman Leroy used to shoot pool with. Virgil recently led a drug bust in a back room at a bowling alley, where he seized ten thousand dollars' worth of marijuana. The newspaper had a picture of him holding up the bags of grass and grinning widely. Right now, Leroy can imagine Virgil breaking down the door and arresting him with a lungful of smoke. Virgil would probably have been alerted to the scene because of all the racket Norma Jean is making. Now she sounds like a hard-rock band. Norma Jean is terrific. When she switches to a Latin-rhythm version of "Sunshine Superman," Leroy hums along. Norma Jean's foot goes up and down, up and down.

"Well, what do you think?" Leroy says, when Norma Jean pauses to search through her music.

"What do I think about what?"

His mind has gone blank. Then he says, "I'll sell my rig and build us a house." That wasn't what he wanted to say. He wanted to know what she thought—what she *really* thought—about them.

"Don't start in on that again," says Norma Jean. She begins playing "Who'll Be the Next in Line?"

Leroy used to tell hitchhikers his whole life story—about his travels, his hometown, the baby. He would end with a question: "Well, what do you think?" It was just a rhetorical question. In time, he had the feeling that he'd been telling the same story over and over to the same hitchhikers. He quit talking to hitchhikers when he realized how his voice sounded—whining and self-pitying, like some teenage-tragedy song. Now Leroy has the sudden impulse to tell Norma Jean about himself, as if he had just met her. They have known each other so long they have forgotten a lot about each other. They could become reacquainted. But when the oven timer goes off and she runs to the kitchen, he forgets why he wants to do this.

❧ ❧ ❧

The next day, Mabel drops by. It is Saturday and Norma Jean is cleaning. Leroy is studying the plans of his log house, which have finally come in the mail. He has them spread out on the table—big sheets of stiff blue paper, with diagrams and numbers printed in white. While Norma Jean runs the vacuum, Mabel drinks coffee. She sets her coffee cup on a blueprint.

"I'm just waiting for time to pass," she says to Leroy, drumming her fingers on the table.

As soon as Norma Jean switches off the vacuum, Mabel says in a loud voice, "Did you hear about the datsun dog that killed the baby?"

Norma Jean says, "The word is 'dachshund.'"

"They put the dog on trial. It chewed the baby's legs off. The mother was in the next room all the time." She raises her voice. "They thought it was neglect."

Norma Jean is holding her ears. Leroy manages to open the refrigerator and get some Diet Pepsi to offer Mabel. Mabel still has some coffee and she waves away the Pepsi.

"Datsuns are like that," Mabel says. "They're jealous dogs. They'll tear a place to pieces if you don't keep an eye on them."

"You better watch out what you're saying, Mabel," says Leroy.

"Well, facts is facts."

Leroy looks out the window at his rig. It is like a huge piece of furniture gathering dust in the backyard. Pretty soon it will be an antique. He hears the vacuum cleaner. Norma Jean seems to be cleaning the living room rug again.

Later, she says to Leroy, "She just said that about the baby because she caught me smoking. She's trying to pay me back."

"What are you talking about?" Leroy says, nervously shuffling blueprints.

"You know good and well," Norma Jean says. She is sitting in a kitchen chair with her feet up and her arms wrapped around her knees. She looks small and helpless. She says, "The very idea, her bringing up a subject like that! Saying it was neglect."

"She didn't mean that," Leroy says.

"She might not have *thought* she meant it. She always says things like that. You don't know how she goes on."

"But she didn't really mean it. She was just talking."

Leroy opens a king-sized bottle of beer and pours it into two glasses, dividing it carefully. He hands a glass to Norma Jean and she takes it from him mechanically. For a long time, they sit by the kitchen window watching the birds at the feeder.

Something is happening. Norma Jean is going to night school. She has graduated from her six-week body-building course and now she is taking an adult-education course in composition at Paducah Community College. She spends her evenings outlining paragraphs.

"First you have a topic sentence," she explains to Leroy. "Then you divide it up. Your secondary topic has to be connected to your primary topic."

To Leroy, this sounds intimidating. "I never was any good in English," he says.

"It makes a lot of sense."

"What are you doing this for, anyhow?"

She shrugs. "It's something to do." She stands up and lifts her dumbbells a few times.

"Driving a rig, nobody cared about my English."

"I'm not criticizing your English."

Norma Jean used to say, "If I lose ten minutes' sleep, I just drag all day." Now she stays up late, writing compositions. She got a B on her first paper— a how-to theme on soup-based casseroles. Recently Norma Jean has been cooking unusual foods—tacos, lasagna, Bombay chicken. She doesn't play the organ anymore, though her second paper was called "Why Music Is Important to Me." She sits at the kitchen table, concentrating on her outlines, while Leroy plays with his log house plans, practicing with a set of Lincoln Logs. The thought of getting a truckload of notched, numbered logs scares him, and he wants to be prepared. As he and Norma Jean work together at the kitchen table, Leroy has the hopeful thought that they are sharing something, but he knows he is a fool to think this. Norma Jean is miles away. He knows he is going to lose her. Like Mabel, he is just waiting for time to pass.

One day, Mabel is there before Norma Jean gets home from work, and Leroy finds himself confiding in her. Mabel, he realizes, must know Norma Jean better than he does.

"I don't know what's got into that girl," Mabel says. "She used to go to bed with the chickens. Now you say she's up all hours. Plus her a-smoking. I like to died."

"I want to make her this beautiful home," Leroy says, indicating the Lincoln Logs. "I don't think she even wants it. Maybe she was happier with me gone."

"She don't know what to make of you, coming home like this."

"Is that it?"

Mabel takes the roof off his Lincoln Log cabin. "You couldn't get *me* in a log cabin," she says. "I was raised in one. It's no picnic, let me tell you."

"They're different now," says Leroy.

"I tell you what," Mabel says, smiling oddly at Leroy.

"What?"

"Take her on down to Shiloh. Y'all need to get out together, stir a little. Her brain's all balled up over them books."

Leroy can see traces of Norma Jean's features in her mother's face. Mabel's worn face has the texture of crinkled cotton, but suddenly she looks pretty. It occurs to Leroy that Mabel has been hinting all along that she wants them to take her with them to Shiloh.

"Let's all go to Shiloh," he says. "You and me and her. Come Sunday."

Mabel throws up her hands in protest. "Oh, no, not me. Young folks want to be by theirselves."

When Norma Jean comes in with groceries, Leroy says excitedly, "Your mama here's been dying to go to Shiloh for thirty-five years. It's about time we went, don't you think?"

"I'm not going to butt in on anybody's second honeymoon," Mabel says.

"Who's going on a honeymoon, for Christ's sake?" Norma Jean says loudly.

"I never raised no daughter of mine to talk that-a-way," Mabel says.

"You ain't seen nothing yet," says Norma Jean. She starts putting away boxes and cans, slamming cabinet doors.

"There's a log cabin at Shiloh," Mabel says. "It was there during the battle. There's bullet holes in it."

"When are you going to *shut up* about Shiloh, Mama?" asks Norma Jean.

"I always thought Shiloh was the prettiest place, so full of history," Mabel goes on. "I just hoped y'all could see it once before I die, so you could tell me about it." Later, she whispers to Leroy, "You do what I said. A little change is what she needs."

"Your name means 'the king,'" Norma Jean says to Leroy that evening. He is trying to get her to go to Shiloh, and she is reading a book about another century.

"Well, I reckon I ought to be right proud."

"I guess so."

"Am I still king around here?"

Norma Jean flexes her biceps and feels them for hardness. "I'm not fooling around with anybody, if that's what you mean," she says.

"Would you tell me if you were?"

"I don't know."

"What does *your* name mean?"

"It was Marilyn Monroe's real name."

"No kidding!"

"Norma comes from the Normans. They were invaders," she says. She closes her book and looks hard at Leroy. "I'll go to Shiloh with you if you'll stop staring at me."

⸱⸱⸱ ⸱⸱⸱ ⸱⸱⸱

On Sunday, Norma Jean packs a picnic and they go to Shiloh. To Leroy's relief, Mabel says she does not want to come with them. Norma Jean drives, and Leroy, sitting beside her, feels like some boring hitchhiker she has picked up. He tries some conversation, but she answers him in monosyllables. At Shiloh, she drives aimlessly through the park, past bluffs and trails and steep ravines. Shiloh is an immense place, and Leroy cannot see it as a battleground. It is not what he expected. He thought it would look like a golf course. Monuments are everywhere, showing through the thick clusters of trees. Norma Jean passes the log cabin Mabel mentioned. It is surrounded by tourists looking for bullet holes.

"That's not the kind of log house I've got in mind," says Leroy apologetically.

"I know *that*."

"This is a pretty place. Your mama was right."

"It's O.K.," says Norma Jean. "Well, we've seen it. I hope she's satisfied."

They burst out laughing together.

At the park museum, a movie on Shiloh is shown every half hour, but they decide that they don't want to see it. They buy a souvenir Confederate flag for Mabel, and then they find a picnic spot near the cemetery. Norma Jean has brought a picnic cooler, with pimiento sandwiches, soft drinks, and Yodels. Leroy eats a sandwich and then smokes a joint, hiding it behind the picnic cooler. Norma Jean has quit smoking altogether. She is picking cake crumbs from the cellophane wrapper, like a fussy bird.

Leroy says, "So the boys in gray ended up in Corinth. The Union soldiers zapped 'em finally. April 7, 1862."

They both know that he doesn't know any history. He is just talking about some of the historical plaques they have read. He feels awkward, like a boy on a date with an older girl. They are still just making conversation.

"Corinth is where Mama eloped to," says Norma Jean.

They sit in silence and stare at the cemetery for the Union dead and, beyond, at a tall cluster of trees. Campers are parked nearby, bumper to bumper, and small children in bright clothing are cavorting and squealing. Norma Jean wads up the cake wrapper and squeezes it tightly in her hand. Without looking at Leroy, she says, "I want to leave you."

Leroy takes a bottle of Coke out of the cooler and flips off the cap. He holds the bottle poised near his mouth but cannot remember to take a drink. Finally he says, "No, you don't."

"Yes, I do."

"I won't let you."

"You can't stop me."

"Don't do me that way."

Leroy knows Norma Jean will have her own way. "Didn't I promise to be home from now on?" he says.

"In some ways, a woman prefers a man who wanders," says Norma Jean. "That sounds crazy, I know."

"You're not crazy."

Leroy remembers to drink from his Coke. Then he says, "Yes, you *are* crazy. You and me could start all over again. Right back at the beginning."

"We *have* started all over again," says Norma Jean. "And this is how it turned out."

"What did I do wrong?"

"Nothing."

"Is this one of those women's lib things?" Leroy asks.

"Don't be funny."

The cemetery, a green slope dotted with white markers, looks like a subdivision site. Leroy is trying to comprehend that his marriage is breaking up, but for some reason he is wondering about white slabs in a graveyard.

"Everything was fine till Mama caught me smoking," says Norma Jean, standing up. "That set something off."

"What are you talking about?"

"She won't leave me alone—*you* won't leave me alone." Norma Jean seems to be crying, but she is looking away from him. "I feel eighteen again. I can't face that all over again." She starts walking away. "No, it *wasn't* fine. I don't know what I'm saying. Forget it."

Leroy takes a lungful of smoke and closes his eyes as Norma Jean's words sink in. He tries to focus on the fact that thirty-five hundred soldiers died on the grounds around him. He can only think of that war as a board game with plastic soldiers. Leroy almost smiles, as he compares the Confederates' daring attack on the Union camps and Virgil Mathis's raid on the bowling alley. General Grant, drunk and furious, shoved the Southerners back to Corinth, where Mabel and Jet Beasley were married years later, when Mabel was still thin and goodlooking. The next day, Mabel and Jet visited the battleground, and then Norma Jean was born, and then she married Leroy and they had a baby, which they lost, and now Leroy and Norma Jean are here at the same battleground. Leroy knows he is leaving out a lot. He is leaving out the insides of history. History was always just names and dates to him. It occurs to him that building a house out of logs is similarly empty—too simple. And the real inner workings of a marriage, like most of history, have escaped him. Now he sees that building a log house is the dumbest idea he could have had. It was clumsy of him to think Norma Jean would want a log house. It was a crazy idea. He'll have to think of something else, quickly. He will wad the blueprints into tight balls and fling them into the lake. Then he'll get moving again. He opens his eyes. Norma Jean has moved away and is walking through the cemetery, following a serpentine brick path.

Leroy gets up to follow his wife, but his good leg is asleep and his bad leg still hurts him. Norma Jean is far away, walking rapidly toward the bluff by the river, and he tries to hobble toward her. Some children run past him, screaming noisily. Norma Jean has reached the bluff, and she is looking out over the Tennessee River. Now she turns toward Leroy and waves her arms. Is she beckoning to him? She seems to be doing an exercise for her chest muscles. The sky is unusually pale—the color of the dust ruffle Mabel made for their bed.

"The Pond," from *Clear Springs*

Here we find Mason's mother on a real-life fishing expedition in the pond behind her old homestead. It is a fish—and a story—of epic proportions.

It had been an unusually hot summer, and my mother had gotten out of the habit of stirring about, although she still drove to her garden at the farm each morning. When she lived at the farm, she had kept active all summer, but at the new house, she felt inhibited from going outside. There were so many houses around, with people to see her and make her feel self-conscious. She was stiffening up with arthritis, and her muscles were still weak from her stroke a year ago. The doctor told her she had severe osteoporosis, but he didn't seem to think that was unusual for someone her age—seventy-seven. Her daughters nagged at her about exercise. They went on and went on about muscle tone and skeletal support. It made her tired to listen to them.

Now that it was autumn, the weather was a little cooler, and she longed to go fishing. Her daughters had given her a new rod-and-reel for her birthday over a year ago, but she had hardly made use of it. She knew the fish were growing big. When Wilburn restocked the pond, just before he died, he had included two five-pound catfish.

One sunny day in early October, after her dinner at noon, she impulsively went fishing. Leaving the dirty dishes on the table and the pots and pans on the counter, she stowed her tackle box and her rod-and-reel in the car and drove to the farm. She parked the car in the shade by the stable, near her garden, and headed across the soybean field toward the pond. She knew the fish would be biting. She was quicker in her step than she had been lately, but she picked her way carefully through the stubbly field. The soybeans had been recently harvested, but she did not know if the men who leased the land had gathered the popcorn they had planted in the back fields. It had been several years since she had been across the creeks to the back acreage.

She was walking through the field behind Granny's house. Only one car was in the driveway, and she did not see any of the renters. The trampoline in the yard reminded her of a misshapen hospital cot. The black dog chained to the wash-house regarded her skeptically, pawed at the ground, and sat down lazily. With his chain, he had worn away her grapevine and turned the grass into a crescent of dirt. The old place had so much time and heart invested in it, too much to comprehend. Now it seemed derelict and unloved.

She was out of breath when she reached the pond, but she recovered quickly in the warm air. The leaves on the trees along the creek were beginning to turn yellow and brown. The pond was full and still. The pondweed had diminished somewhat this year because Don had released two grass-eating carp into the water. They were supposed to eat their weight in pond-weed daily. She had told Don to make sure they were the same sex. She didn't want the pond overrun with carp, which could be a worse calamity than pondweed.

She felt good, eager to fish. She baited her hook with a piece of a chicken gizzard she had bought the week before. It was ripe, a piece of stink bait to lure a catfish. After wiping her hands on the grass, she cast out and reeled in slowly. It was pleasant to stand on the bank and watch the arc of her line fly out. She was standing at the deep bend of the pond, near the old lane. The water was exceptionally high, nearly reaching the rim of the pond. The wind was blowing from the east, and her floater drifted to the left. She reeled it toward her.

Lately she had been reviewing her life, reflecting on the hardships she had endured. She bridled at the way the women always had to serve the men. The men always sat down in the evening, but the women kept going. Why had the women agreed to that arrangement? How had they stood it? What if she had had an opportunity for something different? Wilburn, amazed by her paintings, once said, "Why, if you'd had a chance, there's no telling what you could have accomplished." She didn't know. The thought weighed her down, taunting her with something lost she could never retrieve, like a still-born child.

After a while, she got a bite. Her cork plunged down and then took off. A fish was carrying the bait across the pond, against the wind, rippling the water, flying across. She reeled in and felt the fish pull steady. It was a big one, but she didn't allow her hopes to rise yet. It seemed heavy, though. She worked it back and forth, feeling the deep pleasure of hooking a fish. It grew lively then. It was a fighter. As it resisted, she gradually realized its strength. She was afraid her line wasn't strong enough to bring it in. She would have to play it delicately.

She had never felt such a huge fish pulling at her. With growing anticipation, she worked the fish for an hour or more. But time seemed to drift like a cloud. She thought of LaNelle's Lark at the bottom of the pond. Wilburn had sunk the dilapidated car at the high end of the pond to reinforce the levee. Its hulk would be like a cow's skeleton, she thought. She did not allow the fish to take her line near that area.

She thought she knew exactly which fish she had hooked. She had had her eye on it for years. It was the prize fish of the whole pond. She had seen this great fish now and then, a monster that would occasionally surface and roll. It would wallow around like a whale. Since the first time she'd seen it, she had been out to get the "old big one." Her quest had become legendary in the family. "Mama's going to get that old big fish," they'd say. But she hadn't imagined this would be the day. It was as though the fish had been waiting for her, growing formidably, until this day. It had caught *her* by surprise.

Slowly, the fish lost its strength. She could see its mouth as she drew it nearer, as it relaxed and let her float it in. The fish was gigantic, more immense than any fish she had ever caught. From the feel of it and now the glimpse of it in the murky water, she thought it might weigh thirty pounds. If only she could see Wilburn's face when she brought this fish in.

She had never landed a fish larger than eleven pounds. She had caught a ten-pound catfish at a pay-pond once, and she had hooked the eleven-pounder in this pond. She knew that landing this one would be a challenge. She would have to drag it out, instead of raising it and flipping it out of the water.

Finally, the fish was at the bank, its mouth shut on the line like a clamp-top canning jar, its whiskers working like knitting needles. It was enormous. She was astonished. It touched the bank, but without the smooth glide of the water to support it the fish was dead weight. She couldn't pull it all the way up the bank. She couldn't lift it with her rod, nor could she drag it through the weeds of the bank. She was more worn out than the fish was, she thought. She held the line taut, so that the fish couldn't slip back in the water, and she tugged, but it didn't give. The mud was sucking it, holding it fast. Its head was out of the water, and with those whiskers and its wide wraparound mouth, it seemed to be smiling at her. She stepped carefully through scrubby dried weeds and clumps of grass, making her way down the shallow bank toward the fish. Knots of pondweed bordered the water. Gingerly, she placed her left foot on a patch of dried vegetation and reached toward the fish.

The patch appeared solid. For a fraction of a second, the surprise of its give was like the strangeness of the taste of Coca-Cola when the tongue had expected iced tea. The ground gave way under her foot and she slid straight into the pond. It wasn't a hard fall, for her weight slid right into the water, almost gracefully. On the way, she grabbed at a willow bush but missed it. She still had hold of the line, even though her rod-and-reel slipped into the water. She clutched at dried weeds as she slid, and the brittle leaves crumpled in her hands. Then the fish was slipping back into the water, dragging the rod. She snatched the rod and felt the fish still weighting the end of the line. Quickly, she heaved the rod to the bank. She caught hold of the fish and held it tight, her fingernails studding its skin.

She was gasping at the chill of the water. She could not touch bottom. She was clutching the edge of the bank, and the water was up to her neck.

She hadn't imagined the pond was so deep next to the bank. The fish in her hands, she hugged the bank, propping herself against it with her elbows. She tried to get a toehold against the side of the pond, but as she shifted her weight, the solid matter fell away and her foot seemed to float free. She kept a tight hold on the fish, pointing its head away from her so it would not grab her fingers. Sometimes a channel catfish would grip bait and not let go, even after the fish was dead. It could bite a person's finger off.

She still couldn't touch the bottom, but she balanced herself against the side of the pond and held the fish's head out of the water. The water helped buoy the weight of the fish. The fish gaped, and the baited hook floated for a moment. The hook was not even sunk into its flesh. Then the fish clamped onto the hook again.

The fish was a fine one, she thought. It would make good eating. She was pleased, even amazed that she had caught it. It had lost much of its strength. She would have to wait for it to die. When the mouth stayed open, it would be dead, even if it still seemed to be breathing.

She managed to scoot it up onto the bank, inching it in front of her. She laid it in the ooze, placing it by the gills. Its gills were still working, its mouth loosened now. She held it down hard against the mud. The fish gaped, and she lessened her pressure. She floundered in the water, repositioning herself against the muck. She realized the water no longer seemed chilly.

The water was high, submerging the lower branches of the willow bushes. The willows were only a few feet away, but she did not want to get near those bushes. She was sure there were snakes around the roots of the willows. The snaky tendrils of the pondweed brushed her legs. She kicked and stirred the water while holding on to a tuft of grass.

To make her way to the shallow end, she would have to maneuver around the willows. But she would have to launch too far out into the pond to do that. She wasn't sure she could swim, yet her clothes did not feel heavy. She was wearing her old tan stretch-knit pants and a thin blouse and a cotton shirt and tennis shoes.

She noticed it was shady in the direction of the shallow end, so she decided to stay where she was, where she could feel the sunshine. She expected that someone would see her presently and come to help her out. With difficulty, she twisted her body toward the road, where cars were passing. She let out a holler. More cars passed. She hollered again. The cars were driven by the blind and the deaf. Their windows were rolled up tight.

"Hey!" She let out a yodeling sound, and then a pig call. "Sooeeee!" She tried all the calls she knew, calls she used when she had to reach the men working in the fields, sounds that could carry across creeks and hollers. "Sook, cow!" she called, as if summoning a herd of milk cows.

There was no one at the house now, but she thought the renters would be there soon. The car she had seen was gone. Her car gleamed fire-red at the stable. In the smooth surface of the pond before her, stretching toward the soybean field and then the road, she saw the upside-down reflection of the chicken-feed mill. The sky was bright autumn blue, and the reflection of the tower was like a picturesque postcard, still and important-looking.

Balancing against the bank in the water up to her neck, she gazed across the field toward the houses and the road. In that panorama, her whole life lay before her—a rug at the foot of the feed-mill tower. She saw her own small house in the clump of trees. The bulldozer still had not come to demolish it. She was sure the house could be fixed up, if she could only tend to it. Leaving it vacant had caused it to deteriorate. The loss of her house probably hurt her more than anything about the farm. But she couldn't keep everything up. It was too much for her. She'd had the stable repainted—a clear red—but it needed more work. Her thoughts weighed her down with the heaviness of the farm's history. Her memories mixed together in a mosaic of hard bits, like chicken grit. She saw the calves, the horses, the corncrib, the gardens, the henhouses, and other buildings no longer there. She saw the onions and potatoes she stored in one of the stalls. She saw mules and tractors and bonfires of leaves. What she saw before her eyes now was the consequence and basis of her labor. Years of toil were finished now; sometimes she wondered what it had all been for.

She seized a clump of grass but could not nudge her weight onto the bank. It was like trying to chin herself on a high bar. She did not have the energy. Then the grass pulled loose. The fish gaped again, and she managed to push it farther up the bank. She avoided its mouth.

Time passed. For a while, she lay horizontal in the water, clutching grass; then she rested vertically against the sludge of the bank. When occasionally her grip loosened, she had to dog-paddle to keep afloat.

She was panting. She held herself steady until she gathered her strength, then she tried again to pull herself up. She could not. The water seemed quite warm now. She thrashed, to scare off snakes. If she could grab a willow branch, she was sure she could pull herself out, but the thought of snakes underwater around the willow roots made her tremble. Snapping turtles were there too, she felt sure.

⁐ ⁐ ⁐

The shade covering the shallow end had grown deeper and longer now. She needed to stay here in the sun.

A pack of coyotes could eat a person. Wilburn had said that was not true, but she believed it was. Last year, one of the neighbor women carried dinner to the farmhands at work in one of her back fields. She parked her car on a lane beside the field, and as she started toward the gate with the dinner she saw some coyotes running at her, a whole caboodle of them. She raced back to the car and slammed the door just in time. The coyotes clambered all over the car, sniffing.

Sometimes the siren of a passing ambulance started the coyotes howling. All along the creek, a long ribbon of eerie sound followed the siren. If the coyotes found her in the pond, she could not escape. They might smell the fish, she thought. That would draw them like bait. Her dread hardened into a knot. She thought she ought to pray. She hadn't been to church much lately. She had trouble hearing, now that they had a microphone. Its squealing hurt her ears.

Cars passed. She thought she saw her son's van under the trees. She thought he might be sawing wood. She hollered to the air. After a while, she could tell that what she had thought was the van was only some scrap metal glinting in the sun.

The soybeans had been harvested only a week before, and the combine had missed multitudes of beans. She could see clumps of them dotting the field. There was so much waste. It bothered her. The land itself was washing into the creek. She pictured herself in the pond, washing over the levee in a hard rain and then sweeping on down through the creek.

If Wilburn came along and saw her here, he would grin at her and say, "What are you fooling around in the pond for? Got time on your hands?"

She wondered what it would be like to while away the hours in a country club swimming pool. She had never had time to idle like that. She did not know how people could piddle their lives away and not go crazy. She had stopped going on the senior-citizen bus tours because they wasted so much time at shopping malls. She told them she'd rather eat a worm.

She recalled falling into water before—it was familiar. She was a little thing, fishing in Panther Creek with her grandmother and aunt. Suddenly she slid off a log, down the bank, and into the water. Mammy Hicks and Aunt Hattie laughed at her. "You got wet, didn't you?" Hattie said, bobbing her pole. A whole life passed between those two splashings.

Her hands were raw. She thought she could see snakes swirling and swimming along the bank some yards away. She had never seen a cottonmouth at this pond, but a snake was a snake, poisonous or not. She shuddered and tightened her grasp on the grass. She kicked her feet behind her. Her shoes were sodden.

A pain jerked through her leg—a charley horse. She waited for it to subside. She did not know how much time had passed, but the sun was low. She was starting to feel cooler. Her legs were numb. She realized she could be having another stroke. For the first time, it occurred to her that she might really be stranded here and no one would know. No one knew she had come fishing.

She scrambled clumsily at the bank. Now she knew she had to get out. No one was going to come for her. She knew she should have tried earlier, when she had more strength, but she had believed someone would spot her and come to help her. She worked more industriously now, not in panic but with single-minded purpose. She paused to take some deep breaths. Then she began to pull, gripping the mud, holding herself against it. She was panting hard. Little by little, she pulled herself up the mud bank. She crawled out of the water an inch at a time, stopping to rest after each small gain. She did not know if she felt desperation. She was so heavy. Her teeth were chattering from the cold, and she was too weak to rise. Finally she was on the bank, lying on her belly, but her legs remained in the water. She twisted around, trying to raise herself up. She saw a car turn into the driveway. She hollered as loud as she could. Her teeth rattled. After a moment, the car backed up and drove away.

The western sun was still beating down. She lay still and let it dry her. As her clothes dried, she felt warmer. But her legs remained in the water, her shoes like laden satchels. She pulled and pulled and crawled until her legs emerged from the water. She felt the sun drawing the water from her clammy legs. But as the sun sank, she felt cooler. She crawled with the sun—moving with it, grabbing grass.

When she finally uprighted herself, the sun was going down. She stood still, letting her strength gather. Then she placed one foot in front of her, then the other.

She had to get the fish. Stooping, she pulled it onto the grass, but she could not lift it, and she knew she could not pack it to the car. It was dead, though its gills still worked like a bellows, slowly expanding and collapsing. It had let go of the hook. Leaving the fish, she struck out across the soybean field toward the car. No one was at the house. She reached the car. Luckily, the key had not washed out of her pocket while she was in the pond. In the dim light, she couldn't see how to get it in the ignition. For an interminable time, she fumbled with the key. Then it turned.

Instead of following the path around the edge of the field, she steered the car straight across the beanfield. She stopped before the rise to the pond and got out. As she climbed toward the pond, her feet became tangled in some greenbrier vines and she fell backwards into a clump of high grass. Her head was lower than her feet. She managed to twist herself around so that she was headed up the bank, but she was too weak to stand.

She lay there in the grass for some time, probably half an hour. She dozed, then jarred awake, remembering the fish. Slowly, she eased up the bank and eventually stood. When she reached the fish, it appeared as a silhouette, the day had grown so dark. She dragged the fish to the car and heaved it up through the door, then scooted it onto the floorboard behind the driver's seat. She paused to catch her breath.

The sun was down now. In the car, she made her way out of the field to the road. Cars were whizzing by. She was not sure her lights were working. They seemed to burn only dimly. She hugged the edge of the narrow road, which had no shoulders, just deep ditches. Cars with blazing headlights roared past. She slowed down. By the time she got into town, the streetlights were on. She could not see where to turn into her street. A car behind her honked. Flustered, she made her turn.

When she got home, the kitchen clock said 7:25. She had been at the pond for seven hours. She opened the back door, and Chester the cat darted in, then skidded to a stop and stared at her, his eyes bugged out. She laughed.

"Chester, you don't know me! Do I smell like the pond?"

Chester retreated under the kitchen table, where he kept a wary lookout.

"Come here, baby," she said softly. "Come on." He backed away from her.

She got into the shower, where she let hot water beat on her. Memories of the afternoon's ordeal mingled in her mind like dreams, the sensations running together and contorting out of shape. She thought that later she would be angry with herself for not pulling herself out of the pond sooner—

she could have ventured into those willow bushes—but now she felt nothing but relief.

After she was clean and warm, she went to the kitchen. Chester reappeared. He rubbed against her legs.

"Chester," she crooned. "You didn't know me." She laughed at him again.

She fed Chester and warmed up some leftovers for her supper. She hadn't been hungry all those hours, and she was too tired to eat now, but she ate anyway. She ate quickly. Then she went out to the garage and dragged the fish out of the car.

She wrestled it into the kitchen. She couldn't find her hatchet. But she thought she was too weak to hack its head off now. Using the step stool, she managed, in stages, to get the fish up onto the counter. She located her camera. The flash didn't work, but she took a picture of the fish anyway, knowing it probably wouldn't turn out. She didn't know where her kitchen scales were— lost in the move somewhere. She was too tired to look for them. She found her tape measure in a tool drawer.

The fish was thirty-eight and a half inches long. It was the largest fish she had ever caught.

"Look at that fish, Chester," she said.

With her butcher knife, she gutted the fish into a bucket. The fish was full—intestines and pondweed and debris and unidentifiable black masses squished out.

She could feel herself grinning. She had not let go of the fish when she was working it, and she had gotten back home with the old big one. She imagined telling Wilburn about the fish. He would be sitting in front of the TV, and she would call him from the kitchen. "Just wait till you see what I reeled in at the pond," she would say. "Come in here and see. Hurry!" He would know immediately what she had caught. She had a habit of giving away a secret prematurely. Her grinning face—and her laughing voice— gave her away. When she had a surprise for the children, she couldn't wait to tell them. She wanted to see their faces, the delight over something she had bought them for Christmas or some surprise she had planned. "Wake up, get out of bed. Guess what! Hurry!"

Joe Ashby Porter

"Bowling Green"

Joe Ashby Porter's main piece of Kentucky ground is east and a bit north of Mason's, but Porter's people are more than likely to be outlaws who inhabit a Gothic universe of murder and mayhem and revenge. If you were to meet the mild-mannered, attractive, well-groomed Porter, you might be surprised that he has fathered such awful offspring, especially if you knew his credentials. Born in Madisonville in 1942, he studied at Harvard and Cambridge (as a Fulbright Fellow), earned an M.A. and a Ph.D. from the University of California at Berkeley, and has taught in the Department of English at Duke since 1980. We all know we can't trust appearances; Porter knows what evil lurks in the heart of every man and woman, and he reveals it to us in stories in which evil is made flesh.

His first book, *Eelgrass* (1977), is about flower children of the 1960s waltzing in Neverland. *The Kentucky Stories* (1983) brings us into the gritty real world of treachery, murder, and madness. "Bowling Green" is a Gothic tale told by a strange-looking woman about revenge on a college boy who goes to Western Kentucky State Teachers College (now Western Kentucky University). The boy, who according to the very involved narrator, Lena Toombs, "always did set himself a little above people," also got in the habit of using women and then dropping them. You decide if his punishment fits his crime.

So, you come from there, did you? Maybe they told you about R.W. Pritchett—maybe he's there now, and you saw what he had on him. Well, I don't want to know anything about that fool's doings. But I can tell you this: nothing would've happened if he'd stayed there and tended his own business. This place could have gotten along without him and his red Pontiac, I daresay! Why, I'd been glad to see him gone in the beginning, and that Lois Meeker, she had stopped crying about him, at least. You know, we all thought we was lucky to get through high school, but R.W., R.W. just couldn't wait to go off to college. He always did set himself a little above people. I told him when he left he'd do best to stay away, but no, he had to come traipsing back, didn't he? Well, I'm not a bit sorry for what happened—ask me, he deserved more than he got, and then some.

I'm Lena Toombs, and don't think I don't know how I look. You can say I'm a redhead but that's about as far as you can go. I cut it close to the back of my head because it frizzes up so, and I let it bunch out on top so I can hide my razor in it. My daddy calls me "scarecrow," and people think my nose makes me look like a weasel. Why, I used to spit whenever I saw myself in a mirror, and I'm squint to boot. I'll marry me some old geezer that don't care one of these days. Meantime, homely as I am, when I'm down to the river there's always somebody or other waiting, and I've never spent much time talking about the weather either.

If you're back through there, I hope you'll tell this story and teach some of those college boys a lesson. I understand the college is real pretty, though. They have girls there too, don't they—learning to be schoolteachers and such? Maybe I'll get to see it before I'm dead and gone.

R.W. was just a kid like the rest of us when the Pritchetts first come here, even if they did have the best bottom land. He grew to be a nice-looking boy—not as handsome as Lois's brothers, but nice-looking, and congenial. When he was older, he'd meet me down on the bank now and again like the others. But even then he was beginning to get some outlandish notions, and don't think I didn't try to straighten him out. As long as I can remember I've been trying to talk some sense into people. Many's the time I've had to grit my teeth to keep from giving R.W. a good smack up side of the head. And when that damn cousin of his come here one summer talking all about Bowling Green, and R.W. brought *him* down to the river, why I laughed right in his face, I said, "I'm very sorry, but you better go on back where you come from, unless you want to just sit over there and watch R.W. and me do some country loving." "Lena, Lena," he started in, but I only laughed the more.

I don't mind telling all this, because I don't regret it. I don't do things I'll regret, not like most. When R.W. started courting Lois Meeker, and he kept on coming to see me, I didn't mind a bit, and I didn't mind telling her, either. I don't need to keep anybody's dirt for them. It was partly for his good I told her anyway—I didn't want him to turn sheepish and bad. The thing is, it didn't bother her after all, she had gotten so sick over him. There was craziness on her mother's side, and I don't think she's ever been quite right, even for a Meeker. I've had my eye on her for a long time. She ought to have known that if R.W. Pritchett was going to college, he sure didn't aim to marry the likes of her!

There's Meekers all up and down this river, as I hear. People say they come crawling up out of the mudflats at night. Lois's daddy runs the ferry. It don't make him any living to speak of, so he runs in liquor from the next county—and when they can't live on that sometimes the boys thieve. They're the lowest breed around here, but oh my they're lookers—purest black hair, big dark eyes, eyelashes so long and thick it makes them look sleepy, and the whitest softest baby skin you ever saw—it reminds you of old river clay, it's always so damp and cold. It don't seem right.

Lois used to walk sort of hunched over forward. She never did curl her hair, so it hung straight down from her head and swung back and forth when she walked. It looked wild to me, but men liked it. When she was growing up she had a little more flesh on her than me—but that's not saying much, is it? She was always the opposite of me: she didn't talk much, and she didn't want to look you in the eye. She was knock-kneed, too, and she had a snub nose.

Like I say, R.W. took it into his head to court her. They had their own place they'd go to, up a way under the cliffs. She was practically a virgin—she'd only had to do with her brothers. Sometimes when R.W. was with her I'd hear her moaning and howling, and after he'd gone home she'd sit out on the rocks in the river by herself. I'll say this much for him: he always told her he was going away, and he never come close to talking about marrying her. It was her, with her crazy foolishness, that kept hoping against hope—she never let on, but I know she really thought she'd hold him. People always do that—they believe what they want, they say the sun's about to shine when it's getting darker every minute. I wanted then to beat her black and blue for her craziness—sitting out there on the rocks talking to herself. But it wasn't my place, and I don't know as it would have done a whole lot of good. Anyway, one fall he left out of here, like he always said he would.

He left early one morning in an old pickup, headed for Bowling Green, and I said good riddance. Lois mooned up and down the street all day. I was home—I had work to do—but I saw her out the window, hunched over and whispering and playing with her hair like that. She made me so nervous I had a chew of my daddy's old Rough Country. Well, on toward evening I saw her stand still for a while, and then she started up the road away from town. I supposed she was going up to Robbie Baird's to see about some sewing, but after a while I got to feeling funny, so I went up there myself. Robbie was just coming in from the fields, and she hadn't laid eyes on Lois. Robbie says she's never seen me so mad. I lit out as fast as I could go, and I caught up with Lois about three quarters of a mile up. She was walking fast, with her head down, and she wouldn't slow when I called her. When I got up with her I said, "Lois Meeker, you damn fool, where do you think you're going?" Of course I knew what she would say. How far is it—eighty, ninety miles? I pulled her down and beat her in the face till she was out cold.

I must have knocked some sense into her, because after that she managed to get along. She cried a good deal at first, but after a while she seemed to give up. All along I was telling her, "He's never coming back, he's never coming back," because his family had moved away after he left. Nobody here had enough money to buy the farm or even rent it, so the Pritchetts just locked up the house and left. It's the one off to the left down river. It's run down now, and the youngsters have started to break into it at night for the beds. It's an awful shame for that land to go to waste so. Of course R.W. stayed there when he come back, and he shingled the roof, but he didn't farm any. Anyhow, after all the Pritchetts was gone, Lois would go over and sit on their porch sometimes. And also, she started spending time by the river, up under the cliffs where she had used to go with R.W.

Well, R.W. was away for almost two years, and it seemed like he had taken the weather with him. A few weeks after he left, the hail beat down all the crops, and the next year the same thing happened. Besides that, they opened a mine up in the next county, and did something to the water so we haven't had any fish. Nobody had enough to eat, and I guess the Meekers was hurt most. Lois got almost as thin as me, and then she started to puff up and I knew she was eating an awful lot of clay.

Ever hear of river beans? Why, it's just clay done up with pork and to-mato sauce. Most people eats it plain, though, when they do eat it. I eat me a little now and then, when I'm feeling particularly low. It does taste a little like beans, but more like river water. I bring a little bowl of it back to the house and eat it while it's still cold. It feels good going down, and it sits nice and heavy on the stomach. It makes you real sleepy—I usually don't get through more than a cupful or so. But it's not too good for you, and most around here don't eat much of it, except the Meekers. I guess they could live on it if they had to, being river people. Anyway like I said, Lois spent a lot of time up under the cliffs, and when I saw she was beginning to bloat out I imagined she was going there to eat clay by herself. I didn't go up there, so that I didn't find out just exactly what she was up to.

I'll tell you, though, I felt sorry for the poor thing. Seth said she wouldn't have a thing to do with him or anybody else—said she just didn't feel like it. He thought she'd got uppity from R.W., but I knew she was still grieving some. Judy Weldon that handles the mail said Lois had been sending some letters to him, but that he hadn't answered, and she'd finally stopped writing. The trouble was, she didn't have nothing to occupy herself. Me, I spend half the day housecleaning and cooking, but those Meekers is satisfied with a roof over their head. Then too, Lois wasn't the kind to do any visiting among the other women. I didn't owe her anything, but it hurt me to see her drag-ging herself around like that. I got her to come sit with me now and again, just to fill up some of her time.

I remember once I told her I'd heard about her letters, and I asked her what she expected. She looked real sullen, and said she didn't expect a thing. But after a while she got to looking so sad, with those big Meeker eyes, I had to come over and put my arms around her. I just said, "Don't take on, now." Then she said, "He snuck away, Lena, like some old dog that's afraid he'll get whipped. He couldn't bring himself to tell me goodbye." And then in a minute she said, "I'd rather he'd died than to have left me that way. That's all I told him, in every letter I wrote. I told him I wished he'd die for doing me that way." Still, I know she hoped he'd come back and marry her.

R.W. said he come here that summer because he wanted to be by himself— here, of all places! He said he thought college was too hard for him, and maybe he wasn't meant to go there anyway, and he had to study all summer long or he'd fail it for sure. No, he couldn't stay with his family, because they would "distract" him. Well, he got a little "distracted" here, I think! I could have told him that he'd have better gone any place but here—for his own sake, not to mention anybody else's. But my advice wasn't wanted. Most people just itch to go to ruin. And if he couldn't bear to be anywhere else, I could have told him it wouldn't help any to show up with that red Pontiac, or wearing those loud argyle socks. I guess he hoped it would keep up his spirits, though—he looked tired and about five years older instead of two.

He didn't intend to see anybody, at least in the beginning. He'd even brought a bunch of canned goods so he wouldn't need to go to the store for a while. Somebody noticed the car up by the house, and called the constable to see who it was, and that's how we knew he was back. When I heard it I took out for the Meekers' fast as I could go. Seth, the oldest boy, was all sprawled out on the front porch sound asleep in the middle of the day. Sometimes I hate to see him, he's such a handsome good-for-nothing thing. Well, I knew I couldn't wake him up, so I barged right on in.

There's not much to that little old house. It's up on stilts, like the dock, out over the water beside the ferry line. There's holes in it big enough for a cat to jump through, and you have to watch your step because the floors is all damp and scummy. The parlor was empty and I could see the kitchen was too, so I banged on the bedroom door. Lois was in there, and she said, "Is that R.W.?"

"Not hardly!" I said. "Not hardly, it's not! It's just plain Lena Toombs," I said. I said, "It's just plain Lena Toombs, Lois, me that always has to tend to other people's rat-killing because they won't tend to it themselves." I was mad. I told her to come out from behind that door but she just said, "Go home, Lena. I don't want you to bother me any more." I'll tell you one thing: if she'd have come out and faced me then, I'd have done more than bother her! Lord, the thanks! I was shaking, and I had my razor out, ready to go after anybody.

I stared at that door for a while, and then I gave it a good kick, and I said, "I'll be more than relieved, Lois Meeker, to wash my hands of your foolishness. But before I go, there's one thing I have to say: you'd do best to forget R.W. Pritchett's name. He'll never do right by you. So if I was you I'd just stay in that bedroom so long as he's here." And then I marched myself straight home.

She did stay in the house at least during the daytime from then on. Maybe she thought everything would be fine if only R.W. would come to her. And then maybe she just felt like hiding. At night, of course, she'd go up under the cliffs. But he didn't come looking for her there either, for the time being.

After a week or so R.W. asked me to come cook and keep house for him, since he'd found out he couldn't manage on his own. I wasn't in a mood to do him any favors, but I couldn't help feeling a little sorry for him. When he'd cock his head to the side, with the silly grin of his, I knew he was ashamed of how he'd done at college. Still, I kept tight-lipped and waited. It wasn't my place to stir up anything until I knew what was in his mind. I didn't even say anything about those loud clothes or the way he had cut his hair all short so you could see his scalp through it, and shaved off his sideburns. It was none of my concern if he wanted to look like a fool.

Every day save Sunday I'd go over there at noon and stay till five or so. I made him dinner and supper, and in between I did housecleaning or what have you, and sometimes I'd help him practice his great long lists of questions and answers. But I figured that wasn't all he wanted me for, and sure enough after a day or two he tried to get me into the bedroom. I let him know right then that if that's what he wanted he'd have to pay extra: I hadn't wasted my time pining after him. Well, he wasn't expecting that. He looked at me sort of funny, and then he shrugged and stuck his nose in a book. Then in a few minutes he put his head down on the table like he was thinking. I was going about my business, whistling and shaking my head. But I was really watching him, and do you know what?—he was sort of frowning and mouthing things to himself without making a sound—just like Lois Meeker! I remember to this day how peculiar he looked. Well, after a while he sat up, and told me to name my price; his voice was kind of husky. So after that almost every day we'd go to bed directly after dinner. He'd brought some French ticklers and such back with him, but I thought they were more trouble than they were worth, really.

One thing, though: sometimes he'd shut his eyes, and then I'd poke at him till he looked at me again. If I do it in the daylight, I want you to look me straight in the eyes. There's no getting around it: it's me, Lena Toombs.

Sometimes he just wanted to talk—in fact, I got the feeling he wanted me more for that than for anything. I ought to have charged him for talking, too, but I was curious to see what he'd say. I'd fix some lemonade and we'd sit us in the glider under the trees to the side of the house. It's pretty—you can look at the crabapple thicket across the river. I kept thinking he was going to ask me about Lois, but he never did. Maybe he wanted me to bring it up—well, like I say, I was keeping myself tight-lipped. We didn't talk about the old days either. Instead, he might tell me about college, or lots of times he'd complain about how hard it was to make a doctor (that's what he wanted to do). I'd say, "If it's that hard, you better not do it!" and he'd say, "No, Lena, no, I think I better." "Well, then," I'd say, "you better do a little more studying at it, and a little less gabbing and mooning. You need to get yourself straightened out, young man, is what I mean." He'd give a kind of a slow smile and sigh and lean back. He'd look up at the sky and he'd say, "You're right, Lena, I know you're right." Then why did he go on that way, I'd like to know? He'd make me mad and I'd say, "I never heard of anybody coming *here* to learn to doctor, anyway!"

I'll give him credit, though: he did seem to get a good batch of studying done at first. And I was pretty sure he was staying home nights. My house is that one up there, and from my bedroom window you can see all the way down the street to the river, so I'd have known if he'd have been slipping over to the Meekers' or the cliffs either. Lois must have heard through her brothers that R.W. had settled in for the summer, and that I was working for him. Everybody in town knew it, and some of them would talk about me because like I say food was scarce and R.W. and me (and my daddy of course) was the only ones that had all we wanted. Not that Lois would have been jealous, unless I mistake her. No, she wouldn't have minded if he'd have carried on with every woman in town, so long as he came back to her in the end. Or maybe in her crazy way she wanted to give up on him, but couldn't do it while he was still here.

He aimed to leave on September first. It was early in August he started to fidget and slack off in his studying. He'd just lay around the house dreaming. And then he'd be whispering things to himself, exactly like Lois. (You know, sometimes I got the feeling he was doing it to irk me into mentioning her name.) I'd clear my throat or snap my fingers and point at his books, but he didn't pay me much mind, and sometimes he'd have tears in his eyes. And then sometimes he'd race around in that red Pontiac his daddy had given him for college. It made me sick, it was such foolishness. Who did he think he was? College my foot! I told him I aimed to stop coming if he kept on, and I felt like it, I'll tell you. What did he do? He laughed at me, and said he'd have the law on me because he'd already given me my pay. He was only joking, though: I could tell he didn't much care whether I stayed or left. I cussed him out good then, I told him he'd come to naught. By the middle of August he'd stopped even pretending to study. I stayed on anyway. I had some idea of what was brewing. Of course I didn't know it would happen the way it did.

By this time it was me that had to get him into the bed instead of the other way around, but anyway I kept after him because I thought it was good for him. I guess by then I just wanted to keep him "distracted" till September. I remember it was one Thursday afternoon, and I'd had a particularly hard time getting him worked up, but we'd finally got going strong. He was laying all stretched out while I cleaned him up, when we heard this soft little noise from the kitchen. It sort of went "Creak . . . creak. . . ." Both of us tiptoed in there, and it was Seth Meeker stealing food out of the frigidaire.

To this day I remember how they looked at each other—R.W. standing there naked as a jaybird, and Seth all crouched back in the corner. Seth mustn't have been at the clay like Lois—he was thin, and that soft face of his was whiter then ever. From where I stood I could see him easing his hand toward the switchblade in his pocket. Still, I didn't think he'd start anything—Meekers fights like animals when they have to, but they'll slink away if they can. Besides, R.W. must have been a good forty pounds heavier.

They looked at each other for the longest time, and then R.W. said, "I'd be happy for you to have what food you want, Seth. Now come on and have a drink old buddy." Seth started to relax a little then. He said he was obliged and for us to go on about our business. But R.W. said no, we'd all have us a drink right then. Pretty soon we was all talking and joking. R.W. said, "Seth, why don't you and Lena have a go—be my guest." It was high-handed of him, but I didn't care. R.W. came in the room with us and sat in the easy chair, laughing and yelling things out, and drinking more. Toward dark a hailstorm come up, and Seth had to leave. The two of them stood on the porch for a while, joking and slapping each other on the back. Before Seth left I heard him say, "You ain't forgot old Lois now have you, R.W.? She ain't said boo to nothing in pants since you been gone. And she's up there under the cliffs just about every night now, you hear?" He had to run for it then, because the hail had already started.

R.W. sat on the porch for a smoke, and meantime I was in the parlor practically jerking my hair out. What was I to do? But finally I said to myself that nothing aimed to happen that night anyhow because of the storm. So I sat out with R.W. for a while, and sure enough pretty soon he went in and went to sleep—I listened outside his door just to be safe. I put a washtub over my head and ran home. It had just cleared off when I woke up the next morning. That was a Friday—don't ask me if it was the thirteenth because I don't remember.

I thought I'd best be to the Pritchett house early, so I went directly after I'd cooked breakfast for my daddy, and what do you think? R.W. was already up and hard at work, studying to beat the band. It appeared to me to be a little late for that. I don't mind telling you, it didn't look like a good sign. He ate a sandwich and then went straight back to work. He hadn't said two words to me all day, and so I thought I'd talk to him at supper. I did myself proud with that supper—it was the last meal I cooked for him. I don't care much about food myself—I guess you can tell by looking, can't you! While he was eating his pie I said to him, just like that, "You mean to see her tonight?" He looked at me like he'd never seen me before. "Well, Lena," he said, "well, Lena, what's it to you?" So then I had my say.

"Never mind what it is to me," I said. "Never you mind that. Lena Toombs can take care of herself, which is what I wish other people could do, and if they could, things would be a lot easier for me. What is it to me? It's not one damn thing in the world to me, except I can't abide people making a mess of each other, I wish I could for my own sake. No sir, don't go worrying your head about Lena," I said, "no, just you keep your mouth shut and hear me out what I have to say, and what I've been expecting I'd be brought to say before I got you away from here, the more fool you for coming back anyway!

"You did wrong, R.W. Pritchett," I said, "you did wrong before you left in the first place. Oh I know you never told her you aimed to marry her, and I know you always told her you was going. But that wasn't enough—you know how she gets things into that fool Meeker head of hers. You let her hope for things! You let her when it was your place to keep her from it! And if you didn't know it then, I'm telling you now and you better listen good."

I said, "She'd just about gotten over you—it took her long enough—when you come waltzing back here. What do you suppose she thought, I'd like to know. Well, that's all water under the bridge. What you've got to do now is start taking care of what you do, for once in your life. With all your college ideas, maybe you need somebody to remind you this is a lonesome little old river town, and you don't forget about people here so easy—people sticks in your mind whether you like it or not. And we have to keep on getting by some way, even when you're up there at college, did you ever think about that? I guess you don't aim to come back here and doctor, and I guess that's why you think you can get away with anything you want, long as you're here, and then pick up and go. Well, Lena's here to tell you you can't! And you can laugh at me when you get back there, but right now you better pay close attention: if you don't aim to do right on your own steam, I swear I'll do everything in my power to make you do right. What I mean is this: if you go up there and see her tonight, you better get good and clear in your head what you aim to see her for. And if it's wrong you better keep yourself to home, young man. Because I tell you it won't do for you just to have a quick go at her for old times' sake. It wouldn't matter if it was me, but for

Lois Meeker it won't do, because she don't have good sense—neither of you do. I'm going home now, and I'm leaving you to get straight about what you have to do. But it better be right, and if it's wrong, you better drive out of here tonight, without waiting for morning. That's what I've got to say."

That surprised him—I guess he'd forgotten what I could be like. He didn't laugh though. In fact he sort of frowned and looked serious. He looked me in the eye, and I didn't think I saw any of that old sheepishness. I went home and set myself down to watch.

Now there was a full moon, so I could see clear, and along toward nine o'clock there he was, crossing the street, headed up toward the cliffs. I saw him stop in the middle of the street and look at my house, like he was trying to see if I was watching. That decided me I'd best follow him. I stuck my razor back in my topknot, and set out. He was walking slow—I guess he was still studying about what he ought to do—so before he got to the cliffs I was close on him without him knowing it. He was walking along with his head down and his hands in his pockets, and every once in a while he'd shrug his shoulders and kick a rock or something. I hunt some with my daddy so I knew how to follow him real soft.

The rest of what happened is sickening. Myself, I don't even like to think about it much. Most people act like it never happened, and I don't blame them. It did happen though—there's no getting around it.

You ought to see the place to get a good picture of it. The ground slopes up from the river toward the base of the cliff. It's solid clay, so there's not much growing on it. About ten feet from the cliff it levels off, and there's a kind of a shelf back up under the overhang—you almost feel like you're in a cave.

R.W. walked out onto the claybank, where the ground starts to rise, and I crouched back in some bushes. The moon was low northwest, shining straight into that cleft. Still, from where I was you couldn't tell whether there was anybody up there or not. R.W. walked halfway up, and then he stopped. I felt like running out and grabbing him then, but I didn't. It appeared he was looking around for her, but didn't see her yet. "Hoo-oo, Lois," he said. Then I heard her voice coming from up there—it sounded kind of low and thicklike. "What's your business out here R.W. Pritchett," she said. And then I heard her say, "You better go on back to town." It sounded like she was crying or whining. But you might have known: R.W. didn't turn back, he started walking again right on up the hill.

I crept out into the open and followed him. It was awful quiet, but there was a bullfrog down in the river grass, and I'd take a step or two whenever he'd croak. But Lois must have heard R.W. coming on, because she yelled out, "What are you doing to me!" Those were the last words she ever said in her life. Lord, she was a miserable crazy thing—always was, but R.W. didn't help any.

He got up to the level ground, and he was still looking around for her, and then he walked forward toward the cliff face out of my sight. I said to myself that something awful peculiar was going on, so I run off to the side a little to get against the rock and I come up close to them that way. I didn't see her yet. He was standing there staring down toward the ground, not moving at all.

Don't ask me how I knew it, but right then and there I decided it wouldn't make him any difference if I walked right up to him, so I did. It was high time somebody did something, anyway. When I got there I saw what he was looking at, and why he hadn't seen Lois at first. Because she was down in front of him, lying in a sort of shallow grave. She had gotten so fat I might not have recognized her if I didn't know who it was, and of course R.W. only remembered her when she was thinnish. She had her mouth shut, but she kept making a coughing or a sort of little whimpering sound. And every time, all that flesh would shake like pudding. She had clay on her face and hands. She didn't even notice me peeping over the edge—she was looking straight at R.W., and tears was running down the sides of her face. I never saw such a mess in all my life.

Well, I looked at him and what do you think: He had his eyes closed, and he'd started to ease back away from the grave. Then he just turned around and went off down the hill at a fast walk. I didn't know what to do. Lois had closed her eyes too, and the tears was pouring out. She was nodding her head like she wanted to say, "I knew it, I knew it." Maybe that was what she was saying—she had started whispering like she always did. So then I ran down after R.W. "No sir!" I said, "no sir! You don't walk away like that." I whipped out my razor and held it on him. I said, "Now you march yourself right back up there, or you'll wish you had!" He looked real stupid, like he was drunk. He didn't seem to know what was happening, but I gave him a good push to get him moving, and we went back up there.

You guessed it: she had already killed herself with that awful old long switchblade of Seth's, that she had brought with her. R.W. looked at her, and his eyes got big, but he still had that fool's look on his face. And then he shut his eyes again, and he put his hands over his damn ears!

I was so mad I couldn't have told you what I'd do next. I probably should have killed him too and thrown him in there with her, but I didn't. I got him by the hair and pulled him down on his back there beside the grave and I held my razor against his neck so he couldn't move. He was just lying there and shaking all over, and he still had his eyes squinched shut. I straddled him and just looked at him for a while. A lot of things run through my head—I don't mind telling you I thought about cutting off his goddamn ears that wouldn't listen when they should. But then I thought of what to do. I reached down and got that switchblade out of her. And then I yelled at him, to make sure he heard me this time. I said, "I'm aiming to hurt you, R.W. and if you move—you feel this razor under your goddamn ear?" I tore off his shirt, and then I cut right into his chest, the way you cut something in a tree. I cut "B.G." for Bowling Green, for all his foolishness. I cut it in capital letters. I had to keep mopping him up to see what I was doing. He kept yelling for me to stop. I think he must have gone sort of crazy, because he kept talking about Lois. I left him there and I went home. He must not have died from it—in the morning I saw the Pontiac was gone. He must have made it to some place up the road and got taken care of.

The next day when I went back up under the cliff with the Meeker boys to see to Lois I found out where all that clay she'd been eating had come from. Seth said, "She's done gnawed out her own grave, ain't she?" You could see the teeth marks all over the sides and bottom. It made me feel kind of funny. None of the Meekers could afford a coffin, so we just buried her right there. It didn't matter: animals can't smell things through that river clay the way they can through regular dirt.

I don't know whether R.W. went back to college and made a doctor or not, and I don't want to know. I said I don't want to hear anything about his doings. I've stopped troubling about such as Pritchetts or Meekers either. I do know he'll carry my mark for his folly on him till his dying day.

Sena Jeter Naslund

from *Ahab's Wife*

In 1988, when William Ward published his nearly comprehensive study of Kentucky writing, Sena Jeter Naslund was not even mentioned in a footnote. The reason, I'm sure, is that despite the fact that she had already written and published many stories, she had no book in print. Indeed, her first book of short stories, *Ice Skating at the North Pole,* came out in 1989, followed by two novels, both published in 1993, *The Animal Way to Love* and *Sherlock in Love;* these were followed by another book of stories, *The Disobedience of Water,* in 1999, the same year her blockbuster, *Ahab's Wife,* was published. With *Four Spirits,* her new book based on the church bombing that killed four little girls in her own hometown (she was born in Birmingham in 1942), she has been on a popular and critical roll.

Despite her acclaim and the incredible demands on her time, she is still writing and teaching at the University of Louisville, where she has been a professor of English since 1972. She is also an editor of the *Louisville Review* and heads a new limited-residency writing program at Spalding University that attracts talented writers from all over the country. In 2005 she was chosen to be Kentucky's poet laureate for two years, a selection that honors the award at least as much as the award honors Naslund. To honor her adopted state of Kentucky and her residency here for more than thirty years, she decided to give Ahab's wife a Kentucky connection. According to Naslund, Una, Ahab's wife, whom Melville barely mentions in *Moby Dick,* was born in Kentucky but moved to New England to live with relatives in a lighthouse. When she is sixteen, she decides to disguise herself as a cabin boy and go a-whaling. She has exciting adventures and then meets and marries Captain Ahab. According to Naslund, she decides to return to Kentucky for her confinement. But this is not your mother's pregnancy; she gets personally involved with the slavery controversy in this fiercely divided state on the eve of the Civil War.

I did not consult Ahab about my decision to spend my pregnancy in a rough Kentucky cabin, with my mother, instead of staying in the gracious home of a captain's wife on Nantucket. But I wrote him, of course, and sent the letter after him on the ship called the *Dove,* so he could imagine me aright.

That time spent with my mother outdoors in the sweet summer and golden Kentucky autumn was augmented by our indoor companionship of sewing baby smocks and cooking and reading again those great works of literature my mother had brought with her to the wilderness, green-bound books I had read as a child or she had read to me.

Sometimes my mother and I stood and looked at our faces together in the oval mirror she had brought with her from the East. Along with her library chest of books, the mirror with its many-stepped molding distinguished our frontier cabin from others. Thus, elegantly framed, my mother and I made a double portrait of ourselves for memory, by looking in the mirror.

❧ ❧ ❧

When in mid-December the labor began but tried in vain to progress, my mother went from our cabin, driving the old mare in the black buggy through a six-inch crust of snow, for the doctor. In my travail, I scarcely noticed her leaving. When my mother did not come home and did not come home, and the pains were near unbearable and the chill was creeping across the cabin floor and into my feet as I paced, I grasped the feather bed from my bunk and flung it atop her bed. In desperation, between spasms, I gathered all the gaudy quilts in the house, and then, leaving the latchstring out so that I would not have to venture from my nest when she returned, I took to my childbirth bed. There, softness of two mattresses comforted me from beneath and warmth of myriad quilts, a cacophony of colors, warmed me from above, but still I worked my feet and legs and twisted my back.

Despite the heat of my labor, I could feel my nose turning to ice, long and sharp as a church steeple all glazed with frost. *Parsnip!* I thought of; frozen and funny—a vegetable on my face! I chortled and then prayed, wondering if prayer and laughter gurgled up, sometime, from the same spring. *Let nose be parsnip, parsnip be steeple, steeple be nose—whatever that protuberance, it is frozen to the very cartilage. Warm it! Save me, gods and saints!*

Wild and crazed by pain, my thoughts leaped about in antic dance, circling one picture after another. Nose! Steeple! Parsnip! My desperate, laughing prayer from within that quilted hump below its parsnip was only that I should be delivered and nothing at all for the welfare of the rest of the world.

And yet I wanted to wait for my mother's return, and I was afraid because I had little idea of how to catch the baby. So even as I prayed, I prayed against myself, that time would not pass nor take me any closer to the port of motherhood. I thought of Ahab, as if his ship were wallowing, going neither forward nor drifting back but immobile in a confused sea. Sometimes I slept a little.

During an exhausted respite from the pains that wrung me, and yet amid my anxiety for my too-long-absent mother, I thought I heard the door creak open and an attendant puff of colder cold, but sleep claimed me again. In

468   *The Kentucky Anthology*

my sleep Zephyrs roamed the room. Their cheeks were bloated with frosty breath, which they jetted through pursed lips across the tip of my nose, down the part of my hair, and into my ears.

Then there came such a pounding at the door that I thought, *Volcanos! It will burst through!*

"Open the door," they shouted. "Give her up now!" And terrible pounding of closed fists on my boards.

"Pull the latchstring," I called, for terrifying as they sounded, I didn't want my door shattered by their anger, nor did I want to leave the bed. Seeing how humped I was, wouldn't any being attached to human voice pity me? Around me, the cabin was almost black, as I had left no candle burning, and the windows had been shuttered for the winter. The fire was no more than red-glow.

"No latchstring out!" one man called. And gruffer voices growled without human language. So I lifted the covers and stood by the bed, but before I did their bidding, I covered my warm spot atop the two feather beds with my quilts. Slowly I crossed the dim cabin—I imagined a dark ghoul crouching along the wall—harbinger of pain to come?—but I opened the door and faced the snow. As though frozen in the icy air, a group of six, all bundled up in wool and fur, stood around a torch of blazing pine knot.

"Her tracks come to your door, Madam," one said. "Give her up, now."

These bounty hunters seemed to lick their mouths where frost was caked in their long mustaches and beards. They were like ice demons, but my innocence made me brave, for I harbored no runaway slave.

"I am in childbirth at this very moment." They could clearly see my great roundness in my flannel gown. "I'm waiting my mother and the doctor. Have you seen them?"

One of the six was much smaller than a normal man. His head rose only to the waists of the others, and he wore the pelt of a wolf. I would have thought the man a child, but his face was heavily bearded, and the hair of his face joined and blended with the wolf fur. The ears and snout of the wolf hooded his head, and the wolf's ivory teeth were fastened in the man's hair. Were he not diminutive, he would have suggested a frontier Hercules cloaked in skin of wolf instead of Nemean lion. The dwarfish wolf-man held the high-lifted, blazing pine knot, big as a thigh, in the center of the group. As he lifted his torch higher, the pack stretched to see beyond me into my house. Beyond them, in that flickering, orange light, I could see bare footprints in the snow, small ones, such as a woman might make, and indeed they led toward my door, at least to the great mauled patch where their boots were shifting and scratching.

"We must search your house."

The frigid wind swept over my skin like icy water, and then hot water poured from between my legs and wetted my gown and the floor. I stepped back.

"Look, you," I cried. "My water's breaking!" I would use my shame to rebuff them.

"Still, we'll have the wench, and you must yield her up."

"Look in my house, if you like," I replied, resigned. "But I must go to my bed."

And I did, sniffing back my fear, and wanting my mother, and watching them. From the big torch, which they stuck in a snowbank, they each lighted a taper of fat-pine kindling and entered my house, closing the door. They held up the flaming sticks like candles and filled the cabin with light. Deep in my bed, I wondered, *Will these ruffians stay while my sweet babe comes out?* The room glowed, and rosin-scented smoke curled to the ceiling. *Among these demon-angels, is there a father who might help me?* But the thought of their awful paws between my thighs frightened me so much I would not ask. I lay gasping and groaning while they looked around and beneath the furniture. There was little place for concealment in the room.

"Search under the bunk."

The dwarf dropped to all fours, and then he truly looked like a wolf snuffing under the beds. And when he stood up again, he seemed a magic wolf, trained to walk unnaturally in houses, on his hind legs. One hunter opened my sea chest, which I knew to be empty, and peered in.

"You have a hill of cover upon you."

"The lass is a mountain in herself, Jack," another said quietly, and I heard the Scotch burr in his voice.

"Could you bring in wood for me? afore you leave?"

The rough-spoken man put his hand on my cover to jerk it back in his search, but the Scotsman restrained the hand and said, "No, Jack. Be leaving her her warmth now, and let's be off." I have always thought the Scotsman would have brought in wood for me, but because he knew the men to be mean and ready for roughness of unspeakable kinds, he set them on the hunt again.

"Sometimes they walk backward in their trails," the dwarf added persuasively, "to throw us off the chase." I started at his voice—soft as fur. "She's not here," he added, in the same caressing tone. Pivoting in a furry blur, he scampered across the room to the door.

A pack following their leader, the hunters clomped after the wolf-cloaked dwarf, and as they passed through the door, they doused their firebrands, each stick hissing as it entered the snow. From the drift, the Scotsman took up the blazing torch, the pine knot whorled like a hip joint. Then someone eased the door shut, and the cabin was utterly dark again.

My fear seemed to have stilled my labor. I listened to the crunch of the men's boots going toward the river, which was frozen solid. At a distance, they sounded almost merry, like Christmas revelers, rather than a cruel posse on a deadly hunt for a human being.

Their coming and going had let out all the warmth from the fire, which was sunk almost to embers, no bigger than eyes. Though my labor stood still, and I did not knead the covers or corkscrew my back, I quivered and shook—whether with fear that the men might come back or with dread that my baby was to be welcomed only by my ignorance and the winter's cold, I don't know. If I did not die of childbirth, I and my child would likely freeze to death. I knew if I rubbed myself that friction would warm me a bit, but I was too fearful to make the effort. Involunteer, I lay and quivered and shivered. It seemed, after a long time, that the bed itself was cold and also shivering.

Typhoon sleep enswirled my mind and I dreamed—of the dwarf, his eyes brown and warm as ancient amber, beautifully human in his animal face. Did he know the midwife's art? The dream dwarf asked me my name. "Una!" I said sharply and woke myself.

The pain was hard, tight and dark within me. I lay still except for my involuntary shivering and the bedding shivering on its woven ropes in return. The fire had fallen to ash; the last ember eye had closed.

I shivered and the bed shivered, till finally in my delirious state, the bed seemed to be offering a signal, and I thought it was a friendly signal, that it, too, was cold, and I was not alone. Finally, thinking that if *somehow* I *should* live, I should not want to do so without a nose, and if I did not cover it, mine might freeze solid and crack off, falling like a tree cut at its base, I reached up for the edge of the covers and pulled them over my head. Fingering that vulnerable member, I said, *Thou shalt not freeze—not at least if I've brains enough to pull thee under cover!* Then I smiled, to speak to my nose in the voice of Quaker English. *Art turning into Ahab?* I asked. *Nose first?* And, under the quilts, I thumped myself there till I did sting with the feeling, and tears squeezed from my eyes.

But the tears were for the loneliness of the gesture, not for the stinging, but for my longing for my husband. If Dr. Carter was not to be found, what harm or danger prevented my mother's return? I realized cold was but a cloak for the more fearsome specter: aloneness.

As I continued to thump my nose, then it was I heard a voice, coming, it seemed, from my own belly! Or from my back? Within my cave in the bed. I opened my eyes to look down my body, to see if somehow I had, unknown, produced a vocal babe. Under the covers, the blackness of the cabin—the fire having gone totally out—was compounded to the most profound degree.

What had my babe said?

I waited in the dark, but heard nothing. I felt my belly; the babe was yet within. I shivered. Yes, the bed shivered.

"O, Natural Vibration!" I said aloud, but did not know how to further address a Vibration. And so I laughed, an unearthly, merry peal.

Then, it occurred to me to jiggle the bed. I did shake the mattresses upon their web of rope, and in return, from beneath me—a jiggle. Complexing the signal, I jiggled twice—and twice the bed jiggled in return. I skipped ahead in my addition and jiggled seven times for the days in the week. When seven jiggles, to the very count, came back, despite my crazy dilemma, I giggled.

And then the voice, low as though filtered through baffles, said, "We be lots warmer, we put our skins together."

"Lazarus, come forth," I commanded and laughed joyfully, till a birth pain cut me short.

I was not alone.

From between the two mattresses, under my back, I felt her body moving. And though I saw nothing, I imaged with my inward eye her fingers grope the edge, her head and neck thrust through, and then in a smooth lunge—so as not to disturb me on the upper mattress—she slid out onto the floor, her landing muffled by the braided rug. I pictured her quite flat as though passed through the wringers over a washtub, and then puffed up to normal, once free of her compression. Lifting up the side of my cover, I welcomed her, emissary of the lost tribe, into my tent.

Though she had run far in the snowy night, she was wearing but a shift, and her body was colder than mine. I turned to her, and she curved her small self; lean and taut, to my belly as though it were a great hot rock. I bent her close to me and she pulled herself yet closer so that our bosoms touched, and I rubbed her back, and *she* rubbed the flat space between my shoulder blades and all down my spine, and what with the friction of it and the two of us constantly moving, we did become warmer. And then I kissed her on the cheek, and she did me, and it was settled that we were sisters and more than that, for the spirits of sisters are not always married.

Before I had seen either her face or the smooth cheek I had kissed, my labor seized me. I needed to turn on my back, and needed to bear down and needed desperately to lift my knees—oh, let some contortion expel this babe!—let me thrust my legs straight. Again, I needed to draw them back and thrust, and coil and uncoil, and again. After much of this labor, during a lull, I learned her name, and she said that she would go out to the woodpile and I said that she must wrap herself in the top two quilts.

She slid out from our bed, and, still not visible in the darkness, carefully drew off the top layers of cover, wrapped herself, crossed the floor, and passed through the door. So quickly did my state vacillate now, between dozing and consciousness, that I am ashamed to say that I kept no vigil for her but awoke when she returned. From the moonlight reflected by the snow, I saw her figure in the door opening, one arm curled up carrying the logs, the other free to reach back. With the closing of the door, her image was lost to me again, but I pictured her by sound. When she straightened her arms, the wood rolled down to the hearth, and the rumble of the pieces jouncing each other, bruising and kissing the bark of their fellows and tumbling onto the hearthstones, was as pleasant and promising as any sound I know.

After she had kindled a blaze for us, in the warm glow of the fire, I could see her—Susan—moving about the room, enfolded by the quilts, the red patch-blocks catching the fireglow with their congenial color. The dark curve of her head and her small pigtails sticking up, which I had known by feel in the bed, I saw in silhouette.

Soon, I discerned her face and believed it to be the color of dark walnut. Her lips, leaning over me, her lips very even in the fullness of the upper and lower lip, and most generous, shaped words: "You be all right, soon now. Push on, now." Her dear lips pushed the air when she said *push* in a soft puff of encouragement. "You sure to live." Her hands briskly rubbed my belly, so fast and light that I could not feel pain where her fingers shimmied.

"You be all right. You be all right."

"You must reach inside me," I said.

"I afeared," Susan answered, but she did not refuse.

"Give me your hands." I took them and kissed her fingertips. "Now," I said, "reach in."

Susan nodded yes and, between my tented knees, bent her head to the work; her short pigtails marched in a single row over the top of her head. Quicker than a gasp, I saw ancient helmets with their row of short, stiff horsehair, line drawings of warriors in Mother's *Iliad for Boys*.

"I not want to hurt you." Her voice was a sweet whisper of kindness. Through it ran the silver vein of intelligence.

I told her I couldn't feel. I smiled as I lied. That the feeling was elsewhere.

We screamed together. The screams tore out of us.

She tore the baby out of me.

"Aloft! Aloft!" I shouted, and she held him up by his heels, the purple cord spiraling down.

When he cried, our screams sank to silence, and each of us snuffled back tears. Together we sounded like a quiet surf. Spent.

"You be all right."

And I was.

We named the baby Liberty, but he was listless and did not try to suckle me. Though I had no belief, I bargained with God, offered my life instead, but the universe did not listen. I planned how Susan could have taken my baby with her, had I died. Found sanctuary from the cold as soon as they crossed into freedom. But my baby died.

Susan stayed with me.

That night with the wind howling above the snow-laden roof, I thought of wind in canvas, at sea, and of Ahab, sailing the South Seas. Standing at the rail each morning, Ahab surely would think that each new day the sun might be message-boy with news of a child for his old age. Sleepless, lying on my back, with both hands and groping fingers, I searched the loose flesh of my belly—a husk, my fruit stolen away. I had only disappointment and an empty womb to offer. In his age, with passion, Ahab had given me seed; I in my youth had failed to birth a thriving child.

The only comfort was to turn and curl toward the warmth of Susan's dark body, radiant beside me in the bed. I nestled against her as though she were my husband, mother, sister, shadow, angel.

∽∽∽ ∽∽∽ ∽∽∽

In three days, the snow had still not melted, but the river had begun to break up. Those days! I will not tell of them now. Imagine Christ crucified and not yet risen.

Imagine him *comforted* in the bowels of hell by an angel, who was neither named nor imaged in the Gospels. But such a one was she who was small and dark, her hair standing up in pigtails. We wrapped the baby in soft white lamb's wool and placed him tenderly under the snow not far from the mound where the men had stuck their torch.

When neighbors came across the snowy yard, I quickly hid Susan in the sea chest I had used to transport my goods from Nantucket to Kentucky. These neighbors said that my father's old buggy, driven by my mother, had turned over through the office of a deep rut hidden under the snow; and my mother had frozen before anyone found her. Her skin had turned black from the freezing. Black, like a cinder, one neighbor said, before they could stop her describing.

I heard Susan sob once from inside the green-painted chest, so great was her sympathy for me. For myself, the quick and caring and grieving part of me already frozen beyond feeling, I wanted not my mother so much as that hidden person who could sob for her.

"Take the baby," I wailed, "for he's dead, too!"

The neighbors and I agreed that the ground would surely thaw enough to dig in three days, whereupon someone would come for me, and we would have the funerals.

"You and your news of death, leave me!" I blazed at them. "Take the second corpse and leave me!"

When they had reluctantly gone—I stood before the closed door and watched their progress in the snow—then, as I turned, up from the sea-green trunk rose Susan, like a dark waterspout unwinding grief for me. I watched the flowing of her tears, but my own were unshed. Instead, I felt my thudding heart, a pump whose shaft was sunk in a dry well.

In her gush of tears, Susan said though she had never had a child, she had had a loving mother, left behind in slavery.

"Your mama be black like my mam," she sobbed.

I reached out my hands and arms to enclose and comfort her, while she yet stood in the chest. I envisioned my mother's cheek—leather-slick as well as black. Feeling myself to be a jointed doll, stiff and unnatural in my movement, a wooden thing, I reached for Susan.

"Your mother lives," I said.

My bodice was soaked with her weeping, and though I could not cry, my swollen breasts unloosed my milk, which mingled with her tears.

"We ain't got but one mam," she wailed. "Never be no other."

Standing knee-deep in the chest, like a spent jack-in-the-box, she leaned on me and sobbed—for her mother, not mine.

≈ ≈ ≈

Susan had left her mam for the sake of freedom, but for my sake she lingered, even though the river ice was thawing.

"You stay with 'em?" she asked anxiously, referring to when the neighbors would return.

"No. I'll stay here."

"You don't care for them folks?"

"I don't know them."

"But they be good to you."

"I know."

I got slowly out of bed and held out my hand to her. I took her to the mirror and framed both our faces. She looked solemnly at us.

"I think we look alike," I said.

She did not laugh. "How that?"

"I think we both will go where we will go and do what we will do."

For three days, we prepared for Susan's journey. When the neighbors returned, she folded herself back into the Nantucket sea chest.

≈ ≈ ≈

Like a stone statue I walked away from my cabin with them. Like a juggernaut, that stone car pulled forward relentlessly by the Hindi, I was pulled forward, arms outstretched, by my neighbors. I do not know how my adamantine body was able to bend enough to sit in the wagon.

The world was a vast whiteness barred by the black trunks and limbs of trees. Half a world away, did Ahab stand on the wooden deck, feet firmly planted, watching some mournful scene? Perhaps a sailor, fallen, sewn into canvas, was sinking into the water. I seemed to feel the pitching of the *Pequod*. Did Ahab also mourn? I fastened my gaze on the brown haunches of the two horses, and their color was a relief from the world of alabaster and ebony.

⁊⁊⁊

Beside the coffin of my mother I held the body of my boy in my arms. Susan and I had cocooned him in wool, and the neighbors had added batts of cotton to try to soften him for me, and they had wrapped him again in white crochetwork, and so he seemed larger, as though he had grown. Yet I could feel the stiff, unbending hardness. Slaunchwise, across my bosom, his little fleecy oblong looked the picture of a cloud. His face was covered. They had bound this cloudy shape with string, a little parcel of mortality.

I laid him down beside that bundle of sheet-shroud they said was my mother. I committed him to her care, and them both, their coffin lidded, down into a muddy grave.

Anger that she should have died lay in my left hand and sorrow, for him, in my right. Someone had knitted black mittens for me, and within their muffling wool, over the mud-stained grave, sorrow clasped anger and anger sorrow, with all their might, till they were the same. I would not move from my clenching till they shoveled clean snow over the brown smear.

After that, I looked skyward. I wondered if the universe was punishing me.

⁊⁊⁊

That night, Susan and I stood on the banks of the river, which was moving blackly with its load of white ice floes. The floes were flat on the top and big as the floor of my cabin. Some were as big as a river barge. They all moved downstream in a ghostly procession, separated by jagged black lines where the water was bare. The edges crunched when they touched and hissed when they swept by. In the center of the river, where the current ran swifter, a band of floes moved much more quickly than those near the sides.

The moon was full, which would make the footing easier for Susan, for she must jump from floe to floe to cross the river. We stood alone—hand in hand at the edge of the water, our skin separated by the wool of our mittens. No other eyes, no other soul, would watch her go. Silence, stillness, cold. They chimed about us as one snowy chord.

Susan and I had fashioned her a coat from a quilt, and called it a Joseph's coat, because it was truly of many colors, and I had given her my own knitted cap and, under the patchwork coat, an oat-colored sweater. In a cloth bag, she carried some cooked potatoes and johnnycake and a pair of my mother's shoes. She wore another pair of Mother's shoes, and we had driven nails from the inside so that the soles would prick into the slippery ice and keep her feet from sliding. Around her neck, in a tiny gathered bag, she carried a lock of my baby's hair, for he was born with hair and it was red as flame. I have a lock of it, too, intertwined with one of Susan's, but I do not have a lock of my mother's hair. I'd given Susan my red mittens; I wore the new black ones. We loosened our grip on one another's hand.

When I saw Susan step upon the ice, I bit my lower lip till the blood flowed down my chin and crusted in the cold. Here the riverbank was no higher than a step, as from house to yard. In the moonlight, new snow like sugar glittered atop the sheet of ice lying along the bank. Behind her, in a lengthening path, Susan's footprints indented the sparkling snow. She moved toward the center of the river as calmly as though crossing a broad moonlit road cut through the brush and trees of the wilderness.

When she came to the first black edge, she stepped across the open water as though it were a mere stream. The next floe was smaller, and the next even smaller; they dipped or tilted slightly when she stepped onto them. The spans of open water between them seemed wider and wider, and sometimes she waited for the current to bring the ice rafts closer together. Then she leapt the narrowed fissure and walked on.

It seemed to me Susan was walking on clouds in a black sky. There *were* clouds in the sky, but they stayed far from the moon and did not block her benevolent light. I blessed the moon that held up her lantern for us. Over the water, from seeming cloud to cloud, some silvery, some gray, some white and bright as mirrors for the moon, Susan stepped across the black water.

As the current accelerated and the spaces between floes widened, Susan ran and jumped from raft to raft; my heart hung in the air with her. In the center of the river, the swifter current zipped the ice rafts downstream, with Susan standing on one of them. Her arms fluttered once for balance, twice.

I began to walk downstream and then to run to keep up with the central river as it swept Susan's floe downstream. She never turned to look at me, nor did I want to distract her, and I never called any words of encouragement except as the mind blazes out messages brighter than a lighthouse.

Fly! Fly! as she leapt and landed, the floe she landed on already taking her downstream.

At last the treacherous midsection of river was traversed. She was far from me now—a dark upright using the flatness: flying and landing, running and leaping, from floe to floe. I saw shapes in the ice rafts, mostly like enormous animals, flat, not like a natural swan or bear but flat as a cookie animal or a tin weathervane. Near the other side, approaching a bend, she had to wait for her floe to come close to the bank. Holding the stitch in my side, I continued walking as rapidly downstream as I could till I came to a high but tangled shoreline that thwarted me. Soon the current would sweep Susan's floe beyond my sight. *O, carry her close, carry her close, now,* I prayed to the ice, and I prayed that Susan would not feel herself passing beyond my sight and take the risk of trying to jump ashore when the gulf remained too great. The floe that wheeled her toward the far shore was like the palm of a hand, open and presentational.

Patient Susan! Her ice raft nudged the shore, and she jumped. Even as her shoes landed on the snowy bank, she turned and looked exactly where I stood. Together we lifted our arms, blowing each other a kiss across the water, for we had not kissed on parting, saving it till she should be safe, and trusting the sweet air to be our go-between. And then one shout, though it was small from the distance, from Susan: *Freedom!*

Lucinda Dixon Sullivan

from *It Was the Goodness of the Place*

Lucinda Dixon Sullivan, a very talented Kentucky-born latecomer to the high art of writing good fiction, was once a student of Sena Jeter Naslund's in the Spalding University writing program. In this elegant and sad story of passion, murder, and salvation set in the fully realized towns of Milan and Hickman, you will find an emerging writer who has already written a book of epic dimensions that most veteran writers would envy. Sullivan introduces her two principal protagonists with surcharged sexuality and a confidence and deftness reminiscent of *A Long and Happy Life,* Reynolds Price's 1962 debut novel.

The skirted fenders and tank of Gabe Phillips' new Indian Chief motorcycle were red as apples and glowed like Chinese lacquer. On Gabe's instruction, Lucy Clement hiked her leg up behind the cycle's black leather seat that was big as a saddle and clambered over. Gabe pointed to the fold-out kick start pedal so she wouldn't scrape her leg. But who wouldn't risk it at the chance for a ride? The Indian Chief's suspension was so springy that when Lucy mounted, it bounced under her added weight. The thing not only felt alive, it was frisky as a summer pony.

Lucy wiggled herself into a comfortable position behind Gabe. Her arms slid forward naturally and latched around him at the waist. She seemed to fit precisely, like the shiny chrome cables and linkages that connected parts to the cycle's chassis.

It was a hot, dry, blue-white July day in 1934, and Lucy didn't care if she was wearing her best skirt. Sixteen-year-old Lucy would have this adventure no matter what her daddy said. Before she gave Gabe the go-a-head, she pulled her skirt hem down until it all but covered the brown-and-white saddle oxfords which she had only recently scuffed to her satisfaction. The skirt was made of soft, fern green and gray plaid challis, and Lucy set almost as much store by it as Gabe did by his cycle. Besides, if Lucien Clement found out that she was racing around Milan County glued onto Gabe Phillips' back like "some tacky piece of Boxtown trash," what Lucy was wearing wouldn't make her father's wrath less thunderous or Gabe's company more suitable in her parents' eyes.

Gabe could hardly get started for bragging to Lucy about the Indian Chief's particulars. His cheeks were this minute as shiny-apple red as the motorcycle's paint while he showed off a "mounted shift lever." What Lucy loved was that Gabe loved it. He was eighteen years old and she, after years of studying Gabe, had never seen his face light up like this. For the first time ever, Gabe seemed simply to have no notion of the fact that his right leg was crippled.

They were at a pull-off way out at the end of Rose Hill where Milan started to thin out and blend into the countryside when fields expanded and stretched the houses farther and farther apart until turrets on the old, painted Victorian homes pulled away from their foundations and became silos on the horizon, near the enlarging barns.

Lucy's stomach hitched when all Gabe's noisy throttling and choking of the engine gave way to motion. But the very next minute they glided off the shoulder and headed down the road, then Lucy eased. Gabe would keep her safe. She could feel his back muscles flex against her chest. He leaned forward into the wind against them and she held tight, bending the reed of herself to the whistling reed of him.

They were headed toward the river gorge. The road was narrow but newly paved, one of the few county roads that wasn't a simple strip of oiled gravel. Lucy looked away to her right.

Already there was a backdrop of faraway palisades behind the unrolling fields. Gabe speeded up, gaining on the open country. The wind scrubbed against them hard but was no match for their red engine. It was exhilarating. Her red hair was liquid like the engine. Lucy laughed, head back, and caught cup after cup of warm summer in her mouth and swallowed, spitting out her curls. She and Gabe were flying. The trees were all one stripe of green against a wall of rock.

Without thinking more, Lucy brought an arm back and unbuttoned her blouse one-handed.

She untucked Gabe's shirt tail and raised his shirt as high as she was able. Lucy leaned forward and reclaimed her earlier hold, daringly atingle, skin to skin, brushing through the air. Gabe briefly pressed a hand on her re-locked fist, then they went faster still. Yes, oh yes oh yes. This was what she wanted. She and Gabe would fly and her life would be like this.

Michael Dorris

"The New York Hat"

In 1997 Michael Dorris ended his too-short life alone in a motel room in New Hampshire, estranged from his wife and accused of indiscretions with his children. It was a sad conclusion for the talented writer, born in Louisville in 1945 and reared by his devoted mother and aunt. He graduated from St. Xavier High School in 1963, earned a degree in classical languages from Georgetown University in Washington, D.C., and studied anthropology at Yale in order to research his American Indian ancestors on his father's side. While in Alaska in 1971, he was able to adopt an Indian boy—one of the first adoptions by a single male on record. Because of his mother's prenatal consumption of alcohol, the boy suffered from fetal alcohol syndrome. In 1989 Dorris wrote *The Broken Cord,* a prizewinning account of his son's problems with the disease. He married the author Louise Erdrich in 1981, and the couple coauthored several books. His works include a collection of short stories, *Working Men* (1993), and *Paper Trail* (1994), a collection of essays that includes "The New York Hat," about a happier time in his life.

My maternal grandmother was a small, heavy woman, born in Henderson, Kentucky, who wore her gray hair coiled in a bun at the base of her neck and had fierce hazel eyes and thick black brows behind the lenses of her rimless glasses. She was queen of our house, demanding no less than total respect from the rest of the world. If any visitor was so foolish as to come to call without bringing some small token of homage for her—a cutting from a special flowering plant, a lace handkerchief, a straw fan—she refused to emerge from her bedroom. The rest of us made small talk with the offending guest, hoping that the slam of dresser drawers, the loud play of a radio, the prolonged sighs broadcast through the closed door, would go unnoticed.

My grandmother had survived all but one of her eleven brothers and sisters and expected that now, in her late seventies, she was owed celebration, especially on formal occasions. Every Easter, my Aunt Marion's friend Mrs. Shreck constructed from flour and icing a large lamb reclining in a field of spiky green meringue. With wool of shaved coconut, raisin eyes, a smiling maraschino mouth, and—the most realistic touch—a pink strawberry cake interior, the lamb was ceremoniously displayed in the center of the dining room table.

"It's too pretty to cut," my grandmother annually pronounced, and so the lamb remained, growing stale and stiff, then fragile, as we went about our lives around it. The weather warmed and the grass softened. Humidity caused the coconut to swell and drop like an aura. Finally, sometime around Decoration Day, gravity would prevail and, with an audible thud, the creature's head would fall off.

My grandmother expected and received an azalea for the 4th of July, a new dress for her birthday, lily of the valley scent in commemoration of her wedding anniversary, and cash on Thanksgiving, but Christmas was the crowning feast, for on Christmas my Aunt Ginny took the train from New York and brought with her, among other things, a gift for my grandmother from Bonwit Teller.

෨ඬ෨ඬ෨ඬ

I knew Aunt Ginny's story by heart: In 1945, at the end of her third decade and shortly before I was born, my mother's eldest sister, Virginia, took the train from Louisville to New York on a vacation with her friend, Linda Lee. They ate at automats in order to have enough money to stay at the Algonquin, locale of the round table they'd heard about on the radio. Out of curiosity they read the want ads in the *Times,* where Linda's eye was caught one day by "Reputable Theatrical Firm Needs Secretaries." Aunt Ginny had been a slave to the Louisville Little Theater for years, a star in its productions, a constant presence backstage, and so when Linda read her the ad she cried, "It's fate!" and went to be interviewed.

"I was so enthusiastic," she always added when reporting this part of the tale. "I told them 'I love the theater, I love it!' Only after they'd hired me did the boss remember to ask, 'Can you type?'"

Aunt Ginny intended to work a week, as a lark, at the United Booking Company, which scheduled Broadway shows for out-of-town performances, but from her first day she was in her element. She found an apartment in a five-story walk-up on Jones Street in Greenwich Village. To pay the rent, she put in a forty-hour week plus weekends and holidays and spent every spare minute at the theater, standing or seated in the highest balcony.

After World War II, business on Broadway boomed. The demand for tickets exceeded the span of a normal working day, so Aunt Ginny started moonlighting in theaters and was there when *South Pacific* hit big and the steady mail order stream became a flood. Each night she'd watch the show from behind the exit curtains; in three and a half years, she never missed her favorite number, "There Is Nothing Like a Dame." But when, around the same time, she met James Michener at a party, she refused his offer of a drink. Enzio Pinza he wasn't.

Over the years, Aunt Ginny gained a reputation as someone who knew the intricacies of selling blocks of seats to parties and groups. She knew the view of the stage from every seat, was familiar with the idiosyncrasies of each playhouse, and was mesmerizing—equally to the president of a Hadassah in New Jersey and to me, sitting at her feet in our living room—with her synopses spanning a seasonful of the shows she had seen or a new outline she had just read. She had leaped when an executive assistant position opened with the Shubert Organization.

"They wanted a man to handle it," she always added. "Well, P.S., I got the job. From then on it was a whole different ball game. I had responsibility, handled millions of dollars' worth of business. And I got a raise, too."

"How much?" I once asked her.

"Oh, honey, I don't know! The thing is, I didn't care." Aunt Ginny caught her breath, struck all over again by the perks. "I'd have worked for nothing because I got free tickets."

Then she paused. "There was a time I couldn't get along financially, so I thought I'd join the ushers' union. I had no fear of anything." She raised her fist, a familiar gesture. "I walked New York at any hour. But then I found out I'd have to start in second balcony, as an usher I mean." She shook her head, reflecting. "I couldn't do it. I'm scared to death of steps."

When Aunt Ginny talked about her employers at the Shubert Organization, they became real, characters in the drama of her life. I could see Mr. Lee, a small-boned gentleman in a dapper dark suit and brown derby, his hair blacked and face heavily made up to look tan. "He loved the theater, worshipped the stars. He and I were kindred spirits!"

In her work, which was on the order of a daily devotion, Aunt Ginny read scripts, argued with producers, arranged rehearsal space, saw every show at least once, and did her best to keep them playing through her monomaniacal attention to sales. She met and sparred with everyone from production consultant Eleanor Roosevelt (*Sunrise at Campobello*) to star Rosalind Russell (*Wonderful Town*).

She moved uptown, changed buildings as each was torn down or went co-op. She had strong, enduring friendships, but no time for romance, unless one counted her triumphant affairs with New York or the "other town" in her life, Paris, whose streets she walked on five vacation visits—with tears of happiness streaming down her cheeks.

ᘓᘓ ᘓᘓ ᘓᘓ

By the time Aunt Ginny arrived on the train for her annual visit from New York, the box of gifts from my father's mother was under the tree. A red wool stocking with white piping sewed by my seamstress mother hung from the mantel of the fake fireplace, officially there for the cheer and pleasure of our dog, Jerry. Nothing was out of place, but for some reason on the Christmas I was fourteen I didn't take any permanence for granted. I watched each member of my family with the appreciation of distance, with the kind of homesickness one anticipates before ever leaving home. In the warm room flickering with colored lights from the tree, we gathered after dinner to sit around my grandmother's chair. We knew each other so well that every routine was practiced, a ritual, casually affectionate, and I caught a glimpse of that fragile, fleeting construction of blood and intersecting time, of family.

As the youngest member, I was given my present first—much more than what I'd hoped for: a secondhand office typewriter, tall and shiny black, its alphabet a careful, precise pica on yellowing white keys. Everyone was delighted at my surprise, took their thanks proudly. One by one, my mother and aunts opened their gifts—powders and scarves and rose sachets and Santa Claus earrings—each exclaiming that she had received exactly what she wanted.

My grandmother was last and she waited, patient and appraising, pretending that she had forgotten that her turn had not yet come. There was a moment of silent anticipation. Aunt Ginny left the room and then returned bearing the large violet-strewn container she had carried all the way from New York. We had pooled our Christmas funds and had heard described what was inside, but we hadn't actually seen it.

I remember that a flush spread along my grandmother's neck as she busied herself with layers of tissue paper, taking her time at unwrapping. Suddenly her hands froze, then lifted from the box a hat of purple crushed velvet. Around its border, at intervals, were pure white feathers arranged as half-wings. It was a hat from outer space, a hat of the imagination, larger than life—a hat so different from anything we had ever seen that we could only marvel.

My grandmother recovered first.

"Oh, my," she said. "My stars." She straightened her shoulders, lifted her chin, kept her lips steady. Raising both hands, their skin fine and crossed with tiny wrinkles, she set the hat firmly on her head. Then, expertly aiming its matching pin, she fixed it in place and arranged the flowered net veil about her face. She posed, a lady about town, a dowager, for a moment the complete collection of all her aspirations. Her eyes, however, were masked. Perhaps they watched for our reaction, or perhaps, just for that one instant, they were closed.

Linda Bruckheimer

from *Dreaming Southern*

Americans have been going west since the first Europeans landed on the East Coast and began looking for a better life beyond the sunset. Until the 1890s, when the frontier was officially closed, there was always a place to go. For a long time, Kentucky was the West; then it filled up. Even Daniel Boone said it was getting too crowded for him and moved to Missouri, when that was the frontier. In the twentieth century, the West still beckoned. When movies got big and Hollywood became the movie capital of the world, people—young people, especially—went west to become glamorous, famous, and rich. The luster of the Golden West may have dulled a bit with the dusking of the twentieth century, but it is still there; and, with her husband, Roy, beckoning from afar, Lila Mae Wooten has loaded up her four children in a 1953 Packard and started the epical trek across the land, the way it used to be before interstates and fast food chains. Linda Bruckheimer, a native Kentuckian who now lives part-time in Kentucky and part-time in Los Angeles, where her husband, Jerry Bruckheimer, produces blockbuster films, has written a road trip novel, *Dreaming Southern* (1999), that takes us not only to California but also back in time. This is a comic trip with serious overtones that eventually gets to California. Linda Bruckheimer's delightful novel will let you take a trip west and stay home at the same time.

Usually Lila Mae Wooten had to scream bloody murder before her kids would pay any attention to her at all. But she was desperately trying to turn over a new leaf, so she pushed the accelerator of the swamp-green 1953 Packard to the floor and smiled at them in the rearview mirror.

"Well, here it comes, kids—the Kentucky state line!" She had already told them five or six times that the state line was coming up very soon, but they still hadn't given her the type of response she had hoped for.

"Take a look at them tobacco fields and that blue grass . . ." she continued. "It might be years and years before you see 'em again, if ever—*if ever*." Lila Mae spoke very dramatically, arching her crescent eyebrows and sighing deeply. She was wearing a print housedress and simulated pearls, and her hair had just been tinted Polynesian Spice. Supposedly, it was the exact same color that Rita Hayworth used, but Lila Mae was afraid it was way too loud. "Come on, kids, it ain't right to just drive across like we don't give a hoot. . . ."

Determined to snag their attention come hell or high water, she said, "I swear there's an awful noise comin' from the trailer. Maybe I should pull over right before we cross the state line and double check." When that didn't work, she took a quick peek in the rearview mirror to see exactly what type of situation she was dealing with, then started to sing: "Oh, the sun shines bright on my old Kentucky home!"

Finally, Becky Jean stopped flipping the pages of her *Modern Screen* magazine and huffed, "We *heard* you the first time. What do you expect us to do, bawl our eyes out?" A pretty girl and the eldest of Lila Mae's four children, she had a heart-shaped, Miss America face and a rosebud mouth that was usually in one stage or another of smirk. Her caramel hair—flecked with gold and swirling around her shoulders—was styled in a perfect pageboy fluff, and she was wearing pink velveteen pedal pushers and ballerina flats. Looped around her wrist was a sterling-silver Speidel ID bracelet engraved: TO BECKY JEAN, LOVE YA, GLEN.

"Besides," Becky Jean said in a nonchalant drawl, "what's the big deal about a stupid old sign?"

"What's the *big deal?*" Lila Mae craned her neck and gawked into the backseat. "If this ain't your idea of a big deal, leaving the state you grew up in—probably *forever*—then I don't know what is. I swanee!" No wonder I have to exaggerate everything, Lila Mae thought, there's no way to get through to them kids normally.

"You act like we're moving to Mars or something," Becky Jean griped. Naturally, her mother, the queen of dramatic rigamaroles, wanted to depart Kentucky in a blaze of ceremonies and turmoil. The best thing to do when she was in a tizzy, which was fifty percent of the time, was to simply give her the cold shoulder. Shutting the *Modern Screen,* Becky Jean bent down and opened her cosmetics case, where she kept perfumes and dusting powders, two novels, half a dozen movie magazines, Tigress by Fabergé, and Can Can Dancer Red, a newly purchased lipstick the color of communion wine. Lila Mae said she'd better not catch Becky Jean wearing the lipstick unless she wanted to be taken for a brazen hussy, and she didn't want her daughter to wear the perfume, either, since she thought it would attract men like flies.

Locating the *Photoplay* with Natalie Wood on the cover, Becky Jean straightened up, made a sassy puff of a noise, and picked up where she left off. "What do you expect, anyway? Marching bands with tubas and trombones? Sheet cakes, confetti, tearful mourners?"

"Mouth off all ya want, Miss Smarty Pants." Lila Mae gave her a mournful warning. "Someday when I'm gone, you'll be sorry you didn't pay more attention to your heritage."

When they were mere yards from the state line, Lila Mae stopped the car, then took a deep breath and stared sadly at the crystal-white clouds and neon-blue sky. A chestnut thoroughbred galloped across a green meadow and a trio of Kentucky cardinals flitted past the last seasonal vestiges of crape myrtle. Swagged over the gently rolling hills of a horse farm were low, billowy vapors of Ohio Valley fog. Lila Mae gazed at the scene as if she'd never see another horse or bird or swatch of fog for the rest of her life.

Just when she started to get all choked up, she thought about Loretta Nutt, a woman who'd lost not only her beloved husband but all of her limbs in a horrible train wreck. Even with all that going against her, the woman had managed to raise six kids, worked full time in a dime store, and had even written an entire novel with a pencil in between her teeth! Lila Mae didn't know Mrs. Nutt personally, but she had read all about her in *Reader's Digest*. So, if a handicapped person could manage all that, then surely, Lila Mae thought to herself, she could handle a car trip across country with a few high-strung, smart-alecky kids.

Just thinking about the amazing woman gave Lila Mae a sudden gust of optimism. Jabbing the accelerator, she glanced in the mirror to see if she looked as good as she felt; then she tooted the horn several times and began to sing, her voice bellowing and vibrating like Ethel Merman's and her fist whipping the air like a spirited bandleader's. "Cal-i-fooorn-ia, heeere we come, riiiight back where we started from. . . ."

Ralph Cotton

from *While Angels Dance*

Ralph Cotton, a native of Louisville and the author of a dozen and more novels about the Old West, takes Jeston Nash, the hero of his trilogy of Western novels, through a series of fast-action adventures. This is the original Old West of Missouri, Kansas, Nebraska, Wyoming, and Texas, and the time is the lawless era between 1860 and 1900. The Civil War is still raging, and Jeston is a Kentuckian who kills a Union soldier over a horse trade in Louisville and, like a latter-day Huck Finn, heads west to find safety, a new identity, and a new life. Once in Missouri, he hooks up with his Aunt Zerelda and her two sons, Frank and Jesse James. Now unfettered by "civilization," his dark passions are unleashed, and he descends into his own heart of darkness. When you finish a Ralph Cotton Western, you know you've read a great story told by a master storyteller. If it's action with a Western accent you want, along with good craftsmanship, depth, and wisdom, you can't do better than Ralph Cotton. Over and over, Cotton proves that he is no mere "Western" writer; he is a very good writer who writes great Westerns. This is how Jeston introduces himself in 1994 in *While Angels Dance,* the first novel of the trilogy.

When I first took up with my cousins, Jesse and Frank, and the Youngers, the Millers, and that bunch, I was on the run same as them. We were all young, full of spit and fire back then; but they'd thrown in with Quantrill's guerrilla forces and already learned to slip around by the skin of their necks, while I still worked with Pa, tending the fields and handling horses. By the time we met up, they were miles ahead of me when it came to living on the run.

Riding under a black flag had taught them some hard lessons. Getting caught meant death, stretching rope with their toes pointing to the ground—no trial, no nothing. It was a plain and simple fact; knowing it kept them sharp eyed and lean.

Myself, I'd had the misfortune of killing a Yankee soldier over a horse swap, and though the killing was self-defense, I didn't stick around to explain. Since Kentucky was a neutral state, that is, being kicked back and forth between Sherman's Yankees and Hunt Morgan's rebel forces, you could stumble into more trouble in two minutes than you could crawl out of in a hundred years.

So I lit out of Kentucky late at night on a freight train in the dead of winter, with a broken jaw, four copper pennies, and a wrinkled up letter in the pocket of Pa's old mackinaw. Had it not been for killing that soldier, I would've played out my life helping Pa turn forty acres of dark earth into corn and tobacco. I would have done so proudly, but it just wasn't meant to be.

I never knew that young soldier's name or much else about him. He was a big ole Irish boy, bad tempered and dumb as a stump. The truth is, I had cheated him a little on the price, but that's just horse trading. It was nothing worth killing or dying over, and I knew it. When I saw he wasn't happy with the trade, I even gave him back his money and the receipt for his horse just to avoid trouble. But then as I turned to walk away, all of a sudden he jumped me from behind.

There was just the two of us in that livery stable, and he wasn't fighting like a man out to settle a dispute. I knew right off that he meant to kill me, and he would have . . .

But the next thing I knew, a woman screamed at the sight of me staggering out covered with blood, and my pa came running, looped my arm across his shoulder, and pulled me into an alley beside the mercantile building.

"Listen to me," he'd said, helping me out of my bloody coat and into his warm mackinaw. "It don't matter where you go . . . just go! If they catch you, they'll hang you." He took off his slouch hat and shoved it down on my head.

I needed to think, but my thoughts were addled. All I could picture was a blue uniform and hard knuckles pounding my face. I remembered wrapping my hands around a pick handle somehow, and to this day I recall the sound of it slicing through the air as I swung it again and again.

From around the corner of the alley, voices split the darkness, and I heard horses jolt noisily to a halt near the livery stable. "Who did this?" I heard a soldier yell in rage. "Where is he?"

"They're coming," Pa said. Steam gushed in his breath like smoke from a bellows, "Get out of here!"

"My horses!" I said, and my jaw made a sound like rocks crunching together. The pain nearly blinded me.

Pa shoved me away that night with tears in his eyes. "Damn them horses, that's what got you in this mess," I heard him say, as boots pounded across wooden planks, and I took off through the alley out of town.

I glanced back once, saw Pa slip into my blood-splattered coat, and I wondered why he did it. It was only when I'd reached the woods outside of town and heard the volley of rifles that I realized Pa had given his life to save me.

⧼⧽ ⧼⧽ ⧼⧽

The letter in Pa's mackinaw was from my Aunt Zerelda Samuel, Frank's and Jesse's mother, and the only kin who'd kept in touch since Ma's death. She'd

Ralph Cotton   489

written to Pa to tell him they'd moved to Nebraska Territory bcause of the war. All I could think of that night was to find my kinfolk as quickly as I could. I needed help, my jaw being broken, and I needed a place to settle in and put the violence behind me. I knew nothing else to do but hop trains, sleep in haylofts, and suck eggs when I could I steal a few here and there.

I must've been a sorry sight the day I showed up in the Samuels' front yard, but Aunt Zerelda, or "Ma Samuel" as she asked to be called, took me in and cared for me like I was one of her own. "Look here," she said to Doc Samuel, after I'd cleaned up and gotten some hot stew in my belly, "he looks enough like Jesse to be his brother."

Old Doc, Jesse's and Frank's stepfather, was a good hand at mending and healing, and as soon as I got my strength back and rested a couple of days he went to work, cutting, cracking and realigning my face. When he'd finished, he carved a small chunk of wood, fitted it between my teeth to hold my jaws slightly open, and tied a strong sling round my face from under my chin to the top of my head. I went three weeks bound that way, but it was worth it. Except for a lump of crooked bone that still pains me in cold weather, old Doc did a fine job repairing my jaw.

"It ain't perfect," he'd said, the day he removed the sling. I spit out the chunk of wood and worked in my jaw carefully. Doc tipped my head back, studying my face through his spectacles, "But you'll soon be able to chew, cuss, and spit tobacco. Can't ask for more'n that, can ya?"

"Reckon not," I'd said, touching my jaw carefully while examining it in a hand-held shaving mirror. I glanced up at Doc and managed a stiff grin.

Living on stew, tea, and molasses until I could bite down on something solid, I lay around like a sore cat for another five or six weeks before I ever met my cousins. With the war pressing hard on the Southern Regulars, guerrilla forces shouldered more and more of the fighting. Quantrill's men were so heavily pressed along the border that Jesse and Frank only slipped home now and then.

I could tell it troubled Ma Samuel, her boys off fighting and she and old Doe forced off their land in Missouri because of the evacuation order, Order Eleven. They called Order Eleven "The Devil's Prayer," for it ran decent folk out of Cass, Bates, and Jackson counties, and left their homes and holdings at the mercy of red-legs, Yankees, and thugs. But the Samuels were a strong family, closely knit. And hard pressed as they were, they never whimpered; they hung on and made do.

I have a soft spot a mile wide when it comes to my kin. I always did. So no matter what's said of the James brothers, in their defense, they were just what times turned them into—no better, no worse. True, they could be cruel as a killing frost outside our own circle, but to our own kind, our brothers-in-arms, Frank and Jesse James were the kind of friends you'd willingly die for, because you knew they would do the same for you without batting an eye. And that's the long and short of it.

‹∞› ‹∞› ‹∞›

Until news of my being at the Samuel farm reached Jesse and Frank through the grapevine, they had probably forgotten they had a cousin over in Kentucky. When they heard of my presence they approached me cautiously. I didn't know till Frank told me about it months later: they'd watched the house for days, leery of a trap. When they did venture in, it was sudden and silent.

I'd been drawing a fresh bucket of water from the well; the only sound in the stillness of morning was the squeaking crank handle and the clucking of chickens scratching in the dirt. Then all at once behind me, a horse nickered low, and the single heavy thud of a hoof jarred the ground. I froze, felt the skin ripple on my neck, and wondered in that split second how the hell a rider could've slipped in without them chickens raising a fuss.

"Let me give you a hand, Cousin," said a voice at my shoulder, and I spun around facing Frank James. He stood so close I could see the tiny veins in his eyes.

Frank could lock on to your eyes like a coiled viper, and though I learned to overcome it in time, that day at the well, off guard, I just stood there staring, dumbfounded by the sudden appearance of this stranger with a friendly smile and a voice like gravel wrapped in silk. And behind him . . . less than fifteen feet . . . not one rider . . . but six! They'd slipped in as quiet as smoke, and sat there atop their horses, looking hard eyed and evil.

There was not enough room to look down between Frank and me, but had I been able to, as I learned seconds later, I would have seen his gun poised an inch from my heart. "You seem a little tense, Cousin," Frank said. He reached past me and hefted the bucket in his left hand without taking his eyes from mine. "They're not working you too hard here, are they?" When he stepped back with the water bucket, I saw the brass framed Colt come down from my chest.

I couldn't answer; I just stared back and forth between Frank and the others, truly stunned. Either I'd gone stone deaf, or this bunch had just materialized out of the morning mist.

The riders sat watching me with eyes like gun sights; nothing stirred but their breath in the chilled air. Then behind me, once again I heard a hoof thud against the ground, and without turning from Frank and the others, I knew that someone else had crept in. Knowing it, I felt like a lapdog stalked by a pack of timberwolves. Apparently this bunch could slip around as they pleased.

Frank smiled as his pistol disappeared beneath his frock coat. "Come around here, Jesse," he said. "Meet our cousin."

"So you're Jeston Nash," said a quiet voice, and I watched Jesse circle the well and rein his bay gelding between me and the others. His eyes shifted about the yard as he spoke. Unlike Frank who could stare in your eyes till your nose bled, I noticed Jesse couldn't keep his eyes still for a second. His eyes searched everything around him, pinned everything in its place, and checked back like a schoolmaster to see what'd changed. "I hear you've been hiding out here a while," he said.

I hadn't thought of my being there as "hiding out," but that's what I was doing. Once that woman saw Pa's body, she had to say it wasn't he who killed the soldier; and that being the case, I was on the run and hiding out, no different than Jesse, Frank, and these others. I just hadn't heard it put that way, and it took a second of consideration before I answered. "I reckon so."

Jesse leaned down slightly and stared me straight in the eyes. I noted our striking resemblance and wondered for a second if one of our fathers hadn't jumped the fence some years back. "That makes you an outlaw . . . don't it?" He reached down a gloved hand and smiled. I glanced at the others; they sat silent as stone. Beside me, Frank nodded his head as if settling something of great importance.

"I reckon it does," I said, reaching my hand to Jesse's.

Behind him, the others seemed to ease down in their saddles. Jesse saw how closely I watched them, and he nodded toward them over his shoulder. "They're kind of a loud bunch, ain't they?" His smile widened.

"Yeah," I said, feeling a little red-faced. Frank reached over and slapped me on the back, and in a second we all laughed like fools.

It might seem strange that after taking the precautions of watching the house and checking me out before making their presence known, once they rode in, looked me in the eye and shook my hand, they took me at face value, no questions asked.

But that's how it was in them days of bitter madness during the great civil conflict. You learned to size a feller real quick. If he was a friend, you could tell it in his eyes; and if he shook your hand you could tell if he meant it. I reckon Jesse and Frank must've seen all they needed to know about me that day by the well. I was young, inexperienced, and without a friend in the world; but I was blood kin, at a time when being kin meant everything.

And I learned a lot about Jesse that day by shaking his hand. Jesse's handshake had been strong, but cautious, as if any second his hand might disappear, leaving you holding nothing but air. Over the years I'd come to learn that's how it was with Jesse; his handshake fit him from the ground up.

Gayl Jones

from *Mosquito*

The elusive, reclusive, and highly praised author Gayl Jones was born in 1949 in Lexington, the daughter of a cook and a housewife. She attended Connecticut College and earned a Ph.D. at Brown University; she then taught at the University of Michigan, which she left to move with her new husband, Bob Higgins, to Paris, where they lived for some ten years. In 1988 they moved to her hometown, where her husband's violent nature and erratic demands sometimes caused him to clash with the police. On February 20, 1998, they barricaded themselves in their home against police who were trying to serve Higgins with an arrest warrant on a Michigan weapons charge. The house began to fill with natural gas, in an apparent suicide attempt, and the police burst in as Higgins cut his own throat; he died later that night. Jones was taken to a mental hospital and placed under a suicide watch.

In the 1970s Gayl Jones published two novels and a short story collection that established her as a bold, new voice in contemporary fiction. Her stories often dealt with the degrading sexual relations between sometimes violent black men and their submissive women.

Corregidora (1975) is about a blues singer consumed by her hatred of the slave owner who fathered both her grandmother and her mother. In a review in the *Courier-Journal,* John Filiatreau called the novel "what may well be the finest and most unflinchingly honest book ever written about black men and women, their history and their souls." Her second novel, *Eva's Man* (1976), is the story of a prostitute whose own sexual odyssey is characterized by fear, self-loathing, and loneliness and who, in an act of desperation, kills her latest lover. *The Healing* (1998), her third novel, is told by a faith healer who travels from town to town, commenting on everything from Clark Gable movies to the tools of the cosmetology trade. *Mosquito,* published in 1999, is about Sojourner Nadine Jane Johnson, also known as Mosquito, who makes her living as a truck driver. The story is set in a Texas border town, where Mosquito gets involved in "the new underground railroad," which provides sanctuary for Mexican immigrants. She develops a romance with Ray, a nonviolent revolutionary and philosopher. The conclusion to the novel is a good example of the energy and power of Jones's writing.

People thinks that I am Mrs. Mendoza. Ray and I encourages the thought and likes to tease peoples. Everybody that comes in the restaurant I praises Ray to them and tells them he's like a Aztec god, and he's always telling peoples I'm like a African goddess. I has seen photographs of some African goddesses and they does kinda resemble me, or I should say I kinda resembles them. I kinda likes the fact that they is goddesses that I resembles. However, I am still a Perfectability Baptist. All my peoples is Baptists except them who is Catholics, and the ones who ain't Catholics is African Methodist Episcopals and there is a few Witnesses for Jehovah amongst us, and they says that some of us ancestors was Mohammedans and us mighta even had some Buddhists. My uncle Buddy Johnson, rumor has it, were the first amongst us to become a Perfectability Baptist. We have even added Gladys Knight Pipism to the church. Originally Perfectability Baptism combined only Southern Baptism, Holler Roller Theology, Scientific Christianity, and African Methodist Episcopalism.

"Do not submit to your own ignorance"; the motto of the Daughters of Nzingha is actually derived from a speech given by Malcolm X. That is what is different about the Daughters of Nzingha. They don't just include wisdom derived from Afro-womanhood but also includes Afro-manhood wisdom books in they archives, books which I has in my memory. I first heard that quoted by the Daughters of Nzingha, though, in a newsletter as one of the requirements for being an archives keeper. To tell you the truth, I am an archives keeper and I have been submitting to my own ignorance since preschool. I still submits to my own ignorance unless I'm in the presence of someone who refuses to allow me to submit to my own ignorance. I try not to submit to other people's ignorance, but I have certainly been known to submit to my own ignorance. Of course, once I knows it for the ignorance it is, I stops submitting to it. Perhaps that is why they allows me to be a archives keeper.

Some members of the Perfectability Baptist Church are Negroes, others is colored people, others is blacks (with a small *b*), others is Blacks (with a big *b*), others is Afro-Americans, others is African-Americans (hyphenated), others is African Americans (unhyphenated), others is Just Plain Americans, others is New World Africans, others is Descendants of the Victims of the African Diaspora Holocaust, others is Multiracialists, others is Multiethnics, others is Sweeter the Juice Multiracial Multiethnics (these are people like myself who have other races and ethnic groups, like Mexicans, Irish, Greeks, and Italians in they ancestry but who resemble pure African gods and goddesses), others is Cosmopolitan Neo-Africans, others is African-Internationalists, others is African Memphians from the Republic of New Africa Memphis and drapes theyselves in the Africa Memphis flags, 'cause when I give them some of my Republic of Texas literature that talked about gringos freeing theyselves from imperial Mexico they decided to form they own Independent African Republic in Memphis, not the whole state but just they own city, though like the Texans they still considers theyselves to be Americans but not citizens of the "corporate United States."

There is some members of the Perfectability Baptist Church, though, who don't believe that we should keep Gladys Knight Pipism as part of the official church doctrine. They don't want people to think that we are the William Faulkner Stereotypical Colored Peoples Southern Baptist Church. They don't want people to think that we're silly, even if they do believe in Keep on keeping on. Cayenne Goodling wanted us to add some of the doctrines of the Church of Elvis, but we ain't that silly. There is some members of the church, myself included, that believes we should add to us church doctrine Mama Didn't Raise No Foolism. Since I don't have any children of my own, they have made me a Official Mama of the Perfectability Baptist Church, which ain't the same as a matriarch, 'cause they is also Official Papas of the Church. I ain't allowed to tell other peoples children Mama Didn't Raise No Fool, though. We is modernists and you can't just be telling other people's childrens they ain't been raised to be a fool.

Ain't James Brown have a song say "Papa Don't Raise No Fool"? I think that you can acknowledge that they is a subtle difference to Mama didn't raise no fool and Papa don't raise no fool. When peoples talks about the difference between masculine and feminine languages, I thinks you can see the difference in saying Mama didn't raise no fool and Papa don't raise no fool. Papa don't raise no fool is the language of command. Mamas just tells they children that they didn't raise no fool. I am glad they have named me one of the Official Mamas of the Church and not the Official Fool.

The church still don't allow no women preachers but they lets us along with the mens who ain't official preachers to assume the role of griots in our various African Diaspora communities. I am the official griot to the small New World African community of Cuba, New Mexico. We might tell warrior stories or culture stories or children's stories or whatever stories we wants to tell. We are not required just to tell stories that have to do with Perfectability Baptist theology, though most of us have at least got to mention the Perfectability Baptist Church. We is also required to be as much listeners as we is storytellers. And if peoples asks us questions while we is telling stories, we's got to answer them questions. If we prefers not to answer them questions or ain't got no answers for them questions, then we has got to say so and include it in us stories. As storytellers we has got to know that the listener is as important to the story as the storyteller. As for the other Ray being a Aztec god and me being a African goddess and us being married, we just gets playful with the peoples. I uses my name Nadine for the restaurant name and the other Ray uses his whole name, so the restaurant's name is Nadine and Ray Mendoza's. That is why the peoples thinks that I'm Mrs. Nadine Mendoza when my true name is who I am.

Most people still calls me Mosquito, and they don't know my full name. You know a lot of people don't even know what your full name is, either Ray, even the other Ray, and I had to tell him your full name is Ray Guerrero Sacerdote Ku'oko'a-Maikai. I know it is because you have the same name as your aunt Electra, whose story I know as well as my own because of all the documents that Amanda Ku'oko'a-Maikai Mariner Wordlaw has sent me to read aloud and keep them in my memory. I have in my memory all the mystical and prophetic writings of your aunt Electra and all of her other writings and all the documents. I have also in my memory all of the documents of the Spiritual Mother project. I has got so many auditory memory obligations: to you and your people, to Monkey Bread and the Daughters of Nzingha, and even to being an Official Mama of the Perfectability Baptist Church. I gots to keep the official doctrine of Mama and Papa Didn't and Don't Raise No Fool in my auditory memory to keep us childrens from becoming fools and to help them that is fools already, as well as all the stories and histories of everybody of color who sends they stories and histories to the Daughters of Nzingha archives, and to be able to distinguish between the stories that is wisdom stories and them that is trickster stories, and also to be able to think deep. Monkey Bread refers to me as the worthy listener when she is not calling me Nadine. Even though I am a griot for the Perfectability Baptists, Monkey Bread still prefers to refer to me as a listener.

I know how people of color is about stories, though. If the African traditional story about wisdom and its many variations can come all the way from Africa to America and be told to me by my Papa Didn't Raise No Fool Neither Daddy, who has as much Mexican in him as African, and my mama, whose maternal grandmother looks just like Miguelita, the crazy gringa I told you about but my maternal great-grandmother was sane and "went for black," as my mama says, with a sane mind, can tell me stories of an uncle Bud and aunt Blossom, escaped slaves from slavery times, and stories about my granny Jane, who looked just like a African and who kept on keeping on and who kinda remind me of Kate Hickman in one of my favorite books I reads and about John Free who fought in the Civil War and also wrote letters for colored soldiers and Big Warrior the Seminole African who fought with the Seminoles in Florida and about Africans of the warrior class; this letter would be too long if I tells you their story, including all the other stories in my auditory memory—not the same Uncle Bud as the Uncle Bud World War II Uncle Bud but Aunt Blossom's Uncle Bud of slavery times, but Mama says they is many Buds and Blossoms in us family—then I knows that in your African-Mexican village you can hear tales about a Mrs. Nadine Mendoza of Cuba, New Mexico, so I wants you to know the truth of the story, for the purposes of the revolution, you know what I mean, Ray, even though I know that you more than anybody knows me for who I really am.
Sojourner Nadine Jane Nzingha Johnson

George Ella Lyon

from *Borrowed Children*

Most people think of George Ella Lyon as an author of children's books. Indeed, she is, but she's much more. She's a poet, a teacher, a playwright, and an author of books for readers of all ages. Hailing from Harlan County, she holds degrees from Centre College, the University of Arkansas, and Indiana University, where she wrote her dissertation on Virginia Woolf. She has taught at the University of Kentucky, Transylvania University, Centre College, and Radford University. She has taught at the Appalachian Writers Workshop in Hindman for many years. Her poetry collections include *Mountain* (1983) and *Catalpa* (1993). Her children's books include *Father Time and the Day Boxes* (1985), *Come a Tide* (1990), and *Mama Is a Miner* (1994). Her *Borrowed Children* (1988) is a novel for young adults, and *With a Hammer for My Heart* (1997) is a novel for adults. She credits her mountain background with having given her the gifts, especially the penchant for storytelling, to be a writer. In an interview published in the *Kentucky Review* in 2000, she said that in the mountains "you ask directions, you get a story." There are now two writers in the Lyon family. In 2004 her husband, Steve Lyon, a musician and composer, published *The Gift Moves,* an impressive debut novel of fantasy and myth for young people and adults. The selection below is from George Ella Lyon's *Borrowed Children.*

It's Friday. Fridays are the best days because we know Daddy is coming home. He works all week cutting timber on Big Lick Mountain—too far to come back to Goose Rock every night. I wish he could. The house lights up when Daddy's here.

Even now, just knowing he's on his way, chores seem easier and we don't quarrel. I've been taking care of my little sisters, Anna and Helen, but they've been happy—Helen stringing spools on yarn, Anna looking at the new Sears-Roebuck catalogue. "Wish Book," Daddy calls it. "Wishes are free," he says. "Look your fill." And we do. They've got things on those slick pages that Goose Rock's never seen: clothes washers, typewriters, electric lights. But Anna looks at dolls.

"I'd give a bushel of money for that bride doll," she says, pointing to a tall one got up in wads of lace.

"And what would you do with her? She'd be thick with coal dust in no time." In Goose Rock coal dust is as common as dirt.

"I'd keep her under my pillow," Anna insists.

"And squash her flat as a board."

"Oh, Mandy . . ."

"Remember what Daddy said about Miss Snavely and the Wish Book. You don't always get what you order."

"What did he say?"

"Said she ordered a suit, and when it came, her heart broke because it didn't have that pretty man in it."

"That's just a story," Anna argues. "Nobody's that dumb."

"No? Then what are they doing here, stuck between two mountains with nothing but a Wish Book to look at?"

"We're not dumb and we're here."

"That's because we follow the timber."

"Maybe it's the trees that are dumb," Helen suggests.

"That's it exactly," I tell her. "Dumb maple! Dumb walnut! Knot-head pine."

We're all laughing when Ben bursts in.

"Mandy, I've got to talk to you," he says, his breath coming in heaves. "Right now. Private." He motions me out on the porch.

Ben is fourteen, tall and skinny like me, but that's okay for a boy. He's been running, and his hair looks like a blackbird about to take off.

"I'm listening," I say, glancing through the window to make sure the girls don't knock over a lamp or something.

"You know those lunches Mama packs us in school-time—ham biscuit, a jar of milk? Well, that's all right here in Goose Rock, but when you go to Manchester to school . . . why, there's boys eating steak between white bread, Mandy, and not out of paper sacks either. They say you can buy that bread sliced and it tastes just like cake. And there we sit with dry biscuits and hard ham. So me and David—I don't know which of us first—we just thought we'd go to the hotel one day and try out lunch there."

I can't believe it. David's two years older than Ben and so crazy about Polly Anderson I didn't know he'd even noticed the Asher Hotel. I've wanted to eat there ever since I first laid eyes on it—white and tall and fancy, like a hotel in New York. I've read about New York, you know. And that's the kind of place I belong. But I'd be too scared—not of the hotel people but of Mama and Daddy—to ever just walk in.

"Well, what was it like?"

"You never saw a thing like it," Ben says, his blue eyes warming, "unless it was in the dining car bound for Memphis. Tablecloths and silver dish covers, hot meat and potatoes with the butter standing. Why, we ate so much, David said he slept through the next hour of school. Not me. And Mr. Asher told us to come back to the hotel any time we wanted, he was proud to do business with Mr. Perritt's sons."

"Proud to take Daddy's money, you mean." Ben's face whitens. I didn't mean to make him feel worse. "That's pretty bad," I say, "but anybody can slip up once. Daddy'll get over it."

"But it wasn't just once," Ben says, his voice rising. "We went there the whole last month of school, Mandy, and that's how come Mr. Asher sent Daddy a bill. It's come today. Mama said she couldn't think what we owed the hotel for."

"And she's not opened it?"

"I reckon not. I can still sit down."

"Well, try not to worry," I tell him. "It may blow over."

His eyes follow mine to a thunderhead along the ridge.

Without a word, he bolts off the porch, then lopes across the yard and through the narrow meadow to the shed. I expect that's where he ran in from. Had to go talk to Welkie about the bill before he talked to me. Welkie's a horse. Ben gets more comfort out of any kind of creature than most people do from best friends.

He's going to need comfort too. Money is already a problem around here. Sawmill business is down because of something called the Depression, and Mama is expecting another baby. Don't ask me why. A baby is the last thing we need.

So it's going to hit hard, this bill from the Asher Hotel. Ben and David never should have done it. As long as they did, though, I wish they'd taken me along. I'm the one who would appreciate it. Boys judge a meal by how well it covers the plate.

It's getting dark as a cellar out here and it's only six o'clock. Daddy says these are dog days—hot enough to make anybody pant. But now a wind's come up and the forsythia bush skitters against the porch. Mama calls to ask if I see Daddy, and I go in, watching the curtains blow at the window.

"Not a sign," I tell her.

He should be here by now. The table's laid, the dumplings puffing up in the chicken broth. Mama's lit the lamp above the gold-rimmed tureen on the table.

"It's chipped but it's gold," she says, patting the graceful lid, "and older than any of us. Came over with the Ezelles from France, packed in feathers."

My grandmother Omie was an Ezelle, and Mama always says this whenever we have chicken and dumplings or stew or whatever requires the tureen. I like to think of the Ezelles themselves packed in feathers.

I follow her back to the kitchen. It's strange—I'm taller than she is now. I check the part in her hair. Always straight. Everything about her is neat, plump, and pretty. Where did she get a daughter like a clothesline pole?

Sweat beads on her forehead as she mixes the cornbread batter.

"No point in baking this till your father gets here. Go see if you see him coming."

As I pass through the parlor, Helen reaches for something in the catalogue, Anna jerks it back, and the thin page rips.

"She's tearing up my dolls!" Anna hollers.

"Mine, too!" Helen holds the crumpled paper close.

"Take them outside, Amanda," Mama says. "Leave the catalogue and go watch for Daddy. It'll help him get home. Somebody watching always does."

So we troop out to the porch. Thunder rumbles like empty coal cars. Just as we reach the rail, the rain comes down in buckets and lightning bleaches the dirt road in front of our house. All of a sudden there's a shriek, Helen grabs me around the waist, and Anna starts pointing and screaming. I look where she's looking and see a horse and rider blurred by the slant of rain.

"It's all right," I begin.

"But *look* at him," Anna splutters. "It can't be Daddy. He doesn't have a . . ."

Then I see what she sees. The figure sits high, his body covered in a cape. And where his head should be, there's nothing. It's like in the Sleepy Hollow story—but this time it's coming at a gallop directly for us.

The screen door bangs and I feel Mama behind us. I reach for her hand, but she's already holding Helen's, so I grab the rail. The figure is getting close now, swaying and gleaming.

Not a one of us moves and even Helen is quiet. The figure slows, dismounts, and leads the horse toward the porch. Mama takes a step forward, drawing herself up. "Come no farther," she commands.

Then the rider throws back its shoulders and laughs. It keeps coming. The cloak slips down, a head emerges, and it's Daddy, his smile wide, his glasses all steamed up.

I almost cry, I'm so glad it's him, but Helen buries her face in my skirt. Mama moves toward him, not yet ready to laugh.

"Jim," she says, "what on earth do you think you're doing, scaring the children to death?"

Now he's up on the porch, water pouring off the cloak, and him still shaking with laughter.

"Just trying to keep dry," he says. "I cut a piece of cloth off a log tarp. Never dreamed it would give these girls a fright. I couldn't see them through the rain."

"Well, they could see you," Mama says, "and you could have been the Devil himself." She's trying to brush water off his face. "I'll call one of the boys to come get Midge."

"That's all right, Rena." Daddy lays a dripping hand on her shoulder. "I'll walk on down to the shed."

Mama doesn't smile till his back is turned, and then it's a slow smile, like the sun coming up.

"You girls get on in the house now," she says. "It's so damp out here you could catch your death."

John Hay
"Renascence"

Although John Hay has published four popular children's books and several superb stories in the *Sewanee Review* and other periodicals, he is surely one of Kentucky's best-kept secrets. Born in Frankfort in 1944, he grew up on nearby Scotland Farm caring for horses. He holds a bachelor's degree from the University of the South, a master's degree in writing from Hollins College, and a J.D. from the University of Louisville. He has received a number of awards for his writing and continues to live and write and care for the horses on the family farm. "Renascence," which first appeared in the 2002 issue of Brescia University's literary magazine, *Open 24 Hours,* demonstrates that he is a writer with major talent.

There are many stories—to hear a gentler one than this, we must earn it. You can try an antique, leather-bound book on the Renaissance full of riches, but the cosmos demands the oblique. The rhythms of life demand discrimination. The broad gestures of language can only hope to be generous. My travels are inward now, connected with something electrical: the light bulb burning in the empty kitchen, the gas stove burning the edges of the fat pizza, the burning starlight, the dull eyes of Deliberator, the blind stallion racing across the field. The stallion is satisfied in his travels across the field. He will stop at the fence on a dime. He is burning or cold at the shiver of a mare, or a fat cob of corn. He is only a stallion. He looks to breed his mare, Dusty Dream, as his kind have looked for a thousand years. I am not a blind stallion. Is my friend Candice a blind mare? Do I look for loving arms today? I have been alone for awhile since my loved-one passed on. The pizza is in the oven, and starlight is seething at the edge of the cheese. Candice is coming to lunch.

I am singing in the key of blue. If you flinch at a caustic thought or two, off the cuff and lazy, forgive me. I am singing a song in the key of yellow. If I offend, know that I am but a friend of someone who is living out a thought. . . .

But wait! The moments come and go . . . Candice wheels in. Her red car sweeps down the lane, a quarter mile away, makes fresh tracks in the deep, sparkling snow. Candice. A young woman I've known only a little while. Maybe twenty-eight, she is. A success with her own company, a painter in her spare time. Landscapes.

I have been sifting through books to clarify the useless and left them scattered. Candice wants to know me, and I her, of course. If I leave the books out, will she be scanning titles, looking for her own brand in me? Branded. Sizzling, permanent. Well, all right, you might say, people have got to look at something. But for today, no books. Let the pizza be enough for her, all vegetables in the snow-covered kitchen looking out over the empty, white, rolling, monastic hills of Kentucky. It is a warm, easy kitchen with an ancient, wooden table. Will she worry then if the vegetable knife decapitates a bug?

No, not Candice. She isn't like that. She is sensitive (not issue bound), and she is charming. Charming because what she is makes charm happen—courteous, bright, kind, seeking. Doomed, possibly, I think, as I sift through the books.

One eye on the window, I track her in the red car. She slides at the big curve, a long, graceful, slow-motion slide to the ditch. Maybe she was testing the snow against her speed—having fun. Now in the ditch she revs it up—spinning—rich, black earth shoots from the back tires flying into the field. Back on the road, she is out to check the damage. From my perspective: dark red coat, bright red car, white field, black dirt—color and stillness. She drives on, curving toward me, slower now.

I imagine her thoughts by the thousands tumbling off in the wind: honey bees, five hundred Luna moths on the wing, birds of paradise, dying house flies toddling behind like penguins, a mantis with a mouth full of broken wings trying to pray, all drags against the wheels. We know them all. I meet her at the car. Hands in my pockets against the wind. Nimbly, she is out in a heartbeat, warm smile, a greeting of goodness, reaches to give me a gentle hug. I barely get my hands out of my pockets in time.

"Well, I'm here. Nice place, this open country of yours."

We have been together a couple of times before, Candice and I. One night, talking along the edges of history, I mentioned the color black. In passing, only. Black absorbs the spectrum of light, takes it all in. Symbol of wisdom in some ancient circles, the resplendent inner state. Said no. Candice. Black was only evil, cruelty and darkness to her. Different tradition, different scholar, different book, different symbol. Candice and I, two people talking. Symbols! But what of the real thing?

We have chatted about everything from the roll of dice to the diffusion of intent. We went to a movie, tainted as usual, funny a bit. But there you go! Culture. We kissed gently at her door in the city. She seems everything a man could want. I see her standing there in the snow like, well, like the Duchess of Earl: you know the Duke of the song, his loved-one—hair swept back, quick to laugh, curving tenderly in her tight winter coat.

In the house, I smell pizza and say, "pizza!" and run. She gets it, and is right behind me. I throw open the hot oven door. She tosses me her colorful, blue and green and saffron glove, and the pizza is saved in a heartbeat.

In by the fire while the pizza cools. She picks up a book and asks with her eyes, "What is this?"

"A poet from Deya," I say.

"I see by the cover," she says.

"Don't open it now," I say. "Better for another time." Too beautiful, I tell myself, as I set it aside for her, this book. The delicate spiritual and physical love between man and woman. Too beautiful for Candice today. She would lose herself in that mood.

I am in a wing-backed chair by the open fire, and she is up looking about. She stops and turns her head toward me over her shoulder as if I whispered her name. Her eyes smile to me, looking to weigh anchor. Alight? Energy floating in the space? Are those her deep intentions? Now, she seems more a chandelier.

∞ ∞ ∞

I could add warmth to this story for you, but warmth that might drug us, and in wearing off turn to ice. I could spend time with conversation over lunch, but instead I'll pass on her fugitive thought, like a finch at dawn, that the condition of people is not all it is cracked up to be, even the seeming best of it. She is beginning to turn inward. "What is the trip you are taking?" she asks again.

I could tell you of being with her on the big, golden sofa as the afternoon wore on, and how high her wool skirt hiked when she tucked her leg under her, how warm the wood fire, how compatible we were, how tenderly she kissed me moments after her long, eloquent sentence describing the lace ice flows at the falls of Tourgunn and how the sun beat upon them. How, in essence, she offers her warmth to me, herself . . . maybe just for holding each other closely. How yes rustles in us. How I lean back without accepting her lovely offer. No feeling of separation. Only I know I don't accept her willing gesture—silence awhile. We wait.

"What is this trip you're taking?" she asks.

"You know what," I say. "Isn't it strange who we are."

"Very strange." She smiles.

It occurs to me, I say, that people are made of their conditioning since childhood and before. That struggling persons might have held them, brought them up, as they say. Good intentions, I ask, does it matter much? I ask: who bought their books, defined their words, offered them too much in the way of bad food and facts?

Who slaked their inborn, tender, loving thirst for peace with raw opinion, and with chemicals like Old Man Alcohol the Insidious? Heirlooms of
emotion drift from mind to mind, I say. The trivial intellect talks on and on.
Born where, who from, to what club, religion? Random experience, mixed
with a little honey, but not honey enough. Honey? A different food, I say.

"I suppose," she says.

And there is more. I say.

I talk about the animal within, and the false self that commands us without us commanding it. The preposterous fear and laziness within humanity,
the senses unhinged, the ungainly carnivorous engagement with the intellect, emotion, food and sex, without understanding or finesse. The thousand
and one degrees of murder, there within the thoughts. All in the course of a
day, these thoughts, drifting in and out of the being, until the food of the
soul flutters against a stone vase.

"Well," she says. "Some people more than others." She steams up a bit.
Defensive. "This is not new."

And I agree with her, yes, but it is subdued, truncated. It is only the one
who really listens, who acts upon the knowledge, who makes a tremendous,
conscious effort as rare as peace. Pedantry like barnacles hangs upon human
history—only the deep freshness of spring for one or so. Whole civilizations
live and die, and not one person makes the effort. I tell her.

"I think maybe you are an arrogant son-of-a. . . . A waste." She tells me.

I don't mind her words, though ease is better, but what can I do? She
apologizes briefly, unconvincingly because of her darkening mood. But I
know what she means, and I tell her so to ease the break between us: she
didn't really think that of me, just of the ideas, etc. etc. Talk.

Quiet now. Maybe she's remembering her poor Aunt Alice who, in her
mind, was a saint. Maybe she is thinking of herself and the good job she has
done so far. Maybe she doubts them both. But it sinks in today, as it does
with almost all of us, someday. She knows there is something missing; she
knows there is weakness in herself; with her life before her eyes in an expanded second, maybe she shuffles over all the people she knows and finds
them confused and struggling. They put forward at times their best face,
their stiff upper lip, their faith in hope, their faith in their new shoes—but
floundering.

"Ego," she says.

"It seems to me," I say, very gently this time. "That people use the weapons of the ego to fight the ego. And so, stalemate."

The afternoon is not going the way she had imagined it—edging up the
avenue in her red car at the height of her poetic understanding in the rolling
white, elegant hills of Kentucky, engaging the warm, open fire and the home-

made pizza and an equal of sorts, me; all the rhythms of her reality were tenderly opened to be confirmed. She is disappointed. This is hard, maybe even shallow, earthbound.

She says: "Doesn't everyone complain this way? Thinking people? Your ideas are not so rare. Of course we are up against it in an imperfect world."

She wants companionship today. Love the way she knows it. And now a moody day, chilled by the intellect. She is right in a way, you know; why chill tenderness between people? Why? Answer me that. Is there a time when that chill could be kindness?

"Ego." I say. "Too easy. It is deeper than a personal, imaginative view of the word. It seems to me that any change would be beyond the skill of definition, or a rendition of beauty, beyond carte blanche, beyond the northern lights or rose buds, beyond ecstasy." Naturally.

"How about beyond magniloquent wheelbarrows?" she asks and smiles. "Are you a surrealist?"

I laugh. "Beyond them, too." Yes, quick and funny—she is—in deciding to cut back at me. I don't answer her surrealist parry. It isn't a moment for intellectual play, that is, in my cynosure—my court, as they say. I could say: why go beyond the real anyway? I could point out that almost the whole world is surreal, and leave it at that. I don't. Too easy.

She becomes quiet again. It is one of those fine, sparse, uncompressed days, one of those days when it is possible to hear the faint, calming sounds of the distance: the warble of a yellow dog chanting to be free, the bluster of an invisible train.

She finally speaks, not so much to me as to the smoldering logs. "Am I a little harsh too? I know. I am. You are trying to talk about what we are like inside. Just that."

I say truly, yes, but only yes, to soften things, I guess. She leans against me, her cascading hair against my neck; an ideal she is: thoughtful, warm, interested. No groveling over the pizza, even inwardly—abstemious, healthy. Her body begins to imprint her thin, soft, blue dress, nothing special, just ongoing in the warmth of the fire. Fresh. Her lips part slightly, her shoe falls from her foot to the floor.

I look at her against me. My feeling: respect, tremendously, like seeing a work of art in progress, but a greater thing, a human being struggling in that manner, a sculpture with invisible chips of stone flying away like startled birds into oblivion leaving only the fillet, the truth, the immortal. The chisel allows the breeze to seep into the pores, deep into the cells, the kiss from the cause of life. Not mortal like a pizza or a winter coat, not dumb as they are dumb, not an idiot of faith or imagination.

I heave a cedar log into the fire. The sparks begin to snap, the cat scurries, and I know she will gallop on to the kitchen to gnaw a crust of pizza from the table. But if I put her out today, well, she will get knocked up in a heartbeat—regularly, that drive, with nothing much in between but food and sleep.

I sit down again with Candice.

"There is a good chance you will waste your life," I say.

She grabs for her shoe, quick, smooth, like catching a fly on the wing and looks straight into my eyes. Boldly, ankle to knee, hem of dress falling to her thighs, shoe to foot. Internally, on her way out the door. She catches herself. I'm not surprised. She is too smart to miss anything, to let chances go by, and not thin-skinned, not weak like the run of the mill, just relatively so.

"You don't get off so easy." She leans back and smiles. She has gathered her aplomb in a heartbeat. Nothing fake about it. "You are going on a trip. Or did you say you've been? We have brought this up several times. You don't tell where or why. Tell me now."

I say. My trip? 1 am not going where the cat goes, I tell Candice, or where the fine, dun mare wants to go, which is to the feedbag or to the stallion or to sleep. Most of the day the cat likes to torture and kill and devour and sleep. People can sleep all of the day and do their dirty work consuming in a somnambulist trance. Rather like us. She flinches, restraint, she listens. The cat would be as fat as a swine eating its carrion if I would let her. If I would let her, the beautiful, dun mare would eat until her legs would lock into pegs and she would jerk along on all fours like a frozen spider— "foundered" as they say on the farm. Tears would come to the dun mare's eyes. And the cat would cry softly. If they were given all of what they want.

I say. We try to understand the cat and the dun mare, and take care of them. It is people who have the capacity for consciousness. If we are foundered, we can cure it. When the cosmos loves us, we can see our hidden faults and turn against them. Who can change to become lovable in that invisible realm? Our trip is not the trip of the animal, so we must know our history, our resumé of muscle and blood. The trip is the trip which nobody takes. Yet someone will—always—because it can be done, I propose to her.

She leans toward me; she holds her ground with the strength of her mind. There is an unnatural steadiness in her eyes. She puts her hand on my knee showing me she isn't afraid. Her eyes go soft, as if the imprint of some fresh Mona Lisa was coming through, but distantly, not for me. She doesn't really like me anymore.

She starts to speak. She stops. Her hand is on my knee. Light years stretch away leaving only the moment. Warmth. Thin, silver bracelet at her wrist. Beauty. In that gentle hand, wrist bent as if holding a brush, afternoon peace.

She says: "How about if we just hold each other? How about that, tenderly, with respect and love. We can drink dark tea, talk of the ups and downs of childhood. We can discuss religion and poetic living and take a walk in these empty hills. Love would freshen around us and we could talk of houses with white blossoms. How about it? We could start with holding each other, maybe just kiss the afternoon away."

Tears well into her eyes. They are wet with tears, brimming. She brushes them away with the hand that had been on my knee. She seems to have gone too far into the emotions she has mothered so long, too far into that intuitive sense of what is missing from the mundane.

She hears the soft tick of the iron clock and it jolts her. Somewhere in her heart she knows the whisper of something completely whole, entirely beautiful that must be found within. She holds her hand gently at her neck as if closing the collar of a coat against a cold wind.

I tell myself, "I love her." Naturally. To her I give another feeling, truly: "All you say is beautiful."

She's up and moves closer to the fire with a clumsy turn of her body as if too many words have cut off her circulation. All the talk has cut off mine. I stretch, and take a deep, slow breath. She turns her back to me and pretends to watch the fire. She is thinking again, naturally.

"You know what, I'm tired of you," she says. "Tired of your implications that go nowhere, tired of your talk, tired of losing this beautiful December afternoon. I'm leaving. Don't walk me out. But with your permission I will walk out and sit on the hill out there." She turns to the window, her back to me. "If you don't mind, I would like to be there alone before I go." I nod my assent. For her, I want everything. She is everyone. Naturally.

"Of course," I say. At that, she gathers that dark red, sleek, form-fitting, wool coat and is out the door in a heartbeat.

rଙ୬ rଙ୬ rଙ୬

Smoke tree holding a leaf. Gray. Winter. Night falling from far away. The light, like rest. The horses will be waiting as is their habit. Now and then the cat bounds from footprint to footprint, or trots along beside me on the white, white frozen snow. She is a good mouser, happy, always alert and interested, never bored.

The dun mare, Dusty Dream, is against the fence waiting for me. She holds in profile like a bronze statue, a streak of alabaster against the snow, but a statue for a moment only. Nickering in that deep, tender voice, shifting from foot to foot, the clear, winter breeze touching her mane, her head rising and falling, whirling with her ears back to scatter the restless mares waiting behind her, and making the full circle with a kind expression, ears up for me. I lean my head against hers, my cheek against her cheek, and we are still for a moment. As I carry in the bale of grass hay, she nuzzles me aside for the first fleck. Gently. A fine mare, strong, involved.

Deliberator! There he is, the huge, blind, black thoroughbred stallion. Blind, with a stallion's beauty of the highest. Is the dun mare more beautiful? Watching her, well, yes, but. . . . What is beauty? Love itself? So then. His tail, long and full and dark, brushes the white snow. Perfectly formed he is, no weight but what he needs for peace. He knows I am near. He whirls and lifts his front feet into the air and whirls again and makes for the fence at a gallop—no sight for the bare trees, the violet sky, the jagged fences and the drunken hills—they go on forever—no sight for the winter day—completely within, he comes charging.

I scan the horizon to freshen my view of the evening. I see Candice in the far distance, a little, dark red brush stroke. I forget her in this time with the horses. Naturally I miss her, but I forget her now. Nothing harsh. Let her be.

Deliberator slides to a stop—the fence—his chest bowing in the plank, snow powdering the air, pure and true—the snow—as the sparkles float and fall and remain in me fresh forever. I throw the hay. He knows it. He waits. He swings away and swings back. Dancing. He is fun loving, inclines to joy. He is dancing. To play. Naturally. He waits until I touch his face. I pat his face and smooth his long wild, elegant forelock. He has no fear, no haste. He cares deeply for this moment, and every other. I rub his nose on both sides with my open hands. He lifts his head sharply and looks over my shoulder. He cannot see, and yet. . . . He leans back into my hands, gently. I brush his cheeks and around his eyes with my hand. In time he steps away. No division. He is awake when others sleep. He is blind to the things of the day. Inside he is all sparkles soothing him, like snow sparkles hanging languidly in the evening air. He is old. I have known him all of my life. And these are the things that he whispered to me over the long years, forever.

❦ ❦ ❦

A year passes. Again it is December. Again. Snow. In that I have lived fully, retreated for some of my needs, come forward for others. A year can be a long, engaging time for some of us. Again a violet sky. All different, all better. Following that same timeless lead. Love? Let it be nameless, that force. Naturally. Strong. I feel. As always now, detaching from the dross. Coming up from the barn I see the cat against a pane of glass that must be a hundred years old, the waves in the glass give her a diffuse air, as if maybe she is dying and going away. But none the less for wear in that journey. Naturally. She declined to trot with me to the barn because of the bitter wind. Naturally.

I come to the door. There is a note from Candice. I have to think twice. I have not seen her, nor heard of her, since that day she left me in the afternoon, long ago. It is folded and says, from Candice. I take off my glove to unfold it. In fresh ink it reads:

> Come on out the ridge
> And find me,
> I'll be the one in the black coat
> On the white hill
> With a sleigh.

In a heartbeat, I begin to think. She is stepping into another room. That room is on her way to becoming uncluttered. Her coat, the one she wears, might be any color, a brush of red, but she paints it black for me in her poem—the resplendent inner, symbolic black of which we chatted. Her hill is pure, and that is the white thought of which she speaks, not cold snow forever melting. I'll make a bet there is no sleigh; she speaks instead of action, an effort onward. She invites me to join her in that trip. Sustenance between us. Naturally. Yes, she'll be out there alone, no little sleigh, I'll bet; I'll wager what's in my pocket: a piece of string, my pet frog, the little raft I fashion to head out on the broad Mississippi.

Silas House

from *Clay's Quilt*

Silas House of Lily, in the Kentucky mountains, was one of the biggest literary discoveries of the late twentieth century in Kentucky—and American—letters. The publication of his first novel, *Clay's Quilt,* in 2001 was greeted with almost universal enthusiasm and approval. Lee Smith called him "a young writer of immense gifts," and Robert Morgan said that he was "one of the truest and most exciting new voices in American fiction." The novel is focused on Clay Sizemore, who has lost both parents by the time he is four; he has to learn that, like a quilter who takes odd pieces of cloth and sews them into a beautiful quilt, he must learn to shape a life for himself out of the bits and pieces of himself and his experiences with people who love and care for him.

His second novel also received general acclaim by readers and critics alike. *A Parchment of Leaves* (2002) proves that his first novel was not a fluke and that he has talent and staying power. In this novel House shows the range of his talent by writing a historical novel set in the early 1900s and by taking on the persona of Vine, a young Cherokee woman who is determined to have her white man, regardless of the barriers and consequences. The title of his third novel, *The Coal Tattoo* (2004), comes from the dark imprint left on the miners who survive a mine collapse. In Black Bank, however, everyone is marked by coal, including the two very different sisters, Anneth and Easter, whose lives are at the core of the story and who can't live together or apart. It is exciting to watch such a young writer as House grow into a major author. The selection below is the prologue to *Clay's Quilt;* it narrates the accident that will determine a young boy's future.

They were in a car going over Buffalo Mountain, but the man driving was not Clay's father. The man was hunched over the steering wheel, peering out the frosted window with hard, gray eyes. The muscle in his jaw never relaxed, and he seemed to have an extra, square-shaped bone on the side of his face.

"No way we'll make it without getting killed," the man said. His lips were thin and white.

"We ain't got no choice but to try now," Clay's mother, Anneth, said. "We can't pull over and just set on the side of the road until it thaws."

Clay listened to the tires crunching through the snow and ice as they moved slowly on the winding road. It sounded as if they were driving on a highway made of broken glass. On one side of the road there rose a wall of cliffs, and on the other side was a wooden guardrail. It looked like the world dropped off after that.

They met a sharp curve and the steering wheel spun around in the man's hands. His elbows went high into the air as he tried to straighten the car. The two women in the back cried out "Oh Lord!" in unison as one was thrown atop the other to one side of the car. Anneth pressed her slender fingers deep into Clay's arms, and he wanted to scream, but then the car was righted on course. The man looked at Anneth as if it were her fault.

The women in the back had been carrying on all the way up the mountain, and now they laughed wildly at themselves for being scared. They acted like going over the crooked, ice-covered highway was the best time they had had in ages, and the man kept telling them to shut up. It seemed they lit one cigarette after another, so many that Clay couldn't tell if the mist swirling around in the cab of the car was from their smoking or their breathing.

The heater in the little car didn't work, and when one of the women hollered to the man to give it another try, the vents rattled and coughed, pushing out a chilling breeze. Clay could see his own breath clenching out silver in front of him until it made a white fist on the windshield. The man wiped the glass off every few minutes, and when he did, he let out a line of cusswords, all close and connected like a string of paper dolls.

Anneth exhaled loudly and said, "I'd appreciate it if you didn't cuss and go on like that in front of this child."

"Well, God almighty," the driver said. "I ain't never been in such a mess before in my life."

Clay knew that his mother was getting mad because a curl of her hair had suddenly fallen down between her eyes. She pushed it away roughly, but it fell back again.

"They ain't no use taking the Lord's name in vain. I never could stand to hear that word," she said. She patted Clay's hands and focused on the icy highway. "Sides, you ought to be praying instead of handling bad language."

"Yeah, you're a real saint, ain't you, Anneth Sizemore?" the man said, and a laugh seemed to catch in the back of his throat. He pulled his shoulders up in a way that signaled he was ready to stop talking. Clay watched him hold tightly to the steering wheel and look out at the road without blinking. He knew this man somehow, but couldn't figure how exactly, and he didn't feel right with him. He wished that his father had been driving them. He reconsidered and simply wished he could put a face to the word *daddy*. He was only four, but he had already noticed that most of his cousins had fathers, while his was never even spoken of. He wondered if his father would smell so strongly of aftershave, like this man, and have a box-bone in his cheek that tightened every few minutes. He started to ask his mother about this but didn't. He had so many questions. Today alone, he couldn't understand what all had gone on.

Clay looked out at the snow and wondered if the world had stopped. Maybe it had frozen, grown silver like the creek water around the edges of rocks. They had not met one car all the way over the mountain, and the few houses they passed looked empty. No tracks on the porches, no movement at the windows. Thin little breaths of black smoke slithered out of chimneys, as if the people had left the fires behind.

The windows frosted over again, and Anneth took the heel of her gloved hand and wiped off the passenger window so they could look out. The pines lining the road were bent low and pitiful, full of clotted ice and winking snow. Some of the trees had broken in two. Their limbs stuck out of the packed snow like jagged bones with damp, yellow ends bright against the whiteness. There was not so much sunshine as daylight, but the snow and ice twinkled anyway. The cliffs had frozen into huge boulders of ice where water had trickled down to make icicles.

"Look," Anneth said, "them icicles look like the faces of people we know."

She whispered into Clay's ear and pointed out daggers of ice. The one with the big belly looked like Gabe. One column of ice looked like a woman with wigged-up hair, just like his aunt Easter. There was even one that favored the president, who was on television all of the time. Clay put his hands inside hers. The blue leather gloves she had on were cold to his bare hands. He didn't move, though, and hoped the warmth of her fingers would seep down into his own.

"I need to get this baby some mitts," Anneth said, to no one in particular. The women were singing, and the driver was ignoring every one of them. "His little hands is plumb frostbit."

She undid the knot at her neck and slid the scarf around her collar with one quick jerk. The scarf was white, with fringes on each end. She shook out her hair and picked at it with one hand. The car was filled with the smell of strawberries. She always washed her hair in strawberry shampoo, except on Fridays, when she washed it with beer. She took his hands and lay the scarf out across her lap, then wound the scarf round and round his hands, like a bandage.

"I'm awful ashamed to have on gloves and my baby not," she said as she worked with the scarf. "There," she said. There was a fat white ball in Clay's lap where his arms should have met.

One of the women in the back put her chin on the top of the front seat. "I hain't never seen a vehicle that didn't have a heater *or* a radio. This beats it all to hell."

The man shot her a hateful look in the rearview mirror.

She fell back against her seat and began to sing "Me and Bobby McGee." The other woman joined in and they swayed back and forth with their arms wrapped around each other's necks. Their backs smoothed across the leather seat in rhythm with the windshield wipers. They snapped their fingers and cackled out between verses.

"Help us sing, Anneth!" one of them cried out. "I know you like Janis Joplin."

Anneth ignored them, but she hummed the song quietly to Clay, patting his arm to keep in tune.

The man said that he would never make it off the downhill side of the mountain without wrecking and killing them. There was more arguing over the fact that they couldn't pull over. They would surely freeze to death sitting on the side of the road. They were on top of the mountain now, far past the row of houses. There was nothing here but black trees and gray cliffs and mountains that stretched out below them. Everybody started talking at once, and it reminded Clay of the way the church house sounded just before the meeting started.

Clay looked over his mother's shoulder at the women. One of the women was looking at herself in a silver compact and patting the curls that fell down on either side of her face. She snapped the compact shut with a loud click and looked up at him happily.

"Don't worry, Clay," she said. "We'll make it off this mountain." He could see lipstick smudged across her straight white teeth.

The other woman stared blankly into space, and it took her a long moment to realize that Clay was studying her. She was beautiful, much younger than his mother, but as Clay looked at her, she aged before his eyes. Her face grew solid and tough, her skin like a persimmon. Her eyes looked made of water, her nose lengthened and thinned, and her mouth pinched together tightly. He caught a glimpse of what would never become of her, because she was killed that day, alongside his mother and the man driving the car.

The man's voice was suddenly harsh. "Well, I was good enough to take you over there, now dammit. I need to pull off and calm down some," he said loudly. "My nerves is shot all to hell."

"I'll never ask you to do nothing else for me, then," she said with disgust. "I ain't worried about myself—I have to get this baby home."

"Hellfire, I'd rather be home, too, but this road is a sight," he said. "You ought not got that child out in this. I'm pulling over, and that's all there is to it."

"Go on, then," Anneth shouted in a deep voice. She turned toward the window and didn't speak to him again.

"Let's just set here a few minutes and figure something out," the driver said.

The shoulder widened out and they could see the mountains spread out below. The white guardrail was wound about by dead vines that showed in brown places through the thick snow. The mountains looked like smudges of paint, rolling back to the horizon until they faded into one another in a misted-over heap.

Anneth wiped the icy window off once more and said, "Look how peaceful. Look at them mountains, how purple and still."

Clay knew that the mountains looked purple under that big, moving sky, but they didn't look still at all to him. They seemed to be breathing—rising so slowly, so carefully, that no one noticed but him. He watched them, concentrating the way he did when he was convinced a shadow had moved across his bedroom wall. It seemed to Clay that they rose and fell with a single pulse, as if the whole mountain chain was connected.

Everyone had grown silent looking out at the hills, and later this struck Clay as strange. They were all accustomed to seeing hills laid out before them, but there was something about this day, something about how silently the mountains lay beneath the snow.

It was so quiet that Clay was certain that the end of the world had come. Everybody on earth had been sucked up into the sky in the twinkling of an eye. He was used to hearing people talk about the End and the Twinkling of an Eye; his Aunt Easter constantly spoke of such things. She looked forward to the day when Jesus would part the clouds and come after His children. "Rapture," she called it, and the word was always whispered. Easter said if you weren't saved, you'd be left behind.

He pressed against his mother and felt the warmth of her body spread out across his back. She ran her fingers through his hair and began to hum softly again. He could feel the purr of her lungs against his face. It was the same song the women had been singing. Clay knew it by heart. He'd watched his mother iron or wash dishes while she listened to that song. Sometimes she would snatch him up and dance around the room with him while the song was on the record player. She had sung every word then, singing especially loud when it got to the part about the Kentucky coal mines. The vibration in her chest was as comforting as rain on a tin roof, and he fought his sleep so that he could feel it. She must have thought he was asleep, too, because finally she took her hand from his head and stopped humming.

She pressed her face to the window, leaning her forehead against the cold glass. "I ain't never seen it so quiet on this mountain," she said.

That was the last thing Clay was aware of, but afterward, he sometimes dreamed of blood on the snow, blood so thick that it ran slow like syrup and lay in stripes across the whiteness, as if someone had dashed out a bucket of paint.

Dwight Allen

"Fishing with Alex," from *The Green Suit*

Dwight Allen, with one novel to his credit at the beginning of his writing career, is a man who has been involved in the literary world for some time, studying the art of writing at Iowa and practicing a bit of writing and fact-checking at the *New Yorker*. In 2000 he brought together some of his previously published stories into a book that chronicles the activities of a prominent, upper-middle-class family in his hometown of Louisville. It is not quite a novel, but all the pieces focus on the members of the Sackrider family and, in particular, Peter Sackrider. For Peter the book is a series of experiences that mature him—sort of. It is a comfortable read, and for anyone familiar with Louisville in the sixties, it evokes memories of things past.

When my sister was a sophomore in college, in Philadelphia, she fell in love with a sallow-skinned, lank-haired boy whose chief interest in life was the effects of hallucinogens on the neurochemistry of white rats. This was in 1973. Ed was two years older than Alex, and when he dropped her, she came unglued. She left school and returned home to Kentucky. One morning in March, after eating half a grapefruit and casting a cold eye on the saucer of vitamin pills my mother had set before her, she went back upstairs, swallowed most of a bottle of barbiturates, and sat down in the reading chair in my bedroom. By the time my mother found her, Alex was in a stupor; her head lolled, her hands were clammy, her blood was pooling, not moving. My mother, who had been on her way to church to tag items for a bazaar, called an ambulance and got Alex to the hospital, where her stomach was pumped. Later, the doctor put her in Queen of Peace, a columned and porticoed institution that sat on a hill about a mile from the new county zoo. Because the windows to the rooms were sealed shut, it was unlikely that a patient would hear an elephant trumpet or a peacock shriek or a lion roar. But Alex said there was a man in her morning group therapy class who complained that the animals kept him awake every night. As for Alex herself, she heard nothing at night, just a whispering in her head, like a breeze passing through fir trees.

A few days after my sister entered Queen of Peace, I took the bus home from college. My father picked me up at the depot downtown. I asked how Alex was, and he said, "Your mother thinks she might be hypoglycemic." I looked puzzled, and he said, "Something about a low level of sugar in the blood." He didn't tell me what he thought. Three stoplights later, we fell silent. Eventually, he turned on the radio. The car filled with opera—it was a Saturday—and then he dialed around until he got a basketball game. "Now here's something in English," he said.

My father led me into the hospital and up a broad, curving staircase, which I pictured women in long dresses descending, on their way to meet men who wouldn't have resembled me or my father in his raincoat that looked as if he'd slept in it. At the top, Dad remembered that my mother had sent along a sack of vitamins for my sister. He left me at Alex's door and went back to the car to fetch the sack.

My sister was sitting up in bed. Next to her, on the nightstand, was a fish bowl, and above her, on the white wall, was a small plaster crucifix; the bony Jesus, his head downcast, looked as if he'd given his last cry. Alex wore a black shawl over a white blouse that was buttoned to the throat. I'd never seen the shawl. It made her look dramatic, in a formal kind of way, like someone in a painting from another century and another country. Alex had always liked to dress up, and I thought it was a good sign that she hadn't stopped. I didn't know if it was a good sign that she'd tied her hair back, leaving her brow so exposed.

"Don't worry, Peter," she said gamely. "I'm just having a run-of-the-mill nervous breakdown. Isn't that right, fishy?" She tapped on the bowl. The goldfish, the only truly bright spot of color in the room, streaked away. It was a gift from Bobby Tarr, a guy Alex had dated in high school.

"Mom thinks I'm chemically unbalanced," Alex said. "And spiritually at sea. And that I go out with the wrong boys." She looked out the window. It was an erratic mid-March afternoon, full of clouds one moment and bursts of sunlight the next.

"What do you think?" I touched the too-small black beret on my head. I'd bought it at a thrift shop. I'd hoped it would make me look worldly.

"I don't know," she said. "I guess some of my boyfriends haven't turned out too hot." She glanced toward the doorway, as if love might be there, waiting.

I saw a wimpled nun walk past, then another. I expected to see a third—didn't nuns travel in threes?—but she didn't materialize.

I said, "You've had some OK boyfriends. What about Bobby?" Bobby was three years older than Alex; he'd dropped out of college by the time she met him. At the moment, he was the leader of a band called the Tarrdy Boys and clerking in a store on Bardstown Road where you could buy incense and peasant shirts and Tarot cards, among other things.

"Bobby can be nice," Alex said. "But I'm just one of his chicks."

"And Mac?" Mac, whose actual name was Eldon McRae, was my age. Alex had first gone out with him when she was a sophomore in high school and he was a senior. Mac was shy and awkward, except on the basketball court, where he became someone who could make fallaway jumpers with his eyes half-closed. Alex found Mac's shyness appealing—that and his soft, blond, almost feminine looks. Mac felt flummoxed by his shyness, and as a result, he drank more than was normal in our group. When he drank, he sometimes did stupid, shy-boy sorts of things. Once, he tried to pole-vault into Alex's second-story bedroom, using a long metal rod he'd stolen from a construction site. He'd risen briefly into the air, like a pioneer of flight, and then had fallen on his shoulder, dislocating it. Like me, Mac had been a solid B-minus student, and we'd ended up at the same college, a boys-only institution, on a mountain in Tennessee.

"Mac got so bombed sometimes," Alex said, "he missed my face completely when he tried to kiss me." I saw her watching Mac's face float by again.

"Well, anyway," I said, "Mac said to say 'Hi.'"

"'Hi' back." Alex gazed at her fingers, which a flare-up of eczema had reddened, and made a church out of them, loosing silence upon the room. She was burrowing into herself, her nose leading the way. She had the Sackrider family nose. The sharp tip suggested that it would be worth your while to tell her a joke or a story.

"How are the nuns?" I asked.

"Les zéros?" She roughened the r expertly; she used to practice her French in the shower, bouncing accents argus off the tiles. "They're watchful."

My father appeared in the doorway, the sack of vitamins in one hand and a tweed motoring cap in the other. The cap was a Christmas present from my mother, something to make him look more sporty. He was a judge, and as a rule he dressed like one, though he sometimes failed to notice that his dark suit coat didn't match his dark suit trousers. After all, there were motions and petitions to be pondered, precedents to be considered.

Dad told me he was going to wait outside in the car. "I don't want to intrude on your discussion," he said, stooping to kiss Alex on the forehead. "We love you, Moony Tooth." My father had a whole hatful of names for my sister: Izzy Woo, Alexosaurus, Babes, Miss Graham Cracker. The last was derived from Alex's full name, Alexandra Bell Sackrider.

After my father left the room, Alex said, "Dad told me a story about how some East Coast girl had snubbed him when he was in college and how he'd been down in the dumps for days. Then he came back home for Christmas, and he saw Mom at a party, standing under mistletoe."

"Mom under mistletoe? Wasn't she a member of a Trotskyite cell back then?"

"Allegedly," Alex said. "Anyway, Dad kissed her. 'I took the liberty,' was how he put it, 'and I started living again.'"

"Didn't it take Dad about seven years to persuade Mom to marry him?"

"He left that part out," Alex said. The goldfish darted around the bowl, filling the room with its agitation. "I guess he was trying to tell me to hang in there." She pulled her shawl more tightly around her shoulders.

Ten minutes later, when I left Alex's room, it was snowing. It shouldn't have been snowing in Kentucky in mid-March, when green was surging through everything, but there the flakes were, all fat and wet. They fell on my face, like kisses from somebody—an aunt, say—who hadn't seen me in an age.

I found my father in his gray three-on-the-tree Chevrolet Biscayne, a car as unstylish as his old raincoat. He was leaning his forehead against the steering wheel.

When I got in, Dad sat up straight and adjusted his cap. The steering wheel had left a mark on his brow. "I was thinking of that fish Alex caught in Lake Cumberland. Fall of sixty-two. You remember that?"

I remembered our fishing guide, a narrow, dilapidated man named Bristow who rolled his own cigarettes. He was so quiet that he'd essentially finished talking for the day after he'd said "Morning" to you.

"Alex was the happiest girl in the state when she caught that fish," my father said. "A little old crappie. And now she's inconsolable because of this fellow Ned."

"Ed." I watched the snow fall, as thick as a plague of moths. "But I doubt it's just him."

"What else do you think it is?" He pushed his glasses up his nose. Maybe my father loved the world too much to imagine that someone's sorrow could lead her to want to vanish, to forgo the chance to drop a line in the water once more.

I said, "Sometimes you lose your grip and you start sliding down the slope and you can't stop."

"Yes," my father said. "You need something to hang on to when it gets rough." He fired up the Biscayne, turned on the windshield wipers. "Isn't it peculiar, this snow?"

⁘ ⁘ ⁘

Several weeks later, when every dogwood in Jefferson County was in bloom, Alex sat at the table in my parents' kitchen, smoking one of Willie's Salems. Willie, who had worked for our family since before I was born, sat across from Alex, snapping the ends off green beans. There was sunlight in the room, a springtime flood of it. It washed over the cut-glass sugar bowl and

Dwight Allen 519

the three china monkeys (See No Evil, etc.) on the lazy Susan, over the faint hairs on Alex's wrist, and over the cast-iron pot Willie dropped the beans into.

"Last night I dreamed I was on a Greyhound," Alex said, "and this soldier kept falling asleep on my shoulder. And when I'd wake him, he'd scratch his head and say, 'Excuse me, ma'am, is this the Silver Dog to Bozeman?'"

I thought it was a good sign that Alex was having travel dreams. Since coming home from Queen of Peace, she'd rarely ventured out of the house, except to see her therapist. Once she'd driven to Frisch's Big Boy and ordered a cheeseburger and a shake, but had left before the curb girl could deliver the food. On another afternoon she'd gone with Bobby Tarr and his friend Pipe Cleaner Man to see a show at the planetarium.

"Don't talk to no soldiers on Greyhounds is my advice to you," Willie said. Willie handed out advice without much prompting. She snapped the stem off a bean. "You getting ready to leave us, Alex?"

"I'm just telling you my dream," Alex said. Cigarette smoke hung around her like a cloud, then slid out the window. She looked pale and a bit undernourished, but not without resources. I watched her trying to work out things behind her large brown eyes. A thought sped by; she touched her temple. Another thought, a longer one, it seemed, unfurled itself and lingered near the corner of her mouth, which curled downward.

"What do you think I should do, Willie?" Alex asked.

"Well," Willie said, "if I was you, I wouldn't be sitting here in my bedclothes at three in the afternoon with the sun shining. That's first. And second, I don't know that I'd be fooling with that boy Bobby and his friend, the one that looks like a Halloween skeleton."

"Pipe Cleaner Man," I said.

"He has a good heart," said Alex, who was drawn to socially marginal boys, boys whose brows were unclear, boys who liked to sleep in their labs with their rats and gels. "He can't help how he looks."

"All that reefer don't improve him any," Willie said. "And you neither." Her eyes, bloodshot from too much work or too many cigarettes, aimed daggers at me.

"I wonder what Bozeman is like," Alex said, giving the lazy Susan a push. The three monkeys glided by, two of them clearly grinning.

"Never heard of it," Willie said.

"Cowboys, rednecks," I said. "What would you be thinking of Montana for?"

"Bobby's sister lives there," Alex said. "She's a weaver."

"Cowboys, rednecks, and a weaver," I said, reaching for one of Willie's Salems.

"You can leave your money on the table," Willie said to me, carrying the pot of beans over to the stove. She was short and wide, a formidable squarish shape, like something not easily knocked over, though she walked on the sides of her feet and her white shoes were split at the seams.

"What about New York?" I said to Alex. I was thinking of moving there when I graduated from college, later that spring. "We could go together, find an apartment."

"I hear they got rats as big as suitcases in New York," Willie said. "Rats that eat children." She took an onion out of a bowl on the counter and slipped off its brown jacket.

"New York's too close to Philadelphia," Alex said, looking out the window. Our mother was kneeling at the edge of the garden, her trowel flashing in the sunlight. Hugo, our old dachshund, lay nearby.

"Where would you go, Willie," Alex asked, "if you were trying to think of someplace to go?"

"Walter took me to Chicago once," Willie said, "but I didn't think much of it." Walter was Willie's husband; he worked in a mattress factory and shot more pool than Willie believed was good for him. "When I was a girl, I used to like to visit my Great-aunt Alberta down in Hardin County. She had a horse and some Seckel pear trees. Sometimes she'd wrap the pears in newspaper and stick them in a drawer to let them ripen." Willie pushed chopped onion off the cutting board into the pot of beans. "But Hardin County might be a little slow for you."

Alex rubbed her temple with an index finger; a thought had lodged there, apparently. "Maybe I should be a nun."

"You're just talking," Willie said. "Anyhow, you ain't Catholic."

"The Episcopal Church has nuns," Alex said. We were Medium High Church Episcopalians, except for my mother, who practiced Episcopalianism but kept her ears open to the teachings of Baptist fundamentalists and Catholic mystics who lived on nuts and berries.

"You got to stay in the nunhouse on Saturday night if you're one of them," Willie said.

"Mac asked after you," I said, blowing a smoke ring that wobbled over the lazy Susan before collapsing.

Alex peered at me through the haze of smoke and sunlight. "How come you keep promoting Mac?"

"He's my friend," I said. "He likes you."

"Is that the boy who tried to fly into your window like he was some kind of spirit?" Willie asked.

"The same," Alex said. "If drunks had wings."

"Yeah," Willie said. "Then they could fly upside down and sing to you like Smokey Robinson."

Alex studied her hands. Eczema had chewed up her fingers, but they still flexed and wandered and grasped. Outside, sunlight washed over the figure of my mother kneeling among columbine and coralbells, Hugo dozing in the abundant green grass. Alex said, "Maybe I'll go get dressed and play some piano."

⸎ ⸎ ⸎

"Pigs are smart, you know," Mac said. He was telling Alex about Ben Franklin, a pig he'd kept as a pet for most of our last semester in college. We were in a johnboat on a lake east of Bardstown—my father in the bow, Alex and Mac in the middle, and myself in the stern, my hand on the tiller of a six-horse-power engine. It was a hot late-June afternoon, the sky the color of steam, no more than a shred of breeze. None of us had caught anything in the three hours we'd been on the lake. Alex and Mac still had lines in the water, but only my father, who secretly believed that catching a fish could make your blood rush and your soul expand all at once, fished as if he meant it. He was using a green popping plug, something that had worked for him on other occasions. Twenty times, the plug fell out of the sky into dark, weedy water near the shore, and twenty times my father slowly reeled in, flicking his rod now and then so that the open-mouthed lure made a sound—*bup-bup*—intended to excite bass. And twenty times the plug reached the boat slathered in algae.

"Where did the pig sleep?" Alex asked. She lifted her bait out of the water—a night crawler that resembled a knot of blanched viscera—and then dropped it back in.

"He slept in my dorm room in a box, until he got too big. I got him a student ID with his picture on it." Mac grinned. The sun had turned his fair skin a bright pink. His little blond mustache, which he'd worked on for months, was barely perceptible.

"Maybe I should try one of those weedless jigs," my father said. He opened his tackle box and took out a yellow-skirted lure. I saw a hawk cruise the pines at the far end of the lake, then dive out of sight.

"Is that the end of the story?" Alex asked. "I bet not. I bet that pig didn't live happily ever after." She glanced at Mac from underneath her baseball cap.

"I sort of donated him to my cultural anthro class," Mac said. "I gave him to my professor. We were studying hunting cultures and how they relate to animals."

"So then you barbecued him," Alex said.

"Eventually, yeah," Mac said, sighing a little. "But first I had to shoot him and cut his throat. Except I screwed up and missed the jugular. So then the pig gets up all of a sudden, all zonked on adrenaline, and starts flying around the pen in the professor's yard, splattering blood everywhere. And everybody in the class is silent, like this is a secret ceremony or something."

"The class watched you do this?" Alex asked.

"Pig Killing 101," I said.

"Yeah," Mac said. "So the professor and I caught the pig and cut the vein. I needed a keg of beer when it was over."

My father cast his yellow-skirted jig toward a stump, the monofilament gleaming as it arced across the water. It was possible that he hadn't heard Mac.

"What was the hardest part?" Alex asked Mac. Her knee was almost touching his, and she moved it away. "Shooting the pig? Slicing his throat? Or eating him?"

"Shooting him, I guess," Mac said, glancing at me. Mac had omitted from his account the fact that he'd been near tears as Ben Franklin flung himself around in that last mad rush of adrenaline, and the fact that it was the professor who had finally cut the jugular. "You're supposed to shoot him between the eyes. It's cleaner that way. But the pig wouldn't stand still while I was trying to sight him in. He kept moving his head back and forth, like he was on amphetamines, sniffing the dirt. I kept waiting for him to look at me." Mac didn't say that his hand had been shaking and that his first shot had hit the pig in the shoulder.

"If I'd been that pig," Alex said, "I would've looked at you. I would've wanted you to feel all my dying pig thoughts." She stared at Mac.

"Yeah," Mac said, turning away.

Alex reached over and pressed the sunburned flesh above his knee with her thumb. "You're going to fry, if you don't watch it."

My father reeled in his jig, and proposed that we move toward the end of the lake that lay in shade.

We scooted across the water, stirring up a breeze. Mac put a fresh night crawler on his hook and offered to put one on for Alex, but she said she'd do it herself. When I turned off the engine and we began to drift through the shade, my father said, "There's a fish waiting for you here, Moony Tooth."

"If you say so, Dad." Alex tossed her rebaited line into the water, and set her elbow on her thigh and her chin on her fist.

My father's yellow jig flew toward a fallen tree near the shore and the bass that surely slept there.

Mac watched his bobber. "Come on, fish. Bite."

A dragonfly landed on the bill of Alex's cap, its four wings in repose. "I've decided to move to Montana," she said.

My father reeled in his lure, which wiggled like a grass-skirted dancer. I could see him pondering the distance between Kentucky and Montana. He and my mother had wanted Alex to stay in-state for a while, spend a semester at U of K or U of L. "Long enough for her to get her feet on the ground," my mother had said. When I'd argued that I thought Alex had her feet on the ground—I'd still hoped she'd come to New York with me—my mother had replied, "Do you know what you're talking about? Depression doesn't just go away, like the chicken pox. It follows you around, and then one day it's sitting on your chest again and you can't breathe." My mother talked with her face turned aside, as if to spare me some of her indignation. "Can you imagine what it would be like for your sister to fall ill in a desolate place like Montana, where she doesn't know a soul, except for Bobby Tarr's sister?"

The dragonfly flew from Alex's cap. I considered the distance between Montana and New York, and I thought I saw Mac calculating the distance between Montana and Nashville, where he would begin work later that summer, selling pool tables for his father, who owned a chain of billiards stores in the mid-South. Anyway, I saw Mac's pink face darken, as if some slim hope had fled. Alex had a hold on Mac's imagination, the more so since she'd tried suicide. It was as if she knew things now—what pigs felt, why space curved.

"Montana," Mac mused. "Do they have daily mail delivery in Montana?"

"Are you going to write to me every day, Mac?"

Mac stroked the fuzz on his upper lip and studied his bobber.

My father looked out across the lake, which was flat and glaring where the sun struck it. Perhaps he was thinking of the winter he'd spent in Wyoming. He was fresh out of college then. Having been deemed unfit to serve in the Army—his eyesight was unacceptable, he was thinner than a darning needle—and having no good idea of how he should spend his professional life, he took a job at a private school in Sheridan founded by an oilman's wife. Dad had told Alex and me this story at dinner a few nights before. "Oh, it was as cold as Billy Blue," he'd said. "I thought spring would never come. I couldn't wait to get back to Kentucky." When he'd finished the story, Alex said, "I'll be sure to take some warm clothes with me, if I decide to go."

Now my father removed his glasses and cleaned them on his shirt. The lake was still. All the dull weight of the afternoon seemed to lie on it. Then Alex's bobber went under and her rod bent. The line ran parallel to the boat, then doubled back. Her face was intent, as if she were in the grip of a revelation.

The fish she pulled out of the water was a silvery yellow, with dark stripes. It wasn't much longer than her hand.

"A bluegill," my father said. "You saved us from being skunked, Moony Tooth."

"A lunker," Mac said.

"It's not always the size that counts," Alex said, grinning, showing Mac some of her fine, straight teeth.

"That line's older than my grandmother," Mac said, grabbing hold of the fish as it twisted in the air.

"Still applies," Alex said.

Mac wrestled with the hook—it was in deep—until the bluegill squirted out of his hands, landing on the slatted floor of the boat. I picked it up, felt the muscle bunched beneath its scales, then watched it shoot out of my hands. Alex took off her baseball cap and scooped the fish into it. Her loosened hair fell across her face.

"I've got a hook disgorger somewhere," my father said.

"That's OK, Dad," Alex said. "I can do it." She pushed her hair out of her face and bent over the fish, which she held on her lap in the cap. "Don't look at me like that," she said to the fish, working the hook back and forth. When the hook finally came free, she placed the fish back in the water carefully, as if she were setting a vase of flowers on a table.

"Go!" she said.

Crystal Wilkinson

"An Introduction to *Blackberries, Blackberries*"

A bright new African American voice in Kentucky is that of Crystal Wilkinson, who describes herself in *Blackberries, Blackberries* as "a black, country girl" who "grew up in rural Kentucky, and teaches creative writing." Born in Hamilton, Ohio, she went to live with her Wilkinson grandparents on their sixty-four-acre tobacco farm in Casey County when she was six. She has been director of the Carnegie Center for Literacy and Learning in Lexington and serves as chair of the creative writing department for the Kentucky Governor's School for the Arts. She is a charter member of the Affrilachian Poets, a group of performing African American poets from the South. She has written two very fine books that indicate a first-rate, original talent at work: *Blackberries, Blackberries* (2000) and *Water Street* (2002). In her introduction to *Blackberries, Blackberries,* she provides more details about who she is.

I grew up on a farm in Indian Creek, Kentucky, during the seventies. I swam in creeks and roamed the knobs and hills. We had an outhouse and no inside running water. Our house was heated by coal and wood-burning stoves and we lived so far back in the woods that we could get only one television station. But it was a place of beauty—trees, green grass and blue sky as far as you could see. I am country.

Being country is as much a part of me as my full lips, wide hips, dreadlocks and high cheekbones. There are many black country folks who have lived and are living in small towns, up hollers and across knobs. They are all over the South—scattered like milk-thistle seeds in the wind. The stories in this book are centered in these places.

As a girl, there was an extreme urgency to grow up as soon as possible. Being a woman was something that I longed for. I remember sitting quietly watching the way my grandmother put on lipstick, circling her lips just so. I studied my mother's walk, how it changed when she was all dressed up for church. I eavesdropped in on "women's business." Listened to the music my aunts and older cousins made with their voices. Observed the way my cousin's hand rested in the deep curve separating her waist and hip while her other hand moved in the air when she was most passionate about something. I watched how these beautiful women wore their countryness, wore their womanness. How they interacted with men, children and each other. I wanted to learn all the ways of womenfolk, to capture all the secrets. What I didn't know then was that a woman's life is never cut and dried. Never plain and simple, not as a girl, not as a full-fledged woman.

These stories come from the ordinary and the extraordinary. From black, country women with curious lives. From struggle, from fear, from love, from life, from the gut, from the heart. Black and juicy, just like a blackberry.

"Spoiled," from *Water Street*

A note in *Water Street* explains the relationship between Wilkinson's life and her fiction. Calling the book a work of fiction, she continues: "I spent many summers in Stanford, Kentucky, a place I considered my second home. This book is set there but the characters portrayed here and the events that take place on these pages should not be construed as real." They are, she reminds us, "the product of my imagination." She is echoing poet Marianne Moore's definition of poetry as "a place for the genuine," which Moore further describes as "imaginary gardens with real toads in them." Wilkinson's imaginative use of Stanford could be described as "a real town with imaginary people in it."

～∞～

Maxine Mason heard someone say once that mothers spoil their sons and raise their daughters. She turned that thought around and around in her head like that spinning wheel at the county fair, but she had never birthed daughters. Mouse was her only child. Still warm from the dryer, she folded Mouse's blue jeans . . . She smelled them, ran her cheek up and down the leg of the denim, folded his sports shirts, careful to turn down the collars. It was something she had done even when his clothes were much smaller. She had found herself fascinated with the tiny tennis shoes, the pastel terry cloth snap-ups that came in colors that reminded her of Easter. The fuzzy blue snowsuit that she bundled him in the day he came home from the hospital. He had been hot and sweaty when she unzipped him. The snowsuit had been too much for September. Could a mother ever do *too much*?

You're always fussing over him. Let him walk, Maxine. Put him down. Tie the boy's shoes? Hell, he's ten years old! When's he gonna learn to tie his own damn shoes?

She remembers Mouse's tiny, brown feet the day of his birth. How his feet and his hands were the only brown parts of him. He had been premature and so small that Maxine could nearly hold him in one hand. Five pounds, three ounces. His skin was wrinkled those first few days, looking just like a

Crystal Wilkinson 527

mouse. He was named Monte after Eugene's father but the nickname stuck all these years.

Eugene's sister, Cookie, stood over Maxine's hospital bed, two thick braids snaking down and back on either side of her head. Flailing arms, bracelets clanging and bright yellow dress flashing like a caution signal all over the room.

"That ain't Gene's baby! That baby don't look nothing like my brother! Not one thing on him. That baby's got a white daddy somewhere."

Her loud, red mouth focusing on Maxine with all its fury.

But at the moment she held her son in her arms and looked into his eyes, Maxine was in love. Not a romantic love, but almost. It hadn't mattered that Gene acted a fool. That he accused her of lying down with some white man just because his crazy sister said so. Now she wondered if all the accusations had come from his own guilt. Maybe he was messing around even then. It hadn't mattered that it took the boy two months to turn the color of the dark beer his daddy drank on Saturday nights.

It was what Maxine sensed behind those little eyes on that first day that mattered: that knowing thing that had started between them even before he was born. The moment she knew that it was a little miracle forming in her belly. The moment Mouse was born, Maxine knew her baby recognized her as being someone who belonged to him for life. It was a hushed pact between them. A vow of sorts. Something she thought would always be. But that was before this new space opened up. Before the unraveling started. Before this new thing threatened to swallow her whole.

"That boy can't fix his own supper plate. A damn shame. You done spoiled him. Rotten to the core. Ain't never gonna be no count to nobody. Some kinda mama's boy fool his whole damn life."

Gene had always been jealous of the looks that crossed between Maxine and Mouse. Knew from day one that a big part of his woman was gone forever. Knew he could never compete with her mothering no matter how hard he tried. A thread had already been pulled.

Before the baby came things had been different.

Baby, can you wear the orange sweater? I like to see you in that.

Every time they headed out to dinner or to a dance Gene would ask her to wear special things for him. They had never had a marriage filled with negligees or sexy frills but there had been something alive there once. Sometimes Maxine would be sitting in the living room reading a book, naked from the waist down, wearing only one of Gene's favorite bras or one of his T-shirts. The memory of legs locked, Gene's hands moving across her, tweaked some dormant feeling buried beneath her maternal self, but she stuffed it back in neat, tidy, like a starched white blouse being tucked into a skirt. That was before the phone started ringing in the middle of the night before Gene came home late smelling of perfume with lie after lie after lie. Maxine rested her elbows on the dryer, while the rest of the wash dried. Let the warm hum of it take her off somewhere. Followed it wherever it wanted to go.

It wasn't until Gene came home from the service that she had started liking him. He had been just one of the other boys in high school. Tall, dark, bow-legged. Played a little basketball. Got good grades. But really not the kind of guy that too many girls noticed back then. After high school, Maxine worked as a secretary at the American Greetings factory in Danville. Gene came home from the service. A man with four years of serving his country but nobody in Stanford needed his help. So he had turned to factories for work. He met Maxine again when he came into the factory to fill out an application. He came home a different man than Maxine had remembered. A different look in his eye. He was confident and that made him attractive.

What about our time?

Maxine was at the stove mashing up a potato for Mouse. Peeling all the brown skin off, mashing up every bit with a fork. It was a simple task but she concentrated hard, just making sure there was nothing for him to choke on. Before the question, Gene had come through the front door without a greeting. He missed the softness of Maxine's arms around him. He missed her mouth on his before he crossed the threshold.

But what about our time?

Maxine was a blur. He had become accustomed to seeing just the back of her body scooting from room to room. Hands elbow-deep in laundry, her backside bent over the crib, a glimpse of the way her short-cropped hair graced the nape of her long neck. Even at night it was only her back that he saw. Her bare arms and shoulders, the color of baked piecrust. A taste of her neck exposed just above the lace collar of her nightgown. Night after night he reached out to her.

Please Gene not tonight.

Or, at the exact moment that he had finally convinced her to let him just hold her, the baby's cry would intrude.

It was odd, but just when Mouse was finally growing up, just then was when Maxine was about to need Gene again. That's when he had begun to be drawn to the streets, to the bootleg house, to the other women. That's when he had given up trying.

You don't need me Maxine, you got your man right in there.

That night when Mouse was sixteen and Maxine had put Gene out, Eugene pointed his long, dark finger toward Mouse's room. And walked out the door.

This done gone on too long. I ain't cut out for this kind of life. That's our child, Maxine Jean. I love him too. But I'm your husband; I needed a wife.

Maxine pulled another load of clothes out of the dryer.

Spoil their sons and raise their daughters?

She had never had a daughter. She wondered how a girl child would have been different. Would she have loved her any less? The space between Mouse's joyous entrance into this world and this person he had become was an expansive gap. So wide Maxine felt sometimes she would fall over into the space and find herself surrounded by darkness and alone. She saw herself ending up in a hospital. Heartbreak manifesting itself into ulcers or full-blown heart trouble.

Her husband was spending his nights with Honey. He was gone. And Mouse was growing up on her. She had gone from knowing everything to knowing nothing. Her evenings were spent alone. Every time the phone rang it was for Mouse. Girls needing his company. She could hear the pleading in their voices reminding her too much of herself. Junior and Peanut calling him to the hill and wanting to "shoot some hoops." Always something, somebody.

Mouse always comes to dinner waiting for him in the oven. His mother is always waiting on the couch. Seeing him safely in. He retreats to his room and shuts the door, not to be seen until the next morning. All she ever sees is his back and the occasional shrug of his shoulders, or the occasional kiss on the cheek she receives when she questions him. When she pleads for a piece of his time. He will be leaving her house soon, too, following in his father's footsteps.

Maxine is in mourning, grieving for the tiny hands and feet that she used to kiss. She hears little slippered feet pattering down the hallway. Feels little chubby arms wrapped around her knees. Hears the incessant questions.

Mommy, how does the rain stay in the sky before it falls? Is the moon really made out of cheese? Will you play with me?

Sixteen years move in slow motion; then catch speed, fast, like the pages of a book being flipped. At night it is not Gene she misses but the closeness of Mouse. His limp body on her lap, asleep. His head on her breasts. His eyes closed. Long eyelashes. She kisses his sleeping face. Smells baby smells.

She folds his underwear. White, with dark green ovals and octagons. She holds them in the air. Clean. Looks at them and shakes her head. Too big. Much too big.

She hears him before he comes in. Hears his footsteps, slapping against the sidewalk. His long feet slapping, slapping. She has prepared a speech, a good talking to. The back door opens. She feels his hands on her shoulders but she dares not turn around. She feels his kiss on her cheek, thinks there was a hint of stubble. Smells beer on his breath.

"Dinner still in the oven?" he says.

She keeps still, to keep from crumbling. Closes her eyes and takes in his voice. Deep. Scratchy. Some strange voice that she has yet to fully recognize. Some strange man who refuses her, shuns her sweetness.

Barbara Kingsolver

"Rose-Johnny"

Barbara Kingsolver, one of Kentucky's most distinguished contemporary authors, was born in Annapolis, Maryland, in 1955, but she moved when she was two with her family to Carlisle, Kentucky, where she grew up. She holds degrees in biology and English from Depauw University and the University of Arizona. She became a celebrated author with the publication of her first novel, *The Bean Trees* (1988), which is the story of a young Kentucky woman, Taylor Greer, who moves west to Tucson and acquires an unusual family that includes an orphaned baby girl she names Turtle, a Guatemalan refugee couple, a single mother, and several elderly neighbors. She soon becomes involved in the sanctuary movement in support of undocumented aliens. This was only the beginning of a lifetime of work and writing in support of liberal causes as a writer and activist. In her acknowledgments in *Small Wonder* (2002), a book of essays, she thanks her mother, who "never once told me not to stick my neck out." Sticking her neck out has earned her and her books a fiercely dedicated following. *The Poisonwood Bible* (1998) is a cautionary tale told by the wife and four daughters of Nathan Price, a devout evangelical Baptist who takes his family with him on a mission to the Belgian Congo in 1959 and learns a thing or two about cultural values.

Her other books include *Animal Dreams* (1990), which involves an environmental catastrophe; *Another America* (1992), a collection of poems; *Pigs in Heaven* (1993), a novel about the risks of love that moves from rural Kentucky and the southwest to Heaven, Oklahoma, and the Cherokee Nation; *High Tide in Tucson* (1995), essays on family, community, and the natural world; *Holding the Line: Women in the Great Arizona Mine Strike of 1983* (1996); and *Prodigal Summer* (2000), which weaves together three love stories in the mountains and small farms of southern Appalachia. In this novel a character speaks of a theme that runs throughout all Kingsolver's wise and important books: "Everything alive is connected to every other by fine, invisible threads. Things you don't see can help you plenty, and things you try to control will often rear back and bite you, and that's the moral of the story." If we are to survive, we all may have to learn this lesson. Another related theme is that if we humans are in right relationship to nature, we are likely to be in right relationship to each other and treat each other decently and fairly. "Rose-Johnny," from *Homeland and Other Stories* (1989), is a poignant story about love and acceptance and fairness as it is played out in a small Kentucky town.

Rose-Johnny wore a man's haircut and terrified little children, although I will never believe that was her intention. For her own part she inspired in us only curiosity. It was our mothers who took this fascination and wrung it, through daily admonitions, into the most irresistible kind of horror. She was like the old wells, covered with ancient rotting boards and overgrown with weeds, that waited behind the barns to swallow us down: our mothers warned us time and again not to go near them, and still were certain that we did.

My own mother was not one of those who had a great deal to say about her, but Walnut Knobs was a small enough town so that a person did not need to be told things directly. When I had my first good look at her, at close range, I was ten years old. I fully understood the importance of the encounter.

What mattered to me at the time, though, was that it was something my sister had not done before me. She was five years older, and as a consequence there was hardly an achievement in my life, nor even an article of clothing, that had not first been Mary Etta's. But, because of the circumstances of my meeting Rose-Johnny, I couldn't tell a living soul about it, and so for nearly a year I carried the secret torment of a great power that can't be used. My agitation was not relieved but made worse when I told the story to myself, over and over again.

She was not, as we always heard, half man and half woman, something akin to the pagan creatures whose naked torsos are inserted in various shocking ways into parts of animal bodies. In fact, I was astonished by her ordinariness. It is true that she wore Red Wing boots like my father. And also there was something not quite womanly in her face, but maybe any woman's face would look the same with that haircut. Her hair was coal black, cut flat across the top of her round head, so that when she looked down I could see a faint pale spot right on top where the scalp almost surfaced.

But the rest of her looked exactly like anybody's mother in a big flowered dress without a waistline and with two faded spots in front, where her bosom rubbed over the counter when she reached across to make change or wipe away the dust.

People say there is a reason for every important thing that happens. I was sent to the feed store, where I spoke to Rose-Johnny and passed a quarter from my hand into hers, because it was haying time. And because I was small for my age. I was not too small to help with tobacco setting in the spring, in fact I was better at it than Mary Etta, who complained about the stains on her hands, but I was not yet big enough to throw a bale of hay onto the flatbed. It was the time of year when Daddy complained about not having boys. Mama said that at least he oughtn't to bother going into town for the chicken mash that day because Georgeann could do it on her way home from school.

Mama told me to ask Aunt Minnie to please ma'am give me a ride home. "Ask her nice to stop off at Lester Wall's store so you can run in with this quarter and get five pound of laying mash."

I put the quarter in my pocket, keeping my eye out to make certain Mary Etta understood what I had been asked to do. Mary Etta had once told me that I was no better than the bugs that suck on potato vines, and that the family was going to starve to death because of my laziness. It was one of the summer days when we were on our knees in the garden picking off bugs and dropping them into cans of coal oil. She couldn't go into town with Aunt Minnie to look at dress patterns until we finished with the potato bugs. What she said, exactly, was that if I couldn't work any harder than that, then she might just as well throw *me* into a can of coal oil. Later she told me she hadn't meant it, but I intended to remember it nonetheless.

⸎ ⸎ ⸎

Aunt Minnie taught the first grade and had a 1951 Dodge. That is how she referred to her car whenever she spoke of it. It was the newest automobile belonging to anyone related to us, although some of the Wilcox cousins had once come down to visit from Knoxville in a Ford they were said to have bought the same year it was made. But I saw that car and did not find it nearly as impressive as Aunt Minnie's, which was white and immense and shone like glass. She paid a boy to polish it every other Saturday.

On the day she took me to Wall's, she waited in the car while I went inside with my fist tight around the quarter. I had never been in the store before, and although I had passed by it many times and knew what could be bought there, I had never imagined what a wonderful combination of warm, sweet smells of mash and animals and seed corn it would contain. The dust lay white and thin on everything like a bridal veil. Rose-Johnny was in the back with a water can, leaning over into one of the chick tubs. The steel rang with the sound of confined baby birds, and a light bulb shining up from inside the tub made her face glow white. Mr. Wall, Rose-Johnny's Pa, was in the front of the store talking to two men about a horse. He didn't notice me as I crept up to the counter. It was Rose-Johnny who came forward to the cash register.

"And what for you, missy?"

She is exactly like anybody's mama, was all I could think, and I wanted to reach and touch her flowered dress. The two men were looking at me.

"My mama needs five pound of laying mash and here's a quarter for it." I clicked the coin quickly onto the counter.

"Yes, ma'am." She smiled at me, but her boots made heavy, tired sounds on the floor. She made her way slowly, like a duck in water, over to the row of wooden bins that stood against the wall. She scooped the mash into a paper bag and weighed it, then shoved the scoop back into the bin. A little cloud of dust rose out of the mash up into the window. I watched her from the counter.

"Don't your mama know she's wasting good money on chicken mash? Any fool chicken will eat corn." I jumped when the man spoke. It was one of the two, and they were standing so close behind me I would have had to look right straight up to see their faces. Mr. Wall was gone.

"No sir, they need mash," I said to the man's boots.

"What's that?" It was the taller man doing the talking.

"They need mash," I said louder. "To lay good sturdy eggs for selling. A little mash mixed in with the corn. Mama says it's got oster shells in it."

"Is that a fact," he said. "Did you hear that, Rose-Johnny?" he called out. "This child says you put oster shells in that mash. Is that right?"

When Rose-Johnny came back to the cash register she was moon-eyed. She made quick motions with her hands and pushed the bag at me as if she didn't know how to talk.

"Do you catch them osters yourself, Rose-Johnny? Up at Jackson Crick?" The man was laughing. The other man was quiet.

Rose-Johnny looked all around and up at the ceiling. She scratched at her short hair, fast and hard, like a dog with ticks.

When the two men were gone I stood on my toes and leaned over the counter as far as I could. "Do you catch the osters yourself?"

She hooked her eyes right into mine, the way the bit goes into the mule's mouth and fits just so, one way and no other. Her eyes were the palest blue of any I had ever seen. Then she threw back her head and laughed so hard I could see the wide, flat bottoms of her back teeth, and I wasn't afraid of her.

When I left the store, the two men were still outside. Their boots scuffed on the front-porch floorboards, and the shorter one spoke.

"Child, how much did you pay that woman for the chicken mash?"

"A quarter," I told him.

He put a quarter in my hand. "You take this here, and go home and tell your daddy something. Tell him not never to send his little girls to Wall's feed store. Tell him to send his boys if he has to, but not his little girls." His hat was off, and his hair lay back in wet orange strips. A clean line separated the white top of his forehead from the red-burned hide of his face. In this way, it was like my father's face.

"No, sir, I can't tell him, because all my daddy's got is girls."

"That's George Bowles's child, Bud," the tall man said. "He's just got the two girls."

"Then tell him to come for hisself," Bud said. His eyes had the sun in them, and looked like a pair of new pennies.

Aunt Minnie didn't see the man give me the quarter because she was looking at herself in the side-view mirror of the Dodge. Aunt Minnie was older than Mama, but everyone mistook her for the younger because of the way she fixed herself up. And, of course, Mama was married. Mama said if Aunt Minnie ever found a man she would act her age.

When I climbed in the car she was pulling gray hairs out of her part. She said it was teaching school that caused them, but early gray ran in my mama's family.

She jumped when I slammed the car door. "All set?"

"Yes ma'am," I said. She put her little purple hat back on her head and slowly pushed the long pin through it. I shuddered as she started up the car.

Aunt Minnie laughed. "Somebody walked over your grave."

"I don't have a grave," I said. "I'm not dead."

"No, you most certainly are not. That's just what they say when a person shivers like that." She smiled. I liked Aunt Minnie most of the time.

"I don't think they mean your real grave, with you in it," she said after a minute. "I think it means the place where your grave is going to be someday."

I thought about this for a while. I tried to picture the place but could not. Then I thought about the two men outside Wall's store. I asked Aunt Minnie why it was all right for boys to do some things that girls couldn't.

"Oh, there's all kinds of reasons," she said. "Like what kinds of things, do you mean?"

"Like going into Wall's feed store."

"Who told you that?"

"Somebody."

Aunt Minnie didn't say anything.

Then I said, "It's because of Rose-Johnny, isn't it?"

Aunt Minnie raised her chin just a tiny bit. She might have been checking her lipstick in the mirror, or she might have been saying yes.

"Why?" I asked.

"Why what?"

"Why because of Rose-Johnny?"

"I can't tell you that, Georgeann."

"Why can't you tell me?" I whined. "Tell me."

The car rumbled over a cattle grate. When we came to the crossing, Aunt Minnie stepped on the brake so hard we both flopped forward. She looked at me. "Georgeann, Rose-Johnny is a Lebanese. That's all I'm going to tell you. You'll understand better when you're older."

When I got home I put the laying mash in the henhouse. The hens were already roosting high above my head, clucking softly into their feathers and shifting back and forth on their feet. I collected the eggs as I did every day, and took them into the house. I hadn't yet decided what to do about the quarter, and so I held on to it until dinnertime.

Mary Etta was late coming down, and even though she had washed and changed she looked pale as a haunt from helping with the haying all day. She didn't speak and she hardly ate.

"Here, girls, both of you, eat up these potatoes," Mama said after a while. "There's not but just a little bit left. Something to grow on."

"I don't need none then," Mary Etta said. "I've done growed all I'm going to grow."

"Don't talk back to your mama," Daddy said.

"I'm not talking back. It's the truth." Mary Etta looked at Mama. "Well, it is."

"Eat a little bite, Mary Etta. Just because you're in the same dresses for a year don't mean you're not going to grow no more."

"I'm as big as you are, Mama."

"All right then." Mama scraped the mashed potatoes onto my plate. "I expect now you'll be telling me you don't want to grow no more either," she said to me.

"No, ma'am, I won't," I said. But I was distressed, and looked sideways at the pink shirtwaist I had looked forward to inheriting along with the grown-up shape that would have to be worn inside it. Now it appeared that I was condemned to my present clothes and potato-shaped body; keeping these forever seemed to me far more likely than the possibility of having clothes that, like the Wilcox automobile, had never before been owned. I ate my potatoes quietly. Dinner was almost over when Daddy asked if I had remembered to get the laying mash.

"Yes, sir. I put it in the henhouse." I hesitated. "And here's the quarter back. Mr. Wall gave me the mash for nothing."

"Why did he do that?" Mama asked.

Mary Ella was staring like the dead. Even her hair looked tired, slumped over the back of her chair like a long black shadow.

"I helped him out," I said. "Rose-Johnny wasn't there, she was sick, and Mr. Wall said if I would help him clean out the bins and dust the shelves and water the chicks, then it wouldn't cost me for the laying mash."

"And Aunt Minnie waited while you did all that?"

"She didn't mind," I said. "She had some magazines to look at."

It was the first important lie I had told in my life, and I was thrilled with its power. Every member of my family believed I had brought home the laying mash in exchange for honest work.

I was also astonished at how my story, once I had begun it, wouldn't finish. "He wants me to come back and help him again the next time we need something," I said.

"I don't reckon you let on like we couldn't pay for the mash?" Daddy asked sternly.

"No, sir. I put the quarter right up there on the counter. But he said he needed the help. Rose-Johnny's real sick."

He looked at me like he knew. Like he had found the hole in the coop where the black snake was getting in. But he just said, "All right. You can go, if Aunt Minnie don't mind waiting for you."

"You don't have to say a thing to her about it," I said. "I can walk home the same as I do every day. Five pound of mash isn't nothing to carry."

"We'll see," Mama said.

That night I believed I would burst. For a long time after Mary Etta fell asleep I twisted in my blankets and told the story over to myself, both the true and false versions. I talked to my doll, Miss Regina. She was a big doll, a birthday present from my Grandma and Grandpa Bowles, with a tiny wire crown and lovely long blond curls.

"Rose-Johnny isn't really sick," I told Miss Regina. "She's a Lebanese."

❧❧❧

I looked up the word in Aunt Minnie's Bible dictionary after school. I pretended to be looking up St. John the Baptist but then turned over in a hurry to the *L*'s while she was washing her chalkboards. My heart thumped when I found it, but I read the passage quickly, several times over, and found it empty. It said the Lebanese were a seafaring people who built great ships from cedar trees. I couldn't believe that even when I was older I would be able, as Aunt Minnie promised, to connect this with what I had seen of Rose-Johnny. Nevertheless, I resolved to understand. The following week I went back to the store, confident that my lie would continue to carry its own weight.

Rose-Johnny recognized me. "Five pounds of laying mash," she said, and this time I followed her to the feed bins. There were flecks of white dust in her hair.

"Is it true you come from over the sea?" I asked her quietly as she bent over with the scoop.

She laughed and rolled her eyes. "A lot of them says I come from the moon," she said, and I was afraid she was going to be struck dumb and animal-eyed as she was the time before. But, when she finished weighing the bag, she just said, "I was born in Slate Holler, and that's as far from here as I ever been or will be."

"Is that where you get the osters from?" I asked, looking into the mash and trying to pick out which of the colored flecks they might be.

Rose-Johnny looked at me for a long time, and then suddenly laughed her big laugh. "Why, honey child, don't you know? Osters comes from the sea."

She rang up twenty-five cents on the register, but I didn't look at her. "That was all, wasn't it?"

I leaned over the counter and tried to put tears in my eyes, but they wouldn't come. "I can't pay," I said. "My daddy said to ask you if I could do some work for it. Clean up or something."

"Your daddy said to ask me that? Well, bless your heart," she said. "Let me see if we can't find something for you to do. Bless your little heart, child, what's your name?"

"Georgeann," I told her.

"I'm Rose-Johnny," she said, and I did not say that I knew it, that like every other child I had known it since the first time I saw her in town, when I was five or six, and had to ask Mama if it was a man or a lady.

"Pleased to meet you," I said.

We kept it between the two of us: I came in every week to help with the pullets and the feed, and took home my mash. We did not tell Mr. Wall, although it seemed it would not have mattered one whit to him. Mr. Wall was in the store so seldom that he might not have known I was there. He kept to himself in the apartment at the back where he and Rose-Johnny lived.

It was she who ran the store, kept the accounts, and did the orders. She showed me how to feed and water the pullets and ducklings and pull out the sick ones. Later I learned how to weigh out packages of seed and to mix the different kinds of mash. There were lists nailed to the wall telling how much cracked corn and oats and grit to put in. I followed the recipes with enormous care, adding tiny amounts at a time to the bag on the hanging scales until the needle touched the right number. Although she was patient with me, I felt slow next to Rose-Johnny, who never had to look at the lists and used the scales only to check herself. It seemed to me she knew how to do more things than anyone I had ever known, woman or man.

She also knew the names of all the customers, although she rarely spoke to them. Sometimes such a change came over her when the men were there that it wasn't clear to me whether she was pretending or had really lost the capacity to speak. But afterward she would tell me their names and everything about them. Once she told me about Ed Charney, Sr. and Bud Mattox, the two men I had seen the first day I was in the store. According to Rose-Johnny, Ed had an old red mule he was in the habit of mistreating. "But even so," she said, "Ed's mule don't have it as bad as Bud's wife." I never knew how she acquired this knowledge.

When she said "Bud Mattox," I remembered his penny-colored eyes and connected him then with all the Mattox boys at school. It had never occurred to me that eyes could run in families, like early gray.

Occasionally a group of black-skinned children came to the store, always after hours. Rose-Johnny opened up for them. She called each child by name, and asked after their families and the health of their mothers' laying hens.

The oldest one, whose name was Cleota, was shaped like Mary Etta. Her hair was straight and pointed, and smelled to me like citronella candles. The younger girls had plaits that curved out from their heads like so many handles. Several of them wore dresses made from the same bolt of cloth, but they were not sisters. Rose-Johnny filled a separate order for each child.

I watched, but didn't speak. The skin on their heels and palms was creased, and as light as my own. Once, after they had left, I asked Rose-Johnny why they only came into the store when it was closed.

"People's got their ways," she said, stoking up the wood stove for the night. Then she told me all their names again, starting with Cleota and working down. She looked me in the eye. "When you see them in town, you speak. Do you hear? By *name*. I don't care who is watching."

⋘ ⋘ ⋘

I was allowed to spend half an hour or more with Rose-Johnny nearly every day after school, so long as I did not neglect my chores at home. Sometimes on days that were rainy or cold Aunt Minnie would pick me up, but I preferred to walk. By myself, without Mary Etta to hurry me up.

As far as I know, my parents believed I was helping Mr. Wall because of Rose-Johnny's illness. They had no opportunity to learn otherwise, though I worried that someday Aunt Minnie would come inside the store to fetch me, instead of just honking, or that Daddy would have to go to Wall's for something and see for himself that Rose-Johnny was fit and well. Come springtime he would be needing to buy tobacco seed.

It was soon after Christmas when I became consumed with a desire to confess. I felt the lies down inside me like cold, dirty potatoes in a root cellar, beginning to sprout and crowd. At night I told Miss Regina of my dishonesty and the things that were likely to happen to me because of it. In so doing, there were several times I nearly confessed by accident to Mary Etta.

"Who's going to wring your neck?" she wanted to know, coming into the room one night when I thought she was downstairs washing the supper dishes.

"Nobody," I said, clutching Miss Regina to my pillow. I pretended to be asleep. I could hear Mary Etta starting to brush her hair. Every night before she went to bed she sat with her dress hiked up and her head hung over between her knees, brushing her hair all the way down to the floor. This improved the circulation to the hair, she told me, and would prevent it turning. Mary Etta was already beginning to get white hairs.

"Is it because Mama let you watch Daddy kill the cockerels? Did it scare you to see them jump around like that with their necks broke?"

"I'm not scared," I murmured, but I wanted so badly to tell the truth that I started to cry. I knew, for certain, that something bad was going to happen. I believe I also knew it would happen to my sister, instead of me.

"Nobody's going to hurt you," Mary Etta said. She smoothed my bangs and laid my pigtails down flat on top of the quilt. "Give me Miss Regina and let me put her up for you now, so you won't get her hair all messed up."

I let her have the doll. "I'm not scared about the cockerels, Mary Etta. I promise." With my finger, under the covers, I traced a cross over my heart.

⋙ ⋙ ⋙

When Rose-Johnny fell ill I was sick with guilt. When I first saw Mr. Wall behind the counter instead of Rose-Johnny, so help me God, I prayed this would be the day Aunt Minnie would come inside to get me. Immediately after, I felt sure God would kill me for my wickedness. I pictured myself falling dead beside the oat bin. I begged Mr. Wall to let me see her.

"Go on back, littl'un. She told me you'd be coming in," he said.

I had never been in the apartment before. There was little in it beyond the necessary things and a few old photographs on the walls, all of the same woman. The rooms were cold and felt infused with sickness and an odor I incorrectly believed to be medicine. Because my father didn't drink, I had never before encountered the smell of whiskey.

Rose-Johnny was propped on the pillows in a lifeless flannel gown. Her face changed when she saw me, and I remembered the way her face was lit by the light bulb in the chick tub, the first time I saw her. With fresh guilt I threw myself on her bosom.

"I'm sorry. I could have paid for the mash. I didn't mean to make you sick." Through my sobs I heard accusing needly wheezing sounds in Rose-Johnny's chest. She breathed with a great pulling effort.

"Child, don't talk foolish."

⋙ ⋙ ⋙

As weeks passed and Rose-Johnny didn't improve, it became clear that my lie was prophetic. Without Rose-Johnny to run the store, Mr. Wall badly needed my help. He seemed mystified by his inventory and was rendered helpless by any unusual demand from a customer. It was March, the busiest time for the store. I had turned eleven, one week before Mary Etta turned sixteen. These seven days out of each year, during which she was only four years older, I considered to be God's greatest gifts to me.

The afternoon my father would come in to buy the vegetable garden and tobacco seed was an event I had rehearsed endlessly in my mind. When it finally did transpire, Mr. Wall's confusion gave such complete respectability to my long-standing lie that I didn't need to say a word myself in support of it. I waited on him with dignity, precisely weighing out his tobacco seed, and even recommended to him the white runner beans that Mr. Wall had accidentally overstocked, and which my father did not buy.

Later on that same afternoon, after the winter light had come slanting through the dusty windows and I was alone in the store cleaning up, Cleota and the other children came pecking at the glass. I let them in. When I had filled all the orders Cleota unwrapped their coins, knotted all together into a blue handkerchief. I counted, and counted again. It was not the right amount, not even half.

"That's what Miss Rose-Johnny ast us for it," Cleota said. "Same as always." The smaller children—Venise, Anita, Little-Roy, James—shuffled and elbowed each other like fighting cocks, paying no attention. Cleota gazed at me calmly, steadily. Her eyebrows were two perfect arches.

"I thank you very much," I said, and put the coins in their proper places in the cash drawer.

During that week I also discovered an epidemic of chick droop in the pullets. I had to pull Mr. Wall over by the hand to make him look. There were more sick ones than well.

"It's because it's so cold in the store," I told him. "They can't keep warm. Can't we make it warmer in here?"

Mr. Wall shrugged at the wood stove, helpless. He could never keep a fire going for long, the way Rose-Johnny could.

"We have to try. The one light bulb isn't enough," I said. The chicks were huddled around the bulb just the way the men would collect around the stove in the mornings to say howdy-do to Mr. Wall and warm up their hands on the way to work. Except the chicks were more ruthless: they climbed and shoved, and the healthy ones pecked at the eyes and feet of the sick ones, making them bleed.

I had not noticed before what a very old man Mr. Wall was. As he stared down at the light, I saw that his eyes were covered with a film. "How do we fix them up?" he asked me.

"We can't. We've got to take the sick ones out so they won't all get it. Rose-Johnny puts them in that tub over there. We give them water and keep them warm, but it don't do any good. They've got to die."

He looked so sad I stood and patted his old freckled hand.

I spent much more time than before at the store, but no longer enjoyed it particularly. Working in the shadow of Rose-Johnny's expertise, I had been a secret witness to a wondrous ritual of counting, weighing, and tending. Together we created little packages that sailed out like ships to all parts of the county, giving rise to gardens and barnyard life in places I had never even seen. I felt superior to my schoolmates, knowing that I had had a hand in the creation of their families' poultry flocks and their mothers' kitchen gardens. By contrast, Mr. Wall's bewilderment was pathetic and only increased my guilt. But each day I was able to spend a little time in the back rooms with Rose-Johnny.

There were rumors about her illness, both before and after the fact. It did not occur to me that I might have been the source of some of the earlier rumors. But, if I didn't think of this, it was because Walnut Knobs was over-run with tales of Rose-Johnny, and not because I didn't take notice of the stories. I did.

The tales that troubled me most were those about Rose-Johnny's daddy. I had heard many adults say that he was responsible for her misfortune, which I presumed to mean her short hair. But it was also said that he was a colored man, and this I knew to be untrue. Aunt Minnie, when I pressed her, would offer nothing more than that if it were up to her I wouldn't go near either one of them, advice which I ignored. I was coming to understand that I would not hear the truth about Rose-Johnny from Aunt Minnie or anyone else. I knew, in a manner that went beyond the meanings of words I could not understand, that she was no more masculine than my mother or aunt, and no more lesbian than Lebanese. Rose-Johnny was simply herself, and alone.

And yet she was such a capable woman that I couldn't believe she would be sick for very long. But as the warm weather came she grew sluggish and pale. Her slow, difficult breathing frightened me. I brought my schoolbooks and read to her from the foot of the bed. Sometimes the rather ordinary adventures of the boy in my reader would make her laugh aloud until she choked. Other times she fell asleep while I read, but then would make me read those parts over again.

She worried about the store. Frequently she would ask about Mr. Wall and the customers, and how he was managing. "He does all right," I always said. But eventually my eagerness to avoid the burden of further lies, along with the considerable force of my pride, led me to confess that I had to tell him nearly everything. "He forgets something awful," I told her.

Rose-Johnny smiled. "He used to be as smart as anything, and taught me. Now I've done taught you, and you him again." She was lying back on the pillows with her eyes closed and her plump hands folded on her stomach.

"But he's a nice man," I said. I listened to her breathing. "He don't hurt you does he? Your pa?"

Nothing moved except her eyelids. They opened and let the blue eyes out at me. I looked down and traced my finger over the triangles of the flying-geese patch on the quilt. I whispered, "Does he make you cut off your hair?"

Rose-Johnny's eyes were so pale they were almost white, like ice with water running underneath. "He cuts it with a butcher knife. Sometimes he chases me all the way down to the river." She laughed a hissing laugh like a boy, and she had the same look the yearling calves get when they are cornered and jump the corral and run to the woods and won't be butchered. I understood then that Rose-Johnny, too, knew the power of a lie.

⁂ ⁂ ⁂

It was the youngest Mattox boy who started the fight at school on the Monday after Easter. He was older than me, and a boy, so nobody believed he would hit me, but when he started the name calling I called them right back, and he threw me down on the ground. The girls screamed and ran to get the teacher, but by the time she arrived I had a bloody nose and had bitten his arm wonderfully hard.

Miss Althea gave me her handkerchief for my nose and dragged Roy Mattox inside to see the principal. All the other children stood in a circle, looking at me.

"It isn't true, what he said," I told them. "And not about Rose-Johnny either. She isn't a pervert. I love her."

"Pervert," one of the boys said.

I marveled at the sight of my own blood soaking through the handkerchief. "I love her," I said.

I did not get to see Rose-Johnny that day. The door of Wall's store was locked. I could see Mr. Wall through the window, though, so I banged on the glass with the flats of my hands until he came. He had the strong medicine smell on his breath.

"Not today, littl'un." The skin under his eyes was dark blue.

"I need to see Rose-Johnny." I was irritated with Mr. Wall, and did not consider him important enough to prevent me from seeing her. But evidently he was.

"Not today," he said. "We're closed." He shut the door and locked it.

I shouted at him through the glass. "Tell her I hit a boy and bit his arm, that was calling her names. Tell her I fought with a boy, Mr. Wall."

The next day the door was open, but I didn't see him in the store. In the back, the apartment was dark except for the lamp by Rose-Johnny's bed. A small brown bottle and a glass stood just touching each other on the night table. Rose-Johnny looked asleep but made a snuffing sound when I climbed onto the bottom of the bed.

"Did your daddy tell you what I told him yesterday?"

She said nothing.

"Is your daddy sick?"

"My daddy's dead," she said suddenly, causing me to swallow a little gulp of air. She opened her eyes, then closed them again. "Pa's all right, honey, just stepped out, I imagine." She stopped to breathe between every few words. "I didn't mean to give you a fright. Pa's not my daddy, he's my mama's daddy."

I was confused. "And your real daddy's dead?"

She nodded. "Long time."

"And your mama, what about her? Is she dead too?"

"Mm-hmm," she said, in the same lazy sort of way Mama would say it when she wasn't really listening.

"That her?" I pointed to the picture over the bed. The woman's shoulders were bare except for a dark lace shawl. She was looking backward toward you, over her shoulder.

Rose-Johnny looked up at the picture, and said yes it was.

"She's pretty," I said.

"People used to say I looked just like her." Rose-Johnny laughed a wheezy laugh, and coughed.

"Why did she die?"

Rose-Johnny shook her head. "I can't tell you that."

"Can you when I'm older?"

She didn't answer.

"Well then, if Mr. Wall isn't your daddy, then the colored man is your daddy," I said, mostly to myself.

She looked at me. "Is that what they say?"

I shrugged.

"Does no harm to me. Every man is some color," she said.

"Oh," I said.

"My daddy was white. After he died my mama loved another man and he was brown."

"What happened then?"

"What happened then," she said. "Then they had a sweet little baby Johnny." Her voice was more like singing than talking, and her eyes were so peacefully closed I was afraid they might not open again. Every time she breathed there was the sound of a hundred tiny birds chirping inside her chest.

"Where's he?"

"Mama's Rose and sweet little baby Johnny," she sang it like an old song. "Not nothing bad going to happen to them, not nobody going to take her babies." A silvery moth flew into the lamp and clicked against the inside of the lampshade. Rose-Johnny stretched out her hand toward the night table. "I want you to pour me some of that bottle."

I lifted the bottle carefully and poured the glass half full. "That your medicine?" I asked. No answer. I feared this would be another story without an end, without meaning. "Did somebody take your mama's babies?" I persisted.

"Took her man, is what they did, and hung him up from a tree." She sat up slowly on her elbows, and looked straight at me. "Do you know what lynched is?"

"Yes, ma'am," I said, although until that moment I had not been sure.

"People will tell you there's never been no lynchings north of where the rivers don't freeze over. But they done it. Do you know where Jackson Crick is, up there by Floyd's Mill?" I nodded. "They lynched him up there, and drowned her baby Johnny in Jackson Crick, and it was as froze as you're ever going to see it. They had to break a hole in the ice to do it." She would not stop looking right into me. "In that river. Poor little baby in that cold river. Poor Mama, what they did to Mama. And said they would do to me, when I got old enough."

She didn't drink the medicine I poured for her, but let it sit. I was afraid to hear any more, and afraid to leave. I watched the moth crawl up the outside of the lampshade.

And then, out of the clear blue, she sat up and said, "But they didn't do a thing to me!" The way she said it, she sounded more like she ought to be weighing out bags of mash than sick in bed. "Do you want to know what Mama did?"

I didn't say.

"I'll tell you what she did. She took her scissors and cut my hair right off, every bit of it. She said, 'From now on, I want you to be Rose and Johnny both.' And then she went down to the same hole in the crick where they put baby Johnny in."

I sat with Rose-Johnny for a long time. I patted the lump in the covers where her knees were, and wiped my nose on my sleeve. "You'd better drink your medicine, Rose-Johnny," I said. "Drink up and get better now," I told her. "It's all over now."

∽ ∽ ∽

It was the last time I saw Rose-Johnny. The next time I saw the store, more than a month later, it was locked and boarded up. Later on, the Londroski brothers took it over. Some people said she had died. Others thought she and

Mr. Wall had gone to live somewhere up in the Blue Ridge, and opened a store there. This is the story I believed. In the years since, when passing through that part of the country, I have never failed to notice the Plymouth Rocks and Rhode Islands scratching in the yards, and the tomato vines tied up around the back doors.

∽∽∽ ∽∽∽ ∽∽∽

I would like to stop here and say no more, but there are enough half-true stories in my past. This one will have to be heard to the end.

Whatever became of Rose-Johnny and her grandfather, I am certain that their going away had something to do with what happened on that same evening to Mary Etta. And I knew this to be my fault.

It was late when I got home. As I walked I turned Rose-Johnny's story over and over, like Grandpa Bowles's Indian penny with the head on both sides. You never could stop turning it over.

When I caught sight of Mama standing like somebody's ghost in the front doorway I thought she was going to thrash me, but she didn't. Instead she ran out into the yard and picked me up like she used to when I was a little girl, and carried me into the house.

"Where's Daddy?" I asked. It was suppertime, but there was no supper.

"Daddy's gone looking for you in the truck. He'll be back directly, when he don't find you."

"Why's he looking for me? What did I do?"

"Georgeann, some men tried to hurt Mary Etta. We don't know why they done it, but we was afraid they might try to hurt you."

"No, ma'am, nobody hurt me," I said quietly. "Did they kill her?" I asked.

"Oh Lordy no," Mama said, and hugged me. "She's all right. You can go upstairs and see her, but don't bother her if she don't want to be bothered."

Our room was dark, and Mary Etta was in bed crying. "Can I turn on the little light?" I asked. I wanted to see Mary Etta. I was afraid that some part of her might be missing.

"If you want to."

She was all there: arms, legs, hair. Her face was swollen, and there were marks on her neck.

"Don't stare at me," she said.

"I'm sorry." I looked around the room. Her dress was hanging over the chair. It was her best dress, the solid green linen with covered buttons and attached petticoat that had taken her all winter to make. It was red with dirt and torn nearly in half at the bodice.

"I'll fix your dress, Mary Etta. I can't sew as good as you, but I can mend," I said.

"Can't be mended," she said, but then tried to smile with her swollen mouth. "You can help me make another one."

"Who was it that done it?" I asked.

"I don't know." She rolled over and faced the wallpaper. "Some men. Three or four of them. Some of them might have been boys, I couldn't tell for sure. They had things over their faces."

"What kind of things?"

"I don't know. Just bandanners and things." She spoke quietly to the wall. "You know how the Mattoxes have those funny-colored eyes? I think some of them might of been Mattoxes. Don't tell, Georgeann. Promise."

I remembered the feeling of Roy Mattox's muscle in my teeth. I did not promise.

"Did you hit them?"

"No. I screamed. Mr. Dorsey come along the road."

"What did they say, before you screamed?"

"Nothing. They just kept saying, 'Are you the Bowles girl, are you the Bowles girl?' And they said nasty things."

"It was me they was looking for," I said. And no matter what anyone said, I would not believe otherwise. I took to my bed and would not eat or speak to anyone. My convalescence was longer than Mary Etta's. It was during that time that I found my sister's sewing scissors and cut off all my hair and all of Miss Regina's. I said that my name was George-Etta, not Georgeann, and I called my doll Rose-Johnny.

For the most part, my family tolerated my distress. My mother retrimmed my hair as neatly as she could, but there was little that could be done. Every time I looked in the mirror I was startled and secretly pleased to see that I looked exactly like a little boy. Mama said that when I went back to school I would have to do the explaining for myself. Aunt Minnie said I was going through a stage and oughtn't to be pampered.

But there was only a month left of school, and my father let Mary Etta and me stay home to help set tobacco. By the end of the summer my hair had grown out sufficiently so that no explanations were needed. Miss Regina's hair, of course, never grew back.

Chris Holbrook

"First of the Month"

Chris Holbrook is an award-winning young writer who grew up in Soft Shell in Knott County, but he has lived long enough to see and chronicle the changes that have come to Appalachia in his time—some good and some not. Many of his characters leave home to find better jobs and lives elsewhere, then return hopefully to a reality of unemployment and springs poisoned by runoff from strip mines. Sometimes the people who stay behind must compromise to survive, some living from one welfare check to the next.

I despise the first of the month. You can't get on the road for the welfare cases. I see Dougie Johnston at the mouth of Brushy Creek. I try to just cruise on by, like I don't see him standing there in his black turtleneck sweater and oversize camouflage pants and chewed up Reds cap stuck backwards on his head that he found in the middle of the road somewhere.

He stares me down, not even holding his thumb out, just standing there, pitiful, waiting. I go on by for a ways, make it almost, but then I look in the rear view mirror and my foot hits the brake in spite of what I want, and he comes running up to the pickup and hops in the cab like my long lost pal.

"I didn't think you seen me for a minute," he says. "I sure do appreciate you stopping."

"Yeah, man," I say. "No problem."

"Where you headed?" he asks.

"County Market."

"That's lucky for me."

He sits crouched up, hands on his knees, looking straight ahead. He doesn't move the whole ride. But he talks. That's how he gets around you. "Your wife all right?" he asks.

"Why wouldn't she be all right?" I snap. "There ain't been nothing in the paper about her not being all right, not that I know of."

"I reckon," Dougie says.

I don't speak again for a while. I'm remembering Roberta when we were first married. I'm remembering the secondhand trailer we lived in the first five years, how we went without water when the pipes froze, without electricity when I was out of work. I'm thinking how what got us through was having to pull together so hard just to scrape by. I'm thinking about us now, how we come and go, say "hello" and "thank you" and "excuse me" to each other like strangers.

We ride up Polk Mountain, lay over for a loaded down Mack we meet in a switchback curve. The driver pulls his horn. I recognize the name "Black Cat" painted on the truck's door, wave my arm out my window, and yell, "Hey, Patton."

Near the mountaintop I pull off to view the strip site. This is one of John Winfrey's biggest operations. Half the mountain, two thousand acres, has been honed down. I sit for a while and watch the D-9 dozers and backhoes gouging up coal, the endloaders scooping it into the Mack trucks. The smell of diesel fuel rises on a little breeze, and I can feel the rumble of heavy equipment right in my chest.

"Sure is something," Dougie says.

For a second I'd forgot he was in the truck with me. I don't answer, just put her in gear and head on down the mountain.

We drive through Palestine, row on row of tiny box-frame houses propped on stilts on the hillside above the old C&O railway spur. Each one is like the other, two windows to a side, no porch, rusty metal stovepipes sticking through gray tarpaper roofs. A few of the houses that are still yet lived in have been kept up, but most of them are falling in on themselves. There's talk of opening up a section of the old deep mine, restoring the company commissary and a few of the old houses and running tours through. I'd like to get in on that.

We bypass the county seat and head out on Highway 1 to the County Market. The parking lot is filled with rolling wrecks, just bits and pieces of cars, not one of them whole. I find a space next to the war monument, a World War II Howitzer, shut her off and start to climb out, but before I do old Dougie says reckon I couldn't let him have a dollar or two.

It ain't like I didn't expect it, but even so it pisses me off. I grew up with this boy. I know his people. My daddy and his daddy both worked in the mines. My daddy stove his leg up under a shuttle car. His daddy claimed black lung. Claimed it. I ain't saying a lot of folks don't deserve them benefits. I ain't saying that at all. But they's some that don't. Some that cheat and lie. I don't mind a feller getting what's coming to him. And I don't mind helping a feller out. It ain't that at all. But when my daddy couldn't hump no more, he didn't stick out his thumb for a free ride. He borrowed on the home place, leased some machinery, and put us boys to work.

We had fifty acres in the head of Bear Creek, a good lot of timber and a four foot seam of coal just under the ridge. We hauled out the timber on twenty-five acres, then we stripped it. Daddy said that busted leg was the best thing that ever happened to him, made him start relying on himself instead of other people. I think about that when Dougie Johnston asks me couldn't I let him have a dollar or two. I think, "By God, I never took Dougie Johnston to raise." And I say it too.

"By God, Dougie, I ain't took you to raise."

Dougie just nods and slides out of the cab. "We thank you for the ride," he says. I feel a little bit bad then, so I pull a couple of ones from my billfold and start to hand them over. He doesn't even blink, just reaches his hand to take them, and I realize I'm not sticking up for what I believe. So I pull the bills back and stick them in my shirt pocket. I know how that must look, but a man's got to stick up for what he believes.

⁓ ⁓ ⁓

Alicia Wingate's list is filled with last minute party items—5 pounds of butterfly shrimp, 5 jars of smoked herring in sour cream, 4 jars of black olives/pitted, 5 jars of marinated artichoke hearts, 3 pounds of ripe lemons. The word "ripe" is underlined. It's a testament to progress that a grocery in this part of the state would stock such items. Ten years ago it would have been unheard of. Strides have been made.

Now and again I catch sight of old Dougie Johnston as I make my way through the aisles. I see him pilfering through the rolls of unsliced bologna, squeezing the loaves of day old light bread, sniffing the packs of discount chicken wings. He's among his own today. The store's full of cases just like him—skinny, scraggly haired men and obese women trailing screaming kids; grandmaws and grandpaws doddering along behind, toothless, bent over, broken down, uneasy so far from the head of the holler. You can always tell when the welfare checks have come out.

One old codger pops up in my face as I'm ordering my butterfly shrimp. "Use a good knife, buddy?" he asks. He has two used pocket knives in the palm of his hand. They look like something hammered together in a sweat shop in Pakistan. The grips are plastic. The blades are black with tarnish. "Give you a good deal," he says.

"No, I got a good knife," I answer and turn away to watch the lady weigh out my shrimp.

"Well," he says, "I reckon if a man's got a good knife, he don't need another'un." He doesn't go away though. He stands next to me and stares at that iced shrimp piling up on the scales. "Them are shore big crawdads," he says. I glance over to see if he's joking. I can't tell, and the glance is all he needs to start in. "I recollect the feller went swimming in a creek full of crawdads," he says. He pauses. His eyes go blank for a second. He's trying to tell a joke, but he's lost the thread of it.

I take a good look at him while he's off trying to find his thoughts. I've never seen such a beat-up looking face. The skin is peppered with flecks of coal dust. The lines in it could be hundreds of years old, but I take him to be about sixty. He has big hands for a little man. They're callused all over, not just the palms. The fingers, the thumbs, and the heels are all covered with thick, dead horns of skin. His nails are long and broken. They are dirty and blackened with injury. His eyes lose some of their blankness while I stare at him.

"That time I never even heard no noise," he says, almost in a whisper, "just felt all the air blow out of the hole." Then he blinks, and his eyes are all clear. "Use a good knife?" he asks.

"No," I say and take my shrimp and get away. I don't know what old hurt was coming back on him. I don't need to know. Every face in this store has got some old hurt ready to flare up.

I'm not surprised when Dougie Johnston hails me in the parking lot and asks if I'm heading back toward the county seat. I lie and say I'm not.

◦◦◦ ◦◦◦ ◦◦◦

I've hauled for John Wingate for ten years. I drive my own truck, mine and the bank's. Roberta and I are looking to build on Millionaire's Ridge. We're not millionaires, but we've done all right. We've got a twenty-foot pontoon on Laurel Lake. She drives a Camry. I've got this new Dodge Ram. All this comes from work.

When the coal run out on that first twenty-five acres, I talked Daddy into mining the other half. He was reluctant. "What's the use of being land poor?" I asked him. He'd grown up in them hills, he said. Hated to see it all go. But he finally saw the profit. We were still hauling coal out of there when he died.

Little brother and I got joint ownership of the land. I sold my share of the equipment to him and started trucking, but I've got a scheme to develop that property. A couple of tracts have been leveled enough for a trailer park or a shopping plaza. All I need is a little working capital. Little brother and me are both mortgaged to the hilt. Red ink goes with the territory.

Millionaire's Ridge is a prime example of what can be done with reclamation. It rises 2,000 feet above sea level, even with being stripped. The highway going up was once an access road. The house lots are in what was once a mining pit. There's a highwall at the north end that keeps the wind down. The slag has been dozed over and fill dirt brought in and fescue planted. There's a buttress built all around the ridge to keep the whole thing from sliding off. And the view is tremendous. You can look down on the center of town, on the other ridges that have been stripped and reclaimed, made even and level and grassy. There's the beginning of a horse trail that goes for twenty miles across the county and links up with seven different strip sites. There's room for pasture land now, or golf courses, or trailer parks.

Roberta's Camry is parked in the Wingate's driveway, behind Alicia's 321 BMW and in front of a Nissan 300Z and a new Cadillac El Dorado. I park my pickup on the shoulder of the road.

I don't know the girl who answers the door. She's about eighteen, dressed in cutoff jeans, a tie-dyed tee shirt, and a pair of bright red Chuck Taylor high top sneakers. She has blonde hair done up in corn rows. She backs out of the doorway and yells over her shoulder. "Alicia, there's a guy here." I push on through before she has a chance to confirm my admittance. I lug the groceries down the hall to the kitchen.

Alicia Wingate and Roberta are seated at the kitchen table. I almost drop the beer when I see Alicia's face. I almost say, "My God, what happened to you?" Both her eyes are blacked. Her nose is bandaged and swollen. I almost say, "What'd you tangle with?" But before I do, I remember Roberta saying something about plastic surgery, and I just nod. But my face has given me away. Alicia's hand flutters up to cover her nose. Roberta glares.

John comes in from the patio to rescue the moment. "Rick," he says, "this is Ann Marie Morehead." He turns to the girl who wasn't sure I should be in the house. "Ann Marie is here with the Christian Appalachian Project." Then he puts his hand on my arm and says, "Ann Marie, this is Rick Baker, one of my best men." Ann Marie cocks her head back, goes "ah" to herself, like now she understands, and reaches out her hand. I wipe mine on my pants before I shake.

I can feel Roberta watching me. I don't want to mess up again and make us look bad. I'm relieved when John steers me out to the patio. I don't know either of the guys out there, but they have the look of capital about them. The young guy, Steve Thompson, is the son of one of John's old buddies who John is teaching the coal business. I pair him with the Nissan.

The other guy, Louis Kellum, is dressed like a rich cowboy, leather sports coat and a pair of thousand dollar ostrich skin boots. He has something like a cowboy accent, like I think one would be, but it's a little too slick. I figure he drives the Cad.

We stand around for a while and talk. Steve Thompson seems all right. He and John talk golf. When John mentions how nice it'd be to have a course in the county someday, a real course, not some par three, I take the opportunity to mention how ripe this county is for development. "All kinds of possibilities," I say. Louis Kellum snorts and looks off across the ridge tops.

"I've been thinking about some development of my own," I say, and I outline my plans for a trailer park. John hears me out. Steve Thompson looks interested, but Louis Kellum keeps his back turned, keeps staring across the ridges.

"Minimum investment, low maintenance and good returns over the long term," I say, looking directly at Steve Thompson.

John pats me on the back before I finish and says, "How about checking on the refreshments."

෨ ෨ ෨

In the kitchen the ladies are slicing lemons into pitchers of ice water and artificial sweetener. Ann Marie is telling about her social service work. She has a way of turning everything she says into a question.

"It's worse than you imagine?" she says. "A dozen people sometimes in a rusty trailer? Or a shack no bigger than this kitchen?"

Alicia nods.

"Whatever we do, it's just never enough? And in the end they resent us?"

"There's just so much built-in failure to overcome," Alicia says. She sighs a little, brings a tissue to her bandaged nose. "Am I right, Roberta? You're from here. You've had to overcome your background."

"Oh yes," Roberta says, then covers her mouth with her fingers.

"What do you think, Rick?" Alicia asks. "Is Ann Marie wasting her time?"

I stare at Roberta for a moment. Her cheeks have been shaded to points, her hair trimmed short of her collar and styled into a silver stranded helmet, like Alicia's. Her eyebrows are plucked thin and drawn into arches. She smiles like her jaw is broken.

"Welfare kills the gumption in people," I say, without really thinking, "so does your volunteer programs." The room gets quiet. I pause to consider what I've said, try to remember who I'm talking to. The CAP girl sits forward in her chair, chewing a thumbnail, frowning. I realize my mistake. "Why, honey," I say, "you're not wasting your time. Long as you feel good about what you're doing."

They all scowl. I shuffle my feet a little. "Don't pay no attention to me," I say. I take a full pitcher of lemonade and a few glasses then head for the outdoors.

෨ ෨ ෨

"Incentives," John is saying. "If we're going to attract new industry to this area, we need to offer incentives."

"Amen to that," I say.

"Incentives in the form of tax breaks. Of cost reduction. We've got to offer recreational facilities and better schools. We've got to improve our infrastructure. We've got to give corporate America a reason to locate here."

The women come out to join us. Alicia sets extra glasses on the patio table and goes to stand next to John. Roberta stays clear of me. When she glances in my direction, there's nothing in her eyes I know how to read.

I once heard that love is just hormones. People fall in love for the high and fall out of love when the high wears off. That's the reason so many marriages fail in the first two years. The high wears off.

I don't know about Roberta and me. We've been together for fifteen years, and I can't say at this moment whether I'm in or out of love with her.

Roberta is smiling her broken-jawed smile. She's not a homely woman, but there's something about the way she stands, with her shoulders slightly stooped, that next to Alicia Wingate makes her look not as good. It may be the way I look at her. It may be the way I look next to John Wingate. I feel bad. When I reach for the pitcher of lemonade, I'm just clumsy enough to tip it over. It shatters against the deck, a splatter of fine crystal, lemon slices, and ice cubes.

The back of my neck gets hot. I kneel to pick up the pieces of glass. Roberta brings a towel from the kitchen to help mop up. I watch her face as we work. I wish she'd look at me.

Alicia brings a fresh pitcher. Nobody mentions my mishap, and after a while I feel like I'm among friends again.

Roberta and I stand together for a minute, watching John and Alicia slow dance across the deck. John sings softly in Alicia's ear, and Alicia giggles in a way I would've never thought she could. Steve Thompson and the CAP girl whisper to each other and stare off over the ridge tops, holding hands. Louis Kellum hangs on the rail, keeping to himself.

The CAP girl wanders back into the house, then Roberta makes her getaway. When Kellum drains his glass and goes inside, I corner Steve Thompson. I tell jokes and get him to laugh. I get him to tell jokes, and I laugh. I agree with his politics. I admire his car. I cross over to his religion. Then I get down to business. Within half an hour we have a verbal commitment to a written commitment to an agreement that will be mutually beneficial to both of us, but mostly to me. We raise our glasses of lemonade and drink to prosperity.

The CAP girl returns. John and Alicia are still dancing, so I excuse myself and head inside. When I enter the kitchen, I hear Roberta's muffled voice mingled with Kellum's snaky cowboy drawl. Kellum has his arms around Roberta, and Roberta is pushing him away. I can't tell if she's laughing or crying.

Kellum is already on the floor by the time I feel my fist smash into his face. I've not punched anyone since I was in the army. I feel none of the wild release of adrenaline. The flash of anger that set me off becomes a steady ache inside my gut.

The next thing I know the party has moved indoors, and I'm the center of attention. For some reason I think about the old codger in the County Market, about the years he must've spent in the mines to get that face of his, about the busted joints and cracked bones he must've suffered and about the memory of pain that's all he's left with for all his work.

I help Kellum to his feet, offer him a handkerchief for his busted nose, dust him off. He pushes me away and stalks out of the kitchen. I see lost opportunity on Steve Thompson's face. When I look at John, his face gets hard, and for a minute I feel like I'm on the job and he's about to come down on me.

I say my apologies as much as I can. I say I'm sorry about the pitcher I broke. I say I'm sorry about the mess in the kitchen. I tell Steve Thompson we'll have to talk business sometime. I tell John Wingate I'll see him Monday. I say to Alicia, "Thank you for having us." I say to the CAP girl, "It's been nice to meet you." I say, "I'm sorry we have to go now."

We leave Roberta's Camry blocked by all that rolling money and climb into the pickup. Roberta's quiet. I look at her, and I think, "Lord, what just happened?"

Before we even get close to home, I see a figure on the roadside. Who else but Dougie Johnston? He's lugging a sack full of groceries back to Brushy Creek. He steps off the road when he sees us coming. I tap the brakes.

I see Roberta tense as Dougie climbs into the cab. He smiles at both of us, nods to Roberta, and settles in next to the door, keeping a polite distance.

Right off Dougie asks Roberta how her dad has been. She tells him about his bursitis, and Dougie says how he reckons he ought to stop by and visit. Roberta asks Dougie how his mom and dad are, and Dougie says, "Oh, about the same." By the time we pass through Palestine, Roberta has relaxed a little. She and Dougie talk family all the way up Polk Mountain.

I pull over when we get to the mouth of Brushy Creek. Roberta manages a weak smile as Dougie gets out of the cab. "Thank you for the ride," he says, and for a second I think he's going to put the touch on me, but he just tips the brim of his cap at Roberta and heads up the holler with his sack full of groceries. I think about going after him, maybe slipping him a few dollars. It would help him out. It would make me feel better.

I shut off the truck when Roberta says, "Come on, let's go." I can feel her staring at me, but I just sit there, thinking things over. She settles in on her side of the cab to do her own thinking. It gets dark. We watch the moon come up over Auglin Mountain. The outfit that stripped it has yet to do any reclamation. The bare knobs of rock shine white as bone in the full moon's light. I hear a dragline start up on a strip job five miles away. I think about all the money to be made in this world. I wonder if I'll have a job on Monday or a wife.

Gayle Compton
"Long Distance to Detroit"

Gayle Compton was born and grew up in a coal camp in Pike County. With lively humor, good will, and respect, he writes poems and stories about the mountain people and their way of life, including the ones who move to Detroit and sometimes have difficulty communicating with their loved ones back home.

MILDRED (answering the telephone): Charlie Bob Tucker's residence.

OPERATOR: I have a collect call from Ms. Irene Sweeney, Peabrook, Kentucky. Will you accept the charges?

MILDRED: Yes, mam, put her on.

IRENE: Hello, Mildred? Is that you? Well, it's about time. I been trying to get a hold of you for over a week now. Ever time I call up there I get a place name Joe's Pool Hall and a feller named Eightball that sounds for the world like your Charlie Bob. I hated to call collect but I wanted to ask you about that old ironing board you got stored down at Mommy's. I called three times yesterday and got a funeral home and some smart aleck that tried to make me a deal on a casket. He sounded just like your Charlie, too. Reckon everybody up there talks just alike. Just this morning I called the same number and got Tucker's Whorehouse. What kind of place *is* Detroit anyhow?

MILDRED: Oh, Irene, it's just so nice here. You'd love it. We all just got back from a weekend at Boblo Island and . . .

IRENE: Well, I just hope you're having better weather for it than we are. Don't know from one minute till the next what it's going to do down here. Saturday it was just as warm! People out plantin' their peas and onions, and that old Nadine Thacker out in them shorts mowing her yard and showing her hind end. Next day we got a tornader. Why honey, yesterday it was snowing and thundering and lightning all at the same time! Hail balls big enough to knock the winder lights out. They can call it El Nino if they want to, but we didn't have weather like this, Mildred, until they started putting up all them old rockets and saddlelights, going to Mars, messing with the Ozarks and walking around on the moon. Course, Homer says ain't nobody never been on no moon. He says they just took them pitchurs in a desert somers. Where's this Boblo Island?

MILDRED: Oh Irene, dear, it's my favorite place in Michigan. Me and Charles, we took the kids and got on this big boat—

IRENE: I heard about Charlie Bob getting his back hurt on that night watching job up yonder. A body can't be too careful. To beat it all, Homer's hurt his back too. Pulled it picking up a case of beer the wrong way. I doubt if he'll ever work again. He's getting him a lawyer. Lord, he gets on my nerves sometimes! He's not even suppose to *be* here. No! He moved back in about a month atter we started getting our checks. Said he missed his family so bad he couldn't hardly stand it. All he does, Mildred, is lay around and eat and work on that old motorcycle of his'n. He's got it scattered all over the house. The other day he had the motor baking in the oven and the pistons boiling in my big kettle on the cookstove. Only God knows why. He claims he's crippled but you ought to see the way he acts when that old sorry Nadine comes on the place. That Nadine's no count. Just like her mother. Mayfern was the same way. Had six young'uns and nary a one of them had the same daddy. She paid for it though. That's the very reason that last child of hers, bless his sweet heart, was born afflicted and marked by a bullfrog. How's your young'uns?

MILDRED: Fine as can be, and loving their new school. Billy got sick on us, though, on the boat over to Boblo I—

IRENE: You know, Mildred, I don't know what I'm going to do with Eugene. Stands up and sasses me and won't go to school a-tall. It don't do no good to whup him. This morning I gave him his lunch money and laid out his clothes but I bet you he ain't in two miles of a schoolhouse. Up yonder under the third railroad bridge is where you'll find him. Up there fishing or down at the pizza house gambling on them old machines. I've worried and I've prayed but it don't do no good. Last time he brought his report card home he had four Fs and a D. Even Homer jumped onto him over that. Homer told him he was spending too much time on one subject. I tell you a body can do just so much for a young'un. I told him I wasn't going to raise no re-tard. He worries me. Like when I sent him to the store the other day to get me a box of Brillo pads. You know what he said to his own mother? He said if I was going to wear them things I could go get 'em myself.

I blame the schools for a lot of it. They don't teach them nothing these days and times except how to play ball and with one another. And they don't make 'em mind. And that old Madeline O'Hair what took prayer out of the school is at it again. This time she's going to try to stop them from playing Christian songs on the radio and taking all the good religious programs off the TV. It's a shame, and she'll get her way, too. I always get such a good blessing out of Ernest Angley. Can you pick up Brother Angley in Detroit? I'll tell you one thing. I'm hanging on to all my good Ralph Stanley records.

Lord, it makes me boiling mad! They claim she's hid out somers and it's a good thing for her. She's going to keep it up until some good Christian hunts her down and blows her brains out. How's Ruby and them?

MILDRED: Ruby's been kind of sick. Still, she went with us all when we went to Bob—

IRENE: Well, I've requested prayer for all of youins. Lord, Mildred, I meant to write and tell you what a good meeting we had over at Brother Bill Dick Robinson's church Wednesday night. You talk about a time! We had us a healing service and then a casting out of demons. Brother Harlis Damron was there and prayed for Sister Williams. Prayed for her nervous headaches and her yaller janders. I got my hemorrhoids prayed for. Then Harlis tried on poor old Kenis Fouts, Lou Ann's hunchback husband. You know Kenis. They've had him all over creation with that hump trying to get him healed. Harlis prayed until he was as blue in the face as a grampus but the hump wouldn't budge. Harlis finally told him that it just wasn't the Lord's will for him to be healed. Told him that hump was put there for a purpose. Said the Lord worked in mysterious ways and that hump of his'n was a blessing.

Then they brought in this puny little feller from Slickrock that was possessed with demons. That's when everybody started gathering in. Never seen so many people. You can talk about the crowd that's drawed in by a funeral or a singing if you want to. Ain't nothing packs 'em in like a service where they're casting out devils. Homer even went! I don't remember the man's name, but Mildred he was pitiful. It would scare you to look at him. They lit in on him around nine o'clock and at two the next morning they was still at it. Sister Williams said she counted thirteen demons cast out of him. Pervis Mullins was there and kept track. He swears they was fourteen in all. Some said thirteen. Some fourteen.

MILDRED: Did they get them all?

IRENE: Well, almost. They got 'em all except one demon.

MILDRED: One demon?

IRENE: One demon. Brother Harlis said it was an alcoholic demon. He prayed and sweated and went on forever, seemed like, but the demon wouldn't give. Hung on like a cat on a curtain. Brother Harlis said an alcoholic demon is the worst kind. He said he would rather cast out ten lust demons than just one common ordinary alcoholic demon.

MILDRED: We saw a man put me in mind of Brother Damron when we went over to Bo—

IRENE: Well, when we found out that last 'un was an alcoholic demon we all knowed we'd be up all night. Jimmy's Patty went home and brought back a cake she'd baked and some refreshments. That's when Patty Harmon told Patty Sue that if she'd knowed Jimmy's Patty was going to try to run things, she would have just stayed at the house. That's when Patty Sue told Jimmy's Patty what Patty Harmon said and Patty told her what she thought about her right there in the church house. Lord, Patty was mad!

I was so plagued I left before they cast out that last devil, but Pervis stayed until it was delivered. He said you couldn't see it on account of it was a spirit, but you could *feel* it. He said they was four dogs got atter it and chased it to the hills. But you can't believe everything Pervis Mullins says. It coulda been just three dogs instead of four. I hated to leave when I did cause it was one of the few times I've got Homer in church. Homer says he ain't never going back, though, cause somebody stoled his coat. Have you fellers caught that old flu yet?

MILDRED: No, but I did catch a little head cold after getting wet on our way back from B—

IRENE: Everybody's been just about dead with the flu here. All except me. The way they keep letting them Japs and Russians and that bunch come over here it's a wonder we're not all dead. The TV is calling this new flu the Shanghai Flu. Now, if that ain't Russian I don't know what is. No, I ain't had no flu, thank the Lord, but I still have to watch my gall bladder and I got these big pones on my legs and I've been having them old sinking spells again. It scares me to death.

Oh Lord, Mildred honey, did I tell you how bad off our Wilma Lou's been? Female trouble, if you know what I mean. Lord yes! We had her down to the Mud Creek Clinic last week. The doctor gave her a good going over but you couldn't understand nary a word he said, hardly. All them big words. He asked us if Wilma Lou had ever had intercourse. Mildred, I didn't take no chances. I told him if that medical card would pay for it to go ahead and give it to her.

Mildred . . . Mildred? (to silence on the other end).

Hmph! Musta got cut off. It's just as well. All Mildred wants to do anyway is brag and carry on about that old boat. If the truth's knowed, she ain't never been out of Detroit, let alone took a boat ride to Michigan. She can keep her stupid ironing board!

Chris Offutt

from *The Good Brother*

In the August 16, 1998, issue of the *Lexington Herald-Leader,* Art Jester, the book editor, announced excitedly that Chris Offutt had moved back to his native Rowan County, calling him "the outstanding Kentucky-born writer of his generation." He included a quick rundown of the forty-year-old writer's achievements: teaching at the universities of New Mexico and Montana; three acclaimed books: *Kentucky Straight* (1992), a collection of stories; *The Same River Twice* (1993), a memoir; and *The Good Brother* (1997), his first novel; and coveted awards and grants from the Guggenheim Foundation and the National Endowment for the Arts. Jester quoted Offutt, who said that he had become so homesick he decided it was time to move his wife, Rita, and his two sons back to his Kentucky homeland. Offutt said: "For the last few years I felt that I wasn't connected. Now I'm complete."

It was a beautiful dream. But it didn't last; things were not the same. His hometown of Haldeman had all but disappeared. His childhood chums had gone on to other lives. Then the April 18, 2002, *New York Times* had a feature article on Offutt headed, "Learning Not to Trespass on the Gently Rolling Past"; there was a sidebar that read, "A Kentucky Son Finds the Hills No Longer Cradle Him." Offutt was ready to move on again, this time to teach in the writers' program at the University of Iowa. Noting that Offutt had stayed only one year, the *Times* concluded: "The experience burned his boyhood home to the ground like dry woods." In his own book about the aborted move home, *No Heroes: A Memoir of Coming Home* (2002), Offutt said it more effectively. You can go home again, he said, but you'll live to regret it. Some Kentucky readers of the book were not very kind. In an April 13, 2002, column in the *Herald-Leader,* Cheryl Truman wrote that "Kentucky is used to being portrayed as a state of toothless illiterates," but, she added, "What we are not used to is having Kentucky portrayed this way by a Kentuckian." It's dangerous for Kentuckians to be openly critical of their homeland. Nevertheless, Offutt's magnificent talent for writing is a priceless gift to Kentuckians.

In addition to the books already mentioned, there is a recent collection of short stories, *Out of the Woods* (1999), about Kentuckians who leave home and wish they hadn't. *The Good Brother* is about Virgil Caudill, the good brother who, according to the code of the hills, has to avenge the murder of his hell-raising brother. The first chapter is just a start.

❧

Virgil followed the rain branch off the hill and drove to the Blizzard post office. The mail hadn't come yet and he continued past, giving a general wave to the crowd that gossiped in the glare of April sun. He drove up a steep hill to the county line. It was only two miles from the house he'd grown up in, but he'd never crossed it.

He parked by the edge of the cliff. The color of the air was brighter at the top. Clay Creek ran through the hollow with purple milkweed blooming in the ditch. When Virgil was a kid, he and his brother had walked its slippery bank, gathering enough empty pop bottles to buy candy when they reached Blizzard's only store. Virgil wished he and Boyd could do it again but people had stopped throwing pop bottles away when the deposit rose to a nickel. The store closed when the owner died. Boyd was dead now, too.

Virgil tried to imagine the land when it was flat across the hilltops, before a million years of rain chewed the dirt to make creeks and hollows. Clouds lay in heaps like sawdust piles. He figured he was seeing out of the county and he wondered if hawks could see farther, or just better. The world seemed smaller from above. The dips and folds of the wooded hills reminded him of a rumpled quilt that needed smoothing out.

Cars were leaving the post office, which meant the mail truck had arrived. A titmouse clung to a tree upside down, darting its head to pick an insect from a leaf. Pine sap ran like blood from a wound in the tree. Virgil drove down the road and parked in willow shade beside the creek. A tattered flag dangled above the post office, fastened permanently to a hickory pole. Every morning the postmaster, a white-haired man named Zephaniah, dragged the flagpole from the post office and slipped one end into a hole in the earth beside a fence post. He buckled a leather belt around the flagpole and the post. At day's end he stored the pole inside.

Instead of a system of organized boxes, Zephaniah had laid out a few narrow tables to correspond roughly with the surrounding terrain—two hollows, a hill, and a creek. He arranged the day's mail in stacks that represented the location of each family's house in the community. Virgil leaned on the narrow shelf that protruded from the arched hole in the wall where Zephaniah worked. The shelf's edge was round and smooth from years of use.

"Flag's looking kindly ragged, ain't it," Virgil said.

"Government never sent a new one this year."

"Can't you tell them?"

"Could."

The screen door banged as a man from Red Bird Ridge came in.

"Mail run yet?" he said to Virgil.

"Just did."

"I ain't seen you since . . ."

The man adjusted his cap, looked at the floor, and rapidly scratched his sideburn. The last time they'd met had been at Boyd's funeral. Virgil didn't know how to ease the man's discomfort.

"Well, a long while went by since I seen you," the man said.

He stepped to the window and looked through the mail that Zephaniah had gathered for him.

"Write me a order, will you, Zeph?"

"How much?"

"Ten dollars even. Mamaw owes the doctors that much a month."

"Which doctor?"

"I don't know, that clinic in town. The one everybody goes to."

"Rocksalt Medical?"

"Reckon."

Zephaniah filled out the form, printing carefully. When he finished, he waited, and Virgil knew that Zephaniah would stand there all day rather than insult the man by asking him to write his name on the money order.

"Go ahead and sign it for me, Zeph."

Zephaniah wrote the man's name at the bottom of the money order, and asked for eleven dollars. The man placed three fives on the shelf.

"Buying money sure ain't cheap," he said.

"Best to have a checking account," Zephaniah said.

"None of my people have fooled with banks and I ain't about to start now."

"Need an envelope?"

The man nodded. Zephaniah wrote the address on a pre-stamped envelope and made change. The man went outside and spoke to Virgil through the screen. "Come here a minute."

Virgil went to the door. The man pressed his forehead to the screen, his skin pushing through the mesh in tiny squares. "I knowed your brother," he said. "You tell your mama I'm sorry."

Virgil never knew what to say back. The man looked up and down the creek before speaking in a ragged whisper. "It was a Rodale done it. Billy Rodale."

The man walked swiftly to his truck.

Virgil leaned against the wall and inhaled as deeply as possible. He let the air out in a long slow breath. Across the road, green tendrils of forsythia bushes dragged the creek.

"Virge?" said Zephaniah. "You all right?"

"Yeah. Just sick of it."

"Of what?"

"You know. Boyd and all."

"People feel bad."

"You didn't hear what he said."

"I heard. Ears is the last thing I got left that works."

"Well, I'm sick to death of it. I know who it was. The whole damn creek does, and I don't need everybody telling me. They figure I don't know since I ain't done nothing."

"A man like him ain't worth worrying about. He's the reason for the flag problem."

"What?"

"I ain't asked for a new flag because I don't want to draw attention. When I retire, this post office will shut down. Only reason it's open now is folks buying money orders. Half this creek pays their bills through me. We're showing a profit here, which ain't exactly something the government is used to."

"So why close down?"

"Because profit ain't what they go by."

"What is?"

"If I knew that, I'd be President."

Fifty years ago the post office building had housed the company store for the town of Blizzard. The community had run on scrip issued by the mineral company. Now the mines were empty and the town was gone, along with its barbershop, saloon, train station, and doctor. Most of the families were gone, too. The remaining people still walked off the hillsides for money orders, another form of scrip.

"If they shut this down," Virgil said, "there won't be much left of here."

"Church and grade school," Zephaniah said. "I've throwed hours of thought at it. Blizzard's old and wore out, and the government's getting rid of it. They ain't too many to care about us. I'd say even God was right mad the day he laid this place out. It's as slanty a land as ever was."

"Maybe you could get a petition."

"Who'd sign it, Virge? You can't turn in a petition full of X's. They'd say if these people can't read or write, what do they need a post office for? No, Virge. Blizzard's done."

Zephaniah stood with his shoulders slumped, his arms hanging straight as if held by weights. He suddenly seemed what he was—short and old.

"I could retire now," he said. "I'm tired enough, but I'm the last man with a job. That's why I keep working. If I stop, the town stops."

"Well."

"It burnt my daddy up that I never left out of here. He died still mad over it. I know they's some saying you ort to take care of that Rodale boy for killing Boyd. More say it than don't, my opinion. But I say get yourself out of here, and I don't mean Rocksalt, either. There's Mount Sterling to think on, even Lexington. No sense going to the state pen over your brother."

Virgil couldn't imagine leaving Blizzard. He'd lived here thirty-two years. Boyd was the restless one, the wild brother, the one who'd leave one day. Virgil had grown up letting Boyd do the talking and later the running around acting crazy. He drove fast, drank hard, played cards, and chased women. Finally, Boyd had done the dying.

The narrow hall seemed to squeeze Virgil and he felt a need for breath that he couldn't quite get. He was thirsty. He stumbled outside and smelled honeysuckle vine along the creek. He drove down the road and up the steep dirt lane of his home hill. In his mother's house, he turned on the faucet and let it run to bring water from deep in the earth. He drank two cups fast. His body recognized the water, its cold taste the most familiar sensation he'd ever known. He breathed through his nose as he drank, his chin and shirt wet.

He was drinking his fourth cup when he noticed his mother and sister watching from the doorway. He set the cup in the sink.

"Mom," he said. "I ain't going to that post office no more."

His mother's face didn't change, but the expression of her eyes did. Virgil recognized it as the look she got when Boyd said something outrageous, but she had never regarded Virgil in this manner. He leaned on the sink and looked through the window. It was cracked from the beak of a cardinal that had repeatedly attacked its own reflection.

"Where's the mail at anyway?" his sister said.

"I left it."

"Well, shoot, Virgie." Sara turned to their mother. "I'll send Marlon directly. I'm glad I married somebody who's got some sense, even if it's just to pick up the mail."

"I just don't like hearing that old gossip down there's all. You go, Sara. You'd talk a bird out of its nest."

"What were they saying?" Sara said.

Beside her, their mother waited without speaking. She had spent most of her life in just such a stance—silent in the kitchen, waiting for news that was invariably bad.

"You don't really want to know, do you?" Virgil said.

Sara nodded.

"They say that Wayne girl is pregnant," he said.

"No!"

"Sure is."

"Which one?"

"Up on Redbird Ridge."

"I know that," Sara said. "They ain't but one bunch of Waynes. I mean which girl?"

"The littlest."

"Lord love a duck, she ain't but fourteen."

"Well," Virgil said.

"Whose is it? Anybody say?"

"They's no question of that."

"Well, who?"

"I hate to be the one to tell you, Sara. But it was your Marlon done it."

Sara's face changed color. Her breath rasped into the air. Their mother glanced at her as if to make sure Sara wasn't going to collapse, then studied Virgil carefully.

"Sara, honey," she said. "I believe he's telling a story."

Sara grabbed a sponge and threw it, bouncing it off his chest and leaving a wet mark on his shirt.

"If you went for the mail," Virgil said, "you'd know true gossip from wrong."

"If you can't fetch mail," Sara said, "you at least can mow the yard."

Boyd had taken care of the yard and retrieved the mail. Four months after his death, the family was still trying to divvy up chores.

The Dramatic Tradition
in Kentucky

This is a short chapter because Kentucky has produced relatively few good dramatists. Playhouses in Kentucky, especially on college campuses, originally preferred to present plays written by Greek, English, or European playwrights (such as Sophocles, Aeschylus, Shakespeare, Marlowe, Congreve, Goldsmith, Sheridan, and Ibsen) or American playwrights (such as Clyde Fitch and William Vaughn Moody). In Kentucky theaters, even well into the twentieth century, producers and managers were reluctant to provide a venue for homegrown talent. It was safer to go with Eugene O'Neill, Arthur Miller, or even Tennessee Williams than to risk failure with an unknown local playwright. One of the earliest playwrights with a Kentucky pedigree was Charles T. Dazey, who was born in Illinois of Kentucky parents and who spent much of his boyhood with his grandparents in Bourbon County. Dazey wrote popular melodramas such as *In Old Kentucky* (1892), a play centered around a horse race and featuring such stereotypes as a mountain lass, an aristocrat from the Bluegrass region of the state, an unprincipled villain, a good-hearted moonshiner, and a colorful colonel; the plot line includes a mountain feud and a horse race won by the mountain lass masquerading as a jockey. The characters are painted in broad strokes appropriate for the acting style of heavy declamation and exaggerated gestures.

Ann Crawford Flexner (1874–1955) was a step up in talent and achievement. Born in Georgetown, Kentucky, she graduated from Vassar in 1895, married Abraham Flexner, and lived in Louisville until 1905, when she moved to New York, where most of her plays were produced. Her greatest success was her dramatization of Alice Hegan Rice's *Mrs. Wiggs of the Cabbage Patch* in 1904. One of her later plays was *Aged 26* (1936), based on the love affair of John Keats and Fanny Brawne. Another playwright was Thompson Buchanan (1877–1937), who grew up in Louisville and became a drama critic for the *Louisville Herald*. After 1903 he lived in New York, where he wrote his greatest success, *A Woman's Day* (1909), in which a young woman fights successfully for her husband's affections against a determined rival. After World War I he became head of the editorial staff of Goldwyn Pictures in New York.

Cleves Kinkead (1882–1955) was a Louisville native who tried law, politics, and journalism before he turned his hand to writing plays, only one of which had much success. *Common Clay* is about Ellen Neal, a poor young girl who struggles for social respectability. It won a number of prizes and had successful runs in Boston, New York, and London, and was made into a movie two times. In 1930 Constance Bennett played the lead in a popular sound production. Other Kentucky authors who wrote dramas and who deserve a modest mention are Cale Young Rice and Olive Dargan. Both were more successful as poets. They wrote closet dramas, which were poetic plays designed mainly to be read and not performed. (Today they are neither read nor performed.) And there was D. W. Griffith (1875–1948), a native of Oldham County, who should be acknowledged not only as the "inventor" of Hollywood, as some theater historians label him, for his pioneering techniques in producing, directing, and editing films, but also as an actor and playwright for some ten years before he turned to film. Until he began making his own films, he sold "scenarios"—crude story outlines or treatments— to Biograph in New York. For his own films he wrote much of what we would call a book or script today.

In recent years Kentucky's resident theaters have sporadically encouraged playwrights in the state to submit plays for possible production. Actors Theatre of Louisville, founded in 1963, has from time to time produced plays by Kentuckians, particularly since the start of the Humana Festival of New American Plays. Eben Henson's Pioneer Playhouse in Danville and the Horse Cave Theatre in Hart County have also supported regional playwrights. In June 1994, for example, *Piggyback,* Sallie Bingham's play about the Kentucky poet and balladeer John Jacob Niles and his relationship with the photographer Doris Ulmann, premiered at the Horse Cave Theatre under the direction of Pamela White. The Louisville-born playwright Naomi Wallace has had several of her plays performed at Actors Theatre, including *One Flea Spare, The Trestle at Pope Lick Creek,* and *Slaughter City U.S.A.,* which is based on a lengthy strike at a local packing plant. Naomi Wallace is a member of Louisville's affluent and controversial Wallace family, widely known for opposing the Vietnam War and supporting labor rights, women's rights, African American rights, and gay rights, and her plays usually court controversy. In 1999 Wallace won one of the coveted MacArthur Foundation's "genius grants," worth almost $300,000.

A local poet, college professor, and playwright who has had some success with his plays is Jerry Rodgers, a native of the Louisville suburb of Okolona. Like most playwrights, Rodgers has a desk full of unperformed and unpublished plays. His lucky break came in early 1976, when the director of a project on women and employment for the Louisville YWCA asked him to write a short play about the problems of a man and a woman working together in a Louisville factory. The result was *Chat,* a twelve-minute play about a woman's first day on the job as a forklift operator. Funded by the Kentucky Humanities Council, it was first performed in May 1976 at the Louisville-based Marley Cooling Tower Company, a firm employing 250 male sheet-metal workers and 25 male supervisors—and facing federal affirmative action requirements. Word got around about the unusual production, and the March 14, 1977, issue of *Business Week* carried a two-page review of it. Although *Chat* was written for that one performance, it proved so effective that it has since played before audiences ranging from the Louisville Archdiocesan Task Force on Women to the International Women's Year Convention in Lexington. Writing social service dramas was not all Rodgers wanted to do with his talent, and he has since written a number of plays, mostly satirical, that have Louisville settings and subjects.

Another local playwright, originally from Barbourville in the Kentucky mountains, is Patricia Ramsey, whose *A Killin'* has won a number of regional awards. The play is both a heartbreaking story about a mining family and a protest against unsafe conditions in Kentucky's deep coal mines.

A Louisvillian who made a significant contribution to American theater was John Mason Brown (1900–1969). He took his first job in the theater as a drama critic for *Theatre Arts Monthly Magazine* in the 1920s and spent most of his life writing drama criticism for a succession of newspapers and magazines, including the *New York Evening Post,* the *New York World Tele-gram,* and the *Saturday Review of Literature,* where he was also associate editor. He was, moreover, the author of twelve volumes on theater and drama.

Brief mention should be made of the outdoor dramas that have popped up sporadically throughout Kentucky, especially in the 1960s and 1970s. Robert Emmett McDowell's *Home Is the Hunter* is a tribute to Harrodsburg, which bills itself as "the first permanent settlement west of the Allegheny Mountains," and to such feckless pioneers as Captain James Harrod, George Rogers Clark, Daniel Boone, and Captain John Floyd. Other outdoor dramas include *The Jenny Wiley Story, The Legend of Daniel Boone, Wilderness Road,* and Paul Green's *The Stephen Foster Story,* the most successful and enduring of Kentucky's outdoor pageants, performed each summer in Bardstown.

John Patrick

from *The Teahouse of the August Moon*

Four twentieth-century playwrights who have enjoyed international recognition are Marsha Norman, Jane Martin, George C. Wolfe, and John Patrick, whose story begins here. Born John Patrick Goggan in 1906 in Louisville, he wrote plays that had little to do with his native state. He was abandoned by his parents when he was a small boy and grew up in foster homes and boarding schools. In his teens he became a hobo, and at nineteen he was a radio announcer in San Francisco, where he legally dropped his last name. After service in World War II he made a name for himself as the author of *The Hasty Heart* (1945) and the Pulitzer Prize–winning *Teahouse of the August Moon* (1952). Patrick also wrote numerous screen adaptations, including *The President's Lady* (1953), *High Society* (1956), and *Some Came Running* (1959). He committed suicide in November 1995 in a nursing home in Florida at the age of ninety.

The Teahouse of the August Moon was by far Patrick's most successful play. It is a satire about the inability of American occupation forces to understand their defeated enemy, the Japanese in a remote village on Okinawa, well enough to "reconstruct" them and teach them American values of democracy and industry or how to run a successful farm. Our guide in the play is an Okinawa native, Sakini, who, he says, is eager to learn from the Americans.

SAKINI. Juicy-fruit. (*He takes the gum from his mouth and puts it in a match box and restores it to a pocket in his shirt.*) Most generous gift of American sergeant. (*Resumes original posture of dignity.*)
Lovely ladies—kind gentlemen.
Please to introduce myself.
Sakini by name.
Interpreter by profession.
Education by ancient dictionary.
Okinawan by whim of gods. (*He kneels.*)
History of Okinawa reveal distinguished record of conquerors.
We have honor to be subjugated in 14th century by Chinese pirates.
In sixteenth century by English missionaries.
In eighteenth century by Japanese warlords.
And in twentieth century by American Marines.

Okinawa very fortunate.
Culture brought to us . . . not have to leave home for it.
Learn many things.
Most important that rest of world not like Okinawa.
World filled with delightful variation.
Illustration.
In Okinawa . . . no locks on doors.
Bad manners not to trust neighbors.
In America . . . lock and key big industry.
Conclusion?
Bad manners good business.
In Okinawa . . . wash self in public bath with nude lady quite proper.
Picture of nude lady in private home . . . quite improper.
In America . . . statue of nude lady in park win prize.
But nude lady in flesh in park win penalty.
Conclusion?
Pornography question of geography.

But Okinawans most eager to be educated by conquerors.
Deep desire to improve friction.
Not easy to learn.
Sometimes painful.
But pain makes man think.
Thought makes man wise.
Wisdom makes life endurable.

Marsha Norman

from *Getting Out*

Marsha Norman, who was born in Louisville in 1947, won the Pulitzer Prize for Drama in 1983 for *'Night, Mother*. After she earned degrees from Agnes Scott College and the University of Louisville, she worked with mentally disturbed children at Central State Hospital in Anchorage, taught in the Jefferson County Public Schools, and edited the "Jelly Bean Journal," the children's supplement of the old *Louisville Times*. Her first play, *Getting Out*, premiered at Actors Theatre of Louisville in 1977. Other plays by Norman include *Third and Oak: The Laundromat, Third and Oak: The Pool Hall* (1978), and *D. Boone* (1992). *Getting Out* is about life inside a women's correctional institution. Here is how the play begins—with a monologue delivered through a loudspeaker.

These announcements will be broadcast beginning five minutes before the house-lights come down for Act I. A woman's voice is preferred, a droning loudspeaker tone is essential.

LOUDSPEAKER: Kitchen workers, all kitchen workers report immediately to the kitchen. Kitchen workers to the kitchen. The library will not be open today. Those scheduled for book checkout should remain in morning work assignments. Kitchen workers to the kitchen. No library hours today. Library hours resume tomorrow as usual. All kitchen workers to the kitchen.

Frances Mills, you have a visitor at the front gate. All residents and staff, all residents and staff . . . do not, repeat, do not, walk on the front lawn today or use the picnic tables on the front lawn during your break after lunch or dinner.

Your attention please. The exercise class for Dorm A residents has been cancelled. Mrs. Fischer should be back at work in another month. She thanks you for your cards and wants all her girls to know she had an eight-pound baby girl.

Doris Creech, see Mrs. Adams at the library before lunch. Frances Mills, you have a visitor at the front gate. The Women's Associates' picnic for the beauty school class has been postponed until Friday. As picnic lunches have already been prepared, any beauty school member who so wishes may pick up a picnic lunch and eat it at her assigned lunch table during the regular lunch period.

Frances Mills, you have a visitor at the front gate. Doris Creech to see Mrs. Adams at the library before lunch. I'm sorry, that's Frankie Hill, you have a visitor at the front gate. Repeat, Frankie Hill, not Frances Mills, you have a visitor at the front gate.

Jane Martin

The Deal

Actors Theatre of Louisville is the home theater for the elusive Jane Martin, the pen name of a playwright who, so far, has refused to identify herself (or himself). All we know is that her scripts appear mysteriously at ATL from time to time and are accepted and produced on its stage, generally with great popular and critical success. Her agent at ATL is Sandy Speer, the executive director of the theater, who handles all her professional and business work. Everyone is quite certain that Speer is not Jane Martin. Most of her plays have been published; they include *Talking With* (1983), *What Mama Don't Know* (1988), and *Kelly and Du* (1993), all of which have been brought together in *Jane Martin: Collected Plays, 1980–1995. The Deal* is one of Martin's short plays—a very short one. It was commissioned and first produced by ATL in the Humana Festival of New American Plays, March 2000. It is part of a dramatic anthology titled *Back Story,* which is based on characters created by Joan Ackerman.

Ainsley sits at a kitchen table with nine glass-bottled beers on it.

AINSLEY: I never drank nine beers before. I feel strangely free. Ethan, bring me my toe out of the refrigerator, will you? I like to see my toe when I'm drunk.
   (He brings the toe. It's in a ziplock sandwich bag.)
   Thanks. Two and a half years old, an' I cut this baby clean off with a snow shovel the night Momma went to the hospital to have you. You ingrate. One of a thousand sacrifices, baby brother. If ol' Reuben hadn't a come along drunk as a lord, I might have bled to death, but, more importantly, I would never, never have played the oboe. Did you know Reuben played with the Boston Symphony Orchestra for thirty years? That old drunk, who would have thought it. He's got crystal pure tone. You play a duet with Reuben, you downright feel fucked. He's eighty-one years old come November.
   (She opens the ziplock and dumps the toe into her hand.)
   They sewed this baby on an' it lasted fourteen years till it snapped off that time I fell when I was doing cross-country. I believe the moral to be that you can't put something broken back together. Not in the long run.

This has proved true in all three of my romantic relationships. In each one, we split an' then came back together an' then broke off forever. The toe knows.

(She puts it back in the bag.)

I wonder how it came to be that I'm a supporting role even in my own life. I mean I thought I'd star in my life, but it hasn't worked out that way. You're the star of my life, brother mine. Whatever I am it's in relation to you. Second oboe. You know people hear about my toe before they hear about me? I meet 'em an' they say, "Oh, sure, you're the one keeps her toe in the refrigerator." Second fiddle to my own body parts. At what point, Ethan, is it determined in your own life whether you are to be a first chair or just a general all-purpose oboist? I believe it was when you were born, Ethan, and I wasn't allowed to go to the hospital. I was not . . . among the chosen, though I did, however, achieve self-mutilation with the snow shovel. Well, "They also serve who only bleed and wait," right? I believe I'll put my claim to fame back in the freezer compartment and fix you some dinner. What, dearest Ethan, would you like for dinner? I was once offered admission to the Boston Conservatory of Music, and though our family mythology would have it that I gave it up on your behalf, my sad, wild brother, I actually declined on the basis that it was a hell of a lot of money just to come out playing second oboe. It seemed a . . . pretension to be expensively trained to be ordinary. Oh, it's best to know who you are . . . or so they tell you.

George C. Wolfe

from *The Colored Museum*

In New York, Frankfort-born George Wolfe was the talk of the town for much of the 1990s as he wrote, produced, and directed some of the most daring and successful shows in years, such as *The Colored Museum, Jelly's Last Jam, Bring in 'da Noise, Bring in 'da Funk,* and *Angels in America.* Then in the spring of 1997 he suffered kidney failure and spent a year on three-times-a-week dialysis. He kept his condition mostly a secret until he received a kidney transplant in March 1998. During the dialysis period he was hopping around like a completely healthy man, not only running New York's Public Theater but also directing the musical *On the Town,* the opera *Armistad,* and *Macbeth* at the Public with Alec Baldwin. Where did he get all that talent and energy? Possibly from his mother, he told a writer for the *New York Times* in November 1998, whom he adored and whose motto was "Keep going no matter what." Wolfe was the third of four children and grew up in Frankfort, where his father worked for the Department of Corrections and his mother was principal of an all-black school that he attended.

One summer when he was twelve he went with his mother to New York, she to work on her doctorate in education and he to see the town. He saw Pearl Bailey in *Hello Dolly!* and a new production of *West Side Story,* and those experiences changed his life. Then he went to an integrated high school in Frankfort and was traumatized by the size of the place and all those white people, he said. He began to stutter. The next summer his mother went to graduate school in Ohio, and he took a course in the theater program there. Again his life was transformed. He got rid of his stutter and returned to high school in Frankfort and became a campus leader. After high school he went to Pomona College, then taught acting and began writing and directing in the Los Angeles area, and in 1979 he moved to New York. Wolfe enrolled in New York University's program in dramatic writing and musical theater and started writing *The Colored Museum,* a satire on black stereotypes. It was a hit. He began his takeover of New York. This passage from *The Colored Museum* is his original take on the gruesome slave traffic.

❦

(Blackness. Cut by drums pounding. Then slides, rapidly flashing before us. Images we've all seen before, of African slaves being captured, loaded onto ships, tortured. The images flash, flash, flash. The drums crescendo. Blackout. And then lights reveal MISS PAT, *frozen. She is black, pert, and cute. She has a flip to her hair and wears a hot pink mini-skirt stewardess uniform.)*

(She stands in front of a curtain which separates her from an offstage cockpit.)

(An electronic bell goes "ding" and Miss Pat *comes to life, presenting herself in a friendly but rehearsed manner, smiling and speaking as she has done so many times before.)*

Miss Pat: Welcome aboard Celebrity Slaveship, departing the Gold Coast and making short stops at Bahia, Port Au Prince, and Havana, before our final destination of Savannah.

Hi. I'm Miss Pat and I'll be serving you here in Cabin A. We will be crossing the Atlantic at an altitude that's pretty high, so you must wear your shackles at all times.

(She removes a shackle from the overhead compartment and demonstrates.)

To put on your shackle, take the right hand and close the metal ring around your left hand like so. Repeat the action using your left hand to secure the right. If you have any trouble bonding yourself, I'd be more than glad to assist.

Once we reach the desired altitude, the Captain will turn off the "Fasten Your Shackle" sign . . . *(She efficiently points out the "FASTEN YOUR SHACKLE" signs on either side of her, which light up.)* . . . allowing you a chance to stretch and dance in the aisles a bit. But otherwise, shackles must be worn at all times.

(The "Fasten Your Shackles" signs go off.)

Miss Pat: Also, we ask that you please refrain from call-and-response singing between cabins as that sort of thing can lead to rebellion. And, of course, no drums are allowed on board. Can you repeat after me, "No drums." *(She gets the audience to repeat.)* With a little more enthusiasm, please. "No drums." *(After the audience repeats it.)* That was great!

Once we're airborne, I'll be by with magazines, and earphones can be purchased for the price of your first-born male.

If there's anything I can do to make this middle passage more pleasant, press the little button overhead and I'll be with you faster than you can say, "Go down, Moses." *(She laughs at her "little joke.")* Thanks for flying Celebrity and here's hoping you have a pleasant takeoff.

(The engines surge, the "Fasten Your Shackle" signs go on, and over-articulate Muzak voices are heard singing as Miss Pat *pulls down a bucket seat and "shackles-up" for takeoff.)*

Voices:
GET ON BOARD CELEBRITY SLAVESHIP

GET ON BOARD CELEBRITY SLAVESHIP
GET ON BOARD CELEBRITY SLAVESHIP
THERE'S ROOM FOR MANY A MORE

(*The engines reach an even, steady hum. Just as* MISS PAT *rises and replaces the shackles in the overhead compartment, the faint sound of African drumming is heard.*)

MISS PAT: Hi. Miss Pat again. I'm sorry to disturb you, but someone is playing drums. And what did we just say . . . "No drums." It must be someone in Coach. But we here in Cabin A are not going to respond to those drums. As a matter of fact, we don't even hear them. Repeat after me. "I don't hear any drums." (*The audience repeats.*) And "I will not rebel."

(*The audience repeats. The drumming grows.*)

MISS PAT: (*Placating*) OK, now I realize some of us are a bit edgy after hearing about the tragedy on board The Laughing Mary, but let me assure you Celebrity has no intention of throwing you overboard and collecting the insurance. We value you!

(*She proceeds to single out individual passengers/audience members.*)

Why the songs *you* are going to sing in the cotton fields, under the burning heat and stinging lash, will metamorphose and give birth to the likes of James Brown and the Fabulous Flames. And you, yes *you*, are going to come up with some of the best dances. The best dances! The Watusi! The Funky Chicken! And just think of what *you* are going to mean to William Faulkner.

All right, so you're gonna have to suffer for a few hundred years, but from your pain will come a culture so complex. *And,* with this little item here . . . (*She removes a basketball from the overhead compartment.*) . . . you'll become millionaires!

(*There is a roar of thunder. The lights quiver and the "Fasten Your Shackle" signs begin to flash.* MISS PAT *quickly replaces the basketball in the overhead compartment and speaks very reassuringly.*)

MISS PAT: No, don't panic. We're just caught in a little thunder storm. Now the only way you're going to make it through is if you abandon your God and worship a new one. So, on the count of three, let's all sing. One, two, three . . .

NOBODY KNOWS DE TROUBLE I SEEN

Oh, I forgot to mention, when singing, omit the T-H sound. "The" becomes "de." "They" becomes "dey." Got it? Good!

NOBODY KNOWS . . .
NOBODY KNOWS . . .

Oh, so you don't like that one? Well then let's try another—

SUMMER TIME
AND DE LIVIN' IS EASY

Gershwin. He comes from another oppressed people so he understands.

FISH ARE JUMPIN' . . . come on.
AND DE COTTON IS HIGH.
AND DE COTTON IS . . . Sing, damnit!

(*Lights begin to flash, the engines surge, and there is wild drumming.* MISS PAT *sticks her head through the curtain and speaks with an offstage* CAPTAIN.)

MISS PAT: What?

VOICE OF CAPTAIN (*O.S.*): Time warp!

MISS PAT: Time warp! (*She turns to the audience and puts on a pleasant face.*) The Captain has assured me everything is fine. We're just caught in a little time warp. (*Trying to fight her growing hysteria.*) On your right you will see the American Revolution, which will give the U.S. of A. exclusive rights to your life. And on your left, the Civil War, which means you will vote Republican until F.D.R. comes along. And now we're passing over the Great Depression, which means everybody gets to live the way you've been living. (*There is a blinding flash of light, and an explosion. She screams.*) Ahhhhhhhhh! That was World War I which is not to be confused with World War II . . . (*There is a larger flash of light, and another explosion.*). . . Ahhhhh! Which is not to be confused with the Korean War or the Vietnam War, all of which you will play a major role in.

Oh, look, now we're passing over the sixties. Martha and the Vandellas . . . "Julia" with Miss Diahann Carroll . . . Malcom X . . . those five little girls in Alabama . . . Martin Luther King . . . Oh no! The Supremes broke up! (*The drumming intensifies*.) Stop playing those drums! Those drums will be confiscated once we reach Savannah. You can't change history! You can't turn back the clock! (*To the audience.*) Repeat after me, I don't hear any drums! I will not rebel! I will not rebel! I will not re—

(*The lights go out, she screams, and the sound of a plane landing and screeching to a halt is heard. After a beat, lights reveal a wasted, disheveled* MISS PAT, *but perky nonetheless.*)

MISS PAT: Hi. Miss Pat here. Things got a bit jumpy back there, but the Captain has just informed me we have safely landed in Savannah. Please check the overhead before exiting as any baggage you don't claim, we trash.

It's been fun, and we hope the next time you consider travel, it's with Celebrity.

(*Luggage begins to revolve onstage from offstage left, going past* MISS PAT *and revolving offstage right. Mixed in with the luggage are two male slaves and a woman slave, complete with luggage and I.D. tags around their necks.*)

MISS PAT: (*With routine, rehearsed pleasantness.*)

Have a nice day. Bye bye.
Button up that coat, it's kind of chilly.
Have a nice day. Bye bye.
You take care now.
See you.
Have a nice day.
Have a nice day.
Have a nice day.

Mary Anderson

from *A Few Memories*

There is one area in American theater history to which Kentucky has made a significant contribution—actors for the stage, the radio, the big screen, and the little screen. Who doesn't know these names: Patricia Neal, Victor Mature, Tom Cruise, Ned Beatty, Ashley Judd, Irene Dunne, Harry Dean Stanton, Una Merkel, Arthur Lake. Well, maybe you don't know some of them, but they all belong to Kentucky-born actors.

Another actor who once called Kentucky home was Mary Anderson. Who was she? She was the most acclaimed and popular actor of her day. In fact, there used to be a theater in downtown Louisville named the Mary Anderson Theatre. She was born in Sacramento in 1859 but grew up in Louisville and considered it her hometown. She was sixteen when she made her debut as Juliet in 1875 at the old Macauley's Theatre on Fourth Street, and within a few years she was the toast of the English-speaking stage, with her picture on the cover of *Harper's Weekly*. In 1896, after she had retired and married and moved to England, she published her autobiography, *A Few Memories*. She died in England in 1940. In the excerpt below, she recalls how, after months of studying Shakespeare's plays at home, she persuaded her stepfather to take her to see the owner of Macauley's Theatre and ask him to give her a part in a play. That part happened to be Juliet, and she was on her way to almost instant stardom.

One morning, on returning from the old cathedral after my daily visit, I met Dr. Griffin in front of the manager's house. Neither of us had seen Mr. Macauley since our introduction to him some months before. "Let us call and ask if he can give me a start," said I; "something tells me there may be an opportunity for a first appearance." He acceded. Mr. Macauley received us cordially, and seemed pleased and relieved when Dr. Griffin proposed his giving me a trial at his theatre. "Why," said he, "this is luck! You have come to help me out of a difficulty. The star I have this week is playing to such poor 'business' that unless he gets one good house before the week is out he may be unable to leave the town. To-day is Thursday; now, if you could act something on the night after to-morrow! Of course I will pay you nothing. I will only give you the theatre, actors, music, etc., gratis. I am certain that in

581

my way of advertising I could crowd the house for that night. I will furnish you with appropriate costumes; but I fear it is very short notice. Could you act on Saturday night?"

Could I? Here was my tide, and, with my mother's consent, I meant to take it at the flood! That had to be gained before an answer could be given. Leaving Dr. Griffin to talk over the rehearsal, etc., I ran through the streets, and reached home panting for breath. Though startled at the suddenness of the offer, my mother gave her full permission. So it was all arranged in a wonderful way! That Thursday was one of the happiest days of my life, filled as it was with brightest hope and anticipation. Only one black cloud hung over it: the thought of Nonie and my grandparents, who were all very dear to me. Had I known then that I would never again see the face of the former— that he would die, my mother and I far away from him, and that almost until his death he would refuse to forgive or see me unless I abandoned the stage life which he thought so injurious, nay, sinful—I would even then have renounced what was within my grasp. This estrangement saddened many years of my life, and has cast a shadow over all the otherwise bright and happy memories of him who was the father, friend, and playmate of our childhood's days.

A rehearsal—the only one—was called for the next morning. On my way to the cathedral I was enchanted to see posters on the fences with the following announcement:

THURSDAY, NOVEMBER 25, 1875.
AMUSEMENTS.
MACAULEY'S THEATER.

Saturday Evening—Miss MARY ANDERSON, a young lady of this city, will make her first appearance on any stage as Juliet in Shakespeare's *Romeo and Juliet*; MILNES LEVICK as Mercutio, and a powerful cast of characters.

As I was in the quiet church the hour for rehearsal struck, and I started for the theatre in a radiant frame of mind. Passing with my people through the darkened house and private boxes covered with their linen dusters, I found myself for the first time upon the stage. How strange and dream-like it seemed, that empty theatre, lighted only here and there by the faint glimmer of the gray day without, bereft of all the eager faces it had always been peopled with! And the stage! How dismal it was with the noisy patter of the rain on its tin roof, a small gas-jet burning in the centre, throwing a dingy light on the men and women (they did not relish the extra rehearsal) gloomily standing in the wings! Could they be the brilliant, sparkling courtiers I had seen but a few nights before blazing in jewels and wreathed in smiles? On seeing me, all looked surprised. Some made remarks in whispers, which I felt to be unkind; others laughed audibly. Scarcely sixteen, my hair in a long braid, my frock reaching to my boot-tops, tall, shy, and awkward, I may have given them cause for merriment; but it was as cruel, I thought, as underbred, to make no effort to conceal their mirth at my expense. However, their rudeness was salutary in its effect, putting me on my mettle before the work began. The stage-manager clapped his hands for Act I. The actors immediately rattled off their lines, making crosses and sweeps down the stage quite different from the business I had arranged. I was bewildered, and asked them to go through the play as they proposed doing it at night, and to allow me, at least in my own scenes, to follow the only "business" I knew. "Oh, bother!" said one of the actors, who did not remark the tall figure of the manager at the back of the dark theatre, "I acted in this play before you were born, and I, for one, don't mean to change what I have always done." To have all I had arranged in my sanctum thus upset in every detail threw me out so hopelessly that I was unable to go on with the rehearsal. Mr. Macauley's voice put an end to the awkward pause, saying that he had not thought it necessary to ask them, as old actors, to do all in their power to aid a girl who was then standing on the stage for the first time; and he added, "I must request now that you follow the business she knows, and that you try to be obliging." The sulkiness that followed this rebuke was damping, but the rehearsal proceeded more smoothly.

They were, with three exceptions, the most dogged, coldly uninterested set of people I have ever met, sneering at my every movement or suggestion. It was a relief to turn from them to that excellent artist and true gentleman, Milnes Levick, and to watch the earnest care with which he rehearsed every line. Most play-goers in America know how full of charm and originality is his reading of this difficult character. His interest in my work, and his almost fatherly kindness, I shall never forget. From that day we became friends, and he has no warmer admirer of his sterling qualities as man and actor than the unknown Juliet of that November morning. At last the rehearsal, so full of torture and disappointment to me, came to an end. With one blow all my beautiful ideals had been dashed to the ground. It was a rude awakening from a long dream, and my heart was sore and heavy as I trudged home through the rain, longing to hide myself in the friendly den, and find relief in tears.

There had been so many humiliations, such cold, cruel treatment from nearly all the actors, that I dreaded the coming of Saturday, when I should have to encounter their sneering faces again. Still, it did come, and my mother and I found ourselves walking to the theatre in the crisp air of a starry winter night. After the sad experience of the day before, I was hardly hopeful enough to be nervous.

The borrowed robes were quickly donned. They fitted well, with the exception of the white satin train (the first I had ever worn), which threatened every moment to upset me. The art of make-up was unknown to me, and ornaments I had none. When Juliet was called to await her cue, what a transformation in the scene! The actors, in velvets and brocades, were gay and excited, some of them even deigned to give me a condescending nod, while the gloomy stage of the day before was flooded with light, life, and animation. I became feverishly anxious to begin. It was hard to stand still while waiting for the word. At last it came: "What, ladybird! God forbid! where's this girl? what, Juliet!" and in a flash I was on the stage, conscious only of a wall of yellow light before me, and a burst of prolonged applause. Curiosity had crowded the house. "Why, it's little Mamie Anderson. How strange! it's only a few months ago since I saw her rolling a hoop!" etc., were some of the many remarks which, I was afterwards told, ran through the audience.

The early, lighter scenes, being uncongenial, I hurried through as quickly as possible. Even these were well received by the indulgent audience. But there was enthusiasm in the house when the tragic parts were reached. Flowers and recalls were the order of the evening. While things were so smiling before, they were less satisfactory behind, the curtain. The artist who had acted in the play before my birth forgot his words, and I had to prompt him in two important scenes. In the last act the lamp that hangs above Juliet, as she lies in the tomb, fell, and burned my hands and dress badly, and, to make matters worse, Romeo forgot the dagger with which Juliet was to kill herself, and that unfortunate young person had, in desperation, to despatch herself with a hair-pin. But in spite of much disillusion, a burned hand and arm, and several other accidents, the night was full of success, and I knew that my stage career had begun in earnest.

Contemporary
Nonfiction

At this stop on our Kentucky journey, I have prepared a feast of nonfiction to satisfy every palate. Here are writings for your enjoyment ranging from Dr. Thomas Clark's description of pioneer life to the sportswriter Jerry Brewer's homecoming piece. There are even a few Kentuckians who leave home temporarily to write about other places. There will also be some new voices who will celebrate Kentucky as a state of admirable diversity.

Few historians merit mention in a literary anthology, but Kentucky has been blessed for over two hundred years with historians who were also good writers, from John Filson to Thomas D. Clark. For the record, here are a few recent historians whose names should be noted: J. Winston Coleman, James C. Klotter, Lowell H. Harrison, John E. Kleber, and Martin F. Schmidt. Some of these historians have even been known to try their pens at poetry and fiction.

I wish I could have found a place for one of Kentucky's most interesting and little-known writers, J. Ross Browne, who left the state when still a young man, signed aboard a whaling ship off New England, and later wrote a book about his experiences, *Etchings of a Whaling Cruise* (1846), which apparently influenced Melville when he was writing *Moby Dick.* Clay Lancaster (1917–2000), the influential Lexington-born scholar and architectural historian who wrote books on subjects ranging from the Japanese influence in America to the architecture of Kentucky, deserves some space. So does the renowned authority on urban affairs, Grady Clay, who has lived in Louisville since 1939 and analyzed the city from its courthouse to its alleys. He authored *Close-Up: How to Read the American City* in 1973. Even new areas of research and writing should be noticed—such as health and wellness, a whole new genre of professional and popular writing. One of the authorities in this burgeoning field is the Louisvillian Bryant Stamford, who not only writes books about the subject but has a weekly syndicated column called "The Body Shop." Unfortunately, I can't include everyone who deserves to be in this chapter or in this book, but I think you'll agree that, as a writerly state, we've come a long way from the time when Kentucky was wilderness.

Straddling the fence between fiction and nonfiction is Kentucky's folk culture, which not only undergirds the fiction of such writers as Jesse Stuart,

James Still, and Bobbie Ann Mason but also has become a respectable area of study, as evidenced by folklore programs and curricula in several of Kentucky's colleges and universities. An especially fertile area of folklore centers around ghost stories, which have been collected by such academic and popular authors as Leonard Roberts in eastern Kentucky, Kenneth and Mary Clark, Lynwood Montell in southern Kentucky, and Louisville's David Dominé, whose *Ghosts of Old Louisville* became a local best seller when it was published in July 2005.

Surely, Kentucky's Holy Threesome are Horses, Religion, and Food. Some people would also add bourbon and tobacco, although the latter has recently slipped in use and popularity, and bourbon is often included with food. To tell the truth, in Kentucky not many people are directly affected by horses except on Derby Day, when all Kentuckians become horse people and experts on thoroughbred racing. That leaves religion and food as the passions of most Kentuckians. A onetime Kentucky import from Georgia, Willie Snow Ethridge, wrote in *I'll Sing One Song,* a hilarious tribute to her adopted state, that "hostesses here, I fear, devote more thought to food than to religion." Next to the Bible, the cookbook is surely the most popular book in Kentucky. Indeed, the cookbook is probably more often read. Dozens of cookbooks are issued annually by women's clubs, hotels, restaurants, professional groups, schools, churches, and just about any organization with more than a dozen members. Such names as Cissy Gregg, John Egerton, Sarah Fritschner, and Richard T. Hougen—not to mention Kentucky-born Duncan Hines—are household words. Perhaps the food expert who spans the broadest range is Camille Glenn, who grew up in the early twentieth century in Dawson Springs, where her father owned and operated a popular spa for affluent city people. Glenn's expertise and tastes encompass, on the one hand, French cuisine (she studied at the Cordon Bleu in Paris and taught French cooking in Louisville for many years) and, on the other, Southern country cooking that she learned at her mother's side in Hopkins County. As she wrote in *The Fine Art of Delectable Desserts:* "Cooking does take time, as does everything else worthwhile. Don't count the hours ever. If you cook well, the fruits of your labor will delight all those who gather at your table. Have you ever noticed the voices when the food is good? They don't talk—they chatter—they purr. Those hours you forgot to count will reap many happy returns."

In an article in the *Clark Times,* a publication of the Kentucky Historical Society Foundation, even Dr. Thomas D. Clark became a food expert when he speculated on the history of burgoo. Tracing its roots to Virginia's Brunswick stew, he writes that the scrumptious Kentucky version "originated back in the days when hunters counted up their day's kill in the thousands of squirrels, and when pigeons flew throughout the woods in veritable clouds, and bear, deer, buffalo, and hundreds of turkeys were available." In a sidebar he provides a handy recipe for a hostess who is expecting a crowd for dinner. The ingredients consist of the following: "800 lbs. beef, 200 lbs. fowl, 168 gallons tomatoes, 36 gallons corn, 350 lbs. cabbage, 6 bushels onions, carrots [presumably to taste], 1,800 lbs. potatoes, 2 lbs. red pepper, 1/2 lb. black pepper, 20 lbs. salt, 8 oz. angostura, 1 pint Worcestershire, 1/2 lb. curry powder, 3 quarts tomato catsup, and 2 quarts sherry. Mix and cook over a slow fire for 22 hours." If you make this recipe, you may never have to cook again.

Kentuckians have always loved their state inordinately, but they are also firmly grounded in their counties, communities, towns, and cities. In the first few selections we travel all over the state with natives and visitors who give us a taste of what writers in the nineteenth century called "the odd corners" of Kentucky. Along the way we meet the genius Guy Davenport and the gonzo journalist Hunter Thompson, as well as several minority voices.

I suppose it has always been true that people who are in power don't want to share it. The powerless have to demand power to obtain it. In retrospect, of course, it seems incredible that any society ever condoned slavery or female subjugation, or child labor, or segregation, or any form of discrimination. Although we have made remarkable progress, the goal of a completely just society has not yet been reached. Two selections near the end of this chapter are about recent and current struggles for equality: for the disabled and for gays and lesbians.

Thomas D. Clark

from *A History of Kentucky*

The dean of Kentucky historians, Thomas Dionysius Clark, was born in Mississippi in 1903. After a brief sojourn in Lexington in the late 1920s to pick up a master's degree, he had the good sense to move to Kentucky permanently in 1931, remaining there until his death on June 28, 2005. What he accomplished as Kentucky's preeminent historian in over three quarters of a century is amazing: as a teacher, writer, lecturer, collector, faculty leader, and inspiration for generations of Kentuckians at the University of Kentucky, and as father of the state archives, the UK Library Special Collections, and the University Press of Kentucky. Two excerpts give a brief sample of Clark's readable style of writing history: the first is from his classic *History of Kentucky* (1937), in which he discusses the social side of pioneer life.

With all the trials and tribulations characteristic of settling a new country, where both animal and human kingdoms conspired against them, the Kentucky pioneers were not without their lighter and happier moments. Distinction in social rank was the exception rather than the rule, for one man's rifle was as effective as another's, if both were good shots.

It is a matter of history that on the American frontier there were fewer women than men and that this condition naturally led to whirlwind courtships and hurried marriages. A single woman was a highly coveted prize by every bachelor, and no woman, regardless of her homeliness of appearance or state of decrepitude, was forced to remain single for any length of time. Widows hardly donned their weeds before being "spoken for."

When courtships resulted in marriage, the whole community prepared to celebrate, for frontier weddings were generally accompanied by as much ritual, pomp, and ceremony as a royal nuptial. The bridegroom's friends gathered at his father's house, and from there they proceeded to the home of the bride. The party timed itself to arrive at the scene of the wedding shortly before noon, for the wedding was allowed to interfere in no way with the customary infare following the ceremony.

The wedding party constituted in reality a frontier dress parade. Guests were clothed in garments ranging from the typical deer skin and linsey woolsey, worn by the hunters as everyday clothing, to that of frayed and faded silks, of another day and another land, worn by some of the ladies. Most of the women, however, dressed in homespuns, and, in some cases, coarse linsey woolsey "Sunday" dresses, trimmed with ruffles taken from former-day finery. A miscellaneous collection of buttons and buckles "from over the mountains" served as ornaments.

After the wedding ceremony, the bridal party went from the home of the bride to that of the groom, where the infare was served. A cavalcade set forth, the young males of which performed numerous antics to the amusement of their lady escorts. Often a young gallant would purposely frighten the horse of his partner to hear her scream and to give him opportunity to rush to her rescue. Occasionally, the wedding party was a victim of practical jokers who preceded it and threw obstacles in the way by cutting down trees or tying grapevines across the path. When the merrymakers neared their destination, two of the more daring boys were singled out to "run for the bottle." This feat (which was really a horse race in the woods) required expert horsemanship, for the run was through the forest, over fallen trees and under low-hanging branches.

At the bridegroom's home, the infare consisted of nearly every kind of food known to the frontier. There were venison, beef, pork, and fowl. Vegetables, such as cabbage and potatoes, were present in abundance. There were biscuit and hoecakes, treacle (molasses), honey, sweetened corn meal mush, and milk. The "bottle" was passed freely, for the feast was a merry affair. Individuals traded witticisms; toasts were drunk to the newlyweds; jokes were told at the expense of the bridegroom; and, inevitably, prophecies of large families were made—prophecies which were soon fulfilled.

When the wedding banqueters had finished their revels at the festal board, the musicians, led always by the fiddler, struck up a merry tune for the dance, which lasted for hours. A unique dance was developed on the frontier in the well-known "square dance," and the Virginia reel was a favorite in some communities. Fiddlers confined their selections to favorite frontier "breakdown" tunes such as *Billy in the Low Ground, Fisher's Horn Pipe,* and *Barbara Allen,* tunes which still enliven dance parties of many Kentucky communities. In the midst of the evening's gaiety (about nine o'clock), a deputation of young ladies stole the bride away and put her to bed in the bridal chamber. This room was most often in the loft, which was reached by climbing a peg ladder to the hatch in the ceiling of the "big" room. When the ladies had finished their task, a group of young men stole the bridegroom away and saw that he was placed snugly beside his bride. Then the party continued until later in the evening, when the merrymakers returned to the kitchen for sustenance. In this lull the bride and bridegroom were not forgotten. A party climbed aloft with food and "Black Betty," the bottle, to minister to the hunger and thirst of the newlyweds.

Weddings were not always free of unfortunate consequences, for often there were those in the community who had been overlooked when the invitations were made. They felt that this snubbing justified revenge, and the favorite trick of the jealous ones was the shearing of tails, foretops, and manes of the wedding attendants' horses. Many were the revelers who returned home in an evil mood because some sneaking neighbor had disfigured their saddle horses.

from *The Kentucky*

This selection, from Clark's book *The Kentucky* (1942), in the American Rivers series, takes us on a trip with him on the midnight special out of Lexington into the mountains at Blackey.

The Kentucky country presents a veritable kaleidoscopic pattern of life. Its modern story is a long one, and there are countless details in it, but with all this it is never dull. The range of the story runs all the way from one of luscious living in grand country mansions and economic self-sufficiency of the land to one of abject poverty in a coal-mining village hovel. Upstream the Kentucky's valleys are being subjected to new types of culture. Highways and railroads have completely remade the transportation story. Today the "outside" is not so far away as it once was. Where once "push" boats were shoved on their heavy and tedious way mile after mile up the treacherous Middle Fork to Hazard and Whitesburg from market towns downstream, trains and motor trucks now go out from Lexington, Louisville, and Cincinnati loaded with freight for the highland towns. Long coal trains come roaring westward to Lexington and Louisville with thousands of tons of soft coal from the eastern Kentucky mines.

In the Lexington bus station and at the Union Station which serves the Louisville and Nashville Company's eastern branch, dozens of anxious people sit with tired and strained faces. They hold on to precious packages bought in the city or keep an eye on a battered suitcase parked in the corner. They are on their way to the hills. The "midnight special" which runs out of Lexington to Blackey up the river is a rolling museum in rural culture. This little train puffs along with its three or four cars, dragging itself over the steep grades up through Beattyville to Jackson to Hazard and to Blackey. Drowsy mountain passengers loll or toss restlessly in their cramped sleeping positions on the narrow seats. The next morning, as the mist lifts a bit at daybreak and the little engine shoots its smoke and steam high overhead, the

North Fork appears alongside the grade. Soon there is a jerk, a screeching of brakes, and the train comes to a stop. Coal miners pile on by the dozen, each man carrying a huge dinner pail. Each of these buckets contains enough flat biscuits and large slabs of meat to feed a dozen Lexington businessmen on a picnic. Miners, however, must eat because their work is heavy. They are a boisterous, rugged crowd of public workingmen who do not have the shy hesitancy of the men who till the hillside farms. Association with each other in industrial labor has put a wire edge on the native son. The train lurches forward in its heavy start upgrade; the front door of the coach swings open with a violent crash and sticks in the bracket which holds it open. A rowdy miner stands in the door with his big aluminum dinner bucket swinging on his arm. The door swings open just as he tries to take hold of it and causes a moment of surprise, and then he yells, "Boys, this door knows when a big shot is coming through." Back in the coach a sharp-tongued wit yells in a high mountain voice, "Hit jest opens that-away fer pretty women and children." Soon a crap game is going in the rear of the vestibule, and then all of a sudden the train stops and the miners file out, and life aboard settles down to its former state of quietness.

Occasionally a missionary rides this famous midnight special out of Lexington, or some good Samaritan hovers protectingly over an emaciated child. Or that courageous soldier against congenital eye infections, Miss Linda Neville, rides deep into the hill country on her mission of mercy. One rides along on this train, feeling the union of every rail lifting the coach up and setting it down with monotonous regularity. Interesting faces come through the door at every trail-crossing flag stop. Then the visitor begins to speculate on what this part of the American scene really means. Along the railroad and the graded and surfaced highway which runs roughly parallel to the river, life is rapidly becoming brackish. Industrialism with its "jenny barns" and its age of flashy life values is pouring a new culture into the old and static society of the landlocked Appalachians. Pioneer America is being subjected to the modern pattern without first having gone through the important intermediary stage of being conditioned for it. Folk culture of the mountains has sometimes of late years become strangely intermingled with that of workaday industrialism. The whole thing presents the appearance of a fine piece of period furniture which has been smeared with bright red paint in order to give it life.

Folklore people have piled into the settlement schools to examine, at first hand, primitive America. Most of the people who have founded the settlement schools, and who have given all their energies to promote them, have known what they wished to accomplish. But some of the people who have rushed in to study the folk in their natural habitat have confused the scene. Where there has been an absence of a clearly defined folk culture they have planted one, and now in some cases they, who lack the power of discrimination and a knowledge of population, do not actually know what is indigenous and what is history. Al Capp with his Li'l Abner Yokum strip has sent visitors into the Kentucky hills looking for "presarved" turnips, Hairless Joes, and two-fisted mammies, but his strip is a gross libel on a virile race of rural Americans. Then there has come the great racial conjurer who has planted the Anglo-Saxon theory good and strong, and even the natives like to believe this. To them it is some sort of vague racial pat on the back, and they have found it a delightful excuse behind which they hide in a moment of defensive confusion. Religious messiahs of all known brands have wandered into the upriver country to solve the spiritual problems of the people. They have carried only a part of one solution with them, and almost always they have come away with fragmentary results. This will always be true until some leader who can see the pattern as a whole comes along.

In Lexington the Mountain Club holds its annual meetings, and the Sunday papers publish long columns about its social affairs. Prominent businessmen in all the Bluegrass towns are there to attest their pride in the place of their origin. If these people stopped in the mountains, as John Fox, Jr.'s linchpin theory would have it, because they lacked initiative, then this generation has mustered enough spunk to push on in effective strides. One wonders, when reading special sociological reports on the Bluegrass population or hearing a scientific scholar report on population movements between the regions, what this intersectional mixture will become.

A Bluegrass girl announces her marriage in a central Kentucky paper. Her husband is a mountaineer. Or a mountain girl announces that she has married a Bluegrass boy, and the theory of strict sectional conformity of *The Heart of the Hills* is ignored. It is true that these things are indicative of rapid changes in much of the upriver country, yet enough of the old is still left behind to make of it a land of eternal surprise and fascination. . . .

The story of the land along the Kentucky River is made up of all these things which have served as marks of regional distinction, but there are many more. The history of the Kentucky in comparison with that of other rivers might lose some of its major significance, but even this would only be a relative matter. The story of this river is completely American, and its people have both preserved and created at least three distinct aspects of American culture. Other rivers have stretched their history over larger patterns, but none has exceeded it in the intensity of interesting native background. Any comparison between it and other rivers would again call for a verse from Samuel Woodworth's famous song which eulogized the old huntsmen who stood guard with their long squirrel rifles atop the ramparts of Jackson's famous line across the Plains of Chalmette:

> We are a hardy, freelorn race,
>   Each man to fear a stranger,
> Whate'er the game we join in chase,
>   Despising toil and danger;
> And if daring foe annoys,
>   Whate'er his strength and forces,
> We'll show him that Kentucky boys
>   Are "alligator horses."
> O Kentucky, the hunters of Kentucky,
>   The hunters of Kentucky!

John Fetterman

Another capable guide to the hills and mountains of southeastern Kentucky is John Fetterman, the late newspaperman and photographer. In the 1960s Fetterman recorded the hardscrabble lives of the mountain people who lived along Stinking Creek in Knox County, a creek possibly named for the foul odors caused by the rotting carcasses of game animals thrown into it by pioneer hunters. Fetterman based *Stinking Creek* (1967), a book of photographs and reportage, on numerous visits and interviews with the citizens of what was then a remote, almost inaccessible part of Kentucky. In these two selections we witness a baptism by total immersion and visit a country store.

⌀

from "Shall We Gather at the River," Chapter 6, *Stinking Creek*

On the day of the baptizing the creek bank was crowded with the congregation and bystanders. A swinging bridge which crosses at that point groaned on its supporting rusty steel cables as watchers gathered on it to seek a vantage point. It was a hot Sunday morning when even the big purple flies seemed loathe to expend sufficient energy to fly.

But the congregation was eager and happy, pushing to the very edge of the creek through the scrub sycamore and willow growth, ignoring the gray, sticky mud, and moving closer to the sanctified spot where sixteen souls were about to step nearer the Kingdom of Heaven.

The sixteen were all young people, gathered in a knot by the creek. Some of the girls wore tinted, transparent raincoats over their dresses, the coats tied tightly about them against the turbid yellow water of the creek. The older children were quiet and willing; the little ones gathered about Preacher Marsee, their eyes wide with apprehension as they wondered at the fervor of the singing that arose from the multitude gathered at the creek bank.

Suddenly, Preacher Marsee, in a white shirt open at the throat, led his converts into the creek. He was at the head of the long winding line, as those to be baptized followed one by one, each holding hands with both the person in front and the person in back. The young people entered the creek downstream from the crowd, then waded up to the spot where the water deepened to waist height on the smaller ones. Preacher Marsee led the new members of his flock, carefully feeling the way with his feet, smiling, his face

594

turned upward into the scalding sun. Preacher Marsee was collecting the fruits of his two weeks of struggle with evil in the hot little box that was Salem Baptist Church in midsummer.

When he reached the baptizing hole, Preacher Marsee turned and brought the first child to his side. Placing a napkin over the little girl's face, Preacher Marsee said in a voice that was ecstatic to the point of almost sounding like a series of gasps:

"Upon this profession of faith in Christ as your Saviour and Lord, and in obedience to His command, I baptize you my sister, in the name of the Father and the Son and the Holy Ghost."

With that, he plunged the child beneath the murky water, lowering her backward so that the water closed over her face with a quick gush, then raised her quickly.

As the child went beneath the water, a chorus of voices shattered the quiet of the congregation as a hymn began:

> *"Shall we gather at the river,*
> *The beautiful, the beautiful river . . ."*

One by one the line edged nearer Preacher Marsee as he repeated the ritual: "Upon this profession of faith . . ."

A boy or a girl was plunged into the yellow stream. And the chorus resumed:

> *"Shall we gather at the river*
> *That flows by the throne of God."*

For Preacher Marsee it was a moment of triumph. In two short weeks his apprehensions as to the success of a revival had been swept away in a victory for his Maker. Now in the role of spokesman for a conqueror, he exulted. He clasped a boy to him, and before performing the ritual of baptism, turned to the crowd, and cried: "I feel so good. I could do this all day. Thank God! Whole families saved!"

And when the next convert stepped forward, Preacher Marsee cried, "The angels are hovering over this creek today, and the Lord is looking down."

As the believer was plunged into the water, the voices on the bank sang:

> *"Shall we gather at the river,*
> *The beautiful, the beautiful river . . ."*

And from those on the bridge, the hymn echoed along the narrow valley:

> *"Shall we gather at the river*
> *That flows by the throne of God."*

When the last of the sixteen young residents of Stinking Creek were baptized, they waded out of the creek and into the arms of their weeping parents. Some—the very young—trembled as though from a chill—but more from excitement—as their wet bodies were embraced by the emotional throng.

Preacher Marsee, the last to emerge from the creek, stepped out onto the bank elated and flushed with success. He held out his hand in greeting, but a quick sad look played upon his face, now wet with perspiration and red from the sun and heat.

"Thank you. Thank you," he cried to the searing blue sky. He paused a moment, and his voice was a whisper when he added, "We have only touched the hem of His garment today."

from "Shady School,"
Chapter 7, *Stinking Creek*

The children of Stinking Creek are beautiful—strikingly, physically beautiful. Their faces are open and frank, and they reflect the round, fair features of their English, Scottish, and Irish ancestors. Even when filthy and clothed in rags stiffened with accumulations of grease and grime, mountain children bring you up short with their wide trusting eyes and their angelic, innocent, naïve friendliness.

Despite shortages of food, proper medical attention, and lack of sanitation, the children of Stinking Creek appear to bloom with a sweetness that defies their heritage. But while their physical beauty is exceptional, their intellectual world is shabby.

In the county seat that serves Stinking Creek, a man who stood high in school administration once said, "I don't know whether we can ever do anything for those people up the hollows."

Whether anything can or cannot be done, one thing is apparent: No one has ever tried to do anything. . . .

from "The Young People,"
Chapter 8, *Stinking Creek*

Entering and trading at Ellis Messer's store is an unvarying ritual. You step up from the dusty road and into the comparative gloom of the interior and nod to the men and boys reclining on the cow-feed bags. Then you walk directly to the bright red Coca-Cola cooler squatting against the wall. You always have a pop first. If children come along, they walk silently to the cooler and await the signal to reach in.

Pop flows freely on Stinking Creek. Youth drink eight or ten bottles a day. The tiniest youngster can gulp down a king-size bottle in minutes. The selection is a thoughtful and unhurried decision. You lift one large hinged lid and peer inside. Diet Rite, Dr. Pepper, Tab, Mountain Dew. You drop the lid, lift the other lid and examine the contents of the other half of the cooler. Seven-Up, Coca-Cola, Grape, Orange. The crimped top of the pop bottle is lifted on an opener nailed to the wall; the top clatters into a cardboard box on the floor, and the customer takes a deep, long pull from the bottle. Then, accompanied by his silent children, he walks over to examine the delicacies on the metal bakery shelf. "Have a cake if you want," the head of the house says. Like flickers of spring lightning, young fingers snatch the cookies and cakes from their resting place and tear off the clear plastic covers. The craving for the sting of carbonated beverages and the lingering sweetness of the little cakes and assorted fruit bars is constant. . . .

The biggest trading day in Ellis Messer's store is on check day when the dollars sent to fight poverty come pouring in. Crisp, heavy paper checks, perforated to be processed by electronic machines later in Washington or the state capital. The checks protrude proudly from the shirt pockets of the men and burn impatiently in the apron pockets of the women. Check day is the day to pay up last month's credit that has been carefully added and double-checked by Ellis Messer.

Ellis keeps his records in a worn blue looseleaf notebook, and each page represents a customer on credit. Purchases are entered with a heavy pencil. When you pay up, Ellis adds the figures, takes the welfare check, and subtracts the amount needed to restore the customer to debt-free independence. When the customer can't write, Ellis witnesses the X used to endorse the check. As he hands the change over, Ellis pulls the customer's page from the notebook, ceremoniously folds it into a small square, and hands it over. "You might check that when you get time," he says. "If I made a mistake you know where you got it." The figures are rarely checked, for two reasons. Folks on Stinking Creek trust Ellis Messer, and many customers can't read the rows of numbers anyway.

With pop and cake consumed and last month's credit disposed of, the time to trade has come. Ellis and his customer regard each other unblinkingly across the counter: the customer silent and studying the shelves; Ellis solemn and waiting, one arm resting on the pan of the ancient scale.

The trading is time-consuming, deliberate, and deadly serious. The conversation is brief and to the point, and for a time gossip and matters of less import are put aside.

"You got flour?"

"Plain or self-rising?"

A pause for reflection, as though there might be a remote chance that on some eventful day the self-rising might be selected. "Give me a sack of plain."

Ellis fetches the flour in its white bag and enshrines it on the counter between himself and the customer.

"Got ary cornmeal?"

"Yep."

"Two sacks."

The yellow paper sacks are brought to the counter and hefted into place beside the flour.

"Got ary light bread?"

"Got Kern's sliced."

"Give me a cake of that."

The bread joins the selected groceries on the counter.

"You got lard?"

"It's went up five cents."

A pause, while the customer studies the pastoral illustration on the Commonwealth Life Insurance Company calendar on the front wall.

"Two boxes."

The staples are taken care of first—always the flour, cornmeal, lard, and pork side meat, a white, salted chunk of meat wrapped in a brown paper that quickly absorbs the grease. The pile of groceries grows steadily. The trading pace slows as the customer carefully regards his accumulated purchases piled reassuringly on the counter between the two men like a monument to the astuteness of the buyer. The customer rocks slowly on his heels and lets his eyes play over the groceries he has bought, measuring the provisions against the demands of the young uns at home, the remains of his welfare check, and the length of time until the next check will be deposited in his mailbox.

The customer moves cautiously from the field of necessity into the treacherous area of luxury. He glances down at his children standing quietly beside him, their bright, wide eyes straining to see upon the high counter. The provider reads a plea in their young faces. Prudence is swept aside by a swell of love and of pride. There ought to be something a man can do for the young uns.

The customer looks at his children a few moments, then turns solemnly to Ellis. "You got Kool Aide?"

"Got the sweetened kind. What flavor you like?"

"Strawberry," the man says, checking his selection with a quick downward glance. The laughing eyes of his brood confirm the decision.

Ellis has his pencil in his hand, but he has not yet turned to the customer's place in the blue looseleaf notebook. He knows the trading is not yet completed.

The customer hesitates, and hooks his thumbs into the bib of his overalls. Ellis waits patiently. He knows the struggle going on in the man's mind and how it will end. It is check day. The old woman and the young uns have been good this month. Hell, a man's got to do what he can for his own kind. And do it while he can, because he might not be able to do for them tomorrow.

The customer walks over to a lone angel-food cake. Its sticker says fifty-nine cents. The man hefts it, walks erectly back to the counter past his adoring children, and places the cake on top of the groceries.

"How much is that?" he asks,

"Fifty-nine cents," Ellis confirms.

"Put it down, too."

Ellis knows the trading is done. He opens the notebook and begins the meticulous entry of the purchases against next month's check.

The trading is ignored by the men and boys who shift their weight on the cow-feed sacks, and talk. They appear unaware of the constant trading at the counter a few feet away—unless a customer wants a sack of cow feed. Then they rise while Ellis or his boy, Kenneth, drags a sack from the pile and carries it out to be hoisted onto the back of a mule or into a car or pickup truck. The men and boys settle back immediately, and although sack after sack disappears during the day, the number of available seats appears to decrease only slowly. When the supply of cow-feed seats dwindles to almost nothing, upended soft-drink cases are pressed into service.

The cow-feed sacks are a pleasant place to sit, and the store has a warm earthy smell of seasoned wood and people. In winter, the black stove gurgles defiance at the howling weather, and in summer drafts of cool air sometimes fan through the store.

The boys and men talk of hunting, of dogs, of things they have seen on the mountain that rises skyward behind the store. They talk and gossip and wink at the children who come in, and chide the old people. There is an unfailing and sincere respect for old people on Stinking Creek. The young boys laugh and joke with them, but their laughter is never of derision; rather it is like fond chuckling at an errant child.

So when spry Aunt Louisa Sizemore comes in pertly and orders her trading goods in authoritative and certain tones, the boys laugh at Ellis Messer's quick compliance, and tell her, "You'll never eat all that, Aunt Louisa."

Louisa Sizemore is ninety-nine. "At least that's what I think I am," she says.

When there are no customers and all the welfare checks have been safely deposited in the wooden cash drawer, Ellis leans on the counter and listens to the young men talk. He grew up in the hollow and has heard the stories many times, but he always listens and shows appropriate wonder at each repeated tale.

Kathy Kahn

"How I Got My Schoolgirl Figure Back"

Kathy Kahn is a freelance journalist, author, community organizer, and country singer from the mountains of northern Georgia. Kahn conducted a series of interviews for her oral history *Hillbilly Women* (1985), and one of her subjects was the labor organizer Granny Hager. Born and bred in the coal camps of eastern Kentucky, Granny Hager brought an eloquent voice to the black-lung controversy of the 1960s. She tried desperately to get the coal miners of Perry County to organize a union to obtain a living wage and decent working conditions in the mines. In the selection that follows, we witness the age-old struggle between miners and mine operators through the eyes of Granny Hager.

At one time we was solid union here. But what the coal operators did, they would come around and say, "Well boys, I'm losing money, I just can't work it this way. If you all will take a cut, we'll work on, and if you don't, we're going to have to shut down."

Naturally the men would take a cut. First thing they knew, they were down to working for nothing. They were working for seven, eight dollars a day. And that's the way the coal operators busted the union and got the men to work for nothing.

So we set up. I believe it was about '62. We set up the Appalachian Committee for Full Employment. The United Mine Workers Union in New York sent a man in here, to see what we could do undercover, see if we could get the miners organized and then bring it all out in the open.

We talked up this roving picket idea, and we went to work. Where we knowed there was un-union mines, we went in time enough to catch the day shift as it went in and the night shift as it went out. We'd ask the miners to sign the checkoff, to come out with us for more money. Well, most of them would sign it, you see, and they'd turn around and go back home, they wouldn't go back in the mine.

One morning real early, we decided to leave out from the union hall in a motorcade and go out and picket. We left the union hall at two-thirty that morning to hit Southeast Coal Company in Knott County. Me and Ashford Thomas, we was riding in the front car and we dropped in over there. But when we'd got about fifteen miles from the mines, the snow was just about that deep and that high. And, boy, did we have a narrow road to drop down into the mines.

So me and Ashford and the rest went on. Whenever nobody else wouldn't ride in the front car going in, me and Ashford, that was all the sense we had, we'd take the lead. So we caught the night shift as it went out and the day shift as it went in.

Well, Southeast, they was a hundred and thirty-seven men a-workin' up there. We asked them to sign the checkoff. And a hundred and thirty-six of them signed it and come back with us. There wasn't but one that wouldn't sign it.

So now the UMW was supposed to give the union men each a twenty-five-dollar check. And from then on the union was supposed to give them fifty dollars a week to feed their families on as long as they stayed out.

That evening we went back on down to the union hall. We'd always go down there after one of these runs and make our plans for the next morning. Well, we decided we'd hit Charley Combs's mine over on Big Creek the next morning.

When the morning come, we changed our mind and decided to go back up the other way again. So back we went, but we didn't do so good this time.

Just as soon as we got out of the driveway at the union hall, they was a whole bunch of highway patrols fell in behind us. And they cut in between our cars. They tried to arrest Ashford. He walked down to their car and they said something or other smart to him. He told them, he said, "If you were standing out there and helping us fight for our rights you'd be better off, instead of guarding scabs for them to go in the mines and work."

Well, one word brought on another, and one of them highway patrols, he jumped out. He said to Ashford, "I'll knock your brains out and put you in that car." Ashford, he said, "You'd better get somebody to help you." He was a little bitty gadget, but it took three of them highway patrols to put him in that car. And they started off to Whitesburg with him. They got about three miles from Whitesburg and the patrol stopped. They said, "Now, Mr. Thomas, we're going to let you go back home. But we don't want to catch you on nary another picket line." Ashford said, "If that picket line's down there when I get down there, you'll catch me in it. And if it hain't," he said, "you'll catch me in the first one that leaves in the morning."

And we had a snoop somewhere in the bunch from then on. We'd say we was going one place and then the next morning we'd head out for another place, trying to throw the highway patrols off. But, the next morning when we formed that motorcade, they knowed exactly where we was going and they would tell us so. We never did catch the one that it was.

We wasn't getting nowheres fast, you see, because we had somebody asneakin' on us. So at one meeting everyone had their say about it. I'm always the least sayer in the bunch; I'm the biggest mouth, but when I get up I hain't got much to say. Well, I got up. Berman Gibson said, "Granny, you look like the devil." I said, "I *feel* like the devil. I'll tell you the truth, it's got to be a man that's tipping the thin gray line off to us." That's what they call the highway patrols here. "If we find out who that man is, we don't want none of the men in our way." I said, "All you women that'll help me take him out of here, hold your hands up." They every one of them women held their hands up. And we really meant it; as much as we'd went and starved and suffered and waded in the snow and stood in it. I really meant I would try to take him out of there, and I knowed with a little help I could.

Well, Berman Gibson, he took over to handle the union's money, a-goin' to get it and paying these men. Well, the men never did get more than twenty-five dollars, but we knowed it was supposed to be more. So the men figured we wasn't going to make it, we wasn't going to accomplish nothing. Gradually the men started going back to work, on account of their families suffering, they couldn't stay out on twenty-five dollars. The International wouldn't come to us until all the men all over Perry County come out. If we could have got them out then the UMW might have come to us.

We never did get a union back in here. It's still here in some of the mines, but it's not carried out like it should be. In other words, it's a bunch of dues-paying scabs, is what we call them. These little mines still work for whatever they want to pay them.

One morning, the day after one of our meetings, I got up and somebody had set fire to some pine grass out there by the bathroom—I've always had to have a outdoor bathroom—and it burned right up to the porch here. It's lucky for me it burned out. A-tryin' to burn me out.

Then one day I come in and laying over there on the far side of the railroad tracks was some dynamite. They was going to dynamite the railroad out here in front of my house just to scare me away. But it was wet or something, it went out. I've really had it on this riverbank.

After Ab passed away in '62, I come up with forty-eight years he'd worked in the mines. In January of '70, I got the form that you fill out to apply for black lung benefits. So I filled out the form. It passed on about two months, they put it on the radio and in the paper—all that had signed up for benefits—the men would have to come to Hazard and *re*-sign. The widow women they'd call in later to the Social Security office to *re*-fill out their forms.

So I go down and I do that. They wanted to know about the death certificate. Well, I thought, then I goes to the funeral home. And the funeral director, he fills out a card for me and I send it in. When it comes back from the Social Security it comes back that Ab died of "general hardening of the arteries."

Then the Social Security called me back in. "You've got nothing to go on, Mrs. Hager. So you's as well as forget about it. You'll not hear from us no more."

I come back home and I was studying what to do next. Then I got another notice to come back in. I went back in and they said, "Mrs. Hager, you'll have to come up with your husband's work record."

I said, "I can come up with nineteen years and a half that he worked at Alloi's, at Columbus Mining Company."

"Columbus Mining Company don't exist," they said. "We can't find it."

I knew it was a lie because back a mile and a half below town those mines worked for about forty years. Right near there they had a Columbus Mining Company.

So I went over to Columbus Mining Company, where it used to be, to Floyd Hurst and he give me Ab's work record, put it down year, month, and all that he worked. Well, I take that back to the Social Security. Passed on a right smart bit I never heard from them.

Then they called me back in again. They said, "We found out Columbus Mining Company *do* exist, but you've got to get the signatures of two or three men that worked with him."

I went over to Reverend Charley down in Wiley Cove. He put down that he pulled coal with Ab for fifteen years or more. I went to another man and he put it down that he chalk-eyed for Ab in the mines for ten years or more. That's where, like a man has a great big place in the mines with different rooms and they hire these men to load the coal for them. They call it chalk-eyeing. Then I went to the man that weighed the coal when it come out to the tipple. So he put it down that he weighed coal for Ab for twenty-five years or more at Columbus Mining Company, Number Four, at Alloi's. And he even put Ab's check number down.

Well, it went and it went and I didn't hear from it. So then I got another letter out of the post office to come in. This time they said, "You're going to have to come up with some doctor's records."

"Doctor Snyder out here doctored him when he got mashed up in the mines," I said. "He's got X-rays but he won't give them to me. He did tell my husband he might live several years if he didn't go back in the mines no more, that his lungs was too bad to go back. And," I said, "he's got the X-rays, but I can't get them."

"Well, people don't keep X-rays."

Then I went to the black lung meeting at Horse Creek. I was supposed to be a witness against Social Security, the way they were a-doin' me. I got over there and when I got up to introduce myself, I didn't know what to say, the first time being on television. We was in a big old basement and there wasn't standing room, there wasn't standing room upstairs and all around that building. Some just couldn't get in hearing hardly of the microphones. So I didn't hardly know what to say.

Well, there was a bunch of pretty good-sized women there. And after I introduced myself I said. "Well, I'll tell you women: if you want to get your schoolgirl figure back, like I got it, you come to Hazard and sign up for something at the Social Security office. And," I said, "when I get through telling you how many trips I made and had to walk it all those miles, you'll understand how *I* got *my* schoolgirl figure back."

I poured it on them pretty heavy. The lawyer asked me did I think it was the fault of the Social Security. "Why are they holding your money up like this, Mrs. Hager?"

I said, "Because the coal operators would rather give them fifty thousand dollars of money to knock me out as to pay what I'd get each month the rest of my life, what time I live. The coal operators is a-payin' the Social Security Board off, for, in nineteen and seventy-three, January the first, the coal operators is going to have to take over and pay. And don't you think the Social Security Board hain't swallering it all, too."

So I talked at the meeting about them—the Social Security Board—and finally they sent a guy out here and he said they'd found all of Ab's X-rays down at the Miners' Hospital. I signed a paper and they took it back. That was on the fourteenth of November, 1970. And then, the seventh of January, 1971, I got my first check.

Now really, I wish something would break in these mountains. I wish something would turn up, or fall out of the sky, or wherever it might come from, that we could wake these mountain people up till they would stand up for their rights and fight for what is honest and just and due them. They's so many of us poor people, I don't care how many big shots there is, if the poor people would stand up, we can run those big shots under the bed.

I've done more work since I got my black lung check than I did before I got it. I have walked in the rain and in the snow ever since I got that check, a-contactin' people about how to get theirs.

Well, I'll tell you, I get awfully bad wore down. I think, well, I'll set down, I won't try no more. But will power keeps me going. And living in hope one or two people will do something about their black lung benefits. I don't get one penny out of it, I don't *want* one penny out of it. The good Lord has made a way that I've got enough to live on now. I never did wear no clothes, but if I got something to eat and can stay warm, that's all I care for.

Well, I'm a-tryin' to put all my time into this, a-tryin' to help the people who have black lung, and the widows. So I don't want no pats on the back, I don't want no reward for it. All I want is for people to get up and move forward and try to help theirselves.

Patricia Neal

from *As I Am*

Patricia Neal is a celebrated screen actress who hailed from Packard, now an abandoned coal town in Whitley County, on the Tennessee state line. Here is Packard, where she was born in 1926 and which she left as a teenager, as she remembers it in her autobiography, *As I Am* (1988).

Packard, Kentucky, is a ghost town now—gone, gone forever—even the house where I was born. But it was once a fertile and thriving boomtown, just below the Mason-Dixon line, nurturing many families like ours on the deep veins of coal that wound down into the bowels of the earth. In 1926 the town was about three hundred wooden houses along a web of dirt roads that etched their way through knobby grasslands over the rolling hills. The church and the general store were the hubs of activity, as they were in every small town in America. The men, when they were not working, would gather at the storefront and swap tales. It was like a village green except the front of the store was just a slab of cement, the only sidewalk in town. There was a well where you could pump water. There was one boardinghouse and a schoolhouse. And, of course, a Baptist church.

Only a few decades away from the Civil War, the Old South still clung to its cobwebs and conventions. Women and men, blacks and whites, bad and good. Everyone had his or her place. The railroad tracks separated the sheep from the goats among the townsfolk with a biblical severity. Women were never permitted to enter the mine shafts, a primal territory of the male. The church unquestionably chose sides. The whites sat on the ground floor and the blacks were restricted to "nigger heaven."

My family did not venture firsthand into the mine shafts, but the aura was there—dark miner, covered with soot—white miner, covered with the details of management.

My father moved through our town like a white god in a native village. He was manager for the Southern Coal and Coke Company and totally beloved and respected by all his friends and all who worked for him. At harvest time the local farmers could not wait to give him their first melons and corn. They would never allow other hunters on their land, but gave him permission to enter their sanctuary for quail or pigeon as if his gun did not kill. His physical dimensions can only be described as—shall I say it?—fat! He was a great fat man. But it was absolutely right. His body complemented an immense spirit that seemed to wrap itself around everyone. When I am asked why I wanted to be an actress, I always say, "I don't really know, I just did." But I think I wanted to have everybody love me, the way they loved my Daddy.

His name was William Burdette Neal, but he was called "Coot" by all. As a baby he was very "cute" and the description became a nickname that stuck to him for life. I loved my father. I looked for his faithful response in the eyes of many men. None could say "forever" as he did.

My father had long roots in the South, five generations that I know. He was born in 1895 in Pittsylvania County, Virginia. His mother was Lucy Fitzgerald and his father was William David Neal. They owned a tobacco plantation between Chatham and Danville, Virginia, and had one daughter and five sons.

My mother was Eura Mildred Petrey. She was the daughter of Pascal Gennings Petrey, who was the town doctor in Packard. In my parents' relationship two very American strains met—the tobacco farmer and the country doctor.

Eura caught her first sight of William at a railroad depot during the closing days of World War I. She had gone to meet a friend and Daddy had just returned from his mother's funeral with his sister, Maude. Later, Mother was invited to a game of rook, a hot card game of that era, that was sponsored by a local schoolteacher named Bertha Snyder. Mother never let us forget that name. Coot was invited to attend on the arm of this hostess, who had set her consoling eyes on the young Virginia boy. But it was love at first sight across the rook board for Mother and Daddy. She said she saw it in his great brown eyes, and it was sealed forever as he spoke in his thick Virginia accent, "No faya tawkin' 'cros'th' boawd!" So they got up and *tawked* in the garden. They started dating immediately. The number-one hit tune of the time was a Hawaiian melody with the meaningful sentiment, "Your big brown eyes have such linger lovely." Mother played that song to death on her Victrola.

The Petreys enlarged their family to four daughters when my mother was sixteen. My mother's new baby sister, Virginia Siler, was the light of her eyes and awakened her young maternal heart. She doted on her, changed her, dressed her up every day and curled her hair, and mourned her as deeply as any mother when the baby tragically died at eighteen months. Mother never returned to school after this incident, perhaps to my advantage, for she was then available to the courting ways of my father. He and Mother got married on November 5, 1918, the week that the Armistice was signed.

Mother and Daddy anticipated their firstborn, Margaret Ann, with elaborate preparations and great emotion. Mother borrowed a bassinet that had come all the way from a friend in Toledo, Ohio. It might as well have come from Paris. It was trimmed with dainty lace and a bridal veil net that went clear to the floor. Margaret Ann was a gorgeous baby and the nurses triumphantly wheeled her all over the hospital. Daddy wept with pride.

I didn't have the advantage of such a debut. I was born at home, with only our doctor present. On January 20, 1926, totally out of character, I slipped quietly into the world. Mother says I was her easiest birth, but she was distressed by my totally bald head. When Margaret Ann toddled into the room, she took one look at me in the bed with my mother and said, "Well, if it isn't *Bill!*" I was, fortunately, christened Patsy Louise by my Aunt Ima's choice, but for many years Bill was my name. Wasn't that good of her?

My maternal grandfather, Dr. Petrey, whom we called Pappy, had his office in back of the general store. Pappy was an astonishing man. I enjoyed him so much. I'd sit with him on the porch swing, trying to absorb his talk about the black-eyed pea crop, the nutritious value of corn bread or the new president-elect, Franklin Delano Roosevelt. He was very religious and often gave homilies in church. Frequently he had his Bible out to talk to me about God. "Patsy, remember what the psalmist says: 'He changes a desert into pools of water, and streams of water into a dry land . . . a fruitful land into saltness for the wickedness of them that dwell in it.'" My eyes would grow as big as saucers and he would see that I had been duly affected. "Never forget the wisdom of the Bible, Patsy Lou."

"But how can I possibly remember all that?" I would ask quite sincerely.

"Never mind," he would scowl. "Get a bookmark."

My mother and my aunts, Ima and Della, adored Pappy. The three daughters courted his darling, affectionate nature by spoiling him to death. When he returned home hot and tired, one of them would come to wipe his face with a cool cloth, another to comb his hair, and the third to fetch him cold lemonade. He thrived on being the center of so much devoted attention.

He came from German farm people. He was reared in a family of eleven and they worked hard. Any son who left the farm had to be very determined, and Pappy had set his sights on medical school. He got a teaching job to support himself and finally earned a diploma from Louisville Medical College, first in his class. He set up practice in Packard.

Pappy took his Hippocratic oath as a religious vow and gave his life for it. When I was ten years old he was operated on for a prostate condition. He was cautioned not to risk a night call for at least three months. One of the farmers called him in the wee hours, begging him to come and treat his sick child. "Just this one time," said Pappy, and off he went in the buggy. The next night he became desperately ill himself and was rushed to the hospital. The doctor was not an ideal patient. "They are giving me too much of this newfangled shot. If only I could treat myself. I have had such marvelous luck with pneumonia patients." He was put under an oxygen tent, but he stayed alert in those last days. The nurse noticed that he was trying to brush his hair. It was beautiful, black with a few gray streaks, and he wore it in a pretty pompadour in the fashion of the day. The nurse asked, "Oh, are you getting all fixed up today?" He answered, "Why shouldn't I? This is Sunday." It was almost as if he were expecting a caller. When the visitor came, it was not a death anyone might have expected. Pappy's expression changed. His face beamed with an unearthly recognition and he cried out in such joy, "My mother! Oh, my mother!" Then he went to her.

My grandmother, Flora Jane Siler, came from neighboring Williamsburg, Kentucky, where the English Silers had gravitated. She was related to almost everybody in that town. Mammy, as she was called, and the young country doctor produced a family of daughters. The first was Della, next came Eura, who was my mother, then Ima and, many years later, the beloved baby sister, Virginia Siler. I am told the girls were named after the Hoggs, an oil-rich Texas family whose children were called Ima Hogg, Eura Hogg and Bea Hogg, who was, unfortunately, a boy. Mammy was a fine seamstress. She made embroidered blankets, really beautiful work. She kept a flock of chickens and she would wring their necks herself with her bare hands. The half-dead things would run around the yard for about five minutes before they dropped. We would have those to eat. The more fortunate birds laid eggs and were kept for loftier purposes—Mammy's glorious angel food cake. If they eat cake in heaven, it must be her recipe.

But Mammy was not a heavenly lady. My mother never remembers Mammy picking her up or offering her any manifestations of love. She describes her as being cold as a cucumber. When Mammy punished, she took a whip. It was horrendous how she would whip my mother. Mammy cast a strong, hard shadow and Mother still shivers in the coldness of that shade. Mammy was not a tender grandmother, either. She stayed with us quite a lot after Pappy died. I remember when my sister would sit on the porch with her beau, Mammy was always at the window with her eyes peering through the blinds to see what was happening. She was always thinking that we were thinking dirty thoughts.

Still, I liked her very much. We did seem to speak the same language. She may have sensed that I was straining at the fetters that had shackled her all her life. Then again, maybe I liked her because she never spanked me.

Once a year we would visit Grandpa Neal's farm in Virginia. Grandpa Neal grew tomatoes, cucumbers, sweet potatoes and all kinds of vegetables, but his main crop was tobacco. The immense barns were perfect for hide-and-seek, and running and jumping onto the stuffed wagons was paradise. I still treasure a photograph of my brother, Pete, taken when he was two or three, standing in his play yard—a wagonload of tobacco.

I remember summer vacations, when Grandpa's watermelon patches would yield their harvests of pink and yellow fruit. I do say yellow! There *is* such a thing! The black families in service would pack a whole wagonload onto a cart and bring them into the backyard. We would cut the melons and eat just the heart out of them. The rest was cast away.

The farmhouse was white wood. Its central sitting room was shrouded with sheets and was never used by anybody but elegant friends and the vicar because it was "too good." The house had a great porch swing where we would sit on sultry summer evenings and rock back and forth, watching the fireflies. Sometimes the only breeze was created by the gentle to-and-fro of the swing. Hot. Hot. Hot. So hot that it was almost ecstatic.

The center of the household at that time was my grandfather's new wife, Miss Mollie. My real grandmother, Lucy Fitzgerald, had died suddenly from a heart attack. She was an enormously fat, enormously beautiful woman who worked like a man and ate like a man. She just dropped over dead one day while she was sitting on a chair in the kitchen. She left a tremendous gap in my grandfather's life, and her picture over his bed. Miss Mollie was at least fifteen years younger and hardly a beauty. Her chin stuck out and she wore thick glasses. She would always call him with a certain majestic air: "Mistah Neal, Mistah Neal!" I think it is astonishing to go to bed with your husband, still call him "Mistah" and have Lucy Fitzgerald Neal looking on.

Miss Mollie was a fabulous cook. The coal stove crackled early in the morning with kingly portions of bacon, sausages, eggs, hot biscuits and grits. She and Grandpa Neal would rise early to share in the chores of the farm. At noon she would summon everyone with a weighty bell to come to a bountiful dinner of smoked ham or roast possum and vegetables from the garden, which was right next to the family graveyard.

The farm also boasted an exotic form of life I have seen only in this part of the South. There were tiny holes in the earth, and whenever we saw one, we would burst into a kind of singsong: "Doodle bug, doodle bug, hurry back home, your house is on fire and your children will burn." The ground around the hole would swell as a tiny creature ruptured the earth in a frenzy of panic. To our delight, they would surface one by one, great round bugs from some secret hiding place. With godlike blessing we would allow them to return to their holes unmolested. Why does my mind jump suddenly to the hand of my Uncle Fitz's wife slamming an insulting blow on a Negro face? The vulnerable bodies of those tiny frightened bugs and the eyes of the black woman darting in contempt—flashes of the soul of my southern childhood. The fragrant perfume of the mimosa with its fernlike fingers . . . the voluptuous roses . . . the joyfully vulgar sunflowers. And those plump yellow watermelons, oozing with a sweetness and a promise that eating alone could never satisfy.

Verna Mae Slone

from *What My Heart Wants to Tell*

Verna Mae Slone, who was born in 1914, has lived all her life in Knott County, where she wrote her first book, *In Remembrance* (1977), when she was sixty-three. Since then she has published several more books of memoirs and autobiographical fiction, including *What My Heart Wants to Tell* (1979) and *Rennie's Way* (1994). For several years she also wrote a column for the Hindman-based *Troublesome Creek Times,* which was founded in 1980 and calls itself "The Voice of Knott County." In the March 31, 1982, issue she writes about pets and laments that the housing project where she lives forbids them. She remembers a dog her brother Owen owned when he died and how much his dog mourned him. The dog attended the burial and refused to leave. He also refused to eat or drink and eventually died. She wrote *What My Heart Wants to Tell* for her grandchildren and to honor her father, Isom B. Slone, whom everyone called Kitteneye. This is her account of his birth in 1863 and how he came by his name.

It was so cold that February morning in 1863, the wind almost bounced off the sides of the hills as it roared its way up Caney Creek and up the mouth of Trace, whirling the icy snow around the log cabin. It was an angry wind that bent its fury against the sturdy logs, trying to find a crack or hole between the wood so as to get to the woman and little seven-year-old boy inside. But the cabin had withstood many such winds. It was built in 1809 by Shady Slone, and was now owned by his grandson Jim Slone. Jim's wife Frankie and ElCaney were safe and warm inside.

Frankie had listened to the winds last night. She had not slept very much. The cabin seemed so empty with only the two of them. She was used to all three beds being full. Her older boys had gone to Walker Town (now Hazard) to swap her hand-tied lace for some salt and coffee.

She laughed at herself when she remembered the coffee and how she had cooked the first batch she had ever seen. The peddler had said, "It's good with fresh meat." And so she had used it as a spice. Of course the meat had to be given to the dogs and they did not like it either.

The wind whistled through the "noise maker," which Jim's great-grandfather had once helped him to make. They had clipped the hairs from a horse's tail and fastened them tightly between the logs, where they were pinned together at the corners of the cabin. The hairs were placed in groups of one, two, and three, and were so arranged that the wind blowing through them made a musical sound. Frankie did not like to listen to the whining, sad, musical tones. It reminded her of death and the scary stories Jim's great-grandmother had told of the "wee folks in Ireland."

Frankie reminded herself she must get up. ElCaney would soon be awake. He had been a little sick all winter, a bad cold that just would not go away. She had made catnip tea several times and ginger tea, adding a little whiskey to the tea, and had rubbed his chest and feet with the juice of a roasted onion. Nothing had seemed to help. The boy said the onion made him stink.

Frankie got up slowly and put her dress on. Going to the hearth with her shoes in her hand, she took the poker and pushed at the "fore log" that was now very near burned in two. By raising first one end and then the other, using the poker as a lever, she pushed the half-burned log back against the "back log" and then placed a fresh log across in front. She counted the logs left in the pile. Only three, but that would be enough; the boys would be home this evening or tomorrow anyway.

She picked up the water bucket and saw that the water had frozen solid.

"Well, it will take too long to melt that," she thought. She slipped her feet into her shoes and reached for an empty bucket. It was her milk bucket, but the cow was dry now, so she could take it and go to the spring for water.

As she raised up, a pain struck her in the back and moved on around in front, down low. She clasped her hands against her body and said, "Oh, no, it can't be that; the baby han't due till April or the first of May. Jest an upset stomach; we've been eating too much of the same thing."

All the "sass" had been gone since just after Christmas and there was no more hog meat, just a few more shucky beans. She wouldn't dare eat any more of the "taters"; they had to be kept for seed.

There was one more shoat to kill. That was why the boys had gone after the salt. She should have killed it in January. "Everybody knowed a hog did not mend any during February," but she had wanted to keep this one until Jim came home. But it did not look like he would come home soon, and if she did not kill the hog now there would not be enough of the cold weather left to cure the meat.

"Well, a good mess of fresh meat shore would taste good, Jim or no Jim."

As she lifted the heavy latch to open the door, she saw a long hickory stick learning against the side of the house. Nick had cut that the other day for ElCaney to ride as a horse. She took the hickory stick in one hand and the bucket in the other, and using the "horse" as a cane, she braced herself against the wind and started to the spring.

As she looked up she saw a beautiful red bird sitting in a low branch of the "weepin' willer"; she hurriedly repeated, almost without thinking, "I wish the war would soon be over and Jim would be back home." Then she thought, "I wonder how many red birds I have made that same wish on. Well, a red bird shore is a purty thing. I have heard of some people eatin' them. I'd starve 'fore I would."

When she got to the spring, a thin sheet of ice had frozen over the top. She took her stick and tapped lightly on the ice and dipped her bucket in. Turning, she hurried back up the path. She saw that she had forgotten to close the door behind her after she had come out. As she set the bucket of water down on the side of the table, another pain hit her, much harder than the first. And as she grasped the edge of the table for support, she knew she had been fooling herself. It was her time, and the baby was saying, "Here I come, ready or not."

She filled the iron teakettle with water and set it before the fire, off to one side. Here it would soon be warm and out of her way, so she could bake some bread. She thought, "I will need all the strength I can muster, so I won't take time to fix a plum out-and-out mess; I will just make a snack for me and ElCaney."

The thought never entered her mind to be afraid; it was just something that had to be done. "Women were made to bear children; children, the Good Book had said. . . . in pain shall you bear them." Of course she did not enjoy pain, but it was something to be gotten over with. She tried to keep her mind on the great joy she would have when it was over.

She mixed a little cornmeal with a pinch of salt and soda, and mixed it with a little water, making a very thick paste. Then she took a board from behind the wood pile stacked in the corner of the room. This board was about three feet long, eight inches wide, and one inch thick. One side of it had been made very smooth. She placed this board at a forty-degree angle before the fire, propping it up by placing a smaller one behind it.

She divided the cornmeal dough into two patties and placed them on the hot board. On the other end of the board she put two large slices of dried beef, sprinkling them with the last of the salt. Soon the cabin was filled with the smell of food, a good appetizing odor that would have brought water to anyone's mouth.

It wasn't long before ElCaney woke up. "Oh, Maw, I smell hotcakes and meat, and I shore am hungry."

"Well, jump up, son, and eat. Don't mind putting your shoes on, fer soon as you eat you have to go back to bed."

"Oh, Maw!"

"You know I mean what I say and I say what I mean."

After they had eaten, she made ElCaney go back to bed.

"Turn ye face toward the wall and don't look around till I tell ye," said Frankie.

"But, Maw, why?"

"Do as I say and no 'why' to it." She wished Caney wasn't here; he was too young.

"You know I told you how the ol' Hoot Owl was goin' to bring us another little'un."

"Yeah, but, Maw, you said it would be after we had our corn all dug in, and Maw, it's still winter outside."

"Well, Caney, me or that ol' Hoot Owl, one or t'uther got mistook, fer he is bringin' that young'un now."

Although Caney was only seven, he knew far more about births than his mother realized. A mountain boy lives so close to nature that he learns many things at an early age.

Another pain came so hard and sharp that she sank to the floor, caught her breath, and murmured, "Please God, let me keep my mind, so I can take care of this little'un You're sending me." She realized the baby was being born. She could not even get to the bed, and pulling Caney's pallet before the fire, she braced herself for the coming of her child.

In less than an hour, Caney, still facing the wall, heard a small, weak cry almost like a kitten and he said, "Can I look now, Maw?"

"Now listen, Caney, and listen good. Ye take that hickory stick Nick cut fer ye a hoss and knock down some of them wearin' things hangin' on that 'are pole and ye bring me my underskirt, that white'un, and bring me some twine from that wood box under the bed. And reach me the knife from the table."

"Shore, Maw."

"And hurry, son."

And Caney scrambled from the bed, feeling very important as he got all the things his maw had asked for. Still hearing the small whimpering voice, he could not believe it was a baby's, it was so low and weak.

It seem to him like hours before his mother called him to her side and showed him what she had wrapped in her white underskirt. And when he looked he almost gasped.

"But, Maw, it's so puny."

"Yeah, under three pounds is my guess, but ye know he has this whole big world to grow in. He is almost as small as a kitten."

And ElCaney answered, "Kitten, Maw! Why he han't as big as a kitten's eye."

And that, my dear grandchildren, is how my father became known as Kitteneye. Although the name written in the Good Book was Isom B. Slone, he was to be stuck with the name Kitteneye all his born days.

Linda Scott DeRosier

from *Creeker*

Linda Scott DeRosier has deep roots in Appalachia reaching back to the early 1800s. She was born in a log house at Two-Mile Creek in the mid-twentieth century and grew up in a closely knit family and community, which has been lovingly and realistically detailed in her memoir, *Creeker: A Woman's Journey* (1999). It is an inspiring story of a woman whose girlhood ambition was to get married and have four children, whose names she had already picked out. Her dream, she says, was thwarted because she was a scrawny girl, not the full-figured woman that local boys found most attractive. She changed her plans and became the first person in her family to attend college, eventually earned a Ph.D., and became a college professor in psychology. Her second book, *Songs of Life and Grace* (2003), is about her parents and their lives. In an essay in the spring 2000 issue of the *Register of the Kentucky Historical Society*, she asserts emphatically the importance of her family and background. "It has always seemed to me that you cannot ever really 'go' anywhere until you establish pretty firmly where you come from." She sympathetically deconstructs parents and other relatives in this passage from *Creeker*.

My momma was the single most intelligent human being I have ever known. When you consider that I have spent my entire adult life in higher education, that is saying quite a lot. It is not, however, an overstatement. Although children are likely to overestimate the power of their mother, let me suggest that every person who ever had contact with my momma would attest that she was, indeed, exceptionally bright. The tragedy is that, with all that capacity, she could never think her way out of the trap that was her life.

Momma was the youngest of nine children born to a most unusual family. Every one of her brothers and sisters was extremely intelligent, but not one of them had a lick of common sense. All three of my mother's brothers were drunks. In Bible-thumping, whiskey-hating, local option territory, they did not just drink; they were dead-dog-get-down-lay-in-the-bed-for-days drunks. The females in the family did not have a drinking problem, perhaps because they were all fundamentalist Christians who never had a drink in their lives.

My momma was brilliant and spirited and passionate in a time and a place where a woman was allowed to be none of those things. She graduated from high school, passed the state teachers' exam, and was given a teaching appointment in a one-room schoolhouse on Hurricane Creek near her homeplace around on Greasy. She saved her salary, bought a car—an act absolutely unheard of in that time and place—and proceeded to get herself engaged no fewer than five times in three years before she met and married my daddy, whom she had known less than a month. Daddy was good-looking, funny, and had a car. What more could a country girl want?

Maybe if she had known him a little longer, she might have made a better choice. It's hard to figure out what *better* might have been, since Daddy made a better living, loved my momma more, and treated her better than anybody she might ever have expected to meet. That does not mean, however, that he was good for *her*. They lived together nearly sixty years, but they were just about as different as two folks could be. Daddy's world was extremely small, and, with my mother in the center of it, he could not have been happier. My momma, however, was Sarah Bernhardt performing in a small-town dinner theater; she was much too big for the stage. You see, my mother was very special and not the least bit like any other mother in our little community.

In those days, birth control often was not used successfully. Girls married early, began having babies immediately, and continued to bear a child every year or so until "the change" took them out of the babymaking business. After their first child was born, most women pulled their hair back in a bun, wore no makeup, affected big aprons from sunup to sundown, and generally adopted a very matronly appearance.

Not so with my mother. She put on bright-red lipstick first thing in the morning, chain-smoked Camels, and wore short shorts in the summertime— red short shorts. Momma was five feet, eight inches tall with chestnut hair that, much to her sorrow, had darkened as she aged. Stories and pictures suggest that she was quite a blond beauty in her youth, and I think that image, internalized in her early years, was with her until she died. She was more than a little outrageous for Two-Mile, since early on she was the only wife and mother who smoked cigarettes or drove a car. Leonie Wallen got her driver's license when I was in high school, and Pat Pelphrey (Ronalta Mae's mother) learned to drive along with Ronalta Mae in 1957, but nobody's mother smoked but mine.

The group of high-school girls just ahead of me, Bonnie and Betty Holbrook (Gwen's older sisters) and Roma Lou Ward (Easter's older sister), spent countless hours at my house, where they could confide in Momma and smoke cigarettes. There was overmuch listening to country music on the radio and laughing about exploits of one or another while Momma washed or ironed or canned or cooked. Momma carried on a veritable salon for teenagers, and at the time I resented their presence and was jealous of the attention they received from my mother. However, upon reflection, it is clear to me that Momma needed contact with people who still had some life left in them, and there was little of that to be found in her peers on the creek.

Although her given name was Grace Mollette, when she was eighteen or so Momma gave herself the middle name "Jean" after the movie star Jean Harlow. Shortly after she married Daddy, she inserted the letter Y into her first name, thus christening herself Grayce Jean Mallette Preston. Throughout her life, Momma explained that she changed the spelling of her first name to avoid being confused with another Grace Preston who lived nearby, but I doubt that was the case. I think she just wanted to have a name all her own.

Still another difference between my mother and the other mothers on the creek was that my momma never sat down in front of the fire or on the porch and just rested. There was always a magazine, book, or crossword puzzle in Momma's lap. I believe we were the only house in the community that subscribed to magazines, and, whenever we did not have physical work to do, all four of us could most often be found either reading something or napping. My family's attitude toward reading differed from that of almost everybody else because we never saw reading as a chore; it was a reward for getting our work finished. The attitude of a lot of homefolks was that folks only read things that were assigned for school, so reading was not seen as a pleasurable activity. My parents were in agreement with the community on one thing, however; they all believed that reading was a waste of time when there were chores to be done, an indication that the reader was not doing his or her share of the work necessary for survival.

Sometimes Momma went out of her way to work harder than was necessary. She was proud of using only paste wax on our linoleum floors because she believed those who used "liquid" wax were just too lazy to get down on their hands and knees and put forth the elbow grease to shine off the paste. Momma made that old house sparkle, and she was a good cook too—not as good as Aunt Exer, of course, whose biscuits and dumplings would float right away if you didn't hold them down. That the women of the community were able to excel at domestic tasks is in a way miraculous, since they were cooking on coal stoves where the heat regulation was none too precise and were keeping house without benefit of vacuum cleaners or store-bought cleaning products. When Momma got married, housekeeping became her sole occupation. She was teaching when she married Daddy, and they were married five years before I was born. Despite Daddy's many lay-offs at the mines, Momma never worked a day after they married. After Sister and I turned out the way we did (both fully employed), the subject of working women often surfaced in our conversations with our parents. Daddy's invariable opinion was "A man oughtn't to have to come home to a goddamn bowl of chili." Momma would quickly agree, and that was the end of that. Although early in their marriage there was plenty of physical work to use up my mother's energy, later in her life she had huge blocks of time that she filled with crossword puzzles, trash novels, TV soap operas, and an increased monitoring of her many illnesses, both real and imagined. Although Momma had a tendency toward hypochondria early on, it was full-blown by the time she was forty. During the course of her life, I do not recall her admitting to one day of good health.

One late summer afternoon when I was about eight years old, Momma, Sister, and I finished our chores and walked down to Leonie Wallen's store for a Pepsi-and-peanuts break. On the way home we decided to drop by and sit for a spell with our across-the-road neighbors, the Holbrooks. I can still picture the three of us climbing exuberantly up the embankment to where Aunt Exer and three of her children were drinking iced tea while relaxing on the porch. When we got about five yards from where Aunt Exer was sitting, she said, "Well, how are you, Grayce?" My mother, who up to that point had been moving along robustly, suddenly slowed her pace, slumped, and began to limp along, dragging her feet, as if it were all she could do to transport herself to the porch. Bernhardt *way* off-Broadway.

Daddy knew *exactly* what it took to make him happy, and he quietly and methodically went about getting it. Momma never had any notion what it would take to satisfy her, so she wanted everything and more—and nothing was ever enough. Her dissatisfaction was complicated by her steadfast refusal to admit to herself or anybody else that her life was not perfect, so she was never able to see what void needed filling, which in turn led to her lifelong inability to find contentment. She was fond of saying, "I have never had one moment of depression in my life." This statement was usually sandwiched between descriptions of her chronic insomnia and reports of this or that joint "going out."

My mother had lupus, which lends itself to a variety of authentic physical difficulties, so there can be no doubt that her health problems were numerous and genuine. Yet it also seems to me that the lack of intellectual stimulation or purpose in her life led to an exaggeration of her many ailments. In my opinion, just as my mother needed a name of her own, she also needed a life of her own. My poor old momma was a freight train that never could get to the station. She had a formidable intelligence and absolutely nowhere to focus it that would have been considered appropriate in that time and place.

From my mother I learned what not to do. At every juncture of my life when faced with a decision on how to proceed, I have asked myself, "What would Momma do?" Once I have answered that question, I have usually gone the opposite way. Her life has stood as an example to me of what can happen when a woman steps away from the center of her life in order to make room for a man to occupy it. However worthy my daddy was of my mother's full concentration, there was not enough substance there to sustain a woman like my momma. I got from her my curiosity and my desire to go everywhere, know everything, and sample all that is out there. From my daddy, I learned to be satisfied with what life brings me while I am trying for something more. Daddy also gave me my judgment, my sense of humor, and my ability to make myself happy wherever I happen to end up. . . .

A significant part of the decade between my seventh and seventeenth birthdays was spent in fairly close proximity to my 'cross-the-road neighbors and fairly close kin, Aunt Exer and Uncle Keenis Holbrook and their baby daughter, Gwen, who is my second cousin and oldest friend. Aunt Exer was a Ward, one of my paternal grandma's sisters, who had married Uncle Keenis when she was just a girl.

The only thing that can be said about my Aunt Exer Holbrook is that she was one truly admirable human being. I do not recall ever hearing her say an unkind word to or about anybody. Whenever Gwen and I would fight, she would caution, "Now, you girls don't be ugly." She was the youngest of the Ward sisters—Grandma Alk, Daddy's mother, being the oldest—and she and Uncle Keenis bought and moved into Pop Pop's house when Grandma Alk died. She sort of took Grandma Alk's place there on the creek, especially for Sister, who was only a baby when our grandma died. Uncle Keenis always said that the first time he laid eyes on Aunt Exer, he told all present that was the very girl he was going to marry, so after that it was all predestined.

Uncle Keenis Holbrook was a true character and formed the ground for many of the stories of my youth. Yes, his name was Keenis, pronounced just the way penis is pronounced, and no, as far as I know nobody ever alluded to the similarities between those two words. You have to remember that this was in the forties and fifties. As best I can recall, the "p" word was never spoken or written, so my neighbors and I were completely unaware of its existence. At least I was. I might also point out that in my home community, Penix—pronounced "pen (as in pigpen) ix"—was a common name, and nobody ever made jest of that either. It was not that we did not make earthy allusions—boys named Dick and Peter, as well as the Titlow family, had a hard row to hoe—we just were not aware of "proper" names.

Uncle Keenis was a deacon in the United Baptist Church, and he took his religion seriously enough to refrain from cussing. However, a man had to have *something* to say in the face of adversity. "Dang" just did not cut it, so Uncle Keenis frequently used the term "Hell-o!" with the accent on the first syllable. On other occasions he would say "Hell-o Pete!" After he had put in his day's work, plowing or planting, Uncle Keenis was best known for lounging in one of the two front-porch swings and calling out to Aunt Exer in the kitchen, "Ek, brang me a drank o' water." When Gwen and I would get too het up over something, he would quiet us by saying "Hush Gwan. You're aworryin' me."

He worked sporadically at a number of different jobs, from mining coal to selling vacuum cleaners, and brought back stories from all of these excursions. Uncle Keenis was a remarkable storyteller, and his recounting of experiences enlivened my imagination and filled my childhood. He traveled more than most of the folks on Two-Mile and, through his big tales, painted for us a vivid picture of the world he saw. I think each of us who knew him came away with our personal favorite among Uncle Keenis's sayings. Among Sister's favorites is Uncle Keenis's oft-repeated description of traffic over on U.S. Route 23 ten miles west of us: he would surmise, "Hell-o, I bet she's bumper-to-bumper on twenty-three." Abiding forever in my memory is his recounting—on many occasions—of a visit with relatives in Nashville, when he attended the Grand Ole Opry in Ryman Auditorium. As he spoke of country music stars Minnie Pearl, Roy Acuff, and Little Jimmy Dickens, he would pause dramatically for effect, give the listener a meaningful look, and declare: "Hell-o, I looked 'em right in the eye!" Uncle Keenis was a born raconteur and had a story to fit any occasion.

Most evenings in good weather, a number of us would gather on his big front porch to sing gospel songs and yell back and forth across the road to the group sitting in the opposite yard—ours. Such a practice was not considered at all inappropriate, since we were accustomed to shouting at each other in order to carry on conversations when we were working on different rows in the fields. In addition, one of the best things about having a house with a porch facing the main road was that it enabled us to talk with anybody who happened to walk up or down the road past our houses. We knew everybody who went by, and it would have been considered rude on the part of both parties not to shout greetings across the hundred yards or so that separated us. Even if we didn't know the person walking by, it would have been deemed impolite not to call out "Hidie" to him or her.

When I was going out with Billy Daniels, who lived over on Pigeon Roost, I would walk out in my yard all dressed up on a summer's eve to be greeted by Uncle Keenis's hollering, "I smell Bee Branch!" which predictably cracked up everybody on both sides of the road. I always yelled back to correct him about the Bee Branch/Pigeon Roost mix-up, but it did no good; he got the laugh anyway.

There was never any agreement about who would be included on which porch, since the entire evening ritual was never formalized, so I probably spent as much time on the Holbrook porch as I did on my own. The staple of such evenings was the telling of tall tales. Somebody always commented, "The first liar ain't got a chance," as everybody tried to outdo each other with their stories. It would be hard for me to exaggerate the importance of what got passed on at these little informal gatherings of friends and family of all ages, because virtually all the values that guided my early life were learned in that way.

One illustration of the respect for position (age and kinship) over book-learning happened when I was in the fifth grade. Uncle Keenis, for some reason, had been to Baltimore, a very unusual circumstance because, unless they worked away, most of our people hardly traveled outside the county, much less the state. Shortly after his return, several of us were sitting around on his front porch listening as he regaled us with descriptions of his adventures in the big city. As he was telling the story, he happened to mention that Baltimore was the capital of Maryland. I said I didn't think so; I thought the capital was Annapolis. He said I was wrong, and nobody else took a position either way. I was certain I was right; so I ran across the road to my house, found the information in my geography book, and carried it back with me to prove I was correct. I opened the book and showed everyone that it said the capital of Maryland was Annapolis. Uncle Keenis glanced at my book, said, "No, it's Baltimore," and continued with his tale. Everybody accepted his declaration as the final word, and that was the end of the story. Book-learning was not very credible on Two-Mile Creek.

Harry M. Caudill

from *Night Comes to the Cumberlands*

One of the most eloquent voices of the southern mountains was the Whitesburg lawyer, legislator, and author Harry M. Caudill, who was born in Letcher County in 1922 and died in 1990. Late in his life he taught history at the University of Kentucky. His great contribution to Kentucky letters, however, is in his articles and books depicting the robbing and raping of the mountain riches by wealthy coal and timber companies and the robber barons who led them. One of the most influential books in American reform writing is *Night Comes to the Cumberlands: A Biography of a Depressed Area* (1963), which focused the nation's attention on the plight of the dispossessed poor in one of the nation's richest regions. After Caudill's death, the *Courier-Journal* referred to the book in these words: "Once in a while a book appears that so captures the minds of readers that it alters history and shapes how a group of people are viewed." Another important book is Caudill's *My Land Is Dying* (1971), which exposes the ravages of strip-mining on land and people. With his polemical writing, his powerful oratory, and his courage, he became the most eloquent and effective advocate for the exploited and powerless people of the Kentucky mountains. He also wrote a novel, *The Senator from Slaughter County* (1973), in which he used fiction to influence reform. His first novel, *Dark Hills to Westward: The Saga of Jennie Wiley* (1969), turns back to the struggle between native Indians and white settlers shortly before Kentucky became a state. The focus is on the historical Jennie Wiley, a white woman who saw three of her children slaughtered by the Indians and who escaped from captivity after almost a year of degradation and abuse. His lasting influence, however, is seen in the agenda he suggested for the Appalachian Regional Commission, a federal agency (or "Authority," as he calls it) that his persuasive books and essays helped establish. Although there is still much work to be done, at least some of the vision and plans he presented near the end of *Night Comes to the Cumberlands* have become reality.

Any plan to lift the plateau or to enable the plateau to lift itself must encompass a broad scheme to expand and improve its schools. No longer do its unschooled citizens constitute a drag on Kentucky alone. The family car and the American road transmit the social and economic shortcomings engendered by poor highland schools into every part of the nation. The glitteringly attractive states of California, Hawaii, Arizona, Florida, Massachusetts, Illinois, Ohio, New York, Pennsylvania and Michigan can ill afford the burdens imposed upon them by the influx of uneducated and untrained citizens. It is increasingly apparent that in the future there will be little place anywhere in our country for men or women who have nothing to sell except the services of unskilled minds and hands.

The Authority should encourage the state to modernize its archaic school administrative machinery and to tighten controls over expenditures. In justice the nation cannot be expected to assist the state with funds until reasonable safeguards have been enacted to assure that the new money does not finance fetid local political dynasties or filter into graft-hungry pockets. Research by state agencies has amply demonstrated the nature of the needed reforms. None of them are radical and, indeed, all of them would be deemed conservative in any progressive state. When the safeguards have been provided the Authority should help the counties to finance enough spacious and attractive school buildings to house the region's pupils. As one of the conditions precedent for Federal aid the school boards should be encouraged to locate their schools so as to serve the population centers envisioned by the Authority's master plan. Attractive schools in the major towns and in areas slated for industrial and agricultural development should serve as additional magnets to draw people out of the territories scheduled for conversion into forests and lakes.

The upgrading of schools will constitute one of the most tenacious problems confronted by the Authority. Like the others it cannot be solved quickly or easily. As the region's economic props diversify and as emphasis shifts away from social isolation to something approaching normal community life in urban centers and on productive farms, the popular interest in schools can be expected to grow. It may be anticipated that as the general economic level of the inhabitants rises a deepening awareness of education's importance to present and future will be manifested.

Nor will the improvement of conventional education alone suffice. A system of manual training schools is urgently needed. It can scarcely be disputed that the education of masons, mechanics, carpenters and machinists is of cardinal importance. Such schools would afford many youths who find little of interest in the academic classroom an opportunity to acquire useful and profitable skills. The training of knowledgeable workmen would gradually overcome one of the region's most serious stumbling blocks to industrial diversification. At the same time the advantages of such skills to departing mountaineers can hardly be overstated.

Another major problem to which the Authority would have to address itself lies in the landlocked inaccessibility of the plateau. Modern highways into the area on several fronts are indispensable to its orderly development. Their location should be included in the master plan lest expensive roads and bridges be lost by submergence. Financial assistance for their construction will have to be extended to the state.

The mountaineer has become depressingly defeatist in attitude. Company domination and paternalism and two decades of uninspired Welfarism have induced the belief that control of his destiny is in other hands. To replace this defeatism and dejection with zeal may prove difficult indeed, but upon its accomplishment all other facets of revival will eventually hinge.

The first step in this direction should be to organize projects on which the idle men could work. The Authority should set to work on a wide variety of undertakings. Central junk- and trash-disposal centers should be established and satisfactorily maintained. Roads, schools and dams should engross the labors of others. Practically all the region's timberland would benefit by clearing and replanting operations conducted under the supervision of foresters. The construction of decent public buildings in the planned towns is imperative.

On the whole there is an infinity of desperately needed tasks. To the inevitable cries of "boondoggling" and the more coherent objections to the creation of a new Federal bureaucracy, the answer is compelling: the taxpayers of the nation are already supporting the plateau through a wide range of cash and commodity handouts; the cost is already staggering. The additional expense of maintaining Federal works projects would not be grievous while it would have the advantage of tangible and beneficial results. The present program sustains life but creates nothing. A works program could at least build stepping-stones upward out of the abyss.

Finally I would remind churchmen across the land that the plateau is a great and baffling challenge to them and to their institutions. To thousands of mountaineers the balms of religious associations are virtually unknown. It is among such as these that the Galilean labored so long ago. In their suffering today the highlanders are both a summons and a reproach to the nation's churches.

Indeed, in a broader context, the highlander is a challenge to all Americans everywhere. His sorrowful history has deposited him as a material and spiritual orphan on the nation's doorstep. He will not go away, and, unless he is helped, his situation will not improve. In his mute suffering he appeals to the mind and conscience of his country. He and his tattered land await the genius and glory of America the Beautiful. We will continue to ignore them at peril to ourselves and our posterity.

David Dick

"Goats and Purple Martins," from *Peace at the Center*

In recent years David Dick, the former CBS correspondent, journalist, educator, and author, and his wife, Eulalie Dick, have traipsed all over Kentucky in pursuit of interesting characters to write about. Although born in 1930 in Cincinnati, he moved with his mother to her native Bourbon County when he was eighteen months old. While exploring the waters of the commonwealth in *Rivers of Kentucky* (2001), he meets a gallery of colorful people—rich and poor, famous and unknown—and he shares them with his readers. In his autobiographical *Follow the Storm* (2002), Dick's work as a news reporter takes him from Cape Horn to Jerusalem, from turkey hunting in Mississippi to a 1973 reunion of Jefferson Davis descendants, where he meets the New Orleans–born beauty who later became his wife. His *Jesse Stuart: The Heritage* (2004) is a biography and celebration of Kentucky's beloved writer that shows us Stuart and his books, inside and out. "Goats and Purple Martins," from *Peace at the Center* (1994), introduces us to Jimmy Williams, a good-hearted, generous man you are not likely to forget. Jimmy and his wife, Wilma, live in Plumville, near Maysville, in Mason County.

About six miles east of Maysville on KY 10, up the hill from the head of Bull Creek, through the community of Plumville is where Jimmy and Wilma Williams live. Jimmy trains goats to pull wagons loaded with children. It's kind of funny to see people's reactions when a wagon pulled by goats heads in their direction. It's generally an occasion for smiles. For Jimmy, who's been using goats to pull things since he was 14 years old, it produces some money but mostly satisfaction now that he's going to be 64 years old this year. Fifty years can make a man turn to goats and pretty much stick with them.

"It's not a big money-making thing . . . we do it just because we love it," says Jimmy, sitting in the coolness of his side porch on a lazy late summer Sunday afternoon. Jimmy's goats (Saanens, Toggenburgs, and French Alpines) seem to *want* to pull wagons filled with children because the goats love it too. Or they love Jimmy, and whatever he wants is what they want.

"They love to do it . . . they know when I put the big collar on them and open up the gate they go straight to the trailer and to their own stall."

Everybody at the Salt Lick Homecoming or the Morehead Harvest festivals this year saw Jimmy and the Toggenburg pair—Tom and Jerry—pulling "kids" at a dollar a ride. Those goats had as much character as Clydesdales, and Tom and Jerry looked as majestically poised in their harness as horses in a Sugar Bowl commercial. One thing about Jimmy and Wilma—they don't work the goats too long on Saturdays, and never on Sundays. Jimmy and Wilma attend church across the Mason County line in Wallingford, which is in Fleming County.

The French Alpine pair, Jim and Jeff, and the Saanen pair, Chip and Dale, and the spare goat, who else but Randy, enjoy their Sundays off too. But they don't mind coming to the gate to visit with a stranger. Each with his bell ringing (all of them ringing loudly at the same time tells Jimmy there's a dog inside the electric fence), these goats are friendly to a fault, or a goatee. True, they like to nibble at a stranger's pant leg, and, yes, the French Alpines might make a visitor think the short, sharp horns are about to come a little too close to the groin for comfort, but the way the goats take to Jimmy is good for the soul. Restores faith in peace at the center.

"They're just like babies," says Jimmy as his hand cups around Chip's face (or was it Dale?). "They depend on me to tell 'em where to go . . . keep 'em straight . . . do what I want 'em to do."

"Here, shake hands with me," says Jimmy to one of the French Alpines, and Jim (or was it Jeff?) sticks out a leg for shaking. When Jimmy Williams was growing up in Lewis County, he trained goats to pull firewood to the house.

"What about billy goats?"

"Never keep 'em."

"I've heard they smell real bad."

"You can smell 'em from here to way over there past that purple martin house," says Jimmy.

"Do goats eat tin cans?"

"Had a woman ask me that once. I said 'look at his mouth.'"

"Why, he doesn't have any teeth on top," said the woman.

"Can you imagine a goat eatin' a tin can?" Jimmy asked her.

When they retire, Jimmy and Wilma would like to travel up to the Amish country of Pennsylvania or the Blue Ridge Mountains or maybe go down to Nashville to visit the Grand Ole Opry. Or they might just stay home in Kentucky. But for now, when Jimmy's not carpentering for an insurance company, they love to pull children in a homemade goat wagon; it doesn't matter if it's a birthday party, a day care center, or a vacation Bible school. Summer festivals in Kentucky are special fun.

"Look at those goats pulling that wagon! Look at those red hats they're wearing!"

"Can I ride too, Mister?"

"Cost you $1," says Jimmy.

Sometimes, if a "kid" doesn't have a dollar, Jimmy will say: "Jump up on this wagon."

"Jimmy, do you ever wonder about that expression, 'separating the sheep from the goats,' as if to say, sheep are good, but goats are bad?"

"Yep," says Jimmy with a shy and knowing smile.

∞ ∞ ∞

The telephone rang, and it was Jimmy talking.

"I want to do something nice for you."

"Why that's mighty nice, Jimmy, what is it?"

"You remember when you were up here last year, and we were sitting there talking, and you admired my martin house?"

"Yessir."

"Well, I'm going to build you one."

"My goodness."

"It'll have 16 rooms and I'll paint it any color you want it."

"Jimmy, that's about the nicest thing anybody's ever done for me, and I want you to know how much I appreciate it."

"No problem."

Jimmy Williams went to work as the winter of 1993–1994 piled snow 25 inches deep around his shop on the edge of Plumville in Mason County. The temperature plummeted to 30 below zero, but the big stove in Jimmy's shop kept him warm as he painstakingly began cutting the wood to build one of Longfellow's "half-way houses on the way to heaven!"

The dimensions were precise, and the work proceeded accordingly: 16 rooms—each six inches in, six inches across, six inches high, with individual entrances two-and-one-half inches in diameter. The holes were slightly higher than the recommended one inch up from the floor.

"I've had trouble with the babies falling out," said Jimmy, so he's begun raising the holes a trifle to try to prevent disasters.

Next, he built an air shaft through the center of the apartment house, and he constructed vents under the eaves of the roof, which he made from metal so as to give a nice sound on rainy nights, although birds might not take on so about this sort of thing the way some humans do out in the country.

"What color did you say you'd like for it to be?" Jimmy wanted to know.

"How about white with a green roof?" That's the color of our house, and I thought it would look nice if the birds had the same decoration.

"Done."

Jimmy was waiting for me in his shop at Plumville on the Ides of March, the birthday of my wife, who from this day forward would be connected in my mind with the return of the purple martins. I got to thinking, if she precedes me, I'll feel her presence with the annual reappearance of the blue-black birds from Latin America, where she and I once worked. Should I precede her, she would witness the arrival of the first swallows and remember how our lives always hinged on hope.

In the words of James Fisher and Roger Tory Peterson: "No philosophers they, they live and die in a drama of colors and shapes and music that makes philosophers of us."

Jimmy helped me load the purple martin house into the front seat of the car. It was a tight fit with no room to spare.

"Well, Jimmy, I suppose our paths will cross many times this year at the community festivals."

"Oh, yes."

"Will you be bringing Tom and Jerry again to pull the wagon for the children?"

"No. Jerry died of pneumonia this winter past, and Tom, he's not well."

"I'm sorry. Then, who'll be the team of goats this year?"

"It'll be the Saanens, Chip and Dale. Randy will be the spare. They're all ready to go." Later, Jimmy said there'd also be Jim and Jeff, and probably a new Tom and Jerry.

"So long, Jimmy . . . I'm on my way home."

Jimmy made me promise to sneak his telephone number into the next thing I wrote about him—(606) 564-9812—shhhhhhhh: I told him the editor would probably throw it out, but Jimmy whispered, "I hope not."

Cousin Marvin and Reda came over and helped us raise our new purple martin house on Plum Lick to a height of about 14 feet above the ground on a six-by-six post. Jimmy had said to be sure to locate it away from trees, because the martins don't prefer to share their perching with every Tom, Dick, and Harry.

On March 25, about two-dozen swallows returned to Jimmy's house at Plumville, but here on Plum Lick we are still looking at what appear to be mixed sparrows and ugly starlings. I guess we can't blame the purple martins. How were they supposed to know?

Jimmy said that when his flock arrived they ran the other birds off. Maybe next year our purple martin house will be listed with the better travel agencies down south.

Muhammad Ali,
with Richard Durham

from *The Greatest: My Own Story*

One man who needs no introduction is Muhammad Ali, a man of strength, intelligence, cunning, and principle who rose from a black ghetto in West Louisville to become not only one of the best-known athletes of the century but ultimately a global spokesman for peace, tolerance, and reconciliation. In *The Greatest: My Own Story* (1975), the autobiography he wrote with his friend Richard Durham, Ali recalls the pride he felt after winning an Olympic gold medal in 1960 and how, after an episode of racism and intimidation in his hometown, his feelings turned to shock, pain, and bitterness. This excerpt concludes with his violent encounter with a motorcycle gang and a thug named Frog, whose deeds cause Ali to commit a desperate act.

So what I remember most about the summer of 1960 is not the hero welcome, the celebrations, the Police Chief, the Mayor, the Governor, or even the ten Louisville millionaires, but that night when I stood on the Jefferson County Bridge and threw my Olympic Gold Medal down to the bottom of the Ohio River.

A few minutes earlier I had fought a man almost to the death because he wanted to take it from me, just as I had been willing to fight to the death in the ring to win it.

It had taken six years of blood, blows, pain, sweat, struggle, a thousand rounds in rings and gyms to win that medal, a prize I had dreamed of holding since I was a child. Now I had thrown it in the river. And I felt no pain and no regret. Only relief, and a new strength.

I had turned pro. In my pocket was my agreement with the ten Louisville millionaires, our "marriage contract" for six years. I felt as sure as day and night that I would one day be the World Heavyweight Champion. But my Olympic honeymoon as a White Hope had ended. It was not a change I wanted to tell the world about yet. I would be champion. My own kind of champion.

The honeymoon had started when my plane touched down at Standiford Field. They opened the door and my mother rushed up to hug me. Then my brother Rudy and Dad. I had been gone for twenty-one days, the most time I'd been away since the day I was born.

Then came the celebrations: the long police escort all the way downtown; black and white crowds on the streets and sidewalks; WELCOME HOME CASSIUS CLAY signs from my classmates at Central High; the Mayor telling me the Olympic Gold Medal was my key to the city; plans under way for me to have my picture taken with President Eisenhower.

Time magazine saying: "Cassius never lets his Gold Medal out of his sight. He even sleeps with it." They were right. I ate with it, and wouldn't stop sleeping with it even though the sharp edges cut my back when I rolled over. Nothing would ever make me part with it. Not even when the "gold" began to wear off, leaving a dull-looking lead base. I wondered why the richest, most powerful nation in the world could not afford to give their Olympic champions real gold.

One Kentucky newspaper described my medal as "the biggest prize any black boy ever brought back to Louisville." But if a white boy had brought back anything better to this city, where only race horses and whiskey were important, I hadn't heard about it.

In later years, when I fought and did exhibitions around the world, in Zurich, Cairo, Tokyo, Stockholm, London, Lima, Dublin, Rio de Janeiro, I was given welcomes and celebrations that were much greater, more colorful. But when you've been planted like a tree in one town, and suddenly become recognized and acclaimed by the other trees, it is unlike any other experience you are likely to have. In fact, I'd written a poem about it on the plane, "How Cassius Took Rome," which I sent to the black newspapers and later recited to my classmates, a poem expressing my love for Louisville.

And although I was still hit with some of the same race hostility I'd known all my life, my spirits were so high I felt whoever was against me would change. Even those whose resentment made them go through the acknowledgments half-heartedly or with no heart at all. Those who came only out of curiosity, and looked disgusted when they learned they had to honor a black boy.

I was deeply proud of having represented America on a world stage. To me the Gold Medal was more than a symbol of what I had achieved for myself and my country; there was something I expected the medal to achieve for me. And during those first days of homecoming it seemed to be doing exactly that.

I remember the crowds that followed us down the street where we lived. The porch of our house was decked with American flags, and my father had painted the steps red, white and blue. Photographers yelled, "Hold it! Hold it!" And I posed for a minute, arm-in-arm with my father as he sang "The Star-Spangled Banner" in his best Russ Columbo style. We stood proud. Everybody cheered.

Through most of that summer the crowds kept coming around the house. Louisville lit up. Congratulations every day from city officials. Even handshakes from the Chief of Police. A slap on the back from the Governor of Kentucky, who reminded me, "Boy, I know you proud of that name 'Cassius Clay.' I know you proud to carry that name."

In the evenings we sifted through offers from professionals to "manage" me. One telegram from Archie Moore: IF YOU DESIRE TO HAVE AN EXCELLENT MANAGER CALL ME COLLECT. From Rocky Marciano: YOU HAVE THE PROMISE. I CAN GIVE YOU THE GUIDANCE. From Cus D'Amato, Floyd Patterson's manager. From Pete Rademacher, former Olympic Champion. We examined every offer until a lawyer came representing ten (later eleven) Louisville millionaires, who put together the contract my father and family approved. It was to run from 1960 to 1966, and it did. The main feature was a $10,000 advance. The Louisville group, to start off, was to get 50 percent of all my earnings, in and out of the ring. At the time, $10,000 seemed to me a huge amount. The only frame of reference I had to "big" sums of money was the worn-down little house we lived in. Sold to us on installment for $4,500, it was taking my father his lifetime to pay for it. Most of the $10,000 went to repair and pay off the house.

In those first days after my return from Rome, I was proud to boast of my millionaire sponsors. It looked like solid evidence that the pain and struggle I had undergone to win national Golden Gloves titles, state and AAU championships had brought me to a point where I could make money from boxing, not only for myself but for my backers. I felt fortunate having so many people in town who wanted to give me what they called the "right kind of moral and ethical environment" for launching a career. As far back as I could remember, boxing was associated with stories of "gangster control," "fixed fights" and "back-door deals," some of it brought out by Kefauver Committee investigations while I was fighting in the Golden Gloves.

The Sunday after I signed, the Reverend Isaiah Brayden, of the Ship of Zion Baptist Church, preached a sermon about it, and said, "May Cassius Clay be eternally grateful for what those kind Christian millionaires are doing for his black soul." Every newspaper account I read described the event in the holiest light, with ten white angels tending charity in the jungle. Not as the good, hard, common-sense business deal it was.

And if I could not always manage to act humble and thankful, maybe it was because, even though arithmetic was not my best subject at Central High, I could figure that $10,000 from ten millionaires who had shared equally in the funds (Bill Faversham got in free) meant that each had chipped in $1,000. (A little more, but not much, was later added to cover training fees before my second fight; after that, the money rolled in.) If $1,000 each had come from poor people like my father, I would have felt humble. But I had been around Louisville hotels and the Kentucky race tracks, and I had seen rich guys, without shedding a tear, blow that much in a weekend on a girl friend or lose twice that on a long-shot horse. And I was different from the Kentucky horses. I would win. More and longer. . . .

Ronnie King was one of my best friends from the time I started in junior high school to my second fight with Liston. He had an uncle he called "Tootie" who operated a dry cleaner's in Louisville, and he was always talking about him. "Tootie gonna take me fishing" . . . "Tootie goin' hunting" . . . "Tootie got a motorcycle." So I just named him "Tootie."

When I first met him, I was walking to enroll in classes in DuVall Junior High School, way down in the West End of Louisville on 34th Street, about fourteen blocks from my home. He was walking with his grandmother, a heavyset lady with gray hair. She introduced us and said, "Well, will you walk with my little grandson?"

So Tootie and I walked on together. "This is my lunch," he said, noticing me looking at a paper bag he was holding. "You want it?"

"What is it?"

"Aw, an ole hamburger," he answered, frowning. "My mother always makes me take hamburger sandwiches on this homemade wheat bread with mustard and onions and a pickle. And I want me a peanut-butter bun and some cookies and milk. I don't want this."

This boy must be crazy, I thought to myself. A big ole fat juicy beefburger, onions, pickle, and he's talking about he want some cookies and a peanut-butter bun.

"How much you want for it?" I asked.

"Gimme a nickel."

I gave him a nickel and took the sandwich. At lunchtime he came out with a peanut-butter bun, cookies and milk, and he was happy. I still had a nickel change from my lunch money, so I bought a couple of cartons of milk to go with my beefburger.

Every morning for almost two years after that, I'd be on the corner just in time, waiting to get that beefburger. If I missed him in the morning, I'd catch him in the lunchroom. We got to be pretty tight.

Since we both lived in the same district, we were assigned to the same classroom and we got seats right by each other. He was always a little smarter than me. He could read fast, spell good, add and subtract. I had my mind so wrapped up in boxing, I didn't work too hard in school. All I could think about was getting home, getting on my bike and going to the gym. I'd be shadowboxing from the minute I woke up in the morning. And I'd stop in a little drugstore, get a carton of milk and break two raw eggs in it because someone had told me this would help build up my wind and my lungs.

So Tootie did most of my schoolwork for me. A lot of times I'd look over and ask, "What's the answer to number four?" Or, "What's the answer to test number six?" And he'd always give me the answers. This is how I got by.

After school Tootie would come with me and my brother to the gym. We would ride all the way on my bicycle, one of us trotting while the other two rode, then switching around, taking turns.

This went on for about four years and we became fast friends. Ran with the gang together; fought in the streets together; sought girls together. We'd even gone into boxing together, but Tootie quit early. He got tired of getting his long nose bloody, his big eyes puffed: he said it jeopardized his chances of ever becoming a hustler, a career which brought him to an early death, fighting over a woman on a New York street.

I was thankful that he was by my side now. I had gym buddies like Jimmy Ellis, Donnie Hall, Tommy Jones, Maceo Bell and my own brother who, by ring rules, were far better fighters. But Ronnie was a natural demon by street rules, with the knack of making all his brawls seem like life-and-death choices. And so far, faced with such alternatives, most of his opponents had chosen "life" without a fight. . . .

I remember how relieved I felt when I got within sight of the bridge. The rain had slackened, and I decided it was safe to swing from the passageways and hit the bridge from Main Street.

It turned out to be a mistake. No sooner had I struck the street than I heard wild, faraway screams. "There they is! There them niggers!" A woman's high-pitched cry. "You black bastard! We got yo' ass!" Frog's bellow.

At first I could only see Frog's machine. He had apparently sent his scouts to check the route to the black neighborhood, but he was cunning enough to suspect that I might try to get over the bridge into Indiana, and had come to seal it off. Comparing our relatively slow speed with his, and judging the distance to the bridge, it was obvious Frog would be on our backs by the time we made the top.

Ronnie leaned over, his face, like mine, wet far more from sweat than from rain. "They want you the most. Not me. You go up ahead. I'll be behind. You dig?"

I dug it. We hit the bridge and I began weaving from side to side, Ronnie dropping behind me, slightly to my right. I glanced over my shoulder, could see still another hog now, directly behind Frog. Kentucky Slim.

But Ronnie was right. Frog was almost parallel with him yet ignoring him, still concentrating on me, whirling his chain like a cowboy ready to lasso a loose steer. "Hey, Olympic nigger! So you a fighter—"

He may have said more, but with perfect timing and in a coordinated move Ronnie leaped off his machine, hurling it with all his strength underneath Frog's front wheel. Frog saw it too late, made a frantic jerk, cut to the left, skidded up against the cement mortar, smashing himself and his woman on the bridge column. The woman let out a painful scream. Badly hurt and bleeding, her blouse ripped, she scrambled over to help Frog, who hung dazed against the rail.

Kentucky was coming up behind them, whirling the same kind of chain, aiming at my head. Then and there occurred one of the two split-second moves in my life without which my career would have been forever altered. The second happened during my first championship fight with Sonny Liston, when in the fifth round, with my eyes blinded and burning from something on Liston's glove, Angelo Dundee pushed me back in the ring only a split second before the referee was about to award the fight to Liston. That incident was highly publicized. The first was here on Jefferson County Bridge.

Slim whipped his doubled-up chain at my head. Instead of slashing my face, the chain wrapped around my shoulders. Instinctively, I shot my hand out and gripped the chain and jerked with all my might. The force snatched Slim off his hog and hurled us together in a violent impact. His head struck mine and stunned me, but not enough to stop me from smashing my fist into his face. His body hit the ground, blood spurted from his nose, his empty hog careened over to the rail.

The woman was screaming, "They gonna kill Frog! They gonna kill Frog!"

Ronnie had a half nelson around Frog's neck, choking him, his blotched face even more distorted by the veins popping from his temples. The switchblade was pressed against his throat. "Get back! I'll cut his goddamn neck off! Get back!" He started ripping Frog's leather jacket as though it was tissue paper.

The girl dropped down on her knees, sobbing and pleading. Two other riders were coming up, one I remember with a flaming red, polka-dot neckpiece and a World War II German helmet.

I shouted to the girl, "Tell 'em stay off the bridge. Get 'em off the bridge!"

She sprang up, flew down to the end of the bridge, waving her arms. "Y'all go back! Go back!"

They slowed down, but kept creeping up cautiously.

"Let Frog tell 'em. Loosen up so Frog can tell 'em," I told Ronnie.

He eased his grip. Frog sucked in all the breath he could, and with more force than I expected he cried out, "Y'all g'on home! G'on! G'ON!"

For a second his riders just paused at the bottom of the bridge, confused. "What you want us to do, Frog?"

The girl shouted back, "Do what Frog tells y'all! You hear? Do what he tells you!"

The rider in the German helmet pulled out what looked like a .45, and I kept my eyes on his face for the slightest flicker of what he might do. They could have overwhelmed us for certain. But just as certain they knew Ronnie would rip Frog's jugular vein.

"Lighten up," I whispered to Ronnie. Frog was our only hope. "Let Frog talk."

Frog screamed, a throaty, desperate gurgle. "I done told y'all, g'on back! G'on back home. You too, Slim! G'on!"

Slim pulled himself together like a drunkard and limped with his machine back to his battalion. They consulted briefly, looked up at us, then slowly retreated down the street.

I didn't move. Just watched until I heard the girl crying, "They gone now. What you gone do with us?"

Ronnie released Frog and let him crawl over to his wheel. Like a hunter who chased what he thought would be a bunny rabbit, only to corner it and discover it to be a tiger, Frog's single thought now was escape. His girl struggled to help him mount the hog, but he kept slipping off. I stood there looking at them, feeling no anger, pity or hatred, just tension. Neither of them could ever make the hog go without our help. I moved over to the girl, and she cringed as though she expected me to hit her.

"Help us get off." She spoke very low, very desperate. "We ain't comin' back. Honest! We'll keep goin'."

I straightened the bent fenders so they wouldn't rub against the wheels, and fixed Frog's fingers on the handlebars. He was weak, unsteady, coughing as though his throat was still in Ronnie's grip. His blood, oozing through the shredded slits Ronnie's blade had made in his jacket, soaked all the way through my T-shirt as I helped him.

Ronnie and I held the hog on each side steady enough to run it down the incline and give it a mighty push. The electric starter was shot, but the hog sputtered, caught and slowly moved off, swaying a little. We watched to see if Frog would regroup the gang. But what the girl had said was true. Frog rode by them and they all fell in behind. We stood there until they disappeared, until all we could hear was rain and the shuffle and rattle of trains on the Kentucky side.

"Better get the hell away from here." Ronnie was wiping his knife on his sleeve like a violin bow. "My bike's wrecked." He surveyed what was left of it, a mass of twisted metal. Then something about my face must have stopped him. "You hurt? Goddamn—they got you?"

I shook my head. Physically, I had come off better than I expected, but the miserable pain in my head and stomach that I felt in the restaurant had returned. Give-and-take punches, like the blows exchanged with Frog's battalion, are bearable. But I was feeling the aftereffects of the blows I'd taken from The Owner, the Mayor, the millionaires.

"Let's wash off all this mess. You'll feel better," Ronnie concluded. We tested my bike to see if it would carry us both. "We get the blood off, we feel better."

I followed him down to the river, and hung the Olympic medal on a pier piling, the red, white and blue ribbon thick with Frog's blood. Some of it had stained the gold.

Ronnie picked it up tenderly. Even before washing himself, he washed the medal. Rubbed the luster back into the gold, rinsed the blood off the ribbon and hung it lovingly around his own neck.

I stopped and watched. This was the first time the Gold Medal had been away from my chest since the Olympic judge hung it there that day I stood on the podium, a Russian on my left, a Pole on my right. And for the first time I saw it as it was. Ordinary, just an object. It had lost its magic. Suddenly I knew what I wanted to do with this cheap piece of metal and raggedy ribbon. And as soon as I knew, the pain in my stomach eased.

We quickly rinsed, and Ronnie put the medal back around my neck, followed me to the bridge to get the bike.

I remember thinking that the middle of the Ohio was probably the deepest part, and I walked over to the center of the bridge. And Ronnie, with that extra sense people have who have known and loved each other for a long time, anticipated my actions. Dropping the bike, he ran toward me, yelling. But I had snapped the ribbon from around my neck. I held the medallion just far enough out so that it wouldn't tangle in the bridge structure, and threw it into the black water of the Ohio. I watched it drag the red, white and blue ribbon down to the bottom behind it.

When I turned, Ronnie had a look of horror in his eyes. "Jesus. Oh, my God!" Then tears came down his cheeks. "Oh, my God. You know what you did?"

"It wasn't real gold. It was phony." I tried to put my arms around him. He was wet and cold and stiff. "It was phony."

Virginia Honchell Jewell

In the far western Kentucky county of Hickman, Virginia Honchell Jewell did an unusual profile of her adopted county—"a collection of historical sidelights," she calls her book, *Lick Skillet and Other Tales of Hickman County* (1986). She graduated from Murray State University with a degree in journalism and has been a reporter, editor, and writer for the *Hickman County Gazette* and a stringer for the *Paducah Sun Democrat* and other regional papers. Here are two of her stories: a piece about growing marijuana for the government during World War II and a portrait of a storyteller from the Tarheel community.

⌔⌔⌔

"Growing Marijuana," from *Lick Skillet and Other Tales of Hickman County*

"We had no idea we were growing what is now known as marijuana," Edna Humphreys stated in amazement. "But the government contracted with farmers all over the county to grow hempseed as part of the war effort."

That was in 1942; the nation had been catapulted into a worldwide conflict. The supply of Manila hemp for rope and cordage from the Philippines and jute from India was cut off because of war on the high seas. Kentucky was asked to produce 33,000 acres of hemp that year with the county allotted 800 of those acres. Kentucky had for many years been the chief hemp producing state in the nation as the Bluegrass region was particularly suited for the crop. Rope and bagging factories were early sources of employment as the state developed but it is believed the crop had never before been grown in Hickman County.

The local agricultural board urged that farmers voluntarily sign hemp contracts but it was announced that if sufficient acreage was not contracted, the Department of Agriculture would demand it. In March of 1942 County Agent Baker Atterbury explained that seed saved during the 1942 statewide harvest season would plant a half-million acres for fiber the next year. He not only encouraged the growing of hempseed but also the production of soybeans and castor beans for oil to defeat the Axis powers.

"We grew an acre or more and tended it by hand," Mrs. Humphreys said. "It had to be kept clean much like corn. At harvest time when the seeds were ripe, we cut the plants and when dry enough we flailed them with sticks onto a huge sheet of muslin. There were strict rules about growing the crop and we were urged to save every seed. They resembled seed from the okra plant."

In October of that first growing year, farmers were cautioned not to thresh hemp too soon after it had been shocked as this resulted in the loss of a large number of seed. On November 5, the county agent was lamenting that "over 80% of the hemp shocks blew over last week in a storm." Farmers were counseled to prop up the shocks to keep the seed from sprouting.

Three-fourths of all the hemp produced that first crop year in the Purchase was grown in Hickman and Fulton Counties and the county's allotment was almost doubled the next year.

Edward Bugg, chief clerk with the Agricultural Adjustment Administration during that time, said the crop was strictly controlled and supervised. Farmers were required to have narcotic permits to grow the plants but no one ever suggested using it as a narcotic, he said. However, he added, it became apparent that hemp plants had a drugging effect. "Doves flocked to the fields where the plants were shocked and couldn't be scared away with gunfire."

Mrs. Humphreys said a neighbor used plant stems to make a hog bed in his shed. Shortly afterward, he discovered his pigs were asleep and couldn't be aroused. A veterinarian, called to the scene, recognized that the animals were on a "high." After the pigs were dragged out into the fresh air and the stems disposed of, the animals rallied.

"The Tarheel Philosopher," from *Lick Skillet and Other Tales of Hickman County*

Arthur Bugg, a delightful teller of tales and philosopher of Tarheel community, had a yarn for most every occasion. One dealt with the custom of driving buggies and wagons through ponds to swell the wooden wheels and spokes to keep them intact. His tale went this way:

"One day Ole Man Jackson pulled up with his horse and buggy at the pond out here and asked if it was very miry.

"'No,' I said.

"'Do you care if I drive my buggy through it to swell my wheels?'

"'No,' I answered and went on to the house.

"About the time I got to the porch I heard him squall. I didn't go back till after he left and there his hat was floatin' in the water. He didn't ask if the pond was deep—just wanted to know if it was miry."

Tarheel is the area north of New Chapel Church. Various explanations have been given as to how it got its name—one being that it was settled by North Carolinians.

A small, wiry man, Arthur Bugg had a whole passel of tales which popped out with the slightest encouragement just like dandelions with the first spring sunshine. One such yarn was about his days at Marvin College where he walked or rode his horse three miles to attend school during the winter months—"after the corn was gathered." One of the older boys "who was making a preacher" nearly got caught eating an apple during "time of books." Rather than face "'Fessor Browder" with the apple, the young man swallowed the rest of it—core and all—choking as a result. "They beat him on his back till he was black as a spade."

Next Sunday the hapless student preached at New Chapel. Twelve-year-old Arthur said, "Hello Apple Core," when he saw him at the door. "My daddy nearly wore the socks off me."

Another tale dealt with a drunken loafer who bought fifty cents worth of gunpowder at the Hailwell general store in the early 1900s. He wandered outside the store where he secretly exchanged the gunpowder for sawdust.

Later he came back in to warm himself. The other bystanders were aware that he had purchased the gunpowder and kept urging him to stay away from the stove. Feigning irritation, he whirled suddenly and threw the contents of the sack into the open door of the heating stove, instantly scattering all the customers, including one who ended up headfirst in a huge box with only his peg leg sticking out.

Although he spent nearly all of his 93 years on Tarheel land originally owned by his grandfather, he did for a time live in Oakton and often passed the time of day at the Hailwell store. Virgil Clark ran the store, he said, and sold everything from drygoods to fancy groceries and cultivators. The store also served as a voting precinct and housed the post office.

He remembered when there were seven or eight passenger trains a day passing through the Tarheel area. He chuckled to himself about Fred Ball, a conductor who would stop anywhere on the line to let people on or off. Ball said it was an accommodation train and "if it wasn't going to accommodate the people, they ought to take it off." "When my brother had appendicitis, the train stopped to take him on his cot to the hospital in Cairo."

"And if I wanted to go Paducah or Cairo, I didn't have to go into town; I just flagged the train right out here at Hot Box Hill."

The hill was so named because a storm sewer ran under the track at the crest of the hill. It was a dandy place to stop for water to cool the axle's "hot box" and also to get a good downhill start afterward.

At age 15 he saw his first electric lights in Clinton. He had gone to town on Saturday night to get his hair cut and ended up walking all over town to gape at the lights.

Arthur Bugg would strike up a conversation with anyone. Once he encountered an untalkative fellow bus traveler. "I was determined to make him talk and said 'I ain't no stranger—just an old friend you haven't seen in a long time.'"

"I've had a good life," he reflected, "done as I pleased and don't have any kick comin'."

Arthur who lost an arm in a powder plant accident, said "I've plowed with a mule all day many a day and enjoyed it."

"I never was much of a hand to want something I had to die to get."

Jo Anna Holt Watson

from *A Taste of the Sweet Apple*

Jo Anna Holt Watson, or "Pig," as she is nicknamed by Joe Collins, the black major-domo of Grassy Springs Farm, is the narrator of the memoir *A Taste of the Sweet Apple* (2004), which reads like an enchanted novel. Her eccentric and delightful family has lived on this magical piece of Kentucky for generations, and she had the good fortune to be born before the arrival of television into an affluent family of colorful relatives and servants three generations deep—all of them master storytellers. Indeed, they are so good that she sometimes turns the narrative over to her long-winded Aunt Tot or to Doc, her opinionated, impulsive physician-father, or, more likely, to Joe, her childhood mentor and surrogate father.

This unconventional household is, moreover, surrounded by vividly sketched neighbors and townspeople in Woodford County and Versailles who fill out Watson's panorama of connected lives in the mid-twentieth century. Who can forget the police chief, a chubby young man nicknamed Scooter, or the friendly telephone operator, Elsie Mae, or Big Tootsie Sizemore, owner of the Sweet Shop? Who wouldn't want to eavesdrop at Ginny Rae's Beauty Shoppe or visit Ocean Frog's Grocery Store? And then there is Pig's Aunt Sudie Louisa. Pig makes the introduction.

My Aunt Sudie Louisa was named the prettiest girl in the Bluegrass by the *Sun* weekly newspaper in 1922. Decades later, that coveted article describing her golden curls and sparkling blue eyes still provided daily nourishment for her soul. "After all these years, that little piece from the *Sun* is still stuck in Sudie's craw," Doc mused. "When in God's name will it end?"

Aunt Sudie was the most offended by my appearance and she was the most vocal. "The child looks like an urchin from the Orphan's Home, or worse, like one of those dirty little things from the alley behind the filling station." Each morning Sallie Gay or Eva Belle brushed and braided my unruly shock of light hair and tied me up with pretty bows, but long before noontime the bows had flown off and I never replaced them. When Sudie Louisa got herself going on my peculiar style of beauty, that pink manicured hand flew to her breast as if another hot flash was coming on. "She runs around under that awful hat with dirty hen feathers and whenever she gets the chance she trails behind those mules, of all things, with Joe Collins, and she's up to *something* down in the cellar with those neighbor boys, too," she whispered as the eyes narrowed into a squint. "If she belonged to me, I would be looking into that cellar business, believe you me." Sudie never failed to add, "I'm here to tell you, no child of mine would ever be allowed to look that way."

Doc said, "There's a great deal of truth to what Sudie says since she has no children, and furthermore, if the Lord had seen fit to grant her issue, she would have powdered and painted the poor little devils and set them up on a shelf in the Chippendale corner cupboard where no dust could get at them. The Lord knew what He was doing there and I'll give Him credit for that one!" There was no way on the face of this earth I was ever going to be found sitting up on the shelf of Aunt Sudie Louisa's fine Chippendale corner cupboard. I planned to farm.

Doc warned, "Ginny Rae's Beauty Shoppe dyes and ammonia cold waves will eventually fry every living strand of hair from all their heads." Occasionally, Ginny Rae *did* hang too long on the telephone line while the color worked its magic. When the result was a bluish or pastel pink head, she didn't charge full price and she painted nails Arden Pink to match. Ginny Rae's was not the only salon in the town, but her popularity had soared since Miss Alma Tuttle's tragic episode with the ammonia permanent-wave solution at Razor's Beauty Shop, where solution was applied full strength and left on entirely too long with heartbreaking results. Just as Doc warned, ammonia singed most of the hair right off Alma's head. Her husband Hiram rushed her to Doc's office, where he prescribed sedatives for the both of them and treated Miss Alma's blistered scalp with ointments, to be applied regularly each week, with the head left uncovered to get the air. Aunt Sudie Louisa sighed, "Just lay me down to die if that ever happens to me. Everyone knows my hair is my crowning glory." Aunt Tott vowed to have herself done thereafter over in Lexington "in a professional salon." But loyal Sallie Gay said, "We should go right on back to Ginny Rae's where we belong." Their hearts ached for poor Alma. "She tries so hard to go on, bless her heart, just *bless her heart.*"

When Ginny Rae's Beauty Shoppe turned my Aunt Sudie's hair pink it put me in mind of our old mule Kate, who had a pinkish purple birthmark that started at the left nostril and ran all the way up her long face, through her bad eye that was stuck half open. I mentioned this one evening at the supper table and it caused Sudie Louisa to tune up and cry, but she cried at the drop of a hat. Doc said her crying was "just another one of Sudie's attention-getters." Sallie Gay said, "Your aunt is beside herself, just being mentioned in the same breath as that one-eyed mule, and rightly so I might add." "My bridge club girls still call me, Beauty, I'll have you know!" Sudie Louisa sobbed. And she was quick to add, "Beauty is one cross you will never have to bear or my name's not Sudie Louisa Harriss Holt Hall!" I named my barren old roan after Sudie Louisa, but she was offended by that too, and thereafter never once asked about her namesake, Hot Flash. Doc was right; there was just no pleasing Sudie.

Everybody knew Sudie Louisa's first and only husband, Clinton Hall, ran off less than three years after they married, to hire on as a ranger working for the West Virginia State Parks. "Of all the godforsaken places to run to, just so he could get shed of Sudie," Doc declared. "Sitting up in a goddamned watchtower outside Elton, West Virginia. If that isn't the last of pea-time and the first of frost, you tell me what is. Sudie Louisa walked through the woods and picked up a broken reed when she found Clinton. He was never much force." But nobody blamed the man for leaving the hellcat Sudie, and Clinton never once failed to send a two-pound box of Whitman's Sampler to the family at Christmas.

After he high-tailed it off to West Virginia, Sudie stayed at our house for almost a year, claiming that a virtual army of doctors, lawyers, judges, and even policemen, wanted to force their intentions upon her. Doc said, "I suspect the only man in town to telephone Sudie in a year or more is Albert Potter down at the courthouse." He leaned back in his leather chair and laughed: "Seems sister failed to pay her property taxes, and after several notices came to her in the mail, poor Albert, the County Clerk, rang her up and asked if she could bring a check down." Doc laughed so hard he had to take off his tortoise-shell glasses and wipe his eyes. "Sudie says she knows exactly what Potter and the men who gathered outside the courthouse want from her. And what's more, she told me, 'I don't even walk on that side of the street anymore, so that should fix their kind!' Oh Lord, Lord, Lord, what is to become of Sudie Louisa?"

But even before poor Clinton fled, Sudie's delusions were flourishing, and she even managed to be insulted by the town's only Jewish shopkeeper, a small, well-mannered gentleman who owned the dry goods store. His shop was located midway between the Rexall Drug Store and Tootsie Sizemore's Sweet Shop down on Main Street, and early each morning, before the traffic started moving, he stepped through his front door with his broom and painstakingly swept the pavement all the way from his shop down to the drug store. Sudie's business with the druggist was concluded by eight-thirty that fresh summer morning and she set out for The Sweet Shop up the street.

The little shopkeeper rested his broom, bowed, and smiled at her, "Good morning to you, Missus." He said, "And how's your *Nubble* today?" "My *what?*" "Your *Nubble*, Missus, how's your *Nubble?*" he said again, smiling and drawing closer to her. She threw out her purse to fend off his vile advances as she staggered back toward the shelter of the drug store. "Police,

police, help," she whimpered. The poor man's wife stepped into the street looking totally bewildered and wondering why her gray-haired husband was pursuing Missus Sudie down the Main Street with his broom. He caught up with Sudie Louisa as she blew through the front door of the Rexall Drug Store and into the arms of the pharmacist; then she streaked for the safety of the prescription desk in the rear of the store, and the poor man sank into a chair at the nearest ice-cream table and tried to catch his breath. With trembling hands, he removed his gold-rimmed eyeglasses and pulled a handkerchief from his vest pocket. He dabbed at the perspiration that streamed into his eyes despite the cool morning, wiped his face, and began to wring the handkerchief in his hands. He shook his head back and forth pleading for someone to help him understand. "Oh, Missus, Missus, *Missus* . . ." he repeated over and over while the druggist ran to the telephone. "Central, get Doc and the police."

Within minutes, the shops on Main emptied into the street to form a lively parade. Customers poured out of The Sweet Shop with donuts and sweet rolls in their hand. The old maid Taylor sisters down at The Style Shop held hands and peeped through a crack in their door. Shopkeepers and the lecherous men who loitered in front of the courthouse hankering after Sudie Louisa and the boys from the pool hall stood chattering out on the sidewalk just like they did on December 7th, when the Japanese bombed Pearl Harbor! That evening, Doc had to administer a sedative, and Aunt Sudie had to be reminded of Clinton's membership in the Lodge in Lexington, where members were always respectfully addressed as *Noble*. "That tacky Lodge business," Doc said, "was typical of Clinton's need to belong to something, *anything* Sudie Louisa couldn't get her hands on. Poor ordinary son of a bitch runs around with a fez on his head and calls himself *Noble*. Deliver me."

Poor Sudie, she was always out of sorts about something or other. She was offended by the way people in the little town dressed or by their unfortunate deformities, and she took their innocent remarks to be insults. She had a way of silently clearing her throat and looking off to the left while she lovingly patted the pearls that hung loosely above her breastbone. "I just look the other way when I see that albino child they call Snowflake coming. If I don't run into him mopping the floor at the drug store, I have to look at him when we play cards at Edith's, where he works around the yard. Emile hired him to work in his chambers down at the courthouse, maybe because it's dark in the courthouse, and they say he can't tolerate the sun."

She was offended by the boy's appearance and she feared him, too. She was afraid of a frail little boy because he was different, because, to her, he was ugly and the child of mixed blood, because he was neither white nor black. She looked askance and wagged her forefinger back and forth: "He has no right to know my name, I don't mind telling you. 'How do you do, Miss Sudie,' he likes to say." She said it with a smirk. "He has no right knowing my name much less say it out loud and to my face."

Lord love him, the hapless child she took off on was only nine or ten years old and virtually an orphan. Joe Collins named him Snowflake. "That boy's neither fishes nor fouls, Pig. He's a palomino, you understand." Joe had a way of just slipping off the right word sometimes. It was a little confusing but I never said anything about it. Palomino is pretty close to albino.

Doc said he knew for a fact that the night watchman at Grissom's Lumberyard was the boy's father and his mother was a beautiful, bright young woman who worked as a nurse's aide in the hospital. He said, "The boy's father, LD, is worthless, but in many ways the bastard's brilliant. He can fix anything mechanical, any kind of motor, anything with moving parts, no matter how difficult. I believe he could fix my stethoscope or take the microscope in the office apart and put it back together blindfolded. Strangest thing I've ever seen, but he's a no-good, and there's no help there for Snowflake, I can tell you." Doc looked puzzled when he talked about the man's "lack of common sense" that relegated him to a night watchman's job while the weird and wonderful part of his brain ran like a fine Swiss clock. "What the hell," he mused, "I guess he's an idiot and a genius all at the same time. Regardless, the boy will spend his life sweeping floors and mowing lawns and trying to stay out of the sun, unless someone gives him a hand. It's just a shame; the child is as smart as a whip."

It never once occurred to me when I saw him sitting on the porch at Ocean Frog's store most mornings, with a grown man's hat pulled down over his pale eyes and dressed in a long-sleeved shirt, that he felt stuck tight between worlds of black and white, caught like the three-hundred-pound man who found himself trapped between the cold stone walls of Fat Man's Misery, a mile deep underground at Mammoth Cave. As I went inside to get my Orange Crush at Ocean Frog's, we smiled and spoke, but we never talked to each other like I talked to Ocean Frog or to Joe or to the hired men settling onto the truck bed. I never said more to him than "How you doing?" and he would say "Oh, fair, thanks." One morning as I waited for Joe out on Frog's porch, he offered me a stick of Juicy Fruit Chewing Gum. The fingers that held the package were long and tapered, freckled and pinkish, and the back of his smooth hand was rose-pink under the cuff of his blue work shirt. I reached for the stick of gum and looked up into his pastel eyes. He was smiling, his teeth were straight and white behind freckled lips, and he gently nodded his head. He had his mother's beauty and his daddy's peculiar brain. He swept floors for Ocean Frog in order to buy chewing gum, maybe an Orange Crush or an RC, and he offered that chewing gum to me.

Some years later, the men down at Ocean Frog's store would be calling him "Dr. Lewis Daniel Moore." Doc had cared enough to offer the bright young man a helping hand, and long after my daddy's death the letters continued to arrive regularly, first from his school in Ohio and then from the young doctor himself.

It took many years for Sudie's disposition to improve but improve it did. She actually mellowed in her sunset years, finally gave her hair a rest, letting it go gray and then white. She grew a bit plump, like a soft buxom quail, as did my dear Aunt Tott: plump little quail sitting in their white wicker rocking chairs on the broad porches or at the card table, laughing and gossiping, and still playing cards with a vengeance. I can see them now, patting their breasts and fanning with the score pad, leaving the roost to fan and stroll around a bit, and then, just like little feathered birds, flutter down again into their seats to resume their bidding. Perhaps it was the passage of time that took the edge off my Sudie's terrible disposition and gave her a trace of sentiment toward the last. Joe said, "Time can do that . . . if you *live* long enough." Aunt Tott called it "Sudie's benign retirement."

When she was about eighty, she met an orphan boy called Toad. "They called him Toad," Sudie told me, "called him that just for meanness, that poor little orphan thing and I'm here to say, the Orphan's Home people had no business farming out that child to strain himself in the Ice House, of all places; heaving fifty- or hundred-pound blocks of ice onto the back of the truck, then lugging them off again and into The Rexall Drug Store so everybody could sit back and enjoy a Co-Cola. I don't think even soaking wet he weighed more than one of those big blocks, and the poor frail thing worked all day long winter and summer, and then, if you can believe it, they sent him over to Floyd's Pool Hall to clean until ten o'clock at night. It made my heart *ache* to look into those eyes—eyes that said 'hungry for love,' and I know very well why the fat jailer adopted him. Your father always said the fat ones dig their graves with their teeth and he did just that, dropped dead at thirty-eight years old in front of the courthouse. Oh, to be thirty-eight again, just for a day. Well, that's what most of their kind do when they are on the public payroll. That jailer and his wife, Erline Hines, they grazed at the public trough like they both had a tapeworm. Anyway you look at it, they were as common as cat hair and couldn't wait to take in little Toad to do the cleaning in that nasty jailhouse. He would have been better off staying in the Orphan's Home, where at least he could have a hot meal and a nice clean bed."

My childless Aunt Sudie adopted little Toad Tuttle and loved him in her mind, but it was late, more than fifty years too late. It was at this time that Sudie's oscillating electric fan began to play well-known Episcopal hymns. As the hymns droned in the background, she fingered her string of pearls and smiled. She liked to sing along and many times I found her happily seated by the remarkable Anglican fan, humming along and remembering the plight of that sad little boy called Toad. "Fairest Lord Je-ee-sus, fairer than the meh-eh-dows, hum dah dah dah and the mor-ning sun. Je-ee-sus is fair-er-er, Jee-sus is bri-hite-ter than all the dah da heaven can boast."

Harlan Hubbard

from *Shantyboat*

Harlan Hubbard lived an independent life in the woods longer than did Henry David Thoreau, who spent only a little more than two years at Walden Pond. Born in 1900 in Bellevue, across the Ohio River from Cincinnati, Hubbard was a loner who didn't marry until he was forty-three; then he and his new wife, Anna Eikenhout, a retired librarian, built a shanty boat, which they maneuvered over the next seven years down the Ohio and Mississippi Rivers, stopping each spring to squat and raise a garden, then resuming their river journey. In 1952 they moved to Payne Hollow, a spot in Trimble County near Milton on the Ohio River, built a house, and lived there the rest of their lives. She died in 1986, and he followed less than two years later.

As Hubbard once said, they had all the conveniences of the eighteenth century—including a violin, which he played, and a grand piano, which Anna played. He also wrote several books, including *Shantyboat* (1953) and *Payne Hollow* (1977), which detail their experiences and his meditations about their lives on the river and in their riverside home. This excerpt from *Shantyboat* describes the Ohio River, Payne Hollow itself, and the process of making maple syrup.

The river is a world in itself, separated from the country through which it flows by invisible walls. Its seasons are not the same as those of the country inland. The river air is softer, a little misty always, except in those times when all the land is scoured by the north wind. Even then, if the shantyboater has chosen his winter harbor well, the wind roars through the trees overhead, and the sun warms his sheltered deck.

When we first came to the river in autumn, the brilliant coloring and stark contrast of the hills were left behind. The green willows changed to gold, faded and scattered their thin leaves as imperceptibly as the course of the sun moved southward. On sunny days the pale yellow shores seemed afloat on the heavy blue water. In the mild air, the migrating birds lingered, softly whistling fragments of their summer songs.

In the nights of summer and autumn, the colder air descended to the river, and we enjoyed a little summer fire when it would be unthought of on the hilltops. In cold weather, however, the water tempers the air. Riverbank gardens often flourish long after the first official frost. Snow melts sooner there, and the river road is bare when the higher roads are coated with ice.

It was a peculiar springtime along the river after the flood. While the hills and fields were becoming green with opening buds and new grass, the receding waters left a dead shore. The stark, muddy trees were draped with trash which floated into them at different levels. The banks were slimy as the primeval shores, and the odor of spring, there, was the odor of decay. Yet the river elms were the first to show a tinge of warmth in their black ranks, and along the creeks the maples flowered before one suspected that spring was astir.

The tips of trees which were above water had sprouted green buds, but the lower branches were lifeless after the river fell. The crest of the flood was marked by a distinct line, spring above and winter below. Slowly the lower part began to show the fresh green of spring, but by then it was early summer above. We found a little redbud tree below the flood line, where none should be, flowering long after the redbuds had faded from the hillsides.

The most natural undertaking at this season is a garden, and it was more by instinct than design that we went up on the hillside above the railroad, since the riverbank would not be dry enough for several weeks, and tentatively cleared a little patch of ground. The owner was unknown to us, but he must have been easygoing and tolerant, for no one ever questioned our gardening there, any more than they had our squatting on the riverbank. We burned the brush and dry weeds, removed some of the stones and bricks which were remnants of an old house that once stood there. The soil was rich and black, for the original forest, which still flourished on the higher slopes, had once extended almost down to the river.

It was pleasant to work up there on the green hillside, away from the desolation which surrounded the boat, looking over the wide river where wind and swirling current made an ever-changing pattern. The warm sun stirred us as it did the growing things, and we responded by extending our garden. We planted lettuce, spinach, peas, beets, and carrots, a little early for some of it, perhaps, with cold rains and frost almost sure to come. Experience has taught us little, for we are still "sooners." Often it pays, the earlier plantings doing as well, or better, than the more cautious later ones.

Our riverbank gardens in succeeding years have been almost as haphazard as this first one. When we are drifting down the river in the wintertime, absorbed in our voyage and the strange shores we pass or linger at, a garden, if thought of at all, is so remote that we even consider drifting on through the summer, or at least until late spring. But when the first warm days come, we begin to pick out possible garden sites, only in fun, of course. At length, however, we give way to the influence of the spring sun, and the desire for some fresh green lettuce, and think seriously about gardening.

It has not been difficult to find a suitable place even in a strange country.

There are marginal bits of land everywhere and good-natured, generous owners who are glad to see it put to use. Extra work is usually required to clear the ground and keep down weeds, and there is the risk of an unexpected summer overflow, but the reward is a rich, vigorous soil, needing no fertilizer, and the satisfaction which must always be attendant on making waste land bear fruit. . . .

It was not a long voyage down to Payne Hollow, but we had never seen such a shore along the Ohio. It rose sharply from the river without the usual fringe of willows. The hardwood forest trees and stones of all sizes from the rugged hillside came down to the water's edge. The natives call such a shore the Narrows, rather "Narrs."

We landed at Payne Hollow with great expectations. How good it was to have a sandy beach, and solitude!

We explored our new territory with the eagerness of castaways on their desert island. The freedom of the river was still with us. We occupied the shore as naturally as the driftwood and river sand, though of course the land belonged to someone, and we were ready to decamp at the least suggestion.

The nearest road or house being a mile away, no one came to the riverbank in those inclement days of late winter. Powell, the hunter, in fresh clean overalls, stopped by on his Sunday forays into the woods, but he was the aborigine and disturbed the solitude no more than did the ducks on the river.

The small upland creek which came down Payne Hollow—it was never called Payne Creek or given any other name that we heard—had cut through a high range of hills which paralleled the river. At its mouth a narrow strip of sandy bottomland, covered with last year's broken cornstalks, extended along the river, tapering to a point above and below the creek where the Narrows rose steeply from the water's edge. Farther back from the river, against the wooded hillside and higher than the field next to the willows, was another strip of tillable ground, not recently cultivated. We thought this would be a good place for a garden.

Winding through the bottomland, the course of the creek was marked by two rows of water-loving trees, and where it entered the river a pair of cottonwoods formed a gigantic gateway. The creek had high mud banks at this low stage of the river, but its clear water flowed over shelving rock. A few rods from the river, under a tall sycamore whose exposed roots formed a weird Gothic canopy, was the spring, pouring forth in great volume.

Downstream from the creek, at the higher level, was a stone foundation. The house which once stood there might have been carried away by some high flood. Prowling among the briars, we came upon the root cellar mentioned by Art Moore, its low door like the hidden entrance to a cave. Within it was a rather spacious dome, the stones well-laid, plastered and whitewashed. A stone shelf ran all around. There was an air hole at the top, which was at ground level. This cellar was enough to tempt one to rebuild there.

We followed the trace of a road along the creek which farther up ran over a shallow bed of broken stones. The hollow widened out into a level field in the midst of which stood a well-built fireplace and chimney of stone. Except for some unevenness of ground and a few scattered stones, no trace of a house remained. Against the hill was a tobacco barn, evidently of later date than the chimney and still in use. Here the creek divided and the old road, following neither branch, began its sloping climb to the ridge.

We, the latest inhabitants of Payne Hollow, came upon other sites of dwellings, perhaps a square of rough-laid stone overgrown with new forest, or an old well. Later the natives told us that there had been a small settlement at Payne Landing. The farmers used to bring their stock and produce down to the steamboat. Near the landing once stood a rude warehouse and a small corral. Many wagonloads of peaches had been brought down from the ridge and shipped from there. The road must have been much better in those days, for in our time it was too rough for even an apple.

In this year winter ran its full course. The smoke from our blazing fires was ever carried downstream with the south-flowing current. March was past the season for ice in the river, but the water was low and clear, the air very cold. One night we awoke dismayed to hear the crunching sound of ice, made by the scattered floes as they crashed into our boat and scraped along its length. In a few days the river was nearly full of floating ice. A solid mass of it extended out from shore. I hauled the johnboat out on the bank, and kept a little duck pool open around the boat.

Remembering the advice of Andy, which was repeated by the local river authority—who was Cleo's father, the old pilot—we determined to pull the boat out on the bank if the river froze into a solid sheet of ice. Some straight young sycamores to be used as skids were located. No actual preparations were necessary, however, for the March sun checked the formation of solid ice. After a few days the running ice vanished as suddenly as it had appeared, and the river was again open for navigation.

Thinking that all danger was past, I took away the protecting boom from the outside of the hull. The nights turned cold again, and large sheets of very thin ice formed in the river. One morning in a stiff west wind, about an acre of this ice, as thin and transparent as window glass, was blown in to the boat, and as it drifted along, its saw edge cut a narrow groove the length of the hull, thus doing more damage than the heavier ice had. It was remarkable how fast this sheet ice was moved toward the shore and our boat by the crossriver wind. There was nothing on the ice to catch the wind, but the rippling wind waves at its edge, and friction of the wind across its surface must have created a continuous force which set the sheet of ice in motion.

These cold nights and thawing days made us think of maple syrup, or it may have been the hard maple trees we saw on the steep Narrows upriver from our landing. In a previous spring, living then at the studio in Fort Thomas, we had boiled some sap, and still had the wooden tubes I had whittled out and used as spigots. I now made a few more and we gathered together all available buckets, cans, jars, and utensils—there was no dump to draw on now, no gas station from which to get discarded oil cans. Nineteen trees were tapped and our makeshift sap buckets hung out. The hillside was rough and very steep; so the gathering of sap and carrying it in was a difficult and un-certain performance, even though the trees were concentrated in a small area near the bottom of the hill. The fire was built in the woods, close to the river, at the end of a little path which ran along the shore from Payne Hollow.

The season for syrup making did not last long. We continued our sugar camp for nine days, boiling down nine washboilerfuls of sap, each of which made about a quart of syrup.

These were special days. It was a joy to be working in the winter woods, above the river, building huge fires. I would roll in some logs and big chunks of hardwood on the last trip before bed time. Then I walked back to the boat through the dark, starry woods by a path soon well-known. In the morning the sap was still steaming, half boiled down. As we finished off this, the sap buckets were emptied into a wash tub for a new batch. It was convenient to take our midday meal up to the camp, to watch carefully the last of the boiling, exciting for us novices, and to start afresh. Our dinner was often shad broiled over the coals and potatoes and corn dodgers baked in the ashes. The new syrup was delicious with the hot bread.

While cutting wood near our sugar camp one day I saw, standing up-right among the old leaves—it still seems the most unlikely object to find there—a grinder. It was just what we were looking for to grind our corn and wheat, an old hand-power coffee mill, the kind once used in grocery stores, with a wheel on each side to serve as crank and flywheel. The coffee beans were put in a hopper in the center. The hopper had a bell-shaped cover, missing in our model, as was one of the wheels. Originally a bright red, it had been repainted gray, unfortunately. Yet it worked, and it was not too rusty. Our grinding of corn and wheat became much easier and faster, and the meal and flour finer. Later we found other things to grind.

Who left the grinder on that uninhabited hillside is still something of a mystery. Powell said that Art Moore had camped there, and had made the path to the spring. His campsite, close to our sap-boiling fire, was still marked. We thought he might have used the grinder in some process of his distilling.

During our syrup making we explored all the hillside. Halfway up, on a narrow shelf, was an overgrown clearing and the remains of a house. Above this the slope became even more steep, ending in a palisade of bare rock. It was more like mountain than river country. Almost at the crest of the hill a strong spring flowed out from under the rock. This water had been piped to the farm on the hillside clearing below by a rude aqueduct which we followed down through the steep woods. It was made of the trunks of straight trees, mostly ash, which had been split and hollowed into rude troughs with an ax. At the end was a large, hollowed-out log to receive the water. All this might have been done in pioneer times, or even in the stone age, but later we met the man who, with his boys, had made the clearing and piped the water.

Following the brow of the hill, thick with cedars, an almost sheer drop to the river on one hand, farm land on the other, past a log cabin in good condition but unoccupied, we came to a weatherbeaten farmhouse which had long stood on this windy point. With its cluster of pine trees, it was a landmark from the river, which was spread out before it as on a map. We wondered how anyone could live an ordinary life with such an outlook constantly before him, with so much of the world at his feet.

"Winter Birds"

Hubbard also kept a journal, which was published shortly before he died. The Hubbards were cordial hosts to those who could find them nestled in their home, which was almost inaccessible. On a visit I made to Payne Hollow in the summer of 1984, Anna taught me how to snap green beans, which I found to be a useful skill. Hubbard was also a superb painter, mostly of riverscapes, steamboats, and landscapes, which he would sell to his guests. Except for modest book royalties, his paintings were his only cash crop and supported his meager needs for soybeans, medicine, and house repairs. Here is his poetic meditation on birds in winter.

I sit at the window
on a winter morning, writing,
the cheery stove behind me.
Outside in the half light
snow falling gently
a host of little birds
is breakfasting on seeds and grains
I have put out for them;
juncos and sparrows
scratch in the snow for cornmeal;

on the old stump are titmice and nuthatches;
chickadees hovering on the fringe
wait their chance undaunted
by the larger birds.
Where is the cardinal?
They all peck and squabble
snatch a sunflower seed and fly away
returning for another one.
When a downy woodpecker appears
the smaller birds scatter—
but now comes a redbelly;
he sits in the middle of things unmolested
feeding alone and in no hurry
while the others wait.
How bright his red patch
stands out against the snow!

For many years I have watched
this unchanging spectacle of winter,
and the same birds will be pecking
at what they can find after I am no longer
here to see them.
This is a disquieting thought
difficult to accept
for I would like to watch the friendly birds
winters without end;
yet I know I must die—
every living thing dies
according to the inexorable law
of Earth. Even so I do not mourn—
having fed with the chickadees
on the Bread of Life
I am assured that all is well
and I need not be concerned
about immortality.

Hunter S. Thompson

from *Kingdom of Fear,* Part One, "When the Going Gets Weird, the Weird Turn Pro"

Hunter Thompson invented what he called Gonzo, or Outlaw, Journalism, a kind of irreverent, in-your-face, iconoclastic journalistic aberration, and for that reason he is a well-known writer. Actually, it can be a very effective form of reportage. In *The Great Shark Hunt* (1979), he defines his invention as a combination of a master journalist's talent, an artist's and photographer's eye, and an involved participant. *Hell's Angels: A Strange and Terrible Saga* (1966) is based on his participation in the controversial motorcycle club and conversations and interviews with its members. He went to Las Vegas to cover a desert motorcycle race and attend a seminar on illegal drugs, the principal sources for his *Fear and Loathing in Las Vegas: A Strange Journey to the Heart of the American Dream* (1972). In the 1970s he also wrote articles for *Rolling Stone.* Born in Louisville in 1937, he lived recently in seclusion in Montana until his suicide early in 2005. The personal essay below, "When the Going Gets Weird, the Weird Turn Pro," is from *Kingdom of Fear: Loathsome Secrets of a Star-Crossed Child in the Final Days of the American Century* (2003).

There are no jokes. Truth is the funniest joke of all.

—Muhammad Ali

The Mailbox: Louisville, Summer of 1946

My parents were decent people, and I was raised, like my friends, to believe that Police were our friends and protectors—the Badge was a symbol of extremely high authority, perhaps the highest of all. Nobody ever asked *why.* It was one of those unnatural questions that are better left alone. If you had to ask *that,* you were sure as hell Guilty of *something* and probably should have been put behind bars a long time ago. It was a no-win situation.

My first face-to-face confrontation with the FBI occurred when I was nine years old. Two grim-looking Agents came to our house and terrified my parents by saying that I was a "prime suspect" in the case of a Federal Mailbox being turned over in the path of a speeding bus. It was a Federal Offense, they said, and carried a five-year prison sentence.

"Oh no!" wailed my mother. "Not in prison! That's insane! He's only a child. How could he have known?"

"The warning is clearly printed on the Mailbox," said the agent in the gray suit. "He's old enough to read."

"Not necessarily," my father said sharply. "How do you know he's not blind, or a moron?"

"Are you a moron, son?" the agent asked me. "Are you blind? Were you just *pretending* to read that newspaper when we came in?" He pointed to the *Louisville Courier-Journal* on the couch.

"That was only the sports section," I told him. "I can't read the other stuff."

"See?" said my father. "I told you he was a moron."

"Ignorance of the law is no excuse," the brown-suit agent replied. "Tampering with the U.S. Mail is a Federal offense punishable under Federal law. That Mailbox was badly damaged."

Mailboxes were huge, back then. They were heavy green vaults that stood like Roman mile markers at corners on the neighborhood bus routes and were rarely, if ever, moved. I was barely tall enough to reach the Mail-drop slot, much less big enough to turn the bastard over and into the path of a bus. It was clearly impossible that I could have committed this crime without help, and that was what they wanted: names and addresses, along with a total confession. They already knew I was guilty, they said, because other culprits had squealed on me. My parents hung their heads, and I saw my mother weeping.

I had done it, of course, and I had done it with plenty of help. It was carefully plotted and planned, a deliberate ambush that we set up and executed with the fiendish skill that smart nine-year-old boys are capable of when they have too much time on their hands and a lust for revenge on a rude and stupid bus driver who got a kick out of closing his doors and pulling away just as we staggered to the top of the hill and begged him to let us climb on. . . . He was new on the job, probably a brain-damaged substitute, filling in for our regular driver, who was friendly and kind and always willing to wait a few seconds for children rushing to school. Every kid in the neighborhood agreed that this new swine of a driver was a sadist who deserved to be punished, and the Hawks A.C. were the ones to do it. We saw it more as a duty than a prank. It was a brazen Insult to the honor of the whole neighborhood.

We would need ropes and pulleys and certainly no witnesses to do the job properly. We had to tilt the iron monster so far over that it was perfectly balanced to fall instantly, just as the fool zoomed into the bus stop at his usual arrogant speed. All that kept the box more or less upright was my grip on a long "invisible" string that we had carefully stretched all the way from the corner and across about 50 feet of grass lawn to where we crouched out of sight in some bushes.

The rig worked perfectly. The bastard was right on schedule and going too fast to stop when he saw the thing falling in front of him. . . . The collision made a horrible noise, like a bomb going off or a freight train exploding in Germany. That is how I remember it, at least. It was the worst noise I'd ever heard. People ran screaming out of their houses like chickens gone crazy with fear. They howled at one another as the driver stumbled out of his bus and collapsed in a heap on the grass. . . . The bus was empty of passengers, as usual at the far end of the line. The man was not injured, but he went into a foaming rage when he spotted us fleeing down the hill and into a nearby alley. He knew in a flash who had done it, and so did most of the neighbors.

"Why deny it, Hunter?" said one of the FBI agents. "We know *exactly* what happened up there on that corner on Saturday. Your buddies already confessed, son. They *squealed* on you. We know you did it, so don't lie to us now and make things worse for yourself. A nice kid like you shouldn't have to go to Federal prison." He smiled again and winked at my father, who responded with a snarl: "Tell the Truth, damn it! Don't lie to these men. They have *witnesses!*" The FBI agents nodded grimly at each other and moved as if to take me into custody.

It was a magic moment in my life, a defining instant for me or any other nine-year-old boy growing up in the 1940s after World War II—and I clearly recall thinking: *Well, this is it. These are G-Men. . . .*

WHACK! Like a flash of nearby lightning that lights up the sky for three or four terrifying split seconds before you hear the thunder—a matter of *zepto-seconds* in real time—but when you are a nine-year-old boy with two (2) full-grown FBI agents about to seize you and clap you in Federal prison, a few quiet zepto-seconds can seem like the rest of your life. . . . And that's how it felt to me that day, and in grim retrospect, I was right. They had me, dead to rights. I was Guilty. Why deny it? Confess Now, and throw myself on their mercy, or—

What? What if I *didn't* confess? That was the question. And I was a curious boy, so I decided, as it were, to roll the dice and ask *them* a question.

"Who?" I said. "What witnesses?"

It was not a hell of a lot to ask, under those circumstances—and I really did want to know exactly who among my best friends and blood brothers in the dreaded Hawks A.C. had cracked under pressure and betrayed me to these thugs, these pompous brutes and toadies with badges & plastic cards in their wallets that said they worked for J. Edgar Hoover and that they had the Right, and even the duty, to put me in jail, because they'd heard a "Rumor in the neighborhood" that some of my boys had gone belly up and rolled on me. *What?* No. Impossible.

Or not *likely,* anyway. Hell, Nobody squealed on the Hawks A.C., or not on its President, anyway. Not on Me. So I asked again: "Witnesses? What Witnesses?"

❦ ❦ ❦

And that was all it took, as I recall. We observed a moment of silence, as my old friend Edward Bennett Williams would say. Nobody spoke—especially not me—and when my father finally broke the eerie silence, there was *doubt* in his voice. "I think my son has a point, officer. Just exactly who *have* you talked to? I was about to ask that myself."

"Not Duke!" I shouted. "He went to Lexington with his father! And not *Ching*! And not *Jay*!—"

"Shut up," said my father. "Be quiet and let *me* handle this, you fool."

And that's what happened, folks. We never saw those FBI agents again. Never. And I learned a powerful lesson; Never believe the first thing an FBI agent tells you about anything—especially not if he seems to believe you are guilty of a crime. Maybe he has no evidence. Maybe he's bluffing. Maybe you are innocent. Maybe. The Law can be hazy on these things. . . . But it is definitely worth a roll.

In any case, nobody was arrested for that alleged incident. The FBI agents went away, the U.S. Mailbox was put back up on its heavy iron legs, and we never saw that drunken swine of a substitute bus driver again.

Guy Davenport

Everybody said that Guy Davenport was a genius. He even won one of the MacArthur genius grants to prove it. Certainly, he was one of the most radically original, surprising, witty, quirky, learned, difficult, and sensual writers of his time. Born in South Carolina in 1927, he received undergraduate degrees from Duke and Oxford, where he was a Rhodes Scholar, and a Ph.D. in English from Harvard. He came to the University of Kentucky in 1963 and taught there until his MacArthur grant made him financially independent, and he resigned. He lived in Lexington until his death on January 4, 2005. He wrote poems, short stories, essays, reviews, and translations. Most of his works were amalgams that displayed his broad learning, from ancient history, music, and art to the contemporary and avant-garde. His ambitious works obliterate time, place, and form, uniting it all as one piece of art. Consequently, his works, especially his poetry and fiction, can be obscure, exasperating, and puzzling for many readers and critics. For the determined and classically educated reader, however, the reward is highly satisfying.

Two examples of Davenport's work are unusually clear and straightforward, yet they suggest the range of his interests, from the circumcision of male gentiles to his friendship with two other Kentucky geniuses, the blazingly original photographer Eugene Meatyard and the saintly sinner and impishly contemplative Trappist monk Thomas Merton. Both pieces are taken from *The Hunter Gracchus and Other Papers on Literature and Art* (1996), a gathering of studies, reviews, essays, commentaries, and entries from his journals. Gracchus, the name of a noble Roman family just before the Christian era, is synonymous with the search for truth, meaning, and virtue. One imagines that Davenport saw himself as just such a hunter in all his creations, fiction and nonfiction, mundane and ethereal.

⚬⚭⚬

from "Journal I" in *The Hunter Gracchus and Other Papers on Literature and Art*

The circumcision of gentiles in the United States is a cruel and useless mutilation. Michel Tournier in *Le Vent paraclète* likens it to removing the eyelids. It is an ironic turn of events. The circumcision of the Old Testament was a slicing away of the merest tip of the foreskin, the *akroposthion* as the Greeks called it. In the Hellenizing period of the first century C.E. (see Maccabees) the rabbinate changed over to total removal of the prepuce, to make a more decisive symbol. Gentiles began to circumcize fairly recently: a Victorian attempt, one among many, to prevent masturbation. (A. E. Housman was circumcized at thirteen.) It is done nowadays by parents so ignorant that they don't know it doesn't need to be done, and doctors, always ready for another buck, recommend it on hygienic principles. It is difficult to think of another such institutionalized gratuitous meanness, the brutal insensitivity of which enjoys universal indifference. A Tiresian conundrum: a male who has never known the sensuality of a foreskin, both for masturbation and for making love, cannot know what he has been so criminally bereft of.

ఞఞ ఞఞ ఞఞ

If Jews returned to cutting away the wedding ring's worth of flesh (as with Michelangelo's David, who has almost all of a foreskin, and as with Abraham, Isaac, and Jacob)—a nicely revolutionary recovery of archaic truth—perhaps American parents would quit agreeing to the mutilation of their children's bodies. But as long as Ann Landers et Cie. continue to idiotize the populace with a rancid puritanism, maiming boys will continue.

from "Tom and Gene" in *The Hunter Gracchus and Other Papers on Literature and Art*

Ralph Eugene Meatyard met Thomas Merton on January 17, 1967, at the Trappist monastery of Our Lady of Gethsemani near Bardstown, Kentucky. The day was bright and cold. The next day Merton wrote his friend Bob Lax that he had been visited by "three kings from Lexington," as Michael Mott records in his biography. Tom's letters to Lax were always madcap and full of private jokes, so that why we were cast as the Magi must remain a mystery. We brought no gifts, we came in Gene's car, and we were decidedly remote in religion: Gene, I think, was a lapsed Methodist; Jonathan Williams a very lapsed Episcopalian; and I a Baptist who would figure in Tom's judgment as the only real pagan he had ever met.

Tom was grateful that we weren't pious. His life was bedeviled by people who had read a third of *The Seven Storey Mountain* and wanted to say they had met him. Just why we made our visit I'm not certain. Jonathan Williams was well into his ongoing enterprise of meeting every person worth knowing on the face of the earth, and had remarked that he "had no sense of Merton the man" and wanted to look in on him. Jonathan was at the time on a weeklong visit at my house, showing slides and giving readings at the University of Kentucky. Some years before he had introduced me to Gene Meatyard, optometrist and photographer. Gene and I had become friends, and I had begun urging him to photograph literary figures. Eventually he photographed Louis Zukofsky, Wendell Berry, James Baker Hall, Jonathan Greene, and Hugh Kenner, among others. It was therefore as a portraitist that he was along. I was there because Tom had read my poem *Flowers and Leaves* (to his fellow monks, at table, moreover; the silent Trappists may hear secular writing while they eat, and it was one of Tom's chores to read to them).

This frosty January day has become magic in my memory. Merton met us at the lodge. He was dressed in dungarees, sweater, and hooded jacket. He looked like a cross between Picasso and Jean Genet. He got into Gene's car to guide us to his cement-block one-room cabin in the woods in back of the abbey. Tom had just before this become a desert father, the first in a thousand years. He remarked wryly that the abbot suspected him of having orgies there. (Joan Baez had been a visitor a short time before, against all rules: two signs along the approach to Gethsemani warned away the female sex—the first read NO LADIES PERMITTED, the second NO WOMEN.) Tom and the abbot had had disagreements about the rules for a desert father, especially about Tom's growing predilection for visiting people in Louisville and Lexington. "Who's to say," Tom countered, "if Saint Anthony didn't take the streetcar into Alexandria when he'd had it with his loneliness?"

The hermit's cabin had its bed zoned from the rest of the inside by a Mexican blanket. We got to see the bed—spartan to be sure when Tom reached under it to bring out a half bottle of the local bourbon. There was an oil stove for heat as well as a handsome fireplace. A few sacred icons, all folk art, were on the walls. The books were largely poetry. I noted letters on his desk from Marguerite Yourcenar and Nicanor Parra. Tom Merton knew no strangers; we settled in to good talk as if we had known each other for years.

Gene had begun the conversation as we got out of the car. His incredibly sharp eyes had seen a rock by a pine tree near the cabin porch, and he remarked casually that it had been photographed by someone and used on the cover of a New Directions book. Tom had taken the picture. So Gene and Tom first met as fellow photographers. And it is not every day you meet someone who can identify from a phenomenal visual memory a rock among rocks and a pine among pines. (I once needed Gene to identify a man in his thirties of whom I had only a photograph at age ten. This was at an airport; Gene identified him as he emerged from the plane.)

My notes say that at some point Tom did a dance, which he said was Chilean, though I now cannot remember any music or Tom dancing. He made drawings for us by dipping weeds in ink and slapping them onto a sheet of typing paper. He drew a horse, very Zen in its strokes. We had arrived at eleven, having been lost for an hour on Kentucky back roads; the matter of lunch arose. Tom served us goat cheese made at the abbey, packets of salted peanuts, and jiggers of bourbon. Jonathan asked at this epicurean meal what Tom was writing. He was writing what came to be Section 35 of *Cables to the Ace* (1968). Would we like to hear some of it?

He read: "C'est l'heure des chars fondus dans le noir de la cité. Dans les caves, les voix sourdes des taureaux mal rêvés! l'océan monte dans les couloirs de l'oeil jusqu'à la lumière des matins: et ils sont là, tous les deux: le Soleil et le Franc-Tireur."

My notes say: Gene photographed as we talked. For the rest of their friendship, up until Tom's departure for the East, Gene photographed.

Tom's bladder needed frequent relief. The outhouse was the home of a black snake. Tom instructed us, if we wanted to use this amenity, to kick the door first and shout, "Get out, you bastard!" In the afternoon we walked up the hill to the reservoir—the Monk's Pond of Tom's magazine—and it was on this walk that he talked about *Flowers and Leaves* and suggested that Jonathan consider becoming a Trappist. In the summer, he said, there was nude bathing in the pond for those so minded, and he remembered swimming there with the Stephen Spenders.

My notes say: A warm, generous, frank, and utterly friendly man.

We left at four, having been given bread from the refectory and having been introduced to Brother Richard, who, clerking in the abbey's cheese shop, was allowed to talk.

When Bonnie Jean Cox later met Tom, she whispered to me, "This is not the man who wrote *The Seven Storey Mountain*," as indeed he wasn't. It was Bonnie's observation, when we heard of Tom's death in Bangkok, that he had held out his hand to God on his arrival in heaven and hooted, "Hello you old son of a bitch!"

Tom's reputation was already myth in these last two years of his life when Gene Meatyard was one of his closest friends. Gene, merriest of men and with a wicked sense of humor, delighted in my telling him that I had been to an English Department cocktail party where some visiting scholar was impressing us with his inside dope about Father Marie Louis, Order of the Cistercians of the Strict Observance. Did we know—few did—this English prof asked us in awed tones, that Merton had retreated from the monastery, incredibly disciplined as it was (sign language only, vigils at the altar through the night, incessant prayer and unremitting study), for a bare hut in a Kentucky forest, where he'd grown a long beard, and where absolutely no one saw him. He communicated only with God.

This professor was enjoying himself immensely, imparting privileged information to the ignorant.

At an opportune moment, I said, watching the ghastly look that grew on his face: "Tom Merton was by the house day before yesterday, turning up on my porch after a phone call from the bus station. He was in mufti: tobacco-farmer field clothes, with a tractor cap. He made quite a dent in my bottle of Jack Daniels, and was excited to find that I had a text of Bernardus Silvestris's

De Mundi Universitate, about which we had a lively discussion. We also talked about Buster Keaton and the superiority in comic genius of the silent film over the talkies, Charles Babbage, French painting, and Lord knows what else, including Catalan, a dictionary of which he'd hoped I could lend him."

It was quite clear that the professor took me to be not only a fool but a jackanapes, and soon after this I was told that one of my department who listened to this drivel reported me to the administration as a fraud. (I had just come to the university, and was suspect for various other reasons.)

I am sorry that I could not have recounted a later appearance of Tom in Lexington, when he, Gene, an editor of *Fortune* and Columbia classmate of Tom's, and I went to lunch at the Ramada Inn. The editor of *Fortune* had rented a car at the airport, wrecked it, and had minor cuts and bruises, enough to have bloodied his clothes. He sported a bandage around his head and invited second looks. Gene was in a neat business suit. Tom was, as before, dressed as a tobacco farmer. The four of us were served with the utmost courtesy, beginning with martinis, which Tom downed four of. One of Tom's topics at this meal was the architecture of Buddhist temples.

It is my guess that Tom was, like Saint Paul, all things to all men. The pious monk of the professor at the cocktail party certainly existed. He was indeed the vigilant before the altar in the cold watches of a winter's night. He was also the man who asked Joan Baez to take off her shoes, as he hadn't seen a woman's foot in years. He showed me where she'd danced in the wheat field for him, barefoot and singing. He had a healthy distrust of the trendy and velleitous in religion. He winced when pious visitors from the world hunted him down. One Sunday afternoon he, Gene, Bonnie, and I walked to the remotest part of a field, in hiding from the inevitable elbow swingers. "Even so," he said, "it was here that a car stopped, and a family got out, and before I could get away they held up their infant son dressed in a Trappist habit." It was this same afternoon that we learned that Tom gave lectures to the abbey on Eastern religions. He'd looked at his watch, said, "Damn! I have to jack-rabbit over to the big house and do the Sufis," and trotted off at a lively pace, shouting that he'd be back in fifty minutes.

Gene Meatyard was at this time deep into Zen, which he saw as a philosophy relevant to his art as well as to his life. Zen was, however, but one of many of Gene's concerns. He was, when he met Tom Merton, one of the most distinguished of American photographers, all the more distinguished and typically American for being invisibly in a Kentucky university town. He was known to the members of the Lexington Camera Club, which was, with Van Deren Coke, Guy Mendes, James Baker Hall, and Robert C. May among its members, one of the epicenters of American photography. He had a large circle, or circles, of friends. Born in 1925 in Normal, Illinois (he treasured that name), he invented himself. He was deeply, eclectically educated, despite a typical high school and Williams College. When he met Tom Merton he was married to the charming and beautiful Madeleine ("Mattie") and had three children, Mike, Chris, and Melissa. Their home, which Tom visited frequently, was as friendly and comfortable a place as a home can be. While bearing the stamp of all the Meatyards' hobbies, it was Gene's hand that one saw traces of everywhere—his *objettrouvé* sculptures, his collection of rare recordings of jazz, his books and photographs.

The laughable was Gene's passion. He had a notebook full of peculiar names which led, in time, to the idea of Lucybelle Crater and her daughter Lucybelle Crater (a misremembering of Flannery O'Connor's Lucynelle Crater and her daughter Lucynelle Crater). One of Lexington's citizens at the time was Carlos Toadvine, whose stage name was Little Enis. Gene was fascinated with his own name, Meatyard, and was delighted when I pointed out that it is the Middle English *meteyeard,* or yardstick, cognate with *Dreyfus.* And that his first name is properly pronounced *Rafe.* He approved of Edward Muggeridge's changing his name to Eadweard Muybridge.

My first response to Gene's photographs was to see them as images parallel to Henry James's evocation of hallucinations—the blurred, half-recognizable face in the shadows. I did not know at the time that Gene had worked in many styles, that he had made documentary studies as brilliant as Margaret Bourke-White's and had begun as a fairly traditional modernist, echoing Minor White and Charles Sheeler. All the Merton portraits belong to a period of experimentation in which Gene was exploring his own mastery of the camera. He would take pictures seemingly offhandedly, without looking in the viewer. There was an afternoon of talk with Tom at Gene's house in which he took some amazing photographs all but secretly. I was aware that the camera was there on its tripod and that Gene fiddled with it from time to time.

There were also elaborate stagings and poses. There was an afternoon when Gene took Tom and me to an abandoned farm, standing us under a clothesline, having us peer into a rain barrel, posing us back to back like duelists. This was at the time that the Anglican Bishop Pike had wandered off into a desert in the southwest, and the papers were full of speculation as to his whereabouts. "All bishops are mad," Tom offered.

Joseph Phelps

"He Saved Others"

The quest for ultimate meanings is not restricted, of course, to seekers like monks, ministers, rabbis, priests, and so on; but they are the ones who are most likely to write on the subject. Thomas Merton, the Trappist monk at Gethsemani, near Bardstown, was perhaps the best-known spiritual writer in Kentucky in the second half of the twentieth century. In sermons, readings, homilies, and the religious petitions and proclamations of many religious groups, Kentuckians for over two hundred years have heard men and women of the spirit speak on holy days. The form most familiar to the vast majority of Kentuckians, however, has been and is the service dominated by the sermon, which in most Protestant churches follows the pattern dominant at least since the sixteenth century: text or scripture, doctrine, application, and response. Although sermons were often collected and printed in book form in the nineteenth and early twentieth centuries, other forms of recording and retrieval have made such collections rare today. A recent sermon preached by the Reverend Joseph Phelps, pastor of Highland Baptist Church in Louisville, represents the continuing vitality of the sermon, still the most common literary form in this state and in the nation. Even in this abbreviated form, his sermon displays the common structure, beginning with the text from scripture.

Text: Luke 23: 33–43

If you were to pick a text that best depicts who Jesus is and what He stands for, which one would you choose?

Those who developed the calendar for the Christian year made an interesting choice for the last Sunday of the year, referred to as Christ the King Sunday. It is a scene from the end of the gospels, made vividly graphic last year by Mel Gibson's movie, *The Passion,* where Jesus is crucified between two thieves.

Notice the consistent, mocking focus of the onlookers. The religious leaders scoff, "he saved others, let him save himself." So too the soldiers taunt, "If you are the King of the Jews save yourself." Even the thief hanging next to Jesus echoes the theme. "Are you not the Messiah? Save yourself and us!"

The focus is on what Jesus can or can't do for himself. "Jesus, can you save yourself? Can you save your own body, your reputation, your control of the situation? Can you win, can you silence these cocky, arrogant taunters? Can you show us what a king looks like?"

In ninth grade we elected a king and queen for our end of the year school dance. My friends and I voted for John, a handsome, popular, fun guy to be our king. But then, to poke fun at the girls in our class and to add some color to the occasion, we stuffed the ballot box with votes for Theresa, an overweight, unattractive wallflower of a girl.

Midway through the dance the chaperons stopped the music to announce the Class King and Queen. We clapped loud when John's name was announced. When Theresa was named Class Queen we roared with delight. Theresa, not knowing it was a joke, also jumped for joy, adding to our sick pleasure.

Then the lights dimmed, the slow music began, and a spotlight welcomed the traditional dance of the Class King and Queen. In that moment, John panicked. "Dance with Theresa? I'd never hear the end of it. I've got to save myself." And in a flash, John bolted for the exit and was not seen for the rest of the evening.

Even dumb ninth grade boys know when a joke has gone badly. We were stunned, frozen in time. Then out of the darkness stepped Chet, the handsome quarterback of the football team and one of the other nominees for Class King. Chet offered his hand to Theresa, led her into the spotlight, where they danced and talked like Cinderella and Prince Charming through several songs in the evening.

Theresa changed that night. She became happier and more confident. But a lot of us standing in the shadows changed that night too. We learned who the real king of our class was, and what a king looks like. We learned that the crown belongs on the head of those who worry less about saving themselves, and more about saving others.

"He saved others," they mocked, while Jesus continued to hang on the Cross. Despite what was happening to Him, Jesus' focus remained steadfast on God and others. "Father, forgive them, for they know not what they do." Instead of saving himself as they dared Him to do, He saved others.

However we interpret and apply the story of the Cross of Jesus, we all agree on this: Jesus died to save others. However we think of the mystery of His blood atoning for our sins, we agree that Jesus' laying down His life affects us, transforms us, calls us.

We hear the text, and once again see Him on the Cross, and suddenly "the veil in the Temple is torn from top to bottom," the heavens are opened, and we see: Caesar is not king; Herod is not King; Pilate, the religious leaders and soldiers don't rule the world. The One whose hands are strapped to the Cross is the One who is King of all. Jesus Christ is King. His love, shown finally and fully on the Cross, is the essence of life—our individual lives and the life of this world. In the end, the world is transformed by love alone. "He saved others," they said in derision. Truer words have never been spoken.

The question today is: has He saved you? Have you felt the love of God as it is made visible in the Crucified One come personally to you just as you are, to bless you, welcome you, and lift you up?

Hafiz, the 14th Century Sufi mystic and poet, writes of *The God Who Only Knows Four Words:*

> Every child has known God,
> Not the God of names,
> Not the God of don'ts,
> Not the God who ever does anything weird,
> But the God who only knows four words
> And keeps repeating them, saying:
> "Come dance with me."
> Come
> Dance.

No magic prayers make it happen. Just two simple words in response. "Yes. Thanks."

Paul Quenon

from *Holy Folly*

The religious life, whether clerical or lay, is not all pious seriousness. Humor, which is surely a divine gift that humans need to endure the vicissitudes of their lives, is as much a part of life lived inside a monastery as it is outside. Here is an excerpt from the diary kept by Brother Paul Quenon, one of the novices who studied under Father Louis, as Thomas Merton was known at the Abbey of Gethsemani. Brother Paul's diary is the first part of a three-part collection of light and serious writings by three monks, who, in addition to Brother Paul, are Brother Guerric Plante and Father Timothy Kelly, a former abbot at Gethsemani. Through Brother Paul's diary, *Holy Folly: Short and Tall Tales from the Abbey of Gethsemani* (1998), you can enjoy the drama and comedy of life inside the monastery without having to wear the monk's cowl.

⚮

January 4, 1984—

Some pipes broke last week in the vacated Retreat House, because it was left unheated. Today a pipe broke alongside the tunnel. Charlie Boon was called in to dig with his backhoe, which crouches like Behemoth the Dragon outside the entrance. The basement is filled with sulfuric fumes of sewer gas. Will the night be filled with phantoms?

⚮ ⚮ ⚮

January 6, 1984—

Brother Andrew, one of the cooks, tells me when things used to disappear from the ice box, they would always assume the culprit was Father Idesbald (now deceased). About age 80-going-on-14, he would take generously from the plates and trays prepared for others with their names on it. One day Brother Maurice, a cook, walked into the kitchen and found Father Idesbald peering into the refrigerator. Maurice gave him a swat on the rear. Idesbald grabbed a butcher knife and brandished it at Maurice. When Andrew walked into the kitchen, Maurice was backed up against the oven laughing uncontrollably.

⚮ ⚮ ⚮

January 7, 1984—

Jeff Fagenbush, a young temporary resident, has decided to give up his comic books. The inspiration came to him suddenly, during Mass, and he turned over the whole collection to Brother Anthony—a collection he has assembled over many years. In the world of comic book collectors, it would be worth much. Jeff was baptized the Sunday before Christmas. He has been at the monastery since early November. He lives in the vacated Retreat House, and works with Brother Ambrose in the kitchen, as well as in the Farms Building where cheese is packed.

Jeff is 23. He was kicked out of every year of school he attended since 6th grade, the year his father left home. He has been in prison, and now is a fugitive from the law. Brother Ambrose has been helping him and his older brother, John Joseph, for years, getting them out of trouble. Now he has them both baptized. The change in Jeff since coming here has been noticeable, although he still likes to wear tight patchy jeans.

So who has the comics? I do. I got them from Anthony. Now you know the worst about me.

John Joseph Fagenbush, the older brother of Jeff, came here first with his uncle, a truck driver. John did not have the faintest idea of what kind of a place a monastery might be. He had never even heard of the term. The sign at the entry gate particularly frightened him: NO ENTRANCE UNDER PAIN OF EXCOMMUNICATION. He had no idea what excommunication meant. All he knew is that it didn't sound good—like you might get shot. His uncle drove him up, opened the gate, backed up, then bolted forward at full roar past the threatening sign. John yelled: "Hey! this isn't funny anymore, stop!" and ducked beneath the dashboard.

They went to the cheese packaging to make the regular mail delivery. That is where John first met Ambrose. He began asking him questions, and when he asked what a monk is, Ambrose explained how the word comes from the Greek word *monos,* meaning alone. "Monks are called that because they live in solitude." John said: "You are not alone because you live with God." After that, Ambrose took real interest in John.

At Christmas time Ambrose sent him a Gethsemani Farms fruitcake, and invited him back. John did not respond. He said: "I figured all those monks are queer and someone was liable to grab me." His Grandma told him he ought to at least go back and thank Ambrose. He did. After that, the visits were more frequent, especially since there was livestock and things rare for a young man from the city.

Once Ambrose was called out to handle a neighbor's horse, that was in heat and particularly difficult to control. John, hearing new words, got them tangled up in describing the animal to two of our hired men from neighboring farms:

"Yes sir, that was a mean old stud-mare."

They howled and said: "I'd be mean too, if I was a stud-mare!"

At that time Jeff, John's brother, had blond hair down to his waist, and could not stand staying around the monastery more than 2 or 3 days.

Both of the Fagenbush boys seem devoted to their Grandma. She is a lovable person, who was the best influence they ever had. She says she can raise a garden as good as any man, smokes incessantly, and wheezes badly. She married three times, and can take care of herself. She will, by their account, use a skillet on the side of a man's head if she wants to.

It was thanks to her that John and Jeff were put in jail. They had robbed a liquor store, returned home and got drunk on the takings. Soon they got into a brawl, and Grandma called the police.

Her husband killed her son (the father of John and Jeff) in order to stop a fit of violence. Jeff thus witnessed the murder of his own dad. His father had been prevented from visiting his own children, and had become so irate that Grandma had to flee to a neighbor's. And when he tried to pursue her he was stopped with a shot in the back.

❧ ❧ ❧

One reason Ambrose is so devoted to the poor is that he was so poor himself. As a child of a Mexican family, he had lived in a house with a mud floor. All might have died of typhoid if a Baptist minister had not found them and helped them out. They were poor, but had dignity. When Ambrose's sister came back from the store one day with more money than she had gone with—the clerk had given the wrong change—their mother made her go back and return it, even though that was all the money they had in the house.

Ambrose will do almost anything to help the poor, including using the monastery's resources to do it—much to the chagrin of the Cellerar and Department Heads. One day the Cobbler found all the boots missing from the shoe shop. It took no time to guess where they might have gone. When approached, Ambrose answered: "Why should the monks be wearing $40 shoes when a family in the neighborhood has no shoes at all?"

The fact the boots would not fit the kids was of no consequence to him. He had them stuff paper in the toes and heels.

The electrician keeps his shop carefully locked against Ambrose, and speaks of him as "Robin Hood."

There was one time when it seemed to Ambrose we had too many toilets, and much to the dismay of the plumber, one disappeared from what is euphonically called The Grand Parlor. He had taken it to a poor neighbor who was building a new house.

Unfortunately for me because that particular toilet was my favorite. . . .

Evening. March 1, 1984

For the first time in the history of our monastery, a group of women ate in our community refectory. They were the Cistercian nuns, here for the Regional Meeting of the Order. I sat with Mother Miriam from Redwoods Monastery, who paused for a moment in the conversation because she wanted to absorb, she said, "the atmosphere of the place where so many monks for so many years ate and listened to the reading, laughed and performed public penance." (The refectory was scene for certain penances assigned for an offense, such as eating in the middle of the room, under the eyes of all, seated on a very low stool.)

During our meals a book is publicly read over the microphone. I told her the story of the time one of the innocent souls doing the reading from a biography of St. Jerome came upon the episode of Jerome's sexual temptations. The monk read a passage describing St. Jerome having a fantasy about being locked, he read, in a garden full of "courtesans," except that he pronounced it "Cartesians." Everyone was discreetly silent until one lone voice from the adjoining Infirmary Refectory let out a yelp of laughter. We all assumed it was Father Louis, for he ate in the Infirm Refectory. Father Louis however claimed it was Brother Fidelis. Brother Fidelis in turn claimed it was Father Louis.

                                                          ⌘ ⌘ ⌘

March 11, 1984—

Ambrose's friend, James Reed, went home today to Beaver Dam, Ky. In prison his name was Goober. He seemed sad to leave, he liked it here.

Yesterday at work in the kitchen he kept his leg propped up on a stool, and limped when he walked. I asked him what happened. He said he was walking along the road to New Haven, and some driver nearly knocked him off the road. Goober swore at him, and the guy stopped the car and got out to fight. He was drunk. The two got to tussling, and the man kicked Goober in the shins with his hard toe boot. In the end Goober, a rather short guy, got the better of him and had the man pinned down. The fellow got in his car and drove away. Goober hitched a ride to the monastery: "Strange neighborhood here!"

He seems such a gentle fellow. I'm sure he will be back.

                                                          ⌘ ⌘ ⌘

March 17, 1984—

For several weeks now Ambrose has been out of the leg cast, but is having much pain. He holds the tip of his tongue to his upper tooth when he takes a step.

He said James Reed phoned and said he has almost decided to become a monk. . . .

Jan. 2, 1987—

According to the Rule of St. Benedict, a monk has no claims of ownership over anything, not even over his own body. This was put to the test in a rather literal way for Father Matthew. This, by his own account, is what happened:

"I went to renew my drivers license in Bardstown. At the bottom of the sheet a question: 'Do you want to will your body to Science?'"

"I thought: Not a bad idea!"

"So I filled out the form. And forgot about it."

"Weeks later, in casual converse with the Abbot: 'By the way, I gave my body to Science.'"

"'No you didn't. You have no jurisdiction over your body.'"

"'The Loretto nuns (neighbors) do it. And any way, it's all done.'"

"'Well, go and undo it.'"

"So I had to go back to the woman and get my body back. 'I have no jurisdiction over it,' I told her." . . .

Conclusion

John Joseph Fagenbush lives a free life, sort of like a street monk. He takes part time jobs and works in soup kitchens, sleeps in a tent and travels about the country from one work pool to another. Last time I saw him he was cooling his feet in a public fountain in Louisville talking to an old man.

Jeff Fagenbush acquired a degree in electrical engineering in Texas, married and has two children. He works for a trucking firm in Colorado.

Brother Ambrose still works in the kitchen, but less frequently now, thanks to a relative temporarily employed in his place. He has slowed down but may in fact never die, and it is a mystery to the kitchen crew where he spends his time. Perhaps he is in solitude at the hermitage, or fixing it up, or fixing houses for poor neighbors, or maybe the hermitage is for one of the black, Mexican or a recovering drug addict, or he is getting a kid out of jail for stealing a car, or . . .

Abraham Flexner

from *I Remember*

Not everyone who has lived in Kentucky over the past two hundred years has been the stereotypical white, Christian male, yet, except for the slave narratives of antebellum Kentucky, few minority voices have been heard in our literature. In the mid-nineteenth century, large numbers of Irish, German, and Jewish immigrants began coming to America and to Kentucky. One of the best-known Jewish families in Louisville were the Flexners, who within a generation were producing sons and daughters who became leaders in their fields. Three sons of Morris and Esther Abraham Flexner, immigrants from Bohemia and Alsace, for example, were all born in Louisville: Simon in 1863, Bernard in 1865, and Abraham in 1866. Simon became a research pathologist and author. Bernard became a prominent lawyer, Zionist, and author. Abraham became a physician, medical school reformer, and author of an autobiography, *I Remember* (1940), from which the following excerpt is taken. He describes his mother's and his aunt's immigration to the United States in 1855 during the antiforeigner riots in Louisville. After a delay in New York, the two young women came to Louisville, where Abraham's mother met and married her husband, Morris Flexner.

About this time there had been antiforeign and anti-Masonic riots in Louisville, so that instead of going immediately to their uncle the two girls remained in New York with another relative, who was a tailor and who gladly welcomed them. Approximately a month later they went to Louisville, arriving there on October 15. They were very happy in those early days in Louisville, but they soon learned that in the Louisville of that time one must shift for oneself. Their uncle had a large wholesale and retail china establishment. Their aunt was an accomplished seamstress who made all the clothes required by her own family and often also made clothes for others. Very soon my mother undertook the housekeeping, while her sister became a seamstress. Toward spring, however, my mother decided that she too would become an earner in order that she might accumulate something for herself and likewise from time to time send helpful remittances to her family in the "old country." Her Paris training enabled her to become a seamstress in a somewhat fashionable cloak establishment, spending the whole day at work and being accompanied home by a nephew of the proprietor of the establishment. At their uncle's home they met many of the young Jewish merchants or peddlers, who used to spend the Jewish holidays and week ends in the large city. She felt a certain contempt because the clothes worn by the girls and women in Louisville were, from the standpoint of style and finish, so much inferior to what she had seen and worn in Paris. She did not remain a seamstress long. My father had been in the habit of making purchases of her uncle, and before the winter was over he and my mother became engaged. By this time my father felt himself almost a "rich man," to use my mother's words. They were married on September 13, 1856, and were in a position to equip a small house comfortably and tastefully. Much of the furniture which they purchased for their start in life still remains in our family. My mother was always proud of the fact that it never "went out of style."

I was born in 1866, the sixth of nine children—seven boys and two girls. After the panic of 1873 our living conditions had to be materially altered, but, although the successive houses in which we lived became for many years smaller and smaller and our way of living simpler and simpler, there was nothing either in the atmosphere or the appearance of the home to suggest the poverty and hardship in which we grew up. I am still at a loss to understand the courage and confidence with which my parents contemplated the future of their large family. I do not recall a single word of complaint. They did not bemoan their fate; never a word of bitterness or envy escaped either. It made no difference to them that others were more fortunate or successful. They had pitched their own ideals incredibly high, and no pressure of external circumstances, no temporary expedient to which they had to resort, such as putting the older boys to work to help support the family, ever lowered their aims even for the time being; nor did they lean on others. I marvel, as I look back, at their confidence and serenity. What spiritual force sustained them? Religion? Perhaps—certainly to some extent it was a source of comfort. But at bottom they, like other pioneers, relied on themselves. They faced facts, endured, clung to ideals, and acted fearlessly, persistently, confidently. "They can," as Virgil says, "because they think they can." Throughout this long and dreary period they instinctively dealt with their children in such wise as to develop both initiative and intimacy. At an early age, for example, we began to be affected by the rationalistic spirit of the time. Our parents remained to the end of their lives pious Hebrews, attending the synagogue regularly and observing religious feasts. They saw us drift away into streams of thought and feeling that they did not understand. They interposed no resistance. For us Herbert Spencer and Huxley, then at the height of their fame and influence, replaced the Bible and the prayer book; never a word of remonstrance, inquiry, or expostulation escaped our parents. They were shrewd enough to realize that their hold upon their children was strengthened by the fact that they held them with a loose rein. In consequence, we had no secrets from them. They knew where we were and where we were going, and they made our friends, from a world alien to them, welcome in our home and at our table. It did not trouble my mother later that two of her sons married Christian girls, who became not daughters-in-law, but daughters.

Even after my father's death, when the dark age became for almost fifteen years darker and darker, my mother quietly, resolutely, and without sentimentality persisted in the belief that somehow and some day the ambitions that she and my father had entertained would be realized, as indeed they were. To their joint purpose she clung quietly but fixedly. Despite humble origin and a difficult life, she was absolute mistress of herself, her family, and every situation which arose. As her children advanced in life she naturally met, both in Louisville and in the East, to which one by one her children drifted, people of far different background and way of living from that to which she had been accustomed, She manifested neither the slightest awkwardness nor self-consciousness, but preserved under all circumstances absolute simplicity and sincerity. It has always made us happy to know that she lived long enough to witness the successful working-out of the ideals which had governed her and my father. In my opinion, none of her children equaled her in respect to native endowment.

Alanna Nash

from *The Colonel*

Country music is a big business in Kentucky. Bill Monroe, Randy Atcher, John Jacob Niles, Loretta Lynn, Ricky Skaggs, Tom T. Hall, Pee Wee King—these are some of the Kentuckians who have made big names for themselves as composers and performers in country and folk music. Probably the most popular performer in this state, however, was a native of Tupelo, Mississippi, whose grandfather lived in Louisville. Yes, Elvis was—and still is—big in Kentucky. In 2003 Bobbie Ann Mason published a biography of Elvis. In the same year, Alanna Nash, who has made a big name for herself by writing about country music and musicians, published a biography of Colonel Parker, Elvis's manager, that is really about Elvis. After all, who would Colonel Parker have been without Elvis? This is Nash's dramatic account of Elvis's death—if you believe he's really dead.

On the sweltering evening of August 15, 1977, Elvis Presley slipped out of his blue silk lounging pajamas, and with the help of his cousin Billy Smith, climbed into a black sweat suit emblazoned with a Drug Enforcement Agency patch on the back, a white silk shirt, and a pair of black patent boots, which he wore unzipped due to the puffy buildup of fluid in his ankles.

At 10:30, after a night of motorcycle riding with girlfriend Ginger Alden, the singer stuffed two .45-caliber automatic pistols in the waistband of his sweatpants. Then he donned his blue-tinted, chrome sunglasses—custom-made, with the trademark "EP" spanning the bridge and the "TCB" logo on the earpieces, by California optician Dennis Roberts—to slide behind the wheel of his Stutz automobile. With Alden, Smith, and Smith's wife, Jo, in tow, Elvis steered his way to the office of his dentist, Dr. Lester Hofman, in East Memphis. A crown on Presley's back tooth needed fixing, and he wanted to tend to it before he left the following evening for Portland, Maine, the first date of a twelve-day tour.

When the couples returned to Graceland around midnight, Elvis and Ginger went upstairs, and the Smiths retired to their trailer on the property. Sometime around 2:00 A.M., Elvis spoke with Larry Geller. Geller recalls his friend was "in a very good mood, looking forward to the tour, and making plans for the future." Around 4:00 A.M., Elvis still felt energetic enough for a game of racquetball, and phoned Billy and Jo to join him and Ginger. As the foursome went out the back door and down the concrete walkway to Elvis's racquetball building, a light rain began to fall.

"Ain't no problem. I'll take care of it," Elvis said, and put out his hands as if to stop it. Miraculously, Smith remembers, the rain let up. "See, I told you," Elvis said. "If you've got a little faith, you can stop the rain."

Despite his sudden burst of energy, Elvis was exhausted from several days of a Jell-O diet, the latest in a series of desperate attempts to trim him down enough to fit into his stage costumes. He tired quickly on the court, and the couples resorted more to cutting up than concentrating on their game, mostly swatting each other with the ball. After ten minutes, they took a break, then returned to the court. But they quit a second time when Elvis misjudged a serve and hit himself hard in the shin with his racquet.

Limping into the lounge, Presley fixed himself a glass of ice water and then moved to the piano and began singing softly, ending with "Blue Eyes Crying in the Rain."

Afterward, upstairs in the house, Smith washed and dried his cousin's hair. As they talked, Presley again obsessed about *Elvis: What Happened?*, which had hit the bookstores two weeks before. Yelling wildly, out of his head, Elvis fumed he'd bring Red, Sonny, and Dave Hebler to Graceland, where he'd kill them himself and dispose of their bodies. Then his mood dimmed, and he rehearsed a speech he planned to give from the stage if his fans, shocked to learn their idol spent $1 million a year on drugs and doctors, turned on him in concert. "They've never beat me before," he said, "and they won't beat me now." Billy knew what he meant: "Even if I have to get up there and admit to everything."

Numb, frightened, and weary from dread, he cried pitifully, shaking. Billy petted him, cooed baby talk to him. "It's okay," Billy soothed. "It's going to be all right." As Smith went out the door, Elvis, the cousin who was more like a big brother, turned to him. "Billy . . . son . . . this is going to be my best tour ever." At 7:45 A.M., the singer took his second "attack packet" of four or five sleeping pills within two hours. The third would come shortly afterward. He'd had no food since the day before.

Sometime around 8:00 A.M., Elvis climbed in bed with Ginger. As she recalled, she awakened in the tomblike room—always kept at a chilly sixty degrees—to find her aging boyfriend too keyed up to sleep, preoccupied with the tour. "Precious," he said, "I'm going to go in the bathroom and read for a while." Ginger stirred. "Okay, but don't fall asleep."

"Don't worry," he called back. "I won't."

Behind the bathroom door, Elvis picked up *A Scientific Search for the Face of Jesus,* a book about the Shroud of Turin, and waited for his pharmaceutical escort to slumber.

As Elvis's day was ending in Memphis, the Colonel's was already in full swing in Portland, the big man holed up in the Dunfey Sheraton and riding herd on Tom Hulett, Lamar Fike, George Parkhill, and Tom Diskin to oversee every detail of Elvis's two-day engagement there. Fike had flown in from Los Angeles on the red-eye and immediately went to work setting up the security and arranging the hotel rooms for the band and crew. Then he grabbed a quick bite to eat and went to bed.

Just before noon, Billy Smith walked over to Graceland and spoke with entourage member Al Strada, who was packing Elvis's wardrobe cases. Smith inquired as to whether anyone had seen the boss. Al said no, that Elvis wasn't to be awakened until 4:00 P.M. Billy wondered aloud if one of the Stanley brothers had checked on Elvis and started up the stairs to do so himself. No, if they ain't heard from him, God, let him rest, he thought. He needs it.

At 2:20 in the afternoon, Ginger turned over in Elvis's huge bed and found it empty. Had he never come back to sleep? She noticed his reading light was still on and thought it odd. Ginger knocked on the bathroom door. "Elvis, honey?" No response. She turned the knob and went inside. Elvis was slumped on the floor, angled slightly to the left. He was on his knees, his hands beneath his face, in a near praying position, his silk pajama bottoms bunched at his feet. Inexplicably, he had fallen off the toilet and somehow twisted himself into the grotesque form. But why hadn't he answered? Ginger called again. "Elvis?" He laid so still, so unnaturally still.

Now Ginger bent down to touch him. He was cold, his swollen face buried in the red shag carpet, blood dotting the nostrils of his flattened nose, his tongue, nearly severed in two, protruding from clenched teeth. His skin was mottled purple-black. She forced open an eye. A cloudy blue pupil stared back at her lifelessly.

Elvis Presley was dead at the age of forty-two.

Wade Hall

from *The Rest of the Dream:*
The Black Odyssey of Lyman Johnson

The abolition of slavery in 1863 and 1865 did not make the freedmen and freed-women full citizens of the United States. It took another hundred years for full equality to become the law of the land. Two of Louisville's prominent African American leaders after World War II were Lyman Tefft Johnson and Mae Street Kidd. Both were subjects of oral biographies that I wrote with their cooperation in the 1980s and 1990s. Johnson was born in 1906 in Columbia, Tennessee, where his father was principal of the local school for blacks and one of the best-educated men in Columbia, black or white. After earning undergraduate and graduate degrees in history from Virginia Union University and the University of Michigan, Johnson came to Louisville in 1933 and began a thirty-three-year career at all-black Central High School. Almost immediately he began to fight for equal rights, and in 1949 he was the plaintiff in the lawsuit that opened the University of Kentucky to African Americans. In 1979 the university that fought to keep him out awarded him an honorary doctor of letters degree. He died in Louisville in 1997. In the following passage Dr. Johnson tells how his grandfather obtained his freedom and his wife's freedom before the Civil War.

My father's father was a carpenter and a slave. He never learned to read or write, but he was an excellent carpenter so he must have known how to figure. He had to have a lot of native ability to pick up a trade like that and excel in it. People could tell him what they wanted built, and he could build it. He was a smart man—smart enough to buy himself out of slavery.

He did such good work that his master hired him out to work for other people repairing and building houses. When the master got paid for my grandfather's work, he would sometimes share part of it with him to keep his incentive up. My grandfather quietly saved what he was given. Of course, he didn't have access to banks, so he must have hidden it in little cans under the apple trees or some place like that. One day, apparently kidding his master, he must have said: "Massa, would you sell me? If somebody offered you a good price, would you sell me?" The master said, "Oh, yeah." My grandfather said: "I thought you liked me. I didn't think you'd sell me." The master said: "Oh, yes I would. If the price was right, you'd go like all the rest of my slaves. But don't worry right now. As long as you satisfy the people you're working for and as long as you behave yourself, I won't put you on the block."

My grandfather brought up the subject several times, and finally the master admitted that if anybody offered him $1,300 he would sell him. This was around 1849. One day my grandfather walked in and said to the master, "There's a fellow I know that wants to buy me." The master said, "Well, tell him to send me $1,300 and he can have you." My grandfather was all set. In a few days, he came to the master and said, "That man I told you about that wants to buy me, well, he sent you $1,300." So he counted out $1,300 that he'd picked up out of those cans under those trees. The master took his money and said: "Well, if he trusted you with this much money, I'll trust you to go on over there and turn yourself in to him. You're through here. Get going." "Yes sir," my newly freed grandfather said, "but the man said he'd like to have a receipt." So the white man sat down to write a receipt. He looked up at the freedman. "Now, whose name do I put down as your new owner?" My grandfather said, "Put down 'Dyer Johnson!'" The man started to write it down, then looked up suddenly and said, "But that's you." "That's right," Grandfather said. "Put *my* name down as my new owner!" So the slaveowner said, "Well, I said I'd sell you for $1,300 and so I will." He wrote "I sell Dyer Johnson to Dyer Johnson" and signed his name. My grandfather reached down for the document and was a free man from then on.

But he wasn't finished with his buying. Three or four years later he bought his wife, my grandmother, whom he had married while he was a slave. After he became a free man, he wasn't allowed to see his wife. Slaveholders were suspicious of free blacks. I imagine Grandmother's owner said to him: "Don't you come around here any more. You're a free man, and you might give my other slaves screwy ideas about freedom. You'd bother them." Grandfather said: "But you let me marry Betty. She's my wife." Her owner said: "Yeah, but she's still a slave. She's still my property. I can't let her off the place. Don't come back to see her." Finally, however, he talked her owner into selling her to him. Before he could claim her, the agreement was that he had to buy a little piece of property and build a house on it. Within a year he had bought some ground and built a one-room log cabin. That cabin is still standing. It's part of the house I was born in and grew up in.

So Grandfather bought Grandmother from her mistress and took her to live in that log cabin—both of them free people of color more than ten years before the Civil War freed all the slaves. They were impatient to be free. They couldn't wait. Maybe that's where I got my own sense of justice, my own impatience with the law's long delay. Because my grandmother was an invalid, my grandfather bought her cheap—for only $300. The bill of sale does not warrant that she is sound of body. This is the way it reads.

State of Tennessee. Maury County. Know all men by these presents that I, Nancy White, of the state and county aforesaid have this day sold and do hereby convey to Dyer Johnson, a free man of color, to his heirs and assigns forever for the sum of $300 to me paid one Negro slave named Betty, age about thirty years, of mulatto color. I warrant the title of said slave to said Dyer Johnson, his heirs and assigns against the lawful claims of all persons but I do not warrant the said slave Betty to be a healthy and sound woman. May 10, 1852. My hand and seal. Nancy White.

Below this she drew a little seal and wrote in the middle of it "seal." The sale is attested to by somebody named I.B. Hamilton and W. Watson. They were the witnesses. It was important that Grandfather have this bill of sale. Technically, she was still a slave. The bill of sale simply transferred her ownership to another person who happened to be her husband and my grandfather. She was legally a slave till she was freed by the Thirteenth Amendment to the Constitution. Till then, anyone owning this document could have legally sold her.

I imagine my grandfather must have kidded her about how cheap she was. He had cost $1,300 while she had cost only $300. Despite the refusal of her owner to warrant that she was "a healthy or sound woman," she was quite a bargain! She lived to be almost eighty and had three healthy children. Her daughter lived to be eighty-three, and her two sons reached ninety and ninety-two.

How do I feel about this piece of paper in my hands? How do I feel about the fact that my grandparents—on both sides—were slaves? My mama and papa taught me that a person should never be ashamed of where he comes from. It's not my fault that my grandparents were slaves. I make no apology for it to anybody. It's the other side that should be apologizing. I tell other black people not to pity themselves because they once were slaves. "Many whites were slaves too," I say. "In the days of ancient Rome, many Greek scholars were enslaved by Roman generals who would take them to Rome to teach their children. So don't feel sorry for yourself. White intellectuals once were slaves to their inferiors." So I remind black people that Rome was a drop down from the Greeks in culture. But when Caesar got to England and saw those little stringy-haired, blond, pale-faced English children, he almost cried to see how backward they were. "It is a disgrace that these children are so dirty and dumb," he said. I tell black people that history makes the whole racial eugenics argument absurd—the idea that black people are inferior because they can't help it.

Slavery, of course, wherever and whenever it existed, was an evil. But

American slavery was a compounded evil because it was based almost exclusively on race. In other parts of the world, slavery was not racial. The Arabs took black and white slaves. Indentured servants in early America lived almost in slavery, but they were at least term slaves. They agreed to serve a man for a period of time, usually seven years, in return for passage to America and maybe other considerations. On the other hand, to be a life slave in this country was to be black. The life of a white indentured servant was often not any better than that of a black slave. Sometimes their indenture was arbitrarily extended by their masters on some flimsy excuse. Then when they were old and worthless, they would be thrown out. Nevertheless, their children weren't handicapped by a black face. It's taken a long time to get Negroes themselves to believe that they are not inferior simply because they are Negroes. That is the legacy of slavery in this country.

Fortunately, my grandfather and grandmother didn't let their black faces discourage them. They set an example for my father, who then set an example for my generation. Grandpapa worked hard to make a good life for his wife and their three children born after she left the plantation. But when he died in 1873, he had nothing to leave them, except that one-room cabin and the ground it was on. I never knew what made Grandmother Johnson an invalid. I was told it was a frailness, but I never heard its source.

So Dyer Johnson died and left an invalid wife, three children ten to thirteen years old, and whatever was in that cabin. They had no Social Security, no food stamps, no retirement funds. The children were too young to do steady work, and Grandmother was unable to. They were in utter, dire poverty. I'm sure they scratched around in the dirt and grew what vegetables they could. Maybe they had chickens and a milk cow. Neighbors—black and white—helped too. They would come by and leave little sacks of food. "Here, Aunt Betty," they'd say, "here's a little something to cook." And they'd give her a handful of sweet potatoes or beans or collard greens, whatever they had to spare. She'd cook whatever she had and whatever she was given, and she and the three children would sit around the table and eat till it was gone. It usually wasn't very much. Then she'd say: "Children, that's all we have today. Now, go on out, but don't tell anybody you're hungry."

When my Uncle Will was about twelve, he got a job as a handy boy in a wholesale grocery store. He swept the floors, helped move the goods around, and stocked the shelves. He'd go to work right after school and would work till closing time. He and the owner were usually the last two people to leave the place at night. As they left, the man would say: "Well, Will, we put in a good day today. You've done a good job. Now, Will, what do you think Aunt Betty wants for tomorrow?" Uncle Will would say, "Mr. Sloane, Mama says can you spare a little piece of bacon?" Mr. Sloane would say, "Yes, Will, and you tell Aunt Betty how much we think of her and hope she's feeling better." All the time he'd be getting out his big butcher knife and reaching up and cutting off a little slab of bacon. And that was Uncle Will's pay for the day. The next day they'd go through the same little act. Mr. Sloane would say: "Will, you did a nice job today. Tell your mother what a good workman you are. What does Aunt Betty want tomorrow?" And Uncle Will might say, "Mama wants to know could you spare a few beans?" And the white man would get out a little bag and put some beans in it, and that would be Uncle Will's pay for that day. In that way Uncle Will provided the main foodstuffs for the family—a little meal, a little flour, some beans, a piece of bacon.

Uncle Will was the youngest of the three children—two years younger than my papa—but he could do more hard work than Papa. As a boy father was kind of frail, though he eventually grew more vigorous. Uncle Will was the mainstay of the family. A white man out in the country furnished him a mule, a plow, a wagon, the seed cane, fertilizer, and the land. My uncle furnished the labor, and when the cane was cut, they split it in half. That was usually the way sharecropping worked. The cane crop was big that year, and it was backbreaking work. My papa helped with some of the labor, but he couldn't do much or he would be laid up for weeks. Uncle Will wouldn't let his mother or sister help. "You can't go to the fields," he'd say. "That isn't your place." So my uncle raised the sorghum, cut it, and hauled it to the mill. He was a man who had muscle *and* brains. But for the grace of God he might have stayed a sharecropper all his life. He might never have bloomed out.

But he had brains, and they helped take him to college. This is how he got there. Uncle Will's share of the syrup made from the sorghum crop was one-fourth. He had given one-half of the cane to the landowner. Then he took his half to the sorghum syrup mill and had it squeezed and the juice cooked down until it became molasses. Then he had to give half of the syrup to the mill owner. So he wound up with a fourth of the original crop. Still it was a lot more than he, his mother and brother and sister could eat at home. So he started to college on the excess.

In those days it was about forty-eight miles from Columbia to Nashville on an old dirt road. I imagine Uncle Will hitchhiked to Nashville by wagon. There were buggies on the road too, but I don't think anybody in a buggy would have picked him up. He probably hitched a ride on a wagon being sent to Nashville to pick up supplies. One more little Negro boy on a supply wagon wouldn't have overloaded the mules. So Uncle Will arrived at Roger Williams University in Nashville, one of those schools set up in the South by northern churches after the Civil War to educate the freedman and his children.

When he got to the campus, he went to the president's office and said, "Professor, I want to go to school, but I don't have anything but molasses."

Uncle Will must have had rags on his back, but he had a beautiful countenance and light shining through his eyes. The president didn't know whether he was naive or just bold, but he was apparently impressed with the young man before him. And he said: "You are the kind of person we want here at Roger Williams. I think we can find enough money to take care of you." And that poor country boy who could only offer a few gallons of molasses to pay his tuition and board went to college—and finally became a college president. That story has been in the recesses of my mind a long time. It's one I've wanted to unload on blacks and whites. Young men like Booker T. Washington and my Uncle Will rewarded those dedicated teachers who came down from the North to teach the illiterate freed slave and his children. And such rewards they were—the awakening of a whole race of people!

I don't know how many buckets of molasses got transferred from Columbia to Nashville to pay Uncle Will's expenses. But I do know he got a good education at Roger Williams, good enough that Brown University validated his work there and took him into graduate school. He later returned to teach at Roger Williams and was president when the school folded about 1915. At that time one of his former students, who was president of Morehouse, said: "Professor Johnson, I want you to move down here to Atlanta and teach our students. I've worked under you. Now would you mind if we turned things around and have you work for me?" My uncle taught there till he retired and moved back to Columbia to live out his remaining years with his brother, my father. He lived to be ninety-two. When I was growing up, he was always a glamorous somebody to me. He never married. He'd say: "I don't need any children. My brother and sister have so many they can't feed and clothe and educate them all, so I'll just adopt some of them." And he did a marvelous job of helping us all.

Uncle Will was an inspiration to me. I could sit for hours and listen to him tell stories about his life. One story he told me the last year of his life shows how much he loved his mother. One time she whipped him for something he didn't do. Something went wrong, he said, and his mother satisfied herself that neither of the other children had been responsible. So she called Will in and said, "Now, Willie, you know you did it." He said, "No, Mama, I didn't do it." She said: "Willie, it has to be you. You must be lying, and I will not tolerate lying from one of my children." They went round and round for a few minutes. She accused him, and he denied it. Again and again. The more she accused and he denied, the more convinced she became that she was right. Finally, she said: "All right, Willie, I'm not going to punish you for doing it, but I am going to punish you for lying about it. Hand me that switch over there. I'm going to whip you for lying." Uncle Will said he handed her the switch, but she was so frail she could hardly raise it up, and when she brought it across his backsides, he could hardly feel it. But just to give her satisfaction he pretended he was being hurt. "Even though I was innocent," he said, "I would never reject her effort to straighten me out. So I stood there and she switched—or tried to switch—me good for something I never did."

Grandmama Johnson did her best not only to feed and clothe but to educate her children. She sent them to school in the Baptist church her husband, my grandpapa, had given the land for. It was next door—just across the fence—from where they lived. When it got lunch time, the other little children sat on benches in the yard and ate lunches they brought from home. But Grandmama told her children: "Now, don't stand around when the other children start to eat. You get over that fence and come home. If I've got anything to eat, we'll eat it together. If I don't have anything, we'll all just sit here till the lunch period is over. I don't want you hanging around and begging for something to eat. And when you go back to school, don't tell anybody you're hungry. Just say you went home to eat because you live so close."

The little Negro children went to school in that church on weekdays. The teacher was one of my papa's older cousins named Edmund Kelly. He had been born a slave but had run away, and the underground railroad had got him all the way to Massachusetts. He was found to be a brilliant fellow, and the people there gave him a first-class education. About six years after slavery ended, he came back down to Columbia to live with his kinpeople and to teach in that little school in the Baptist church. The facilities were improvised and primitive. The little children sat on the bare church benches. But that didn't matter. It was a school—the first one for black children in that town. And Edmund Kelly was a dedicated teacher. It must have been ironic and aggravating to the white people who had known him when he was a slave. He came back talking with a northern accent. After ten years in northern schools taught by teachers motivated by the zeal of religion, he was speaking correct grammar, pronouncing his words correctly, putting "r's" in his words, and teaching Negroes right out of slavery to do the same thing. He didn't get any regular pay. He got whatever handouts the black parents could afford. He did what he did out of a love for his people. He is one of the unknown heroes of American history.

from *Passing for Black: The Life and Careers of Mae Street Kidd*

Mae Street Kidd was a sassy, no-nonsense, independent woman who was always dressed and groomed as if she were on her way to church. She was born in 1904 in Millersburg to a white father, Charles Robert Jones, and an African American mother, Anna Belle Leer. She attended the Lincoln Institute in Simpsonville; then, at twenty-one, she moved to Louisville to work for the black-owned and -operated Mammoth Life Insurance Company. During World War II she served in England with the American Red Cross. From the mid-sixties to the mid-eighties, she served as a Democrat in the Kentucky General Assembly, where she spearheaded several landmark bills, including Kentucky's official ratification of the Thirteenth, Fourteenth, and Fifteenth Amendments to the U.S. Constitution, which freed the slaves and gave them their citizenship rights. She died in 1999 in Louisville. In the passages below from *Passing for Black: The Life and Careers of Mae Street Kidd* (1997), she recalls her childhood in Millersburg, her parents, her resistance to segregated transportation, and how she lived her life as an almost-white woman.

⚬❈⚬

When my mother was about twenty-four years old, she married a black man named James William Taylor. I was two years old and my brother George William was four. He was the finest stepfather I could hope for. Everyone called him Willie but me. I called him Wowley, the name I called him when I was a baby. He called me Sister and was very fond of me. I think he called me Sister because that's what he wanted his own children to call me. He considered me his own daughter, but he never tried to boss me. He was gentle with all of us. Sometimes he would speak sternly to us, but he never whipped us. He left that up to Mother. Of course, she would have done that anyway. He let Mother raise me her way and never interfered when she was reprimanding me. He was a wonderful man, always a gentleman. He was easy to get along with and did whatever Mother wanted to do. I never heard them argue or fight. He was a man of few words. He sometimes liked a little bourbon, but I never saw him drunk or violent. He was a trustee of the CME Church and became a thirty-second degree Mason.

He and my mother worked hard to provide for our family. He and another man leased some land and had a ten-acre tobacco base. Tobacco was his cash crop, and that's what we lived on. When he got older, he stopped his tobacco farming and started a chicken business. He raised them in large brooders where their feet never touched the ground. When they got big enough to eat, he and Mother would kill and dress the chickens for customers. People would call in their orders for so many chickens, and when they arrived, the chickens would be dressed and ready to go.

We were a family that provided for ourselves, and we raised most of what we ate. Mother was an industrious woman and a wonderful homemaker. We had chickens for eating and for eggs. We raised our own hogs and killed them when it got cold and we could keep the meat from spoiling by salting it down or smoking it. We ate vegetables out of our garden for half a year, and in the winter we ate what Mother had canned and preserved. About the only foods we bought at the grocery store were flour, sugar, coffee, and salt. Mother was also a very good quilter. In the wintertime I used to help her piece quilt tops by the fireplace. Then we put up the quilting frame, and with the help of her mother-in-law, we made each top into a quilt by sewing them to a backing with a cotton batting in between. I still have some of her beautiful quilts, and they are treasures. Since I've become almost blind, I'm afraid people will steal from me; so when my sister was here the last time, I told her to take my favorite one, called the Double Wedding Ring.

My mother and my stepfather's mother were very good friends. They lived close to our house in Shippsville, and we did a lot of things together—quilting and preserving and cooking. Mrs. Taylor lived in an old frame house with lots of land around it. We were a family-oriented people and often ate dinner and supper with each other. We didn't entertain friends very much but were always having family gatherings, especially at Thanksgiving and Christmas. My stepfather and my mother owned jointly the house we lived in. She had her own income but shared it with him when he was short.

I was already in school when my half brother, Webster Demetrius Taylor, and half sister, Mary Evelyn Taylor, came along. I think they were a surprise to Mother because she was forty-two when Demetrius was born and forty-three when Mary Evelyn was born. As I have said, we all considered ourselves one family, even though my brother George and I carried our father's name of Jones. It was not unusual in those days for the children of a white father and a colored mother to take the father's name and be acknowledged in the community. Of course, we were not taken into our father's home and raised as his legitimate children, but everyone knew who we were.

Now I'm getting into a murky area that I don't know much about. People did not talk about matters of sex and children of mixed relationships. My mother never, ever mentioned my father. Of course, when I got up some size I was curious about my real father, but I never asked her about it. It wasn't considered any of my business. I do know, however, that my mother was born on a farm in Harrison County, which adjoined Bourbon County. It may have been a farm owned by my father's family, and she may have worked in the house as a cook or maid. Now I'm speculating because I don't know anything for sure, but she and my father may have gotten to know each other because they both were growing up on the same farm—she as a black servant girl and he as the rich white farmer's son. Look at the situation. She was a very pretty girl, almost white. He was a good-looking young white boy. White men liked to seduce pretty colored girls. That's why we had so many beautiful, light-skinned Negro children in Millersburg. Maybe one day she noticed him and he noticed her. You can guess what happened. A young colored servant girl did whatever the white boss, or the white boss's son, said. Maybe as time went on they fell in love. I believe they did because they had two children, and their relationship must have continued for a number of years—else my mother would have married before she did. They both knew from the beginning that he *couldn't* marry her. She surely knew that even if he could, he *wouldn't* marry her. After all, he was from a rich, land-owning family, and it would have destroyed his future. Mixed-race marriages were not possible, according to the law or the custom. The custom was that white men seduced young women of color, and sometimes the two young people were deeply in love. Sometimes their relationships continued for a long time, sometimes throughout their lives. It was very common. When you're young and in love, you don't worry about society's prejudices and laws. Who knows? Their relationship may have continued for a long, long time—maybe after he married a white woman and after she married a black man. We do know that it lasted long enough for two children—my brother George and me—to be born.

Nobody in my family ever mentioned my father to me. The situation that my family and I were in was considered just as natural as the trees around our house. They were just there, and I never asked who planted them or where they came from. What little knowledge I had of my father and his family came from older women of color. I'd be at somebody's house and we'd be talking—a little girl and an older woman—and she'd say, "Mae, I do declare you're just like your grandmother Elizabeth Jones. You look like her. You act like her. You even put powder and rouge on your face like her." I grew up knowing not to ask my mother or my stepfather about my real father. Nothing was ever said by either one of them about it. Indeed, I don't think it bothered Mr. Taylor that my mother had two children by a white man before he married her. It was not that uncommon. And what could he have done anyway?

I'm hesitant to talk about my blood father because light people of color like me are sometimes accused of bragging about their white blood. I had nothing to do with my racial makeup. I didn't choose my mother or my father. I know almost nothing about my father, except that he was a white farmer from Harrison County, Kentucky, and his name was Charles Robert Jones. That much is on my birth certificate. I do know that he eventually married a white woman and had another set of children by her, and they and their mother used to come visit my mother, who was very friendly with his white family. But I never wanted anything to do with them. I was hurt that he couldn't or wouldn't acknowledge me openly as his daughter. It was a painful part of my childhood, but I got over it.

I only saw my father one time. It was after I was grown and living in Louisville. I was visiting my mother in Millersburg and was in the post office when he came in. A friend who was with me said, "Mae, see that white man over there at the counter? That's your father." I looked over at him but didn't say anything. He made no move to speak to me, and I didn't speak to him. He left the post office and then came back in almost immediately. Again, he looked over in my direction but didn't say anything. He stood without moving for a minute or two, then left again. I believe he recognized me and came back in to take a second look at his daughter. No, I wasn't resentful that my own father didn't speak to me. At that point in my life, I didn't give a damn! It was too late to make a difference to me. I remember that everyone in my father's family was crazy about my brother George. They provided some support for him and recognized him as a member of the family among themselves. It is possible, of course, that my father gave my mother some money for my support, but if he did, she never told me. All I know is that my father never made an effort to get to know me, and I never tried to get to know him. I was never interested in becoming friendly with any of my father's people. I didn't care anything about them. I didn't hate them. I had no feelings about them at all. For me, they simply didn't—and don't—exist. . . .

It should be apparent if you've listened to me thus far that I am not one to be shoved around. I stand up for what is right. In my articles, in my speeches, in my business and professional work, in my political career—in all my activities I have been a supporter of equal rights for all. My civil rights work has taken the form of words. I have spoken in schools, churches, and clubs trying to get people to register to vote. I pushed for equal rights in the Kentucky General Assembly. As a businesswoman I expected fair treatment and said so, even though I didn't usually receive it. But perhaps my most important service to my sex and to my race is my life, which I have tried to live as an example of what a black person could achieve—not just any black person—but a black woman from a modest background who had to pull herself up.

Let me give you a few examples of how I refused to accept second-class citizenship. I don't intentionally put myself in a position where someone can insult me. On the other hand, I'm not going to be subservient to anyone. If I have to set you straight, I'll do it in a rational, intelligent way. I don't go around ranting and raving. Before my brother Webster Taylor and I went overseas during World War II—he was with a black Signal Corps unit and I was with the American Red Cross—we decided to visit our mother in Kentucky. He met me in Washington, where I was preparing for my work overseas, and we boarded a train. Webster and I were comfortably seated in a Jim Crow car as was the custom. Webster was dark brown and I was light enough to pass for white. Soon after the train pulled out of the station, the conductor came up to me and said, "Young lady, you'll have to move to another coach." I looked at him, said nothing, and resumed talking with my brother.

About an hour later, while we were passing through Virginia, the conductor came back and said, "Lady, I'm sorry to have to disturb you, but you're going to have to move to another coach." I looked him squarely in the eye and said, "Please leave me alone. I'm comfortable where I am." I knew, of course, that he assumed I was white and had gotten on the black coach by mistake. I didn't budge from my seat. I didn't offer him an explanation. He must have given up because he never bothered me again, and I rode with my brother until our trip ended in Millersburg. That's the way I took my stand.

Sometimes it's almost funny the way the subject of my race comes up. One day when I was in the hospital after my stroke, a nurse said, "Mrs. Kidd, are you mixed up?" She was embarrassed because she didn't quite know how to say it. I knew what she meant, but I said, "Mixed up about what, honey?" Another nurse said, "Oh, Mrs. Kidd, what she means is 'Do you have white blood in you?'" I laughed and said, "I think the question is 'Do you have black blood in you?'" Then I went on and told her I was of mixed blood. She certainly embarrassed herself more than she embarrassed me.

Even people who should know better have questioned my color preference. One afternoon near the end of my lunch break at Mammoth, I was in downtown Louisville on Fourth Street window shopping. I happened to pass two black schoolteachers I knew very well, and I spoke to them. Neither one answered. I was a very sensitive young woman, and their snub hurt me, so I walked up to them and said, "I spoke to you ladies and you didn't say anything. Didn't you hear me? Is something wrong?" One of them said, almost in a whisper, "Oh we thought you were passing." I said, "Passing? Passing? Passing for what?" She said, "Oh, you know—passing for white." I said, "Ladies, noooooo, I'm not trying to pass for white. If anything, I've been passing for black all my life because I'm almost 90 percent white." I believe they really thought I was trying to pass for white and that made them angry, and they intentionally snubbed me because they were darker than me. They didn't have the option they assumed I had. It's so very obvious that I'm so much whiter than I am black that I have to pretend to be black. But I can truly say I've never been ashamed of my mother's blood that made me legally a Negro. I loved her so much I didn't care what kind of blood she had or what kind of blood she gave me. I would never have turned my back on my dear mother. I remember an old movie from the fifties called *Imitation of Life*. It's about a young light-skinned woman named Sarah Jane, who rejects her black mother and passes for white. I cannot imagine doing a thing like that to my mother. I'm proud to be who she made me—a person of mixed blood who happens to be mostly white. When people ask me what I am, I say, "American." That's all I need to say.

Anne McCarty Braden

from *The Wall Between*

Black people were always in the forefront of the battles that freed them and later earned them their citizenship rights. From William Lloyd Garrison and John Brown to the Louisville journalists and civil libertarians Carl and Anne McCarty Braden, however, many white people of conscience and goodwill have been their able supporters. In 1954 the Bradens sought to enable a black couple to live in an all-white neighborhood in Shively, a Louisville suburb, by buying a house on their behalf. The house was dynamited. The Bradens were accused of being Communists and became pariahs in their hometown. Carl Braden was indicted for sedition and jailed. Anne Braden, who was born in Louisville in 1924 and grew up Anniston, Alabama, chronicled their struggles to help tear down the remaining walls of segregation in Louisville in her highly acclaimed memoir, *The Wall Between* (1958). In the excerpt below she reconstructs their decision to become involved in the struggle against segregated housing.

It was on a beautiful spring day in 1954 that this story begins—one of those days in early March when the earth throbs with the promise of new life and it is hard to believe that all is not right with the world.

I had been to town and my husband, Carl, had stayed home to take care of our two children, Jimmy, two and a half, and Anita, a year old, and to wait for a friend, Andrew Wade, who had called the day before to say he was coming by to see us.

When I came in, Carl followed me into the kitchen where I was putting groceries away.

"Darling," he said cheerfully, "we're going to buy a house."

I stopped dead in my tracks. We had bought the house we were living in only two years before and had paid no more than a few hundred dollars on the $6,500 mortgage. Carl's salary as a newspaperman was adequate for our needs, but we rarely had any money left after living expenses were paid, and our savings were practically nil. A new house at this point was utterly fantastic.

"Buy a house?" I exclaimed. "Oh, Carl!"

"Sure," he insisted. "Don't you want to?"

"What are you talking about, Carl?" I asked. "We can't buy another house, and anyway I like this house." The house we lived in was a small four-room cottage, and it had been a little crowded since Anita's arrival over a year before. In addition to our own children our family included Sonia, Carl's sixteen-year-old daughter by a previous marriage. But at that very moment we were in the process of converting the unfinished attic into two more rooms. It seemed to me this would make the house quite sufficient for our family and even for the new baby we were hoping would soon be on the way.

"But this house will be in the country," Carl went on, his eyes twinkling. "Wouldn't you like that?"

I looked at him in confusion, and he evidently realized he had joked long enough. His face suddenly became serious.

"No," he explained. "Andrew Wade wants us to buy a house and transfer it to him. He'll put up the money for the down payment of course."

Immediately I understood. Andrew Wade was a Negro. We were white. Louisville was a segregated town—a town of unspoken restrictive covenants long after restrictive covenants had been declared non-enforceable by the Supreme Court of the United States.

"What's the problem?" I asked. I knew the answer. The question was almost rhetorical.

"He's been looking for a house for months," Carl said. "He's got a little girl two years old—just Jimmy's age—and his wife is pregnant. They've been renting a little apartment and they're crowded up. He's looked all over the Jim Crow sections and there just aren't any new houses for sale. They haven't built any new houses for Negroes here to amount to anything since the war. He could get an old house, but that's not what he wants. And anyway the down payment on those old houses is too much, and he doesn't have much money saved. His wife has her heart set on a new little ranch-type house out in a suburb. There are hundreds of them going up in all directions from town, you know. He's tried to buy several of them, but every time when they find out it's a Negro negotiating for the house, the deal gets squashed. He's got a real problem. He wants us to help him." Carl's face was quite serious now.

"What did you tell him?" I asked.

"I told him of course we would," Carl replied. "But he said for me to talk it over with you and he'd come back tomorrow to get a final answer. He didn't believe me when I told him I could speak for you too because I knew what your answer would be. But I did know."

I smiled. Of course Carl knew what my answer would be. We had been married six years, and there was no doubt in the mind of either of us as to where the other stood on this question. Never had either of us refused to act when someone asked us to help in any effort to break down segregation. These were things that were understood between us. They needed no discussion.

"Of course you knew," I said. "He didn't need to come back for an answer."

That was all. The decision was made. It was as simple and natural as breathing, for any other answer would have been unthinkable. I went back to my chores—putting groceries away, preparing supper, thinking of other things—little knowing that Carl and I had just made one of the major decisions of our lives.

Only twice after that did I ever hesitate or express any doubt about our decision. Once was several weeks later when Andrew was having difficulty settling on the particular house he wanted to buy and in which suburb. I suggested that perhaps he would like to buy in our neighborhood. It was not in the country, and the houses were not ranch-type, but they were relatively new little frame houses—sparkling white with red, green, or blue roofs and shutters. There were already Negroes living in the next block and in several other blocks close by, for this was the old section of town into which Negroes had been moving for a number of years; he might perhaps have bought a house in our block himself. I did not analyze my doubts, but I had some vague feeling that the atmosphere in our block would be more congenial for him and, if any of the neighbors did object to his presence, we would be there to try to influence people to be friendly. I will never forget his dignity as he turned down my proposal.

"No," he said, "we want to get out of town where the children will have more room to play. And my wife has her heart set on a stone ranch-type house. We're not looking for an easy way out. Some of the people where we move may be hostile, but we can take a few hurts and rebuffs. In time they'll come around to being friendly."

I realized that he neither needed nor wanted my maternalistic efforts to protect him and his family. I never mentioned my proposal again.

The other time I expressed a passing doubt about the project on which we were embarking was on that same afternoon when Carl first presented it to me. Carl had gone into the living room to play with the children. I was busy with supper. Carl's job at the newspaper was a night one, and there were therefore only two evenings a week when he could be at home. Supper on his off-nights was always something of an occasion, and I usually tried to prepare something he especially liked. That night I was frying chicken, taking great care to see that each piece was cooked just right. Suddenly as I was turning the chicken in the skillet—and almost like a premonition of things to come—I felt a shadow of a cold chill pass over me. I went into the living room.

Carl and the children were sitting on the floor, all three of their heads bent over a blockhouse Carl was helping them build on the rug. The children's blond heads made a sharp contrast to Carl's. His hair—although it was already streaked with some gray, and would be much grayer before the next two years had passed—was still predominantly black.

"Carl," I said, "this is legal, isn't it?"

Carl stopped work on the blockhouse and looked up at me. He appeared baffled. He had obviously dismissed the subject of Andrew Wade and a house from his mind, as he always dismisses a matter once a decision is made; he did not realize immediately what I was talking about.

"Is what legal?" he asked.

"This buying a house for Andrew. I mean we can't get into any trouble, can we?"

"Oh, sure not," he replied confidently. "There'll be some people who won't like it of course, but it's completely legal. You've got a right to sell property to anybody you want to."

His tone was contagious. I nodded and went back to my cooking. The cold chill had passed now, and I never felt it again.

I doubt that it was a premonition. Nothing in my experience has ever indicated that I have any psychic powers. It is more likely that I was sensing some way the magnitude of the thing we were about to do.

I did not see it consciously. Neither Carl nor I nor Andrew ever considered for an instant the possibility that what did happen later might happen. Louisville's race relations, such as they were, had always been quiet. There had been no open clashes. One man wanted a house. We were helping him get it. It seemed a small thing.

And yet, in that step, three powerful worlds were coming into contact. There was the world of Andrew Wade. There was the world of Carl and me. And there was the world of segregated Louisville—complacent, self-satisfied, locked in a fancied security. It was strange we did not see it; it was strange we did not sense it except for that shadowy chill that passed over me in our kitchen that night; for it is easy to see now that when these three worlds met in a decisive course of action, there were bound to be far-reaching repercussions.

Georgia Davis Powers

from *Celia's Land*

Like her friend Mae Street Kidd, Georgia Davis Powers was active in politics, and she served in the Kentucky General Assembly from 1968 to 1989. She was the first woman and the first African American to serve in the state senate. She was born in 1923 in Springfield and later came to Louisville to attend and graduate from both Central High School and Louisville Municipal College. In the 1960s she became a force in local politics, serving as a campaign head for a number of Democratic candidates for public office. In *I Shared the Dream* (1995) she recalls her active role in the major civil rights campaigns and marches and her friendship with the movement's national leaders, including Dr. Martin Luther King. Her most recent book is *Celia's Land* (2004), a historically accurate novel based on the life of her great aunt, Celia Mudd, who was born a slave in Nelson County in 1859 and who, after receiving her freedom, chose to remain with the Lancaster family, who had formerly owned her. When Sam Lancaster dies and leaves Celia the family's 840-acre farm, the Lancaster family contests the will. The passage below shows the racial tension in Bardstown as Celia prepares to leave for the courthouse and the trial by an all-white male jury to determine who will inherit the property—a white relative or a black ex-slave.

Celia awoke abruptly after a fitful sleep that climaxed with dreams of an angry crowd storming the farmhouse. Even half conscious, she knew it was simply her imagination running wild. Nevertheless, the first thing she did on rising was rush to the window and peek outside. Nothing had changed, of course. From the front of the two-story house she could see the courtyard, the open gate at the edge of the property, and beyond it Plum Run Road winding toward town. The only person around was Young Sam, her half-brother humming absently as he led a buggy out of the barn.

In her dream, the mob had surrounded the building, torches blazing, taunting Celia to come out and meet her maker. Some wore Klan hoods or masks, but most of the faces were recognizable in the flickering light. Horrified, she recognized neighbors, white folks who had never expressed anything remotely like this kind of rage. And respected pillars of Bardstown, people who had always treated her with, if not convincing respect, at least a formal civility. Now they were out for blood.

It was very much like one of those terrible tales she too often read in the papers. Usually, the victims were ripped from jail in the middle of the night, then strung up at the edge of town and left for children to see on the way to school the next day. In Shelbyville, not much more than a year ago, Jimbo Fields and Clarence Garnett had been lynched from a railroad trestle less than a mile from the center of town. The next day they were still hanging when Methodists from all over the state arrived for their convention. It was a gruesome reminder of southern "justice," and what could happen to Negroes when whites needed someone to blame. They were just boys, teenagers accused of killing a white man who sometimes shared a bed with their mother. But no trial was ever held; the jail had been stormed within days of their arrests.

No one had threatened Celia—at least directly. But whenever she thought about the trial that would begin today, she couldn't help but suspect that if the verdict went in her favor, night riders might some day come for her and her family. Dozens of colored folks had met Judge Lynch in just the last few years. In fact, things recently seemed to be getting worse rather than better. Forty years after The Emancipation Proclamation, and it still wasn't always safe to be free and colored in Kentucky.

"Mornin', Miss Cely," shouted Young Sam from the yard. "When we goin' to town?"

The words jerked Celia back to reality, reminding her that, no matter what her private paranoia, this day couldn't be avoided. It had been coming for almost a year, ever since the moment Boss Sam Lancaster signed his will. Sometimes she wondered whether—if she'd known what he was planning to do—she could or would have tried to stop him. Very likely, Sam wouldn't have taken kindly to such talk. Even on his best days, when he wasn't raving on about his brother's greed or some plot against him, the old man wasn't one to accept advice once his mind was made up. And though he'd said in his final months that she was the only person on earth he truly trusted, he rarely let Celia forget she was also his servant.

But Celia was no longer anyone's servant. She was the mistress of this house—for now. And as such, she had no time to become paralyzed by nightmares.

"Mornin'," she replied, waving at the shy, sturdy young fellow. Very much like his father, Young Sam was large, light skinned, and handsome. Also like Jack Barnes, the quiet giant who'd married their mother after the Civil War, he treated Celia with a deference that made her feel both responsible and oddly maternal.

"Things won't get started 'til about ten," she explained. "Lawyers don't keep the same hours as us farm folk."

Sam guffawed, half-embarrassed because he was having a joke at the expense of those intimidating men in their high collars and stiff suits. "I know it," he said. "But Mama say you got to talk with Mista Halstead. She tol' me to git Ezekiel hitched up and be ready to go by nine."

"Well, Mama knows best." The remark carried a hint of skepticism he didn't catch. She turned away from the window, grabbed her housecoat, and rushed through the dining room. Beyond it was the breezeway that connected the main house to the kitchen. She could hear clattering dishes and smell sausage on the fire.

"Mama, you cookin' already?" she said loudly.

"Somebody's got to get this family going," came the familiar voice. Rolling her eyes, Celia marched into the room to find her mother happily setting the table.

Celia had asked Emily Barnes to stay over last night, but hadn't counted on her taking charge of the house. She should have known better. At 69, Emily was as over-active as ever. She lived on a five acre plot down the road, managing not only to take care of her own home and keep her good-natured, though somewhat lazy man in line, but also help sister Annie with cooking down at the Talbott Tavern and keep Celia on her toes. Sometimes it was irritating having her mother set the pace. Emily could barely read. She knew nothing about business, and didn't understand how difficult it was to manage an 840 acre farm, with a foreman, Jim Hardy, who wasn't yet used to being told what to do by a Negro woman he didn't even consider his equal. But then again, Emily's specialty had always been getting people—especially men—to do what she wanted, an area in which Celia had little experience.

Nat W. Halstead was a perfect example. As executor of Sam's will, the prominent Bardstown lawyer was supposed to be representing Celia's interests in the trial. But he rarely discussed it with her, preferring to develop strategy with Sam's cousin, Button Willett. When she asked him to explain exactly what Robert Benjamin Lancaster, Sam's brother, was trying to prove in court, he simply told her not to worry. "He's just jealous of your good fortune," Halstead said, using the just-folks manner that worked so well in the courtroom. "So he's claiming that the will isn't legal. Robert never did agree with anything else Sam did. Why in heaven would he start now? You let us handle it, Miss. The law is men's work."

But it's my life, she'd thought at the time. I'm the one everybody in town is whispering about. I'm the one they think stole this white man's inheritance. She hadn't said anything, though, and might have entered the county courthouse without understanding the real issues if it hadn't been for her mamma. One day, as Halstead and his friends were leaving the Talbott Tavern, Emily ambushed him outside, sweet as pie but impossible to shake.

Without a hint of aggression, she nevertheless managed to make it clear that if Halstead didn't want to bring his main client into his full confidence, maybe her daughter needed another lawyer. That would be very sad, she said coyly, since he had always been such a friend to the Negro and was obviously the best person they could hope to find. It was part threat—and part seduction.

The next day Halstead was at the Lancaster farm, having tea and outlining the entire history of the case. What Robert's lawyers hoped to prove, he explained, was that his brother hadn't been competent to understand the will he had signed. They wouldn't make any direct attack on Celia in court, but would attempt to show that Button Willett had arranged everything and that the people who witnessed the will weren't qualified to know whether Sam was right in the head. They would bring in doctors and friends to say he was basically crazy. Why else would he leave almost everything he had to a Negro servant?

It wasn't a bad argument. She could hardly believe what Sam had done herself.

"You go back and get into that pretty blue dress," commanded Emily, sweeping back a whisp of wavy grey hair. Celia could still see hints of the light brown that had undoubtedly helped make her a striking sight in her youth. "And don't forget a coat. It may look like summertime, but it's still February."

"Sure, Mamma. But you told Young Sam I had to talk with Mister Halstead today. I thought we had everything worked out."

"Sure, all them men got things worked out for themselves. But this is your land now, Cely, and you got to make sure that old boy knows who he's working for. People are sayin' you tricked Boss Sam."

"I know what they're saying."

"All right, then. So, he got to defend you, and show them folks you're a fine woman who took care of that old man and that's all."

Celia wanted to argue. But what was the point? For Emily, the issue wasn't what a judge or jury thought, but what people in Bardstown believed. As she saw it, Celia's honor was on trial. In a way, she was right. But a lawyer couldn't do much in the court of public opinion. That was a case Celia would have to win on her own.

The outfit Emily wanted her to wear was a light blue ankle-length dirndl of chambray cotton. Looking it over, she agreed. It was suitably dignified, yet quite fetching. But it needed something more—a small brooch pinned close at her neck. She'd already polished her black leather shoes, and set aside her lucky scarf, dark blue checkered and only slightly worn.

While dressing, her mind raced over the same questions she had been asking herself for weeks. Could they win against such a formidable opponent and his herd of lawyers? Robert Lancaster had spared no expense on his legal team. But more important, would the jury be fair? Could a group of white folks, trying to decide between the rights of a Negro servant and the charges of a respected banker, see the truth and do what was just? Did her dedication to Boss Sam and the whole Lancaster family for all those years count for anything?

Looking in the mirror, she carefully examined what the jurors would see. She wasn't used to evaluating her own appearance. She was unable to escape the feeling that she was giving in to the sin of pride. But today everything had to be just right. Her soft Negro hair, held in place with small combs, was neatly pulled back into a chignon at the nape of her neck and poufs of hair on each side of her head. Her suitably modest outfit, fitting perfectly on her slight frame, gave the impression of quiet elegance and piety. Could the jury and townsfolk believe that she had taken advantage of a dying man? It didn't seem possible. Yet, when land and money were involved, people usually suspected the worst.

Once satisfied that she was ready, she returned to the breezeway and ate quietly as Emily prepared for the trip. Afterward, she decided to visit her old cubicle behind Boss Sam's bedroom, walking back through the formal dining room on the way. Sitting at the long dinner table, Jim Hardy nodded somberly as she passed. The stoic foreman, who used to take meals with Boss Sam and the white guests who often stayed at the farm, now preferred to eat alone. Since Sam's death there had been few visitors. Even Robert Hagan, the sour old coot who'd lived there for over a year during Sam's last days, had moved out. The relationship between Hardy and Celia had always been cordial, despite his treating her like a subordinate, and he showed no inclination to leave. But since he'd learned the details of the will, his attitude toward Celia had subtly shifted. Submerged superiority had been replaced by nervous discomfort.

"Will you be coming with us?" Celia asked, hoping a smile would dispel the tension.

"No, ma'am. I got to see to the horses first. You go ahead."

She didn't believe the excuse, but let it pass. It certainly didn't surprise her that Hardy wanted to keep his distance. Riding into Bardstown with the community's most notorious resident could easily open him to attack. But if he was going to remain foreman, assuming she was still running the household after the trial, they would have to get beyond this troubling unease.

In the tiny room, Celia sat on the bed and closed her eyes. She knew the place by heart: a narrow bed, by the wall, a marble-top table with a crock pitcher and wash basin, and her primitive, hand carved rocking chair. This dim, windowless space had been her private world. In a way, it was her prison from the age of 13, when Ann Lancaster had brought her in from the old, two-room slave cabin. A few months after Sam passed on, she'd moved into his old room, the bedroom across the hall from the parlor.

As she sat in her rocking chair in front of the fireplace fingering her rosary, she prayed for Missus Ann, her earliest master and teacher. She prayed for Ann's son, the troubled man-child Mart, who had never completely emerged from the shadow of two domineering brothers; he'd died in her arms nine years ago. She most definitely prayed for Sam. Ah, Boss Sam! She couldn't remember a time when he wasn't at the center of her life, either as the object of her girlish infatuation, as mentor and boss, or the architect of her fate.

May God grant them peace, she whispered, shocked at the struggle to hold back tears. They weren't her blood. But, in a sense, they'd become part of her family. How strange. Once masters, now the dear departed.

Before she knew it, Emily was calling her to the buggy. Young Sam had meanwhile changed into button shoes and a too-tight Mayfield suit on loan from his father, Jack Barnes, who lived down the road. Holding the reins, he reached down to help Celia aboard, his eyes wide as he contemplated his first time in the Nelson County Courthouse. The impressive new building had been constructed less than ten years before, replacing the old stone courthouse that had stood at the center of Bardstown for more than a century. . . .

Approaching the county courthouse, she sat erect, determined not to betray her apprehension. The streets were packed, a tangle of horses, buggies, and whispering, finger-pointing pedestrians. The curious had come from as far as Louisville, some 40 miles away. A large contingent had also made the trip from Marion County, drawn by the fact that one of its prominent citizens, Robert Lancaster, was the plaintiff. Most considered the outcome of the proceedings a foregone conclusion. R. B. Lancaster was, after all, the only legal heir. Blood kin. And Celia Mudd was just a nigger, a former slave at that. Still, the air bristled with anticipation. The atmosphere combined the rough-and-ready gaiety of a carnival with the anxious energy of a high-stakes horse race.

Young Sam reined Ezekiel to a halt directly in front of the building. For a moment, no one moved. Celia turned her head slowly, taking in the cluster of lawyers, white matrons in their bustled overskirts and high top shoes, sour-faced husbands, and her own clan, much more modestly attired as they huddled beside the door. Everyone was watching her. The total silence was unnerving. But she forced back a nervous frown, took a deep breath, and nudged Sam to get moving.

Leaping off, he rushed round to the brick sidewalk, helping her and Emily down from the buggy. As he did that, Celia could feel his whole body shaking. "Don't fret, little brother," she whispered. "At least we've got God on our side." Though she didn't really believe that God took sides in court, she knew it would calm him.

Then she linked arms with her mother and walked defiantly through the crowd.

Cass Irvin

from *Home Bound: Growing Up with a Disability in America*

Cass Irvin is a Louisville quadriplegic who uses a wheelchair. Her brave struggles for access and fair treatment are detailed in her inspiring autobiography, *Home Bound* (2004). The passage below shows how the tables are turned when, disabled though she is, she is able to help her father at the end of his life. The moral? At some point in life, everyone becomes disabled.

In the summer of 1991, Daddy got pneumonia, and I knew when he left the hospital he was going to need more help. I called three nurses I knew from my NOW chapter and learned everything I could about his condition and what he could expect. One nurse taught me all about sleep apnea; she wanted him to be in her sleep apnea program in Louisville. He wouldn't go. Another friend suggested a breathing clinic in Bowling Green. He would not do that either.

The one thing I could do was get him home health services. When Daddy left the hospital, he was on oxygen; from home health services, he was eligible for a nurse once a week and home health aides three times a week. He accepted the help more willingly when he found out he did not have to pay for it.

He, like my mother, did not mind people working for him. It was hard on him to be "helpless"; he preferred to think he could still do it all. I remember how I was treated whenever I have approached the medical community: I become a "helpless cripple" incapable of knowing what is right for me, because of either their attitude or my intimidation. I become a patient.

"Patient" connotes a person unable to speak on his or her own behalf. A patient fears not so much lifestyle change as a loss of self. The fear is justified. People who preach cure play into this belief. Everyone will not be cured, but everyone can use personal assistance.

Having home aides was good for Daddy's ego. He was an interesting character, colorful, worldly, and intelligent. He was a good conversationalist and admired for his experiences. People loved talking to him and often asked his advice on everything from sex to gardening. He lectured several nurses about planning for their financial futures. Everyone, of course, thought he was handsome.

He enjoyed the visits and the help, although he griped about not being able to do things for himself. He felt he did not need a bath three times a week, because he was not working hard enough to build up a sweat, so he especially griped during the showers. Sometimes he joked with his female aides that it would be fun if they joined him. One day, in a particularly grumpy mood, Daddy muttered through the whole shower. Since he had a new aide that day, John tried to explain that Daddy did not like the state he was in. Her response was, "Mel, you don't like Kentucky?" Daddy looked at John and just rolled his eyes.

He also griped that in thirty days the agency had sent nineteen different aides. Poor planning, he complained. "If the aide has never been here before, they get lost," he complained. "They stop and call me for directions. All that wastes time and gas and wear and tear on their car." I was more concerned that no single person was seeing him on a regular basis. How could anyone mark a change in his condition?

Since John and I went to his home often, we met many of his aides. Even though they were capable help, it was hard for me to leave Daddy and go back to Louisville. Usually it would be late afternoon, the sun beginning to go down—a beautiful, melancholy time of day. One sunny afternoon I sat on the screened porch talking with Daddy while John loaded the van. Daddy was in his usual place on the porch, in a chair near the back corner, near the deck overlooking the lake. While we talked, I watched hummingbirds come to the feeders hanging from the deck behind his shoulder.

Daddy would complain and then apologize—"I'm not telling you something you don't already know." I was shocked to hear him apologize. He was not used to being "helpless" and did not know what to expect. It was the first time, I think, that he understood what my life had been like. "I need someone like John," Daddy said, and he was right. He needed someone who cared how he was and worked with him to have the best, healthiest life possible. As John and I drove away, I felt pulled in two directions—toward work and toward my dad.

During the Christmas holidays in 1991, Daddy went into the hospital with pneumonia again. This time we did not know if he would come out. If he could get stronger, his doctor said, maybe he could fight it off. But Daddy was very weak and the prognosis grave. He was in the hospital three weeks; John and I went to Cumberland as often as we could, spending most afternoons at the hospital and evenings getting the place ready for when he came home.

He could not live alone anymore. He could not dress himself, get out of bed by himself. I suggested he move back to Louisville to Kenwood so we could take care of him here, but he refused. Cumberland was his home.

If I could have done it by myself, I would have moved down there with him and taken care of him. But I am a quadriplegic, and any taking care of I do is going to be through someone else's hands. Juanita had family in Louisville, and John had his son on the weekends. I could not make such a commitment for them.

We began looking for someone to stay with him. His doctor wanted him stronger before he left the hospital, but Daddy wanted to go home. I think he thought he could manage on his own. I was on the phone for days trying to track down a personal attendant, and finally I got a tentative yes from a woman named Jean.

That night Daddy called from the hospital. He was tired of being there, he told me. They could not help him anymore. He was not going to get any better. I told him the doctor had said he thought he could get Daddy into the next available Medicare bed. That was a big issue with Daddy—expense. But he wanted to go home.

I explained that we did not have anyone yet to stay with him and begged him to wait and talk to his doctor in the morning. He told me he had told his doctor he was checking himself out tomorrow, with or without medical permission. How could I stop him?

Luckily that tentative yes from Jean became a firm agreement, but she could not start for a couple of days. The next day we got up and dressed, finished cleaning up, and got his room ready. About eleven, we got a phone call from the hospital to tell us Daddy was leaving the hospital and on the way home.

⁊ ⁊ ⁊

We heard the dogs barking way up at Keane's farm, and then Daddy's three dogs chimed in. Daddy arrived in a huge red-and-white ambulance, no flashing lights, no sirens. John had moved our van to the next-door neighbor's drive and parked Daddy's Blazer out of the way. The ambulance pulled in; the doors opened. Even before the stretcher appeared, Daddy was hollering at his dogs to stop barking. The minute they heard his voice, they got more excited. Finally, the attendants slid the stretcher out. There sat my daddy, propped up in a hospital gown, his eyes looking enormous because of his trifocal glasses and his frailty—roaring.

I cannot describe the look on Daddy's face when he saw he was home again. He surveyed his surroundings, told the ambulance drivers what to do, what to get out of the ambulance. He warned them about the ramped steps, pointed out and explained his garden, and finally directed them to his bedroom.

I hate to admit that my dad, far from politically correct when it comes to disability, taught me about language that day. From the beginning of my disability work with ALPHA, I have been involved with language, grappling with words like "invalid," "crippled." Words are so important that *The Disability Rag* came out with consciousness-raising bookmarks that explained why words like "victim," "confined," and "wheelchair bound" are incorrect. Wheelchairs are *not* confining. In fact, I could not go anywhere without mine—unless someone is willing to carry me. "Victim" is an emotional term that conjures up tragedy; the real tragedy is that society does not see us as okay the way we are—disabled. Most terms used for people with disabilities are medical, clinical, derogatory.

One word we have not found a substitute for is "homebound." As a child in the fifties and sixties, when I was considered "homebound," I did not think the label fit. Agencies define homebound people as those who cannot leave home. I could leave home whenever someone would take me.

My friend Sanda Aronson and I have discussed this term at length. Sanda, a visual artist, is founder and executive director of the Disabled Artists' Network out of New York. She has been an art teacher and is a veteran of the feminist art movement of the 1970s. She has an environmental disability, so she does not leave home. She has chronic fatigue syndrome and is an allergic asthmatic. Because society has not figured out how to deal with her disabilities, she is considered "homebound."

My dad taught me a different definition of homebound. That last night when he called me and said he was checking himself out of the hospital, I knew he was determined to be home. He demanded it and he got it. When I saw him pop out of that ambulance I thought, My father is homebound. He was bound and determined to be home.

One week after leaving Daddy with Jean, his live-in attendant, I got a call from his friend Millie, from his house. Jean had called her and said she could not do the work; she was quitting. Millie had been a "girlfriend" of my father's and had helped him in the past, so I asked if she could stay until John and I could get there. Since it was the weekend, we had John's son, Erik, and could not leave Louisville until the next evening, Sunday. Millie said she would stay and we talked awhile about how Daddy was taking all this. "He thinks she quit because she just needed some money, and once she got paid . . ."

Juanita went to Cumberland with us. She was prepared to stay if we did not find a better solution by the next weekend, when we had to return to Louisville to Erik. She liked my dad, who called her Barbara because he thought she looked like a Barbara. Juanita thought that was funny.

With Juanita at Cumberland, John would be totally responsible for my personal assistance at home. John is a good personal assistant and when we went on trips he was my PA, but taking care of both me and Erik on weekends would be hard for him.

Daddy had checked himself out of the hospital to come home to die. When he was still alive a week later, he began asking why was it taking so long. He told John he wanted to go outside and freeze to death. "Mel," John had to tell him, "the low tonight is only going to be forty."

Our worst problem was that Russell County had no hospice service, which meant no one told us what to expect or gave us guidance. Daddy got worse. He still had pneumonia, so he could not breathe well. Nurses and aides came for an hour or two each day, but all they could do was try to make him comfortable. He could never get comfortable.

Daddy began having trouble sleeping and would call out at night. We got a baby monitor, so he could whisper and we could hear him. Soon he began calling out about every twenty minutes, although he did not realize it was that often. Since Juanita, a heavy sleeper, did not wake up, John got up for Daddy all night long and got no sleep. We asked the agency to send someone to stay overnight.

The day Daddy died, Juanita got up early as usual, before Mark, the overnight person, left. John and I got up midmorning; it would be noon before I could get dressed and up in my chair.

By early afternoon, the aide had come and gone. John and I headed for town in the van to run errands. In the middle of the road, close to town, was a cardboard Porter Paint box, open, upside down—in perfect condition.

"John," I said.

"No!" he exclaimed. "We're not going to go back and get it."

"I know, I know. But it is in good shape. We could use a box like that."

He knew I was kidding. We went to the bank on the far side of town, where I went in, and to the store, where I did not have to go in, and to the drugstore. On our way out of town, we passed the Porter Paint box again. It was still in the *middle* of the road, still upside down, still in perfect condition. Evidently, everyone had driven around it.

When we got back to the cottage, Daddy was the same so I decided the Porter Paint box wasn't an omen. At about nine o'clock, Mark arrived. I greeted him, and John walked with him into Daddy's room, filling him in on Daddy's present condition.

I went to the master bedroom and sat by the big window overlooking the lake. The first time we came here, John was excited about the window until we realized it was set so high I could barely see out of it. Now I looked for stars and the moon and thought, How remarkable, I am here with the first most important man in my life, Daddy, and with John, who I hope will be the last most important man in my life.

From Daddy's bedroom over the baby monitor, I could hear John and Mark were mumbling. Then John said quietly but firmly, "Cassie, come in here. *Now.*"

How ironic that most of what I had learned about disability issues, many of the connections I had made, benefited my dad. I had studied all my life, prepared all my life, for this job—daughter. Daddy gave me the resources to have a life and I had given back to him the only way I could.

Fenton Johnson

from *Geography of the Heart*

Fenton Johnson is as much a daring pioneer of unexplored wilderness as Daniel Boone ever was. He is an openly gay man who exposes himself to homophobia and twisted religious zealots who write letters to the newspaper saying, "Jesus hates fags." Born into a large Catholic family of nine children in New Haven in 1953, he attended local Catholic schools, then graduated from Larue County High School. His college degree is from Stanford University, and he has studied at the prestigious Iowa Writers Workshop. He now teaches writing at the University of Arizona. His books include *Crossing the River* (1989), *Scissors, Paper, Rock* (1993), and *Keeping Faith: A Skeptic's Journey* (2003). When Fenton Johnson was asked in a recent interview if he planned ever to move back home to Kentucky, he gave an equivocal response, saying he loved the Kentucky landscape and Kentuckians and he took it all with him when he was away.

In 1987 he met Larry Rose, who was HIV-positive. They lived together for four years, during which Johnson says he learned how to love unconditionally and how to live after a lover dies. In 1996 he published *Geography of the Heart: A Memoir*, which tells of his life with Rose. In the excerpts below Johnson tells of meeting Rose, portrays their life together, and finally describes how he copes with his great loss and carries on with his life.

August 1987: In my early thirties I decided certain things about my life. Two years earlier I'd bailed out of a relationship with a kindhearted, thoughtful man—a fine companion for summer days and winter nights, but not a life partner. I'd spent the intervening time in desultory dating, but opportunities for romance don't present themselves often to writers, introverted curmudgeons who work at home. More to the point, everywhere I turned I encountered the inexorable law of desire: those whom I wanted didn't want me; those who wanted me I didn't want.

Enough such hopeless affairs and I decided this: single, childless, I would close up emotional shop, to put myself out into the world and see where it might take me. I was thirty-four and aging as fast as the rest of us; I needed to spend some time alone, letting my heart repair itself. I packed up my meager belongings and stored them in a friend's basement. I arranged to house-sit for a friend, to be followed by a residency at a nearby artists' colony. I'd spend the year floating and writing. I turned my back on love.

A month later Larry Rose entered my life.

Romance and sleep, in this they are alike: Each arrives only when you're looking the other way.

෬ ෬ ෬

We met at the reception following the memorial service for a former roommate of mine (as so often happens: Death provides humus for love). At the time I was catering to my worst instincts by flirting with a lawyer with whom I associated money, intellectual prowess, power; all the requirements, I thought then, for true love.

The lawyer placed his hand on my arm. "I really enjoy talking with you. Maybe we should get together sometime."

"Sure," I said. "Let me give you my phone number."

He took my number, tucked it in his pocket, and produced a business card. "Sometime soon." Then he glanced across the room. "Oh, if you'll excuse me. I have to go check with my boyfriend."

I watched him go. I turned around to find Larry at my side.

෬ ෬ ෬

A letter to a friend;

> Dear B.,
>
> I went to an old roommate's memorial service on Saturday and met two guys—a lawyer whom I'm really attracted to, and a Berkeley High School English teacher named Larry Rose, who's really attracted to me. So I came home and placed this bet with myself: The phone will ring on Tuesday, and it will be the Berkeley High English teacher.

The phone rang Monday, and it was Larry. . . .

Not long after Larry and I moved in together: a summer evening when he was at his healthiest, and it was possible to believe that we would be given two or six or ten years together in the three-bedroom apartment with the great view and the aging cat. We were sitting on the deck not long before sunset, watching the fog peer over the hills. The moon, thinnest of Arabian crescents, was descending into the weird red cage of the radio tower that squats on Twin Peaks. Larry brought out the camera—he wanted to send his parents pictures of the view from the new apartment.

He took photos of the view, then we clowned for each other in front of the camera—more pictures for the overflowing box that now sits at one end of my desk. I waggled my fingers above my head and mugged for Larry, then it was his turn. He stuck his fingers in the corners of his mouth and eyes and pulled his face into a wacky grin, all squinty eyes and bared teeth, while in the background the slip of a moon tangled itself in the radio tower's webbing of cables and girders.

Afterward we wrapped ourselves in blankets and watched as the moon freed itself of the radio tower and sank into the fog. We talked a little about this and that—nothing important; end-of-the-day partner talk. I wasn't paying much attention. I was thinking about all kinds of pressing matters— what I was going to work on tomorrow and the impossible deadline I was facing and how was I going to make time for Larry amid all this work that was supposed to have been done yesterday, and somewhere in the middle of my thoughts he spoke up and said something like this: "Love is like a ripe peach. You take it when and where you find it, there's no point in letting it sit around. If you're lucky enough to come across it, you'd better enjoy it right then and there."

Later that summer, when he grew really, evidently, seriously ill, I thought, as little as possible but inevitably, of what would become of me after he died. I figured, of course, that a relatively young person who'd lost a great love would have a chance at such a love again—after all, that would be only fair. Then Larry died, and time and more time passed, and I came to understand how fairness has nothing to do with how and when love arrives; that I can be grateful for love only when and while it's happening, when it's quite literally in the hand.

಄ ಄ ಄

Surely we are all dealing with this, HIV-negative or HIV-positive, irrespective of our gender or sexualities: incorporating loss into life; substituting for the myth of control a reality that embraces light *and* dark, love *and* grief, life *and* death.

In the earliest years of the epidemic in San Francisco, this was the party line that we were all engaged to support: HIV-positive men would live forever, had as much claim as any of us on the myth of immortality. New drugs or new therapies, or old drugs and old therapies, or crystals or visualization, or simply our ignorance of the long-term workings of the virus gave us the right to this hope.

All this was true, except for one small problem: The emperor had no clothes. The myth of immortality was just that, as much a myth for the HIV-negative as the HIV-positive, as much a myth for you as for me.

Before helping Larry die, I considered the myth that I would live forever (when I considered it at all) as necessary insulation that enabled me to carry on with daily life. Now that I have been brought to understand how we all live continually in the presence of death, insulation is not an option.

We are all survivors, after all, we are all mourners on this mortal earth, who choose daily the measure of our participation (or lack thereof) in the world's fate, which is to say its mortality, which is to say its grief. It's just that HIV, with its extended incubation period, its prolonged illnesses, its often horrifying complications, its impact on close-knit neighborhoods and communities, is forcing gay men of my generation to acknowledge what our life-and-youth-obsessed society prefers to deny.

"Write about the courage it takes to live in denial," a straight friend urges me, meaning, I suppose, the willpower required to live as if one has a long-term future when so many signs point to the contrary. I think of David Weissman's short film *Song from an Angel*, in which Rodney Price, founder of the 1970s theater troupe Angels of Light, sings from his wheelchair, less than two weeks before his death, an original song entitled "I've Got Less Time Than You" ("If I look thinner / Take me to dinner / 'Cause I've got less time than you, oh yeah / I've got less time than yo-oo-ou").

How is it possible to deny an illness for which one takes medication every four hours? The wisest people of my life, positive or negative, are living not in denial but in acceptance, a state not of forgive and forget but of forgive and remember. This, it strikes me, is the mourner's most difficult and necessary of tasks, the holding in the heart of these contradictory imperatives: forgive and remember; accept and never shut up.

Grief is love's alter ego, after all, yin to its yang, the necessary other; like night, grief has its own dark beauty. How may we know light without knowledge of dark? How may we know love without sorrow? "The disorientation following such loss can be terrible, I know," Wendell Berry wrote me on learning of Larry's death. "But grief gives the full measure of love, and it is somehow reassuring to learn, even by suffering, how large and powerful love is."

⁓ ⁓ ⁓

Enough time passes and I discover that I no longer measure time against how long it's been since Larry died.

My mother returns to visit San Francisco. We are driving north to Muir Woods to seek out the earliest spring wildflowers, which she has taught me to appreciate.

In our relationship I have always been in charge of raising emotional issues. Though she has known for many years that I'm gay, until Larry's death she found it difficult to speak to me of such matters, partly from fear of intruding past the wall I myself had maintained for so long, partly because (like all who were raised without such words) she has had to learn and grow comfortable with a new vocabulary to describe my life and her place in it ("my gay son," "his partner, who died of AIDS"). A country woman with little more than a high school education, she traveled very little until late in her life, but she has taught herself that new vocabulary. In part it is her experience learning it—in staying open to what her heart tells her is right and true—that has kept her young.

Now for the first time I can recall, she broaches the subject of my emotional life. She speaks in that lovely, circuitous, Southern narrative style— she begins by asking after Larry's mother, then after his family, then she reminisces briefly about his visit to Kentucky, then she talks of her visit to San Francisco in the summer before he died, when Larry drove up the coast to rescue us when my car battery died. After she has laid the groundwork by telling these stories, she takes up the heart of what she wants to say—the point of her remembering:

"I always thought of myself as tolerant and open-minded. I grew up with people who were gay, though of course back then we didn't use that word. I knew some people in our town were gay, everyone knew they were gay, but I didn't think much about that one way or another. Just live and let live, that's my way of being in the world. And then you told me you were gay, and I guess I'd suspected it all along, and I just prayed that you'd stay healthy and find yourself a place where you could be happy. I prayed for all that and I was glad to see you get yourself to San Francisco, to a place where you could live in peace and be yourself. I was happy about that, but it wasn't until I met you and Larry and spent time with the two of you together that I understood that two men could love each other in the same way as a man and a woman."

This speaking is the sacred thing, the gift from the dead to the living.

෬෧ ෬෧ ෬෧

Of Larry's tightly bound family triangle, the mother endures.

I stay in touch with Kathy, who resists my gentle encouragement to form a life apart from her memories. From time to time she has sent me money, which for the most part I have accepted graciously, though occasionally my stubbornness asserts itself and we reenact uncomfortably familiar scenes in which I resist her generosity. She has accepted, I think, that I am not and cannot be a replacement for her son. For my part, I have accepted that there is no love worth the name without responsibility. We strive to find some kind of balance; more often than not we succeed.

෬෧ ෬෧ ෬෧

I love better now, more wholly and completely, not because I have learned some exotic technique but because I know death.

More than four years since Larry's death, making love: My friend is stocky and tall, as tall as I but otherwise built unnervingly like Larry and with a shock of salt-and-pepper hair that is thicker even than Larry's was. Smart and big hearted and handsome as a mountain range and I tell him exactly that, I tell him this is fine because he is who he is and I am who I am, I would have nothing different from the way things are, right here, right now in this present perfect moment.

Before knowing Larry I would have wanted more. If I'd understood what I'd been given, it would have been only dimly, and I would never have found the courage to speak aloud my happiness in the moment. Now I try to pay more attention—I am a good student, if a little slow, and Larry was, after all, a teacher. These days I take care to give voice to my good fortune.

◌◌◌ ◌◌◌ ◌◌◌

Today is a blindingly clear winter day in San Francisco. I climb to the hill above my apartment, from which it's almost possible to believe I might count the blades of grass on Mount Tamalpais, some ten miles distant. The low-slanting winter light reflects from the pastel houses of the city with such purity and directness that one would think this image would be burned into memory. And yet I could return to my apartment and in five minutes forget the salmon pink of the tower on the old Sears building on César Chavez Street, or the thin line of gilt that gleams from the steeple of St. James on Guerrero. Whereas the violets in the gardens of the French hotel where Larry and I spent our last night together—delicate lavender, lustrous from the damp of an evening thundershower—these I can evoke as clearly as if I were walking now a path that is years distant, while upstairs in his balconied room Larry lies dying. What is more to the point is the way those violets evoke themselves, planting themselves in memory and denying the possibility of forgetting.

◌◌◌ ◌◌◌ ◌◌◌

I am in France, driving Larry south and west from Tours, along the banks of the Loire. Two days later he will be dead, impossible to believe then or now, but in this moment we are driving, we are fleeing south and west, to Nantes, the Atlantic, the Gironde, the Pyrenees, Spain, Morocco, we will run as far as we can, as far as it takes. The Loire flows on our left, a broad, silvered ribbon reflecting the towering pastels of this Fragonard sky. On our right yellowing poplars shiver behind limestone-walled villages and ornate châteaux.

I drive until I am blinded by tears—Larry is so quiet, so ill. Under the crenellated medieval towers of Langeais I stop the car and turn to him. "Are you in pain?"

"No."

"We could turn back."

He presses his finger to my lips. "I'm happy being quiet here with you."

This is what I am trying to learn, the lesson Larry was teaching: the sufficiency and necessity of being quiet here with you.

But we have no choice but to cross that river, to turn and head back. Life takes the shape of an hourglass: focusing down, past and future falling away until there is nothing but this moment, this present place, the two of us amid this ancient, pastoral, autumnal countryside. Surely this is as close as I will get—surely it is as close as anyone could bear—to love pure as sunlight; to our reason for being alive.

And the sun sinks lower in the sky, the light fails, time is running out; a day, a life is racing to its end. The sunlight slants across the reed-choked Indre, shining white on the raked and graveled paths of Azay-le-Rideau, this fantasy castle. A swan sinks on extended wings, his double rising to meet him from the depths of the lake's emerald mirror. He lands, and the château's slate-sheathed towers shatter, ripple, then reassemble their inverted perfection. Stark, sharp shadows of osiers, black rapiers against green water, Larry and I set out to walk the symmetrical paths except that he cannot lift his swollen feet, shoes scrape gravel and so he turns back to the car. I turn to follow, then crouch to take up a handful of pebbles, to lodge in memory the feel of this place that I will surely never touch again in the presence of this man, this friend of my youth. The rough and raked stoniness grates against my palms, the gravel runs through my fingers but it is the thin, serpentine-flecked dirt of San Francisco, and I am standing on the hill above the apartment where I now live, where I have lived alone since Larry died. The bright white bowl of the city spreads out below. To the north the copper-red towers of the Golden Gate Bridge rise against the tawny Marin headlands.

I am in California, not in France. It is years later, I am here and he is not but love goes on, this is the lesson that I have taken, for a comfort that must and will suffice. In grief there is renewal, of love and so of life.

Jerry Brewer

"Hello from a Kentuckian"

Jerry Brewer, a Paducah native who joined the *Courier-Journal*'s staff as a sports writer in late 2004, was clear about his feelings for the state. This is an October 2004 column in which he introduces himself to his fellow Kentuckians and tells of his homecoming. Where once "success was an exit sign," Brewer realizes that Kentucky is indeed where he wants—and needs—to be. It is a fitting conclusion to this chapter of nonfiction writing.

The dream always involved leaving this state. Kentucky was home, sure, and I loved it. We all did. But it would've been nice if home had a subway or some palm trees or a pro sports team, even a bad one.

Success was an exit sign. Aspiration demanded it. As children growing up in Paducah, Ky., we looked yonder and tripped over home. We must have forgotten home was there, right there. Ouch.

I was the worst. Live in Kentucky? Nah. The big-timers don't live in Kentucky. New York. Los Angeles. Chicago. That's where I wanted to be. That's where everyone expected me to be.

While moving last week, I found my high school yearbook—Paducah Tilghman, 1995–96, senior year—and re-read some of my classmates' notes.

"I hope you work for 'The New York Times' and win the Pulitzer someday," Lee Ann Massey wrote.

Out came the giggles.

Guess I'll have to win that Pulitzer at The Courier-Journal. Guess I'll have to win that Pulitzer back home, not out yonder. Guess I've truly discovered the allure of our state.

This is your new sports columnist typing. Here are the particulars: 26 years old, been in Orlando the past 3½ years, began career in Philadelphia, earned journalism degree at Western Kentucky University.

I'm here to inform you, challenge you, entertain you, irritate you and inspire you. We're going to argue, but you always get the last word. Some of us might never understand each other, but that's life. We're going to laugh and cry, and during the best times we might do both at once.

At this time, though, I'm just writing as a giddy Kentuckian, full of hope. Home always was a retirement option, not a career possibility. I always wanted to escape from you, not write to you.

Now I'm back and feeling fortunate. This is right. Somewhere along a path that introduced me to Donovan McNabb's brilliance, to Tracy McGrady's smooth flair, to Florida's football supremacy, right got lost. Right became the mission, not the experience. Right became about the future's promise, not today's joy.

I was a maniac, chasing something I couldn't see. Then I tripped again. Finally, I realized home should be kept in a safer place. It was a marvelous revelation.

In the past, I was a child thinking as a child, ignoring obvious signs. Since departing, lips of this arrogant dreamer have touched Bluegrass upon every return. When outsiders started the Kentucky jokes—one friend called it "Kenyucky" (grrrr)—this flee spirit would turn angry, start getting possessive and protective. When Nappy Roots made it big, this underestimating fool immediately put them among the top five rap groups.

One of those dudes was in my art appreciation class at Western. We didn't appreciate anything about that class. He used to try to sell me Nappy demo tapes for $10. I declined. I didn't know his group would be amazing. I misjudged the prowess of Kentuckians again.

We're special. Maybe we should say that more often. We're underrated and understated. Maybe we should flaunt a little more.

We're crazy and obsessive, Wildcats and Cardinals and Hilltoppers and Colonels and Racers and Eagles controlling our lives. We're always trying to keep a Hoosier or Bearcat down, but we appreciate their fight. If our primary squabbles revolve around college basketball and horse racing, we're a little bit off, but we're an OK group.

So to end this hello, I must say one final thing. After all that youthful arrogance and desire to run away, these final words are appropriate.

Please forgive me, Kentucky. I need you. Now I know, I need you.

A Shower of Poets
Contemporary Kentucky Poetry

In its annual anniversary issue in February 2005, the *New Yorker* devoted 14 lines to a loose sonnet (irregular iambic pentameter and a couple of near rhymes) by Seamus Heaney, the Irish poet who won the Nobel Prize for Literature shortly after his visit to Bellarmine University in 1994. (We assured him that he would win the prize after the Nobel Committee heard that he had won Bellarmine's prestigious Guarnaschelli Award.) The issue also carried a 16-line free verse poem by Linda Gregg and Jorie Graham's "Praying," a whopping 77 lines of wisdom and warning about global warming and other impending disasters. And those 107 lines are all the poetry in a total of 262 pages, which left generous space for ads, essays, cartoons, and stories. The issue is a prose master's paradise.

I pondered the paucity of poetry, then decided that poetry must be on the decline in New Yorkerland. It may be, but it's certainly alive and flourishing in Kentucky, and has been ever since the Drunken Poets of Danville got us off to a fast start. I'll bet Kentucky has more living and recently living poets per square mile than any other state or nation. Alas, there isn't room enough in this anthology for all of them, but I can put in a good sampling. Poets, you know, don't need a lot of space to say a lot.

This final section, "A Shower of Poets," covers Kentucky from Maysville to Mayfield, from Henderson to Hindman, like a gentle spring rain that brings the land to life. I hope you meet some new friends along the way—perhaps friends that you'd like to revisit. It is a challenging and, I hope, rewarding trip, one worth your time and effort, one that you can take again at any point and any time you choose.

Albert Stewart

"The Poet as High-Diver Perhaps"

It is fitting that we begin our poets' tour of Kentucky with Albert Stewart, born in 1914 at Yellow Mountain in Knott County. He studied at Hindman Settlement School, Berea College, and the University of Kentucky; he later taught at Kentucky, Morehead State University, and Alice Lloyd College. He founded and for twelve years edited *Appalachian Heritage,* where he nurtured other poets and writers. A poem, he once wrote, is "one of man's most vital undertakings." In the following poem he suggests that the poet, like the high diver, is also in a dangerous business.

Hand over hand, foot over foot, up
the laddered slope—it is a mountain
you are climbing—grasping, holding,
pushing, staying: a closeness in sinew,
touch, a friendly oxygenation.

Roots, delicate as eye veins, break
rock, digest stone, feed gardens of
blossoming, colored gems.
Oh, arbutus, showy orchis, diatoms,
flowering, singing, in and out of
you all the way up still.

Those are marvelous crystals that are
your eyes. Bright memory chips swarm
your electric brain. Your skin is a
slipcase, waterfilled. Emblems of
ancient oceans, transformed, enjoined,
teeming, swim. You are the fable of
a far journey: sacred, arcane.

You reach the top, stand poised.
The mountain is high, remote, the
horizon farther. You look out.
The space is too wide. There is too

much air. The distance down is not
the same as the distance up. You are
stripped, naked, in wide new light.
You are lost and in love.

(But oh the faery bells tinkling, tingling,
and oh the wild apple scent along the way
        oh the wild bloom in the blood, the
            sweet remembering bone)

At last, by this,
you have come to where you are.
You have no wings.
You must leap out from here and
freefall all the way down to
where it is.

John Filiatreau

"Ode on a Writer's Block"

Now we stop off in Louisville, where John Filiatreau used to write for the *Courier-Journal* and apparently learned a thing or two about writer's block.

Look, he does not write.
Cut off his head.
Better he should turn up somewhere dead
than live without the words
that used to dance down
like water
so clear so pretty
so full of joy,
remember? But now
he does not write.
He thinks to write and then does not.
Look how he sizzles with guilt
yet he refuses to write
though he is burned up
with not writing. He and the world
are not speaking just now.
Of course the world will not relent,
ever; and he is stubborn
when he is not writing.
You see the outlook is not hopeful.

Does a horse get up and run?
Does a leaf seek sun?
Does a bird take flight?
But look, he does not write:
Cut off his head.
One who so lacks generosity
that he nurses a grudge
of such deep silence

all night long
and cannot force himself to budge
when silence is wrong,
is ready to be dead.

We have offered him suicide,
but he declines;
the notion intrigues him
but he cannot produce
a proper note;
and he wants assurances
that in light of the eloquence of his death
his poems will at last be read—
Why else be dead? You see
how tangled is his reticence,
how cold his bed. Do him a favor.
Cut off his head.

Betty Layman Receveur

"Kentucky Woman"

Betty Layman Receveur was first and last a poet, whether she called a piece of her writing poetry or a historical novel. She was a proud seventh-generation Kentuckian and showed her pride in poetry and prose, including this poem about an ancestor looking out from a tintype portrait.

❧

You look out across
genetic memory
tin preserved
rimmed and honored
atop polished cherry.
da Vinci would have
painted your
wide-planed face
strong as hickory
eyes deepset
that whisper of
the others gone before.

Unknown hand
browned ink
forever at your back
lest you forget
as if you could
the echo of my blood
and bone
three times removed
child of
child of
child.

You speak to me
of Etta, daughter of

Anna, daughter of
Mariah, of women
who could match the land
and give each day its due
of blood-rich womb and
roughened hands
and finally of time
the cruelest thing of all.

Jonathan Greene
"The Album"

Although not a native Kentuckian, Jonathan Greene has contributed significantly to Kentucky's literature as a poet and as a publisher. His Gnomon Press, based in Frankfort, has published poetry and prose by some of Kentucky's best-known authors. His poem about a family photograph album for sale at an auction focuses on the brevity of life and identity.

In the wedding pictures
it's so clear no one knows
what's happening. There is
a levity & a hidden gravity,
both unreal. And plenty of food
in the background.

It is wonderful to be foolish
& rash. Otherwise, great things
would be left undone. And yet
few can survive it.

Frayed, dust-covered,
left in the empty house
whose walls blotted
dark recriminations,
echoes of voices
breaking, going
hoarse.

Who will bid on this
dreambox, will unknowingly
inherit this album full of
strangers smiling nakedly
into oblivion.

Miriam Woolfolk

"Railroad Man's Daughter"

In this poem Miriam Woolfolk, who lives in Lexington, pays tribute to her father, a railroad worker, and to a time when trains could take you anywhere you wanted to go.

(In memory of my father, Edward J. Lamy,
  who worked for the L&N Railroad, 1914–67)

Small hand in yours, we caught the train
as hissing steam swirled to and fro.
The scenery blurred through drops of rain

that pelted on the thick window
and sent the wet streaks slithering past.
We heard the crossing bells. The glow

that circled from the lamp was cast
above our heads. The clickedy-clack
of wheels wove rhythms unsurpassed

to those whose love of train and track
is inbred, or inherited.
Many's the time I've wandered back

in dreams, recalling from the dead
dear past those days of other rides
and places we once visited.

The little girl that in me hides
still lives, still wants to travel far,
from mountain peak to ocean tides.

Oh, I could go by plane or car,
but how I'd love to catch a TRAIN—
if it could take me where YOU are.

"His Land"

This poem of regular iambic tetrameter couplets honors the faithful Kentucky farmer. Like many of Kentucky's fine poets, Woolfolk is a longtime member of the Kentucky State Poetry Society.

There is a certain artistry
to plowing fields. His eye can see
deep patterns woven in the earth,
his cloth of life. He finds rebirth
each growing season. Planting seed,
he prays for rain and hopes his need
is greater than the ones who pray
for solid sunshine every day.

Weeds are his dragons. Hoe and spray
his weapons, and the pests that prey
on crops keep him in anxious wait
right through the harvest. He is late
to dinner, work seems never done,
too tired to watch the setting sun,
but farming-blood runs in the vein.
He'll likely plant next year again.

Aleda Shirley

"One Summer Night"

In this poem Aleda Shirley remembers a summer night in Oakland, in Warren County, when she was a girl and surrounded by her loved ones—and ice cream, a moon, and a mimosa tree.

The sherbet-colored lawn chairs arranged
themselves in pairs, like dancers,
and my grandfather rattled his newspaper,
cigarette smoke curling like a bad mood around him.
This was how it was twenty years ago
in Oakland, Kentucky: my uncles telling jokes
as they took turns turning the ice cream freezer,
my grandmother drying her hands on her apron
and, there, by the door, my mother talking softly
to her sisters about a time longer ago than this one
I long for. Slow, like a slow dance:
my cousins and I waded through green shadows
and touched the tips of honeysuckle
to the tips of our tongues. The walnut,
heavy with fruit, was a ship with tall pink sails,
the patio a kind of shore and the adults calling
Girls, ice cream the light of a lighthouse
beaming across dark distance. Night fell
gently as if it were bending down to look
in our faces; waving sparklers
we filled the air with rhinestones, so profuse
and lovely they had to be fake.

Odd now to think no one had walked
on that moon rising in the mimosa's shallow limbs
and off to understand how, much more than that night, I want
to know they want it back as much as I do. For this
I would forfeit my dozen cities, even the loveliest one;

the thin clear goodnight the child calls
from across the street; my lover's hand
on my upper arms as he rises above me in the dark.
I'd give up the secrets I've coaxed from memory's
closed fist and the ability to articulate them.
Though not the desire.

Virginia Pile

"Lost Children"

Virginia Pile of Hardinsburg, in Breckinridge County, remembers a childhood lost
to time.

Under the dark cedars
the yard is starred with June fireflies.

Brother's handsome face
is grimaced with laughter.
He crushes fireflies

against his brass buttons,
the bib of his overalls
armoured like an officer's pallettes,
his eyes reckless with denials.

My little sister's pure face alit,
chants, *catch me, catch me,*

daring to be free, to be caught.
I, pursuing, afraid in the dark.

Running, she leaves me behind
in fallow dusk.
Buddy calls, his baby hands
clutch and rip my loosened sash,

bares small sharp teeth in his baby face,
stumbles in his dark unremembered void
of evening yard, crying
that he might be left alone.

The tall presence of the man no longer in the house,
filling the doorway, his hat
like none the tenants wore,

a gray hat of wool, not rain-crumpled, sun-bleached,
taller than the others, shadowing the door,
the house a silence between him and our mother,
wearing the hat then, the suit,

carrying the big leather bag, not as before,
with the case of fertilizer samples,
and promised gifts of bitter horehound,
but snapped and locked against us now.

We raised our wonder-rounded eyes,
questioning time leisurely, receptively,
awaiting answers, fulfillment.
Looking up, we saw our father's face
dark eyes, the stranger hat,
and looking away in our careless leisure,
innocent of time—days, years, or forever—
and looking back, he is gone.

Lampkin light we have run down the lane,
over the culvert of sleeping trolls,
and back to the safeness of the yard,

our mother and grandmother calling us in.
my brother's buttons burn with
blue, dying lights of fireflies.
Our faces laughing like clowns,
we can no longer see one another's eyes.

Jeffrey Skinner

"Stay"

Jeffrey Skinner, a husband and father, paints a Louisville street scene with people that he knows will not stay—except in his poem. Skinner is a professor of English and the director of creative writing at the University of Louisville. His collections include *Late Stars* (1985) and *The Company of Heaven* (1992).

A clearance sale banner has broken free and risen
momentarily into clouds: *Everything Goes.* Cool air,
Canadian import, silvers the look of grass
and branch, each leaf a tuning fork set humming,
each shadow exact, razor-cut. Across the street
Frank rakes his hosta bed; the scritch
of tines jerks up my dog's head briefly. But it's
a known sound, and she sinks back
into the furred rumple of dream. My daughters
have entered their teens intact, whole shells, rarely
found, waiting to be lifted and filled with a new
element, air breathers now. Everyone alive
is arrayed. I don't say joyous, I say singular
constellation. And I want everything
to stay as it is: stay, cloud pinned
over the slaughterhouse on Market Street,
stay voices of men laying concrete on Mossrose.
Stay Sarah, whose body has sifted mine fifteen years.
Stay sober mind, stay necessary delusions.
Stay shadows, air, rake, dog. Good stay. Good.

Lee Pennington

"Of Earth"

A native of Eastern Kentucky, Lee Pennington now lives and writes in Middletown and is a longtime professor of English at Jefferson Community College, where he also nurtures new poets. This poem is a dirge for the death of spring and for one who loved the seasons of life.

I remember spring of year
When she would go to fields of growing corn
And on her knees in fresh plowed earth
Would place her ear to stalks to hear
Young blades' noisy growth.

Once the snow came late.
April blooms died where death is cold.
She came weeping from winter's delay
Carrying on her back the load
Of the world now white and dead.

Now she too must hear the wind—
Being so much of earth—
Must hear the hemlock needles
Whet against the stone
Where restless moonlight
Gives the shadows birth.

Leonard A. Slade Jr.

"For My Forefathers"

Formerly a professor of English at Kentucky State University in Frankfort, Leonard Slade was born in North Carolina and now writes poetry and teaches in Albany, New York. He has published numerous collections of poems, including *Another Black Voice* (1988), *The Beauty of Blackness* (1989), *Pure Light* (1996), and *Lilacs in Spring* (1998). His poems have been praised by such luminaries as Maya Angelou and Gwendolyn Brooks. This poem is a tribute to his ancestors, who survived slavery on faith and hope.

⋘

For my forefathers
Whipped from Africa
Where children cried
but ships sailed on
And plantation owners were animals
their roars echoing three-hundred years.

For my forefathers
Whose fingers pierced cotton bolls
Beneath the sun roasting human flesh
And darkness told master
to rape black women
for labor and profit.

For my forefathers
Whose masters cursed the North
And justified the South
And debated Lincoln vs. Douglas
And cited slaves in the Bible
And returned to Africa for more.

For my forefathers
Who couldn't read or write
But heard freedom ringing

After Lincoln's Emancipation Proclamation
That taught me to watch
And pray for a new day.

For my forefathers
who loved me.

Catherine Sutton

"Buzzard's Roost"

Catherine Sutton's poem is a lament for the African American women who washed the clothes and served the whites of Louisville in 1880—and for those who still do. She has been a member of the faculty and staff of Bellarmine University for many years.

In 1880, 64% of all working women in Louisville,
Kentucky were servants or laundresses.

Housewives and servants passed laundry out the
back door into the hands of black women who never
saw a starched collar or tucked sleeve on anyone
in Bug Alley or Buzzard's Roost where twelve
families clutched at thirteen brittle rooms.

Each apartment, one room wide, was a mine shaft
collapsing on the solid darkness and frail children,
battered as the cook stove and the debris on which
people sat and slept. Hung loosely on the back gallery
porches, the outside wooden stairs led to the dirt
yard and the one tap at 136 West Jefferson.

The laundresses of Buzzard's Roost carried water
past the overflowing privy, up the rotting stairs
before they could boil, scrub, rinse clothes to the
brightness black women made from their own lives.
On clotheslines in the yard, woven among the sheds
and stables, they hung white flags and told each
other the truths beneath the facts I've read

in the 1880 census. Arms raised to ropes strung above
their heads, stood: Mary Thomas, single, four boys,
none still alive. Jennie Reed, a roomer, age 29,
three children. Lizzie Lewis age 64, six children,

four still living. Nellie Simpson, Head of House,
her daughter, 17. All the "best grade of colored girl"

as the want ads required. These dark rolls of microfilm
excavate the site now wiped clean by a Travel Lodge
where black women climb the outside stairs unfurling
clean linen in each room, banners shining for their
mothers who send a bold, white signal from the yard.

Frank X Walker

"Black Box"

Founder of the Affrilachian writers' movement, which is composed of African American writers of the Appalachian Mountains, Frank X Walker is a poet and teacher whose work is a model and an inspiration for younger poets. The first selection, "Black Box," paints an ironic family portrait of burley farmers who will lose their youth and lives to the tobacco that once supported them.

in the photo
only suspenders, a black leather belt
and the shadow under a hat
are darker than your face
a charcoal reservoir for the sun

a handrotted filterless cigarette dances
at the edge of your smile
like a ghost
the child cradled at your hip
is wringing her tiny hands
unable to look away to the camera
she is only four
but she recognizes the devil
on your lips

acres and acres of your life
hang from the top rails
inside the tobacco barn
this was suppose to be a victory photo
so you allow yourself the pleasure
of a special blend
savoring the raw strength
of its unknown toxins

next to you
in my father's arms

my entire hand gripping the expanse
of his thumb
I am fully focused
on the mysterious blinking eye

none of us seem to know
that the smell of burley can get under your skin,
    way under
or that the black box would capture
more light than the obituary

"God's House," from *Buffalo Dance*

This is a section from Walker's long poem about York, the body servant to William Clark, who accompanied Meriwether Lewis on the journey of discovery to the West Coast.

◦✇◦

The expedition left the Louisville, Kentucky, area
near the Falls of the Ohio on October 26, 1803.

When we first left Kentucke
the trees had commenced to dressing up
the fall harvest an the garden
was already full a pumpkins an squash.

Massa Clark didn't ask me to go on no expedition.
He just say "pack" an pointed to the door.
So I gather up what little I got an more than I can carry a his
an head off to a sail-bearing keelboat
where his friend Massa Lewis is waiting.
That boat was so big
you could lay any ten a the sixteen men on board
or eight a me head to toe an still have enough
room for the dog.

We start out on the Ohio an swing up the old man a rivers.
When we gets to the mouth a the dark woman
they calls the Big Muddy
we sets up winter camp a good canoe ride from Saint Louie.

That spring when the rains come we cross the Misssissippi
an commence to climbing the M'soura
an float right up through heaven on earth
more sky than I ever seen, rocks as pretty as trees
an game so plentiful they come right down to the river bank
an invites they selves to dinner.

Now, I ain't what you would call
a scripture quoter, but the first time
I seen the water fall at M'soura,
felt a herd a buffalo stampede
an looked down from top
a Rock Mountains, it was like church.

An where else but God's house can a body servant
big as me, carry a rifle, hatchet ana bone handle knife
so sharp it can peel the black off a lump a coal
an the white man
still close his eyes an feel safe, at night?

Jane Mayhall

"Shaking the Tablecloth"

A native of Louisville, Jane Mayhall has lived in New York City most of her life. When she writes poems, however, she often returns to her girlhood and the common domestic rituals that have been seared into her memory.

Some pleasures come undiluted; on October mornings
when the sun aimed its last, cumulated gold
over our depleted grape arbor, the baked raisins
turned black, wizened solar memories, the air at the edge
of town coming on with a sauterne bite of cold,
and the Kentucky sky high in a preternatural, almost
a Tiepolo blue, my mother would go to the open
kitchen door, with one of our two surviving tablecloths
under her arm and, leaning out, would shake out crumbs.

Even when there were not crumbs, the ritual of morning
from last night's supper was her excuse to feel the air,
and look on past fences to the bold, emblazoned woodland,
and unlock her eyes to the wanton circumference of the world.
I saw her shaking the white linen she had washed and ironed,
gazing beyond. It was a great chance she had every day
to do something ritualistic and free; and like wine
poured over me, intoxicated credence, faith.
That a shook cloth had in it all that distancing.

Ron Seitz

A Louisville native and former Bellarmine University professor, Ron Seitz, and his wife, Sally, were close friends of the Trappist monk and writer Thomas Merton, whose untimely death in 1968 left memories and a void that Seitz has turned into numerous poems. The first poem is a canticle to his lost friend.

✸

"Thomas Merton: A Signature"

THOMAS MERTON
the shade of my hulk amove in time
a shadow cast forward to envelope my spirit
a spectre cloak to wrangle my weight upon the pavement
the heavy gravemark I carry aback all these years
an echoed tome that will not still the tomb

THOMAS MERTON
his life a fleet phantom passing-thru
a memory vision'd Cold Mountain climb
a longday lone monk tracery Way
a cowl scrawl of cryptic cables to what Ace

THOMAS MERTON
his face flesh caught framed by space
an ear to the hidden rhythms of a voice
so weary with write waiting the call
to mark the void with silent song
to initial empty his portrait a Person

THOMAS MERTON
a motioned body blanking white this page
of what   of why   and Who
here announced to audience always
One and None

"Found Note of a Monastery Escapee"
A Confession of Sorts

out of Kentucky on down

to Arkansas in April
hailing shacks and poverty
rags and sticks singing
the cottonfield dynasty of Mammy

across Texas to visions
west and lost Pueblo tombs
reaching high to cold mortuary
starry and ancient

Aida's blond warrior march
wading the Rio Grande shoeless
through Tijuana to triumph
with Mexico

tequila's sad sweat of dust
raining rose petals and maidens
chanting a hot bordello
burro joke of domino trumpets

tramping it South to tropic
Acapulco's Aztec sun
shining Inca idol temples
tangled in jungle ruins

ranting a tribal ritual
of poetry and countless guitars
burying silence
in psalmbooks of the skull

R. Meir Morton

"Interview with an Aging Idol"

Victor Mature, the original Hollywood "hunk," was from Louisville. R. Meir Morton of Louisville decided to do an imaginary interview with the actor. First, she did some research, and then she cast the results as a monologue; and so we have her poem. It's amazing how much a good poet can get into a short poem.

The producer called me up, said:
Would you consider playing the father
in a remake of your old film?
I said I'd play the mother
if the price were right.
I looked at the script, my role
was meaningless, unnecessary.
All I do is run around in a robe
with a towel wrapped around my head.
Hey, I could have phoned the part in.

I'll tell you how it started.
I went out to Hollywood, just looking.
Ran into this guy who asked me to read
for the Pasadena Playhouse.
Next thing I knew I was on stage.
Then the movie magazines dubbed me The Hunk.
Hunk of Junk, I called it.
I never said I was a great actor,
got trunkloads of reviews to prove it.

If it hadn't been for one hometown girl
I never would have left.
I went to this debutante thing,
asked her for a dance.
She said she wasn't dancing with the son
of an immigrant.

I promised myself I would leave town,
make it big. And I did.

Those were the days, I really miss them.
Back then you could jump in a convertible,
wheel around to see the old gang.
Memories, I have lots of good ones.
I'd love to do it all over again,
even the mistakes.
A magazine called, wanted to know
if I was dead.
I told them, No.
If you are going to write about me
get some pictures from the old days.
That's how I'd like to be remembered.

Jane Gentry

"A Garden in Kentucky"

You've seen the gardens. An elderly couple has moved into town to be close to their children. They miss the earth's seasonal rotation of seeds into fruit and more. So, bit by bit, they bring the farm to town, complete with a rooster. What you get is a contented couple and a fine poem by Jane Gentry of Versailles.

Under the fluorescent sun
inside the Kroger, it is always
southern California. Hard avocados
rot as they ripen from the center out.
Tomatoes granulate inside their hides.
But by the parking lot, a six-tree orchard
frames a cottage where winter has set in.

Pork fat seasons these rooms.
The wood range spits and hisses,
limbers the oilcloth on the table
where an old man and an old woman
draw the quarter-moons of their nails,
shadowed still with dirt,
across the legends of seed catalogues.

Each morning he milks the only goat
inside the limits of Versailles. She feeds
a rooster that wakes up all the neighbors.
Through dark afternoons and into night
they study the roses' velvet mouths
and the apples' bright skins
that crack at the first bite.

When thaw comes, the man turns up
the sod and, on its underside, ciphers
roots and worms. The sun like an angel

beats its wings above their grubbing.
Evenings on the viny porch they rock,
discussing clouds, the chance of rain.
Husks in the dark dirt fatten and burst.

"The Drum Majorette Marries at Calvary Baptist"

You've seen the drum majorette on the football field in all her glittery glory; and
when she marries she takes it all with her—and Gentry's poem tells the score.

She goes blind down the aisle.
Candles prick the twilight
banks of gladioli, fern, and baby's breath.
Abloom in polyester peau de soie,
she smiles a starlet smile, clings
to her wet-eyed daddy's beef.
The organ metes her steps in groans.
Her mother wrings a tissue in her lap.
The groom, monolith to the white cloud
she is, waits at the altar. His Adam's
apple bobs. He is a straight, black
prop incidental to this script.

Outside, night falls over the tableau
the flashbulbs freeze as the couple
ducks through showers of seed
and runs for the idling limousine.
Before the door clicks shut on all her gauze,
in the strange light the white dress
seems to drift like petals piece by piece,
until out of the net the drum majorette
pumps her knees. Her trim boots dart,
her white gloves slice
at cacophonies of dark.
Her silver whistle flashes, shrills.

Eve Spears

"The Daughter"

Eve Spears grew up in Jesse Stuart country in northeast Kentucky, but she lived most of her life in Georgetown, Kentucky, where her husband, Woodridge, taught at the college. She grew up in a culture in which the folkways of growing food and cooking, of worshiping and playing, were their way of life. Ballads and folksongs from England, Scotland, and Ireland were still being sung. It's hard to read this poem, with its balladlike rhyme of *abcb* and its story about a dying woman and her mysterious mother, without wanting to sing it.

What is the time, O Mother, dear Mother,
Since I came to bide the night with you?

Only an hour or so until morning,
Only an hour and the night will be through.

What is the noise that I hear in the door-yard?
Is somebody coming or going away?

It's only the old hound turning around, dear,
Only the old hound facing the day.

Was that a door that opened, dear Mother,
Or was it but my imagining?

Only a shutter a-blowing, my darling,
Only a shutter it sounded to me.

Oh, listen, dear Mother, a step on the stairway,
A step so light. I hear it again.

It's only the old house a-settling, my darling,
A sign in the summer it's going to rain.

A sign of rain and a moving about me,
Tell me, oh, tell me, who stays for the night?

It's just my old mother so restless and weary,
So painful her bed and so long is her fight.

Why do the corners grow darker, dear Mother,
And why does the wind cry lonesomely?

Your eyelids are heavy, so sleep, my sweet darling;
Only the wind can see, can see.

Woodridge Spears

"Interleaf"

The second half of the Spears writing team is Woodridge Spears, who, like his wife, is from Jesse Stuart country. His poetry tends to be academic and occasionally laden with remote allusions, but this one is just as dark and foreboding as his wife's poem.

For Eve
November night unlike those former hours,
The stern with rain and heavy hours ago:
Eleventh month and drawing to the bound,
November night and mild-remembered,
Summer-mild to come at this, the waning.

The garden of the bright red bird is dark,
A willow darkness fringes all the runs,
Lost sometime color of the tangled vine,
A window darkness, utter, still prevails.

Motion mild speaks over the night, and speech
Recedes at last to river, river tones
That lap at passing, lap, and double on,
Water mild as blessing sound, and gone.

Settle for you the music of the light,
Mild night, chosen bird, mirrors in the dark:
River, river of blessed sound,
Accept the invocation of the breath
Not as a prayer, not as a prayer to death.

Quentin Howard
"Going Home"

Quentin Howard is one of the three Pikeville poets gathered here, so named for
their frequent publishing in the Pikeville College literary magazine, *Twigs,* edited by
Bruce Bennett Brown. In this selection Howard accompanies a Vietnam War veteran home on a train that carries the ghosts of veterans of more than one war.

The C & O train, nosing through canyons of rock,
Noisily enters Floyd County, late
Going eighty-two miles southeast from Ashland.

Fetid shacks, perched on gray cliffs
Reflect as mansions in the still dead river below.

My head splits with clacks of wheels on rainy rails.
(I wish I could escape the rain.)

With every stop, there are thirty-two, empty feelings
    claw at my insides,
Knowing I am getting closer home.

I am glad the fly-specked window
    further distorts my face.

I escape by watching the river mansions.
Suddenly, the pale woman in an ermine cloak
With swollen lips the color of overriped grapes
Drops tears from powder-puff eyes,
Walks on the river, still beckoning me to follow.

At Dwale, the nineteenth stop,
A black-shawled purple lady laboriously climbs aboard.
Empty booths call to her but she comes to me
Enticed by my uniform and overseas stripes.

I feel her bony hips.
Her questioning eyes stare through me.

I wade quickly away from the river where I was baptized.

"My only grandson, my Bobby," the dry wrinkled lips move.
"You must have seen him at Brestogne?"
"Brestogne? What a strange name. I only remember Tay
    Ninh Province."
"But why?"

Tears form but do not drop from eyes too old.
I offer her no sympathy.
Inwardly, I laugh as I turn back to the dead river.

Suddenly, I see brass bands on parade,
Welcoming home a war hero.
There is no sound, because
There are no brass bands in my home town.

Lillie D. Chaffin

Born in Pike County in 1925, where she lived most of her life, Lillie D. Chaffin is perhaps best known as an author of children's books, including *Bear Weather* (1969), a verse story about a mother bear and her cub in winter, which was selected as one of the fifteen best juvenile books of 1969. She also wrote deceptively simple and cynical poems for adults.

"Stance"

"Never spread your legs except
in your own bedroom," Mama
cautioned. "Never sit and do
a long legged dance as men'll
think you're working yourself up
for them, and don't stick out
your tongue or your chest. Ladies
never beg attention." I walked
about knock-kneed, hump-backed,
dry lipped, now and then wishing
the message would move out
or over long enough and
far enough that I might do
a natural thing or two.

"Sunning"

"It's not decent," Mama said, "to go
out naked. You put on another
princess slip right now, or stay at home.
You can't be sunning yourself, and that's
final."
　　　　It was Mama's last word on
between-the-leg exposure, but dark
days have dulled that tenderness. Questioning
that anyone cares to peek through this

skirt, I send all my selves out to eyes
of varied critics who want my poems dressed
in old styles, need lines freshly struck
in blood—menstrual or heart-stabbing—
crave revised proverbs, question mechanics,
deny metaphors . . .
                              If my poems indecently
give glimpses of old skeletons and new skin,
these people don't know me, Mama. If they attack
words which keep sunlight and shadows in
balance, how I let air circulate without
burning my lips, you must know that I
always wear my photo gray lenses.

Carolyn Wilford Fuqua

"Hair"

Carolyn Wilford Fuqua of Hopkinsville found inspiration for this poem in the Bible, specifically in Second Samuel 14:25–26: "Now in all Israel there was none to be so much praised as Absalom for his beauty; from the sole of his foot even to the crown of his head there was no blemish in him. And when he polled [trimmed] his head— now it was at every year's end that he polled it; because the hair was heavy on him, therefore he polled it—he weighed the hair of his head at two hundred shekels, after the king's weight." Absalom was the rebellious third son of King David, and he challenged his father in battle several times. His long hair eventually caused his death during an attempted retreat, when it was caught in the branches of a tree, hanging him.

Absalom, Absalom,
King's son, Absalom,
Beautiful in Israel,
Beautiful as a stag in the forest,
      in King David's oak forest,
Each year's end
Cut his princely hair.
When it weighed heavy upon him
      like a crown,
He cut the black cloud, curling crisply,
Weighed it upon the king's scales,
(Two hundred shekels on the king's scales)
      each year's end.

Absalom, Absalom,
King's foe, Absalom,
Crafty in Israel
Craved his father's crown;
At four years' end
Had stolen the hearts of the men of Israel.
      "Absalom is king at Hebron!"
      Absalom, Absalom,

King's woe, Absalom,
Riding in the king's forest,
Prisoner of his pride in the forest,
Hung high from the oak
By crisply curling hair
(Two hundred shekels' worth on the king's scales)
Prey to Joab's darts, three darts
To the heart of David's son
        still alive in the oak
He dies under blows from ten young men.

"May all who rise against you
Be like that young man,
O King!"

But the father covered his face.
        "O my son Absalom,
        My son,
        My son!"

Reid Bush

"April"

Reid Bush was born across the Ohio River in southern Indiana. He lived in California as a youth, then went to school in Arkansas, Indiana, and Kentucky. He has lived in Kentucky since 1969 and has been married to a Kentuckian for a long time. He has children living in five states and Malaysia. He was an English teacher at various levels until he retired in 2000.

What I love most in April's
how its best days warm the grass
so much you stop walking
or planting or mulching
or playing catch with a kid—
or whatever you're doing—
and just lie down flat in it.

And as you lie there—
body spread out and adrift
under an April sky—
you feel so satisfied
that all that's left to want
is to stay there forever.

And you feel light,
                lifted,

knowing some day you will.

Bruce Bennett Brown

"Blue-Fall"

One of the least-known of Kentucky's important literary figures is the reclusive Bruce Bennett Brown of Zebulon, near Pikeville, in Pike County. In the 1960s and 1970s at Pikeville College he was editing *Twigs,* one of the most lively and experimental literary magazines in the country, which published established, well-known writers alongside fresh and fragrant talent. He has written some of the most brilliant and original—sometimes enigmatic—poetry of anyone in Kentucky. In addition, he is a master of two almost extinct genres—the diary and the personal letter. The poem below is but a nugget of the riches in his trunk.

Dreadful is the singing of the hymn
in this chilly afternoon before the oblong
blunted tale becomes a bell,
walking in a peal unshaped
three colors make a sound you say:
freckled egg in the shaded nest,
history of the flapping flock
and the flight
and the light
slanted right,
rain cuts the sparrow down to size.

You talk confusing things
about leaving here for France,
questioning the architecture of
the human column,
how soon the low wind again over emptiness
and the trembling setting in,
the cherry in the wooden bowl
splits its final seed.

We give enough attention to the dry moon,
listening for the catch in the blood
and the floating leaves,

a lost bee from the hive
a hand flung up for speech
and is that Silence forever and right now.

Don't leave the cry open with a why.
Let the cry close.
In the courtesy of country places
your hands quiet the furious fruit
and the last whimper of the sun.
You would not try to spell my curses
or my praise.
My private language
is my own worn book.

You will stay and be,
will doubt and hold out.

Dreadful is the singing of the hymn
and the terrible gesture of amen,

    the echo and the scream lead out the
    celebration

Jim Wayne Miller

"The Brier Losing Touch with His Traditions"

No Kentucky poet has been more beloved than Jim Wayne Miller, a native of North Carolina who attended Berea College and, after graduating with a Ph.D. in German from Vanderbilt, spent the rest of his career at Western Kentucky University, where he wrote poetry about the southern Appalachians and where he promoted and supported other poets and prose writers who wrote about his cherished mountains. For many of his poems, he invented a persona called "the Brier," a native of the mountains much like Miller himself who loves the old ways and crafts and tries to come to terms with progress and the new ways. The Brier in this poem learns to play the role of traditional mountain craftsman when he makes chairs to sell to the public. It's good marketing, but is he being true to himself?

Once he was a chairmaker.
People up north discovered him.
They said he was "an authentic mountain craftsman."
People came and made pictures of him working,
wrote him up in the newspapers.

He got famous.
Got a lot of orders for his chairs.

When he moved up to Cincinnati
so he could be closer to his market
(besides, a lot of his people lived there now)
he found out he was a Brier.

And when his customers found out
he was using an electric lathe and power drill
just to keep up with all the orders,
they said he was losing touch with his traditions.
His orders fell off something awful.
He figured it had been a bad mistake
to let the magazine people take those pictures
of him with his power tools, clean-shaven,
wearing a flowered sport shirt and drip-dry pants.

So he moved back down to east Kentucky.
Had himself a brochure printed up
with a picture of him using his hand lathe,
bearded, barefoot, in faded overalls.
Then when folks would come from the magazines,
he'd get rid of them before suppertime
so he could put on his shoes, his flowered sport shirt
and double-knit pants, and open a can of beer
and watch the six-thirty news on tv
out of New York and Washington.

He had to have some time to be himself.

Logan English
"The Wind That Shakes the Barley"

Logan English was Bourbon County's poet-errant, a man who loved Kentucky but who could never live for very long in the land that formed and nourished him and provided him with material for his poetry, plays, and songs. He was a strolling player, a singing poet, a lyrical dramatist, a thespian whose love for the state lasted as long as his life. He was most influenced by his grandfather, a Baptist minister, and the tenants who worked his family's farm when he was a boy. In his epic poem "No Land Where I Have Traveled," he recalls his Kentucky roots, his birth in Henderson, his boyhood years and young manhood at Wyndhurst, the English-LaRue homestead near Paris, Kentucky, the beloved land from which he was always departing in anger and frustration and to which he was always returning in love and acclamation. This was his place on earth, where "the truth is in the soil." The first poem is about the universal subject of love.

If by chance I have slipped
My hand into your heart—

Then I would dress you in silk:
White silk with a great, soft
Blue about your throat;
A golden girdle beneath your
Breasts in the manner of
The ancient Greeks; a purple trim
About the hem brushing
The golden sandals of Io.

But like the sun we rage
At the moon and fall asleep
When the opportunities arise.

Just so: you have filled my
Mind with possibilities
That only Titania could imagine.

Like Helen and Paris;
Hero and Leander
    (whose souls loft above
      the stormy seas of the Hellespont)
The lost lovers of history & myth
Have entered our frailty.

But when I first saw the shimmering
Barley of your hair;
Looked into the China of
Your eyes: I knew the wind was in
My hand and I could shake the barley.

"Beware You Sons of Sorrow"

Another—*the* other—universal subject is war. This poem is an irregular sonnet about the irony and waste of war that only a philosopher could write.

Oh beware you sons of sorrow; oh beware
You sons of death! It is the dead, who died
Quickly, that war serves best; for they wear
Their illusions to the end. But they who tried
To understand war's majesty and came
Home, brought with them the broken shell
Of an empty dream. "We kept alive the flame
Of Freedom," they would say—but, in the well
Dark place of their deepest minds, the Siren's song
Is tuneless and honor is left behind to bleach
With the bones of those who died under the long
Shadow of man's neglect. And if war did teach
The gentle art of peace—then, long ago,
The guns were silent as the river's flow.

Maureen Morehead

One of Kentucky's most talented poets, Maureen Morehead writes about agonizing emotions and early loss with perfect control. She holds graduate degrees in English and composition from the University of Louisville and teaches in the Jefferson County school system. The first poem is from *Our Brothers' War,* a collection of poems and stories that she and Pat Carr, who has taught English at Western Kentucky University at Bowling Green, based on actual letters and diaries from the period of the American Civil War. Morehead's second poem is about a more recent, and devastating, loss.

"Why I Stopped Writing in My Diary"

It was May when we married.
I was sixteen.
The peach trees were in bloom,
and the white peony.

Now I am grown.
When I look in the glass,
it is an ordinary sparrow
that I see,
small and rent and wary.

The woman making poems
from my small parcel of diaries
has learned that Willis died quickly,
an artillery shot to the head,
that I told no one
but my children.

Forgive me.
Have you noticed
when someone you love dies
it is the sound of his boots upon gravel
that you wait for,

and the lost timbre of his voice
to restore you—

I wrote Mr. Lincoln,
asking that I might cross, both going
and coming, my enemy's lines.
Thus, I have traveled forthright

to the tomb of my dear husband.
I intend to bring him home
as soon as I am able.

"Driver's License"

I was swimming at the Y today,
a little earlier than usual,
when the sun, still low,
rose through the three windows
to the right, then the left, of me,
casting rectangles of light
on the bottom of the pool
where I saw the shadows of my arms
like quick dark birds across the deck of our house,
and that dream I want to forget,
my son in biology class,
the tall curved windows admitting light,
and when they pull out the drawer,
he is eight with that crooked smile
and I know he will not move again.
   When we bought this lot,
I could not sleep for days—
a pond lay beyond the trees, and our son,
I knew, would inevitably go there,
who is a month from sixteen
whose knees nearly touch the dashboard
as we drive through Louisville.

Cora Lucas

"April Furlough"

A native of Louisville, Cora Lucas wrote her first poem when she was seven. Her
mother's tragic early death and her father's piano performances (he was a piano
graduate of the Conservatory Verdi in Milan) are recurring themes in her poetry.
The wife of a Louisville surgeon, she and her husband, a soldier, lived through
World War II. In this poem about the constancy of love and loss she recalls a furlough when her husband returned home briefly to see her and their young daughter,
who is now grown and caring for her widowed mother.

Cold April furlough
the wool warm embrace
after months of waiting
how trim the khaki
the Sam Brown belt
how firm the muscles
in long-deferred love.

The toddler behind bars
in the play-pen
kissed and fondled but left
to her own amusement
while mother and father
unleashed their longing.

Ripened years
flattened now into albums and slides
slick surfaces older eyes
scour deep for answers,
a certain way of looking
at transformations:
growth, change, death.

Now the child
prepares the guest room for mother

kissed and hugged, advised to rest
with books   with wool warm
surplus army blankets.

These comforts have boundaries.

Through stair rails
she hears the din, laughter,
knows love cannot close the distance
from that April furlough.

Leatha Kendrick

"Postcard"

Leatha Kendrick, the mother of three daughters, lives with her husband in eastern Kentucky. Her poetry has been published widely in such periodicals as *Connecticut Review* and the *American Voice*. She has taught creative writing at the University of Kentucky and Morehead State University and has been coeditor of *Wind Magazine*. Robert Morgan has said that she gives "a fresh voice to the poetry of motherhood and family." In this poem she writes a postcard to her late mother while driving one of her daughters through an everlasting landscape.

dear Mother, I've found the blank space underneath the sky,
the world without you—bounded, thin, and blazing.
Months before the heart's failure carried off your shut
mouth or your closed eye flashed wide to death
we were already retreating from each other
faster than the two ends of the universe.
I'd barely learned to write to you again.
Gone, you plunge back toward me—
the reverse of flight puts you briefly
in my hand. So here I am turning the world
on its face, poor false front, its blue and green,
as garish through my windshield as those scenes we'd pick
to send home from the beach: "Wish you were here!" I am
driving the youngest girl to school or to piano, the sky
the hill the flower by the roadside and the names you gave them
not disappearing! Leaping out, stubborn, bright. The world so vivid, nothing
ends.

Charlie Hughes

"Mundy's Landing"

Charlie Hughes is a Lexington poet, a writer of fiction, and the editor of *Wind Magazine,* the venerable periodical founded years ago by the indefatigable Quentin Howard, who put his resources and his life into one of the best of our literary journals. His is a tradition being honored and built upon by Hughes. The dark, haunting memories of childhood are the subject of many of his poems, including this one about the night noise in a new house, a defiant, protective mother, a son, and an absent husband and father.

⚬✖⚬

What I remember is the brightness,
every light in the house,
and my reflection beside my mother

in the dark mirror of each bare window,
no curtains yet in our first night
in that house, and my mother

illuminated at the window, alert,
standing with legs defiantly apart,
and the .38 automatic in her hand.

She'd heard a noise, she said.
Later she told how she'd cocked
the pistol before the window,

slid the cold metal sleeve back
over the barrel like a foreskin,
an invitation to whatever or whoever

lurking beyond the porch.
She never said where you were
that night Daddy. I never asked.

John Spalding Gatton

"Called"

A native of Louisville and a professor of English at Bellarmine University, John Spalding Gatton is an academic writer who also writes occasional poems, like these heartrending lines about the early death of a friend.

Somewhere, a phone is ringing.
    —He's gone.
    —I know.
    —The service is Tuesday at 11 at the cemetery, at . . .
    —I know. I bought the plot.

    —You're welcome to go with us   or on your own.
    —Whatever.
    —So, then, we'll see you Tuesday.   I'm truly sorry.
    —Good night.
I lift the receiver.
—He's gone.
I know the rest.
Unconscious, we embrace inevitable truths that,
Conscious, we would vigorously deny.

You were so anal.
The day the spot appeared,
You picked up boxes at the store,
And started packing books,
First individually wrapped in tissue and newsprint
("hospital corners," you blithely called the folds),
Then taped and labeled.
The cartons, too, their contents tightly ordered,
You sealed with plastic crosses
And catalogued in precise capitals
On top
And

All
Four
Sides.
—You never know how the movers will stack them, you
    explained.
Christ,
When I told you to let go,
I didn't mean
Of
Life.

Charles Semones

Charles Semones would have been a major poet no matter where he was born. Fortunately for us, he was born in 1937 in Mercer County, which over the past forty and more years he has written into a poetic landscape that he calls "the Sabbath Country," which is as real and as vivid as Faulkner's Yoknapatawpha County in Mississippi. The author of several volumes of poems, including *Witch Cry* (1973), *Homeplace* (1993), *Hard Love* (1994), and *Afternoon in the Country of Summer* (2003), Semones is like no other poet you've ever read, even though one critic called him "an improbable cross between James Still and James Thurber." Such an association honors Still and Thurber as much as it honors Semones. The following poems will introduce you, rather inadequately, to the country of his youth, his maturity, and his imagination—the Sabbath Country. First is an overview from birth to death.

"The Sabbath Country"

To be born in that country was to come alive
screaming for mercy. Cut loose, we blinked
in the frantic light and looked around.
We drank our meals of milk and grew sturdy.

Pubescence seized us early. Legends
and old wives' tales kept us scared and proper.
Old men turned scriptural in dog days
and thumped out warnings of the Lord.
In our imaginings, we saw Him large with anger.
But we were young and lusty and liked to tease.
We tunneled deep into haymows, deep into love.
Sin reddened around us like tomatoes.
We were heedless of the ripening.

Suddenly, it seemed, the light failed, and the wind
came up menacing. Thunder snarled along the paths
of heaven. Flowers withered in a gust. Old hounds
dreamed, sinister, in chimney corners.
All night long there was a whining sound.

To grow old in that country was to hurt with idleness.
We felt the creek turn cold. Our Sunday afternoons
droned sad. Clouds loomed tall to westward and the dusk
came early. We lighted lamps and counted secret guilts
like old coins. We did not go into darkened rooms
and attics. For each of us, in time, a bed was made.
The tender wives of our young manhood haunted us.
We recalled the cries that terrified us when our sons were born.

When we died, our mothers reappeared with fingers
quick as birds, and draped the laughing mirrors.

"Christmas Eve in Kentucky"

for M.R.

The earth, after several hard freezes in a row, is ready to accommodate
the heavy snow the weatherman predicted on the newscast at 6 o'clock.
As far back as late September, *The Old Farmer's Almanac* told us
this would happen. Directly overhead, the full moon of Advent
is close to bursting. The moonwash illuminates the hills and bottomland
for miles around. Distant farmhouses—century-old two-storied clapboard
and new low-slung ranch-style—are wrapped in strings of blinking lights,
inviting any travelers, a man and wife, say—and she with child—who, far
from home and cold and hungry, might be out this late. They could warm
themselves and share a cornucopia of food at any farmer's table.

On Deep Creek Hill, the Baptist bell,
stock-still, holds back its hallelujahs. The church is darkness-filled and
getting cold.
Earlier, we had candle-glow and carols by a country choir, the prayers of
the faithful,
and the ancient story of the Lord's Nativity retold. Afterward, we who
heard it
went out, sad, into the night, steadying our candles, knowing Peace on
Earth is still
a hollow phrase on Christmas cards, the rattle of a gourd, and nothing
more.

Westward, the sky banks low and starts to bulge into an overhang of
snow-clouds.

Old barns loom spectral, shaping rectangular shadows on the landscape.
Each one could be Bethlehem's stable, preparing for a miracle at midnight.
There is the shuffling of animals, anxious in their stalls. They sense the
    annual visitation
of shepherds, wise men, and a host of angels. In the distance, house by
    house,
the lamps in windows are turned off. Soon Santa Claus will be along. He
    was seen
on radar, crossing the Canadian border into North Dakota at 8 o'clock.
They told it on a TV bulletin at 10, and children headed straightaway to
    bed.
 Come morning, snow will be falling, carloads of kinfolk will be coming
    out from town,
and on Deep Creek Hill there'll be the glorious commotion of the Bap-
    tist bell.

Roberta Scott Bunnell

A friend once suggested that Roberta Scott Bunnell was a poor man's Dorothy Parker. I said, "Roberta can write rings around Parker." No one can write bittersweet poems about love and life with more incisiveness than Roberta Scott Bunnell. Born in 1910 in Paducah, she attended Logan College in Russellville and later the University of Louisville. She worked for many years at radio stations in Louisville. She has published in *Cosmopolitan, Saturday Evening Post,* and *McCall's,* as well as in a multitude of local and regional publications. Gregg Swem, a former arts writer for the *Courier-Journal,* has written a one-woman show based on Bunnell's life and poetry called *Roberta . . . Dahling.* Her poems are both sad and amusing.

"Four-Letter Word"

One night you left in anger
And told me where to go,
And ever since, I've been there,
I thought you'd like to know.

"What If"

What if the phone suddenly rings
some late and lush spring night
when I'm alone . . . and I should hear
his voice again . . .
saying "Hello!"
What if I could answer, coolly,
"How have you been?" and chat
awhile about ordinary things . . .
And then hang up, and put
the night latch on . . .
and murmur idly, to myself
"Well that, I guess, is that"
. . . and go to bed—and wait
impatiently for the dawn.

"Sonnet"

How odd that I can see you on the street
and have no feeling should we chance to meet,
except a passing moment of concern
that eyes, once tender, suddenly would turn
the other way to keep from meeting mine;
and strange that I can come upon some line
we read together in a well-loved book
and turn the page without a second look
or hear a song we heard when first we met
and have no aching feeling of regret.
And yet, just now, my eyes were stung with mist
of tears, because I happened on a list
of laundry that I sent one day for you:
shirts—8; shorts—6; socks—4; pajamas—2.

"If I Should Be the First to Leave"

If I should be the first to leave, and you
Should lay me in a quiet resting place,
Where I must be content to sleep alone
Without the comfort of your loving face
Beside me, as accustomed I have grown—
O, rest I could, and possibly delight
Staying for awhile in solitude,
Peaceful and free in that eternal night—
Except for one, insistent, chilling thought:
That should you find some other after me
(Which, in itself, I'm willing to admit
Is only fair, and readily agree),
That she—not I—would then be justly due
To spend the last, unending night with you.

Dot Gibbs

Welcome to the enchanted world of Louisville's Dot Gibbs, who, while her husband was busy as an executive with a large printing company, spent her time seeing God in such ordinary things as sweet pea vines, dragonfly wings, and green peas in pods. Her companion in literary history may well be William Blake—the one who wrote "The Lamb" and "The Tyger." Here is a sampling of the epiphanies that Dot Gibbs found in nature and made into poems.

"Spinning Threads as Spiders Do"

You know how the sweet pea vine
spins green threads
like curly pig tails
to twine around fences

and grape vines spin tails
to hold grapes high
for the sun to warm and ripen
to purple, red and green

I seek morning beauty
and the soft twilight
spinning threads around beauty
with mind and heart strings

Man from earth's dust began
let's gather and around the fence twine
this flowered May Day of spring
and of the wonder of sweet peas sing.

"Dragonfly Wings"

Making dragonfly wings
is one of God's
most beautiful things
and laying green peas in pods.

Patricia Ramsey

"Harlan County Cat"

Patricia Ramsey is a native of Barbourville and grew up among Elizabethan ballads and folklore transplanted to Appalachia. She has taught in the public schools of Jefferson County, served as a counselor at Indiana University Southeast, and been a poetry therapist at the Southern Indiana Mental Health and Guidance Center in Jeffersonville. She is also a playwright and has won several prestigious awards with her play about coal mining in eastern Kentucky, *A Killin'*. In this poem she returns to her native mountains to take a stand against the giant, destructive "cats" that eat up the hills.

⌘

In the early morning
when mists hang wet spiderwebs
in hollows of dead leaves,
        wind sings
under and through rock cliffs
where ancient seas once raged,
the unmoccasined coon and badger
cross and recross the forgotten trails of men
        the silent trails to empty mines.
        Against the gray sky
stands a monstrous cat
its mouth hanging loose,
a few boney trees
dangling from its jaws.
(Someone said it can take a 125 cubic yard bite
        . . . that's half a mountain.)
Downstream from Decatur's Woods
everything is dead or dying.
The cat hunches over the countryside,
over the laurel and dogwood and mayapple
and even the blackbird flees the preying cat,
        deserts the land of acid water
        and bitter despair.

Half the mountain is gone
and more than half the people.
                    Lord,
you think we got nine lives?

Prentice Baker

"The Delusion"

A native of Leitchfield, in Grayson County, Prentice Baker was an office worker at the L&N Railroad by day and a poet by night. Although he has lived in the city most of his life, his poems recall his boyhood and youth in rural Kentucky. *Down Cellar,* a collection of his poetry, was published in 1973. This poem is a festival of country living and loneliness.

You are just in time for supper. You look tired;
There is pollen dust on your shoes.
Wave the moths from the screen; come in; sit.
Join me at corncakes and buttermilk,
Fried ham and gravy and shelly beans.
Then I will look into your clear eyes,
Reading the well-earned comfort of poor years
Lived richly. How genuine is your laughter!
We'll light a kerosene lamp for novelty.
A while, perhaps, you will honor me by pretending
I could be, or I might be or have been
The man to fill whatever lack you've found,
And I, delude myself that loneliness
Would slip away into our night-ringed fields
Could you remain; but this it never would.
There are fireflies over the tiger-lilies,
Over the clematis purpling the west fence.
It has been pleasant, your visiting with me,
And I will walk the gravel road with you,
Counting the dim white heads of Queen Anne's Lace
Blown in the drafty dusk among the weedstalks
Scornful of numbering, all the way to your house.
It may be that the dusk scorns loneliness
And the one goodnight kiss of our pretense.

Mary O'Dell

"Road Trip"

As I'm sure Mary O'Dell will agree, you're never too young or too old to write and enjoy poetry. Every age has its gifts and its visions. O'Dell, a native Appalachian now living in Louisville, is president of Green River Writers, an important support group for writers of all ages, and the author of some five volumes of verse. The fifth volume, *Living in the Body*, is the source of the poem below about living fully every moment of life.

(for Michelle)

Child of my long lover gone away
you are what I have now
yet I risk your limbs with my bad driving.

We run this midnight artery through some high state
until we swerve into a roadhouse, dimly lit.
We are looking to hear
    Turn around, go back to your lives.

But no one speaks our language.
No one speaks at all.

And so, forsaking that dim incandescence
we bore through darkness terminal as the good death.
Tonight is all we have.
Wild country waits.

Mary Ann Taylor-Hall

"Bunting"

Novelist and short-story writer Mary Ann Taylor-Hall of Sadieville is also a very fine poet, as the following imagist-tinged, philosophical poem will show. Responding to the aborted life of a bird and the plaintive night cries of animals in distress or dying, she experiences only temporary consolation in the thought that "we are all one thing" and finishes the poem with its big question unanswered—or perhaps unanswerable.

1

the feathers of the indigo bunting the cat killed
shine in the morning wind like broken mirrors
smithereens the green-black wings once scalloped
a little dip of breeze the life wanted to fly
the body knew how the life went out
on breath and did not come back the torn
blue chest had a long song it would sing

2

the distant high thrilled yelping in the night
means something is being taken from us
for food I suppose or play a possum perhaps
or some small dog lost in terror in the dry creek bed
but in the morning an indigo bunting sings
in the maple wood the cat purrs in a patch of sun
life goes on goes on we are all one thing
what our bodies breathe out goes through plants
they take from it what they need then give it back
whereupon it travels into other bodies
there is no comfort in this thought I'm leaving
something out I don't know what

Ann Jonas

"Making Coffins"

Ann Jonas is a poet's poet—one whose craftsmanship is sure, whose focus is certain, and whose control is total, whether she is writing about urban life or a casket maker in Wendover, in the mountains of eastern Kentucky.

I never did charge a man in my life
for making a coffin, and never had
a man offer me nothin'. I wouldn't
have took it if they had.
—Cecil Morgan, Wendover, Kentucky

Making coffins goes on year round.
Ain't over and done with
like spring planting.
If I had my pick,
I'd sooner be at it in fall.
Too hot in the shed when the sun's up,
too cold when the snow's up.
Fall suits me fine; trees turn color.
Count on Mother Nature.
She comes through every year.

Not people.
A body could up and pass on
middle of the night; a granny, say.
When they're old and paining,
ain't so bad. But could be a young chap
strong as heartwood, lungs give out.
Or buddies together in a mine.
Or some little kid fall in a well.
Could be a car wreck. Old jalopies,
when they hear a train whistle,
they go to pieces right on the track.

I make coffins for friends, kin,
altogether strangers.
Ain't hard to make. Average coffin
runs you fifteen-inch deep,
twenty-five wide at the feet; ten, head.
Takes a plane, two handsaws—
twelve-point, eight-point—
hammer, square.
That, poplar boards—all you need.
And nails.

Times I wonder why we can't stay on
at this good place
till we get the hang of it.
Seems like I study on that
whenever I see a dandelion ball
blow away in the wind.

Main thing—I stick to one rule:
no warped boards, no knots.
I don't want my work looking shoddy
in the sight of the Lord.

Vivian Shipley

"The Last Wild Horses in Kentucky"

Vivian Shipley was born in Chicago but grew up in Kentucky in and around Hardin County, where her family were farmers—"hillbillies," she fondly calls them. She was educated at the University of Kentucky in the 1960s and received her Ph.D. from Vanderbilt in 1975. Since 1969 she has taught at Southern Connecticut University, where she also edits the *Connecticut Review*. Her poems have appeared in numerous prestigious periodicals and have been collected under such titles as *Poems Out of Harlan County* (1989), *Fair Haven* (2000), and *When There Is No Shore* (2002). Her poems are filled with allusions to her Kentucky childhood: "No Connecticut roots, / my mind's back in Cecilia, Kentucky, the cellar house / where Grandma kept green mason jars she'd filled last fall." The following poem involves another return to Kentucky.

We stand at the bus stop. Eyeing my son and me,
the other children are quiet and they look hard.
It's not their first day of class. My fingers tighten
over my hand at six years: cowbarn, outhouse, backdoor,
cornbread, woodpile, chickenhouse. I rode a plowhorse
named Snip, no big yellow bus. Our greyhound, Queenie,

uncurled from under a forsythia bush outside the kitchen,
leaping to race me, but my father held her by the collar.
Before I rode off, he told me about the last wild horses
in Kentucky. Scoured out of hills, they were roped,
tied down, nostrils clamped shut. Their neck veins pulsed
like salmon jumping upstream. The mares all aborted.

I know beyond that word. Hanging limp as morning
wet grass, my son's hands are smooth not toughened
from milking a cow as mine were by the time I went
to first grade. I want to double fence a pasture to protect
him like my father did to keep our stallions apart in order
to keep them spirited for breeding. Eric waits, but strains

to see beyond the corner as I pull him back, fearing roads
I cannot see him travel. The day must come when I'll force
his snowsuited body out, without immunity, into January
mornings so cold milk jugs would freeze if I left them out
on doorsteps. Can I be ready with a message to pin on him
as his boots scale snow, tracking maps I have not traced?

Boarding the bus, Eric twists around to me from the landing
and I reach out to touch his shoulder, then stand waving him
out of sight. My stomach cupped in hands, I bow my head
and let my son go. Knowing how wild horses are broken,
I pray he will remember the soles of his bare feet running
through bluegrass blooming over hills in Hardin County.

Charles Williams

"Upon Discovering That My Daffodils
Were Taking Leave without a Word"

Munfordville attorney Charles Williams, who holds degrees from Duke University and the University of Kentucky, finds poems in his travels, his law practice, and the flora and fauna of his native Hart County.

I do not know the way back to the gate.
I know the way the daffodils have come.
Creeping, exploding through green-ridden winter,
The mystery-driven face,
This force that moves me even on my way.
Odd, that it should take me to a gate,
The way I watched the daffodils go last spring,
Processions of an April afternoon,
Unspoken riddles from another tongue.

Donald H. Vish

Donald Vish is a lawyer, a nature lover, and a photographer who, he says, enjoys the company of good books and good friends. He has, to my knowledge, just one book to his credit; but it is a delight. *Prideful Violets* (2001) contains thimble-sized poems filled with wit and wisdom, plus short, witty paragraphs, an "impolitical dictionary," and various other odds and ends that will mostly surprise and please you. Here are two examples of his short poems.

"Regret"

To marry or
To marry not
I haven't chosen yet.
But I know
The way I go
Will lead me to regret.

"Ryker's Ridge"

"Trust Jesus," said the faded sign
Above the covered bridge.
I did and so my horse and I
Set out for Rykers Ridge.

Trust Jesus, know that God provides,
Put all your faith in Him
But if you're going to Rykers Ridge
You better learn to swim.

Sarah Gorham

"Honeymoon, Pleasant Hill"

Sarah Gorham is a fine publisher and a fine poet. Her poems have appeared in such places as the *Nation, Paris Review, Poetry,* and *Antaeus.* She has also published several collections: *Don't Go Back to Sleep* (1989), *The Tension Zone* (1996), and *The Cure* (2003). She is cofounder and editor-in-chief of Sarabande Books in Louisville. In the following poem she and her new husband have fun at the old Shaker settlement near Harrodsburg.

Poor sinners, we wandered too far,
lured by those trim Shaker fences
like lace on the good mother's slip.

We slumped in chairs meant to straighten the spine.
Ran our fingers over testicle-shaped finials,
our palms down the Trustees' railing,

smooth as a woman's thigh.
Damn that was good pie, we exclaimed
to the waiter in his Shaker smock.

He cracked a smile (only three survive
in upstate Maine), and kept that
Shaker food coming. Baby

corn, vegetables soaked in lemon oil,
mashed potatoes swollen
around our steak. We tossed and turned the night,

our Shaker beds sheeted too tight—
and woke to labor that zig-zag dance.
First a hum from inside out, then the verse

pitched from brother east to sister west,

against the boards faster, the telltale
thump, heels dug in for good purchase.

Finally, the dousing with an ecstatic shout.
(So sure the Shakers were their Godly Version
would bear the future out.)

Boynton Merrill Jr.

Born in Boston in 1925, Boynton Merrill Jr. served in the navy during World War II, then earned a degree from Dartmouth College. In the early 1950s he moved to Henderson, Kentucky, to manage his mother's family farm. He soon became involved in real estate development and poetry. In 1976 he published both *A Bestiary*, a collection of poems, and *Jefferson's Nephews: A Frontier Tragedy*, a highly praised historical study of the gruesome murder of a family slave by two nephews of Thomas Jefferson living in far western Kentucky in the early nineteenth century. Two of the poems below are word portraits of a writer and a teacher, and the third is a sonnet about the ravages of time.

"The Writer"

With words for wings life is a magic flight.
Without them we can have no soul or mind.
We may with words take fear out of the night
And soar where we might else have been confined.

"The Teacher"

Words are the way that wisdom kisses you,
Sighing in your ears, shining in your eyes.
I bring you ideas pure and true
And warn you of false lovers' lies.

"Yesterdays"

Old sadness grown familiar has no pain.
Good years of friendship, kindnesses, and dreams,
When gradually lost cannot be had again.
Gone too are strength and grace, or so it lately seems.
But keep some glories well-remembered yet:
The brave words said, the deeds you dared to try,
The storm that turned to prism at sunset,
The lover kissed that smiled and stayed nearby,

Your child that went away to be a lark,
A few blue aging years away, and soared,
Flew vivid skies that you had feared were dark
And blessed your later life with sweet accord.
The other hoped-for joys that never came;
Forget such sorrows now. Time is to blame.

Hortense Flexner

Hortense Flexner, who spent most of her life in Louisville, was a graduate of the University of Michigan and worked as a journalist early in her career. She wrote several competent plays and popular children's books, and her collections of poetry—*Clouds and Cobblestones* (1920), *The Stubborn Root* (1930), and *North Window* (1943)—were reviewed favorably in several publications. She published numerous poems in national magazines, including the *New Yorker*. After her death in 1973 at the age of eighty-eight, several of her admirers published additional volumes of her poetry. Many of her poems, including the three below, were short, light poems with serious intent.

"Belief"

In six gold weeks of summer
The stripèd bee,
Still eager for more roses,
And sunny paths of clover sweetness,
Dies,
Believing that flowers are eternal.

"Complaint"

Creator—so we call Him and believe,
Whose vast intention and accomplished feat
Made life a theme, He had but to conceive
And we have had forever to repeat.

"Weary Phoenix"

Amid the flames, self burned, the great bird dies,
White embers wait his new birth as a nest,
But if he said, "Perhaps I shall not rise,
I think of sleep—perhaps the ash is best."

Joy Bale Boone

"The Supper"

A native of Evanston, Illinois, Joy Bale Boone married Dr. Garnett Bale of Elizabethtown in the early 1930s and lived most of her life in Kentucky. She became one of the state's leading advocates for the prevention and treatment of heart disease and for women's rights, as well as a major promoter of Kentucky's literary culture. In the early 1960s she was a cofounder of *Approaches,* a magazine of poetry by Kentuckians, which later evolved into *Kentucky Poetry Review.* In 1997 she became the first Kentucky poet laureate to be chosen under upgraded guidelines that specified that the office could be held by a writer in any genre, from poetry to fiction, and the laureate would be the state's active spokesperson for the literary arts. After her first husband's death, she married George Street Boone of Elkton and lived there and in Glasgow until her death in 2002. This poem is a tribute to her two daughters and four sons; it recalls the suppers around the table when they were young and when they returned for visits.

There are good late afternoons
when reverence shields our table
as an altar, when chipped plates
gleam as meissen in anticipation
of boys recounting hours away,
girls returning home in multiplicity,
wedging extra chairs around an oval
where milk and love were daily spilt
in tangled years of sixteen hands.

More daily, now, we are alone, two,
head and foot of table, pass to me,
please; no hands impatiently reaching
for bowls or silver once unsafe from
sand boxes and kits of tools.
The sun sets from an old angle,
a bit left of your right shoulder,
casting light on an oval altar
without need of consecrated light.

There are good late afternoons
when reverence shields our table.

James Baker Hall

"Stopping on the Edge to Wave"

James Baker Hall was named Kentucky poet laureate in 2001. A native of Lexington born in 1935, he has been a poet, novelist, photographer, and professor of writing at the University of Kentucky. In addition to his novels, he has published short stories in such periodicals as the *Saturday Evening Post, Shenandoah Review,* and the *Paris Review.* His poems have appeared in the *Sewanee Review, Southern Poetry Review,* and *Poetry.* The poem below, which first appeared in the *New Yorker,* is a daring, cutting-edge look into the presumed abyss.

> . . . light is on the edge—the last thing we know
> before things become too swift for us.
> —C. S. Lewis

The scene always takes place
at the gate, outside the wall,
and the assumption always is—

I can no longer even remember.
It's more a condition, like light—
Our condition always is

That I have the key
That you have the key
That we know what we are doing there

or here or anywhere. There is no key.
We stand atop whatever we can find
to climb up on, arm in arm,
peering over the wall.
There is no wall.

What is it then?
What is it we hope

to see on the other side? The vacant
streets lined with buildings. Nothing
moves, there is no color. Over the cobblestones nothing
moves, there is no sound. Behind the brick walls nothing
moves, as if we'd stopped off
in a photograph
on our way—

Where?

There is no where
and no when. As in a picture
of such emptiness, as if to speak
of such emptiness—nothing moves

at the center.
It is the light.
There are no sides.
The light falls

from the buildings into the streets
and keeps falling.
What more could we have
come all this way to know, hoping
to find our way

back to the room
of flowers, the bed,
the familiar stories? Everything

on the edge is familiar
where nothing is

the last thing we see,
like this light,
before things get too swift
for us. We thought we were

alone and indeed there is no other.
It is the light waving back.

We thought all things
change and indeed

there are no streets, no buildings.
The light falls
on white egrets
next to black
cattle grazing. The pasture falls

down to the sea. The light
has come all this way
bearing us with it. Each morning
at our backs the crater, each night
the sea. We are farther back
than we know. Nothing

does move—
in the form
of a white bird
it lifts off
and flies away
into itself

taking us with it, light
and then dark and then light
again, farther than we can see—
The sky
empty—

Joe Survant

"In Malay Forests"

Selected as the Kentucky poet laureate for 2003–5, Joe Survant, a graduate of the University of Kentucky and the University of Delaware, teaches contemporary literature and creative writing at Western Kentucky University. He has published three collections of poetry: *We Will All Be Changed* (1995), *Anne & Alpheus* (1996), and *The Presence of Snow in the Tropics* (2001), which is based on a year he spent with his family teaching at the Universiti Sains Malaysia, where he learned to tread lightly and carefully among the snakes and other denizens of the forest.

Fear of snakes
sends us highstepping
up the trail.
Overhead
a Tualong tree
outstrips its rivals
for air and light
despite the strangler fig
growing from a crotch
at 200 feet.

All around,
that silent life
rises and falls
beneath the airy bodies
of leaves.
Lianas, rattans, and creepers
send dense signals
where the slower self
still reads the book
of bramble and briar
and heartwood's sap
rises in tides
where no moon shows
nor any hand
leaflike goes.

Richard Taylor

"Upward Mobility"

A professor of English at Kentucky State University in Frankfort, Richard Taylor also owns a bookstore and writes poetry, including *Bluegrass* (1975) and *Earth Bones* (1979). *Girty* (1977) is a long narrative poem about a renegade white man who went to live with the Seneca Indians and took on their ways and attitudes against the encroaching whites. For his two years as poet laureate, 1999–2001, Taylor was also an eloquent spokesman for literature throughout Kentucky.

In a dialogue between the poet and a rock—yes, a rock—in his ironically named "Upward Mobility," Taylor pokes fun at human pride and conceit. In this poem the complacent rock is perhaps wiser than the almighty man.

⌘

for A. R. Ammons

Given your druthers,
I said to the rock,
what is it you would most
like to have that is man's?
Is it a tower of bone
from which to lord it over the others?
Is it reason, virtue, a face
that is the mirror of God's,
an opposable thumb?

Oh no, said the rock.
Those heights where the air
is anemic are nothing to me,
and dialectic puts me to sleep;
give me wind any day over babble.
Having little use for the upright,
I prefer proneness, my niche
on the slopes, sedentary ways.
Admitting that much is beyond
my grasp, still I know God's face
at the head of the hollow

is a craggy wonder.
When it rains, when it washes,
I take note of the flow,
but mostly I keep to my stratum,
resting frugal and flat.
All right, mundane. But
indispensably mundane.

Tony Crunk
"Reliquaria"

Tony Crunk is one of three young Kentucky poets who have won the coveted Yale Younger Poets competition in recent years. A native of Hopkinsville, Crunk earned degrees from Centre College, the University of Kentucky, and the University of Virginia. He has taught at the University of Montana and Murray State University and now teaches at the University of Alabama in Birmingham. His church-drenched Baptist boyhood in western Kentucky is the material out of which he has written an impressive collection, *Living in the Resurrection* (1995). In these unapologetically spiritual poems, there are echoes of familiar passages from hymns and the Bible; but these old words and images are placed in new settings that startle and illuminate. The result is a gentle, aching, restrained poetry filled with paradox and irony but no condescending satire. His people retain the dignity of vagrant yet redeemed souls this side of the Resurrection. In this poem a man carefully prepares his way into the hereafter, regardless of which way he will go.

1. *Found Hand-Painted on a Tin Flue Cover*

Ribbon of black crape
draped on a door knob

like broken strings
hanging from a loom

with the words: Weep not.
What do I need of this world?

2. *S. P. Dinsmoor Describes His Tomb*

I have made myself a coffin with a glass lid.
By the door of my grave house

I have set a cement angel and a stone jug.
When I see the host coming down, the lid will fly open

and I will sail out into the air like a locust.
If I am called above, the angel will help me on my way.

If I have to go below, I will grab my jug
and fill it with water somewhere on the road down.

Meantime, every day I pray—O Lord
teach me that I am but earth,

a hollow vessel of clay,
only a wisp of thy breath against my emptiness.

3.

They have yet to figure out
the name of the church

two men diving in Barkley Lake
around Cain's Mill a few years ago

found the whole steeple of
cross and all

half-buried in the mud shallows.

Davis McCombs

When he won the Yale Younger Poets contest, Davis McCombs was working as a guide and "parking-lot guy" at Mammoth Cave National Park, near his home in Munfordville. He was somewhat overqualified for his work, with degrees from Harvard and the University of Virginia and a writing fellowship from Stanford. His long familiarity and love for the cave, however, provided him with the inspiration and subject for his prizewinning collection, *Ultima Thule* (2000), a term that originally referred to the place nearest to the North Pole that people could live. McCombs uses it to refer to what was the most remote area of Mammoth Cave to be explored and mapped—what he calls "both a beginning and an end." In these two fourteen-line stanzas, the speaker is the famed slave guide Stephen Bishop, who explored and mapped a large portion of the cave system in the mid-nineteenth century before he died at thirty-seven.

"Candlewriting"

Childhood was a mapless country, a rough
terrain of sinks and outcrops. Not once
did I suspect the earth was hollow, lost
as I was among the fields and shanties.
I remember the wind and how the sounds
it carried were my name, meant me, *Stephen* . . .
called out over the cornfield where I hid.
There was no sound when candlesmoke
met limestone—just this: seven characters
I learned to write with a taper on a stick.
What have they to do with that boy in the weeds?
Am I the letters or the hand that made them?
A word I answer to and turn from, or the flame
that holds the shadows, for a time at least, at bay?

"Fame"

It was the night before the night before last
when I sat so deep in thought by the fire.
The Doctor boasts I was the merest germ

of a man when he bought me. Through him,
I was able, in time, to acquire a knowledge
of science, a considerable degree of culture.
Through him, my fame—the subject of articles,
my map distributed widely. But fame,
like the fire in the hearth, must be fed:
a bundle of twigs soon needs a log to stay
alight. And then full thirty cords of oak.
I am ever in search of exploits, discoveries.
Some nights I wake in darkness to know
a greater darkness waits. A hillside. A mouth.

Maurice Manning

"First"

A recent winner of the Yale Younger Poets prize is Maurice Manning, a native of Danville, with degrees from Earlham College, the University of Kentucky, and the University of Alabama, where he received his M.F.A. in 1999. He now teaches at Indiana University. *Lawrence Booth's Book of Visions* (2001) is a collection that the poet W. S. Merwin calls "an outrageous, lit-up, wide-ranging sequence of poems" gathered loosely around a gothic pilgrim possessed by visions. In his second book of poems, *A Companion for Owls* (2004), Manning assumes the persona of Daniel Boone as he explores and tries to understand the wilderness of Kentucky. In this poem, Boone has his first view of the new land.

Arriving, we walked down as if we were hill-born
and bred to know only hills, so that the end of hills
was surprising, rolling out before us like a woman's
skirts gathered and fanned across her lap, like loosely
folded fabric, like calico: spotted and patchworked
as if some big-fingered god had gently smudged
the world he made. Our horses and our dogs paused.
We had not expected glory and it stopped us dead,
which is not altogether uncommon: Moses spying
Canaan, for example, must have first stood silent
before waving his people ahead, the land smothered
in half shadow, half-light like velvet, and steadied
himself, one hand firm on his staff, the other reaching
to his brow, wiping his gray hair back. So I walked
into Kentucky barefooted and clumsy as if I had
sneaked out of school to cheat my lessons and come
upon a girl waiting for me behind a beech tree,
wondering where on earth I'd been. I stood still
on the invisible line and spit across it onto the new
map, making my first mark, wondering if I could
keep such a dark and bloody secret to myself.

"Testament"

Here Boone considers his brother's directions for his burial and thinks about his own.

Squire's boys laid him in a cave for several days
granting him one final whim: that if his spirit
were unfettered by the earth, it might be free
to visit them and tell them all the wonders
of the other side. It was a tenderly
foolish plan, but death promotes such schemes.
Still, one will make provisions, and I have cast
my lot in that regard. One day in Osage
country I was hunting with Derry, my sole
companion now for fifteen years, and death
dealt me a fever which I thought would be
the end. So Derry bore me on his shoulders
and took me to a bluff above the river,
and I said, plant me here when I am gone.
But I love the God-made world so much that I
recovered to hunt again. Yet I know my days
are winding down; I will go and not return.
My estate is a simple matter to resolve—
I leave my rifle to whoever wants it.
Don't dress me up for death, leave me naked
and fill my box with mast: I'm taking seeds
to heaven in case God needs more trees. When I swim
the pitch-hewed river, bury me beside
Rebecca; and when his days run out of numbers,
bury Derry next to me.

Kathleen Driskell

"Old Woman Looks out Window"

A young poet who is beginning to make a name for herself as a writer, a teacher, and a promoter of writers and writing is Kathleen Driskell, a professor of English at Spalding University in Louisville and a founder of the Kentucky Writers' Coalition. She has published a number of poems in literary journals and has edited *Kentucky Writer's Directory* (1999) and *Place Gives Rise to Spirit* (2001). The poem below appeared in the fall 1990 issue of *Kentucky Poetry Review,* which was dedicated to the North Carolina author Fred Chappell, under whom Driskell studied at the University of North Carolina at Greensboro.

Rosebushes webbed with silkworm nests
remind me of the cauliflower stumps left
after I could not keep the crows away.
My snap beans are sure to be thick with weeds,
caterpillars eating up the vines. I'm glad
I can't see it now. For two days,
there has been a fly in my water glass.
I had to hide it well. I want to call the nurse,
ask her to pick it out and lay it on the sill to dry.
I want to know if the sun will give back its life
or shrivel it like a raisin, but she will not
do that for me. It would not be clean.
She wants to keep dirt and earth away from me
and she tells my doctor not to let me go home.
He does not know how much she hates the rough look
of my hands, how she uses a sharp tool to twist
the black from under my fingernails. I study her motion,
but turn deaf to her talking. I know she would be worthless
turning a spade. Her pale skin would blister
in one summer noon.

Joe Bolton

"Tropical Courtyard"

I'd like to pay homage to a young man who, sadly, did not survive the demons, the passions, the impulses that perhaps gave him the sensibility to become a great poet. In his twenty-eight years, however, he wrote some very moving and astounding poems. Joe Bolton was born in Cadiz in 1961 and studied at the University of Arizona, where he earned an M.F.A. He taught at the University of Florida in Gainesville and published two collections of poetry, *Breckinridge County Suite* (1987) and *Days of Summer Gone* (1990). *The Last Nostalgia: Poems 1982–1990* was published posthumously in 1999. He took his own life in March 1990. The country of his poetry extended from his own rolling hills and river valleys of western Kentucky down to the languid Gulf Coast and the tropical tangles of Florida.

It is a rage against geometry:
The spiked fans of the palmetto arcing
Like improvised brushstrokes in the light breeze;
Late shadowplay, somewhere a dog barking.

Against the height of new and old brick walls,
Confounding stone, transplanted pine and palm
Lift in imperfection, as heavy bells
That would force order fade into the calm

Of azure and a faint scent of musk.
(Is it eucalyptus or just the past?)
There's nothing in this warm, vegetal dusk
That is not beautiful or that will last.

Abigail Gramig

"Chuck Autumn"

If Abigail Gramig is any indication, the new generation of Kentucky poets is ready to assert itself. Still in her early twenties and a recent graduate of Bellarmine University, she has already demonstrated remarkable maturity and originality in her first collection of poems, *Dusting the Piano* (2004). She is a protean poet with a unique voice and many faces and disguises. In her youthful poems she has created an enchanted garden of delights and insights written in compact free verse. In this new poem she assumes the disguise of a college professor who sees and understands why her nursing students are smoking cancer-causing cigarettes outside her office window between classes.

⸙

The start of school.
Outside my office window
nursing students gather.
A flock of blue-swathed smokers.
Girls mostly, all cigarettes and scrubs.

I don't begrudge them their relief
the white paper hanging from lower lips.
Or poised between middle and forefinger,
the ash end growing longer and eventually
falling under the thick tread of their sneakers.

My grandmother used to smoke.
For so many years she filled those hurried
hands, fingers with tense nicotine.
All this until she got cancer
and I watched her hair and weight fall away.
It didn't take very long.

It is hard work,
learning to take care of people.
So I give them permission,
more so than to the deep, ever-brooding

English students I'm used to.
After all, nurses know the eventual effect
of their stress relief, the piecemeal decline
that will surely come
after a while.

They drop what's left of their cigarette breaks
into a sand-filled cement planter
and disappear into the doors of my building,
back to class.
I watch one, a pediatric nurse
in Charlie Brown scrubs—
he and Lucy frozen in that hopeful moment
just before she yanks the football away
and Chuck goes flying.

Frederick Smock

"Kentuckie"

Frederick Smock is a professor of English and writer-in-residence at Bellarmine University, where Abigail Gramig was his student. Still a young man himself (he was born in 1954), he is a vital link between the aging contemporary poets of this gathering and the fledgling writers in his classes waiting to put their inspired words into print for all of us to read. Smock has published several collections of poems: *12 Poems* (1991), *Gardencourt* (1997), *Guest House* (2003), and *The Good Life* (2000), the last from which this poem was taken. "Kentuckie" is a summation as well as a good ending for this anthology. Moreover, it is a fit beginning for the stories, essays, plays, novels, and poems yet to come from this good land and its people.

What was that blurred quiver
of light I half-glimpsed,
walking in Cherokee Park, where
three hundred years ago
Indians of five nations came to hunt?
High up on a ridge,
a bare knuckle of land over rock,
in amongst the trees and fallen leaves—
an ashwood bow drawn—
a breath held against that moment
the grouse steps gingerly around
the may-apple—then the letting out
of breath, the arrow quick as a wish
finding the heart of the heart
of the matter, and dropping,
plump, to the ground,
to the dark and bloody ground,
three hundred years ago.

Appendix
Biographies

Muhammad Ali. Born Cassius Clay in an African American neighborhood in West Louisville, Ky., on Jan. 17, 1942, the son of Cassius Marcellus Clay Sr. and Odessa Grady Clay, Muhammad Ali is one of the best-known names in the world. He grew up when Louisville was still a segregated city. He began his rise to athletic fame in 1954, when he started training as a boxer at Columbia Gym. By the time he had graduated from Central High School in 1960, he had won two national Golden Glove tournaments and two national AAU titles. Shortly after graduation, he won the Olympic gold medal in boxing as a light heavyweight. On Feb. 25, 1964, he defeated Charles "Sonny" Liston in Miami for the heavyweight championship. Already such words as cocky, brash, outspoken, controversial, flamboyant, and uppity were being used to describe the Louisville Lip with the lethal left jab. From then until the early 1980s, Ali would challenge the roster of heavyweight contenders, including Floyd Patterson, Joe Frazier, Jimmy Ellis, George Foreman, Leon Spinks, and Larry Holmes. He would usually win. The morning after he knocked out Liston, he announced his earlier conversion to the Nation of Islam, and within two weeks he had officially changed his name to Muhammad Ali. He became even more controversial when on April 28, 1967, asserting that he was a conscientious objector, he refused induction into the military service. He was subsequently indicted for resisting the draft and found guilty, a verdict that was overturned by the U.S. Supreme Court on June 28, 1970. After losing his championship to Larry Holmes on Oct. 2, 1980, he retired in 1981 with a record of fifty-six wins and five losses and thirty-seven knockouts. Despite the onset of Parkinson's disease, he became a global goodwill ambassador for his country and his religion during the 1980s. The apex of his fame was reached symbolically when he lighted the flame to signal the beginning of the 1996 Summer Olympics in Atlanta. In 1999 the Kentucky Athletic Hall of Fame designated him Kentucky Athlete of the Century. In mid-2005 the Muhammad Ali Center in downtown Louisville was nearing completion. He was renowned for the clever verses he wrote extolling his strength and beauty, which he would recite to taunt and soften up his opponents before a match. In 1975 he published *The Greatest: My Own Story,* which he wrote with Richard Durham, and painted a self-portrait of a man who could, in his words, "float like a butterfly, sting like a bee."

Dwight Allen. Born into a prominent Louisville family in 1951, Dwight Allen received a B.A. from Lawrence University and an M.F.A. from the University of Iowa Writers Workshop. For ten years he worked as a fact-checker and staff writer at the *New Yorker.* He has published stories in the *Southern Review, Missouri Review, Georgia Review,* and other magazines and anthologies. In 2000 he brought his stories together as a loosely constructed but engaging autobiographical novel, *The Green Suit,* which chronicles the adventures and misadventures of his alter ego, Peter Sackrider; his sister; and a menagerie of relatives and friends in the late 1960s and 1970s in a city very much like Louisville. Living now with his wife and son in Madison, Wis., he is a talented writer whose emerging talent bodes well for his literary future.

James Lane Allen. Born Dec. 21, 1849, near Lexington, Ky.; died Feb. 18, 1925, in New York City. James Lane Allen was the seventh of seven children and the first Kentucky writer to support himself with his writing. He received B.A. and M.A. degrees from Transylvania University (then called Kentucky University), and for more than a dozen years he was a teacher in private schools and colleges in Kentucky, Missouri, and West Virginia. In the mid-1880s he began to publish stories and essays in *Harper's, Atlantic Monthly, Century,* and other popular American magazines. His best-selling books include *Flute and Violin and Other Kentucky Tales and Romances* (1891), *The Blue-Grass Region of Kentucky* (1892, nonfiction), and *A Kentucky Cardinal* (1894), the story of a young, idealistic man in love with a realistic woman. Allen traveled widely and in 1893 moved to New York, where he lived the remainder of his life.

Mary Anderson. Born July 28, 1859, Sacramento, Calif.; died May 30, 1940, Broadway, Worcestershire, Eng. When Mary Anderson was one, the family moved from California to Louisville, where she attended the local Catholic schools until she was fourteen; she then persuaded her mother to allow her to study at home. Her study consisted mostly of memorizing lines from the plays of Shakespeare, the favorite author of her stepfather, Dr. Hamilton Griffin, whom her mother had married after the death of her father, a Confederate soldier, in 1863. Despite opposition from her mother's strict Catholic family to her plans for becoming an actress, she pursued her dream and at sixteen, with only two days' notice, made her debut at Louisville's Macauley's Theatre on Nov. 27, 1875. Soon she was the toast of the American- and English-speaking stage. After she married Antonio de Novarro, a wealthy New Yorker living in England, she retired at thirty and moved with her husband to the small English village of Broadway, having won acclaim in the United States, Britain, and Ireland. She wrote two autobiographies, *A Few Memories* (1896) and *A Few More Memories* (1936). Throughout her life she kept in close touch with her Kentucky relatives and left to the Franciscans her property near New Albany, Ind., now the Mary Anderson Center for the Arts.

Harriette Simpson Arnow. Born July 7, 1908, Wayne County, Ky.; died March 21, 1986, near Ann Arbor, Mich. Arnow attended Berea College 1924–1926 and received her B.A. from the University of Louisville in 1930. In the early 1930s she taught in public schools in Pulaski County and in Louisville. In 1935 she moved to Cincinnati to work and write short stories and to complete her first novel, *Mountain Path* (1936), the first of her Kentucky Trilogy, which also included *Hunter's Horn* (1944) and *The Dollmaker* (1954), one of the most powerful and underrated novels in American literature. It depicts the trials and tribulations of a Kentucky family that moves to Detroit during World War II to find work and thereby loses its soul. Its hero, Gertie Nevels, is one of the strongest, most clearly delineated characters in American fiction. It was made into a superb TV movie in 1983, with Jane Fonda as Gertie. Arnow's other works include three social histories of the Cumberland River region of Kentucky, *Seedtime on the Cumberland* (1960), *Flowering of the Cumberland* (1963), and *Old Burnside* (1977). In 1939 she married Harold B. Arnow, and they lived for several years on a farm in Pulaski County; then in 1944 they moved into a housing project in Detroit, where Harold Arnow worked for the *Detroit Times.* In 1955 *The Dollmaker* won the National Book Award for fiction. She and her family lived near Ann Arbor from 1951 until her death.

John James Audubon. Born April 26, 1785, in St. Domingue (now Haiti); died Jan. 27, 1851, in New York City. Audubon was born the illegitimate son of a French naval officer and slave trader and his mistress, who died shortly after her son's birth. He grew up in France with his father's family and came to America in 1803 to manage a farm his father owned in Pennsylvania. His love of the outdoors and his pastime of sketching birds, which he had pursued in France, were enlarged by the American forests and new varieties of birds he encountered. In 1808 he married a neighbor's daughter, Lucy Bakewell, and they moved to Louisville, where he and a partner, Ferdinand Rozier, also a Frenchman, had opened a store the previous year. Audubon indulged his passion by exploring the woods around Louisville and observing, killing, and drawing birds. In 1810 he met the Scottish ornithologist Alexander Wilson, who came through Louisville to sketch birds and to sell subscriptions for a book of birds he planned to publish. Audubon had until then done his bird drawings for enjoyment; now he began to see their commercial potential. The business in Louisville did not prosper, and Rozier and Audubon moved their families downriver to Henderson and opened a store there. Audubon continued to tramp the woods and draw birds;

and the business failed again. Then in 1817 he moved his family back to Louisville, where he supported himself by painting portraits and teaching art. Two years later the Audubon family left Kentucky, moving first to Cincinnati and a year later to Louisiana. His masterpiece, *Birds of America,* an oversized, four-volume set of hand-colored prints, was published in parts between 1827 and 1838. In the 1840s he published the five-volume *Quadrupeds of America.* Both the birds and the quadrupeds were reissued later in various sizes and editions. In the 1830s he also published a sort of artist's autobiography, *Ornithological Biography,* which includes his experiences and impressions of Kentucky. Many of his original works are on view at the John James Audubon Memorial Museum, at the Audubon State Park in Henderson.

Prentice Baker. Prentice Baker was born on a farm near Hardinsburg, Ky., in April 1923. He graduated from Leitchfield High School in 1940 and was employed in a Kentucky state job for over two years. From 1943 until his retirement some thirty-eight years later, he worked in the home office of the Louisville and Nashville Railroad in Louisville. He has written his finely crafted poems since he was a boy, when his mother, a schoolteacher, encouraged him to write, and has published in several periodicals, including *Approaches, Roanoke Review,* and *Kentucky Poetry Review.* In 1973 a collection of his poems was published by Kentucky Poetry Press under the title *Down Cellar.* What he admires most in life, he says, are "solitude, order, and honesty," and, in writing, "understatement, the oblique approach, and the random rhyme."

Wendell Berry. Wendell Erdman Berry, Kentucky's agrarian poet-philosopher, was born in Louisville on August 5, 1934, and grew up in Henry County. He was educated at Millersburg Military Institute and received a B.A. in 1956 and an M.A. in 1957, both from the University of Kentucky. He also studied creative writing at Stanford University as a Wallace Stegner Fellow in the late 1950s. In 1960 he published his first novel, *Nathan Coulter,* which began his chronicle of fictional Port William, a small village on the Kentucky River, based on Port Royal, his hometown. Since then he has published poetry, essays, short stories, and novels that develop and promote the good life, according to Berry's vision of right relationship to the land. His other books include *The Broken Ground* (1964, poems), *A Place on Earth* (1967, a novel), *The Unsettling of America* (1977, essays), *The Wild Birds* (1986, short stories), and *Jayber Crow* (2000, a novel). He has taught at Georgetown College, New York University, and the University of Kentucky. In 1957 he married Tanya Amyx, and they have a son, Den, and a daughter, Mary Dee. Since 1965 he and his family have lived on a small working farm near Port Royal.

Sallie Bingham. Sarah "Sallie" Montague Bingham was born Jan. 22, 1937, in Louisville during the great Ohio River flood. Her family's communications companies included the *Courier-Journal, Louisville Times,* two radio stations, and a printing business. She graduated from Radcliffe College in 1958 and published her first novel, *After Such Knowledge,* in 1960. Her short stories have been published in such magazines as the *Atlantic, Mademoiselle,* and *Redbook;* some of them have been gathered in three collections: *The Touching Hand* (1967), *The Way It Is Now* (1972), and *Transgressions* (2002). Two of her plays, *Paducah* (1984) and *Piggyback* (1994), were premiered by the Kentucky Repertory Theatre at Horse Cave, then known as Horse Cave Theatre. In the mid-1980s she established the Kentucky Foundation for Women to support and promote women writers. She lives in Santa Fe.

Harold Blythe (*See also* Charlie Sweet Jr.). Harold Blythe was born in Louisville on Dec. 11, 1944, and holds degrees from Kentucky Southern College, the University of Florida, and the University of Louisville, where he was awarded a Ph.D. in 1972. With Charlie Sweet, a fellow professor of English at Eastern Kentucky University in Richmond, he has written popular short stories and detective stories under the pen names Hal Charles and Brett Halliday. He has taught literature and writing at the University of Florida, the University of Louisville, Adrian College in Michigan, and, since 1972, at Eastern Kentucky, where he has won numerous classroom and campus awards. With his writing partner he has published dozens of short stories and mysteries in magazines ranging from *Ellery Queen's Mystery Magazine* to *Home Life* and *Kentucky Monthly.*

Joe Bolton. Born 1961 in Cadiz, Ky.; died March 1990. Joe Bolton received an M.F.A. from the University of Arizona and taught there and at the University of Florida. He published numerous poems in a variety of magazines and two collections of poetry, *Breckinridge County Suite* (1987) and *Days of Summer Gone* (1990). He was twenty-eight when he took his own life. In 1999 the University of Arkansas Press published a posthumous collection, *The Last Nostalgia: Poems, 1982–1990,* edited by Donald Justice.

Joy Bale Boone. Born Oct. 29, 1912, Chicago; died Oct. 1, 2002, Glasgow, Ky. Joy Bale Boone grew up in Evanston, Ill., and attended the Chicago Latin School and the Roycemore School for Girls. While en route with her mother to Florida in the early 1930s, they stopped in Elizabethtown, where she met Shelby Garnett Bale, a physician; she married him in 1937. Three years after her husband's death in 1972, she married George Street Boone of Elkton and lived there and in Glasgow, Ky., until her death. She was the mother of six children (all with her first husband), three of whom became physicians. Throughout her life she was active in health and women's issues, in literature, and in education, and she served several years as president of the Friends of Kentucky Libraries. In 1987 she became the founding chairperson of the Robert Penn Warren Committee at Western Kentucky University. She was active in efforts to promote reading and writing among Kentuckians of all ages, and in 1964 was a founder of *Approaches,* a magazine of Kentucky poetry. In 1975 she relinquished the primary editorship to Wade Hall, who renamed the periodical *Kentucky Poetry Review.* A collection of her poems, *Never Less Than Love,* appeared in 1970, and in 1974 she published *The Storm's Eye: A Narrative in Verse Celebrating Cassius Marcellus Clay.*

Anne McCarty Braden. Anne Braden, who was born in Louisville in 1924 and grew up in Anniston, Ala., became, with her husband Carl Braden, a leading civil rights advocate in Kentucky. In 1954 the couple's role in helping an African American couple buy a house in an all-white neighborhood of Shively led to their arrest for sedition after the house was bombed. She has continued her outspoken support for human rights since her husband's death in 1975. Her book about her life and support for human justice, *The Wall Between,* was published in 1958 and reissued in 1999 with a foreword by the civil rights leader Julian Bond. In 2002 a biography of her by Catherine Fosl, *Subversive Southerner: Anne Braden and the Struggle for Racial Justice in the Cold War South,* was published by Palgrave Macmillan.

Jerry Brewer. Born Jan. 21, 1978, in Madison, Tenn., Jerry Brewer moved with his family to Paducah when he was four. He graduated from Paducah Tilghman High School and in 2001 received a degree from Western Kentucky University. He has worked at the *Philadelphia Inquirer* and *Orlando Sentinel* and is now a sports columnist for the *Courier-Journal* in Louisville.

Bruce Bennett Brown. A native of Pike County, Bruce Bennett Brown spent forty years "in all facets of education, county government, editing and research," and as he writes from Raccoon, "I am now retired and writing full time." He was associated with Pikeville College for many years in various positions. His poem "Blue-Fall" has been set to music by the composer Don Malone.

William Wells Brown. Born a slave in 1814 on the John Young farm, near Lexington, Ky.; died Nov. 6, 1884, in Cambridge, Mass. His mother was named Elizabeth, and his father was probably a white relative of his owner. As a boy he was moved with his owner's family to a farm near St. Louis. In 1834 he escaped from an Ohio River steamboat to Ohio, where he was befriended by a Quaker abolitionist named Wells Brown, whose name he adopted out of gratitude. He moved to northern Ohio and worked on a Lake Erie steamboat. He soon became an outspoken abolitionist and conductor of slaves to freedom in Canada. He later moved to various cities in New York and Massachusetts and lived for several years in Europe as a popular spokesman for abolition. In 1847 he published *Narrative of William W. Brown, a Fugitive Slave, Written by Himself;* and in 1853 he published a controversial novel, *Clotel; or, The President's Daughter,* based on Thomas Jefferson's rumored relationship with Sally Hemmings, one of Jefferson's slaves—a relationship that has been rather conclusively confirmed by recent scholarship. He also wrote a play about his escape to freedom and books about the history of American slavery and black soldiers in the Civil War. He was one of the earliest and most eloquent voices of the African American experience.

Linda Bruckheimer. Born 1945 in Kentucky. Linda Bruckheimer's family was like thousands of other Kentucky families who fell on hard times in their native state and headed west to California; but fortunately for Kentucky, she has returned, at least part-time. She and her husband, the TV and film producer Jerry Bruckheimer, divide their time between Los Angeles and their estate near Bloomfield, where Linda Bruckheimer spearheaded a successful drive to restore and preserve the community's heritage. Indeed, she is a woman with a passionate double mission, writing and preservation. Sometimes she mixes both in the same book. Her first novel, *Dreaming Southern* (1999), was a best seller that draws on her experiences growing up in Kentucky and moving to California. Her second novel, *The Southern Belles of Honeysuckle Way* (2004), continues the adventures of the Wooten family as three daughters try to save the old family place from greedy developers. Bruckheimer takes time from her writing to be an active board member of the National Trust for Historic Preservation. She has served as the West Coast editor of *Mirabella* and has produced two award-winning specials for PBS.

Roberta Scott Bunnell. Born Dec. 9, 1910, in Paducah, Roberta Scott Bunnell attended Logan College in Russellville and, later, the University of Louisville. Since 1935 she has lived in Louisville, where she worked at radio stations WAVE and WKLO and was active in the local arts and literary scene. She did an early show for women on WKLO and became the station's continuity and public service director. In addition to regional magazines, she has published poems in *Cosmopolitan, McCall's,* and the *Saturday Evening Post.* In 1972 she published *Eavesdropper,* a selection of her poems, which the former *Courier-Journal* writer Gregg Swem has adapted for the stage.

Ben Lucien Burman. Born Dec. 12, 1895, in Covington, Ky., of Jewish immigrant parents; died Nov. 12, 1984, in New York City. Burman attended Miami University of Ohio, served in the U.S. Army in France during World War I, and was seriously injured at Soissons in 1918. After graduation from Harvard in 1920, he worked as a journalist for several prominent newspapers and in 1927 married the artist Alice Caddy, who illustrated many of his books, including the popular Catfish Bend series of animal fables that he wrote near the end of his life. During World War II, as a newspaper and magazine correspondent, he traveled to Brazzaville, Congo, where he wrote a book, *Miracle on the Congo,* about the Free French forces based in the former French colony, for which he was later awarded the French Legion of Honor. Most of his books are about rivers and the people who live on them and along their banks. Two of his river novels were made into movies, *Mississippi* (1929), which was filmed as *Heaven on Earth,* and *Steamboat Round the Bend* (1933), which starred Will Rogers. Other books by Burman include *Blow for a Landing* (1938), *Everywhere I Roam* (1949), and *The Four Lives of Mundy Tolliver* (1953).

Reid Bush. Born in rural southern Indiana on Feb. 22, 1934, Reid Bush has lived since 1969 in Kentucky, where he has served as a minister and an educator. His early schooling occurred in southern California; then he came east to Arkansas for college, and finally to Indiana and Kentucky for graduate school. He's married to a Kentuckian and claims to have children living in five states and Malaysia, grandchildren living in four states and Malaysia, and a dog born in Shively. His poems have appeared in the *American Voice, Louisville Review,* and elsewhere. Poet and critic Richard Taylor called each poem in Bush's 2005 collection, *What You Know,* "a verbal journey with contractions and expansions in the poet's mind that take us, accordion-like, to new destinations." Since his retirement, Bush has been writing more and even better poetry.

William O. Butler. Born 1791 near Nicholasville, Ky.; died Aug. 6, 1880, in Carrollton, Ky. William Orlando Butler was a man of many vocations—soldier, lawyer, politician, and poet. He graduated from Transylvania University in 1812, studied law for a while, then enlisted for duty in the War of 1812 and was wounded at the River Raisin. He was also with General Jackson at the Battle of New Orleans. After the war he settled permanently at Carrollton; and in July 1821 his most famous poem, "The Boatman's Horn," was published in the *Western Review,* a monthly magazine published in Lexington. It was subsequently published as the title poem of a collection of his verse, *The Boatman's Horn and Other Poems*. In 1839 he was elected to Congress, and he later ran unsuccessfully for governor of Kentucky and for vice president of the United States. John Wilson Townsend wrote in 1913 that, although "'The Boatman's Horn' will keep his name green for many years," some of his other poems "are not to be utterly despised."

Pat Carr. Born in 1932 in Grass Creek, Wyo., Pat Carr earned two degrees from Rice University and a Ph.D. from Tulane. She has taught at Rice, Texas Southern, Dillard, the University of New Orleans, and the University of Texas at El Paso. From 1988 until the mid-1990s she taught at Western Kentucky University at Bowling Green. She is the author of criticism, stories, and poems. With Maureen Morehead she published a cycle of Civil War stories and poems, *Our Brother's War* (1993). Her short stories have appeared in *Kansas Quarterly, Yale Review, Best American Short Stories,* and other places. Her story collections include *Beneath the Hill of the Three Crosses* (1970), *The Women in the Mirror* (1977), and *Night of the Luminarias* (1986). She now lives with her husband in Arkansas.

Harry M. Caudill. Born May 3, 1922, in Letcher County, Ky.; died Nov. 29, 1990, near Whitesburg, Ky., of a self-inflicted gunshot wound. The voice and conscience of the Kentucky mountains, especially the poor and dispossessed, Harry Monroe Caudill had been suffering from Parkinson's disease and other ailments when he ended his life. The author of some ten books, including fiction and nonfiction, numerous essays, and many impassioned letters to newspapers, he is best known for his groundbreaking call for reform and restoration of his beloved southern mountains, *Night Comes to the Cumberlands: A Biography of a Depressed Area* (1963). His other books include *Dark Hills to Westward: The Saga of Jennie Wiley* (1969), a novel about a pioneer woman captured by Indians; *My Land Is Dying* (1972), an indictment of strip-mining; and *A Darkness at Dawn: Appalachian Kentucky and the Future* (1976), a profile of a stricken country and a road map for reform. He was a practicing lawyer for more than a quarter century and, near the end of his life, taught history at the University of Kentucky. His polemical writing was impatient and forceful. A letter to the *Courier-Journal* of Feb. 13, 1978, ended: "For $500.2 billion a year we get a government of dullards, by dullards and for dullards." He couldn't have said it more directly.

Madison Cawein. Born March 23, 1865, in Louisville; died Dec. 8, 1914, in St. James Court, Louisville. Before his death at forty-nine, with thirty-six volumes of poetry to his credit, he had become a popular and widely praised American poet. Unfortunately, his Victorian sentiments, traditional versification, and forced rhymes did not survive very far into the twentieth century, and he is today little more than a footnote in American literary history. Both his parents were descended from recent German immigrants. His father was a colorful jack-of-all-trades, from baker and chef to patent medicine doctor and resort hotel owner. After graduating from the renowned Male High School, Cawein became a cashier at Newmarket, a Third Street gambling establishment, where betting on horses thrived. When his first volume of poems, *Blooms of the Berry* (1887), was published, the editor of *Harper's Monthly* praised him effusively as a new kind of "Western" poet whose poetry was different from that written in New England: "Here is a fresh strain; the effect of longer summers and wider horizons; the wine of the old English vine planted in another soil, and ripened by a sun of Italian fervor, has a sweetness and fire of its own." But his enchanted fields and forests could not thrive in the age of realism.

Lillie D. Chaffin. Born 1925 in Varney, Pike County, Ky.; died Oct. 27, 1993, in Huntington, W.V. Lillie Chaffin (Lillie D. Chaffin Kash) published some sixteen books of fiction and poetry for children and adults, mostly about her native Appalachia and its people. A graduate of Pikeville College, she worked as a teacher and librarian in Pike County schools until her retirement in the late 1970s. Her short stories, poems, and educational articles appeared in anthologies, textbooks, magazines, and newspapers. Her books for children include *Bear Weather* (1969), which was named by the *New York Times* as one of the best juvenile books of that year, and *John Henry McCoy* (1971), which won the annual Best Book for Young Readers Award given by the Child

Study Association of America. Her collection of poems, *A Stone for Sisyphus* (1967), based on Greek mythology, won an award from the International Poetry Society. She served as an associate poet laureate of Kentucky and has received various awards and honors from Alice Lloyd College, Pikeville College, and Eastern Kentucky University.

Hal Charles (*See* Harold Blythe; Charlie Sweet).

Billy C. Clark. Billy Curtis Clark was born in 1928 near Catlettsburg, Ky., on the Big Sandy River, a community that he has used frequently—often calling it Sourwood—as the setting and inspiration for his fiction, poetry, and autobiographical works. He was the first member of his family to complete high school; then he served for four years in the U.S. military during the Korean War. As a veteran he enrolled at the University of Kentucky in 1953 and began his career as a published author with a collection of short stories, *A Heap of Hills* (1956). At Kentucky he studied with Hollis Summers. In five years Clark would publish five more books, including *Song of the River* (1957), a novel he had written in high school. In 1960 he published his best-known and most beloved book, a fictionalized autobiography, *A Long Row to Hoe*, which chronicles his hardscrabble life through high school. Another popular book is *Sourwood Tales* (1968), a collection of stories about life in Sourwood during the Great Depression. More recent books are *To Leave My Heart at Catlettsburg* (1999), a gathering of poems, and a novel, *By Way of the Forked Stick* (2000). Clark taught for many years in the University of Kentucky community college system at Somerset. Since 1986 he has been writer-in-residence at Longwood University in Farmville, Va. As a writer he has earned many awards and honors; but the most visible is the Billy C. Clark Bridge over the Big Sandy River, connecting Kentucky and West Virginia. In recent years the Jesse Stuart Foundation has reissued Clark's books, with the intention of keeping them all in print permanently. That is a recognition that few writers ever receive.

George Rogers Clark. Born Nov. 19, 1752, in Albemarle County, Va.; died Feb. 13, 1818, at Locust Grove, near Louisville. George Rogers Clark, a son of the Virginia aristocracy, was educated by tutors and at the age of twenty became a land surveyor. In 1774 he began his military career as a member of an expedition against the Shawnees. In the Kentucky country he became a surveyor for the Ohio Company and a leader in the effort to organize the new land as Kentucky County, Virginia. In 1778 he led a small army of soldiers and civilians down the Ohio River to the Falls of the Ohio, where he established a small settlement of civilians on Corn Island, the beginnings of Louisville; he then resumed his secret mission to dismantle British influence on the Western frontier at Kaskaskia, Vincennes, and Cahokia. He later led assaults on Britain's Indian allies, including a major attack on the Shawnees at Piqua, near present-day Springfield, Ohio. In 1781 Clark was appointed a brigadier general by Governor Thomas Jefferson of Virginia and established Fort Nelson at the Falls. In 1784 Clark surveyed land for the town of Clarksville, in what would become the state of Indiana, and in 1803 he moved to Clark's Point there, where he lived until a stroke disabled him in 1809. At that time he moved to Locust Grove, the home of his sister Lucy Clark Croghan, outside Louisville, and lived there until his death in 1818. As a military man he was lucky but valiant and helped secure the Western frontier for the fledgling United States of America.

Thomas D. Clark. Thomas Dionysius Clark was born in Louisville, Miss., on July 14, 1903, and died in Lexington, Ky., on June 28, 2005. He spent most of his life in Lexington, Ky., where he taught history at the University of Kentucky and became the dynamo that led to the founding of the Kentucky State Archives, the University Press of Kentucky, and the Special Collections division of the University of Kentucky King Library—to list but a few of his highly visible achievements. His intangible influence as a history professor was most widely felt as he taught thousands of Kentuckians to take pride in their state's history and heritage and to safeguard it. His influence as a scholar-historian was even broader as the author of authoritative, readable, and eloquent books. Starting in 1933 with *The Beginning of the L&N* and continuing into the twenty-first century, he published books about Kentucky and the south that are essential to understanding these vital parts of the American experience. Such books as these are familiar (and well-thumbed) in professional as well as amateur historians' libraries: *A History of Kentucky* (1937), *The Rampaging Frontier* (1939), *Pills, Petticoats and Plows* (1944), *The Southern Country Editor* (1948), *The Great American Frontier* (1975), and *Footloose in Jacksonian America* (1990), the story of the life and travels of Robert Wilmot Scott. Dr. Clark's most recent book is *The People's House: Governor's Mansions of Kentucky* (2002), written with Margaret A. Lane. He graduated from the University of Mississippi in 1928; he received his M.A. from the University of Kentucky in 1929 and his Ph.D. from Duke University in 1932. In addition to the University of Kentucky, he taught at Memphis State University, Indiana University, Harvard, Duke, North Carolina, Tennessee, Wisconsin, Stanford, and many other schools. He received numerous honorary degrees and awards, including a Guggenheim Fellowship, and was Kentucky's historian laureate. His life and works are awe-inspiring achievements and worthy of emulation.

Milton Clarke. Milton Clarke was born into slavery about 1820 in Madison County, Ky., and escaped across the Ohio River into Ohio about 1840. With his brother Lewis, who had escaped earlier, he lectured at antislavery rallies and helped other slaves escape from Kentucky to Canada. According to *Narratives of the Suffering of Lewis and Milton Clarke, Sons of a Soldier of the Revolution, During a Captivity of More Than Twenty Years among the Slaveholders of Kentucky, One of the So Called Christian States of North America. Dictated by Themselves,* published in Boston in 1846, the two brothers were grandsons of Samuel Campbell, a slaveholder of Madison County, and a half-white slave woman named Mary. Their mother was Letitia ("Letty") Campbell, a slave to her own father. Their father was a white man named Clarke from Scotland, a weaver and a veteran of the American Revolution who had settled in Kentucky around 1800 and married Letitia, on the promise that she would be freed at Campbell's death. Apparently, the heirs destroyed the will that would have freed Letitia and her children, and instead, they were sold at auction, along with the other slaves of the estate. In his narrative Milton gives a heartrending account of the sale of his mother, a brother, a sister, and himself; their removal to a new home in Lexington; and his later escape to freedom.

Henry Clay. Born April 12, 1777, in Hanover County, Va.; died June 29, 1852, in Washington, D.C. Henry Clay was easily Kentucky's best-known citizen in the period before the Civil War, and he offered himself to the nation three times for the presidency, but the nation declined each time. His father, a Baptist minister and farmer in Virginia, died when Clay was four; his mother remarried and, when her son was fifteen, moved with her new husband to Versailles, Ky. Clay stayed behind until he had obtained a sufficient classical and legal education as a copyist and protégé of George Wythe, a law professor, and as a clerk in the law office of Robert Brooke, a former governor. In 1797 he moved to Lexington and became a successful lawyer. Over the years he served in the Kentucky legislature, in the U.S. Congress as congressman and senator, as secretary of state to John Quincy Adams, and as leader of the Whig party. Clay came to prominence during the period before the Civil War known as the Golden Age of American Political Oratory, and he proved to be one of the most accomplished orators of his day.

Irvin S. Cobb. Born June 23, 1876, in Paducah; died March 10, 1944, in California. Irvin Shrewsbury Cobb once wrote that "in my youth, I was the Younger Bohemian Set of Paducah." Perhaps he was. But he was also a good journalist. As a teenager he was a reporter and comedy writer for local and regional papers, and at nineteen he became editor of the *Paducah News*. In 1900 he married Laura Spencer Baker of Savannah, who encouraged him to try his journalistic talents in New York. Leaving his wife and their daughter with her parents, he left for New York with two hundred dollars in his pocket. After two fruitless weeks trying to get an interview with an editor, he decided to write the executive editors of thirteen of the leading newspapers in the city. To these editors he sent the same letter, which emphasized his candor, down-home humor, and desperation, and he received offers from five of them. He accepted the offer from the *Evening Sun*. His first job was editing telegraph dispatches. His break came when he was working as a reporter on the early morning edition and received a murder story over the telephone. Instead of turning his notes and draft over to a rewrite man, he wrote and edited the story himself. It appeared on the front page, and in a single day his name was being called all over New York. Cobb soon began to write stories about small-town life in Paducah following the Civil War, and the *Saturday Evening Post* began publishing them. In 1912 he joined the staff of the *Post* and during World War I represented the *Post* as a war correspondent in Europe. In the 1920s he sold several scripts to Hollywood, and in 1934 he and his family moved to California, where he appeared in several movies, including *Steamboat Round the Bend,* based on the novel by his fellow Kentuckian Ben Lucien Burman. One of his early collections, *Back Home* (1912), features his Paducah stories and made the town nationally famous. For much of the first half of the twentieth century, he was one of the most successful and best-paid popular writers in the country. His other best-selling books include *Old Judge Priest* (1916), *Speaking of Operations* (1916), and *Snake Doctor* (1923). Near the end of his life he published his autobiography, *Exit Laughing* (1941), which introduced him to a new generation of readers. The marker on his grave in Paducah reads: "Back Home."

Gayle Compton. Born at Big Shoal, an early coal camp in Pike County, Ky., on Nov. 3, 1944, Gayle C. Compton is a graduate of Pikeville College with a B.A. in English. Through the years, he has been a high school English teacher, a coal miner, and a mail carrier, and for ten years he worked in radio broadcasting as a manager, announcer, and general factotum. He is now service coordinator for Whayne Supply Company in Pikeville. He has published poems and stories in *Wind, Kentucky Poetry Review, Appalachian Heritage, Ideals,* and *Kudzu,* the literary magazine at Hazard Community College, which gave him their 2005 Kudzu Prize. Among his other honors are the Plattner Award for three years from *Appalachian Heritage* and first prize in numerous Kentucky State Poetry Society competitions. He is preparing a collection to be called *Black Lung Washing Machine: The Peabrook Stories.*

Joseph S. Cotter Sr. Born Feb. 2, 1861, near Bardstown, Ky.; died March 14, 1949, in Louisville. Joseph Seamon Cotter Sr., one of Kentucky's first acclaimed African American poets, was the son of a poor woman who had been a slave at Federal Hill in Bardstown and moved to Louisville when her son was an infant. The boy proved to be very precocious and learned to read when he was four. He dropped out of school in the third grade to do odd jobs to help support the family. Later he attended Louisville's first night school for blacks and earned his high school diploma in his early twenties. He obtained a teacher's certificate and soon became a prominent high school principal in the city's black schools. In 1938 he became a member of the Louisville Board of Education. His writing talent developed while he was still young, and he soon became a nationally known poet. His first book of poems, *A Rhyming* (1895), was followed by *Links of Friendship* (1898). Other works include *A White Song and a Black One* (1909) and *Collected Poems* (1938). His single work of fiction is *Negro Tales* (1912), and his only play is *Caleb: A Play in Four Acts* (1903). Cotter was a progressive civic leader who espoused, among other causes, the idea that blacks should own their houses—a movement that led to the building of single-family houses in the Parkland neighborhood and to the naming of a later development the Cotter Homes. His son, Joseph Seamon Cotter Jr., was a promising poet who died of tuberculosis at age twenty-three.

Ralph Cotton. A native of Caneyville, Ky., where he was born March 16, 1945, Ralph Cotton grew up in Louisville and attended public schools and, after receiving his high school GED from the U.S. Army, enrolled at Jefferson Community College. He has also been schooled by an incredible variety of jobs, including ironworker and bridge builder, second mate on a commercial barge, teamster, horse trainer, and lay minister in the Lutheran church. He is also one of America's most popular and prolific writers of Western novels, with over thirty books in print. He says he taught himself how to write fiction by reading and studying paperbacks while working on riverboats up and down the Mississippi. In addition, he learned a lot about writing from such masters as Twain, Melville, Conrad, and Hemingway. Three of his novels—*While Angels Dance* (1994), *Powder River* (1995), and *Price of a Horse* (1996)—follow the adventures of Jeston Nash, the Kentucky-born outlaw hero of the series. His flight from a Kentucky "Eden" frees him of the restraints of family and society and even his real name. Cotton uses the rough, tough, violent West as the setting for parables of our time. In his novels he shows himself to be not merely a "Western" writer, but a good writer who writes Westerns. For some forty years he has been married to Mary Lynn Branch of Louisville and is the father of four children and grandfather of five. He and his wife currently live in Spring Hill, Fla.

Alfred Leland Crabb. Born Jan. 22, 1884, in Warren County near Bowling Green, Ky.; died Oct. 1, 1979, in Lexington, Ky. Crabb attended the local public schools and the nearby normal school; then he earned a B.A. and a Ph.D. from Peabody College and an M.A. from Columbia University. During his long career as an educator, he was principal of schools in Paducah and Louisville, a professor of education and history, and a dean at what is now Western Kentucky University. From 1927 until 1950, when he retired, he was a professor at Peabody College. He wrote a number of histories and textbooks, but he is remembered today for his eleven historical novels, including *Home to Kentucky* (1953), about Henry Clay, and *Peace at Bowling Green* (1955), which follows a pioneer family from the early nineteenth century to the start of the Civil War. Like all good writers of historical fiction, he created fictional characters to live among well-known historical personages.

Tony Crunk. Tony Crunk, born in Hopkinsville, Ky., in 1956, studied religion, philosophy, and English at Centre College, the University of Kentucky, and the University of Virginia. He has held a variety of jobs through the years, clerking at Big Daddy's Liquors in Nicholasville, doing editorial work at the Methodist Publishing House in Nashville, and teaching writing at the University of Virginia, the University of Montana, and Murray State University. Since 2000 he has taught in the Department of English at the University of Alabama in Birmingham. He has published poetry in the *Paris Review, Poetry Northwest, Quarterly West,* and *Virginia Quarterly Review.* In 1994 he won the Yale Younger Poets competition with his first book of poems, *Living in the Resurrection,* in which he used his Baptist boyhood in western Kentucky as the material out of which he wrought an impressive gathering of poetry. He has also published two children's books, *Big Mama* (2000) and *Grandpa's Overalls* (2002). He will have three new books published in 2005: *Parables and Revelations* and *Cumberland,* both poetry; and *Railroad John and the Red Rock Run,* a children's book.

Olive Tilford Dargan. Born 1869 in Grayson County, Ky., at Tilford Springs, near Leitchfield; died 1968 in the North Carolina mountains. Olive Tilford Dargan wrote plays, poems, and, using the pen name Fielding Burke, proletarian novels in the 1930s. When she was ten, her family moved to the Missouri Ozarks, where she began teaching school at thirteen. Later she studied at the Peabody Conservatory in Baltimore and at Radcliffe College. When she was nineteen she married a South Carolina native, Peagram Dargan, and they moved to New York to become writers. In 1906 they bought a farm near Bryson City, N.C., to which she moved after her husband drowned off the coast of Cuba in 1915. Her early poetic dramas presaged her later interest in social causes. *The Mortal Gods* (1912) is about the exploitation of the working class in an industrialized society; and *Flutter of the Gold Leaf* (1922) shows her interest in liberal causes. She turned from closet dramas to poetry with *Path Flowers and Other Poems* (1914); *Cycle's Rim* (1916), a sequence of sonnets on the death of her husband; and *Lute and Furrow* (1922), which along with a collection of her stories and sketches, *Highland Annals* (1925), indicated a change in focus to the dirt farmers of the South. In the 1930s she became one of the most effective writers of proletarian fiction in such novels as *Call Home the Heart* (1932) and *A Stone Came Rolling* (1935), both of which portray poor North Carolina farmers and mountain people. Her last book was *Innocent Bigamy and Other Stories* (1962), which she published when she was ninety-three.

Guy Davenport. Born Nov. 23, 1927, in Anderson, S.C.; died Jan. 4, 2005, in Lexington, Ky. One of the most learned and gifted American writers of the second half of the twentieth century, he was a poet, critic, short story writer, essayist, translator, artist, book illustrator, book reviewer, and, from 1963 until he won a MacArthur fellowship in 1990, a professor of English at the University of Kentucky. He held degrees from Duke; Oxford, where he was a Rhodes Scholar; and Harvard, where he earned his Ph.D. in 1961. His books include *The Intelligence of Louis Agassiz* (1963), *Sappho: Songs and Fragments* (1965, a translation), *Tatlin!* (1974, stories), *Da Vinci's Bicycle* (1979, stories), *The Geography of the Imagination* (1981, essays), *The Cardiff Team* (1996, stories), and *The Hunter Gracchus and Other Papers on Literature and Art* (1996). Among his many honors are an O. Henry Award for his short stories and the Morton Douwen Zabel Award for fiction. In 1998 he was elected a fellow in the American Academy of Arts and Sciences. He was one of the most esoteric, challenging, and learned writers of his time.

Gwen Davenport. Born Oct. 3, 1910, in Colon, C.Z.; died March 23, 2002, Louisville. Gwen Leys Davenport wrote a handful of books but created one character who left the pages of one of her novels and became part of the American folk landscape. Mr. Belvedere was created in her third novel, *Belvedere* (1947), which is set at the end of World War II and concerns a child-hating male author who answers an ad for a baby-sitter in the *Saturday Review.* Her other novel with a Kentucky setting is *Family Fortunes* (1949), set in the Bluegrass region of central Kentucky. Her last book, *Time and Chance* (1993), was set in England in the 1830s. She also published fiction and essays in such magazines as *The New Yorker, Reader's Digest, Saturday Evening Post, McCall's,* and *Holiday.* In 1937 she married John Davenport and settled permanently in Louisville.

Jefferson Davis. Born June 3, 1808, at Fairview, Todd County, Ky.; died Dec. 6, 1889, in New Orleans. Jefferson Davis, the only president of the Confederate States of America, was the son of Samuel Emory Davis, a captain in the Revolutionary War, and Jane Cook Davis. In 1810 the family moved from Kentucky to Louisiana, then to Mississippi. He attended St. Thomas School in Springfield and Transylvania University in Lexington, and he graduated from the U.S. Military Academy at West Point in 1824. He married Sarah Knox Taylor, daughter of Zachary Taylor of Louisville, the future president, in 1835; she died three months later of malaria. In 1845 he married Varina Howell of Natchez, Miss. He fought in the Mexican War, served in the U.S. House of Representatives and the Senate and as secretary of war, and resigned his seat in the Senate on Jan. 21, 1861, when Mississippi seceded from the Union. At the first meeting of the Confederate Congress in Montgomery, Ala., on Feb. 9, 1861, he was named president of the Confederacy and served in that office until he was captured in Georgia on May 10, 1865, as he and his family were attempting to flee to Mexico. After he was released from prison at Fortress Monroe in Virginia in May 1867, he traveled for a couple of years and then settled at Beauvoir, overlooking the Gulf Coast near Biloxi, Miss., where he spent the remainder of his life. In 1881 he published the two-volume *Rise and Fall of the Confederate Government.*

Linda Scott DeRosier. Born the daughter of a coal miner and a former schoolteacher on Greasy Creek in Johnson County, Ky., in 1941, Linda Scott DeRosier attended Pikeville College and Eastern Kentucky University and received a Ph.D. from the University of Kentucky, where she "fell in love with ideas." She taught at Kentucky State University and was director of the Institute for Appalachian Studies at East Tennessee State University before she became a professor of psychology at Rocky Mountain College in Montana. She was married at nineteen, divorced, and then married the president of East Tennessee State, with whom she moved west. She tells her own inspiring story in *Creeker: A Woman's Journey* (1999), which the state historian, James Klotter, has called "a thoughtful, powerful, and realistic perspective on what it meant to grow up female in Appalachia." In 2003 she published *Songs of Life and Grace,* a family memoir based on letters, interviews, and memories of her father and mother.

Jude Devereaux. Jude Devereaux, the pen name of Jude Gilliam White, was born Sept. 20, 1947, in Louisville, the daughter of Harold J. White, an electrician, and Virginia Berry Gilliam. She received a B.A. from Murray State University in 1970 and later attended the College of Santa Fe and the University of New Mexico. She was an elementary school teacher from 1973 to 1977. Since 1976 she has devoted her time and talents to writing and has become one of the most popular writers in the world. Since her first novel, *The Enchanted Land* (1978), she has authored more than twenty-four *New York Times* best-sellers, and there are more than thirty million copies of her books in print. Especially popular are her historical romances, which include *A Knight in Shining Armor* (1989) and the James River Trilogy: *Counterfeit Lady* (1984), *Lost Lady* (1985), and *River Lady* (1985). She once told *Contemporary Authors* the reason she gave up the classroom for literature: "I wanted to write about women who had some power, who could create things, could make things happen."

David Dick. Born Feb. 18, 1930, in Cincinnati, David Dick moved with his mother to her native Bourbon County when he was eighteen months old. After earning a B.A. and an M.A. from the University of Kentucky, he worked as a writer and on-air journalist for WHAS Radio and Television in Louisville from 1959 to 1966, when he was employed by CBS News and stationed in Washington, D.C. He later worked in CBS News bureaus in Atlanta and Dallas and covered wars in El Salvador, Nicaragua, and Beirut, as well as Argentina's invasion of the Falkland Islands. After retiring from CBS, he taught journalism and directed the School of Journalism at the University of Kentucky. His books include *The View from Plum Lick* (1992), *Follow the Storm* (1993), *Peace at the Center* (1994), *The Scourges of Heaven* (1998), and *Jesse Stuart: The Heritage* (2004). He lives with his wife and coauthor Eulalie on a farm in central Kentucky that has been in his family since 1799.

Charles Dickens. Born Feb. 7, 1812, at Landport, near Portsmouth, Eng.; died June 9, 1870, at Gadshill, near Rochester, Eng. Charles Dickens was one of the most popular and successful novelists in the English language, the author of such standard works, most of them published serially in periodicals, as *Oliver Twist* (1837–1838), *A Christmas Carol* (1843), *David Copperfield* (1849–1850), *A Tale of Two Cities* (1859), and *Great Expectations* (1860–1861). In 1842 he traveled around the United States, including Kentucky, where he advocated an international copyright to protect authors' rights and the abolition of slavery. Later that year he published an account of his experiences and impressions in *American Notes*.

Michael Dorris. Born Jan. 13, 1945, in Louisville; died April 11, 1997, in Concord, N.H., a presumed suicide. Winner of the National Book Award in 1989 for *The Broken Cord*, Michael Dorris was a successful novelist, essayist, critic, and educator. His father died in the service in World War II, and Dorris was raised in the Crescent Hill neighborhood of Louisville by his mother and an aunt. He attended local Catholic schools and graduated from St. Xavier High School in 1963. He majored in classical languages at Georgetown University and went to graduate school at Yale to study theater but switched to anthropology to study his American Indian (his father's) ancestors. In 1971, as a single man, he adopted an Indian boy, who, he soon discovered, was afflicted with fetal alcohol syndrome, a consequence of the alcoholism of the boy's mother. He told his son's story in *The Broken Cord*. In 1981 he married Louise Erdrich, an author who also has American Indian ancestry. Together they wrote several books, including *The Crown of Columbus* (1991), a novel about Christopher Columbus. Their unusually close relationship apparently unraveled, and the couple were separated at the time of Dorris's suicide. Among his other books are a novel, *A Yellow Raft in Blue Water* (1987); a collection of essays, *Paper Trail* (1994); and his last novel, *The Cloud Chamber* (1997).

Kathleen Driskell. Kathleen Driskell is a native of Louisville who studied with Fred Chappell at the University of North Carolina at Greensboro, where she earned her M.F.A. in creative writing and was poetry editor of the *Greensboro Review*. She was a founder of the Kentucky Writers' Coalition in 1996 and teaches creative writing at Spalding University, where she also serves as associate program director for the brief-residency M.F.A. in Writing Program. She has published *Laughing Sickness* (1999), a book of poetry, and edited *Place Gives Rise to Spirit: Writers on Louisville* (2001). In 1995 she coedited, with Sena Jeter Naslund, *High Horse: Contemporary Writing by Spalding University's M.F.A. Faculty*. Her poems have appeared in such magazines as the *Southern Review*, *American Voice*, *Connecticut Review*, *Gulfstream*, and *Mid-American Review*. She has won grants for her poetry and fiction from the Kentucky Arts Council and the Kentucky Foundation for Women and prizes from the Associated Writing Programs and the Frankfort Arts Foundation.

Leon Driskell. Born 1932 in Athens, Ga.; died Feb. 19, 1995, in Louisville. Leon V. Driskell wrote poems, books, stories, critical articles, and book reviews and was a dedicated professor of English at the University of Louisville. He attended the University of Georgia and earned a Ph.D. in English at the University of Texas. Before coming to Louisville, he taught at the University of Texas, Birmingham-Southern College, and the University of Cincinnati. He published poems and stories in such magazines as the *Carolina Quarterly, Georgia Review,* and *Kentucky Poetry Review.* Several of his stories were listed in *Best American Short Stories.* He was coauthor, with Joan Brittain, of *The Eternal Crossroads: The Art of Flannery O'Connor* (1971), and in 1983 he published *Passing Through,* a critically acclaimed series of connected stories about the fictional Waters family in Owen County, Kentucky. He was not a prolific writer, but what he wrote was choice.

Logan English. Born 1928 in Bourbon County, Ky., at Wyndhurst, the family farm; died 1983 at Saratoga Springs, N.Y., after a car accident. Logan English was a folksinger, composer, and poet who spent his life leaving Kentucky and returning to it. He received a B.A. from Georgetown College and an M.F.A. from Yale and was a veteran of the Korean War. He sang in Carnegie Hall twice and had a radio show on WBAI in New York. He produced concerts from coast to coast and directed the American Hootenanny Festival. He recorded six albums, including *Kentucky Folk Songs and Ballads.* During his career as a musician, he met and became friends with Woody Guthrie, Bob Dylan, and Judy Collins. He acted in several plays on Broadway, including *St. Joan,* and in an off-Broadway production of *No Time for Sergeants.* In 1982 he told Gregg Swem, a writer for the *Courier-Journal,* that the two vital influences on his developing sensibilities were his Grandfather Eberhardt, a Baptist minister, and the tenants who worked his family's farm. His grandfather's pulpit performances and the songs of the field hands as they herded cattle and stripped tobacco shaped his love for folk music and theater. His long autobiographical poem, *No Land Where I Have Traveled: A Kentucky Poem,* was published in 1979. It was reprinted in 2001 by Larkspur Press. In a verse letter to his mother, which concludes the poem, he laments the death of his father sixteen years before: "Sixteen years. And now it is spring again in Kentucky. / If one longs for Kentucky all year, one aches for her in / the spring. No land where I have traveled is more fair."

John Fetterman. Born 1920 in Danville, Ky; died 1975. A Kentucky native, a freelance writer, and a longtime staff member at the *Courier-Journal,* John Fetterman knew his state intimately and thoroughly. In *Stinking Creek* (1967), he offers an up-close portrait of the mountain people of the Knox and Clay Counties border country by a man who got to know them by living with them and listening to them talk. It is not merely a sociological study but also a look at the soul of these isolated people, as they were in the mid-1960s.

John Filiatreau. John Filiatreau was born in Louisville on Sept. 18, 1949, and attended the Passionist Seminary in Warrenton, Mo. He later attended the University of Louisville for two years and received an M.F.A. in poetry from the University of Massachusetts. From 1968 to 1990 he was a writer and columnist for the *Courier-Journal.* He is now an editor for the Presbyterian Church USA in Louisville.

John Filson. Born Dec. 10, 1753, in East Fallowfield, Pa.; died ca. Oct. 1, 1788, near Cincinnati. John Filson was a historian, teacher, surveyor, mapmaker, and the author of the first history of Kentucky. He arrived in the Kentucky country in the fall of 1783 and began to acquire and survey land and to interview earlier pioneers for a book about the new territory. In 1784 he published in Wilmington, Del., *The Discovery, Settlement, and Present State of Kentucke,* which is more a promotional tract than a history. It is often referred to as Filson's *Kentucke.* It featured an appendix, "The Adventures of Colonel Daniel Boon," which singled Boone out and made him famous as a representative of the Kentucky frontiersman. It was an immediate best seller, and soon editions appeared in French and German. Filson made several more trips to Kentucky to survey and sell land; then in 1788 he surveyed a road from Lexington to the mouth of the Licking River, where he was one of the founders of Losantiville, which became Cincinnati. He and his investment partners purchased some eight hundred acres of Ohio land north of the Ohio River, and he disappeared while exploring the area, presumably killed by the Indians.

Abraham Flexner. Born Nov. 13, 1866, in Louisville; died Sept. 21, 1959; buried in Cave Hill Cemetery. Abraham Flexner, a pioneer in education reform, earned degrees from Johns Hopkins University, Harvard University, and the University of Berlin. His influential *Flexner Report*, as it was commonly called, was published in 1910 as *Medical Education in the United States and Canada* and led to many reforms in medical education. In 1930 he became the first director of the Institute for Advanced Study at Princeton. His tribute to Louisville and Kentucky is contained in his autobiography, *I Remember* (1940), which was expanded and published posthumously as *Abraham Flexner: An Autobiography* (1960).

Hortense Flexner. Born 1885 in Louisville; died 1973 in Louisville. Hortense Flexner received a B.A. and an M.A. from the University of Michigan and began her writing career on the old *Louisville Herald.* Her plays include *The Broken God* (1915) and *The New Queen* (1920). *Wishing Window* (1942), about two French children at the time of the Nazi invasion of France during World War II, is but one of her several popular books for children. Her poetry collections include *Clouds and Cobblestones* (1920), *The Stubborn Root* (1930), and *North Window* (1943). The *Saturday Review of Literature* noted in 1943 that "if perhaps her poetry is too much preoccupied with bitter inquiry and unresolved speculation, it is always interesting, always provocative." Her poems were frequently published in *The New Yorker.* Some of her best poems were gathered in 1963 in *Selected Poems,* with a foreword by Laurie Lee.

Charles Bracelen Flood. A nationally acclaimed author of fiction and nonfiction, Charles Bracelen Flood is a transplant from New York to Kentucky. In 1975 he met and fell in love with Katherine Burnam, a native of Richmond, Ky.; they married and have lived in Kentucky ever since. He is a graduate of Harvard, where he studied under John Ciardi and Archibald MacLeish. At twenty-three he broke into the literary scene with a best-selling novel, *Love Is a Bridge* (1953), followed by other novels, including *A Distant Drum* (1957) and *Tell Me, Stranger* (1959). He has also written nonfiction books on Vietnam, Hitler, and Robert E. Lee. Published in 1981, *Lee: The Last Years* was a popular and critical success. It is a book that focuses, Flood says, on "a remarkably little-known chapter in the life of a remarkably well-known name."

John Fox Jr. Born Dec. 16, 1862, near Paris, Ky., at Stony Point in Bourbon County; died July 8, 1919, at Big Stone Gap, Va. One of the first writers to treat the people of the southern Appalachians sympathetically, John Fox Jr. studied for two years at Transylvania University and graduated from Harvard in 1883. He worked for brief periods as a reporter for the *New York Sun* and the *New York Times* and studied law at Columbia; but poor health caused him to return to Kentucky in 1885, where he joined his family in pursuing real estate and mining interests near Big Stone Gap. Several walking tours of the Kentucky-Virginia border country, particularly the counties of Letcher, Harlan, Leslie, and Perry, made him familiar with the Kentucky mountain people and their culture. Encouraged by a former professor at Transylvania, James Lane Allen, he began writing short sketches of mountain life and in 1892 published his first short story, "A Mountain Europa," in *Century* magazine. He was soon publishing fiction and nonfiction pieces in *Scribner's, Ladies' Home Journal, Harper's Weekly,* and *Harper's Monthly.* In 1895 he published his first book, a collection of stories called *A Cumberland Vendetta,* and in 1897, his first novel, *The Kentuckians,* set principally in the Bluegrass. Other popular books included *The Little Shepherd of Kingdom Come* (1903), which was probably the first American novel to sell more than a million copies; and *The Trail of the Lonesome Pine* (1908), a love story based in part upon his own experiences. In 1908 he married Fritzi Scheff, a Viennese opera singer, but they divorced four years later. In July 1919 he developed pneumonia while on a fishing trip and died at his home in Big Stone Gap. He is buried in Paris, Ky.

Carolyn Wilford Fuqua. During the 1970s and 1980s, Carolyn Wilford Fuqua of Hopkinsville was a frequent contributor to *Approaches* and its successor, *Kentucky Poetry Review.* Not only was she a fine poet in those years, but she also traveled and once taught creative writing to students at Ricks Institute in Monrovia, Liberia, where she discovered at least one emerging poet, "an 18-year-old tribal lad who has a great gift for freshness." She was also a painter, a gardener, and an actor who performed with the Pennyrile Players, a local drama group.

Lucy Furman. Born June 7, 1869, in Henderson, Ky.; died Aug. 25, 1958, in Cranford, N.J. After her parents' deaths, she grew up in Evansville, Ind., and attended the Sayre School in Lexington. During her visits across the Ohio River to Henderson, she collected material for a series of short stories she published in *Century* magazine, which were later reprinted in her first book, *Stories of a Sanctified Town* (1896). Some ten years later, while she was visiting a former Sayre classmate, Katherine Pettit, at the Hindman Settlement School, she became interested in the Kentucky mountain people and culture and remained at the school as a teacher and a housemother for the male students for seventeen years. She wrote realistic and positive sketches of her experiences in several popular books, including *Mothering on Perilous* (1913), *Sight to the Blind* (1914), *The Quare Women* (1923), and *The Glass Window* (1925). In 1924 she returned to Henderson, where she became active in the Anti–Steel Trap League of Washington, D.C., and lectured throughout Kentucky against the use of steel traps. In 1934 she moved to Frankfort, where she lobbied the General Assembly for anti–steel trap legislation and wrote editorials on the subject—with little success. In 1953 she moved to Cranford, N.J., to live with a nephew and died there in 1958.

John Spalding Gatton. Born March 20, 1947, in Louisville, John Spalding Gatton received a B.A. from the Catholic University of America, an M.Litt. from the University of Dublin, Trinity College, and his Ph.D. from the University of Kentucky. He taught English as a second language in Dublin and Paris and acted with Le Café-Théâtre Anglais in Paris. At the University of Kentucky he taught in the English Department and in the Honors Program; at Virginia Military Institute he also taught in the English Department. Since 1989 he has been a professor of English at Bellarmine University, where he has directed eleven plays. He has written professional articles on such subjects as Oscar Wilde, Natalie Clifford Barney, staging violence in medieval drama, Lord Byron's historical tragedies, and Delacroix's interpretations of Byron's poetry. He has written entries on Byron as a poet and as a prose writer for two volumes of the *Dictionary of Literary Biography.* He also wrote entries for *The Kentucky Encyclopedia* and *The Encyclopedia of Louisville* on several writers and on the history of theater in Louisville. In 1992 New York University Press published *Adventures of the Mind,* his annotated translation of *Aventures de l'esprit* by Natalie Clifford Barney. He has recently completed a book on Lord Byron's London and has published poems in several journals, including *Kentucky Poetry Review.*

Jane Gentry. Jane Gentry was born in Athens, Ky., on Feb. 9, 1941. She earned her B.A. from Hollins College, her M.A. from Brandeis University, and her Ph.D. from the University of North Carolina at Chapel Hill. She is now a professor of English at the University of Kentucky, where she teaches poetry workshops and honors colloquia. She has published poems in *Southern Poetry Review, Sewanee Review, American Voice,* and other journals. In 1995 the LSU Press published *A Garden in Kentucky,* a much-praised and oft-quoted collection of her poems. She has two forthcoming collections, *A Year in Kentucky: A Garland of Poems* and *Portrait of the Artist as a White Pig.* In 1986 she received the University of Kentucky Alumni Association's Distinguished Teacher Award.

Dot Gibbs. Born 1910 in Louisville; died in Louisville in the mid-1980s. Dorothy Barr Gibbs attended Logan College in Russellville and married Walter Gibbs, a printing company executive, in 1930. She was the mother of six children, all of whom she celebrated in her poetry. Occupied with rearing her large family, she became a serious poet fairly late in life. Encouraged by her oldest son, Packy, she took a course in creative writing at the University of Louisville under

Harvey Curtis Webster; she published her first poem in 1965 in *Approaches: A Quarterly of Poems by Kentuckians,* edited by Joy Bale of Elizabethtown. Some of her poems were collected in *Not Forgotten Blue* (1977). Her poems invite readers into an enchanted, mystical world charged with divinity—from a speckled turkey egg all the way up to the moon. The landscape of her poetry is a place where children sing and play in divine innocence and abandon.

Janice Holt Giles. Born 1905 in Altus, Ark.; died 1983 in Knifley, Ky. Janice Holt Giles had the good fortune to be riding a bus near Bowling Green in the summer of 1943 when she met Henry Giles, a soldier from nearby Adair County, and she was smitten by him and he by her. They corresponded during the remainder of the war and married in Louisville, where she was working as a secretary to the dean of the Louisville Presbyterian Seminary, immediately upon his return to Kentucky. Soon they moved to his home community of Knifley, in Adair County, and she developed the people and folk culture of her husband's south-central Kentucky into some of Kentucky's best-loved books, including *The Enduring Hills* (1950), *Miss Willie* (1951), *Tara's Healing* (1951), *The Kentuckians* (1953), *Hannah Fowler* (1956), *The Believers* (1957), and *Shady Grove* (1967). But neither did she neglect her native Arkansas and Oklahoma, where she grew up in a family of schoolteachers; her books about the West include *Johnny Osage* (1960), *Savanna* (1961), and *Voyage to Santa Fe* (1962). Among her nonfiction books are *40 Acres and No Mule* (1952), *The Kinta Years* (1973), and *Wellspring* (1975). She also wrote several books with the assistance of Henry Giles. The Giles Foundation was established in 1996 to preserve the Gileses' literary legacy and to restore their log home near Knifley.

Caroline Gordon. Born Oct. 6, 1895, in Todd County, Ky.; died April 11, 1981, in San Cristobal, Mex. Caroline Gordon grew up at her mother's ancestral seat, Merrymount, in Todd County, and was taught at home by her father and later at his school for boys in Clarksville, Tenn. She received a B.A. from Bethany College in 1916 and taught school and worked as a journalist for several years. In 1924 she married her fellow Kentuckian Allen Tate, one of the Vanderbilt "Agrarian" writers. Her first novel, *Penhally* (1931), chronicles an affluent Kentucky family like her own from antebellum plantation days to the early twentieth century. In 1934 she published her popular novel *Aleck Maury, Sportsman,* which is based on her reactionary father and his old-fashioned ways. Her other books include *The Garden of Adonis* (1937) and *The Women on the Porch* (1944). Her short stories were collected in *The Forest of the South* (1945), *Old Red* (1963), and *The Collected Stories of Caroline Gordon* (1981), a signature volume with her usual characters and themes as each generation copes, or fails to cope, with the changing times.

Sarah Gorham. Born in 1956, Sarah Gorham is a poet in the grand tradition of the poet as soothsayer, the bardic voice that shows us our world and ourselves in ways that science and technology cannot. It is the poetry of honesty, insight, and revelation that is aware of other poets and traditions but speaks in its own unique way, frequently in an oracular voice of parable and philosophy. As she writes in *The Tension Zone* (1996): "I want truth with grass / stains, truth with sticky feet." She has published in such prestigious journals as *Poetry, Nation, Antaeus, Kenyon Review,* and *Poetry Northwest,* whose Carolyn Kiser Award she won in 1990. She has received awards from the Kentucky State Arts Council and the Kentucky Foundation for Women; and she has been in residence at the Yaddo and McDowell writers' colonies. Moreover, she is a cofounder of Sarabande Books, based in Louisville and publisher of quality books that sometimes sell in respectable numbers and sometimes merely seek, in the words of John Milton, "fit audience though few." She has displayed her poems admirably in two other collections, *Don't Go Back to Sleep* (1989), her first volume, and *The Cure* (2003), which the novelist Dwight Allen called "a brave, eloquent, stirring book." She is married to the poet Jeffrey Skinner, with whom she edited *Last Call: Poems on Alcoholism, Addiction, and Deliverance* in 1997. She is the mother of two daughters.

Sue Grafton. Sue Grafton was born in Louisville in 1940 and was educated in the local schools and at the University of Louisville, from which she received a B.A. She is the author of novels, TV screenplays, and, since 1982 (when she published the first of her abecedarian series,

"A" Is for Alibi), best-selling mysteries starring Kinsey Millhone, a California-based private eye who has become one of the most famous fictional detectives of either gender. By 2004 she had worked her way through the alphabet to *"R" Is for Richochet.* Before she started her sinister alphabet, she wrote traditional novels, such as *Keziah Dane* (1967) and *The Lolly-Madonna War* (1973), and television plays, such as *Killer in the Family,* which starred Robert Mitchum. In her *Courier-Journal* review of *"O" Is for Outlaw,* which is partly set in Louisville, Mary Caldwell called Grafton "the Sara Lee of the publishing world," with "a very narrow range: good, better, best." Indeed, Grafton is not the first of the female sleuth writers, but she is surely near the head of the lineup.

Abigail Gramig. Born in Louisville on Jan. 15, 1980, Abigail Gramig is a young poet whose formal education includes Assumption High School and Bellarmine University, from which she received a B.A. Her first collection of poetry is a chapbook of some twenty-nine pages, *Dusting the Piano* (2004), an enchanted garden of delights and insights articulated expertly in compact, lyrical free verse. She is a protean poet of many faces and disguises, and she chooses subjects as old as Homer and as current as the latest TV installment of *Will and Grace.*

Jonathan Greene. Jonathan Greene, born in 1943, is a Frankfort poet, book designer, and publisher. His poetry has been published by small presses with limited runs and high standards and includes *The Reckoning* (1966), *The Lapidary* (1969), and *The Quiet Goods* (1979). As a book designer and publisher, he founded Gnomon Press and has edited and published fine Kentucky writers ranging from Richard Taylor to James Still.

Granny Hager. Granny Hager is a good example of one of the remarkable developments in contemporary writing, the emergence of the voices of plain people, who heretofore would have been silent. Using an as-told-to method of transmission, the subject tells her or his story to another person, who transcribes and arranges the subject's words into a meaningful, coherent narrative. It is a form of creative oral biography that has flowered especially since the invention of the portable tape recorder, which has increased the collection of the life stories of semiliterate and, frequently, illiterate people. It is a genre that goes back to the slave narratives written by ex-slaves or told to educated abolitionists. Granny Hager probably knew little or nothing about her literary antecedents, but this Hazard native did not have to do research to tell about her experiences. She simply searched her memory and told her story to Kathy Kahn, a political activist. Hager was born and bred in the coal camps of eastern Kentucky. In 1962 her husband died of pneumoconiosis, or black lung disease, caused by the black dust from the soft bituminous coal mined in the southern Appalachians. That year she joined with thousands of other eastern Kentuckians to form the Appalachian Committee for Full Employment, whose mission was to end job discrimination, increase the power of unions, and improve working conditions for miners. Their strategy involved strikes and confrontations with mine owners and their supporters.

Eliza Calvert Hall. Born Feb. 11, 1856, in Bowling Green, Ky.; died Dec. 20, 1935, in Dallas, Tex. Eliza Caroline Calvert Obenchain wrote under her maiden name, Eliza Calvert Hall. She was born into one of the pioneer families of Bowling Green; she attended Western College in Cincinnati and taught until she married William Alexander Obenchain in 1885. She was the author of poems, stories, and essays about western Kentucky that appeared in such periodicals as the *New York Times, Scribner's, Cosmopolitan,* and the *Ladies' Home Journal.* Her support for women's rights to vote, to marry and divorce, and to own property set her apart from most men and women in her community—and state and nation. It is a subtle theme that runs throughout her most popular story, "Sally Ann's Experience," which was collected as part of *Aunt Jane of Kentucky* (1907). She also published a sequel, *The Land of Long Ago* (1909), and other books, but none achieved the popularity of *Aunt Jane.* She did, however, publish the nonfiction *Book of Hand-Woven Coverlets* (1912), which is a standard work on the folk craft of weaving.

James Baker Hall. James Baker Hall was born in Lexington in 1935 and attended the University of Kentucky and, like three other young Kentucky writers of his age—Wendell Berry, Ed McClanahan, and Gurney Norman—also attended Stanford as a Wallace Stegner Fellow and earned an M.A. there in 1961. Photography has been a passion of his from an early age, and he worked with Gene Meatyard, the distinguished Lexington photographer; he later taught English and photography at M.I.T. and at the University of Connecticut. He now teaches creative writing at the University of Kentucky. His first novel, *Yates Paul, His Grand Flights, His Tootings* (1963), was influenced by photography; it has been described as a comic novel about "several kinds of darkrooms." His next novel was *Music for a Broken Piano* (1983), set in western Massachusetts among a colony of liberal young people of various persuasions. His short stories have been published in the *Saturday Evening Post, Shenandoah Review, Chicago Review,* and *Paris Review.* When he was well into his thirties he began writing and publishing his poems in such periodicals as the *Sewanee Review, Southern Poetry Review, Hudson Review, The New Yorker,* and *Poetry* and has collected them into several volumes.

Wade Hall. Born in Alabama on a farm near Union Springs on Feb. 2, 1934, Wade Hall holds degrees from Troy University and the University of Alabama and a Ph.D. from the University of Illinois. He served in the U.S. Army from 1954 to 1956, mostly in Germany. He has taught at Troy University, the University of Alabama, the University of Illinois, the University of Florida, Kentucky Southern College, and Bellarmine University. He is the author of numerous poems, reviews, and essays in various periodicals and has written some twenty books and monographs, including *The Smiling Phoenix: Southern Humor, 1865–1914* (1965), *The Truth Is Funny: A Study of Jesse Stuart's Humor* (1970), *The High Limb: Poems* (1973), *The Kentucky Book* (1979), *The Rest of the Dream: The Black Odyssey of Lyman Johnson* (1988), *A Visit with Harlan Hubbard* (1996), *Passing for Black: The Life and Careers of Mae Street Kidd* (1997), *James Still: Portrait of the Artist as a Boy in Alabama* (1998), *Conecuh People: Words of Life from the Alabama Black Belt* (1999), and *High Upon a Hill: A History of Bellarmine College* (1999). For the past thirty years he has aggressively collected books about Kentucky and the south, picture postcards, photography, American sheet music and recordings, folk art, quilts, and American letters and diaries—all of which are being deposited at several museums and archives. He has lived in Louisville since 1962.

Elizabeth Hardwick. Elizabeth Hardwick was born July 27, 1916, in Lexington, and, as she told a writer for the *New Yorker* in July 1998: "I am not sorry to have grown up in Lexington, so long as I didn't have to stay there forever. I remember the streets, the drugstores, Woolworth's, the mad preacher in front of the courthouse saying things like 'Christ don't care about cute, remember that, folks.'" In her first novel, *The Ghostly Lover* (1945), and in her early short stories she appears to be a "Southern" writer, but, as she remarked to an interviewer for the *Paris Review* in 1985, "being a Southern writer is a decision, not a fate." Indeed, she had the family and educational background to be a Southern or a Kentucky writer. She was one of ten children in her Lexington family and had deep Kentucky roots, and she earned two degrees from the University of Kentucky. Then she decided to go to New York, and there she became a writer in many genres, with a broader view and more cosmopolitan subjects. For seventeen years she wrote reviews, essays, and short stories for the *Partisan Review.* A *New York Times* reviewer of *Sight Readings: American Fictions* (1998), a collection of her essays, notes that they "provide the reader with a bright, breezy window on a century of American writing" and then names some of the writers she had reviewed: Edith Wharton, Henry James, John Updike, Philip Roth, and John Cheever. She had, indeed, broadened her horizons. She married one of the best American poets of the twentieth century, Robert Lowell, and helped found a spicy alternative to the *New York Times Book Review* and other national reviews, the *New York Review of Books,* which published some of her best essays, including one datelined Selma, Ala., March 22, 1965, which began: "What a sad countryside it is, the home of the pain of the Confederacy, the birthplace of the White Citizens Council." In the summer of 1966 she went to the Watts area of Los Angeles to report on the aftermath of the riots there. In addition to her fiction and social and literary criticism, for which she won a Guggenheim Fellowship, she was a drama critic and in 1967 won the George Jean Nathan Award for Dramatic Criticism. Her other books include two novels, *The Simple Truth* (1955) and *Sleep-*

less Nights (1979), and two collections of essays, *A View of My Own* (1962) and *Bartleby in Manhattan* (1983).

John Hay. John Williams Hay is one of Kentucky's most talented, underrated, and underknown authors, despite the fact that he is a well-known author of children's books. He was born in Frankfort on July 31, 1944, and grew up on nearby Scotland Farm caring for horses. He holds a B.A. from the University of the South at Sewanee, an M.A. in writing from Hollins University, and a J.D. from the University of Louisville. He has published four children's books: *Rover and Coo Coo* (1986), *Mama, Were You Ever Young?* (1989), *Shell of Wonder* (1990, with Mary Belle Harwich), and *How to Be Full with Beauty* (1991). *Rover and Coo Coo,* a frontier story based on the author's great-great-great-grandfather's frontier experiences, won the Friends of American Writers Juvenile Fiction Award. He has also won an honorable mention in *Best American Short Stories* for "High," which appeared in the *Sewanee Review* in the summer of 1972. He has had poetry and three short stories in *Open 24 Hours,* a publication of the creative writing program at Brescia University in Owensboro. He is writing and living on Scotland Farm, at work on a longer piece.

Will Shakespeare Hays. Born July 19, 1837, in Louisville, at Hancock and Main Streets, about a block from the Ohio River; died July 23, 1907, in Louisville. William Shakespeare Hays was a journalist and a songwriter who wrote more than 350 songs, which sold millions of copies in sheet music. He attended Hanover College, and after graduating from Georgetown College, he became a clerk on a riverboat. He wrote river columns for several Louisville newspapers before and during the Civil War and became river editor of the *Courier-Journal* after the war. Some of his popular songs were "Evangeline," "The Drummer Boy of Shiloh," "My Sunny Southern Home," "Write Me a Letter from Home," and "We Parted by the River Side." Although he was a Southern sympathizer, before the war he wrote "The Union Forever for Me," which became popular on the Union side. According to the actress Kittie Blanchard, she sang Hays's new song "When Sherman Marched Down to the Sea" at the old Louisville Theater in the spring of 1865 before an audience of cheering Union soldiers that included General Sherman. Although Hays claimed to be the author of "Dixie," there is yet no credible evidence to support this. His most popular song by far was "Mollie Darling," which he published in 1871. According to Hays, he sold the song to a New York publisher for twenty-five dollars, which he gave to a poor woman he met on the street to bury her dead child. In a newspaper article in 1898 he said: "No, I never made any money out of my songs. I don't want to, either. It's enough pay for me to hear people singing them, and know that I have made somebody happy." He is buried in Cave Hill Cemetery.

Josiah Henson. Born a slave June 15, 1789, in Charles County, Md.; escaped from Kentucky with his family to Canada in Oct. 1830; died a free man in Dresden, Ont., May 5, 1883. Josiah Henson—ex-slave, Methodist preacher, educator, and Underground Railroad activist—grew up in Maryland and was a trusted overseer and servant to his master, who sent him to Kentucky. After his Kentucky master, Isaac Riley, almost sold him on a trading trip to New Orleans, he decided that he must try to run away. In October 1830 he escaped from Riley in Daviess County, crossed the Ohio River with his wife and four children, and reached Canada on October 28. He established Dawn, a community for runaway slaves near Dresden, Ont., and helped over one hundred slaves escape from Kentucky. He tells the story of his life in one of the nation's best-known slave narratives, *The Life of Josiah Henson, Formerly a Slave, Now an Inhabitant of Canada, as Narrated by Himself* (1849). According to Harriet Beecher Stowe, his book influenced her novel *Uncle Tom's Cabin* (1852), especially the character of Uncle Tom.

Chris Holbrook. Chris Holbrook was born in 1961 and grew up in Soft Shell, Ky., in Knott County. He earned a B.A. at the University of Kentucky and an M.F.A. at the University of Iowa. His stories have appeared in such periodicals and anthologies as *Groundwater, Home and Beyond, A Gathering at the Forks, A Kentucky Christmas,* and *Kentucky Voices.* He has won first place awards in contests held by *Louisville Magazine* and *Now and Then.* He has held residency fellowships at the Fine Arts Work Center in Provincetown, Mass., and at Yaddo in Saratoga

Springs, N.Y. He has won two Al Smith Fellowships from the Kentucky Arts Council and the Chaffin Award from Morehead State University. He has taught at Alice Lloyd College and is now an assistant professor of creative writing at Morehead. Gurney Norman has called his stories of contemporary Appalachia "consummate literary artistry." Ed McClanahan calls his stories in *Hell and Ohio: Stories of Southern Appalachia* (1995) "trenchant, unflinching." He lives with his wife and daughter in Pippa Passes.

Silas House. Silas House was born in Lily, Laurel County, Ky., where his family has lived for generations, in 1971. He attended Sue Bennett College and graduated in English from Eastern Kentucky University. He is married to Teresa and is the father of two young girls, Cheyenne and Olivia. He's worked as a Wal-Mart cashier, a cook, a waiter, a busboy, a satellite installer, a data entry clerk, and, when *Clay's Quilt* (2001) was published, he was delivering mail to about eight hundred mailboxes in and around Lily. Needless to say, he was an immediate celebrity, known even to people who don't read many novels. *Clay's Quilt* is, in the words of House, "about a young man who was orphaned as a child and is being brought up by his aunt and uncle." It's about Generation X coming of age in the Kentucky mountains, blending the old with the new. His second novel, *A Parchment of Leaves* (2002), is the story of Vine, a Cherokee who leaves her people for a white man she thinks she loves in the early twentieth century. It pays tribute to the author's great-grandmother, a Cherokee, and to his own family. The setting for his next novel, *The Coal Tattoo* (2004), is Black Banks, a coal mining town in east Tennessee, where the two protagonists, Anneth and Easter, are two very dissimilar sisters who can't live together or apart. The title refers to the indelible mark left on coal miners caught in a mine collapse, but it also describes the cultural mark left on all the people of the mining communities. House has received a number of honors, including the James Still Award from the Fellowship of Southern Writers and the Chaffin Award from Morehead State University, and he was named a finalist for the Southeast Booksellers Association fiction award. His is a new, vigorous, and authentic voice from the southern mountains—one that is worthy to follow the likes of James Still, Harry Caudill, and Albert Stewart.

Quentin Howard. Born Sept. 10, 1918, in Pike County near Meta, Ky.; died April 1998 in Pike County. Quentin Howard lived in Kentucky almost all his life. He attended local schools and earned a B.A. from Morehead State University and an M.A. from Vanderbilt. He was a teacher and a school principal for some thirty years. He published poems, stories, and articles in the *New York Times, Grit, Christian Science Monitor,* and several literary magazines. He started his own "little" magazine, *Wind,* in April 1971 and ran it on a shoestring, which he provided, for more than twenty years. (It was revived and continued for seven years under the editorship of Charlie G. Hughes in Nicholasville.) He was pleased to publish established poets like James Still, Jesse Stuart, and Jim Wayne Miller; but he delighted in discovering and publishing unknown authors. It was a labor of love that he felt was sufficient reward in itself. Occasionally, he would get recognition that made him proud, such as *Wind's* designation by *Writer's Digest* in the mid-1980s as one of the nation's ten top small literary magazines.

Harlan Hubbard. Born Jan. 4, 1900, in Bellevue, Ky., across the Ohio River from Cincinnati; died Jan. 16, 1988, at Payne Hollow, near Milton. Harlan Hubbard—artist, writer, naturalist—fled the noise and confusion of the modern world and found peace with his wife and companion, Anna, on a few acres of land along the south shore of the Ohio River several miles downriver from Madison, Ind. Unlike Thoreau's two-year retreat to Walden Pond in the mid-nineteenth century, Hubbard's sojourn in the woods was not a calculated experiment in living. It was living. It was not an easy living or even a comfortable one. It was living on the land and living, to a great extent, off the land and the river. He didn't have much money, but he had all he needed to pay his taxes and for an occasional visit to the doctor and for a few foodstuffs he couldn't grow or harvest from the river, like a sack of soybeans that Anna could find infinite ways to use. He once sold a riverscape painting to a city visitor for two hundred dollars and asked, "How long do you think this money will last us?" Without waiting for a reply, he answered, "Oh, about six months." After Anna died in 1986, he had his dog Ranger for company and sometimes unexpected guests who trekked through the woods a couple of miles to his enclave. But Hubbard didn't start out as an irresponsible adult Huck Finn. He was from a middle-class family with two brothers who moved to New York and Hollywood and succeeded in the twentieth century's quest for wealth and power. Indeed, after his father died in 1907, he moved with his mother to New York, where he attended high school in the Bronx and later the National Academy of Design in New York, and, back home, the Cincinnati Art Academy. He and his mother returned to Kentucky in 1919 and settled in Fort Thomas, where he made a spartan living as a carpenter. In 1929 he began keeping a journal in which he recorded his rejection of an industrial, consumer society and his love for painting, writing, music, and the natural world. In 1943 he married Anna Eikenhout, a Cincinnati librarian originally from Michigan, and the following year they built a shanty boat and began a slow voyage down the Ohio and Mississippi Rivers and through the Louisiana bayous, ending in 1951, when they returned to Payne Hollow, where they would live the rest of their lives. In addition to his journals, he published *Shantyboat* (1953), *Payne Hollow* (1974), and, posthumously, *Shantyboat in the Bayous* (1990).

Virginia Cary Hudson. Born 1894 in Versailles, Ky.; died 1954 in Louisville. Virginia Cary Hudson was a precocious little girl growing up in the beautiful Bluegrass town of Versailles at the turn of the twentieth century. Her daughter, Virginia C. Mayne, said her mother had written a number of comic personal essays about her girlhood for school assignments and put them away in a trunk. Eight years after her mother's death in 1954, Mayne published them as *O Ye Jigs and Juleps!* (1962), which became a runaway best seller, with almost half a million copies sold in one year. Two volumes of her later writing, penned when she lived in St. James Court in Louisville as the wife of Kirtley S. Cleveland, were also published posthumously as *Credos and Quips* (1964) and *Flapdoodle, Trust, and Obey* (1966). The commercial success of these three books is a cautionary tale against destroying family papers before they are read.

Charlie Hughes. Charlie Hughes was born in Lexington, Ky., on Feb. 29, 1944, and was raised on a farm near Harrodsburg. In 1967 he received a B.A. in chemistry from Transylvania University and an M.A. in toxicology from the University of Kentucky in 1985. He worked as an analytical chemist at the University of Kentucky for thirty years. He edited *Wind* magazine from 1993 to 2000. His work has been published in such journals as *Kentucky Poetry Review, Cumberland Poetry Review, Hollins Critic, Kansas Quarterly,* and the *Journal of Kentucky Studies.* He is a coeditor of two collections, *Groundwater: Contemporary Kentucky Fiction* (1992) and *Best of Wind* (1994), and the author of *Shifting for Myself* (2002), a collection of his poems.

Gilbert Imlay. Born ca. 1754 in New Jersey, Gilbert Imlay served in the War for Independence and by about 1783 was in Kentucky and beginning to acquire vast land grants. By 1786 he had apparently left the state and in the early 1790s was in Europe courting Mary Wollstonecraft, by whom he had an illegitimate daughter. He abandoned them both, leaving Wollstonecraft to eventually marry William Godwin. Although Imlay remained in Kentucky for little more than two years, he produced two important books about the new country. *Topographical Description of the Western Territory of North America* (1792) is a promotional book that praises the land, its resources, and its potential. His second book, a novel, *The Emigrants,* published in London in 1793, is the sentimental story of an English merchant who moves his family to Louisville.

Cass Irvin. Cass Irvin is a native of Louisville and a graduate of Kentucky Southern College and the University of Louisville. She has been a quadriplegic since she contracted polio at age nine while attending a Girl Scout camp; however, she shows convincingly in her memoir, *Home Bound* (2004), that with reasonable assistance, disabled people like herself can become enabled and live fulfilling and productive lives. This book is the sensitive yet hard-nosed account of the frustrations, the embarrassments, the humors, and the triumphs of a woman who wanted to live a good life—and how she did. In Louisville she has served as executive director of Access to the Arts, Inc., and has written frequently for the *Disability Rag* and *Ragged Edge.*

Virginia Honchell Jewell. Virginia Honchell Jewell lives in Clinton, the seat of Hickman County, in far western Kentucky. This historic county, which borders the Mississippi River, provided the subject matter for her two books: *Lick Skillet and Other Tales of Hickman County* (1986) and *The Cat and the Pillow Slip and More about Hickman County, Ky.* Born in Huntington, W.V., in 1924, she spent her early years in West Virginia and moved with her family to Barlow, Ky., at age twelve. She is a graduate of Murray State University, where she studied journalism under the late Dr. L. J. Hortin. After marrying Ramer B. Jewell, she moved with him to Hickman County, where she has lived for almost sixty years. She has been a contributor to the *Hickman County Gazette* for many years and has written for other area newspapers. She played the organ for over fifty years at her church and has been active in promoting the Hickman County Museum in Clinton. She has a son and a daughter and five grandchildren.

Fenton Johnson. Born into a large Catholic family of nine children in New Haven, Ky., in 1953, Fenton Johnson attended local parochial schools, then graduated from Larue County High School. He holds a degree from Stanford University, and he also studied at the prestigious Iowa Writers Workshop. He now teaches in the writing program at the University of Arizona. His books include *Crossing the River* (1989), *Scissors, Paper, Rock* (1993), and *Keeping Faith: A Skeptic's Journey* (2003). In 1996 he published *Geography of the Heart: A Memoir,* which tells of his relationship with an HIV-positive man who dies of AIDS. Johnson is a frequent contributor to such national publications as the *New York Times Magazine.*

Lyman Tefft Johnson. Born June 12, 1906, in Columbia, Tenn.; died Oct. 3, 1997, in Louisville. A civil rights leader and educator, Lyman Tefft Johnson was born, as he once said, during "the darkest days" of segregation and discrimination. His father was principal of the local "colored" school, and all four of his grandparents had been slaves—that is, until his paternal grandfather, a skilled carpenter, had done extra work and saved enough money to buy freedom for himself and his wife. In 1930 Johnson graduated from Virginia Union University in Richmond with a degree in Greek. In 1931 he earned an M.A. in history from the University of Michigan. Two years later he arrived in Louisville to begin a thirty-three-year career teaching history, economics, and mathematics at Central High School, where he became an inspiration and a role model for his students. Before he retired, he spent seven years in school administration and four years as a member of the Jefferson County Board of Education. While serving as president of the Louisville Association of Teachers in Colored Schools between 1939 and 1941, he led the movement to equalize the salaries of black and white teachers. In 1949 he was a plaintiff in the lawsuit that opened the University of Kentucky to African Americans. In 1979 the University of Kentucky awarded him an honorary D.Litt.; and in 1980 the Jefferson County Board of Education named a school in his honor. In 1936 he married Juanita Morrell, with whom he had a daughter, Yvonne, and a son, Lyman Morrell Johnson. He is the subject of an oral biography, *The Rest of the Dream: The Black Odyssey of Lyman Johnson,* by Wade Hall.

Thomas Johnson Jr. Born ca. 1760 in Virginia; died before 1830 in Danville, Ky. Known as Kentucky's first poet as well as the "Drunken Poet of Danville," Thomas Johnson Jr. arrived in Kentucky in 1785 and settled in the frontier town of Danville. He immediately gained a reputation as the maker of coarse, satirical verses, which he collected into a thirty-six-page booklet, published in 1795 and titled *The Kentucky Miscellany.* It is one of the rarest of Kentucky books. Only two copies of the first edition are known to exist, though copies of the three following editions, ending with the fourth edition of 1821, are occasionally obtainable. The University of Kentucky Libraries has printed a facsimile of the fourth edition as No. 11 in their Occasional Papers Series. Although the date of his death is unknown, it was probably before 1830. He was buried in an unmarked grave.

Annie Fellows Johnston. Born May 15, 1863, in Evansville, Ind.; died Oct. 5, 1931, at her home, "The Beeches," in Pewee Valley, Ky. Annie Fellows Johnston attended the public schools of Evansville and spent one year at the University of Iowa, 1881–1882; she then returned to Evansville as a teacher and office worker. In 1888 she married her second cousin, William L. Johnston, a widower with three children. After her husband died in 1892, she began to write children's stories and novels to support her family, her first work being *Big Brother* (1893). On a trip to Pewee Valley, near Louisville, in 1894, she became enamored with the community and the people; and when she met a little girl named Hattie Cochran, who was visiting her grandfather, an ex-Confederate colonel named George Weissinger, she was inspired to write a novel, *The Little Colonel* (1896); this was the first of the twelve volumes that make up the Little Colonel Series. In 1893 she moved to Pewee Valley and bought a home, "The Beeches," where she lived until her death. Although she wrote other novels, the Little Colonel stories made her one of the most popular writers of her time. She transformed Pewee Valley into the fictional Lloydsboro, Ky., and Hattie Cochran into Lloyd Sherman, the five-year-old girl whose adventures she tells as she grows up. In 1929, shortly before her death, she published *The Land of the Little Colonel,* which describes in words and photographs the real people and places of Pewee Valley.

Ann Jonas. A native of Missouri and a graduate of Goodman Theatre in Chicago, Ann Jonas is a longtime Kentuckian who lives in Louisville. Her poems have appeared in a variety of journals, including the *American Voice, Kentucky Poetry Review, Louisville Review, Southern Review,* and *Southern Humanities Review.* She is the recipient of the Cecil Hemley Memorial Award of the Poetry Society of America, The Henry Rago Memorial Award of the New York Poetry Forum, and the Poetry Prize of the Caddo National Writing Center. She has also received residency grants from Yaddo and the Kentucky Foundation for Women. Some of her poems have been published in *So Small This Arc* (2003).

Gayl Jones. Born in Lexington in 1949, Gayl Jones earned her B.A. in English at Connecticut College in 1971 and her graduate degrees in creative writing at Brown University. In 1975 she began teaching English and African American studies at the University of Michigan. In three years, from 1975 through 1977, she published three explosive and powerful books that earned her acclaim and controversy: *Corregidora* (1975), *Eva's Man* (1976), and *White Rat* (1977). In the 1970s she won many prestigious awards, including the Breadloaf Writers' Conference Award, the Shubert Grant for Playwriting, and a National Endowment for the Arts fellowship. Implicit in all her novels, short stories, and poems is the victimization of blacks by whites. One of the central leitmotifs of her fiction is how slavery, miscegenation, incest, and female exploitation have sullied black male-female relationships down to the present. *Song for Anninho* (1981) is an epic poem set in colonial Brazil. Her other books include *The Healing* (1998) and *Mosquito* (1999).

Kathy Kahn. Kathy Kahn (Skye Kathleen Moody) is a writer, community organizer, and country singer originally from Washington State. In the 1960s and 1970s she lived and worked in southern Appalachia, where she helped organize factory and mine workers and fought for improved health conditions and welfare rights for poor and working people. A play version of *Hillbilly Women* has been performed at Actors Studio in New York. She is also the author of *Fruits of Our Labor: U.S. and Soviet Workers Talk about Making a Living,* published by Putnam in 1982.

Leatha Kendrick. Leatha Kendrick is the author of two books of poetry: *Heart Cake* (2000), in which Molly Peacock has said she "mixes the ingredients of love and death and transforms them into the food of celebration," and *Science in Your Own Back Yard* (2003), a selection of her poems that were based on her experiences with breast cancer. She is a former editor of *Wind* magazine and coeditor (with George Ella Lyon) of *Crossing Troublesome: 25 Years of the Appalachian Writers Workshop* (2002). She also wrote the script for a documentary about the photographer Doris Ulmann entitled *A Lasting Thing for the World,* which aired on Kentucky Educational Television. Her poems and essays have appeared in the *Louisville Review, American Voice, Nimrod, Connecticut Review,* and other places. She has taught creative writing at the University of Kentucky, the Carnegie Center for Literacy and Learning, and the Appalachian Writers Workshop. She has received grants from the Kentucky Arts Council and the Kentucky Foundation for Women. She received her M.A. from Vermont College and now lives in eastern Kentucky.

Mae Street Kidd. Born 1904 in Millersburg, Ky.; died 1999 in Louisville. Mae Street Kidd was the daughter of a white father, Charles Robert Jones, and an African American mother, Anna Belle Leer. She attended the Lincoln Institute in Simpsonville; then at twenty-one she moved to Louisville to work for the black-owned Mammoth Life Insurance Company. During World War II she worked for the American Red Cross in England. From the mid-1960s to the mid-1980s she was a Democrat in the Kentucky General Assembly, where she worked on several landmark bills, including Kentucky's official ratification of the Thirteenth, Fourteenth and Fifteenth amendments to the U.S. Constitution. She is the subject of Wade Hall's 1997 oral biography, *Passing for Black: The Life and Careers of Mae Street Kidd.* Of her light skin color, which would have allowed her to "pass" for white, she said: "I never tried to be anything I wasn't. I have tried to fulfill my life in trying to be who I am, and that includes the color of my skin."

Barbara Kingsolver. Barbara Kingsolver, one of Kentucky's most distinguished contemporary authors, was born in Annapolis, Md., in 1955, but moved when she was two with her family to Carlisle, Ky., where she grew up. She holds degrees in biology and English from Depauw University and the University of Arizona. She became a celebrated author with the publication of her first novel, *The Bean Trees* (1988). So began a lifetime as a writer and activist for liberal causes. Other works include *Animal Dreams* (1990), *Another America* (1992, poems), *Pigs in Heaven* (1993), *High Tide in Tucson* (1995, essays), *Holding the Line: Women in the Great Arizona Mine Strike of 1983* (1996), *The Poisonwood Bible* (1998), *Prodigal Summer* (2000), and *Small Wonder* (2002). Kingsolver's novels, stories, poetry, and essays are on the cutting edge of contemporary literature.

J. Proctor Knott. Born Aug. 29, 1830, in Marion County, Ky.; died June 18, 1911, in Lebanon, Ky. Although J. Proctor Knott was a prominent politician in both Kentucky and Missouri, serving Kentucky as governor and congressman, he is now remembered almost solely for a comic speech he made in the U.S. House of Representatives in 1871 that mocked legislation providing federal aid for a railroad to be built to Duluth, in northern Minnesota. In addition to his government service, he practiced law and taught for several years at Centre College in Danville.

Abraham Lincoln. Born Feb. 12, 1809, near Hodgenville, Ky., to Thomas and Nancy Hanks Lincoln; died April 15, 1865, in Washington, D.C. Most Americans consider Abraham Lincoln our greatest president because he freed the slaves and made the Union indivisible. His story is the ultimate American Dream: from log cabin to White House. When Lincoln was seven, his family moved from Kentucky to southern Indiana, then to Illinois. He moved from New Salem to Springfield, Ill., in 1837 to study and practice law. He served as a Whig in the Illinois legislature and in 1846 was elected to the U.S. House of Representatives. In 1856 he joined the new Republican Party and lost his race for the U.S. Senate in 1858 to Stephen A. Douglas, but he was nominated by the Republicans for president in 1860 and won. He was well into his second term when he was assassinated at Ford's Theater in Washington by John Wilkes Booth. Ironically, Booth, a Southern partisan, killed the man who would have made easier the South's transition back into the Union, as Lincoln's "Second Inaugural Address" proposed. Lincoln's ties to his home state were strong throughout his life. After the death of his mother in Indiana, his father married Sarah Bush Johnston of Elizabethtown. Lincoln's wife, Mary Todd, whom he married in 1842, was from Lexington; and his principal law partner, William Herndon, was from Greensburg. His political mentor was Kentucky's Henry Clay. Not only was Lincoln a great statesman; he was also an eloquent writer, as his letters and speeches attest.

Edwin Carlile Litsey. Born June 3, 1874, at Beechland in Washington County, Ky.; died Feb. 3, 1970, in Lebanon, Ky. Although Edwin Carlile Litsey spent all his adult life as a banker in Lebanon, during his lifetime he was a popular poet and fiction writer. His heavy doses of sentimentality and preachiness, however, have made his works almost unread in the twenty-first century. In 1898, when he was twenty-four, he published his first book, a fantasy novel, *The Princess of Gramfalon.* Most of his subsequent books were set in his native south-central Kentucky. Some of his popular books include *The Race of the Swift* (1905), *The Man from Jericho* (1911), *Grist*

(1927), and *Stones for Bread* (1940), the story of two lonely brothers. In 1954 Litsey and Jesse Stuart were appointed joint poets laureate of Kentucky.

Sarah Litsey. Born June 23, 1901, in Springfield, Ky.; died ca. 1998 in Connecticut. Sarah Litsey, the daughter of Edwin Carlile Litsey, graduated from the Louisville Collegiate School in 1920 and studied at the Sargent School for Physical Education in Cambridge, Mass. She married Frank Nye, the son of the popular humorist Bill Nye, in 1933, and lived in Connecticut the remainder of her life. Her novels include *There Was a Lady* (1945), *The Intimate Illusion* (1956), and *A Path to the Water* (1962). She published poems and short stories in numerous magazines, including the *Saturday Evening Post, McCall's, Poetry, Cosmopolitan,* and *Kentucky Poetry Review.* Her first two novels and many of her poems were set in Kentucky. For many years she was an instructor at the Famous Writers School in Westport, Conn.

John Uri Lloyd. Born April 19, 1849, in West Bloomfield Township, N.Y.; died April 9, 1936, in Van Nuys, Calif. When John Uri Lloyd was four years old his family moved from New York State to Petersburg in Boone County, where his father became a surveyor and teacher. Lloyd was educated in private schools in Petersburg, Burlington, and Florence. At fourteen he became a pharmacist's apprentice and spent the rest of his life as a pharmacist and a scientist. He became a famous chemist and plant scientist as well as a renowned novelist. His best-known novel is *Stringtown on the Pike* (1900), which is set in Florence. His other novels include *Etidorpha, or The End of the Earth* (1893), *Warwick of the Knobs* (1901), *Red Head* (1903), and *Felix Moses: The Beloved Jew of Stringtown* (1930). Most of his fiction deals with the history and folk culture of northern Kentucky.

Cora Lucas. Born June 26, 1910, in Louisville; died 1985 in Louisville. Cora Lucas was the only child of Theodore Graf, a concert pianist, and Etelka Sever. From age seven she wrote poems and stories, which she published in local, regional, and national magazines. She received a B.A in German and an M.S. in social work from the University of Louisville. For thirteen years she was a family counselor and district supervisor at the Family Service Organization in Louisville. She was married to Dr. Marvin Lucas, a Louisville surgeon, for forty years. They were parents of two daughters. Some of her poems were collected in *This Rented House* (1982), from the Kentucky Poetry Press.

George Ella Lyon. Born in Harlan, Ky., in 1949, George Ella Lyon now lives in Lexington. For the past twenty-five years she has been an authentic and eloquent voice of the southern Appalachians. She received her undergraduate degree from Centre College, an M.A. from the University of Arkansas, and her Ph.D. from Indiana University. She has published books of poetry, short stories, and numerous books for children and young adults, including *Mountain* (1983); her poetry includes *Father Time and the Day Boxes* (1985), *A Regular Rolling Noah* (1986), *Dreamplace* (1999), and *Weaving the Rainbow* (2004). She has taught at the Community College of the University of Kentucky, Indiana University, Centre College, Radford University, and Transylvania University.

Maurice Manning. Maurice Manning is the third Kentuckian to win the Yale Younger Poets prize. Born in 1966 in Danville, Ky., he has earned degrees from Earlham College, the University of Kentucky, and the University of Alabama, where he received his M.F.A. in 1999. He now teaches in the Department of English at Indiana University. His two books of poetry are *Lawrence Booth's Book of Visions* (2001) and *A Companion for Owls* (2004).

Jane Martin. Jane Martin is the pseudonym of a Kentucky playwright who came to national prominence for *Talking With,* a collection of monologues that premiered in the Actors Theatre of Louisville's 1981 Humana Festival of New American Plays. Since its New York premiere at the Manhattan Theatre Club in 1982, *Talking With* has been performed around the world, winning the Best Foreign Play of the Year Award in Germany from *Theatre Heute* magazine. Other Actors Theatre of Louisville premieres of Jane Martin plays include the following: *Vital Signs* (1990 Humana Festival); *Cementville* (1991 Humana Festival); *Keely and Du* (1993 Humana Festival), which was nominated for the Pulitzer Prize in Drama and won the American

Theatre Critics Association Award for Best New Play; *Jack and Jill* (1996 Humana Festival), which won the American Theatre Critics Association Award for Best New Play; *Mr. Bundy* (1998 Humana Festival); *Anton in Show Business* (2000 Humana Festival), which won the American Theatre Critics Association Award for Best New Play; *Flaming Guns of the Purple Sage* (2001 Humana Festival); and *Good Boys,* which premiered at the Guthrie Theatre in 2002. Martin's most recent play, *Flags,* premiered at Mixed Blood Theatre Company in Oct. 2004.

William F. Marvin. Born 1804 in Leicestershire, Eng.; died July 12, 1879, in Danville, Ky. This latter-day Drunken Poet of Danville, William F. Marvin came to Danville as a young man, perhaps in time to know Thomas Johnson Jr., the first Drunken Poet of Danville. One hopes their paths crossed at a local pub in time for them to trade ribaldries. Marvin made his living as a shoemaker, and his nights he spent making verses while drinking and debauching. On one occasion he is said to have tried suicide using his shoe knife but was dissuaded. He was sober enough, however, to serve in the Mexican War, which generated his first and only volume of poems, *The Battle of Monterey and Other Poems* (1851). The title work is a lengthy metrical romance and almost unreadable, but his shorter verses are often lyrical and witty. He published later poems in the local paper, the *Kentucky Advocate,* which apparently remain uncollected.

Bobbie Ann Mason. One of Kentucky's best-known and most celebrated contemporary writers is Bobbie Ann Mason, who was born in Mayfield, in western Kentucky, on May 1, 1940, the daughter of Wilburn and Bernice Christie Lee Mason. She grew up on the family's fifty-four-acre dairy farm and attended the University of Kentucky, the State University of New York at Binghamton, and the University of Connecticut, where she received her Ph.D. in 1972. Her first books were nonfiction and somewhat scholarly. With the appearance of her first short story in *The New Yorker* in 1980, her fiction career took off, and she began publishing in such magazines as the *Paris Review, North American Review, Redbook, Atlantic, Mother Jones,* and *Harper's.* Many of these stories were collected in *Shiloh and Other Stories* (1982) and *Love Life* (1989). Her first novel, *In Country* (1985), was in 1988 made into a successful film, much of which was shot near Paducah. Her later fiction and nonfiction works have added luster to her reputation. Some of these are *Spence + Lila* (1988), *Feather Crowns* (1993), *Midnight Magic* (1998), *Clear Springs* (1999), and *Elvis Presley* (2002), an incisive biography of the singer.

Jane Mayhall. Born in Louisville in 1919, Jane Mayhall attended Black Mountain College in North Carolina and has taught at the New School for Social Research, Hofstra University, Morehead State University, and the Summer Writers' Workshop at Hindman Settlement School. Her fiction and poems have appeared in the *New Yorker, Paris Review, Yale Review,* and elsewhere. She has lived in New York City most of her life, but many of her poems recall incidents of her Kentucky childhood. During her long bohemian life in New York, she and her late husband, Leslie Katz, knew the friendship and company of such luminaries as Arthur Miller, James Agee, Walker Evans, Lincoln Kirstein, Ned Rorem, Conrad Aiken, May Swenson, Allan Gurganus, and Carl van Vechten. Of her recent collection of poems, *Sleeping Late on Judgment Day* (2004), a reviewer for the *Courier-Journal* said that through her poems "a mature poet invites us to share the intensity and passion of her life from youth to old age." He added, "It is a feast that you will enjoy if you savor her words slowly and responsibly—like food and drinks prepared carefully with exotic ingredients and surprising combinations."

Ed McClanahan. Ed McClanahan was born in 1932 in Brooksville, in Bracken County, Ky., and attended college at several institutions, including Washington and Lee in Virginia and Miami University in Ohio. He received an M.A. in English at the University of Kentucky in 1958 and began teaching at Oregon State University. A novella from which his first novel, *The Natural Man* (1983), evolved won him a Wallace Stegner Fellowship to Stanford University, where he studied, taught, and wrote for nine years. *The Natural Man* was a critical and popular success. *Harper's* called it "graceful and splendid"; Ken Kesey called it "joyous, unprecedented, heart-warming." Other critics compared his raunchy, comic growing-up saga of a bookish adolescent in Needmore, Ky., to J. D. Salinger's *Catcher in the Rye*. In addition to writing, McClanahan has taught at the University of Kentucky and in regional writing workshops; he has also written a number of magazine pieces, which he collected as *Famous People I Have Known* (1985). In 1996 he published *A Congress of Wonders,* a collection of three stories about the adventures of his con-man hero, Philander Cosmos Rexroat, set in the mid-1940s in his fictional Burdock County.

Davis McCombs. Born in Munfordville, Ky., in 1969, Davis McCombs has already won enough awards and honors to satisfy poets three times his age. He has studied at Harvard, the University of Virginia, and Stanford, where he was a Wallace Stegner Fellow, 1996–1998. In 1993 he won the $15,000 Ruth Lilly Poetry Prize at Indiana University. In 1999 he won the Yale Younger Poets award. His winning collection was published as *Ultima Thule* in 2000 by Yale University Press. The judge, W. S. Merwin, called his poems "quiet, understated, delicate as a hand exploring a tunnel in the dark"—appropriate imagery to describe a poet who has also served as a parking lot attendant and guide at Mammoth Cave National Park near his home. Indeed, the poems were inspired by McCombs's experiences in the cave and by the career of Stephen Bishop, a slave guide at the cave in the mid-nineteenth century.

Robert Emmett McDowell. Born April 5, 1914, in Sentinel, Okla.; died March 29, 1975, in Louisville. Although he was born in Oklahoma, Robert Emmett McDowell's roots were deep in Kentucky history, and he spent most of his adult life writing and editing historical articles and books, notably writing for the *Filson Club History Quarterly.* His historical novel, *Tidewater Sprig* (1961), concerns the Bullitt County salt springs. *City of Conflict* (1962) is a history of Louisville during the Civil War. *Home Is the Hunter* is a play, which premiered in 1963, that tells the story of the building of the first permanent settlement in Kentucky at Harrodsburg. In 1971 he published *Re-discovering Kentucky: A Guide for the Modern Day Explorer.* He also wrote Kentucky-based detective stories, including *Bloodline to Murder* (1960) and *Portrait of a Victim* (1964).

Boynton Merrill Jr. Boynton Merrill Jr. was born Oct. 21, 1925, in Boston, Mass., and was educated in the public schools of Newton, Mass., at Deerfield Academy, and at Dartmouth College, from which he received a B.A. in American literature in 1950. In 1952 he married Frances M. Royster in Henderson, Ky., where he still lives, writes, manages family property, and is active in civic organizations. On family farms he has grown products from fruit and nuts to timber. He served in the U.S. Navy from 1944 to 1946. He has published numerous articles, reviews, lectures, poems, and books on history and architecture, including the acclaimed *Jefferson's Nephews: A Frontier Tragedy* (1976), *A Bestiary* (1976, poems), *Old Henderson Homes and Buildings* (1985), *A Calling* (1997, poems), and *Sonnets for Gerontion* (2000).

Thomas Merton. Born Jan. 31, 1915, in Prades, France; died Dec. 10, 1968, in Bangkok, Thailand. Thomas Merton was a Trappist monk (known as Father Louis in the monastery), a theologian, and one of the most widely read spiritual writers of the twentieth century. He attended Clare College at Cambridge University and received a B.A. and an M.A. from Columbia University. Following his conversion to Catholicism in 1938, he taught English at Bonaventure University in Olean, N.Y., for a year and a half. On Dec. 10, 1941, he entered the Abbey of Our Lady of Gethsemani near Bardstown, Ky. Because of his literary background and his talents, he was encouraged by his superiors to write. In 1948 he published *The Seven Storey Mountain,* an autobiography, which chronicles his spiritual odyssey that led to the monastery. It was a sensational best-seller and has become a classic that still inspires its readers. Other important books by Merton include *The Sign of Jonas* (1953), *Conjectures of a Guilty Bystander* (1966), *Selected Poems* (1967), and *Faith and Violence* (1968). He was accidentally electrocuted while attending an ecumenical conference in Bangkok.

Jim Wayne Miller. Born Oct. 21, 1936, in Leicester, N.C.; died Aug. 18, 1996, in Bowling Green, Ky. A poet, novelist, and educator, Jim Wayne Miller received a B.A. in English literature from Berea College in 1958 and a Ph.D. in German and English literature from

Vanderbilt University. He served two years as a German instructor at Ft. Knox and became a professor of German at Western Kentucky University, where he also taught writing and folklore. His collections of poetry include *Copperhead Cane* (1964), *Dialogue with a Dead Man* (1974), and *The Mountains Have Come Closer* (1980), which won the Thomas Wolfe Award. *Newfound* (1989), his first novel, is set in Appalachia. His play, *His First, Best Country,* which he based on his novel of the same title, premiered at the Horse Cave Theater in 1992. He died of lung cancer at the age of fifty-nine.

Carolyn Lott Monohan. Born Christmas Eve 1922 in Covington, Ky.; died Oct. 1996 in Louisville. Carolyn Lott Monohan attended Louisville public schools and studied at the University of Louisville and Bellarmine College. She and James Lott, whom she married in 1943, were parents of Sharon, Bruce, and David. She was widowed in 1974, and in 1979 she married Thomas Monohan, who died in 1987. Her poems have appeared in numerous periodicals and books, including *Approaches, Christian Century, Green River Review, Handsel, Kentucky Book, Kentucky Poetry Review, Southern Poetry Review, Vanguard, Twigs, Wind,* and *Connecticut River Review.* She served as a deacon at Louisville's Douglass Boulevard Christian Church, for which she also wrote many hymns.

Maureen Morehead. Born March 28, 1951, in St. Louis, Maureen Morehead moved with her family to Kentucky in 1965, when her father took a position with the University of Kentucky School of Dentistry. She earned M.A. and Ph.D. degrees from the University of Louisville, with her thesis and dissertation directed by Sena Jeter Naslund. Her poems have appeared in numerous journals, including *Poetry, American Poetry Review, Black Warrior Review, Louisville Review, California Quarterly, Iowa Review, Kentucky Poetry Review,* and *Southern Poetry Review.* She has published three books: *In a Yellow Room* (1990), *Our Brothers' War: Civil War Stories* (1994, with Pat Carr), and *A Sense of Time Left* (2003). She lives in Louisville and teaches English in the Jefferson County public schools and in the brief-residency M.F.A. in Writing Program at Spalding University.

R. Meir Morton. Born in Louisville in 1930, R. Meir Morton has been active as a poet and musician for many years. She has taught at the Louisville Music Conservatory and at Bellarmine University and has been a poetry editor and columnist. She has long been active in the Kentucky State Poetry Society and has served as its president. She was designated poet laureate of the Kentucky Federation of Music Clubs in 2001 and has published nine books of poetry. "Interview with an Aging Idol" was a fourth place winner in the 1996 contest of the National Federation of State Poetry Societies and was published in *Kentucky Poems* (2002).

James H. Mulligan. Born Nov. 21, 1844, in Lexington, Ky.; died 1915 in Lexington. James H. Mulligan was a lawyer, judge, diplomat, Kentucky legislator, and comic poet; but he is remembered now solely for a poem he read at a Chamber of Commerce banquet at the Phoenix Hotel in Lexington. In February 1902, after finishing his humorous address in prose, he pulled from his pocket—as if it were an afterthought—a piece of paper and began to read what is now the best-known poem (if the term is used liberally) in the large library of Kentucky verse. It is a poem he named simply "In Kentucky." It begins, "The moonlight falls the softest / In Kentucky," and ends, "And politics—the damnedest / In Kentucky."

Alanna Nash. Born in Louisville in 1950, Alanna Nash is one of the foremost authorities on American country music and pop culture. She earned an M.A. from the Columbia University Graduate School of Journalism. Her books include *Dolly* (1978); *Behind Closed Doors: Talking with the Legends of Country Music* (1988); *Golden Girl: The Story of Jessica Savitch* (1988), which was the basis for the feature film *Up Close and Personal; Elvis Aaron Presley: Revelations from the Memphis Mafia* (1995); and *The Colonel: The Extraordinary Story of Colonel Tom Parker and Elvis Presley* (2003), winner of the 2004 Belmont Book Award, which is presented annually to the author of the best book about country music. The award was presented to Nash by the singer Brenda Lee, a member of the Country Music Hall of Fame. A feature writer for *Entertainment*

Weekly, USA Weekend, and the *New York Times,* Nash was named one of the "Heavy Hundred of County Music" by *Esquire.*

Sena Jeter Naslund. Sena Jeter Naslund was born in 1942 in Birmingham, Ala. She received her B.A. from Birmingham-Southern College and an M.A. and Ph.D. from the University of Iowa's Writers Workshop. She is a Distinguished Teaching Professor at the University of Louisville and the program director of Spalding University's brief-residency M.F.A. in Writing Program. In 2003 she was Vacca Professor, along with her husband, the physicist Dr. John C. Morrison, at the University of Montevallo in Alabama. Her fiction has appeared in the *Paris Review, Georgia Review, Iowa Review, Michigan Quarterly Review,* and elsewhere. She is the author of *Ice-Skating at the North Pole* (1989), *Sherlock in Love* (1993), *The Animal Way to Love* (1993), *The Disobedience of Water* (1999), *Ahab's Wife* (1999), and *Four Spirits* (2003). She is a recipient of the Harper Lee Award. All of Naslund's books have received critical acclaim; but with the publication of *Ahab's Wife* and *Four Spirits,* she has joined the league of major contemporary American writers. *Ahab's Wife* is an impressive amplification and a passionate fleshing out of Melville's bare mention of the wife that the captain of the *Pequod* left behind when he went on his mad quest for Moby Dick. *Four Spirits* is an epic rendering of the civil rights struggles of the 1960s that focuses on Birmingham and tragically climaxes with the racist bombing of the Sixteenth Street Baptist Church on Sept. 15, 1963. It is a towering achievement in American fiction that only a native of that strife-torn city could have written.

Patricia Neal. The celebrated actress Patricia Neal was born Jan. 20, 1926, in Packard, Whitley County, Ky. She studied drama at Northwestern University, then worked as a model before her Broadway debut in *The Voice of the Turtle* in 1946. Her first film, *John Loves Mary,* was released in 1949. Her brilliant performance in *A Face in the Crowd* in 1957 placed her in the front row of film actors, and her stellar work in *Hud* in 1963 won her the Academy Award for Best Actress. She suffered a series of severe strokes in 1965 but miraculously recovered to play a lead in the 1968 production of *The Subject Was Roses,* which earned her another Oscar nomination. In 1953 she married the British author Roald Dahl, from whom she was divorced in 1983. She is the mother of five children. Her autobiography, *As I Am,* was published in 1988.

John Jacob Niles. Born April 28, 1892, in Louisville; died March 1, 1980, at Boot Hill Farm, near Lexington. As a folk-song collector, composer, and performer, John Jacob Niles is one of the brightest stars in the American musical sky. His singing voice was as authentic and unique as it was arresting. He electrified audiences with his high tenor and sometimes falsetto-sounding performances in person and on recordings. His entire family in Louisville was musically talented in various ways. With relatives who had earned recognition as composer, organist, pianist, cello manufacturer, folksinger, and square-dance caller, Niles could hardly have avoided a vocation in music. After Henry Watterson, the editor of the *Courier-Journal,* encouraged him to study music, he became a student at the Université de Lyon and, later, the Schola Cantorum in Paris and the Cincinnati Conservatory of Music. During World War I he was a pilot in France. In 1921 he worked as a master of ceremonies in a nightclub. He began to give public singing performances and helped popularize folk music throughout the century, giving his last concert at Swannanoa, N.C., in 1978. Before World War I and during the late 1920s and early 1930s, he collected and recorded folk songs in eastern Kentucky and the southern Appalachians. During his lifetime he arranged or composed more than one thousand folk songs, Christmas carols, and war songs. His best-known songs included "I Wonder as I Wander," "Black Is the Color of My True Love's Hair," "Jesus, Jesus, Rest Your Head," and "The Hangman." At fifteen he composed "Go 'Way from My Window." Many of his songs were included in the *Ballad Book of John Jacob Niles* in 1961. Niles earned a lofty place among the top American composers and performers.

Cotton Noe. Born May 2, 1864, in Thompsonville (now Fenwick), Washington County, Ky.; died Nov. 9, 1953, in Beverly Hills, Calif. The poet and educator Cotton Noe attended the local schools in Springfield and Perryville, then went away to Franklin College in Indiana, Cornell

University, and the University of Chicago. After practicing law in Springfield for four years, he began his teaching career, becoming a member of the faculty at Cumberland College and Lincoln Memorial University. He taught at the University of Kentucky from 1908 until his retirement in 1934. In 1926 he was made Kentucky's first poet laureate by the General Assembly. His poetry was published in several volumes, including *Tip Sams of Kentucky* (1926) and *The Valley of Parnassus* (1953). He moved to southern California for his health in 1934 and lived there until his death in 1953.

Gurney Norman. Gurney Norman was born in 1937 in Grundy, Va., but he grew up near Hazard and attended the Stuart Robinson Boarding School in Letcher County for most of his elementary and high school education. He earned a degree in journalism at the University of Kentucky, where he wrote short stories for *Stylus,* the campus literary magazine. He attended Stanford University on a Wallace Stegner Fellowship, then spent two years in the U.S. Army. In the mid-1960s he edited the *Hazard Herald* and began writing short stories that would eventually be published as *Kinfolks* in 1977. By 1968 he was back in California working on the *Whole Earth Catalog,* for which he wrote his first and most famous novel, *Divine Right's Trip,* which was published in its final issue. The novel was later reprinted in book form by Gnomon Press in 1990. In recent years he has taught writing at the University of Kentucky and helped produce documentary films for Kentucky Educational Television. One of the major influences on Norman's fiction has been the high example and skilled craftsmanship of the late Appalachian author James Still.

Marsha Norman. Marsha Williams Norman was born in Louisville on Sept. 21, 1947, the daughter of Billie and Bertha Williams. After graduating from Durrett High School, she earned a B.A. at Agnes Scott College in Georgia in 1969 and an M.A. in theater at the University of Louisville in 1971. She held several jobs in Louisville before she turned to full-time playwriting in 1976, including work with mentally disturbed children at Central State Hospital, teaching in the Jefferson County public schools, and serving as project director for the Kentucky Arts Commission. Her close association with Actors Theatre of Louisville began with her first play, *Getting Out,* in 1977, which portrays the struggle of a woman to go straight after being released from prison. Her 1982 play about a daughter's suicide, *'Night, Mother,* won the Pulitzer Prize for drama. It was made into a film in 1986. She has also written television plays and a novel, *The Fortune Teller* (1987).

Mary O'Dell. Mary E. O'Dell, a poet and short story writer, was born in Beckley, W.V., on Sept. 8, 1935, and moved to eastern Kentucky when she was fifteen. She now lives in Louisville. She received a B.A. from Transylvania University and an M.A. and Rank I in elementary education from Western Kentucky University. She taught remedial reading in elementary school until 1987, when she took early retirement to devote more time to her writing and to fostering other writers. In 1984 she founded Green River Writers, which is dedicated to discovering, promoting, and supporting writers in all genres through readings, retreats, seminars, and workshops. Her recent poetry collections include *Poems for the Man Who Weighs Light* (1999), *Living in the Body* (2002), and *The Dangerous Man* (2003). Her poetry and prose have appeared recently in *Place Gives Rise to Spirit: Writers on Louisville* (2000), *Tobacco: A Literary Anthology* (2004), *The Encyclopedia of Louisville* (2001), *Glimmertrain,* and *American Voice.*

Chris Offutt. Chris Offutt grew up in Haldeman, Ky., in rural Rowan County, a former mining community of some two hundred people. He attended Morehead State University and received an M.F.A. from the writing program of the University of Iowa in 1990. His memoir, *The Same River Twice* (1993), focuses on his relationship with his wife, Rita Lily, and her support for his writing. His story collection, *Kentucky Straight* (1993), portrays rustic Kentuckians with honesty and sympathy. In 1994 he moved from Iowa to Montana; then in the fall of 1998 he returned to Kentucky to teach at Morehead State. His disappointments with his homeland are chronicled in *No Heroes* (2002), which earned him disdain from some of the home folks. His other books include a novel, *The Good Brother* (1997), and *Out of the Woods* (1999), a collection of stories. He won the 1994 Jean Stein Award for Fiction.

Theodore O'Hara. Born Feb. 11, 1820, in Danville, Ky.; died June 6, 1867, in Guerrytown, Ala. Theodore O'Hara was a journalist, lawyer, soldier, and a sometime poet who is remembered for one poem, "The Bivouac of the Dead," whose lines are often inscribed on the tombstones of soldiers and on bronze tablets in military cemeteries, particularly the second quatrain of the second stanza: "On Fame's eternal camping ground / Their silent tents are spread, / and Glory guards with solemn round / the bivouac of the dead." O'Hara graduated from St. Joseph College in Bardstown in 1839, studied law, and was admitted to the bar in 1842. In June 1846 he joined the Kentucky volunteers in the Mexican War and was discharged in 1848 with the rank of major. In 1847 he wrote his famous poem for the interment in the Frankfort Cemetery of Kentuckians killed in the Battle of Buena Vista. Before the Civil War he worked as a reporter for the Frankfort *Yeoman* and the *Louisville Daily Times;* after the war he edited the *Mobile Register.* During the war he fought with the Alabama 12th Infantry, on the Confederate side. He spent the last several years of his life in Columbus, Ga., and Guerrytown, Ala.

John Patrick. Born 1905 in Louisville; died 1995 in Delray Beach, Fla. John Patrick Goggan—he later dropped his last name—was abandoned by his parents and raised by foster parents. He attended Our Lady of Holy Cross College in New Orleans and began his career as a scriptwriter for NBC Radio in San Francisco from 1933 to 1936. His first produced play was *Hell Freezes Over,* a flop directed by Josh Logan on Broadway in 1935. His other plays include *Curious Savage* (1950) and *The Hasty Heart* (1945), which was based on his experiences in an ambulance unit in World War II. In 1949 it was made into a movie with Ronald Reagan. The apex of his career was reached in 1953, when *The Teahouse of the August Moon* won the Pulitzer Prize for Drama. Brooks Atkinson praised the play in the *New York Times* as "not only amusing but enchanting, and perhaps illuminating as well." He also worked on more than two dozen screenplays from the 1930s through the 1960s, including *Three Coins in the Fountain* (1954), *Love Is a Many-Splendored Thing* (1955), and his own *Teahouse of the August Moon* (1956), which starred Marlon Brando. At ninety he committed suicide at an adult-care center.

Lee Pennington. Lee Pennington was born May 1, 1939, at White Oak, Greenup County, in northeastern Kentucky. He attended elementary and high school in Greenup County and received degrees from Berea College and the University of Iowa. He also attended the University of Kentucky and San Diego State and has received honorary degrees from World University at Danzig, N.Y., and the Academy of Southern Arts and Letters. He has held a variety of jobs and positions, ranging from farmer, sports editor, and encyclopedia salesman to professor at Southeast Community College in Cumberland, Morehead State University, Jefferson Community College, and Eastern Kentucky University. He has won numerous awards and honors and was named poet laureate of Kentucky in 1984. His poems and short stories have appeared in dozens of magazines, including *American Bard, Southern Poetry Review, Kansas Quarterly, Mountain Life and Work, Bluegrass Woman,* and *Appalachian Review.* He has published many books of poetry, drama, photography, and criticism, including *Scenes from a Southern Road* (1969), *Appalachia, My Sorrow* (1971), *I Knew a Woman* (1980), and *Thigmotropism* (1993). He has also produced many video documentaries, and his own plays have been performed at the University of Kentucky, Jefferson Community College, Poets Theatre in New York, and elsewhere.

Thomas Perkins. Born in Bridgewater, Mass., in 1756; died in Danville, Ky., fall 1786. Thomas Perkins is the presumed author of a letter written in Danville on March 1, 1785, to a friend in his native Massachusetts that describes his recent wilderness trip through the Cumberland Gap. Generally unknown to historians of the early West, his "Letter from Kentucky," as the editor of the *Boston Magazine* titled it in the Sept. 1785 issue, contains a valuable eyewitness account of the dangers and privations of the Cumberland Gap route from Virginia to Kentucky. Perkins graduated from Harvard in 1779, tutored the children of John and Abigail Adams for about a year, moved to Virginia in 1782 to conduct a private school, and finally came to Kentucky, where he settled and practiced law briefly until his death in late 1786.

Cordia Greer Petrie. Born Feb. 12, 1872, near Merry Oaks in Barren County, Ky.; died 1964 in Louisville. In 1922 Cordia Greer Petrie shared the backwoods persona that she had been portraying around Kentucky for years, Angeline Keaton, with the world when she published a small book called *Angeline at the Seelbach,* in which the title character recalls her family's experiences when they make their first trip from Bear Holler in Barren County to Louisville and stay at the city's most luxurious hotel, the Seelbach. It immediately became popular locally and nationally and went through more than thirteen printings. The humor was in the character, her rural Kentucky "hillbilly" dialect, and her hilarious adventures when she stepped outside Bear Holler. Her second adventure came in 1923, with *Angeline Doin' Society,* and was followed by seven more adventures. In 1925 Angeline went to the Derby. Petrie based her comic dialect on speech she had heard in Barren County and in the mountain counties where she lived with her physician husband in the first decades of the century. To enhance the character, Petrie overdressed herself in tacky, unfashionable, homemade clothes and performed Angeline's adventures before live audiences all around Kentucky and beyond. Unlike her stage character, she was an educated society woman who graduated from Eminence College and whose husband had graduated from the University of Louisville Medical School. They had moved to Louisville in 1920. She was the original who preceded other rustic monologists, including such later Grand Ole Opry radio stars as the Duke of Paducah and Minnie Pearl.

Joseph Phelps. Born Dec. 21, 1954, in Erie, Pa., Joseph Phelps has been pastor of Highland Baptist Church in Louisville since 1997. For some eighteen years he led several churches in Texas and was founding pastor of the Church of the Savior in Austin, where he was also the founding president of Capital Area Foodbank. He received an M.Div. from Southern Baptist Theological Seminary in Louisville and a D.Min. from Austin Presbyterian Theological Seminary. He is the author of *More Light, Less Heat: How Dialogue Can Transform Christian Conflict into Growth.*

Virginia Pile. Virginia Pile was born and raised in a log house her great-grandfather built in Breckinridge County, the setting for much of her writing. She published poetry and short fiction in many literary journals. Her play, *Hunting Moon,* a story of the founding of Hardinsburg and Breckinridge County, is presented annually. She attended the University of Kentucky and traveled abroad in pursuit of subjects for her poems, sketches, and watercolors.

Joe Ashby Porter. Joe Ashby Porter was born in Madisonville, Ky., in 1942. He has studied at Harvard, Oxford (on a Fulbright), and the University of California at Berkeley, where he earned his Ph.D. in 1972. He has taught at the University of Virginia, the University of Baltimore, Towson State, Shoreline Community College, Murray State University, and since 1980 at Duke University. He has published short fiction in such periodicals and anthologies as the *Harvard Advocate, Best American Short Stories '73, Antaeus, Iowa Review, Wind, Ploughshares, Contemporary American Fiction,* and the *Minnesota Review.* His books include *Eelgrass* (1977), *The Drama of Speech Acts: Shakespeare's Lancastrian Tetralogy* (1979), *The Kentucky Stories* (1983), *Lithuania* (1990), *Resident Aliens* (2000), and *Touch Wood* (2002). He told the *Courier-Journal*'s book editor, Sallie Bingham, in 1983 that, for him, Kentucky is "a state of mind" and that he writes about his home state because its history and geography are "complicated" and its heritage is "mixed and rich." Among his many awards are a National Merit scholarship, an NEA Fellowship Grant, an NEA/PEN Syndicated Fiction Award, and a 2004 Academy Award in Literature from the American Academy of Arts and Letters.

Georgia Davis Powers. Georgia Davis Powers was born in Springfield to Ben Gore and Frances Walker Montgomery on Oct. 29, 1923, and, after a tornado destroyed their two-room cabin, grew up in Louisville as the only girl in a family of eight brothers. Her father enameled bathtubs for the American Standard Company for over forty years. She attended Virginia Avenue Elementary School, Madison Junior High School, Central High School, and Louisville Municipal College. Before finding her vocation in politics, she held many jobs, from riveting during

World War II to supervising at the U.S. Census Bureau. In 1962 she became active in politics as a campaign worker for candidates at local, state, and national levels. By 1964 she was active in the civil rights movement and organized the Allied Organization for Civil Rights, which supported a public accommodations bill in the Kentucky General Assembly. She was one of the organizers of the March on Frankfort, which drew more than ten thousand participants. In 1967 she was elected to the Kentucky State Senate, where she was known as "the conscience of the Senate" and served for twenty-one years. While in the Senate she was a major force behind the passage of laws on open and low-cost housing and GED validation, as well as the resolution that gave Kentucky's approval, at long last, to the Equal Rights Amendment to the U.S. Constitution. In 1995 she published *I Shared the Dream,* a memoir of her work with Dr. Martin Luther King and other local and national civil rights leaders. In 2004 she published *Celia's Land,* a historical novel based on the real-life struggle of her great-aunt Celia Mudd Crawford, an ex-slave who inherited an estate from a white man in Nelson County and then had to fight in court for five years to retain her inheritance.

Paul Quenon. Paul Quenon is a Trappist monk who lives in the Abbey of Gethsemani, near Bardstown. He entered this Roman Catholic religious order when he was a teenager. His novitiate was spent studying under the renowned poet and philosopher Thomas Merton, who was known as Father Louis in the monastery. Brother Paul is a poet, photographer, and editor of *Holy Folly: Short and Tall Tales from the Abbey of Gethsemani* (1998), to which he contributes a selection from his seriocomic diary about life within the monastery. The publisher, Black Moss Press, describes this book in these carefully selected and accurate words about the monks and their vocation: "*Holy Folly* is their take on life behind the walls of this place. A portrait of the richly pious life of monks faithfully following the monastic rule, but not without a little fun along that terribly rigid road to Heaven." Brother Paul Quenon is also the author of *Terrors of Paradise* (1995), a poetic take on his life in the monastic community.

Patricia Ramsey. Patricia Stamper Ramsey was born in 1933 in Barbourville, in the Kentucky mountains. She has taught in the public schools of Jefferson County, served as a counselor at Indiana University Southeast, and been a poetry therapist at the Southern Indiana Mental Health and Guidance Center in Jeffersonville. *A Killin',* her play about a Kentucky coal mining family, won Best Play in Community Theatre for 2005, given by the Kentucky Community Theatre Association. She has also won best play contests sponsored by the Old Louisville One Act Play Festival and the Kentucky Playwrights Festival. Her play *The Farm* was chosen in 2005 by the Louisville Repertory Theatre to be produced in its New Play Festival. In 2005 she was awarded a playwriting grant from the Kentucky Arts Council.

Betty Layman Receveur. Born Oct. 25, 1930, in Louisville; died Dec. 22, 2003, in Salem, Ind. Betty Layman Receveur was the daughter of Russell and Georgia Heyser Layman and was reared by her paternal grandparents, Frank Fuller and Addie Shelton Layman. She attended Louisville public and parochial schools and credited the Dominican nuns for instilling in her respect for the English language and a love of literature. In 1945, at the age of fourteen, she married Donald Receveur, with whom she had three sons. Although she completed only one semester of high school, she grew up with a passion to read and to write that stayed with her all her life. She kept her writing flame alive as a faithful member of the Louisville Writers Club for almost forty years. As she told the *Courier-Journal* in 1979, "My great fear as a child was that I would read all the books in the world and there would be nothing left to read." With neither high school diploma nor college degree, she wrote and published numerous poems and five superb novels, three of them historical romances—*Sable Flanagan* (1979), *Molly Gallagher* (1982), and *Carrie Kingston* (1984)—and two of them novels of historical fiction about the settling of Kentucky, of which she was proudest—*Oh, Kentucky!* (1990) and *Kentucky Home* (1995). Her fierce pride in being "a seventh-generation Kentuckian," as she often bragged, is reflected in the meticulous research that buttressed her Kentucky novels and the extreme care and pain she took in making sure that her characters would come alive on the page for present and future readers. That she succeeded is the legacy she wanted.

Alice Hegan Rice. Born Jan. 11, 1870, in Shelbyville, Ky.; died Feb. 10, 1942, in Louisville. Alice Hegan Rice wrote some twenty books, but her stellar success was *Mrs. Wiggs of the Cabbage Patch* (1901). The novel featured the popular combination of humor and pathos embodied in poor but optimistic Mrs. Wiggs and her fatherless family, fictional residents of Louisville's Cabbage Patch community south of Oak Street and west of Sixth Street. Based on Mary Bass, a real resident of the neighborhood, Mrs. Rice's novel exploited the new reform movements aimed at improving the quality of life in poor urban areas. Mrs. Wiggs is a struggling widow with five children; but in her sordid world the sun is always shining behind the clouds. The novel spawned a stage play and four film versions, the best of which was the 1934 production with W. C. Fields and Zasu Pitts. Her other books include *Lovey Mary* (1903) and *Mr. Opp* (1909), the sequels to *Mrs. Wiggs*; *Mr. Pete & Co.* (1933), a tale of the Louisville waterfront; *My Pillow Book* (1937), a book of devotions; and *The Inky Way* (1940), her autobiography. In 1902 she married Cale Young Rice, a poet and playwright who was somewhat less successful commercially than his wife. She received an honorary D.Litt. from the University of Louisville in 1937.

Cale Young Rice. Born Dec. 7, 1872, in Dixon, Ky.; died Jan. 24, 1943, in Louisville. Cale Young Rice had a much better formal education than his wife, Alice Hegan, whom he married on Dec. 18, 1902; but she was the better writer, critically and commercially. Rice received degrees from Cumberland University in Tennessee and Harvard, where he studied under the renowned philosophers William James and George Santayana. He taught English at his alma mater in Tennessee for one year, then moved to Louisville, where he met Alice Hegan. His first book, *From Dusk to Dusk* (1898), was followed by almost forty volumes of poetry, fiction, and verse dramas. Although the *New York Times* called him a poet without inspiration in 1921, his books were usually favorably reviewed, especially in England, but their sales were modest. He and his wife were active in Louisville's social, intellectual, and artistic life; he served as the first president of The Arts Club and as a member of the board of the J. B. Speed Art Museum. He was also a member of the Poetry Society of America. After his wife died in early 1942, he sold their spacious home in St. James Court in Louisville and moved into a nearby apartment, still writing but despondent over her death. On the night of Jan. 23–24, 1943, he shot himself and died.

Clara Rising. A native of Mississippi, Clara Rising has traveled extensively with her army husband, now retired; but one of her favorite places is Kentucky, where she has lived and raised and ridden horses for many years. She has an M.A. in creative writing from the University of Louisville and a Ph.D. from the University of Florida. In her first novel, *In the Season of the Wild Rose* (1986), she brings the Civil War alive through the swashbuckling career of John Hunt Morgan and his Raiders. Her later books also unwrap the past in dramatic and exciting ways, from the age of Pericles in *The Birth and Death of Athenian Democracy* (2004) to *The Taylor File: The Mysterious Death of a President* (2004), which chronicles the forensic investigation that led to the 1991 exhumation in Louisville of the twelfth president of the United States, Zachary Taylor.

Elizabeth Madox Roberts. Born in 1881 in Perryville, Ky., near the Civil War battlefield; died spring 1941 in Orlando, Fla. Elizabeth Madox Roberts may not be the greatest author that Kentucky has produced, but she surely has written some of the greatest fiction ever written by a Kentuckian. Her scope, for example, is not as broad as Robert Penn Warren's, and neither is her depth. But two of her novels deserve to be placed close to his on the Kentucky shelf: *The Time of Man* (1926), the brave, heartbreaking odyssey of a poor tenant family and their daughter; and *The Great Meadow* (1930), which is easily the greatest novel ever written about the Kentucky frontier years from 1774 to 1781. When she was about three, her family moved to Springfield, which she considered her home for the rest of her life. Afflicted with tuberculosis and other breathing ailments, she was plagued by ill health throughout her life. After she completed high school in Covington in 1900, she enrolled at the University of Kentucky; but she soon had to return home to Springfield, where she taught in local public and private schools until 1910, when she again had to withdraw and go to live with her sister in Colorado, where the climate was allegedly salutary for tubercular patients. There she wrote verses that were published in 1915 as *In the Great Steep's Garden.* In January 1917 she enrolled at the University of Chicago, where she became friends with such talented young writers as Glenway Wescott, Yvor Winters, and Monroe Wheeler, and where she met such midwestern luminaries as Edgar Lee Masters, Vachel Lindsay, and Carl Sandburg. During her Chicago period, she published poetry in such national magazines as the *Atlantic Monthly* and *Poetry,* whose editor, Harriet Monroe, became her friend. In 1921 she returned to Springfield and began writing the poems, stories, and novels that would secure her exalted place in Kentucky letters. A list of her books is impressive: *Under the Tree* (1922, poetry), *The Time of Man* (1926), *My Heart and My Flesh* (1927), *The Great Meadow* (1930), *A Buried Treasure* (1931), *The Haunted Mirror* (1932, stories), *He Sent Forth a Raven* (1935), *Black Is My True Love's Hair* (1938), *Song in the Meadow* (1940, poetry), and *Not by Strange Gods* (1941, stories). In little more than twenty years, counting her sojourn in Chicago, she wrote a lifetime of books. Moreover, the recognition and awards she received were generous. *The Time of Man* was a Book-of-the-Month-Club selection, and *The Great Meadow* was a selection of the Literary Guild at a time when the book clubs served millions of readers. In 1928 she won the John Reed Memorial Prize from *Poetry* magazine, and in 1931 a prize from the Poetry Society of South Carolina. In 1932 her short story "The Sacrifice of the Maidens" won the O. Henry second prize. In 1981, on the occasion of the one hundredth anniversary of her birth, a national conference was held in her honor at St. Catharine College near Springfield, and the *Kentucky Poetry Review* published a special issue devoted to her unpublished poems, *I Touched White Clover.* Her stories, novels, and poems still merit careful reading—even in the twenty-first century.

Christian Schultz. Although little is known about Christian Schultz, his *Travels on an Inland Voyage through the States of New-York, Pennsylvania, Virginia, Ohio, Kentucky and Tennessee, and through the Territories of Indiana, Louisiana, Mississippi and New-Orleans, Performed in the Years 1807 and 1808; Including a Tour of Nearly Six Thousand Miles, with Maps and Plates* (1810) suggests that he was a native of New York and a well-educated, talented writer and adventurer whose curiosity and skills resulted in one of the most detailed and colorful early travel narratives about the western and southern frontiers. Like a lot of young men from the coastal states, he was probably lured by the sheer adventure of the frontier, as well as the prospects for exploiting its wealth in land and natural resources.

Ron Seitz. Born Sept. 19, 1935, in Louisville, Ron Seitz attended a variety of schools, from Occidental College in Los Angeles to the Army Security Agency Institute, before earning his B.A. in psychology from Bellarmine College and his M.A. in creative writing from the University of Louisville. At various times he has taught at Las Sendas Cultural Studies Center in Arizona, Red Mountain Academy in Phoenix, St. Catharine College in Kentucky, St. Meinrad Archabbey Graduate School in Indiana, the University of Louisville, and, from 1962 to 1988, as a professor of English at Bellarmine. In addition to broadsides and publications in numerous anthologies and periodicals, his books include *The Gethsemani Poems* (1985), *Cables across the Ohio* (1990), *Poet Pray: A Song of New Harmony* (1991), *Song for Nobody: A Memory Vision of Thomas Merton* (1993), and *Bad Meat: For James Laughlin* (1997). His poems have appeared in numerous journals, including *America, Commonweal, Evergreen Review, Harper's, Monks Pond, Kentucky Poetry Review,* and *Wind.* His grants and awards include those from the Robert Lee Blaffer Trust Foundation for the Arts, the George W. Norton Foundation for the Arts, the Blackhawk Colorado Artists Workshop; and the Abbey of Gethsemani Fund for the Arts.

Charles Semones. Born in the community of Deep Creek in western Mercer County, Ky., on Aug. 25, 1937, Charles Semones attended the county public schools and Campbellsville College and Eastern Kentucky State Teachers College. His teaching career as an instructor in the language arts was spent in the middle schools of Nelson and Mercer Counties. He spent two years in the U.S. Army. He has published poems in many publications, including the *American Voice, Approaches, Kentucky Poetry Review, Arts across Kentucky, Chattahoochee Review, Kansas Quarterly,* the *Mennonite, Wind,* and *South Carolina Review.* He has published three books of poetry: *Witch Cry* (1973), *Homeplace* (1993), and *Afternoon in the Country of Summer: New and Selected Poems* (2003), which was chosen as the winner of the Kentucky Literary Award for Excellence in Poetry for 2003. His collection of personal essays is *A Storm of Honey: Notes from the Sabbath Country* (2004).

Vivian Shipley. Born in Chicago but raised in Kentucky, Vivian Shipley's family have been farmers—she describes them lovingly as "hillbillies"—for several generations. In her poetry and elsewhere she speaks fondly of growing up in the Kentucky mountains. She received her B.A. and her M.A. from the University of Kentucky in 1964 and 1967 and her Ph.D. from Vanderbilt University in 1975. Since 1969 she has taught at Southern Connecticut University, which has named her a Distinguished Professor. In addition to her teaching and writing, she is also editor of the *Connecticut Review,* a journal of poetry, prose, and art. Her poems have appeared in many periodicals, including the *Vanderbilt Review, American Scholar, Iowa Review, Nebraska Review, Prairie Schooner,* and *Comstock Review.* Her poetry has been collected under the following titles: *Jack Tales* (1982), *Poems Out of Harlan County* (1989), *Devil's Lane* (1996), *How Many Stones?* (1998), *Crazy Quilt* (1999), *Fair Haven* (2000), and *When There Is No Shore* (2002). Her awards include the Sara Henderson Hay Prize for Poetry from the *Pittsburgh Quarterly,* So to Speak Poetry Prize from George Mason University, the Readers' Choice Award from *Prairie Schooner,* and the Ann Stanford Poetry Prize.

Aleda Shirley. Born into a military family (her father was in the U.S. Air Force) on May 2, 1955, in Sumter, S.C., Aleda Shirley grew up all over the South and in the Philippines; her father's people, however, have lived in Kentucky since the late eighteenth century. She graduated from the University of Louisville in 1975. Her first collection of poetry, *Chinese Architecture* (1986), won the Poetry Society of America's First Book Award. Her second book, *Long Distance,* appeared in 1996. Her poems have been published in *Poetry, American Poetry Review, Virginia Quarterly Review, Georgia Review, Shenandoah, Poetry Northwest,* and other periodicals. She has won awards and fellowships from the National Endowment for the Arts, the Kentucky Arts Council, the Kentucky Foundation for Women, and the Mississippi Arts Commission. She has also been project director for *All Write!,* a program of the Mississippi Arts Commission that promotes literacy and creative writing in state prisons. She is now writer-in-residence at Millsaps College in Jackson, Miss.

Jeffrey Skinner. Jeffrey Skinner, professor of creative writing at the University of Louisville, has published a number of poetry collections, including *Late Stars* (1985); *A Guide to Forgetting* (1988), which was a National Poetry Series selection; *The Company of Heaven* (1992); *Gender Studies* (1999); and *Salt Water Amnesia* (2005). His poems have appeared in such periodicals as the *Atlantic Monthly, New Yorker, Nation,* and *Georgia Review.* He is also a playwright. Three of his plays have been finalists in the Eugene O'Neill Theater Conference competition, and his one-act *Delta Waves* won the 1991 Market Theater short play competition. His full-length play *Fortunate Son* was given a staged reading at the O'Neill Center as part of the 2002 Local Playwrights Festival. He has received grants from the National Endowment for the Arts, the Howard Foundation, the Ingram Merrill Foundation, and the Kentucky Arts Council. He has been awarded residencies at Yaddo, McDowell, and the Fine Arts Work Center in Provincetown, Mass. In 1997 he was the Frost House poet-in-residence, and in 1998 he served as the American writer-in-residence at the annual Arts Festival in County Kildare, Ireland. In 2002 he served as poet-in-residence at the James Merrill House in Stonington, Conn. Over the years Skinner has made his living in a variety of ways, including working as a social psychologist, actor, waterfront director, factory stock man, and private detective. He is married to the poet and publisher Sarah Gorham, with whom he founded Sarabande Books and edited *Last Call: Poems on Alcoholism, Addiction, and Deliverance* (1997). He is the father of two daughters.

Leonard A. Slade Jr. Leonard Slade was born in 1942 on a peanut, cotton, and corn farm near Conway, N.C. The oldest of nine children, he attended a traditionally black college, Elizabeth City State University in North Carolina, and received his Ph.D. in English at the University of Illinois. He is currently a professor of Africana studies, adjunct professor of English, and past chair of the Department of African Studies at the State University of New York at Albany. He has published some ten books of poems and professional writing, and his work has appeared in numerous reviews and journals. From 1965 to 1988 he was a professor of English and an administrator at Kentucky State University in Frankfort.

Verna Mae Slone. Verna Mae Slone was born in 1914 in Knott County, where she has lived all her life. She is an author, a craftswoman, a collector of mountain culture, and the mother of five sons. She has written several books about mountain life and culture, much of it autobiographical, including *Common Folks* (1978), *What My Heart Wants to Tell* (1979), *Sarah Ellen* (1982), and *Rennie's Way* (1994), a revised and expanded version of *Sarah Ellen.* She once said that she didn't start writing until she was past sixty, and that she started writing "to show the other side of mountain life." Indeed, she has presented a positive image of her people and their culture, without softening their hardships. As a mountain culture preservationist Slone is without equal. While not suggesting that mountain people of today should try to live like their ancestors, she tells them to be proud of them and their folkways and skills, and to keep their spirit alive and use what is useful. In *Rennie's Way,* for example, she presents folklore not as static museum exhibits but as vital parts of mountain life of the past. The spirit of community, if not the form, is something young people can practice, even in the twenty-first century.

Harry Smith. According to *Fifty Years of Slavery in the United States,* Harry Smith was born a slave in Nelson County, Ky., in 1815. This slave narrative, which was published in 1891, over a quarter century after President Lincoln's Emancipation Proclamation, is related in the third person, with Smith telling his own story as if he were someone else. Smith probably related his life story to another person, who wrote it as if it were a biography and not an autobiography, hence the use of the third person. The authorship attribution to "Harry Smith," therefore, is awkward and incorrect. Nevertheless, even though the origin of this narrative is murky and it came too late to benefit the antebellum abolition movement, it is still one of the most detailed and dramatic stories of slave life extant. There are funny stories and incidents of violence. There are poor whites and rich whites, "good" masters and "bad" masters. Indeed, Smith does not run away and remains a slave until the end of the war. Lincoln's proclamation did not affect slaves in states like Kentucky, which, though divided, were not officially in rebellion against the Union. Smith would not have been freed until the Thirteenth Amendment officially took effect on Dec. 18, 1865. In fact, Smith tells us that he left the Salt River toll gate where he worked, some twenty-three miles south of Louisville, on April 1, 1868, and moved to Indianapolis. He later moved to Osceola County, Mich., where he apparently lived the rest of his life.

Frederick Smock. Frederick Smock, born in 1954, is the author of several books of poems, including *12 Poems* (1991); *The Good Life* (2000); *Poems* (2002), a bilingual English-Russian book; and a travel memoir, *This Meadow of Time: A Provence Journal* (1995). He was the founding and only editor of the *American Voice,* the Louisville-based literary journal that for some fifteen years published some of the best poetry and fiction of the late twentieth century. Following the shutdown of the journal, he edited a selection of poetry, *The American Voice Anthology of Poetry* (1998). His work has appeared in *Poetry, Iowa Review, Orion, Southern Review,* and elsewhere. He is poet-in-residence at Bellarmine University, where he teaches creative writing and literature. He has also taught summer classes in Denmark. He has received an Al Smith Fellowship, the Frankfort Arts Foundation Prize, and the Jim Wayne Miller Prize.

Eve Spears. Born Jan. 11, 1908, in Carter County, Ky.; died Sept. 20, 2003, in Georgetown, Ky. Evalena Gilbert Spears was born at the mouth of Everman's Creek in Carter County, the sixth child in a family of five boys and two girls. She attended school in Grayson and later in Greenup

County, where her family moved when she was seven to work a tobacco farm on Laurel Creek. She completed Greenup High School and later studied at Wilmington College in Ohio, Ohio University, and Morehead State. She received an M.A. from the University of Kentucky. For almost forty years she taught in the public elementary schools of the counties of Fayette and Greenup, where in the 1932–33 academic year her superintendent was the Kentucky writer and educator Jesse Stuart. In 1935 she married the educator and poet Woodridge Spears, with whom she had twin sons, Philip and Richard, and a daughter, Sandra. Her poems echo the joys, sorrows, humor, and pathos of her own life and reflect the culture of the two sections of Kentucky where she lived all her life, the northeastern Kentucky hills and the central Kentucky Bluegrass. Her poems sometimes rhyme like folk ballads and sometimes throb like primitive free verse. She published poems in such journals as *Appalachian Heritage, Lyric, Kentucky Poetry Review,* and *Twigs.* She published three books of poetry: *Laurel Creek* (1972), *A Stranger to Myself,* and *A Cloud of Laurel* (1988). The poet and critic Hollis Summers said he was "enormously moved" by "A Cloud of Laurel," the eleven-page title poem of her 1988 collection.

Woodridge Spears. Born Jan. 22, 1913, Woodridge Spears was a son of Greenup County and the eastern Kentucky hills, and his life spanned most of the twentieth century. He received his Ph.D. from the University of Kentucky and taught at Georgetown College for most of his career. The depth and breadth of his knowledge and scholarship sometimes baffled his students and colleagues. He was not only a poet and professor but also a skilled linguist, whose expertise included Latin, Italian, Greek, and Swahili. His books of poetry included *The Feudalist* (1946), *River Island* (1963), and *The High Places* (1994). He also edited a collection of poems by the great-granddaughter of Henry Clay, *The Circling Thread: Poems by Susan Clay Sawitsky* (1984). In 1935 he married the poet and educator Eve Spears; they had two sons, Philip and Richard, and a daughter, Sandra. He died Oct. 4, 1989, in Georgetown, several years before his wife.

Henry T. Stanton. Born June 30, 1834, in Alexandria, Va.; died May 8, 1898, in Frankfort. One of Kentucky's most popular poets in the nineteenth century, Henry T. Stanton was born in Virginia but was brought by his family to Maysville, Ky., when he was only two years old. He was educated at Maysville Academy and at West Point and served in the Confederate Army during the Civil War. After the war he practiced law and was the editor of the *Maysville Bulletin* until 1870, when he moved to Frankfort to become chief assistant to the state commissioner of insurance. In 1871 he published his first volume of poetry, *The Moneyless Man and Other Poems.* He had written the title poem for a wandering elocutionist—a melodramatic performer who used exaggerated postures and gestures and vocal extremes—who appeared in Maysville one day and pleaded with Stanton to write him a poem that would wring tears from his audience. Stanton, apparently rising to the challenge, pulled out all the lachrymose stops he knew and, in the words of a contemporary critic, "brought all Kentucky to the mourners' bench." It was a triumph that he would regret the rest of his life, for it stamped him indelibly as the author of this bathetic poem—and nothing else. He did write several novels and publish another collection of poems, *Jacob Brown and Other Poems* (1875), and he edited the *Frankfort Yeoman* and became land commissioner under President Cleveland. Another collection of poems was published posthumously, *Poems of the Confederacy* (1900). Of course, some shallow readers took it seriously and loved it; but he was labeled for time and eternity as a one-poem man, the author of "The Moneyless Man."

Albert Stewart. Born July 17, 1914, at Yellow Mountain, Knott County, Ky.; died April 1, 2001, Knott County. Albert Stewart is sometimes called the patron saint to two generations of Kentucky Appalachian writers. He was a poet, an editor, a teacher, an inspiration, and a role model for his students. He even provided an outlet for young poets and prose writers—older ones, too—when he founded *Appalachian Heritage: A Magazine of Southern Appalachian Life and Culture* during his tenure as an instructor at Alice Lloyd College at Pippa Passes. After twelve years under his editorship, the magazine was moved to Berea College at the time of his retirement. Stewart attended Hindman Settlement School, where he knew the prominent authors Lucy Furman and Ann Cobb, who showed him the cultural heritage of the Appalachians and how it could be used in literature. He later received a B.A. in English from Berea College and an M.A. from the University of Kentucky. He served in the U.S. Navy during World War II. In addition to Alice Lloyd College, Stewart taught at Morehead State, where he started summer writing workshops taught by successful regional authors. At that time he edited an annual anthology of poems and short stories he named *Kentucky Writing*. Stewart also organized a summer writing program at Hindman Settlement School that became the prestigious Appalachian Writers Workshop. He published numerous poems, reviews, and essays and in 1962 a collection, *The Untoward Hills*, which has become a Kentucky classic. In 1994 he published a second volume of poetry, *The Holy Season: Walking in the Wild*. In 1983 he donated his three-hundred-acre farm and home, in which he was born and lived until he died, to the University of Kentucky for research and preservation.

Martha Bennett Stiles. Martha Bennett Stiles was born in 1933 in Manila, P.I., and reared in Virginia. At the College of William and Mary she won the James Bryan Hope Award for poetry. She graduated with a B.S. in chemistry from the University of Michigan, where she won Avery Hopwood Awards for essays. Until her marriage she worked as an analytical chemist for DuPont; then she and her husband bought a Bourbon County horse farm and moved to Kentucky in 1967. She has taught creative writing at the Universities of Kentucky and Louisville and received prizes for fiction from the Frankfort Arts Council and grants from the Kentucky Arts Council. Her publications include *Lonesome Road* (1998), a novel; more than sixty articles and stories in the *New York Times, Esquire, Georgia Review*, and other periodicals; three picture books, including *Island Magic* (1999), winner of the Detroit Working Writers Millennium Award; three novels for intermediate readers; and four novels for young adults, including *Darkness Over the Land* (1966), an American Library Association Notable Book, and *Kate of the Still Waters* (1990), winner of a Society of Children's Book Writers/Judy Blume Award. In 1978 she was awarded a citation from Central Missouri State University "in Recognition of Distinguished Contribution to Children's Literature."

James Still. Born July 16, 1906, in Lafayette, Ala.; died April 2001 in Hindman, Ky. During the sixty-plus years that James Still lived, taught, and wrote in Kentucky, he became the most eloquent voice of the southern Appalachians in all genres—poems, stories, novels, folktales, and children's stories. The body of his work is fairly small but choice. The son of an Alabama veterinarian (his father called himself "a horse doctor"), Still graduated from Lincoln Memorial University in 1929 and earned graduate degrees from Vanderbilt University and the University of Illinois. He served six years as a librarian at the Hindman Settlement School in Knott County and remained, with occasional short and protracted absences, as an informal writer-in-residence there until his death. Until his later years, when he lived primarily in a house in Hindman owned by the settlement school, he lived in a log cabin on Dead Mare Branch. Despite the image he sometimes cultivated, he was never a hermit. He served two years in the U.S. Army during World War II, and he made many excursions out of the mountains to travel in Latin America and to write at various writers' colonies in New England and elsewhere. He also welcomed hordes of visitors who beat a well-worn path to his cabin door. He taught at Morehead State for several years. He published his first poem in the *Virginia Quarterly Review* in 1935 and his first short story in *Atlantic Monthly* in 1936. His books include *Hounds on the Mountain* (1937, poems), *River of Earth* (1940, a novel), *On Troublesome Creek* (1941, stories), *Pattern of a Man* (1976, stories), *Sporty Creek* (1977, a novel), *Jack and the Wonder Beans* (1977, a folktale), *The Run for the Elbertas* (1980, stories), and *From the Mountain, From the Valley* (2001, poems). Everything he published he had crafted to near perfection.

Harriet Beecher Stowe. Born June 14, 1811, in Litchfield, Conn.; died July 1, 1896, in Hartford, Conn. Harriet Elizabeth Beecher Stowe was born and reared in a strict Calvinist family in Connecticut. In 1832 she moved with her family to Cincinnati, where her father, Lyman Beecher, was president of Lane Theological Seminary and where she taught in a girls' school and began to write sketches of New England life. In 1836 she married Calvin E. Stowe, who taught in her father's seminary. She probably conceived the idea of writing a series of sketches on slavery from the antislavery atmosphere of her father's school. Furthermore, she was separated from the slave state of Kentucky by a narrow band of the Ohio River, and she apparently took advantage of visits to Kentucky to observe the slave system up close. Several of her characters in *Uncle Tom's Cabin* (1852) may be based on real people she met in Kentucky or on slave narratives like those of Josiah Henson and Lewis Clarke. More probably, she combined her impressions of actual slaves with those she read about and reimagined them as Uncle Tom, Little Eva, George Harris, and other characters. It is also likely that at least once she witnessed a slave auction in front of the Maysville courthouse. Certainly she remembered the Kentucky mansions, the owners, and the slaves she visited and the Kentucky landscape she traveled through when she sat down to create the Kentucky setting for her story. When she and her husband moved to Maine in 1850, she had stored up images and impressions that she could use when she started writing her antislavery sketches for the *National Era,* an abolitionist newspaper in Washington, D.C. These loose sketches make it obvious that she had no grand design to write a unified novel; but the serialized sketches became so popular that a book publication became inevitable. Despite the structural weaknesses of the novel, Stowe puts believable human faces on the slavery system; and the impact of the story was immediate and powerful. Its effect on American—even world—history is undeniable. A close, unbiased reading shows that although she is clearly against slavery, her book is not anti-Southern. It is antislavery. Indeed, she opposed slavery on moral and religious grounds because she believed that it corrupted and enslaved both the master and the slave. After all, the most sadistic, heinous character in the book is Simon Legree, and he's from Vermont.

Jane Stuart. Jane Stuart, the daughter of Jesse and Naomi Deane Stuart, was born in 1942 in Greenup County. She received a B.A. in Greek and Latin from Case-Western Reserve University. She received an M.A. in classics and a Ph.D. in Italian from Indiana University. She is both a poet and a fiction writer. Her poetry books are *A Year's Harvest* (1957), *Eyes of the Mole* (1967), and *White Barn* (1973). Her novels are considerably stronger than her poetry: *Yellowhawk* (1973); *Passerman's Hollow* (1974); *Land of the Fox* (1975), a psychological portrait of a woman who is driven to the edge of madness by the noises and pressures of city life; and *Gideon's Children* (1976), a collection of character sketches. In recent years she has been living at her home at W-Hollow in Greenup County.

Jesse Stuart. Born Aug. 8, 1906, in Greenup County, Ky.; died Feb. 17, 1984; buried in Plum Grove Cemetery, near W-Hollow, Greenup County. Although Jesse Stuart was not Kentucky's greatest writer, he was the most prolific and the one that people most admired, even loved. He was a man of the soil who never lost his common touch and never forgot where he came from. Indeed, even though he did a lot of traveling in Kentucky and around the world, his home was always in W-Hollow, Greenup County. It was the place he left and the place he came back to. Born into a family of illiterate or near-illiterate people, he valued, preached, and practiced education his entire life. He graduated from Greenup High School in 1926 and from Lincoln Memorial University three years later; then he returned home to teach what he'd learned. Within a few decades he had taught in one-room schools, served as a principal and school superintendent, taught at universities at home and abroad, and performed lectures and readings before thousands of students and fans. In addition, he had used his experiences as building blocks for his finest tribute to American education, *The Thread That Runs So True* (1949), one of the most inspirational grassroots novels ever written. A list of his books is a road map of his life: *Harvest of Youth* (1930), a collection of personal poems; *Man with a Bull-Tongue Plow* (1934); *Album of Destiny* (1944); *Kentucky Is My Land* (1952); and *Hold April* (1962). He revisits his youth in such children's books as *The Beatinest Boy* (1953) and *A Penny's Worth of Character* (1954). His explicit autobiography is *Beyond Dark Hills* (1938); but he appears in all his fiction as well, from *Trees of Heaven* (1940), his first novel, to *Taps for Private Tussie* (1943). *God's Oddling* (1960) is a gift to his father. *The Year of*

My Rebirth (1956) is his gift to life—a life that he reclaimed after suffering a major heart attack in 1954. As if his books were not gifts enough, he gave his property to Kentucky for a nature preserve in 1980. He was worn out and used up when he finally succumbed in 1984, but he left behind a living body of works that will keep him alive and passionate for life each time we open one of his books.

Lucinda Dixon Sullivan. Lucinda Dixon Sullivan is a native Kentuckian, raised in Bowling Green. She attended the University of Kentucky, married, mothered, worked, and returned to college to graduate from the University of Louisville. After she received an M.F.A. from Vermont College in 1992, she made an impressive debut as a novelist with a tough and heartwarming first novel, *It Was the Goodness of the Place* (2003), which was lauded by critics and fellow writers alike. Sena Jeter Naslund wrote that "through the pity and terror of the story, *It Was the Goodness of the Place* illumines the inherent worth of human potential." Dixon's stories and essays have appeared in the *Louisville Review; Place Gives Rise to Spirit,* an anthology of personal essays on living in Louisville; and elsewhere. She is married to Richard M. Sullivan, a Louisville attorney.

Hollis Summers. Born June 21, 1916, in Eminence, Ky.; died Nov. 14, 1987, in Athens, Ohio. Hollis Spurgeon Summers grew up in Madisonville, received a B.A. from Georgetown College in 1937, an M.A. in 1943 from the Bread Loaf School of English of Middlebury College in Vermont, and a Ph.D. from the University of Iowa in 1949. He began his teaching career at Holmes High School in Covington, taught ten years at the University of Kentucky, and then taught at Ohio University until his retirement in 1986. His first book of poetry, *The Walks Near Athens* (1959), was followed by *Someone Else* (1962), *Occupant, Please Forward* (1976), and *Dinosaurs* (1977). His novels include *City Limit* (1948), *Brighten the Corner* (1952), and *How They Chose the Dead* (1973). He earned many awards for teaching and writing, including a grant from the Fund for Advancement of Education in 1951, a *Saturday Review* award for poetry in 1957, several distinguished professor awards, and an honorary D.Litt. from Georgetown College in 1965. In 1978 he was a Fulbright lecturer in New Zealand. The spring 1981 issue of *Kentucky Poetry Review* was dedicated to Summers.

Joe Survant. Born in 1942, Joe Survant is a native of Owensboro and received an M.A. and a Ph.D. from the University of Delaware. Since 1970 he has been a professor of English at Western Kentucky University and director of the writing program there since 1994. His poetry has been published in such magazines as *Chelsea Poet and Critic, Kentucky Poetry Review, American Voice,* and the *Sow's Ear Poetry Review.* His poetry has been collected in *Anne & Alpheus, 1842–1882* (1996), *The Presence of Snow in the Tropics* (2001), and *Rafting Rise* (1999), a collection of narrative poems set in the Green River Basin in 1916. He was appointed Kentucky's poet laureate in 2003.

Catherine Sutton. Catherine Sutton was born on Feb. 14, 1947, in Louisville. After receiving her B.A. and M.A. from the University of Louisville, she earned a Ph.D. at Indiana University. She has been teaching and working as an administrator at Bellarmine University since 1994. She has published poetry in the *American Voice, Poet & Critic, Mississippi Valley Review, Kentucky Poetry Review,* and other journals. She has recently taken up the violin, to which she now devotes most of her creative energies.

Charlie Sweet (*See also* Harold Blythe.). Born in Bristol, Conn., on Sept. 8, 1943, Charles A. Sweet Jr. is a professor of English at Eastern Kentucky University, where he frequently writes as half of a team (with Harold Blythe) variously bylined Hal Charles or Brett Halliday. He holds degrees from Washington and Lee University and Florida State University, where he received a Ph.D. in 1970. Since then he has taught at Eastern Kentucky, winning numerous teaching awards and writing dozens of professional papers, textbooks, and writing guides. Outside the academic community he is best known for the short stories and detective stories that he and Harold Blythe have published in magazines ranging from *Ellery Queen's Mystery Magazine* to *Kentucky Monthly.*

Allen Tate. Born Nov. 10, 1899, in Winchester, Ky.; died Feb. 9, 1979, in Nashville, Tenn. When John Orley Allen Tate was three, his parents moved to Ashland. He attended Cross School for Boys in Louisville, Ashland High School, and Georgetown University Prep School in Washington, D.C. In 1918 he entered Vanderbilt, where he would get to know such prominent professors and fellow students as Robert Penn Warren, Merrill Moore, John Crowe Ransom, Andrew Lytle, and Donald Davidson—a veritable hotbed of talent. In 1924 he moved to New York and established himself as a talented poet, critic, and biographer, with a central focus on the Civil War and its aftermath. In 1928 he won a Guggenheim Fellowship, which took him to France and England for almost two years, during which time he became acquainted with such giants of modern literature as T. S. Eliot, Gertrude Stein, and e. e. cummings. In February 1930 he returned to his home, Benfolly, on the Cumberland River in Tennessee and opened his own version of a Parisian salon and writers' retreat. In later years he was a writer-in-residence at Princeton and lecturer at Oxford. He held teaching positions at many schools, including Southwestern College in Memphis; the University of the South, where he edited the *Sewanee Review* for several years; the University of North Carolina at Greensboro; and the University of Minnesota. Tate's signature poems include "Ode to the Confederate Dead" and "The Swimmers." His best-known novel is *The Fathers* (1938), which is set in antebellum Virginia. His two incisive Civil War biographies are *Stonewall Jackson, the Good Soldier* (1928) and *Jefferson Davis: His Rise and Fall* (1929). In 1924 he married Caroline Gordon, the Kentucky-born fiction writer, with whom he had one daughter; with his third wife he fathered three sons. He is known famously as one of the leaders of the New Criticism, which emphasizes close textual analysis, and as one of the twelve southern "Agrarians" who contributed their neoconservative essays to *I'll Take My Stand* (1930), their statement of beliefs about literature, art, and culture.

Richard Taylor. Richard Taylor was born in Louisville in 1941, grew up in the Crescent Hill neighborhood, and graduated from Atherton High School in 1959; he received a B.A. from the University of Kentucky in 1963, an M.A. from the University of Louisville in 1964, and a Ph.D. from Kentucky. Between those degrees, he also took a law degree at Louisville, although he has practiced very little. Instead, he became a writer and a professor of English at Kentucky State University in Frankfort, where he lives with his family and, with his wife, Elizabeth, also operates Poor Richard's Books, which offers new and antiquarian books. His works include *Bluegrass* (1975), *Earth Bones* (1979), *Stone Eye* (2001), *In the Country of Morning Calm* (2001), and *Braintree: Fifteen Poems* (2004). He has also written *Girty* (1990), a novel. He was appointed poet laureate of Kentucky in 1999.

Mary Ann Taylor-Hall. Born in Chicago, poet and fiction writer Mary Ann Taylor-Hall holds degrees from the University of Florida and Columbia University. She has taught at Auburn University, the University of Kentucky, Miami University, and Transylvania University. She has published short fiction in the *Sewanee Review, Colorado Quarterly, Kenyon Review, Paris Review,* and elsewhere. A collection of her short fiction, *How She Knows What She Knows about Yo-Yos,* was published in 2000. Her first novel, *Come and Go, Mollie Snow,* was published in 1995. She lives with her husband, the poet James Baker Hall, near Sadieville, Ky.

Julia A. Tevis. Born Dec. 5, 1799, near Winchester, Ky.; died 1880, in Shelbyville, Ky. When she was seven Julia Ann Hieronymous moved with her parents from Winchester, Ky., to Winchester, Va. In 1813 the family moved to Washington, D.C. Julia was educated under private teachers and in several finishing schools, where she learned not only how to become a lady, but, as she later recalled, "music, drawing, and French, with various kinds of embroidery." At twenty, in Wytheville, Va., she began a sixty-year career as a teacher. She later taught at Abingdon, Va., where she met and married a young Kentucky Methodist minister, the Reverend John Tevis. After their move to his hometown of Shelbyville, Ky., she founded one of the oldest Protestant female finishing schools in the Mississippi Valley, Science Hill Academy, which opened on March 25, 1825, and continued, after it was sold to W. T. Poynter in 1879, until it closed in June 1939. By the first quarter of the twentieth century, Science Hill had become one of the country's foremost college preparatory schools for women. In 1878 Julia Tevis opened a charming and spacious window on the education of young women from affluent American families when she published her autobiography, *Sixty Years in a School-Room.*

Walter Tevis. Born Feb. 28, 1928, in San Francisco; died Aug. 9, 1984, in New York. When he was ten Walter Tevis moved with his family from San Francisco to Kentucky, where his father had been born in Madison County. Tevis graduated from Model High School in Richmond, then served for two years in the U.S. Naval Reserve in the Pacific. In 1949 he received his B.A. in English from the University of Kentucky. After he had taught high school English at Science Hill, Hawesville, Carlisle, and Irvine, he returned to the University of Kentucky to earn his M.A. in English. Later, he was awarded an M.F.A. at the University of Iowa. In the fall of 1958 he joined the faculty of the University of Kentucky's Northern Kentucky extension, now Northern Kentucky University. Later he taught creative writing at Ohio University in Athens; then in 1978 he resigned from teaching and moved to New York to become a full-time writer. He had been writing and publishing occasionally since he studied for his M.A. at Kentucky and took a class under the journalist-novelist A. B. Guthrie. He supported himself in those days as a worker in a poolroom near the campus. It was there that he learned about pool and wrote a pool hall story that appeared in *Esquire* in 1953. Eventually he would develop the plot and publish the blockbuster novel *The Hustler* (1959), which was made into a movie starring Paul Newman and Jackie Gleason. His second novel, *The Man Who Fell to Earth* (1963), is the science fiction story of a man who is sent from the dying planet of Anthea to Earth to prepare a place for his planet's survivors. It won the Little Green Man citation as the best science fiction novel of the year. His other books include *Mocking Bird* (1980), another science fiction novel; *Far from Home* (1981), a collection of short stories; *The Steps of the Sun* (1983); *The Queen's Gambit* (1983); and *The Color of Money* (1984), a sequel to *The Hustler,* which continues the pool hall hustling adventures of Fast Eddie Felson and Minnesota Fats. It was made into a 1986 movie with Paul Newman and a Louisville native, Tom Cruise.

Hunter S. Thompson. Born July 18, 1937, in Louisville; died Feb. 20, 2005, in Woody Creek, Colo. Hunter Stockton Thompson did something that few writers accomplish. He invented and practiced a new genre of writing: a personal, rough, angry, strident, in-your-face, involved, rule-breaking form called gonzo journalism in which the writer is heavily, often violently, involved in his subject. Thompson lived and wrote on the edge; he was, as he once called himself, "a connoisseur of edge work." It started, he said, when he was sent by *Scanlan's* magazine to cover the Kentucky Derby. He had been drinking and drugging and carousing and couldn't write a straight dispatch according to the rules and by the deadline, so he suddenly started tearing out pages from his notebook that contained his random raw observations. He numbered them and sent them off, assuming that was the end of his career in journalism. But no. His raw, rough-edged rants were published and he found himself a winner. He tried out his invention in a protracted edition when he lived and traveled with the Hell's Angels for more than a year and wrote it up as *Hell's Angels: A Strange and Terrible Saga* (1967). He was at full throttle when he wrote *Fear and Loathing in Las Vegas: A Savage Journey to the Heart of the American Dream* (1972). It is presented in the form of a drug-ridden road trip from Los Angeles to Las Vegas, a final jab at Richard Nixon. His other titles, each suggesting similarly abrasive content, include *The Great Shark Hunt* (1979), *The Curse of Lono* (1983), *Generation of Swine* (1988), *Songs of the Doomed* (1990), and *The Rum Diary* (1998). During a tribute to Thompson in Louisville shortly after he shot and killed himself at his Colorado retreat, Ron Whitehead, a local poet and friend of Thompson, offered these words written by a twenty-three-year-old Thompson while he was living in Bermuda: "If I could think of a way to do it right now, I'd head back to Louisville, sit on the porch drinking beer, drive around Cherokee Park for a few nights, and try to sink back as far as I could into the world that did its best to make me. It's not hard to get tired of interminable palms and poinciana, and I could do at the moment with a single elm tree on a midnight street in the Highlands."

Alexis de Tocqueville. Born 1805 in Verneuil, near Paris, France; died 1859 in Cannes, France. Alexis de Tocqueville published in 1835–1840 *Democracy in America,* one of the most incisive and influential books ever written about American politics and society. He was raised by his father's tutor, Abbé Lesueur, an elderly priest who taught his pupil a devout religious faith, which he modified after reading Descartes and other philosophers. He studied law in Paris, 1825–1827, and attended lectures on the history of civilization at the Sorbonne by François-Pierre Guizot, under whose influence he wrote a pamphlet in which he advocated the emancipation of slaves. For almost a year, in 1831 and 1832, he traveled throughout the United States, observing the habits and attitudes of its citizens, with his friend Gustave de Beaumont, ostensibly to study the American prison system but actually to study the nation's culture and political system, which resulted in his publication of *Democracy in America.* In 1835 he married Mary Mottley, an Englishwoman. He died on his estate in Cannes.

Donald H. Vish. Donald Vish, a lawyer, photographer, and writer, was born in 1945 at Ft. Benning, Ga. He graduated from Bellarmine College in 1968 with a degree in English. In 1970 he received his J.D. with honors from the Brandeis School of Law at the University of Louisville. From 1989 to 1991 he was associate solicitor for the U.S. Department of the Interior in Washington, D.C. From 1976 to 1984 he was an adjunct associate professor of law at the University of Kentucky. In addition to his professional writing in law, he has published a collection of his poems, *Poems and Musings* (2001). He now practices law privately with Middleton Reutlinger in Louisville.

Frank X Walker. Born in Danville, Ky., in 1962 to Frank Wesley and Faith Smith Walker, Frank X Walker has the distinction of having cofounded a literary movement with two other African American professors and poets, Kelly Norman Ellis and Nikky Finney, who teaches at the University of Kentucky and is the author of *Rice* (1995). It has evolved into a school of writing called Affrilachian, a combination of African and Appalachian, which produces a unique voice in American letters. Appropriately, Walker's first book of poetry is entitled *Affrilachia,* published by Old Cove Press in 2000. It is a much-acclaimed collection of thirty-eight poems about family and social issues and has been staged as a musical. Walker enrolled at the University of Kentucky to study engineering, but, after taking several courses with the author Gurney Norman, he switched to English. Norman has called Walker "a modern bard" with "a marvelous literary voice, one of clarity, honesty and naturalness." In 2004 Walker published *Buffalo Dance: The Journey of York.* Walker has served as director of the King Cultural Center at the University of Kentucky and as director of the Governor's School for the Arts.

Robert Penn Warren. Born April 24, 1905, in Guthrie, Todd County, Ky.; died Sept. 15, 1989, in Stratton, Vt. Robert Penn Warren, the most gifted and versatile writer that Kentucky has produced, was one of the major American writers of the twentieth century. He was a master of all the literary genres, from poetry and short stories to novels and essays. After attending the public schools in Guthrie, he attended Vanderbilt University, from which he graduated summa cum laude in 1925. At Vanderbilt he was a member of the literary group "The Fugitives" and contributed to their journal, the *Fugitive.* Along with Allen Tate, John Crowe Ransom, Donald Davidson, and others, he belonged to another Vanderbilt social and political group called "The Agrarians," which called for a literary and social return to the values and standards of the South's nineteenth-century rural culture. In 1927 he received an M.A. in English from the University of California at Berkeley. He continued his studies at Yale and Oxford, where he was a Rhodes Scholar. He began his teaching career at Louisiana State University in 1934 and founded the *Southern Review* with his fellow Rhodes Scholar and critic Cleanth Brooks, a native of Murray, Ky. Warren later taught at the University of Minnesota for nine years and in 1951 went to Yale, where he remained until he retired in 1973. Some of his most important books are *Night Rider* (1939), *All the King's Men*

(1946), *The Circus in the Attic and Other Stories* (1948), *World Enough and Time* (1950), *Brother to Dragons* (1953, a play), *Band of Angels* (1955), *The Cave* (1959), *Flood* (1964), and *A Place To Come To* (1977). In 1938 he coauthored, with Cleanth Brooks, *Understanding Poetry*, a textbook that fostered the New Criticism and its emphasis on close reading of literary texts. He won the Pulitzer Prize three times and is the only writer to have won it for both poetry and fiction. His stellar career as a teacher and writer spanned several generations and climaxed in 1986, when he was appointed as the first U.S. poet laureate. After he left Guthrie to study at Vanderbilt as a youth, he never returned to Kentucky to live permanently. Except for *All the King's Men,* which is set in Louisiana, he turned to Kentucky, however, almost every time he wrote a story or a poem or a novel. Kentucky's pivotal and turbulent history and its rich heritage were overflowing reservoirs from which he drew inspiration and subject matter. To echo the wording of his 1977 novel, it was a place he came to frequently when he sat down to write. In 1987 Western Kentucky University established the Center for Warren Studies, and in 1989 the citizens of Guthrie completed the restoration of his birthplace.

Jo Anna Holt Watson. Born and reared in Woodford County, Ky., Jo Anna "Pee Wee" Holt Watson is not only a superb writer but an entrepreneur and a passionate recycling advocate. She was co-owner of Bandana Yardbirds, a company that used scrap, overruns, and discontinued garden tool parts to produce whimsical birdlike yard sculptures. She was once described by the *Atlanta Constitution* as a woman who travels across the country in a blue blazer and a straw hat "preaching the gospel of recycling." She is also a photographer, gardener, avid sportswoman, horse trials judge, and creator of *Plumline,* a television series focusing on political and social issues. She is as well a fourth-generation Kentuckian and a self-proclaimed Yellow Dog Democrat. In 2004 Sarabande Books of Louisville published her best-selling, critically acclaimed family memoir, *A Taste of the Sweet Apple.* She lives in Louisville with her Airedale terrier, Harrie Holt, and her Welsh terrier, Maggie Tarbell.

Henry Watterson. Born Feb. 16, 1840, in Washington, D.C.; died Dec. 22, 1921, in Jacksonville, Fla. For over fifty years, Henry Watterson was editor of the *Courier-Journal* and one of the most influential editorial voices in the United States. He was born into a political family (his father was a congressman from Tennessee) and retained a passionate interest in politics and politicians all his life. Except for William Henry Harrison, he knew personally all the American presidents from John Quincy Adams to Franklin Delano Roosevelt. During the Civil War he edited the *Rebel,* the most widely read newspaper in the Confederate Army. After the war he moved to Louisville and took over the combined *Courier* and *Journal,* which became the *Courier-Journal* on Nov. 8, 1868, under the ownership of Watterson and Walter N. Haldeman. He used his editor's chair to promote the policies and candidates of the Democratic Party and to preach the gospel of the New South, whose basic tenets were that the South must abandon its slave-ridden past; adjust to the new social, cultural, and economic realities; and compete with the North for industry. In 1918 he sold the *Courier-Journal* to Robert Worth Bingham, whose family owned and operated the newspaper until 1986, when it and the *Louisville Times* were sold to the Gannett Corporation. Watterson was the author of two books. In 1882 he published a collection of light and humorous writing, *Oddities in Southern Life and Character,* which was designed, so he says in the preface, to promote "a better understanding and reconciliation among classes of people hitherto kept asunder by misconceptions and prejudices the most whimsical." In 1919 he published his two-volume autobiography, *Marse Henry.*

Amelia B. Welby. Born Feb. 3, 1819, in St. Michael's, Md.; died May 3, 1852, in Louisville. Amelia B. Coppuck Welby was one of the most popular poets of the mid-nineteenth century. Her *Poems by Amelia* was published in 1845, and by 1860 it was in its seventeenth printing. Even Edgar Allan Poe praised her poetry in a glowing review. Unfortunately, most of her poetry is, by today's standards, superficial, sentimental doggerel about love, children, nature, religion, and, especially, death. Whatever her subject, she caressed it until she smothered the life from it. Indeed, as Mark Twain said of Emmeline Grangerford, a sentimental poet he satirizes in *Huckleberry Finn,* regardless of where Amelia started one of her poems, it usually ended in the graveyard. As a wise (anonymous) critic once said, a sentimental poet is one who tries to love her or his subject more than God does. Nevertheless, Welby is important as a cultural indicator of the popular literary taste of her day.

Crystal Wilkinson. Born in Hamilton, Ohio, in 1962, Crystal Wilkinson came to Kentucky when she was six to live with her Wilkinson grandparents on their tobacco farm in Casey County. This is, indeed, an important part of who she is. She told a writer for the *Courier-Journal* in December 2002 that she had "as perfect a childhood as anyone could ask for," and added, "I was free to take advantage of the land, and let the land take advantage of me." She graduated from Casey County High School at sixteen and received a degree in journalism in 1985 from Eastern Kentucky University. She has also been the director of the Carnegie Center for Literacy and Learning in Lexington and serves as chair of the creative writing department for the Kentucky Governor's School for the Arts. She is a charter member of the Affrilachian Poets, a group of performing African American poets from Appalachia. Her coming-of-age essay, "One Affrilachian's Journey Home," was included in the anthology *Confronting Appalachian Stereotypes.* Her books include *Blackberries, Blackberries* (2000) and *Water Street* (2002). Morris Grubbs, who edited *Home and Beyond: An Anthology of Kentucky Short Stories,* included her story "Humming Back Yesterday." He has called her "the most exciting new voice in Kentucky writing right now."

Charles Williams. Born in Munfordville, Ky., near the Green River, Charles Dowling Williams is Kentucky's answer to Wallace Stevens. Both became lawyer-poets, Williams several generations after Stevens. They share an interest in poetry that is sensual, lyrical, intellectual, and transcendently mortal. Williams graduated from Duke University with majors in history and psychology, with thirty-three hours in English and thirty hours in religion. After he received his J.D. from the University of Kentucky, he joined the law firm in Munfordville started by his grandfather in 1902. He has published poetry in various periodicals and the following books: *A Pause amid Bloodbaths; Uncle Jim's Green River Diary* (1996); *A Man of the Courts* (1999), a career biography of his father, Davis Williams, that is also a social and anecdotal history of Hart County and nearby counties; and *Out of Green River Kitchens* (2004), a lyrical collection of recipes good for the body and the soul.

Robert Burns Wilson. Born Oct. 30, 1850, near Parker, Pa.; died March 31, 1916, in Brooklyn, N.Y. Robert Burns Wilson was orphaned at ten and raised by his grandparents in Wheeling, W.V. In 1871 he moved to Pittsburgh to study art, and the following year he moved to Louisville. In 1875 he moved to Frankfort, where he did portraits in oil, crayon, and charcoal and painted landscapes in watercolor. In 1885 he published a poem, "When Evening Cometh On," in *Harper's* magazine. He wrote a poem, "Remember the Maine," shortly after the sinking of the battleship during the Spanish-American War. It was set to music and became the most famous battle song to come out of the war. He published three books of poetry: *Life and Love* (1887), *Chant of a Woodland Spirit* (1894), and *The Shadows of the Trees* (1898). In 1904 he and his wife and daughter moved to Brooklyn, where he thought he could sell his art better than in Kentucky. He wrote old-fashioned, traditional poems filled with archaic words and mawkish sentiments. Sad to say, he was a better artist than poet.

George C. Wolfe. George Wolfe was born in 1955 in Frankfort and graduated from Frankfort High School in 1972. He received a B.A. in directing from Pomona College and an M.F.A. in Dramatic Writing/Musical Theater from New York University and thereafter became a playwright and librettist. He is one of the most successful African American playwrights and directors working in New York. He is best known for his Broadway musical *Jelly's Last Jam,* which ran from 1991 to 1993. One of his big successes was his play *The Colored Museum* (1986). In a short time he has won a long list of awards, including an Obie Award in 1990. He had several Tony Award nominations in 1992. He has received grants from the Rockefeller Foundation, the National Endowment for the Arts, and the National Institute for Musical Theatre. He was the 1986 recipient of a CBS/ Foundation of the Dramatists Guild Playwriting Award for *The Colored Museum.*

Miriam Woolfolk. Born in Louisville on Feb. 14, 1926, Miriam Lamy Woolfolk attended local schools and during World War II worked in the magazine department of the L&N Railroad Company before moving in 1951 to Lexington, where her late husband, Patch G. Woolfolk, was professor of animal sciences at the University of Kentucky. She has been a poet since the second grade, when one of her poems appeared in the *Longfellow Announcer,* the school paper. Since then, she has pursued poetry and painting, sometimes combining the two arts in one book. Her publications include *Kentucky's Covered Bridges, Seasons, Little Book of Drawings,* and seven poetry chapbooks. She has been active in the Kentucky State Poetry Society for many years, serving as its president and as editor of its journal, *Pegasus.* Her poems have appeared in numerous regional and national journals, including *Twigs, Kentucky Poetry Review, Approaches, Old Hickory Review, Kudzu,* and *Wind.*

Bibliography

Ali, Muhammad, with Richard Durham. *The Greatest: My Own Story.* New York: Random House, 1975.

Allen, Dwight. *The Green Suit.* Chapel Hill: Algonquin Books, 2000.

Allen, James Lane. *Flute and Violin and Other Kentucky Tales and Romances.* New York: Harper and Brothers, 1891.

Anderson, Mary. *A Few Memories.* New York: Harper and Brothers, 1896.

Andrews, William L., ed. *The Oxford Companion to African American Literature.* New York: Oxford University Press, 1997.

Arnow, Harriette Simpson. *The Dollmaker.* New York: Macmillan, 1954.

———. *Old Burnside.* Lexington: University Press of Kentucky, 1977.

Audubon, John James. *Delineations of American Scenery and Character.* New York: G. A. Baker and Company, 1926.

Baker, Prentice. *Down Cellar: Poems.* Louisville: Kentucky Poetry Press, 1973.

Berry, Wendell. *A Timbered Choir: The Sabbath Poems 1979–1997.* Washington, D.C.: Counterpoint, 1998.

———. *What Are People For?* New York: Farrar Straus and Giroux, 1990.

Bingham, Sallie. *Transgressions: Stories.* Louisville: Sarabande Books, 2002.

Bolton, Joe. "Tropical Courtyard." In *The Last Nostalgia: Poems 1982–1990,* ed. Donald Justice. Little Rock: University of Arkansas Press, 1999.

[Boone], Joy Bale. *Never Less Than Love: Poems.* 1970.

Braden, Anne. *The Wall Between.* New York: Monthly Review Press, 1958.

Brewer, Jerry. "Hello from a Kentuckian." *Courier-Journal,* November 1, 2004.

Brown, Bruce Bennett. "Blue-Fall." In *Contemporary Kentucky Poetry,* ed. Joy Bale et al. Elizabethtown: Friends of Kentucky Libraries, 1967.

Brown, William Wells. *Narrative of William W. Brown, a Fugitive Slave, Written by Himself.* Boston: The Anti-slavery Office, 1847.

Bruckheimer, Linda. *Dreaming Southern.* New York: Dutton, 1999.

Bunnell, Roberta Scott. *Eavesdropper: Poems.* Louisville: Kentucky Poetry Press, [1972].

Burman, Ben Lucien. *It's a Big Country: America Off the Highways.* New York: Reynal and Co., 1956.

Butler, William O. "The Boatman's Horn." *Western Review,* July 1821. Reprinted in *The Poets and Poetry of the West,* ed. William T. Coggeshall. Columbus, Ohio: Follett and Foster, 1860.

Carr, Pat, and Maureen Morehead. *Our Brothers' War.* Louisville: Sulgrave Press, [1992].

Caudill, Harry M. *Night Comes to the Cumberlands.* Boston: Little, Brown, 1963.

Cawein, Madison. *Undertones.* Boston: Copeland and Day, 1896.

———. "Waste Land." *Poetry,* January 1913.

Chaffin, Lillie. "Stance" and "Sunning." *Kentucky Poetry Review* 22, no. 1 (Spring 1986).

Charles, Hal (Harold Blythe and Charlie Sweet). "Horn of Plenty." *Kentucky Monthly,* February 2005.

Clark, Billy C. *Sourwood Tales.* New York: G. P. Putnam's Sons, 1968.

Clark, George Rogers. *Col. George Rogers Clark's Sketch of His Campaign in the Illinois in 1778–79 with an Introduction by Hon. Henry Pirtle, of Louisville and an Appendix Containing the Public and Private Instructions to Col. Clark and Major Bowman's Journal of the Taking of the Post St. Vincents.* Cincinnati: Robert Clarke and Co., 1869.

Clark, Thomas D. *A History of Kentucky.* New York: Prentice-Hall, 1937.

———. *The Kentucky.* New York: Henry Holt, 1942.

Clarke, Lewis, and Milton Clarke. *Narratives of the Sufferings of Lewis and Milton Clarke, Sons of a Soldier of the Revolution, During a Captivity of More Than Twenty Years among the Slaveholders of Kentucky, One of the So Called Christian States of North America. Dictated by Themselves.* Boston: Bela Marsh, 1846.

Clay, Henry. *The Life and Speeches of the Hon. Henry Clay.* Ed. Daniel Mallory. New York, 1844.

Cobb, Irvin S. *Old Judge Priest.* New York: George H. Doran, 1916.

Compton, Gayle C. "Long Distance to Detroit." *Appalachian Heritage,* Fall 1991.

Cotter, Joseph S., Sr. *Sequel to the Pied Piper of Hamelin and Other Poems.* New York: Henry Harrison, 1939.

———. *A White Song and a Black One.* Louisville: Bradley and Gilbert, 1909.

Cotton, Ralph. *While Angels Dance: The Life and Times of Jeston Nash.* New York: St. Martin's Press, 1994.

Crabb, Alfred Leland. *Peace at Bowling Green.* Indianapolis: Bobbs-Merrill, 1955.

Crunk, Tony. *Living in the Resurrection.* New Haven: Yale University Press, 1995.

Dargan, Olive Tilford. "We Creators." In *The Lyric South,* ed. Addison Hibbard. New York: Macmillan, 1928.

Davenport, Guy. *The Hunter Gracchus and Others Papers on Literature and Art.* Washington, D.C.: Counterpoint, 1996.

Davenport, Gwen. *Belvedere.* Indianapolis: Bobbs-Merrill, 1947.

Davis, Jefferson. *The Rise and Fall of the Confederate Government.* 2 vols. New York: D. Appleton, 1881.

DeRosier, Linda Scott. *Creeker: A Woman's Journey.* Lexington: University Press of Kentucky, 1999.

Deveraux, Jude. *River Lady.* New York: Pocket Books, 1985.

Dick, David. *Peace at the Center: Essays.* Paris, Ky.: Plum Lick Publishing, 1994.

Dickens, Charles. *American Notes for General Circulation.* London: Chapman and Hall, 1842.

Dorris, Michael. *Paper Trail: Essays.* New York: HarperCollins, 1994.

Driskell, Kathleen. "Old Woman Looks Out Window." *Kentucky Poetry Review* 26, no. 2 (Fall 1990).

Driskell, Leon. *Passing Through.* Chapel Hill: Algonquin Books, 1983.

English, Logan. "The Wind That Shakes the Barley" and "Beware You Sons of Sorrow." *Kentucky Poetry Review: Logan English Memorial Issue* 19, no. 2 (Fall 1983).

Fetterman, John. *Stinking Creek.* New York: E. P. Dutton, 1967.

Filiatreau, John. "Ode on a Writer's Block." *Kentucky Poetry Review* 20, no. 2 (Fall 1984).

Filson, John. *The Discovery, Settlement, and Present State of Kentucke.* Wilmington, Del.: James Adams, 1784.

Flexner, Abraham. *I Remember: The Autobiography of Abraham Flexner.* New York: Simon and Schuster, 1940.

Flexner, Hortense. *Selected Poems.* London: Hutchinson, 1963.

Flood, Charles Bracelen. *Lee: The Last Years.* Boston: Houghton Mifflin, 1981.

Fox, John Jr. *Christmas Eve on Lonesome, Hell-Fer-Sartain and Other Stories.* New York: Charles Scribner's Sons, 1913.

Fuqua, Carolyn Wilford. "Hair." *Kentucky Poetry Review* (Spring 1973).

Furman, Lucy. *Mothering on Perilous.* New York: Macmillan, 1913.

Gatton, John. "Called." *Kentucky Poetry Review* 28, no. 1 (Spring 1992).

Gentry, Jane. *A Garden in Kentucky.* Baton Rouge: Louisiana State University Press, 1995.

Gibbs, Dot. *Not Forgotten Blue: Poems.* Louisville: Kentucky Poetry Press, 1977.

Giles, Janice Holt. *The Believers.* Boston: Houghton Mifflin, 1957.

Gordon, Caroline. *The Collected Stories of Caroline Gordon.* New York: Farrar, Straus and Giroux, 1981.

Gorham, Sarah. *The Cure.* New York: Four Way Books, 2003.

Grafton, Sue. *"O" Is for Outlaw.* New York: Henry Holt, 1999.

Greene, Jonathan. *Inventions of Necessity.* Frankfort: Gnomon Press, 1998.

Grubbs, Morris Allen. *Home and Beyond: An Anthology of Kentucky Short Stories.* Lexington: University Press of Kentucky, 2001.

Hall, Eliza Calvert. *Aunt Jane of Kentucky.* Boston: Little, Brown, 1907.

Hall, James Baker. *Stopping on the Edge to Wave.* Middletown, Conn.: Wesleyan University Press, 1988.

Hall, Wade. *Passing for Black: The Life and Careers of Mae Street Kidd.* Lexington: University Press of Kentucky, 1997.

———. *The Rest of the Dream: The Black Odyssey of Lyman Johnson.* Lexington: University Press of Kentucky, 1988.

Hardwick, Elizabeth. "Evenings at Home." *Partisan Review,* 1948. Reprinted in *Kentucky Story,* ed. Hollis Summers. Lexington: University of Kentucky Press, 1954.

Hay, John. "Renascence." *Open 24 Hours,* 2002.

Hays, William Shakespeare. *Poems and Songs.* Louisville: Charles T. Dearing, 1895.

Henson, Josiah. *Father Henson's Story of His Own Life.* Boston: John P. Jewett, 1858.

Holbrook, Chris. *Hell and Ohio: Stories of Southern Appalachia.* Frankfort: Gnomon, 1995.

House, Silas. *Clay's Quilt.* Chapel Hill: Algonquin Books, 2001.

Howard, Quentin. *Tell Me No Sad Tale.* Pikeville, Ky.: Wind Press, 1976.

Hubbard, Harlan. *Shantyboat: A River Way of Life.* Lexington: University Press of Kentucky, 1977.

———— "Winter Birds." *Kentucky Poetry Review* 23, no. 2 (Fall 1987).

Hudson, Virginia Cary. *O Ye Jigs and Juleps!* New York: Macmillan, 1962.

Hughes, Charlie G. "Mundy's Landing." *Kentucky Poetry Review* 28, no. 1 (Spring 1992).

Imlay, Gilbert. *Topographical Description of the Western Territory of North America.* London: J. Debrett, 1792.

Irvin, Cass. *Home Bound: Growing Up with a Disability in America.* Philadelphia: Temple University Press, 2004.

Jewell, Virginia. *Lick Skillet and Other Tales of Hickman County.* Union City, Tenn.: Lanzer Printing Company, 1986.

Johnson, Fenton. *Geography of the Heart: A Memoir.* New York: Scribner, 1996.

Johnson, Thomas, Jr. *The Kentucky Miscellany.* Lexington, 1821.

Johnston, Annie Fellows. *The Little Colonel.* Boston: Page Company, 1896.

Jonas, Ann. "Making Coffins" (published as "Making Caskets"). *Kentucky Poetry Review* 20, no. 2 (Fall 1984).

Jones, Gayl. *Mosquito.* Boston: Beacon Press, 1999.

Kahn, Kathy. *Hillbilly Women.* New York: Doubleday, 1973.

Kendrick, Leatha. *Heart Cake.* Abingdon, Va.: Sow's Ear Press, 2000.

Kingsolver, Barbara. *Homeland and Other Stories.* New York: Harper and Row, 1989.

Kleber, John E., ed. *The Encyclopedia of Louisville.* Lexington: University Press of Kentucky, 2001.

————. *The Kentucky Encyclopedia.* Lexington: University Press of Kentucky, 1992.

Knott, J. Proctor. "The Duluth Speech." In *Oddities in Southern Life and Character,* ed. Henry Watterson. Boston: Houghton Mifflin, 1883.

Lincoln, Abraham. *Complete Works of Abraham Lincoln.* Ed. John C. Nicolay and John Hay. 12 vols. New York: F. D. Tandy, 1905.

Litsey, Edwin Carlile. *Spindrift: Verses and Poems.* Louisville: John P. Morton, 1915.

Litsey, Sarah. "Star Reaper: A Ballad of Kentucky." *Scribner's Magazine,* April 1930.

Lloyd, John Uri. *Stringtown on the Pike: A Tale of Northernmost Kentucky.* New York: Dodd, Mead, 1900.

Lucas, Cora E. *This Rented House.* Louisville: Kentucky Poetry Press, 1982.

Lyon, George Ella. *Borrowed Children.* New York: Orchard Books, 1988.

Manning, Maurice. *A Companion for Owls: Being the Commonplace Book of D. Boone, Long Hunter, Back Woodsman, etc.* Orlando: Harcourt, 2004.

Martin, Jane. *The Deal.* In *Humana Festival 2000: The Complete Plays.* Hanover, N.H.: Smith and Kraus, 2000.

Marvin, William F. *The Battle of Monterey and Other Poems.* Danville, Ky.: A. S. M'Grorty, 1851.

Mason, Bobbie Ann. *Clear Springs: A Family Story.* New York: Random House, 1999.

————. *Shiloh and Other Stories.* New York: Harper and Row, 1982.

Mayhall, Jane. "Shaking the Tablecloth." *Kentucky Poetry Review* 20, no. 2 (Fall 1984).

McClanahan, Ed. *The Natural Man.* New York: Farrar, Straus and Giroux, 1983.

McCombs, Davis. *Ultima Thule.* New Haven: Yale University Press, 2000.

McDowell, Robert Emmett. *Tidewater Sprig.* New York: Crown, 1961.

Merrill, Boynton, Jr. *Callings.* Evansville, Ind.: Buttonwood Press, 1999.

————. *Sonnets for Gerontion.* Evansville, Ind.: Evansville Bindery, 2000.

Merton, Thomas. *The Collected Poems of Thomas Merton.* New York: New Directions, 1980.

————. *Selected Poems.* New York: New Directions, 1967.

————. *The Seven Storey Mountain.* New York: Harcourt, Brace, 1948.

Miller, Jim Wayne. *The Brier Poems.* Frankfort: Gnomon Press, 1997.

Monohan, Carolyn Lott. *A Grace of Wings: Poems.* Louisville: Kentucky Poetry Press, 1984.

Morehead, Maureen. "Driver's License" and "Why I Stopped Writing in My Diary." *Poetry* 162, no. 6 (September 1998).

Morton, R. Meir. *Prize Winning Poems of a Kentucky Poet.* Louisville: Fleur de Lis Poetry Press, 2003.

Mulligan, James H. "In Kentucky." *Lexington Herald,* February 12, 1902.

Nash, Alanna. *The Colonel: The Extraordinary Story of Colonel Tom Parker and Elvis Presley.* New York: Simon and Schuster, 2003.

Naslund, Sena Jeter. *Ahab's Wife; or, The Star-Gazer.* New York: William Morrow, 1999.

Neal, Patricia, with Richard DeNeut. *As I Am: An Autobiography.* New York: Simon and Schuster, 1988.

Niles, John Jacob. *Brick Dust and Buttermilk: Poems.* Frankfort: Boone Tolliver Press, 1977.

Noe, James T. Cotton. *Tip Sams of Kentucky, and Other Poems and Dramas.* Lexington: Canterbury Club, 1926.

Norman, Gurney. "Death in Lexington." *Iron Mountain Review* 13 (Spring 1997).

———. *Kinfolks.* Frankfort: Gnomon Press, 1977.

Norman, Marsha. *Getting Out.* New York: Avon Books, 1980.

O'Dell, Mary. *Living in the Body: Poems by Mary O'Dell.* Lewiston, N.Y.: Edwin Mellen Press, 2002.

Offutt, Chris. *The Good Brother.* New York: Simon and Schuster, 1997.

O'Hara, Theodore. *O'Hara and His Elegies,* ed. George W. Ranck. Baltimore: Turnbull Brothers, 1875.

Patrick, John. *The Teahouse of the August Moon: A Play.* New York: G. P. Putnam's Sons, 1952.

[Perkins, Thomas.] "Letter from Kentucky." *Boston Magazine,* September 23, 1785.

Petrie, Cordia Greer. *Angeline of the Hill Country.* New York: Thomas Y. Crowell, 1925.

Phelps, Joseph. "He Saved Others." A Sermon Preached by the Reverend Joseph Phelps, Highland Baptist Church, Louisville, Nov. 21, 2004.

Pile, Virginia. *Cedarsong.* Middletown, Ky.: Grex Press, 1998.

Porter, Joe Ashby. *The Kentucky Stories.* Baltimore: Johns Hopkins University Press, 1983.

Powers, Georgia Davis. *Celia's Land.* Louisville: Goose Creek Publishers, 2004.

Quenon, Brother Paul, Brother Guerric Plante, and Father Timothy Kelly. *Holy Folly: Short and Tall Tales from the Abbey of Gethsemani.* Windsor, Ont.: Black Moss Press, 1998.

Ramsey, Patricia. *Shoring Up: Poems.* Louisville: Kentucky Poetry Press, 1974.

Receveur, Betty Layman. "Kentucky Woman." *Kentucky Poetry Review* 20, no. 2 (Fall 1984).

Rice, Alice Hegan. *Mrs. Wiggs of the Cabbage Patch.* New York: Century, 1901.

Rice, Cale Young. *Seed of the Moon.* New York: Century, 1929.

———. *Selected Poems and Plays.* New York: Century, 1926.

Rising, Clara. *In the Season of the Wild Rose.* New York: Villard Books, 1986.

Roberts, Elizabeth Madox. *The Great Meadow.* New York: Viking, 1930.

———. *Song in the Meadow: Poems.* New York: Viking, 1940.

———. *The Time of Man.* New York: Viking, 1926. Reprint, Lexington: University Press of Kentucky, 2000.

———. *Under the Tree: Poems.* New York: B. W. Huebsch, 1922.

Schultz, Christian, Jr. *Travels on an Inland Voyage through the States of New-York, Pennsylvania, Virginia, Ohio, Kentucky and Tennessee and through the Territories of Indiana, Louisiana, Mississippi and New-Orleans; Performed in the Years 1807 and 1808; Including a Tour of Nearly Six Thousand Miles.* 2 vols. New York: Isaac Riley, 1810.

Seitz, Ron. *Death Eat.* Cincinnati: Spotlight Press, 1987.

———. *Song for Nobody: A Memory Vision of Thomas Merton.* Liguori, Mo.: Triumph Books, 1993.

Semones, Charles. *Afternoon in the Country of Summer: New and Selected Poems.* Nicholasville, Ky.: Wind Publications, 2003.

———. "Christmas Eve in Kentucky." *Kentucky Monthly,* December 2003.

Shipley, Vivian. *Fair Haven.* Mobile, Ala.: Negative Capability Press, 2000.

Shirley, Aleda. *Chinese Architecture: Poems.* Athens: University of Georgia Press, 1986.

Skinner, Jeffrey. *The Company of Heaven.* Pittsburgh: University of Pittsburgh Press, 1992.

Slade, Leonard A., Jr. *Elisabeth and Other Poems.* New York: McGraw-Hill, 1999.

Slone, Verna Mae. *What My Heart Wants to Tell.* Lexington: University Press of Kentucky, 1979.

Smith, Harry. *Fifty Years of Slavery in the United States of America*. Grand Rapids: West Michigan Printing Co., 1891.

Smith, James. *An Account of the Remarkable Occurrences in the Life and Travels of Col. James Smith (now a citizen of Bourbon County, Kentucky) During His Captivity with the Indians, in the Years 1755, '56, '57, '58 & '59*. Lexington: John Bradford, 1799.

Smock, Frederick. *The Good Life*. Monterey, Ky.: Larkspur Press, 2000.

Spears, Eve. *A Cloud of Laurel: Poems*. Louisville: Kentucky Poetry Press, 1988.

Spears, Woodridge. "Interleaf," *Kentucky Poetry Review* 28, no. 1 (Spring 1992).

Stanton, Henry T. *The Moneyless Man and Other Poems*. Baltimore: H. C. Turnbull, 1871.

Stewart, Albert. "The Poet as High-Diver Perhaps." *Kentucky Poetry Review* 28, no. 1 (Spring 1992).

Stiles, Martha Bennett. *Lonesome Road*. Frankfort: Gnomon Press, 1998.

Still, James. *From the Mountain, From the Valley: New and Collected Poems*. Lexington: University Press of Kentucky, 2001.

———. *Pattern of a Man and Other Stories*. Frankfort: Gnomon Press, 1976.

———. *River of Earth*. New York: Viking, 1940. Reprint, Lexington: University Press of Kentucky, 1978.

Stowe, Harriet Beecher. *Uncle Tom's Cabin*. New York, 1852.

Stuart, Jane. *Gideon's Children*. New York: McGraw-Hill, 1976.

———. "Plum Grove Cemetery." *Kentucky Poetry Review* 20, no. 2 (Fall 1984).

———. "Song of the Blackbirds." *Kentucky Poetry Review* 20, no. 2 (Fall 1984).

———. *White Barn*. Frankfort: Whippoorwill Press, 1973.

Stuart, Jesse. *Man with a Bull-Tongue Plow*. New York: Dutton, 1934.

———. *The Thread That Runs So True*. New York: Charles Scribner's Sons, 1949.

———. *The Year of My Rebirth*. New York: McGraw-Hill, 1956.

Sullivan, Lucinda Dixon. *It Was the Goodness of the Place*. Louisville: Fleur-de-Lis Press, 2003.

Summers, Hollis. *Standing Room: Stories by Hollis Summers*. Baton Rouge: Louisiana State University Press, 1984.

Survant, Joe. *The Presence of Snow in the Tropics*. Singapore: Landmark Books, 2001.

Sutton, Catherine. "Buzzard's Roost." *Kentucky Poetry Review* 28, no. 1 (Spring 1992).

Tate, Allen. *Collected Poems 1919–1976*. New York: Farrar, Straus and Giroux, 1977.

Taylor, Richard. *The Country of Morning Calm*. Monterey, Ky.: Larkspur Press, 1998.

Taylor-Hall, Mary Ann. "Bunting." *Open 24 Hours,* 2002.

Tevis, Julia A. *Sixty Years in a School-Room*. Cincinnati: Western Methodist, 1878.

Tevis, Walter. *The Color of Money*. New York: Warner Books, 1984.

Thompson, Hunter S. *Kingdom of Fear: Loathsome Secrets of a Star-Crossed Child in the Final Days of the American Century*. New York: Simon and Schuster, 2003.

Tocqueville, Alexis de. *Democracy in America*. 1835, 1840. Trans. Arthur Goldhammer. New York: Library of America, 2004.

Townsend, John Wilson. *Kentucky in American Letters, 1784–1912*. 2 vols. Cedar Rapids, Iowa: Torch Press, 1913.

Vish, Donald H. *Prideful Violets: Poems and Musings*. 1st Books Library: www.1stbooks.com, 2001.

Walker, Frank X. "Black Box." In *Tobacco: A Literary Anthology,* ed. Edmund August. Nicholasville, Ky.: Wind Publications, 2004.

———. *Buffalo Dance: The Journey of York*. Lexington: University Press of Kentucky, 2004.

Ward, William S. *A Literary History of Kentucky*. Knoxville: University of Tennessee Press, 1988.

Warren, Robert Penn. *The Circus in the Attic and Other Stories*. New York: Harcourt, Brace and World, 1947.

———. *The Collected Poems of Robert Penn Warren*. Baton Rouge: Louisiana State University Press, 1998.

———. *Now and Then*. New York: Random House, 1978.

———. *World Enough and Time: A Romantic Novel*. New York: Random House, 1950.

Watson, Jo Anna Holt. *A Taste of the Sweet Apple*. Louisville: Sarabande Books, 2004.

Watterson, Henry. "On the Death of Carrie Nation." *Courier-Journal,* July 13, 1911.

Welby, Amelia B. *Poems by Amelia.* Boston: A. Tompkins, 1845.
Wilkinson, Crystal. *Blackberries, Blackberries.* London: Toby Press, 2000.
———. *Water Street.* London: Toby Press, 2002.
Wilson, Robert Burns. *Life and Love.* New York: Cassell, 1887.
Wolfe, George C. *The Colored Museum.* New York: Grove Press, 1988.
Woolfolk, Miriam. "His Land." *Kentucky Poetry Review* 23, no. 1 (Spring 1987).
———. "Railroad Man's Daughter." *Kentucky Poetry Review* 20, no. 2 (Fall 1984).

Copyrights and Permissions

Greene, Jonathan. "The Album," from *Inventions of Necessity* by Jonathan Greene, used by permission of Gnomon Press.

Hall, James Baker. "Stopping on the Edge to Wave," reprinted by permission of the author.

Hardwick, Elizabeth. "Evenings at Home." Reprinted by permission of the author.

Hay, John. "Renascence," reprinted by permission of the author.

Holbrook, Chris. "First of the Month," from *Hell and Ohio, Stories of Southern Appalachia* by Chris Holbrook, used by permission of Gnomon Press.

House, Silas. From *Clay's Quilt.* © 2001 by Silas House. Reprinted by permission of Algonquin Books of Chapel Hill.

Howard, Quentin. "Going Home," reprinted by permission of Glenn Gibson.

Hubbard, Harlan. "Winter Birds," reprinted by permission of *Kentucky Poetry Review.*

Hudson, Virginia Cary. Reprinted with the permission of Scribner, an imprint of Simon & Schuster Adult Publishing Group, from *O Ye Jigs and Juleps!* by Virginia Cary Hudson. Copyright © 1962 Virginia Cleveland Mayne; copyright renewed © 1990 by Beverly Cary Mayne Kienzie.

Hughes, Charles. "Mundy's Landing," reprinted by permission of the author.

Irvin, Cass. Pages 216–223 from *Home Bound: Growing Up with a Disability in America* by Cass Irvin. Reprinted by permission of Temple University Press. © 2004 by Cass F. Irvin. All rights reserved.

Jewell, Virginia Honchell. "Growing Marijuana" and "The Tarheel Philosopher," from *Lick Skillet and Other Tales of Hickman County,* reprinted by permission of the author.

Johnson, Fenton. From *Geography of the Heart: A Memoir* by Fenton Johnson. Copyright 1996 by Fenton Johnson. Reprinted with permission of Scribner, an imprint of Simon & Schuster Adult Publishing Group.

Jonas, Ann. "Making Coffins," reprinted by permission of the author.

Jones, Gayl. From *Mosquito* by Gayl Jones. Copyright © 1999 by Gayl Jones. Reprinted by permission of Beacon Press, Boston.

Kahn, Kathy. "How I Got My Schoolgirl Figure Back," from *Hillbilly Women* by Kathy Kahn, copyright © 1973 by Kathy Kahn. Used by permission of Doubleday, a division of Random House, Inc.

Kendrick, Leatha. "Postcard," from *Heart Cake,* reprinted by permission of Sow's Ear Press.

Kingsolver, Barbara. "Rose-Johnny" (pp. 203–25) from *Homeland and Other Stories.* Copyright © 1989 by Barbara Kingsolver. Reprinted by permission of HarperCollins Publishers Inc.

Lucas, Cora. "April Furlough," reprinted by permission of Coretta Lucas Wolford.

Manning, Maurice. "First" and "Testament," from *A Companion for Owls,* copyright © 2004 by Maurice Manning. Reprinted by permission of Harcourt, Inc.

Martin, Jane. *The Deal,* reprinted by permission of Alexander Speer, the copyright holder for Jane Martin. Caution: The amateur and stock acting rights to this work are controlled exclusively by The Dramatic Publishing Company, without whose permission in writing no performance of it may be given. Royalty must be paid every time the play is performed whether or not it is presented for profit and whether or not admission is charged. A play is performed any time it is acted before an audience. All inquiries concerning amateur and stock rights should be addressed to Dramatic Publishing, P.O. Box 129, Woodstock, IL 60098.

Mason, Bobbie Ann. "Shiloh," *Shiloh and Other Stories* reprinted by permission of International Creative Management, Inc.

Mason, Bobbie Ann. From *Clear Springs* by Bobbie Ann Mason, copyright 1999 by Bobbie Ann Mason. Used by permission of Random House, Inc.

Mayhall, Jane. "Shaking the Tablecloth," reprinted by permission of the author.

McClanahan, Ed. From *The Natural Man,* used by permission of Gnomon Press.

McCombs, Davis. "Candlewriting" and "Fame," from *Ultima Thule,* Yale University Press, 2000, reprinted by permission of Yale University Press.

Merrill, Boynton, Jr. "The Writer," "The Teacher," and "Yesterdays," reprinted by permission of the author.

Merton, Thomas. "To the Monastery," from *The Seven Storey Mountain* by Thomas Merton. Copyright 1948 by Harcourt, Inc.; copyright renewed 1976 by the Trustees of the Merton Legacy Trust; reprinted by permission of the publisher.

Merton, Thomas. "A Practical Program for Monks" by Thomas Merton, original by Cesar Vallejo, from

Index